Nora Roberts

Three Complete Novels

Also by Nora Roberts

Honest Illusions
Private Scandals
Hidden Riches
True Betrayals
Montana Sky
Born in Fire
Born in Ice
Born in Shame
Daring to Dream
Holding the Dream
Finding the Dream
Sanctuary
Homeport
Sea Swept
Rising Tides
Inner Harbor
The Reef
River's End
Jewels of the Sun
Carolina Moon

Writing as J. D. Robb

Naked in Death
Glory in Death
Immortal in Death
Rapture in Death
Ceremony in Death
Vengeance in Death
Holiday in Death
Conspiracy in Death
Loyalty in Death
Witness in Death

Nora Roberts

Three Complete Novels

Honest Illusions

Private Scandals

Hidden Riches

G. P. Putnam's Sons New York

G. P. Putnam's Sons
Publishers Since 1838
a member of
Penguin Putnam Inc.
375 Hudson Street
New York, NY 10014

Published simultaneously in Canada

Library of Congress Cataloging-in-Publication Data

Roberts, Nora
[Novels. Selections]
Three complete novels / Nora Roberts.
p. cm.
Contents: Honest illusions—Private scandals—Hidden riches.
ISBN 0-399-14627-X
1. Philadelphia (Pa.)—Fiction. 2. Antique dealers—Fiction. 3. Magicians—Fiction. 4. Thieves—Fiction. I. Title.

PS3568.O243 A6 2000 00-028058
813'.54—dc21

Printed in the United States of America
9 10

Book design by Patrice Sheridan

Contents

Honest Illusions

To Bruce, Dan and Jason,

the magic in my life

Part One

O brave new world,
That has such people in't!
—William Shakespeare

Prologue

The lady vanishes. It was an old illusion, given a modern twist, and never failed to leave the audience gasping. The glittery crowd at Radio City was as eager to be duped as a group of slack-jawed rubes at a dog and pony show.

Even as Roxanne stepped onto the glass pedestal she could feel their anticipation—the silvery edge of it that was a merging of hope and doubt glued together with wonder. The inching forward in the seat ranged from president to peon.

Magic made equals of them all.

Max had said that, she recalled. Many, many times.

Amid the swirl of mist and the flash of light, the pedestal slowly ascended, circling majestically to the tune of Gershwin's *Rhapsody in Blue.* The gentle three-hundred-and-sixty-degree revolution showed the crowd all sides of the ice-clear pedestal and the slender woman atop it—and distracted them from the trickery at hand.

Presentation, she'd been taught, was often the slim difference between a charlatan and an artist.

In keeping with the theme of the music, Roxanne wore a sparkling gown of midnight blue that clung to her long, willowy form—clung so closely that no one studying her would believe there was anything under the spangled silk but her own flesh. Her hair, a waterfall of flame curling to her waist, twinkled with thousands of tiny iridescent stars.

Fire and ice. More than one man had wondered how one woman could be both at the same time.

As in sleep or a trance, her eyes were closed—or seemed to be—and her elegant face was lifted toward the star-pricked ceiling of the stage.

As she rose, she let her arms sway to the music, then held them high above her head, for showmanship and for the practical necessity that underscores all magic.

It was a beautiful illusion, she knew. The mist, the lights, the music, the woman. She enjoyed the sheer drama of it, and was not above being amused by the irony of using the age-old symbol of the lone, lovely woman placed on a pedestal, above the common worry and toils of man.

It was also a miserably complex bit of business, requiring a great deal of physical control and split-second timing. But not even those fortunate enough to be seated in the first row could detect the intense concentration in her serene face. None of them could know how many tedious hours she had put in, perfecting every aspect of the act on paper, then in practice. Unrelenting practice.

Slowly, again to Gershwin's rhythm, her body began to turn, dip, sway. A partnerless dance ten feet above stage, all color and fluid movement. There were murmurs from the audience, scattered applause.

They could see her—yes, they could see her through the blue-tinted mist and spinning lights. The glitter of the dark gown, the flow of flame-colored hair, the gleam of that alabaster skin.

Then, in a breath, in a gasp, they could not. In less time than it takes to blink an eye, she was gone. In her place was a sleek Bengal tiger who reared on his hind legs to paw the air and roar.

There was a pause, that most satisfying of pauses to an entertainer where an audience held its stunned collective breath before the applause thundered, echoing as the pedestal descended once more. The big cat leaped down to stalk stage right. He stopped by an ebony box, sent up another roar that had a woman in the front row giggling nervously. As one, the four sides of the box collapsed.

And there was Roxanne, dressed not in shimmery blue but in a silver cat suit. She took her bows as she'd been taught almost from birth. With a flourish.

As the sound of success continued to pound in her ears, she mounted the tiger and rode the beast offstage.

"Nice work, Oscar." With a little sigh, she bent forward to scratch the cat between the ears.

"You looked real pretty, Roxy." Her big, burly assistant clipped a leash to Oscar's spangled collar.

"Thanks, Mouse." Dismounting, she tossed her hair back. The back-stage area was already hopping. Those trusted to do so would secure her equipment and guard it from prying eyes. Since she'd scheduled a press conference for the following day, she would see no reporters now. Roxanne had high hopes for a bottle of iced champagne and a stingingly hot whirlpool bath.

Alone.

Absently she rubbed her hands together—an old habit Mouse could have told her she'd picked up from her father.

"I've got the fidgets," she said with a half laugh. "Had them all damn night. It feels like someone's breathing down my neck."

"Well, ah . . ." Mouse stood where he was, letting Oscar rub against his knees. Never articulate under the best of circumstances, Mouse fumbled for the best way to phrase the news. "You got company, Roxy. In the dressing room."

"Oh?" Her brows drew together, forming the faint line of impatience between them. "Who?"

"Take another bow, honey." Lily, Roxanne's onstage assistant and surrogate mother, swept over to grab her arm. "You brought down the house." Lily dabbed a handkerchief around the false eyelashes she wore onstage and off. "Max would be so proud."

The quick twist in Roxanne's gut had her willing away her own tears. They didn't show. They were never permitted to show in public. She started forward, moving into the swell of applause. "Who's waiting for me?" she called over her shoulder, but Mouse was already leading the big cat away.

He'd been taught by the master that discretion was the better part of survival.

Ten minutes later, flushed with success, Roxanne opened the door of her dressing room. The scent hit her first—roses and greasepaint. That mix of fragrances had become so familiar she breathed it in like fresh air. But there was another scent here—the sting of rich tobacco. Elegant, exotic, French. Her hand trembled once on the knob as she pushed the door fully open.

There was one man she would forever associate with that aroma. One man she knew who habitually smoked slim French cigars.

She said nothing when she saw him. Could say nothing as he rose from a chair where he'd been enjoying his cigar and her champagne. Oh, God, it was thrilling and horrible to watch that wonderful mouth quirk in that very familiar grin, to meet those impossibly blue eyes with her own.

His hair was still long, a mane of ebony waving back from his face. Even as a child he'd been gorgeous, an elegant gypsy with eyes that could freeze or burn. Age had only enhanced his looks, fining down that compelling face, the long bones and shadowy hollows, the faint cleft in the chin. Beyond the physical, there was a drama that shivered around him like an aura.

He was a man women shuddered over and wanted.

She had. Oh, she had.

Five years had passed since she'd seen that smile, since she'd run her hands through that thick hair or felt the searing pressure of that clever mouth. Five years to mourn, to weep and to hate.

Why wasn't he dead? she wondered as she forced herself to close the door at her back. Why hadn't he had the decency to succumb to any of the varied and gruesome tragedies she'd imagined for him?

And what in God's name was she going to do with this terrible yearning she felt just looking at him again?

"Roxanne." Training kept Luke's voice steady as he said her name. He'd watched her over the years. Tonight he'd studied her every move from the shadows of the wings. Judging, weighing. Wanting. But here, now, face to face, she was almost too beautiful to bear. "It was a good show. The finale was spectacular."

"Thank you."

His hand was steady as he poured her a flute of champagne, as hers was when she accepted it. They were, after all, showmen, cast in an odd way from the same mold. Max's mold.

"I'm sorry about Max."

Her eyes went flat. "Are you?"

Because Luke felt he deserved more than the slash of sarcasm, he merely nodded, then glanced down at his bubbling wine, remembering. His mouth curved when he looked back at her. "The Calais job, the rubics. Was that yours?"

She sipped, the silver sparkled on her shoulders as she moved them in a careless shrug. "Of course."

"Ah." He nodded again, pleased. He had to be sure she hadn't lost her touch—for magic or for larceny. "I heard rumors that a first edition of Poe's *House of Usher* was lifted from a vault in London."

"Your hearing was always good, Callahan."

He continued to smile, wondering when she'd learned to exude sex like breath. He remembered the clever child, the coltish adolescent, the irresistible bloom of the young woman. The bloom had blossomed seductively. And he could feel the pull that had always been between them. He would use it now, with regret, but he would use it to gain his own ends.

The end justifies everything. Another of Maximillian Nouvelle's maxims.

"I have a proposition for you, Rox."

"Really?" She took a last sip before setting her glass aside. The bubbles were bitter on her tongue.

"Business," he said lightly, tapping out the stub of his cigar. Taking her hand, he brought her fingers to his lips. "And personal. I've missed you, Roxanne." It was the truest statement he could make. One flash of sterling honesty in years of tricks, illusions and pretense. Caught up in his own feelings, he missed the warning flash in her eyes.

"Have you, Luke? Have you really?"

"More than I can tell you." Swamped by memories and needs, he drew her closer, felt his blood begin to pump as her body brushed his. She'd always been the one. No matter how many escapes he'd accomplished, he'd never freed himself from the trap in which Roxanne Nouvelle had caught him. "Come back to my hotel." His breath whispered over her face as she went fluidly into his arms. "We'll have a late supper. Talk."

"Talk?" Her arms wound sinuously around him. Her rings flashed as she dipped her fingers into his hair. Beside them the makeup mirror over her dressing table reflected them in triplicate. As if showing them past, present, future. When she spoke, her voice was like the mist she'd vanished into. Dark and rich and mysterious. "Is that what you want to do with me, Luke?"

He forgot the importance of control, forgot everything but the fact that her mouth was an inch from his. The taste he'd once gorged on was a wish away. "No."

He dropped his head toward hers. Then his breath exploded as her knee shot up between his legs. Even as he was doubling over, she slammed her fist onto his chin.

His grunt of surprise, and the splintering of wood from the table he smashed on his way down gave Roxanne enormous satisfaction. Roses flew, water splashed. A few slender buds drifted over him as he lay on the dampening carpet.

"You . . ." Scowling, he dragged a rose from his hair. The brat had always been sneaky, he remembered. "You're quicker than you used to be, Rox."

Hands on her hips, she stood over him, a slim, silver warrior who'd never learned to sample her revenge cold. "I'm a lot of things I didn't used to be." Her knuckles hurt like fire, but she used that pain to block another, deeper ache. "Now, you lying Irish bastard, crawl back into whatever hole you dug for yourself five years ago. Come near me again, and I swear, I'll make you disappear for good."

Delighted with her exit line, she turned on her heel, then let out a shriek when Luke snagged her ankle. She went down hard on her rump and before she could put nails and teeth to use, he had her pinned. She'd forgotten how strong and how quick he was.

A miscalculation, Max would have said. And miscalculations were the root of all failures.

"Okay, Rox, we can talk here." Though he was breathless and still in pain, he grinned. "Your choice."

"I'll see you in hell—"

"Very likely." His grin faded. "Damn it, Roxy, I never could resist you." When he crushed his mouth to hers, he tossed them both back into the past.

1

1973, near Portland, Maine

"Hur-ry, hur-ry, step right up. Be amazed, be astounded. Watch the Great Nouvelle defy the laws of nature. For one small dollar, see him make cards dance in midair. Before your eyes, right before your astonished eyes, see a beautiful woman sawed in two."

While the barker ran through his spiel, Luke Callahan slithered through the carnival crowd, busily picking pockets. He had quick hands, agile fingers and that most important asset of a successful thief, a complete lack of conscience.

He was twelve.

For nearly six weeks he'd been on the road, on the run. Luke had big plans to head south before the steamy New England summer became a frigid New England winter.

He wasn't going to get very far with pickings like this, he thought and nipped a billfold from the sagging overalls pocket. There weren't many of those who had come to ride the Tilt-a-Whirl or challenge the Wheel of Fortune who had more than a few creased dollars on them.

Now, when he got to Miami, things would be different. In the shadows behind the milk bottle toss, he discarded the imitation leather wallet and counted his take for the evening.

Twenty-eight dollars. Pathetic.

But in Miami, that land of sun, fun and high rollers, he'd clean house. All he had to do was get there first, and so far he'd managed to squirrel away nearly two hundred dollars. A little more and he'd be able to afford to take the bus at least part of the way. A Greyhound, he thought with a quick grin. He'd leave the driving to them, all right, and take a break from hitching rides with stoned-out hippies and fat-fingered perverts.

A runaway couldn't be choosy about his mode of transportation. Luke was already aware that a ride from an upstanding citizen could lead to a police report or—nearly as bad—a lecture on the dangers of a young boy leaving home.

It was no use telling anyone that home was much more dangerous than the perils of the road.

After flipping off two singles, Luke tucked the rest of his take into his battered chukkas. He needed food. The smell of hot grease had been tantalizing his stomach for nearly an hour. He'd reward himself with an overcooked burger and fries, and wash it all down with some fresh lemonade.

Like most twelve-year-old boys, Luke would have enjoyed a ride on the Whip, but if there was a longing in him toward the spinning lights, he covered it with a sneer. Jerks thought they were having an adventure, he mused while sour grapes stuck in his throat. They'd be tucked in their beds tonight while he slept under the stars and when they woke up Mommy and Daddy would tell them what to do and how to do it.

No one would tell him any of those things ever again.

Feeling superior in every way, he tucked his thumbs in the front pockets of his jeans and strutted toward the concession stands.

He passed the poster again—the larger-than-life-sized picture of the magician. The Great Nouvelle, with his sweep of black hair, flowing moustache, his hypnotic dark eyes. Every time Luke looked at the poster he felt himself being pulled toward something he couldn't understand.

The eyes in the picture seemed to look right into him, as if they could see and understand much too much about Luke Callahan, late of Bangor, Maine, by way of Burlington and Utica and Christ knew where because Luke had forgotten.

He almost expected the painted mouth to speak and the hand that held the fan of cards to shoot out, snatch him by the throat and pull him right inside that poster. He'd be trapped there forever, beating on the other side of that pasteboard the way he'd beat on so many of the locked doors of his childhood.

Because the idea gave him the willies, Luke curled his lip. "Magic's bunk," he said, but he said it in a whisper. And his heart pounded hard as he dared the painted face to challenge him. "Big deal," he went on, gaining confidence. "Pulling stupid rabbits out of stupid hats and doing a few dumbass card tricks."

He wanted to see those dumbass tricks more than he wanted to ride on the Whip. More even than he wanted to stuff his mouth with ketchup-dripping fries. Luke wavered, fingering one of the dollars in his pocket.

It would be worth a buck, he decided, just to prove to himself that the magician was no big deal. It would be worth a buck to sit down. In the dark, he mused as he drew out the crumpled bill and paid the price. There were bound to be a few pockets he could slip his nimble fingers into.

The heavy canvas flap swung shut behind him and blocked out most of the light and air from the midway. Noise battered against it like rainfall. People were already crowded on the low wooden seats, murmuring among themselves, shifting and waving paper fans against the stifling heat.

He stood in the back a moment, scanning. With an instinct that had been honed sharp as a switchblade over the past six weeks he skipped over a huddle of kids, crossed off a few couples as being too poor to net him anything but his admission price and cagily chose his marks. The situation called for him to look to women, as most of the men would be sitting on their money.

"Excuse me," he said, polite as a Boy Scout, as he squeezed in behind a grandmotherly type who seemed distracted by the antics of the boy and girl on either side of her.

The moment he was settled, the Great Nouvelle took the stage. He was dressed in full formal gear. The black tux and starched white shirt looked exotic in the heat-drenched tent. His shoes gleamed with polish. On the pinkie of his left hand he wore a gold ring with a black center stone that winked in the stage lights.

The impression of greatness was set the moment he faced his audience.

The magician said nothing, yet the tent filled with his presence, swelled with it. He was every bit as dramatic as his poster, though the black hair was shot with glints of silver. The Great Nouvelle lifted his hands, held them palm out toward the audience. With a flick of his wrist, his spread, empty fingers held a coin. Another flick, another coin, and another, until the wide vee's of his fingers were filled with the gleam of gold.

Luke's attention was snagged enough for him to lean forward, eyes narrowed. He wanted to know how it was done. It was a trick, of course. He was all too aware the world was full of them. He'd already stopped wondering why, but he hadn't stopped wondering how.

The coins became colored balls that changed size and hue. They multiplied, subtracted, appeared and vanished while the audience applauded.

Pulling his eyes from the show was difficult. Lifting six dollars from Grandma's purse was easy. After tucking his take away, Luke slid out of his seat to move into position behind a blonde whose straw purse was sitting carelessly on the floor beside her.

As the sleight of hand warmed up the audience, Luke pocketed another four dollars. But he kept losing his concentration. Telling himself he'd wait before hitting the fat lady to his right, he settled down to watch.

For the next few moments, Luke was only a child, his eyes wide with amazement as the magician fanned the cards, passed his hand over their tops, and his other hand over the bottoms so that the spread deck hung suspended in the air. At a stylish movement of his hands, the cards swayed, dipped, turned. The audience cheered, wholly intent on the show. And Luke missed his chance to clean house.

"You there." Nouvelle's voice resounded. Luke froze as he felt those dark eyes pin him. "You're a likely-looking boy. I need a smart . . ." The eyes twinkled. "An honest boy to help me with my next trick. Up here." Nouvelle scooped up the hanging cards and gestured.

"Go ahead, kid. Go on." An elbow rammed into Luke's ribs.

Flushing to his toes, Luke rose. He knew it was dangerous when people noticed you. They would notice him all the more if he refused.

"Pick a card," Nouvelle invited as Luke climbed onstage. "Any card."

He fanned them again, outward to the audience so that they could see it was an ordinary deck. Quick and deft, Nouvelle shuffled them, then spread them on a small table.

"Any card," he repeated, and Luke frowned in concentration as he slid one from the pile. "Turn toward our gracious audience," Nouvelle instructed. "Hold the card facing out so all can see. Good, excellent. You're a natural."

Chuckling to himself, Nouvelle picked up the discarded pack, manipulating it again with his long, clever fingers. "Now . . ." His eyes on Luke, he held out the deck. "Slip your card in anywhere. Anywhere at all. Excellent." His lips were curved as he offered the deck to the boy. "Shuffle them as you please." Nouvelle's gaze remained on Luke as the boy mixed the cards. "Now." Nouvelle laid a hand on Luke's shoulder. "On the table, if you please. Would you like to cut them, or shall I?"

"I'll do it." Luke laid his hands over the cards, certain he couldn't be tricked. Not when he was so close.

"Is your card the top one?"

Luke flipped it up, grinned. "No."

Nouvelle looked amazed as the audience tittered. "No? The bottom one, perhaps?"

Getting into the spirit, Luke turned the deck over and held the card out. "No. Guess you screwed up, mister."

"Odd, odd indeed," Nouvelle murmured, tapping a finger to his moustache. "You're a more clever boy than I imagined. It seems you've tricked me. The card you chose isn't in that deck at all. Because it's . . ." He snapped his fingers, turned his wrist, and plucked the eight of hearts out of thin air. "Here."

While Luke goggled, the audience broke into appreciative applause. Under the cover of the sound, Nouvelle spoke quietly.

"Come backstage after the show."

And that was all. Giving Luke a nudge, Nouvelle sent him back to his seat.

For the next twenty minutes, Luke forgot everything but the magic. He watched the little redheaded girl dance out on the stage in spangled tights. Grinned when she stepped into an oversized top hat and changed into a white rabbit. He felt adult and amused when the girl and the magician staged a mock argument over her bedtime. The girl tossed her curling red hair and stomped her feet. With a sigh, Nouvelle whipped a black cape over her, tapped three times with his magic wand. The cape slithered to the floor, and the child was gone.

"A parent," Nouvelle said soberly, "must be firm."

For a finale, Nouvelle sawed a curvy blonde in a skimpy leotard in half. The curves and the costume had elicited a great deal of whistling and cheers.

One enthusiastic man in a paisley shirt and starched bell-bottom jeans leaped up, shouting. "Hey, Nouvelle, if you're done with the lady, I'll take either half!"

The divided lady was pushed apart. At Nouvelle's command, she wriggled her fingers and toes. Once the box was pushed back together, Nouvelle removed the steel dividers, waved his wand and threw open the lid.

Magically reassembled, the lady stepped out to a round of applause.

Luke had forgotten all about the fat woman's purse, but decided he'd gotten his money's worth.

As the audience filed out to take a ride on the Loop De Loop or gawk at Sahib the Snake Charmer, Luke sidled toward the stage. He thought maybe, since he'd been a kind of assistant for the card trick, that Nouvelle would show him how it was done.

"Kid."

Luke looked up. From his vantage point, the man looked like a giant. Six feet five inches and two hundred and sixty pounds of solid muscle. The smooth-shaven face was as wide as a dinner plate, the eyes like two raisins stuck slightly off center. There was an unfiltered cigarette dangling from the mouth.

As ugly went, Herbert Mouse Patrinski had all the bases covered.

Luke instinctively struck a pose, chin jutted forward, shoulders hunched, legs spread and braced. "Yeah?"

For an answer, Mouse jerked his head and lumbered away. Luke debated for less than ten seconds, then followed.

Most of the tawdry glamour of the carnival faded to gray as they crossed the yellowed and trampled grass toward the huddle of trailers and trucks.

Nouvelle's trailer looked like a thoroughbred in a field of hacks. It was long and sleek, its black paint gleaming in the shadowy moonlight. A flourish of silver scrolled on the side proclaimed THE GREAT NOUVELLE, CONJURER EXTRAORDINAIRE.

Mouse rapped once on the door before pushing it open. Luke caught a scent that reminded him oddly and comfortingly of church as he stepped inside behind Mouse.

The Great Nouvelle had already changed out of his stage tux and was lounging on the narrow built-in sofa in a black silk dressing gown. Thin plumes of smoke curled lazily upward from a half a dozen incense cones. Sitar music played in the background while Nouvelle swirled two inches of brandy.

Luke tucked his suddenly nervous hands in his pockets and gauged his surroundings. He knew he'd just walked into a trailer but there was a strong illusion of some exotic den. The scents, of course, and the colors from the plush, vivid pillows heaped here and there, the small richly woven mats tossed helter-skelter over the floor, the draping silks over the windows, the mysterious dip and sway of candlelight.

And, of course, Maximillian Nouvelle himself.

"Ah." His amused smile half hidden by his moustache, Max toasted the boy. "So glad you could join me."

To show he was unimpressed, Luke shrugged his bony shoulders. "It was a pretty decent show."

"I blush at the compliment," Max said dryly and waved with the back of his hand for Luke to sit. "Do you have an interest in magic, Mr. . . . ?"

"I'm Luke Callahan. I figured it was worth a buck to see some tricks."

"A princely sum, I agree." Slowly, his eyes on Luke, Max sipped his brandy. "But a good investment for you, I trust?"

"Investment?" Uneasy, Luke slid his eyes toward Mouse, who seemed to be hulking around, blocking the door.

"You took several more dollars out with you than you came in with. In finance we would call it a quick upward turn on your money."

Luke resisted, barely, the urge to squirm and met Max's eyes levelly. Well done, Max thought to himself. Quite well done.

"I don't know what you're talking about. I gotta take off."

"Sit." All Max did was utter the single syllable and raise one finger. Luke tensed, but sat. "You see, Mr. Callahan—or may I call you Luke? A good name that. From Lucius, the Latin for light." He chuckled, sipped again. "But I digress. You see, Luke, while you were watching me, I was watching you. It wouldn't be sporting of me to ask how much you got, but an educated guess would put it at eight to ten dollars." He smiled charmingly. "Not at all a bad turn, you see, on a single."

Luke narrowed his eyes to slits. A thin trail of sweat dribbled down his back. "Are you calling me a thief?"

"Not if it offends you. After all, you're my guest. And I'm being a remiss host. What can I offer you as refreshment?"

"What's the deal here, mister?"

"Oh, we'll get to that. Indeed, we'll get to that. But first things first, I always say. I know a young boy's appetite, having been one myself." And this young boy was so thin

Max could all but count the ribs beneath the grubby T-shirt. "Mouse, I believe our guest would enjoy a hamburger or two, with all the accompaniments."

" 'Kay."

Max rose as Mouse slipped out the door. "A cold drink?" he offered, opening the small refrigerator. He didn't have to see to know the boy's eyes cut to the door. "You can run, of course," he said casually as he took out a bottle of Pepsi. "I doubt the money you have tucked in your right shoe would slow you down very much. Or you can relax, enjoy a civilized meal and some conversation."

Luke considered bolting. His stomach rumbled. Compromising, he slid an inch closer to the door. "What do you want?"

"Why, your company," Max said as he poured Pepsi over ice. His brow lifted a fraction at the quickly smothered flash in Luke's eyes. So, he thought as his own mouth grimaced. It had been that bad. Hoping to signal the boy that he would be safe from that sort of advance, Max called for Lily.

She stepped through a curtain of crimson silk. Like Max, she was also in a robe. Hers was pale pink and trimmed with fuchsia feathers, as were the high-heeled slippers on her feet. She tapped over the scattered rugs in a wave of Chanel.

"We have company." She had a pipy voice that seemed to be stuck in perpetual giggle.

"Yes. Lily, my dear." Max took her hand and brought it to his lips, lingered over it. "Meet Luke Callahan. Luke, my invaluable assistant and adored companion, Lily Bates."

Luke swallowed a hard knot in his throat. He'd never seen anything like her. She was all curves and scent, her eyes and mouth exotically painted. She smiled, batting incredibly long lashes. "Pleased to meet you," she said, and snuggled closer to Max when he slipped an arm around her waist.

"Ma'am."

"Luke and I have some things to discuss. I didn't want you to wait up for me."

"I don't mind."

He kissed her lightly, but with such tenderness, Luke's cheeks went hot before he looked away. *"Je t'aime, ma belle."*

"Oh, Max." That French business always made Lily's toes curl.

"Get some sleep," he murmured.

"Okay." But her eyes told him, quite clearly, that she would wait. "Nice meeting you, Luke."

"Ma'am," he managed again as she swayed back through the red curtain.

"A wonderful woman," Max commented as he offered Luke the glass of Pepsi. "Roxanne and I would be quite lost without her. Wouldn't we, *ma petite?*"

"Daddy." On a little huff of breath, Roxanne crawled under the curtain then popped to her feet. "I was so quiet, even Lily didn't see me."

"Ah, but I sensed you." Smiling at her, he tapped a finger to his nose. "Your shampoo. Your soap. The crayons you've been drawing with."

Roxanne made a face and shuffled forward in her bare feet. "You always know."

"And I always will know when my little girl is close." He lifted her up and settled her on his hip.

Luke recognized the kid from the act, though she was dressed for bed now in a long ruffled nightgown. Bright, fiery red hair curled halfway down her back. While Luke sipped his drink, she twined an arm around her father's neck and studied their guest with wide, sea-green eyes.

"He looks mean," Roxanne decided, and her father chuckled and kissed her temple.

"I'm sure you're mistaken."

Roxanne debated, then temporized. "He looks like he could be mean."

"Much more accurate." He set her down and ran a hand over her hair. "Now say a polite hello."

She tilted her head, then inclined it like a little queen granting audience. "Hello."

"Yeah. Hi." Snotty little brat, Luke thought, then flushed again as his stomach growled.

"I guess you have to feed him," Roxanne said, very much as though Luke were a stray dog found rooting through the garbage. "But I don't know if you should keep him."

Torn between exasperation and amusement, Max gave her bottom a light swat. "Go to bed, old woman."

"One more hour, please, Daddy."

He shook his head and bent to kiss her. *"Bon nuit, bambine."*

Her brows drew together, forming a faint verticle crease between them. "When I grow up, I'll stay up all night when I want."

"I'm sure you will, more than once. Until then . . ." He pointed toward the curtain.

Roxanne's bottom lip poked out, but she obeyed. She parted the silk, then shot a look back over her shoulder. "I love you anyway."

"And I you." Max felt that old, always deep warmth flutter into him. His child. The one thing he had made without tricks or illusions. "She's growing up," Max said to himself.

"Shit." Luke snorted into his Pepsi. "She's just a kid."

"So it seems, I'm sure, to one of your vast years and experience." The sarcasm was so pleasant, Luke missed it.

"Kids're a pain in the butt."

"In the heart, quite often," Max corrected, sitting again. "But I've never found one that gave me any discomfort in another part of the anatomy."

"They cost money, don't they?" A trickle of old anger worked its way into the words. "And they get in the way all the time. People have them mostly because they get too hot to think about the consequences when they screw around."

Max stroked a finger over his moustache as he picked up his brandy. "An interesting philosophy. One we'll have to discuss in depth sometime. But for tonight . . . Ah, your meal."

Confused, Luke looked at the door. It was still closed. He heard nothing. Only seconds later there was the scrape of feet and the single quick rap. Mouse entered carrying a brown bag already spotted with grease. The smell had saliva pooling in Luke's mouth.

"Thank you, Mouse." Out of the corner of his eye, Max noted Luke restraining himself from snatching the bag.

"You want me to hang around?" Mouse asked and set the food on the small round table that fronted the sofa.

"Not necessary. I'm sure you're tired."

" 'Kay. Good night then."

"Good night. Please," Max continued as Mouse closed the door behind him. "Help yourself."

Luke shot a hand into the bag and pulled out a burger. Striving for nonchalance, he took the first bite slowly, then, before he could stop himself, he bolted the rest. Max settled back, swirling brandy, his eyes half closed.

The boy ate like a young wolf, Max thought as Luke plowed his way through the second burger and a pile of fries. Starved, Max imagined, for a great many things. He knew perfectly well what it was to starve—for a great many things. Because he trusted his instincts, and what he believed he saw behind the sly defiance in the boy's eyes, he would offer a chance for a feast.

"I occasionally do a mentalist act," Max said quietly. "You may not be aware of that."

Because his mouth was full, Luke only managed to grunt.

"I thought not. A demonstration then, if you will. You've left home and have been traveling for some time now."

Luke swallowed, belched. "Got that one wrong. My folks have a farm a couple miles from here. I just came for the rides."

Max opened his eyes. There was power in them and something that made the power more acute. Simple kindness. "Don't lie to me. To others if you must, but not to me. You've run away." He moved so quickly, Luke had no chance to avoid the hand that clamped like steel over his wrist. "Tell me this, have you left behind a mother, a father, an aged grandparent with a broken heart?"

"I told you . . ." The clever lies, the ones that he'd learned to tell so easily, withered on his tongue. It was the eyes, he thought on a flutter of panic. Just like the eyes in the poster, which seemed to look into him and see everything. "I don't know who my father is." He spat it out as his body began to vibrate with shame and fury. "I don't figure she knows either. She sure as hell don't care. Maybe she's sorry I'm gone 'cause there's no one around to fetch her a bottle, or steal one for her if she ain't got the money. And maybe that bastard she's living with is sorry because he doesn't have anybody to knock around anymore." Tears he wasn't even aware of burned in his eyes. But he was aware of the panic that had leaped like a dragon to claw at his throat. "I won't go back. I swear to God I'll kill you before you make me go back to that."

Max gentled his hand on Luke's wrist. He felt that pain, so much like his own at that age. "The man beat you."

"When he could catch me." There was defiance even in that. The tears shimmered briefly, then dried up.

"The authorities."

Luke curled his lip. "Shit."

"Yes." Max indulged in a sigh. "You have no one?"

The chin with its faint cleft firmed. "I got myself."

An excellent answer, Max reflected. "And your plans?"

"I'm heading south, Miami."

"Mmmm." Max took Luke's other wrist and turned his hands up. When he felt the boy tense, he showed his first sign of impatience. "I'm not interested in men sexually," he snapped. "And if I were, I wouldn't lower myself to pawing a boy." Luke lifted his eyes, and Max saw something there, something no twelve-year-old should know existed. "Did this man abuse you in other ways?"

Luke shook his head quickly, too humiliated to speak.

But someone had, Max concluded. Or someone had tried. That would wait, until there was trust. "You have good hands, quick agile fingers. Your timing is also quite keen for one so young I could make use of those qualities, perhaps help you refine them, if you choose to work for me."

"Work?" Luke didn't quite recognize the emotion working through him. A child's memory is often short, and it had already been a long time since he'd known hope. "What kind of work?"

"This and that." Max sat back again, smiled. "You might like to learn a few tricks, young Luke. It happens we'll be heading south in another few weeks. You can work off your room and board, and earn a small salary if you deserve it. I'd have to ask that you refrain from lifting wallets for a time, of course. But I doubt if anything else I'd ask would cramp your style."

His chest hurt. It wasn't until he'd let out a breath that he realized he'd been holding it until his lungs burned. "I'd, like, be in the magic show?"

Max smiled again. "You would not. You would, however, assist in the setting up and breaking down. And you would learn, if you have any affinity for such things. Eventually, you may learn enough."

There had to be a catch. There was always a catch. Luke circled around the offer as a man might circle a sleeping snake. "I guess I could think about it."

"That's always wise." Max rose, setting his empty snifter aside. "Why don't you sleep here? We'll see where we stand in the morning. I'll get you some linens," Max offered, and walked out without waiting for a response.

Maybe it was a scam, Luke thought, gnawing on his knuckles. But he couldn't see the trap, not yet. And it would be good, so good, to sleep inside for once, with a full stomach. He stretched out, telling himself he was just testing his ground. But his eyelids drooped. The candlelight played hypnotically over them.

Because his back still troubled him, he shifted to his side. Before he let his eyes close again, he judged the distance to the door in case he had to get out quickly.

He could always take off in the morning, he told himself. No one could make him stay. No one could make him do anything anymore.

That was his last thought as he tumbled into sleep. He didn't hear Max come back with a clean sheet and the pillow. He didn't feel the slight tug as his shoes were removed, and placed beside the sofa. He didn't even murmur or shift as his head was lifted and laid, quite gently, on the linen-cased pillow that smelled faintly of lilacs.

"I know where you've been," Max murmured. "I wonder where you'll go."

For another moment he studied the sleeping boy, noting the strong facial bones, the hand that was clutched in a defensive fist, the deep rise and fall of the frail chest that spoke of utter exhaustion.

He left Luke to sleep and went to Lily's soft, waiting arms.

2

Luke awoke in stages. He heard the birds chattering outside first, then felt the sun warm on his face. In his mind he imagined it to be gold and liquid with a taste like sweet honey. He caught the scent of coffee next and wondered where he was.

Then he opened his eyes, saw the girl and remembered.

She was standing between the round table and the sofa where he was sprawled, her lips pursed, her head tilted as she stared at him. Her eyes were bright and curious—a not entirely friendly curiosity.

He noted there was a faint dusting of freckles over the bridge of her nose that he hadn't seen when she'd been onstage or in the candleglow.

As wary as she, Luke stared back, slowly running his tongue over his teeth. His toothbrush was in the denim knapsack he'd stolen from a K Mart and hidden in some bushes nearby. He was fastidious about brushing his teeth, a habit which grew directly out of his paralyzing fear of the dentist. Particularly the one his mother had dragged him to nearly three years before. The one with breath fouled by gin and knuckles covered with coarse black hair.

He wanted to brush his teeth, to gulp down some of that hot coffee and to be alone.

"What the hell are you looking at?"

"You." She'd been thinking about poking him and was a little disappointed that he'd awakened before she'd had the chance. "You're skinny. Lily said you have a beautiful face, but it just looks mean to me."

He felt a wave of disgust, and of confusion at being called beautiful by the curvy Lily. Luke had no such twisted feelings about Roxanne. She was what his stepfather called a class A bitch. Of course, Luke couldn't remember any woman Al Cobb hadn't considered one kind of bitch or another.

"You're skinny *and* ugly. Now, beat it."

"I live here," she pointed out grandly. "And if I don't like you I can make my daddy send you away."

"Big freaking deal."

"That's bad language." She gave a prim, ladylike sniff. At least she thought it was.

"No." Maybe if he shocked her angelic ears, she'd take off. "Big fucking deal is bad language."

"It is?" Interested now, she leaned closer. "What does fucking mean?"

"Christ." He rubbed the heels of his hands over his eyes as he sat up. "Get out of my face, will you?"

"*I* know how to be polite." And if she was, Roxanne thought she might get him to tell her what the new word meant. "Because I'm the hostess, I'll get you a cup of coffee. I already made it."

"You?" It bothered him that he hadn't heard her rattling around.

"It's my job." She strutted importantly to the stove. "Because Daddy and Lily sleep late in the mornings, and I don't like to. I hardly ever need any sleep. I didn't even when I was a baby. It's metabolism," she told him, pleased with the word her father had taught her.

"Yeah. Right." He watched her pour the coffee into a china cup. Probably tasted like mud, Luke thought, and looked forward to telling her so.

"Cream and sugar?" She chanted the words, like a peppy flight attendant.

"Lots of both."

She took him at his word, then, with her tongue caught between her teeth, brought the brimming cup to the table. "You can have orange juice, too, with breakfast." Though she didn't particularly like him, Roxanne enjoyed the idea of playing the gracious hostess, and imagined herself wearing one of Lily's long silk gowns and teetering on high heels. "I'll make my special one."

"Great." Luke braced to wince at the taste of the coffee and was surprised when it went down smoothly. It was a bit sweet, even for his taste, but he'd never had better. "It's pretty good," he muttered, and Roxanne granted him a quick smile that was innately female.

"I have a magic touch with coffee. Everyone says so." Enthusiastic now, she popped slices of bread into the toaster, then opened the fridge. "How come you don't live with your mother and father?"

"Because I don't want to."

"But you have to," she pointed out. "Even if you don't want to."

"The hell I do. Besides I don't have a father."

"Oh." She pressed her lips together. Though she was only eight, she knew such things happened. She herself had lost a mother, one she had no memory of. Since Lily had slid so seamlessly into the gap, it wasn't a loss that jarred her. But the idea of being without a father always made her sad—and scared. "Did he get sick, or have a terrible accident?"

"I don't know or give a good damn. Drop it."

Under any other circumstances, the sharp tone would have loosened her temper. Instead, it sparked her sympathies. "What part of the show did you like best?"

"I don't know. The card tricks were pretty cool."

"I know one. I can show you." Carefully, she poured juice into crystal glasses. "After breakfast I will. You can use the bathroom back there to wash your hands 'cause it's almost ready."

He was a lot more interested in emptying his straining bladder and, following the direction of her hand, found the closet-sized bathroom behind the red curtain. It smelled of woman—not the heavy, cloying scent that often trailed around his mother, but sweet, luxurious femininity.

There were stockings draped over the rung of the narrow shower stall, and a floral box of dusting powder and a big pink puff sat on a crocheted doily on the back of the toilet. In the corner was a small wedge of counter space that was crowded from edge to edge with bottles and pots and tubes.

Whore's tools, Cobb would have called them, but Luke thought they looked kind of nice and pretty jumbled there, like a garden he'd seen on his travels, where flowers and weeds had run wild together.

Despite the clutter, the room was scrupulously clean. A far cry, he realized as he scrubbed hot water over his face, from the filthy bathroom in the filthy apartment he'd escaped from.

Unable to resist, he peeked into the medicine cabinet. There were men things in there. A razor, shaving cream, after-shave. There was also a spare toothbrush still in its box. The terror of cavities overpowered any sense of guilt he might have had as he made use of it.

It wasn't until he was back in the hall, wondering if he could take a chance and poke around a bit that he remembered his shoes.

He was back in the living area like a shot, diving under the table and checking his stash.

As calm as a queen on her throne, Roxanne sat on a satin pillow and sipped her juice. "How come you keep your money in your shoe when you've got pockets?"

"Because it's safer there." And it had been, he noted with relief. Every last dollar. He slid up into his seat and looked at his plate. There was a piece of toast in the center of it. It had been mounded with chunky peanut butter, drizzled with what looked like honey, sprinkled with cinnamon and sugar, then cut into two neat triangles.

"It's very good," Roxanne assured him, taking dainty bites of her own.

Luke bit a triangle in two, and was forced to agree. She smiled again when he'd finished the last crumb.

"I'll make more."

An hour later, when Max pushed through the curtain, he saw them sitting hip to hip on the sofa. His little girl had a short pile of bills at her elbow and was expertly shifting three cards over the table.

"Okay, where's the queen?"

Luke blew the hair out of his eyes, hesitated, then tapped the center card. "I know it's there this time, damn it."

Smug, Roxanne flipped over the card, then giggled when he swore again.

"Roxy," Max said as he crossed to them. "It's quite rude to fleece a guest."

"I told him Three Card Monte was a sucker's game, Daddy." All innocence, she beamed up at her father. "He didn't listen."

He chuckled and clucked her on the chin. "My little swindler. How did you sleep, Luke?"

"Okay." He'd lost five bucks to the little cheat. It was mortifying.

"And I see you've eaten. If you've decided to stay, I'll give you over to Mouse shortly. He'll put you to work."

"That'd be good." But he knew better than to sound anxious. When you sounded anxious, that was when they pulled the rug out from under you. "For a couple days, anyhow."

"Splendid. A free lesson before we begin." He paused to pour coffee, sniff appreciatively then sip. "Never bet on the house game unless losing is to your advantage. Will you need clothes?"

Though he couldn't see how losing could ever be an advantage, Luke didn't comment. "I've got some stuff."

"All right then, you can go retrieve it. Then we'll get started."

One of the advantages of being a boy like Luke was that he had no expectations. Another might have anticipated touches of glamour, or adventure, perhaps a bit of jolly camaraderie of carny life. But in Luke's philosophy, people generally got less than they paid for of the good things, and more than they could handle of the bad.

So when he was put to work by the taciturn Mouse lifting, hauling, cleaning, painting and fetching, he followed orders without complaint or conversation. Since Mouse had little to say for himself, Luke was able to keep his own counsel and observe.

Life in a carnival wasn't glamorous, he noted. It was sweaty, and dirty. The air snapped with the scents of frying food, cheap cologne and unwashed bodies. Colors that looked so bright at night were dingy in the light of day. And the rides that seemed so fast and fearsome under a starry sky appeared tired, and more than a little unsafe under a hard summer sun.

As for adventure, there was nothing exciting about scrubbing down the long black trailer, or helping Mouse change the spark plugs in the Chevy pickup that hauled it.

Mouse had head and shoulders under the hood, and his tiny eyes were slitted nearly closed as he listened to the idling engine. Occasionally he would hum a little tune, or grunt and make a few more adjustments.

Luke shifted from foot to foot. The heat was terrible. Sweat was beginning to seep through the faded bandanna he'd tied around his head. He didn't know a damn thing about cars, and didn't see why he needed to when he wouldn't be able to drive one for years and years. The way Mouse was humming and fiddling was getting on his nerves.

"It sounds okay to me."

Mouse blinked his eyes open. There was grease on his hands, streaked on his moon pie face, smeared on his baggy white T-shirt. He was quite simply in Mouse heaven.

"Missing," he corrected, then closed his eyes again. He made minute adjustments, as gently as a man in love would initiate a virgin. The engine purred for him. "Sweet baby," he said under his breath.

There was nothing in Mouse's world more fascinating, or seductive, than a well-oiled machine.

"Jesus, it's just a stupid truck."

Mouse opened his eyes again, and there was a smile in them. He was barely twenty, and because of his size and plodding manner, had been considered a freak by the other children in the state home where he'd grown up. He neither trusted nor liked a great many people, but he'd already developed a tolerant affection for Luke.

There was something about his smile—it was slow and pure as a baby's—that made Luke grin back. "You done yet or what?"

"Done." To prove it Mouse closed the hood, then rounded it to take the keys from the ignition and pocket them. He'd never forgotten the surge of pride he'd felt when Max had trusted him with the keys for the first time. "She'll run fine tonight when we head to Manchester."

"How long are we there?"

"Three days." Mouse took a pack of Pall Malls from his rolled sleeve, shook the pack and nipped one out with his teeth before offering the pack to Luke. Luke accepted it as casually as possible. "Hard work tonight. Loading up."

Luke let the cigarette dangle from the corner of his mouth and waited for Mouse to light a match. "How come somebody like Mr. Nouvelle's in a cheap carny like this?"

The match flared as Mouse touched it to the end of his cigarette. "Got his reasons."

He held the match to the tip of Luke's, then leaned back on the truck and began to daydream about the long, quiet drive.

Luke took an experimental puff, choked back a hacking cough and made the mistake of inhaling. He coughed hard enough to make his eyes water, but when Mouse glanced his way, he struggled for dignity.

"Not my usual brand." His voice was a thin squeak before he took another determined drag. This time he swallowed the smoke, gagged and fought a sweaty battle to keep from losing his lunch. It felt as though his eyes were rolling back in his head to meet his rising stomach.

"Hey. Hey, kid." Concern at the green tinge of Luke's skin had Mouse slapping a fist to his back hard enough to take Luke to his knees. When he vomited weakly, Mouse patted his head with a greasy hand. "Holy cow. You sick or something?"

"Do we have a problem here?" Max crossed to them. Lily broke from his side to crouch beside Luke.

"Oh, honey. You poor thing," she crooned, rubbing a hand up and down Luke's back. "Just stay down there, sweetie, till it passes." She spotted the smoldering cigarette that had dropped from Luke's hand and clucked her tongue. "What in the world was this child doing with one of those awful things?"

"My fault." Mouse stared miserably at his own feet. "I wasn't thinking when I gave him a cigarette, Max. It's my fault."

"He didn't have to take it." Max shook his head as Luke braced himself on his hands and knees and struggled with the nausea. "And he's certainly paying for it. Another free lesson. Don't take what you can't hold."

"Oh, leave the child be." Her mothering instinct on overdrive, Lily pressed Luke's clammy face to her breast, where he breathed in a heady mixture of Chanel and sweat. Holding Luke close, Lily glared at Max. "Just because you've never been sick a day in your life is no reason to be unsympathetic."

"Quite right," Max agreed and hid a smile. "Mouse and I will leave him to your tender care."

"We'll fix you up," she murmured to Luke. "You just come with Lily, honey. Come on now, lean on me."

"I'm okay." But as he dragged himself to his feet, his head spun in counterpoint to his roiling stomach. The sickness spread its slippery fingers through him so expertly, he had no room for embarrassment as Lily half carried him back to the trailer.

"Don't you worry about a thing, baby doll. You just need to lie down awhile, that's all."

"Yes, ma'am." He wanted to lie down. It would be easier to die that way.

"Now, you don't have to ma'am me, honey. You call me Lily just like everybody." She had him tucked under one arm as she opened the trailer door. "You lie right on down on the sofa and I'll get you a nice, cold cloth."

Groaning, he collapsed facedown and began to pray with a fervor he'd just discovered that he wouldn't throw up again.

"Here you go, baby." Armed with a damp cloth and a basin—just in case—Lily knelt beside him. After slipping the sweaty bandanna from his head, she laid the cloth over his brow. "You'll feel better soon, I promise. I had a brother who got sick the first time he smoked." She spoke quietly, in that soothing sick-room voice some women assume so naturally. "But he got over it in no time."

The best Luke could manage was a moan. Lily continued to talk as she turned the cloth over and stroked his face and neck with it. "You just rest." Her lips curved as she felt him drifting off. "That's the way, honey pie. You sleep it out."

Indulging herself, she brushed her fingers through his hair. It was long and thick, and smooth as silk. If she and Max had been able to make a child together, he might have had hair like that, she thought, wistful. But as fertile as her heart was to love a brood of children, her womb was sterile.

The boy did have a beautiful face, she mused. His skin gold from the sun and smooth as a girl's. Good strong bones beneath it. And those lashes. She let out another sigh. Still, as appealing as the boy was, and as much as her soul ached to fill her life with children, she wasn't certain Max had done the right thing by taking him in.

He wasn't an orphan like Mouse. The child had a mother, after all. As hard as her own life had been, Lily found it next to impossible to believe that a mother wouldn't do all in her power to protect, to shelter, to love her child.

"I bet she's frantic for you, baby doll," Lily murmured. She clucked her tongue. "You're hardly more than skin and bones. And look here, you've sweated right through this shirt. All right then, we'll slip you out of it and get it washed up for you."

Gently, she tugged it up his back. Her fingers froze on the damp cloth. Her quick, involuntary cry had him moaning in his sleep. As tears of grief and rage sprang hot to her eyes, she slid the shirt back down.

Max stood in front of the mirror he'd set on stage and rehearsed his sleight-of-hand routine. He watched as the audience would watch as coins slipped in and out of his fingers. Max had performed his version of the Sympathetic Coins countless times, enhancing it, refining it as he did with every trick and illusion he'd learned or invented since he'd first stood on the corner of Bourbon and St. Louis in New Orleans, with his folding table, his cardboard box salted with coins, and the Cups and Balls.

He didn't often think of those early days now, not now that he was a successful man, past forty. But the bitter, desperate child he had been could sneak back to haunt him. As it had now, in the guise of Luke Callahan.

The boy had potential, Max mused as he split a gold coin into two, then three.

With a little time, care and direction, Luke would make something of himself. What that something might be, Max left up to the gods. If the boy was still with them when they reached New Orleans, they would see.

Max lifted his hands, clapped them together, and all coins save the one he'd started with vanished.

"Nothing up my sleeve," he murmured and wondered why it was that people always believed it.

"Max!" A little out of breath from her dash across the fairgrounds, Lily hurried toward the stage.

For Max it was, always was, a pleasure to watch her. Lily in snug shorts, snug T-shirt, with her painted toes peeking out of dusty sandals was a sight to behold. But when he caught her hand to help her onto the stage and saw her face, his smile faded.

"What's happened? Roxanne?"

"No, no." Shaken, she threw her arms around him and held tight. "Roxy's fine. She talked one of the roustabouts into giving her a ride on the carousel. But that boy, Max, that poor little boy."

He laughed then and gave her a quick, affectionate hug. "Lily, my love, he'll be queasy for a while, and perfectly miserable with embarrassment for a great deal longer, but it'll pass."

"No, it's not that." Tears already rolling, she pressed her face into his neck. "I had him lie down on the sofa, and when he fell asleep I was going to take off his shirt. It was all sweaty, and I wanted him to be comfortable." She paused and took a deep, steadying breath. "His back, Max, his poor little back. The scars, old scars and new welts that have barely healed. From a strap, or a belt, or God knows." She rubbed tears away with the heels of her hands. "Someone must have beaten that boy horribly."

"His stepfather." Max's voice was flat. The emotions pumping through him required the most finite control. Memories, however vicious, he could battle back. But the rage for the boy all but defeated him. "I'm afraid I didn't believe it was that serious. Do you think he should see a doctor?"

"No." With her lips pressed tight, she shook her head. "It's mostly scars, awful scars. I don't understand how anyone could do that to a child." She sniffled, accepted the handkerchief Max offered. "I wasn't sure you'd done the right thing by taking him in. I thought his mother must be desperate for news of him." Her soft eyes hardened like glass. "His mother," she spat out. "I'd like to get my hands on that bitch. Even if she didn't use the strap herself, she allowed this to happen to her own little boy. Well, she ought to be beaten. I'd do it myself if I had the chance."

"So fierce." Gently Max cupped her face in his hands and kissed her. "By God, I love you, Lily. For so many reasons. Now go fix your face, make yourself a nice cup of tea so you'll be calm. No one will hurt the boy again."

"No, no one will hurt him again." She curled her fingers around Max's wrists. Her eyes were hot with passion now, and her voice amazingly steady. "He's ours now."

Most of Luke's nausea faded, but his embarrassment peaked as he awakened to find Lily sitting beside him, drinking tea. He tried to make some excuse, but she spoke cheerfully over his stammerings and made him a bowl of soup.

She continued to talk as he ate, bright, sunny conversation that nearly convinced him no one had noticed that he'd disgraced himself.

Then Roxanne burst in.

She was dusty from head to toe, the hair Lily had braided so neatly that morning in wild disarray. There was a fresh scrape on her knee, and a long jagged tear in her shorts. The ripe scent of animal followed her into the trailer. She'd just finished playing with the trio of terriers from the dog show.

Lily gave the grubby girl an indulgent smile. Next to seeing a child eat, Lily loved to see them covered with dirt as evidence that they had played hard and well.

"Is that my Roxy under there?"

Roxanne grinned, then reached into the refrigerator for a cold drink. "I rode on the carousel forever, and Big Jim let me toss the rings as long as I wanted." She glugged down grape Nehi, adding a rakish purple moustache to the dirt. "Then played with the dogs." She turned her gaze on Luke. "Did you really smoke a cigarette and get sick all over?"

Luke bared his teeth, but didn't speak.

"What'd you want to do that for, anyway?" she went on, bright as a magpie. "Kids aren't supposed to smoke."

"Roxy." Her voice a trill of cheer, Lily hopped up and began to nudge the girl toward the curtain. "You have to get cleaned up."

"But I just want to know—"

"Hurry up now. It'll be time for the first show before you know it."

"I only wondered—"

"You wonder too much. Now scoot."

Annoyed with the dismissal, Roxanne shot a look of dislike at Luke, and met one equally unfriendly. Doing what came naturally, she stuck out her tongue before flipping the curtain behind her.

Torn between laughter and sympathy, Lily turned back. "Well now." Luke's anger and humiliation were so clear on his face. "I guess we'd better get busy." She was too wise to ask him if he felt up to the night's work. "Why don't you run over and tell one of the boys to give you some flyers to pass out once people start dribbling in?"

He shrugged his shoulders by way of agreement, then jerked back as Lily's hand shot toward him. He'd expected a blow. She could see that by the dark, fixed look in his eyes. Just as she could see that look turn to blank confusion when what she gave him was a fast, affectionate ruffling of his hair.

No one had ever touched him like that. While he stared up at her, stunned, a knot formed in his throat, making speech of any kind impossible.

"You don't have to be afraid." She said it quietly, as though it were a secret between only them. "I won't hurt you." She slid her hand down to cup his cheek. "Not now. Not ever." She would have liked to have held him then, but judged it too soon. He couldn't know, as she did, that he was her son now. And what belonged to Lily Bates, she protected. "If you need anything," she said briskly, "you come to me. Understand?"

He could do no more than nod as he scrambled to his feet. There was a pressure in his chest, a dryness to his throat. Knowing he was perilously close to tears, he darted outside.

He'd learned three things that day. He supposed Max would call them free lessons, and they were three he would never forget. First, he would never again smoke an unfiltered cigarette. Second, he detested the little snot-nosed Roxanne. And third, most important, he had fallen in love with Lily Bates.

3

Summer heated up as they traveled south. Portland to Manchester, on to Albany, and then Poughkeepsie, where it rained hard for two miserable days. Wilkes-Barre, then west to Allentown, where Roxanne had the time of her life palling around with twin girls named Tessie and Trudie. When they parted two days later, amid tears and solemn vows of eternal friendship, Roxanne had her first taste of the disadvantages of life on the road.

She pouted for a week, driving Luke crazy with praise for her lost friends. He avoided her whenever possible but it was difficult, as they were all but living under the same roof.

He bunked with Mouse under the capped bed of the truck, but a good many of his meals were taken in the trailer. And more than once, he found her waiting to spring out at him when he stepped out of the bathroom.

It wasn't that she liked him. In fact, she had developed the bone-deep disgust that neither yet recognized as natural sibling rivalry. But since her experience with Tessie and Trudie, Roxanne had come to crave companionship of her own age.

Even if he was a boy.

She did what little sisters have been doing to big brothers since time began. She made his life hell.

From Hagerstown to Winchester, from there to Roanoke and on to Winston-Salem, she nagged him unmercifully, dogged his footsteps and pestered relentlessly. If it hadn't been for Lily, Luke might have fought back. But for reasons that eluded him, Lily was crazy about the little brat.

Proof of that affection was obvious during a run-through of the performance in Winston-Salem.

Roxanne's messing up the timing, Luke thought smugly as he watched the rehearsal while loitering in the tent. Skinny twerp couldn't get anything right today. And she was whining.

The poor rehearsal gave him hope. He could do the trick a lot better than she could. If Max would give him the chance. If Max would just teach him a little. Luke had already practiced some of the flourishes and stage moves in front of the tiny bathroom mirror.

All he needed was for prune-faced Rox to get some incurable disease, or have a tragic accident. If she was out of the picture, he could slip right in and take her place.

"Roxanne," Max said patiently, interrupting Luke's thoughts. "You're not paying attention."

"I am too." Her lip poked out; her eyes filled. She hated being cooped up in this hot old tent.

"Max," said Lily, coming up to the stage. "Maybe we should give her a break."

"Lily." Max was struggling to keep his temper.

"I'm tired of rehearsing," Roxanne continued, lifting her flushed, miserable face. "I'm tired of the trailer, and the show and everything. I want to go back to Allentown and see Tessie and Trudie."

"I'm afraid that's impossible." Her words had wounded Max's pride and opened up a hole for guilt to seep into. "If you don't want to perform, that will be your choice. But if I can't depend on you, I'll have to replace you."

"Max!" Appalled, Lily took a step forward, only to freeze in place when Max held up a hand.

"As my daughter," he continued while a single tear trickled down Roxanne's cheek, "you're entitled to as many temper tantrums as you like. But as my employee, you will rehearse when rehearsals are called. Is that understood?"

Roxanne's head dropped. "Yes, Daddy."

"All right then. Now, why don't we take a moment to regroup. Dry your face," he began and tucked a hand under her chin. "I want you to . . ." He trailed off and pressed his palm to her brow. His stomach took a nosedive to his knees and froze there. "She's burning up," he said in an odd voice. "Lily." And the Great Nouvelle, Conjurer Extraordinaire, looked toward his lover helplessly. "She's ill."

"Oh, little lamb." Instantly, Lily was on her knees, checking for fever herself. Roxanne's brow was hot and clammy under her hand. "Baby, does your head hurt? Your stomach?"

Two big tears plopped on the stage floor. "I'm okay. It's just hot in here. I'm not sick, I want to rehearse. Don't let Daddy replace me."

"Oh, that's nonsense." Lily's busy fingers were checking for swollen glands. "No one could replace you." Tucking Roxanne's head on her shoulder, Lily looked up at Max. He was white as a sheet. "I think we should go into town and find a doctor."

Speechless, Luke watched Max carry a weeping Roxanne away. His fondest wish had come true, he realized. The brat was sick. Maybe she even had the plague. Heart thumping, he raced out of the tent and watched the plume of dust as the truck raced off.

She might die before they even got into town. That thought brought on a shiver of panic that was followed hard on the heels by a hideous guilt. She'd looked awfully small when Max had carried her out.

"Where'd they go?" Mouse demanded, puffing a bit as he'd raced over when he'd heard his beloved engine start.

"Doctor." Luke bit down hard on his lip. "Roxanne's sick."

Before Mouse could ask any more questions, Luke dashed away. He hoped if there really was a God He'd believe he hadn't really meant it.

It was two terrifying hours later before the truck returned from town. As it pulled in, Luke started toward it, but his heart stopped when he saw Max take a limp Roxanne from Lily's arms and walk with her toward the trailer.

"Is she . . ." His throat closed on the "D" word.

"Sleeping." Lily gave him a distracted smile. "I'm sorry, Luke, you better run along now. We'll be busy for a while."

"But—but—" He got his feet moving and dogged Lily to the trailer. "Is she, I mean . . ."

"It'll be rough for a few days, but once the crisis passes, she'll do."

"Crisis?" His voice was a croak. Jesus please us, it *was* the plague.

"It's so miserably hot, too," she murmured. "Well, we'll make her as comfortable as we can while it lasts."

"I didn't mean it," Luke blurted out. "I swear I didn't mean to make her sick."

Though her mind was elsewhere, Lily paused at the door. "You didn't, honey. Actually, I suspect Roxy got more from Trudie and Tessie than a vow of endless friendship." She smiled as she stepped inside. "Looks like she got a bonus of the chicken pox."

Luke's mouth dropped open as Lily closed the door in his face.

Chicken pox? He'd practically died of fright, and all the little brat had was the damn chicken pox?

• • •

"I can do it." Luke stood stubbornly in center stage, scowling as Max continued to manipulate the cards. "I can do anything she can do."

"You're far from ready to perform." Max set the cards on the folding table, did a flashy turnover.

It had been three days since Roxanne had been put to bed, hot, itchy and miserable. And at every opportunity during that time span, Luke had been singing the same tune.

"You just have to show me what to do." He'd badgered Mouse to teach him the oversized-hat trick, and had run headlong into a wall of insurmountable loyalty. "I heard you tell Lily that there's a hole in the act with Roxanne sick. And she won't be able to be in the show for at least ten more days."

Toying with the idea of adding a bit of close-up conjuring to offset Roxanne's absence, Max began to set up a variation of Aces High. "Your concern for her health is touching, Luke."

His color rose as he jammed his hands in his pockets. "I didn't make her sick." He was almost sure of that now. "And it's just the chicken pox."

Dissatisfied with the sleight of hand, Max set the cards aside. The boy had a sturdy mind, Max mused, and could be trusted with something as basic as the oversized hat.

"Come here." Luke took a step forward; when his gaze clashed with Max's, something in the man's eyes made Luke suppress a shudder. "Swear," Max said, his voice deep and commanding in the dusty tent. "Swear by all you are and all you will be that you will never reveal any of the secrets of the art that are shown to you."

Luke wanted to grin, to remind Max that it was only a trick after all. But he couldn't. There was something here bigger than he could imagine. When he could speak, his voice was a whisper. "I swear."

Max took another moment to study Luke's face, then nodded. "Very well. This is what I want you to do."

It was so simple really. When Luke discovered how remarkably simple it all was he was amazed that he, or anyone else, could have been duped. He hated to admit it to himself, and refused to admit it to Max, but now that he knew how Roxanne had become the rabbit, how she had disappeared from under the cape, he was a little sorry.

Max gave him no time to grieve over the loss of innocence. They worked, repeating the sequence for more than an hour. Perfecting the timing, choreographing each move, removing bits of business that had suited Roxanne and replacing them with some that fit Luke.

It was tiring work, unbelievably monotonous, but Max refused to accept anything less than perfection.

"How come you go through all this for a bunch of hicks? For a lousy buck they'd be satisfied with a couple of card tricks and a rabbit in a hat."

"I wouldn't. Perform for yourself first, and you will always do your best work."

"But you, with the stuff you can do, you don't have to be in a two-bit carnival."

Max's lips curved under his finger as he smoothed his moustache. "Your compliment, however ill phrased, is appreciated. It's a mistake to believe anyone has to be anywhere they don't choose to be. I find a certain pleasure in the gypsy's life. And, as you are obviously unaware, I own this two-bit carnival."

He swung his cape over Luke, snapped his fingers twice, then chuckled when the shape under the black material stayed in place. "A good magician's assistant never misses a cue, however distracted he might be."

There was a quick huff of breath from under the cape, and the shape dissolved. Far from displeased with Luke's progress, Max thought the boy would do. He would use Luke's cockiness, his hunger and defiance, along with that underlying vulnerability. He would use all that Luke was, and in turn he would give the boy a home, and a chance to choose.

A fair bargain, Max considered. "Again," he said simply as Luke stepped onto the stage from the wings.

After another hour, Luke wondered why he'd wanted to be a part of the act in the first place. When Lily walked into the tent he was on the verge of telling Max exactly what he could do with his magic wand.

"I know I'm late," she began as she hurried forward. "Everything's running behind today."

"Roxanne?"

"Hot and cranky, but bearing up." Worry creased Lily's brow as she looked over her shoulder. "I hate leaving her alone. Everyone's tied up right now, so I . . . Luke." Instantly Lily's brow cleared. "Honey, you'd be doing me such a huge favor if you'd go sit with her for an hour or so."

"Me?" She might as well have asked him to eat toads.

"She could really use the company. It takes her mind off the itching."

"Well, yeah, but . . ." Inspiration hit. "I'd like to, but Max needs me to rehearse."

"Rehearse?"

No mentalist could have read Luke's mind more clearly. Max smiled, setting a friendly hand on the boy's shoulder. Progress, he thought briefly. Luke had tensed at the touch only for a moment. "Meet the newest member of our happy crew," he said to Lily. "Luke's going to fill in tonight."

"Tonight?" Alerted, Luke swung about so he faced Max. "Just tonight? I haven't been sweating through all this practice for one night."

"That remains to be seen. If you do well tonight, there'll be tomorrow night. It's what we call a probationary period. In any case, we've rehearsed enough for the moment, so you're quite free to entertain Roxanne." There was a twinkle in his eye as he leaned toward the boy. "You gambled against the house again, Luke. You lose."

"I don't know what the hell I'm supposed to do with her," Luke muttered as he clumped offstage. Lily sighed at his language.

"Play a game with her," she suggested. "And, honey, I really wish you wouldn't swear around Roxy."

Fine, he thought and continued out of the shadowy tent into the white flash of sunlight. He wouldn't swear around her. He'd swear at her.

He tugged open the trailer door and headed straight for the refrigerator. The impulse to check over his shoulder as he reached for a cold drink was still strong. Luke always expected someone to leap out and smack him for taking food.

No one did. But he was still faintly embarrassed by his actions during the first week with Max. He'd come into the trailer alone and found a big bowl of leftover spaghetti. He'd wolfed it down cold, stuffing himself, the memory of so many hungry days clawing at him.

He'd waited to be punished. Waited to be told he could have nothing more for a day, or even two. As his mother had done to him so many times. Preparing for it, he'd secreted candy bars and sandwiches into his knapsack.

But he hadn't been punished. No one had mentioned it.

Not one to press his luck, Luke wrapped a piece of bread around some lunch meat and gulped down the makeshift sandwich before going back to Roxanne.

He moved quietly, another habit he'd developed out of necessity. As he started down the narrow hallway, he could hear Jim Croce's sly ballad of Leroy Brown. Roxanne sang along with the radio, adding a warbling soprano.

Amused, Luke peeked in the doorway. She was lying flat on her back, staring up at the ceiling as the radio played beside her. A small round table beside the bed held a pitcher of juice and a glass along with some bottles of medication and a deck of cards.

Someone had tacked posters to the walls. Most were magic-related, but the glossy one of David Cassidy made Luke want to puke. It only proved girls were hopeless.

"Man, that's gross."

Roxanne shifted her eyes and spotted him. She nearly smiled, that desperate was she for diversion. "What's gross?"

"That." He gestured toward the poster with his Coke. "Hanging that pussy teeny-bopper star on your wall."

Satisfied with the jibe, Luke gulped down Coke as he studied her. Her white skin was blotchy, spotted with ugly red sores. They were all over her face, too, which Luke thought was *really* gross. He wondered how Lily and Max could stand to look at her.

"Boy oh boy, you got that shit all over, don't you? Makes you look like something out of 'Creature Feature.' "

"Lily says they'll go away soon and I'll be beautiful."

"They'll *probably* go away," he said, tingeing his voice with enough doubt to make Roxanne's brow crease with worry. "But you'll still be ugly."

She forgot all about the horrible itching on her stomach and pushed herself to a sitting position. "I hope I give you the chicken pox. I hope you get spots all over—even on your weenie."

Luke choked on his drink, then grinned. "Tough break. I had them already. Chicken pox is for babies."

"I'm not a baby." Nothing could have infuriated her more. Before Luke could dodge, she leaped up and launched herself at him, fists hammering. His Coke bottle flew, hitting the wall and spraying Coke everywhere. It would have been funny, in fact he let out one bray of laughter before it struck him how frail she was. Her arms were like little burning sticks.

"Okay, okay." Because he figured he'd had one close call with wishing her dead, he didn't want to take a chance on giving her some kind of seizure. "You're not a baby. Now get back into bed."

"I'm tired of bed." But she stumbled back into it, prompted by his not so gentle shove.

"Well, tough. Shit, look at this mess. I guess I have to clean it up."

"Your fault," she said and, prim-mouthed, looked determinedly out of the window, an old woman's pose in a child's body. Grumbling all the way, Luke went off to find a rag.

After he'd mopped up the spill she continued to ignore him. As strategies went, it was inspired.

He shifted from foot to foot. "Look, I took it back, didn't I?"

Her face turned a fraction in his direction, but the ice didn't thaw. "Are you sorry you said I was ugly?"

"I guess I could be."

Silence.

"Okay, okay. Jeez. I'm sorry I said you were ugly."

The faintest hint of a smile. "And you're sorry you said David Cassidy was gross."

Now he grinned. "No way."

Her lips curved in response. "I guess that's okay, since you're just a boy." The small taste of power had been pleasant. Hoping to milk it, Roxanne widened the smile. Even at eight, there was power in it. She was, after all, her father's daughter. "Would you pour me some juice?"

"I guess."

He poured some from pitcher to glass and handed it to her.

"You don't talk very much," she said after a bit.

"You talk too much."

"I have lots to say. Everyone says I'm very bright." She was also horribly bored. "We could play a game, if you'd like."

"I'm too old for games."

"No, you're not. Daddy says no one ever is. That's why people get suckered into Three Card Monte or the Cups and Balls on street corners and lose their money." She caught the brief flicker of interest on his face and pounced. "If you play Go Fish with me, I'll teach you a card trick."

Luke hadn't survived to the age of twelve without knowing how to bargain. "Teach me the card trick, and then I'll play."

"Nuh-uh." Her smile was smug, a younger, only slightly more innocent version of a woman's who knew she'd trapped her man. "I'll *show* you the trick, then we'll play. Then I'll teach you how to do it."

She picked up her rubber-band-bound deck from the table, riffled it with considerable skill. Caught, Luke sat on the edge of the bed and watched her hands.

"Now this is called Lost and Found. You pick any card you see, and name the card out loud."

"Big-deal trick if I'm telling you the card," Luke muttered. But when she riffled the deck again, he chose the king of spades.

"Oh, you can't have that card," Roxanne told him.

"Why the hell not? You said any card I saw."

"But you couldn't see the king of spades. It's not there." Smiling, she flipped the cards again, and Luke's mouth fell open. Damn it, he'd just seen that king. How had she gotten rid of it?

"You palmed it."

Her grin was wide and pleased. "Nothing up my sleeve," she said and, setting the pack down on her lap, held up both hands to show them empty. "You can pick another one."

This time, eyes sharp, Luke picked the three of clubs. With a showy sigh, Roxanne shook her head.

"You keep picking missing cards." A slow flip, and Luke saw that not only was the three missing, but the king was back. Frustrated, he made a grab for the pack, but Roxanne swung them up over her head.

"I don't believe it's a regular deck."

"Not believing is what makes magic magic." Roxanne quoted her father with great seriousness. She gave the pack a sharp riffle, then spread it faceup on the sheets. A wave of her hand to point out both cards Luke had chosen were among the fifty-two.

He huffed out a breath, defeated. "Okay, how'd you do it?"

Grinning again, she executed a nearly successful turnover. "First, Go Fish."

He would have told her to go to hell. But more than the satisfaction of telling her off he wanted to know how the trick was done.

After two games of fish, he unbent enough to get them both a snack of cold drinks and cookies.

"I'll show you now," Roxanne offered, pleased that he hadn't nagged. "But you have to swear never to tell the secret."

"I already took the oath."

Her eyes narrowed. "When? How come?"

He could have bitten off his tongue. "At rehearsal, a little while ago," he said reluctantly. "I'm filling in until you're not full of spots."

Her lip poked out. Slowly, she picked up the cards and began to shuffle them. It always helped her to think if she did something with her hands. "You're taking my place."

"Max said there was a hole in the act without you. I'm filling it." Then with a diplomacy he hadn't been aware of possessing, he added, "Temporarily. That's what Max said. Maybe just tonight."

After another moment of consideration, she nodded. "If Daddy said so, it's okay. He said he was sorry about telling me he'd replace me. That nobody ever would."

Luke had no idea what it would be like to be loved that way or to have that much trust. Envy was a fist punching his heart.

"Here's what you have to do," Roxanne began, drawing his attention back to her. "First you have to set the cards up in a riffle pack." She dealt out two heaps and began to teach him with all the patience of a first-grade teacher instructing a student on how to print his name.

She ran through the trick twice, step by step, then handed him the pack. "You try."

As Max had said, the boy had good hands.

"This is cool," he murmured.

"Magic's the coolest."

When she smiled, he smiled back. For a moment, at least, they were simply two children with a good secret between them.

4

Stage fright was a new and humbling experience for Luke. He was set, cocky, even eager as he waited in the wings. His secondhand tuxedo, hastily altered by Mama Franconi's nimble fingers, made him feel like a star. Over and over in his head he ran through the blocking, his moves, his patter while Max warmed up the crowd with some sleight of hand.

There was nothing to it, he thought. It would be a grade A cinch that would earn him an extra ten bucks a night as long as Roxanne remained covered with those little red welts. If the doctor's prognosis ran true, that would mean a hundred dollars for Luke's Miami fund.

He was congratulating himself on his good fortune and sneering at the pop-eyed group of rubes in the front row when Mouse tapped him on the shoulder.

"Cue's coming up."

"Huh?"

"Your cue." Mouse jerked his head toward the stage where Lily was flouncing in her spangled tights, adding a little hip motion for the men in the audience.

"My cue," Luke said as his bowels turned to ice water and his heart became a hot little ball in his throat.

Having been prepared for this possibility by Max, Mouse gave a grunt of assent and shoved Luke onstage.

There was a titter of laughter as the thin boy in the baggy tux stumbled on. In contrast to his shiny black lapels, Luke's face was sheet white. He missed his mark, and his first line. The best he could manage as his back ran with what any pro could have told him was flop sweat was to stand rock still while his eyes darted wildly over the grinning faces of his first audience.

"Ah." Smooth as the silk he'd caused to appear and vanish. Max strode to him. "My young friend seems to be lost." To the audience it appeared that Max stroked a friendly hand over Luke's hair. They didn't see the agile fingers pinch hard at the back of the boy's neck to shock him out of opening-night jitters.

Luke jerked, blinked and swallowed. "I, ah . . ." Shit, what was he supposed to say? "Lost my hat," he finished in a rush, then went from white to red as the chuckles bounced toward the stage. The hell with them, he told himself and straightened his shoulders. In that moment, he was transformed from a frightened little boy to an arrogant young man. "I got a date with Lily. Can't take a beautiful woman dancing without my hat."

"A date with Lily?" As rehearsed, Max looked surprised, then annoyed, then sly. "I'm afraid you must be mistaken, the lovely Lily is engaged for the evening with me."

"Guess she changed her mind." Luke grinned, and hooked his fingers around his lapels. "She's waiting for me. We're going . . ." A little flourish, and a big red rose popped out on his lapel. "Out on the town."

The scattering of applause for his first public magic trick beckoned like a seductive woman.

Luke Callahan had found his calling.

"I see." Max shot a sideways glance at the audience. "Aren't you a little young for a woman of Lily's charms?"

He was rolling now. "What I lack in years I make up for in energy."

This remark, delivered with a sneer, brought a loud guffaw from the audience. Luke felt something shift inside him at the sound. As it settled comfortably into place, the sneer turned to a grin.

"But of course, a gentleman can't escort a lady out on the town without his hat." Max rubbed his hands together and glanced stage left. "I'm afraid that's the only hat I've seen tonight." The key light swung on the oversized top hat. "It's seems a little large, even for one with your swelled head."

Rocking back on his heels, Luke tucked his thumbs in his waistband. "I'm on to your tricks, old man. It'll go easier on you if you change my hat back the way it was."

"I?" Eyebrows lifting, Max placed a hand to his breast. "Are you accusing me of sorcery in order to spoil your evening with Lily?"

"Damn right." It wasn't precisely the line as rehearsed, but Luke delivered it with relish as he stalked over and tapped the rim of the hat. "Just get on with it."

"Very well then." With a sigh for the boy's obvious lack of manners, Max gestured. "If you'd be so kind as to step into the hat." He smiled as Luke eyed him owlishly.

"Okay, but no funny business." Agile and quick, Luke hopped inside. "Remember, I'm on to you."

The moment Luke's head disappeared below the rim, Max whipped out his magic wand. "And presto! Suitable magic." He reached in the hat and pulled out a white rabbit. As the audience roared their approval, Max tipped the hat toward them so they could see for themselves that it was quite empty. "I doubt Lily will be interested in a night on the town with him now."

Responding to cue, Lily sauntered out. One look at the wriggling rabbit in Max's hand made her shriek. "Not again!" Exasperation clear on her face, she turned to the audience. "That's the fourth rabbit this month. Let me tell you, ladies, don't get yourself hung up on a jealous magician." Amid the laughter, she turned to Max. "Change him back."

"But, Lily—"

"Change him back right this minute." She fisted her hands on her glitter-slicked hips. "Or we're through."

"Very well." With exaggerated reluctance, Max slipped the rabbit back into the hat, sighed, then tapped the rim twice with his wand. Luke popped up, fury on every feature.

The audience was still applauding as Luke scrambled clear of the hat, fists raised. Then there were gales of laughter as they spotted the white cottontail strategically placed on the back of his tux.

It hadn't taken Luke long to learn how to milk a bit. His head craned, he turned three circles, struggling to get a look at his own rear.

"A slight miscalculation," Max apologized when things quieted. "To prove no hard feelings, I'll make it disappear."

Lily pouted prettily. "You promise?"

"On my honor," Max swore, placing a hand over his heart. He whipped off his cape, swirled it over Luke, then passed his wand over the silk-shrouded form. Even as the cape began to drift toward the floor, Max took up a corner and swung the silk high.

"Max!" Lily gasped out his name, horrified.

"I kept my word." He took a deep bow toward her, then the cheering audience. "The tail's gone. And so is the presumptuous brat."

As Lily and Max segued into the finale, Luke stood in the wings. Transfixed. They were applauding. They were cheering. For him. Luke leaned forward in the wings, staring at Max as he prepared to saw Lily in half.

It was only for the barest of instants that their eyes met, held. But in that instant there was such a wealth of understanding, and joy, that Luke felt his throat burn.

For the first time in his life he began to love another man. And there was no shame in it.

Luke haunted the midway. It was long after the last show, but he still carried the sound of applause and laughter inside his head, like an old song that kept repeating its melody over and over.

He'd been somebody. For a few brief moments, he'd been someone who'd mattered. Before the baffled eyes of dozens of people, he'd vanished.

And they'd believed.

That was the secret, Luke thought to himself as he strutted along past the tired carnies who were still rambling out their spiel to the dwindling crowd. Making people believe an illusion was reality, if only for a split second. That was power, true power that went beyond fists and fury. He wondered if he would be able to explain to anyone that it was all in the mind. And his mind was now so full of that power it felt as though it might split apart, and light would spill out, hot and white.

He knew Max would understand the sensation, but he wasn't ready to share what was inside him with anyone. For tonight, this first night, it was his alone.

The ten dollars Max had given him after the last show crinkled against his fingers when he slipped a hand into his pocket. The urge to spend it was amazingly strong—stronger than the hunger he'd learned to ignore. He stared at the blur of lights from the Ferris wheel, heard the rumble of cars whirling on the Crack the Whip. Tonight he could ride them all.

The little figure in jeans and a baggy shirt darted across his vision, made him stop, then frown, then swear.

"Roxanne! Hey, hey, Rox!" He scrambled after her, grabbing her arm. "What the hell do you think you are doing out?"

She'd thought about it all right. She'd thought about being cooped up in bed feeling miserable while Luke took her place onstage. She'd thought about how endless the days had become, and how itchy the nights. And she'd thought about the fact that they would be in New Orleans, the summer season behind them, before she was clear of spots.

"I'm going for a ride."

"Like hell."

Her pale face flushed with angry color. "You can't tell me what to do, Luke Callahan. Not now, not ever. I'm going for a ride on the Ferris wheel, right now."

"Look, little miss shit for brains." But before he could finish the thought, she'd rapped him hard in the stomach with her elbow. She was off and running before he caught his breath. "Goddammit, Roxy." He snagged her again only because she got stuck in line. He started to tug her out, but this time she rounded on him with teeth.

"You crazy or what?"

"I'm going for a ride." She folded her arms over her thin chest. The colored lights played over her face, making her blotches eerily festive.

He could walk away. She certainly would tell no one he'd seen her. After all, she wasn't his responsibility. But for reasons he couldn't begin to fathom he stuck by her side. He'd even reached for his money to pay their fares when the operator, who knew Roxy well, waved them both on.

Like a princess granting an audience, Roxanne nodded to Luke. "You can ride with me if you want."

"Thanks loads." He dropped down beside her and waited for the clang of the safety bar.

Roxanne didn't squeal or gasp as the wheel started its backward ascent. She merely sat back, closed her eyes and let a small, satisfied smile play around her lips. Years later, Luke would look back on that moment and realize that she had looked like a satisfied woman relaxing in an easy chair after a long day.

She didn't speak until the wheel had completed a full revolution. When she did, her voice was oddly adult.

"I'm tired of being inside. I can't see the lights, I can't see the people."

"It's the same every night."

"It's different every night." She opened her eyes then, emeralds in which all the colors around them flashed. She leaned forward against the bar, and the wind rippled her hair back witchlike into the sky. "See that skinny man down there, the one with the straw hat? I've never seen him before. And that girl in the shorts carrying the stuffed poodle? I don't know her either. So it's different." As they climbed again, she threw her face back to the stars. "I used to think that we'd go right up through the sky. That I could touch it and bring it back down with me." She smiled a little, just old enough to be amused at the childishness of the thought—and child enough to wish it could be true. "I wanted to do it. Just once."

"A lot of good it would do you down here." But he smiled as well. It had been a long time since he'd ridden a Ferris wheel. So long he could barely remember the sensation of having his stomach drop away and his body circling fast to catch up.

"You did a good job tonight, with the act," Roxanne said suddenly. "I heard Daddy say so when he was talking to Lily. They thought I was asleep."

"Yeah?" He struggled to feign indifference.

"He said that he'd seen something in you, and you didn't disappoint him." Roxanne lifted her arms straight up. The rush of air felt glorious on her itchy skin. "I guess you're going to be part of the act."

The ripple of excitement Luke felt had nothing to do with the quick downward drop. "It's something to do." He shrugged to show insouciance. "As long as I'm hanging around." When he glanced over she was watching him, measuring.

"He says you've done things, seen things you shouldn't have. What things?"

Humiliation, anger and a sick sense of horror collided inside of him. Max knew,

Luke thought. Somehow he knew. He felt his skin heat up, but his voice was cool. "I don't know what you're talking about."

"Yes, you do."

"If I do, it's none of your business."

"If you stay with us, it is. I know all about Mouse and Lily and LeClerc."

"Who the hell's LeClerc?"

"He cooks for us in New Orleans and helps Daddy with the cabaret act. He robbed banks."

"No shit?"

Pleased that she'd snagged his full attention, Roxanne nodded. "He's been to prison and everything 'cause he got caught. He taught Daddy how to open any lock there is." Because she felt like pulling away from him, she rounded back. "So, I should know all about you, too. That's the way it works."

"I haven't said I'm staying yet. I got plans of my own."

"You'll stay," Roxanne said half to herself. "Daddy wants you to. And Lily. Daddy will teach you magic if you want to learn. Like he teaches me. Only I'll be better." Her lashes didn't even flutter at his snort of derision. "I'm going to be the best."

"We'll see about that," he murmured as they wheeled into the sky. He turned his face to the wind. When he did, he almost believed that what he had done was nothing, nothing compared to what he could do.

5

Luke's first impression of New Orleans was a jumbled whirl of sounds and scents. While Max, Lily and Roxanne bedded down in the trailer, he'd been curled in the cab of the truck, bored into patchy sleep by the sound of Mouse's tuneless humming. They'd argued about the radio since Shreveport, but Mouse stood firm. He refused to have any noise that would interfere with the pleasure of listening to his engine.

Now other sounds had begun to drift into Luke's logy brain. Voices pitched high and shrieking laughter, the clashes of sax and drum and trumpet. As he floated awake, he thought they were back at the carnival. He could smell food, a spice on the air and the underlying reek of garbage gone ripe in the heat.

Yawning, he opened his eyes and blinked out his open window.

People, masses of people, streamed past in the streets. He saw a juggler who looked like Jesus tossing bright orange balls that glowed in the dark. An enormously fat woman in a flowered muumuu was doing a solo boogie to the backwash of Dixieland that poured through an open doorway. He smelled hot dogs.

The circus is in town, he thought as he struggled to sit up.

And he saw they had left the traveling carnival behind to join a more massive and more permanent one.

"Where are we?"

Mouse negotiated the truck and trailer through the narrow streets. "Home," he said simply as he drove past Bourbon Street toward Chartres.

Luke couldn't have said why the word made him grin.

He could still hear the music, but it was fainter now. There were fewer people walking along these quieter streets. Some were heading to the action, some away. In the flickering lights of the streetlamps, he caught glimpses of old brick buildings, of flower-drenched balconies, of cabs hurrying by with fares and of figures curled up to sleep in doorways.

He didn't see how anyone could sleep with the music, the smells, the unbelievable heat. His own fatigue had vanished, to be replaced by a clenching impatience with the way Mouse was creeping along.

Luke wanted to get where they were going. Wherever it was.

"Jesus, Mouse, you go any slower, we'll be backing up."

"No hurry," Mouse said, then stunned Luke by stopping completely in the middle of the street and getting out.

"What the hell are you doing?" Luke scrambled out himself to see Mouse standing by an open iron gate. "You can't leave that thing sitting in the middle of the road. You'll bring the cops."

"Just refreshing my memory." Mouse stood, stroking his chin. "Gotta back her in."

"Back *what?*" Luke's eyes popped wide. He did a quick dance of disbelief toward the gate and back to the truck. "Back that thing in here?" Luke scanned the opening between two unforgiving brick walls, then turned to judge the width of the trailer. "No way in hell."

Mouse smiled. His eyes glowed like a sinner's who'd just found religion. "You just stand out here, in case I need you." He sauntered back to the truck.

"Can't be done," Luke called after him.

But Mouse was humming again as he began to maneuver the truck and trailer across the narrow street.

"You're going to hit. Jesus, Mouse." Luke braced for the sound of scraping metal. His mouth dropped open when the big black trailer slid into the opening as easily as a hand into a glove. As the truck backed in behind it, Mouse glanced over at Luke. And winked.

It was a fine thing. For some reason the parking of the truck and trailer struck Luke as an event as fine as Christmas, or the opening day of a new baseball season. His own laughter rocked him back on his heels while he stood blinded by the headlights.

"Man, you are number one," Luke shouted as Mouse climbed out of the truck. Then he whirled like a boxer at the ready when a light flashed on in the house beside them. "Who's that?" he demanded of Mouse as he spotted a figure in the doorway.

"LeClerc." Jiggling the keys in his pocket, Mouse moved forward to shut the iron gates to the courtyard.

"So, you've returned." LeClerc stepped down, and in the backwash of light Luke saw a small man with gray hair and a full beard. He wore a snowy white athletic T-shirt and baggy gray trousers held up with a hunk of rope. His voice was touched with a slight accent, not the fluid drawl of Max's, but something sharper that seemed to add syllables to words. "And you're hungry, yes?"

"Didn't stop to eat," Mouse called out.

"Good you didn't." LeClerc came forward, his gait stiff and uneven. Luke saw that he was old, older than Max by a decade or more. The boy's impression was of an ancient face, a tattered leather map scored with hundreds of deeply traveled roads. The brown eyes were wide-set and shrewd under wiry brows.

LeClerc saw a slim young boy with a beautiful face dominated by wary eyes. A boy who was poised on the balls of his feet as if to run, or to fight.

"And who would this be?"

"This is Luke," Max said as he stepped out of the trailer with a dozing Roxanne in his arms. "He's with us now."

Something passed between the two men that seemed all the more intimate with being left unsaid.

"Another one, eh?" LeClerc's lips curved briefly around the stem of the pipe he kept clenched permanently between his teeth. "We'll see. And how is my *bébé?*"

Heavy-eyed, Roxanne held out her arms and was gathered up to LeClerc. She settled against the bone and sinew as though he were a feather pillow. "Can I have a beignet?"

"I make just for you, don't I?" LeClerc pulled the pipe out of his mouth to kiss her cheek. "You are better, *oui?*"

"I had the chicken pox forever. I'm never, never getting sick again."

"I make you a *gris-gris* for good health." He settled her comfortably on his hip as Lily stepped out. She carried a heavy makeup bag over one arm of her flowing negligee. "Ah, Mademoiselle Lily." LeClerc managed to bow despite the child on his hip. "More beautiful than ever."

She giggled and held out a hand for him to kiss, which he did with smooth aplomb. "It's good to be home, Jean."

"Come in, come in. Enjoy the midnight supper I make for you."

At the mention of dinner, Max too stepped down from the trailer and greeted LeClerc as he led the way across the courtyard, where roses and lilies and begonias bloomed in profusion, up a short flight of steps and through a door that opened into the kitchen. There a light was burning to shine on the polished surfaces of white tile and dark wood.

There was a small hearth of bricks that had been smoked from red to a comfortable rose gray. Atop it stood a plastic glow-in-the-dark statue of the Blessed Virgin, and what looked like an Indian rattle dressed with beads and feathers.

Though it was too miraculously cool inside for Luke to believe the bricked oven had been used, he would have sworn he caught the tantalizing odor of bread just baked.

Dried bouquets of spices and herbs hung from the ceiling, along with dangling ropes of onion and garlic. Gleaming copper pots were suspended from iron hooks above the stove. Another pot, with steam puffing out, sat on the back burner. Whatever was simmering inside smelled like paradise.

A long butcher-block table had already been set with bowls and plates and brightly checked linen napkins. Still carrying Roxanne, LeClerc reached inside a cupboard for another place setting.

"Gumbo." Lily sighed as she slipped an arm around Luke's shoulders. She wanted badly to welcome him home. "No one cooks like Jean, honey. Just wait until you taste. If I don't watch myself, I'll be popping right out of my costume within a week."

"Tonight you don't worry, you just eat." LeClerc set Roxanne down in a chair, then picking up two thick cloths, hefted the pot from the stove.

Luke watched, fascinated, as the tattoo which wound from bony wrist to bony shoulder rippled and danced. They were snakes, Luke realized. A nest of vipers in faded blue and red that twisted and twined over the leathered skin.

They all but hissed.

"You like?" LeClerc's eyes were merry as he studied Luke. "Snakes, they are quick, and cunning. Good luck for me." He made a sibilent sound as he darted his arm toward Luke. "Snakes won't do for you, boy." He chuckled to himself as he dished up the thick, spicy gumbo. "You bring me a young wolf, Max. He'll bite first."

"A wolf needs a pack." Casually, Max lifted a basket from the table and uncovered a golden loaf of bread. He offered the basket to Lily.

"What am I, LeClerc?" Wide awake now, Roxanne was spooning up her gumbo.

"You." The leathery, lined face softened as he passed his wide, gnarled hand over her hair. "My little kitten."

"Just a kitten?"

"Ah, but kittens are clever and brave and wise, and some grow to be tigers."

That brightened her look. She slanted her eyes toward Luke. "Tigers can eat wolves."

When the moon had begun to set, and even the echoes of music from Bourbon Street had faded, LeClerc sat on a marble bench in the courtyard, surrounded by the flowers he loved.

It was Max who owned the house, but it was Jean LeClerc who had made it a home. He'd taken long-ago memories of a cabin in the bayou, and flowers that had run wild, blossoms his mother had tamed in plastic pots, the smells of potpourri and spice, of colored cloths and polished woods, and had mixed them together with Max's need for elegance.

LeClerc would have been happy back in the swamp, but he wouldn't have been happy without Max, and the family Max had given him.

He smoked his pipe and listened to the night. The faintest breeze rustled the magnolia leaves, stirring the heat and promising rain much as a teasing woman might promise a kiss. The dampness that was gradually wearing away the brick and stone of the French Quarter hung like a mist in the air.

He didn't see Max approach, nor did he hear him, though his hearing was keen. He felt him.

"So." He puffed on his pipe and studied the stars. "What will you do with the boy?"

"Give him a chance," Max said. "The same as you gave me a lifetime ago."

"His eyes want to swallow everything he sees. Such appetites can be difficult."

"So I'll feed him." There was a hint of impatience in Max's voice as he joined LeClerc on the bench. "Would you have me send him away?"

"It's too late to be practical now that your heart's involved."

"Lily's attached," Max began and was cut off by LeClerc's rumbling laugh.

"Only Lily, *mon ami?*"

Max took time to light a cigar, draw in smoke. "I'm fond of the boy."

"You love the boy," LeClerc corrected. "And how could it be otherwise, when you look and see yourself? He makes you remember."

It was difficult to admit it. Max knew when you loved you could also hurt and be hurt. "He makes me remember not to forget. If you forget all the pain, the loneliness, the despair, you forget to be grateful for the lack of it. You taught me that, Jean."

"So good, my student is now the master. This contents me." LeClerc turned his head and his dark eyes gleamed through the shadows. "Will it content you when he outreaches what you are?"

"I don't know." Max looked down at his hands. They were good ones, agile, quick and clever. He was afraid what it would do to his heart when they slowed. "I've begun to teach him magic. I haven't decided if I'll teach him the rest."

"You won't keep secrets from those eyes for long. What was he doing when you found him?"

Max had to smile. "Picking pockets."

"Ah." LeClerc chuckled over his pipe. "So, he is already one of us. Is he as good as you were?"

"Every bit as good," Max admitted. "Perhaps better than I at that age. Less fear of reprisal, more ruthless. But there is a long leap between lifting wallets at a carnival and picking locks at grand houses and fine hotels."

"A leap you made gracefully. Regrets, *mon ami?*"

"None." Max laughed again. "What's wrong with me?"

"You were born to steal," LeClerc said with a shrug. "Just as you were to pull rabbits out of hats. And, apparently, as you were to take in strays. It's good to have you home."

"It's good to be home."

For a moment they sat in silence, enjoying the night. Then LeClerc got down to business.

"The diamonds you sent from Boston were exceptional."

"I preferred the pearls from Charleston."

"Ah, yes." LeClerc sighed out smoke. "They were elegant, but the diamonds had such fire. It pained me to take money for them."

"And you got . . . ?"

"Ten thousand, only five for the pearls, despite their elegance."

"The pleasure of holding them outweighs the profit." He remembered, with pleasure, how they had looked against Lily's skin for one glorious evening. "And the painting?"

"Twenty-two thousand. Me, I thought it a clumsy work. Those English painters had no passion," he added, dismissing the Turner landscape with a shrug. "The Chinese vase I hold awhile longer. Did you bring the coin collection with you?"

"No, I didn't get it. When Roxanne took sick, I canceled that engagement."

"Best." LeClerc nodded and smoked. "Worry for her would have distracted you."

"I would hardly have been at my best. So, until the vase is placed, that makes the tithe . . . thirty-seven hundred." A glance at LeClerc's scowl made Max smile. "So little to resent so much."

"By the end of the year, you'll have thrown fifteen thousand away at least. Add this to each year you've been taking ten percent to ease your conscience—"

"A gift to charity," Max interrupted, amused. "I don't do it to ease my conscience, but to appease my soul. I'm a thief, Jean, an excellent one who thinks nothing of the people from whom I steal, but quite a bit about those I see who have nothing worth stealing." He studied the glowing tip of his cigar. "I may not be able to live with the morality of others, but I must live with my own."

"The churches you give your tithe to would damn you to hell."

"I've escaped from worse places than the hell priests imagine for us."

"It's not a joke."

Max smothered a smile as he rose. He knew that LeClerc's religion ran the gamut from Catholicism to voodoo, and any handy superstition in between. "Then think of it as insurance. Perhaps my foolish generosity will ensure us both a cooler place in the hereafter. Let's get some sleep." He laid a hand on LeClerc's shoulder. "Tomorrow I'll tell you what I've planned for the next few months."

Luke knew he'd found heaven. There was no list of chores the next day so he was free to wander the house, which he did gobbling beignets he'd snatched from the kitchen. The trail of powdered sugar in his wake dribbled through the first floor, up the stairs, onto one of the long flower-twined balconies and back again.

He couldn't believe his good fortune.

He'd been given a room of his own, and had spent a great deal of a wakeful night looking, touching. The high, carved headboard had fascinated him, as had the soft sheen of the wallpaper and the muted pattern of the rug. There was a huge cupboard that Max had called an armoire. Luke figured it would hold more clothes than any one person would need in a lifetime.

And there were flowers. A tall blue vase was filled with them. He'd never had flowers in his room before, and though he knew he should dismiss them as sissy, their fragrance brought him a deep and secret pleasure.

Luke drifted through the house as soundlessly as smoke. He wasn't sure of LeClerc as yet and easily avoided the man while he made his explorations.

The furnishings reflected Max's elegance. It gave Luke a sense of his mentor, though he didn't recognize the French and British antiques. What he saw were graceful gleaming tables, curvy sofas, pretty china lamps and peaceful landscapes.

As much as he liked the house, Luke found his favorite spot on the balcony outside his room. From there he could smell the heat of the flowers and the street. He could watch people snapping pictures and searching for souvenirs.

He couldn't help but notice how careless people were with their wallets. Women with their shoulder bags dangling, men with their cash tucked into the back pocket of their bell-bottoms. A pickpocket's paradise. If Miami didn't pan out, Luke decided he could do very well here, supplementing his salary as a sorcerer's apprentice.

"You got sugar all over," Roxanne said from behind him.

Luke tensed. He snuck a look down at his hands and saw with disgust that the evidence was all over his fingers. Hastily, he wiped them on his jeans. "So?"

"LeClerc'll get mad. Sugar draws bugs."

He wiped his hands again, because they'd grown damp. "I'll clean it up."

She joined him at the rail, looking pretty and prim in a yellow shorts set. "What're you doing?"

"Just looking."

"Daddy says we can take the whole day off. Tomorrow we have to start rehearsing the new cabaret act for the club."

"What club?"

"The Magic Door. We work there." She began to play with the flowers that twined along the rail. "We can do bigger illusions there than at the carnival, and sometimes Daddy goes over during the day and does close-up work for some of the customers."

LeClerc's annoyance and any possible reprisals shifted to the back of Luke's mind. He didn't know what his place would be in a cabaret act, but he was going to make sure he had one. "How many shows a night?"

"Two." After plucking a clematis bloom, she tried to wind the slim stem around her ear. "Eight and eleven. We're the headliners." She wrinkled her nose. "I have to take a nap after school every day. Like a baby."

Luke wasn't the least bit concerned about Roxanne's problems. "Does he keep in the card tricks?"

She patted the flower as she wandered back into Luke's bedroom to study the result in the mirror. "Oh, he'll make up other ones."

Luke nodded and began to plan. He was getting pretty good at the tricks he'd wheedled Roxanne into showing him. And he'd been practicing at least an hour a day with the Cups and Balls. He just needed to show Max. He couldn't bear it if they cut him out of the act now.

"Daddy gave me money for ice cream." She poked her head back out the French doors. "You want to go get some?"

"No." Luke was much too busy to be distracted by a treat and an eight-year-old's company. "Take off, will you? I have to think."

"More for me," Roxanne shot back, barely controlling a pout.

The minute he was alone, Luke dug out his cards and began to practice. He'd hardly begun to set up Aces High when he was distracted again.

It was the voice. He'd never heard anything like it. He tried to brush it out of his mind, but it kept flowing back. A rich, heartbreaking alto that seemed to be singing just for him. Unable to resist, he walked back out on the balcony.

He spotted her instantly. A woman in a flowing flowered dress, a red turban over her head, her skin gleaming like ebony. She stood on the corner, a cardboard box at her feet as she sang swaying gospel a cappella.

He couldn't turn away, the sound all but hypnotizing him. This was true beauty. Even as he realized it, it reached deep inside him to a place he didn't know existed.

That voice rang out over the Quarter. It never paused or hesitated when she drew a small crowd. She never glanced down when coins thudded into the box.

It made his skin prickle and his throat ache.

On impulse he dashed back inside and dug out the bag he'd secreted under his pillow. From it he took a crumpled dollar. His heart was still soaring to the music as he raced out of the room and down the stairs.

He saw Roxanne in the hallway, sweeping up powdered sugar while LeClerc stood behind her, lecturing.

"You eat in the kitchen, not all over the house. You be sure you get all those crumbs, you hear?"

"I'm getting them." She lifted her head to stick her tongue out at Luke. His heart was so full of the music, his brain so dazzled by the idea that Roxanne was taking the blame for him, he missed the last step. On a muffled cry, he threw out a hand to save himself.

For Luke it happened in slow motion. He saw the vase, the faceted crystal alive with sunlight, filled with bloodred roses. In horror, he saw his own hand sweep at it, watched it teeter even as he scrambled for balance.

His fingers brushed it. He felt the cool glass on his skin and let out a groan of despair as it slipped away.

The sound of the vase shattering on the hardwood was like a volley of pistol shots. Luke stood frozen, the glistening shards at his feet, and the smell of roses heavy in the air.

LeClerc was swearing. Luke didn't have to understand French to know the oaths were strong and furious. He didn't move, didn't bother to run. He was braced for a blow, had already taken that part of himself that felt pain and humiliation away. What stood there was a silent shell that would refuse to care.

"You run through my house like a wild Indian. Now you break the Waterford, you bruise the roses and you have water all over my floor. *Imbécile!* Look what you've done to my beauties."

"Jean." Max's voice was hardly more than a whisper, but it cut through the old man's tantrum.

"The Waterford, Max." LeClerc crouched down to save his roses. "The boy was running like hounds of hell were after him. I tell you he needs to be—"

"Jean," Max said again. "Enough. Look at his face."

With roses dripping from his hands, LeClerc glanced up. The boy was ghost white, his eyes dark and glazed over with something too deep to be termed fear. With a sigh, he straightened. "I'll get another vase," he said quietly and walked away.

"Daddy." Shaken, Roxanne gripped her father's hand. "Why does he look that way?"

"It's all right, Roxy. Run along."

"But, Daddy—"

"Run along," he repeated, and gave her a nudge.

She stepped back into the parlor, but she didn't go far. For once her father was too intent on someone else to notice.

"You disappoint me, Luke," Max said quietly.

Something flickered in Luke's belly, and showed briefly in his eyes. An oath, a blow wouldn't have touched him, but the simple sadness in Max's voice cut deep.

"I'm sorry." The words burned like acid in his icy throat. "I can pay for it. I have money."

Don't send me away, his heart begged. God, please don't send me away.

"What are you sorry for?"

"I wasn't looking where I was going. I'm clumsy. Stupid." And all the rest he'd been accused of during his twelve short years. "I'm sorry," he said again, becoming more desperate as he waited for the blow. Or worse, so much worse, a shove out the door. "I was hurrying because I thought she might go away."

"Who?"

"The woman. Singing on the corner. I wanted to . . ." Realizing the absurdity of it, Luke looked helplessly at the bill still crumpled in his hand.

"I see." And because he did, Max's heart all but broke. "She often sings there. You'll hear her again."

Fresh terror swam into his eyes as he looked back at Max. It was so much more frightening to hope. "I can—I can stay?"

On a long breath, Max bent down and picked up a piece of shattered crystal. "What do you see here?"

"It's broken. I broke it. I never think about anyone else but myself, and I—"

"Stop it."

The sharp order had Luke's head snapping up. Somewhere inside he began to tremble as he realized he couldn't hide from this. When Max hit him it wouldn't just be the physical pain, it would shatter his hopes as completely as he'd shattered the vase.

"It's broken." Max said, struggling for calm. "And it's quite true you broke it. Did you mean to?"

"No, but I—"

"Look at this." He held the piece of glass toward Luke. "It's a thing. An object. Something anyone with the price can own. Do you think you mean less to me than this?" When he tossed it aside, Luke couldn't hold the trembling inside any longer. "Do you think so little of me that you believe I'd strike you for breaking a glass?"

"I don't..." Luke's breath began to hitch as the pressure in his chest spread like brushfire. He couldn't stop the hot, hateful tears from spilling out. "Please. Don't make me go."

"My dear child, can you have been with me all these weeks and not know I'm different from them? Did they scar you that badly?"

Beyond words now, Luke only shook his head.

"I've been where you've been," Max murmured, and took the next step by gathering Luke against him. The boy stiffened, the primitive fear running deep. Then even the fear crumbled as Max eased him down on the steps and rocked him. "No one can make you go back. You're safe here."

He knew he should be humiliated, blubbering like a baby against Max's shirt. But the arms around him were strong, solid, real.

What kind of a boy is it, Max wondered, who can be so moved by a song that he would part with one of his precious dollars to pay for it? How deeply could such a boy be hurt by casual cruelty, and the lack of choice?

"Can you tell me what they did to you?"

Shame welled up, and the need—oh the need for someone to understand. "I couldn't do anything. I couldn't make it stop."

"I know."

The old angers simmered out even as the tears fell. "They beat me all the time. If I did something, if I didn't do it. If they were drunk, if they were sober." His fists clenched against Max's shirt like small balls of iron. "Sometimes they'd lock me up, and I'd beat on the closet door and beg them to let me out. I couldn't get out. I could never get out."

It was hideous to remember that, weeping hysterically in the dark coffin of the closet, with no hope, no help, no escape.

"The social workers would come, and if I didn't say the right thing, he'd take after me with the belt. The last time, that last time before I left, I thought he was going to kill me. He wanted to. I know he wanted to—you can tell when it's in their eyes, but I don't know why. I don't know why."

"It wasn't your fault. None of it was your fault." Max stroked the boy's head and fought back his own demons. "People tell their children there are no monsters in the world. They tell them that because they believe it, or they want the child to feel safe. But there are monsters, Luke, all the more frightening because they look like people." He drew the boy back to study his wet, ravaged face. "You're free of them now."

"I hate him."

"You're entitled to that."

There was more. He wasn't certain he dared speak of it. The shame was black and oily. But with Max's eyes so quiet and intense on his, Luke stumbled through it. "He—he brought a man one night. It was late and they were drunk. Al went out and locked the door. And the man—he tried—"

"It's all right." He tried to gather Luke close again, but the horror had the boy scrambling back.

"He put his fat hands on me, and his mouth." Luke wiped his own with the back of his hand. "He said how he'd paid Al, and I was supposed to do things to him, and let him do them to me. And I was stupid, 'cause I didn't know what he meant."

There were no tears now, but a rage, burning dry. "I didn't know until he got on top of me. I thought he was going to smother me until..." The sheer terror of it boomeranged back. The sweaty skin and the stink of gin, the greedy hands groping.

"Then I knew, all right. I knew." His hands clenched and unclenched, leaving deep crescents in his palms. "I hit him, and I hit him, but he wouldn't stop. So I bit and I scratched. I had his blood all over my hands, and he was holding his face and screaming. Then Al came in, and he beat me for a long time. And I don't remember—I don't know if..." That was the worst, the not knowing. It was a shame he couldn't speak out loud. "That's the night he wanted to kill me. That's the night I left."

Max was silent for a long time, so long Luke was afraid he'd said too much, much too much to ever be forgiven.

"You did everything right." There was a heaviness in Max's voice that had tears stinging Luke's eyes again. "And I can promise you this. No one will ever touch you in that way again, while you're with me. And I'll teach you the way out of the closet." Max's eyes came back to Luke's and held. "They may lock you in, but they won't keep you there."

Luke tried to speak, but the words caught in his throat before he forced them out. His life depended on the answer. "I can stay?"

"Until you want to go."

His gratitude was so huge, he thought it might burst from him like light. Like love. "I'll pay for the vase," he managed. "I promise."

"You already have. Now, run wash your face. We'd best clean this up before LeClerc has another tantrum."

Max sat on the steps as Luke bounded up them. From her hiding place in the parlor, Roxanne heard her father sigh. And she wept.

6

Over the next few days, Luke felt his way carefully. He was unsure of LeClerc, and knew only that the Cajun was in charge of the house. Luke did his best to keep out of the way. He never made the mistake of dropping crumbs through the house again.

He went shopping with Lily, carrying boxes and bags for her up and down the steamy streets. He sat patiently in boutiques as she picked over new clothes, stood by while she oohed and aahed over trinkets in windows.

His love for her was deep enough to have him tolerating her choosing outfits for him. So deep that he hardly winced at the paisley shirts she bought him. If he had free time, he haunted the Quarter, content to explore, to listen to the street musicians, to watch the artists work around Jackson Square.

But the best time for Luke was when they rehearsed.

The Magic Door was a cramped, dim club that smelled of the whiskey fumes and smoke that had soaked into the walls for decades. On those hot afternoons, the shades would be drawn against the sun and the tourists. The air conditioner made grinding sounds that were more industrious than the resulting puff of tepid air it produced. The ceiling fan did a bit more, but with the stage lights lit, the club was like a small furnace.

The walls were papered in red and gold velvet, the wall behind the bar mirrored to give the illusion of space. It was like being a bug inside a decorated box, and the forgetful child who'd captured you had neglected to punch holes in the top.

Luke loved it.

Every afternoon, Lester Friedmont, the manager, would sit at the front table, nursing a beer and the short stub of a lit cigar. He was a tall man who carried all of his extra weight in his belly. Invariably he wore a white short-sleeved shirt, with a tie and matching suspenders. His black laced shoes were always shined. His thinning hair was slicked back and gleamed wetly under the lights. He looked at his world through the smudged lenses of heavy black glasses perched on the end of his angular nose.

A fat calico cat he called Fifi would prowl around his legs, waddle off to nibble from the dish set under the bar, then prowl back again.

Friedmont kept a phone on the table. He had the ability to watch the rehearsal and add his comments, harass whoever was cleaning the club and talk on the phone simultaneously.

It took Luke several afternoons to realize that Friedmont was a bookie.

No matter how often they would run through a bit, Lester would hoot and shake his head. "Jesus please us, that was a good one. You going to tell me how you did that one, Max?"

"Sorry, Lester. Trade secret."

So Lester would go back to taking bets and scratching his belly.

Max planned to start off the act with sleight of hand, and some colored scarf tricks, similar to what he'd done in the carnival. Then he wanted to add his own version of the Floating Ball before bringing Roxanne out for his new Levitating Girl. He'd added a spin to sawing a woman in half by using a vertical box and cutting Lily into three parts. It was nearly perfected.

He was trying Luke out in bits and pieces. He had no doubts about the boy's quick mind and quick hands. Now he was testing Luke's heart. "Watch," he said to Luke. "Learn."

Standing center stage, Max pulled silks out of his pocket; color after vivid color poured out. Luke's lips began to twitch. He didn't understand that what he was seeing was pure timing. The longer the bit lasted, the longer the audience would laugh—and be misdirected.

"Hold out your arms," Max ordered, then draped the scarves over Luke's arms seemingly at random. "We'll have music to go with this. Lily?"

She turned on the tape recorder. "The Blue Danube."

"The waltz is slow, lovely," Max said. "The gestures mirror it." His hands flowed over the scarves, lifted, fell as he walked around Luke. "And, of course, if I've chosen a beautiful woman from the audience to stand in your place, this adds to the showmanship, and the beauty of the illusion. And her reaction will cue the audience to theirs." A snap of the wrist and Max plucked the end of a scarf, as he whipped it back, the others followed, all neatly tied together, scarlet to yellow, yellow to sapphire, sapphire to emerald.

Luke's eyes popped wide an instant before his grin spread.

"Excellent." Max scooped up the scarves, balled them into a colorful orb as he spoke. "So you see, even in such a small trick, showmanship, stage presence, is every bit as important as dexterity. To do a trick well is never enough. But to do it with a flourish . . ." He tossed the ball into the air, the scarves, no longer joined, floated down.

Nearby Roxanne giggled and clapped her hands. "I like that one, Daddy."

"My best audience." He bent down to pick up the silks. "Show me."

Roxanne rubbed her hands together, gnawed on her lip. "I can't do as many yet."

"What you can, then."

Nerves and pride jangled together as she chose six of the scarves. Turning to the imaginary audience, she tugged each between her hands then waving each in the air draped them on Luke's arms. There was an undeniably feminine touch to her gestures that made Max smile as she turned her hands over and under the silks. Though she moved to the music as she executed a series of slow pirouettes around Luke, her concentration was total. There was no such thing as a small trick in Roxanne's world. They were all huge.

Facing Luke again, she smiled, skimmed her hands over the scarves once more, as a woman might stroke a cat, then taking the end, she whirled them over her head. She laughed in triumph as she wound the tied scarves around her shoulders.

"Well done." Max scooped her up to kiss her. "Quite well done."

"She's a pistol, Max," Lester called out. "You ought to let her try it out in front of a crowd."

"What do you say, Roxanne?" Max stroked a hand over her hair as he set her down. "Ready to try a solo?"

"Can I?" Her heart leaped into her eyes. "Daddy, please, can I?"

"We'll try it out in the first show, then we'll see."

She let out a shriek and raced to Lily. "Can I wear earrings? Real ones? Can I?"

She smiled at Max over Roxanne's head. "You can pick out the ones you like best."

"The ones in the window down the street. The blue ones."

"Take twenty minutes, Lily," Max suggested. "A woman needs at least that much time to choose accessories for her costume." And he wanted a moment alone with Luke.

"So." As Roxanne dragged Lily out, Max picked up a deck of cards. He began to do one-handed cuts. "You're wondering why a little girl can do something you can't."

Luke flushed, but his chin stayed up. "I can learn anything she can."

"Possibly." To entertain himself, Max fanned the cards. "I could tell you it's a mistake to use her, or anyone, as a yardstick for yourself. But you wouldn't listen."

"You could teach me."

"I could," Max agreed.

"I already know some. I've been practicing."

"Indeed." Raising a brow, Max offered the cards. "Show me."

Nerves dampened his fingertips as Luke shuffled the cards. "It won't be as good, because you know how I'll do it."

"Ah, there you're wrong. A magician's best audience is another magician. Because they understand the purpose. Do you?"

"To do a trick," Luke responded, struggling to concentrate on the cards.

"As simple as that? Sit," Max suggested. Once they were seated at one of the tables, he chose a card from the pack Luke held out. "Anyone can learn to do a trick. It only takes an understanding of how it works, and a basic skill that can be refined with practice. But magic." He glanced at the card, then slipped it back into the pack. "Magic is taking what's real and what's not, and blending them into one, for a short period. It's causing someone who doesn't believe to blink in amazement. It's giving people what they want."

"What do they want?" Luke shuffled the cards, tapped the top, then turned over Max's card. His heart swelled at Max's nod of approval.

"Excellent. Do another." He sat back as Luke fumbled through a one-handed cut. "What do they want? To be duped, to be fooled, and amazed. To watch the astounding happen under their nose." Max opened his hand and showed Luke a small red ball. "Right before their eyes." He slapped the ball on the table, then took his other hand from under the wood. The ball was there, his other hand empty. Luke grinned and set the cards for Aces High.

"You palmed it," Luke said. "I know you did, but I didn't see."

"Because I looked at you, in your eyes. So you looked in mine. Always look them in the eye. Innocently, smugly, however you choose. But look them in the eye. This makes an illusion honest."

"A trick's a cheat, isn't it?"

"Only if you can't make them enjoy the deception." He nodded again when Luke drew the four aces from the top of the shuffled deck. "Your mechanics are good, but where is your flair? Where is that drama that tells the audience it's not simply a well-practiced trick, but magic? Again." he said, shoving the cards toward Luke. "Astound me."

Max watched the concentration come into Luke's eyes, heard the two deep indrawn breaths as he prepared.

"I want to do the first one again."

"All right. Let me hear your patter."

Luke's color came up, but he cleared his throat and dived in. He'd been practicing for weeks. "I'd like to show you a few card tricks." He did a fair Russian shuffle, and a snappy turnover. "Now, not many magicians will tell you what they're going to do beforehand. But I'm just a kid. I don't know any better." He fanned the cards face out toward his imaginary audience so they could identify it as an ordinary deck. "I'm going to ask this gentleman here to pick a card, any card at all." Luke spread the cards facedown on the table, waited a beat while Max reached for one. "That one?" he said and looked uneasy. "You sure you want that one?"

Playing along, Max inclined his head. "Indeed I do."

"You sure you wouldn't rather take this one?" Luke tapped the end card. "No?" He swallowed audibly when Max held firm. "Okay. Remember, I'm just a kid. If you'd show the card to the audience. Make sure I don't see it," Luke added as he tried to crane his neck to get a glimpse of the card. "Good." His voice shook. "I guess you can put it back in, anywhere, anywhere at all. Then you can shuffle them—unless you want me to," he asked hopefully as he gathered the cards.

"No, I believe I'll do it myself."

"Terrific." He heaved a sigh. "Once they're shuffled, I'll cut the cards and magically reveal the one this fine gentleman chose." He reached in his pocket, pulled out an invisible handkerchief and wiped his brow. "I think that's enough. Really, really, you've done enough." Luke snatched the deck back. After setting it on the table, he waved his hands over it and mumbled. "Almost got it. And!" He cut the cards and held one up in triumph. At the gentle shake of Max's head, he looked crestfallen. "That's not it? I was sure I did this right. Hold on a minute." He set the cards back, mumbled over them again, and again chose incorrectly.

"Something must be wrong with this deck. I don't think your card's there at all. I think you cheated." He rose, incensed, and stalked toward the audience. "And someone out here must be working with you. You there." He pointed a finger at Lester, who was busily taking bets. "Come on, give it up."

"Give what up, kid?"

"The card. I know you've got it."

"Hey." Lester cocked the phone on his shoulder and held up both hands. "I ain't got no card, kid."

"Oh no?" Luke reached down past Lester's bulging belly under the waistband of his slacks and pulled out a nine of diamonds. "Guess you were just on your way to a poker game."

While Lester howled with laughter, Luke held the card overhead for the audience to identify. "Thank you. Thank you. Hey, you've been a good sport," he said to Lester. "Why don't you stand up and take a bow."

"Sure, kid, sure." Amused, Lester rose. "You got an up-and-comer here, Max. You sure as hell do."

The compliment had Luke beaming. But it was nothing, nothing compared to hearing Max laugh.

"Now." Max rose to drop a hand on Luke's shoulder. "That's showmanship. Let's see if we can work it into the act."

Luke's jaw dropped to his knees. "No shit?"

Max ruffled Luke's hair, pleased that the boy didn't stiffen at the touch. "No shit."

It wasn't a long trip from New Orleans to Lafayette. With Mouse at the wheel of the dark sedan, Max could sit back, close his eyes and prepare. Stealing wasn't so different from performing. Or it had never been for him. When he had first begun, so many years ago, he'd blended the two skills. That had been a matter of survival.

Now, older, more mature, he separated his performances from his thievery. That, too, was survival. As his name became more well known, it would have been reckless to steal from his audience.

Max was not a reckless man.

Some might have pointed out that he no longer had to steal to keep food in his belly or a roof over his head. Max would have agreed. He also would have added that not only was it difficult to break a habit of such long standing, particularly when he was so skilled, but he enjoyed stealing.

As a child who had been abused, abandoned and unloved, stealing had been a matter of control, and of defiance.

Now, it was a matter of pride.

He was, quite simply, one of the best. And he considered himself gracious enough to choose his marks carefully, taking only from those who could afford to lose.

It was rare for him to work this close to home. Max considered it not only risky but messy. Still, rules were made to be broken.

With his eyes shut, he could conjure the flash and beauty of the aquamarine and diamond necklace. All that icy blue and white. For himself, he preferred hot gems. Rubies, sapphires, deep, rich colors that held passion as well as glory. But personal taste often had to be set aside for practicality. If his information was correct, those emerald-cut aquamarines would bring a hefty sum once they were popped free of their setting.

LeClerc already had a buyer.

Even after the tithe, and expenses, Max calculated there would be a nice chunk left over for Roxanne's college fund, and for the one he'd recently started for Luke.

He smiled to himself. Irony rarely escaped him. He was a thief who worried about interest rates and mutual funds.

Too many hungry years had taught him the value of investments. His children wouldn't go hungry, and they would have a choice over which path they took.

"This is the corner, Max."

Max opened his eyes and noted that Mouse had the car idling at the curb. It was a quiet neighborhood, tree-lined, with big, elegant houses shielded by leaves and flowering shrubs.

"Ah, yes. The time?"

Mouse checked his watch as Max did. "Two-ten."

"Good."

"The alarm system's really basic. You just snip both red wires. But if you're not sure, I can come do it for you."

"Thank you, Mouse." Max pulled on thin black gloves. "I believe I can handle it. If the safe is as LeClerc led me to believe, I'll need only seven or eight minutes to open it. Meet me back here at precisely two-thirty. If I'm more than five minutes late, you leave." When Mouse only grumbled, Max tapped his shoulder. "I have to be able to count on you for that."

"You'll be back," Mouse said and hunched down in the seat.

"And we'll be several thousand dollars richer." Max slipped from the car and faded into the shadows.

Half a block down, he vaulted over a low stone wall. There were no lights on in the three-story brick house, but he made a circuit just to be sure before locating the alarm box. Once the red wires were snipped, he didn't hesitate. Mouse was never wrong.

He took his glass cutter and suction cup from the soft leather pouch at his waist. Clouds dancing over the moon kept the light shifting, but he needed none at all. If he'd been struck blind, Max could have found his way in or out of a locked door.

There was a quiet click as he reached in and undid the latch. Then silence. As always, he listened to it, let it cloak him before he stepped inside.

He could never describe to anyone the feeling that rose inside him each and every time he stepped into a dark, quiet house. It was a kind of power, he supposed, in being where you weren't supposed to be, and going undiscovered.

Silent as a shadow, he slipped through the kitchen, into the dining room and into the hall.

His heart beat fast. A pleasant feeling, one he knew was similar to the anticipation of good sex.

He found the library exactly where LeClerc had told him it would be, and the safe, hidden behind a false door.

With a penlight clamped between his teeth and a stethoscope pressed near the lock, Max went to work.

He was enjoying the job. The library smelled faintly of overblown roses and cherry tobacco. A light breeze was tapping the branches of a chestnut against the window. He imagined, if he had the time, he'd find a brandy decanter close by and could indulge in a sip or two before going on his way.

The third of the four tumblers fell into place, with eight minutes to spare. Then he heard the whimpering.

Braced to run, he turned slowly. Using the penlight, he scanned toward the sound. A puppy, no more than a few weeks old, stood watching him. With another whimper, he squatted and piddled on the Turkish carpet.

"A little too late to ask me to let you out," Max murmured. "And I'm sorry, but I can't afford the time to clean up after you. You'll just have to take your lumps in the morning."

Max worked on the fourth tumbler as the pup waddled over to sniff his shoes. With a satisfied sigh, he opened the safe.

"Fortunately for me, I didn't plan this job a year from now, when you'd be big enough to take a bite out of me. Though I do have a scar on my rump from a poodle not much bigger than you."

He bypassed stock certificates and opened a velvet box. The aquamarines gleamed up at him. Using the penlight and a jeweler's loupe, he checked the stones, gave a satisfied sigh.

"Lovely, aren't they?" He slid them out of the box and into his pouch.

As he bent to give the puppy a farewell pat on the head, he heard the rustle on the stairs. "Frisky?" It was a female voice, pitched to a stage whisper. "Frisky, are you down here?"

"Frisky?" Max said under his breath, giving the dog a sympathetic stroke. "Some of us are forced to rise above our names." He clicked the safe shut, then faded back into the shadows.

A middle-aged woman with her hair in a sleep net and her face gleaming with night cream tiptoed into the room. The puppy whined, slapped his tail on the rug, then started in Max's direction.

"There you are! Mama's baby!" Less than a foot away from Max, she scooped the dog up. "What have you been up to? You naughty dog." She gave him loud kisses as the pup tried to wriggle away. "Are you hungry? Are you hungry, honey bunny? Let's give you a nice bowl of milk."

Max closed his eyes, wholeheartedly on the side of the dog, who yipped and tried to gain his freedom. But the woman clung tight, bundling Frisky to her breast as she started out toward the kitchen.

Since that meant Max couldn't get out the way he'd come in, he eased up a window. If his luck held, she would be too involved with the pup to notice the nice, neat hole in the beveled glass kitchen door.

If it didn't, Max mused as he tossed a leg out the window, he'd still have a head start.

He closed the window after him and did his best not to trample the pansies.

Luke couldn't sleep. The idea of performing the next night had him tied up in knots of exhilaration and terror. The what-ifs plagued him.

What if he fumbled. What if he forgot the trick. What if the audience thought he was just a dumb kid.

He could be good. He knew that inside him was the potential to be really good. But so many years of being told he was stupid, worthless, good for nothing, had left their mark.

For Luke there was only one way to deal with insomnia. That was food. He still believed the best time to feast was when no one was around to tell him not to.

He pulled on a pair of cutoffs and moved silently downstairs. Images of LeClerc's barbecued pork and pecan pie waltzed through his head.

The sound of LeClerc's voice made him stop, and swear. He was far from sure of the old man. But when he heard Max's laugh, he crept closer.

"Your information is always reliable, Jean. The blueprints, the safe, the gems." Max cupped a brandy in one hand, the jewels in the other. "I can't complain overmuch about one small dog."

"They didn't have a dog last week. Not even five days ago."

"They have one now." Max laughed and drank more brandy. "Who hasn't been housebroken."

"Thank the Virgin he didn't bark." LeClerc added bourbon to his coffee. "I don't like surprises."

"There we part ways. I like them very much." And the light of success glowed in Max's eyes, even as the necklace shimmered in the overhead light. "Otherwise, a job would become routine. And routine too easily becomes a rut. So, will they miss them by morning, do you think?" He held the necklace up, letting gems drip through his fingers. "And will the fact that these were payment for a gambling debt prevent them from reporting the loss?"

"Reported or not, they won't be traced here." LeClerc started to raise his coffee cup in toast, then stopped. His eyes narrowed as he set it on the table. "I'm afraid the walls have at least two ears tonight."

Alerted, Max glanced up, then sighed. "Luke." He said the name, and gestured toward the shadows. "Come into the light." He waited, gauging the boy's face as Luke walked into the kitchen. "You're up late."

"I couldn't sleep." Despite his attempt not to, Luke couldn't stop himself from staring at the necklace. It was a matter of trust, pure trust, that allowed him to look back at Max and speak. "You stole them."

"Yes."

With a tentative finger, Luke reached out to touch one pale blue gem. "Why?"

Max leaned back, sipping brandy and considering. "Why not?"

Luke's lips twitched at that. It was a good answer. One that satisfied him more than a dozen heartfelt justifications. "Then you're a thief."

"Among other things." Max leaned forward then, but resisted the urge to lay a hand over Luke's. "Do I disappoint you?"

Luke's eyes filled with a love he had no words to express. "You couldn't." He shook his head in frantic denial. "Ever."

"Don't be sure of that." Max touched his hand briefly, then picked up the necklace. "The vase you broke that day was a thing—so is this. Things are worth only as much or as little as people believe." He closed his hand over it, bumped his fists together, then opened both hands. Empty. "One more illusion. My reasons for taking what others value are mine. One day I may share them with you. Until then, I'll ask you not to speak of it."

"I won't tell anyone." He'd have died first. "I can help you. I can," he repeated, furious with LeClerc's derisive snort. "I can make good money picking pockets."

"Luke, there's no such thing as bad money. But I'd prefer you didn't pick pockets unless it's part of a performance."

"But why—"

"I'll tell you." He gestured for Luke to sit, and the gems were back in his hand. "If you'd continued at the carnival, you might very well have been caught. That would have been untidy, and unfortunate."

"I'm careful."

"You're young," Max corrected. "I doubt if it occurred to you to wonder if the people you took from could afford to lose what you slipped from their wallets." He shook his head before Luke could speak. "And your need was great at the time. It isn't great now."

"But you steal."

"Because I choose to. Because, quite simply, I enjoy it. And for complex reasons you—" He broke off and chuckled softly. "I started to say that you wouldn't understand. But you would." His eyes darkened. "I was hardly older than you when LeClerc found me. I was hustling nickels and dimes with the Cups and Balls, card tricks. Lifting wallets. I, too, had escaped from the kind of nightmare no child should experience. Magic sustained me. So did stealing. I had a choice, and I chose to hone my craft on both paths. I don't apologize for being a thief. Every time I steal, I take back something that was stolen from me."

He laughed and sipped. "Oh, what a psychiatrist would make of that. No, I don't apologize, but neither will I play modern-day Fagan with you. I'll give you magic, Luke. And when you're older, you'll make your own choices."

Luke thought it over. "Does Roxanne know?"

For the first time a flicker of doubt showed on Max's face. "I see no reason why she should."

That made it better. For Luke, knowing something Roxanne didn't made all the difference. "I'll wait. I'll learn."

"I'm sure you will. And speaking of that, we should begin to see to your education."

Luke's enthusiasm suffered a direct hit. "Education? I'm not going to school."

"Oh, but you are." Casually, Max handed the necklace to LeClerc. "The paperwork should be simple enough. I think he should be my cousin's boy, recently orphaned."

"It'll take me a week," LeClerc stated. "Maybe two."

"Excellent. Then we'll be set for fall classes."

"I'm not going to school," Luke repeated. "I don't need school. You can't make me go."

"On the contrary," Max said mildly. "You will go to school, you certainly need it and I most assuredly can make you go."

Luke was prepared to die for him, would have been delighted with the opportunity to try. But he was not willing to suffer through several hours of boredom five days a week. "I won't go."

Max only smiled.

7

Luke went to school. Pleas and bargains and threats fell on deaf ears. When he discovered even the soft-hearted Lily was against him, Luke surrendered.

Or pretended to.

They could make him go. At least they could make him get dressed, heft a bunch of stupid books and head toward school under LeClerc's eagle eye.

But they couldn't make him learn anything.

The smirky way Roxanne showed off her A's and gold stars began to tick him off. It really got his goat when she'd smile at him as Max or Lily voiced their approval. And each night the little brat would sit backstage, industriously doing her homework between acts.

Max had expanded her bit with the scarves.

Luke knew he could get A's. If he felt like it.

It wasn't any big deal—just numbers on a paper—but to prove that he couldn't be bested by some snotty, monkey-faced girl, he studied for a geography test.

It wasn't so bad, really, studying about the states and capitals. Especially when he started counting up how many of those states he'd visited.

Afterward he couldn't wait to show off. But he made himself stay cool. If his geography test with the bright red A on it happened to slip out of his notebook backstage, it wasn't his fault.

He nearly exploded with impatience until Lily spotted it and scooped it up.

"What's this?" He saw Lily's eyes go wide and bright with an emotion he'd seen so rarely he blushed to his toes. It was pride. "Luke! This is great! Why didn't you tell us?"

"What?" The foolish grin that spread over his face ruined his show of indifference, but he shrugged anyway. "Oh, that. No big deal."

"No big deal?" Laughing, she squeezed him against her. "It's a huge deal. You didn't miss one. Not even one." With one arm still slung around him she called Max away from a discussion with Lester. "Max, Max, honey, come see this."

"What do I have to see?"

"This." Triumphant, Lily waved the test in front of him. "Look what our Luke did, and never said a word to anyone."

"I'd be glad to look, if you'd hold it still." His brow lifted as he glanced down at Luke. "Well, well. You've decided to apply your brain after all. And with excellent results."

"It's no big thing." He hadn't known it could be. "It's just memorizing."

"My dear boy." Max reached out and flicked a finger down Luke's cheek. "Life is just memorizing. Once you learn the trick, there's very little you can't do. You've done well. Quite well."

As they moved off to prepare for the next act, Luke stood still, absorbing all the pleasure. It dimmed only a little when he turned and saw Roxanne studying him with wise eyes.

"What the hell are you looking at?"

"You," she said simply.

"Well, cut it out."

But even when he stalked away, she continued to look after him. As she would with anything that puzzled her.

School wasn't so bad. Luke discovered he could tolerate it, and rarely hooked more than one or two days a month. His grades were good. He might not have gotten consistent A's like Roxanne, but he copped his share.

Luke wasn't a quick study in all things. It took a black eye and a bloodied lip before that last revelation came to him.

Walking home bruised, disgusted and minus three dollars and twenty-seven cents spending money, he plotted revenge. He'd have taken them, he thought. He'd have taken all three of the bastard creeps if the principal, Mr. Limp Dick, hadn't come along and broken things up.

Actually, if Mr. Rampwick hadn't spotted the tussle, Luke would have been sporting two black eyes at the very least, but adolescent pride colored the event differently. He just hoped he could get cleaned up at home before anyone saw him. He wondered if he could cover the worst of the damage with greasepaint.

"What did you do?"

Luke cursed himself for scowling down at the sidewalk instead of keeping a lookout. Now he'd all but run into Roxanne.

"None of your goddamn business."

"You've been fighting." Roxanne swung her pink bookbag over her shoulder and planted her fists on her hips. "Daddy won't like it."

"That's tough shit." But it worried him. Was Max going to punish him? Max wouldn't hit him—he'd promised he wouldn't. As much as Luke longed to believe that, a part of him still doubted. And feared.

"Your lip's bleeding." Sighing, Roxanne dug into the pocket of her blue skirt for a tissue. "Here. No, don't wipe it with your hand, you'll just smear it." Patient as an old woman, she dabbed at the cut herself. "You'd better sit down. You're too tall for me to reach."

Grumbling, Luke dropped down on the steps of a shop. He wanted a minute anyway, to prepare for Max and Lily. "I can do it myself."

She didn't complain when he snatched the tissue. Roxanne was too interested in studying his eye, where a bruise was already blooming. "Did you make somebody mad?"

"Yeah. They were mad because I wanted to keep my money. Now shut up."

Her eyes narrowed. "They? They beat you up and took your money?"

The humiliation of that stung more than his eye. "That creep Alex Custer sucker-punched me. I'd have held my own if he hadn't had two of his slimy pals holding me down."

"Where'd they go?" She was revved now, and surprised Luke by bounding up from the stoop. "We'll go get Mouse and take care of them."

"We, shit." He grinned and turned his split lip into fire. "You're just a kid—a girl kid. Hey!" He grabbed at the shin she kicked. "What the hell?"

"I can take care of myself," she pointed out grandly. "You're the one with the smashed-up face."

"And the broken leg," he said, amused despite himself. She looked hot and ready and oddly dangerous. "And I can take care of myself, too. I don't need help."

"Yeah, right," she shot back, mimicking him. But she took a deep breath, letting the autumn breeze cool her heated cheeks. "Anyway it's better not to fight. It's more fun to be smarter."

"Smarter than Alex?" Luke hooted. "A head of cabbage is smarter than him."

"Then be a head of cabbage." She sat again, devious rather than angry. "We'll scam him," she said, with quiet relish.

"What's this 'we' shit again?" But he was interested.

"You don't have enough experience to do it on your own. You've got to do the con so he doesn't know he's been conned." She brushed her skirt smooth and put her flexible mind to work. "I know his little brother, Bobby. He's always pinching girls and stealing food." Roxanne smiled slowly. "Well, I was thinking about doing this job on Bobby, but I guess you could have it for Alex."

"What?"

"I'll show you later. We have to get home. They'll start to worry."

He didn't nag her only because he didn't want to seem too interested. And secondly, he was worried about the reaction when he walked in the kitchen door. He'd probably get yelled at, he decided, dragging his feet. Or worse, infinitely worse, Max would give him that long, slow look and say those awful words.

You disappoint me, Luke.

They did yell when he followed Roxanne in the kitchen door. All of them at once, but it was hardly what Luke had expected.

"Happy birthday!"

He jumped back as though he'd been struck. They stood around the kitchen table, Max, Lily, Mouse, LeClerc, with a big lushly iced cake lit with candles. As he gaped, dumbfounded, Lily's beaming smile turned to an "o" of dismay.

"Baby! What happened?" Max halted Lily's forward rush by snagging her wrist. His eyes stayed on Luke's, and while there was a flicker of anger, his voice was calm.

"Had a tussle, did you?"

Luke only shrugged, but Roxanne picked up his banner. "There were three of them, Daddy. That makes them cowards, doesn't it?"

"Indeed." He leaned forward, gently cupping Luke's chin in his hand. "Choose your odds more carefully next time."

"Try this." LeClerc chose a bottle from a shelf and shook some of the contents on a clean cloth. When he pressed it to Luke's swollen eye the worst of the ache faded. "Three?" he said and winked. "This is some of their blood on your shirt, *oui?*"

It was the first time he'd ever felt LeClerc's approval. Luke risked opening his lip again and sneered. "Damn right."

"Well," said Lily, "you've just given us as big a surprise as we planned to give you. I hope ours is better. Happy birthday, baby."

"Better blow out the candles," Max suggested when Luke merely stood, staring. "Before we burn down the house."

"Don't forget to make a wish." This from Roxanne, who was angling herself into the frame as Mouse focused a camera.

He only had one, and that was to belong. It seemed that had already been granted.

The dazzling excitement of his first birthday cake, of opening presents that had been bought just for him, wiped all thoughts of Alex and revenge out of his mind.

Roxanne was more single-minded.

Two days later, Luke found himself in the middle of a sting that could bring him great satisfaction, or a broken face.

He had to admit it was clever. Even—to borrow one of Roxanne's ten-dollar words—diabolical. Following Roxanne's advice, Luke made certain Alex and his two juvenile henchmen saw him saunter into a market on the corner a block from school. He paid for the bottle of grape Nehi—Alex's personal favorite—popped the cap and took a long swig as he stepped back out.

Then he pretended to spot Alex for the first time, forced himself to appear afraid. Like a shark scenting blood, Alex needed no more than that to pursue.

Little peabrain had it right, Luke thought as he darted down an alleyway, uncapping the vial that held one of LeClerc's home remedies.

With quick hands, Luke dumped the strong laxative into the Nehi. He trusted Roxanne knew what she was doing, and that he wasn't about to kill anyone. Though his conscience wouldn't have suffered overmuch.

Stuffing the empty vial back in his pocket, he whirled, as if in panic. He'd chosen the blind alley cold-bloodedly. They might pound on him again, but at least one of them would pay for it later.

"What's the matter, fart breath?" Seeing his quarry pinned, Alex puffed out his chest and grinned. "Lost?"

"I don't want any trouble." Luke buried pride under vengeance and made his voice and hands shake. "I ain't got no money left. I spent it on this."

"No money?" Alex grabbed the bottle before shoving Luke back against the wall. "See if he's lying, Jerry." Alex took a long pull on the spiked soft drink and grinned under a purple moustache.

Luke whimpered, allowing the other boy to poke and prod through his pockets. He wanted to make sure Alex emptied the bottle.

"He's got nothing," Jerry announced. "Give me a sip, Alex."

"Get your own." Alex tilted the bottle back and drained it. "Now." He tossed the bottle aside. "Let's kick ass."

But this time Luke was ready for them. When you couldn't fight, you ran. He ducked his head and plowed into Alex's gut, knocking one boy into the other until the three of them wobbled like a house of cards. He dashed to the mouth of the alley. He was faster, he knew, and could have gotten away before they'd sorted themselves out to come after him. But he wanted them to chase him. A little exercise, he thought, should get things moving through Alex's system.

He led them on a chase, toward Jackson Square and down Royal, skidding around the corner at St. Ann and hotfooting it over to Decatur. A glance back showed him Alex's face was sheet white and running with sweat. Luke made it to his own courtyard and was debating whether to race out and continue, when Alex groaned and clutched his belly.

"Hey, what's the matter?" Jerry pulled at him. "Come on, man. He's getting away."

"My gut! My gut!" Alex dashed toward some rhododendrons and squatted.

"Je-sus!" Jerry shouted in disgust. "That is gr-oss."

"Can't, can't," was all Alex could say as LeClerc's laxative purged him pitilessly.

"Oh, look!" Roxanne popped out of nowhere to point. "There's a boy in the bushes doing number two. Mommy!" She squealed in a baby-doll voice. "Mommy, come quick."

"Come on, Alex, *jeez,* come on." After a quick look around, both Jerry and his companion left the groaning Alex and took off for safer ground as several adults began to hurry over.

With a careless smile on her face, Roxanne strolled into the courtyard. "That's better than punching him," she said to Luke. "He'd forget about that, but he won't ever forget about this."

He had to grin. "And you said I was mean."

From the balcony Max had seen most of the little drama, and had heard all he needed to hear. His children, he thought with a warm glow of pride, were coming along nicely, very nicely indeed. How pleased Moira would have been with her girl.

It wasn't often he thought of his wife, that redheaded firebrand who'd zoomed so quickly in and out of his life. He'd loved her—oh yes, he'd loved her with a kind of greedy wonder. How could he have done otherwise when she'd been beautiful and fearless?

Even after all the years that had passed he found it difficult to believe that all that flash and dash had been snuffed out. So quickly. So uselessly.

A burst appendix. She'd been too impatient to complain about the pain—and then it had been too late. A frantic rush to the hospital, the emergency surgery, hadn't saved her. She'd streamed out of his life, leaving him with the most precious thing they'd made together.

Yes, he was certain Moira would be proud of her daughter.

Turning back into the bedroom, he watched Lily slip an extra pair of his argyle socks into his overnight bag.

Lily. Even her name made him smile. Sweet, lovely Lily. A man could hardly curse God when he'd been given two such glorious women to love in one lifetime.

"You don't have to do that for me."

"I don't mind." She checked his shaving kit to be certain it contained fresh razors before packing it. "I'm going to miss you."

"I'll be back before you know I'm gone. Houston's practically next door."

"I know." She sighed and snuggled against him. "I'd just feel better if I were going with you."

"Mouse and LeClerc are quite enough protection, don't you think?" He kissed her again, one temple, then the other. His Lily had skin as smooth as the petals of her namesake.

"I suppose." She tilted her head, letting her eyes close when he skimmed his lips down her throat. "And someone has to stay with the children. Do you really think the job will be worth a quarter of a million?"

"Oh, at a minimum. These oil men like to put their spare change into art and jewelry."

The idea of that much money excited her, but not nearly as much as what Max's clever tongue was currently doing to her ear. "I locked the door."

Max chuckled as he pressed her down on the bed. "I know."

There was plenty of time during the short flight from New Orleans to Houston, with Mouse at the controls of the Cessna, to go over the blueprints again. The house they would hit a few hours later was huge, a sprawling fifty-five hundred square feet.

The blueprints Max was currently poring over had cost a little more than five thousand in bribes. It was an investment Max calculated well worth the ultimate payoff.

The Crooked R Ranch, as it was overcutely named, was loaded with nineteenth-and twentieth-century art, heavy on the American and Oriental, all of which had been chosen for the owners by agents. It had been purchased not for its aesthetic value or simple beauty but as an investment.

A good one, Max had no doubt. It was about to make him a great deal of money.

There was jewelry, too. The list Max had obtained—from a file drawer in Security Insurance, Inc.'s home base in Atlanta—contained enough baubles and beads to stock a modest jewelry store.

Since his marks were heavily insured, Max figured Security's loss would be his gain. And after all, insurance was a bet, between insurer and insuree. Eventually someone had to lose.

Max glanced up and grinned at LeClerc. The Cajun's knuckles were white as he gripped his armrest. Around his neck were a silver cross, a gold ankh, a crystal talisman and an eagle feather. There were rosary beads, a black rabbit's foot and a pouch full of colored stones in his lap.

LeClerc covered all the bases when he flew.

Because LeClerc's eyes were tightly closed, and his mouth moving in silent prayer, Max said nothing as he rose to pour a small brandy for both of them.

LeClerc downed the brandy. "It's unnatural for a man to be in the air. He dares the gods."

"He dares them every time he takes a breath. I'm sorry to subject you to something you dislike, but my absence in New Orleans couldn't possibly go unnoticed if we'd taken the time to drive."

"Your magic makes you too famous."

"I'm nothing without it. And there are advantages to fame. It's becoming quite the thing for the more important hostesses to invite me to dinner parties, as a guest." He pulled a coin out of the air and began to manipulate it through his fingers. "With the hopes that I'll entertain her, and her party, in the parlor."

"Like a juggler," LeClerc said in disgust, but Max only shrugged.

"If you like. I'm always willing to pay for a well-presented meal. And I'm more than paid back in kind with the contacts I've made. Our friends in Houston were delighted with my impromptu performance at a soiree in Washington last year. How fortunate for us that they'd decided to visit their cousin the senator."

"More fortunate for us that they're in Europe now."

"Much more. Though it's not much of a challenge to steal from an uninhabited house." He moved his shoulders again and turned one coin into two.

They picked up a limo at Hobby, and Mouse donned his chauffeur's cap and jacket for the drive. The long stretch limousine would be less conspicuous in the rich neighborhood than an unmarked sedan.

And Max preferred to travel well whenever possible.

In the backseat, to the strains of a Mozart cantata, he checked his tools one last time.

"Two hours," he announced. "No more."

LeClerc was already slipping on his gloves—an old firehorse who hears the alarm bells and quivers for the harness.

It had been months since he had heard the tumblers click and fall, months since he had had the pleasure of opening the door of a safe and reaching into the darkness beyond. For the long summer, he had been celibate—at least figuratively—and was anxious for the romance of theft.

Without Max, he knew this pleasure would be lost to him by now. Though they never spoke of it, they both knew that LeClerc was slowing down. A younger man would have fit the triangle made up of himself, Mouse and Max more practically. And that day would come. Already he accompanied Max only on less arduous jobs. If the oil man's house hadn't been empty, LeClerc knew he would be at home waiting, as Lily was waiting.

But he wasn't bitter. He was grateful for the opportunity of one more chance at the thrill.

They purred up the sweeping drive, past a statue of a nude boy holding a carp. When the Texans were in residence, Max imagined the carp would vomit water into the birdbath.

"A lesson for you, Mouse. Money can't buy taste."

When they parked in front of the house, the men moved in silence. Max and LeClerc walked to the trunk, Mouse lumbered off to deal with the security system. It was pitch dark, without even a hint of moon.

"Lots of land," LeClerc murmured, pleased. "Lots of big trees. The neighbors must need binoculars to peek in each other's windows."

"Let's hope no one's playing Peeping Tom tonight." Max took a large velvet-lined box from the trunk, and a roll of soundproofing often used in theaters.

And they waited.

Ten minutes later, Mouse hurried back. "Sorry. Was a pretty good system. Took some time."

"No apologies necessary." Max felt the familiar tingling in his fingertips as he approached the front door. Taking out his packet of picks, he went to work.

"Why fool with that? Have Mouse break it in. The alarm's down."

"Lacks finesse," Max muttered, his eyes half closed, his mind inside the tumblers. "There . . . only a moment more."

He was as good as his word. Minutes later they stood inside a dazzling three-story black-and-white marble foyer, facing a reproduction of Venus and an indoor goldfish pond.

"Jeez," was all Mouse could think of to say.

"Indeed. It nearly makes one want to pause and reflect." Max glanced toward an enormous coatrack made of steer horns. "Nearly."

They separated, LeClerc going up the wide curving stairs toward the bedroom safe and milady's jewels, Mouse and Max covering the first floor.

They worked smoothly, cutting paintings from what Max considered overly ornate frames and rolling them inside the velvet box. Sculptures of bronze and marble and stone were wrapped in the thick soundproofing.

"A Rodin." Max paused a moment to teach. "A truly remarkable piece. See the movement, Mouse? The fluidity, the emotion of the artist for his subject."

Mouse saw a funny-looking glob of stone. "Ah, sure, Max. It's neat."

Max could only sigh as he tucked the Rodin reverently between folds of the heavy cloth. "No, not that one," he said when he noted the bronze work Mouse was holding.

"It's real heavy," Mouse told him. "Solid. Must be worth a lot."

"Undoubtedly, or it wouldn't be in this collection. But it lacks style, Mouse, and beauty. It's much more important to steal the beautiful than the valuable. Otherwise, we'd be robbing banks, wouldn't we?"

"I guess." He moved to the next room and came back hefting a Remington piece of a cowboy astride a bucking horse. "How about this one, Max?"

Max eyed it. A good piece and probably as heavy as a truck. Though it wasn't to his personal taste, he could see Mouse was drawn to it. "Excellent choice. Best take it out to the limo as it is. We're nearly done here."

"We're well done," LeClerc stated, striding downstairs and tapping his bulging pouch. "I don't know what Madame and Monsieur took to Europe, but they left behind plenty of baubles for us." It had been difficult to ignore the negotiable bonds and cold cash he'd found in the twin safes, but Max was superstitious about stealing money. LeClerc never sneezed on anyone's superstitions. "Look at this one."

He pulled out a blinding array of diamonds and rubies worked into a three-tiered necklace. With a grunt Max took it and held it up to the light. "How can one take such beautiful stones and make something so hideous from them? The lady should thank us for never having to wear this again."

"Must be worth fifty thousand, at least."

"Hmmm." Possibly, Max thought and wished for his loupe. He would choose a few of the choicer stones and have a more suitable necklace made for Lily. A check of his watch, and a nod. "I believe our shopping spree is over. Shall we load up? I believe we can be back home in time for brunch."

Part Two

A devil, a born devil, on whose nature
Nurture can never stick; on whom my pains,
Humanely taken, all, all lost, quite lost . . .
—William Shakespeare

8

When Luke was sixteen, Mouse taught him to drive. They did a lot of bumping and grinding on the back roads, and once, when Luke attempted to shift, steer and brake at the same time, nearly ended up in a swamp. But Mouse had an endless store of patience.

Getting his driver's license was a momentous occasion for Luke, that giant step toward reaching the manhood he was beginning to crave. But even that paled against another momentous occasion. His date with Annabelle Walker that included the fantasy roller coaster of *Star Wars,* two giant tubes of popcorn and an evening ending in sex in the backseat of the secondhand Nova he'd bought with his savings.

Neither Annabelle nor the Nova were strangers to the backseat boogie. But it was Luke's first time, and for him, the dark road, the music of the cicadas in counterpoint to all the gasps and grunts, the miraculous feel of Annabelle's braless breasts in his hands were as romantic and majestic as the Taj Mahal.

Annabelle might have been considered easy, but she only crawled into the backseat with a boy if he was cute, if he treated her well and if he was a good kisser.

Luke qualified on all counts.

When she let him under her T-shirt to sample those generous, milk-white globes, he thought he'd found heaven. But when she tugged down the zipper on his Levi's and took hold, he understood the gates of paradise were swinging open.

"Christ, Annabelle." He fumbled with her jeans while she jackhammered him toward delirium. He'd hoped she'd let him touch, but he'd had no idea a handful of dates and an evening watching worlds being saved would convince her to let him do the big IT.

Still he wasn't one to miss an opportunity once it was presented. Max had taught him that much.

"Let me . . ." Let him what he wasn't precisely sure, but he got his hand inside her lacy red panties.

Wet, hot, slippery. His blood swam wildly downstream from his head to his crotch, throbbing there in a jungle drumbeat that set the rhythm for his seeking fingers. Annabelle's pleasure sounded in a low hum that became quick greedy moans, desperate pants, delightful little whimpers. Her generous hips arched and fell, slapping against the tattered seat of the Nova. The windows Luke had rolled up against the chill of oncoming winter fogged up, turning the car into a steamy sauna that smelled of sex.

He could feel, actually feel her muscles contract around him as she pitched higher and happily came in his hand.

His breath hitched in and out as he struggled toward something that had been only a dark dream punctuated by locker-room talk.

With his face pillowed between her breasts, one hand busily working her, he tugged his hips free of the Levi's. The sensation of being inside of a woman this way was nearly enough to shatter his control. Yet a part of him, some small corner of his brain, remained cool, oddly detached, even amused.

Here was Luke Callahan, bare-assed in his '72 Nova, with the Bee Gees warbling on the radio—Christ, did it have to be the Bee Gees?—and Annabelle spreading her legs in her best cheerleader style beneath him.

His cock felt like a rocket, huge and hot, vibrating on the launching pad of his arousal. He could only hope lift-off didn't occur prematurely.

It wasn't skill which had him giving her more than the other boys she'd dated. It was pure inexperience mixed with healthy curiosity and a love of beautiful things. Feeling all that hot moisture, feeling a female form tremble and buck beneath his was one of the most beautiful things Luke had ever experienced.

"Oh, baby." A veteran of close-quarters sex, Annabelle wriggled and shifted and locked her legs around his hips. "I can't wait. I just can't."

Neither could he. Blind instinct had him driving himself into her. Control that was as much instinct as the tutelage of four years had him holding back that need for instant release. He worked them both into a delirious sweat before letting go. The last thing he heard was her calling out his name. She all but sang it.

Courtesy of Annabelle, he would return to school Monday with a reputation a growing boy could be proud of.

The house was dark but for a light left burning in the kitchen when he arrived home, smelling of sex and sweat and Annabelle's Charlie cologne.

He was grateful no one was up to greet him. Even more was he grateful that he'd been given every other weekend off from the club to, as Max put it, develop a well-rounded social life.

He sure as hell was feeling well rounded tonight.

He opened the fridge and drained a pint of orange juice straight from the bottle. He was grinning still, and humming the Eagles' "Witchy Woman" under his breath when he turned and spotted Roxanne in the doorway.

"That's disgusting." She inclined her head toward the bottle he held.

She'd sprung up over the years, as he had. But while Luke skimmed under six foot yet, and was no more than average height for his age, Roxanne was the tallest girl in her class—taller, in fact, than most of the boys. Most of it was leg, as showed now in the short nightshirt she wore. Since her hair was neatly brushed, something Luke knew she did every night before bed, he assumed she'd yet to go to sleep.

"Stuff it." He smiled and set the bottle on the counter.

"Maybe someone else wanted some." Though she wasn't in the least thirsty, she marched to the refrigerator and searched. As she chose a Dr Pepper, she wrinkled her nose at Luke. "You smell." Sniffing the air she caught, among other things, the fading hint of Annabelle's cologne. "You went out with *her* again."

Roxanne hated Annabelle Walker on principle. The principle being that she was petite and blond and pretty, and that Luke spent time with her.

"What's it to you?"

"She bleaches her hair and wears her clothes too tight."

"She wears sexy clothes," Luke corrected, feeling an expert on the subject. "You're just jealous because she's got tits and you don't."

"I'll get them." On the cusp of thirteen, Roxanne was mortified by the snail's pace of her feminine development. Almost all the girls in her class had at least the buds of breasts, and she was still as flat as LeClerc's breadboard. "When I do, they'll be better than hers."

"Right." The idea of Roxanne with breasts amused him. Initially. When he began to think about it, it became uncomfortably warm. "Beat it."

"I'm getting a drink." She poured Dr Pepper into a glass to prove it. "I don't have a bedtime on Saturday nights."

"Then I'm going." How was a guy supposed to float around on a cloud of lust with that little whiner around? he wondered as he strode out and up the stairs. Not wanting to miss a moment of the indulgent dream he had planned, Luke stripped and plopped naked onto the bed.

He'd gotten used to the scent and feel of clean sheets, though he'd yet to take them for granted. It was a rare thing for him to go to bed hungry, and for long periods of time he'd forgotten what real fear was.

In the past four years, he'd traveled over most of the eastern United States, had performed in fallow fields, in dingy clubs and on polished stages. The previous summer after Max—with some regret—had sold the carnival, they'd traveled to Europe, where Max had added to his reputation as a master magician.

He could speak French, haltingly, and had learned to make the cards dance. As far as he could see, he had it all. Life was perfect, Luke thought as he drifted to sleep.

So he was stunned when he woke in a cold sweat an hour later with a whimper in his throat.

He'd been back, all the way back to that cramped two-room apartment. Al's belt had whipped like a razor across his skin, and there'd been nowhere to run, nowhere to hide.

Sitting up, Luke gulped in huge breaths of the heavy, autumn air and waited for the shaking to pass. It hadn't happened in months, he told himself as he rested his head on his knees. Months and months without his subconscious zapping him back there. He'd thought he'd beaten it. Each time weeks or months passed without one of those hideous dreams he was sure it was behind him.

Then it would pop back, like a cackling gremlin out of a closet, to taunt and torture.

He wasn't a kid anymore, Luke reminded himself and stumbled from the bed. He wasn't supposed to have nightmares and wake up shaking and wanting Lily or Max to come and make it all go away again.

So he'd walk it off. Luke pulled on pants and told himself he'd walk over to Bourbon and back and shake off the sticky dregs of the nightmare.

When he reached the bottom of the steps he heard the high-pitched scream and the muffled mutter of voices. Glancing into the den, he spotted Roxanne seated cross-legged on the floor, a bowl of popcorn on her lap.

"What're you doing?"

She jolted, but didn't take her eyes off the screen. "I'm watching 'Terror Theater.' *Castle of the Walking Dead.* This count guy's embalming people. It's neat."

"Gross." But he was caught, at least enough to sit on the end of the couch and dip a hand into Roxanne's popcorn. He was still feeling shaky, but before Christopher Lee got what was coming to him, had fallen asleep.

Roxanne waited until she was sure he had, then, leaning her cheek against the cushion on the couch, reached up to stroke his hair.

"They're growing up on us, Lily."

"I know, honey." She sighed as she settled into the brightly painted horizontal box. They were rehearsing alone in the club, a new bit Max called the Divided Woman.

"Roxy's going to be a teenager." Max clamped the locks into place while doing a stylish turn around the box for the benefit of the potential audience. "How much longer are the boys going to stay away?"

Lily smiled and wriggled the feet and hands that stuck out of the holes in the box. "Not much longer. Don't worry, Max, she's too smart to settle for anything less than exactly what she wants."

"I hope you're right."

"She's her father's daughter." Lily made the appropriate whimpers and moans while Max demonstrated the keenness of the blade of a jewel-encrusted scimitar.

"By that you mean she's stubborn, ambitious and one-track-minded."

Lily was silent as Max went through the routine of cutting the box apart and then joining the halves together. Then she asked, "You're not sad the kids're growing up, are you, sweetie?"

"Maybe a little. It reminds me I'm getting older. Luke driving a car and chasing girls."

"He doesn't have to chase them." Lily's brow creased in annoyance. "They throw themselves at him. Anyway," she sighed, "they're good kids, Max. A terrific pair."

Half of that terrific pair was two blocks away, running a brisk game of Three Card Monte. A flood of conventioneers had poured into town. Roxanne simply didn't have the willpower to resist.

She was neatly dressed in pink jeans and matching jacket, a flowered shirt and snow-white sneakers. Her hair was pulled back in a bouncy ponytail, and her face was scrubbed clean of everything but freckles.

She looked like a sweet, wholesome, all-American girl. Which was precisely her intention. Roxanne knew the value of illusion and imagery.

She'd already taken in over two hundred, though she made certain to hit no one mark too hard. She wasn't doing it for the money—though she was every bit as fond of what money could buy as her father. She was doing it because it was fun.

Once again she slapped three cards on the little folding table. She took the five-dollar bet from her current mark—a portly man in an aloha shirt—flipped the cards facedown and began to manipulate them. And the rest of the crowd.

"Keep your eye on the black queen. Don't blink. Don't sneeze. Keep watching her. Keep watching." Her small, long-fingered hands moved like lightning. And, of course, the queen was already palmed.

She took in another fifty, paid out twenty of it to maintain good community relations. Somewhere close by a street-corner musician blew a lonely trumpet. Roxanne decided it was time to close down and move on.

"That's all for today. Thank you, ladies and gentlemen. Enjoy your stay in New Orleans." She started to scoop up the cards when a hand clamped over her wrist.

"One more game. I didn't get to try my luck."

It was a boy of eighteen or nineteen. Under his faded jeans and Grateful Dead T-shirt was a wiry build—all lean muscle. His shaggy hair was a golden blond, a scruffy halo around a narrow face of sharp angles. His eyes, a deep, dark brown, were locked on Roxanne's.

He reminded her of Luke—not in looks but in that inner wildness and potential for mean. His voice didn't sound like New Orleans. It didn't sound like anywhere at all.

"You're too late," she told him.

His hand remained firmly locked around her wrist. When he smiled, showing perfect, even white teeth, her nerves jangled. "One game," he said. "I've been watching you."

It was nearly impossible for Roxanne to resist a direct challenge. Instinct told her to, but pride was stronger.

"I've got time for one. The bet's five dollars."

With a nod, he pulled a folded bill from his back pocket and laid it on the table.

Roxanne laid the cards down, two red queens with the black in the center. "Watch the black lady," she began as she flipped the cards over. In a split-second decision she opted not to palm it, but to face the challenger even up. She shifted the cards in an ever-increasing rhythm, and kept her eye on the boy.

He wasn't new to the game. She'd been in it herself too long not to recognize a pro. Roxanne bet her ego against the five-dollar bill.

Though she hadn't looked at the cards since she'd begun, she knew exactly where the black queen hid. "Where is she?"

He didn't hesitate, but tapped a finger against the left-hand card. Before she could turn it up herself, he snagged her wrist again. "I'll do it." He flipped up the queen of hearts.

"Looks like my hand's quicker than your eye."

Still holding her hand aloft, he turned up the other cards. He blinked once when he saw the black queen was exactly where she'd begun. In the center.

"Looks like," he murmured. His eyes narrowed as he watched her slip his five and the cards into a bag she'd put under the table.

"Better luck next time." She folded the table, hitched it under her arm and started toward the Magic Door.

He didn't give up that easily. "Hey, kid. What's your name?"

She slanted him a look as he fell into step beside her. "Roxanne. Why?"

"Just like to know. I'm Sam. Sam Wyatt. You're good. Real good."

"I know."

He chuckled, but his mind was working on the possibilities. If he could lure her into a less crowded area, he could get his five back, and the rest of her take as well. "You took them smooth. What are you, twelve, thirteen?"

"So?"

"Hey, that's a compliment, sweetheart."

He saw her preen, just a little. Whether it was in response to the compliment, or to the fact that a boy his age would call a twelve-year-old "sweetheart," he wasn't sure. Either way, it was working.

"I was in New York a few months ago. There was a guy working a corner there, taking in five, six hundred a day. He wasn't any better than you. How long you been on the grift?"

"I'm not a grifter." The idea that she could be mistaken for a common con artist had Roxanne bristling. "I'm a magician," she informed him. "Working that crowd was a kind of rehearsal." She smiled to herself. "A paying rehearsal."

"A magician." Sam noted that the pedestrian traffic was thinner here. He could see no one who would give him any real trouble when he snatched the kid's bag and ran. "Why don't you show me a trick?" He put a hand on her arm and prepared to shove her to the ground.

"Roxanne." Scowling, Luke loped across the street. "What the hell are you doing? You're supposed to be at rehearsal."

"I'm going." She scowled right back, furious that he'd come along just when she was going to try her hand at flirting. "You're not there either."

"That's beside the point." He'd noted the table and bag and guessed what she'd been up to. It annoyed the hell out of him that she hadn't cut him in. Pushing that aside for now, he sized up Sam. In the way of the male animal, his hackles rose.

"Who's this?"

"A friend of mine," Roxanne decided on the spot. "Sam, this is Luke."

Sam flashed an easygoing smile. "How's it going?"

"Okay. You're not from around here."

"Just got into town a couple days ago. I'm traveling around, you know?"

"Right." Luke didn't like him. The greedy look in Sam's eyes didn't match the generous smile. "We're late, Roxy. Let's go."

"In a minute." If Luke was going to treat her like a baby, she'd damn well show him she was her own woman. "Maybe you'd like to hang out, Sam. Watch the rehearsal. We're right down there at the Magic Door."

It didn't look like he was going to get his hand on the bag, but Sam wasn't one to give up. The encounter with Roxanne had to be worth something. "That'd be great. If you're sure it's okay."

"It's fine." She took his hand and led him to her father.

Sam knew how to be charming. The veneer of affability, manners and deprecating good humor was as much a part of the game as a marked deck. Sam sat in the Magic Door and applauded, expressed astonished disbelief and laughed at all the right places.

When Lily extended an invitation to dinner, he accepted with shy gratitude.

He found LeClerc old and stupid, Mouse slow and stupid, and went out of his way to make a good impression on both.

Afterward, he made himself scarce for a day so as not to seem too forward. When he showed up at the Magic Door to watch a show, he was greeted warmly. He made certain Lily saw him carefully counting out enough change to buy a soft drink.

"Max." She tugged on his arm when he came backstage, leaving Luke in front to do his five-minute sleight of hand. "That boy's in trouble."

"Luke?"

"No, no. Sam."

"He's hardly a boy, Lily. He's nearly a man."

"He's barely older than Luke." She peeked out, spotted Sam at the bar and noted that he was nursing the same watered-down Coke. "I don't think he has any money, and nowhere to go."

"He doesn't seem to be looking for work." Max knew he was being harsh, and had no real clue as to why he felt so reluctant to offer this helping hand.

"Honey, you know how hard it is to find any. Couldn't you find something for him?"

"Perhaps. Give me a day or two."

A day or two was all Sam needed. To cap his image, he curled up to sleep in the Nouvelle courtyard one night, making sure he was discovered in the morning.

Fully awake, he kept his eyes closed, watching under his lashes as Roxanne darted out of the kitchen door. He groaned, shifted, then blinked his eyes open on a muffled cry of alarm when she spotted him.

"What're you doing?"

"Nothing." He rolled up a tattered blanket and scrambled to his feet. "I wasn't doing anything."

Brow puckered, she came closer. "Were you sleeping out here?"

Sam moistened his lips. "Listen, it's no big deal, okay. Don't say anything."

"Don't you have a room?"

"I lost it." He shrugged, managing to look brave and hopeless at the same time. "Hey, something'll turn up. I just didn't want to be out on the street all night. I didn't figure I'd bother anybody here."

She had her father's heart. "Come on in." She held out a hand. "LeClerc's fixing breakfast."

"I don't need a handout."

Because she understood pride, she softened further. "Daddy can give you a job. I'll ask him."

"You would?" He slipped a hand into hers. "Man, I'd really owe you, Rox. I'd owe you big."

9

There was very little Max denied Roxanne. It was because of her that he hired Sam Wyatt, despite an odd reluctance to add the boy to his entourage. He gave Sam a job hauling props, an occupation Sam knew was beneath his dignity and abilities.

But Sam had instincts as well. His told him that joining the Nouvelle troupe could be the gateway to much bigger and much better things. They were saps, all of them. Even as he derided them he detested them for taking him in off the street like some lost mongrel dog. But for Sam the long con had more appeal than the short shuffle. He could be patient.

He spent hours loading and unloading equipment, polishing the boxes and hinges Max used for various routines. He vowed to pay the old man back one day for offering him such demeaning work but he was unflaggingly kind and attentive to Roxanne and shyly flattering to Lily. Sam had long ago decided that the real power in any group was held by the women.

He didn't make the mistake of competing with Luke. He doubted it would be wise to openly antagonize the person Max considered a son, but the enmity Sam nursed for Luke saw him through the menial, boring days. The fact that the antagonism was shared made it all the better. Neither could have said why, but they had detested each other on sight. One let his feelings bubble to the surface, the other secreted his away, hoarding hate like a miser hoards gold.

Sam looked for the day when he made that gold pay.

In the meantime he was satisfied with his toehold, and with the fact that they were about to spend a week in LA.

Max was pleased with the upcoming trip as well. They would have the opportunity to perform at the Magic Castle, attend a dinner party hosted by Brent Taylor, movie star and amateur magician, and Max would have the pleasure of showing his family some of the glitter of Hollywood.

He also intended to take some of the more expensive glitter back cast with him. Beverly Hills, and its mansions filled with treasures, was going to add to an already lucrative gig.

He had two houses targeted, and would choose between them after he had arrived in Los Angeles and had cased the areas firsthand.

They took over several rooms at the Beverly Hills Hotel. It amused Max to watch Luke charm the bellman and the chambermaid with a few pocket tricks. The boy had learned, he thought. And learned well.

He arranged an elaborate lunch at Maxim's, treating his family and all the members of his troupe down to the lowliest back-door boy. Afterward he sent Lily and Roxanne shopping.

"Now then." Max lit a post-meal cigar. "Mouse and I have some business to attend to, but the rest of you have the day free to explore, sightsee, whatever strikes your fancy. I'll need everyone bright-eyed for rehearsals at nine A.M. tomorrow."

While the others left, Luke shifted chairs to sit next to Max. "I need to talk to you."

"Of course." Recognizing both nerves and determination, Max lifted a brow. "Is there a problem?"

"I don't think it's a problem." Luke took a deep breath and dived. "I want to go with you." He shook his head before Max could speak. He'd been preparing this speech for days. "I know the routine, Max. You and Mouse are going out to case a couple of houses. You'll already have most of the important stuff. A copy of the insurance lists, blueprints, the schematics of the security systems, an idea of the basic household routine. Now you'll do some checking firsthand and decide when and where to hit."

Max brushed at his moustache. He wasn't certain if he was annoyed or impressed. "You've been keeping up."

"I've had four years to study the routine while I've waited for you to let me in."

Max tapped away cigar ash before taking a considering drag. "My dear boy—"

"I'm not a boy anymore." Luke's eyes flashed as he leaned closer. "You either trust me or you don't. I have to know."

Max puffed out a breath and held his silence while the waiter cleared the dishes. "It's not a matter of trust, Luke, but of timing."

"You're not going to tell me you're trying to save me from a life of crime."

Max's lips twitched. "Certainly not. I've never been a hypocrite, and I'm as egocentric as any father, hoping his son will follow in his footsteps. But . . ."

Luke laid a hand on Max's wrist. "But?"

"You are still young. I'm not sure you're ready. To be a successful thief takes maturity, experience."

"It takes balls," Luke put in and made Max throw back his head and laugh.

"Oh, indeed it does. But besides that, a certain amount of skill, finesse, coolheadedness. In a few more years you may ripen, but for now—"

"What time is it?"

Distracted, Max blinked, then glanced down at his watch. Or where his watch should have been. "I always said you had good hands," he murmured.

"Don't have the time?" Luke turned his wrist. The sunlight glinted off the gold of Max's Rolex. "It's nearly three. I guess you'd better pay the check and get going." Luke signaled for the waiter himself. Absently, Max reached inside his jacket for his wallet. And came up empty.

"A little short?" Luke smiled and took Max's wallet out of his own pocket. "This one's on me. I happen to have come into some money recently."

Point taken, Max thought and smiled at Mouse. "Why don't you take the afternoon off as well? Luke can drive me."

"Sure, Max. I can go over and see those footprints at the Chinese place."

"Enjoy yourself." With a sigh, Max held out his hand for his wallet. "Ready to go?" he asked Luke.

"I've been ready for years."

Beverly Hills appealed to Luke. Not like New Orleans with its party streets and decaying glamour. That was the only place he would ever consider home. But the wide, palm-lined avenues and fantasy aura of houses tucked onto hilltops in the smog-misted distance was like a movie. He supposed that was why so many movie stars chose that section of real estate to live.

He tooled along, following Max's directions. He noted the occasional police cruiser. No scratched and dusty cars for the cops here. Each one was glittering clean in the afternoon sun.

Most of the estates were tucked behind high walls and hedges. Twice as they circled around they passed one of the buses that toured movie stars' homes. Luke wondered why anyone would pay for the ride when all they would really see would be stone walls and the tops of trees.

"Why," Max asked as he opened his briefcase, "do you want to steal?"

"Because it's fun," Luke answered without thinking. "And I'm good at it."

"Mmmm." Max could only agree that it was best to spend your life doing something you enjoyed and were skilled at. "The bellman who brought up our bags and was so entertained by your pocket tricks. He had a watch and a wallet. Did you take them?"

"No." Surprised, Luke turned his head to stare. "Why would I?"

"Why wouldn't you is more to the point." Max loosened his tie and folded it inside the case.

"Well, hell, it's no fun if it's that easy. Besides he was just some guy trying to make a living."

"One could argue that a thief is also just some guy trying to make a living."

"If that's all I wanted, I could knock over some convenience store."

"Ah, so you'd consider such an enterprise out of the question."

"It's low-class."

"Luke." Max sighed as he folded his crisp white shirt into the case. "You do make me proud."

"It's like magic," Luke said after a moment. "You want to do the best you're capable of. If you're going to dupe somebody, then you ought to do it with some flair. Right?"

"Precisely right." Max slipped into a short-sleeved polyester shirt in screaming checks of green and orange.

"What are you doing?"

"Just donning the appropriate costume." Max added a Phillies baseball cap and a pair of mirrored sunglasses. "I do hope I look like a tourist."

Luke pulled up at a stop sign and took the time to study Max. "You look like an idiot."

"Close enough. See the tour bus halfway down the block. Pull up behind it."

Obeying orders, Luke parked the car, but he scowled down at the fielder's cap Max held out to him. "Pittsburgh. You know I'm not a National League fan."

"Tough it out." Max wound binocular and camera straps around his neck. "This here's Elsa Langtree's house," Max said in a thick Midwestern twang as he pushed out of the car. He added a whistle before jockeying with the other tourists for a peek through the wrought-iron gate. "Man oh man, is she something!"

Luke picked up on the tone and craned his neck. "Hell, Daddy, she's old."

"She can retire in my neck of the woods anytime."

This brought a few chuckles from the rest of the crowd before the tour guide began his routine. Stepping back, Max circled the bus and climbed nimbly on its roof while the rest of the tour listened and snapped pictures. Max used the telescopic lens on his camera to take shots of the wall, the three-story colonial house, its outbuildings, the outdoor lighting.

"Hey, buddy." The bus driver squinted up from under the bill of his cap. "Get the hell down from there, will ya? Christ, there's one in every crowd."

"I just wanted to see if I could catch a look at Elsa."

"Come on, Daddy. Jeez, you're embarrassing me."

"Okay, okay. Oh, wait! I think I see her. Elsa!" he shouted, using the confusion as people scrabbled back to the gate to take the last of his pictures.

While the driver cursed and threatened, Max climbed down. He offered a sheepish grin and an apology. "I've been a fan for twenty years. Even named my parakeet after her."

"Yeah, she'd be thrilled."

With obvious reluctance, Max let Luke drag him back to the car. "Wait till I tell the boys back in Omaha. Just wait."

"Did you get what you needed?" Luke asked.

"Oh, I imagine so. We'll take a look at one more. Lawrence Trent's home isn't on the tour, but he's reputed to have an excellent collection of nineteenth-century snuff-boxes."

"What does Elsa have?"

"Besides the obvious feminine charms?" Max adjusted the radio and found some Chopin. "Emeralds, my dear boy. The lady is particularly fond of emeralds. They match her eyes."

Max was fond of emeralds as well. Once LeClerc had arranged for the pictures to be developed, it was obvious that Trent's estate would be the easier mark. Max needed little else to decide him. He'd go for the stones.

"Heels, Roxanne?"

Roxanne stood proudly in the wings, teetering a bit on her new inch-high pumps. "I'm practically a teenager," she told her father.

"I believe we have several months yet before that momentous occasion."

"That's hardly any time. And besides, they punch up the costume." She turned, carefully, in her blue spangled leotard. "And the extra inch gives me more stage presence." If her breasts were going to take forever to develop, at least she'd take advantage of her height. "Making a good impression here at the Magic Castle's important, isn't it?" She smiled winningly.

"Naturally." And they had thirty seconds to cue. "I don't suppose you brought along any spare shoes."

Her smile widened before she kissed his cheek. "We're going to knock them dead."

Perhaps it was a trick of those lights, or his own thoughts, but for a moment when the curtain went up he saw her as a woman grown, slim and lovely, glowing with confidence, her eyes glinting with secrets only the female heart ever truly understands.

Then she was just his little girl again, wearing grown-up shoes and charming the audience with her skill with the silks. Moments later the silks were pooled at her feet, and she turned to her father, prepared to be put into a trance for his new levitation routine, a combination of the old broomstick illusion and the floating girl.

The music cued. "Für Elise." Slowly, gracefully, Max passed his hands in front of her face. Her head swayed. Her eyes drooped closed.

He used brooms with sparkling brushes, wanting beauty as well as drama. The first he placed between her shoulder blades, then taking a step stage left, held out his arms, gesturing. As if weightless, her legs began to rise, straight and extended, until her body was parallel to the stage. He used the other broomstick to sweep, over and under. Her long, already dramatic mane of red hair tumbled downward. When he removed the only brace, passing both brooms to a waiting Lily, the crowd was already applauding.

To the liquid strains of Beethoven, Roxanne began to revolve. The light changed to gold as her body turned, tilted, became vertical a foot above the stage. He brought her down gently, inch by inch, until her feet touched the stage.

And he awakened her.

Roxanne opened her eyes to a thunder of applause. Already in her mind, there was no sweeter sound.

"Told you, Daddy," she said under her breath.

"So you did, my sweet."

Sam watched from backstage and shook his head. It was all a scam, he thought. What pissed him off the most was that no one would let him in on the secret of how it was done. It was just one more thing the Nouvelles would have to pay for eventually.

All he needed was a couple of the steps, then he imagined he could duplicate it, or any of the other tricks, if he chose to. It amazed him, and appealed to his sense of greed, that people would actually pay good money to watch someone pretend he could do what couldn't be done.

There had to be a way to cash in on it, he considered. He lit a cigarette and watched Luke make his entrance. Big fucking deal, he thought. The bastard thought he was hot shit, standing out there in the spotlight, getting the applause and the attention.

The day would come, Sam told himself, when he would have all the attention. Because when you had that, you had power. And that was what Sam wanted most.

"Mr. Nouvelle." The moment the performance was over Brent Taylor, the actor with matinee-idol looks and a cream-rich baritone voice, sought Max out in his dressing room. "I have never, never seen better." Taylor pumped Max's hand enthusiastically.

"You flatter me, Mr. Taylor."

"Brent, please."

"Brent, then, and you'll call me Max. It's a bit cramped in here, but I'd be honored if you'd join me in a brandy."

"My pleasure. The transformation routine." Taylor continued while Max poured. "Simply marvelous. And the levitation was spectacular. I'm anxious for my dinner party so that we'll have more time to discuss magic."

"I'm always happy to discuss magic." He offered a snifter full of Napoleon.

"And perhaps we could also discuss the magic of the small screen. Television," Taylor said when Max merely smiled politely.

"Yes, I'm afraid I have little opportunity to watch it. My children now, they're experts."

"And impressive magicians in their own right. I imagine they'd be delighted to try their luck in a television special."

Max gestured for Taylor to sit on the small settee and took his own seat in front of the makeup table. "Magic loses power on film."

"It can, of course. But with your sense of theater, it could be marvelous. I'll be frank,

Max. I've been given an opportunity by one of the networks to produce a series of variety specials. I'd like very much to produce an hour of 'The Amazing Nouvelle.' "

"Max." Luke paused, one hand on the door. "I'm sorry. There's a reporter from the *LA Times*."

"I'll speak with him in a moment. Brent Taylor, Luke Callahan."

"A pleasure to meet you." Taylor rose to shake Luke's hand. "You have a lot of talent—it's not surprising when you've been taught by the best."

"Thanks. I like your movies." Luke glanced from Taylor to Max. "I'll ask him to wait at the bar."

"That's fine."

"An amazingly good-looking boy," Taylor commented when Luke left them alone. "If he decides not to follow in your footsteps, I could get him six roles tomorrow."

Max smiled and studied his nails. "I'm afraid he's quite determined to follow in mine. Now, as to your offer..."

Luke could hardly bear to wait. There was no time to speak to Max privately until after the second show. The moment Max slipped into his dressing room, Luke pounced.

"When are we going to do it?"

"Do?" Max sat at the makeup table and dipped his fingers into cold cream. "Do what?"

"The television thing." Excitement shimmered around him as he stared at Max's reflection. "The special Taylor wants to produce. Would we do it here, in LA?"

With deliberate strokes, Max creamed off greasepaint. "No."

"We could do it on location in New Orleans." He could already see it—the lights, the cameras, the fame.

Max tossed aside used tissues. "We're not doing it, Luke."

"We should probably cut out any close-up work, but we could fill in..." He trailed off, excitement fading into astonishment. "What? What do you mean we're not doing it?"

"Just that." Max loosened the tie of his tux before rising to change. "I turned it down."

"But why? We'd reach millions of people in one evening."

"Magic loses impact on film." Max hung up his jacket and went to work on the studs of his shirt.

"It doesn't have to. We could do it live. Lots of times they have a studio audience."

"Our schedule wouldn't permit it in any case." Max placed the studs in a small gold box. A movement of *Swan Lake* wafted out when he opened the lid.

"That's bull." Luke's voice quieted as something other than confusion worked into him. Max hadn't met his eyes once, not once since they'd come into the room. "It's all bull. You're not doing it because of me."

Deliberately, Max closed the lid on the music. "That's a remarkably foolish idea."

"No, it's not. You don't want that kind of exposure, not with me along. Just like you turned down the Carson show last year. You don't want to do TV because you think that son of a bitch might see me, him or my mother, and make trouble. So you're saying no to the kind of stuff that would put you over the top."

Max stripped off his tuxedo shirt and stood in a white undershirt and dress pants.

Out of habit, he hung the shirt on a padded hanger, brushed a finger down the pleats. "I make my own choices, Luke, for my own reasons."

"Because of me," Luke murmured. It hurt, this pressure in the chest, this twisting in the gut. "It's not right."

"It's right for me. Luke." Max reached out to touch his shoulder, but Luke jerked away. It was the first time in years the boy had made that sharp, defensive movement. That, too, hurt. "There's no need to take it this way."

"How am I supposed to take it?" Luke demanded. He wanted to smash something, anything, but managed to clench his fists at his sides. "It's my fault."

"Blame doesn't enter into it. Priorities do. You may not be quite old enough yet to understand that, or that time passes. In another two years, you'll be eighteen. If I choose to accept an offer to do television at that time, I'll do so."

"I don't want you to wait. Not for me." His eyes were bright and furious. "If there's trouble, I'll handle it. I'm not a kid anymore. And for all we know, she's dead. I hope to God she's dead."

"Don't." Max's voice was sharp as a sword. "Whatever she did or didn't do, she remains your mother, and gave you life. Don't wish for death, Luke. It comes to all of us soon enough."

"Do you expect me not to hate her?"

"Your feelings are your responsibility. Just as my decisions are mine." Suddenly tired, Max scrubbed his hands over his face. He'd known the time would come to speak of it. The time always came for what you dreaded most. "She isn't dead."

Luke's body coiled like a whip. "How do you know?"

"Do you think I would take chances with you?" Furious at having to explain himself, Max snatched a clean shirt from the hanger. "I've kept track of where she is, how she is, what she's doing. One move toward you, one, and I'd have taken you where she couldn't find you."

All of the anger drained out of Luke, leaving him empty and miserable. "I don't know what I'm supposed to say to you."

"There's nothing you have to say. I did what I did, and will continue to do, because I love you. If I have to ask anything of you in return, I'll ask you to be patient for two short years."

Shoulders slumped, Luke poked at the pots on Max's dressing table. "I'll never be able to pay you back."

"Don't insult me by trying."

"You and Lily . . ." He picked up a jar, set it down again. Some emotions were too huge for words. "I'd do anything for you."

"Then put this out of your mind for now. Go and change. I have work to do yet tonight."

Luke looked up again. Max wondered how it could be that the boy could turn into a man in the short time they'd stood inside that cramped room. But it was a man who turned to him now, his shoulders broad and erect, his eyes no longer bright, but dark and direct.

"You're going to do the Langtree job tonight. I want to go with you."

Max sighed and sat to remove his stage shoes. "You're making things difficult this evening, Luke. I indulged you before, but there's a big step between casing a job and executing one."

"I'm going with you, Max." Luke stepped forward so that Max was forced to tilt back his head to meet Luke's eyes. "You're always talking about choices. Isn't it time you let me start making some of my own?"

There was a long pause before Max spoke again. "We leave in an hour. You'll need dark clothes."

Max was grateful that Elsa Langtree didn't collect the small fru-fru dogs many actresses found fashionable. Elsa's eccentricities ran toward collecting men—younger and brawnier as the years passed. She was currently between husbands number seven and eight, having recently divorced a professional linebacker. Wedding plans were underway with her current amour, a twenty-eight-year-old bodybuilder.

Elsa was forty-nine and counting.

While her taste was admittedly poor in men, it was otherwise flawless. A fact that Max pointed out to Luke as they climbed over her eight-foot security wall.

"The wealthy often lose perspective," Max said softly as they hurried across the trim lawn. "But as you'll see, the house Elsa had built about ten years ago is simply lovely. She hired decorators, of course. Baxter and Fitch, quite good. But she inspected and approved every swatch, every piece, every detail personally.

"How do you know all this?"

"When one prepares to break into a home, it's imperative to know all about the inhabitants, as well as the structural layout." He paused in the shelter of some mimosa trees. "There, as you see, is an excellent example of Colonial architecture. Very traditional lines, slightly fluid and feminine and perfectly suited to Elsa."

"It's big," Luke remarked.

"Naturally, but not ostentatious. Once we're inside, you will speak only when absolutely necessary, stay beside me at all times and follow my instructions to the letter, and without hesitation."

Luke nodded. Anticipation was bubbling in his blood. "I'm ready."

Max found the alarm system camouflaged by the window boxes off the rear patio. Following Mouse's instructions, he unscrewed the shield and snipped the proper wires. Fighting impatience, Luke waited while Max replaced the screws and moved to the terrace door.

"Etched glass, cut and designed by an artist in New Hampshire," Max murmured. "A crime to damage it." Instead of using his cutter, he took out his picks and went to work on the two locks.

It took time. As the minutes clicked by, Luke heard every sound in the air. The faint hum from the pool filter, the rustle of night birds in the trees, the quiet click of metal on metal as Max finessed the locks. Then the whisper of success as Max slid the door open.

Now, for the first time, he felt what Max always experienced. That thrumming excitement of walking inside a locked house, that eerie pleasure of knowing people slept inside, the itchy power of moving through the darkness to take the prize.

They walked silently, single file through the spacious drawing room. A light scent of mums, a whisper of female perfume lingering. With the blueprints clear in his mind, Max headed for the kitchen, and the door that led to the basement.

"Why—"

Max shook his head for silence and moved downstairs. The walls were paneled in dark pine. A pool table stood in the center of the main room and was surrounded by weight equipment. An oak bar dominated one wall.

"Play room," Max said quietly. "To keep her men happy."

"She keeps her jewelry down here?"

"No." Max chuckled at the thought. "But the breaker box is. The safe is a time release. Quite sophisticated and difficult to crack. Of course, if the power's off..."

"The safe will open."

"Bingo." Max creaked open the door of the utility room. "Isn't this handy?" he said to Luke. "All neatly labeled. Library." He flipped the breaker. "That should do it." He turned to Luke with a smile. "People so often hide their safe among their books. It's interesting, don't you think?"

"Yeah." Inside his gloves, his hands were sweating.

"How do you feel?"

"Like I did the first time I climbed into the backseat with Annabelle," Luke heard himself say, then flushed.

Max pressed a hand to his heart but couldn't hold back the quick chuckle. "Oh yes," he managed after a moment. "A very apt analogy." Turning, he led the way back up the stairs.

They found the safe in the library, behind a gorgeous O'Keeffe. With the time release negated, it was as simple to open as a child's puzzle box. Max stepped back and gestured to Luke.

From father to son, he thought proudly while Luke removed the jeweler's boxes from the safe. The narrow beam of his penlight shone on the gems when Luke opened the tops.

They were beautiful. That was all Luke could think as he stared down at the sparkle of stones, magnificently set in gold and platinum. That he didn't think at all of their monetary value in that first instant would have pleased Max enormously.

"Not yet," Max said with his mouth close to Luke's ear. "What shimmers is often paste." He removed a loupe from his pouch and, handing the light for Luke to hold over the gems, examined them. "Gorgeous," he murmured, sighing. "Simply gorgeous. As I said, Elsa has exquisite taste." He closed the safe and levered the painting back over it. "It's a shame to leave the O'Keeffe behind. But it seems only fair, don't you think?"

Luke stood with thousands of dollars in emeralds in his hands. And grinned.

10

The trick of pulling off a clean scam, as far as Sam was concerned, was to exploit the weakest link. In the short time he'd been with the Nouvelle troupe, he had made himself available for all and any jobs, kept an eager smile on his face and a word of flattery ready on his tongue. He had listened sympathetically when Lily told him about Luke's past and won her heart by inventing a story of a dead mother and a brutal father—which would have surprised his parents, who lived in a modest home in Bloomfield, New Jersey, and who had never in the sixteen years he'd lived under their roof raised an angry hand to him.

He'd hated the suburbs, and for reasons that had baffled both of his quiet, hard-working parents, had despised them, their life-style and their modest ambitions.

Throughout his teenage years, he had broken their hearts with defiance and rebellion. He'd stolen the family car for the first time at fourteen and had headed for Manhattan. He might have made it, if he'd bothered to pay the toll at the tunnel. The cops brought him back to Bloomfield, surly and unrepentant.

He became adept at shoplifting, stealing watches, costume jewelry, department store makeup. He'd box the merchandise neatly in a leather suitcase he'd lifted, then sell it all at a discount to schoolmates.

Twice he broke into school and vandalized it, for the pleasure of breaking windows or busting water pipes. He was clever enough not to brag about his exploits, and was so charming to his teachers, they never glanced in his direction.

At home he was a hellion, driving his mother to tears on a regular basis. His parents knew he stole from them, a twenty would be missing from a wallet, knickknacks would disappear, a piece of jewelry would vanish. They couldn't understand why he felt compelled to take when they provided well for him. They didn't understand that their son didn't particularly like to steal. But he liked, very much, to hurt people.

He refused to go to counseling sessions, or if they did manage to drag him to the therapist, he would sit sullenly and speak not at all. When at sixteen his mother had refused to allow him the use of her car, he had responded by striking her, splitting her lip and bruising her eye. Then he had calmly taken up the keys, walked out the door and driven away.

He'd ditched the car near the Pennsylvania border, and he'd never gone back.

He never thought about his parents. No memories played through his mind of Christmases or birthdays, trips to the shore. For Sam, they meant less than nothing, and therefore didn't exist.

The Nouvelles were providing him with some pocket change, an excellent front and the time to plan another score. Because he was able to use them, he despised them as much as he had despised the quiet couple who'd given him life.

For reasons he didn't understand, or try to explore, he hated Luke the most. Because he sensed that Roxanne had developed a childish crush on Luke, Sam set about wooing her away.

He also considered her the weakest link.

He gave her time and attention, listened to her ideas, complimented her magic skills. He flattered her into showing him a few tricks and gradually built up her trust and affection for him.

He was dead sure of her loyalty, and toward the end of his second month in New Orleans, decided to put it to use.

He'd often walk out to meet her on her way home from school, a habit that had endeared him to both Max and Lily. It was a chill, damp winter, and people hurried along the streets, seeking the comfort of home. It was easy to spot Roxanne, strolling slowly along the sidewalk, keeping out of the thin rain by walking under the overhanging terracing while she looked in shop windows. Many of the shopkeepers knew her well and would welcome her in if she came to browse.

She handled what she touched with respect and admiration, often asking questions and storing the knowledge away.

She was still two blocks away when he saw her, the bright hair and deep blue jacket shining out of the gloom. He'd already chosen his mark and, as he walked to meet her, was in the best of moods.

"Hey, Rox, how was school?"

"It was okay." She smiled up at him, just old enough, and certainly female enough, to be flattered by the attentions of a nineteen-year-old man. The heart inside her stubbornly undeveloped breast picked up its rhythm.

One of the shops along Royal was stocked with more junk than treasure. There were some interesting pieces, most of them inexpensive. The woman who ran the shop took merchandise on consignment, and supplemented her income by reading tarot cards and palms. Sam had chosen the shop because the proprietor usually worked alone, and because Roxanne often stopped in for a reading.

"Want to get your cards read?" He grinned at her. "Maybe you can find out how you did on that test?"

"I never ask dumb stuff like that."

"You could ask her about a boyfriend." He sent her a look that had her pulses jittering, and opened the door before she had a chance to move on. "Maybe she'll tell you when you're going to get married."

Roxanne stared down at her shoes. "You don't really believe in the cards."

"Let's see what she tells you. Maybe I will."

Madame D'Amour sat behind the counter. She had an angular, heavily rouged face dominated by dark brown eyes. Today she wore one of her many turbans, a purple one that covered all but a few wisps of her mercilessly dyed ebony hair. She added heavy rhinestone earrings that fell nearly to the shoulders of her purple caftan. Around her neck were several silver chains. Bracelets jangled on both wrists.

She was somewhere in her sixties and claimed to be descended from gypsies. It might have been true, but regardless of her heritage, Roxanne was fascinated by her.

As the bells on the door jingled, she glanced up and smiled. Colorfully illustrated tarot cards were on the counter before her, arranged in a Celtic cross.

"I thought my little friend would visit me today."

Roxanne moved closer so that she could study the cards. It was overly warm in the shop, but she never minded. It always smelled wonderful from the incense Madame burned and the woman's generous use of perfume.

"Did you come to shop," Madame asked her, "or to seek?"

"Do you have time for a reading?"

"For you, my love, always. Perhaps we can share some hot chocolate, *oui?"* She glanced over at Sam, and her smile dimmed a bit. There was something about the boy she couldn't like, despite his open, friendly smile and pretty eyes. "And you? You have a question for the cards?"

"That's okay." He made his smile sheepish. "I guess it spooks me a little. Go ahead, Rox, take your time. I've got to go pick up some stuff at the drugstore. I'll meet you back home."

"Okay." As Madame scooped up the cards and rose, Roxanne moved toward the curtain that separated the shop from the back room. "Tell Daddy I'm coming."

"Sure. See you." He started toward the door, stopping when he heard the curtain whisk closed. His smile was no longer friendly as he deliberately opened the outside door, letting the bells jangle, then shut it again. Moving quickly, he skirted the tables loaded with trash and treasures and headed for the counter. Beneath it was a painted cigar box where Madame kept the day's receipts. The haul wasn't huge—business was slow on rainy winter days, but Sam scooped out everything, down to the last penny. He stuffed bills and change into his pocket, glanced quickly around to see if anything else was worth his time. He would have preferred smashing some of the glass and china. That made a statement. Instead, he filled his jacket pockets with some of the smaller knickknacks. Carefully holding the bells still, he eased the door open, slipped out and closed it slowly, quietly behind him.

Over the next week, Sam hit four more shops in the Quarter. When it was to his advantage, he enlisted Roxanne's help, wandering into stores with her and waiting while she, a familiar face in the district, caught the clerk's attention. He'd stuff whatever was handy into his pockets, whether it was a valuable Limoges box or a cheap souvenir ashtray. Once he was lucky enough to clean out another cash drawer when Roxanne was taken in the back to be shown a porcelain doll that had just been shipped in from Paris.

It didn't matter to Sam how much his loot was worth. What he enjoyed most was knowing that the wide-eyed, trusting Roxanne was his unwitting partner. No one would accuse Maximillian Nouvelle's little darling of lifting trinkets. As long as he was with her, he could line his pockets to his frigid heart's content.

But the best part of that New Orleans winter was seducing Annabelle away from the lovesick Luke.

It was easy, as easy as his compulsive and mean-spirited shoplifting. All he had to do was watch, listen and take advantage of opportunities offered.

Like most young lovers, Luke and Annabelle had their share of spats. Most of them revolved around the limited amount of time Luke had to entertain her, and her increasing demand for every moment of his day. She nagged at him to skip rehearsals, to bow out of performances so that he could take her to a party, to a dance, for a ride. Maybe he was being led around by his hormones, but Luke was too professional an entertainer—and too dedicated a thief—to cancel a performance or a heist, even for Annabelle.

"Listen, I can't." Luke blew out an impatient breath and shifted the phone to his other ear. "Annabelle, I explained all this days ago."

"You're just being stubborn." Through the receiver the tears in her voice came clearly. And made Luke feel like sludge. "You know Mr. Nouvelle would understand."

"No, I don't," Luke responded—because he hadn't asked Max to understand, and had no intention of doing so. "It's not my weekend off, Annabelle. I have a commitment to the act."

"I guess it means more to you than I do."

Naturally it did, but Luke doubted it would be wise to say so. "It's something I have to do."

"Lucy's party's going to be the biggest one of the year. Everybody's going to be there. Her dad even hired a live band. I'll just die if I miss it."

"Then go," Luke said between his teeth. "I told you it was okay with me. I don't expect you to sit home alone."

"Oh, sure." Derision, on the shrill side, joined the tears. "Go to the biggest party of the year without my boyfriend." She sniffled, then put all the wheedling at her disposal into her voice. "Oh, please, honey, couldn't you just get out of the first show? It wouldn't be so bad if we went to it together, then you had to leave."

It was tempting, as the Crack the Whip had once been tempting not so many years ago. It promised excitement, a fast, breathless ride. Luke hadn't changed so much in the last years that he didn't know when to resist the offer of pleasure.

"I'm sorry, Annabelle. I can't."

"Won't." The single word was ice.

"Listen," he began, then winced as the crash of the receiver echoed in his ear. "Christ," he muttered and dropped the phone on the hook.

"Women trouble?" It appeared as though Sam was just wandering in from the kitchen, an apple in one hand. In truth, he'd eavesdropped on the entire conversation, and was already formulating plans.

"They don't understand anything." It wasn't usual for Luke to confide in Sam, but he was just angry and frustrated enough to dump on the first available ear. "How the hell am I supposed to screw around with everyone's schedule just because Lucy Harbecker's having some party?"

Sam nodded in sympathy and bit into his apple. "Hey, she'll get over it." He gave Luke a friendly punch in the arm. "And if she doesn't, there are plenty of babes in the woods. Right?" He winked and started upstairs. It looked as though he needed to shake loose from tonight's show. Sam had a party to go to.

A faked fever and sick headache were all he needed. While Luke was preparing to warm up the audience at the Magic Door, Sam knocked on Annabelle's door. She answered it herself, her eyes puffy from weeping and bad temper.

"Oh, hi, Sam." She sniffled and smoothed at her hair. "What're you doing around here?"

"Luke sent me." With an apologetic smile, he brought his hand from behind his back and offered a clutch of painted daisies.

"Oh." She took the flowers and sniffed at them. They were nice, but they didn't make up for missing the biggest night of the year. "I guess he's trying to make up."

"He's really sorry. Annabelle. He felt bad about you missing the party."

"Me too." Her eyes hardened, then she sighed and shrugged. Her parents were out for the evening, her own night was ruined and all she had to show for it was a bunch of stupid flowers. "Well, thanks for bringing them by."

"My pleasure. It's not exactly a hardship to bring flowers to a beautiful woman." Admiration, with a touch of lust, showed in his eyes before he looked hurriedly away. "I guess I should take off. You've got things to do."

"No, not really." She was flattered by the look, touched by the fact that he'd tried to conceal it. With the long, dull night stretched in front of her, it seemed foolish to shut the door on an attractive male. "Maybe you'd like to come in for a Coke or something. Unless you've got plans."

"That'd be nice, if you're sure it's okay with your folks."

"Oh, they're out, won't be back for hours." She batted her eyes at him. "I'd really like some company."

"Me too." He closed the door behind him.

He played shy at first, keeping plenty of distance between them on the couch while they drank Cokes and listened to records. Gradually, he moved to sympathetic confidant. He was careful to stop just short of criticizing Luke, aware of how easily Annabelle could turn on him. Under the guise of making up to her the missed party, he invited her—with just a touch of awkwardness—to dance.

She found his shy admiration sweet and snuggled her head against his shoulder as she swayed over the rug. When his hand began to move rhythmically up and down her spine, she only sighed.

"I'm so glad you came by," she murmured. "I feel so much better."

"I hated to think about you being alone and upset. Luke's so lucky to have a girl like you." He swallowed, making sure it was audible. When he spoke again, his voice was unsteady. "I, ah, I think about you all the time, Annabelle. I know I shouldn't, but I can't help it."

"Really?" Her eyes were shining as she tilted back her head to look at his face. "What do you think about me?"

"About how beautiful you are." He brought his mouth close to hers, felt her shudder. It amused him how easy women were. Tell them they were beautiful, and they believed anything you said. "When you come over to the house, or to the club, I can't keep my eyes off you." He touched his lips to hers, just a whisper then, as if coming to his senses, jerked back. "I'm sorry." He dragged a trembling hand through his hair. "I should go."

But he didn't move, only stood, staring at her. In a moment it was she, as he had hoped, as he had planned, who stepped to him, who wrapped her arms around his neck. "Don't go, Sam."

He was cute, he was nice to her and he was a good kisser. Annabelle's requirements had just been met.

When he had lowered her to the couch and had her, his body shuddered from the climax. But it shuddered more from the pleasure of knowing he had taken something that had been Luke's.

While Sam was making Annabelle moan on the faded cabbage roses of her mother's couch, Madame walked backstage of the Magic Door. It disturbed her to be the bearer of bad tidings. It was something she did not so much for the other merchants in the Quarter, not so much even for herself, but for Roxanne.

"Monsieur Nouvelle."

Max glanced up from the sketches he was making and saw Madame in his dressing room door. Real pleasure brightened his eyes as he rose, taking her hand to kiss. "Ah, Madame, *bonsoir, bienvenu*. It's a delight to see you again."

"I wish I could say I had come to watch the performance, *mon ami*, but I have not." She saw the smile in his eyes fade to concern.

"There's a problem."

"*Oui*, one I must pass to you, with regret. We may speak?"

"Of course." He closed the door, ushered her to a chair.

"Early this week, my store was robbed."

Perhaps it was ironic that anger should fill him at the idea, when he himself was a thief. Max didn't consider it so. Madame was a friend, and a friend who could ill afford a robbery. "What did you lose?"

"A hundred dollars, more or less, and several trinkets. It is an inconvenience, monsieur, not quite a tragedy. I reported it, of course, and of course, there was little to be done. When one is in business, one learns to accept losses. I would have thought little more about it, but a day or two later, I heard that two more shops—the New Orleans Boutique on Bourbon and Rendezvous on Conti—had also been robbed, of small amounts to be sure. One day later, the shop next to mine took a loss—not quite so small. Several valuable porcelain pieces were taken, as well as several hundred in cash."

Max brushed a finger over his moustache. "Did anyone see the robber?"

"Perhaps." Madame toyed with the amulet that rested on the red silk bodice of her flowing caftan. "Perhaps not. As we merchants conferred to complain about our troubles, it came out that someone we knew had been in the shop each time the losses occurred. Coincidence, perhaps."

"Coincidence?" Max arched a brow. "An unlikely one to be sure. Why do you come to me with this, Madame"

"Because the visitor to each of the shops was Roxanne."

Madame pressed her lips tight as she saw Max's face change. Gone, vanished was the concern, the interest, the obvious desire to help. In its place was a dangerous rage that burned out of his eyes. "Madame," he said in a voice no louder than a whisper and as frightening as a sword. "You dare?"

"I dare, monsieur, because I love the child."

"Yet you accuse her of sneaking into your shop, stealing from those who love and trust her?"

"No." Madame's shoulders lifted. "I do not accuse her. She would not take what was mine when in her heart she knows she had only to ask to be given. She was not alone on these visits, monsieur."

Battling rage, Max shifted to pour brandies for both of them. He waited to speak until he had offered a snifter to Madame and had taken his own first sip. "And who was she with?"

"Samuel Wyatt."

Max digested the information and nodded. He only wished he could say he was surprised. Only wished he didn't feel the inevitability of it. He had taken the boy in, done his best by him, but he had known, somehow he had known that it would not be repaid in kind.

"You will give me a moment?" He moved to the door and called for Roxanne. Still in costume, she came to her father's dressing room. Her smile blossomed when she spotted Madame.

"You came!" She scooted over to kiss the woman's cheek. "I'm so glad you did. You can see the new illusion. Luke and I did it for the first time to an audience in the early show. We did it well, didn't we, Daddy?"

"Yes." He shut the door, then crouched down to lay his hand on her shoulders. "I have something to ask you, Roxanne. Something important. You must tell me the truth, no matter what."

The smile died out of her eyes, turning them solemn and a little frightened. "I wouldn't lie to you, Daddy. Not ever."

"You were in Madame's shop early this week?"

"On Monday after school. Madame read the cards for me."

"You were alone?"

"Yes—when she read the cards, I mean. Sam went with me, but he left."

"Did you take anything from Madame's shop?"

"No. I think I might buy the little blue bottle, the one with the peacock on it?" She looked at Madame for confirmation. "For Lily's birthday, but I didn't have my money with me."

"Not buy, Roxanne. Take."

"I . . ." Her mouth quivered open as she understood. "I wouldn't take from Madame, Daddy. How could I? She's my friend."

"Did you see Sam take anything, from Madame, or any of the other shops he visited with you this week?"

"Oh, Daddy, no." The idea had tears swimming in her eyes. "He couldn't."

"We'll see." He kissed her cheek. "I'm sorry, Roxanne. You have to put it out of your mind until after the show, and be prepared to accept the truth, whatever it is."

"He's my friend."

"I hope so."

It was after one when Max opened the door of Sam's room. He saw the figure under the covers and moved quietly to the side of the bed. Wide awake, Sam shifted, blinked his eyes sleepily open. Moonlight slanted over his face.

"Feeling better?" Max asked.

"I think so." Sam offered a weak smile. "I'm sorry I let you down tonight."

"That's a small thing." Max switched on the light, ignoring Sam's grunt of surprise. "I'll apologize in advance for this intrusion. It's quite necessary." He walked to the closet.

"What's going on?"

"There are two ways to look at it." Max pushed aside hanging clothes. "Either I'm defending my home, or I'm doing you a grave disservice. I sincerely hope it's the latter."

"You've no right to pry into my personal things." Sam leaped out of bed in his underwear and grabbed at Max's arm.

"By doing so I may save your reputation."

"Come on, Sam." Embarrassment evident by the redness in his cheeks, Mouse stepped into the room to pull Sam aside.

"You fucking creep, take your hands off me." Sam jerked and bucked, and Mouse held firm. The fury that always bubbled beneath the surface burst out of Sam when he saw Max reach for a box on the closet shelf. "You goddamn bastard, I'll kill you for this."

Calmly, Max took the lid off the box and studied the contents. Cash was neatly stacked and bound with rubber bands. Some of the trinkets on the list Madame had given him were there as well. Others had probably been sold, Max assumed. There was a heaviness around his heart as he looked over at Sam.

"I took you into my home," Max said slowly. "I don't expect gratitude for that since you worked for your room and board. But I trusted you with my child, and she trusted you as her friend. You used her, and in such a way that you've stolen a piece of her childhood along with these. If I were a man of violence, I would kill you for that alone."

"She knew what I was doing," Sam spat out. "She was part of it. She—"

He broke off as Max struck him hard across the face with the back of his hand. "Perhaps I'm a man of violence after all." He stepped forward so that his eyes were close to Sam's. "You'll take your clothes and leave tonight. I'll give you what pay you have owed to you. You'll not only leave this house, but the Quarter. Understand me, I know every inch of the Vieux Carré. If you're still in it by dawn, I'll know. And I'll find you."

He turned and, taking the box, started out. "Let him go, Mouse. See that he packs his things and his things only."

"You'll pay, you bastard." Sam wiped at the blood on his lip. "I swear to Christ, you'll pay."

"I have," Max said over his shoulder. "By subjecting my family to you."

Sam grabbed a pair of jeans off the back of a chair. He sneered at Mouse while he tugged them on. "Get your rocks off watching me dress, faggot?"

Mouse flushed a little, but said nothing.

"I'll be glad to get the hell out of here anyway." He pulled out a shirt. "The past couple of months I've been bored out of my gourd."

"Then get moving." Luke stood in the doorway. His eyes glittered. "It'll give us time to fumigate the stink in here from a creep that uses a little kid to cover his ass."

"Don't you think she liked to be used?" Grinning a challenge, Sam stuffed his remaining clothes in a denim laundry bag. "That's what females like best, asshole. Just ask Annabelle."

"What the hell does that mean?"

"Well now." Sam shrugged into the jacket Lily had bought for him. It would keep him warm through the winter. "Since you ask, maybe you'd be interested to know that while you were being the good little trouper tonight, I was busy fucking your girl's brains out." He saw the fury on Luke's face, and the disbelief. His lips spread over his teeth. "Right on that ugly flowered couch in the living room." Sam's grin was hard and cold as ice. "I had her out of those red lace panties in five minutes. She likes to be on top best, doesn't she? So you can give it to her real deep. That mole under her left tit's sexy as hell, don't you think?"

He braced, eager for a fight, as Luke leaped at him. But Mouse moved fast, grabbing

Luke and dragging him toward the door. "It's not worth it." Mouse kept saying. "Come on, Luke, let it go. It's not worth it." Sam's laugh echoed after them as Mouse shoved Luke toward the stairs. "Go out and cool off."

"Get the hell out of my way."

"Max wants him to go." Mouse stood firm at the top of the stairs. He would, if he had to, knock Luke down them. "That's all he wants. You go outside, take a walk. I gotta make sure he goes."

Fine, Luke thought. Dandy. He'd go out all right. And he'd wait for Sam. He stormed down the steps and out into the courtyard. His blood was up, boiling Irish in his veins. His fists were already curled and ready. He planned to wait on the street, follow Sam for a block or two, then beat the shit out of him.

But he heard her crying. He was turned toward the street, his body braced, his mind full of violence. She was crying as if her heart were broken, curled up on a stone bench by the dormant azaleas.

Perhaps if she'd been given to tears, Luke could have ignored it and gone about his business. But in all the years he'd lived with the Nouvelles, he'd never once heard Roxanne cry since her bout with chicken pox. The sound of it reached inside and took him by the heart.

"Come on, Roxy." Awkward and out of his depth, Luke walked to the bench and patted her head. "Don't do that."

She kept her face pressed against her knees and sobbed.

"Jesus." However reluctant he was, Luke found himself sitting beside her and drawing her into his arms. "Come on, baby, don't let him make you cry like this. He's a bastard, a freaking creep." He sighed and rocked and found himself gradually calming. "He's not worth it," he said half to himself, realizing Mouse's words had been right on target.

"He used me," Roxanne murmured against Luke's chest. She had control of the sobbing now, and nearly felt strong enough to stop the tears. "He pretended to be my friend, but he never was. He used me to take things from people I cared about. I heard what he said to Daddy. It was like he hated us, like he'd hated us all along."

"Maybe he did. What do we care?"

"I brought him home." She pressed her lips together. She wasn't sure she could forgive herself for that. "Did he—did he really do that with Annabelle?"

Luke let out a breath and settled his cheek against Roxanne's hair. "I guess he probably did."

"I'm sorry."

"If she'd let him, just like that, I don't think she was really mine anyway."

"He wanted to hurt you." She stroked her finger down Luke's arm, comforted. "He wanted to hurt everybody, I guess. That's why he took things. It's not like what Daddy does."

"Uh-uh," Luke said absently, then froze. "What?"

"You know, stealing. Daddy wouldn't steal from a friend, or from somebody who'd get hurt because of what he took." She yawned. The crying jag had tired her out. "He takes jewels and stuff like that. It's always insured."

"Jesus Christ." He pushed her off his lap so that she landed hard on her rump on the bench. "How long have you known about all that? How long have you known what we're doing?"

She smiled indulgently, her swollen eyes sparkled with moonlight. "Always," she smiled simply. "I've always known."

Sam left the house, but he didn't leave the Quarter. Not when he had a score to settle. There was only one way he could have been found out so completely. Roxanne had ratted on him.

It was easy to convince himself that she'd known what he was doing from the beginning. She'd waltzed into those shops, and had waltzed out again, making it all so slick. And then, she'd turned on him, so that he'd been kicked out of a warm bed, humiliated. She'd have to pay for that.

He waited for her. He knew the route she took to school. He'd even walked her there himself from time to time, trying to be nice to her. Trying to be nice, Sam thought, grinding a fist into his open palm. Look how she'd paid him back.

He spent several cold hours huddled in an alley trying to keep out of a thin, chill drizzle. He hated being cold.

It was one more thing she'd pay for.

He spotted her and drew back a little. There was no need for the precaution, he noted. She was dragging along, her knapsack over her back, her eyes cast down. He waited, and when she was close enough, pounced.

Roxanne didn't even get out a scream when she was grabbed from behind and yanked into the alley. Her fists came up—she was a natural fighter—but they lowered again when she saw Sam.

Her eyes were still puffy. She resented that. Resented that he'd driven her to tears. But they were all used up. Her chin leveled, and her eyes, perfectly dry, gleamed dangerously up at his.

"What do you want?"

"A nice little talk. Just you and me."

There was something in his face that made her want to run, something she hadn't seen in it before. There was hate, yes, but there was a dullness about it. Like a rusty razor that would infect as well as slice.

"Daddy told you to leave."

"You think that old man scares me?" He shoved her, surprising more than hurting her as she slammed back into the wall. "I do what I want, and what I want right now is to settle up with you. You owe me, Rox."

"Owe you?" Forgetting surprise, forgetting the ache where her shoulder had bumped stone, she pushed herself away from the wall. "I brought you home. I asked Daddy to give you a job. I helped you, and then you stole from my friends. I don't owe you jack."

"Where are you going?" He shoved her back into place when she tried to stalk past him. "Off to school? I don't think so. I think you should spend some time with me." He slid a hand around her throat. She would have screamed then, loud and long, but she couldn't draw enough air. "You ratted on me, Rox."

"I didn't," she managed to whisper. "But I would have if I'd known."

"Same thing, isn't it?" He shoved her again so that her head knocked painfully into the wall.

Fear had her reaching up, without thought, without warning and raking her nails down his face. He howled, his grip loosened. She nearly made the mouth of the alley before he caught her.

"You little bitch." He was breathing hard as he sent her sprawling. There was anger, there was pain, but there was also excitement. He could do whatever he wanted with her, anything, everything, and no one would stop him.

Her head was swimming. She saw him coming as she pushed herself up on her hands and knees. He was going to hurt her, she knew, and it was going to be really bad. Aim low, she told herself, and hit him hard.

She didn't have to. Even as she was bracing for the attack, Luke flew into the alley. He made a sound in his throat as he leaped on Sam. A sound Roxanne could only describe as wolfish.

Then there was the thud of fists against flesh. She managed to gain her feet, though her legs wobbled. She looked first for a weapon, a plank, a rock, a piece of metal. In the end she settled for the lid of a garbage can and, hefting it, advanced on the fight.

It took her only a moment to see that Luke didn't need her help. He was straddling Sam now and methodically, mercilessly, pounding his fists into Sam's face.

"That's enough now." She tossed the lid aside to use both hands on Luke's pumping arms. "You've got to stop. We'll get in trouble if you kill him." She had to get down so that Luke's fierce eyes could meet hers. "Luke, Daddy wouldn't want you to hurt your hands."

Something about the cool, logical tone had him looking down. His knuckles were bruised and raw and bloody. He had to laugh. "Right." But he touched one of those bleeding hands to her face. He'd been furious about Annabelle, but that was nothing, nothing compared with what he'd felt when he'd seen Roxanne on the ground and Sam looming over her. "Are you okay?"

"Yeah. I was going to go for his balls, but thanks for beating him up for me."

"No problem, I enjoyed it. Go pick up your bookbag. Wait for me on the sidewalk."

"You're not going to hit him again, are you?" She glanced down dispassionately into Sam's battered face. Unless she missed her guess, his nose was broken, and he'd lose a couple of teeth.

"No." He jerked his head toward the mouth of the alley. "Go on, Rox. Wait for me."

With one last glance at Sam, she turned and walked away.

"I could kill you for touching her." Luke leaned down close. "You come near her or any of my family again, and I will kill you."

Sam struggled onto his elbows when Luke rose. His face was on fire, his body felt as though it had been hit by a truck. No one, no one, had ever hurt him before.

"I'll pay you back." His voice was a croak that made Luke's brow lift in derision.

"You can try. Free lesson, Wyatt, quit while you're able to walk away. Next time I'll break more than your nose."

When Luke left him, Sam curled up in a ball to try to stop the pain. But it ate through him, tangling with the hate. One day, he promised himself as he wept and dragged himself to his feet. One day, they'd all pay for hurting him.

11

Paris, 1982

"I'm not a child anymore." Roxanne's temper was up. It snapped in her voice, sizzled in her eyes as she whirled from her view of Paris in the spring.

"I'm aware of that." In deliberate contrast, Max's tone was mild. He seemed completely unaffected by his daughter's fury as he added a dash of cream to his strong French coffee. The years had turned his hair to a gleaming pewter.

"I have a right to go with you, a right to be a part of it."

Max spread butter generously on his croissant, nibbled, then dabbed his lips with a linen napkin. "No," he said, smiled sweetly and continued to eat.

She could have screamed. God knew she wanted to—scream and rant and rave. And that sort of behavior would hardly convince her father that she was a competent adult, ready to assume her place in his business.

The parlor of their suite at the Ritz was beautifully appointed, sumptuous in comfort. In her flowing silk robe splashed with vivid flowers, the discreet emeralds winking at her ears, the intricate French braid spilling down her back, she looked as though she belonged there.

But Roxanne's heart and soul longed for dark alleys, sooty rooftops. The blood that pumped through her veins under that lily-soft skin was the blood of a thief. She only needed to convince her father it was time for her debut.

"Daddy . . ." She topped off his coffee, giving him another engaging smile. "I understand you only want to protect me."

"A parent's most important job."

"And I love you for it. But you have to let me grow up."

He looked at her then. Though his lips remained curved, his eyes were unbearably sad. "All the magic at my disposal couldn't have stopped you from that."

"I'm ready." She took advantage of his long sigh, cupping his hand in hers, leaning forward. Her eyes were soft again, her smile persuasive. "I've been ready. I'm every bit as good as Luke—"

"You have no idea how good Luke is." Max patted her hand and went back to his breakfast. How often had they had this discussion? he wondered, since she had announced at the tender age of fourteen that she was ready to join his after-hours show? He'd had no idea she'd even known what he did when the spotlights dimmed and the crowds went home.

Roxanne's eyes iced over. Max nearly chuckled. Such was a woman's magic, he thought. "However good he is," she said, "I can be better."

"It's not a competition, my love."

He was wrong there, Roxanne mused as she sprang up to pace the room again. It had been a competition, a fierce one, for years. "It's because I'm not a man." There was bitterness in every syllable.

"That has nothing to do with it. I take some pride in considering myself a feminist." Max sighed again, pushing his plate aside. "You're too young, Roxy."

That was the wrong button to push. Outraged, she spun around. "I'm nearly eighteen. How old was he when you took him with you the first time?"

"Years older," Max murmured. "Inside. Roxanne, I want you to go to college, learn the things I can't teach you. Discover yourself."

"I know who I am." Her head came up, her shoulders straightened. Max saw a glimpse of the woman she would be. The pride burned so hot and fast it caused his eyes to swim. "You've taught me everything I need to know."

"Not nearly enough," Max said quietly. "Lily and I have kept you close, perhaps too close, because we couldn't bear to do otherwise. We only want you to take a step away, on your own. If you come back, I'll be content it's right for you."

"What about what I want?" she demanded. "I want to be there when you go to Chaumet, when you open the safe. I want to know what it feels like to stand in the dark and hold the Azzedine diamonds in my hands."

Max understood, only too well. He could regret that he'd told her about the jewels, their history, their spectacular beauty and the mystique that went along with the glittery stones. But there was little room for regret in his life.

"Your day will come, if it's meant to. But not this time."

"Damn it, I want—"

"Your wants have to wait." His tone was flat and final. Only he knew how relieved he was when the knock on the door interrupted them. He gestured for Roxanne to answer it and went back to his coffee.

She managed to fight her fury back, to open the door with a pleasant smile on her face. It faded immediately when she saw Luke. The look she aimed at him was sharp enough to cut bone.

"Got turned down, did you?" He grinned, tucked his hands in his pockets and strolled past her. The teasing, feminine scent of her perfume kindled an instant fire in his blood. He'd learned he couldn't ignore it, but he could keep her from seeing his reaction to her, and making him pay for it.

"Max." He poked through the silver basket of pastries and helped himself. "I thought you'd want to know, the rest of the equipment finally arrived."

"Ah, at last." With a nod he gestured for Luke to sit. "Have some coffee. I'll go check it myself. You can keep Roxanne company."

Damned if he wanted to be alone with her. It was hard enough in the day-to-day order of things. But he knew, he damn well knew, she was wearing nothing under that robe. "I'll go with you."

He was half out of his chair when Max stood and pushed him down again. "No need. Mouse and I can make sure everything's in order. We should be able to rehearse this afternoon." He moved to the mirror to straighten his tie and brush at his moustache.

Didn't they realize the sparks they set off each other? Max wondered. An innocent bystander could go up in flames. Youth, he thought with a sigh and a smile. In the mirror, he could see their reflections, both of them tensed as alley cats with most of the room between them.

"If Lily wakes soon, tell her to enjoy her morning. We'll meet at La Palace at two." He crossed over to kiss his daughter's cheek. "*Au revoir, ma belle.*"

"We're not finished with this."

"Two o'clock," he said. "Meanwhile you two should go out, take a walk in the Paris sunshine."

The minute the door closed behind her father, Roxanne rounded on Luke. "I'm not going to be left behind this time."

"It's not up to me."

She marched to the table where he sat, slapped her palms down on the linen cloth hard enough to make the china rattle. "And if it were?"

He looked her square in the eyes. He could have strangled her for becoming so beautiful. And she'd done it slowly, insidiously over the last few years, sneaking up on him like a thief to steal his breath away with a look. "I'd do exactly what Max is doing."

That hurt. She sucked in her breath on the sharp pain of betrayal. "Why?"

"Because you're not ready yet."

"How do you know?" She tossed her head back. The light through the windows shivered over her hair and turned it to flame. Luke was afraid she'd read the passion in his eyes. "How do you know what I'm ready for?"

It was a direct challenge. Much too direct. His palms dampened. "Heisting jewels from the Trimalda villa's a far cry from scamming tourists with the Cups and Balls, Rox." Needing a prop, he picked up his coffee. Years of training kept his hand steady. He could make her angry, he knew. It was best. As long as she was angry he could keep his hands off her. He hoped.

"I'm every bit as good as you, Callahan. You didn't even know how to riffle a deck until I taught you."

"It must be tough to know you've been outreached."

Her skin went ice-white then flushed deeper than the roses on the table between them. She straightened, and to his misery, Luke saw every curve of her body beneath the robe. "You witless bastard. You couldn't outreach me if you were standing on stilts."

He only smiled. "Who got the most press the last gig in New York?"

"An idiot who has himself chained in a trunk and gets tossed in the East River is bound to get press." How she hated the fact that the escapes he'd gravitated to were spectacular. Every time he'd lock himself into another box, she was torn in two parts—one thrilled by his skill and his daring, the other disgusted by it.

"I got the press for getting out," he reminded her, and took out one of the French cigars he'd developed a fondness for. "For being the best." He flicked on his lighter and puffed smoke from the cigar. "You should be content with your pretty illusions, Rox, your pretty boyfriends—" All of which he'd like to murder. "Leave the dangerous work to those of us who can handle it."

She was quick. He'd always admired that in her. He barely had time to shoot up a hand and catch her fist before it plowed into his nose. Still gripping her curled fingers, he rose. They were face to face now, bodies almost brushing.

She felt a tingle skitter along her spine. A yearning bloomed inside like a flame she'd never been able to stamp out. She wanted to hate him for it.

"Watch your step." The warning was quiet, telling her she'd managed to fan the fires of his temper if nothing else.

"If you think I'm afraid you'll hit me back—"

He shocked them both by catching her chin in tensed fingers, holding her face close. Her lips parted as much in surprise as anticipation. Her mind went blessedly blank.

"I could do worse." He ground the words out. They tasted like glass in his throat. "And we'd both pay for it."

He shoved her away before he did something he'd never forgive himself for. As he strode to the door, he tossed back a clipped order. "Two o'clock. In costume." And slammed the door behind him.

When she realized her knees were shaking, Roxanne lowered herself into a chair. After several deep breaths, she rubbed a hand along her throat until she could swallow over the obstruction lodged there. For an instant, just a flashing instant, he'd looked at her as though he realized she was a woman. A woman he could want. A woman he did want.

On another shaky breath, she shook her head. That was ridiculous. He'd never thought of her as anything but a necessary nuisance. And she didn't care. She'd long ago gotten over that silly childish crush.

She wasn't interested in men anyway. She had bigger plans.

Damn if she was going to wait through four years of college before she implemented them. Her lips firmed. Damn if she was going to wait another week.

It was time to flesh out the idea that had been brewing in her mind. Past time. Smiling to herself, she brought her long legs up, crossed them and casually reached for the cigar Luke had left burning. She sat back, blowing smoke rings at the ceiling. And plotted.

Luke could only thank God he had so much on his mind. Between preparing for the gig at La Palace and the job at Chaumet, he didn't have time to dwell on Roxanne.

Except at three A.M., when he'd awake in the cold sweat of frustration from dreams of her. Incredibly clear, incredibly provocative dreams of that long, white body wrapped around his. Of that glorious hair spread over a patch of dewy green grass in some secluded glade. Of those witchy eyes, clouded with passion.

If there was a hell, Luke was certain he would burn for those dreams alone. He'd been raised with her, for Christ's sake, and was the closest thing to a brother she had. The only thing keeping her safe from him was the idea he'd fixed in his head that doing what he wanted to do would be a kind of spiritual incest.

And the certainty that she would laugh at him, that the laugh would rake him clean to the bone, if he let his feelings show.

He had to get out, he realized when he'd paced the length and width of the room a dozen times. A nice long walk before dinner, a stroll in the Parisian twilight. He grabbed his black leather bomber jacket and paused in front of the mirror long enough to run fingers through his hair.

He didn't notice the changes in himself over the years. So much was the same. His hair was still dark, still thick, still worn dramatically long to curl over his collar, or to be caught in a queue. His eyes were still blue, and the length of his sooty lashes had ceased to embarrass him. He'd learned that his poetically good looks could charm women who put stock in such things. His skin remained smooth, with long bones pressed taut against it. Once in his teens he'd grown a moustache, but it hadn't suited him. Now his mouth was unadorned.

He'd broken his nose once in an escape, but it had healed straight. That was a slight disappointment.

At twenty-one he'd grown into his full height of six-one, and his body was rangy. The haunted look that had come over him so often during childhood came only rarely now. The years with Max had taught him control, physical, mental, emotional. He was, and always would be, grateful for that.

And given time, given will, he would break clear of the shackles his feelings for Roxanne had clamped on him.

Turning away from the mirror, he went out, started down the long, carpeted hallway toward the elevators. He glanced briefly at the pretty blond maid pushing her cart.

Time for a check for extra towels, mints on the pillow. The child who'd once slept in ditches had become so used to such luxuries he barely noted them.

"Bon soir," he murmured with a casual smile as he passed her.

"Bon soir, monsieur." Her smile was shy and swift before she knocked on a door across the hall.

Luke was nearly to the elevators when he stopped dead. That scent. Roxanne's scent. Damn her, was he so bedazzled he could smell her everywhere? He shook himself loose, took another step and stopped again. His eyes narrowed as he turned around and studied the maid, who was fitting her master key into the lock.

Those legs. His teeth set as he studied the long slim legs beneath the discreet black skirt of the uniform.

Roxanne's legs.

She was easing the door shut behind her when he slapped a hand against it. "What the hell do you think you're doing?"

She blinked up at him. *"Pardon?"*

"Cut the crap, Roxanne. What's the deal?"

"Shut up." She hissed the words as she grabbed his arm and pulled him inside. She was furious, but that could wait. First she wanted answers. "How did you know it was me?"

He could hardly tell her he'd have recognized her legs anywhere. So he lied. "Give me a break. Who do you think you're fooling with that getup?"

The fact was, it was perfect. The short sassy blond wig changed her looks dramatically. Even her eye color was different. Colored contacts, he imagined, that turned emerald into smoky brown. She was skilled enough with makeup to subtly change the tone of her skin, the shape of her face. She'd added a bit of padding to her hips and, Luke was certain, was wearing one of those clever bras that should have been illegal.

They pushed up and padded and made a man's mouth water for what was essentially a mirage.

"Bull." Her voice was still an incensed whisper. "I spent ten minutes in Lily's room and she didn't recognize me."

Because she hasn't been drooling over your legs for the past two years.

"I did," he said and left it at that. "Now, what the hell are you doing in here?"

"I'm stealing Mrs. Melville's jewelry."

"Like hell."

Her eyes flared. They might have been brown, Luke thought, but they were Roxanne's.

"Leave me alone. I got in here, and I'm not walking out empty-handed. I planned it out down to the last detail, and you're not spoiling it for me."

"And what are you going to do when Mrs. Melville screams down the *gendarmes?*"

"Look shocked and appalled and outraged, of course. Like every other guest in the hotel." Turning away, she went directly to the dresser. She took a hankie from her pocket, using it to ensure against fingerprints as she opened drawers.

He made a sound in his throat that was equal parts amusement and disgust. "You think you're going to find her stuff just lying around in a drawer? The Ritz has a safe downstairs for that."

Roxanne sent him a withering look. "She doesn't keep it downstairs. I overheard her arguing with her husband the other night. She likes to keep it close so she can pick through it when she's dressing each evening."

It was good, Luke mused. Very good. He searched around for another flaw. "What are you going to do if one of them walks in while you're pawing around?"

"I won't be pawing around." Moving quickly, competently, she closed a drawer. "I'm here to turn down the bed. What's your excuse?"

"Okay, Rox, enough's enough." He grabbed her arm. "We've planned out the Chaumet job for months. I'm not having one of your two-bit games spoil it."

"One has nothing to do with the other." She jerked away from him. "And it's not two-bit. Have you seen the rocks that woman wears?"

"Could be paste."

"That's for me to find out." With one brow arched, she took a jeweler's loupe from her pocket. "I've been around Max nearly eighteen years," she said as she slipped it back in place. "I know what I'm doing."

"What you're doing is getting the hell out—" He broke off when he heard a key rattle in the lock. "Oh, shit."

"I could scream," she said pleasantly. "Claim you'd pushed your way in and attacked me."

There wasn't time for rebuttal. He shot her one fulminating look, then took his only option. He dived under the bed.

With her tongue tucked in her cheek, Roxanne began to turn down the bedclothes. She straightened when the door opened, and blushed prettily.

"Oh, Monsieur Melville," she said in heavily accented English. "I should . . . come back?"

"No need, honey." He was a big, brawny Texan in his fifties, and the damn French food gave him indigestion. "You just keep on with what you're doing."

"Merci." Roxanne smoothed the spread and fluffed pillows, well aware Melville's eyes were riveted to her posterior.

"Don't recall seeing you in here before."

"This is not . . ." She leaned over the bed a little further. Might as well give the randy old guy his money's worth, she thought. "My floor usual." Enjoying her character, she turned, slanting him a look from under her lashes. "You would like more towels, monsieur? I can get you something?"

"Well now." He leaned down to tickle her chin. There was a whiff of bourbon on his breath, not entirely unpleasant. "What you got in mind, sugar cakes?"

She giggled and fluttered her lashes again. "Oh, *monsieur.* You tease me, *oui?*"

He'd sure as hell like to, he thought. Unwrapping a pretty little package like this would be a hell of a lot more fun than the opera his wife was dragging him to. But it would also take time. Indigestion forgotten, he decided he could make time for a little slap and tickle.

"I've had this hankering for French pastries." Melville patted her bottom, and when she tittered, gave her breast a light squeeze. From under the bed, Luke was sure he was growing fangs.

Blushing and breathy, Roxanne stared up at Melville with big, brown eyes. "Oh, *monsieur.* You Americans."

"I'm not just American, sweetie. I'm a Texan."

"Ah." She let him nibble at her neck while Luke lay helpless, his fists clenched. "Is it true what they say about Texans, *monsieur?* That everything is . . . bigger."

Melville let out a hoot and kissed her hard on the mouth. "Damn straight, sugar. Why don't I let you find out?" He forgot about his wife as well as his stomach and started pushing her down on the bed. Luke braced, ready to pounce.

"But, *monsieur,* I'm on duty." Roxanne struggled away, still giggling. "I will be discharged."

"How about when you're not on duty?"

Playing the Texan's image of French tart to the hilt, she flushed again, and caught her bottom lip flirtatiously between her teeth. "Perhaps at midnight we could meet." Her lashes fluttered. "There is a little café close—Robert's?"

"Well now, I think I could manage that." He pulled her close again to give her padded hips a squeeze. "You keep an eye out for me—what's your name, darling?"

"It's Monique." She trailed her fingers over his cheek. "I will wait for midnight."

He gave her another pinch and a wink before strolling out dreaming of young French sex.

Roxanne plopped onto the bed and howled with laughter.

"Oh yeah, it's a riot," Luke muttered as he crawled out. "You let that sleazeball paw all over you, practically crawl on top of you, and it's a laugh a minute. I should spank you."

Still holding her sides, she let out a last sighing laugh. "Oh, grow up." Then she sucked in her breath when Luke snagged her arm and hauled her to her feet. She recognized real fury when she saw it, and bit off any protest.

"You seem to have done enough growing up for both of us. Damn good at that, weren't you, Rox? How many of those smart college guys you date have you let put their sweaty hands all over you?"

This time her blush was genuine. "That's none of your business."

"The hell it's not. I'm—" Crazy about you. The words nearly tumbled out before he choked them off. "Somebody has to look out for you."

"I can do that fine for myself." She elbowed him away, horrified that her spine was tingling. "And for your information, flea brain, he didn't have his hands on *me.* I've got enough padding where he was groping to stuff a mattress."

"That's beside the point." He grabbed for her hand, but she shoved him away. "Roxanne, we're getting out of here. Now."

"You go. I'm getting what I came for." Prepared to take her stand, she tossed her head back. "I want it more than ever. That cheating bastard is going to buy his wife a whole new basket of jewelry. Serves him right—going off to meet some little French tootsie at a cheap café."

Despite himself, Luke chuckled and ran a hand through his hair. "You're the French tootsie, Rox."

"And I'm the one who's going to make him pay for adultery." Her gaze sharpened. There was enough deviousness in the look to elicit Luke's reluctant admiration. "And what's he going to say about me? He'll talk about walking in on a maid, describe me—but not in too much detail, because he'll be guilty and scared. It's better this way than if he'd never seen me at all." She marched to the closet and, scanning the top shelf, grinned. "*Et, voilà.*"

She had to stretch to reach the three-tiered jewelry box.

"God, Luke, it must weigh twenty pounds." Before he could assist her, she set it on the floor and crouched beside it. "Mine," she said in a warning hiss, slapping his hand away. She took a set of picks from her pocket, chose one and went to work on the lock.

It took her forty-three seconds—Luke timed her. And he was forced to admit that she was better, much better, than he had imagined.

"Oh, my." Her heart did a quick jig as she opened the top. Sparkles, gleams, shines. She felt like Aladdin exploring his cave. No, no, she thought, like one of the forty thieves. "Aren't they gorgeous?" Indulging herself, she dipped her hand in.

"If they're real." It wasn't possible to completely staunch the familiar tingle, but he kept his voice brisk. "And a pro doesn't drool over the goods."

"I'm not drooling." Then she laughed again, turned that glowing smile on him. "Maybe a little. Luke, isn't it fabulous?"

"If..." His voice cracked. He had to clear his throat. "If they're real," he repeated.

Roxanne only sighed at his lack of vision and pulled out the loupe. After examining a chain of sapphires and diamonds, she sat back on her heels. "They're real, Callahan." Moving briskly now, she examined piece after piece before wrapping them in towels. "I wouldn't say the diamonds are better than second water—probably third, but that'll do. I make it to be oh, a hundred and sixty, hundred and seventy thousand net?"

He'd figured the same himself, but didn't want to tell her how closely their thoughts had meshed. Instead, he hauled her to her feet. He wiped the box clean, then using a towel, set it back in place.

"Let's go."

"Come on, Luke." She blocked the door, and her eyes were laughing. "At least you can say I did good."

"Beginner's luck." But he grinned back at her.

"Luck had nothing to do with it." She stabbed a finger at his chest. "Like it or not, Callahan, you've got a new partner."

12

"You're not being fair."

Roxanne stood in her father's dressing room in full costume. The spangles and beads on her strapless emerald gown shivered from the lights, and her indignation.

"I proved myself," she insisted.

"You proved you're impulsive, reckless and stubborn." After adjusting the cuff of his tuxedo shirt to his liking, Max met her furious face in his mirror. "And you are not, I repeat not, going on the Chaumet job. Now, I have ten minutes to cue, young lady. Is there anything else?"

In that moment she was plunged back into childhood. Her bottom lip quivered as she dropped into a chair. "Daddy, why don't you trust me?"

"On the contrary, I trust you implicitly. You must trust me, however, when I tell you you're not ready."

"But the Melvilles—"

"Were a risk you should never have taken." He shook his head as he crossed over to take her drooping chin in his hand. He knew—who better?—what it was like to covet those shiny toys, to crave the excitement of stealing in the dark. How could he expect a child of his blood to be any different?

And, truthfully, he was enormously proud of her. Warped, he supposed with a half smile. But a father's pride was a father's pride.

"*Ma belle,* I will tell you this. Never, never muddy your own pond."

Roxanne arched a brow. "I don't recall you putting the jewels back, Daddy."

Caught, he ran his tongue around his teeth. "No," he agreed, drawing the word out. "One shouldn't look a gift diamond in the mouth—so to speak. Still, what you acquired is a fraction of what we hope to acquire tonight. It's been months in the planning, Roxanne. The timing is calculated to the instant. Even if I wanted to add you, or anyone, on at this point, it would tilt those very delicately balanced scales."

"It's an excuse," she tossed back, feeling like a little girl forbidden to attend a party. "Next time you'll have another."

"It's the truth. Next time there'll be another truth. When have I ever lied to you?"

She opened her mouth, closed it again. He'd evaded, avoided and toyed with veracity. But lied to her? No, never. "I'm as good as Luke."

"He used to say the same thing about you, onstage. Speaking of which..." He took her hand, lifting her before kissing it lightly. "We have a show to do."

"All right." She opened the door, then glanced over her shoulder. "Daddy, I want my share of the hundred and sixty."

He grinned, ear to ear. Had a father ever had so perfect a child? "That's my girl."

The audience at La Palace was studded with film stars, Paris models and those rich and glamorous enough to rub elbows with them. Max had created a show sophisticated and complicated enough to entertain the discriminating. It wasn't possible for Roxanne to walk through the act with her mind on something else.

As she had been trained, she put everything aside but the magic. It was she who performed the Floating Balls illusion now, a slim woman in shimmering emerald. Watching her, Luke realized she looked like a long-stemmed rose—that sinuous green, the fiery hair. The audience was as captivated by her beauty as by the silvery balls that swayed and danced inches above her graceful hands.

He liked to tease her, of course, that her illusions were all glitz and no meat. But the truth was she was extraordinary. Even knowing what went on behind the trick, he was caught.

She lifted her arms. Three balls shimmered along each arm, from shoulder to wrist. While Debussy played, Lily draped emerald silk over them, stepped back out of the light. By turning her arms over, palms up, Roxanne had the silk drifting to the floor. And there, where the shining globes had been, white doves perched.

The audience exploded as she took her bows and exited. Luke was there in the wings, grinning at Roxanne as Mouse coaxed the doves into their cage. "Birds are okay, Rox, but if you worked with a tiger . . ."

"Kiss my—" She broke off only because Lily had followed her off and was already clucking her tongue.

"Don't start." She gave them both affectionate pats on the cheek. "Mouse, honey, you keep these two in line. I've got to go back for this set." She gave an exaggerated sigh. "I swear, Max never stops thinking of ways to cut me into pieces." After a last lingering look at Luke, she walked on, into Max's applause.

"You know what's wrong with her, don't you?" Roxanne said under her breath.

"Nothing's wrong with Lily." Luke's lips curved as he watched Max roll into a flashy routine that began with shooting fire from his fingertips and would end with his cutting Lily into thirds with laser beams.

"She worries about you, God knows why."

That got under his skin, touched on the guilt that always hovered there. "She's got nothing to worry about. I know what I'm doing."

She whirled on him then, struggling back her own needs. Show business was too much a part of what she was to allow her a tantrum in the wings. She spoke her mind, but in whispers. "You always know, don't you, Luke? You've been doing what the hell you pleased since Max and Lily took you in. Damn you, they love you, and it's eating Lily up that you keep pushing."

He shut down his emotions. It was the only way to survive. "It's what I do. You make pretty balls float in the air. I break out of chains. And all of us steal." His eyes flashed down to hers. "It's what we do. It's what we are."

"It wouldn't cost you anything to cut that part of the act."

The look held, a moment, two. She thought she saw something there, just behind his eyes, that she would never understand. "You're wrong," he said simply and walked away.

Roxanne turned quickly to the stage. Because she wanted so badly to go after him, to beg. She knew it would do no good, nor did she expect it to. Luke was right. They did what they did. Lily was able to understand and appreciate the thievery. She would have to learn to do the same with Luke's escapes.

He would always be the lone wolf LeClerc had called him all those years ago. He would go his way when he chose. Always with something to prove, she thought now.

And the truth was, the truth she hated to admit, was that the finale of tonight's show worried her nearly as much as it worried Lily.

She fixed a smile on her face so that neither Max nor Lily could see she was upset. She could control the outward signs of agitation. That was simple mind over matter. But she couldn't stop the image that was running over and over in her brain.

Luke's version of Houdini's Water Torture Escape. Only in that endless loop in her brain, he didn't break free.

It always brought down the house, Max thought as he turned the spotlight over to Luke. No one, not even Lily, knew what it had cost him to hand Luke the finale. But it had been time, Max mused, flexing his still nimble fingers, for youth to take center stage.

And the boy was so talented. So driven. So . . . magical.

The idea made Max smile as the curtain was lifted to reveal the glass water chamber. The boy had designed it himself, painstakingly. The dimensions, the thickness of the glass, even the brass fittings shaped like wizards and sorceresses. Luke knew to the pint how much water it contained to allow for displacement when his body was lowered, chained into it.

He knew to the second how much time it required for him to free himself from the chains, from the handcuffs, from the manacles that secured him to the bolts at the chamber's sides.

And he knew how much of a grace period his lungs would allow him if something went wrong.

In her costume change of sheer draping white, Roxanne stood beside the water chamber. Despite her thundering heart her face was serene. It was she who slipped Luke's wide-sleeved shirt away so that he stood stripped to the waist.

She didn't look at the scars that crisscrossed white over his tanned back. Not once in all the years they'd been together had she mentioned them. Whatever locks she could open, she wouldn't touch the bolt on his pride.

It was she who stood calmly by as two volunteers from the audience locked the heavy chains around him. When his arms were crossed over his chest and bound there, the steel cuffs fastened over his wrists, his bare feet were attached by the ankles with manacles to a slab of smooth wood.

There were cellos playing, low, ominous, as the platform Luke stood on was lifted into the air.

"It's been said," he began in a voice that floated over the heads of the audience, "that the Great Houdini lost his life due to the injuries incurred in this escape. Since his death, it has been a challenge to every magician, every escape artist, to duplicate the escape, and make it his own by triumphing over it."

He glanced down and there was Mouse, embarrassed as hell in his *Arabian Knights'* outfit, holding a huge mallet. "Hopefully, we'll have no need for my friend with the muscles to break the glass." He winked down at Roxanne. "But perhaps I'll have need for the lovely Roxanne to give me a little mouth-to-mouth."

Roxanne didn't care for the ad-lib, but the audience laughed and applauded.

"Once I'm lowered into the chamber, it will be sealed, airtight." The audience gasped as the platform turned over, pivoted. Luke was facing them again, but upside down. He began to take deep breaths, filling his lungs. Roxanne took over the patter.

"We ask for silence during the escape, and that you direct your attention to the clock." At her cue, a spotlight hit a large clock face at the rear of the stage. "It will begin ticking off the seconds the moment Callahan is immersed in the chamber. Ladies and gentlemen..." Luke was lowered inch by inch toward the surface of the water. Roxanne kept her eyes and her mind riveted on the audience. "Callahan will have four minutes, and four minutes only, to escape from the chamber, or we will be forced to break the glass. A doctor is standing by in case of accident."

Now she had to turn, to throw out her arm for showmanship as Luke's head broke water. She watched him lower until his body was immersed, heard the thud as the platform fit snugly into place on top of the tank. His hair swirled, floating, as his eyes, brilliantly blue, met hers.

Then the thin white curtain lowered, covering all four sides of the chamber.

The clock began to tick.

"One minute," Roxanne announced in a voice that revealed nothing of her inner turmoil. She imagined Luke out of the cuffs. Willed him out of them. He would already be unlocking the chains.

There were murmurs from the audience as the clock rounded two minutes. Roxanne felt the sweat spring cold on her palms, the back of her neck, the small of her back. He was always out in three, three-twenty tops. She could see vaguely through the white cloth a shadow of movement.

He had no way to call for help, she thought frantically as the clock neared the three-minute mark. No way to signal if his lungs hitched and ran out of air. He could die before they ripped the curtain aside, before Mouse could smash the glass. He could die alone and in silence, chained to his own ambition.

"Three minutes," she said, and now hints of her fear leaked through and caused the audience to lean forward.

"Three twenty," she said and turned panicked eyes to Mouse. "Three twenty-five. Please, ladies and gentlemen, remain calm. Remain seated." She gulped in air, imagining Luke's lungs searing. "Three minutes, forty seconds."

A woman in the back began to shout hysterically in French. It caused a chain reaction of alarm to ripple along the rows until the audience was abuzz. Many had leaped to their feet as the clock neared the four-minute mark.

"Oh, Mouse, God." With eight seconds to go, Roxanne tossed showmanship aside and ripped at the curtain. It came tumbling down just as Luke shouldered the platform aside. He surfaced, sleek as an otter, and sucked in a greedy breath. His eyes were alight with triumph as the audience erupted with shouts and applause. It had been worth the extra thirty seconds he'd waited, freed, beneath the water.

He stood, dragging air in, one hand lifted. He was already planning to add that little extra bit of drama to the next show. Hooking his arms around the platform, he rode it up away from the chamber and down again to the stage. He stood dripping, taking his bows.

On impulse he grabbed Roxanne's hand, bending gallantly over it and kissing her fingers to the delight of the romantic French.

"Your hand's shaking," he noted under the cover of applause. "Don't tell me you were worried I wouldn't make it out."

Rather than snatch her hand back as she would have preferred, she smiled at him. "I was afraid Mouse would have to break the glass. Do you know how much it would cost to replace?"

"That's my Roxanne." He kissed her hand again. "I love your avaricious mind."

This time she did pull her hand away. His lips had lingered on her skin too long for comfort. "You're dripping on me, Callahan," she said, and stepped back to let him take the spotlight alone.

It killed Roxanne to have to sit and wait. It was degrading, she thought, pacing the parlor while Lily sprawled comfortably on the couch and watched an old black-and-white on TV.

It was like sitting by the phone for hours and hoping the jerk who took you out to the movies would call and ask you out again. Making a woman wait was so typically male.

She said as much to Lily and was answered by a murmur of agreement.

"I mean, they've done it since the dawn of time." Roxanne plopped into a chair, rose restlessly again to pull open the sheer drapes to watch the City of Lights twinkle. "Cavemen went off hunting and left the women by the fire. Vikings raped and pillaged while the womenfolk stayed home. Cowboys rode off into the sunset, men went down to the sea in ships and soldiers marched off to war. And where were we?" Roxanne demanded, her vivid floral robe swirling as she spun around. "Standing on widow's walks, waiting at train stations, wearing chastity belts or sitting by the damn phone.

"Well, I don't want to let a man dictate my life."

"Love." Lily blew her nose heartily as the credits rolled. "It's love that dictates, honeybunch, not a man."

"Well, the hell with that."

"Oh, no. It's the best there is." Lily sighed, satisfied with the romance, the tragedy and the good cry. "Max is only doing what he thinks is right for you."

"What about what I think is right?" Roxanne demanded.

"You'll have all the time in the world for that." Lily shifted, tucking her favorite robe—a peacock silk trimmed in pink ostrich feathers—under her. "The years go so fast, Roxy. You can't imagine it now, but before you know it they start whizzing by. If you don't have love in them, you end up empty. Whatever you choose as right, if love's sprinkled through it, it will be right."

There was no use arguing with Lily, Roxanne thought. She was a bred-in-the-bone romantic. Roxanne prided herself on being a more practical woman. "Didn't you ever want to go with them? Didn't you ever want to be a part of it?"

"I am a part of it." Lily smiled, looking young and pretty and content. "My being here's part of it. I know Max'll walk in that door, and he'll have that look in his eyes. That look that says he's done just what he wanted to do. And he'll need to tell me, to share it with me. He'll need me to tell him how smart and clever he is."

"And that's enough?" Despite her love for both of them, Roxanne found it amazing, appalling. "Being a sounding board for Max's ego?"

Lily's smile faded. The flash in her eyes turned the soft blue to marble.

"I'm exactly where I want to be, Roxanne. In all the years I've been with Max he's never once used me, or deliberately hurt my feelings. That may not count for much with you, but for me, it's more than enough. He's gentle and kind and gives me everything I could want."

"I'm sorry." And she was as she reached out to take Lily's hand. Sorry that *she* had hurt Lily's feelings. Sorry, too, that her independent soul couldn't understand. "I'm feeling nasty that they left me behind, and I'm taking it out on you."

"Sweetie, we can't all think alike, or feel alike, or be alike. You..." Lily leaned forward to take Roxanne's face in her hands. "You're your father's daughter."

"Maybe he'd rather have had a son."

Lily's fingers tightened. "Don't even think it."

"Luke's out with him." Bitterness leaked through the crack in her ego. "I'm sitting here twiddling my thumbs."

"Roxy, you're only seventeen."

"Then I hate being seventeen." She sprang up again, silk swirling around her as she marched to the window and threw it open. She drank in air like water. "I hate having to wait for everything, having everyone say there's plenty of time."

"Of course you do." There was a smile on Lily's lips and fresh tears in her eyes as she studied Roxanne. She's so beautiful, Lily thought. So full of needs. How desperate it was to be seventeen. How wonderful and horrible to be caught on that razor's edge of womanhood. "I can give you some advice, but it might not be what you want to hear."

Roxanne lifted her face to the soft spring night and shut her eyes. How could she explain to Lily these burning, pumping needs inside her when she couldn't explain them to herself? "Advice never hurts, taking it often does."

Lily laughed because it was one of Max's sayings. "Compromise." Roxanne groaned at the word, but Lily plowed on. "Compromise isn't so painful if you're the one setting the terms." She rose, pleased when Roxanne turned toward her, a thoughtful gleam in her eyes. "You're a female, do you want to change that?"

Roxanne's lips curved as she remembered her own relief and pride when her breasts had finally begun to bud. "No. No, I don't."

"Then use it, honey." Lily laid a hand on Roxanne's shoulder. "Using it doesn't have to be the same as..."

"Exploiting it?" Roxanne suggested, and Lily beamed.

"That's it. You take advantage of what you've got. Make it work for you. Your brains, your looks, your womanhood. Baby, the women who've done that have been liberated for centuries. Men didn't always know it, that's all."

"I'll think about it." One decisive nod, then she kissed Lily's cheek. "Thanks." She stiffened when she heard the key in the lock, and forced herself to relax. Beside her Lily was already vibrating with excitement. It baffled Roxanne, and delighted her. After all the years they'd been together, she mused as Max swung through the door. He can still make her feel that way.

She wondered, fleetingly, if there would ever be someone who could give her that kind of gift.

Luke strolled in behind Max, grinned and tossed Roxanne a pouch.

"Still awake?" Filled to the brim with his victory, Max was already kissing Lily. "What more can a man want, Luke, than to come home after a successful venture and find two lovely ladies awaiting him?"

"A cold beer," Luke answered as he headed toward the mini-bar. "It must have been a hundred-twenty in that vault once we killed the power." Luke popped open a beer and gulped half of it down his dry throat.

He looked like a barbarian, Roxanne thought, jiggling the pouch in her hand. Dark, sweaty, overtly male. Because watching him made her own throat go dry, she turned back to her father. Now this was a man, she thought, pleased, who understood class. An aristocratic pirate, his moustache gleaming, his black trousers meticulously pressed, the dark cashmere sweater smelling lightly of his cologne.

There were thieves, she decided as she sat on the arm of the couch, and thieves.

"Mouse and LeClerc?" Lily asked.

"Both gone off to bed. I invited Luke in for a nightcap. My dear boy, perhaps you could open a bottle of that Chardonnay we have chilled."

"Sure." While he uncorked the bottle, he glanced at Roxanne. "Don't you want to see what's in the pouch, Rox?"

"I suppose." She hadn't wanted to seem anxious. Certainly didn't want to give either of them too much of a reaction. But when she poured the contents of the pouch in her hand no amount of willpower could still her gasp. "Oh," she said as diamonds sizzled against her skin. And again, "Oh."

"Spectacular, aren't they?" Max took the pouch and poured the remaining stones into Lily's cupped hands. "Russian whites, round cut, perfect quality. What do you say, Luke, a million-five?"

"Closer to two." He offered Roxanne a glass of wine, set Lily's on the table.

"Perhaps you're right." Max murmured a thanks when Luke brought him a glass. "It was tempting to be greedy, I admit. Standing there in that vault." With his eyes closed, he could see it. "All that utilitarian steel gleaming, and inside a treasure trove of emeralds, sapphires, rubies. Ah, Lily, the artistry. Necklaces dripping with color. Square-cut, pear-shaped, baguettes, tiffanies." He sighed. "But these handsome fellows will be much simpler to transport and invest."

Luke remembered one piece in particular, a dramatic symphony of emeralds, diamonds, topaz and amethyst worked into a hammered gold collar in Byzantine style. He'd imagined slipping it around Roxanne's neck, lifting all that heavy hair, fixing the clasp. She'd have looked like a queen wearing it.

He would have tried to tell her that he'd needed to see her wear it, needed to give her something no one else could.

And she would have laughed.

Luke shook his head as Max's voice penetrated his fantasy. "What? Sorry?"

"Something on your mind?"

"No." With an effort of will he banished the image and his scowl. "I'm tired, that's all. It's been a long day, I'm going to turn in."

Maternal instincts were stronger than the flash of gems. Lily forgot about the diamonds sparkling in her hands. "Honey, don't you want a sandwich or something? You hardly touched your dinner."

"I'm fine." He kissed her, the left cheek, then the right, in a habit he'd developed over the years. "Good night, Lily. Max."

"An excellent job, Luke," Max put in. "Sleep well."

He opened the door and tossed a look over his shoulder. They were gathered close. Max in the center with Lily nestled under his arm, Roxanne on the arm of the couch, her head resting against her father's side, her hand full of icy white stones.

Family portrait, he thought. His family. His eyes shifted to Roxanne's, held. He'd do best to remember she was family. "See you, Rox."

He shut the door and walked across the hall to his own room, where he knew he would spend what was left of the night dreaming about a prize much more unattainable than diamonds.

She rubbed his nose in that the very next day. The minute rehearsal was over, Roxanne hopped on the back of a motor scooter behind a blond Adonis. She sent a cheery wave, linked her arms around the French bastard's waist and blasted off into the reckless Parisian traffic.

"Who the hell was that?" Luke demanded.

Max stopped by a flower vendor and purchased a carnation for his lapel. "Who was who?"

"That jerk Roxanne just raced off with?"

"Oh, the boy." Max sniffed the red blossom before slipping the stem through his buttonhole. "Antoine, Alastair, something of the kind. A student at the Sorbonne. An artist, I believe."

"You let her ride off with some guy you don't know?" It was outrageous. It was inconceivable. It was unbelievably painful. "Some *French* guy?"

"Roxanne knows him," Max pointed out. Delighted with life in general, he took a deep breath of air. "When Lily finishes changing, I believe we'll all have lunch in some quaint outdoor café."

"How can you think about eating?" Luke spun on his heel and fought the urge to put his hands around Max's throat. "Your daughter's just driven off with a perfect stranger. He could be a maniac for all you know."

Max chuckled and decided to choose a dozen roses from the vendor's cart for Lily. "Roxanne can handle him perfectly well."

"He was staring at her legs," Luke said savagely.

"Yes, well. It's difficult to blame him. Ah, here's Lily." He presented her with the roses and a sweeping bow that made her giggle.

Roxanne had a perfectly wonderful time. A picnic in the countryside, the scent of wildflowers, a French artist who read her poetry under the shade of a chestnut tree.

She'd enjoyed the interlude, the soft, stirring kisses, the whispered endearments in the world's most romantic language. She slipped back into her room half dreaming, with a secret smile on her lips and stars in her eyes.

"What the hell have you been doing?"

She muffled a shriek, stumbled back and stared at Luke. He was sitting in the chair by the window, a bottle of beer in his hand, the stub of a cigar in the ashtray beside him and murder in his eyes.

"Damn it, Callahan, you scared me to death. What are you doing in my room?"

"Waiting for you to decide to come back."

Once her heart started beating again, she pushed her hair from her shoulders. It was windblown from the drive, and made him think of a woman just rising out of bed after an interlude of hot, reckless sex. It was one more reason for murder.

"I don't know what you're talking about. I've got a good hour before we have to leave for the theater."

She'd let the son of a bitch kiss her. Oh, he knew it. She had that look about her, those soft, swollen lips, the heavy eyes. Her shirt was wrinkled. She'd let him lay her back on the grass and...

He couldn't bear to think of it.

It was bad enough when they were home and she took off with American guys. But French.

Every man had his limit.

"I'd like to know what happened to your brain. What did you think you were doing, going off with some smarmy French creep named Alastair."

"I went on a picnic," she tossed back. "And he isn't smarmy or a creep. He's a sweet, sensitive man. An artist." She threw that out like a gauntlet. "And for your information, his name is Alain."

"I don't give a flying shit what his name is." Luke rose slowly. He was still under the delusion that he had control. "You're not going out with him again."

For an instant she was too stunned to speak. But only for an instant. "Who the hell do you think you are?" She advanced on him to shove the heel of her hand in his chest. "I can go out with whomever I want."

He snagged her wrist and brought her up hard against him. "Like hell."

Her chin snapped up, her eyes sizzled. "Who do you think's going to stop me? You? You've got no say in what I do, Callahan. Not now, not ever."

"You're wrong." He said it between his teeth. His hand had dived into her hair, fisted there. He couldn't seem to stop it. He could smell her, and the lingering tang of grass, of sunlight. Wildflowers. It plunged him into a murderous rage to think someone else had been this close. Close enough to touch. To taste. "You let him put his hands on you. If you do that again, I'll kill him."

She would have laughed the threat off, or shouted it off. But she saw the naked truth in his eyes. The only way to combat the fear that sprang into her throat was with fury. "You're out of your mind. If he put his hands on me it was because I wanted him to. Because I like it." She knew it was the wrong thing to say, but was as helpless to stop fanning the flames as Luke had been to stop them from igniting. "And I want yours off. Now."

"Do you?" His voice was soft, smooth as silk. That frightened her more, much more than his sneering threats. "Why don't we just call this a free lesson?" He damned himself even as he brought his mouth down to cover hers.

She didn't struggle, didn't protest. She wasn't sure she continued to breathe. How could she when the heat flashed so fast and hot it incinerated everything? Even thought. This was nothing, nothing like the soft, gentle kisses of the artist. Nothing like the awkward or arrogant embraces of the boys she'd dated. This was raw, it was primitive, it was terrifying. She wondered if there was a woman alive who would want to be kissed any other way.

His mouth fit over hers perfectly. The scrape of the skin he'd neglected to shave only added to the dizzying knowledge that at last, at long last, she was being held by a man. Naked aggression, frustrated passion, pure rage, erupted from him, into her, creating a kiss beyond anything she'd experienced. That single, wild moment was everything she'd dreamed of.

With his hand still fisted in her hair he dragged her head back. If he was going to hell, he would at least have the satisfaction of knowing it had been worth it. He didn't think, didn't dare to think, but plunged his tongue between her parted lips and filled himself on her.

She was everything he'd imagined and more. Soft, strong, sexy. The moan came from her instant and torrid response. The way her body strained and trembled against his, the way her mouth met demand for hot, violent demand. Her lips clung to his, forming his name. He swallowed her moans like a starving man swallows a crust of bread.

He wanted, desperately wanted, to tumble her onto the bed. To tear her clothes aside and drive himself into her. To feel her arch as she closed around him. He couldn't breathe for wanting it.

It was like being closed in a box. Trapped. Running out of air. His heart and lungs were straining. He had no control over them. No control over anything.

He jerked back, fighting for air, and some rag of sanity. She was still wrapped around him, her eyes dark and heavy, her lips soft, parted and eager for more. Waves of shame and need washed over him, warring tidal waves that had him shoving her roughly aside.

"Luke—"

"Don't." He was hard as iron and twitchy as a stallion. If she touched him now, only touched him, he would take her like an animal. To protect her from that, he cloaked himself with all the fury he felt for what he'd nearly done, and aimed it straight at her. "Free lesson," he repeated and pretended he didn't see her lips part in shock, or her eyes glitter with hurt. "That's the kind of treatment you're asking for if you go out with men you don't know."

She had pride, and was enough of an actress to use it to mask devastation. "Odd, isn't it? You're the only one who's ever treated me that way. And I know you. Or thought I did." She turned her back on him and stared out the window. She wouldn't cry, she promised herself. And if she did, he wouldn't see it. "Get out of my room, Callahan. If you touch me that way again, you'll pay for it."

He was already paying for it, Luke thought. He curled his hand into a fist before he could give into the urge to stroke her hair. To beg. Instead he walked to the door. "I meant what I said, Roxanne."

She aimed a glittering look over her shoulder. "So did I."

13

Roxanne took Lily's advice and compromised with Max—though Roxanne preferred to think of it as a deal. She would register at Tulane University and give her college education serious attention. If after one year she was still determined to join her father's less public show, she would be taken on as an apprentice.

It suited Roxanne perfectly. First, because she enjoyed the process of learning. Second, because she had no intention of changing her mind.

The demands of her stage career and her education had the added benefit of leaving her limited free time. She spent as little as possible in Luke's company.

She would have forgiven him for the shouting, even for the orders. Certainly she would have forgiven him for the kiss. But she would never forgive him for turning one of the most glorious moments of her life into nothing more than a lesson offered from master to student.

She was too professional to allow it to interfere with her work or his. When rehearsal was called, she rehearsed with him. They performed together night after night with none of their inner feelings bubbling up from beneath the slick surface of the act.

If the troupe went on the road, they traveled together without incident—polite strangers who shared a plane or train or car from place to place.

Only once, when Lily expressed concern that Luke's escapes were becoming more complex and more dangerous, did any of the trapped turmoil escape.

"Let him be," Roxanne had shot back. "Men like him always have something to prove."

Her small and sweet revenge was in dating a succession of attractive men. She brought them home often, for dinner, parties, study groups. It gave her a great deal of pleasure to know her current beau—as Lily was wont to call them—was in the audience during the performance. It gave her a great deal more pleasure to know that Luke was aware of it.

She leaned toward the scholarly type, because she was attracted to a keen mind. And, deviously, because she knew that none of Max's prodding had pushed Luke beyond his single year of college. It was so satisfying to mention, casually, that Matthew was a law student, or that Philip was working on his master's in economics.

For herself, Roxanne had chosen to study both art history and gemology. Her purpose, much to Max's delight, was to enhance her knowledge of what she now termed her hobby. If one was going to steal great works of art and fine gems, she'd informed her father, one should have a solid understanding of the background and value of the take.

Max was proud to have a daughter with vision.

He was pleased, too, that his reputation as a performer and respect for his troupe had grown. He treasured his magician-of-the-year award from the Academy of Magical Arts. He no longer found it necessary to avoid national exposure. The Nouvelles had two successful television specials under their belts, and Max had recently signed a contract to write a definitive book on magic.

A month before, he'd relieved a Baltimore matron of an opal and diamond brooch, with matching earrings. He'd used his share of the profits—after tithing—to pay for his research into what had become his biggest interest: the philosophers' stone.

To some it was a legend. To Max it was a goal, one he needed badly now that his dual careers had reached their zenith. He wanted to hold it, that rock that was a magician's dream. Not simply to turn iron into gold, but as a testament to all he had learned, accomplished, taken and given back over his lifetime. Already he had gathered books, maps, scores of letters and diaries.

Tracking down the philosophers' stone would be Maximillian Nouvelle's greatest feat.

Once he had it, he thought—hoped—that he could ease into retirement. He and Lily would travel the world like vagabonds while their children carried on the Nouvelle tradition.

As New Orleans settled down into a chill, rainy winter, Max was at peace with the world. The occasional twinge the damp weather brought to his hands was overcome with a couple of aspirin, and easily ignored.

Roxanne liked the rain. It gave her a cozy, dreamy feeling to watch it patter on the sidewalk, run down the glass of the window. She stood on the covered balcony outside of Gerald's apartment and watched the thin, chilly curtain chase away the pedestrians. If she took a deep breath she could smell the café au lait Gerald was brewing in his tiny kitchen.

It was nice to be here, she thought, taking this rainy night off. She enjoyed Gerald's company, and found him smart and sweet. A man who liked to listen to Gershwin and view foreign films. His little apartment over a souvenir shop was crammed with books and records and VCR tapes. Gerald was a student of the cinema, and had already collected more movies than Roxanne imagined she would see in her lifetime.

Tonight they were going to watch Ingmar Bergman's *Wild Strawberries*, and Hitchcock's *Vertigo*.

"Aren't you cold?" Gerald stood inside the narrow doorway, holding out a sweater. He was perhaps a half inch shorter than Roxanne with broad shoulders that gave the illusion of more height. He had lank, sandy hair that fell—endearingly, she thought—onto his forehead. He had chiseled, leading-man looks that reminded her faintly of Harrison Ford. His mild brown eyes were given distinction by the dignified tortoiseshell glasses he wore.

"Not really." But she came back inside. "It doesn't look like there's a soul in the city tonight. Everyone's snuggled in."

He set the sweater aside. "I'm glad you're snuggled in here."

"Me too." She gave him her lips in a light kiss. "I like it here." They'd been seeing each other on and off for nearly a month, but this was the first time Roxanne had been to his apartment.

It was pure struggling student. Movie posters adorned the walls, the sagging couch was covered with a faded bedspread, the scarred wooden desk shoved into the corner was laden with books. His electronic equipment, however, was state-of-the-art.

"I guess these home-movie things are the wave of the future."

"By the end of the decade, VCRs will be as common as television sets in the American home. Everyone will own video cameras." He grinned and patted his own. "Amateur directors will spring up everywhere." He touched her hair, a wild tangle of curls she'd recently cut to chin length. "Maybe you'll let me make a movie of you sometime."

"Of me?" The idea made her laugh. "I can't imagine."

He could. Taking her hand, he led her to the couch. "Bergman first, okay?"

"Fine." She picked up her coffee and settled back into the crook of his arm. Gerald pushed some buttons on his remote. One to engage the VCR, the other to start the camera he had strategically placed between stacks of books.

Roxanne supposed she was plebeian, but Bergman didn't grab her. Give me a car chase any day, she thought as she struggled to keep her mind on the slow-moving black-and-white art flickering on the screen.

She didn't mind having Gerald's arm around her. He smelled of peppermint mouthwash and mild, inexpensive cologne. She didn't object to the light trail his fingers made up and down her arm. When he shifted to kiss her, she had no trouble tilting her head back and accepting the offer.

But when she tried to ease away, he tightened his hold.

"Gerald." She gave a light laugh as she turned her head away. "You're going to miss the movie."

"I've seen it before." His voice was thick and breathless as he ran kisses down the side of her throat.

"I haven't." She wasn't worried, not really. A little annoyed perhaps that he was making such an obvious and fevered move, but not worried.

"Don't you find it erotic? The imagery, the subtleties."

"Not really." Tedious was what she found it, just as tedious as she found the fact that he was pressing her back against the cushions of the couch. "But then I'm probably too literal-minded." She blocked his mouth, but wasn't quick enough to stop his fingers from fumbling with the buttons of her blouse. "Stop it, Gerald." She didn't want to hurt him, his feelings or otherwise. "This isn't why I came here, and it isn't what I want."

"I've wanted you since the first time I saw you." He managed to pry her legs apart and began to grind his erection against her. Roxanne felt the first licks of panic sneak through the annoyance. "I'm going to get you naked, baby, and make you a star."

"No, you're not." She struggled in earnest when his hand closed over her breast and squeezed. Growing fear had her voice shaking. A mistake, she realized instantly as his breathing quickened with excitement. "Damn it, get off me." She bucked like a bronco, heard her blouse rip.

"You like it rough, baby? That's okay." He grabbed at the zipper of her jeans with sweaty, impatient hands. "That's good. Better visual. We'll watch it after."

"You son of a bitch." She never knew whether it was timing or terror that had her elbow swinging over, knocking hard enough against his temple to make him rear back. She didn't hesitate, but balled her hand into a fist and slammed it against his nose.

Blood fountained out, splattering her blouse, making him yelp like a kicked puppy. His hands flew up to his face, knocking his glasses askew. Roxanne scrambled up, grabbed her canvas bag and brought it against the side of his face in a vicious, two-handed swipe.

His glasses soared across the room. "Hey, hey." Blood dripped through his fingers as he goggled up at her. "You broke my fucking nose."

"You try that again with me, or anyone else I hear about, I'll break your fucking dick."

He started to rise, then sank back down again when she lifted both fists in a boxer's stance.

"Come on," she taunted. There were tears in her eyes now, but they weren't from fear. It was pure rage. "You want to take me on, you bastard?"

He shook his head, grabbing a corner of the bedspread to staunch the flow of blood from his nose. "Just get out. Jesus, you're crazy."

"Yeah." She felt the hysteria bubbling up. She wanted to hit him again, she realized. She wanted to beat and punch and pummel until he was as frightened and helpless as she had been moments before. "You remember that, creep, and stay away from me." She slammed out, leaving him babbling about hospitals and lawsuits.

Roxanne was a block away and searching for a cab when it hit her. Make you a star? Watch it after? A scream of rage burst out as it sank in.

The son of a bitch must have been filming the whole thing.

It was like falling into a nightmare. Though the rain had slowed to a drizzle, it was a cold, miserable night. Nothing could have suited Luke's mood more perfectly.

In his hand was a letter, a letter that had dragged him back over the jagged distance to the past. Cobb. The bastard had found him. Standing in the Nouvelle courtyard with the thin rain sneaking under the collar of his jacket, Luke wondered why he had ever allowed himself to believe in escapes.

No matter how clever he'd been, how successful, how strong, he could be jerked back into that small, frightened boy. It had only taken a few words on paper.

Callahan—long time no see. I'm looking forward to talking about old times. If you don't want to lose your classy situation meet me tonight at ten at Bodine's on Bourbon. Don't try no disappearing act, or I'll have to have a nice, long talk with your pals the Nouvelles. Al Cobb.

He'd wanted to ignore it. He'd wanted to laugh and tear the paper into tiny, insignificant pieces to show just how little it had meant to the man he'd become. But his hands had shaken. His stomach had twisted into slick, tiny knots. And he'd known, as he'd always known, that he couldn't escape from where he'd come from. Or what he'd lived through.

Still, he wasn't a child afraid to face the monster in the closet. He balled the paper into his pocket and stepped toward the street. He'd face Cobb tonight, and somehow find a way to vanish him and everything he stood for.

The rain dampened his jacket, his shoes and his mood. He hunched his shoulders, swore at nothing in particular and started toward the corner. When a cab veered toward the curb, he hesitated, debating about whether it would improve his frame of mind to take a dry ride rather than a wet walk.

He forgot both possibilities as he watched Roxanne alight. She was a handy target for his frustration.

"Back so soon?" he called out. "Didn't your four-eyed friend keep you entertained?"

"Kiss ass, Callahan." She kept her head down as she hurried by him, hoping to slip into the house unseen. But Luke was feeling just ugly enough to taunt her.

"Hey." He snagged her arm and spun her again. "You got some—" He stopped dead when he saw the state of her clothes. Beneath her bright jacket, the boxy cotton blouse was torn and splattered with blood. Panic hammered through him as he grabbed both of her shoulders, fingers digging in. "What happened to you?"

"Nothing. Leave me alone."

He gave her one hard shake. "What happened?" His voice seemed to be caught in his throat, squeezing out over razor blades. "Baby, what happened?"

"Nothing," she said again. Why was she starting to shake now? she wondered. It was all over. Over and done. "Gerald had a different idea on what I was doing in his apartment than I had." She tossed her chin up, ready for a lecture. "I had to disabuse him of the notion."

She heard Luke suck in his breath—not in shock. It was more like an animal snarling.

When she glanced up at his face, her unsteady pulse went haywire. His eyes were like glass, the kind that leaves deep jagged gashes on flesh.

"I'll kill him." His fingers dug into her shoulders hard enough to make her yelp. He released her so quickly, Roxanne stumbled back. By the time she'd regained her balance, she had to run to catch him.

"Luke. Stop this." She snatched at his sleeve. Though her heart dropped to her knees when he rounded on her, eyes glowing, teeth bare, she hung on. "Nothing happened. Nothing. I'm all right."

"You've got blood all over you."

"None of it's mine." She tried a smile, scraping her wet hair out of her face. "Come on, I appreciate the white knight routine, but I took care of it. You don't even know where the jerk lives."

He'd find him. Somehow Luke knew that he could track the bastard down like a wolf tracking a rabbit. But Roxanne's hand was trembling on his arm.

"Did he hurt you?" It was an effort to keep his voice steady and calm, but he thought she needed it. "Tell me the truth, Rox. Did he rape you?"

"No." She didn't resist when Luke's arms came around her. It wasn't fear that was making her shake, she realized. It was a haunting sense of betrayal. She had known Gerald, she'd liked him, and he'd been prepared to force sex on her. "No, he didn't rape me. I swear."

"He ripped your shirt."

This time her smile was a little steadier. "He said I broke his nose, but I think I just bloodied it." She laughed and settled her head on Luke's shoulder. It felt so good to be there, standing in the rain with him, feeling that hard, steady beat of his heart. Whenever things got really bad, she mused, Luke was there. There was a comfort in that. "You should have heard him squeal. Luke, I don't want Max or Lily to know. Please."

"Max has a right—"

"I know." She lifted her head again. Rain trickled down her face like tears. "It's nothing to do with rights. It would hurt him, and frighten him. And it's over now, so what could he do?"

"I won't say anything. If—"

"I knew there'd be an if."

"If," Luke repeated, tucking a finger under her chin, "you agree to let me talk to this creep. Satisfy myself that he's going to stay away from you."

"Believe me, I don't have anything to worry about. He might even take out a warrant so I won't be able to go within five hundred feet of him."

"I talk to him, or I talk to Max."

"Damn it." She sighed, considered her options, then shrugged. "Okay, I'll tell you where to find him, if—"

"Yeah, right. If?"

"You swear it's just talk. I don't want or need you to go beat someone's face in for me anymore." She smiled again and knew they both thought of Sam Wyatt. "I did that all by myself this time."

"Just talk," Luke said. Unless he decided more was necessary.

"Actually, you could do me a favor." She eased away because this was a tough one. "I'm not positive, but I think... from something he said when he was, well..."

"What?"

"I think he had a camera on somewhere. Filming the event, you know?"

Luke opened his mouth, shut it again. Perhaps it was for the best that he was stunned speechless. "Excuse me?"

"He's a film major," she hurried on. "Really hung up on movies, and this video craze. That's why I went to his apartment. To watch a couple of classic films. And he..." She blew out a breath that fogged in the air then washed away in the rain. "I'm pretty sure he had a camera on, so we could enjoy watching ourselves after."

"That fucking perverted asshole."

"Well, yeah, but I was wondering, if you insist on talking to him, if you could make him give you the film or the tape or whatever the hell it is."

"I'll get it. If you ever pull something like this again—"

"I pull?" She slapped her hands on her hips. "Look, peabrain, I was nearly raped. That makes me a victim, get it? I didn't do anything to deserve that kind of treatment."

"I didn't mean—"

"Hell with that. It's just like a man." She whirled away, paced two steps then spun back. "I must have been asking for it, right? I lured that poor, helpless man into my web then cried foul when things got heavy."

"Shut up." He pulled her against him and held tight. "I'm sorry. I didn't mean anything like that. Christ, Roxanne, can't you understand you scared me? I don't know what I'd have done if he'd..." He pressed his mouth to her hair. "I don't know what I'd have done."

"All right." Another tremor hit her, rippling down her spine. "It's all right."

"Okay." He was murmuring, stroking, trying to comfort, even as his mouth sought hers. "No one's going to hurt you again." There was rain on her lips. He kissed it away, gently, sweetly, then went back for more. Her arms came up to wind strong and sure around his neck even as her body melted like wax against him. He gave himself a moment, one glorious moment to hold her, and pretend it could be real.

"Feeling better?" His smile was strained as he drew her away.

"I'm feeling something." Her voice was like the fog that snaked along the ground at their feet. When she lifted a hand to his cheek, he grabbed it, pressed his lips to the center of her palm. She wondered the rain didn't sizzle off as it struck her.

"Rox... we'd better—" He broke off as a man walked through the curtain of rain. Luke started to simply shift Roxanne aside, then he looked at Cobb's face, at Cobb's eyes, and felt his life turn upside down.

How foolish he'd been to forget even for a moment that he had his own demons to face that night.

But if he could do nothing else, he could prevent that ugliness from touching Roxanne.

"Go inside," he ordered.

"But, Luke—"

"Go in. Now." He pulled her toward the gate and the courtyard. "There's something I have to do."

"I'll wait."

"No, don't." When he turned, she had one glimpse of his eyes, and the torment in them.

Luke walked through the rain to confront an old nightmare.

"Been a while, kid." Al Cobb sat in the dingy Bourbon Street strip joint smoking a Camel. It was his kind of setting, the women with tired eyes bumping hips and twirling pasties, the smell of stale drunks and impersonal sex. He'd known Luke would follow him in.

Luke had draped one arm over the back of his chair. He was forcing himself to relax, using every ounce of will to prevent those nasty flash-backs from sneaking into his mind. "What do you want?"

"A drink, a little conversation." Cobb let his eyes crawl over the cocktail waitress's breasts and roam down to her crotch. "Bourbon, a double."

"Black Jack," Luke told her, knowing his usual beer wouldn't have the fire to purge.

"A man's drink." Cobb grinned, showing tobacco-stained teeth. Years of hefting the bottle hadn't been kind to him. Even in the dim light Luke could see the maze of broken capillaries in his face, those twisted red banners of the dedicated drunk. He'd put on too much weight around the middle so that his knit shirt stretched and strained over the girth.

"I asked you what you wanted."

Cobb said nothing as their drinks were set down. He lifted his, took a deep swallow and watched the stage. An improbably built redhead was peeling away a French maid's uniform. She was down to her G-string and a pair of feather dusters.

"Je-sus, look at the tits on that bitch." Cobb downed his drink and signaled for another. He grinned over at Luke. "What's the matter, boy, don't you like looking at boobs?"

"What are you doing in New Orleans?"

"Having me a little holiday." Cobb licked his lips while the dancer bounced her abundant breasts and squeezed them together. "Figured since I was in the neighborhood, I'd look you up. Ain't you going to ask about your mother?"

Luke sipped carefully at the whiskey, letting the heat slide down into his gut and thaw frozen muscles. "No."

"That's unnatural." Cobb clucked his tongue. "She's living in Portland now. We still get together from time to time. She started to charge for it, you know?" He gave Luke a lascivious wink, pleased when he saw the muscles in his jaw clench. "But old Maggie, she's sentimental enough to give me a free pop when I come knocking. Want I should give her your best?"

"I don't want you to give her anything from me."

"You got a shitty attitude." Cobb tossed back more bourbon while the music grew louder, more raucous. One of the men tried to climb onstage and was tossed out. "Always did. You'd stayed around a little longer, I'd have beaten some respect into you."

Luke leaned forward, eyes glittering. "Or you'd have turned me into a whore."

"You had a roof over your head, food in your belly." Cobb shrugged and continued to drink. "I just expected you to pay for it." It didn't occur to him to be afraid of Luke. His memory was keen enough to recall how easily he'd cowed the boy with a few solid whacks of the belt. "But that's behind us now, ain't it? You're a big fucking deal these days. Coulda knocked me over with a whiff of gin when I saw you on the TV." He snorted into his bourbon. "Doing magic tricks for chrissake. Learned how to wave your magic wand, did you, Luke?" He roared with laughter at his own joke until tears sparkled in his eyes. "You and that old man got yourself a couple of prime pieces of ass out of it."

The laughter died into choking when Luke grabbed him by the collar. Their faces were close now, close enough for Luke to smell the whiskey on Cobb's breath over the barroom stink of liquor and smoke. "What do you want?" he repeated, spacing each word.

"You want to take me on, boy?" Always ready to brawl, he wrapped his meaty fingers around Luke's wrists. He was surprised by the strength he found there, but never doubted his own superiority. "Want to go head-to-head with me?"

He did, so badly his body shook with a need as basic as sex. But there was a part of him, buried deep, that was still a terrified little boy who remembered the snap of a leather belt, and the sear of it against tender flesh. "I don't want to be in the same state with you."

"It's a free country." Because he was smart enough to know that a fight wouldn't get him what he'd come for, Cobb jerked away and ordered another drink. "Problem with that is you got to pay for every damn thing. You're making good money with your magic tricks."

"Is that what you want?" Luke would have laughed if disgust hadn't blocked his throat. "You want me to give you money?"

"Helped raise you, didn't I? I'm the closest thing to a father you had."

Now he did laugh. There was enough fury in the sound to have the people nearby glance over warily. "Fuck off." Before he could rise, Cobb took hold of his sleeve.

"I can make trouble for you, and for that old man you're tangled up with. All I got to do is make a couple of calls to some of them reporters. What do you think the TV producers would think once they read about you? Callahan—that's what you call yourself now, ain't it? Just plain Callahan. Escape artist and male prostitute."

"That's a lie." But he'd paled, and Cobb saw it. All those memories flooded back, the fat hands pawing, groping, the sweat and heavy breathing. "I didn't let him touch me."

"You don't know what happened after I kicked you senseless." Cobb was pleased to see the bluff take root. He fed on the horror, the doubt, the revulsion in Luke's eyes. "One way or the other, people'd wonder, wouldn't they? People like that hot little number you were making time with a little while ago. You think she'd let you dip your wick once she found out you were blowing freaking fags when you were twelve?" He grinned, with hate in his eyes. "Don't matter if it's a lie or the God's truth, boy, not once it's in print."

"I'll kill you." Nausea weakened Luke's voice and had sweat pearling on his forehead.

"Be easier to pay me." Confident he could run the show, Cobb took out another cigarette. "I don't need much. Couple thousand to start." He blew smoke in Luke's direction. "Starting tomorrow. Then I'll drop you a line now and then, telling you how much I want and where to send it. Otherwise . . . I go to the press. I'd have to tell them how you sold yourself to perverts, how you took off from your poor, grieving mother, how you got tangled up with that Nouvelle. Seems to me he broke a law or two taking in a runaway. Then again, it might sound like he had other uses for you. You know." He smiled again, satisfied with the revulsion on Luke's face. "I could make people wonder if he didn't get for free what you sold to others."

"Keep Max out of it."

"Be glad to." Cobb spread his hands in cooperation. "You bring me two thousand tomorrow night, right here. That's a show of good faith. Then I'll be on my way. You don't show, I'll just have to make me a call to the *National Enquirer.* I don't guess all the little boys and girls, and their mommies and daddies, would have much use for a magician who had a taste for young meat? Nope." He took another drag. "Can't see you doing another performance for the Queen of England when you're accused of buggery. That's what those limeys call it. Buggery." Cobb laughed again as he rose. "Tomorrow night. I'll be waiting."

Luke sat where he was, fighting just to breathe. Lies, fucking lies. He could prove it, couldn't he? His hand shook as he reached for his glass. No one would believe, could possibly believe that Max had...

Sickened, he pressed the heels of his hands against his eyes.

Cobb was right, once it was in print, once people started to question and whisper, it wouldn't matter. The stain would be there, the shame and the horror.

If he could stand it for himself, he couldn't bear the thought of any of it touching Max or Lily. Or Roxanne. Sweet God, Roxanne. He squeezed his eyes shut as he downed the rest of his whiskey. He ordered another and settled down to get miserably drunk.

She was waiting for him. Roxanne had gone inside and slipped into her room unnoticed. A long, hot bath had soothed most of the aches, and some of the frustrations. Then she'd settled herself on the balcony to wait.

She saw him stumble through the drizzle and fog. Watched him weave and stop, and start again with the exaggerated care of a drunk. Her worry and confusion vanished in a white-hot rage.

He had left her and her humming nerve ends standing in the rain, and had gone off to find a bottle. Or several bottles by the look of him. Roxanne stood, jerked the robe of her belt tight—like a soldier gearing for battle, then rushed down to intercept Luke in the courtyard.

"You imbecile."

He teetered back, tried to maintain balance on the suddenly slanting bricks and grinned stupidly. "Babe, whatcha doing out in the rain? Catch cold." He took a staggering step forward. "Christ you look pretty, Roxy. Drives me nuts."

"Obviously." It didn't seem like much of a compliment when the words were slurred almost beyond recognition. She reached out to grab his arm in reflex when he swayed. "I hope you pay for this in the morning."

"T'morrow night," he muttered while his head went round and round on his shoulders. "Gotta pay tomorrow night."

"You should live so long." She sighed, but took his weight, draping one of his arms over her shoulders. "Come on, Callahan, let's see if we can get a drunk Irishman to bed without waking up the house."

"My great-grandfather came from county Sligo. The old lady told me that once. Did I mention it?"

"No." She grunted a bit with the effort of dragging him toward the side door.

"Supposed to have a voice like an angel. Sang in the pubs, you know." Rain washed over his face, cool and sweet, when his head fell back. "Sumbitch was never my father. Nothing of him inside me."

"No, there's just a gallon of whiskey inside you from the way you stink."

He grinned and bumped heavily against the door before she could open it. "Sorry. You smell good, Rox. Like rain on wildflowers."

"Ah, the Irish poet." And her face flushed as she braced Luke upright with one hand and pushed the door open with the other.

"I'm just as glad you don't have tits like that broad tonight. I don't think I'd like it."

"What broad?" Roxanne demanded in a stage whisper before she hissed out a breath. "Never mind."

"I don't get much of a thrill watching some babe strip when there's a couple dozen guys in the room. One-on-one's more my style, you know?"

"Fascinating." She didn't feel the least remorse when she turned and rammed him into the kitchen counter. "Leaves me in the rain and runs off to a strip joint. You're a prince, Callahan."

"I'm a bastard," he said with drunken cheer. "Born that way, die that way." He reeled around as she tried to steer him toward the back stairs. "Maybe I should just kill him. Cleaner that way."

"No, you promised me you'd just talk to him."

Luke ran a hand over his face to make sure it was still there. "Talk to who?"

"Gerald."

"Yeah, yeah." He tripped on the first step, and though he went down hard, he didn't seem to notice. To Roxanne's dismay he simply stretched out on the staircase and prepared to go to sleep. "It's scary, so fucking scary when he comes at you that way. And you know you might not be able to stop it. Grabbing you, slobbering on you. Oh, Christ..." His voice died to a bleary whisper. "Don't want to think about it."

"Then don't. Think about getting upstairs."

"Gotta lie down," he muttered, all irritation when she pulled and tugged at him. "Let me alone."

"You're not going to pass out here, like the drunken jerk you are. Lily'll worry sick over you if she finds you here."

"Lily." He sighed, crawling up the steps at Roxanne's prodding. "First woman I ever loved. She's the best. Nobody's ever going to hurt Lily."

"Of course not. Come on, just a little further." Her struggles had her robe spreading open. From his vantage point, Luke had an excellent and disturbing view of smooth, white thigh. Even the whiskey couldn't stop his blood from heating. "Going to hell," he said on a groaning laugh as Roxanne shushed him. "Straight to hell. Christ, I wish you'd wear something under your robe once in a while. Let me just—" But as he reached out to touch, just to touch that smooth white skin, he landed with a heap on the top landing.

"On your feet, Callahan," Roxanne hissed in his ear. "You're not going to wake up Max and Lily."

"Okay, okay." He tried to swallow, but his spit tasted like poison. He made it to his knees on his own, then did his best to stand upright when Roxanne dragged him to his feet. "Am I going to be sick?" he asked as nausea curled in his belly.

"I hope so," she said between her teeth as she half carried, half dragged him to his bedroom. "I sincerely hope so."

"Hate that. Makes me feel like that time Mouse gave me my first cigarette. Not getting drunk anymore, Rox."

"Right. Here we—Shit."

He pitched toward the bed. Though she was quick, she wasn't quite quick enough to avoid going down with him. He landed on her with enough force to steal her breath.

"Get off me, Callahan."

His answer was an unintelligible mutter. Because his breath reeked of Jack Daniel's, she turned her head away. His lips nuzzled sleepily at her throat.

"Cut it out. Oh . . . damn." The curse ended on a muffled groan. Pleasure, heavy and dark, crept into her when he cupped a hand over her breast. He didn't grope, didn't squeeze, he simply possessed.

"Soft," he murmured. "Soft Roxanne." His fingers caressed over the thin silk, lazily, absently while his lips rubbed flesh.

"Luke. Kiss me." Her body was already floating as she tried to turn her mouth to his. "Kiss me like you did before."

"Mmm-hmm." He gave a long, windy sigh, and passed out.

"Luke." She shook his shoulders. It couldn't be, she told herself, not twice in one night. But when she took a handful of his hair to pull his head back, she saw that he was out cold. Grinding her teeth and swearing under her breath, she shoved his inert body aside.

She left him sprawled crossways on the bed, fully dressed, and went off to try the time-honored remedy of a cold shower.

14

He nearly killed himself. Between a vicious hangover and a precarious emotional state, Luke found his timing and his equilibrium were off. He knew better. There were rules, hard and fast rules governing the art of escapology. They quite simply fashioned the border between life and death.

But the choice of playing by the rules and ignoring pride left little room for maneuvering. Luke went forward with the escape segment of the first show, allowing himself to be straitjacketed, shackled and leg-ironed before folding himself into an iron chest center stage.

It was hot, black and all but airless inside. Like a tomb, like a vault. Like a closet. As always, he felt that initial bolt of panic. Being trapped.

No way out, boy, Cobb's voice chortled inside Luke's head. *No way out until I let you out. And don't you forget it.*

That old, helpless fear swept into him, grinning masked bandits hunched in the shadows ready to ambush control. He took slow, shallow breaths to beat the nerves back as he worked on freeing his hands.

He could get out. He'd proven time and time again that no one would keep him locked up ever again. Focusing, focusing, he turned the next corner.

Cobb was waiting for him.

I got the key, you little bastard, and you'll stay right where I put you. It's time you remember who's boss around here.

The image of the closet came back, the small boy sobbing, beating his bound hands raw against the door. Luke's breath hitched as his heart knocked fitfully against his ribs, echoing in his spinning head. The lingering nausea churned in his stomach like a sea of acid. Fear came back, skittering like tiny insects along his sweaty skin.

He hissed with pain as the irons bit into his wrists. For one blind moment, he fought them like a desperate man fighting his shackles on his way to the gallows. And he smelled the coppery scent of his own blood.

Breathing too fast, he told himself, unnerved by the helpless, whooshing sound of his own lungs struggling for oxygen. Calm down, damn it, calm down.

He twisted his body, the familiar and expected twinge as he manipulated his joints helped. His shoulder shifted into an impossible position, allowing him to slither and slide in the straitjacket.

The pounding at his temples had him cursing Jack Daniel's. He was forced to stop again, to gather enough composure to float by the pain.

He was light-headed, a sensation that reminded him too vividly of his condition the night before—and Roxanne. The flashes came, even when he fought to hold them back and concentrate on freeing his arms. Her skin, that soft white skin and his hands moving over it. Her body, curved and yielding under his.

Oh God, Jesus God, had he seduced her, had he used his own turmoil and drink as an excuse to act on the fantasy that had been plaguing him for years?

The sweat was running off Luke in thin hot rivers. He'd lost track of the time, a huge mistake. If he'd had the breath left he would have cursed himself. By the time he was free of the straitjacket, his tortured muscles and joints were screaming. He had only to beat on the box—beat on it as he had once beat on a closet door.

They'd open it, let him out, let him gulp in fresh air. His head lolled back, rapping sharply against the side of the trunk. White-hot pain seared into his head, and images danced behind his closed eyes.

Cobb leering, spouting gut-clenching lies.

He could take care of Cobb, Luke promised himself as he grayed out. It only took money.

Roxanne. Those pictures of Roxanne on the tape he'd terrified out of Gerald. He could hear the sound of her blouse ripping, the muffled demands to be released. He could see the spray of blood, almost smell it as she'd fought herself free.

And how she'd looked, bloody Christ, how she'd looked standing there, fist clenched and ready, body poised like an Amazon, valor shimmering around her and fear and rage shining in her eyes.

He'd wanted to hold her then, to stroke the tremors away. Just as he'd wanted to beat the already bruised and battered Gerald to a slimy pulp.

But as furious as he'd been, he'd been equally ashamed. Had he, blind with drink and lust, done to Roxanne what Gerald had only attempted?

No. He was being a fool. Hadn't he awakened, sick, aching *and* fully dressed? Right down to his shoes. The taste in his mouth hadn't been Roxanne, but the dead skunk flavor of stale whiskey.

Desire and blackmail. Well, neither were worth dying for. He lifted an unsteady hand and slapped himself hard, once, twice so that the shock of pain cleared most of the mists in his brain.

He went to work on the leg irons, sipping cautiously at the thinning air.

"It's too long." Roxanne heard the skitter of panic in her own voice as she grabbed at her father's sleeve. "Daddy, he's two full minutes over."

"I know." Max closed a hand that had gone ice cold over his daughter's. "He has time yet." There was no use telling her that he'd taken one look at Luke's pale, hollow-eyed face in the dressing room and had demanded he cancel his part of tonight's performance.

Just as there was no use telling her that Luke had overruled him. The boy was a man now, and the lines of power were shifting.

"Something's wrong." She could imagine him unconscious, smothering helplessly. "Damn it." She whirled around, intending to streak to the wings to snatch the keys from Mouse. Before she'd taken a step, the lid to the box crashed open.

Suitably impressed, the audience applauded. Drenched with sweat, Luke took his bows and filled his starving lungs. When Max saw him sway, brace himself, he signaled to Roxanne and immediately stepped forward to distract the crowd with sleight of hand.

"Idiot. Jerk. Flea brain." She hurled insults between the clenched teeth of a bright smile as she took his arm and led him offstage. "What the hell were you trying to do?"

Lily was right there with a tall glass of water and a towel. Luke gulped down every drop. The fact that he still felt faint mortified him.

"Get out, mostly," he said as he rubbed sweat from his face. When he staggered, Roxanne wrapped her arms around him. Her heart beat like thunder in her ears as she continued to berate him.

"You had no business going in there tonight after spending last night in a bottle."

"My business *is* going in there," he reminded her. It felt good, too good, to have her holding him steady. He pulled away and headed for his dressing room. Like an angry terrier, Roxanne stayed on his heels.

"Show business does not mean you have to kill yourself. And if you—" She stopped at the door to his dressing room. "Oh, Luke, you're bleeding."

He glanced down where the blood seeped from his wrists and ankles. "Had a little trouble with the leg irons." He shot a hand up to stop her before she could rush in. "I want to change."

"You need to have those cleaned up. Let me—"

"I said I want to change." Now it was the cool look in his eyes that stopped her. "I can take care of it myself."

She pressed her lips together to keep them from trembling. Didn't he know that a cold dismissal hurt her a hundred times more than an angry word? Her chin came up. Of course he did. Who knew better?

"Why are you treating me like this, Luke? After last night—"

"I was drunk," he said sharply, but she shook her head.

"Before, you weren't drunk before. When you kissed me."

Little licks of fire curled in his gut. A man would have to be blind not to see what she was offering with her eyes. He felt sick, needy and tired to the bone. "You were upset," he managed with remarkable calm. "So was I. I was trying to make you feel better, that's all."

Pride flared. "You're a liar. You wanted me."

He gave her a smile calculated to insult. He had that much self-control left. "Babe, if I've learned anything in the past ten years, it's to take what I want." His hands curled into fists at his sides, but his eyes stayed lightly amused. "Weave your little fantasy around your pin-striped college boys. Now I've got things to do before the next show."

He closed the door smartly in her face, then leaned heavily against it.

Close call, Callahan, he thought, closing his eyes. In more ways than one. Because his aches were demanding attention, he pushed away to search out some aspirin. He had to go see Cobb, and he would be armed with two thousand dollars and a clear head.

No one knew the value of timing better than Maximillian Nouvelle. He waited patiently through the second show, making no comment, voicing no criticism. He firmly overrode both Lily's and Roxanne's objections when Luke lowered himself into the iron box for the late audience. Max was in a position to know that if a man didn't face his personal demons, he would be swallowed whole by them.

At home, he politely invited Luke into the parlor for a nightcap and moved inside to pour two snifters of brandy before the invitation could be accepted or declined.

"I'm not much in the mood for a drink." Luke's stomach swayed sickly at the thought of alcohol.

Max merely settled into his favorite wing chair, warming the bowl of the snifter in his hands. "No? Well, then you can keep me company while I have mine."

"It's been a long night," Luke began, hanging back.

"It certainly has." Max lifted one long-fingered hand, gesturing to a chair. "Sit."

The power was still there, the same force that had once compelled a twelve-year-old boy to wait by a darkened stage. Luke sat, took out a cigar. He only ran it between his fingers as he waited for Max to speak.

"There are all manner of methods of suicide." Max's voice was mild, like a man settling back to tell a story. "But I have to admit that I consider any and all of them a form of cowardice. However." Gesturing with one hand, he smiled benignly. "A choice of that nature is highly personal. Would you agree?"

Luke was lost. Since he'd learned long ago to be cautious with words when Max was laying a trap, he merely shrugged.

"Eloquently put," Max said with the bite of sarcasm that had Luke's eyes narrowing.

"If you contemplate the choice again," Max continued after a sip of brandy and an "ah" of appreciation for its flavor, "I would suggest a quicker, cleaner method, such as the use of the handgun on the top shelf of my bedroom closet." Before Luke could do more than blink in surprise, Max had lunged forward, one hand still delicately cupped around the glass bowl, the other dragging hard on the collar of Luke's shirt. When their faces were close, Max spoke with a quietly intense fury that mirrored the look in his eyes. "Don't ever use my stage again, or the illusion of magic, for something as cowardly as ending your life."

"Max, for God's sake." Luke felt the strong, wiry fingers close around his throat, squeeze off his words, then release.

"I've never lifted a hand to you." Now the control that had cloaked Max through the second show and beyond began to crack so that he had to rise and turn away as he spoke. "A decade now, and I've kept that promise I made to you. I'm warning you now, I will break it. If you ever do such a thing again, I will beat you sensible." He turned back, measuring Luke with dark, gleaming eyes. "Naturally, I'd be forced to have Mouse hold you down while I did so, but I promise you I know where to strike to hurt a man most."

The outrage came first. Luke sprang to his feet with it, furious dares and denials hot on his tongue. It was then he saw in the flash of the lamplight that Max's eyes weren't gleaming with temper, but with tears. It humbled him more than a thousand beatings would have done.

"I shouldn't have done the bit tonight," he said quietly. "My timing was off. I had problems I wasn't able to push out of my mind. I knew it, but I couldn't . . . I wasn't trying to hurt myself, Max, I swear it. It was stupidity, and pride."

"Amounts to the same, doesn't it?" Max drank again to clear the thickness from his voice. "You drove Lily to tears. That's difficult for me to forgive."

For the first time in years, Luke felt that clammy fear—that he would be turned away. That he would lose what had become so precious to him. "I didn't think." He knew it was a weak excuse. Part of him wanted to pour out his reasons. But if he could do nothing else, he could spare them that. "I'll talk to her. Try to make it right."

"I expect you will." Calmer now, Max reached out to lay a hand on Luke's shoulder. There was comfort in that, and a wealth of understanding that needed no words. "Is it a woman?"

Luke thought of Roxanne, and how his hands burned to touch her. That had been part of what had clogged his brain, topped off by Cobb and too much drink. He could only shrug.

"I could tell you that no woman is worth your life, or your peace of mind. But of course, that would be a lie." His lips curved now, and his fingers squeezed lightly. "There are some, and a man is both blessed and cursed to find them. Would you like to talk about it?"

"No," Luke managed in a strangled voice. The idea of discussing his dark and driving desire for Roxanne with her father had him hovering between a laugh and a scream. "I've got it under control."

"Very well. Perhaps you'd like to hear about the next job."

"Yes. Fine."

Satisfied the air was clear once more, Max sat again, settled back. "LeClerc has come across some interesting information. A certain high-ranking politician keeps a mistress in the rich suburbs of Maryland near our nation's capital." Max paused to drink. Interest caught, Luke reached for his own snifter. His stomach no longer felt like a mine field. "Our public servant is not above accepting bribes—a particularly foul way of making a living in my estimation, but there you have it. In any case, he's wise enough not to use his bonuses to inflate his own life-style and cause speculation. Instead, he quietly invests in jewelry and art, and keeps his investments with his mistress."

"She must be a hell of a lay."

"Precisely." Max inclined his head, brushed a finger over his luxuriant moustache. "It's difficult to imagine why a man who would cheat on his wife and his constituents would then trust the woman who helps him cheat with nearly two million in trinkets." Max sighed a bit, as always baffled and delighted with the capriciousness of human nature. "I would hardly admit this in front of the delightful ladies of our house, but a man is not led by the nose, but by the dick."

Luke grinned. "I thought the way to a man's heart was through his stomach."

"Oh, it is, dear boy, it is. As long as it's by way of the crotch. We are, after all, an animal with intellect, but an animal nonetheless. We bury ourselves in a woman, don't we? Quite literally. How many among us can resist that illusion of returning to the womb?"

Luke lifted a brow. "I wouldn't say that was what was on my mind when I'm bouncing on a woman."

Max swirled his brandy. It had been a roundabout way to get the boy to talk, but Max often preferred a circular route. "My point, Luke, is that at a certain stage—thank God—the intellect clicks off and the animal takes over. If you're doing everything right, you're not thinking at all. Thought comes before—in the attraction, the pursuit, the seduction, the romance. Once a man's inside a woman, once she surrounds him, the mind turns off and control is forfeited. I suppose that's why sex is more dangerous than war, and much more desirable."

Luke could only shake his head. "It's not that difficult to enjoy the experience, and keep your mind focused."

"Obviously you haven't found the right woman. But you're young yet," Max said gently. "Now." He leaned forward. "About our trip to Washington."

It took six months in the planning. Details needed to be refined and polished as carefully as the stage show the Nouvelles would perform at the Kennedy Center.

In April, when the cherry blossoms were in rich and fragrant bloom, Luke traveled to wealthy Potomac, Maryland. Disguised with a pinstriped suit, a blond wig and a trimmed beard, he made the rounds with an eager real estate agent. With a clipped Boston accent, he assumed the identity of Charles B. Holderman, the representative of a wealthy New England industrialist who was interested in a home in D.C.'s elegant suburbs.

He appreciated the trip for what it was, and for the added benefit of distance from Roxanne. She'd taken her revenge in the sneakiest and most effective of ways. By acting as though nothing had ever happened.

Luke hadn't fully relaxed in months, and looked on the trip as a kind of working vacation. There was the added benefit of having a suite of rooms in the quietly dignified Madison, indulging in tourism—he particularly enjoyed the Smithsonian's array of gems—and simply being alone.

He toured the listed houses with the real estate agent, hemmed and hawed over building lots and locations. The questions he asked as the representative of a perspective buyer paralleled what he needed to know as a potential thief.

Who lived in the neighborhood and what did they do? Were there any loud dogs? Police patrols? What company would be recommended for installing a security system? And so on.

Later that day Luke approached Miranda Leesburg straight on. He strolled up her flower-lined flagstone walk and knocked on her oak and stained-glass front door.

He already knew what to expect. He'd studied the pictures of the sharp and sleek thirty-something blonde with a killer body and blue ice eyes. With resignation, he heard the high-pitched barking of a pair of dogs. He'd known she had two Pomeranians, it was just too bad they were yappers.

When she opened the door he was surprised to see the sleek blond hair pulled ruthlessly back in a ponytail and the sharp-featured, canny face damp with sweat. There was a towel around Miranda's neck. The rest of that lush, boldly curved body was snugged into a scant, two-piece exercise suit in vivid purple.

She scooped up both dogs, soothing them against breasts that rose like snowy white moons above the thin swatch of spandex.

Luke didn't lick his lips—but he thought about it. He began to understand why the good senator kept this little prize tucked away.

In photographs she was lovely in a cool, detached and obvious way. In person she shot out enough sex appeal to strike a man blind at sixty paces. Luke was much closer than that.

"I beg your pardon." He smiled and spoke with Charles's Yankee accent. "I'm sorry to disturb you." The dogs were still yapping and he had to pitch his voice over the din. "I'm Holderman, Charles Holderman."

"Yes?" She looked him up and down, much as she might if he were a sculpture she was contemplating in a gallery. "I've seen you around the neighborhood."

"My employer is interested in some property in the area." Luke smiled again. Holderman's proper maroon tie was beginning to strangle him.

"Sorry, my house isn't on the market."

"No, I realize that. I wonder if I might have a moment of your time? We could speak out here if you'd be more comfortable."

"Why would I be more comfortable outside?" She arched one delicately sculpted brow as she sized him up. Young, well built, repressed. She bent down to set the dogs on the polished hardwood—the movement put a marvelous strain on the spandex—and gave them both a little pat on the rump to send them skittering off. With her lover out of town for nearly two weeks on a fund-raising tour, she was bored. Charles B. Holderman looked like an interesting diversion. "What did you want to speak to me about?"

"Ah, landscaping." He managed to keep his eyes from skimming down to the slopes of her breasts. "My employer has very specific requirements for grounds and gardens. Yours comes quite close to meeting them. I wonder, did you construct the rock garden in your side yard yourself?"

She laughed, patting the towel to her breasts, her gleaming midriff. "Darling, I don't know a pansy from a petunia. I use a service."

"Ah. Then perhaps you could give me a name, a number." The ever efficient Holderman took a slim, leather-bound book from his breast pocket. "I'd appreciate it very much."

"I suppose I could help you out." She tapped a finger to her lips. "Come on in. I'll dig up the card."

"That's very kind of you." Luke put the book away and filled his mind instead with the details of the foyer, the front stairs, the size and number of rooms off the hallway. "Your home is lovely."

"Yeah, I had it redecorated a few months ago."

It was all pastels and floral prints. Restful, feminine. The lush body in the vivid slashes of purple added a shock of sex. Like passion in a meadow.

Luke paused to distract himself and admired a Corot painting. "Exquisite," he said when Miranda looked questioningly over her shoulder.

"You into paintings?" She pouted a little as she turned back to his side to study it with him.

"Yes, I'm quite an admirer of art. Corot, with his dreamy style, is a favorite of mine."

"Corot, right." She didn't give a damn about the style, but she knew the value of the painting to the last cent. "I can never figure out why people want to paint trees and bushes."

Luke smiled again. "Perhaps to make people wonder who or what is behind them."

She laughed at that. "That's good, Charles, very good. I keep a card file in the kitchen. Why don't you join me for something cold while I find you your landscaper?"

"It would be a pleasure."

The kitchen carried through the soft, female charm of the rest of the house he'd seen. Potted African violets sat in sunbeams on mauve and ivory tiled counters. The appliances were streamlined and unobtrusive. A round glass table with a quartet of padded ice-cream-parlor chairs stood in the center of the room on a pale rose rug. Incongruously, the hard-edged pulse of Eddie Van Halen's screaming guitar spouted through the kitchen speakers.

"I was working out when you knocked." Miranda moved to the refrigerator for a pitcher of lemonade. "I like to keep in shape, you know?" She set the pitcher down and skimmed her hands over her hips. "That kind of music makes me sweat."

Luke rolled his tongue inside his mouth to keep it from hanging out and answered as Holderman would. "I'm sure it's stimulating."

"You bet." She chuckled to herself as she took out two glasses and poured. "Sit down, Charles. I'll find that card for you."

She set the glasses on the table with a quick chink of glass to glass, then brushed lightly against him as she walked over to a drawer. Her musky scent went straight to his grateful loins. Loins, he thought now, he hadn't been able to put to good use since he'd passed out courtesy of Jack Daniel's on top of Roxanne.

Down boy, he thought and straightened the knot of his tie before reaching for his drink.

"Beautiful day," he said conversationally as she rummaged through the drawer. "How fortunate that you can be home to enjoy it."

"Oh, my time's pretty much my own. I own a little boutique in Georgetown. Keeps the wolf from the door, you might say, but I have a manager that handles the day-to-day nuisances." She took a business card from the drawer and stood flipping the end against her palm. "Are you married, Charles?"

"No. Divorced."

"Me too." She smiled, pleased. "I discovered I like having the house, and my life, to myself. Just how long will you be in the area?"

"Oh, only a day or two longer, I'm afraid. Whether or not my employer purchases property here, my business will be completed."

"Then it's back to . . ."

"Boston."

"Hmm." That was good. In fact, it was perfect. If he'd been staying longer, she would have dismissed him with the drink and the landscaper's card. As it was, he was the answer to a long and frustrating two weeks. Every so often—every so discreetly often—Miranda liked to change partners and dance.

She didn't know him, and neither did the senator. A quick, anonymous fuck would do a lot more for her state of mind than an hour on the damn Nautilus.

"Well . . ." She slid her hand down to rub it lightly over her crotch. "You could say you'll be—in and out."

Luke set down his glass before it slid out of his hand. "In a manner of speaking."

"Since you're here now." Watching him, she slipped the business card down into the triangle of her spandex bikini. "Why don't you take what you need."

Luke debated for nearly a heartbeat. It wasn't going precisely the way he'd imagined. But, as Max was wont to say, an ounce of spontaneity was worth a pound of planning. "Why don't I?" He rose and, moving much faster than she'd given him credit for, hooked a finger under the slanted line of spandex. She was hot and wet as a geyser.

Even as she arched back in shock, the first lusty cry tumbling from her lips, he'd dragged the material down. In two quick moves, he'd freed himself and plunged violently into her. The first orgasm took her by surprise. Damned if he'd looked that clever.

"Oh, Christ!" Her eyes popped wide with pleasure. Then his hands had cupped her hips and had lifted her up in surprisingly strong arms so that her legs were wrapped around his waist. She managed a few gargled gasps and held on for the ride of her life.

He watched her. His blood was pumping hot and fast, his body was steeped in the velvet lightning that was sex. But his mind—that was clear enough so that he could see the faint lines around her eyes, the quick darts of her tongue. He knew the dogs had scrambled in, nervous and curious at the sounds their mistress made. They were crouched under the glass table, yapping.

Van Halen was wailing on the speakers. Luke set his rhythm to theirs, down and dirty. He could count her climaxes, and saw that the third he gave her left her dazed and limp. It was his pleasure to gift her with another before he succumbed to his own. But even as he reached flash point, he had enough control to keep her from rapping her head back against the white oak cabinet door—and enough to prevent her from snatching at his hair and dislodging the wig.

"Sweet God." Miranda would have slid bonelessly to the floor if he hadn't held her up with that easy, eerie strength. "Who'd have thought you had all that under that Brooks Brothers suit?"

"Only my tailor." A bit belatedly, he tilted her head back for a kiss.

"When did you say you had to leave?"

"Tomorrow night, actually. But I have some time today." And he might as well use it to case the house. "Do you have a bed?"

Miranda wound her arms around his neck. "I've got four of them. Where do you want to start?"

"You look pleased with yourself," LeClerc noted when Luke dropped his suitcases in the foyer of the house in New Orleans.

"Got the job done. Why shouldn't I look pleased?" Luke opened his briefcase and took out a notebook filled with notes and drawings. "The layout of her house. Two safes, one in the master bedroom, another in the living room. She's got a Corot in the downstairs hallway and a goddamn Monet over her bed."

LeClerc grunted as he scanned the notes. "And just how did you discover the painting and the safe in her bedroom, *mon ami?*"

"I let her fuck my brains out." Grinning, Luke peeled off his leather jacket. "I feel so cheap."

"Casse pas mon coeur," LeClerc muttered, amusement gleaming in his eye. "Next time I'll see that Max sends me."

"*Bonne chance,* old man. An hour with that lady would have put you in traction. Sweet Christ, she had moves you wouldn't—" He broke off when he heard a sound at the top of the stairs. Roxanne stood there, one hand gripping the banister. Her face was blank, coldly so, but for two flags of color that could have been embarrassment or fury and rode high on her cheeks. Without a word, she turned and disappeared. He heard the echo of her door slamming.

Now he did feel cheap, and dirty. He would have rejoiced to strangle her for it. "Why the fuck didn't you tell me she was here?"

"You didn't ask," LeClerc said simply. "*Allons.* Max is in the workroom. He'll want to hear what you found out."

Upstairs, Roxanne lay prone on her bed, fighting back a horrible urge to hurl breakables. She wouldn't give him the satisfaction. She didn't need him, didn't want him. Didn't care. If he wanted to spend his time screwing overendowed tarts, it was strictly his business.

Oh, but damn him to a fiery hell for enjoying it.

There were a dozen—well, at least a half dozen—men who would be more than happy to relieve her of the burden of her virginity. Maybe it was time to pick one out.

She could brag, too, after all. She could flaunt her sexual exploits under his nose until he choked on them.

No, she'd be damned if she'd make a decision like that out of pique.

And she'd be double damned, she decided, sitting up, if she'd wait in the wings this time while the men had all the fun. When they moved on the house in Potomac, she was going to be right there with them.

Come hell or high water.

"I'm fully prepared, Daddy." Roxanne transferred a neatly folded blouse from her suitcase to a drawer in her room at the Washington Ritz. "And I've kept my part of the bargain." She arranged lingerie tidily in the drawer above. "I've completed my first year at Tulane, with a three point five grade average. I fully intend to do the same when classes start back in the fall."

"I appreciate that, Roxanne." Max stood at the window. Behind him, the Washington summer baked the pavements and rose again in oily waves. "But this job has been months in the planning. It's wiser for you to make your debut, as it were, with something smaller."

"I prefer starting at the top." With the careless precision of the innately tidy, she began to hang dresses and cocktail wear in the closet. "I'm not a novice, and you know it. I've been a part of this aspect of your life—behind the scenes, unfortunately—since I was a child. I can pick a lock as well, and often quicker than LeClerc." Conscientiously, she shook a fold out of a silk skirt. "I know a great deal about engines and mechanics thanks to Mouse." After closing the closet doors, she shot her father a bland look. "I know more about computers than any of you. You know yourself that kind of skill is invaluable."

"And I've appreciated your help in the early stages of this job. However—"

"There's no however, Daddy. It's time."

"There are physical aspects as well as mental," he began.

"Do you think I've been working out five hours a week for the last year for my health?" she tossed back. They'd reached a crossroads. Roxanne chose her path and planted her fists on her hips. "Are you standing in my way because you're having fatherly qualms about leading me down a dishonest path?"

"Certainly not." He looked shocked, then affronted. "I happen to consider what I do an ancient and valuable art. Thievery is a time-honored profession, my girl. Not to be confused with these hooligans who mug people on the street, or bloodthirsty klutzes who burst into banks, guns blazing. We're discriminating. We're romantic." His voice rose in passion. "We're artists."

"Well, then." She crossed over to kiss his cheek. "When do we start?"

He stared down into her smiling, smug face and began to laugh. "You're a credit to me, Roxanne."

"I know, Max." She kissed him again. "I know."

15

The Kennedy Center lent itself to large-scale illusions, as did the network television cameras that were filming the event for a special to be aired in the fall. Max had staged the one-hundred-and-two-minute show like a three-act play, with full orchestra, complex lighting cues and elaborate costumes.

It began with Max alone on a darkened stage, caught in the moonlike beam of a single spotlight. He was draped in a velvet cloak of midnight blue that was threaded with shimmering silver. In one hand he held a wand, also silver, that glinted in the light. In the other he cupped a ball of crystal.

So Merlin might have looked as he plotted for the birth of a king.

Sorcery was his theme, and he played the mystic necromancer with dignity and drama. He lifted the ball onto the crown of his fingertips. It pulsed with lights as he spoke to the audience of spells and dragons, alchemy and witchcraft. While they watched, already snagged by the theatrics, the ball began to float—along the folds of the velvet cloak, above the tip of the magic wand, spinning high above his head at a shouted incantation.

All the while it pulsed with those inner lights, flickering scarlet and sapphire, amber and emerald onto his uplifted face. The audience gasped as the ball plummeted toward the stage, then applauded when it stopped, inches before destruction, to rotate in a widening circle, rising, rising toward Max's outstretched hands. Once more he held it poised on his fingertips. He tapped it once with the shimmering wand and tossed it high. The ball became a shower of silver that rained down on the stage before it went black.

When the lights came up again, seconds later, it was Roxanne who stood center stage. She was all in glimmering silver. Stars glittered in her hair, along the arms the column of sequins left bare. She stood straight as a sword, her arms crossed over her breasts, her eyes closed. When the orchestra began to play a movement from Beethoven's Sixth Symphony, she swayed. Her eyes opened.

She spoke of spells cast and love lost, of witchery gone wrong. As she uncrossed her arms, lifted them high, sparks flew from her fingertips. Her hair, a flame of curls nearly to her shoulders, began to wave in an unseen wind. The spotlight widened to show a small table beside her, on it a bell, a book and an unlit candle. Cupping her palms, she made fire in them, flames rising and ebbing as if breathing. As she passed her hands over the candle, the flames guttered in her palms and spurted from the wick in a shimmer of gold.

A flick of her wrist, and the pages of the book began to turn, slowly, then faster, faster, until it was a whirl. The bell rose from the table between her outstretched palms. As she swayed her hands, it tolled. Suddenly, beneath the table where there had been only space three candles burned brightly. Their fire licked up and up until the table itself was aflame with Roxanne standing behind it, her face washed in its light and shadows. She threw her arms out and there was nothing left but smoke. At the same instant another spotlight shot on. Luke was there, upstage left.

He wore sleek black trimmed in glistening gold. Lily's clever makeup had accented his cheekbones, arched his brows. Nearly as long as hers, his raven hair flowed free. He looked to Roxanne like a cross between a satyr and a pirate. Her traitorous heart gave one thump before she quashed the flicker of need.

She faced him across the stage with smoke twining between them. Her stance was a challenge, head thrown back, one arm up, the other held out to the side. A streak of light shot from her fingertips toward him. He lifted a hand, seemed to catch it. The audience erupted with applause as the duel continued. The combatants moved closer together, whirling smoke, hurling fire as the stage lights came up rose and gold, simulating sunrise.

Roxanne threw her arm over her eyes, as if to shield herself. Then her arms fell limply, her head drooped. The silver gown sparkled, hissing with light while she swayed, as if her body were attached by strings to Luke's hands. He circled her, passing those hands around her, inches from touching. He passed his spread hand in front of her eyes, indicating trance, then slowly, slowly gestured her back, farther back. Her feet lifted from the stage. Her back stayed straight as a spear as he floated her up until she lay on nothing more than wisps of blue smoke.

He whirled once, and when he faced the stage again he held a slim silver ring. Graceful as a dancer, he moved from her feet to her head, sliding her body through the circle. Unrehearsed, he leaned forward, as if to kiss her. He felt her body stiffen as his lips halted a breath away.

"Don't blow it, Rox," he whispered, then whipped off his cape, tossed it over her. It held for a moment before the form beneath it seemed to melt away. When the cape fluttered to the floor, Luke held a white swan cradled in his arms.

There was a crash of thunder from backstage. Luke bent for his cape, praying the damn swan wouldn't take a nick out of him this time. He crouched, swirling the cape over his head. And vanished.

"I didn't care for the ad-lib," Roxanne told Luke the minute she caught up with him.

"No?" He handed off the swan to Mouse and smiled at her. "I thought it was a nice touch. How about you, Mouse?"

Mouse stroked the swan—he was the only one who could without endangering fingers. "Well . . . I guess. Gotta give Myrtle her snack."

"See." Luke gestured after Mouse's retreating back. "Loved it."

"Try it again and I'll do a little ad-libbing myself." She stabbed a finger into his shirt. "You'll end up with a bloody lip."

He caught her wrist before she could storm away. From the sound of the applause he knew that Max and Lily were keeping the momentum high. His own emotions were a rising riot. He wasn't sure he'd ever felt better in his life.

"Listen, Rox, what we do onstage is an act. A job. Just like what we're going to do tomorrow night in Potomac." Some inner demon had him shifting his body, effectively sandwiching her between it and the wall. "Nothing personal."

The blood was humming in her head, but she dredged up a friendly smile. "Maybe you're right."

He could smell her—perfume, greasepaint, the slight muskiness of stage sweat. "Of course I'm right. It's just a matter of—" His breath wolfed out as she rammed an elbow into his gut. She slipped easily away and smiled with a lot more sincerity.

"Nothing personal," she said sweetly. She stepped inside her dressing room, shut—and locked—the door. It was time for a costume change.

The next time she had to deal with him they were nearly nose to nose with only a thin sheet of plywood between them. They were locked in a trick box and had only seconds before transmutation.

"Pull that again, babe," Luke hissed even as they were flipping positions. "I swear I'll hit you back."

"Oh! I'm shaking." Roxanne sprang out of the box in Luke's place to thunderous applause.

They took their bows graciously after the finale. Luke pinched her hard enough to bruise. Roxanne trod heavily on his instep.

He bowed with a flourish, pulling roses out of thin air and offering them to her. She accepted them, but before she could dip into the curtsy, he moved. No way was he going to allow the blow to go unrewarded. He arched her back in an exaggerated dip and kissed her.

Or it appeared to be a kiss to the delighted audience. He bit her.

"You bastard." She forced her throbbing lip to spread into a smile. They stepped back as Max made his final entrance. Luke took Roxanne's hand. His eyes popped wide when she gripped his thumb and twisted.

"Jesus, Rox, not the hands. I can't work without my hands."

"Then keep them off me, pal." She released him, satisfied with the idea that his thumb would be aching every bit as much as her bottom lip. Together they joined Max and Lily center stage for a final bow.

"I love show business," Roxanne said with a breathy laugh.

The pure good humor in her voice scotched Luke's notion of booting her in the rump. He took her hand again, with more caution. "Me too."

She didn't find the benefits too shabby either. The elegant White House reception put the perfect cap on the evening. Max, she knew, was staunchly apolitical. He voted, considering it his right and his duty, but more often than not pulled the lever with the same kind of careless glee with which he gambled.

Max thought nothing of drawing to an inside straight.

It wasn't the politics of Washington that appealed to Roxanne. It was the formal, often pompous ambience those politics generated. A far cry from New Orleans, she thought, admiring the richly dressed and somewhat stuffy dancers swirling around the ballroom floor.

"You seem to have made magic work for you."

Roxanne turned, her pleasant, company smile fading into simple shock. "Sam. What are you doing here?"

"Enjoying the festivities. Almost as much as I enjoyed your performance." He took her hand, bringing her stiff fingers to his lips.

He'd changed considerably. The thin, poorly attired teenager had groomed himself into a slim, impeccable man. His sandy hair was as conservatively cut as the tuxedo he wore. On his hand glittered one discreet diamond ring. Roxanne caught a whiff of masculine cologne as his lips brushed her skin.

He was clean-shaven, as well polished as the gleaming antiques that littered the White House. Like the air they breathed, he exuded the strong, unmistakable aura of wealth and success. And like politics, she thought, beneath that glowing aura, was the faint stink of corruption.

"You've grown up, Roxanne. And beautifully."

She slipped her hand away from his. Her flesh tingled where he'd touched, as if she'd reached too close to a current that might prove fatal. "I could say the same about you."

His teeth flashed. Those he'd lost in his fight with Luke had been nicely replaced. "Why don't you—while we dance."

She could have refused, flatly, politely, flirtatiously. She had the skill for it. But she was curious. Without a word she moved with him out on the floor and joined the flow of dancers.

"I could say," she began, more than a little surprised to find him graceful and accomplished, "that the White House is the last place I would have expected to see you again. But—" She met his eyes. "Most cats land on their feet."

"Oh, I always planned to see you—all of you—again. Odd how fate would make it here in such . . . powerful surroundings." He drew her closer, enjoying the way she held that slim, soft body rigid and still managed to follow his lead as fluidly as water. "The act tonight was quite a step up from those little bits of business at that grimy club in the Quarter. Better even than the show Max devised for the Magic Castle."

"He's the best there is."

"His talent is phenomenal," Sam agreed. He dipped his face down to hers, watched her eyes narrow. The sexual punch was like a brick to the gut. He shifted, just enough so that she'd feel his arousal. "But I must admit it was you and Luke that held me breathless. A very sexy little number that."

"An illusion," she said coolly. "Sex had nothing to do with it."

"If there was a man unstirred when you levitated under his hands, they were dead and buried." And how interesting it would be, he thought, to have her. To feel *her* stir, willing, unwilling, under his hands. A beautiful payback it would be, with the added benefit of hot, greedy sex. "I can assure you, I'm alive."

Her stomach muscles were knotted, but she kept her gaze level. "If you think I'm flattered by the bulge in your pants, Sam, you're mistaken." She had the satisfaction of seeing his lips tighten in anger before she continued. And yes, she noted, his eyes were the same. Sly, canny and potentially mean. "Where did you go when you left New Orleans?"

Now he not only wanted to take her, but wanted to hurt her first. "Here and there."

"And here and there led you..." She gestured. "Here?"

"On a circular route. At the moment, I happen to be the right-hand man of the Gentleman from Tennessee."

"You're joking."

"Not at all." He spread his palm over the small of her back. "I'm the senator's top aide. And I intend to be a great deal more."

It took her only a moment to recover. "Well, I suppose it fits, since politics is the ultimate con game. Won't your past indiscretions interfere with your ambitions?"

"On the contrary. My difficult childhood gives me a fresh and sympathetic perspective on the problems of our children—our most valuable natural resource. I'm a role model—showing them what they can make of themselves."

"I don't suppose you put using an ignorant child to help you steal from her friends on your résumé."

"What a team we made." He chuckled as if his betrayal had been nothing more than a joke. "How much better a team we might make now."

"I'm sorry to say the idea revolts me." She smiled with a flutter of lashes. When she started to step away, he gripped her hand hard enough to make her wince.

"I believe there are some things best left behind the fog of memory. Don't you, Roxanne? After all, if you suddenly felt the urge to gossip about an old acquaintance, I might have to do the same." His eyes were hard as he jerked her closer. To the casual onlooker it would appear they were contemplating a kiss. "I didn't leave New Orleans right away. I made it my business to watch, to ask questions. To learn all manner of things. Unless I'm very much mistaken, you'd prefer those things to be kept quiet."

She felt her color drain. Of all the things she could control, she had never been able to outwit the traitorously delicate skin of a redhead. "I don't know what you're talking about. You're hurting me."

"I'd prefer to avoid that." He lightened his grip. "Unless it were under more intimate circumstances. Perhaps a quiet midnight supper, where we can renew old acquaintance."

"No. I realize it might be a blow to your ego, Sam, but I really have no interest in your past, your present or your future."

"Then we won't talk business." He pressed his mouth to her ear and murmured a suggestion so blatant Roxanne wasn't certain whether to cringe or laugh aloud. She didn't have the chance to do either as a hand gripped her arm and jerked her back.

"Keep your hands off her." Luke's face was alive with fury as he stepped between Roxanne and Sam. He was sixteen again, and ready to rumble. "Don't ever touch her."

"Well, it appears I've stepped on some toes." In marked opposition to Luke's harsh whisper, Sam spoke jovially. He'd been right, after all. Not all the sparks he'd seen flying around onstage had been the result of special effects and magic.

"Luke." Well aware that heads were turning in their direction, Roxanne slipped a hand through his arm. It gave her the opportunity to dig her nails into his flesh. "A reception at the White House isn't the place to cause a scene." She was smiling gaily as she spoke.

"Sensible and beautiful." Sam nodded toward her, but kept his eyes on Luke. It was still there, and Sam was glad of it. The greasy pool of jealousy and hate still lapped in his gut. "I'd listen to the lady, Callahan. After all, this is my turf, not yours."

"Do you know how many bones you have in your hand?" Luke spoke pleasantly while his eyes continued to promise murder. "If you touch her again, you'll find out. Because I'll break each and every one of them."

"Stop it. I'm not a bone for the two of you to snap over." With relief, she saw her father and Lily making their way through the crowd. "Let's get through it, shall we? Daddy!" Bright enthusiasm bubbled out as she turned toward Max. "You won't believe who's here. It's Sam Wyatt. After all this time."

"Max." Smooth as a snake, Sam offered a hand, then took Lily's fingers in his free one to kiss. "And Lily. More beautiful than ever."

"You'll never guess what Sam's up to these days." Roxanne continued to chatter as if they were old, dear friends reunited.

Max wasn't one to hold a grudge. Nor was he a man to let down his guard. "So, you settled on politics."

"Yes, sir. You could say I owe it to you."

"Could you?"

"You taught me showmanship." He grinned, a political poster for success and youthful energy. "Senator Bushfield, sir." Sam waylaid a trim, balding man with tired brown eyes and a lopsided smile. "I imagine you've met the Nouvelles."

"Yes, yes." The Tennessee twang was rich and hearty despite the fatigue on the senator's face. "Delightful show, as I told you, Nouvelle."

"I didn't mention you before, Senator, because I wanted to surprise my old friends." With an amused glance at Luke, Sam laid a hand on Max's shoulder. "I once spent several months as apprentice magician to the master."

"You don't say?" Bushfield's eyes lit with interest.

"But I do." Sam smiled and wove a tale of a confused, disenchanted youth taken in and given direction by the kindness of a generous man and his family. "Unfortunately," he concluded, "I was never adept at performing. But when I left the Nouvelles it was with a fresh purpose." He laughed and ran a finger surreptitiously down Roxanne's spine. "I wouldn't be where I am today without them."

"I'll tell you this." Bushfield thumped Sam paternally on the back. "This boy here's going places. Sharp as a tack and slippery as an eel." He winked at Max. "He may not've been good at hocus pocus, but he sure can charm the pants off the constituents."

"Sam was never lacking in charm," Max said. "Perhaps in focus."

"I'm focused now." He aimed a look at Luke. "I know just how to do what needs to be done."

"The slimy son of a bitch had his hands all over you."

Roxanne merely sighed. It was hard to believe that Luke was playing the same tune. Maybe it was because she'd managed to avoid him for the best part of twenty-four hours. "We were dancing, stupid."

"He was drooling on your neck."

"At least he didn't bite." She shot Luke a superior smile and leaned back. Mouse was driving silently through the suburbs, making slow sweeps of the area around Miranda's house. "Get your mind out of the gutter, Callahan, and back on the job."

"I'd like to know what he's got in his head," Luke muttered. "It's bad luck running into him like this."

"Luck is luck, my boy," Max commented from the front seat. "What we do with it determines whether it's good or bad." Satisfied with the atmosphere, Max stripped out of his suit jacket and the false shirt front that hid a thin black sweater.

In the rear seat, Luke and Roxanne made similar transformations. "Keep away from him."

"Kiss ass."

"Children." Max shook his head as he glanced back. "If you can't behave, Daddy won't take you to find hidden treasure. Thirty-five minutes," he said to Mouse. "No more, no less."

" 'Kay, Max." He slipped the car to the curb, then swiveled around. There was a big, happy grin on his face. "Break a leg, Roxy."

"Thanks, Mouse." She leaned up to kiss him before climbing out of the car.

It was a still, humid night. The light from the thumbnail moon was almost obscured by haze, and the heat hung in the air like a cowl. She could smell roses, jasmine and grass newly mowed, and the damp woody aroma of mulch recently watered.

They moved like shadows over the lawn, slipping past azaleas no longer in bloom and summer perennials just starting to bud. Another shadow streaked past them, causing Roxanne to bump heavily against Luke. Her heart jammed hard at her ribs.

But it was only a cat, racing off to find a stray mouse or a mate.

"Nervous, Rox?" Luke's teeth flashed in the dark.

"No." Annoyed, she hurried on, comforted by the solid bounce of her leather pouch against her thigh.

"They got some woods around here," he whispered close to her ear. "But I doubt there's wolves. A couple wild dogs maybe."

"Get a life." But she looked uneasily into the shadows for yellow eyes or fangs.

As planned, they separated at the east corner of the house, Luke to cut the phone wires, Max to disengage the alarm system.

"It takes a light touch." Max patiently instructed his daughter. "One must not hurry or be overconfident. Practice," he said, as he had done countless times over rehearsals. "An artist can never get enough practice. Even the greatest ballerina continues to take classes all of her professional life."

She watched him spreading and stripping wires. It was a hand-cramping, tedious job. Roxanne held the light steady and watched every move he made.

"There's a unit inside that operates on a code. It's possible, with finesse, to jam it from out here."

"How do you know when you have?"

He smiled and patted her hand, ignoring the grinding ache in his fingers. "Faith, coupled with intuition and experience. And . . . that little light up there will go out. *Et voilà,*" he whispered when the red dot went blank.

"Six minutes gone." Luke crouched behind them.

"We won't cut the glass." Max continued to instruct as he moved to the rear terrace door. "It's wired, you see. Even with the alarm off, it's tricky—and much more time-consuming than picking the lock."

He took out his set of picks, a gift some thirty years before from LeClerc. With some ceremony, he handed them to Roxanne. "Try your luck, my love."

"Jesus, Max, it'll take her forever."

Roxanne took a moment to scowl at Luke before bending to her task. Not even he could spoil the moment for her. She worked as her father had told her. Patiently. With hands as delicate as a surgeon's, she operated on the lock. Her ear close to the door, her eyes serenely closed.

She was imagining herself inside the lock, easing at the tumblers with gentle hands. Shifting, cajoling, maneuvering.

A smile curved softly on her lips as she heard the click. Ah, the power of it.

"It's like music," she whispered, and brought proud tears to Max's eyes.

"Two minutes, thirty-eight seconds." He glanced over at Luke as he hit the button on his watch. "As good, I believe, as you've done."

Beginner's luck, Luke thought, but was wise enough to keep the opinion to himself. They slipped through the door single file, and again separated.

Luke's layout of the house had been so complete they had needed to bribe no one for blueprints. Roxanne's assignment was the paintings. She cut them carefully from their frames and rolled Corots, Monets, a particularly fine Pissarro street scene into the knapsack on her back before joining her father in the living room.

She knew better than to disturb him at work. His fingers flicked at the safe dial. Roxanne thought he looked like Merlin, deftly brewing his spells. Her heart swelled.

They exchanged grins as the door eased open.

"Quickly now, dear." He opened velvet boxes and long flat cases, dumping the contents into her pouch. Wanting to prove she'd learned well, Roxanne removed a loupe and under the beam of her flashlight examined the stones in a sapphire brooch.

"Berlin-blue," she murmured. "With an excellent—"

It was then they heard the yip of a dog.

"Oh, shit."

"Easy." Max laid a quieting hand on her arm. "At the first sign of trouble, you're out the door and back to Mouse."

Her nerves jittered like banjo strings, but loyalty hung tough. "I won't leave you."

"You will." Moving fast, Max emptied the safe.

Upstairs, Luke scowled at the growling Pomeranians. He hadn't forgotten them. He knew, from his own afternoon there, that they made a habit of sleeping on their mistress's bed.

That was why he had two meaty bones in his pouch.

He took them out, freezing when Miranda grumbled sleepily at the dogs and rolled over. Then he crouched, a shadow in the shadows, and gestured with the bones.

He didn't speak, didn't dare take the risk even when Miranda began to snore lightly. But the dogs didn't need any verbal prompting. Scenting the snack, they scrambled off the bed and snapped their jaws.

Satisfied, Luke pulled out the false front on the section of bookshelves and went to work on the safe.

It was a bit distracting having the woman sleeping in the room. Not that he hadn't burgled a home with a woman snoring close by before. But he'd never done so with a woman he'd shared the bed with.

Added an interesting angle, he thought.

And wouldn't you know that the luscious Miranda slept buck naked?

The excitement, always vaguely sexual, that he felt on lifting a lock increased dramatically. By the time he had the safe open, he was rock hard and struggling to hold back laughter at the absurdity of the situation.

He could always climb into bed with her and seduce her while she was half asleep. After all, he had the added benefit of knowing what moves she preferred.

And she'd recognize him in the dark, he had no doubt.

It would be a thrill, undoubtedly, but time was against him.

Of course, there were proprieties and priorities. As Max would have said. Then again, he was the same one who said strike while the iron was hot.

Christ Almighty, Luke thought, his personal iron was currently hot enough to melt stone.

Too bad, baby, he thought, taking a last glance at the sprawled Miranda. He wondered if she'd have considered a quick roll payment for the loss of the jewels. Then he had to stifle another laugh as he hobbled from the room.

"You're two minutes behind." Roxanne stood at the base of the stairs, hissing at him. "I was about to come up." Her eyes narrowed against the dark. "Why are you walking like that?"

Luke only snorted with muffled laughter and kept limping down the stairs.

"Are you hurt? Are you—" She broke off when she saw just what was hampering him. "Christ, you're a pervert."

"Just a healthy all-American boy, Roxy."

"Sick," she tossed back, unreasonably jealous. "Disgusting."

"Normal. Painful, but normal."

"Ah, children." Like a patient schoolteacher, Max signaled. "Perhaps we could discuss this in the car?"

Roxanne continued to whisper insults as they hurried across the lawn. By the time they reached the car, the simple thrill of the entire evening took over. She tumbled in behind Mouse, laughing. She kissed him, even as he drove the car sedately down the street. There was another smacking kiss for Max, and because she was feeling generous—and perhaps just a little vindictive—she turned and pressed her lips firmly to Luke's.

"Oh, God."

"I hope you suffer." Leaning back, she hugged the gem-packed pouch to her breasts. "Okay, Daddy. What do we do for an encore?"

16

Roxanne paced restlessly from beaded lamp shade to picture frame, from crystal wand to jeweled box in Madame's shop. In faded jeans and an oversized New Orleans Saints T-shirt, she looked precisely like what she was. A newly graduated college student waiting for her life to begin.

Madame carefully counted out her customer's change. After thirty years in business she continued to eschew modern distractions such as a cash register. The old, hand-painted cigar box under the counter served her well enough.

"Enjoy," she said, shaking her head as her customer left the shop with a stuffed parrot under his arm. Tourists, she thought, would buy anything. "So, *pichouette,* you come to show me your new college diploma?"

"No. I think Max is having it bronzed." She smiled a little, toying with a china cup that had a chip on its gold rim. "You'd think I'd discovered the cure for cancer instead of slogging my way through four years at Tulane."

"Graduating fifth in your class is not so small potatoes."

Roxanne jerked a shoulder in easy dismissal. She was restless, oh so restless, and couldn't quite find the root of it. "It only took application. I have a good memory for details."

"And this troubles you?"

"No." Roxanne set the cup down and took a steadying breath. "I'm worried about my father." It was a relief to say it aloud. "His hands aren't what they were."

It was something she could speak with no one about, not even Lily. They all knew that arthritis was gaining on Max, swelling his knuckles, stiffening those agile fingers. There had been doctors, medication, massage. Roxanne knew that the pain was nothing compared to the fear of losing what he held most dear. His magic.

"Even Max can't cause time to vanish, *petite.*"

"I know. I understand. I just can't accept. It's affecting him emotionally, Madame. He broods, he spends too much time alone in his workroom and with his research on that bloody magic stone. It's gotten worse since Luke moved out last year."

Madame lifted a brow at the bitterness. "Roxanne, a man becomes a man and needs his own place."

"He just wanted to bring women in."

Madame's lips twitched. "This is reason enough. He's only a short distance, still in the Quarter. Does he not continue to work with Max?"

"Yes, yes." Roxanne waved a hand in dismissal. "I didn't mean to get off the subject. It's my father I'm concerned about. I can't reach him the way I used to, not since he's become obsessed with that damn stone."

"Stone? Tell me what is this stone?"

Roxanne wandered over to the counter. She picked up the tarot deck Madame left there and began to shuffle. "The philosophers' stone. It's a myth, Madame, an illusion. Legend has it that this stone could turn anything it touched into gold. And . . ." She glanced up significantly. "Give youth back to the aged. Health to the ill."

"And you don't believe in such things? You, who have lived your lifetime in magic."

"I know what makes magic work." Roxanne cut the cards and began a Celtic cross. "Sweat and practice, timing and misdirection. Emotion and drama. I believe in the art of magic, Madame, not in magic stones. Not in the supernatural."

"I see." Madame cocked a brow at the cards on the counter. "Yet you seek your answers there?"

"Hmm?" Caught up in interpreting the spread, Roxanne frowned. Then flushed. "Just to pass the time." Before she could gather the cards up, Madame caught her hand.

"A shame to disturb a reading." She hunched over the cards herself. "The girl is ready to become a woman. There's a journey ahead, soon. Both figuratively and literally."

Roxanne smiled. She couldn't help it. "We're taking a cruise. North, up the Saint Lawrence Seaway. We'll perform, of course. Max sees it as a working vacation."

"Prepare for changes." Madame tapped the Wheel of Fortune. "The realization of a dream—if you're wise. And the loss of it. Someone from out of the past. And sorrow. Time to heal."

"And the Death card?" It surprised Roxanne that her skin prickled when she looked at the grinning skeleton.

"Death chases life from the first breath." Madame stroked the card with a gentle finger. "You are too young to feel it whispering at your ear. But this is death that is not death. Go on your journey, *pichouette,* and learn."

Luke was more than ready to go. There was nothing he could think of he'd rather do than get out of town. The latest payment to Cobb sat on his coffee table, addressed and stamped.

The demand for money had been as steady as mortgage payments over the years. Two thousand here, four there, to an average of fifty thousand annually.

Luke didn't mind the money. He had plenty of that. But he'd yet to control that greasy wave of nausea each time he found a plain postcard in his mailbox.

2K, it might say. Or perhaps when Cobb's luck was running thin, 5K, and the post office box. Nothing more.

Luke had had four years to reconsider the extent of Cobb's brainpower. The man was much smarter than Luke had ever given him credit for. A fool would have pushed for the big score and quickly dried the well. But Cobb, good old belt-wielding Al, knew the value of a steady trickle.

So Luke was more than ready to get away—from the postcards, from the dissatisfied tickle at the back of his neck, from worry over Max's overpowering obsession with a nonexistent magic rock.

They'd be too busy on the ship to worry about such things with performances, ports of call and the tidy job they had planned for Manhattan.

When they did have free time, Luke planned to plop himself down by the pool, clamp headphones on his ears, bury his nose in a book while some nubile strolling cocktail waitress kept the cold beer coming.

All in all, life was good. He had a bit more than two million in his Swiss accounts, that much again floating in various stocks, bonds and money markets in the States, along with some modest real estate investments. In his closet hung suits from Savile Row and

Armani, though he still preferred denim by Levi's. Perhaps he was more at home in Nikes, but there were highly polished Gucci shoes in his rack, and a selection of John Lobb boots. He drove a vintage 'Vette and piloted his own Cessna. He indulged in imported cigars and French champagne and had a weakness for Italian women.

All in all, he figured the half-starved pickpocket had turned himself into a discriminating, cosmopolitan man.

What it cost him to maintain the image was a bit of blackmail—and the repression of one small, nagging, incessant need.

Roxanne.

But then, Max had taught him never to count the cost, unless it was pride.

Luke took a mug of coffee onto his terrace to watch the action down in Jackson Square. There were girls in pretty summer dresses, babies in strollers, men with cameras slung around their necks. He spotted three black kids tap dancing. Their feet were moving like fury. Even with the distance, he could hear the cheerful click and clatter of their shoes on the concrete. They'd drawn a crowd, and that pleased him.

The woman he'd heard on that first day in New Orleans no longer sang in the Quarter. He missed the sound of her, and though he'd never quite had the same emotional tug toward anyone else, it satisfied him to see the cardboard boxes of the street performers fill with silver.

Without Max, he thought. Without Max and Lily he could have done much worse than dance for pennies.

That brought a frown to his eyes. He knew why Max was handing over more and more of the sleight of hand and close-up work to him and Roxanne. He thought he even understood why Max was devoting so much of the time he'd once earmarked for preparing the act toward the damn philosophers' stone. And understanding hurt.

Max was getting old, right in front of Luke's eyes.

A knock on the door had him turning reluctantly away from the street scene. But when he opened it, there was only pleasure.

"Lily." Luke bent to kiss her, to breathe in the wonderfully familiar Chanel before taking the various bags and boxes she carried.

"I was shopping." She giggled, patting her fluffy blond hair back into place. "I guess that's obvious. I got the urge to stop by. Hope it's okay."

"It's always okay." He dumped her purchases on an overstuffed chair beside a Belker table. "Ready to give Max his walking papers and move in with me?"

She laughed again, that bubbly, champagne sound that he loved. Past forty now, she remained as lush and pretty as she'd been when Luke had first seen her strut across the stage. It took a bit more woman's magic to maintain the illusion, but Lily had an endless store of it.

"If I did, it would be to give those ladies of yours the once-over as they sashay in and out."

"I'd give them all up, for the right lady."

Lily didn't laugh this time, but there was a different sort of amusement in her eyes. "Oh, I'm sure you would, honey. I'm getting old waiting for you to make the next move. But," she continued before he could speak, "I didn't come by to talk about your love life—fascinating though it may be."

He grinned. "You're going to make me blush."

"Fat chance." She was proud of him, so proud it almost burst her heart. He was tall and trim and gloriously handsome. And more, much more than that, there was a goodness inside of him that she knew she had nurtured herself. "I dropped by to see if you needed any help packing—or if you needed anything while I was shopping. Socks, underwear?"

He couldn't help it. Setting the mug down he cupped her face in his hands and kissed her again. "I love you, Lily."

Pleasure had her cheeks blooming. "I love you, too. I know how men hate to pack and shop for undies and stuff."

"I've got plenty."

"They've probably got holes in them, or the elastic's gone."

Sober-eyed, he lifted a hand in an oath. "I swear to God, I didn't pack a single pair of jocks that I'd be ashamed to wear if I were in an accident."

She sniffed, but her eyes were laughing. "You're making fun of me."

"Yeah. How about some coffee?"

"I'd rather something cold, if you have it."

"Lemonade?" He headed back toward the kitchen. "I must have had a premonition that you'd drop by when I squeezed those damn lemons this morning."

"You made it fresh? Yourself?" She was as proud of that as she would have been if he'd won the Nobel prize.

He took out a squat pitcher of pale green glass and matching glasses. His kitchen was neat and small, with an old-fashioned two-burner gas range and a short, round-edged refrigerator. Lily thought the herbs potted on the windowsill were the sweetest things.

"I know you're competent." It hurt only a little that he could do so easily without her. "You always could do anything you set your mind on." She took the glass he offered and rattled the ice in it, wandered back into the living room. "You have such good taste."

He lifted a brow, noting the way she ran fingertips over the curve of his love seat, the surface of an antique commode. "I got it through osmosis."

"From Max, I know. Me, I have terrible taste. I just love tacky things."

"Whatever I got, I got from both of you." Taking her hand, he drew her down with him on the love seat. "What's this all about, Lily?"

"About? I told you, I just stopped by."

"You've got worry in your eyes."

"What woman doesn't?" But her eyes slid away from his.

He brushed his knuckles over her cheek. It was soft as a baby's still. "Let me help."

That was all it took to crumble the fragile wall she'd managed to build before knocking on his door. Tears blurred her vision as he took her glass, set it aside, then drew her into his arms.

"I'm being silly. I know I am, but I can't help it."

"It's all right." He kissed her hair, her temple, and waited.

"I don't think Max loves me anymore."

"What?" He'd meant to be sympathetic, comforting, supportive. Instead he jerked back, laughing. "What a crock. Oh, shit," he muttered as she dissolved into helpless sobs. "Don't. Come on, Lily, don't cry." Women's tears remained the one thing he had no defense against. "I'm sorry I laughed. What makes you say such a crazy thing?"

"He—he—" It was the best she could do as she wailed against his shoulder.

Change tactics, Luke thought, and stroked her back. "Okay, okay, baby, don't you worry. I'm going to go right over and beat him up for you."

That brought a gurgle of laughter to mix with tears. She wasn't ashamed of the laughter, or the tears. She'd learned never to be ashamed of what felt good. "I just love him so much, you know? He's the best thing that ever happened to me. You don't even know what it was like before."

"No." He sobered, resting his cheek on her hair. "I don't."

"We were so poor. But that was okay, because my mama was wonderful. Even after Daddy died, she held everything together. She'd always see to it there was a little extra, for a movie, or an ice cream. I didn't know, not till later, that she took money from time to time from men. But she wasn't a whore." Lily lifted her tear-streaked face. "It was just a way to take care of her kids."

"Then you can be proud of her."

No mother, she mused, had ever had a wiser son. "I got married before. Max knows about it, but nobody else."

"Then nobody else'll know now, if that's what you want."

"It was a mistake, such an awful mistake. I was just seventeen, and he was so good-looking." She smiled a little again, knowing how silly it sounded. "I got pregnant, so we got married. He didn't like being poor, or having a wife who got sick in the mornings. He knocked me around some."

She felt Luke tense, felt a little curl of shame, and hurried on. "When he kept it up, I told him I was leaving. My mama'd raised me better than to be a punching bag. He told me my mama was a whore and so was I. He beat me good that time, and I lost the baby." She shuddered once, from old memory. "It messed me up inside so they said I wouldn't be able to have another."

"I'm sorry." And helpless, he thought. Completely helpless.

"I'm telling you so that you can understand where I came from. About that time my mother died. I think knowing how hard she'd worked so that I could have good things helped me get strong. So even when he came by and said how he was sorry and he'd never hit me again, I did leave him, and I got work at a carnival. Told fortunes, worked some of the booths. Small cons. That's how I met Max.

"He was magic even back then. Him and little Roxanne. I guess I loved them both so much right off I nearly burst with it. He'd lost his wife, and maybe a little bit of himself, too. And I wanted him, so I did what any smart woman would do and seduced him."

Luke held her closer. "I bet he put up a hell of a fight, didn't he?"

That made her laugh, and sigh. "He could have taken what I gave him and left it at that. But he didn't. He took me in. Treated me like a lady. He showed me the way it's supposed to be between a man and a woman. He made me family. Most of all he loved me—just for me, you know what I mean."

"Yeah, I do. But I don't think it was all one-sided, Lily. I figure you gave as good as you got."

"I always tried. Luke, I've loved him for almost twenty years now. I just don't think I could stand to lose him."

"What makes you think you could? He's nuts about you. That's one of the things that always made me feel the best, the way the two of you are with each other."

"He's pulling away." She took a couple of steadying breaths to strengthen her voice. "Oh, he's still sweet to me, when he remembers I'm around. Max would never hurt me, or anybody on purpose. But he spends hours and hours alone, going through books and notes and journals. That damn stone." She sniffled, digging into her pocket for a lace hankie. "At first I thought it was kind of interesting." She blew her nose. "I mean, suppose there really was such a thing? But he's gotten so caught up in it there's hardly room for anything else. And he's forgetting things." She worried her bottom lip and wrung her hands. "Just little things. Like appointments and meals. We were nearly late for a performance last week because he forgot all about it. I know he's worried because he can't do some of the sleight of hand anymore, and it's affecting his..." She trailed off, wondering how it could be put delicately. "What I mean to say is that Max has always been, well, robust, sexually. But lately we hardly ever... you know."

He did, but devoutly wished he didn't. "Well, I, ah."

"But I don't just mean the performance, so to speak. The romance of it. He doesn't turn to me in the night anymore, or take my hand, or look at me that way." Another tear bloomed over and slid down her cheek.

"He's distracted, Lily. That's all. All that pressure to do another special, to write another book, to go back and tour Europe. Then the jobs. Max has always taken too much on himself in the planning and execution." He wasn't going to mention that on their last job, he found Max standing in front of an open safe as if in a trance. Or that it had taken Max nearly five minutes to come back to himself and remember where he was and what he was doing.

"You know what I think," he said, taking the useless swatch of lace and drying Lily's eyes himself. "I think you're as stressed out as Max is—what with Rox's graduation, getting ready for this summer gig. And I—wait!" He grabbed her hand, turning it palm up. "I see a long sea voyage," he continued as Lily gave a watery chuckle. "Moonlit nights, salty breezes. Romance." He winked at her. "And great sex."

"You don't read palms."

"You taught me, didn't you?" He pressed his lips to her palm, then curled her fingers in his. "You're the most beautiful woman I've ever known, and Max loves you—nearly as much as I do. Hey, don't start dripping again, please."

"Okay." She blinked furiously at tears. "Okay."

"I want you to trust me when I say it's all going to be fine. We're going to get away for a little while, relax and drink champagne cocktails on the poop deck."

"Maybe he does just need to rest." Her shoulders shifted in one last sigh. "I wasn't going to dump on you, Luke, really I wasn't. But I'm awful glad you were here."

"Me too. You dump anytime you like."

"I'm done." Brushing tears from her lashes, she sat up. "Sure you don't want me to pack for you?"

"Already done. I'm as anxious to leave in the morning as you."

"I'm anxious all right." Recovered, she reached for her lemonade and sipped to ease her raw throat. "But I haven't packed a thing. Roxanne's got everything all neat and tidy, and in only two cases. I don't know how she does it."

"The brat's been an organization maniac since she was eight."

"Hmm." She sipped again, watching Luke. "She's not eight anymore. Wait till you see the cocktail dress she bought for the captain's party."

Luke merely shrugged and sat back. "How about you? Any sexy numbers in those bags?"

"A few."

Knowing just how much Lily enjoyed displaying her purchases, Luke played along. "Going to show me?"

"Maybe." She fluttered still damp lashes and turned to set her glass down again. Her glance passed over the letter he'd left on the table, then cut back to it and froze. "Cobb." Nerves fluttered in her throat. "Why are you writing to him?"

"I'm not." With a vicious inner curse, Luke scooped up the letter and jammed it in his pocket. "It's nothing."

"Don't lie to me." Her voice was suddenly brittle as glass. "Don't ever lie to me."

"I'm not. I said I wasn't writing to him."

"Then what's in the envelope?"

His face went blank and still. "It's nothing to do with you."

She said nothing for a moment, but a dozen varied emotions played across her tear-streaked face. "You're everything to do with me," she said quietly as she rose. "Or so I thought. I'd better go."

"Don't." He swore again, violently, and put a hand on her arm. "Damn it, Lily, don't look at me like that. I'm handling this the only way I know how. Leave it to me."

"Of course." She had a way, as certain women did, of being perfectly agreeable, and cutting a man off at the knees. "You'll be at the house by eight, won't you? We don't want to miss the flight."

"Damn it all to hell. I'm paying him, all right? I send him some money now and again and he leaves me alone." His eyes were fierce and deadly. "He leaves all of us alone."

With a nod, Lily sat again. "He's blackmailing you?"

"That's a polite term. A bloodless term." Furious with himself, Luke stalked to the window. "I can afford to be polite."

"Why?"

He only shook his head. Not to her, not to anyone would he speak of it. Not of what had been, nor of the nightmares that plagued him a day or two after he found that plain white postcard in his mailbox.

"As long as you pay him, he'll never go away." Lily spoke quietly from just behind him. Gently, she laid a hand on his back. "He'll never leave you in peace."

"Maybe not. But he knows something I'm ashamed enough of that I'm willing to pay him to keep to himself." The tap dancers had gone off to other pastures, Luke thought. Pigeons fluttered in the park. "And he can insinuate a great deal more, twist lies with truth in such a way that I couldn't live with it. So it costs me a few thousand a pop for this kind of illusionary peace. It's worth it to me."

"Don't you know he can't hurt you anymore?"

"No." He turned back then, torment in every muscle. "I don't. Worse, I don't know who else he could hurt. I won't chance it, Lily. Not even for you."

"I won't ask you to. I will ask that you trust me enough to come to me. Always." She stood on tiptoe to kiss his cheek. "I know I'm silly, flighty—"

"Stop."

She only laughed. "Honey, I know just what I am. And I'm not sorry about it. I'm a middle-aged woman who wears too much makeup and who'll die without letting the first gray hair show. But I stand behind those I love. I've loved you for a long time. You send that check if you feel a need to. And if he asks for more than you can spare, you come to me. I've got my own put aside."

"Thanks." He cleared his throat. "But he doesn't squeeze too hard."

"There's one more thing I want you to remember. There's nothing you've done or could do I'd be ashamed of." She turned and began to gather her bags. "I'd better get on home. It's going to take me half the night to figure out what to pack. Oh, goodness." She pressed her hands to her cheeks. "I have to fix my face first. I can't go out in public with mascara all over." She dashed toward the bathroom, purse in tow. "Oh, Luke, you know you could come on home with me, spend the night in your old room. Might be easier getting things together in the morning."

It might at that, he mused and dipped his hands into his pockets. It would be even better to go home, even if just for one night.

"Let me get my bags," he called out to her. "I'll drive you home in style."

17

The accommodations for the entertainers aboard the *Yankee Princess* weren't quite as luxurious as Roxanne might have hoped. Because of their special guest-star status, they had been given outside cabins—slightly above water level.

The two-berth cabin was tiny enough that she was grateful she wouldn't be required to share its space over the next six weeks. Her practical nature tugged her away from the porthole to unpack the contents of her two suitcases. As a matter of habit, everything was neatly folded or hung in the stationary bureau and gnome-sized closet. She was romantic enough to want to hurry and be on deck when the whistle blew to signal castoff.

She took time to set out the antique bottles and jars she'd collected over the years, all carefully filled with perfumes and lotions. They'd been a bitch to pack against breakage, and she knew plastic would have been wiser. But seeing them there, all those pretty shapes and colors, made her smile. The extra weight and trouble had been worth it.

She checked herself in the mirror first, glad that her hair had grown back to past her shoulders after her rash decision two years before to crop it chin length. It, too, was a great deal of trouble, taking enormous amounts of time to dry and groom. But she was vain enough to consider the time and effort well spent.

Pleased that the piped-in music included a classical station, she touched up her makeup—a bit more bronze shadow on the lids, a whisper of extra blusher along the cheekbones. That wasn't vanity—precisely—she assured herself. Part of the job the Nouvelle troupe had taken on was to mix and mingle with the passengers, to make themselves companionable, presentable and pleasant.

It was little enough to pay for a six-week run on an elegant floating hotel.

Grabbing her roomy canvas bag, she headed out, and up. Boarding passengers were already roaming the narrow passageways, seeking their rooms or exploring. Piles of luggage were stacked in front of cabin doors.

Larceny tugged gleefully at Roxanne's heart. It would be so pitifully simple to pluck a bit here, snatch a bit there. Like picking daisies, she mused, smiling at a round-bellied man in a baseball cap who inched by her.

There'd be time for fun and games, she reminded herself. Six long weeks' worth of time. But this afternoon she was on vacation. She turned at the top of the stairs and wound her way through the Lido Lounge, out to the deck at the stern, where eager passengers were sipping their complimentary cocktails, taking videos or simply leaning at the rail waiting to wave goodbye to the Manhattan skyline.

She took a hurricane glass filled with blush pink liquid from the tray of a waiter and, sipping the oversweet rum drink, sized up her fellow sailors.

At a guess, Roxanne gauged the mean age to be sixty-five. There were a few families with children, a sprinkling of honeymooners, but for the most part there were older couples, elderly singles and a scattering of aging gigolos on the prowl.

"Maybe we should call it the Geriatric Boat," Luke said close to her ear and nearly had her spilling the rum concoction.

"I think it's sweet."

"I didn't say it wasn't." Despite her barbed tone, he slipped a friendly arm around her shoulders. He'd decided if they were going to be in such relatively close quarters for the next few weeks, they should try to be civil. "Check this dude."

He'd bypassed the rum for a bottle of Beck's and gestured with it toward a dapper, silver-haired gentleman wearing a double-breasted navy blazer and natty white trousers. He already had a cluster of admiring female senior citizens around him. "Joe Smooth."

"Of the Palm Beach Smooths," she said, amused. "What do you want to bet he does a mean cha-cha?"

"Probably got a rumba or two in him. And there." He gestured again, using only an arched eyebrow to have Roxanne's gaze shifting. Near the portside rail was a big, frowsy blonde in a shocking-pink jogging suit. She had a camera and a pair of binoculars slung around her neck, and was busily lifting one then the other in between sips of her rum surprise. "Sally Tourist."

"Snob."

He only grinned. "Come on, you pick one."

She scanned the deck, then touched her tongue to her top lip. "Mmm. I'll take him. Tom Terrific."

Luke studied the ship's officer, bronzed and blond and gorgeous in his dress whites. His mood immediately soured. "If you go for that type."

"I do." Unable to resist, she heaved an exaggerated sigh. "Oh, I do. Look, there's Mouse." Roxanne gave a wide wave to bring him over. "What do you think?"

"It's great." His big, pale face was flushed with pleasure. Muscles bulged beneath the cropped sleeves of the flowered shirt Lily had picked for him. "They let me go down in the engine room. I gotta check the equipment for the show and all, but later, they said, I could go up on the bridge and everything."

"They got any women down there?" Luke asked.

"In the engine room?" Mouse grinned and shuffled. "Nah. 'Cept in pictures on the walls."

"Stick with me, pal. I'll find you some real ones."

"Leave him alone, you walking hormone." In defense of Mouse, Roxanne slipped a hand through his arm. "Listen." She squeezed as the ship blew two long blasts. "We're casting off."

"One deck up," Luke murmured when she began to crane her neck.

She looked up and saw them. Lily, looking festive in a flowing blue sundress, Max dashing in an off-white jacket and navy pants, and LeClerc, hovering like a shadow behind them.

"He's going to be fine." Luke took her hand, linking fingers.

"Of course he is." She shook away the seeds of doubt. "Let's go up. I want to get some pictures."

It wasn't going to be a walk on the beach. The first onboard staff meeting dispensed with any notion that the next six weeks would be a free ride. The Nouvelles would give a mini-performance that night to welcome the passengers on board, along with shortened acts from the other entertainers. A French chanteuse, a comedian who spiced up his monologues with juggling and the six-member song-and-dance group who made up the Moonglades.

In addition to their act, they were asked to assist in daily activities from Bingo to shore excursions. When it was discovered that Roxanne spoke fluent French, she was immediately dragooned to help the ship's two interpreters.

Rules were also dispensed. Being friendly and personable with the passengers was mandatory. Being intimate was not. Accepting tips was not permitted, drunkenness was frowned on. Meals were to be taken only after the passengers had dined. And, in the event of trouble at sea, all members of the crew and staff would man the lifeboats only after all passengers were safe.

There was some groaning from the more seasoned members of the staff when weekly assignments were handed out. The cruise director, Jack, a youthful vet with ten years' experience on cruise ships, took it in stride. "If there's anything you need, just ask. And don't pay any attention to these gripers. Most of the extra work with the passengers is pure fun."

"So he says." A tall, slender blonde called Dori aimed a considering smile at Luke. "Let me know if you need any help getting adjusted." She smiled at Roxanne to include her in the invitation. "We've got a very shaky run-through rehearsal scheduled at three-thirty in the movie theater. That's on the Promenade Deck, aft."

"And first show's at eight," Jack finished. "Take some time to get familiar with the ship's layout."

• • •

Roxanne was given a *Yankee Princess* T-shirt in fuchsia, a name tag to pin on and a pat on the back for luck. She toured the ship, rehearsed, then toured the ship some more, answering questions, smiling, wishing passengers a good voyage.

As afternoon slid toward evening, she managed to snag an apple and a few hunks of cheese from the buffet the passengers had decimated and smuggled them into the dressing cum storage room where she and Lily were to change for the first show.

"There's so many of them," Roxanne said over a bite of McIntosh. "And they want to know everything."

"Everyone's so nice and friendly." Lily avoided crashing into a cardboard jail cell and wriggled into costume. "Why, I met people from all over the country. It's really like being on the road again."

"Max likes it, doesn't he?"

"He loves it. He already loves it."

That was enough for Roxanne, even though she had to press a hand to her stomach as the ship rolled. "Do you think this is going to keep up?"

"What, honey?"

"The movement." She blew out a breath, setting the apple aside to reach for her costume.

"Oh, the ship? It kind of feels like being in a cradle, doesn't it? Nice and soothing."

"Yeah. Right." Roxanne swallowed hard.

She managed to get through the first show before the soothing cradle she was in had her dashing down to her cabin. She was just finished being sick when Luke walked in the tiny head.

"I locked the door," she said with all the dignity she could muster while sitting on the floor.

"I know. It took me nearly thirty seconds to open it."

"What I meant was, since I locked it, that probably meant I wanted to be alone."

"Mmm-hmm." He was busy running cool water on a wash cloth. He helped her up and led her out to the bed. "Sit. Put this on the back of your neck."

He did it himself and drew a long, grateful sigh from her. "How'd you know I was sick?"

He flicked a hand over the emerald spangles of her dress. "Your face was the same color as your costume. Dead giveaway."

"I'm okay now." Or she hoped she was. "I'll get used to it." Her eyes were a little more than desperate when she lifted them to his. "Don't you think?"

"Sure you will." It was a rare thing to see Roxanne Nouvelle vulnerable—so rare he had to resist an urge to gather her close and make it all go away. "Take a couple of these." He held out two white pills.

"I don't suppose they're morphine."

"Sorry. Just Dramamine. Down them with a couple of sips of this ginger ale. There you go." As competent as a nurse, he turned the cloth over and pressed the cooler side to her neck again. "If it doesn't let up, the ship's doctor'll take care of it."

"Stupid." More annoyed than embarrassed, she sipped more ginger ale and prayed for it to settle. "I could ride everything in the carnival and never feel a thing. One night on a boat and I'm whipped."

"It'll pass." Since her color was nearly normal again, he judged it already was passing. "If you're feeling shaky, we can cover for you in the second show."

"No way." She rose, willing her legs and her system to steady. "A Nouvelle never misses a cue. Give me a minute." She retreated to the bathroom to rinse out her mouth and check her makeup. "I guess I owe you one," she said when she came out again.

"Babe, you owe me a lot more than one. Ready?"

"Sure, I'm ready." She opened the door, stepped out. "Luke, we don't have to mention this, do we?"

He lifted his brows. "Mention what?"

"Okay." She smiled at him. "I owe you two."

Since there was no recurrence of seasickness over the next day or two, Roxanne was forced to consider that the motion of the boat had only been a contributing factor to the whole that had been made up of stress, rum on a nearly empty stomach and nerves. It wasn't a particularly pleasant admission for a woman who had always prided herself on being able to handle anything that came her way. Her days were too full, however, to allow her to dwell on it.

Jack had been right, she decided. The majority of the work required was pure fun. She enjoyed the passengers, and the games and events scattered through the daily schedule designed to keep them entertained. The rest of her family seemed to be getting into the spirit of things as well. Max and Lily judged a dance contest, Mouse spent most of his spare time haunting the engine room and crew quarters and LeClerc found a trio of poker buddies.

The stress she hadn't been aware of carrying on board with her began to dissipate with each passing hour. It might have faded completely if Roxanne hadn't turned toward the stairway on the Laguna Deck and seen Max standing there, looking lost.

"Daddy?" He didn't respond, so she stepped closer and touched his arm. "Daddy?"

He jolted, and she saw the panic streak into his eyes. In that instant, her blood froze. She saw more in his eyes than panic; she saw total confusion. He didn't know her. He was staring into her face and he didn't know her.

"Daddy," she said again, unable to keep a tremor from her voice. "Are you all right?"

He blinked, a muscle working furiously in his jaw. Like a cloud slowly lifting, the confusion faded from his eyes to reveal annoyance. "Of course I'm all right. Why wouldn't I be?"

"Well, I thought you—" She fought a smile onto her face. "I guess you're turned around. I keep doing that."

"I know exactly where I'm going." Max felt the pulse throbbing at the base of his neck. He could almost hear it. He hadn't known. For a moment, he hadn't been able to remember where he was or what he'd been doing. Stark fear had him snapping at his daughter. "I don't need anyone snooping around after me. And I don't appreciate being nagged about my every move."

"I'm sorry." The color ebbed from her cheeks. "I was just going up to your cabin." There was a book tucked under his arm, she noted. A tattered, antique book on alchemy. "I certainly didn't mean to nag." Cloaked in injured pride, she moved stiffly around him.

A wave of shame had him reaching out. "I apologize. My mind was elsewhere."

She merely shrugged, a distinctly female gesture that could make any man grovel.

He took out his key to open his stateroom door. Mouse, LeClerc and Luke were already waiting.

"All right, my pets." Max pulled out the single chair that stood by the bureau, and sat. "Time to get down to business."

"Lily isn't here yet," Luke pointed out, concerned when Max looked blankly around the room.

"Ah, well."

Roxanne plunged into the uncomfortable silence. "They've already got at least a dozen passengers signed up for the talent show at the end of the week. It should be a kick."

"How much do you want to bet someone does 'Moon River'?" Luke asked.

Roxanne was nervously rubbing her hands together, but she smiled. "No bet. I heard Mrs. Steiner tap dances. Maybe—" She paused, relieved when Lily hurried in.

"Sorry I'm late." She was prettily flushed and weighed down with purse and camera. "They were having an ice-carving demonstration out by the pool, and I got caught up. He made the most incredible peacock." She smiled at Max, who only gestured absently.

"All right then, what have we got?"

LeClerc linked his hands behind his back. "DiMato in cabin seven sixty-seven. Diamond earrings—probably two-carat, Rolex watch and a five-to six-carat sapphire pendant."

"The DiMatos are the ones celebrating their fiftieth wedding anniversary," Roxanne put in, plucking one of the grapes from the fruit basket on the bureau. "The pendant was her anniversary present. They're awfully sweet together."

Max smiled, understanding. "Something else then?"

"Well, Mrs. Gullager in six twenty," Roxanne offered. "A ruby set, cuff bracelet, necklace, earrings. Looks heirloom."

"Oh, she's the dearest thing." Lily sent Roxanne a pleading look. "I had tea with her the other day. She lives in Roanoke, Virginia, with her two cats."

"Another contender?" Max gestured to the room at large.

"There's Harvey Wallace in four thirty-six." Luke shrugged. "Diamond cuff links, stick pin, another Rolex. But . . . Shit, he's such a funny old guy."

"He's nice," Mouse put in. "He told me all about this De Soto he rebuilt in 1962."

"Jamisons," LeClerc said between his teeth. "Cabin seven ten. Diamond ring, square cut, approximately five carats. Ruby ring, possibly Burmese, same carat weight. Antique emerald brooch—"

"Nancy and John Jamison?" Max interrupted. "I had a delightful time playing bridge with them on the Promenade Deck just yesterday. He's in food processing and she owns a bookstore in Corpus Christi."

"Bon Dieu," LeClerc muttered.

"We're a sentimental lot, aren't we?" Roxanne patted LeClerc's hand. "And an embarrassment to you, I'm sure." After choosing another grape, she folded her legs under her. "I don't see how we can steal from people we're all but living with day in and day out. Especially when we like them so much."

Max steepled his hands, tapped his fingers against his chin. "You're quite right, Roxanne. Once an emotional attachment's made, the fun goes out of it." He scanned the room, gauging faces. "Are we agreed then? No marks this week?"

He got a nod from everyone but LeClerc, who only ground his teeth.

"Cheer up." Luke picked up Max's remaining mineral water and toasted. "We've got the best part of six weeks. Someone's bound to come on board we don't like."

"Then we're adjourned."

"Have you got a minute?" Luke asked Max as everyone made to leave.

"Of course."

Luke waited until they were alone, but still took the precaution of keeping his voice low. "Why the hell are you doing this to Lily?"

Max's mouth fell open. "I beg your pardon?"

"Damn it, Max, you're breaking her heart."

"That's absurd." Highly insulted, Max rose from the chair to pick up his book. "Where did you get such a ridiculous notion?"

"From Lily." Too angry for respect, Luke snatched the book away and tossed it onto the bed. "She came to see me the day before we left for New York. Damn you, you made her cry."

"I? I?" Shaken by the thought, Max sat again. "How?"

"Neglect," Luke tossed out. "Disinterest. You're so fucking obsessed with some magical stone, you can't see what's happening in front of your face. She doesn't think you love her anymore. And after seeing the way you behaved toward her over these last couple of days, I understand just how she got the idea in her head."

Very pale, very still, Max stared at Luke. "That is a completely asinine notion. She has no reason to doubt my feelings."

"Really?" Luke sat on the edge of the bed, leaned forward. "When's the last time you bothered to tell her what they are? Have you sat in the moonlight with her and listened to the sea? You know how much she counts on the little things, but have you stirred yourself to give any of them to her? Have you used this bed for anything but sleeping?"

"You go too far." Max stiffened like a poker. "Much too far."

"The hell I do. I'm not going to stand by and see that hurt look in her eyes. She'd crawl over glass for you, and you can't even bother to give her ten minutes of your valuable time."

"You're wrong." Max stared down at his clenched fist. "And if Lily feels as you say, she's quite mistaken. I love her. I've always loved her."

"Could have fooled me. You didn't even look at her when she walked in here."

"That was business," he began, then cut himself off. He'd always prided himself on honesty, in his own way. "Perhaps I've been a bit distracted lately, and more than a little self-involved." He lifted his gaze from his aching hands. "I would never hurt her. I'd cut out my own heart before I'd hurt her."

"Tell her." Luke turned for the door. "Not me."

"Wait." Max pressed his fingers to his eyes. If he'd made a mistake, he'd do whatever was necessary to correct it. The faintest smile touched his lips. And he'd correct it in style. "I need a favor."

The fact that Luke hesitated showed Max just how deep the temper went. And how deep his own sins. "What?"

"First, I'd like to keep this conversation between us. Second, after the last performance tonight, I'd appreciate it if you'd detain Lily, keep her away from the cabin for about thirty minutes. Then I'll need you to be certain she comes directly here."

"All right."

"Luke?"

He had his hand on the door, but paused and glanced back. "Yeah?"

"Thank you. Now and again a man needs someone to make him face his shortcomings, and his blessings. You've done both."

"Just make it up to her."

"Oh, I will." Max smiled then, fully. "That, at the very least, I can promise."

"We done good." Roxanne dropped heavily into a chair in the corner of the disco. The second performance of the evening had gone as successfully as the first.

"We knocked them dead." Luke sat down, stretched out his legs. "Of course, with a crowd this age, that's not too hard."

Roxanne snickered. "Don't be gruesome. Be useful and go get me and Lily drinks."

"Oh, I think I should skip it." Lily looked around the hotly lit room for a glimpse of Max. "You young people should enjoy yourselves."

"No way." Luke grabbed her hand. "You're not ducking out on me without a dance." He pulled her laughing out on the floor where Michael Jackson was telling everyone to beat it.

"That your competition?" Dori plopped down on Luke's vacated chair.

"She's a tough act to follow."

"She's pretty great," Dori agreed and snagged a waitress's attention. "I mean besides being a real sweetheart, just look at that body. Want a drink?"

"Glass of white wine," Roxanne decided. "A pink lady for Lily and a Beck's for Luke."

"Make it two Beck's," Dori said, then leaned over the table again. The music was loud, but not oppressive. There were a smattering of passengers on the dance floor gyrating to Jackson's driving rhythm.

When their drinks were served, she said, "First round's on me. I really like working cruise ships. Most people come on with a mind set to have fun. Makes it easier. And you get to meet so many different types. Speaking of which." She took a deep sip of beer. "What's the story on him?"

Roxanne glanced over to where Luke was twirling Lily under his arm. "Story?"

"I mean, he's gorgeous, dynamic, single. Straight, right?"

Roxanne chuckled. "Definitely heterosexual."

"So how come you haven't jumped on it?"

Roxanne choked on her wine. "Jumped? Jumped on it?"

"Roxanne, he's a mouth waterer." To prove her point, Dori traced her tongue around her lips. "I'd take the leap myself except I don't like to swim in someone else's pool."

After a deep breath, Roxanne shook her head. "You lost me, Dori."

"The two of you. It's so obvious."

"Oh? What's obvious?"

"There's enough sexual friction between you to set the ship on fire."

Since the color was fluctuating in her cheeks, Roxanne hoped it could be blamed on the flashing lights of the disco. "You're reading it wrong."

"Oh yeah?" Dori looked back at Luke, drank, then swiveled back to Roxanne. "Are you saying you don't want him?"

"No. I mean, yes. I mean . . ." She wasn't used to being flustered. "What I mean is things aren't that way with us."

"Because you don't want them to be?"

"Because . . . because they aren't."

"Uh-huh. Well, I don't like to poke my nose in."

Roxanne had to laugh. "Oh, I could see that right off."

"Anyway." Dori grinned engagingly. "If I were to poke it in, I'd offer this simple, time-honored advice. Intrigue, confuse, seduce. And if that doesn't work, jump his bones. Got to go."

"Yeah. See you." Roxanne stared into her wine, drawing lines down the outside of the glass with her fingers. Her thoughts were such that she jolted when Luke and Lily sat down again.

"Oh, that was fun." Nearly out of breath, Lily reached for her drink.

"Finish that off, and we'll do it again."

"Not on your life." She waved a hand. "Go do it with Roxy."

Roxanne choked again and blushed scarlet.

"Take it easy." Luke thumped her on the back. "Want to dance, Rox?"

"No. Ah, maybe later." Her whole body was tingling. Her heart picked up the rhythm of the bass and thudded against her ribs. Sexual friction? Was that what this was? If so, it was deadly. She sipped again, more cautiously. Intrigue. All right, she'd give it a shot. "I liked watching the two of you out there." She touched a hand lightly to the back of Luke's. "You've got some good moves, Callahan."

He stared at her. What was that gleam in her eye? In another woman, he would have taken it as an invitation. In Roxanne, he wondered where she'd bite or scratch first. "Thanks." He picked up his beer and casually checked his watch.

"Got a late date?" Roxanne purred.

"What? No."

Now, wasn't this interesting? Lily mused. A little cat and mouse, with Roxanne in the role of cat. "You two should take a nice stroll out on deck. It's gorgeous tonight."

"Good idea. Why don't we all do that?" Luke grabbed Lily's hand and watched Roxanne warily. He had ten more minutes to detain Lily, then he thought it might be wise to run for his life.

"No, no, I'm a little tired." Lily feigned a huge yawn. "I'll just go down and turn in."

"You haven't finished your drink." Luke sat again, kept his hand firm on Lily's. "And I've been meaning to ask you . . ." What? What? "Ah, if you think it's going to rain tomorrow in Sydney?"

"Australia?" Lily said, big-eyed.

"No, Nova Scotia. We're docking there in the morning. I've, ah, got a couple hours off, and thought I'd go into town and look around."

Why, he's nervous, Roxanne realized, and found it oddly endearing. And exciting. "So do I," she murmured. "Want company?"

"Well . . ."

"I really am tired." Lily yawned again and shook her hand free of Luke's. "Enjoy yourselves."

Shit, Luke thought. He had to hope it was close enough. "I'm a little tired myself." Luke stood as Lily walked off. And made a small, gagging sound when Roxanne rose as well, her body bumping against his.

"A walk on deck would help you sleep better." She tilted her head back so that they were eye to eye and nearly mouth to mouth. He could feel his lips tingle.

"Nope." He thought of all the things he'd like to do with her, to her, in the salt-sprayed moonlight. "I can guarantee it wouldn't. You should turn in, too."

"I don't think so." She trailed a finger down his arm. "I imagine there's someone around who'd like to dance, or walk." She brushed her lips lightly over his. "Good night, Callahan."

"Yeah." He watched her stroll away, then lean over a table where a few of the entertainers were having drinks. He doubted he'd sleep a wink.

Lily unlocked the door of her cabin, smiling at the image of Roxanne and Luke walking hand in hand in the moonlight. She'd waited a long time to see her two children find each other. Maybe tonight, she thought, and opened the door to music, candlelight and roses.

"Oh." She stood there, silhouetted by the backlight from the passageway. Max stepped away from the table where a bottle of champagne was open and waiting. He crossed to her, offering a single pink rose.

He said nothing, only took her hand and brought it to his lips as he eased the door shut behind her. Locked it.

"Oh, Max."

"I hope it's not too late for a small bon voyage celebration."

"No." She pressed her lips together to hold back tears. "It's not too late. It's never too late."

Cupping her face in his hand, he tilted her head back. "My heart," he murmured. His lips were soft and strong against hers. Then the kiss deepened, lengthened as their tongues met in a slow, familiar dance.

When he drew her back, the old twinkle she adored was in his eyes. "Perhaps I could ask one small favor."

"You know you can."

"That crimson negligee you packed? Would you put it on while I pour the wine?"

18

He'd finally figured it out. It took Luke a couple of days, and an equal amount of uncomfortably restless nights, but he finally got a handle on it.

She was trying to drive him crazy.

It was the only reasonable explanation for Roxanne's behavior. It wasn't that she smiled at him so often. It was the *way* she smiled. With that oddly female light in her eyes that was invitation, challenge and amusement melded together. He couldn't even blame the fact that she'd cornered him into one of the ballroom dancing demonstrations—under the guise of staff participation—so that he'd had to hold her in his arms, breathing in the scent of her hair while her hips twitched in a rumba under his hand.

It wasn't possible to point to the fact that she'd run into him that afternoon in Quebec City after completing her role as interpreter on one of the shore excursions—or that she'd made him enjoy being hauled from shop to shop buying gifts and souvenirs, eating ice cream and weaving through crowds of tourists on the long narrow streets to listen to a musician play the concertina.

To be fair, he couldn't blame the fact that she made certain a day didn't pass without giving him one of those light, butterfly kisses that stirred the juices the way a crust of bread would heighten the hunger of a starving man.

No, he couldn't blame any one of those things—until he put them all together with the less tangible but equally effective vibrations she seemed to emit whenever he was within five feet of her.

He grumbled to himself all the way up the outside stairway from the Lido Deck to Promenade, from Promenade to Royal. He wasn't some freaking messenger boy, and he'd nearly told Jack as much. But it would have been hard to explain why he objected so strenuously to asking Roxanne if she'd help greet passengers in the reception line for the captain's farewell party.

They were still docked in Quebec City. From the high rail he could see the pretty hills, the steep streets, the elegance of the towering Château Frontenac. It had been fun to wander through the old town with her, hearing her laugh, watching her eyes light up.

He didn't know how he was going to get through the next five weeks being so goddamn brotherly.

He turned. Most of the deck chairs were empty. Because they wouldn't sail until seven that evening, many of the passengers would stay ashore until deadline. Those who preferred relaxing on board were two decks below, indulging in the delicate pastries being served at tea.

But Roxanne was here, stretched out on a deck chair, mirrored sunglasses shading her eyes, a book in her hands, and an unbearably tiny bikini covering no more than was required by law.

Luke swore viciously under his breath before crossing to her.

She knew he was there, had known from the moment he reached the top of the stairs and turned toward the rail. She'd been staring at the same page in her novel for five full minutes, and was grateful for the time to whip her heart rate under control.

Leisurely she turned the page then reached out for the lukewarm soft drink on the table beside her.

"You like to live dangerously."

She glanced up, arched a brow, then tipped her glasses down just far enough to look over the tops. "Do I?"

"A redhead sitting in the sun's just asking to burn." In truth her skin had neither burned nor tanned. It had simply bloomed, gorgeously, like a ripening peach.

"I don't stay out long." She smiled and pushed her glasses back into place. A healthy ripple of lust swam through her. "And I'm just slathered all over with lotion." Very slowly, she skimmed a fingertip up a glistening thigh. "Did you give Lily the lace fan you bought her?"

"Yeah." To make certain they behaved, Luke tucked his itchy hands in his pockets. "You were right. She was crazy about it."

"See? You only have to trust me."

She shifted, only a little, but he was aware of every muscle, every detail. The tiny hoops in her ears, the glint of the delicate gold chain with its slim amethyst crystal around her neck, the way her hair curled riotously where she tied it on top of her head, the erotic scent of the lotion she'd slicked over her skin.

Murder was too good for her.

"Jack wanted to know if you could do the reception line tonight. One of the girls is fighting off a virus."

"Oh, I think I could manage that." She slid her foot up the chair and lazily scratched her knee. "Want a sip?" She offered the watered-down Coke. "You look hot."

"I'm fine." Or he would be once he managed to move the feet that seemed nailed to the deck by her chair. "Shouldn't you go in and get ready?"

"I've got plenty of time. Do me a favor?" She stretched once, cat-like, before she picked up the bottle of lotion and tossed it to him. "Do my back, okay?"

"Your back?"

"Um-hmm." Shifting again, she lowered the back of the chair, rolled over and snuggled down. "I can't reach it."

He was surprised the lotion didn't geyser out the top as he squeezed the bottle so tightly. "Your back looks fine."

"Be a pal." After pillowing her head on her hands, she sighed like a woman relaxed. But behind the mirrored lenses her eyes were open and watchful. "It wouldn't do for me to ask one of the deckhands."

That did it. Setting his teeth, he crouched down and squeezed lotion on her shoulder blades. She sighed again, her lips curving.

"Feels good," she murmured. "Warm."

"Having the bottle in the sun could account for it." He began to spread the lotion with his fingertips, objectively, he thought. After all, it was only a back. Skin and bone. Soft, satiny skin. Long, delicate bones. She moved sinuously under his hands, and he bit back a moan.

Her toes were curling. His hands were magic on her slippery skin, conjuring up images, lighting fires, fogging the brain. Still, Luke wasn't the only one who knew about image and control. Her voice might have been husky when she spoke, but Roxanne thought that could be attributed to a state of relaxation as easily as arousal.

"You have to unhook the top."

The hands circling her back paused. Her glasses tossed back the reflection of his stunned face. "Excuse me?"

"The top," she repeated. "Unhook it or I'll get a line."

"Right." No big deal, he told himself, but his fingers reached and pulled back from the simple hook twice before he was satisfied with his willpower.

Now Roxanne did close her eyes, the better to absorb each rippling sensation. "Mmmm. You could get a job belowdecks with Inga."

"Inga?" Odd, he didn't think he'd ever noticed how subtly her back tapered down to her waist.

"The masseuse. I had a thirty-minute session last night, but she's got nothing on you, Callahan. Daddy's always admired your hands, you know?" Her chuckle was shaky as he trailed his fingers down to the small of her back. If she didn't laugh, she'd groan. "For entirely different reasons, of course. As for me, I..." She trailed off on a throaty sigh when he smoothed his palms down her rib cage.

Good God, her bones were melting under his hands. It was an impossibly erotic sensation to have her grow warmer, more fluid with each stroke. The nape of her neck tempted him desperately. His mouth watered at the thought of pressing his lips just there, tasting that lotion-slicked skin and feeling her tremble. It took little imagination to conjure a fantasy of her rolling over, that ridiculous band of emerald falling away as she let him explore those sleek curves. She'd groan for him, reach for him, open for him.

And then, at last then...

It was the sound of his own unsteady breathing that pulled him back. His hands were poised on the sides of her breasts, his fingers on the point of sliding beneath to claim that silky fullness.

She was trembling, as obviously and completely aroused as he.

They were on an open deck, he thought in disgust. In full sunlight. Worse, much worse, they were as closely related as two people could be without sharing blood.

He snatched his hands back, capped the bottle after two fumbling attempts. "That'll do it."

Her system shuddered with the broken promise of fulfillment. Roxanne lifted her head, bringing one hand up automatically to hold the loosened top in place, using the other to lower her glasses again. This time the eyes behind them were dark and heavy. "Will it?"

Furious with the ease with which she could undermine his willpower, he clamped tense fingers on her jaw. "I've just seen to it you won't get burned, Rox. Do us both a favor, and keep your distance from the heat."

She forced her lips into a smile. "Which one of us are you afraid for, Callahan?"

Because he didn't know the answer, he pulled back and stood. "Don't push your luck, Roxy."

But she intended to push it, she thought when he strode across the deck and down the iron stairs. She intended to push until it broke, one way or the other.

"Who you mad at, *loup?*"

"No one." Luke stood with LeClerc outside the casino, watching the dancers sway on the postage-stamp dance floor in the Monte Carlo Lounge. The quartet of Polish musicians was playing "Night and Day" with a touch of bebop.

"So why you scowl?" LeClerc yanked at the detested tie he was obliged to wear on this last formal night of the first cruise. "That look in your eye makes the menfolk back away, and the women sigh and shiver."

Despite his mood, Luke's lips twitched. "Maybe that's how I like it. Where's that silver-haired French fox you've been sniffing around?"

"Marie-Clair. She'll be along." LeClerc chewed on his pipe while Luke lit a cigar. "A handsome woman, that. Meat on the bone and fire in the belly." He grinned, making the pipe stem rattle against his teeth. "A rich widow is a gift from God to a man. She has jewelry. Ah." He kissed his fingers and sighed. "Last night, I held her opal pendant in my hand. Ten carats, *mon ami,* perhaps twelve, circled by a dozen ten-point diamonds. But you and the rest, you make me feel guilty for even thinking about taking it from her. So tomorrow, I will bid her *adieu,* and she will go home to Montreal with her opal and her diamonds, with a ruby ring of exquisite proportion, and numerous other treasures that break the heart. Only her virtue will I have stolen."

Amused, Luke laid a hand on LeClerc's shoulder. "Sometimes, *mon ami,* that is enough." He glanced toward the forward entrance of the lounge.

Roxanne stood with her hand being kissed by the ship's first officer. The fact that the man was tall and bronzed and Greek was bad enough. Insult was added to injury by the sound of Roxanne's low laughter.

Her dress was a short, shimmery swath of aquamarine. Without benefit of straps, it left Roxanne's arms and shoulders bare. It dispensed with a back altogether. What little material there was draped low at the hips and stopped teasingly at mid-thigh.

The skin she'd warmed in the sun that afternoon glowed pale gold against the dreamy blue. She caught up her hair in a jeweled pin so that its mass tempted a man to free it and watch it spill fire.

"She's not going to get away with it."

"Eh?"

"I know what she's up to," Luke said under his breath. "And it's not going to work." He stalked off to the bar to indulge in a single whiskey. LeClerc stayed where he was and chuckled.

"It's already worked, *mon cher loup.* The wolf is trapped by the vixen."

Two hours later, Roxanne stood in the shadows behind the stage awaiting her first cue. The show on the last night of the cruise involved all the entertainers. For their part, the Nouvelles intended to leave them gasping.

Max and Lily were cashing in by leading off with one of their variations on the Divided Woman. The moment Lily was put back together for bows, Luke dashed out to keep the crowd warm with patter and pick-pocket routines.

While explaining the escape he planned with handcuffs and a locked trunk, he called for two volunteers from the audience, then proceeded to steal them blind, to the delight of the onlookers.

A shake of hands, and he dangled the first man's watch behind his head, while continuing to distract his two baffled volunteers with the handcuffs he offered for examination. He lifted wallets, penknives and pocket change from under their noses.

"Now, once they're locked on, I'll have thirty seconds. Harry?" He smiled at the short, bespectacled man beside him. "I can call you Harry?"

"Sure."

"Well, Harry, I'm going to want you to time me. Got a second hand on your watch?"

"Oh, yeah." All cooperation, Harry turned his wrist and frowned at his bare wrist.

"He's really good, isn't he?" Dori peeked over Roxanne's shoulder.

Luke finished up the routine, making both men grin sheepishly as he passed back their belongings. The orchestra struck up a lively tune, indicating the finish. "You were great. You can relax now. Take it easy." He winked, handing Harry the tie he'd removed from the man's neck. Then he made a business out of brushing down Harry's shirt, fussing with his jacket, tugging the sleeves.

"What's he doing? Playing valet?" Dori demanded.

"Just watch."

Luke tugged and smoothed and plucked, then stuck out his hand again for a last hearty shake. As Harry turned to walk offstage, Luke grasped the back of his shirt collar. A flick of the wrist and he held Harry's baby-blue Arrow while the man goggled down at his bare chest showing beneath his suit jacket.

"Holy cow! How'd he do that? How'd he get the arms out of the jacket?"

Roxanne laughed, as she did every time she watched Luke pull off that particular trick. "Sorry, trade secret." Roxanne grinned as she left to make her entrance.

She was working with Luke at this point, flying through a fast-moving sleight-of-hand duel from either side of the stage. Her costume mirrored his as well, a tailored tux with spangled lapels. Precision timing was as essential as dexterity. Objects appeared and disappeared out of their hands, multiplied and changed color and size.

To cap off the act, Luke made good on his promise of the trunk escape, cajoling what appeared to be reluctant assistance from Roxanne.

"Come on, Roxy, don't embarrass me in front of all these nice people."

"Do it yourself, Callahan. I know what happened last time."

Luke turned toward the audience and spread his hands. "So she vanished for a couple of hours. I got her back eventually."

"No."

"Give me a break." She shook her head again, and he sighed theatrically. "Okay, just hold up the curtain for me then."

She studied him through narrowed, suspicious eyes. "You just want me to hold up the curtain."

"Yeah."

"No funny business?"

"Absolutely not." He turned to the side with an exaggerated wink.

"Okay. I'll do it, but only because the audience is so great. Tell you what, I'll even do the cuffs for you."

She dangled them, making the audience howl with laughter as Luke opened his eyes wide and patted his pockets.

"Pretty slick, Roxanne."

"I've got plenty of tricks up my sleeves. Assume the position, Callahan."

The music bounced out again as he offered his wrists. With big, exaggerated moves, Roxanne clamped the cuffs, locked them and pulled out a chain to wrap around his hands for good measure. She then turned the trunk in a circle, opening the lid so everyone could see it had four sides and a bottom. Luke climbed in and, taking advantage of his imprisoned hands, she bent to give him a hard kiss.

"For luck." Then she shoved his head down and lowered the top. She fastened the bolts, taking a key from her pocket to lock each one. Using a four-sided white curtain, she stood on the lid, letting the material drop until it had covered everything from her chin down.

"On the count of three," she called out. "One. Two."

Her head disappeared and Luke's popped up. "Three."

The audience erupted with applause, continuing to thunder it out after Luke dropped the curtain. He wore a white tux now, spangled with silver. He took his bow with a flourish before glancing absently over his shoulder. Banging sounded from inside the box.

"Whoops. Forgot something." He snapped his fingers and revealed a key. After using it to unlock the trunk, he pushed the bolts back and threw up the lid.

"Cute, Callahan. Real cute."

He only grinned, reaching down and lifting Roxanne out of the trunk into his arms. She, too, wore a white tuxedo, and now her hands were cuffed and chained. He took a final bow with her in his arms, then carried her offstage.

"Got it?" he murmured.

"Almost. Now."

He turned back toward the applause. He still carried her, only now her hands were free and his were cuffed.

"You could have been a couple seconds faster," he complained when he set her down in front of her dressing room. "You were a beat behind all during the sleight of hand."

"No, you were a beat ahead." She smiled because she'd felt how hard his heart had been thumping when he'd carried her offstage. "Want to fight, Callahan?"

"No. Just work on your damn timing."

"I've got it down," she murmured when he turned away.

She certainly hoped she did. God knew she was nervous as a cat, but it was now or never. For the fifth time, she checked out her appearance in the mirror. Her hair was artfully tousled, her face just touched with the most subtle of cosmetics. The long robe of ivory silk clung lovingly to each curve. She spritzed some scent into the air, then walked through the cloud of fragrance. With her mind made up, she kept walking out her cabin door, down the passageway and across the hall to Luke's.

He'd stripped down to gray sweatpants and was trying to ease his mind toward sleep by working out the bugs in a new escape.

He only grunted when he heard the knock on the door. His absent glance up as the door opened turned into a gape when he saw Roxanne.

"What? What? Is something wrong?"

"I don't think so." She leaned back against the door. It wasn't a provocative move as much as one designed to give her legs a chance to stop shaking. She turned the lock. "I'm working on my timing," she said as she crossed the room. He rose, braced to ward her off. She had only to lay her palm against the bare skin of his chest to break through the guard and make him quiver.

"You were right." She spread her fingers wide over the thud of his heart. The sensation made her bold, reckless, needy. "About my timing? This is something I should have moved on a long time ago."

He could feel his nerves grind and scream like crashing gears. She smelled like sin. "I'm busy, Roxanne, and it's too late for riddles."

"You already have the answer to this one." With a low, careless laugh, she skimmed her hands up his chest to his shoulders. The muscles there were bunched tight. "What do you get when you put a man and a woman together alone, at night, in a small room?"

"I said—" But she moved quickly, and covered his mouth with hers. There was little he could do about the response that leaped into his system, the way a tiger leaps through the open doors of a cage. But he could keep it from going any further. He prayed to God he could.

"There." She brushed her lips over his once, twice, before drawing back just enough to smile into his eyes. "I knew you had the answer."

It cost him dearly, but he let his hands fall away and sidestepped. "Game's over. Now get lost. I've got work to do."

The hurt snuck through, fast as a stiletto, and pierced. Okay, she thought, she might bleed, but she wasn't backing down without a fight. She was at the seduction stage of Dori's advice. Damned if she'd let him see how terrified she was.

"That didn't work very well when I was twelve." She stepped closer, out of the light, into the shadows, effectively maneuvering him into the corner. "It doesn't work at all now. You watch me." The curve of her lips was witchlike, powerful in its confidence. She stepped closer yet so that his hands shot out to take her arms and prevent her body from brushing dangerously against his. "I can feel you watch me when I'm across a room. I can almost hear what you're thinking when you do." Her eyes were like dark, deep seas, and he was already drowning. When she spoke, her voice misted over him like fog. "You wonder what it would be like between us." She cupped a hand on his chin, trailing those long fingers down his jaw. Everything he felt, everything he wanted, careened from his brain to thunder in the blood. "So do I. You wonder what it would feel like to have me, to do all those secret things you've wanted to do. And so do I."

He had to fight every breath into his lungs. Each gulp he took carried the scent of her into his system until he thought he'd explode. If this was seduction, he'd never experienced it before, never imagined she could wrap the hot chains of it so expertly around him. Trapped, was all he could think. He was trapped in a cage of unspeakable needs and the only door out was his own draining will.

The lamplight shimmered in her hair. Before he could think, he'd lifted a hand and had taken a fistful of flame.

"You don't know what I want to do. If you did, you'd run screaming."

Her body leaned forward with a longing much stronger than fear. "I'm not running. I'm not afraid."

"You haven't the sense to be." But he did. He released her hair and shoved her away in one jerky movement. "I'm not one of your trusty college boys, Rox. I wouldn't be polite and make promises and tell you what you think you want to hear. I've got where I came from inside me, and it's staying there, whatever shows on the outside." She saw a flare in his eyes—self-disgust, regret, anger—she couldn't be sure. Then it was gone. "So be a good girl and run along."

She felt the prickle of tears at the back of her throat, but her head remained high, her eyes dry. "I've never been a good girl. And I'm not going anywhere."

He sighed. There was such amused exasperation in it, she winced. "Roxy, you're putting me in the position where I have to hurt your feelings." With legs that felt like brittle glass, he walked over and patted her head. A slap, he knew, would have been less insulting. "I know you worked yourself up to try out this big seduction scene. And I'm flattered, really, that you've got this crush on me."

"Crush?" she managed when she found her voice. He could see by the daggers in her eyes he'd pressed the right button.

"It's sweet, and I appreciate it, but I'm just not interested. You're not my type, babe." He leaned casually against the dresser. "You're pretty, and I'm not going to pretend that I haven't had a couple of interesting fantasies over the years when you've been co-star, but let's get real."

"You..." The stab of rejection nearly brought her to her knees. "You're saying you don't want me."

"That's as clear as it gets." He plucked a cigar off the dresser. "I don't want you, Roxanne."

She would have believed him. His voice was so mild, so insultingly apologetic and understanding. There was a light of amusement in his eyes that sliced like a blade and the faintest of smiles on his lips. She would have believed him. But she saw that his hands were clenched into fists so tight the knuckles were white. He'd already mangled the cigar.

She kept her eyes cast down a moment, knowing she needed that long to put out the gleam of triumph in them. "Well, all right, Luke. I'll only ask one thing."

He took one measured breath, tasted relief. "Don't worry, Rox, I won't mention this to anyone."

"That's not it." She brought her head up and the staggering power of her beauty wiped the easy smile off his face. "The one thing I have to ask you is—prove it."

She reached up and untied the belt at her waist.

"Stop it." He dropped the crushed cigar and backed up. "Christ, Roxanne, what do you think you're doing?"

"Just showing you what you claim not to want." Watching him, she rolled her shoulders and sent the ivory silk slithering to the floor. There was more silk beneath it, a thin chemise of that same soft ivory, trimmed in lace. While he tried to catch his breath, one slender strap slipped seductively from her shoulder. "If you're telling the truth, it shouldn't be any problem. Should it?"

"Get dressed." His voice had thickened like a drunk's. "Get out. Don't you have any pride?"

"Oh, I've got plenty of that." And it swelled as she saw the helpless desire in his eyes. "What I seem to be lacking at the moment is shame." The silk whispered against her flesh as she walked to him. "At the moment," she murmured, winding her arms around his neck, "I don't seem to have an ounce of shame." Tilting her head she nipped at his bottom lip. His groan had her letting loose one low laugh. "Tell me again you're not interested." Her lips parted, full of demands against his. "Tell me again."

"Damn you, Rox." His hands were in her hair again, fisted. "Is that what you want?" He swung her around so that she rammed into the dresser as his mouth plundered hers. "You want to see what I can do to you, what I can make you do?" The part of him that still hoped to survive grasped on to heartlessness to push her away. "You want to be used up and tossed aside?"

She threw her head back. "Try it."

He cursed her, he berated them both, every time he dragged his mouth from hers. The war raged in him even as he pulled her to the bed and tumbled onto the mattress with her. Without care, without compassion, he took his hands over her, ripping the silk, bruising flesh, hating himself for the thrill of excitement that racked him each time she whimpered or moaned.

He'd send them both to hell, he thought. But, by God, they'd take a fast, hot ride through heaven first.

Through a maze of needs and fears she recognized his anger. And his greed. He'd lied, she thought, crying out when his mouth closed hungrily over her breast.

Oh, how he'd lied.

She twined her fingers through his hair and shuddered. This was truth, this desperate, clawing chaos of sensation was truth. All the rest was illusion, pretense, deception.

He was breathless when he lifted his head to stare at her. Breathless and beaten. But somehow the anger had vanished, like a conjurer in a puff of smoke.

Beneath him her body was vibrating, like a finely tuned engine revving to race. He could drive her, that he understood, but he was afraid, horribly afraid that he would lose control until they crashed and burned.

Knowing he was lost, he lowered his forehead to hers. "Oh, Rox," he murmured and stroked his fingers gently over her shoulders.

With no hesitation she wrapped her arms around him. "Listen to me, Callahan, if you stop now, I'll have to kill you."

The laugh was a relief, though it didn't begin to ease the tension balled in his gut. "Roxy, the only way I could stop now is if I were already dead." He lifted his head. She recognized the concentration on his face, the same as she'd seen dozens of times as he prepared for a complicated illusion or a dangerous escape. "We crossed the line, Roxanne. I can't let you go tonight."

Her smile bloomed slowly. "Thank God."

He shook his head. "You'd do better to pray," he warned her, and lowered his mouth to hers.

19

At last. It was the final coherent thought that passed through Roxanne's mind as Luke's mouth fixed hot and open on hers. At long last.

Another woman might have wanted soft words, slow hands, gentle persuasion. She had no need for that now. Every wish she'd ever held close, every fantasy she'd ever woven in secret was granted by the wild, willful demands of his hands and lips.

She gave him the most coveted and elusive gift a woman can grant a man. Complete surrender.

That was her power, and her triumph.

Needs that had budded slyly inside her flashed into full bloom. Fears tangled with them, creating an ache so fierce she shook from it. She hadn't known, not even in her most secret imaginings had she known it was possible to feel like this.

Helpless and strong. Dizzy and sane.

She laughed again, from the sheer glory of it, that reckless, rushing roller coaster ride, speeding uphill, plunging down whippy turns, flashing through dark, dark tunnels of secret desires. She clung, not for support, but to be sure, very sure, he joined her in that same thrilling race.

Every sigh, every gasp intensified his greed. It was Roxanne beneath him, her slim, agile body trembling at his touch, her eager mouth meeting his, her scent crowding reason from his brain.

He didn't need to think—no longer had the faculties to think. Later he would remember Max talking of the animal taking over. But for now, Luke was no more than that, taking what his body so violently craved.

The light still burned brightly, far from loverlike. The spread they'd neglected to turn down was stiff and nubby against flesh. The narrow bed swayed with the roll of the ship. But she arched against him and there was nothing but her, and what she so recklessly offered.

He wanted more, needed more, and tore the tattered remains of her chemise aside to find all of her.

Impatient, urgent, his hand streaked down and found her already hot and wet and waiting. With one rough stroke he drove her hard to a first towering climax.

She felt as though she'd been ripped in two as easily as the ivory silk. Her body jerked, convulsed, exploded before her mind had a chance to catch up. Even as she reared forward, shocked and dazzled, he was shoving her back roughly again, devouring damp, trembling flesh.

She wanted to tell him to wait, to give her a moment to catch her breath and her reason. But he dragged her ruthlessly up again until the breath was sobbing in her lungs and reason was impossible.

Ravenous, he feasted on her breasts, one, then the other, using teeth and tongue and lips so that the answering ache deep in her center spread until even her bones throbbed with it.

"Please." Her hands searched for purchase, fingers gripping urgently in the tousled spread. "Please," she moaned again without shame.

Breath heaving, he dragged the loose sweats over his hips. The blood was pounding in his head, beating mercilessly in his loins. He was quivering like a stallion when he mounted her, then cupped her hips to lift them and plunged deep.

She cried out, arching like a bow when the pain tore through her, a white flash, icy against the heat. Her hips jerked as she sought escape and ripped a moan from him.

"Oh, Jesus, Roxanne." Sweat pearled on his brow as he fought every instinct to remain still, not to hurt her again. "Sweet God."

A virgin. He shook his head in a desperate attempt to clear it even as his body vibrated on the razor's edge between frustration and completion. She'd been a virgin, and he'd slammed into her like a fucking Mack truck.

"I'm sorry. Baby, I'm sorry." Useless words, he thought as he watched the first tears spill over onto her cheeks. He levered his arms, the muscles trembling, and braced himself to slip out of her as gently as possible. "I'm not going to hurt you."

Her breath shuddered through her lips. There was pain yet, radiating pain, and a softer, deeper ache. Mixing through both was a sense of glory not yet reached. She arched her hips instinctively when she felt him retreat from her.

"Don't move." His stomach twisted into slippery knots as she drew him back in. "For God's sake don't..." The rippling pleasure almost drove him mad. "I'm going to stop."

She opened her eyes and locked them on his. "The hell you are." Braced for the next slash of pain, she gripped his hips. She thought she heard him swear. But she couldn't be sure. For there was no pain at all, just a deep, grinding, glorious pleasure. She hurled herself into it, felt it spin and shudder through her system so that there was nothing else, nothing but the wild delight of finding a mate.

He couldn't resist. His body betrayed him, and he thanked God for it. He buried his face in her hair and let her take him.

Her body felt as delicate as glass. She was afraid to move for fear that she would break apart into thousands of glittery pieces. So this was what the poets wept for, she thought. Her lips curved, smugly. It had certainly been nice, though she doubted she'd compose sonnets about the event.

But this part. She sighed and risked moving her hand to stroke Luke's back. This part was lovely, lying here feeling her lover's heart thud fast and hard against hers. She could happily stay just so for days.

But he moved. Roxanne winced as the bed shifted. She was more than a little sore where Luke had invaded her. Not wanting to lose the close, warm feelings, she curled against him as he rolled onto his back.

There weren't names foul enough to call himself, he thought as he stared up at the ceiling. He'd taken her like an animal, without care, without finesse. He shut his eyes. If the guilt didn't kill him, Max would.

Until then, he had to do something to fix what he'd so heedlessly destroyed.

"Rox."

"Hmmm."

"I'm responsible."

Dreaming, she nestled her head more comfortably on his shoulder.

" 'Kay."

"I don't want you to worry about it, or feel guilty."

"About what?"

"This." Impatience shimmering in his voice. Did she have to sound so sleepy, so sexy, so damned satisfied? "It was a mistake, but it doesn't have to ruin anything."

Roxanne opened one eye, then the other. The smile that had curved her lips turned into a frown. "A mistake? You're telling me what just happened here was a mistake?"

"Of course it was." He rolled off the bed, searching for his sweats before his body lured him into repeating it. "In dozens of ways." He looked back at her, setting his teeth. She was sitting up now, her tousled hair falling over her shoulders, curling seductively over her breasts. The stain of blood on the rumpled spread knocked the worst of his mounting desire out of him.

"Really?" The lovely, dreamy feeling had vanished. If Luke hadn't been so involved with cursing himself, he would have recognized the light of battle in her eyes. "Why don't you tell me some of those ways?"

"For Christ's sake, you're practically my sister."

"Ah." She folded her arms, stiffened her shoulders. It would have been a tough stance if she hadn't been buck naked. "I think the operative word there is practically. There's no blood between us, Callahan."

"Max took me in." To help him keep his sanity, Luke yanked open a drawer and found a shirt. He tossed it to Roxanne. "He gave me a home, a life. I've betrayed that."

"Bullshit." She heaved the shirt back at him. "Yes, he took you in and gave you a home. But what happened here was between us, just us. It has nothing to do with Max or betrayal."

"He trusted me." Grimly, Luke stepped over and shoved the shirt over Roxanne's head. She slapped his hands away and sprang to her feet.

"Do you think Max would be shocked and angry because we want each other?" Furious, she yanked the shirt off her shoulders and sent it sailing. "You're not my brother, damn it, and if you're going to stand there and tell me you thought of me as your sister a few minutes ago, you're a goddamn liar."

"No, I didn't think of you as my sister." He gripped her shoulders and shook. "I didn't think at all, that's the problem. I wanted you. I've wanted you for years. It's eaten me from the inside out."

She tossed her head back. The gesture was a challenge, but a soft warmth was kindling inside her. For years. He'd wanted her for years. "So you've been playing games with me, running hot then cold since I was sixteen. All because you wanted me and had it twisted around in your tiny brain that acting on it would be some sort of what—emotional incest?"

He opened his mouth, shut it again. Why did it suddenly sound so ridiculous? "Close enough."

He didn't know what response he expected from her, but it certainly wasn't laughter. She shouted with it until tears sprang to her eyes. Holding her sides, she sat on the side of the bed. "Oh, you jerk."

His pride was at stake. Damned if he'd admit that a naked woman, bowled over with laughter at his expense, could arouse him until he was ready to whimper and beg.

"I don't see that this is a laughing matter."

"Are you kidding? It's a riot." She pushed her hair out of her face and beamed at him. "And terribly sweet, too. Were you protecting my honor, Luke?"

"Shut up."

She only chuckled and scrubbed amused tears from her cheeks. "Think about it, Callahan. Really think for a minute. You're standing there, riddled with guilt over the idea of making love to a woman who used every means available to seduce you, a woman you've known most of your life—one who is not, I repeat, is not in any way, shape or form related to you. A single woman, over the age of consent. You don't think that's funny?"

He shoved his hands in his pockets and scowled. "Not particularly."

"You're losing your sense of humor." She rose then and wound her arms around him. Her naked breasts brushed his chest and she had the satisfaction of feeling his muscles quiver. But he didn't return the embrace. "I guess if you feel this way, I'll have to seduce you every time. I suppose I'm up to it." She nibbled lightly at his lips, smiling when she glanced down between them. "And it appears you are, as well."

"Cut it out." But the order lacked conviction. "Even if I've been off base about that, there are other things."

"Okay." She trailed her fingers down his back, played light kisses over his throat. "Let's hear them."

"Damn it, you were a virgin." He took her arms, pulled her back so he could escape.

"That bothers you?" She pouted a moment, thinking it through. "I always thought men got a charge out of that. You know, the *Star Trek* syndrome."

"What?"

"To boldly go where no man has gone before."

He strangled back a laugh. "Christ." He wished he had a beer—hell, he wished he had a frigging six-pack, but settled on a warm bottle of mineral water. "Look, Roxanne, the point is I didn't do it right."

"You didn't?" She tilted her head, curious. "I can't imagine there are that many ways to do it."

He choked, cautiously set the bottle down again. Not only a virgin, God help him, but impossibly, and yes, damn it, erotically innocent. "What the hell was wrong with all those college boys? Didn't they know what to do with you?"

"I imagine they did—if I'd wanted them to do anything." She smiled again, secure in her power. When she spoke again, her voice was soft. "I wanted you to be the first." She saw the raw emotion in his eyes as she stepped to him again. "I only wanted you."

No one and nothing had ever moved him more. Gently, he touched a hand to her hair. "I hurt you. If you stay with me I'll probably hurt you again. What I said before about what's inside me, it's the truth. There are things you don't know. If you did—"

"I do know." She slid a hand to his back, running fingers over scars. "I've known for years, since the day you told Max. I listened to you. I cried for you. Don't." She wrapped her arms tight around him before he could turn away. "Do you really believe that I'd think less of you because of what was done to you as a child?"

"I'm not good with pity," he said tightly.

"I'm not giving you any." Her eyes were dark and fierce when she tilted back her head. "But understanding, the kind you'll have to take, the kind you can only get from someone who's known you, and loved you all of her life."

Drained, he rested his brow on hers. "I don't know what to say to you."

"Don't say anything. Just be with me."

There was little time to enjoy the sensation of awakening in Luke's arms, and none at all for lazing through the morning. Roxanne took only a moment to cuddle closer as she listened to the announcements from the passageway intercom listing disembarkation structures. One long, sleepy kiss, a few groans of frustration and she was up, tugging on Luke's sweats and the T-shirt she'd rejected the night before. Holding the sweats up to her slim waist with one hand, she cracked open the cabin door and scanned the passageway. Because Luke was laughing behind her, she shot a look over her shoulder.

Her hair was tousled, her face flushed, her eyes heavy and dreamy. She looked, he thought as his breath caught, exactly like what she was. A woman who'd spent the night with her lover.

And he was her lover. Her first. Her only.

"All hands on deck, Callahan." Her voice was morning husky. "See you in fifteen minutes."

"Aye, aye."

Gripping the sweats securely, Roxanne dashed to her own cabin. A stickler for promptness, she reported to the Lido Deck within a quarter hour. Passengers were gathered in the lounges, carry-on and shopping bags pooled around them while they yawned, chatted and waited for their turn to leave the ship. Every few moments the announcement would be made in English, then in French, inviting passengers holding certain colored baggage tags to disembark. They went through red, blue, white, yellow, red with white stripes, white with green stripes. Roxanne shook hands, had her cheek kissed and exchanged hugs while the noise level gradually decreased.

By ten only crew and the small percentage of passengers cruising back to New York were on board. New passengers wouldn't trickle on board until one o'clock. Max took advantage of the lull to call a rehearsal.

It was good to see Max back in stride, she thought. A slower stride than she was used to, but without the hesitation and hitches that had worried her.

She thought she did very well, moving through card tricks, rope tricks and bigger illusions without giving away what was in her mind and heart. Images of Luke tumbling her onto the bed, flashes of memory that brought heat and pleasure were held very strictly under control. She was satisfied that no one knew the dramatic turn her life had taken but herself, and the man who had taken it with her.

But of course love is blind.

Lily sighed every time she glanced in their direction. Her romantic heart wept happy tears. LeClerc's lips twitched. Even Mouse, who'd spent most of his life oblivious to the subtle exchanges between men and women, flushed and grinned.

Only Max seemed oblivious.

"Isn't it wonderful?" Lily sighed again when she and Max took the hour of free time left to them on the nearly deserted Lido Deck with cups of bouillon and herbal tea.

"It certainly is." He patted her hand, thinking she was speaking of the quiet moment, the cooling breeze and the view of Montreal from the port side.

"It's like having your fondest dream come true." She lifted her teacup, her trio of rings sparkling. "I was beginning to think it would never happen."

"It's been a busy week," he agreed. And he hadn't had nearly enough time to continue his research on the philosophers' stone. Perhaps when they docked in Sydney, he could make an excuse not to play tourist and spend a few hours with his books and notes. He was getting closer. He could feel it.

"I wonder if being on a ship like this helped. I mean, in close quarters—sort of in each other's pockets. They couldn't keep avoiding each other."

"Certainly not." Max blinked and frowned. "Who?"

"Roxy and Luke, silly." Bracing her elbows on the table, she sighed dreamily. "I bet they're strolling hand in hand through Montreal right now."

"Roxanne and Luke?" was all Max could think of to say. "Roxanne and Luke?"

"Well, sure, honey. What'd you think I was talking about?" She laughed, enjoying, as women do, that superiority over most males of the species on romance. "Didn't you see the way they were looking at each other this morning? It's a wonder the lounge didn't catch fire with all the sparks flying around."

"They always shot sparks off each other. They do nothing but argue."

"Honey, that was just a kind of mating ritual."

He choked on his tea. "Mating?" he said weakly. "My Jesus."

"Max, baby." Baffled and concerned, Lily took both of his hands. They trembled under hers. "You're not upset, not really, are you? They're so perfect for each other, and so much in love."

"You're saying that he's—that they've—" He couldn't get the words out.

"I wasn't a fly on the wall, but if this morning was any indication, I'd say they've done the deed." She'd kept her voice light, but when Max continued to stare, shell-shocked, her tone changed. "Max, you're not angry?"

"No. No." He shook his head, but had to stand. He walked to the rail like a man in a trance. His baby, he thought as a small piece of his heart ripped away. His little girl. And the boy he'd thought of as his own for so long. They'd grown up on him. Tears started in his eyes. "I should have seen it, I suppose," he murmured when Lily slipped an arm around him.

He shook his head again. The weak-hearted tears were gone as he drew her closer. "Will they have what we have, do you suppose?"

She leaned her head against his shoulder and smiled. "No one could, Max."

That night he came to her. She was waiting for him. No matter how sternly Roxanne told herself it was foolish, she was more nervous now than she had been before. It was a matter of control, she supposed. The night before, that first night, she had mapped the route, and had been so sure of the course.

Tonight, he would be taking her beyond.

She was grateful he hadn't come directly to her cabin after the last show, but had given her time to remove the stage makeup and change from the spangled costume into a simple blue robe. But that time alone had also worked against her, giving her heart the opportunity to beat too fast and hard.

It had been lovely that afternoon. They had done precisely what Lily had imagined for them. Strolling down Montreal's sloping sidewalks, listening to American music pouring through shop doorways, huddling together at a small table of an outdoor café.

Now they were alone again. The bouquet of flowers he'd brought her from a sidewalk vendor stood fragrantly on her dresser. The bed was neatly turned down. The deck swayed under her feet as the ship steamed south.

"It was a good crowd tonight." An idiotic thing to say, Roxanne berated herself.

"Enthusiastic." He flicked his wrist. A single white rosebud appeared in his hand. Roxanne felt her heart melt.

"Thanks." It would be fine, she told herself as she drew in the bud's bouquet. She knew what to expect now, and could look forward to the feel of his hands on her skin, the rough tumble into oblivion. The pain was fleeting after all. Surely a few moments' discomfort was a small price to pay for the lovely aftermath of lying curled in his arms.

He could read the nerves in her eyes as clearly as he could see their color. There was no use cursing himself again for his mindless initiation of the night before. At least he'd had the good sense to do nothing more than hold her throughout the rest of the night.

He touched a hand to her cheek and watched her eyes lift slowly from the rose to his face. He thanked God there was more than fear in them. He could make the fear vanish. He passed a hand in front of her face and made her laugh when she saw the candle between his fingers.

"Clever."

"You ain't seen nothing yet." He crossed to the dresser, slipping a crystal holder he'd palmed from the dining room from his pocket. He set the candle carefully in place, then snapped his fingers. The wick sputtered, caught and glowed.

A bit more relaxed, Roxanne smiled. "Shall I applaud?"

"Not yet." Watching her, he flicked off the lights, removed his jacket. "You can wait till the show's over."

Unconsciously, she brought a hand to her throat. "There's more?"

"Much more." He crossed to her. Perhaps it wasn't quite fair that he should be rewarded rather than whipped for his carelessness last night. But he was going to make it up to her. To both of them. He took the hand that was still splayed against her throat, turned it, pressed his fingers to the cup of her palm, to the fragile wrist where her pulse beat like thunder. "I told you there was more than one way, Roxanne." With her hand still tucked in his, he traced light kisses over her jawline. "But just like magic, showing's better than telling." He saw her lashes flutter down and slipped the rose from her limp fingers. "I won't hurt you again."

Her eyes opened at that. Doubts and needs warred within them. "It's all right," she murmured, and lifted her mouth toward his in invitation.

"Trust me."

"I do."

"No, you don't." He covered her waiting mouth, drawing the kiss out and out until she swayed. "But you will," he said and swept her into his arms.

She braced herself for the onslaught. A part of her burned for the feel of those hard strong hands, that urgent, demanding mouth. But his lips were soft tonight, soft, seductive, even soothing as they whispered over hers. The breathless, confused sound she made in the back of her throat made him smile.

"I have places to take you." His tongue dipped in, toyed with hers. "Magic places."

She had no choice but to follow where he led. Her body was floating before he ended that first, sumptuous kiss. Leaving her lips trembling for more, he took his own on a languorous journey, tasting her skin, lingering at the base of her throat while her pulse fluttered under his mouth like the heart of a caged bird.

The arms that had risen to enfold him went lax. And he knew she was his.

"I want to look at you," he whispered, gently sliding her robe aside. "Let me look at you."

Her beauty scorched his heart, made his blood churn like white water. But in the flickering light he touched her with fingertips only, skimming them over curves and dips, enchanted by the contrast of his flesh against hers, bewitched by the quick tremors each gentle caress tore from her.

"We were in a hurry before." Lowering his head, he gently, very gently laved her aching nipples with his tongue. "Maybe we'll be in a hurry later." When he straightened to look at her, he rolled the damp nipple between his thumb and forefinger pinching, tugging lightly to bring her helplessly to that staggering point between pleasure and pain. "But we'll take our time now, Roxanne." He trailed a finger down the center of her body, enjoying every quiver as he tangled through the soft triangle of hair to stroke the secret sensitive nub.

When her eyes glazed, when her breath caught and he felt the warm flow of her response, his head swam. But he only smiled.

"I want to do things to you. I want you to let me."

When he joined his mouth to hers again, he replaced his fingertips with the rose, sliding the silky petals over her breasts, teasing the nipples with its fragrant smoothness, following those subtle curves over waist and hips.

"Tell me what you like."

The breath shuddered from between her lips. She could see him in the candlelight. His chest was bare now, though she had no memory of him taking the time to shrug out of his shirt. She felt the heaviness of his arousal against her leg, and realized he was as naked as she.

"I can't." She lifted her hand to touch him through air that felt as sweet and thick as syrup. "Just don't stop."

"This?" He slid slowly down, teasing the nub of her breast with his tongue, catching it between his teeth before suckling as if he'd swallow her whole. She moaned, long and deep, thrilling him.

It was torture of the most exquisite. Drugging, aching pleasure glided through her until she thought she would die from it. The bed moaned, gave as he shifted. Her skin hummed under his hands, sang beneath the patient, questing mouth. When his tongue skimmed up her thigh, she understood there was no part of her he wouldn't claim, and nothing she would deny him.

She opened for him on a sigh of acceptance. All at once the soothing warmth exploded into heat, as if a comet had erupted in her and trailed its fire to every cell. Her cry of release trailed into a deep, throaty moan.

Still he was patient, relentlessly patient, stroking her up again, higher, waiting as she drifted down again.

Sighs and moans and whispered promises. The flicker of candlelight and the faintest hint of a moon, the scent of flowers and passion heady on the air. These she would remember, even as her body shuddered from the patient onslaught.

Oh, he did things to her, just as he'd promised. Exquisite, impossible, delicious things.

He showed her what it was to be desired, to be cherished, and at last, at last, what it was to be taken slowly, like sailing down a quiet river into a mist.

He slipped inside her painlessly, perfectly, and she was slick and hot and more than ready. Her body rose fluidly to welcome him. He hadn't known it could be so easy, that he could feel such sweet, sweet pain as she closed around him. The rhythm built, needs swelling like music in his head.

"Roxanne," Her name came hoarsely from his throat. He clung to the reins of his control like a man fighting a wild beast. "Look at me. I need you to look at me."

His voice seemed to come from the end of the long, dark tunnel in which her body was flying. She lifted heavy lids and saw only him. His eyes were a violent blue, like the heat at the center of flame.

"You belong to me now." He crushed his mouth to hers as the climax exploded inside her. Only me, he thought and let himself follow her.

She wasn't sure she could ever move again, but when she did it was to turn her head and seek his mouth. He responded with an unintelligible murmur and rolled to shift their positions.

"Better," she sighed, now that she could breathe again. She rubbed her cheek against his chest, and settled. "I didn't know it could be like that."

Neither had he. But Luke felt it would sound foolish to say it and stroked her hair instead. "I didn't hurt you?"

"No. I feel like . . ." She made a cat-in-cream sound. "Like I've been levitated up to the moon." She stroked a hand down his chest. When she cruised her fingers over his belly, she felt the muscles quiver. Well, well, she thought, smiling to herself. The power wasn't all one-sided. That would have to be put to good use very soon.

"So . . ." She lifted her head and grinned down at him. "Just how many ways are there, anyhow?"

He lifted a brow. "Why don't you give me a couple of minutes, and I'll show you."

Drunk on her own pleasures, Roxanne shifted to straddle him. "Why don't you show me now?" she suggested and closed her mouth over his.

20

Both Luke and Roxanne would have hotly denied any suggestion that they had fallen into a cliché such as a shipboard romance. Sea breezes, brilliant sunsets and moonlit decks might influence others, but never them. They both would have shrugged off the idea of a honeymoon, yet if the honest definition for that time-honored period was an opportunity to discover, to focus on a mate and to enjoy great sex, their honeymoon had cruised into its third week.

Discoveries were made. Much to Luke's relief, he learned that he wasn't a jealous fool. He actually enjoyed the way men's heads turned when Roxanne walked into a room. He could smile when he watched her flirt or be flirted with. Both were a matter of pride and confidence, laced with a touch of arrogance. She was beautiful, and she was his.

Roxanne discovered that beyond the tough, troubled boy she'd known most of her life, the man she'd fallen in love with could be gentle and kind. The veneer of sophistication and charm was a thin coat over a smoldering bed of passions. Yet mixed with those was a keen sense of loyalty and a yearning to love no less than her own.

Both were able to focus on each other, even in a room crowded with people. They didn't need to touch or speak, a look was enough to communicate.

Perhaps that was why the last requirement for a honeymoon fell so naturally into place.

Through this fantasy of days and nights, both agreed there was only one thing missing. They had yet to choose a genuine mark. Their thief's blood grew restless. True, they had stemmed the impatience temporarily by relieving a certain Mrs. Cassell of some antique marcasite and ruby jewelry. Since the old crab had spent her seven days on board the *Yankee Princess* complaining and demanding and making Jack's life as cruise director a living hell, the Nouvelles had considered it a matter of honor to give her something genuine to complain about.

But the job had been so pitifully simple. Roxanne had only to slip into Mrs. Cassell's cabin between cues and snatch the locked jewelry case from among the pile of half-packed luggage. One glance at the mechanism had her altering the plan. Rather than strolling out again and passing the case to Luke, she used one of Cassell's own hairpins to pick the lock. Once the marcasite was snugly in the pockets of her stage tux, she relocked the case, replaced it and slipped outside again.

As planned Luke was just coming through heading aft.

"Problem?"

She smiled. "Not at all." With one brow lifted, she patted her pockets. "I just need to get something from the cabin," she said as he grinned. "I won't miss my cue."

Luke snatched her into his arms for a kiss. His clever fingers dipped into her pockets to take inventory. "You got three minutes, Rox."

It took her less than half that to secure the cache in the false bottom of her makeup case. She had time to freshen the lipstick Luke had smudged and still hit her cue dead on.

They all agreed it was an elegant set, the craftsmanship exquisite, the stones quite good. But the lack of challenge took the sweetness out of it.

The Nouvelles, one and all, yearned for work.

"Maybe we should try something in one of the ports," Roxanne said absently. She and Lily stood on deck. New passengers boarding in Montreal were dribbling out, complimentary cocktails in hand, cameras at the ready. Luke and Mouse had trekked to Olympic Stadium to watch the Expos take on the Dodgers.

"I suppose we could." Lily's mind kept drifting back to Max. She'd stirred awake before dawn and had seen him on the narrow sofa beneath the porthole, his research books spread out around him. He'd been manipulating a coin between his fingers. The second time he'd fumbled and dropped it, she'd seen the pain in his face. A pain she knew she could never ease.

"I was thinking Newport," Roxanne went on. "The place is lousy with mansions. We could at least do some legwork the next time through."

"You're so like him." Lily sighed and turned from the rail. "If you're not in the middle of a project, you're planning one. It's the only way you're happy."

"Life's too short not to enjoy one's work." Her smile was quick and wicked. "God knows I love mine."

"What would you do if it all went away?" Lily's suddenly nervous fingers began to toy with the jade pendant Max had bought her in Halifax. "If you couldn't do it anymore. The magic or the other?"

"If I woke up one morning and it was all gone? If all that was left was the ordinary?" Roxanne pursed her lips in thought, then laughed. At twenty-one, it was impossible to believe that old age would ever apply to you. "Stick my head in the first convenient oven."

"Don't say that." Lily grabbed her hand, squeezing until the bones rubbed. "Don't ever say that."

"Darling, I'm only joking." Surprise widened her eyes. "You know me better. People who do something permanent like that have forgotten that nothing lasts forever. No matter how wonderful, or how awful, if you wait awhile, it changes."

"Of course it does." Feeling foolish, Lily loosened her grip, but her throat remained tight and dry. "Don't pay any attention to me, honey. I think I must be overtired."

Now that Roxanne looked, really looked, she could see the faint shadows beneath Lily's careful makeup. Surprise became concern. "Are you all right? Aren't you feeling well?"

"I'm fine." She'd lived on the stage long enough to show only what she wanted to show. "Just tired—and it's silly—but I think I'm a little homesick. I've had a yen for LeClerc's gumbo for days."

"I know what you mean." Because this so clearly mirrored her own feelings, Roxanne relaxed with a smile. "All this great food, and after a few weeks, you'd offer a hundred dollars for a cheeseburger and fries—and ten times that for an entire day where you didn't have to talk to anyone."

She needed time alone, Lily realized, before she blurted out her fears and miseries. "Well, I'm going to cheat." With a wink, she kissed Roxanne's cheek. "I'm ducking down to the cabin for an hour, giving myself a facial and a foot soak and a chapter of my romance novel."

"You're just saying that to make me jealous."

"Tell you what. Cover for me, and in an hour, I'll do the same for you."

"Deal. Anybody asks, I'll tell them you're tacking loose sequins back on your costume."

"That's a good one." She hurried off, wanting to be behind locked doors before she indulged in a good crying jag.

Alone, Roxanne glanced around the deck. New faces, she thought, new stories. She enjoyed variety, always had. But she couldn't help wishing that Luke was with her rather than chugging beer and damning umpires in two languages. It was more fun with him, studying faces, making up names and backgrounds.

By the time she'd answered the question of what it was like to work on a cruise ship for the tenth or twelfth time, she began to think an hour alone with a mud pack and a romance novel was a pretty good deal.

But she turned, her *Yankee Princess* smile in place, when her name was called yet again. The smile wavered for an instant, then held solidly. She was, after all, a pro.

"Sam. What a small, small world."

"Isn't it?" He might have stepped out of an article on cruisewear in *Gentleman's Quarterly*. His buff-colored trousers had knife-edged pleats that looked sharp enough to draw blood. His shirt was unpressed cotton—the type that cost the earth to look casual. His sockless feet were encased in Docksiders, and his arm was draped around a sleek and polished blonde. She wore billowy silk slacks in an aching blue to match her eyes, with a softly draped blouse in the same shade. Roxanne was more impressed with the simple strand of creamy pearls and their sapphire enhancer that was as big around as Mouse's thumb.

"Justine, darling, I'd like you to meet a very old friend. Roxanne Nouvelle. Roxanne, my wife, Justine Spring Wyatt."

"How nice." Justine offered a pleasant smile that didn't reach her eyes, and a quick firm handshake that pretended to be personable.

The perfect politician's wife, Roxanne decided. "My pleasure."

There were earrings as well, Roxanne noted. Two teardrop-shaped indigo stones dripping from lustrous pearls.

"I was amazed to see you on deck," Sam began. "Doubly amazed to see you're staff."

His gaze skimmed down to the name tag over her breast, lingered, then rose again. "Have you given up the magic business?"

"Not at all. We'll be performing on board for the next few weeks."

"Fabulous." He'd known, of course, had made it his business to know. He hadn't been able to resist the idea of spending a week with the Nouvelles. "Justine, Roxanne is quite an accomplished magician."

"How unusual." Her lips parted in a smile that revealed perfectly aligned teeth. "Do you perform for children's parties?"

"Not yet." Roxanne took a cocktail from a passing waiter's tray. "Is this your first trip on the *Yankee Princess?*"

"On this particular ship, yes. I've done quite a bit of cruising—the Caribbean, the Mediterranean, that sort of thing." She lifted a narrow white hand to toy absently with the enhancer. The diamonds circling the sapphire burst into tiny flames of light that stirred Roxanne's blood. The arousal was as thoroughly sexual as a long, slow, wet kiss.

"How nice." It took most of her control to resist licking her lips. "I hope you'll enjoy this cruise as much."

"I'm sure I will." The sapphire winked like a seductive eye. "I was delighted when Sam suggested this cruise as part of our honeymoon."

"Oh, you're newlyweds." Knowing it was a womanly gesture, considered harmless, Roxanne studied Justine's wedding ring set. Oh yes, she thought, ten carats, emerald cut for the engagement rock, and a nice platinum band studded with channel-set diamonds for the wedding ring. She yearned for her loupe. "How perfectly lovely. Congratulations, Sam."

"Thank you. I'd love to see your family again—and Luke, of course."

"I'm sure you will. Wonderful meeting you, Justine. Enjoy your cruise."

She was smiling when she walked away. At last, they'd found a worthy mark.

Luke took advantage of a lull to bake away fatigue in the sauna belowdecks. He doubted he'd had more than five hours' sleep a night since Roxanne had walked into his room armed with ivory silk and hot-blooded determination.

Not that he was complaining, but the sauna couldn't hurt. If nothing else it would give him a few minutes to clear his head and think through what Roxanne had told him when she'd tracked him down that afternoon.

Mr. and Mrs. Samuel Wyatt.

Of all the cruise ships in all the ports in all the world, he thought with a grimace. Well, hell, they were stuck for the next week. But he wasn't sure he shared Roxanne's enthusiasm for relieving the bride and groom of the lady's glitters.

No, he wanted to take that one slow, and careful, and calculate all the odds.

When the wooden door of the sauna room creaked open, Luke opened one eye. He shut it again and remained leaning against the back wall, the white towel carelessly hooked at his waist.

"Heard you slithered on board, Wyatt."

"And you're still pulling rabbits out of your ass for a living." Sam settled on the bench below Luke. It had taken only a few discreet inquiries to discover where Luke was spending his hour off. "And dancing to the old man's tune."

"Ever learn how to do a one-handed cut?"

"I gave up games quite some time ago."

Luke only smiled. "I didn't think so. You always had lousy hands—not good for much except pushing little girls around."

"You hold a grudge." Sam spread his arms comfortably on the bench. The years had been good to him. He'd jumped on the trend for physical fitness, and his body reflected his daily workouts with his personal trainer. He used his position, and now his wife's money, to indulge in hair stylists, manicurists, spas where they pampered the skin. He'd slipped seamlessly into his image of a young, attractive up-and-comer. Now he had wealth to ice the cake.

"Odd," he continued, "Roxanne doesn't appear to. She was quite—friendly earlier."

It wasn't rage, as it once might have been, that Luke experienced. It was pure amusement. "Pal, she'd chew you up and spit you out."

"Really?" Sam's arms tensed against the baking wood. There was one thing his position and his money hadn't been able to give him. A sense of humor about himself. "I think she might find me more her style than you realize. A woman like Roxanne would appreciate a man of position rather than one who has never been quite able to smooth off those rough edges. You're still a loser, Callahan."

"I'm still a lot of things." Luke opened his eyes and, tilting his head, studied Sam's face. "They did a good job on your nose. Nobody'd know it had been broken." He stretched lazily then climbed down. "Except me, of course. See you around."

Sam clenched and unclenched his fists as the door swung shut behind Luke. It appeared his old friend needed a harder lesson. A telegram to Cobb, perhaps, Sam thought, forcing his angry muscles to relax. It was time to squeeze harder.

He opened his fist and studied the smooth palm where the manicured nails had bitten deep.

Much harder, he decided.

"I tell you it's perfect." Roxanne scowled from face to face. The meeting between shows in her father's cabin was not going according to her plans. "Any woman who wears rocks like that in the afternoon has to be loaded with them. And any woman who'd marry a scum like Sam deserves to lose them."

"Be that as it may." Max steepled his fingers and struggled to focus his concentration. "It's risky to steal from someone you know, and who knows you, particularly in a situation as narrow as this."

"We could do it," she insisted. "LeClerc, if I got you photos and detailed descriptions of some of the better pieces, how long would it take for your contact to make up paste replicas?"

"A week, perhaps two."

She nearly snarled. "If you put a rush on it."

He began to consider. "If we sweetened the pot, four or five days. But, of course, this doesn't include delivery time."

"That's what Federal Express is for. We switch them." She swung back to her father. "The last night of the cruise. By the time Justine gets home and notices any difference, we're clear." She waited impatiently for a response. "Daddy?"

"What?" He jerked himself back, panicking for a moment as he searched for the thread of the conversation. "There isn't enough time to plan properly."

How could he plan when he could barely think? Sweat had begun to trickle cold down his back. They were all looking at him, all staring at him. Wondering.

"The answer is no." The statement whipped out as he sprang to his feet. He wanted them to leave, all of them, couldn't bear to have their pity and curiosity staring him in the face. "That's an end to it."

"But—"

"An end." He shouted it, causing Roxanne to blink and Lily to bite her bottom lip. "I'm still in charge here, young lady. When I want your suggestions and advice, I'll request them. Until then, do as you're told. Is that clear?"

"Very." Pride kept her head high, but there was shocked hurt in her eyes. He'd never shouted at her before. Never. They had argued, certainly, but always with an underlayment of love and respect. All she saw in her father's face was fury. "If you'll excuse me, I'm going to take a walk before the show."

Luke rose slowly as the door slammed behind Roxanne. "I have to go along with your reasons for rejecting the job, Max, but don't you think you were a little hard on her?"

Max rounded on him, his temper a wildly slashing sword. "I don't believe I need your opinion on how to deal with my own child. You may sleep with her, but I'm her father. My generosity to you over the years does not equal the right to interfere with family business."

"Max." Lily reached for his arm, but Luke was already shaking his head.

"It's all right, Lily. I believe I'll take a walk myself."

The sea was splattered with starlight. With her hands clasped tightly on the rail, Roxanne stared out at it. There was a vicious headache behind her eyes, the direct result of refusing the tears that burned them. She would not blubber like a child because her father had scolded her.

She heard the footsteps behind her and turned eagerly. But it wasn't Luke as she hoped. It was Sam.

"Charming," he said and caught the flying ends of her hair. "A beautiful woman in starlight with the sea behind her."

"Lose your wife?" She glanced deliberately behind him before arching a brow. "I don't believe I see her anywhere."

"Justine isn't the kind of woman who needs to be in a man's pocket." He shifted, caging her between his arms as he placed his hands on the rail. A quick bolt of lust twisted through him. She was beautiful, and belonged to someone else. He needed nothing else to covet her. "She's attractive, smart, rich and ambitious. In a few years, she'll be an excellent Washington hostess."

"How you must have charmed her with all those romantic compliments."

"Some women prefer the direct approach." He leaned toward her, stopping only when Roxanne's hand shot up and pushed against his chest.

"I'm not your wife, Sam, but the direct approach is fine with me, too. How's this? I find you revolting, pathetic and obvious. Sort of like a dead skunk on the side of the road." This was said in the most pleasant of tones, with the most pleasant of smiles. "Now, why don't you back off before I have to say something insulting."

"You're going to regret that." His voice was mild as well, for the benefit of the few people strolling the deck. But his eyes had chilled to ice. "Very, very much."

"I don't see how, when I enjoyed it tremendously." Her eyes were as cold as his, but with a shimmer of inner heat that threatened to erupt. "Now, please get out of my way."

Anger veiled discretion so that he gripped her arms and pushed her back. "I'm not through with you."

"I think—" She broke off, shoving Sam aside so that she could scramble between him and Luke. "Don't." She curled fingers around Luke's lapel and spoke between clenched teeth.

"Go inside, Roxanne." He stared at Sam over her head. If eyes were weapons, Sam would already have died a painful death.

"No." She recognized murder in his eye. If she stepped aside she thought it was more than likely Sam would end up overboard. However much the image appealed, she couldn't allow Luke to be responsible. "We have a show in a few minutes. You won't be able to do what you need to do if you break your hand punching in his face." She tossed a furious look over her shoulder. "Get the hell out of here, or I swear, I'll let go of his coat."

"All right. It wouldn't do to cause a scene here. There'll be another time." He nodded at Luke. "Another place."

Roxanne continued to hold on until she saw Sam stroll inside. "Damn you," she hissed.

"Damn me?" His fury still churned like the water in their wake, but he could only stare at her and repeat. "Damn me?"

"Yes. Do you realize what a mess you almost caused?" All the fury and frustration she'd felt since slamming out of her father's cabin shot out and smacked Luke with a bull's-eye. "Just how were we going to explain to Jack, or the captain for that matter, why you beat up a passenger and dumped his unconscious body overboard?"

"He was touching you. Goddamn it, when I walked out he had you trapped against the rail. Do you think I could stand by and watch someone treat you that way?"

"So, what are you, Sir Callahan? My white knight? Let me tell you something, pal." She shoved a finger hard against his chest. "I can slay my own dragons. I'm not some weak, wimpy female who needs rescuing." She poked him again, her nail almost piercing flesh. "I can handle myself. Got it?"

"Yeah. I got it." Because he thought he did, he yanked her against him and kissed her hard until her muffled protest died and her arms came tight around him.

"I'm sorry." Turning her head, she buried her face in his shoulder. "It has nothing to do with that idiot, nothing to do with you."

"I know." He kissed her hair. He'd felt the sting of Max's whip as well, a burn infinitely more painful than any belt Cobb had lifted.

"He hurt me." Because her voice had sounded too small, she pressed her lips together and tried to strengthen it. "He's never hurt me like that before. It wasn't the job, Luke. It wasn't—"

"I know," he said again. "I can't explain it, Rox, except that maybe he's got something else on his mind, maybe he isn't feeling well, maybe a dozen things. He's never come down on you like that before. Don't hold one slip against him."

"You're right." She sighed, drew back. "I'm overreacting." Gently, she lifted a hand to his cheek. "And I took it out on you when you were being such a macho guy. Would you have beat him up for me, baby?"

He grinned, relieved she'd recovered enough to tease. "You bet, doll face. I'd've cremated him."

She gave a quick shiver and lifted her mouth. "Oooh, I just love being kissed by a tough guy."

"Then you're going to get a real charge out of this."

It was one of the most difficult paths Max had ever walked, that narrow carpeted passageway from his cabin to Luke's. He knew his daughter was in there, along with the man he'd considered his son. He lifted his hand to knock, lowered it again. There was pain in his fingers tonight, bone-deep pain. He rapped them hard against the cabin door as if to punish himself.

Luke answered the door. He instantly felt that stiff-necked embarrassment that displayed itself in numbing politeness. "Max? Is there something you need?"

"I'd like to come in for a moment, if you don't mind."

Luke hesitated. At least he could be grateful both he and Roxanne were still fully dressed. "Sure. Would you like a drink?"

"No, nothing. Thank you." He stood miserably just inside the door, his eyes on his daughter. "Roxanne."

"Daddy."

They stood another moment, frozen in a triangle. Three people who had shared so many intimacies. Max found all the speeches he'd prepared had vanished from his brain like smoke. "I'm sorry, Roxy," was all he could think of to say. "I have no excuse."

The stiffness went out of her shoulders. "It's okay." For him, she could set even pride aside. She did so now as she held out her hands and crossed to him. "I guess I was nagging."

"No." Humbled by her easy forgiveness, he brought both her hands to his lips. "You were stating your case, as I've always expected you to do. I wasn't fair or kind." His smile wobbled a bit as he looked up at her. "If it's any consolation, it's the first time in nearly twenty years that Lily's shouted at me and reverted to name calling."

"Oh? Which ones did she use?"

"Jerk was one, I believe."

Roxanne shook her head. "I'll have to teach her some better ones." She kissed him and smiled again. "You'll make it up with her?"

"I think I'll have a better shot if I've made it up with you, first."

"Well, you have."

"Both of you," Max murmured and looked toward Luke.

"I see." Though she wasn't sure she did, Roxanne understood what was needed. "All right then, why don't I go clear your path with Lily?" She touched Luke's arm as she passed, then left them alone.

"There are things I need to say." Max lifted his hands in a rare helpless gesture. "I believe I'll take that drink after all."

"Sure." Luke slid the bottom drawer of the dresser open and pulled out a small bottle of brandy. "No snifters, I'm afraid."

"I can rough it if you can."

Nodding, Luke poured three fingers of brandy into water glasses. "You have some things to say about me and Roxanne," Luke began. "I've wondered why you haven't brought it up before."

"It's hard to admit, but I didn't know how. What I said this afternoon—"

"You were out of line with Rox," Luke interrupted. "Not with me."

"Luke." Max laid a hand on Luke's arm. His eyes were filled with appeal and regret. "Don't close the door on me. I was angry, but anger, contrary to the popular belief, does not always carve out the truth. I sliced to hurt, because I was hurting. I'm ashamed of that."

"Forget it." Uneasy, Luke set the brandy aside and rose. "It was a moment of temper, that's all."

"And do you believe what I said in temper above what I've said and shown you all these years?"

Luke looked back, and his eyes were those of that wild, reckless boy again. "You've given me all I've ever had. You don't owe me anything else."

"A pity people don't realize what power words wield. They'd have more respect for the use of them. It's easier for Roxanne to forgive because she's never doubted my love. I'd hoped that you wouldn't have cause to doubt it either." Max set his brandy, untouched, beside Luke's. "You're the son Lily and I could never make together. Can you understand that there have been entire blocks of time that I've forgotten you hadn't been born to me? And that if I thought of it, it didn't matter."

For a moment Luke said nothing, could say nothing. Then he sat on the edge of the bed. "Yes. Because there were times I nearly forgot myself."

"And perhaps because the lines were blurred in my heart, I found it hard, very hard, to accept what's between you and my daughter."

Luke gave a half laugh. "It gave me some bad moments, so much so that I nearly sent her away." He lifted his head. "I couldn't send her away, Max, not even for you."

"She wouldn't have gone." He understood both of his children. He laid a hand on Luke's shoulder, squeezing though his fingers wept with pain. "Free lesson," he murmured and watched Luke smile. "Love and magic have a great deal in common. They enrich the soul, delight the heart. And they both take unrelenting and unabating practice."

"I'll remember."

"See that you do." Max started toward the door, but stopped when a thought ran through his head. "I would like grandchildren," he said, and Luke's mouth dropped open. "I would like them very much."

21

Sam was quite satisfied with the progress of his plans. He was a highly respected member of the community, a recognizable force in Washington. As the senator's right-hand man, he had his own office, a modestly decorated bastion of masculinity with leather chairs and neutral colors. He had his own secretary, a sharp-minded political veteran who knew exactly what number to call to ferret out information.

Though he would have preferred a zippy foreign make, Sam was forward-thinking and drove a Chrysler. The grass-roots grumbling about buying American was growing. He had plans to be America's favorite son.

According to his timetable, he would slip seamlessly into the senator's position within six years. All the groundwork was there. The years of dedicated public service, the contacts in Washington, in the corporate world and on the streets.

Factoring in his advantages, Sam had nearly tossed his hat into the ring for the most recent election. But patience had won out. He knew his youth would be an initial strike against him, and a good number of bleeding hearts would have interpreted the move as disloyalty to the old fart Bushfield.

So, he bided his time and took his next steps with a cool-eyed look at the nineties. He courted and married Justine Spring, a wealthy department-store heiress with polished looks and impeccable lineage. She championed the correct charities, could plan a dinner party for fifty without turning a hair and had the extra advantage of photographing like a dream.

When Sam had slipped the ring on her finger, he'd known he'd taken another important step. The American people preferred their leaders to be married. With the proper timing, he would campaign for the Senate seat as the devoted father of one, and Justine would be rosily pregnant with their second, and last, child.

He fancied himself a latter-day Kennedy—not the politics, naturally. These were the Reagan years. But the youth, the good looks, the pretty wife and the young, charming family.

It would work because he knew how to play the game. He was climbing the ladder toward the Oval Office with slow, calculated steps, and was already halfway up the rungs.

There was only one niggling sense of failure in Sam's world. The Nouvelles. They were loose ends untied, dangling questions unanswered. He wanted revenge on them for personal reasons, but he needed it for what he considered sharp professional motives. It was important that they be weakened, crushed, so that any vicious truths they might shout about his character would be laughed aside.

He'd had ample time to observe them up close on his honeymoon cruise. Now, cozied into the sumptuous Helmsley Palace in New York, awaiting the parties and celebrations for the Statue of Liberty's one hundredth birthday, he had time to shuffle through his impressions.

The old man looked tired. Sam remembered the lightning-quick movements of those hands a decade before and judged that Max was slowing down. It was interesting as well that the aging magician was spending so much time looking for some mystical rock.

Sam wrote *the philosophers' stone* on Leona's elegant hotel stationery and idly circled it. Maybe he'd have some of his men do some digging into the rock.

There was Lily, as tacky and top-heavy as ever. And as naive, Sam thought, with a smile that curled his lips back from his teeth. He'd made a point of joining her on deck one day, and by the time he'd strolled away, she'd been patting his hand and telling him how glad she was he'd made something good out of his life.

And Roxanne. Ah, Roxanne. If magic existed at all, it existed there. What spell had conjured the skinny, wild-haired girl into a stunning woman? A pity he hadn't had the opportunity to make a few moves in that direction before Justine. He'd have enjoyed seducing her, using her in a way that would shock and disgust his pretty, lukewarm wife.

But no matter how alluring the prospect, he'd had to move carefully there. The incident on ship had very nearly created a scene a public figure—a married public figure—could ill afford.

Which brought him to Luke. Always to Luke. There was the key to the Nouvelles. Sam could dismiss Mouse and LeClerc as callously as he would dismiss servants. They were nothing. But Luke was the lynchpin. Destroying him would put a crack in the wall of the Nouvelles that might never be shored up. It would also be such a sweet, personal triumph.

The business with Cobb wasn't progressing as Sam had hoped. It had taken him years after leaving New Orleans to reach the position where he could afford to hire detectives to investigate Luke's background.

It had cost, and cost dearly, but Sam considered it an investment in the future, and payment for the past. Locating the junkie whore who'd been Luke's mother had been a stroke of luck. But Cobb, Cobb had been icing on the cake.

Sam closed his eyes and drifted out of the elegant suite in the Helmsley, transporting himself to a dank, waterfront bar.

The air smelled of fish and urine, and the cheap whiskey and tobacco consumed by the patrons. Pool balls smacked angrily together across the room, and the men who played cast surly glances at the table as they chalked cues.

A single whore sat at the end of the bar with mean eyes and a preference for Four Roses while she waited to ply her trade. Her eyes skimmed over Sam as he sat in the corner, lingering a moment in consideration, then passed on.

He'd chosen the shadows. A hat was pulled low on his head, and a bulky coat disguised his frame. It was chill enough in the bar with a late-winter wind battering sleet against the windows. But the light sweat of anticipation greased Sam's skin.

He watched Cobb walk in. Saw him hitch up his heavily buckled belt before scanning the room. Once he spotted the figure in the corner, he nodded, strolled with what Sam assumed was meant to be nonchalance to the bar. He brought a glass of whiskey to the table.

"You got business with me?" It was a tough tone, delivered before his first sip of whiskey.

"I have a business offer."

Cobb shrugged his massive shoulders and attempted to look bored. "So?"

"I believe you know an acquaintance of mine." Sam left his own drink untouched on the table. He'd noted, with mild disgust, that the glass was none too clean. "Luke Callahan."

Surprise flickered before Cobb narrowed his eyes. "Can't say as I do."

"Let's not complicate a simple matter. You've been fucking Callahan's mother on and off for years. You lived with them when he was a boy—a kind of unofficial stepfather. At that time, you were doing some unimaginative pimping and dipping your toe into pornography—with an emphasis on children and adolescents."

Cobb's face suffused with color so that the network of broken capillaries flared like torches. "I don't know what that ungrateful shit told you, but I treated him good. Kept food in his belly, didn't I? Showed him what was what."

"You left your mark on him, Cobb. I've seen that for myself." Sam smiled, and Cobb caught a flash of white teeth.

"The boy needed discipline." Whiskey was curdling in Cobb's nervous belly. He sent more down to join it. "I seen him on TV. Big shot now. Don't see him paying me or his old lady back for all the years we did for him."

Sam heard exactly what he'd hoped to hear, resentment, bitterness and envy. "You figure he owes you?"

"Goddamn class A right he does." Cobb leaned forward, but gleaned no more than a vague impression of Sam's face through the smoke and dingy shadows. "If he sent you here to rattle my chain—"

"No one sends me. Callahan owes me, as well. You can be of use to me." Sam reached into his pocket and took out an envelope. After a quick glance around the room, Cobb picked it up. His wide thumb flipped through five hundred in well-used twenties.

"What do you want for it?"

"Satisfaction. This is what I want you to do."

So Sam had sent his dog to New Orleans.

The blackmail wasn't as effective as he'd hoped, Sam mused. The thirty or forty thousand a year was paid without comment. Since Sam had made it his business to know precisely what income Luke reported each year, he would up the ante. There would be a plain white postcard waiting for Luke when he returned to New Orleans. This time the figure on it would be ten thousand.

Sam calculated that a few months of these slim postcard would slide neatly under Luke's foundations. Before long, they would crumble.

It infuriated him. Luke crushed the white square in his fist and hurled it across the room. It terrified him.

Ten thousand dollars. It wasn't the money itself. He had enough of that, and could easily get more. It was the realization that Cobb was not only never going away, but that he was growing greedy.

The next time it could be twenty thousand, or thirty.

Let the fucker go to the press, he thought. The tabloids could have a field day with it.

MASTER MAGICIAN'S SECRET CHILDHOOD

So what?

ESCAPE ARTIST'S LIFE AS A WHORE

Who gave a shit?

THE NOUVELLES' UGLY TRIANGLE
Magician's affair with mentor,
and his master's daughter

Oh, God. Luke scrubbed his hands over his face and tried to think. He was entitled to his life, damn it. The one he'd put together piece by piece since he'd run away from that gin-soaked apartment with his back screaming with pain and the terror of not knowing what they might have done to him after he'd lapsed into unconsciousness.

He would not, could not stand to have what he'd run from dug up and smeared into his face. He wouldn't see the stink of that mud flung at the only people he'd ever loved. And yet. And yet he was losing something of himself every time he answered one of those postcards like a well-trained monkey.

There was one alternative he hadn't yet considered. Luke picked up a teacup, intently studying the delicate design of violets against the cream-colored china. One he'd dreamed about, certainly, but had never put on the floor for a vote.

He could fly up to Maine and lure Cobb out of his hole. Then he could do what he'd yearned to do every time the belt had slashed his flesh. He could kill him.

The cup shattered in his hand, but Luke didn't jolt. He continued to stare down while the image formed more truly in his mind, and the blood welled like a thin smile across his palm.

He could kill.

The pounding on the door jerked him back. The thought was still wheeling like dazzling colored lights in his head as he yanked it open.

"Hi!" Roxanne's hair dripped into her eyes. Her T-shirt clung wetly to her torso. She lifted her lips to Luke's and brought him the scent of rain and summer meadows. "I thought you'd like a picnic."

"Picnic?" He fought hard to bank the violence and smile at her. He glanced toward the torrent falling outside the window as he shut the door behind her. "I guess this kind of weather should cut down on ants."

"Barbecued chicken wings," she said, holding out a cardboard box.

"Oh yeah?"

"The really sloppy kind, and a big bowl of LeClerc's potato salad that I swiped from the fridge, and a very nice white Bordeaux."

"Seems you've thought of everything. Except dessert."

She sent him a long sideways glance as she knelt on the rug. "Oh, I thought of that, too. Why don't you get us a couple of glasses—what's this?" She picked up a shard of broken china.

"I—broke a cup."

When he bent down to pick up the pieces, she spotted the blood on his hand. "Oh, what have you done?" She snatched his hand, clucking over it while she daubed at blood with the hem of her shirt.

"It's just a scratch, doc."

"Don't joke." But she saw with relief that it was, and shallow at that. "Your hands are worth quite a bit, you know. Professionally."

He skimmed a finger down the slope of her breast. "Professionally?"

"Yes. And I do have a personal interest in them, as well." After nibbling on his lips, she sat back on her heels in strategic retreat. "How about those glasses—and a cork-screw?"

Ready to oblige, he rose and started toward the kitchen. "Why don't you dig out a dry shirt? You'll drip on the potato salad."

"No, I won't." The sopping shirt landed a step behind him, splatting on the linoleum.

Luke glanced down at it, then at her. It should be an interesting picnic, he mused. Chicken, potato salad and a wet, half-naked woman. The lingering tension dissolved in a grin. "I love practical women."

It was dark. The shadows were suffocating and stank of sweat. The walls were close on all four sides, and overhead the ceiling dropped low like the lid of a coffin.

There was no door. No latch. No light.

He knew he was naked, for the heat pressed down on his exposed skin like an anvil that throbbed and throbbed under a relentless hammer. Something was crawling over him. For a horrible minute he feared it was spiders. But it was only the creep of his own perspiration.

He tried to be quiet, very, very quiet, but the sound of his labored breathing rattled and whooped with a hollow echo despite the cramped space.

They'd come if he wasn't quiet.

He couldn't stop it. He couldn't stop his panicked heart from booming in his chest or the small animal-like sounds of terror that kept bubbling up in his throat.

His hands were tied. The rope bit into his thin wrists as he twisted and struggled for freedom. He smelled blood and tasted tears and the sweat stung his abraded wrists like a torch.

He had to get out. Had to. There had to be a way to escape. But there was no trap door, no clever mechanism, no slick panel waiting to slide away at his touch.

He was only a boy, after all. And it was so hard to think. So hard to be strong. The sweat froze like tiny balls of ice when he realized he wasn't alone in the box. He could hear the heavy, excited breathing close, could smell the sour stink of gin.

He howled like a wolf when the hands gripped him, his body jerking, bucking, drawing up tight.

"You'll do what you're told to do. You'll do what you're told, you little bastard."

The slash of the belt sliced white-hot pain through flesh, through blood and into bone. And he screamed, and he screamed, and bolted upright. For a moment his dazed eyes saw only the dark. His skin was still shivering against the bite of the belt as hands reached for him.

He jerked away, fists clenched, teeth bared. And saw Roxanne's stunned face.

"You had a nightmare," she said calmly, though her heart was tripping at double time. He didn't look quite sane. "It was a nightmare, Luke. You're awake now."

The madness faded from his eyes before he closed them on a groan. His skin was still quivering when she risked touching a hand to his shoulder. "You were thrashing around. I couldn't bring you out of it."

"I'm sorry." He rubbed his hands over his face, willing the nausea away.

"You don't have to be sorry." Gently, she brushed the sweat-dampened hair from his brow. "Must have been a lulu."

"Yeah." He reached for the bottle and upended a swallow of warm wine into his mouth.

"Tell me?"

He could only shake his head. There were things he could never tell, not even to her. "It's over." But there was a tic in his jaw. Roxanne smoothed her fingers over the movement to soothe.

"Why don't I get you some water?"

"No." He grabbed her hand before she could rise, clinging tight as if he couldn't bear her to be even as far away as the next room. "Just be here. Okay?"

"Okay." She slipped her arms around him.

He'd forgotten they were naked. But oh, the feel of her skin against his was magic, vanquishing those last tattered remnants of the nightmare. Needy, he buried his face into the soft curve of her shoulder.

"It's still raining," he murmured.

"Umm-hmm." Instinctively, she stroked his back, her fingers gliding coolly over the ridges of old scars. "I like the way it sounds, the way it makes the light so soft and the air so heavy."

He watched it fall, still hard and heavy though the thunder had danced on to the west. Beyond the terrace doors his tangle of geraniums stood triumphant against the gloom. "I always liked red flowers best. I could never figure out why. Then one day I realized they made me think of your hair. That's when I knew I loved you."

Her fingers paused, lying still against his back. Her heart broke a little, but sweetly, as it must with joy. "I didn't think you'd ever tell me." On an unsteady laugh she pressed her lips to his throat. "I was considering going to Madame and asking her for a potion."

"You're all the magic I need." He tipped her face back to his. "I was afraid to say it. Those three words are an incantation that releases all kinds of complications."

"Too late." Her lips curved against his. "The spell's already cast. Here." She lifted her hands, palms out, waiting until he placed his against them. "I love you, too. Nothing can change it. No sorcery, no enchantment, no trick of the eye."

Very slowly he slid his fingers between hers so that their spread palms became sturdy, joined fists. "In all the illusions, you're the only truth I need."

He knew then that he would pay Cobb, would dance with the devil himself to keep her safe, to keep what they had unspoiled.

She saw the flash in his eyes, like lightning against a churning sky. His fingers tensed on hers. "I need you, Roxanne." He released her hands to pull her close and press her back onto the rug. "Now. God, now."

Like brushfire, the force of that need burned from him into her, scorching the blood. His desperation tumbled with them over the rug, igniting the spark of hers, fanning the flames higher, brighter, until it was a roar of heat.

His hands were everywhere, streaks of lightning over her flesh that sent hundreds of pulse points thudding. Their playful, good-hearted loving of the afternoon paled like the moon against the sun.

He clasped her hands in his again, holding her arms out to the side as he raced his mouth over her. His teeth scraped, nipped, satisfying an urgent hunger for the taste of flesh. Her hands flexed once, twice, under his grip even as her body greedily absorbed the sensation of being taken, possessed. Devoured.

To want and be wanted like this. She could never explain it, never describe it. Could only thank God for it. When he dragged her higher, into that blinding heat, the pleasure was so intense she felt her soul quake.

More, was all she could think.

She tore her hands free to take them over him, all speed and eagerness. Agile and quick and more than half mad, she rolled on top of him, flesh sliding hot and wet over flesh, mouth meeting ravenous mouth like the clash of bright, dangerous swords.

The power built inside her, sang in her blood, seemed to spark from her fingertips as she felt his muscles bunch and quiver beneath her touch. He'd taught her the magic, tutored her in its varieties. Now, for this moment, the student had become the master.

He groaned, dazed by the suddenness and strength of her assault. Her answer was a laugh, low and breathless and devastating. He would have sworn he smelled hell smoke mixed with that taunting perfume of wild-flowers.

"Roxanne." Her name shuddered through his lips between heaving breaths. "Now. For God's sake."

"No." She laughed again, dipping her head. "Not yet, Callahan. I'm not finished with you yet." She teased his nipple, then slid down, over his rib cage, down his taut belly until an oath exploded from him.

His need was like a wild beast, snapping and clawing for freedom. And she held the whip, tormenting, promising, preventing him from that final burst that would lead to escape.

"You're killing me," he managed.

She trailed her tongue over him. "I know."

And the knowledge made her giddy. Drunk with power, she took him to the thin, quivering edge of relief, then retreated. Witchlike, she slid up his body.

"Tell me again." Her eyes were open and glowing. "Tell me now, when you want me so much it feels like it's ripping you apart. Tell me now."

"I love you." He gripped her hips with unsteady hands when she straddled him.

"Magic words," she murmured and shifted her body up to take him inside her.

When he filled her, when her throbbing muscles contracted to welcome him, she threw her head back with the sheer stunning pleasure of it. For the space of a dozen heartbeats she held him tight inside her, her body angled back and still as a statue.

He'd never forget how she looked, her skin the palest gold and gleaming with damp, her lips full and parted, her eyes closed, her hair tumbling fire down her back.

Then her body shuddered, wracked by a fast, hard orgasm. A slow, sinuous moan slipped from her, but still she didn't move. Then her lips curved, her lids fluttered up to reveal eyes deeper, more beautiful than any emerald he could covet.

She groped for his hands, locked fingers tight and rode him like a woman possessed.

When at last there was no more to take, no more to give, her body flowed like water down to his. The rain had stopped. Watery sunlight crept mystically into the room. He stroked a hand down her hair.

"Move in with me," he said.

She used what was left of her strength to lift her head and arch a brow. "My bags are already packed."

He grinned and gave her pretty butt a light pinch. "Pretty sure of yourself."

"Damn right." She gave him a smacking kiss. "I only have one question."

"What's that?"

"Who's going to do the cooking?"

"Ah." He trailed a finger down her ribs, searching for a foolproof escape. "I burn everything."

Roxanne hadn't been born yesterday. "Me too."

There was an easy way out, he decided. "The Quarter's lousy with restaurants."

"Yeah." Her grin spread. "Aren't we lucky?"

She settled back into his arm. As they lay close in the thin sunlight it seemed possible that the biggest problem they would face would be their appetites.

22

It was as easy as pulling a rabbit out of a hat. They had, after all, lived with each other for years. They knew each other's habits, flaws, eccentricities.

She got up at dawn; he pulled the covers over his head. He took endless showers that used up all the hot water; she took paperback novels into the bathtub and stayed submerged in plot and bubbles until the water turned cold.

He worked out with weights on the living room floor; she preferred the structure of a thrice-weekly exercise class.

The stereo blared with rock when Luke had the controls and ached from the blues when Roxanne had her way.

They did have plenty in common. Neither would have thought of complaining about the need to practice a single routine over and over and over. They both adored Cajun food, movies of the forties and long, meandering walks through the Quarter.

And they both shouted when they argued.

They did plenty of shouting over the next few weeks. They thrived on it. Friction was as much a part of their relationship as breathing, and both would have regretted its loss.

As August steamed through New Orleans, passing toward the blessed relief of fall, they squabbled and made up, snarled and snapped and pushed each other with regularity into frustration and laughter.

For her birthday he gave her a crystal wand, a long, slim staff of amethyst wrapped with thin silver wires and crusted with cabochons of ruby, citrine and deep blue topaz. She set it on a table by the window so that the sun would strike it every day and pulse its magic through the air.

They were wildly in love and shared everything. Everything but the secret Luke paid for every month with a cashier's check for ten thousand dollars.

Max had called a meeting, but he was in no hurry to start. He sipped LeClerc's hot, chicory-flavored coffee and bided his time. It felt good to have his family gathered around him again. He hadn't realized what a blow it would be to have both Roxanne and Luke out from under his roof. Even though they lived only a short walk away, the loss had staggered him.

He felt he was losing so much in such a short span of time. His children, who were no longer children, his hands, with their stiff fingers that so often seemed to belong to a stranger.

Even his thoughts, and that frightened him the most. So often they seemed to float away from him, to hang just out of reach so that he would stop, desperately trying to capture them again.

He told himself it was because he had so much on his mind. That was why he'd taken a wrong turn on his way to the French Market and had ended up lost and disoriented in a city he'd known most of his life. That was why he was forgetting things. Like the name of his stockbroker. Or the cupboard where LeClerc had stored the coffee mugs for years.

But today, having them all around him, he felt more strong, more sure. His voice reflected none of his doubts as he called the meeting to order.

"I believe I have something of interest," he began when the room quieted. "A particular collection of jewelry—" He noted that Roxanne's eyes cut to Luke's. "I've taken a more specific interest in the sapphire portion of this collection. The lady appears to have an affection for this stone, and her jewelry wardrobe—which is extensive—reflects it. There is also a rather elegant pearl and diamond choker that is not to be scoffed at. Naturally, this is only part of the collection, but enough, I believe, for our needs."

"How many pieces?" Roxanne pulled a notebook out of her purse and prepared to scribble information in her own complex code. Max beamed his pride toward his precise and practical daughter.

"Of the sapphires, ten." Max steepled his hands. Odd, now that the game had begun, he no longer felt the ache in them. "Two necklaces, three pairs of earrings, a bracelet, two rings, a pin and an enhancer. Insured for half a million. The choker is valued at ninety thousand, but I believe that to be slightly excessive. Eighty thousand is a more reasonable estimate."

Luke accepted a cookie from the plate Lily passed him. "We got any visuals?"

"Naturally. Jean?"

LeClerc picked up the remote, aimed it toward the television. The set clicked on, then the VCR below it hummed into life. "I have transferred photographs to videotape." As the first picture flashed on, he struck a match and, holding it over the bowl of his pipe, began to suck. "I enjoy these new toys. This necklace," he continued, "is of a conservative design, perhaps lacking in imagination. But the stones themselves are good. There are ten fancy-cut sapphires of a cornflower blue. Total weight, twenty-five carats. The diamonds are very good quality baguettes of a total weight approximately eight point two carats."

But it was the next picture, the enhancer, that caught Roxanne's attention. With a quick sound of surprise she stared at the screen, then at her father.

"Justine Wyatt. If that's not the same piece I saw her wearing on the ship last summer, I'm brain-dead."

"You were never that, my sweet," Max said. "It's precisely the same piece."

The smile started first, spread into a grin, then bubbled out in a laugh of sheer good humor. "We're going to do it after all. Why didn't you tell me?"

"I wanted it to be a surprise." He preened, delighted with her reaction. "Consider it a kind of early Christmas gift, though it will be closer to Easter by the time we have everything in place." He gestured toward the set. "Skip ahead, will you, Jean? We can come back to this. The photos are copied from the insurance file. Our own contribution should be more entertaining."

The pictures zigzagged through fast forward then settled into live-action videos aboard the *Yankee Princess.*

"Home movies." Mouse grinned over a mouthful of cookies. "I took these ones."

"And a budding Spielberg in our midst," Max congratulated.

Indeed, the video was clear as crystal, the picture steady as a rock, the sound perfect. The slow pans, zooms and wide shots flowed together without any of the jerks and jolts of the amateur.

"Oh, look. There's that nice Mrs. Woolburger. Remember, Max. She was in the front row at every show."

"And there's Dori." Roxanne leaned forward, propping her elbows on her thighs. And... oh." She flushed a bit when Mouse's lens zoomed in on the port-side rail, capturing her and Luke in a long kiss.

It was odd and exciting to watch herself skim her fingers up into Luke's hair, to see the way his head tilted so that his mouth could cover hers more truly.

"That's the love interest," Mouse said with a wide grin. "Every good movie's got one."

"Run that part back again." Luke kneaded his fingers over Roxanne's shoulder.

Roxanne snatched the remote before LeClerc could oblige. "Ah, the plot thickens," she murmured as Sam and Justine strolled out on deck. Roxanne inched forward even as the picture focused in on a close-up of the bracelet they'd just studied in the still. The camera followed their progress over the deck, where they chose chairs side by side.

There were none of the secret smiles and lingering touches of newlyweds. Without exchanging a word, they settled back, she with a glossy magazine, he with a Tom Clancy techno-thriller.

"Romantic devils, aren't they?" Roxanne considered as she studied Sam. The breeze was ruffling his hair. He had the light tan of a man used to being outdoors. "The camera's good to him. I suppose that's a political asset."

"Barbie and Ken," Luke commented behind her. "The amazing plastic people."

Mouse thought Sam had shark's eyes, but he didn't say so because he thought the family would chuckle, and he didn't mean it to be funny. In his heart he wished Max had stood by his original decision so that they would all give Sam, his wife and her pretty stones a wide berth. But to Mouse, Max was the smartest person in the world, and it would never occur to him to question or doubt.

As the screen faded to gray, then bled to color again, Roxanne let out a low whistle. "So that's the choker."

"Superb, isn't it? Freeze it there, darling." When Roxanne complied, Max began to lecture like a dedicated professor.

"The choker was a gift from her parents on her twenty-first birthday, four years ago this coming April. It was purchased at Cartier's, New York, for a sum of ninety-two thousand, five hundred and ninety-nine dollars—plus all the accompanying taxes."

"They hose you on that in New York," Luke murmured and received an acknowledging nod from Max.

"I can't believe I missed seeing a piece like that," Roxanne commented.

"She wore it on farewell night." Lily remembered it very well. "I think you and Luke were—occupied—until the show."

"Oh." Roxanne remembered, too, and slid a glance at Luke over her shoulder. "I guess we were."

Luke wrapped an arm around her waist and pulled her back off of the hassock and into his lap. "It's one of a kind, isn't it?"

Max beamed. He'd taught his children well. "Yes, as it happens. That will make it more difficult, though not impossible, to dispose of. I believe that should be enough, Roxanne." The set switched off. He settled back. Max's mind was so clear he wondered if he'd imagined the fog that so often settled over it. "We're awaiting blueprints of the house in Tennessee, as well as the New York pied-à-terre. The security systems on both residences will take some time."

"That'll give us time to enjoy Christmas first." It wasn't a question. For Lily, taking time to enjoy every aspect of the holiday was a sacred trust. "Since we're all here, we can trim the tree tonight." She shot a sly glance at Roxanne and Luke. "Jean's got a roast in the oven."

"With those little potatoes that get all crusty, and the carrots?" Luke felt his stomach, which had made do for two weeks with take-out and one disastrous attempt at fried chicken, give a yearning sigh.

Roxanne elbowed him in the ribs. After all, it had been she who'd fried the chicken. "The man's a walking appetite. We don't need to be bribed to stay."

"It doesn't hurt." Luke sent a beseeching look at LeClerc. "Biscuits?"

"You bet. And maybe enough left over for a doggie bag for a young wolf."

The days to Christmas and the new year passed quickly. There were presents to buy and wrap, cookies to bake. In the case of the Nouvelle/Callahan apartment, there were cookies to burn. The annual magic show to benefit the pediatric wing raised five thousand much-needed dollars. But it was Luke who carried on Max's tradition of entertaining the children who would spend the most magical night of the year confined to bed or wheelchair.

In the hour it took to pluck a coin out of a small ear, or cause magic flowers to spring up out of an empty pot, Luke discovered why Max devoted so much of his time to these children.

They were the most satisfying of audiences. They knew pain, and their reality was often unforgiving. But they believed. For an hour, that was all that mattered.

He dreamed again that night, after leaving those small faces behind. He dreamed, and awakened with his heart pounding and a scream burning his throat.

Roxanne shifted, murmuring in her sleep. He closed his cold fingers over hers and lay, for a long time, staring at the ceiling.

A long, rainy winter clung stubbornly to March. Those entertainers who plied their trade on street corners suffered. In the house on Chartres, LeClerc kept his kitchen cozily warm. Though it stung the pride, he stayed indoors, rarely venturing out even to market. When he did, he felt each gust of wind sneak through his thinning skin and whip straight into the marrow of his bones.

Old age, he thought when he allowed himself to address the issue, was a motherfucker.

When the door opened on a blast of cold wind and chilling rain, he pounced.

"Close the goddamn door. This ain't no cave."

"Sorry."

Luke's apology earned a scowl. He was hatless and gloveless, and wore only a denim jacket as protection from the elements. LeClerc felt bitter envy swirl into his heart.

"You come here for a handout?"

Luke sniffed the air and caught the unmistakable aroma of baked apples. "If I can get one."

"Why don't you learn to cook for yourself? You think you can waltz in here and waltz back out again with a full belly anytime you please? I don't run no soup kitchen."

"It's like this." Since Luke was too used to the rough side of the Cajun's tongue to cower, he poured himself a cup of the coffee warming on the stove. "I figure a man can only be good, really good, at a limited number of things."

LeClerc sniffed. "What you so good at, *mon ami,* you can't boil an egg?"

"Magic." Luke took a teaspoon of sugar, made a fist and poured a rain of white grains into the funnel of his thumb and forefinger. He waited a beat then opened his hands wide to show it empty. LeClerc gave a snort that might have been a laugh. "Stealing." He handed LeClerc back the tattered wallet he'd lifted out of the old man's back pocket when he'd passed to the stove. "And making love to a woman." He picked up his cup and sipped. "But you'll have to take my word on that one, 'cause you ain't getting no demonstration."

LeClerc's leathery face split with a grin. "So, you think you do those things good, eh?"

"I do those things great. Now, how about one of those baked apples?"

"Sit and eat at the table like you been taught." No longer displeased with the company, he went back to kneading his dough. His hands were competent with the homey chore; the snakes twining up his arms slithered. "Where's Roxanne?"

"At that exercise class. She said she might have some lunch with a couple of the other women after."

"So, you're on the prowl, *oui?*"

"I was working out the kinks on this escape, needed a break." He didn't want to admit the apartment seemed empty without her in it. "It'll be ready for Mardi Gras."

"You have only two weeks."

"It's enough. Dangling over Lake Pontchartrain from a burning rope ought to draw a hell of a crowd. Challenger's betting fifty K I don't get out of the cuffs and make it back onto the bridge before the rope burns through."

"And if you don't?"

"Then I lose fifty thousand and get wet."

LeClerc put the dough into a big bowl, covered it. "It's a long drop."

"I know how to fall." He forked warm, spicy apple into his mouth. "I wanted to check over a couple of details with Max. He around?"

"He's sleeping."

"Now?" Luke lifted a brow. "It's eleven o'clock."

"He don't sleep so good at night." Worry creased his brow as he washed clinging dough from his hands, but his back was to Luke. "A man's entitled to sleep late now and again in his own house."

"I didn't mean—he never used to." Luke glanced toward the hallway, realized for the first time how quiet the house was. "He's okay, isn't he?"

Luke stared at LeClerc's rigid back. In his mind he could see Max, working his hands, working his fingers, flexing them, spreading them, manipulating them again and again like a pianist before a performance.

"How bad are his hands?" Luke saw by the slight stiffening of LeClerc's shoulders that he'd hit the mark. The homey scent of spice and apples and bread dough made him vaguely ill as he waited for the answer.

"Don't know what you mean." LeClerc kept his back turned as he shut off the water in the sink and reached for a dish towel.

"Jean. Don't con me. Give me credit for caring as much as you do."

"God damn." But there was no strength behind the oath, and Luke had his answer.

"Has he seen a doctor?" Luke's stomach churned. The fork rattled against his saucer as he pushed it away.

"Lily nagged him to one." LeClerc turned then, his small, dark eyes reflecting all the frustration and emotion he'd suppressed. "They give him pills to ease the pain. The pain in his fingers, *comprends?* Not the pain here." He tapped a fist to his heart. "It doesn't bring the magic back. Nothing will."

"There's got to be something—"

"Rien," LeClerc interrupted. "Nothing. Inside each man is a timetable. And it says this is when his eyes will dim, or his ears clog up. This is the day he will get out of bed with his bones stiff and his joints aching. And today is the day his bladder will fail him or his lungs will go weak, or his heart will burst. The doctors will say do this, take that, but the *bon Dieu* has set the time, and when He says *c'est assez,* nothing can stop it."

"I don't believe that." Didn't want to. Luke scraped his chair back as he rose. "You're saying we've got nothing to do with it, no control."

"You think we do?" LeClerc gave a short bark of a laugh. "That is the arrogance of the young. Do you think it was an accident that you came to the carnival that night, that you found Max, that he found you?"

Luke remembered all too clearly the powerful draw of the poster, the way the painted eyes had seduced him into the tent. "It was good luck."

"Luck, *oui.* It's just another name for fate."

Luke had had enough of LeClerc's fatalistic philosophy. It dug too close to his own deeply buried beliefs. "None of this has anything to do with Max. We should get him to a specialist."

"*Pourquoi?* So he can have tests that break his heart? He has arthritis. It can be eased, but it can't be cured. You're his hands now, you and Roxanne."

Luke sat again, brooding into the black pool of his cooling coffee. "Does she know?"

"Maybe not in her head, but in her heart, she knows. Just as you." LeClerc hesitated. Following instinct, and his own fate, he sat across from Luke. "There is more," he said quietly.

Luke lifted his gaze. The look on LeClerc's face had fear skittering up his spine. "What?"

"He spends hours with his books, with his maps."

"The philosophers' stone?"

"*Oui,* the stone. He talks to scientists, to professors, even to mediums."

"It's caught his imagination," Luke said. "What's the harm of it?"

"Perhaps nothing of itself. This is his Holy Grail. I think if he finds it, he'll have peace. But for now . . . I've seen him stare at the single page in a book, and an hour later, he has yet to turn the page. At breakfast he might ask Mouse to move the parlor sofa under the window. And at lunch he asks why the furniture has been rearranged. He says to Lily we must rehearse this new trick today, and after she waits for him in the workroom, after she goes to find him huddled with his books in the library, he remembers nothing of a rehearsal."

The fear dug in with tiny teeth and claws. "He has a lot on his mind."

"It's his mind that concerns me." LeClerc sighed. He thought his eyes too old for tears, but they prickled hot and had to be fought back. "Yesterday, I found him standing in the courtyard. He was in costume, with no coat against the wind. 'Jean,' he says. 'Where is the van?' "

"The van? But—"

"We have no van." LeClerc kept his eyes level with Luke's. "Not for nearly ten years, but he asks if Mouse has taken it to wash before the show. So, I tell him there is no show today, and he must come inside, out of the cold." LeClerc lifted his cup and swallowed deeply. "Then he looks around him, lost, and I can see fear in his eyes. So I take him inside, up to bed. He asks if Roxanne is home from school, and I tell him no, not yet. But soon. He says Luke must bring his pretty girlfriend back to dinner, and I say *bien,* I will make *étouffée.* Then he sleeps, and when he wakes I think he remembers none of it."

Luke uncurled the hand he'd fisted in his lap. "Jesus."

"A man's body betrays him, he moves slower. But what does he do when it's his mind?"

"He needs to see a doctor."

"Ah, *oui,* and this will be done because Lily will insist. But there's something you must do."

"What can I do?"

"You must see that he doesn't go with you when you fly to Tennessee." Before Luke could speak, LeClerc waved the words back. "He must be a part of the planning, but not the execution. What if he forgets where he is, what he's doing? Can you risk it? Can you risk him?"

"No," Luke answered after a long pause. "I won't risk him. But I won't hurt him, either." He debated for a moment, then nodded. "I think we should—"

"Jean, what is that marvelous bouquet?" Max strolled in, looking so fit and alert that Luke almost dismissed LeClerc's story. "Ah, Luke, so you followed your nose as well. Where's Roxanne?"

"Out with some friends. Want some coffee?" Luke was already up and moving toward the stove. Max sat, stretching out his legs with a sigh. His fingers were moving, moving, moving, like a man playing an invisible piano.

"I hope she doesn't dawdle too long. I know Lily wanted to take her out for new shoes. The child can't seem to keep them on her feet."

Luke's hand jerked. Coffee splashed on the counter. Max was discussing Roxanne as if she were twelve again.

"She'll be along." His heart felt like an anvil in his chest as he carried the coffee back to the kitchen table.

"Have you worked out the bugs in the Water Torture escape?"

Luke wanted to scream at Max to stop, to leap off whatever time machine was holding his mind prisoner. Instead he spoke calmly. "Actually, I'm working on the Burning Rope. Remember?" he prodded gently. "It's set for Shrove Tuesday. Next week."

"Burning Rope?" Max's hand paused. The coffee cup that was halfway to his lips trembled. It was painful to watch his fight to return to the present. His mouth drooped open and hung slack, his eyes darted wildly. Then they focused again. His hand continued to bring the cup to his lips. "You'll draw a good crowd," he said. "The early press is excellent."

"I know. And I couldn't ask for a better cover for the Wyatt job. I want to move on it that night."

Max frowned. "There are a number of small details yet to be worked out."

"There's time." Despising himself, Luke leaned back. He hooked an arm casually over the back of his chair. "I want to ask you for a favor, Max."

"All right."

"I want to pull the job myself." Luke saw the shock on Max's face, the disappointment. "It's important to me," he plowed on. "I know the rules about no job being personal, but this one's the exception. There's a lot of baggage between Sam and me."

"All the more reason not to let emotions cloud the issue."

"They are the issue." At least this much was true. "I owe him. This would go a long way toward paying off old debts." Then he pulled out his trump card, hating himself. "If you don't trust me to carry it off, if you don't think I'm good enough, just say so."

"Of course I trust you. But the point is..." He didn't know what the point was, except that his son was taking yet another step away. "You're right. It's past time for you to try something on your own. You're as good as they get."

"Thanks." He wanted to take those restless hands in his, but only lifted his coffee cup in salute. "I was taught by the best."

"What do you mean you're doing it on your own?" Roxanne demanded. With her gym bag tossed over her shoulder she'd followed Luke from the living room, where he'd dropped his bombshell, into the bedroom.

"Just what I said. It's my show."

"Like hell. We all work together." Despite annoyance, her ingrained tidiness had her unzipping the bag to remove towels and workout clothes. "Daddy wouldn't agree to it."

"He did agree to it." Luke peeled off his denim jacket and tossed it in the vicinity of a chair. It slid off the arm and hit the floor. "It's no big deal."

"It is, too." Roxanne rezipped her bag and set it in its proper place on the closet shelf. She kicked aside a jumble of Luke's shoes. "If we've all been in on the planning stages from the get-go, why do you think you're the only one who gets to have the fun?"

"Because." He dropped down on the bed and tucked his arms behind his head. "That's the way I want it."

"Look, Callahan—"

"You look, Nouvelle." His use of her last name usually made her chuckle. Though her lips twitched, the stubborn chin was still up. "Max and I talked it over. It's cool with him, so let it go."

"Maybe it's cool with him, but not with me." She stuck her hands on her hips. "I'm in, pal. That's that."

His eyes glittered. "I want to do it myself."

"Tough. I want to have straight blond hair but you don't see me whining about it, do you?"

"I like your hair," he said, hoping to distract her. "It looks like a bunch of corkscrews that caught on fire."

"That's poetic."

"I especially like it when you're naked. Want to get naked, Rox?"

"Put a sock in your hormones, Callahan. You're not shaking me loose. I'm going."

"Suit yourself." It didn't matter if she went along or not. But arguing with her about it had taken her mind off Max. "But I run the show."

"In your dreams." She planted her hands on either side of his legs at the foot of the bed. "Full partners all the way."

"I've had more experience."

"That's what you said about sex, but I caught on, didn't I?"

"Now that you mention it." He reared up and made a grab for her. She danced easily out of reach.

"Come here," he demanded.

She tilted her head, sending him a long, seductive smile over her shoulder. "You look strong enough to get up and walk, Callahan. Why don't you come get me?"

He knew how to play the game. After a negligent movement of his shoulders, he gazed at the ceiling. "No thanks. Not that interested."

"Okay. You want to go eat early, avoid the Mardi Gras rush?"

"Sure." Without moving an inch he shifted his eyes down, watched her slowly peel off her shirt. Beneath she wore a thin white cotton athletic bra that should have been as alluring as cold gumbo. The blood drained out of his head and into his loins.

"I feel like something hot." She folded the shirt neatly, laid it on top of the dresser. With deliberate movements she unsnapped her jeans. He heard the quiet rasp of the zipper and concentrated on not swallowing his tongue. "And spicy."

She pulled the denim down, revealing practical cotton briefs in the same snowy white as the bra. Her skin was winter pale and flawless. The jeans went through the same meticulous routine as the shirt.

Idly she picked up her brush, tapping it against her palm. "What are you in the mood for, Callahan?" She strolled just close enough to the bed that when his hand shot out it could grip her arm. She was laughing as she hit the mattress.

"I won," he claimed, rolling on top of her.

"Uh-uh. Tie score." She lifted her head to meet his descending lips with hers. "We're partners. Don't you forget it."

23

Fat Tuesday started off with pancakes. For all LeClerc's talk about luck and fate, he believed in hedging his bets. He'd served pancakes on the last day before Lent as long as she could remember, and Roxanne was practical enough not to thumb her nose at superstition. Her only alteration was to buy a mix rather than slog through LeClerc's complicated recipe.

Her pancakes might have been thin and singed around the edges, but they fulfilled the basic requirements. She managed to chew her way through one of the rubbery disks, but as Luke plowed contentedly through half a dozen, she assumed their luck for the year was set.

And perhaps it was.

The streets and sidewalks of the Quarter were packed with celebrants on this last day of Mardi Gras. The sounds of music and laughter swung up to her balcony as they had for the week of constant partying. Tonight, she knew the volume and the frenzy would increase. Parades, costumes, dancing—that last hurrah before the forty days of sobriety to usher in Easter. But there would also be stumbling drunks, muggers, vicious fighting and a few murders. Behind its beautiful and seductive mask, Mardi Gras could wear a surly face.

Had the evening been free for her, she and Luke might have gone over to the house on Chartres and watched the goings-on from the balcony. As it was, they would be spending most of the night of revelry in Tennessee relieving Mr. and Mrs. Samuel Wyatt of approximately a half of a million in jewels.

Fair trade, Roxanne thought with a smile. The Wyatts would collect on their obscene insurance premiums, balancing that with the sting of having possessions snapped up from under their noses. The Nouvelles would keep the links in an old food chain secure. It wasn't only the Nouvelles who profited, after all.

Roxanne pressed a hand to her queasy stomach. The pancake, she thought, hadn't settled well. She hoped Luke's cast-iron stomach was holding up. The last thing he needed was nausea while he hung upside down above Lake Pontchartrain.

She needed to start over there herself. The escape was due to begin in just over an hour, and Luke would want her close by. The Burning Rope made her uneasy, but she'd grown accustomed to being nervy and tense before one of his escapes.

She picked up her purse, then dropped it again with a moan.

Damn those pancakes! she thought and made a dash for the bathroom.

"She should be here." Torn between concern and annoyance, Luke tried to prepare his mind for the job to come. His body was ready. "Why didn't she just come with me?"

"Because she'd have nothing to do during the setup except worry!" Lily kept an eagle eye on Max, who was granting an interview to one of the television reporters. She had worries of her own. "You concentrate on you," she ordered Luke. "Roxanne'll be along."

"Christ knows how she'd get through now." He scanned the bridge. Behind the barricades people swarmed and jockeyed for a better view. The local authorities had cooperated by closing the bridge to vehicular traffic for the hour Luke required from setup to completion. But that hadn't stopped the crowds. They'd streamed onto the bridge from both sides to press up against the barricades.

Luke wondered idly how many pockets would be picked over the lake that afternoon. He was always willing to lend a hand to an associate.

Where the hell was Roxanne?

He shaded his eyes against the brilliant glare of sun and gave the New Orleans side of the bridge one last look.

Lily was right, he told himself. He had to concentrate on the job at hand. Roxanne would get there when she got there.

At this height over the water, the wind was stiff. He'd factored that in, but he accepted that nature could often play capricious tricks with calculations. That wind was going to batter the living hell out of him.

"Let's do it."

He stepped to his mark. Instantly the crowd began to clap and call out encouragements. The cameras focused. After some delicate diplomacy, it had been decided that Lily would hype the escape rather than Max. She took her mike and, looking splashy in a red jumpsuit, held up a hand for silence.

"Good afternoon, ladies and gentlemen. Today, you're privileged to witness one of the most daring escapes ever attempted. The Burning Rope."

She continued, explaining exactly what would happen and introducing the two police officers, one from New Orleans, one from Lafayette, who examined the shackles and straitjacket Luke would use.

Once Luke's arms were in position, Lafayette cuffed one wrist, looped the chain through and secured the other. The key was held by Miss Louisiana, who'd come to the event decked out in full evening gear and tiara. New Orleans fit the restraint in place.

The rope was tied around Luke's ankles by the current calf-roping champion of the National Rodeo. There was a drumroll, courtesy of the Drum and Bugle Corps of a local high school.

Luke was lowered face first toward the waters of Lake Pontchartrain. Someone in the crowd screamed. Luke blessed them for their timing. There was nothing like a touch of hysteria or a couple of good faints to add to the drama.

A sharp gust of wind slapped his face hard enough to make his eyes water. His body twisted and swayed. He was already working on the cuffs.

He felt the tug when the rope played out. He had five seconds before a volunteer torched the end of the rope and sent the fire crawling toward him. He had to fight a surprising flood of vertigo when the wind cupped him in a playful hand and sent him spinning.

Fucking physics, he thought. A body in motion remains in motion, and he was trapped in a wide pendulum swing that thrilled and delighted the crowd, but made his job that much more difficult.

His satisfaction on freeing his hands was short-lived. He could smell the smoke. Slippery as a snake, he wormed his body inside the straitjacket, felt a bright flash of pain in his abused joints. His fingers went busily to work.

His mind was cold with control. Only one thought intruded, punching through the mechanics of the work like a relentless fist.

He would not stay trapped.

He heard the roar from above when the straitjacket plunged toward the water, empty. The rescue boat bobbing on the lake gave a congratulatory blast of its horn. Though he appreciated the sentiment, Luke was aware it was too early to open the champagne.

On a grunt of effort, he folded at the waist, stomach muscles straining as he levered himself up to fight the cowboy's knots from his legs. He didn't look at the fire, but he could smell it. It was inches away and sneaking closer.

He didn't think he'd die from singed feet, but he figured it would be damn uncomfortable. The clock in his mind warned him that he had minutes only before the fire ate through the rope and sent him diving headlong into the lake.

The cowboy had some tricky moves, Luke discovered. He wished he'd taken LeClerc's advice to slip a knife into his boot. But it was too late for regrets now. He'd manage the knots, or he'd take a swim to cool his hot foot.

He felt the rope give. This final stage took intricate timing. If he released himself too quickly, he'd take a dive. If he waited too long to set up, he'd end his escape with a trip to the burn ward. Neither appealed.

He hooked his hand around the second rope. Misdirection, and the fact that it was thin as wire, had kept the crowd from seeing it. Luke felt the heat from the burning rope smoke his knuckles as he secured his handhold.

He kicked his feet free and began to monkey his way up. From atop the bridge it appeared as though he was climbing on a thin column of fire. Indeed he would require some generous use of LeClerc's salve for singes and burns.

The crowd held its breath, let it out on a gasp each time the wind caught him. When he reached the top, he felt Mouse's good, solid grip on his arms. LeClerc bent down, ostensibly to offer a word of congratulations.

"Got him?" he muttered to Mouse.

"Yep."

"Bien." LeClerc flicked a knife from his sleeve and severed both ropes.

There were shrieks and shudders when the rope of fire fell into the lake.

"Want to pull me the rest of the way up?" Luke nearly had his breath back. He knew the moment the rush of adrenaline faded, he was going to hurt like a mother. With Mouse's assistance he gained his feet. The cameras were already closing in, but Luke was scanning the crowd.

"Roxanne?"

"Must've gotten tied up," Mouse said and thumped Luke hard enough on the back to make him stagger. "Your shirt was smoking," he said mildly and grinned. "That was a neat one, Luke. Maybe we could go to San Francisco and do it on the Golden Gate? Wouldn't that be great?"

"Sure." He passed a hand casually through his hair, just to make sure it wasn't on fire. "Why not?"

Maybe it was stupid, and overly possessive. Maybe it was a lot of unattractive things, but Luke knew only one pertinent fact when he walked into the bedroom, smelling of smoke and triumph, and found Roxanne stretched out on the bed. He was pissed.

"Well, that's really nice." He tossed his keys onto the dresser with a clatter that had Roxanne moaning and opening her eyes. "I figured you had to have been in some sort of a life-threatening accident, and here you are, taking a nap."

She took what she thought was a dreadful risk and opened her mouth to speak. "Luke—"

"I guess it wasn't any big deal to you, the fact that I've been working on this bit for months, that it was probably the biggest thing I've ever done or that you promised you'd be there when I got back up." He stalked to the foot of the bed, scowled briefly, then stalked away. "Just because I needed to concentrate, expected a little support from my woman—"

"Your woman?" That was enough to have her rearing up. "Don't you toss that phrase at me as though I was tucked somewhere between your silk suit and your record collection."

"You're a little higher than my record collection, but obviously my place is a few notches lower."

"Don't be such a jerk."

"Damn it, Rox, you knew this was important to me."

"I was going to come, but I—" She broke off as her stomach roiled. "Oh, shit." She scrambled up and dove into the bathroom.

By the time she'd finished retching, Luke was there with a cool, damp cloth and a repentant attitude. "Come on, baby, back to bed." It seemed her weakened body poured out of his arms and onto the sheets. "I'm sorry, Rox." Gently he bathed her clammy face. "I came in swinging and didn't even take a good look at you."

"How bad do I look?"

"Don't ask." He kissed her forehead. "What happened?"

"I thought it was the pancakes." She kept her eyes closed and her head very still and only opened her mouth wide enough to let the words whisper out. "I was hoping you'd come home green so I'd know it was food poisoning."

"Sorry." He smiled and brushed his lips across her brow again. She was clammy, but he didn't think there was a fever. "I'd say you have one of those twenty-four-hour things."

If she hadn't been so weak, she'd have been insulted. "I never get those."

"You never get anything," he pointed out. "But when something snags you, it snags big time." He remembered her chicken pox, the only childhood illness she'd ever succumbed to. That and the bout of seasickness aboard the *Yankee Princess* were the only times he remembered seeing her down. Until now.

"I just need to rest a little while more. I'll be fine."

"Roxanne." Luke set the cloth aside to take her face in his hands. "You're not going."

Her eyes shot open. She tried to sit up, but he held her in place with only the slightest pressure. "Of course I'm going. This whole gig was my idea in the first place. I'm not missing out on the payoff because I ate a bad pancake."

"It wasn't the pancakes," he corrected. "But it doesn't matter what caused it, you're sick as a dog."

"I'm not. I'm a little queasy."

"You're in no shape to pull a job."

"I'm in perfect shape."

"Fine, we make a deal." He sat back, eyeing her. "You get up now, walk to the living room and back without falling on your face, and we move forward as planned. You don't make it, I go alone."

Because it was a dare, it was irresistible. "All right. Move."

When he rose, she gritted her teeth and swung her legs out of bed. Her head spun, and fresh, nasty sweat popped out on the back of her neck, but she gained her feet.

"No holding on," Luke added when she braced a hand against the wall.

That stiffened her spine. She straightened, walked briskly into the living room. And sank into a chair. "I just need a minute."

"No deal." He crouched in front of her. "Rox, you know you can't do it."

"We could postpone—" She broke off, shaking her head. "No, that would be stupid. I'm being stupid." Weak, frustrated, she let her head fall back. "I hate missing this one, Callahan."

"I know." He picked her up to carry her back to bed. "I guess sometimes things don't work out exactly the way you want." He didn't think it was the time to mention his plans had taken a beating as well. Turning their flush of shared triumph into an evening of romance by asking her to marry him had seemed inspired. Now it would have to wait.

"You don't know the security system as well as I do."

"We've gone over it a dozen times," he reminded her, insulted. "It won't be my first night on the job."

"It'll take you longer."

"Sam and Justine are in Washington. I'll have the time."

"Take Mouse." Sudden panic had her grabbing for his hand. "Don't go alone."

"Rox, relax. I could do this in my sleep. You know that."

"It doesn't feel right."

"You don't feel right," he corrected. "I want you to get some rest. I'll call Lily and have her come by to look in on you. Keep a light burning, babe." He kissed her then, lightly. "I'll be back before sunrise."

"Callahan." She tightened her grip as he eased back. It was foolish, she thought, this awful reluctance to let him go. "I love you."

He smiled and leaned down to kiss her again, the light, friendly kiss of a man who knew he'd have time for more soon. "I love you, too."

"Break a leg." She sighed, and let him go.

Luke loved to fly. From the very first time he'd strapped into the cockpit to take his initial lesson from Mouse, he'd been hooked. It had no longer been a matter of learning a practical skill that could add convenience to both of his careers. It had been, from that soaring beginning, pure delight.

The plane he piloted was registered to a John Carroll Brakeman, a nonexistent insurance executive. To complete the alias, Luke had added a short, trim beard, a three-piece pin-striped suit—with several successful inches of padding beneath it. His black hair was sprinkled with silver at the temples.

When he landed in Tennessee, he logged in, checked his return flight plan and carried his monogrammed briefcase to the spiffy Mercedes 450 he'd rented. He drove it to the Hilton, checked into his reserved suite and left orders not to be disturbed.

Fifteen minutes later, minus the beard, the padding and the silver temples, he hurried down the stairwell to the parking lot. The dark sedan he'd ordered under another alias was waiting. Because it was safer than picking up the keys at the desk, Luke popped the lock, hot-wired the engine and drove serenely away.

Once the job was completed, he would return the sedan to the parking lot and slip back into his room. He would re-don his disguise and check out. Richer by approximately one half a million dollars, he'd fly back to New Orleans. Nothing would connect him with either the alias or the burglary.

A roundabout route, perhaps, but as Max was wont to say, a roundabout route still gets you where you want to go.

Two blocks from Sam's house, Luke parked the dark, nondescript sedan on a tree-lined street. In this suburban paradise, all the lawns were trimmed, the dogs well behaved and the houses respectably dark at one A.M.

Streetlamps pooled light he easily avoided. Clad in black from head to foot, he slipped between shadows. There was a trace of fog that might give him some problems at the airport. But he felt the mist had been custom-made for him. There was a half moon, but its light was trapped behind shifting clouds and the air was sweet with hints of spring.

He circled the Wyatt estate, a sprawling two-story brick with white columns that resembled slender bones in the half-light. There was no car in the drive. The security lights beamed like swords over the lawn and picked up pretty banks of golden daffodils and the tender furled leaves of trees still greening. He was almost sorry that Sam was in Washington. It would have added spice to the sweetness of satisfaction to have stolen in and taken what he wanted while his old enemy snored.

A tall privacy fence guarded the house on three sides, and old leafy trees shielded the front. Luke used both as shelter as he approached.

He missed Roxanne severely when he started on the security. The new computerized systems annoyed him, insulted his creativity. He supposed the numbers and complex sequences appealed to Roxanne's logical mind, but to Luke they took the art of thievery into the ennui of accounting.

Even with her instructions playing in his head, it took him twice as long as it would have taken her to access the code. Still, she didn't have to know.

Satisfied, he chose the rear entrance and handily picked the lock. He preferred the method to jimmying, which any second-rate B&E man could accomplish, and certainly held it above smashing a pane of glass, which took no skill whatsoever.

Luke stepped into a neat sitting room that smelled of lemon oil and wisteria. The old excitement crept up his spine. There was something indescribably arousing about standing in a dark, empty house, surrounded by the shapes and shadows of another person's possessions. It was like being told their secrets.

Luke walked silently from the sitting room, turning left in the corridor toward Sam's office. His fingers were already itching inside the thin, surgical gloves to turn the dial of the safe.

He needed no light. His eyes had had time to adjust, and he knew the square footage of the Wyatt home a great deal better than its owners.

There was a quality of silence to an empty house Luke had always enjoyed. It was a whispering, a humming, an eerily pleasant kind of music the air took on when there was no one inside to breathe it.

He had turned into Sam's office before it struck him that the music was absent. Then the light flashed on, blinding him.

"Well, Luke, come right on in." Sam leaned back in his desk chair, causing the leather to creak. "I've been expecting you. Please." He gestured, and the light glinted off the chrome of the .32 he held. "Join me for a drink."

Luke studied Sam's smile, scanned the smooth surface of the desk where two brandies rested. He imagined it was Napoleon, but doubted its flavor would wash the oily taste of a setup out of his mouth.

"How long have you known?"

"Oh, several months now." With the gun aimed at Luke's chest, he leaned forward to cup his snifter. "I'm ashamed to say I didn't suspect earlier. All this time, I put the Nouvelles' extravagant life-style down to a little blackmail or some short cons. Sit," he invited. "I'm so terribly sorry you came alone."

"I work alone," Luke said, hoping to salvage at least that much.

"You were always pathetically gallant. Sit," he repeated, and his voice was as cold as the chrome of the handgun. Gauging his best chance was to play the scene out, Luke sat. "The brandy's excellent." Sam set aside his snifter to lift the phone. "Don't worry," he said when he noticed the flash in Luke's narrowed eyes. "I'm not phoning the police. I don't believe we'll need them." He punched a series of buttons, waited. "He's here. Yes. Use the back door." He was smiling when he replaced the receiver. "A little surprise. Now what shall we talk about while we wait?"

"You might be able to make breaking and entering stick," Luke said calmly. "There's a possibility of attempted burglary. All of which I can probably finesse into a joke. Poor judgment, I could say, trying to pull a fast one on a childhood rival."

Sam paused a moment as if considering. "I doubt that would work, particularly after I pointed out the pattern. One I admit I didn't catch on to until recently. You son of a bitch," he said with the smile still spread over his face. "You sanctimonious bastards—all of you. Acting outraged because I knocked over a couple of shops while you were nothing but petty thieves and grifters yourselves."

"Not petty," Luke corrected and decided to try the brandy after all. "And never grifters. What do you want?"

"What I've wanted all along. To make you pay. I hated you, right from the start. Keep your hands where I can see them," he warned. Luke shrugged and sipped brandy. "I didn't know precisely why, only that I did. But I believe it was because we were so alike."

Now Luke smiled. "You've got a gun on me, Wyatt. You can kill me or send me to prison. But don't insult me."

"Always cool, and still reckless. It was a combination I might have admired if you hadn't been so disgustingly superior. You held the Nouvelles in the palm of your hand. Oh, I saw the potential even then, but you were in the way."

"Face it, pal." Maybe, just maybe, he could anger him enough to force him into a mistake. "You fucked up."

Sam's eyes glittered, but the gun didn't waver. "What I fucked was your girl. And I seduced Roxanne away from you. Believe me, if I'd realized the potential there, I'd have fucked her rather than—what was her name? Annabelle."

The fury bounded up. Luke had to curl his hand around the arm of the chair to stay seated. "I should have broken more than your nose."

"There, for the first time, you're correct. You should have destroyed me, Callahan, because now, I'll destroy you. Come in, Mr. Cobb."

Now Luke did jerk to his feet. Brandy splashed over his gloved hand. There, in the doorway, was his oldest nightmare.

"I believe you two know each other," Sam continued. Oh, this was rich, he thought. Magnificent. What more could he ask for than to see Luke's face go white? A great deal more, he decided, chuckling to himself. A great deal more. "You might not be aware that Mr. Cobb has been working for me for quite some time now. Help yourself to the bar while I explain a few salient points to our mutual friend."

"Don't mind if I do." Cobb strutted over to the whiskey decanter and poured a double. He liked the idea of sharing a drink with a man of Wyatt's caliber, being invited—after all this time—into his home. "Looks like he's got you by the short hairs, Luke."

"Succinctly put. Now that we're all together, I'll outline the deal." It was perfect, so perfect, Sam could barely keep his voice from shivering with excitement. "It was my idea to have Mr. Cobb contact you and squeeze you for a few thousand a month. Imagine my surprise when you paid quietly and with ease, even when I gave him permission to increase the amounts. Now, how, I asked myself does a man—even one with a certain amount of financial success—pay off blackmail demands in excess of a hundred thousand a year without altering his life-style by even the smallest degree?" Waiting a beat, Sam tapped a finger against his curved lips. "He can't, of course, unless he has another source of income. So, I began tracking you. I still have contacts of my own, you know. Then I laid the bait and watched you nibble. My insurance company, my security system, my schedule. It wasn't difficult to make it seem as though I planned to be in Washington this week."

The first wave of sickness had sweat springing cold to the back of Luke's neck. "You opened the cage door," he managed, "that doesn't mean I'll let it lock behind me."

"I'm aware of that. You see with a clever lawyer you might just wriggle out of the charges. Since you came alone, it would be difficult if not impossible to spread the blame to the Nouvelles. I could simply kill you." Lips pursed, he lifted the gun, sighting in on Luke's forehead. "But then, you'd only be dead."

"Don't kill the golden goose," Cobb said and chuckled at his own wit.

"Certainly not, particularly if you can make him roast slowly."

"And he'll keep paying, too." Cobb poured more whiskey.

"Yes, though not in the way you mean." Sam smiled at Cobb, then pulled the trigger.

The sound of the bullet exploded in the small room. Luke felt it echo through him as if he were a hollow tunnel. Dazed, he watched Cobb stagger, saw the look of surprise on his face, and the blood flow through the neat black hole that had suddenly appeared in his forehead.

The glass of whiskey hit the rug first, rolled unbroken across the bright Turkish carpet. And Cobb fell like a tree.

"That was easier than I imagined." Sam's hand shook once, but it was excitement rather than nerves. "Much easier."

"Jesus." Luke tried to spring to his feet but found his limbs heavy. He rose slowly, like a man fighting his way up through water. The room spun like a carousel and the bright, bloody carpet flew up to meet him.

When he awakened, his head felt clogged. The drummers banging inside it were muffled with wads of cotton wool.

"Obviously you have good stamina." Sam's voice seemed to drift through the mists. "I thought you'd be out longer."

"What?" Wobbly, Luke managed to crawl up on his hands and knees. He had to fight a powerful wave of nausea before he dared lift his head. When he did, he saw Cobb's dead-white face. "Oh, God." Lifting a hand, he wiped the sweat from his face. He was light-headed and sick, but still aware enough to realize he no longer wore his gloves.

"No gratitude?" Sam demanded. He sat behind the desk again, but when Luke focused in, he saw he held a different gun. "After all, the man made your life hell, didn't he? Now he's dead."

"You didn't even flinch." Sam, the gun, the room wavered as Luke fought to clear his head. "You shot him in cold blood and didn't even flinch."

"Thank you. Remember, I can do the same with you—or Max or Lily. Or Roxanne."

He wasn't going to beg, not on his hands and knees. Painfully, Luke pulled himself to his feet. His legs wobbled, adding humiliation to terror. "What do you want?"

"Exactly what I'm going to get. I can call the police now, tell them you and Cobb broke in while I was working late in my office. I surprised you, you pulled a gun. Then you argued between yourselves, and you shot him. During the confusion, I managed to get my gun. This is my gun by the way."

He gestured with a trim .25. He wanted to pull the trigger, wanted badly to pull it and feel that jolt of power again. But that would be too quick. Too quick, too final.

"The other is unregistered, and untraceable—except for the fact that it now has your fingerprints on it. You'll be charged with murder, and with your connection to Cobb, I doubt you'd wiggle out."

He smiled then, hugely. A man dazzled by his own brilliance.

"That's our first scenario," he went on. "Which would play nicely, I believe. I don't like it as much as the second, because it involves me. The second is that you take the body and dispose of it. Then you go."

"Go?" Struggling to remain lucid, Luke dragged a hand through his hair. "Just like that?"

"Exactly. Only you don't go back to New Orleans. You don't contact the Nouvelles. You, quite literally, disappear." The grin on Sam's face spread, erupted into a fast, wild giggle. "Abracadabra." The sound had cold fingers squeezing Luke's spine.

"You're out of your mind."

"You'd like to think so, wouldn't you?" Sam asked, and his eyes glittered. "You'd like to think so because I've beaten you, beaten you at last."

"All of this?" Luke's voice was still slurred from the drug. He spoke slowly, carefully, as if to be certain he understood the words himself. "You planned all this, you murdered Cobb, just to get back at me?"

"Does that seem unreasonable?" Sam leaned back in his chair, swiveled it side to side. "Perhaps I'd think so if I were in your position." He jerked forward again, and had the pleasure of seeing Luke jolt and brace. "But you see, I'm not. I'm in charge. And you'll do exactly as I say. If you don't, I'll have you arrested for murder, and I'll see that Maximillian Nouvelle is investigated for grand larceny—unless I find it more enjoyable to kill him."

"He took you in off the street."

"And kicked me back onto it." The smile on Sam's face twisted into a sneer of disgust. "Don't expect loyalty from me, Callahan, especially if you're not willing to put your own on the line."

"Why don't you just kill me?"

"I prefer the idea of you grubbing for a living in some godforsaken town, having sweaty dreams about Roxanne and the men she'll fill her life with, losing that star you've held on to so tightly over the years. Escape this, Callahan. You go, or the Nouvelles pay, for the rest of their lives. And don't think you can leave now, then reappear in a few weeks. You may slip the noose, but I'll pull it taut around Max's neck, that I promise. I have all the evidence I need to hang him, right in the safe you never had the opportunity to open."

"No one would believe you."

"No? A dedicated public servant with a pristine record? A man who brought himself out of the hell of the streets? Who, though he felt a certain loyalty to the old man, could no longer conceal the facts? And who, recognizing the signs of senility, would plead for confinement in a mental health facility rather than prison?"

That turned fear to ice, a sharp, ragged spear of ice that threatened to draw blood. "No one's going to put Max away."

"That's up to you. Your call, Callahan."

"You've got the hammer." He felt his life slipping through his fingers like sand. "I'll disappear, Wyatt. But you'll never be entirely sure when I'll be back. One night I'll just be there."

"Take your old friend with you, Callahan." He gestured toward Cobb. "And think of me, every day, when you're in hell."

24

Luke knew it was foolishly risky, but risks no longer seemed to matter. He left the second rental car in the hotel parking lot and, using the main elevators in the lobby, rode up to his room. Once inside he pulled a bottle of Jack Daniel's out of a paper sack, set it on the dresser and stared at it.

He stared for a long time before breaking the seal. He tipped the bottle back, taking three long swallows to let the fire burn through the worst of the misery.

It didn't work. He'd already learned from the harsh example of his youth that liquor didn't negate miseries, it only compounded them. But it had been worth a shot.

He could still smell Cobb. The sweat and blood and stench of death clung to his skin. It had been a hideous job, weighing down the body and sinking it into the river.

He'd wanted him dead. God knew he wanted the man dead. But he hadn't known what sudden, violent and pitiless death could do.

Luke couldn't forget how Sam had fired the gun—so casually, as if taking a life was as simple an event as an evening of cards. He hadn't done it out of hate, or for gain or in blind passion. He'd done it thoughtlessly, like a young child might tumble a building of blocks. All because Cobb had been marginally more use to him dead than alive.

Control, Luke thought, easing down on the bed like an old man. All these years he'd thought he'd been in control. But that had been a lie. All along there had been someone behind the scenes, pulling the strings and making a mockery out of what he'd thought he'd made and could make out of his life.

All because of some twisted sense of jealousy, and an overheated grudge due to a broken nose. Anyone standing in that leather and oak office that evening would have seen that Sam was more than ambitious, he was more than cold-blooded. He was crazy. But there was only one person still alive who had seen it.

What could he do? Luke rubbed the heels of his hands over his eyes as if to wipe away the image of what had been so that he could clearly see what had to be.

He'd broken into a private home. If the police knew where to look they would find the trail, and that trail would lead directly back to the Nouvelles. If Luke went to the police with a tangled story of blackmail and murder, whom would they believe? The thief, or the sober citizen?

He could risk that. Though he wasn't certain he could face prison without going mad, he could risk that. But there was a chance Sam would make good on his other threats. Max in a mental ward, Lily devastated, Roxanne ruined. Or perhaps Sam would find murder more to his liking and kill them—kill them with the gun that carried Luke's fingerprints.

That thought brought panic bubbling up so that he grabbed the phone and punched in numbers. His fingers grabbed hard on the receiver. She answered on the first ring, as if she'd been waiting for him.

"Hello . . . Hello? Is anyone there?"

He could see her, as clearly as if he'd conjured her into the room. Sitting up in bed, the phone to her ear and an open book in her lap, an old black-and-white movie flickering on the television.

Then the image was gone, vanished like smoke, because he knew he would never see her that way again.

"Hello? Luke, is that you? Is something—"

He set the phone down, slowly, quietly.

He'd made his choice. To answer her, to tell her would be to keep her and watch her suffer. To leave her, without a word, without a sign, would mean she would grow to hate him, safely.

Like a man already drunk, he rose and brought the bottle back to bed. It wouldn't ease his miseries, but it might bring him sleep.

In the morning, freshly showered, the disguise in place, he checked out of the hotel and headed for the airport. He wanted to live. Perhaps only to make certain, from a distance, that Sam left the Nouvelles undisturbed. And perhaps to bide his time, to wait, to watch and to plan a suitable revenge.

Yet he had no flight plan, no destination. Though he loved to fly, his life was now as empty as the bottle he'd left behind him.

"He should have been back hours ago." Rubbing her damp palms together, Roxanne paced her father's workroom. "Something went wrong. He should never have gone alone."

"It's not his first job, my dear." Max lifted a brightly painted box from a waist-high bench and revealed Mouse's grinning severed head. "He knows what he's doing."

"He hasn't checked in."

"This isn't a weigh station." At a press of a button of the remote concealed in Max's sleeve the head gave a long, echoing moan. Another switch and the eyes rolled left and right, the mouth moved. "Excellent, excellent. Lifelike, don't you think?"

"Daddy." To gain his full attention, Roxanne shoved the box back down over the head. "Luke's in trouble. I know it."

"How do you know it?" He switched off the remote.

"Because no one's heard from him since he left here last night. Because he was due back by six A.M., and it's nearly noon. Because when I called the airport to ask about John Carroll Brakeman, they said he'd filed his flight plan but he'd never shown up."

"Obvious reasons. Just as it's obvious the head is still inside this box." With a show of his old flair, Max plucked the box off the table. The head was gone, replaced by a thriving geranium. "I raised you better than to accept the obvious."

"This isn't a magic trick, damn it." She spun away. How could he play games when Luke was missing? Max laid a hand on her shoulder, and she stiffened.

"He's a bright, resourceful boy, Roxy. I knew the first time I saw him. He'll be back soon."

She hurled his own words back at him. "How do *you* know?"

"It's in the cards." To distract and amuse her, Max pulled a deck from his pocket, whipped them into a fan. But his stiffened fingers couldn't make the flourish. To Max, it seemed as though the cards had come alive to jump gleefully from his hands and scatter. He watched with eyes dulled with horror as they flew out of his grip.

Roxanne felt his heart break as keenly as she felt her own. She crouched to gather the deck and hurried to fill the awful silence.

"I know Luke sometimes breaks routine, but not like this." She cursed the cards, cursed age, cursed her own inadequacy to fill the gap. "Do you think I should go look for him?"

He continued to stare at the floor, though the cards were gone, hidden behind Roxanne's back. Now you see them, now you don't. But Max had a better magic formula. He simply stopped fighting to keep his mind on what was. When he brought his eyes back to his daughter's there was a smile in them, a mild, pleasant, utterly heart-wrenching smile. "If we look hard enough, long enough, we always find what we need. Do you know many people believe there's more than one philosophers' stone? But they've fallen into the trap of the obvious."

"Daddy." Roxanne reached out with her free hand, but Max shook his head, miles away from the daughter who stood watching him with tears in her eyes.

Abruptly, he slammed a book with enough force to make Roxanne jump. There was no smile in his eyes now, but there was passion, and there was desperation. "I've nearly tracked it down now." He held up a ream of notes, shaking them. "When I do, when I finally have it . . ." Gently, he set the papers down, smoothing his aching fingers over them. "Well, the magic will be there, won't it?"

"Yes, it'll be there." She crossed to him to drape her arms around him, press her cheek to his. "Why don't you come upstairs with me, Daddy?"

"No, no, you run along. I have work to do." He sat to pore greedily through ancient books with ancient secrets. "Tell Luke to call Lester," he said absently. "I want to make certain that new lighting equipment's in place."

She opened her mouth to remind Max that the old Magic Door manager had retired to Las Vegas three years earlier. Instead she pressed her lips together hard and nodded. "All right, Daddy."

She climbed the stairs and went to search out Lily.

Roxanne found her in the courtyard, throwing bread crumbs to pigeons.

"LeClerc gets mad at me for doing this." Lily tossed a handful of shredded bread into the air and laughed when the pigeons bumped and squabbled for it. "They get do all over the bricks. But they're so sweet, the way they bob their heads and watch you with those little black eyes."

"Lily, what's wrong with Daddy?"

"Wrong?" Lily's hand froze inside the plastic bag. "Did he hurt himself?" She turned and would have dashed inside if Roxanne hadn't stopped her.

"He isn't hurt. He's down in the workroom going through his books."

"Oh." Relief was so palpable Lily pressed a hand to her heart. She doubted a pigeon's could beat much faster. "You scared me."

"I'm scared," Roxanne said quietly and caused Lily's tentative smile to falter. "He's ill, isn't he?"

For a moment she said nothing. Then the pale blue eyes lost their helpless far-away look. They steadied. "I think we should talk." Lily slipped an arm around Roxanne's waist. "Let's sit down."

Taking charge, she steered Roxanne toward an iron bench beneath the still tender shade of a live oak. The waters of the little fountain tinkled gaily, like a brook over pebbles.

"Give me a minute, honey." She sat, keeping one of Roxanne's hands tight in hers while continuing to throw treats for the birds with her other. "I love this time of year," she murmured. "Not that the heat's ever bothered me like it does some, but spring, early spring is magic. The daffodils and hyacinths are blooming, the tulip stems are poking out. There's a nest in this tree." She glanced up, but her smile was wistful, a little lost. "It's the same every year. They always come back. The birds, the flowers. I can come sit out here and watch, and know some things are forever."

Pigeons cooed and clucked around their feet. From beyond the courtyard gates there was a steady whoosh of traffic. The sun was kind today, softened by a breeze that whispered through tender leaves. From somewhere close by in the Quarter, a flutist played an old Irish tune, "Danny Boy." Roxanne recognized it and shivered, knowing it was a song of death and loss.

"I made him go to the doctor." Lily kneaded Roxanne's hand, soothing as she was soothed. "Max could never hold out against good old-fashioned nagging. They ran tests. Then I had to make him go back so they could run more tests. He wouldn't check into the hospital so they could do everything at once. And I . . . well, I didn't push for that. I didn't want him to go in either."

A pulse began to beat hard behind Roxanne's eyes. Her voice sounded detached, and not at all her own. "What kind of tests?"

"All kinds. So many I lost track. They hooked him up to machines, and they studied graphs. They took samples of blood and made him pee in a cup. They took X rays." She lifted her shoulders, let them fall. "Maybe it was wrong, Roxy, but I asked them to tell me when they found out. I didn't want them telling Max if it was something bad. I know you're his daughter, you're his blood, but I—"

"You didn't do wrong." Roxanne rested her head on Lily's shoulder. "You did exactly right." It took a minute to bolster her courage. "It is something bad, isn't it? You have to tell me, Lily."

"He's going to keep forgetting things," Lily said, and her voice trembled. "Some days he might be just fine, and others, he won't be able to keep his mind focused, even with the medication. It's kind of like a train that jumps off the track. They said it might move real slow, but we should be prepared for times when he won't remember us." Tears slid silently down her cheek and plopped on their joined hands. "He might get angry, accuse us of trying to hurt him, or he might just do what he's told without questioning. He could walk to the corner for a quart of milk and forget how to get home. He could forget who he is, and if they can't stop it, one day he could just go away inside his mind where none of us could reach."

It was worse, Roxanne realized. Much worse than death. "We'll—we'll find a specialist."

"The doctor recommended one. I called him. We can take Max to Atlanta next month to see him." Lily took out one of her useless lace hankies to wipe her eyes. "Meantime he's going to study all Max's tests. They called it Alzheimer's, Roxy, and they don't have a cure."

"Then we'll find one. We're not going to let this happen to Max." She sprang up and would have swayed to her knees if Lily hadn't caught her.

"Honey, oh, honey, what is it? I shouldn't have told you like this."

"No, I just got up too fast." But the dizziness still swam in her head. Nausea clenched in her stomach.

"You're so pale. Let's go in and get you some tea or something."

"I'm all right," she insisted as Lily pulled her toward the house. "It's just some stupid virus." The minute they hit the kitchen door, the scent of the hearty soup LeClerc had simmering on the stove turned her pale skin green. "Damn it," she said through clenched teeth. "I don't have time for this."

She dashed to the bathroom with Lily fluttering behind her.

After she'd finished being sick, she was weak enough not to protest when Lily led her up to bed and insisted she lie down.

"All this worry," Lily diagnosed.

"It's a bug." Roxanne closed her eyes and prayed there was nothing left for her stomach to reject. "I thought it had run its course. Same thing happened yesterday afternoon. By last night I was fine. This morning, too."

"Well." Lily patted her hand. "If you told me you'd gotten sick two mornings in a row, I'd wonder if you were pregnant."

"Pregnant!" Roxanne's eyes popped open again. She wanted to laugh, but it didn't seem particularly funny. "You don't get afternoon sickness when you're pregnant."

"I guess not." But Lily's mind was working. "You haven't missed a period, have you?"

"I haven't missed one, exactly." Roxanne felt the first skip of panic, and something else. Something that wasn't fear of any kind but simple, subtle pleasure. "I'm a little late, that's all."

"How late?"

Roxanne plucked the bedspread with her fingers. "Couple of weeks. Maybe three."

"Oh, honey!" Lily's voice held pure delight. Visions of booties and baby powder danced in her head. "A baby."

"Don't get ahead of yourself." Cautious, Roxanne pressed a hand to her stomach. If there was a baby in there, it was a mean one. That made her lips curve. She wouldn't expect Luke's baby to be sweet-natured, would she?

"They've got those home pregnancy tests now. You could find out right away. This'll knock Luke right off his feet."

"We never talked about it." The fear crept back. "Lily, we never even talked about children. He might not want—"

"Don't be silly, of course he wants. He loves you. Now you stay right here. I'm going down and get you some milk."

"Tea," Roxanne corrected. "I think my system might be able to hold down some tea—a couple of crackers."

"No strawberries and pickle relish?" She giggled when Roxanne groaned. "Sorry, sweetie. I'm just so excited. Be right back."

A baby, Roxanne thought. Why hadn't she considered she might be pregnant? Or had she? She sighed and turned cautiously to her side. She wasn't really surprised by the possibility. And though she thought she'd taken the pill faithfully, she wasn't sorry either.

Luke's baby and hers. What would he say? How would he feel?

The only way to know was to find him.

Reaching over, she pulled the phone onto the bed and dialed.

When Lily came back later with tea, dry toast and a pretty pink rosebud, Roxanne was lying on her back again, staring dully at the ceiling.

"He's gone, Lily."

"Hmmm? Who?"

"Luke's gone." She pushed herself up. Nausea had no chance against the emotions rioting inside her. "I called the airport. He took off from Tennessee at nine thirty-five this morning."

"Nine-thirty?" Lily set the tray on the dresser. "Why, it's after twelve now. It only takes an hour or so to fly back to New Orleans."

"He wasn't headed to New Orleans. I had to do a lot of wrangling to get his flight plan, but I managed it."

"What do you mean he wasn't headed for New Orleans? Of course he was."

"Mexico," Roxanne whispered. "He's going to Mexico."

By the next morning, Roxanne was certain of two things. She was pregnant, and it was possible for a man to vanish from the face of the earth. But what could vanish could be conjured again. She wasn't a second-generation magician for nothing.

She was just zipping her traveling case when she heard the knock. Her first thought, like a flash of lightning, was Luke! She made it from the bedroom to the front door in a dash.

"Where have you—oh, Mouse."

"Sorry, Roxy." His big shoulders slumped.

"It's all right." She mustered up a smile. "Listen, I'm practically on my way out the door."

"I know. Lily said how you were going to Mexico to look for Luke. I'm going with you."

"That's a nice thought, Mouse, but I've already made my plans."

"I'm going with you." He might have been slow, he might have been sweet, but he could also be stubborn. "You're not going all that way alone in your . . . in your condition," he finished on a burst. His face burned beet red.

"Lily's knitting booties already?" But she softened the sarcasm by patting his arm. "Mouse, there's nothing to worry about. I know what I'm doing, and I don't think carrying something the size of a pinprick's going to slow me down."

"I'm going to take care of you. Luke would want me to."

"If Luke was so damn concerned, he wouldn't be in Mexico," she snapped, and was immediately sorry as Mouse's face crumpled and fell. "Sorry. I guess being pregnant messes up your hormones and makes you cranky. I've already got my flight reservations, Mouse."

He wasn't going to budge. "You can cancel them. I'll fly you."

She started to protest, then shrugged. Maybe the company would do her good.

She made it to the ladies' room at the Cancún airport. It occurred to her as she retched that she could almost clock her nausea with a stopwatch. Perhaps the baby had inherited her sense of timing.

When she felt she could stand again, she rejoined a worried Mouse in the tiny, sunwashed terminal. "It's okay," she told him. "Just one of the benefits of expectant motherhood."

"You going to have to do that for nine whole months?"

"Thanks, Mouse," she said weakly. "I needed that."

They spent nearly an hour trying to get information on Luke's plane from the flight tower. Yes, he had been scheduled to land at that airport. No, he had never arrived. He had never come into radio contact or requested permission to divert. He had simply veered off somewhere over the Gulf.

Or, as the cheerful flight dispatcher suggested, into the Gulf.

"He didn't crash, damn it." Roxanne stormed back to the plane. "No way did he crash."

"He's a good pilot." Mouse hustled behind her, patting her shoulder, her head. "And I checked out the plane myself before he left."

"He didn't crash," she repeated. Unrolling one of Mouse's charts, she began to study the lay of the land on the Mexican side of the Gulf. "Where would he go, Mouse? If he'd decided to avoid Cancún."

"I'd make a better guess if I knew why."

"We don't know why." She rubbed the cold bottle of Coke Mouse had bought her against her sweaty brow. "We can speculate—maybe he wanted to cover a trail. We can't call Sam and ask him if his wife's sapphires are missing. There's been no announcement on the news of a burglary, but they often keep the wraps on for a while. If he ran into trouble in Tennessee, he might have decided, for his own idiotic reasons, to head west, let John Carroll Brakeman disappear."

"But why didn't he check in?"

"I don't know." She wanted to scream it, but kept her tone level. "These islands here. Some of them have to have airstrips. Official ones, and not-so-official ones. For smuggling."

"Yeah, sure."

"Okay." She handed the chart to Mouse. "Let's check it out."

They spent three days searching the Mayan Peninsula. They spread Luke's description up and down the coast, slipping money into eager hands and following false leads.

Roxanne's bouts of nausea left Mouse wringing his hands and wishing for Lily. If he tried to fuss or pamper, Roxanne snapped like a terrier. Conversely, her flashes of temper reassured him. He was well aware that given the chance, she would tramp off into the jungle alone, armed with no more than a canteen and a driving need. Until they located Luke, Mouse considered Roxanne his responsibility. When she looked too pale or too flushed, he forced her to stop and rest, bearing her tantrums like an oak bears the tapping of a woodpecker—with silence and grave dignity.

The routine became so set, both of them began to feel they would spend the rest of their lives at it.

Then they found the plane.

It cost Roxanne a thousand American dollars for a ten-minute conversation with a one-eyed Mexican entrepreneur who ran his business out of a sod hut in the Mayan jungle near Mérida.

He pared his nails with a pocketknife while a wary-eyed woman with dusty feet fried tortillas.

"He says he wants to sell, do I want to buy." Juarez tipped tequila into a tin cup, then generously offered Roxanne the bottle.

"No, thanks. When did you buy the plane?"

"Two days ago. I give him good price." He'd all but stolen it, and the satisfaction of that made Juarez expansive to the pretty señorita. "He needs money, I give him money."

"Where did he go?"

"I don't ask questions."

She wanted to swear, but noting the skittishness of the woman by the stove, opted for tact. Her smile was laced with admiration. "But you'd know if he was still in the area. A man like you, with your contacts, you'd know."

"Sí." He appreciated the fact she showed respect. "He's gone. He camps one night in the jungle, then poof." Juarez snapped his fingers. "Gone. He moves softly, and fast. If he knows such a beautiful lady wants him, maybe he moves slower."

Roxanne pushed away from the table. Luke knew she wanted him, she thought wearily. And still, he was running. "Would you mind if I looked at the plane?"

"Look." Juarez gestured, and something in her eyes stopped him from demanding a separate payment for the privilege. "But you won't find him."

She found nothing of him, not even ashes from one of his cigars. There was no sign that Luke had ever sat in the cockpit or held the wheel or studied the stars through the glass.

"We can try north," Mouse said as Roxanne sat in the pilot's seat and stared out at nothing. "Or inland." He was groping, uneasy with the blank, dazed look on her face. "Could be he went further inland."

"No." She only shook her head. Despite the heat hammering down on the roof of the plane, she was too cold for tears. "He left his message right here."

Confused, Mouse glanced around the cockpit. "But, Roxy, there's nothing here."

"I know." She closed her eyes, let the grief tear through her so hope could drain free. When she opened them again, they were clear, and they were hard. "There's nothing here, Mouse. He doesn't want to be found. Let's go home."

Part Three

This rough magic I here abjure.

—William Shakespeare

25

Now he was back. His five-year vanishing act was over, and like the veteran performer he was, Luke had posed his return engagement with a sense of drama and panache. His audience of one was captivated.

For a moment.

The man pressed against her cleverly assaulting her mouth, her mind, wasn't an illusion. He was flesh and blood. It was all so achingly familiar, the good solid weight of him, the taste of his skin, the trip-hammer of her own pulse as those strong, clever fingers crept up to cup her cheek.

He was real.

He was home.

He was the lowest form of life that had ever slunk through the mud.

Her hands tightened in his hair, then yanked with enough strength to make him yelp.

"Jesus, Roxanne—"

But that was all the misdirection she needed. She twisted, shoving her elbow hard into his ribs, popping her knee up between his legs. He managed to block the crippling knee, but she used that same stiffened elbow to catch him hard on the chin.

He saw stars. The next thing he knew, he was on his back with Roxanne straddling him and snarling as her carefully manicured nails shot toward his face.

He gripped her wrists, clamping down before those curled fingers could peel back his skin. They remained in that position, one that brought each uncomfortably sensual memories, breathing hard and eyeing each other with mutual dislike.

"Let me go, Callahan."

"I want to keep my face in the same condition it was when I walked in."

She tried to twist free, but the five years he'd spent doing God knew what hadn't weakened him. He was still strong as a bull. Biting would have been satisfying, but undignified. She settled on disdain.

"Keep your face. It doesn't interest me."

Though he loosened his hold, he remained braced until she stood, with as much grace and arrogance as a goddess rising out of a pool.

He got up quickly, with that eerie speed and economy of movement she remembered too well, and stood on the balls of his feet. Saying nothing, she turned her back on him and poured a glass of champagne. Even as the bubbles exploded on her tongue, they tasted flat and dry. But it gave her a moment, a much needed moment, to lock the last latch on her heart.

"Still here?" she asked as she turned back.

"We have a lot to talk about."

"Do we?" She sipped again. "Odd, I can't think of a thing."

"Then I'll do the talking." He stepped over pooling water and crushed roses to top off his own glass of wine. "You can try something new, like listening." His hand whipped out to snag her wrist before she could toss her wine into his face. "Want to fight some more, Rox?" His voice was low and dangerous and, Lord help her, sent a thrill racing up her spine. "You'll lose. Figure the odds."

They would be against. Temper might urge her to fly biting and scratching into his face, but she'd only end up on her butt again. Still, she had other weapons. And she'd use them all to pay him back for the years he'd left her alone.

"I won't waste good wine on you." When his fingers relaxed, she brought the glass back to her lips. "And my time's even more valuable. I have an engagement, Luke. You'll have to excuse me."

"Your calendar's free until the press conference tomorrow." He lifted his glass in toast. "I already checked with Mouse. Why don't we have a late supper? We can hash things out."

Fury simmered just below flash point. Carefully, Roxanne turned to her dressing table and sat. "No, thanks just the same." Setting her glass aside, she began to cream off her stage makeup. "I'd just as soon dine with a rabid bat."

"Then we'll talk here."

"Luke, time passes." She tossed used tissues aside. He could see that beneath the glamour she'd painted on for the stage, she was only more beautiful. None of the pictures he'd managed to find and hoard over the years came close to what she was in the flesh. None of the longings he'd suffered could equal what speared through him now.

"When it does," she continued, patting moisturizer over her skin, "events either become larger than they were or smaller. You could say that whatever we had has become so small, it's next to invisible. So let's not hash, all right?"

"I know I hurt you." Whatever else he had been prepared to say froze in his throat as her eyes flashed to his in the glass. They were green smoke, and in them the emotions which swirled were painful to watch.

"You have no idea what you did to me." The words were hardly more than a whisper and left him battered. "No idea," she repeated. "I loved you with all my heart, with everything I was or could be, and you shattered it. Shattered me. No, don't." She sucked in her breath, going stiff and still as his hand reached for her hair. "Don't touch me again."

He let his hand hang a bare inch away before dropping it to his side. "You have every right to hate me. I'm only asking you to let me explain."

"Then you ask too much. Do you really think anything you could say would make up for it?" She turned on her seat and rose. She'd always been strong, he remembered. But she was stronger now, and distant as the moon. "That whatever explanation you could conjure up would put things right so I'd welcome you back with open arms and a turned-down bed?"

She stopped herself, realizing she was preciously close to shouting and losing whatever small handhold she had on dignity. "I do have a right to hate you," she said with more calm. "I could tell you that you broke my heart, and I put it back together with a lot of sweat and effort. And that would be true. I can also offer you a more pertinent truth. I simply have no heart where you're concerned. You're smoke and mirrors, Luke, and who knows better how deceiving they are than I?"

He waited until he could be sure his voice would be as even as hers. "You want me to believe you feel nothing?"

"It only matters to me what I believe."

He turned away, amazed that he'd wanted to be close to her for so long and now desperately needed distance. She was right. Time passes. No matter how much magic was left in him, he couldn't wink away the years.

Still, he wasn't going to let the past continue to dictate his future. And he wanted that cool, succulent taste of revenge. For all of those things, he needed her.

"If you're telling me the truth about your feelings, then doing business with me shouldn't be a problem."

"I handle my own business."

"And very well, too." Changing tactics, he took out a cigar and sat. "As I said earlier, I have a proposition for you. A business offer I think you'll be very interested in."

She shrugged and removed the silver stars at her ears. "I doubt it."

"The philosophers' stone," was all he said. The earrings clattered on the dressing table.

"Don't push the wrong button, Callahan."

"I know who has it. I know where it is, and I have some ideas on how to get it." He smiled. "Those buttons suit you?"

"How do you know?"

Perhaps it was the flare of his lighter as he lit the cigar, but Roxanne thought she saw something hot and vicious flash into his eyes. "Let's just say I've made it my business to know. Are you interested?"

She shrugged, picked up her brush and began to pull it slowly through her hair. "I might be. Where do you think it is?"

He couldn't speak. Not when the memories and all the longings that ran through them were flooding him. Roxanne brushing her hair, all rose and gold, laughing over her shoulder. So slender, so lovely.

Their eyes met in the mirror again. The shock of the mutual memory snapped like lightning in the air. Her hand trembled once as she set the brush aside.

"I asked where you thought it was."

"I said I know." He took a long, quiet breath. "It's in a vault in a library of a house in Maryland. It's owned by an old friend of ours." Luke drew in smoke, expelled it in a thin blue cloud. "Sam Wyatt."

Roxanne's eyes narrowed. Luke knew that look, and knew he had her. "You're telling me Sam has the philosophers' stone. The stone Max spent years looking for."

"That's right. It seems to be genuine. Sam certainly believes it to be."

"Why would he want it?"

"Because Max did," Luke said simply. "And because he's convinced it represents power. I doubt he sees anything mystical about it." He shrugged and crossed his legs at the ankles. "It's more a symbol of conquest. Max wanted it, Sam has it. Has had it for the last six months."

It seemed wise to sit again, to get her bearings. She hadn't really believed in the stone. There had been times when she had hated even the legend of it for drawing her father further and further away from his narrowing pinpoint on reality. Yet if it existed...

"How do you know about it, about Sam?"

He could have told her. There were so many things he could have told her reaching back over that five-year gulf. But to tell some was to tell all. He, too, had pride.

"It's my business how. I'm asking you if you're interested in acquiring the stone."

"If I were interested, there's nothing stopping me from acquiring it on my own."

"I'd stop you." He didn't move from his relaxed slouch on the chair, but she sensed the challenge, and the barrier. "I've put a lot of time and effort into tracing that stone, Roxanne. I won't let you slip it out from under me. But..." He turned the cigar to study the tip. "I'm offering you a kind of partnership."

"Why? Why should you offer, why should I accept?"

"For Max." He looked back at her. "Whatever is between us, or not between us, I love him, too."

That hurt. As she absorbed the pain, she gripped her hands together on her lap. "You've certainly shown your devotion over the last five years, haven't you?"

"I offered to explain." He shrugged, reached out for his champagne. "Now you'll have to wait. You can work with me and have the stone, or I'll get it alone."

She hesitated. Her mind was already mulling over the possibilities. It wouldn't be difficult to locate Sam's home in Maryland—not since he was the front-runner in the upcoming senatorial elections. The security would be a little more difficult for precisely the same reason, but not impossible.

"I'll need to think about it."

He knew her too well. "Yes or no, Rox. Now. It would take you months to gather the information I already have. By the time you did, I'd have the stone."

"Then why do you need me?"

"We'll get to that. Yes or no."

She stared at him, at the face she'd known so well. There had been a time when she would have known what he was thinking, and certainly what he was feeling. But the years had made a stranger of him.

That was for the best, she decided. If he remained a stranger she could cope.

"Yes."

The wave of relief was like a flood of fresh air. He could breathe again. His only outward reaction was a slight smile and nod. "Good. There are certain conditions."

Her eyes frosted. "Of course there are."

"I think you can live with them. There's an auction to be held this fall in Washington."

"The Clideburg estate, I know."

"You should also know that the jewelry alone is valued in excess of six million."

"Six point eight, conservatively."

"Conservatively," he agreed and downed the last of his champagne. "I want to hit it."

For an instant she couldn't speak at all. "You're out of your mind." But the excitement in her eyes betrayed her. "You might as well stroll into the Smithsonian and try to cop the Hope Diamond."

"Bad luck." Oh yes, he knew he had her. Rising, he reached for the bottle to pour them both more wine. "I've done quite a bit of the initial research. There are a few bugs to iron out."

"Atomic-sized, I imagine."

"A job is a job," he said, quoting Max. "The bigger the complications, the grander the illusion."

"The auction's in October. That doesn't give us much time."

"Time enough. Particularly if you announce at your press conference tomorrow that you'll be working with a partner again."

"Why in hell would I do that?"

"Because we will, Roxy, onstage and off." He took her hand and, ignoring her resistance, drew her to her feet. "Strictly business, babe. I'm a mystery come back. Put that together with the act we'll create, and we'll be a sensation. And have a tidy diversion in October—in our performance at the gala before the auction."

"You got us booked already?"

He didn't mind the sarcasm, not when he played to win. "You leave that to me. It's all a hook, Rox, the performance, the auction, the stone. When it's all over, we'll both have what we want."

"I know what I want." He still held her hand. She would have sworn she felt the power leaping from his fingers. It was a sensation that both frightened and aroused. "I'm not sure about you."

"You should be." His eyes locked on hers. "You always were. I want you back, Roxanne." He brought her rigid fingers to his lips. "And I've had a long time to figure out how to get the things I want. If you're afraid of that, back out now."

"I'm not afraid of anything." She yanked her hand free of his, tossed up her chin. "I'm in, Callahan. When the job's done, I'll snap my fingers." She did so, in front of his nose. "And you'll be gone. That's what I want."

He only laughed and, taking her by the shoulders, yanked her to him for one short, hard kiss. "God, it's good to be back. Knock them dead at the press conference, Roxy. Tell them you're working on something new. Whet their appetites. Afterward, I'll come to your suite. We can start working out the details."

"No." She pressed both hands on his chest to shove him away. "I'll handle the press, then I'll come to you. Make sure you have enough to keep me interested."

"That I can promise. I'm at the same hotel as you, one floor down."

Some of the color washed out of her cheeks. "How long have you been there?"

"I only checked in an hour before the show." Curious of her reaction, he tilted his head. "Why does that bother you?"

"It just means I'll have to check my locks more carefully."

The smile died out of his eyes. "No lock would keep me out if I decided to come in, Rox. A no from you would. Make it around noon," he said and started toward the door. "I'll buy you lunch."

"Luke." She didn't move toward him. That was something she couldn't give. "Have you seen Lily yet?" When he only shook his head, the heart she thought was so barricaded against him broke a little. "I'll get her for you if you like."

"I can't." In his entire life he'd only loved two women. Facing both on the same night was more than he thought he could handle. "I'll talk to her tomorrow."

Then he was gone, quickly and without another word. Roxanne wasn't certain how long she stood staring at the door he'd closed behind him. She couldn't be sure what she was feeling. Her life had been turned upside down when he'd left her. She didn't think it had righted again by his return. If anything, he'd skewed it in an entirely different manner. This time, it would be up to her to control the angle and degree.

But she was tired. Bone tired. Even the act of changing from her costume to street clothes seemed almost more than she could bear. Her fingers froze on the snap of her jeans when she heard the knock on her door.

If he'd come back, she—but no, she thought with a sneer. Luke wouldn't bother to knock.

"Yes, who is it?"

"It's me, honey." Eyes bright, Lily poked her head in the door. Some of the gleam faded when she scanned the room and found it empty but for Roxanne. "Mouse told me—I waited as long as I could." She stepped in, spotted the mess of water and flowers on the floor. "He is here!" The smile was back and brilliant. "I could hardly believe it. Where's he been? Is he okay? Where is he now?"

"I don't know where he's been." Roxanne picked up her purse, checking the contents to give her something to do with her hands. "He seems fine, and I have no idea where he is."

"But—but—he didn't just leave again?"

"Not the way you mean. He's staying in town, at our hotel. We may have some business to discuss."

"Business?" With a laugh, Lily threw her arms around Roxanne and squeezed. "I guess that's the last thing you two would have to talk about. I can't wait to see him. It's like a miracle."

"More like one of the seven plagues," Roxanne muttered.

"Now, Roxy, I'm sure he must've explained everything."

"I didn't want to hear it." She pulled away, fighting not to resent Lily's easy acceptance. "I don't care why he left or where he was. That part of my life's over."

"Roxy—"

"I mean it, Lily. If you want to kill the fatted calf, go right ahead. Just don't expect me to join the feast." She crouched to toss mangled roses in the trash. "It seems we might be working together, temporarily. But that's all. There's nothing personal between us anymore. That's the way I want it."

"It may be what you say you want," Lily said quietly. "It may even be the way you feel right now. But that isn't the way it is, or ever can be." Lily knelt down to lay a hand on Roxanne's shoulder. "You didn't tell him about Nathaniel."

"No." She tossed a rose aside and stared dully down at the spot of blood where a thorn had pierced her thumb. "I was afraid at first when he said he was at the hotel that he already knew. But he doesn't."

"Honey, you have to tell him."

"Why?" Her eyes burned fierce and furious.

"Luke has a right—"

"His rights ended five years ago. All the rights are mine now. Nathaniel's mine. Damn it, Lily, don't look at me that way." She sprang to her feet to escape the soft, pitying gaze. "What should I have said? Oh, by the way, Callahan, a few months after you took a hike, I gave birth to your son. Looks just like you, too. He's a great kid. Why don't I introduce you to him sometime?" She pressed her hand over her mouth to hold back a sob.

"Don't, Roxy."

"I'm not going to." She shook her head when Lily's arms came around her. "I never cried over him. Not once. I'm not going to start now." But she let herself be comforted, turning her cheek to Lily's shoulder. "What would I tell Nate, Lily? Here's the father I told you had to go away. He's back now, but don't get used to it because he might play now-you-see-him-now-you-don't."

"He wouldn't turn his back on his son. He couldn't."

"I won't risk it." She took a deep breath and stepped back, steadier. "If and when I decide to tell Luke about Nathaniel, it'll be at a time and place of my choosing. I call the shots on this." She gripped Lily's shoulders and held firm. "I want your promise that you'll say nothing."

"I won't tell him, if you promise to do the right thing."

"I'm trying to. Let's get going, okay? It's been a long day."

Hours later, Roxanne stood in the doorway of the room where her son slept. Shadows were just beginning to fade, going pale and pearly in the early dawn. She listened to Nathaniel breathing. Her child, her miracle, her most potent magic. And she thought about the man who slept in a room below, the man who had helped her create a life.

And she remembered how frightened she'd been when she'd sat down to tell her father that she was pregnant. How tightly Max had held her. Unflagging support from him, from Mouse and LeClerc. The booties Lily knitted that had looked like mutant mittens, the wallpaper Mouse had surprised her with for the nursery, the milk LeClerc had forced her to drink.

The day she had felt the baby quicken for the first time. She'd nearly given in and wept then, but she'd held the tears off. Maternity clothes, swollen ankles. That first solid kick that had awakened her out of a sound sleep. Lamaze classes with Lily as her coach. And always that tiny seed of hope that remained planted deep that Luke would come back before their child was born.

But he hadn't. She'd gone through eighteen sweaty hours of labor, at turns terrified and exhilarated. She'd watched their son fight his way from her womb, she'd listened to his first indignant cry.

And every day she'd looked at him and loved him and had seen Luke mirrored in his face.

She'd watched her son grow, and had seen her father swallowed up by the illness no one could fight. She'd been alone. No matter how much love she'd felt in her home, there had been no one to turn to in the night. No arms to come around her and offer her comfort when she wept because her father no longer recognized her.

There was no one to stand with her now, and keep watch over her son as the dawn came up.

26

Lily fluffed her hair, checked her makeup in the mirror of her rhinestone-studded compact, fixed a bright, friendly smile on her face. She rolled back her shoulders, making sure her tummy—which she hated to admit was becoming the teeniest bit of a problem—was sucked in. Only then was she satisfied enough with her appearance to knock on the door of Luke's suite.

It wasn't a matter of being disloyal to Roxanne, she told herself, fidgeting. All she was doing was saying hello—and maybe she'd give the boy a piece of her mind while she was at it. But it wasn't being disloyal, even if her heart was nearly bursting with the sheer joy of seeing him again.

Besides, she'd waited until Roxanne had gone down to her press conference.

By the time she heard the bolt turn, she'd chewed off most of her lipstick. She held her breath, bumped her smile up a few degrees, then stared blankly at the short, dark-haired man who stood on the other side of the threshold. He stared back at her through silver-framed lenses as thick as her thumb. However much Luke might have changed, Lily thought, he couldn't have lost six inches in height.

"I'm sorry. I must have the wrong room."

"Lily Bates!" The voice screamed the Bronx and was as friendly as a pastrami on rye. Lily found her hand clasped and pumped enthusiastically. "I'd recognize you anywhere. *Any*-where! You're even prettier than you are onstage."

"Thank you." Habit had her fluttering her mink eyelashes even as she levered her weight back to prevent him from pulling her into the room. Any woman with a killer body had best have killer instincts as well. "I'm afraid I got the door numbers mixed up."

He kept her hand captured in his and used his other to push up the glasses that were sliding down his prominent hooked nose. "I'm Jake. Jake Finestein."

"Nice to meet you." They continued the little tug-of-war. Lily glanced uneasily over her shoulder, wondering if anyone would come to her aid if she shouted for help. "I'm sorry I bothered you, Mr. Finestein."

"Jake. Jake." He grinned and flashed an amazing set of large white teeth, so straight they might have been surveyed by the Corps of Engineers. "No need for formalities between us, Lily. Wonderful show last night." His black bean eyes, magnified by the thick lenses, beamed up at her. *Won*-der-ful."

"Thank you." She was bigger than he was, she told herself. And certainly outweighed him. His short-sleeved shirt showed puny, toothpick arms and bony wrists. Worst came to worst, she could take him. "I really can't chat now. I'm running late."

"Oh, but you've got time for a cup of coffee." He swung his free hand back to indicate the table laden with pots and cups and covered plates. "And breakfast. I bet you haven't eaten a thing yet this morning. I ordered up some nice bagels. You eat a little bit, have a nice cup of coffee, you relax. Me, I got to eat a little something in the mornings or my system suffers all day. How about some orange juice?" He tugged her in another inch. "They squeeze it fresh."

"Really, I can't. I was just—"

"Jake, will you quit talking to yourself. It makes me crazy." Hair still dripping from the shower, Luke strode out from the bedroom buttoning his shirt. He stopped dead, the annoyance on his face shuddering into blank shock.

"Who needs to talk to himself when he's got a beautiful woman?" Jake's grin twisted into a wince as Lily's fingers tightened on his. "And I mean *bee*-u-ti-ful. We've been having a nice chat. I was just telling Lily she should sit down, have some coffee, maybe a bagel."

"I—I could use some coffee," Lily managed.

"Good, good. I'm going to pour you some. You want cream? Sugar? Sweet'n Low?"

"Yes, fine." She didn't care if Jake poured heavy-weight motor oil out of the pot, she had eyes only for Luke. "You look wonderful." She heard the tears in her voice and cleared her throat to disguise them. "I'm sorry. I'm interrupting your breakfast."

"It's all right. It's good to see you." It was so awful, so hideously polite. He just wanted to stand and stare and absorb everything about her. The pretty, ridiculously youthful face, the silly enameled parrots that swung at her ears, the scent of Chanel that was already filling the room.

"So, sit, sit." Jake made grand gestures toward the table. "You'll talk, you'll eat."

Luke cut his eyes toward the table. "Take off, Jake."

"I'm going, I'm going." Jake fussed with cups and saucers. "You think I'm hanging around to spoil the big reunion? Mrs. Finestein didn't raise any fools. I'm going to get my camera and go take pictures like I was a tourist. Madam Lily." He grasped her hand again, squeezed. "A pleasure, a sincere pleasure."

"Thank you."

Jake sent Luke a last telling look, then walked to the second bedroom and shut the door discreetly behind him. If he pressed his ear to the crack for a few minutes, what harm did it do?

"He's—ah—a very nice man."

"He's a pain in the ass." Luke worked up what nearly passed as a grin. "But I'm used to him." Nervous as a boy on his first date, he shoved his hands in his pockets. "So sit. We'll talk, we'll eat."

Luke's killingly accurate mimicking of Jake had Lily's lips trembling up. "I don't want to take up your time."

He would have preferred being stabbed in the heart. "Lily, please."

"Maybe just some coffee." She made herself sit, keeping the smile planted. But the cup rattled in the saucer when she lifted it. "I don't know what to say to you. I guess I want to know if you're okay."

"I'm all in one piece." He sat as well, but for once his appetite had deserted him. He made do with black coffee. "How about you? Roxanne—well, she wasn't much in the mood to fill me in on everyone last night."

"I'm older," Lily said in a weak attempt at gaiety.

"You don't look it." He searched her face, fighting against emotions that threatened to swamp him. "Not a day."

"You always knew just what to say to a woman. Must be the Irish." She took an unsteady breath and began to pick apart a bagel. "LeClerc's fine. Crankier than he used to be. He doesn't come on the road often now. Mouse is married. Did you know?"

"Mouse? Married?" Luke gave a quick spontaneous laugh that had tears swimming in Lily's eyes. "No shit? How did that happen?"

"Alice came to—to work for us," Lily said carefully. It wouldn't do to say that Roxanne had hired her as Nathaniel's nanny. "She's bright and sweet, and she fell head over heels for Mouse. It took her two years to wear him down. I don't know how many hours she spent helping him tinker with engines."

"I'm going to have to meet her." Silence fell, taunting him. "Can you tell me about Max?"

"He won't get better." Lily lifted her coffee again. "He's gone someplace none of us can reach him. We didn't—we couldn't put him in a hospital so we've arranged for home care. He can't do anything for himself. That's the worst, to see him so helpless. It's hard on Roxanne."

"What about you?"

Lily pressed her lips together. When she spoke, her voice was strong and steady. "Max is gone. I can look into his eyes, and there's no Max there. Oh, I still sit with his body, and feed it or clean it, but everything he was has already died. His body's just waiting to catch up. So it's easier for me. I've done my grieving."

"I need to see him, Lily." He wanted to reach out. His fingers were inches from touching hers before he curled them away. "I know Roxanne might object, but I need to see him."

"He asked for you, dozens of times." There was accusation mixed with the hurt. She couldn't prevent either. "He'd forget that you weren't there, and he'd ask for you."

"I'm sorry." It seemed a pitiful response.

"How could you do it, Luke? How could you leave without a word and break so many hearts?" When he only shook his head, she looked away. "Now I'm sorry," she said stiffly. "I don't have any right to question you. You were always free to come and go as you pleased."

"Direct hit," he murmured. "Much more accurate than anything Rox threw at me last night."

"You devastated her." Lily hadn't known the hot anger was trapped inside until it burst free. "She loved you, since she was a little girl. She trusted you. We all did. We thought something terrible had happened to you. Until Roxanne came back from Mexico we were sure of it."

"Wait." He gripped her hand, holding tight. "She went to Mexico?"

"She tracked you there. Mouse went with her. You have no idea what shape she was in." Frightened, pregnant, heartsick. Lily shook her hand free and rose. Her temper, always so even, was all the more effective when it spiked. "She looked for you, afraid you were dead or sick or God knows. Then she found your plane and the man you'd sold it to. And she knew you didn't want her to find you. Damn you, I didn't think she'd ever get over it." She shoved the chair against the table hard enough to make china rattle. "Tell me you had amnesia. Tell me you got hit on the head and forgot us, forgot everything. Can you tell me that?"

"No."

She was crying now, big silent tears coursing down her face while he looked on miserably.

"I can't tell you that, and I can't ask you to forgive me. I can only tell you that I did what I thought was best for everyone. I didn't see a choice."

"You didn't see a choice? You couldn't see your way clear to letting us know you were alive?"

"No." He picked up a napkin and stood to dab at her tears. "I thought about you every day. In the first year I'd wake up at night thinking I was home, then it would hit me. I'd reach for a bottle instead of Roxanne. I might as well have been dead. I wish I could have forgotten, that I could have stopped needing my family." He balled the napkin in his fist as his voice thickened. "I was twelve before I found my mother. I don't want to spend the rest of my life without her. Tell me what I need to do to convince you to give me another chance."

For Lily love was a fluid thing. No matter how strong the dam, it would always flow free. She did the only thing she could do. She opened her arms and took him into them, rocking and stroking when he buried his face in her hair.

"You're home now," she murmured. "That's what matters."

And it was all there, just where he had left it. The softness, the sweetness, the strength. Emotions rose up in him like a river at flood point. He could only cling. "I missed you. God, I missed you."

"I know." She lowered into a chair and let him lay his head in her lap. "I didn't mean to yell at you, sweetie."

"I didn't think you'd want to see me." He straightened so that he could touch a hand to her cheek, feel that creamy skin. "I never deserved you."

"That's silly. Most people would say we deserved each other." She gave a watery chuckle and hugged him hard. "You'll tell me about it sometime soon, won't you?"

"Whenever you want."

"Later. I just want to spend some time looking at you." Sniffling, she held him at arm's length, studying his face with a mother's eagle eye. "Well, you don't look any the worse for wear." She smoothed the faint lines at the corner of his eyes with her fingertips. "You look a little thinner maybe, a little tougher." With a sigh, she pressed a kiss to his cheek, then fussed the imprint of her lipstick away with her thumb. "You were the most beautiful little boy I'd ever seen." When he winced, she laughed. "Do you still have magic?"

"It kept me alive." He took both of her hands and pressed them to his lips. Shame and simple gratitude ran riot through him. He'd tried to prepare for her anger, for the chill of her resentment, even her disinterest. But he had no defense against the constancy of her love. "You were beautiful last night. Watching you and Rox onstage, it was like the years between never happened."

"But they did."

"Yes, they did." He stood then, but kept her hand in his. "I don't have an incantation to make them disappear. But there are things I can do that might set it right."

"You still love her."

When he only shrugged, she smiled, rose and cupped his face in her hands. "You still love her," she repeated. "But you'll have to have more than a pocketful of tricks to win her back. She's not a pushover like me."

His mouth grimmed. "I can push hard."

With a sigh, Lily shook her head. "Then she'll just push back. Max would say you catch more flies with honey than with a rolled up newspaper. Take it from me, a woman—even a stubborn one—likes to be wooed." He only snorted, but Lily pressed on. "I don't just mean flowers and music, honey. It's a kind of attitude. Roxy needs to be challenged, but she also needs to be courted."

"If I got down on one knee, she'd plant a foot in my face."

Absolutely, Lily thought, but thought it politic not to agree. "I didn't say it would be easy. Don't give up on her, Luke. She needs you more than you could possibly understand."

"What do you mean?"

"Just don't give up."

Thoughtfully, he drew Lily back into his arms. "That's not the kind of mistake I'd make twice. I'll do what needs to be done, Lily." His eyes darkened as he stared at something hateful only he could see. "There are scores to settle."

"And there was a big dog in the park. A gold one. He peed on all the trees."

Roxanne cuddled Nate in her lap, laughing as he recounted his adventures of the morning. "All of them?"

"Maybe a hundred." He looked soulfully into his mother's face with his father's eyes. "Can I have a dog? I'd teach him to sit and shake hands and play dead."

"And pee on trees?"

"Uh-huh." He grinned, turning in her lap to wrap his arms around her neck. Oh, he knew how to charm, she thought. He'd been his father's child since his first toothless grin. "I want a big one. A big boy one. His name's gonna be Mike."

"Since he's already got a name, I suppose we'll have to look into it." She twirled one of Nate's glossy curls around her finger. Much like, she thought wryly, her son twirled her heart around his. "How much ice cream did you eat?"

His eyes widened. "How come you know I had ice cream?"

There was a telltale smear of chocolate on his shirt and a suspicious stickiness on his fingers. But Roxanne knew better than to use such pedestrian clues. "Because mothers know all and see all, especially when they're magicians too."

His lip poked out as he considered. "How come I can never see the eyes in back of your head?"

"Nate, Nate, Nate," she sighed lustily. "Haven't I told you they're invisible eyes?"

Abruptly she dragged him up into her arms, holding him tight with her eyes squeezed shut against tears. She couldn't say why she felt like weeping, didn't want to consider the reasons. All that mattered was that she had her child safe in her arms.

"Better go wash your hands, Nate the Great." Her voice was shaky, but muffled against his neck. "I've got to get to my appointment."

"You said we were going to the zoo."

"And we will." She kissed him, set him on his short, sturdy legs. "I'll be back in an hour, then we'll go see how many monkeys look just like you."

He raced off, laughing. Roxanne stooped to gather the miniature cars, plastic men and picture books that were scattered over the rug. "Alice? I'm heading out. Be back in an hour."

"Take your time," Alice sang back and made Roxanne smile.

Soft-voiced, reliable, unshakable Alice, she thought. Lord knew she would never have been able to continue her work without the steady support of the ethereal Alice.

And to think she'd nearly turned Alice aside because of her frail appearance and whispery voice. Yet out of the legion of prospective nannies she'd interviewed, it had been Alice who had convinced Roxanne that Nathaniel would be safe and happy in her care.

There had been something about her eyes, Roxanne thought now as she walked into the hallway. That pale, almost translucent gray and the quiet kindness in them. Her practical nature had nearly swayed her toward the more prim and experienced applicants, but Nate had smiled at Alice from his crib, and that had been that.

Roxanne still wondered who had done the hiring. Now Alice was family. That single smile from a six-month-old infant had added one more link to the Nouvelle chain.

Roxanne chose the stairs and walked one flight down to face another link. The missing link, she thought nastily and had her shoulders braced when she rapped on Luke's door.

"Prompt as always," Luke commented when he opened the door.

"I only have an hour, so let's get down to business." She sailed past him, leaving a faint trace of wildflowers to torment his system.

"Hot date?"

She thought of her son and smiled. "Yes, and I don't like to keep him waiting." She chose a chair, sat and crossed her legs. "Let's hear the setup, Callahan."

"Whatever you say, Nouvelle." He saw her lips twitch, but she conquered the smile quickly. "Want some wine before lunch?"

"No wine, no lunch." She gestured, a regal flick of the wrist. "Talk."

"Tell me how you played the press conference."

"Where you're concerned?" Arching a brow, she sat back. "I told them I was bringing someone into the act who would dazzle them. A sorcerer who'd been traveling the world learning the secrets of the Mayans, the mysteries of the Aztecs and the magic of the Druids." She smiled faintly. "I hope you're up to the hype."

"I can handle it." He picked up a pair of steel handcuffs from the coffee table and toyed with them as he spoke. "You weren't all that far off. I learned a number of things."

"Such as?" she asked when he handed her the cuffs for inspection.

"How to walk through walls, vanish an elephant, climb a pillar of smoke. In Bangkok I escaped from a trunk studded with nails. And walked off with a ruby as big as your thumb. In Cairo it was a glass box dropped into the Nile—and emeralds almost as green as your eyes."

"Fascinating," she said and yawned deliberately as she passed him the cuffs. She'd found no secret catch.

"I spent nearly a year in Ireland, in haunted castles and smoky pubs. I found something there I'd never found anywhere else."

"Which was?"

"You could call it my soul." He watched her as he snapped the cuffs to his wrists. "I recognized Ireland, the hills, the towns, even the air. The only other place I've been that pulled me that way was New Orleans." He tugged his wrists apart so that the metal snapped. "But that might have been because you were there. I'd take you to Ireland, Rox." His voice had softened, like silk just stroked. "I imagined you there, imagined making love to you in one of those cool, green fields with the mist rising all around like witch smoke and the sound of harp strings sobbing on the air."

She couldn't take her eyes off his, or the image he so skillfully invoked. His magic was such that she could see them, tumbled on the grass, blanketed in fog. She could all but feel his hands on her skin, warming it, softening it as those old needs crackled like dried wood to a hot flame.

She dug her nails hard into her palms, then tore her eyes away. "It's a good line, Callahan. Very smooth." Steadier, she stared back at him. "Try it on someone who doesn't know you."

"You're a hard woman, Roxy." He held the cuffs up by one end and dropped them into her lap. There was a small sense of satisfaction when she smiled.

"You haven't lost your touch here, either, I see. Odd though. If you've been plying your trade so successfully all these years, why didn't I hear about you?"

"I imagine you did." He rose to answer the knock on the door and spoke casually back to her. "You'd have heard of the Phantom."

"The—" She bit her tongue as the room-service waiter wheeled in a tray. Rubbing her palms together she waited while lunch was set up and Luke signed the check. Naturally, she'd heard of the Phantom, the strange, publicity-shy magician who appeared in all corners of the world, then disappeared again.

"I ordered for you," Luke said as he took a seat at the table. "I think I remembered what you like."

"I told you I don't have time for lunch." But curiosity had her wandering over. Barbecued chicken wings. Her lips thinned even as her heartbeat thickened. She wondered how he'd managed it when she knew very well it wasn't on the hotel's menu. "I lost my taste for them," she said and would have turned away but he grabbed her hand.

"Let's be civilized, Rox." He flicked a rose out of the air, offered it.

She took the bud, but refused to be charmed. "This is as good as it gets."

"If you won't eat with me, I'm going to think it's because the menu reminds you of us. And I'm going to think you're still in love with me."

She wrenched away, tossing the rosebud onto the table. Without bothering to sit, she snatched up a piece of chicken and bit in. "Satisfied?"

"That was never a problem with us." Grinning, he handed her a napkin. "You'll make less of a mess if you sit." He lifted his hands. "Relax. Nothing up my sleeve."

She sat and began to wipe sauce from her fingers. "So, you worked as the Phantom. I wasn't sure he really existed."

"That was the beauty." Luke settled back, cocking one foot on his knee. "I wore a mask, did the gig, took a bit extra if something appealed and moved on."

"In other words..." The sauce was damn good. She licked a bit from her thumb. "You went on the grift."

That put the fire in his eyes and, she hoped, in his gut. He shot her a look that could have smelted iron. "It wasn't grifting." Though he had made a few dollars early on with Three Card Monte and the Cups and Balls. "It was touring."

She gave an unladylike snort and went back to her chicken. "Right. Now you've decided you're ready for the big time again."

"I've always been ready for the big time." His only outward sign of annoyance was the tapping of his fingers on his ankles. But she knew him, knew him well, and was delighted to have scored a hit. "You don't want any explanations on where I went or why, so let's just say I was on sabbatical."

"Great word, sabbatical. Covers so much ground. Okay, Callahan, your sabbatical's over. What's the deal?"

"The three gigs hinge together." He poured the golden wine for himself and left her glass empty. "The performance, the auction and the hit. All the same weekend."

She raised her brows. It was the only reaction she chose to give him. "Ambitious, aren't we?"

"Good is what I am, Rox." The smile was a dare, the sort Lucifer might have aimed toward heaven. "As good as ever, maybe better."

"And as self-effacing."

"Modesty's like tact. It's for wimps. The performance is the diversion for the auction." He showed his empty palm, then turned his hand and danced a Russian ruble along his fingers. "The auction draws the eye from the job at Wyatt's." The ruble vanished. After snapping his fingers, he poured three coins into her glass.

"An old trick, Callahan." Willing to play, she dumped the coins into her hand. "As cheap as talk." With a flourish, she turned her palm up to show that the coins had turned into small silver balls. "This doesn't impress."

Damn it, he hadn't realized that disinterest could stimulate. "Try this. You join the luminaries for the auction after our performance. You're an honored guest, anxious to bid on a few baubles."

"And you are?"

"Attending to a few details at the theater, but I'll be joining you. You bid spiritedly against a certain gentleman on an emerald ring, but he outreaches you."

"And what if other attendees covet that ring?"

"Whatever the bid, he'll top it. He's French and rich and romantic and desires that ring for his fiancée. *Mais alors*." Luke slipped into French so smoothly, Roxanne blinked. "When he examines the ring, as a practical Frenchman might, he discovers it to be paste."

"The ring's a fake?"

"That and a number of other items." He linked his hands together, resting his chin on them. Over them, his eyes glowed with that old amused excitement that nearly tricked a grin out of her. "Because, my only love, we will have switched the take in those soft, dark hours before dawn. And while Washington and its very fine police force are abuzz with the daring theft of several million in jewels, we will quietly slip over to Maryland and relieve the aspiring senator of the philosophers' stone."

There was more, a very important more, but he would time the telling as carefully as his staging.

"Interesting," she said in a voice like a yawn, though she was fascinated. "There's just one little detail I don't understand."

"Which is?"

She funneled her hands and poured his coins next to his plate. "How the hell we break into a heavily secured art gallery in the first place?"

"The same way we break into a house in the 'burbs, Roxy. Expertly. It also helps that I have what we could call a secret weapon."

"Secret weapon?"

"Top secret." He took her hand before she could avoid it and raised it to his lips. "I've always been a sucker for the taste of barbecue sauce on a woman's skin." Watching her, he traced his tongue over her knuckles. "Especially if it's your skin. Do you remember the day we had that picnic? We lay on the rug and listened to the rain? I think I started nibbling on your toes and worked my way up." He turned her hand over to scrape his teeth along her wrist. "I could never get enough of you."

"I can't recall." Her pulse jumped and scrabbled. "I've been on a number of picnics."

"Then I'll refresh your memory. We shared this same meal." He rose, drawing her slowly to her feet. "There was rain running over the windows, the light was gloomy. When I touched you, you trembled, just as you're trembling now."

"I'm not." But she was.

"And I kissed you. Here." He brushed his lips over her temple. "And here." Along her jaw. "And then—" He broke off with an oath as a key turned in the lock.

"What a town!" Jake barreled in, laden with shopping bags. "I could spend a week."

"Try another hour," Luke muttered.

"Ooops. I'm interrupting." Grinning, he set his bags down and crossed the room to take Roxanne's limp hand and pump it. "I've been looking forward to meeting you. Would've popped into your dressing room last night, but it would have cost me my life. I'm Jake Finestein, Luke's partner."

"Partner?" Roxanne echoed.

"Roxanne, our secret weapon." Disgusted, Luke sat and poured more wine.

"I see." She didn't have a clue. "Just what's your secret, Mr. Finestein?"

"Jake." He reached around her to cop one of the chicken wings. "Luke didn't fill you in yet? You could say I'm a wunderkind."

"Idiot savant," Luke corrected and made Jake laugh heartily in the peculiar hiccuping rasps that were his own.

"He's pissed, that's all. Thought you'd fall right into his arms. Guy's a pretty good thief, but he doesn't know squat about women."

Roxanne's lips curved in a genuine smile. "I think I like your friend, Callahan."

"I didn't say he was a friend. A thorn in my side, sand in my shoe."

"A fly in his soup." Jake winked and punched at his glasses. "Guess he didn't mention how I saved his life in Nice."

"He didn't mention it."

"You nearly got me killed," Luke pointed out.

"You know how things get twisted up after a few years." Always ready to socialize, Jake poured himself some wine. "Anyway, there was a little disagreement in a club."

"It was a fucking bar fight." Luke gestured with his glass. "Which you started."

"Details, details. There was a matter of an attractive young woman—I mean *a*-ttractive—and a rather overbearing gentleman."

"A hooker and a john," Luke muttered.

"Didn't I offer to beat his price? Business is business, isn't it? It's not like they'd signed a legal contract." Though it still offended his sense of free enterprise, with a sigh and a shrug, Jake continued. "In any case, one thing led to another, and when Luke got in the way—"

"When I stepped in to keep you from getting a shiv under the rib."

"Whatever. There was an altercation. It was me who bashed the big bastard with a whiskey bottle before he slit your throat, and what thanks do I get? I dragged him outside—rapped my shin on a chair, too, and didn't walk right for days. The bruise." He tossed up a hand. "*Oiy!* It was big as a baseball." He scowled at the memory, sipped, then sighed it away. "But I'm rambling."

"What else is new?"

To show there were no hard feelings, Jake patted Luke's shoulder. "I find out Luke here's a magician, and he finds out I'm to computers what Joe DiMaggio was to baseball. A heavy hitter. No system I can't crack. It's a gift." He flashed his militarily aligned teeth and reminded Roxanne of a bespeckled beaver. "God knows where it comes from. My father ran a kosher bakery in the Bronx and had trouble with a cash register. Me, give me a keyboard and I'm in heaven. So one thing leads to another, and we hook up."

"Jake was in Europe running from a forgery rap."

"A slight miscalculation," Jake said mildly, but color rose up his skinny neck. "Computers are my passion, Miss Roxanne, but forgery is my art. Unfortunately, I became overanxious and rushed."

"It happens to the best of us," Roxanne assured him and earned his undying gratitude.

"A woman of understanding is more precious than rubies."

"She's passed precious little my way."

Roxanne arched a brow at Luke. "But you see, Callahan, I *like* Jake. I'm assuming that your skill with computers will get us past the security."

"There hasn't been a system invented that can stop me. I'll get you in, Miss Roxanne, and out again. As for the rest—"

"Let's take it one step at a time," Luke interrupted. "We have a lot of work to do, Rox. Are you up for it?"

"I can hold my own, Callahan. I always have." She turned to Jake with a smile. "Have you ever been to New Orleans?"

"It's a pleasure I'm anticipating."

"We're flying out tomorrow. I'd like you to come to dinner when it's convenient for you." She spared a brief glance for Luke. "I suppose you can bring him along."

"I'll keep him under control."

"I'm sure you will." Taking Luke's glass she clinked it against Jake's and made his beady eyes shine. "I think this is the start of a beautiful relationship." She took one sip before setting the glass aside. "You'll have to excuse me, I have a date. I'll wait to hear from you."

Jake pressed a hand to his heart as Roxanne closed the door behind him. "Oiy! What a woman."

"Make one move in that direction, pal, and you'll be eating all your meals through a straw."

"I think she liked me." Stars glittered behind the thick lenses. "I think she was definitely smitten."

"Check your glands, Finestein, and go get your tools. Let's see how close you can come to Wyatt's signature."

"Even his broker won't know the difference, Luke. Trust me."

"I have to," Luke muttered. "That's the problem."

27

It was perhaps the most difficult role he'd ever played. Certainly it was the most important. Taking a detour on his way from D.C. to New Orleans, Luke arrived at the Wyatt estate in Tennessee with his hat in his hand, and revenge in his heart.

He knew it had to be done, the pleading, the humility, the face of fear. It might have rankled the pride, but keeping the Nouvelles safe well outdistanced the ego. So he would wear a mask—not the literal mask he'd worn off and on over the last five years—but one that would convince Sam Wyatt to accept Luke's return. At least temporarily.

He needed only a few months. At the end of it he would have everything he wanted. Or he would have nothing.

He knocked, and waited. When the uniformed maid answered, Luke ducked his head and swallowed audibly. "I, ah, Mr. Wyatt's expecting me. I'm Callahan. Luke Callahan."

After a brisk nod, she led him down the hallway he remembered and into the office where he had once witnessed a murder, and suffered his own small death.

As he had five years before, Sam sat behind his desk. This time as well as the elegant furnishings there was an oversized campaign poster on an easel. The photographed smile flashed with sincerity and charm. In bold letters outlined in red and blue the caption read:

SAM WYATT FOR TENNESSEE
SAM WYATT FOR AMERICA

In a cloisonné bowl at the edge of the desk was a pile of buttons featuring the same face, the same sentiment.

As for the candidate himself, Sam had changed little. Luke noted that a few silvery hairs had been allowed to glint at his temples, faint lines crinkled beside his eyes as he smiled. And he did smile, hugely. Very much, Luke thought, as a spider might when he spotted a fly struggling feebly in the web.

"Well, well, the prodigal returns. That will be all," he said to the maid, then leaned back, still grinning, when the door shut behind her. "Callahan—you look remarkably well."

"You look . . . successful."

"Yes." In an old habit, Sam turned his wrist so he could admire the gold cuff links winking at his cuffs. "I must say your call yesterday surprised me a great deal. I didn't think you had the nerve."

Luke straightened his shoulders in what he knew would appear to be a pitiful attempt at bravado. "I have a proposition for you."

"Oh, I'm all ears." Chuckling, Sam rose. "I suppose I should offer you a drink." He walked deliberately to the brandy decanter, and his eyes gleamed as he turned back. "For old times' sake."

Luke merely stared at the offered snifter while his breath came quick and loud. "I really don't—"

"What's the matter, Callahan? Lose your taste for brandy? Don't worry." Sam toasted, then drank deeply. "I don't have to doctor your drink to get what I want out of you this time. Sit." It was an order, master to dog. While the fire burned bright in his blood, Luke let the brandy slosh in his glass as he meekly obeyed. "Now..." Sam leaned against the corner of the desk, smiling. "What makes you think I'd let you come back."

"I thought..." Luke drank as if to bolster his courage. "I hoped that it had been long enough."

"Oh no." Reveling in the power, Sam shook his head. "Between you and me it can never be long enough. Perhaps I didn't make myself clear enough—what has it been? Five years ago. It was right here in this same room, wasn't it? Isn't that interesting?"

Idly he wandered to the spot where Cobb had sprawled, bleeding. The rug was new. An Italian antique he'd purchased with his wife's money.

"I don't suppose you've forgotten what happened here?"

"No." Luke pressed his lips together, averted his eyes. "No, I haven't forgotten."

"I believe I told you exactly what I would do if you came back. What would happen to you, and what would happen to the Nouvelles." As if struck with a notion, Sam lifted a finger, tapped it against his lips. "Or perhaps you've lost your enchantment with the Nouvelles after such a long separation. You might not care that I can send the old man to prison, send them all if it comes to that. Including the woman you once loved."

"I don't want anything to happen to them. There's no need for you to take any of this out on them." As if to steady his trembling voice, Luke took another sip. It was damn good brandy, he mused. A pity he couldn't relax enough to enjoy it. "I just want a chance to come home—only for a little while," he added quickly. "Sam, Max is really ill. He may not live long. I'm only asking you to let me spend a month or so with him."

"How touching." Sam moved behind the desk again. Opening a drawer he took out a cigarette. He allowed himself only five a day, and only in private. In today's political climate, smoking was a liability. He might have been well ahead in the polls, but he wasn't a man to take chances with his image. "So, you want to spend time with the old man while he dies." Sam lighted the cigarette, took one deep satisfying drag. "Why in hell should I care?"

"I know—I don't expect you to care. I hoped that since it would be for such a short time. A couple of months." Luke looked up again, his eyes full of pleas. "I don't see how it could matter to you."

"You're wrong. Everything about you, everything about the Nouvelles will always matter to me. Do you know why?" His fierce grin spread into a snarl. "You, none of you, recognized what I had, who I was. You took me in out of pity and tossed me out in disgust. And you thought you were better. You were nothing but common thieves, but you thought you were better than me."

The old anger reared up, nearly choking him. It was the hate that had ripened with it which kept his voice clear.

"But you weren't, were you?" he continued. "You're left without a home, even without a country, and the Nouvelles are saddled with a pathetic old man who can't remember his own name. But here I am, Callahan. Rich, successful, admired and on my way to the top."

Luke had to remind himself of the plan, the long term, the satisfaction of a clever sting. Otherwise he might have leaped up then and there and twisted Sam's neck. Because part of what Sam had said was true. Luke had no home. And Max had lost his identity.

"You have everything you want." Luke kept his shoulders slumped. "I'm only asking for a few weeks."

"You figure that's all the old man has left in him?" Sam sighed, and tipped back his brandy. "A pity. I actually hope he lives a long time yet, a long, long time with his mind vegetating, his body shriveling and the entire situation pulling the heart out of his family."

He smiled suddenly, the glossy politician's smile that lured voters. "I know all about Alzheimer's. More than you might imagine. As I was inspired by Max's predicament, part of my platform has been lending a sympathetic, even a compassionate ear to families dealing with the care and feeding of loved ones with minds like a turnip. Ah!" He laughed at the sudden flash in Luke's eyes. "That offends you. Insults your sensibilities. Well, let me tell you something, Callahan, I don't give a damn about Maximillian Nouvelle or any of the others like him. Turnips don't vote. But don't worry, once I'm elected, we'll continue the . . . illusion," he decided, enjoying the irony of the word. "We'll continue to make promises—even keep a few of them—about research and state funding, because I know how to plan for the long term."

He settled back and let himself project, opening himself to the one man Sam was certain could do nothing to harm him. "The Senate seat's only the next step—the next step toward the White House. Another decade, and I'll have won it all. Once I have control, complete control, things will be run my way. The bleeding hearts will be bled dry, and all those whining special-interest groups can whine themselves into oblivion. In the next century Americans will learn that they have a leader who understands control and power. A leader who knows how to use both and isn't afraid of taking some losses when he does."

His voice had risen, like an evangelist who is bent on saving souls. Luke watched in silence while Sam drew himself in. Sooner or later he would snap, Luke mused. God help us all if Wyatt had any buttons under his thumb when he did.

Sam drew on the cigarette again, then focused back on Luke as he tamped it out. "But I don't imagine you're interested in politics or the fate of a nation. Your interests are more personal."

"I made some money over the last few years." Wanting Sam to see nerves, Luke moistened his lips. "I'll pay you, give you whatever you want for a few weeks with Max and the Nouvelles."

"Money?" Delighted, Sam threw back his head and laughed. "Do I look like I need your money? Have you any idea how much I rake in every month in campaign contributions? That's over and above what I have from my lovely wife."

"But if you had more you—you could increase your television campaign, or whatever it took to make sure the election went your way."

"It's going my way," Sam snapped. His eyes went wide and bright. "Do you want to see the fucking numbers? The people of this state want me, Callahan. They want Sam Wyatt. After I'm finished with him, they wouldn't elect Curtis Gunner dog catcher. I'm winning." He slapped his hands on the desk, scattering ash. "I'm winning."

"A million dollars," Luke blurted out. "Surely you could use a million dollars to make sure. I only want a little time in exchange. Then I'll disappear again. Even if I wanted to stay, if I tried, Roxanne wouldn't have me." He bowed his head, a man defeated. "She's made that clear."

"Has she?" Sam drummed his fingers on the desk. He was calm again. He knew it was important to stay calm. Just as it was important to exploit whatever advantages came your way. "So you've seen her."

"In D.C. I went to her show." Fear radiated from him as he glanced up. "Only for a moment. I couldn't stop myself."

"And your course of true love hit another bump?" Nothing could have pleased him more. But he wondered, because he knew quite a bit about Roxanne, and a small boy named Nathaniel. "And did she catch you up on the highlights of her life during your absence?"

"She would barely speak to me," Luke whispered. "I hurt her, and since I can't explain why I left, she isn't about to forgive me."

Better and better, Sam thought. He didn't know about the child. How much would Roxanne suffer before—and if—she told him. And if she did, how much more would Luke bleed in having to leave again?

He considered it all for a moment. It seemed to him that Luke's return was more satisfying than his staying away altogether. It was, after all, more enjoyable to watch people suffer than to imagine it. And it appeared he could be paid for being entertained.

"A million dollars? Just how did you manage to accumulate so much?" "I . . ." With a hand that shook, Luke set the brandy aside. "I performed."

"Haven't lost the magic touch? I imagine you continued to steal as well." Pleased by Luke's guilty start, he nodded. "Yes, I thought so. A million dollars," he repeated. "I'll have to think about it. Campaign funds are so carefully scrutinized these days. We wouldn't want any hint of graft or corruption to taint my image—especially when Gunner professes to be so squeaky clean. I'd like to . . ." He trailed off as a new idea dawned. It was so perfect, he realized, as if fate had handed him another tool.

"I believe we might be able to make a deal."

With eagerness in his eyes, in his voice, Luke leaned forward. "I'll have the money within a week. I can bring it to you wherever you say."

"The money will have to wait until after the election. I'll want my accountant to find a nice safe channel for it. In the meantime I have work for you. It'll buy you the time you want so badly."

It was a curve Luke hadn't expected. He'd counted on Sam's greed being enough. "Whatever you want."

"You might recall a little incident called Watergate. The burglars there were sloppy. You'd have to be very neat, very clever."

Luke changed gears and nodded. "You want me to steal documents?"

"I have no way of knowing if there are any documents worth stealing. But a man with your connections should be able to manufacture papers, photographs, that sort of thing. And if one can steal, one can also plant."

Folding his hands, Sam inched forward. It was so perfect. With his new tool he would not simply win the election, he would destroy his opponent, politically, personally, publicly.

"Curtis Gunner is the happily married father of two. His record in the State Senate is clean as a whistle. I want you to change all that."

"Change it? How?"

"Magic." Resting his chin on his folded hands, he grinned. "That's what you're best at, isn't it? I want photos of Gunner with other women—with whores. And with other men, yes, with other men." He had to press a hand to his side as giddy laughter shook him at the image. "That will be even more interesting. I want letters, papers documenting his involvement in illegal business deals, others showing he siphoned off welfare money for personal use. That ought to kick his liberal ass. I want you to make them good, unimpeachable."

"I don't know how—"

"Then you'll find a way." Sam's eyes glittered. The power was here, all here, he realized. This time he hadn't even had to look for it. "You want to take your sentimental journey, Callahan, then you pay for it. You put together the faked photos, the papers, receipts, correspondence. I'll give you from now until, we'll say, ten days before the election. Yes, ten days," he murmured to himself. "When this leaks, I'll want it fresh in the voters' minds as they walk behind the curtain to pull the lever." Feeling generous, he inclined his head. "That gives you the same amount of time with the Nouvelles."

"I'll do whatever I can."

"You'll do exactly as I say, or when the time's up, you'll pay. They'll all pay."

"I don't know what you mean."

With a new smile playing around his mouth, Sam lifted his ivory-handled letter opener, testing the tip with his thumb. "You satisfy me with the job I'm giving you. Completely satisfy me. Or everything I threatened you with five years ago will come true."

"You said if I left you wouldn't do anything to them."

With one vicious stroke he stabbed the tip of the letter opener into the padded corner of his blotter. "And you put it all back on the line by coming here. You've tossed the dice again, Callahan. What happens to the Nouvelles depends on just how well you play. Understood?"

"Yeah. Yeah, I understand."

He was going to play, Luke thought. And this time, he was going to win.

"So, so?" Dancing with impatience, Jake trailed Luke to the Cessna.

"So, are my things on board?"

"Yeah, yeah. What happened with Wyatt? Me, I'm just a peon, sure. Just a lowly soldier behind the front lines, just a—"

"An asshole," Luke finished for him. He climbed into the cockpit and began to check gauges. "It went fine," he said when Jake lapsed into offended silence. "If you consider the fact that I had to lower myself to playing the babbling beggar when what I wanted to do was cut out his heart."

"From what I hear, this dude don't have a heart anyway." Jake strapped in, shoved his glasses back up his nose. It was obvious that Luke was in a dangerous mood—which meant the short flight to New Orleans would be an eventful one. As a precaution Jake downed Dramamine and Valium with what was left of his warming orange soda. "Anyway, you got the time you need, right?"

"I got it." Luke broke off to check in with the tower and get the go-ahead for takeoff. As he began his taxi, he glanced at Jake, who was already pale, glassy-eyed and white-knuckled. "I've also got another job for you."

"Oh, good. Yeah, great." In self-defense, Jake closed his eyes when the plane's nose lifted. As he'd told Luke time and time again, he hated flying. Always had, always would. Which was why, he was certain, Luke crammed him into a cockpit on the average of once a week.

"Wyatt's deal included some creative mudslinging." As the plane continued its climb, Luke felt most of his tension draining away. He loved flying. Always had, always would. "It's right up your alley."

"Slinging mud." Cautious, Jake opened one eye. "So what do I know about slinging mud?"

"He wants doctored photographs, papers, business correspondence, putting this Curtis Gunner in a bad light. Illegal, unethical and immoral documents—the kind that lose elections and break up families, destroy lives."

"Shit, Luke, we got nothing against this Gunner guy, right? I know you had to dance with the devil to buy the time you need to put the screws to Wyatt. But, hell, it doesn't seem quite kosher."

After leveling off, Luke drew out a cigar. "Life sucks, Finestein, if you haven't noticed. You do the job, and do it good—with just one small adjustment."

Jake sighed. "I said I was in for the deal, so I'm in. You'll get the stuff—and it'll be hot enough to burn."

"I'm counting on it."

"So, what's the adjustment?"

Luke clamped the cigar between his teeth and grinned. "You don't do it on Gunner, you do it on Wyatt."

"On Wyatt? But you said..." Jake's pale face cleared into a dreamy smile. The Valium was taking hold. "Now I get it. Now I get it. A double cross."

"Christ, you're a quick study, Finestein." His grin was still widening as Luke banked the plane and headed for home.

28

The bedroom Lily and Max had once shared was fully equipped for the care of a patient with severe cognitive impairment. Roxanne had worked closely with hospital staff and an interior decorator to be certain that her father's environment was safe and practical without having the atmosphere of a hospital room.

Monitors and medicines were necessary, but so, in her opinion, were the bright colors and soft materials Max had always loved. A team of three nurses had eight-hour shifts, a physical therapist and a counselor made regular visits. But there were also fresh flowers, plumped pillows and a wide selection of Max's favorite classical music.

A special lock had been installed on the terrace doors to prevent him from wandering out alone. Roxanne had coldly dismissed one doctor's advice to have the windows fixed with bars and had hung new lace curtains instead.

Her father might be a prisoner of his illness, but she wouldn't make him one in his own home.

It pleased her to see the sunlight streaming through the lace at the windows, to hear the muted strains of Chopin as she stepped into her father's room. It no longer ripped so viciously at her heart when he didn't recognize her. She'd come to accept that there would be good days, and there would be bad ones. Now, seeing him sitting at his desk, patiently shifting sponge balls between his fingers, she could feel some small seed of relief.

Today, he was content.

"Good morning, Miss Nouvelle." The first-shift R. N. sat by the window reading. She set the book aside and smiled at Roxanne. "Mr. Nouvelle's taking some practice time before his therapy."

"Thank you, Mrs. Fleck. If you'd like to take a break for ten or fifteen minutes, LeClerc has fresh coffee on."

"I could probably force some down." Mrs. Fleck had twenty years as a nurse, and kind eyes. It had been the eyes more than the experience that had prompted Roxanne to hire her. She hefted her sturdy bulk out of the chair and touched Roxanne's arm briefly as she left the room.

"Hello, Daddy." Roxanne crossed to the desk, bent to kiss her father's cheek. It was too thin, so thin she often wondered how the fragile skin withheld the pressure of bone. "It's a pretty day. Have you looked outside? All of LeClerc's flowers are blooming, and Mouse fixed the fountain in the courtyard. Maybe you'd like to sit down there later and listen to it."

"I have to practice."

"I know." She stood with a hand light on his shoulder, watching his twisted fingers struggle to manipulate the balls. Once he could have snapped his fingers and made fire, but it was best not to think of that. "The performance went well. The finale was especially smooth. Oscar's gotten to be quite a ham, and such a trooper even Lily isn't nervous around him anymore."

She continued to talk, not expecting a response. It was a rare day when Max would stop whatever he was doing to look at her, much less engage in a real conversation. "We took Nate to the zoo. He just loved it. I didn't think I'd ever get him out of the snake house. He's getting so big, Daddy. Sometimes I look at him and can hardly believe he's mine. Did you ever feel that way, when I was growing up? Did you ever just look and feel sort of dazed all over and wonder how that person came from you?"

One of the balls bounced onto the floor. Roxanne bent to retrieve it, then crouched so that her eyes were on a level with Max's as she passed it back to him.

Max's gaze skittered away from hers, like a spider seeking a corner to spin a web. But she was patient and waited until he looked at her again.

"Did you worry all the time?" she asked softly. "In the back of your mind, under and over all the day-to-day business of living? Were you always afraid you'd do the wrong thing, say the wrong thing, make the wrong choice? It never gets easier, does it? Having a child is so wonderful, and it's so scary."

Max's smile bloomed slowly. For Roxanne it was like watching the sun come up over the desert. "You're very pretty," he said, stroking her hair. "I have to practice now. Would you like to come to the performance and watch me saw a woman in half?"

"Yes." She watched him work the balls with his fingers. "That would be nice." She waited a moment. "Luke's back, Daddy."

He continued to work the balls, his smile turning into a frown of concentration. "Luke," he said after a long pause. And again. "Luke."

"Yes. He'd like to see you. Is it all right if I let him visit?"

"Did he get out of that box?" Max's facial muscles began to twitch. The balls scattered, bouncing. His voice rose, petulant and demanding. "Did he get out?"

"Yes." Roxanne took her father's restless hands. "He's just fine. I'm going to see him in a little while. Would you want me to bring him to you?"

"Not when I'm practicing." Max's voice pitched higher, cracked. "I need to practice. How can I get it right if I don't practice?"

"All right, Daddy." To calm him, Roxanne gathered up the balls and set them within reach on the desk.

"I want to see him," Max muttered. "I want to see him when he's out of the box."

"I'll bring him." She kissed the thin cheek again, but Max was already involved with squeezing the sponge balls into his palms.

When Roxanne walked downstairs, she had her strategy mapped out. Luke was back; she couldn't ignore that. Nor would she ignore his tie to Max. But that didn't mean she wouldn't watch him like a hawk when she allowed a visit.

Just as there were certain steps to take toward a job, there were steps to take with Luke. She would work with him because it suited her, because his proposition intrigued her and because unless he'd changed dramatically in the last five years, he was the best. On stage, or opening the securest safe.

So she would use him for her own ends, take her share of the profits and walk away.

Except there was Nathaniel.

Stooping on the second to the last step, Roxanne picked up a tot-sized Ferrari. She slipped it into her pocket, but kept her fingers over it, thinking of the child whose fingers guided it on races across the rug or long rides over the brick courtyard. The child who was even now in his preschool class enjoying the morning with his current best friends. Could she ignore Luke's tie to the child he didn't know existed? Was this an illusion she should maintain for the rest of her life?

More time, she assured herself as she headed back to the kitchen. She needed more time.

It didn't help her peace of mind to find Luke there, sitting at the table as he had so often throughout his life, looking right at home with a cup of coffee in one hand and the last powdery bite of a beignet in the other.

LeClerc was laughing, so obviously pleased to have the prodigal home, so obviously ready to forgive and forget that Roxanne became only more determined to do neither.

"Quite a trick, Callahan, the way you slip through the cracks."

He acknowledged her and the job with an easy smile. "One of the five things I missed most while I was away was LeClerc's cooking."

"This boy was a walking appetite always. Sit, little girl. I fix your coffee."

"No, thank you." She knew her voice was cold, and felt a slight pang when LeClerc's eyes shifted from hers. Damn it, did they expect her to hire a brass band? "If you've finished your *petite déjeuner,* we might get to work."

"Ready when you are." He rose, snatching another pastry from the basket on the table. "I'll just take one for the road." He winked at LeClerc before strolling out the door Roxanne held open. "Does he still do all the gardening himself?" Luke asked as they crossed the flower-decked courtyard.

"Occasionally he lets—" Nate. "One of us help." she finished. "But he's still a tyrant about his roses."

"He hardly looks older. I was afraid." He paused, covering Roxanne's hand as she reached for the doorknob of the workroom. "I don't suppose you could understand, but I was afraid they would have changed. But when I was sitting in the kitchen just now, it was the way it always was. The smells, the sounds, the feel of it, just the same."

"And that makes it easy for you."

He wished he could blame her for twisting the knife so expertly. "Not entirely. You've changed, Rox."

"Have I?" She turned. He was closer than she would have liked, but she wouldn't cringe away, or yearn forward. Instead she stood straight and smiled coolly.

"There was a time I could read everything on your face," he murmured. "But you've pulled a switch. You look the same, you smell the same, sound the same. I imagine if I could take you into bed, you'd feel the same, but you've clicked that one little switch." With his eyes on hers he passed a hand over her face. "Now there's another woman superimposed over the one I remember. Which one are you, Roxy?"

"I'm exactly who I want to be." She twisted the knob and pushed the door open. "I'm who I made myself." She hit the lights and flooded the big workroom with its colored trunks, long tables and clusters of magic. "So, you saw the show. You should have a good idea how I work now. The basic style is elegance, touches of flash, but always with grace and fluidity."

"Yeah, real pretty." Luke bit into the beignet, scattering powdered sugar. "Maybe a little strong on the feminine side."

"Really?" Her brow arched. She picked up a silver dagger with a jeweled hilt she used as a prop. "I suppose you'd prefer strutting across the stage beating your chest and flexing your muscles."

"I think we can come to a happy medium."

Leaning a hip against the table, Roxanne tapped the blade against her palm. "I think we have a miscommunication here, Callahan. I'm the show. I'm perfectly willing to let you stage your comeback as part of the diversion, but I am and will remain in charge of the staging."

"My comeback." He ran his tongue across his teeth. "You're right about one thing, babe. There is a miscommunication. Has-beens have comebacks. I've been bugging their eyes out in Europe."

"Isn't it sweet how so many of those tiny villages still flock to side-shows?"

His eyes narrowed, glinted. "You want to put down that knife and say that?"

She only smiled, running a fingertip along the tip. "Now as I see it, we're doing a one-night-only. The prepublicity should give us enough for a sellout. 'One Night of Magic with Roxanne Nouvelle.'" She tossed her head so that her hair swung out and back. "With a special appearance by Callahan."

"At least your ego hasn't changed. Partners, Roxanne." He stepped closer. "You want top billing, I'll be a gentleman about it. But the sign reads 'Nouvelle and Callahan.'"

She moved a shoulder. "We'll negotiate."

"Look, I'm not wasting time with your petty bullshit."

"Petty? You want to talk petty?" She swung toward him and drove the knife into his heart. The look of stupefaction on his face had her falling back against the table, doubled over with laughter.

"God, what a sucker."

"Cute." He rubbed his chest where the trick knife had thudded. The heart beneath it had stopped dead. "Real cute. Now do you want to get down to business, or do you want to play?"

"Sure, we'll get down to business." She set the knife aside then propped herself up on the table. "It's my show, and it runs an hour forty-five. I'm willing to give you fifteen of it."

"I'll have fifty—including ten minutes for the finale, which we do together."

"You're taking Oscar's place?" When he gave her a blank look, she smiled. "The cat, Callahan. I do a finale with the cat."

"We'll shift that to the last act before intermission."

"Who the hell put you in charge?"

"It's my gig, Roxanne." Leaving it at that, he walked over to one of the brightly painted trunks. It was as tall as he and sectioned into three equal parts. "I want to work in an escape, a multiplication bit I've been working on, one large-scale illusion and a transportation."

To give her hands something to do, she picked up three balls to juggle. "Is that all?"

"No, the finale's separate." He turned back, picked up another ball. Gauging her rhythm, he tossed it in among the three. She picked up the fourth ball without blinking an eye. "I want to do a variation on the broomstick illusion we did on the cruise. I've got most of the kinks worked out already. I'd like to start rehearsing as soon as possible."

"You'd like a lot of things."

"Yeah." He stepped forward and, quick as a snake, slipped his hands under hers to take the balls. "The trick's figuring out when to move and when to wait." He grinned at her through the circling balls. "We can rehearse here, or we can use the house I just bought."

"Oh?" She hated the fact that she was interested. "I figured you'd bunk at a hotel."

"I like my own space. It's a good-sized house in the Garden District. Since I haven't bothered much with furniture yet, we'd have plenty of room."

"Yet?"

"I'm back, Rox." He sailed the balls toward her, but she batted them aside. "Get used to it."

"I don't give a damn where you live. This is business, and a one-shot deal at that. Don't get it into your head that you're coming back on the team."

"I'm already on it," he said. "That's what pisses you off." He held up a hand for peace. "Why don't we see how we manage this? Mouse and Jake already have their heads together over the security angle, and—"

"Hold it." Fired up, she shoved off the table. "What do you mean they have their heads together?"

"I mean, Jake came over with me. He and Mouse went off to talk electronics."

"I'm not having this." She shoved him aside so that she had a clear field to pace. "All right? I'm not having it. No way you're waltzing back here and taking over. I've been running things for over three years. Ever since Max—ever since he couldn't anymore. Mouse is mine."

"I didn't realize he'd become property since I'd left."

Furious, she swung back. "You know very well what I mean. He's *my* family. He's my team. You gave that up."

He nodded. "I gave a lot up. You want to make it personal. Fine. I spent five years doing without everything that mattered to me. Because it mattered to me. Now I'm taking it back, Roxy. All of it." The hell with caution, with courtship, with control, he thought as he grabbed her by the shoulders. "Every last bit of it. Nothing's going to stop me."

She could have pulled away. She could have scratched and bit and fought her way free. But she didn't. Something in his eyes, something wild and desperately unhappy kept her rooted to the spot even when he crushed his mouth to hers.

She tasted the fury and the frustration and something more, a longing too deep for words, too wide for tears. Those old, carefully buried needs fought their way up so that she answered greed with greed.

Oh, how she wanted him still. How she wanted to blank out time and space and simply be again. It was so much as it had been, his taste, the way his mouth slanted over hers, that whip-quick, pulsing excitement that left her body straining urgently toward fulfillment.

But it was not the same. Even as her arms clamped around him she could feel that he was leaner. As if he'd taken a blade and ruthlessly hacked himself down to muscle and bone. Beneath the physical she could sense other changes. This Luke wouldn't laugh as quickly, rest as easily or love as sweetly.

But, oh, how she wanted him still.

He could take her there, on the table where magic had been conjured for a generation. On the floor where enchanter's dust lay scattered. Here and now. And if he did, if he took back what had been lost to him, he might find his salvation. He might find his peace. But even if it brought him hell and chaos, he'd thank God for it. He let his mind wallow in the thought while his hands molded the body that melted so perfectly against his.

She was the only one. The always one. There was nothing and no one to stop him from claiming her again.

Except himself.

"It's the same." He tore his mouth from hers to bury it against her throat. "Damn it, Roxanne, it's the same between us. You know it."

"No, it's not." Yet she clung to him still, wishing.

"Tell me you don't feel it." Furious and frantic, he dragged her back to study her face. He saw what he needed to see there—the heavy eyes, the pale skin, the swollen mouth. "Tell me you don't feel what we do to each other."

"It doesn't matter what I feel." Her voice rose, as if by shouting she could convince herself. "What matters is what is. I'll trust you onstage. I'll even trust you on the job. But nowhere else, Luke. With nothing else ever again."

"Then I'll do without trust." He dipped his fingers in her hair, combing them through. "I'll take what's left."

"You're waiting for me to say I want you." She pulled away, giving herself time for two steadying breaths. "All right, I want you, and maybe I'll decide to act on it. No strings, no promises, no baggage."

He felt like someone was kneading the muscles in his gut as if they were bread dough. "Decide now."

She nearly laughed. There was so much of the old Luke in the command. "Sex is something I'm cautious about." She sent him a level look. "And that's all it would be."

"You're cautious," he murmured, stepping to her again, "because you're afraid it would be a whole lot more." He tilted his head down to kiss her again, but this time she slapped a hand on his chest.

"Is this your answer for everything?"

Because whether she knew it or not they'd made progress, he smiled. "Depends on the question."

"The question is, can we pull off a complicated series of jobs while our hormones are humming?" She smiled back, daring him. "I can if you can."

"Deal." He took her hand. "But I'm going to get you into bed along the way. So, why don't you come to my place. We can . . . rehearse."

"I take rehearsals seriously, Callahan."

"Me too."

With a laugh, she rocked back on her heels, and dipped her hands in her pockets. Her fingers brushed the little car, and she remembered. Too much. The smile died out of her eyes.

"We'll make it tomorrow."

"What is it?" Frustrated that the shutter had dropped between them again, he took her chin in his hand. "Where did you go?"

"I just don't have time to work it in today."

"You know that's not what I meant."

"I have a right to my privacy, Luke. Give me the address, and I'll be there tomorrow morning. To rehearse."

"Fine." He dropped his hand. "We'll play it your way. For now. There's one more thing before I go."

"What?"

"Let me see Max." His temper tripped when she hesitated. "Goddamn it, scrape and claw at me all you want. But don't punish me that way."

"You don't know me at all, do you?" she said wearily. She turned away, walked to the door. "I'll take you up to him."

He'd known it would be bad. Luke had gathered all the snippets from the press on Max's condition, had read everything he could find on Alzheimer's. He'd been sure he'd been prepared for the physical changes, and the emotional ones.

But he hadn't known how badly it would hurt to see the man, that larger-than-life figure from his boyhood, so shrunken, so old and so lost.

He stayed for an hour, in the sunny room with Mozart playing. He talked endlessly, even when there was no response, and he searched Max's face for signs of recognition.

He left only when Lily came in and gently told him that it was time for Max's exercise.

"I'll come back." Luke put his hand over Max's and felt the thready pulse in the narrow wrist. "I've got a couple of new bits you might like to see."

"Have to practice," Max said, staring down at Luke's strong, lean hand. "Good hands. Have to practice." He grinned suddenly. "You have potential."

"I'll be back," Luke said again and walked blindly toward the door. He found Roxanne down in the front parlor, watching the street through the window.

"I'm sorry, Roxy." When he stepped behind her, wrapping his arm around her waist, she didn't object, but gave for a moment, leaning into him.

"There's no one to blame. I tried that route at first. Doctors, fate, God. Even you, just because you weren't here." When he pressed a kiss to the top of her head she squeezed her eyes tightly shut. But they were dry when she opened them. "He's gone somewhere he has to be. That's how I deal with it. He isn't in pain, though sometimes I'm so afraid there's a deeper kind of pain I can't see. But I know how lucky we are to be able to keep him home, and close until he's ready to go away completely."

"I don't want to lose him."

"I know." Understanding was too deep for her to prevent a reaching out. She lifted a hand to the one on her shoulder and linked fingers. Where Max was concerned, she could give without limitation. "Luke, I need to set the rules, and it's not to punish you. I'd like you to see Max as much as possible. I know it's difficult, and it's painful, but I have to believe it's good for him. You were—are—a big part of his life."

"I don't have to tell you how I feel about him, what I'd do for him if I could."

"No. No, you don't." She let out a long breath. "I'll need you to let me know when you'd like to come. Dropping in unannounced disrupts his routine."

"For chrissake, Roxanne."

"There are reasons." She turned, standing firm. "I'm not going to explain myself, I'm just going to set the boundaries. You're welcome here. Max would want that. But on my terms."

"So I make appointments?"

"That's right. Mornings are usually best, like today. Sometime between nine and eleven." When Nathaniel was safely in preschool. "That way we can set rehearsals for the afternoon."

"Fine." He strode toward the door. "Draw me up a goddamn schedule."

Roxanne heard the front door slam. The familiar echo of it nearly made her smile.

29

For the first time in her life, Roxanne suffered from the disapproval of her family. They didn't say she was wrong. There were no lectures, no unsolicited advice, no withholding of smiles or conversation.

She might have preferred that to the murmurs she heard before she walked into a room, the long sorrowful stares she felt behind her back. They didn't understand. She could tell herself that and forgive them—or nearly. None of them had ever found themselves pregnant and deserted and alone. Well, perhaps not really alone, she amended as she propped her chin on her hand and watched Nathaniel play cars in the courtyard. She'd had family, a home and unquestioning support.

But none of it made up for what Luke had done. She'd be damned if she'd reward him by sharing her perfectly beautiful child and risking the steady balance of Nate's happiness.

Why couldn't they see that?

She glanced up when the kitchen door opened, and smiled at Alice as the woman crossed the courtyard. An ally, Roxanne thought, smug. Alice didn't know Luke, had no emotional investment in him. She of all people would agree that a mother had the right to protect her child. And herself.

"There was an awful wreck," Nathaniel told Alice.

Interested, she bent down, her wispy blond hair swung out, her full-skirted cotton dress nearly brushing the bricks. "Looks grim," she agreed in her quiet voice. "Better call nine-one-one."

"Nine-one-one!" Nathaniel agreed, delighted, and began to make siren noises.

"That's the third wreck in fifteen minutes." Roxanne scooted over on the iron bench so Alice could sit. "The fatalities are mounting."

"Those roads are treacherous." Alice smiled her pretty, ethereal smile. "I've tried to educate him on the advantages of car pools, but he prefers traffic jams."

"He prefers traffic accidents. I hope it's not warping his mind."

"Oh, I think we're safe there." Alice took a deep breath to bring in the scent of roses and sweet peas and freshly watered mulch. The courtyard was her favorite spot, a shady summery place designed for sitting and thinking. So typically southern. As a transplanted Yankee, she embraced all that was South with the same fervor a converted Catholic embraces the church. "I thought I'd take Nate to Jackson Square after preschool. Let him run around a little."

"I wish I could go with you. I never feel as though I'm spending enough time with him when I'm prepping for a job."

Alice had accepted all sides of the Nouvelles' professions with philosophical ease. To her they weren't stealing so much as spreading excess profits around. "You're a wonderful mother, Roxanne. I've never seen you let work interfere with Nate's needs."

"I hope not. His needs are the most important thing to me." She laughed as he bashed two cars together and made crashing noises. "Homicidal?"

"Healthy aggression."

"You're good for me, Alice." With a sigh, Roxanne sat back. But she was rubbing her hands together, a sure sign of nerves. "Everything seemed so balanced, so right, so easy. I like routine, you know? I suppose it comes from the discipline of magic."

Alice studied Roxanne with calm eyes. "I wouldn't say you were a woman who disliked surprise."

"Some surprises. I won't have Nate's life disrupted. Or mine either, if it comes to that. I know what's best for him. Damn it, I want to know what's best for him. And I certainly know what's best for me."

Alice was silent a moment. She wasn't a woman to speak without thinking. She gathered those thoughts as carefully and as selectively as she would pick wildflowers. "You want me to tell you that keeping Nate a secret from his father is the right thing to do."

"It is." Roxanne glanced at Nate, cautiously lowering her voice. "At least until I feel it's time. He has no rights to Nate, Alice. He gave them up when he walked away from us."

"He didn't know there was an us."

"That's beside the point."

"It may be beside, or it may be the point. I'm not in a position to know."

"So." Roxanne's lips thinned at the new betrayal. "You're lining up with the rest of them."

"It's not like choosing sides for kickball, Roxanne." Because friendship came first with Alice, she closed a hand over Roxanne's rigid fingers. "Whatever you do or don't do, we're all behind you. Whether we agree or not."

"And you don't."

With a sigh, Alice shook her head. "I don't know what I would do in your position. And only you can know what you really feel in your heart. I can say that in the week since I met Luke, I like him. I like his intensity, his recklessness, his single-minded focus on a goal. Those are some of the same reasons I like you."

"So you're saying I should let him in, trust him with Nate."

It was so hard to give advice, Alice thought. She wondered why so many people thrived on it. "I'm saying you should do what you feel is right. Whatever that is, it won't change one simple fact. Luke is Nathaniel's father."

Luke, Luke, Luke. Roxanne fumed as she watched him run through his Woman in the Glass Box routine with Lily. Mouse and Jake stood off to the side, drawn away from the electronic jammer they'd been tinkering with to watch.

Why was it Luke came back and he was suddenly the sun with all of them revolving like planets around him? She hated it.

It was all wrong. They were rehearsing here, in his barnlike living room with its lofty ceilings and fancy plasterwork. Suddenly they were on his turf, with him calling the shots.

There was rock music on the stereo. He was timing his bit to Springsteen's *Born to Run*. They always worked with classical, Roxanne thought, shoving her hands into the pockets of her sweatpants. Always. It infuriated her further that it suited him, and the illusion.

It was fast, exciting, sexy. Everything he did fit those three words. She knew damn well the audience would love it. That only soured her mood.

"Good." Luke turned to Lily and kissed her flushed cheek. "Time, Jake?"

"Three minutes, forty." He'd already clicked off the stopwatch.

"I think we can shave ten more seconds." Despite the air-conditioning, he was sweating. Still, he liked keeping that particular illusion at a frantic pace, and was revved for more. "Can you handle another run, Lily?"

"Sure."

Sure, Roxanne thought, sneering. Anything you want, Luke. Anytime you want it. Disgusted, she turned away to retreat to the far corner of the room. She'd work through the Spinning Crystal routine she hadn't had time to perfect before the last performance. There, beside the massive stone fireplace, was a long folding table. A number of props were set up there, ready for practicing.

She was particularly pleased with the diamond-shaped crystal, its rainbow facets. It was a good, solid weight in her hands. She imagined the strains of Tchaikovsky, envisioned the shadowy stage, the crisscrossed spotlights softened with blue gel, and herself sheathed from head to foot in pure glistening white.

And swore when Springsteen's primal yell shattered her concentration.

Luke caught the bitter snarl she tossed at him, and grinned. "Mouse, how about setting up for the levitation? I think we've got this one."

"Sure." Mouse lumbered off to oblige.

"Pulling everyone's string, aren't you?" Roxanne said when Luke joined her at the table.

"It's called teamwork."

"I've got another name for it. Worming. Slithering."

"That's two words." He covered her hands over the crystal. "Think of it this way, Rox. Once we pull this off, you'll never have to come within ten feet of me again. Unless you want to."

"I am thinking of that." It was better than thinking of how just the touch of his hands on hers made her blood thicken. "I need to know more about the Wyatt job. You're holding back, and I don't like it."

"So are you," he said evenly. "And neither do I."

"I don't know what you're talking about."

But she'd broken eye contact. "Yes, you do. There's something you're not telling me. Something everyone's holding their breath over. Once you come clean, we'll deal with the situation."

"Come clean?" She cut her eyes back to his, and they were hot and lethal. "Something I'm not telling you? What could it be? Let's see . . . could it be that I detest you?"

"No." He outmaneuvered her by running his hands up her arms while hers were trapped around the crystal. "You've been busy letting me know that for more than a week. And you only detest me when you make yourself think about it."

"But it comes so naturally." She smiled, sweet as a honeyed stiletto.

"Only because you're still crazy about me." He kissed the tip of her nose when she hissed at him. "This is business, right?"

"Yes."

"So let's get down to it." His smile was slow and dangerous. "Then we'll see what comes naturally."

"I want more information."

"And you'll get it. Just like you'll get the stone when it's finished."

"Wait." She grabbed his arm when he started to turn. Unsteady, she set the crystal down again. "What are you saying?"

"That the stone's yours when it's finished. One hundred percent."

She searched his face looking for the truth, wishing she could see him clearly as she once had. "Why?"

"Because I love him, too."

There was nothing for her to say, because that was the truth, and that she could see clearly. Her chest tightened, restricting air as well as words. "I want to hate you, Callahan," she managed. "I really want to hate you."

"Tough, isn't it?" He skimmed a finger down her cheek. "I know, because I wanted to forget you. I really wanted to forget you."

She lifted her eyes to his, and for the first time since his return he saw the opening. He'd wormed his way in all right, he thought with some disgust. Through her love for Max. It wasn't the route he would have chosen.

"Why?" She hadn't wanted to ask, was afraid of the answer.

"Because loving you, remembering loving you was killing me."

That shook her knees and loosened her heart. "You're not going to get to me, Callahan."

"Oh, yeah." He took her hand to lead her to the center of the room. "I am."

"Nearly set." Mouse whistled through his teeth. It was great to have the two of them together again, he thought. Even if they weren't smiling. It embarrassed him to feel the sparks fly from them. It seemed to Mouse that was something that should happen in the dark, when two people were alone. That kind of intimacy was rough on witnesses.

Roxanne lifted her arms so that Mouse could fix his wires. But she never took her eyes from Luke. She hated to admit she liked this particular illusion. It sizzled, and it flowed, it had drama and it had poetry.

Besides, she'd had fun squabbling with him over each and every detail.

"Are we using the music?" she asked.

"Yeah. My pick."

"Why—"

"Because you chose the lighting."

She frowned, but it was tough to argue with quid pro quo. "So what is it?"

" 'Smoke Gets in Your Eyes.' " He grinned when she rolled hers. "The Platters, Rox. It's not classical, but it is a classic."

"If you knew anything about creating a theme, you'd know that the music should be consistent throughout the show."

"If you knew anything about flair, you'd know that the change of pace adds pizzazz."

"Pizzazz." She sniffed, tossed back her hair. "Let's just do it."

"Fine. Cue the music."

She brought her hands up, swayed. He held his out, curling his fingers toward him in invitation. Or in command. Resisting, refusing, she lifted her arm over her face, her palm toward him and turned fluidly to the side. Not a retreat. An allurement. Focused on her, only on her, he mirrored her move, step for step, as if they were bound by invisible threads. Their fingers brushed, lingered, drew away.

Roxanne felt the power ripple through her like wine.

She didn't need her memory of the script to keep her eyes on his. She couldn't have looked away. The concentration on his face pierced her, so it was easy to allow her head to roll loosely, dreamily on her shoulders.

Perhaps she could have won the duel. Or perhaps, in surrender, she already had.

Luke threw up his hands, a dramatic demand which Roxanne resisted by gliding away. Only to stop, poised, when his arms lowered and reached out for her. Slowly, as if caught in a trance, she turned back.

She didn't move when he stepped close. His hand passed in front of her face. Her eyes shuddered closed. Never more than a whisper away from bodies brushing, he circled her. His gestures were long, slow, exaggerated as her feet tipped off the floor, as her hair rained back, as her body lifted.

While the music built, his hands traced her, still that whisper away from contact. Her body quivered, beyond the control of her concentration. She watched him through her lashes, unable to help herself, certain she would scream with need and frustration if those hands continued to skim over her without touching.

He thought he could hear her heart pounding. Barely, he resisted the urge to press his hand over her breast to feel that thud of life. His mouth was dry, and he knew he was breathing too quickly. But he was beyond illusion now.

He'd meant the segment to be romantic, sexual, and had known he would be treading deep water. But he hadn't known how quickly he could drown.

He bent his head toward hers, his lips hovering, so close to tasting. The quiet sound she made as she struggled not to moan roared in his head.

He took her hand, running his fingers over the palm, down the back. When their fingers were linked he, too, began to rise. His eyes were riveted on her face as they lay suspended together. As the music began to fade, he turned his body, cupped a hand under her head and brought his mouth to hers.

Locked together, they tilted toward vertical, bodies revolving. When their feet touched the ground, his arms were still around her and her mouth was still a captive.

Jake clicked off the stopwatch and cleared his throat. "Don't guess anybody cares about time," he murmured and stuck the watch in his pocket. "Radio Shack," he said, inspired. "Come on, Mouse. We gotta get to the mall."

"Huh?"

"The mall, the mall. We need those parts."

Mouse blinked in confusion. "What parts?"

"*Those* parts." Jake rolled his eyes and jerked his head toward Roxanne and Luke. They'd drawn apart now, but only far enough to stare at each other.

"Oh, I need some things, too." Teary-eyed, Lily grabbed Mouse and pulled. "I need lots of things. Let's get going."

"But rehearsal—"

"I think they've got it cold," Jake said and was grinning as they pulled Mouse out of the house.

The silence spun in Roxanne's already dizzy head. "It—it ran long."

"You're telling me." He'd been ready to explode. Now he ran his hands gently up and down her back before freeing her from the levitation harness. "But it's going to be a hell of a finale."

"Needs work."

"I'm not talking about that finale." He released himself. "I'm talking about you and me." Watching her, he skimmed his hands under her sweatshirt and let them roam over the warm, smooth skin of her back. "And this." He kissed her again, softly.

She had no choice but to grip his shoulders for balance. "You're not going to seduce me."

He traced his lips over her jaw, knowing just where to nip to make her shiver. "Want to bet?"

"I can walk away from you anytime." But her body was pressed against his, and her mouth was racing over his face. "I don't need you."

"Me either." He scooped her up and started toward the stairs.

If her body would stop shivering she was sure she'd regain her bearings. For now it seemed best to hold on tight.

She knew what she was doing. God, she hoped she knew. This terrible ragged yearning made everything else seem so small and pitiful. This was all there was, all there needed to be. On a moan, she pressed her face against his neck.

"Hurry," was all she said.

He'd have flown up the stairs if he'd been able. It felt as though he had the way his muscles were quivering and his breath heaving. Once he'd kicked the bedroom door closed behind them, he sought her lips again. He could only thank whatever powers there were that he'd had the foresight to buy a bed.

And a hell of a bed it was. The huge, cushy four-poster gave like a cloud when they fell onto it. He paused for a moment, only a moment, to look down at her and remember—to force her to remember all they had been to each other, what they had done for each other, and to each other, beyond that gulf of five years.

He saw the struggle for denial in her eyes and battered it with a greedy kiss. She wouldn't hold back from him now, he wouldn't permit it. Cuffing her wrists in his hands he drew her arms high over her head. If she touched him he'd ignite like a stick of dynamite. First he wanted to make sure she felt everything he wanted her to feel.

She twisted against his hold, her heart leaping to her throat to bang like a drum in the hollow. He only lowered his lips to it as a prelude to an exploitation of every secret he remembered.

He'd dreamed of this countless times, in countless rooms in countless places. Only this was more potent than any fantasy. The taste of her, rioting through him, was like a feast after years of fasting. He wouldn't deny himself now, or ever again.

She didn't struggle against the flood of sensation. Couldn't bear to. He was giving her back everything he'd taken away, and more. She'd nearly forgotten what it was to crave, and had never really understood what it meant to abandon all will. After so long an abstinence it was so simple, so right, to only feel. Every time his lips found hers, there was a shock of recognition and a shiver of the unknown.

His blood burned when he heard his name tumble from her lips. Each sigh, each moan was a hammer thrust in his gut. Frantic for more, he released her hands to tug at her clothes. He groaned in violent pleasure when he found her gloriously naked beneath.

"Hurry," she said again, tearing his shirt in her rush to be flesh against flesh. The furnace building inside her was nearing flash point. She wanted him in her when it exploded. She wanted him stoking that fire inside her.

He wanted to savor. He needed to devour. Gasping for air, he fought the snap of his jeans while her hands tortured him and her mouth seared like lightning over his shoulders and chest.

He plunged. At the first urgent stroke she came in a geyser of dark, nameless delights. Her body arched, vibrated like a harp string. Air tore from her lungs in a cry that was both pain and triumph.

Then she locked around him, her legs soft as silk, strong as steel. Half mad, he drove himself into her, again and again, until he found his own release, and perhaps his salvation.

He stayed where he was, spread over her, intimately joined. He knew she'd been silent for too long. If things had been as they once were, she would have lifted a hand to lazily stroke his back. She would have sighed and nuzzled or whispered something to make him laugh.

But there was nothing but that long empty silence. It frightened him enough to kindle temper.

"You're not sorry this happened." He curled a hand possessively in her hair to keep her still when he leaned back to look at her. "You might be able to convince yourself of that, but not me."

"I didn't say I was sorry." How difficult it was to be calm when your life had just shifted on its foundations. "I knew it would happen. The minute I walked into my dressing room and saw you again, I knew." She managed what passed for a shrug. "I often make mistakes without being sorry for them."

His eyes glinted before he rolled away from her. "You know just where to hit, don't you? You always did."

"It's not a matter of striking back." She was going to be practical about this. If it killed her. "I enjoyed making love with you again. We were always good in bed."

He snatched her arm before she could reach her knotted sweatshirt. "We were good everywhere."

"Were," she agreed, carefully. "I'll be honest, Callahan. I haven't made much time for this sort of thing in my life since you left."

He couldn't stop it. His ego inflated as helplessly as a balloon swells with helium. "Oh, yeah?"

She couldn't understand how one man could infuriate, arouse and amuse a woman simultaneously. "Don't look so smug. It was my choice. I was busy."

"Admit it." He traced a lazy finger down her breast. "I spoiled you for anybody else."

"My point is." She slapped his hand away before the touch dissolved what was left of pride. "You happened to catch me at a..." Vulnerable wasn't quite the word she wanted. "An incendiary time. I imagine anyone who held the match in the right spot would have set me off."

"If that's the case, you should be pretty well burned out now."

He'd always been quick. She shouldn't have been surprised to find herself on her back again with his hands proving that fires could be kindled out of embers.

"It's just sex," she managed to gasp.

"Sure it is." He laved the damp flesh between her breasts. "And a redwood's just a tree." He used his teeth to torment her nipples until her nails dug crescents into his back. "A diamond's just a rock."

She wanted to laugh. She needed to scream. "Shut up, Callahan."

"Glad to." He lifted her hips and slid gloriously into her.

She didn't think she was burned out. Hollowed out was closer. There didn't seem to be a nerve left in her body. When she managed to open her eyes again, the light had gone rose with twilight. To give her mind a chance to settle, she took note of the room for the first time.

There was nothing in it but the bed where they sprawled and a single enormous chest of drawers in gleaming cherry. Unless you counted the clothes that were tossed over the rugless floor, draped over the doorknob or piled in corners.

How like him, she thought. Just as it was like him to have shifted his body so that hers could curl naturally against it.

How many times had they lain just like this, night after night? There had been a time when she would have drifted right off to sleep, safe, secure, satisfied.

But they were different people now.

She started to sit up. His arm merely tightened around her.

"Luke, this doesn't change anything."

He opened one eye. "Babe, if you want me to prove my point again, I'd be more than happy. You'll just have to give me a couple of minutes."

"The only point we've proved is that we still know how to scratch one another's itch." Most of her anger had died, leaving a gulf of sorrow that was only more potent. "There's no need to—What the hell is this?" She twisted to get a better look at the back of his shoulder.

"It's a tattoo. Haven't you ever seen a damn tattoo?"

"A few in my time." She pursed her lips, studying it in the dimming light. Just above where the scars of his youth began their crisscross on his back was the painted image of a snarling wolf. She didn't know whether to laugh or cry and opted for the former. "Jesus, Callahan, did you go crazy or what?"

It embarrassed the hell out of him. "Tattoos are in."

"Oh, right, and you're Mr. Trendy. Why the hell did you let somebody scar you—" She broke off, appalled. "I'm sorry."

"It's okay." He shrugged and dragged the hair out of his eyes as he sat up. "I was feeling mean one night, a little drunk, a lot dangerous. I decided to get a tattoo instead of looking for a convenient head to bash in. Besides, it reminded me of where I'd come from."

She studied him, the arrogant tilt of the head, the hard gleam of his eyes that warred with the encroaching gloom. "You know, I can almost believe in Lily's amnesia theory."

"Let me know when you want the truth. You'll get every bit of it."

She looked away. It was easy, much too easy for him to pull her in. "It wouldn't make any difference. There's nothing you can say that can wipe away five years."

"Not unless you're willing to let me." He caught her face in his hands, brushing her hair back so that only his fingers framed her. The gentleness he'd forgotten, that she had been certain had burned out of him, was back. Such things were harder to resist than passion. "I need to talk to you, Rox. There's so much I need to say."

"Things aren't what they were, Luke. I can't begin to tell you how much they've changed." And if she stayed, she would say more than was wise before she thought it through. "We can't go back, and I need to consider where we might go from here."

"We can go anyplace. We always could."

"I've gotten used to going on my own." She took a deep breath before shifting away to dress. "It's getting late. I have to go home."

"Stay here." He touched his fingertips to her hair, and tempted her beyond measure.

"I can't."

His fingers curled, tightened. "Won't."

"Won't then." She smoothed down her shirt, rose. It was easier to be strong when she was standing on her feet again. "I run my life now. You can stay or you can go, and I'll deal with the consequences of either. If I owe you anything, it's gratitude for making me tough enough to handle whatever comes." She tilted her head, wishing her heart felt as courageous as the words. "So thanks, Callahan."

Her easy dismissal sliced him open and left him bleeding. "Don't mention it."

"See you tomorrow." She walked from the room, but was running by the time she hit the landing.

30

The house was in an uproar when Roxanne returned. She'd no more than stepped across the threshold when she was caught up in the chaos. While everyone talked at once, she swung Nathaniel up in her arms and kissed him firmly on his pursed and waiting lips, partly in greeting and partly in apology for not being the one to give him his bath and help him into his favored Ninja Turtles pj's.

"Hold on." She settled Nate on her hip, holding up a hand in a futile hope to stem the tide.

Delighted with the confusion, Nate bounced and began to sing a sea chantey about drunken sailors at the top of his voice.

She caught snatches about the telephone, caviar, Clark Gable, San Francisco and Aces High. Her mind, already muddled from her afternoon with Luke, struggled to decipher the code.

"What? Clark Gable called from San Francisco and came over to eat caviar and do card tricks?"

Because Alice laughed, Nate decided it must be a grand joke. Giggling, he tugged on his mother's hair. "Who's Clark Gable, Mama? Who is he?"

"He's a dead man, baby, like certain other people around here are going to be if they don't *shut up!*" Her voice had risen admirably on the last two words. There was a gratifying stunned silence. Before anyone could draw in the breath to start again, she pointed at Alice. Roxanne knew if she couldn't count on Alice for a calm, reasonable explanation, all was lost.

"It really started because of *San Francisco,*" Alice began. "The movie—you know, Clark Gable, Spencer Tracy. You know how the evening nurse likes to watch old movies on the television in your father's room?"

"Yes, yes."

"Well, she had it on while Lily was helping your father eat dinner—"

Lily interrupted by putting her hands over her face and sobbing. Roxanne clicked into panic mode.

"Daddy?" Still gripping Nate, she turned and would have bolted up the stairs if Alice hadn't stopped her.

"No, Roxanne, he's fine. Just fine." For a small, fragile-looking woman, she had a strong grip. She clamped her fingers over Roxanne's arm and held on. "Let me tell you the rest before you go up."

"He started talking," Lily said behind her hands. "About—about San Francisco. Oh, Roxy, he remembered me. He remembered everything."

Nate was so touched by her tears he reached out. Lily gathered him close, rocking and sniffling while Nate patted her cheek. "He kissed my hand—just like he used to. And he talked about a week we'd spent in San Francisco and how we had champagne and caviar on the terrace of our hotel room and watched the fog roll in on the bay. And how—how he tried to teach me card tricks."

"Oh." Roxanne pressed a hand to her lips. She knew he could have moments of clarity but she couldn't quite tamp out that stubborn spark of hope that this one would last. "I should have been here."

"You couldn't know." LeClerc took her hand. He could only think of how it hurt and healed to have sat for a moment with his old friend. "Alice had just gotten off the phone to Luke when you walked in."

"I'll go up." She leaned over to where Nate had tucked his head on Lily's shoulder to comfort. "I'll be in to kiss you good night, knucklehead."

"Can I have a story?"

"Yes."

"A *really* long one, with monsters in it."

"An epic one, with horrible monsters in it." She kissed him and watched his smile bloom.

"Grandpa said I grew a foot. But I only have two."

Tears swam in her eyes as she lowered her brow to her son's. "The third's invisible."

"How come he could see it then?"

"Because he's a magician." She kissed the tip of his nose, then turned to go to her father.

He was wearing a silk robe of royal purple. His hair, a glinting steel gray, was freshly combed. He sat at his desk, much as he had day after day when she visited him. But this time he was writing, using the long, flourishing strokes she remembered.

Roxanne glanced at the nurse who was standing at the foot of the bed filling out the chart. They exchanged nods before the nurse carried the chart out of the room and left them alone.

There were so many things racing through Max's mind. They crashed and boomed together like music. He had to rush to keep up with the notes, to write them down before they faded and were lost to him.

He knew they would fade, and that was his hell. The effort it cost him to fight off the fog, to hold the pen in fingers that cramped with the movement would have exhausted a younger man. But there was a burning in him, bright and hot, that seared beyond the physical. If it hulled out his body, so be it. His mind was his own again. If it lasted for an hour or a day, he wouldn't waste a moment.

Roxanne stepped closer. She was afraid to speak. Afraid that he would look up and that his eyes would pass over her as if she were a stranger. Or worse, as if she were a shade, some transparent illusion that meant nothing more to him than a trick of the eye.

When he did look up, alarm came first. He looked exhausted, so pale and drawn, so horribly thin. His eyes were bright, perhaps overbright, but in them she saw something beyond beauty. She saw recognition.

"Daddy." She tumbled the last few feet to him to fall on her knees with her head pressed to the thin wall of his chest. She hadn't known, hadn't allowed herself to know how much she'd needed to feel his arms around her again. How much she'd missed the feel of his hands stroking through her hair.

Her chest heaved once in an attempt to throw off the pressure building there with a sob. But she wouldn't greet him with tears. "Talk to me, please. Talk to me. Tell me how you feel?"

"Sorry." He bent his head to brush a cheek against her hair. His little girl. It was hard, much too hard to try to remember all the years that had passed between his child and the woman who held him now. They were a mist, a maze, and so he contented himself with accepting her as his little girl.

"So sorry, Roxy."

"No. No." Her eyes were fierce as she sat back on her heels. Her hands squeezed his until they ached, but the pain was sweet. "I don't want you to feel sorry."

She was so unbelievably lovely, he thought. His child, his daughter, her face flushed with determination, tears trembling in her eyes. The strength of her love, the sheer demand of it nearly felled him.

"Grateful, too." His moustache twitched as his lips curved up. "For you. For all of you. Now." He kissed her hands, sighed. He couldn't talk. There was really so little he could talk about. But he could listen. "Tell me what new magic you've conjured."

She curled up at his feet, keeping her fingers linked with his. "I'm doing a variation on the Indian Rope Trick. Very moody and dramatic. It plays well. We set up a videotape so I could review it myself." She laughed up at him. "I amaze myself."

"I'd like to see it." He shifted, tucking a hand under her chin so he could watch her eyes. "Lily tells me you're working on a broomstick illusion."

It took all her will to hold her gaze steady. "You know he's back then."

"I dreamed he was—" And the dream and reality swirled together so that he couldn't be sure. Simply couldn't be sure. "Right here, sitting beside me."

"He comes to see you, almost every day." She wanted to get up, to pace, but couldn't bear to separate her hand from her father's. "We're working together again, temporarily. It was too intriguing a job to pass on. There's to be an auction in D.C.—"

"Roxanne," he interrupted. "What does it mean to you—Luke's coming back?"

"I don't know. I want it to mean nothing."

"Nothing's a poor thing to wish for," he murmured, smiled again. "Has he told you why he left?"

"No. I haven't let him." Restless, she did rise, but couldn't bring herself to move away. "What difference could it make? He left me. He left all of us. Once this job is done, he'll leave again. It won't matter this time, because I won't let it."

"There isn't a magic trick in the book that can shield a heart, Roxy. You have a child between you this time. My grandchild." It pained Max more than he could say that he only had dim memories of the boy.

"I haven't told him." At her father's silence, she whirled around, surprised how ready she was to battle. "You disapprove?"

He only sighed. "You've always made your own decisions. Right or wrong, it's your choice. But nothing you can do will alter the fact that Luke is Nathaniel's father." He lifted a hand to her. "There's nothing you'd want to do to change that."

The muscles in her stomach loosened. The sharp fingers squeezing the base of her neck vanished. Magic, she thought, letting out a long clear breath. Say the magic words. "No, there's nothing I would do to change that." *Oh, I've missed you, Daddy.* She didn't say it, afraid it would hurt him. "It's so hard to be in charge, Max. So bloody hard."

"Easy's boring, Roxy. Who wants to spend their life with easy?"

"Well, maybe just a passing acquaintance."

He was smiling again, shaking his head. "Roxy, Roxy, you can't con me. You thrive on being in charge. The plum doesn't roll far from the tree."

She chuckled, kneeling beside him again. "Okay, maybe. But I wouldn't mind being told what to do—now and again."

"You'd still do what you want."

"Sure." Swamped with love, she threw her arms around him. "But it's more satisfying if someone tries to tell me what to do first."

"Then I'll tell you this. Grudges are bridges with faulty spans. Falling off one is a lot more rewarding then getting stuck on the other side."

"Free lesson?" she murmured and, with a sigh, pressed her cheek to his.

Roxanne was a little wobbly when she left her father sleeping and started back downstairs. He'd been so tired, and with his encroaching fatigue she'd all but been able to see the clouds rolling in again. When she'd tucked him into bed much as she would do for her son, he'd called her Lily.

She had to accept that he might remember nothing in the morning when he awakened. The hour she'd had with him would have to be enough.

Weary and weepy, she paused at the base of the stairs to straighten her shoulders.

She owed her family a solid front, a show of strength. As she walked toward the kitchen, she fixed an easy smile on her face.

"I could smell the coffee all the way..." She fumbled to a halt as her tumbling emotions took one more roll. There, gathered with her family, was Luke, leaning back against the kitchen counter with his hands tucked in his pockets.

Once again, everyone spoke at once. Roxanne only shook her head and marched to the stove to pour coffee. "He's sleeping. Talking all this time tired him out."

"Maybe he'll be fine now." Lily twisted the beads she wore around and around her fingers. "Maybe it's all going to go away." The look in Roxanne's eyes had her glancing away. It was so hard to bury hope, then unearth it again only to feel it die. "It was so good to talk to him again."

"I know." Roxanne cradled the coffee cup in both hands but didn't drink. "We can schedule more tests."

Lily made a tiny sound of distress and immediately began to fiddle with the cow-shaped creamer on the kitchen table. They all knew how difficult and disorienting the tests were for Max. How wrenching they were for those who loved him. "We can hope that the new medication is helping," Roxanne continued. "Or we can leave things as they are."

It was LeClerc who spoke, laying his spindly hand on Roxanne's shoulder to knead out some of the tension. "What do you want to do, *chère?*"

"Nothing," she said on a half sigh. "What I want to do is nothing. But what I think we should do is agree to whatever tests the doctors recommend." She took a deep breath, scanning faces. "Whatever the outcome, we had this evening. We'll have to be grateful for that."

"Can I go sit with him?" Mouse stared down at the toes of his shoes. "I won't wake him up."

"Of course you can." Roxanne waited until Mouse and Alice had left before she turned to Luke. "Why are you here?"

"Why do you think?"

"We agreed you wouldn't drop by for casual visits," she began, only to have the fury in his eyes stop her cold.

"This isn't casual. If you'd like to discuss why, here and now, I'd be glad to." She could still blush, he noted. It was fascinating to watch the color rise, blooming high on her cheeks while her eyes showed temper that had nothing to do with embarrassment. "Added to that," he continued blandly, "when Lily called about Max I wasn't about to sit home marking cards."

"Honey." Lily reached out a tentative hand. "I think Max would want Luke here."

"Max is asleep," she snapped back. "There's no need for you to stay. If he's up to it in the morning, you can have all the time you want with him."

"Damn generous of you, Roxanne."

The weakness showed through only briefly when she pressed her fingers to the thudding in her left temple. "I have to think of Max first. No matter what's between us you have to know I wouldn't keep you from him."

"Just what is between us?"

"I'm hardly going to discuss that now."

Whistling quietly between his teeth, LeClerc began to wipe the stove. He knew he should leave, give them privacy. But it was much too interesting. Lily didn't bother with a diversion. She clasped her hands and watched avidly.

"You climbed out of bed with me and walked away." He pushed away from the counter. "There's no way I'm leaving this unresolved."

"Unresolved?" The irony of it was so sharp she was amazed it didn't slice him into little pieces. But that was fine. She'd do the cutting herself. "You have the nerve to talk to me about leaving something—anything—unresolved? You walked out to do a job one night and never came back. A real clever variation on the old going-out-to-buy-a-pack-of-cigarettes, Callahan. But damn if I can claim to be impressed."

"I had reasons," he tossed out while Lily shifted her eyes from face to face with the eagerness of a tennis buff at Wimbledon.

"I don't give a shit about reasons."

"No, all you care about is making me crawl." He advanced another step and gave serious consideration to strangling her. "Well, I won't."

"I'm not interested in seeing you crawl. Unless it's naked, over broken glass. I went to bed with you, okay?" She pinwheeled her arms to make her point. "It was a mistake, abject stupidity, a moment of mindless lust."

He took a fistful of her sweatshirt. "It may have been stupid and it may have been lust, on both parts, babe. But it wasn't a mistake." His voice had risen to a boom that made her aching head reel. "And we're going to settle this, once and for all, if I have to gag you and cuff you to get you to listen."

"Just try it, Callahan, and all that'll be left of those hands you're so proud of is bloody stumps. So take your threats, and your pitiful..."

But he wasn't listening to her anymore. Fascinated, Roxanne watched the color drain out of his face until it was as white and lax as melted wax. The eyes that were staring over her shoulder darkened to cobalt. "Oh, God," was all he said, and the hand gripping her shirt went limp.

"Mama."

Roxanne's heart stopped, simply stopped at the sound of her son's voice. She turned, certain she heard her bones creak like rusty hinges with the slow, dreamlike movement. Nate was standing in the kitchen doorway, knuckling sleepy eyes with one hand and dragging his battered stuffed basset hound with the other.

"You didn't come kiss me good night."

"Oh, Nate." Cold, she was suddenly so cold, even as she bent to scoop her child into her arms. "I'm sorry. I would have come up soon."

"I didn't hear the end of the story Alice read, either," he complained, yawning and tucking his head in the familiar curve of her shoulder. "I fell asleep before the dog party."

Go Dog Go, Roxanne thought, dazed. Nathaniel did love his Dr. Seuss. "It's late, baby," she murmured.

"Can I have ice cream?"

She wanted to laugh, but it came out perilously close to a sob. "Not a chance."

Luke could only stare, stare at the small boy through eyes that were dazzled and hot and gritty. His heart had dropped to his knees and trembled there, leaving a raw, ragged hole in his chest. The child had his face. His face. It was like looking into a telescope lens, and seeing himself at a distance. In the past. In the past he'd never been given.

Mine, was all he could think. Oh, sweet Jesus. Mine.

After another wide yawn, Nate stared back, all curiosity and sleepy confidence. "Who's that?" he wanted to know.

In all the scenarios that had twisted through Roxanne's mind, introducing her son to his father had never been quite like this. "Ah—he's . . ." A friend? she wondered.

"This is Luke," Lily piped up, rubbing a hand up and down Luke's rigid arm. "He was kind of like my little boy when he was growing up."

"Okay." Nate smiled. All sweetness, no guile. What he saw was a tall man with black hair pulled back in a stubby ponytail and a face as pretty as a prince in one of his story books. "Hi."

"Hi." It amazed Luke how calm his voice sounded when his heart had vaulted back from his feet to lie lodged and swollen in his throat. He needed to touch, was afraid if he tried his hand might pass through the curve of the boy's cheek as in a dream. "You like dogs?" he said and felt incredibly stupid.

"This is Waldo." Always friendly, Nate held out the stuffed toy for Luke's inspection. "When I get a real dog I'm going to name him Mike."

"That's a pretty good name." Luke did touch, just the tips of his fingers to Nate's cheek. The boy's flesh was warm and soft against his.

More sly than shy, Nate cuddled his head against his mother's shoulder and beamed at Luke. "Maybe you'd like some ice cream now."

Roxanne couldn't bear any more—not the pain or the wonder in Luke's eyes or her own terrified guilt. "Kitchen's closed, smart guy." She tightened her grip possessively on her son. The urge to turn and run with what was hers was so cowardly it shamed her. "Lights out, Nate. You have to go to bed before you turn into a frog."

He giggled at that and made respectable frog noises.

"I'll take him up." Lily held out her arms for Nate before Roxanne could protest.

Nate twisted one of Lily's curls around his finger and poured on the charm. "Will you read me a story? I like it best when you read them."

"You bet. Jean?" Lily cocked a brow, amused to note that LeClerc was still wiping the sparkling surface of the stove. "Why don't you come with us?"

"As soon as I finish tidying up." He sighed when Lily narrowed her eyes at him. Too often discretion was a bitter pill to swallow. "I'll come along now."

Never one to let an opportunity pass, Nate began to negotiate as they trooped down the hall. "Can I have two stories? One from you and one from you?"

As Nate's voice faded away, Roxanne stood facing Luke, trapped in the silence.

"I think . . ." She cleared the tremor out of her voice and tried again. "I think I want something stronger than coffee." She started to turn, but Luke's hand whipped out snake-quick and gripped her arm. She felt his fingers press down to the bone.

"He's mine." His voice was low, deadly, terrifying. "Good Christ, Roxanne, that boy is my son. Mine." The force of it struck him so viciously that he shook her. Her head snapped back so that she had no choice but to stare into his ice-pale face. "We have a child, and you kept it from me. Goddamn you, how could you not tell me I had a son?"

"You weren't here!" she shouted, swinging out. The crack of her hand against his cheek stunned them both. Appalled, she pressed her fingers to her lips, then let her arm fall stiffly to her side. "You weren't here," she said again.

"I'm here now." He shoved her away before he did something he'd never forgive himself for. "I've been here for two weeks. 'Don't come by for casual visits, Callahan,' " he ground out, and there was more than fury in his eyes now, there was torment. "You weren't doing that for Max. You were setting up rules so I wouldn't see our son. You weren't going to tell me about him."

"I was going to tell you." She couldn't catch her breath. Never in her life had she feared him, physically. Until now. He looked capable of anything. Of everything. Unconsciously she rubbed the heel of her hand between her breasts as if to force the air in and out again. "I needed time."

"Time." He lifted her off her feet with that quick, baffling strength that both frightened and aroused. "I lost five goddamn years, and you needed time?"

"You lost? You lost? What did you expect me to do, Luke, when you came back into my life? Oh, hello, nice to see you again. By the way, you're a daddy. Have a fucking cigar."

He stared at her for one long frozen moment. Violence leaped through him, a deep, dark need to destroy, to inflict pain, to scream for revenge. He dropped her back on her feet, watched the fear jump into her eyes though she didn't flinch. On a vicious oath, he turned and yanked the door open.

Outside, he dragged in hot, thick air. The scent of flowers spun in his head, seemed to cling to his skin like sticky pollen though he rubbed his hands hard over his face. The pain was so sharp, so sudden, a rapier thrust through the heart that left him shocked and disbelieving while the blood drained.

His son. Luke pressed the heels of his hands against his eyes and uttered a sound that was raw with grief and rage. His son had looked at him, smiled at him and thought him a stranger.

She followed him out. Odd, she was calm now. It wouldn't have surprised her to have him turn on her, strike out at her. There had been that kind of danger in his eyes. She would defend herself if the need arose, but the time for fear had passed.

"I won't apologize for keeping it from you, Luke. I did what I thought best. Right or wrong, I'd do it again."

He didn't turn to look at her, but continued to stare out across the courtyard toward the fountain that played its quiet, liquid song.

They'd made that miracle together, he thought. Conceived the boy in love and laughter and lust. Was that why he'd been so beautiful, so perfect, so incredibly lovely? "Did you know you were pregnant when I left?"

"No." She caught herself rubbing her hands together and made herself drop her arms to her sides. "Right after, though. I was sick that afternoon, remember? It turns out that I was having my morning sickness a little late in the day."

"Trust you not to do the conventional." He jammed his hands in his pockets, struggling, struggling to be calm, to be reasonable. "Was it difficult?"

"What?"

"The pregnancy," he said between his teeth. But he didn't turn to look at her yet. Couldn't. "Was it difficult? You were sick?"

Of all the things she'd expected him to ask, this was the last. "No." Off balance, she pushed a hand through her hair. "I had the nausea for a couple of months, then I breezed through the rest. I've probably never felt better."

In his pockets, his hands curled to fists. "And when he was born?"

"It wasn't a walk on the beach, but I don't feel as though I strolled through the valley of the shadow of death either. Little over eighteen hours, and out popped Nathaniel."

"Nathaniel." He repeated the name in a whisper.

"I didn't want to name him after anyone. I wanted him to have his own."

"He's healthy." Luke continued to stare at the fountain. He could almost see the individual drops as they rose, fell and rose again. "He looks . . . healthy."

"He's fine. He's never sick."

"Like his mother." But he has my face, Luke thought. *He has my face.* "He likes dogs."

"Nate likes most everything. Except lima beans." She let out a shaky breath and took a chance. "Luke," she murmured, touching a hand to his shoulder. He whirled on her so quickly she fell back a step. But when he grabbed her, it wasn't to punish.

His arms simply came around her, bringing her close. His body shuddered once as it enfolded hers. Unable to deny either of them this, she stroked a hand through his hair and returned the embrace.

"We have a son," he whispered.

"Yes." She felt a tear sneak past her defenses, and sighed. "We have a terrific son."

"I can't let you keep him from me, Roxanne. No matter what you think of me, what you feel for me, I can't let you keep me from him."

"I know. But I won't let you hurt him." She drew away. "I won't let you become so important to him that you leave a hole when you go away."

"I want my son. I want you. I want my life back. By God, Roxanne, I'm taking what I want. You're going to listen to me."

"Not tonight." But he already had her by the hand. She swore ripely when he dragged her across the courtyard toward the workroom. "I'm not going through any more emotional wringers tonight. Now let me go."

"I've lived in an emotional wringer for five years." To simplify matters he hauled her off her feet. "You'll just have to tough it out for another hour." Yanking open the door he carried a struggling Roxanne inside.

"How can you do this? How can you behave this way?" She let out a grunt when he dumped her, butt first, onto a workbench. "You just found out about your son, and instead of sitting down and having a calm, adult conversation, you're tossing me around."

"We're not going to have a conversation, calm, adult or otherwise." He snatched up handcuffs and snapped one end over her wrist. "A conversation means two or more people are talking." Quick thinking had him dodging her fist the first time, but it was only a feint. She landed the second and bloodied his lip. "What you're going to do," he said, trapping her hands in front of her and locking them. "Is listen."

"You haven't changed." She would have rolled off the table despite the obvious result of smashing her nose on the floor if he hadn't caught her and secured the loop of the cuffs in a vise. "You're still a bastard, and a bully."

"And you're still a stubborn know-it-all. Now shut up." Satisfied she had no choice but to stay put, he stepped back. Roxanne hissed at him, then fell into an icy silence.

He wanted to talk, she thought. She'd let him talk until his tongue fell out. That didn't mean she had to listen. All of her concentration focused on freeing her wrists from the cuffs. He wasn't the only one with tricks up his sleeve.

"I left you," he began. "I can't deny it. I won't deny it. I left you and Max and Lily and everything that mattered and flew to Mexico with fifty-two dollars in my wallet and the burglar's tools Max had given me for my twenty-first birthday."

Concentration or not, she sniffed at that. "You're forgetting several hundred thousand in jewels."

"I didn't have any jewels. I never got into the safe." Though she turned her head and tried to bite, he caught her chin in his hand and forced her head back until their eyes met. "It was a setup. Are you listening to me? It was a fucking setup right from the start. God knows what might have happened to you if you'd been with me. As bad as it was, I've always been grateful you were sick that day and stayed home."

"Setup, my ass." She twisted away and cursed the fact that she had never been, and would never be, as good as Luke at escapes.

"He knew." The old rage began to burn through him again. With his eyes on middle distance, Luke wiped the blood from his lip. "He knew about the job. He knew about us." He brought his gaze back to Roxanne's face. "He knew all about us."

Something fluttered into her stomach and was ignored. "What are you saying? Are you trying to make me believe that Sam knew we were planning to steal from him?"

"He knew that—he wanted us to."

Her lips thinned and curved without humor. "Just how gullible do you think I am, Callahan? He hinted to me about knowing something years ago, that time we ran into him in D.C. But if he'd known about us, he'd have used it. He'd hardly have wanted us to break into his house and relieve him of his wife's jewelry."

"He never intended for us to take the jewelry. And he used it all right, Rox. He used it to make me pay for being in his way all those years ago. For breaking his goddamn nose. For humiliating him. He used it to hurt the rest of you for having the gall to take him in, trying to help him out, and for rejecting him."

A new sensation was eroding her disdain. And it was cold, very cold. "If he knew for certain we were thieves, why hasn't he pointed his pillar-of-the-community finger at us?"

"You want me to tell you how his mind works? I can't." Fighting for the control to speak calmly, Luke turned away. On the table were three pewter cups and colored balls. He began to work the old routine as he continued. "I can offer an educated guess. If he turned you in, and you didn't manage to beat the rap, all he'd have was the satisfaction of seeing you in prison. With the Nouvelle reputation and celebrity, you'd very likely get a lot of press, maybe a movie-of-the-week." She snorted, but he didn't even glance over. His hands were moving faster, faster. "What he wanted was to see you miserable. And me the most miserable of all. He'd known for a long time. Months at least."

"How? We've never had a whiff of suspicion in our direction. How did some two-bit politician figure it all out?"

"Through me." Luke's hands faltered. He stepped back, flexed his fingers, then began again. "He set Cobb on me."

"Who?"

"Cobb. The guy my mother was living with when I took off." He looked at Roxanne then, his expression carefully blank. "The guy who got off beating me until I passed out. Or locking me up, or cuffing me to the pipes in the bathroom. The one who sold me for twenty bucks to a drunken pervert."

Her face went white and stiff. What he was saying was horrid enough, but hearing it recited in that flat, empty voice froze her blood. "Luke." She would have reached out, but the steel only rattled against the teeth of the vise. "Luke, let me go."

"Not until you hear it. Hear all of it." He picked up a cup again, vaguely surprised to see the faint outline of his fingers against the pewter where he'd squeezed. So the shame was still there, he realized. And it would always be there, like the slight distortion on the carved pewter. "That night—do you remember that night in the rain, Rox? You'd told me about that four-eyed son of a bitch manhandling you. I went crazy because I knew what it was like—to be forced. And I couldn't stand the idea of you . . . of anyone hurting you that way. Then I was holding you. And I kissed you. I tried not to, but I wanted you so bad. I wanted everything about you. And for just a minute, one incredible minute, I thought maybe it would be all right."

"It was all right," she whispered. It felt as though the vise was around her heart, squeezing, squeezing. "It was wonderful."

"Then I saw him." Luke set the cups down again. There was a time for illusion, and a time for truth. "He walked right by us, and he looked at me. I knew it wasn't all right. It might never be. So I sent you away, and went after him."

"What—" She bit her lip, remembering how drunk Luke had been when he'd come home that night. "You didn't . . ."

"Kill him?" He tossed his head up and the smile on his face chilled her. "It would have been simpler all around if I had. What was I, twenty-two, twenty-three? Christ, I might as well have been twelve again, that's how much he scared me. He wanted money—so I gave him money."

She felt a quick twist of relief. "You paid him? Why?"

"So he'd keep what he knew to himself. So he wouldn't go to the press and tell them I'd sold myself."

"But you didn't—"

"What difference did it make what the truth was? I'd been sold. I'd been used. I was ashamed." He looked over again, but his eyes were no longer blank. The swirl of emotion in them battered her heart. "I still am."

"You did nothing."

"I was a victim. Sometimes that's enough." He shrugged it away, but the gesture was jerky. "So I paid him. Whenever he'd send me a postcard, I sent back the amount he'd written on it. When you moved in with me, I always made sure I got the mail. Just in case."

Sympathy dried up into shock. "Wait a minute. Just a minute. You're saying he was still blackmailing you after we were together? All that time, and you didn't tell me?" Pure reflex had her kicking out in his direction. "You didn't trust me enough to share that with me?"

"Goddamn it! I was ashamed, ashamed of what had happened to me, ashamed that I didn't have the balls to tell him to get fucked. I was terrified he'd get tired of yanking my chain and make good on his threat to tell the press that Max had—" He broke off, swearing. He hadn't meant to go quite that far.

Both the shame and the anger clenched in his gut as he waited.

31

Roxanne drew in a long, quiet breath. She was afraid she knew, very much afraid she knew what was coming next. But she had to be sure. "That Max had what, Luke?"

All right, he thought, he'd give her all. There'd be no more question of trust. "That Max had used me sexually."

The angry flush died away until her face was pale as glass. But her eyes glittered, dark as a storm, and as dangerous. "He would have said that? He would have lied that way about you and Daddy?"

"I don't know. I couldn't take the chance, so I paid. And by paying I set myself up for worse."

She closed her eyes. "What could be worse?"

"I said Wyatt set Cobb on me, and Wyatt was calling the shots. I didn't know it, though I should have figured that Cobb wasn't smart enough to pull off something as smooth as the blackmail scam. Whenever they raised the ante, I paid. No questions. That didn't sit well with Wyatt. So he did a little more digging to figure out how I managed to pay upwards of a hundred thousand a year without whining."

"A hundred—" Even the thought choked her.

"I'd have paid twice as much to keep you." When she looked up at him again, he realized that was only half the answer. "And to keep you from seeing I'd been a coward. That someone had forged a chain I couldn't wiggle free from." He turned away and spoke slowly. "I'd been used. I never knew whether Cobb's client got his money's worth out of me, but I'd been used just the same."

"I knew. I told you I'd always known."

"You didn't know what it did to me. Inside. The scars on my back." He shrugged and turned back. "Hell, they're like the tattoo, Roxy. Just a reminder of where I'd come from. But I didn't want you to see past them. I wanted to be invincible for you—for me. It was pride, and Christ knows I paid for it."

She sat quietly now. The cuffs on her wrists were a transient restraint, easily opened with a key. The chains on Luke's pride were made of sterner stuff. "Do you really believe it would have changed anything I felt for you?"

"It changed what I felt *about* me. Wyatt understood that. He used it. And because he was studying every move I made, he saw the pattern. He had months to work out the setup. I guess that's why it was so fucking smooth."

She was no longer struggling, no longer angry. She was simply numb. "He knew you were coming that night."

"He knew. He was waiting for me in his office. He had a gun. I figured he'd kill me and that would be that. Sam didn't want that to be that. He offered me a brandy. The cold-hearted bastard offered me a drink, and he told me what he knew. He painted some pictures of what it would be like if you and Max were sent to prison. He knew Max wasn't so stable, and he taunted me about a lot of things." His mouth grimmed. "I was feeling sick. I guess I thought it was the situation, but it was the brandy."

"He'd drugged you? God."

"While I was sitting there, trying to calculate the odds, Cobb came in. That's when I learned about their partnership. Rox, he told Cobb to pour himself a drink. And then . . . then he killed him. He pointed the gun, he pulled the trigger and he killed him."

"He—" She shut her eyes again, but her vision was clear. She'd begun to see perfectly. "He was going to let you take the fall for murder."

"It was perfect. I passed out, and when I came to, he was holding a different gun." Steadier than he'd expected to be, Luke sat on the bench and lit a cigar as he told her the rest.

"So, I left. I disappeared," he finished. "And I spent five years trying to forget you. And failing miserably. I went all over the world, Rox. Asia, South America, Ireland. I tried drinking myself to death, but I never did like the aftermath of a good drunk. I tried work. I tried women." He slanted her a look. "They worked some better than the bottle."

"I bet."

The chilly annoyance in her tone cheered him. "About six months ago, a couple of things happened. I found out about Max's condition. You'd done a pretty good job of keeping that under wraps."

"My personal life is mine. I don't discuss it with the press."

He studied the tip of his cigar. "I guess that's why I never read anything about Nate."

"I don't share my child with the public."

"Our child," he corrected, looking back at her. He let that simmer while he continued. "The other thing I found out was that Wyatt was running for the Senate in the coming election. Maybe I got jaded over the last five years, Rox. Maybe I just got smart. But I started to think, and I started to wonder. And I started to plan. Running into Jake was handy. Up till then I'd been living on what I could make as the Phantom. I couldn't touch my Swiss accounts because I didn't have the numbers, and there was no way to get them." He grinned. "Until Jake. He went to work on it, and life got easier. Money smooths the way, Rox. And it's going to get me what I want."

"Which is?"

"Besides you." He tapped out his cigar. "Let's call it justice. Our old friend is going to pay."

"This isn't just about the stone, is it?"

"No. I want it, for Max, but no. I've got a way to get him. It's taken me a long time to work it out, and I need you to make it work. Are you still with me?"

"He stole five years from me. Took away my son's father. And you have to ask?"

He grinned, leaning over to kiss her, but she turned her head away. "I want to ask you something, Callahan, so back off."

He eased back an inch. "This far enough?"

"Are you here because I'm a necessary part of the plan?"

"What you are, Roxanne, is necessary." He slipped off the table and turned to run his hands up her outer thighs. "Vital." Because her head was still turned away, he contented himself with nibbling on her earlobe. "I told you there were other women."

"I'm hardly surprised," she said, her voice dry as the Sahara.

"But I didn't tell you that they were poor, pale illusions. Smoke and mirrors, Rox. There was never one day when I didn't want you." He slid his hands to her waist, coaxing her face toward his by running kisses along her jaw. "I've loved you as long as I can remember."

He could feel her softening, warming as he slipped his hands under the sweatshirt to skim fingers along her ribs. "When I left, it was for you. Coming back was for you. There's nothing you can say, nothing you can do that would make me leave you again."

His thumbs just brushed the undersides of her breasts. "I'll kill you if you try this time, Callahan." Desperate, she turned her mouth to his. "I swear it. I won't let you make me love you again unless I'm sure you're staying."

"You never stopped loving me." The excitement was building, unbearably. He cupped her breasts, using his thumbs to tease the nipples into aching points. "Say it."

"I wanted to." Her head fell back with a moan as he pressed his lips to her neck. "I wanted to stop."

"Say the magic words," he demanded again.

"I love you." She would have wept, but the sob turned to a gasp. "Damn you, I've always loved you. I never stopped. Now unlock these stupid cuffs."

"Maybe." He tugged on her hair until her eyes opened and locked on his. The expression on his face had a thrill of panicked excitement ripping up her spine. "Maybe later."

And his mouth came down on hers, smothering any protest and turning shock into churning arousal.

It had gone so quickly the first time, all flash and fire and need. He wanted to do more than savor now. He wanted to take her step by trembling step, inch by aching inch toward madness. And he wanted to shock her, stun her, so that this moment when all the secrets were revealed would be seared into her mind, never to be forgotten.

He skimmed his tongue up the long line of her throat while his hands traced over her, lazily possessive. "If you don't like it, I'll stop," he murmured, nipping at her lips. "Should I stop?"

"I don't know." How could he expect her to think rationally when her head was reeling? "How much time do I have to make up my mind?"

"I'll give you plenty of time."

The marvelous truth was she had no mind, no will, no reason. If this was a matter of power, then she was totally in his. And glorying in it. She would never have believed that helplessness could be erotic. The knowledge that her body was his, utterly, touched off little fires in her blood that burned like a drug. She wanted to be taken, exploited for their mutual pleasure, and in this single private moment, conquered.

A long throaty moan vibrated from her when he tore her shirt down the center. She braced for the onslaught, craved it, but his hands, his mouth, were torturously gentle.

Sensation crashed into emotion, each rising dangerously. Each time, every time she strained toward that final, airless peak, he pulled her back, leaving her gasping and crazed.

It was stunning to watch her, to see everything she felt reflected on her face, to feel every thrill that rocked her body, to hear her murmur his name again and again as the pleasure swamped her.

Her power was all the more potent because she was too dazed to realize she held it. Her surrender made him as much her prisoner as she was his—the completeness of it, and the fearlessness. That she would melt for him made him feel strong as a god, and humble as a beggar.

Slowly, he slid the loose pants down her hips, exploring each newly exposed inch of flesh, pleasuring her with teeth and tongue and clever fingertips until she shuddered violently over the first peak.

"I love you, Roxanne." He pressed her back against the bench. "Always you," he murmured as the hands he'd freed came tight around him. "Only you."

He filled, she surrounded. And they took each other.

It annoyed him that she wouldn't let him spend his nights with her, nor would she spend hers with him. He needed more than the intimacy of sex. He needed to be able to turn to her in the night, to watch her wake in the morning.

But she stood firm, and kept her reasons to herself.

She no longer put any restrictions on his visits to the house on Chartres. There were reasons for that as well. It hurt them all that Max had slipped away again, and each day he was hospitalized for tests was unbearably long. Roxanne knew that having Luke around boosted morale—her own included. And she wanted to give Nate a chance to know him as a man before the boy had to accept him as a father.

Rational or not, any decision she made on allowing Luke back into her life would be focused on her son. Their son.

They worked together. As one week passed into two the act they'd created between them grew slick and flashy. They crafted their job at the auction as meticulously. Roxanne had to admit Luke had entwined all the details as craftily as the Chinese Linking Rings. She was suitably impressed with the first of the forged pieces that arrived from the source he'd commissioned in Bogotá.

"Nice work," she'd told him, deliberately downplaying the craftsmanship in the tiered diamond and ruby necklace. She'd stood at the mirror in his bedroom, draping it around her own neck. "A bit ornate for my taste, of course, but quite good. What did it cost us?"

She was naked, as was he. Luke had tucked his arms behind his head as he'd stretched on the bed and watched her in the glow of the lowering sun. "Five thousand."

"Five." Her brows rose as her practical nature absorbed that shock. "That's very steep."

"The man's an artist." He grinned as she frowned and toyed with the faux stones. "The real one's worth upwards of a hundred and fifty, Rox. We'll cover our overhead nicely."

"I suppose." She had to admit, to herself anyway, that without testing equipment she would have been fooled. Not only did the stones look genuine but the setting was deceptively antique. "When can we expect the rest?"

"In time."

In time, she thought now as she carried two bags of groceries into the kitchen. It was beginning to irk her that Luke continued to be vague. He was testing her, she decided and dumped the bags on the counter. She didn't care for it.

"You got eggs in those bags?" LeClerc demanded, glowering.

She winced, grateful her back was to him, then shrugged. "So, make an omelette."

"Make an omelette, make an omelette. Always the smart talk. Get—out of my kitchen." He waved her off. "I got supper to make for an army."

Which meant only one thing. "Luke's here?"

"You surprised?" He snorted and began to take groceries out of the bag. "Everybody's always here. You call this a ripe melon?" Accusation in every cell, LeClerc held out a cantaloupe.

"How the hell am I supposed to know if it's ripe?" Marketing never put her in a sunny mood. "They all look the same."

"How many times I tell you, smell, listen." He tapped the melon, holding it close to his ear. "Still green."

Roxanne planted her hands on her hips. "Why do you always send me out for fruits and vegetables then complain about what I bring home?"

"You got to learn, don't you?"

Roxanne thought about that a moment. "No." Turning on her heel, she marched out, muttering. The man was never satisfied. Here she'd gone straight from rehearsal to the market, and he didn't even say thanks.

And she hated cantaloupe.

She would have stalked straight upstairs if she hadn't heard the voices from the parlor. Luke's voice. Nate's belly giggles. Moving quietly, she walked to the door and looked in.

They were on the floor together, dark heads bent close, knees brushing. Toys were scattered on the rug, a testament to what her men had been doing while she slaved over melons. Now, Luke was patiently explaining some little pocket trick he'd brought along. The Vanishing Pen, if Roxanne wasn't mistaken. Amused, she leaned against the doorway and watched father attempting to teach son.

"Right under the nose, Nate." To illustrate, Luke tweaked Nate's and made him giggle again. "Right before your eyes. Now, here, let's try it. Can you print your name?"

"Sure I can. N-A-T-E." He took the pen and paper Luke offered, his face screwed in intense concentration. "I'm learning to write Nathaniel, too. Then Nouvelle, 'cause that's my last name."

"Yeah." A shadow passed over Luke's eyes as he watched Nate struggle with the A. "I guess it is." He waited until Nate had completed a very slanted E. "Okay. Now watch carefully." Keeping his movements slow, Luke rolled the pen inside the paper and twisted both ends. "Now, pick a magic word."

"Umm—"

"Nope, umm's not good enough," Luke said and sent Nate off in a fit of fresh giggles.

"Boogers!" Nate decided, delighted to use a word he'd picked up from a sophisticated pal at preschool.

"Disgusting, but it may work." Luke tore the paper in two and had the pleasure of seeing Nate's eyes widen.

"It disappeared! The pen's been disappeared."

"Absolutely." Unable to resist the flourish, Luke held up his hands, turning them, back to front and back again. His son's bug-eyed belief made him feel like a king. "Want to learn how to do it?"

"Can I?"

"You have to take the magician's oath."

"I did that already," Nate said, jaded. "When Mama showed me how to make the quarter go through the table."

"Does she teach you stuff about magic?" He was greedy for anything he could learn about his son's thoughts, feelings, desires.

"Sure. But you have to promise not to tell anybody, even your best friends, 'cause it's secret."

"That's right. Are you going to be a magician one day?"

"Yeah." Unable to keep still for long, Nate bounced his rump on the rug. "I'm going to be a magician, and a race-car driver and a policeman."

A cop, Luke thought, amused. Well, well, where did they go wrong? "All that, huh? Let's see if you can learn this trick before you go win the Indianapolis 500 and chase bad guys."

He was pleased that Nate was interested rather than disappointed when he saw the workings of the trick. It seemed to Luke that he could all but hear the child's mind working it through, exploring the possibilities.

He had good hands, Luke thought as he posed them with his own. A quick mind. And a smile that broke his father's heart.

"This is neat."

"Amazing," Luke said, solemn-eyed, and turned Nate's smile into a grin.

"Amazing neat."

He couldn't help it. Luke leaned down to kiss the grin. "Try it again, slick. Let's see if you can do this with distractions. Sometimes there are hecklers in the audience."

"What's that?"

"Oh, people who yell things or talk too loud. Or . . . tickle you."

Nate gave a squeal of delight when Luke snatched him. After a short, furious battle, Luke let himself be pinned. He grunted with exaggerated bursts as Nate bounced on his stomach.

"You're too tough for me, kid. Uncle."

"Uncle who?"

"Just uncle." Chuckling, Luke ruffled Nate's dark hair. "It means I give up."

"Can you show me another trick?"

"Maybe. What's it worth to you?"

Nate bartered what always worked with his mother and scooted down to give Luke a smacking kiss on the mouth. Dazed by the easy affection, moved unbearably, Luke lifted an unsteady hand to Nate's hair.

"Do you want a hug to go with it?"

"Sure." Luke opened his arms and experienced the unspeakable pleasure of cradling his son. With his eyes closed, he rubbed his cheek to Nate's "You weigh a ton."

"I'm a walking appetite." Nate leaned back to grin down at Luke. "Mama says so. I eat everything 'less it's nailed down."

"Except lima beans," Luke murmured, remembering.

"Yuck. I wish I could make all the lima beans in the whole world disappear."

"We'll work on it."

"I gotta pee," Nate stated, with the carefree childhood habit of announcing bodily functions.

"Don't do it here, okay?"

Nate giggled and held himself uninhibitedly to prolong the inevitable another moment. He liked being with Luke, liked the smell of him that was different from anyone else in his family. Though he'd never had to do without male influence or companionship, there was something different about *this* man. Maybe it was magic.

"Do you have a penis?"

Luke strangled back a laugh because the child was eyeing him owlishly. "I certainly do."

"Me too. Girls don't. Mama neither."

Cautious, Luke tucked his tongue in his cheek. "I believe you're right about that."

"I like having one, 'cause you can stand up to pee."

"It does have its advantages."

"I gotta go." Nate scrambled up, dancing a bit. "You want to go ask LeClerc for some cookies?"

From penises to cookies, Luke thought. Childhood was fascinating. "Go ahead. I'll catch up with you."

Nate turned and spotted his mother, but his bladder was straining. "Hi. I gotta pee."

"Hi yourself. Go be my guest."

Nate trotted off, one hand on his crotch.

"An interesting conversation," Roxanne managed after she heard the powder room door slam.

"Man talk." Luke sat up, grinning. "He's so—" He broke off when Roxanne pressed a hand to her mouth. "What is it?" Alarmed, he rose, trampling a plastic truck as he started toward her.

"Nothing." She wouldn't be able to hold it off this time. Simply wouldn't. "It's nothing." Turning, she bolted up the stairs.

She would have locked herself in her room, but Luke was at the door before she could shove it to. Furious with herself, she whirled away and tossed open the French doors to her terrace.

"What the hell's wrong with you?" he demanded.

"There's nothing wrong with me." The ache was so fierce, so complete she could only combat it with sharp words. "Go away, will you? I'm tired. I want to be alone."

"One of your tantrums, Rox?" His own feelings were brittle as he turned her to face him. Music drifted up from the Quarter, hot driving jazz. It seemed to fit the moment. "Seeing me with Nate get your back up?"

"No. Yes." She jerked away to drag her hands through her hair. Oh God, oh God, she was losing.

The closer she came to the edge, the calmer Luke became.

"I'm going to see him, Roxanne. I'm going to be a part of his life. I have to, and by Christ, I have a right to."

"Don't talk to me about rights," she threw back, humiliated by the catch in her voice.

"He's mine, too. However much you'd like to block that out, it's a fact. I'm trying to understand why you won't tell him I'm his father, I'm trying not to resent that, but I won't stay away because you want to keep him to yourself."

"That's not it. Damn it, that's not it." She rapped a fist against his chest. "Do you know how it makes me feel to see you together? To see the way you look at him?" Tears spilled over, but she fought back the sobs.

"I'm sorry it hurts you," Luke said stiffly. "And maybe I can't blame you too much for wanting to punish me by not letting me be his father."

"I'm not trying to punish you." Desperate to get it all out, she pressed her lips together. "Maybe I am, I'm not sure, and that's the hardest part. Trying to know what to do, what's right, what's best, and then seeing you with him, knowing all that time that was lost. Yes, it hurts me to see you with him, but not the way you mean. It hurts the way it hurts to watch a sunrise, or to hear music. He holds his head the way you do." She dashed furiously at tears. "He always did, and it broke my heart. He has your smile, and your eyes, and your hands. So much smaller, but yours. I used to look at them while he was sleeping, count his fingers and look at his hands. And I'd ache for you."

"Rox." He'd thought, he'd hoped they had passed through the worst of this the night he'd told her everything. "I'm sorry." He reached out, but she pivoted away.

"I never cried over you. Not once in five years did I allow myself a tear for you. That was pride." Pressing the back of her hand to her mouth, she rocked. "It helped me get through the worst of it. I didn't cry when you came back. And when you told me what had happened, I hurt for you, and I tried to understand what you must have felt. But damn you. Damn you, you were wrong." She spun back, clasping an arm around her middle to hold back the worst of the pressure. "You should have come home. You should have come to me and told me then. I would have gone with you. I'd have gone anywhere with you."

"I know." He couldn't touch her now, no matter how much he needed to. She seemed suddenly so fragile that to touch might be to break. He could only stand back and let the storm rage over both of them. "I knew it then, and I nearly did come back. I could have taken you away, away from your family, away from your father. It didn't have to matter that he was ill, that I owed him, all of you, whatever good things I had. I might have risked the fact that Wyatt could have set the cops on me at any time so that they'd hunt me down as a murderer. But I didn't. I couldn't."

"I needed you." Tears blinded her until she covered her face with her hands and let them come freely. "I needed you."

It hurt, oh, it hurt to let go almost as much as it had to hold back. Crying wracked the body, burned the throat, battered the heart. She lost herself in the violence of grief, going limp when his arms came around her, sobbing shamelessly when he lifted her to carry her to bed and cradle her.

He could only hold her as five years of suppressed mourning flooded out. There were no words to comfort. He had known her nearly twenty years and could count on one hand the number of times she'd wept in front of him.

And never like this, he thought, rocking her. Never like this.

She couldn't stop, was afraid she never would. She didn't hear the door open. Didn't feel Luke turn his head, shake it in silent denial as Lily looked in.

Gradually, the wracking sobs turned to dry gasps, and the violent shudders softened to quivers. The hands fisted at his back relaxed.

"I need to be alone," she whispered through a throat dry as dust.

"No. Not again. Never again, Roxanne."

She was too weak to argue. After one shaky sigh, she let her head rest against his shoulder. "I hate this."

"I know you do." He pressed a kiss to her hot, aching temple. "Do you remember that time after you found out Sam had used you. You cried then, and I didn't know quite how to handle it."

"You held me." She sniffled. "Then you broke his nose."

"Yeah. I'll do more this time." Over her head his gaze sharpened like a blade. "That's a promise."

She couldn't think about that now. She felt drained and, oddly, free. "It was easier to give you my body than to give you this." She let her swollen eyes close, soothed by the stroke of his hand over her hair. "I could tell myself it was lust, and if there was still love tangled up with it, I could still be in control. But I was afraid to let you be my friend again." Steadier, she let out a long breath. "Let me get up, wash my face. Leave me alone for a while."

"Rox—"

"No, please." She eased back. It was a point of trust, deeper than any other she'd offered that she let him see the ravage the tears had caused. "There's something I need to do. Take a walk, Callahan. Give me a half an hour."

She kissed him, softly, before he could think of an argument.

"I'll be back."

This time she smiled. "I'm counting on it."

He brought her flowers. He'd realized, a bit guiltily, that he hadn't given Roxanne what Lily would consider a proper wooing either time around. The first time he'd been overwhelmed by her, the second he'd been too tense.

It might have been a little late in the day for the hearts-and-flowers routine seeing as they were lovers, partners and shared a child, but as Max might have said, better late than too soon.

He even went to the front door rather than wandering in through the kitchen. Like a suitor coming to call, he finger-combed his hair and rang the bell.

"Callahan." Roxanne opened the door with a baffled laugh. "What are you doing out here?"

"Asking a beautiful woman out to dinner." He offered the roses, then with a sweeping bow, produced a bouquet of paper flowers that bloomed from the secret pool beneath his shirt cuff.

"Oh." It threw her off—the charming smile, the formal greeting, the armful of fragrant rosebuds and the silly trick. The change in routine automatically triggered suspicion. "What are you up to?"

"I told you. I'm asking you out on a date."

"You—" The laugh snorted out unladylike through her nose. "Right. In twenty years you've never asked me out on a date. What do you want?"

It wasn't easy to court a woman who was glaring at you out of red-rimmed and narrowed eyes. "To take you to dinner," he said between his teeth. "Maybe for a drive afterwards—somewhere we can park on the side of the road and neck."

"There a gas leak in your house, or what?"

"Goddamn it, Rox, will you come out with me?"

"I can't really. I have plans." She did lower her head to draw in the scent of roses. Before she could fully appreciate them, she snapped her head back again. "You didn't bring these to me because I cried, did you?"

Jesus, she was a tough nut. "You'd think I never brought you flowers before."

"No, no, you did." She held back a smile, though she was beginning to enjoy the picture emerging. "Twice. Once when you were two hours late for dinner—a dinner I'd gone to the trouble to cook."

"And you threw them at me."

"Of course. And the second time... Oh yes, that was when you'd broken the little porcelain box Lily had given me for Christmas. So, Callahan, what have you done this time?"

"Nothing, unless it's trying to be nice to an exasperating woman."

"Well, I'm not throwing them at you, am I?" She smiled then, and took his hand. "Come on in. We're having dinner here."

"Rox, I want to be alone with you, not in a houseful of people."

"The houseful of people is out for the evening, and God help you, Callahan, I'm cooking."

"Oh." The depth of his love was proven then and there as he summoned up a smile. "Terrific."

"Yeah, I bet. Let's go into the parlor, I have something for you."

He nearly asked if it was a dose of bicarb, but restrained himself. "If you don't want to go to the hassle of cooking, babe, we could send out." He followed her into the parlor, saw the boy sitting on the edge of the couch. "Hey, slick."

"Hi." Nate studied him for a long moment with a kind of absorbed intensity that made Luke want to squirm. "How come you don't live here if you're my daddy?"

"I—" Rocked straight to the soul, Luke could only stare.

"Mama said you had to go away for a long time 'cause a bad guy was after you. Did you shoot him dead?"

"No." He had to swallow, but couldn't. Both his son and the woman he loved waited patiently. "I thought I might trick him instead. I don't think I'd like shooting anybody." Desperately out of his element, he looked at Roxanne. "Rox." Though his eyes pleaded for help, she shook her head.

"Sometimes stepping out cold's the only way," she murmured. "No rehearsal, Callahan. No script, no props."

"Okay." On watery legs he walked to the couch and crouched down in front of his son. For a moment he was tossed back to his debut performance in a stuffy carnival tent. Flop sweat pooled at the base of his spine. "I'm sorry I wasn't here for you, or for your mother, Nate."

Nate's gaze faltered. His stomach had felt funny ever since his mother had sat him down and told him he had a daddy. He didn't know if it was good funny—the way it felt after Mouse had swung him in circles, or bad, like when he'd eaten too much candy on Halloween.

"Maybe you couldn't help it," Nate murmured, pulling at the threads in the hole worn into the knee of his jeans.

"Whether I could or not, I'm still sorry. I don't guess you need me much, you're pretty grown up and all. We—ah—get along okay, don't we?"

"Sure." Nate poked out his bottom lip. "I guess."

And he'd thought Roxanne was a tough nut, Luke mused. "We could be friends if that's okay with you. You don't have to think of me as your father."

Tears swam in Nate's eyes when he looked up again. His lips quivered and ripped right through Luke's heart. "Don't you want me to?"

"Yeah." His throat ached. His heart healed. "Yeah, I do. A lot. I mean, hey, you're short and ugly now, but I think you've got potential."

"What's potential?"

"Possibilities, Nathaniel." Gently, Luke cupped his son's face in his hands. "Lots and lots of possibilities."

"Potential," Nate repeated, and in an echo of his mother's childhood, savored the word. His smile spread sweetly. "Bobby's father built him a treehouse. A *big* one."

"Oh-oh." Amazed and delighted, Luke glanced back to where Roxanne still stood, holding her flowers. "The kid catches on fast."

"It's that sly Irish blood. A Nouvelle is much too proud to wheedle."

"Wheedle, hell, it's a smart boy who knows when to press his advantage. Right, Nate?"

"Right." He shrieked with pleasure when Luke swung him up. Deciding to go for the gold, he leaned close to Luke's ear and whispered. "Can you tell Mama I should have a dog? A really big dog?"

Luke tilted a finger under Nate's chin so that they grinned identical grins. "I'll work on it. How about a hug?"

"Okay," Nate squeezed his arms hard around Luke's neck. His stomach still felt funny, and the sensation had spread to his chest. But he thought it was a good feeling after all. On a sigh, he settled his head on his father's shoulder, and accepted.

32

"I'm trying to concentrate." Roxanne waved a hand over her shoulder to brush Luke back. He was breathing down her neck.

"I'm trying to ask you out on a date."

"You're certainly hung up on dates these days." She hunched forward, adjusting the light on her father's desk. Spread before her were the blueprints for the art gallery. They had yet to agree on a point of entry. "From the top down, Callahan. It just makes sense. The exhibit's on the third floor, why come in on ground level and climb up?"

"Because that way we can walk up stairs instead of dangling fifteen feet from a rope."

She slanted a look over her shoulder. "You're getting old."

"I beg your pardon. It so happens I'm a parent now. I have to take certain precautions."

"The roof, Daddy Warbucks."

He knew it was the cleanest way, but enjoyed the debate. "We'd have to get Jake up there, too. He doesn't like heights."

"So, you'll blindfold him." She tapped a pencil against the drawing. "Here, east window, third floor. I'm already in, twiddling my thumbs in that storeroom until deadline. I go into the surveillance room at exactly eleven seventeen, which gives me one minute, thirty seconds, and one minute, thirty seconds only, to doctor camera six before the alarm kicks in."

"I don't like the idea of you handling the inside work."

"Don't be such a man, Luke. You know damn well I'm better with electronics. Then I switch the surveillance tapes." Pulling her hair back in one hand, she grinned. "I wish I could see the guard's face when he gets a look at Mouse's video work."

"Only amateurs think they have to be in on the punch line, babe."

"Get bent, Callahan," she said mildly. "To continue, as long as Jake and Mouse have taken care of business, I can deal with the window from inside. In you come, my hero." She fluttered her lashes.

"And we have six and a half minutes to open the display, take the proper loot and replace it with our fakes."

"Then, presto! We're out, leaving not a trace." She ran her tongue over her top lip. "You and I will go back to our hotel room, and fuck like minks."

"God, I love it when you're crude." He rested his chin on the top of her head. "We still need to refine the timing."

"We have a few weeks." She stretched her arms out, then up, to link them around his neck. "And just think of all those lovely, lovely glitters. All ours, Callahan."

He winced, let a quiet breath out between his teeth and straightened. "That's something I've been meaning to talk to you about, Rox." He couldn't predict how she'd react, and took the coward's way by stalling. "Want a brandy?"

"Sure." She stretched again. It was nearly one in the morning. The house was quiet, the hall beyond the office dark with shadows. She thought briefly about seducing Luke on the cushy leather couch, and smiled slowly when he handed her a snifter.

"Sure you want to talk?"

He knew that look, that tone, and nearly escaped into it to avoid the issue. "No, but I think we have to. About the take from the auction."

"Mmmm."

"We're not going to keep it."

She choked on the brandy. Luke thumped her on the back and hoped for the best. "Christ, don't make bad jokes while I'm drinking."

"It's not a joke, Rox. We're not going to keep it."

She, too, knew that look, that tone. It meant Luke had made up his mind about something and was ready to battle. "What the hell are you talking about? What's the point in taking it if we're not going to keep it?"

"I explained that the heist was a diversion for the Wyatt job."

"Of course, and a very profitable one, despite an outrageous overhead."

"Yes, but not monetarily. Not for us."

She drank more brandy, but it did little to relieve the sudden chill in her midsection. "Just what are we going to do with over two million in jewels, Callahan, jewels that are costing us approximately eighty thousand to heist?"

"We're going to plant them. They're very important props for a sting I've been dreaming about for nearly a year."

"A sting." Roxanne rose so that she could walk off her agitation and think. "Sam. You're going to plant them on Sam. This is your justice, isn't it?" Her eyes were hot when she turned back to him. "This is what you'd planned all along."

"I've worked on every angle of this for months. Every piece hinges on the whole of it."

"You've worked on?" A flood of betrayal threatened to swamp her. She fought it back, unsure if she could survive that kind of loss again. "That's why you came back. To hit on Sam."

"You're why I came back." He didn't like the chill in her voice, or the vulnerability he sensed beneath it. And he hated, really hated, explaining himself again. "I told you why I left, Rox, and I can't take those years back. But I'm not losing you again, and I'm not taking any chances with my family." He hesitated. She was likely to slice him into thin, jagged ribbons, but he had to tell her everything. "That's why I went to see Wyatt before I came to New Orleans."

"You've seen him?" Baffled, she dragged a hand through her hair. "You went to see him, and you don't consider that taking chances?"

"I made a deal with him. I'd figured on bribing him with money. A million dollars for a few months' time."

"A million—"

"But he didn't go for it," Luke interrupted. "Or he didn't go for that alone. So we made a deal." Picking up his snifter, he swirled brandy, sniffed, sipped. He enjoyed this part, the way a man enjoyed contemplating a long, stimulating evening with a beautiful woman. "He agreed to give me time, until right before the election, if I came up with compromising photographs of Curtis Gunner. They'd have to be faked, of course, seeing as Gunner's straight as an arrow. Wyatt wants papers, too, implicating Gunner in unethical business deals, and illicit relationships. All I have to do is create them, and plant them right before the voters head off to pull the lever of their choice."

Letting out a long breath, Roxanne lowered to the arm of the sofa. She needed the brandy now, she realized, and tilted back the snifter for a long sip. "That's what it cost you to come back?"

"If I didn't agree, I can't be sure what he might do to you, to Max, Lily, everyone I care about." Luke's eyes locked on hers. "And now there's Nathaniel. There's nothing I wouldn't do to keep him safe. Nothing."

Icy fear rippled down her spine. "He wouldn't hurt Nate. He . . . Of course he would." Roxanne pressed her fingers to her eyes, struggling to justify her conscience with necessity. "I know we have to do whatever needs to be done, but we've never hurt innocent people before. I can't rationalize starting now. We'll find another way." She dropped her hands into her lap. His face was composed again, and cold. "I know we can find another way."

Luke was certain he'd never loved her more than he did at this moment. She was a woman who would protect what was hers, always, and never would she compromise her own code of ethics.

"Jake's already forging documents that I'll plant, along with the take, in Wyatt's safe. They won't be quite what he's expecting," he added before she could protest. "The initial photos Jake's come up with are pretty good, just need a little refining. But all in all, Wyatt looks great. There's one in particular of him in this black leather G-string and boots that I'm real fond of."

"Sam? You're doing the photographs using Sam?" Her lips started to curve, but she stopped the smile, stemmed the admiration. Damn Luke, she thought, she wasn't through yet. "You're double-crossing him, using his own plot to ruin him politically."

"Hey, I've got nothing against Gunner, and plenty against Wyatt. It seemed like solid gold justice to me. In addition to the photos and the documents—some of which will implicate Wyatt in a number of robberies you'll be very familiar with—I've been filtering money into two accounts in Switzerland. Accounts in his name."

"Very clever," she murmured. "You worked it all out. But you didn't bother to fill me in."

"No, I didn't. I wanted to make sure you were in for the long run, Roxanne. I figured the initial plan would challenge you, intrigue you. And I'd hoped by the time I told you all of it, you'd trust me. You want to be pissed because I held back on you, you're entitled. Just as long as you're in for that long haul."

She considered and realized that first hot spurt of anger had eased. Good God, she thought, she hoped she wasn't mellowing. The problem was, she could see it from Luke's side as well as from her own. Not only could she see it, but the simple beauty of the sting enchanted her. She couldn't have planned it better herself.

"From tonight, Callahan, we're in this fifty-fifty, or there's no deal."

"Aren't you going to swear at me, call me at least one name?"

"I'm saving it." She lifted her glass in toast. "To Nouvelle and Callahan."

He tapped his glass to hers and their eyes remained on each other's as they sipped. "Weren't you about to seduce me before I interrupted it?"

"As a matter of fact . . ." She set her brandy aside. "I was."

Luke stood beside Max's chair, looking out of the French doors, wondering what the man saw through the glass. Was it the buildings of the Quarter, the flower-strewn balcony across Chartres, the pieces of gray sky that promised rain? Or was it something else, some long-ago memory of place and time?

Since his relapse, Max's mind had sunk deeper into whatever world it inhabited. He rarely spoke at all now, though he sometimes wept silently. His body was sinking as well, fading away pound by precious pound.

The doctors spoke of plaques and tangles, those primary structural changes found in the brains of Alzheimer patients. Abnormal forms of proteins—tau proteins, B-amyloid, substance P. They meant nothing to Luke, and he'd thought plaques and tangles had sounded like some sort of complex magic trick.

He knew Roxanne had been in to say goodbye and was now down the hall with Nate, overseeing his packing for their week in D.C. Now that he had this moment alone with Max, he didn't know what to do with it.

"I wish you were coming with us." Luke continued to look out the glass. It was so difficult to look at Max, at that blank expression, at the clawed fingers that worked and worked and worked as if manipulating coins. "I'd feel a lot better if I could have gone over the whole plan with you. I think you'd like the act. Drama, emotion, flair. It has it all. I've gone over every detail." Hearing the echo of his mentor's voice in his head, Luke allowed himself a smile. "I know, I know, calculate the odds, then prepare for surprises. I'm going to pay that bastard back for the five years he took from me, Max, from all of us. And I'm going to get you the stone. I'm going to put it right into your hands. If there's any magic in it, you'll find it."

Luke didn't expect a response, but made himself crouch down. Made himself look into the eyes that had once commanded him to come inside a sideshow tent, demanded he take a chance, take a risk. They were as dark as ever, but the power in them was gone.

"I want you to know I'm going to take care of Roxanne and Nate. And Lily and Mouse and LeClerc. Rox would get her back up if she heard me say that; she's been doing a good job of taking care of everything. But she's not going to have to do it alone anymore. Nate calls me Dad. I didn't know that could mean so much." Gently, he covered the gnarled, restless hands with his own. "Dad. I never called you that. But you're my father." Luke leaned forward and kissed the papery cheek. "I love you, Dad."

There was no response. Luke rose and walked out to find his own son.

Max continued to stare through the glass, to stare and stare, even when a tear slipped out of his eye and ran slowly down the cheek that Luke had kissed.

Jake tapped another sequence into his portable computer and let out a crow of delight. "What'd I tell you? What'd I tell you, Mouse? There's always a back door."

"You're in? You're really in?" Filled with admiration, Mouse leaned over Jake's stooped shoulder. "Holy cow."

"The Bank of fucking England." He sniggered, linking his fingers and stretching his hands out to crack his knuckles. "Betcha Charles and Di have an account. Man, oh man, all those pretty pounds sterling."

"Wow." Mouse read the celebrity magazines faithfully, and the Princess of Wales was a favorite. "Can you see how much they have, Jake? You oughta transfer some from his into hers. I don't think he's nice enough to her."

"Sure. Why not?" Jake's fingers poised over the keys, stopping when Alice gently cleared her throat.

"I thought you promised Luke you wouldn't use the computers to poke into anyone's business." She didn't look up, only continued to knit serenely on the sofa at the other end of the suite.

"Well, yeah." Jake's fingers itched. "I'm just practicing is all." He rolled his eyes at Mouse. "Ah, showing Mouse some of the tricks this baby can do since we adjusted her."

"That's very nice. Mouse, I don't think Diana would appreciate you invading her privacy this way."

"You don't?" He glanced over at his wife, who only lifted her head and smiled. "No, I guess not." Defeated, he let out a windy sigh. "We're supposed to be checking the Swiss account," he reminded Jake.

"All right, all right." The keyboard clattered, the modum hummed. "But it just makes me sick, I gotta say. My stomach, I tell you, it feels like I ate some bad whitefish. He wants ten thousand more transferred into that creep's account. I tried to tell him, didn't I try to tell him that I could sneak the money out of some crooked CEO's account instead of bleeding his? But no, oh no. Luke wants to pay for the whole sting. That man is stubborn. *Stub*-born."

"It's a matter of pride," Alice murmured.

"It's a matter of ten fucking thousand." Jake winced and sent her a quick glance. "Excuse my French. It's just that we're not making a dime on this. Not a dime! Don't you think we ought to clear something—cover our overhead, realize a reasonable profit?"

"We're getting satisfaction," Mouse stated and made his wife's heart swell with pride. "That's better than money."

"Satisfaction won't buy you any Italian shoes," Jake grumbled, but accepted that he was outnumbered. Besides, he could always access another account later.

Alice gathered her knitting and rose. It was barely ten, but she was outrageously tired. "I think I'll leave you two to your toys and go on to bed."

Mouse bent to kiss her, stroking a hand down her pale hair. It never failed to amaze him that someone so tiny, so pretty could belong to him. "You want me to order up some tea, or anything?"

"No." What a sweet man he was, she mused. And how thick-headed. She'd all but dangled her knitting under his nose. Deciding it was worth one more shot, she took the bootie she'd completed out of her basket. "I think I'll try to finish the other one of these tonight. It's a nice color, don't you think? Such a pale, pretty green."

"It's real nice." He smiled and ducked his head to kiss her again. "Nate sure likes finger puppets."

"It's not a puppet." As angry as she had ever been with him, Alice set her teeth. "It's a bootie, damn it." With that she swept into the adjoining bedroom and shut the door.

"Alice never swears," Mouse said half to himself. "Never. Maybe I should go see . . ." The revelation hit like a bare-knuckled punch to the jaw. "A bootie."

"A bootie?" Jake's face cracked with a grin. "Well, ain't that some shit? Congratulations, Mouse old man." He jumped up to thump his friend on the back. "Looks like there's a bun in the oven."

Mouse went pale, turned a color similar to the famous bootie, then paled again. "Oh boy." It was the best he could manage as he staggered toward the bedroom. By the time he got the door open and closed again, his palms were dripping sweat.

Alice stood with her back to him, calmly belting her robe. "So, the light dawns," she muttered and walked to the dresser, began to brush her hair.

"Alice." Mouse swallowed so hard his throat clicked. "Are you . . . are we . . ."

It wasn't in her nature to stay angry for long. She loved him too much to try. Her lips curved as she met his eyes in the mirror. "Yes."

"For sure?"

"For absolutely sure. Two home pregnancy tests and an obstetrician don't lie. We're expecting, Mouse." Her voice broke as she dropped her gaze to her hands. "It's okay, isn't it?"

He couldn't answer. His throat was too full of his heart. Instead he crossed to her in three jerky steps. Gently, very gently he wrapped his arms around her, spreading his big hand over her still flat belly.

It was much better than words.

Across the district line in the lush suburbs of Maryland, Sam Wyatt sat at his antique rosewood desk with a snifter of Napoleon brandy. His wife was upstairs in their big Chippendale bed, nursing one of her infamous migraines.

Justine hardly needed the excuse of a headache, he thought as he swirled and sipped the dark amber liquor. He'd long ago lost interest in making love to an icy stick who disguised herself as a woman in designer clothes.

There were other ways to find sexual release, if one was cautious, and paid enough.

He didn't keep a mistress. Mistresses had a habit of growing disenchanted and greedy. Sam had no intention of living with the backlash of a tell-all book after he was in the White House.

And he would be living in the White House, he thought. In the dawn of the twenty-first century, he would be sitting in the Oval Office, sleeping in Lincoln's bed. It was inevitable.

His senatorial campaign was proceeding brilliantly. Every new poll showed him farther and farther in the lead. It would take a miracle for his opponent to close the gap, and Sam had never believed in miracles.

In any case, he had an ace named Luke Callahan up his sleeve. When he chose to play that ace, a week before the election, Gunner would be crushed.

There were only weeks left until that moment of truth, which meant many long days and nights ahead. He'd kissed babies, cut ribbons, roused the common man with speeches glinting with promises, wooed the corporate structure with his stance on private enterprise, charmed women with his easy smiles and lanky body.

Sam considered his rise in political power and prestige a stupendously structured long con.

As he told Luke, he'd deliver on some of the promises, for the con was far from over. He would continue to woo and charm and glad-hand. His image as a self-made man striving to achieve the American dream would hold him in good stead. And his hand-picked staff of advisers would keep him apprised of the proper foreign and domestic policies.

He had only one policy, and that was power.

He had everything he wanted—until he wanted more.

He thought of the stone locked away in his safe. If he had believed in magic he might have considered how so much had fallen into place for him after he'd acquired it. But for Sam, it was simply another victory over an old enemy.

It was true enough that once it had been in his possession the pace of his success had increased. Sam attributed that to luck, timing and his own personal and political skill.

He'd learned a lot from the down-home and popular Senator from Tennessee. He'd sucked up knowledge greedily while playing the man-behind-the-man with the flair of an accomplished thespian—until the opportunity to become *the* man had presented itself.

No one knew that Sam had watched Bushfield die. He had grieved publicly, delivering a moving, tear-choked eulogy, comforting the widow like a son, taking charge of the loose strings of the Senator's duties as the devoted heir.

And he had stood and watched as the Senator had gasped and choked, as his face had burned to purple, as he'd flopped like a landed trout on the floor of his private office. Sam had held the little enameled box containing the nitroglycerin tablets in his hand, saying nothing as his mentor had reached out, his eyes bulging with pain, glazed with confusion.

Only when he'd been sure it was too late had Sam knelt and slipped one of the tablets under the dead man's tongue. He'd made a frantic call to 911, and when the paramedics arrived, they were moved by the urgent way Sam had been performing CPR.

So he had killed Bushfield and had garnered several staunch backers in the medical community.

It hadn't been as thrilling as putting a bullet in Cobb's heart, Sam thought now. But even the passive act of murder had brought its own kind of rush.

Leaning back, he plotted the next round, a spider content to spin his web and wait for the unwary fly.

The arrogance of Callahan's return to the Nouvelle troupe continued to intrigue him. Did the fool actually believe that five years would suffice? Or that money would pay for the insubordination of returning to the stage without permission? Sam hoped so, he dearly hoped so. He hadn't struck out yet because it amused him to lull Luke into complacency. Let him put on his show, Sam mused. Let him try to seduce Roxanne's heart away a second time. Let him try to be a father to his son. Sam enjoyed the idea of the man falling into the bosom of his family, temporarily picking up his career and his life. It would be only sweeter to snatch it all away again.

And he would, Sam thought. Yes, he would.

He'd kept close track of the Nouvelles. He was forced to admit an admiration for Roxanne's style, her flair for larceny. There were carefully documented accounts of her activities in a ledger locked in his safe. They had cost him, but his wife's inheritance allowed for such indulgences.

The time was coming when he would use them. The payment for Luke taking a step into the spotlight without consent would be a high one. And all the Nouvelles would pay for it. And if, as Sam imagined, they believed they could pull off one more heist for old times' sake, they would play directly into his hands.

Because he could wait, he could watch, and he could arrange for the authorities to scoop up all of the Nouvelles after their next job.

That was a very sweet alternative.

He wondered if they would tamper with the auction. It seemed to him that sort of heist held the glamour which appealed to them. He might even let them get away with it. Briefly, very briefly. Then he would snap the jaws of the trap shut, and watch them bleed.

Oh yes, Sam thought, chuckling to himself as he leaned back. It was just that kind of clear thinking that was going to make him an excellent commander in chief.

33

Sam arranged for tickets to the Nouvelles' much-touted Kennedy Center performance. Front row center. Justine sat beside him, draped in silk and sapphires and smiles—the devoted wife and partner.

No one would have guessed they'd come to detest each other.

As the magic unfolded, Sam applauded enthusiastically. He threw back his head and laughed, leaned forward with eyes wide and shook his head in disbelief. His reactions, caught often by the panning television cameras, were as carefully staged as the evening of illusion.

Beneath it, the old jealousy ate at him. Luke was once again the center of attention, the shining star, the holder of power.

Sam hated him for it, as blindly and unreasonably as he'd hated Luke at first sight.

He detested and envied the ease with which Luke drew the audience in, the obvious sexual spark between him and Roxanne, the smoothness with which he could take what could not be and make it so.

But he was the first to rise to his feet when the applause rolled out over the finale. He brought his hands together to join the thunder, and he smiled.

Roxanne looked down at him as she took her bows. Though she lowered her lashes, the venom shot through them. Their gazes held, and for her, for just an instant, they were completely alone. The rage heaved up, volatile as lava, so that she took a step forward, a step toward him, stopping only when Luke's hand linked firmly with hers.

"Just smile, babe." He spoke clearly under the cover of applause and gave her fingers a quick squeeze. "Just keep on smiling."

She did, until at last they walked off the stage together. "I didn't know it would be so hard." Her body trembled from the effort of suppressing the urge to attack. "Seeing him sitting there, looking so pompous and prosperous. I wanted to jump offstage and claw at him."

"You did fine." He rubbed the small of her back, steering her through the wings toward her dressing room. "Phase one, Roxy, and on to the next."

She nodded, then paused with her hand on the knob of her door. "We steal things, Luke. I understand most people wouldn't find that acceptable. But still, what we take are things, easily replaced. He stole time. And love, and trust. None of those can be replaced." She looked back at him over her shoulder, her eyes glinting not with tears or even regret, but with purpose. "Let's get the son of a bitch."

He grinned and patted her butt. Jake was right, he mused. She was a hell of a woman. "Change. We've got work to do."

They attended the post-performance reception, clinking glasses with Washington dignitaries. Luke bided his time, then slipped away from Roxanne. This was a part he had to play alone. As he'd expected, it took Sam only moments to seek him out.

"That was quite a show."

Luke took a champagne flute from a passing tray, letting his fingers shake ever so slightly. "I'm glad you enjoyed it."

"Oh, I did. And I admire your nerve, performing without checking with me first."

"I didn't think—It's been five years." Luke scanned the crowd with nervous eyes, lowered his voice. As if in plea, he clamped a hand over Sam's wrist. "For God's sake, what harm did it do?"

Delighted to have his quarry on the ropes, Sam considered, sipping champagne. "That's yet to be tallied. Tell me, Callahan, what do you think of young Nathaniel?"

This time Luke didn't have to fake the tremor in his hand. It was pure rage. "You know about Nate?"

"I know everything there is to know about the Nouvelles. I thought I made that clear." Absently, he set his empty glass on a tray. "Tell me, have you finished the project I assigned you?"

"Except for some finishing touches." Luke tugged at his tie. "I explained to you every time I checked in that to handle a job like this, to make sure it all holds up to any investigation takes time."

"Time I've been generous with," Sam reminded him, and added a hearty clasp on Luke's shoulder. "And time that's rapidly running out."

"You gave me a deadline. I'll meet it." He glanced around the room again. "I know what's depending on it."

"I hope you do." He held up a hand, warding off Luke's answer. "Two days, Callahan. Bring everything to me in two days, and I might just forget the impertinence you took tonight. Enjoy your evening," he added as he walked away. "Since it's one of the few you have left with your family."

"You were right, pal." Jake, natty in his waiter's uniform, shifted his tray. "He's slime."

"Just don't screw it up," Luke said under his breath. Quick as a flash, he dropped Sam's monogrammed gold cuff link into Jake's plastic-lined pocket.

"Hey, trust me."

"And stop grinning, for Christ's sake. You're a servant."

"So, I'm a happy servant." But Jake did his best to look properly solemn as he strolled away.

An hour later, Jake handed Luke a plastic bag containing the cuff link and a single sandy blond hair.

"Mind how you use them, sport. Don't want it to look too obvious."

"Hell, let's be obvious." There was a grinding in his gut as he held the bag up to study the elegant example of men's jewelry. It was discreet, button-shaped, with the SW swirled fluidly into the gold. If all went well, Luke mused, this little trinket would send Sam Wyatt to hell.

"Have you checked the equipment?" he asked Jake.

"Checked, rechecked. We're on line. Watch this." He picked up a device no bigger than his palm. "Mouse," he whispered. "You read?"

There was a moment's pause, then Mouse's voice boomed out of the transmitter. "Right here, Jake. Clear as a bell."

With a grin, Jake offered the transmitter to Luke. "Better'n *Star Trek*, huh?"

The grinding eased to a pleasant, excited flutter. "I hate to admit it, Finestein, but you're good. We've got fifteen minutes, so keep your butt in gear."

"My butt's always in gear." He grinned and swiveled his skinny hips. "This one's going to be fabulous, Luke. Fab-u-lous."

"Don't count your chickens before they cackle," Luke murmured, quoting Max. He checked his watch. "Roxanne's waiting. Let's move out."

"Saddle up. Wagons ho! Get the lead out." Jake chuckled to himself as they headed for the door.

"Amateur," Luke muttered, but found himself grinning. It was going to be a hell of a night.

The Hampstead Gallery was a three-story, neo-Gothic building tucked behind graceful oaks. On this crisp fall night so near Halloween, the leaves fluttered burnt gold in a breeze that cackled with coming winter, and wisps of ragged fog danced over the concrete and asphalt. Above, the moon was sliced neatly in half, its outline so sharp and keen, it seemed that some passing god might have taken his ax to cleave it. Without clouds to hamper it, the moonglow showered down, white and sweet to silver the trees. But the leaves clung yet to the branches, and provided sheltering shadows.

It was all a matter of timing.

The gallery fronted on Wisconsin Avenue. Washington was not a city that boogied with nightlife. Politics ruled, and politics preferred a patina of discretion—particularly in an election year. At one A.M. the traffic was light and sporadic. Most of the bars were closed.

There was an underbelly of nocturnal activity, the crack houses, the corner drug deals, the hookers who worked the stroll on Fourteenth and those who were addicted to bartering for those temporary pleasures. Nightly murders were as common in this cradle of democracy as campaign promises.

But here in this little corner of the city, all was quiet.

Luke stood in the shadows behind the building, under the grinning gargoyles and lofty pilasters. "This better work, Mouse."

The transmitter around his neck picked up every breath. "It'll work." Mouse's voice was quiet and clear through the mini-speaker. "It's got a range of a hundred feet."

"It better work," Luke said again. He held what looked like a crossbow in his hands.

It was—or had been—just that before Mouse had modified it. It was now a gas-propelled grappling hook. Luke's finger hovered over the trigger while he thought of Roxanne, already curled up inside the third-floor storeroom. He hit the release then watched with boyish pleasure as the five-clawed hook shot up trailing rope. The tiny engine hummed under his hands, vibrating like a cat.

He heard the clink as the spiked metal hit the roof. He switched off the engine before gently, slowly pulling the rope toward him. It went taut when the spikes dug into the weathered brick of the ledge.

Luke tested it, tugging hard, then reached up high enough to swing his legs free of the ground.

"She'll hold. Nice work, Mouse."

"Thanks."

"Okay, Finestein, you go first."

"Me?" Jake's voice piped out in a squeak. His eyes rolled white in a face he'd rubbed liberally with blacking. He looked, pathetically, like a second-rate banjo player in a minstrel show. "Why me?"

"Because if I'm not behind you, poking you in the ass, you won't make it up."

"I'll fall," Jake claimed, stalling.

"Well, try not to scream if you do. You'll rouse the guards."

"All heart. I always said you're all heart."

"Up." Luke held the rope out with one hand and jerked his thumb skyward.

Though his feet were still on the ground, Jake clutched the rope like a drowning man. He squeezed his eyes shut and rose to his toes.

"I'll puke."

"Then I'll have to kill you."

"I hate this part." One last gulp and Jake was shimmying up like a monkey on a vine. "I really, really hate this part."

"Keep going. The faster you climb, the quicker you're on top."

"Hate it," Jake continued to mutter and climbed with his eyes stubbornly shut.

Luke waited until Jake had reached the second story before he began his own ascent. Jake froze like an icicle in a blizzard. "The rope." His voice was a keening whisper. "Luke, the rope's moving."

"Of course it's moving, you jerk. It's not a staircase. Keep going." Luke bullied Jake up another twelve feet. "Grab hold of the ledge, haul yourself over."

"Can't." Jake was praying in the Hebrew he'd learned for his bar mitzvah. "Can't let go of the rope."

"Shit for brains." But this wasn't something unexpected. "Put your foot on my shoulder. There, come on. Feel it?"

"That you?"

"No, it's Batman, asshole."

"I don't want to be Robin anymore. Okay?" Jake put enough weight on Luke's shoulder to make Luke wince.

"Fine. Just get your balance. Keep your weight centered on me and take hold of the ledge. If you don't," Luke continued in the same, calm, unhurried tone, "I'm going to start swinging the rope. Know what it feels like to be hanging three stories up on a rope that keeps swinging so that you bash your face into the bricks?"

"I'm doing it. I'm doing it." With his eyes still shut, Jake uncurled frozen fingers from the rope. His hand scraped brick twice before he got a grip. Indulging in another of those muffled screams, he rolled himself over and landed with a thud.

"Graceful as a cat." Luke swung soundlessly over. "We're up, Mouse." He checked his watch, noting that Roxanne had another ninety seconds before leaving her hiding place. "Do it."

Inside the storage closet that smelled of Mr. Clean and Murphy's oil soap, Roxanne checked the luminous dial of her watch. Rising, working out the kinks that came from sitting for over two hours, she counted down the seconds.

She held her breath as she eased the door open, stepped into the corridor. The darkness here was shades paler than it had been inside. There was a light at the end of the corridor that sent out a pool of pee-yellow to aid the guards on their rounds.

She walked toward it, counting.

Five, four, three, two, one... Yes. A small sigh of satisfaction escaped as the light flickered, died.

Mouse had come through. Moving fast now, Roxanne raced in the dark, past the now blind security cameras toward the surveillance room.

"Goddamn it!" The guard who'd been beating the hell out of his partner at gin swore in the dark and snatched his flashlight out of his belt. "Fucking generator should—ah." He sighed with relief at the electrical hum. The lights flickered back on, the monitors blinked back to life, computers buzzed on. "Better check," he said, but his partner was already dialing the phone.

Lily picked up on the second ring. "Washington Gas and Light, good evening."

"This is the Hampstead Gallery, we've lost power."

"I'm sorry, sir. We have reports of a line down. A crew is being dispatched."

"Line down." The guard broke the connection and shrugged. "Assholes probably won't have it fixed before morning. Fucking electric company, bleeds you dry."

"Generator's handling it." Both turned to survey the monitors. "Figure I'll make my sweep now."

"Right." The guard plopped down in front of the bank of monitors to pour coffee from his thermos. "Watch out for any big, bad burglars."

"Just keep your eyes open, McNulty."

The monitors continued to run their sequences, flipping every few seconds from display to display, shadowy corridor to shadowy corridor. It was enough, to McNulty's thinking, to bore a hole in your head so your brains drained out. He spotted his partner, working the third floor, and flipped him the bird.

It eased the boredom a little.

He started to hum, thought about trying to stack the deck for the next hand of gin. Something on monitor six caught his eye. He blinked, snorted at his own imagination, then made small, strangled sounds in his throat.

It was a woman. But it wasn't. A pale, beautiful woman in a flowing white dress with long silver hair. She faded in and out on the screen. And he could see—Jesus, he could see the paintings right through her. She smiled at him, smiled and held out a beckoning hand.

"Carson." McNulty fumbled with his two-way, but all he got in response to his call was a mechanical buzz. "Carson, you son of a bitch, come in."

She was still there, swaying inches from the floor. He saw his partner as well, starting his sweep of the second floor.

"Carson, goddamn it!"

In disgust, he shoved the two-way back in his belt pouch. His mouth was dry, his heart hammering, but he knew it would be his ass if he didn't investigate.

Roxanne shut off the projector and the hologram of Alice winked off. Once her equipment was back in her bag of tricks, she raced toward the surveillance room. The minutes were ticking away.

Her blood was cool, her hands rock steady as she went to work. She ejected the tape from camera four, replaced it with her own. Following Jake's instructions, she reprogrammed the computer. The camera was now inoperable, but the monitor would continue to show the required sequence. The only difference was, the guards would be watching a doctored tape. It took precious moments to redo camera six and erase the hologram. Even with Jake's expertise there had been no foolproof solution to the time lapse. Those damning thirty seconds where Alice's image had appeared could be fudged somewhat by turning back all the cameras and resetting them. Once the burglary was discovered, and the tapes were examined carefully, the lapse would show.

By then, if all went well, it wouldn't be their problem.

"She should be finished." Luke watched the final second tick away then nodded to Jake. "Jam it."

"My pleasure." Secure now that he had something solid under his feet, Jake withdrew what appeared to be a complex remote control—one of those daunting pieces of home equipment that operated TV, VCR, stereo. He could have adapted it for just that purpose.

On closer look it might have been mistaken for a pocket calculator. Jake's fingers played along the tiny keyboard. Somewhere in the distance a dog began to howl.

"High-pitched frequency," Jake explained. "Going to drive any mutt within a half mile nutso. The security's garbage for fifteen minutes—seventeen at the outside. That's all this baby will last."

"It's enough. Stay up here."

"You bet." He gave Luke a happy salute. "Break a leg, pal."

With a dashing smile, Luke slipped over the side. His feet had no more than touched the window ledge when the pane shot up.

"Christ, what's more romantic than a man swinging in a window on a rope?" Roxanne stepped back to give Luke room to land.

"I'll show you when we get back to the hotel." He stole a moment to kiss her thoroughly. He could feel the excitement drumming, from him to her, from her to him. It had been a long time since they'd worked in the dark together. "Any hitches?"

"Not a one."

"Then let's rock and roll."

"I'm telling you, I saw someone," McNulty insisted.

"Yeah, yeah." Carson gestured toward the bank of monitors. "A floating woman—a *transparent* floating woman. I guess that's why she didn't set off any alarms. Where is she now, McNulty?"

"She was there, damn it."

"Waving to you, right? Well, let's see." Carson tapped a finger on his chin. "Maybe she walked through a wall somewhere. That could be why I didn't see her when I made my sweep. That could be why you didn't see her when you left your post to go ghost-busting, Mc*Nutty*."

"Play back the tape." Seized with inspiration, McNulty punched in rewind on tape six himself. "Prepare to eat your words."

McNulty reran and played back the tape twice, and was going for a third when his partner stopped him.

"You need a vacation. Try St. Elizabeth's. I hear it's real quiet there."

"I saw—"

"I'll tell you what I see. I see an asshole. If the asshole wants to report a floating babe, he's on his own." Carson sat down and dealt himself a hand of solitaire.

Determined, McNulty planted himself in front of the monitors. A tic began to jerk under his left eye as he stared, waiting for the illusion to reappear.

Luke slipped his prized burglar's tools out of his pocket. With the rest of the security conquered, the lock on the display case was a joke. And the laugh would be on Sam.

He chose a pick. His fingers were already itching as he bent to the lock. Abruptly, he straightened, turned to Roxanne and offered the tool.

"Here. You do it. Ladies first."

She started to take the pick, then drew back her hand. "No, no, you go ahead. It's your gig."

"Are you sure?"

"Positive." Then, touching the tip of her tongue to her top lip, she leaned toward him. "Besides," she murmured, voice smoky, "watching you work gets me hot."

"Oh yeah?"

She chuckled, gave him a kiss. "Christ, men are so easy. Lift the lock, Callahan."

She stood behind him while he worked, one hand resting lightly on his shoulder. But she wasn't watching the delicate way he probed and jiggled. Her eyes were on the jewels beyond the glass, glittering brilliantly against the draped blue velvet.

"Oh my. My, oh my, they do shine." She felt the tug, the pull, the unabashed arousal. "I love those pretty stones. All that color, all that flash. Those rubies there. Did you know they've nearly mined all the rubies there are—at least that we know about. That's why they're worth more carat to carat than diamonds."

"Fascinating, Rox." The lock gave. Carefully, silently, Luke slid the glass doors open.

"Oh." Roxanne drew in a deep breath. "Now you can almost smell them. Hot, sweet. Summer candy. Can't we keep—"

"No." He took her backpack from her.

"Just one, Luke. Just that one ruby necklace. We could pop the rocks. I could keep them in a bag and just look at them now and again."

"No," he repeated. "Now get to work. You're wasting time."

"Oh, well. It was worth a shot."

They filled her bag, piece by glittery piece. She was a pro, but she was also a woman, and a connoisseur of gems. If her fingers lingered to caress an emerald here, a sapphire there, she was only human.

"I always figured tiaras were for beauty queens from Texas with two first names," she murmured, but she sighed as she slipped the sparkling circlet in the pack. "Time?"

"Seven minutes, on the outside."

"Good." She took out the Polaroid she'd shot of the display that evening. Working with it, they arranged the faux jewels in their proper place.

"They look good," Luke decided. "Perfect."

"They should, they cost enough."

"I love it when you're greedy. Now, for my favorite part." Taking the Baggie and a pair of tweezers from his pocket, Luke delicately removed the hair he'd picked from the shoulder of Sam's tux. After he'd placed it at the rear on a glass shelf, he poured the cuff link into his palm.

"Pretty fancy duds for a heist," Roxanne commented.

"Let him explain it." Luke wedged it in the thin space between the wall of the case and the bottom shelf, allowing only the faintest glint of gold to show. "Yeah, let him explain it," he said again. "Let's go."

Hands linked, they made the dash from display to window. Roxanne climbed up, swung her legs out, then shot him a smoldering look over her shoulder. "Nice working with you again, Callahan."

Roxanne jammed a loose pin back in her hair. The French twist went with her subtly elegant gray suit in raw silk. She'd put the look together, adding discreet diamond studs, a jeweled lapel pin in the shape of an elongated five-pointed star and black Italian pumps. She considered it suitable for an afternoon at the auction.

Beside her, Lily bubbled over with excitement in a snug hot-pink dress and purple bolero jacket. "I just love stuff like this. All these snooty people with their little numbered cards on a stick. I wish we were really going to buy something."

"They'll be auctioning artwork as well." Roxanne took out her compact, ostensively to powder her nose. She angled the mirror back, searching for Luke in the rear of the room. "You bid on whatever you like."

"I have such bad taste."

"No, you have your taste. And it's perfect." Trying not to be concerned that she couldn't spot Luke, Roxanne snapped the compact closed. "There's no reason we can't have fun while we're here. As long as we get the job done."

"I've got my part cold." Lily crossed her legs and drew some admiring glances from the men down their line of seats.

There was a lot of murmuring going on as people continued to file in and take their chairs. At the front of the high-ceilinged room stood the auctioneer's pedestal, a long, linen-draped display table and two uniformed guards. Armed guards. Along the side sat a Louis XIV desk with a telephone, a computer and stacks of ledgers and notepads. Phone-in bids were encouraged.

Roxanne paged through the thick, glossy catalogue, and like others around her, made notations, circling and checking off items.

"Oh, just look at this lamp!" Lily's enthusiasm was as genuine as the stones in Roxanne's ears, and only made the pretense all the more believable. Several heads turned at her exclamation. "Wouldn't it look perfect in the front parlor?"

Roxanne studied the photo of an Art Nouveau monstrosity and smiled. Only Lily. "Absolutely."

The auctioneer, a short, rotund man who bulged against the gray flannel of his pinstriped suit, took his place.

Curtain, Roxanne thought and sat back, waiting for her cue.

Artwork and antiques took up the opening lots. The bidding was quick if not sprightly, with someone occasionally bold enough to call out his offer rather than lifting the numbered card.

Roxanne began to enjoy the show.

Some shot their cards into the air, others waved them languidly as if the effort of bidding several thousand bored them beyond measure. Some grunted, some barked, some tapped a finger at the air. Adept at interpreting the signals, the auctioneer moved smoothly from lot to lot.

"Oh, look!" Lily gave a squeal of delight as an ornately carved high-boy, circa 1815, was trundled out between two burly men. "Isn't it beautiful, honey? It'd be just perfect for Mouse and Alice's nursery."

Roxanne was still trying to become accustomed to the idea of Mouse's impending fatherhood. "Ah..." The highboy belonged in a castle—or a bordello. But Lily's eyes were shining. "They'll love it," Roxanne stated positively, and hoped to be forgiven.

Lily waved her card in the air before the description was complete, and earned several chuckles.

Indulgent, the auctioneer nodded toward her. "Madam opens the bid for one thousand. Do I hear twelve hundred?"

Lily punctuated each bid with a gasp or a giggle, waving her card like a bayonet. She gripped the arm of the man beside her, squirmed and overbid herself twice. All in all she gained the attention of everyone in attendance.

"Sold, to number eight, for three thousand, one hundred dollars."

"Number eight." Lily turned her card around, squealed when she read the number, then lustily applauded herself. "Oh, that was exciting."

To show her interest, and because the piece caught her eye, Roxanne bid on a Deco sculpture. She found herself flushed with pride when she acquired it for twenty-seven fifty.

"Auction fever," she murmured to Lily, faintly abashed. "It's catching."

"We have to do this more often."

As the afternoon wore on, those interested only in lots already sold drifted out. Others came in. The first lot of jewelry was displayed, a collar of sapphires, citrine and emeralds, accented with full-cut diamonds. Beneath the raw silk jacket, Roxanne's heart began to thud.

"Oh, isn't it elegant?" Lily said in a stage whisper. "Isn't it dreamy?"

"Hmm. The sapphires are indigo." Roxanne gave a little shrug. "Too dark for my taste." She knew they were glass, with a little cobalt oxide added to the strass.

She watched the lots come and go, diamond bracelets that were no more than glittery zircons, rubies that were more glass with gold salts fused with the strass, agate masquerading as lapis lazuli.

She hated to admit it, and would never do so to Luke, but the money had been well spent. Each new piece brought a rustle of excitement from the crowd, and the bidding soared.

She bid on several lots, always careful to gauge the enthusiasm of those who bid against her. Lily commiserated with her each time she dropped out.

And at last, the ring. Roxanne folded out the catalogue where she had darkly circled the photograph. She allowed herself a strangled gasp as the description began and murmured to Lily.

"From Bogotá," she said, excitement vibrating in her voice. "Grass green, absolutely perfect in color and transparency. Twelve and a half carats, mounted *à jour*."

"It matches your eyes, honey."

Roxanne laughed, and leaned forward in her seat like a runner on the mark.

The bidding started at fifty thousand, which separated the mice from the men. After the third offer, Roxanne raised her card and joined in.

When the bidding reached seventy thousand, she spotted him. He wasn't sitting where he'd told her to look for him, which was probably deliberate, to keep her on her guard. He looked artistic and distinguished and nothing at all like Luke. Long brown hair was slicked back into a queue, and a matching moustache adorned his upper lip. He wore rounded spectacles with gold rims and a tailored suit of royal blue set off by a fuchsia shirt.

He bid laconically and steadily, by lifting a finger and ticking it back and forth like a metronome. He didn't glance back even when Lily muffled gasps behind her hands or bounced enthusiastically on her seat. Roxanne pushed, perhaps further than was wise, topping his bid long after it was only the two of them. Caught up in the game, in the challenge, she shot up her card when the offer struck one hundred and twenty thousand.

It was the absolute silence that reigned after her bid that brought her back to reality. That and the vise-like pressure of Lily's fingers over hers.

"Oh, my." Roxanne pressed her hand to her mouth, grateful for once that her coloring brought on blushes. "I lost my head."

"One hundred and twenty-five thousand," Luke stated in a cool, French voice. When the gavel came down he rose. Turning to Roxanne, he bowed smoothly from the waist. "My pardon, *mademoiselle*, for disappointing such a beautiful woman." He strode to the Louis XIV desk, took off his spectacles and began to polish them with a snowy square of white linen. "I will inspect."

"Monsieur Fordener, the auction is still in progress."

"*Oui*, but I always inspect what I acquire, *n'est-ce pas*? The ring, if you please."

As Luke stood behind the desk, holding the ring up to the light, the auctioneer cleared his throat and began the next lot.

"One moment!" Luke's voice snapped like a whip. His eyes behind the clear lenses were cold blue ice. "This is a fraud. This is . . . an insult!"

"Monsieur." The auctioneer tugged at the knot of his tie as people shifted in their seats and muttered. "The Clideburg collection is one of the finest in the world. I'm sure you—"

"I am sure." Luke nodded stiffly. In his hand he held a jeweler's loupe. "This . . ." He held up the ring, pausing dramatically. "Is glass. *Voilà*." He strode onto the stage, sticking the ring under the auctioneer's nose. "Look, look. See for yourself," he demanded, holding out the loupe. "Bubbles, streaks, banding."

"But—but—"

"And this." With a flourish, Luke pulled out an aluminum pencil. Those attending who knew gems recognized it as a method for distinguishing genuine stones from imitations. Luke drew the point of the pencil over the stone, then held it up, showing the shining, silvery line.

"I will have you arrested. I will have you in prison before the day is out. Do you think you can cheat Fordener?"

"No. No, monsieur. I don't understand."

"Fordener understands." He tossed up his head, gesturing to the room. "*Nous sommes trompés!* We are duped!"

In the resulting chaos, Roxanne took the risk of catching Luke's eye. Take your bow, she thought. The curtain was about to go up on the last act.

34

"The papers are full of it." Roxanne nibbled on a croissant as she scanned the headlines. "It's the biggest thing to happen in D.C. since Ollie North."

"Bigger," Luke claimed, pouring more coffee. "People are used to subterfuge and lies in the government. This is a jewel heist. A magnificent one, if I say so myself, and that equals romance, magic. And greed."

"The authorities are baffled," Roxanne read and grinned up at Luke. "They're testing every stone, called in one of the top mineralogists. Of course, all the standard tests were used when the gallery purchased the collection. Polariscopes, dichroscopes, the methylene iodide and benzene bath, roentgen X ray."

"Show off."

"Well, I did spend four years studying." Setting the paper aside, she stretched her arms high. She was still in her robe, and naked under it. It felt wonderful to be lazy, to have this little island of calm before the next bout of excitement.

Over the rim of his cup, Luke watched the robe shift, gape and reveal a tantalizing glimpse of ivory skin. "Why don't we finish breakfast, in bed?"

With her arms still extended, Roxanne smiled. "That sounds—"

"Mama!" Like a rocket out of his adjoining room, Nate shot across the carpet. "I did it. I tied my shoe." Balancing one hand on the table, he plopped his sneakered foot on her lap. "By myself."

"Incredible. The boy's a prodigy." She studied the loose bow that was already becoming undone. "This is certainly a red-letter day."

"Let me see that." Luke nipped Nate at the waist and hauled him onto his knee. "Okay, come clean. Who helped you?"

"Nobody." Eyes wide, Nate stared up into his father's face. While his son was distracted, Luke quickly secured the bow so that it would stay put. "I swear to God."

"I guess you're all grown up then. Want some coffee?"

Nate screwed up his face. "Nah. It tastes yucky."

"Let's see then, what else?" Luke bounced the boy on his knee as he considered. "You know, Rox, it seems to me any kid who can tie his own shoes should be able to take care of a dog."

"Callahan," Roxanne muttered under Nate's enthusiastic cheer.

"You'd feed it, wouldn't you, slick?"

"Sure I would." Eyes solemn, glowing with sincerity and good intentions, Nate nodded. "Every single day. And I'd teach him to sit, too. And to shake hands. And..." Inspiration struck. "To fetch your slippers, Mama."

"After he'd chewed them, no doubt." It would take a harder woman than she to resist two pairs of laughing blue eyes and two crooked smiles. "I'm not sharing the house with some yappy little purebred."

"We want a big, ugly mutt, don't we, Nate?"

"Yeah. A big, ugly mutt." He wound his arm around Luke's neck and looked imploringly at his mother. This was his cue, and performing was, after all, in his blood. "Daddy says they have lots of poor, homeless puppies at the animal shelter. It's like being in jail."

"Low, Callahan, really low," Roxanne said under her breath. "I suppose you think we should go spring one."

"It's the humanitarian thing to do, Rox. Right, Nate?"

"Right."

"I suppose we could look," she began, but Nate was already hooting and leaping off Luke's lap to catch her in a fierce hug. "You two ganged up on me." Over Nate's head she smiled mistily at Luke. "I suppose I'll have to get used to it."

"I'm going to go tell Alice right now!" Nate streaked away, skidded to a halt. "Thanks, Dad." He grinned over his shoulder. "Thanks a lot."

Luke couldn't do much about the grin splitting his face, but he thought it politic to pretend a sudden interest in his breakfast.

"You're going to spoil him."

He moved his shoulders. "So? You're only four years old once. Besides, it feels good."

She rose to walk over and curl on his lap. "Yes, it does. It feels very good." With a little murmur of pleasure she cuddled against him. "I guess we have to get dressed. There's work to do yet."

"I wish we could spend the day with Nate. Just the three of us."

"There'll be other days. Lots of days when this is all over." She smiled, and with her arms linked around his neck, leaned back. "I'd love to see how Tannenbaum's doing right now."

"He's a veteran." Luke kissed her nose. "We should be getting a call within the hour."

"I just hate missing his performance. It should be a once-in-a-lifetime."

Harvey Tannenbaum was indeed a veteran. For more than two-thirds of his sixty-eight years he'd been a successful fence, dealing with only the cream of the crop. To Harvey, Maximillian Nouvelle had been the cream of the cream.

Roxanne's proposition that he come out of his four-year retirement and play a small but pivotal role in an elaborate con had initially thrown him off balance. Then it had intrigued him.

In the end, Harvey had graciously agreed to participate, and to show his sentiments toward Max and the Nouvelles, had taken the job gratis.

He was even looking forward to it.

Certainly it was a new twist for Harvey. It was the first time in his long life he had voluntarily walked into a police station. Certainly the first time he had ever confessed—without duress—a transgression to the authorities.

Since it was the first, and by all likelihood the last, Harvey was playing it for all he was worth.

"I come here as a concerned citizen," he insisted, staring up at the two plainclothes officers to whom he'd been passed by an overworked sergeant. His eyes were sunken, red-rimmed and shadowed, thanks to a dusk-to-dawn movie marathon on cable. He looked, in his baggy suit and wide-striped tie, like a desperate man who'd spent a sleepless night in his clothes.

Only the desperation was an illusion.

"You look worn out, Harvey." Sapperstein, the senior detective, took the compassionate route. "Why don't you let us drive you home?"

"Are you listening to me?" Harvey let his indignation rise. "Hell's fire, boys, I come in here—and it ain't something I do lightly—to give you the tip of a lifetime. All you can do is tell me to go on home. Like I was senile or something. I didn't sleep a wink all night worrying if I had the nerve to do this, and all you want to do is pass me off."

Impatient by nature, irritable by circumstance, the second detective, a basset-eyed Italian named Lorenzo, drummed his fingers on his overburdened desk. "Look, Tannenbaum, we're kind of busy around here today. You know how it is when there's a major jewel heist, don't you?"

"Indeed I do." He sighed, remembering the good old days. "We used to know how to keep the fun in our work. Today, these young guys, it's just business. No flair, no creativity. No, you know, magic."

"Sure." Sapperstein summoned up a smile. "You were the best, Harvey."

"Well, you sure as hell never tagged me, did you? Not that I'm admitting anything, mind, but there are some that might say I handled more ice than a trio of Eskimos."

"Those were the days," the second detective said between his teeth. "Now, we'd just love to sit around and go back down memory lane with you, but we've got work to do."

"I come here to help you fellas out." Harvey folded his arms and kept his wide butt planted. "I'm doing my goddamn civic duty. And before I do it, I want immunity."

"Christ," Lorenzo muttered. "Call the D.A. Harvey wants immunity. Let's get the paperwork moving."

"No need to be sarcastic," Harvey muttered. "Could be I shouldn't be dealing with underlings. Maybe I'll just go to the commissioner."

"Yeah, you do that," Lorenzo invited.

"Put a lid on it," Sapperstein advised. "You got something to say, Harvey, spill it. You look tired, we're tired, and we are pressed for time."

"Maybe you're too busy to hear what I know about the art gallery heist then." Harvey started to heave himself up. "I'll just run along. Wouldn't want to hold you up."

Both detectives' ears perked up. Sapperstein kept his persuasive smile in place. He knew it was probable that Harvey was just blowing hot air. After all, word was that he'd been out of business for a couple years, and he could have been feeling a tug of nostalgia.

Then again...

"Wait." Sapperstein patted Harvey's shoulder to ease him back down. "You know something about that, do you?"

"I know who did it." Harvey's smile was smug. He waited one dramatic beat, deciding he owed Roxanne for offering him the job. "Sam Wyatt."

Lorenzo swore and broke a pencil in half. "How come I get the crazies?" he asked a higher power. "Why is it always me?"

"Crazy? Why you snot-nosed punk. I was passing rocks under cops' noses while you were still pissing your diapers. You can't show more respect than that, I'm out of here."

"Take it easy, Harvey. So you saw senatorial candidate Sam Wyatt steal the Clideburg collection?" This was asked with studied patience by Sapperstein.

"Shit! How could I see him lift them?" Righteous frustration had Harvey tossing up his hands. "What? You figure I stand on street corners and look for thieves? You're not going to hang any accessory bullshit on me. I was home sleeping like a baby when the job went down. And since I wasn't sleeping alone," he added with a wicked grin, "I got me an alibi."

"Then why do you claim that Mr. Wyatt stole the Clideburg collection?"

"Because he told me!" Agitation and excellent projection had Harvey's voice ringing out in the noisy station house. "For Christ sake, put two and two together, will you? Maybe somebody—just for hypothetical purposes we'll say that somebody was me—used to turn over a few rocks for him now and then."

Lorenzo snorted. "You're trying to tell us that you fenced for Sam Wyatt?"

"I said no such thing." Harvey blustered, turned red. "I said hypothetically. If you think you're going to trick me into incriminating myself you've got another think coming. I came in here of my own free will, and I'm walking out the same way. I ain't going to jail."

"Take it easy. Want some water? Lorenzo, get us a cup of water here."

"Sure? Why the hell not?" In disgust, Lorenzo stomped off.

"Now, Harvey." In his best cop-as-diplomat voice, Sapperstein continued. "We're here to listen. That's a fact. But if you're going to make up stories like this about a respected member of the government, you're just going to get yourself in trouble. Maybe you don't like the guy's politics, and you're entitled."

"Politics, balls." Harvey let out his own snort of disgust. "I don't give a flaming shit about his politics. But I'm telling you—hypothetically, got it?"

"Sure, I got it."

"Hypothetically, I've known Sam for a long time. Since he was a teenager. Never cared for him personally, but business is business. Right? Anyway, he used to use me pretty regular. Before he got into politics it was mostly small time, but after, he started hitting bigger targets."

"So you've known Sam Wyatt since he was a kid?" Even Sapperstein's patience could be strained. He took the cup Lorenzo brought back and held it out to Harvey. "Look, you're not doing anyone any good this way—"

"I don't like being pressured," Harvey interrupted. "And that's just what the son of a bitch is trying. Look, I'm retired—hypothetically. And If I want to turn down a job, I turn it down."

"Okay, you turned him down." Sapperstein rolled his eyes. "You're not involved. What do you know?"

"I know plenty. I get a call, right? He tells me he's going to hit the gallery, and I tell him good luck, what's it to me? So he wants me to start working on liquidating the rocks. I give it a pass, and he gets nasty. Starts talking about making it rough for me. You know, I had a kid by my second wife, Florence. He's a dentist on Long Island. Well, Wyatt knows about him and says he'll make things tough. While he's threatening me, he's complimenting me. Telling me how I'm the best and he can't trust any second-rate fence with this kind of merchandise. Reminds me how we worked together before, and how this score's going to set us both up for good."

Harvey drank the rest of his water and sighed. "I gotta say, I've been losing some sleep over this. Wyatt had me worried, and I have to admit, he had me interested. A job like this doesn't come along every day. The commission would set me up good, I've been thinking about moving to Jamaica. It's warm there all the time. Half-naked women everywhere you look."

"Stay focused, Harvey," Sapperstein advised. "What did you do about the job?"

"I played along. First I thought I might do it, then I started thinking how much heat was going to blow when it went down. I'm not as young as I used to be, and I don't need the aggravation. So I figured I'd do the right thing—turn him in, you know? There must be like a reward or finder's fee for that haul. I can do a good deed and make a couple bucks out of it."

"So he passed you the stuff?" Lorenzo spread his hands. "Let's see it."

"Give me a break. I met him yesterday, at the zoo. By the ape house."

"Fine," Sapperstein said, cutting his partner off. "Keep going."

"He tells me he'd pulled it off. He was really high about it, bragging, you know? Never smart to get that emotionally involved with a job. He told me how he'd done it, and how he had planted fakes to buy more time. And he told me he wanted them fenced right after the election."

"That's reaching, Harvey."

"Maybe you think so, but I can tell you something else. The guy's not right. Here." Harvey tapped his head.

Sighing, Sapperstein took up a pad. "What cab company did you use to get to the zoo?" He scribbled the information down as Harvey related it. "What time did you get picked up? How'd you get back?" All this could be easily verified. "Just for argument's sake, how did he tell you he pulled it off?"

Harvey's heart swelled, as it would if he had a fat fish on the line, or a sparkling gem in his hand. In concise phrases he described a break-in so similar to the genuine heist that it would fall beautifully into place during the investigation.

"Pretty slick—and high-tech. Holograms, electronic jammers." It could have worked, Sapperstein thought as his cop's blood began to heat.

"He learned something of magic from these performers out of New Orleans. Lived with them awhile, he told me. They're like famous or something now. Anyway, he used to try to do card tricks."

"You know, even if some of this checks out, it's not enough for us to question Sam Wyatt."

"I know the ropes, kid. I got more." With a flourish worthy of a master, he reached inside his shirt pocket and whipped out a paper folded once. As a force of habit, Sapperstein took it by the edges.

Written on it were descriptions of the Clideburg collection.

"He gave that to me, to help me arrange for the fencing. But he made a big mistake. I don't like threats, and by Christ, I'm retired." He wagged his eyebrows. "Hypothetically."

"Don't get cocky." Lorenzo scowled at the paper Sapperstein was slipping into an evidence bag. "I guess you want me to send that to the lab."

"You get enough pieces, Lorenzo, you've just got to start putting them together. Have them check it for prints. Find out if Wyatt's are on file. While you're at it, see if we can come up with a handwriting sample."

Lorenzo heaved a gusty sigh. "I just heard they lifted a piece from the display at the gallery. Cuff link, gold. Engraved with the initials S W."

Sapperstein's nose all but twitched. "Okay, Harvey, why don't you come over and sit here?" Sapperstein led him away to a bench near the door of the station. "We'll take it from here."

"I get immunity." Harvey clutched Sapperstein's jacket sleeve. "I won't do time for this crap."

"I don't think that's something you have to worry about." With a last pat on the shoulder, the detective walked away. His bland smile vanished when he reached his partner. "I'm going to get all I can on the cuff link. You tell the lab to put a rush on that paper. Bitch later, Lorenzo," he said and there was fire in his eyes. "That old man might just have made our careers."

The old man sat patiently, biding his time. They were wrong, he thought, when they said revenge was sweet. It had a tang. A delicious, lingering tang. And he was enjoying this one for his old pal Max.

"Then it's the last act." She gazed out the window as the wind tossed leaves along the curbs. "I wish Daddy could be here for this one." She shook off the mood, made herself smile. "I hope this doesn't delay our return to New Orleans by more than a day or so. I'd hate to miss Halloween at home."

"We'll make it." Lifting her hand, he kissed it. "That's a promise."

Sam's bags were packed for his trip to Tennessee. He had ten days of campaigning on his schedule, all of which would be spent hand in glove with his staff, and his wife. Justine had already given him trouble over the amount of luggage she claimed to need. She was upstairs, pouting over the ruthless way he'd slashed her four suitcases to two.

She'd get over it, Sam mused. Once she could have Senator and Mrs. Samuel Wyatt printed on her Christmas cards, she'd get over a lot of things.

He was sorry the timing didn't allow him to dole out Luke's punishment immediately. He'd thought he would enjoy stringing out the tension, but it gnawed at him. He wanted to strike quickly, finally.

It should have pleased him that he'd been on target about the Clideburg collection. Sam had no doubt who had engineered the theft. It would be another weight on the scale if he decided to turn his documentation over to the police.

But that would have to wait until Luke had brought him the file on Gunner.

Then he would use these last ten days before the election to secure his place in history.

He ignored the doorbell, leaving that for the servants. His packing was being completed by his valet, but Sam always dealt with the contents of his briefcase personally. His papers, his speeches, the condoms he used religiously in all extramarital affairs, his schedule, pens, notepads, a weighty book on economics. He snapped the locks shut as a maid came to the doorway.

"Mr. Wyatt, the police are here. They'd like to speak with you."

"Police?" He caught the avid interest in the maid's eyes and decided to fire her at the first opportunity. "Show them in."

"Officers." Sam came around the desk to extend his hand to both Sapperstein and Lorenzo. It was a good politician's shake. Firm, dry and confident. "It's always a pleasure to entertain the boys on the force. What can I get you? Coffee?"

"No, thanks." Sapperstein answered for both of them. "We'll try not to take up too much of your time, Mr. Wyatt."

"I'd like to say take all you want, but I'm catching a plane in a couple hours. Hitting the campaign trail." He winked, quick and friendly. "Either of you have friends or relatives in Tennessee?"

"No, sir."

"Well, I had to give it a shot." He gestured toward a chair. "Have a seat, Officer . . . ?"

"Detective Sapperstein, and Detective Lorenzo."

"Detectives." For reasons that baffled him, Sam began to sweat around the collar of his monogrammed shirt. "Why don't you tell me what this is all about?"

"Mr. Wyatt, I have a court order." Sapperstein took it out and paused an extra moment to slip on his reading glasses. "We're authorized to search the premises. Detective Lorenzo and I will head the team that's waiting outside."

"A search warrant?" All of Sam's charm died. "What the hell are you talking about?"

"The Clideburg collection, which was stolen from the Hampstead Gallery on October twenty-third. We have evidence that you're involved in the theft and, by order of Judge Harold J. Lorring, are authorized to conduct a search."

"You're out of your mind." With palms that were suddenly wet, Sam snatched the order from Sapperstein. "This is a fraud. I don't know what game you're playing but . . ." He broke off, sneering. "Callahan sent you. He thought he could rig this whole business to shake me up. Well, he's wrong. You can go back and tell the bastard that he's dead fucking wrong, and I'll bury him for it."

"Mr. Wyatt," Sapperstein continued. "We are authorized to make this search, and will do so with or without your cooperation. We apologize for any inconvenience this causes you."

"Bullshit. Do you think I don't smell a con? You're meat." Triumphant, he jabbed a finger at them. "Both of you. Get out of my house, or I'll call the cops myself."

"You're free to do so, Mr. Wyatt." Sapperstein took the official paper back. "We'll wait."

He wouldn't fall for it. It was a pitiful ploy, Sam told himself as he called through for the office of Judge Harold J. Lorring. By the time he was told a search order had indeed been signed less than thirty minutes before, he was dragging at the knot of his silk tie. He punched the number for his lawyer.

"Windfield, this is Sam Wyatt. I've got a couple of jerks who say they're cops standing in my office with some trumped-up search warrant." He yanked the tie off, threw it. "Yes, that's what I said. Now get your fat ass over here and deal with it." Sam slammed down the receiver. "You don't touch a thing. Not one fucking thing until my lawyer gets here."

Sapperstein nodded. "We've got time." He couldn't help it, something about Sam set him off. He glanced at his watch and smiled. "But I think you're going to miss that plane."

Before Sam could growl out a response, Justine hurried in. "Sam, what in the world is going on? There are two police cars parked in front of the house."

"Shut up!" He sprang at her like a tiger and shoved her toward the door. "Shut up and get out."

"Mr. Wyatt." The maid was nearly swooning with excitement. "You have guests in the foyer."

"Send them away," he said between his teeth. "Can't you see I'm busy?" He walked to the liquor cabinet and poured two fingers of whiskey. He'd lost his head for a moment, but that was all right. Anyone might react the same way under the circumstances. He downed the whiskey and waited for it to settle.

"Officers." With his poster smile back in place, he turned. "I apologize for losing my temper. It was such a shock. It isn't every day I'm accused of robbery."

"Burglary," Lorenzo corrected, for the hell of it.

"Yes, of course." He'd have the man's badge—if it wasn't a fake. "I do prefer to wait until my lawyer arrives, just to verify the procedure. I assure you, you're free to turn the house upside down. I have nothing to hide."

Voices in the corridor had everyone turning. When Luke shoved through the door past the maid, followed closely by Roxanne, Sam's newly regained composure teetered on the edge.

"What are you doing in my house?"

"You called, you demanded I come." Luke slipped a protective arm around Roxanne. "I don't know what you want, Wyatt, but I don't appreciate the tone of your invitation to visit. I . . ." He trailed off, as if spotting the detectives for the first time. "Who are these people?"

"Cops. Nice to see you." Enjoying himself, Lorenzo grinned.

"What is this about?" Roxanne tossed her head up, a lovely, valiant woman obviously running on nerves.

"I'm sorry," Sapperstein stated, "I'll have to ask you both to leave. This is official."

"I want to know what this is all about. You've done something horrible again, haven't you?" She whirled on Sam. "You won't hurt Luke." She gripped his lapels and shook. "You used me once, but never, never again."

"Darling, please." Luke moved to her. "Don't upset yourself. He isn't worth it. He never was."

"I brought you into my home." She shoved Sam back. Only the presence of witnesses kept him from striking her. "I trusted you and my family trusted you. Isn't it enough that you betrayed us all those years ago? Must you still harbor this cancerous hate for us?"

"Keep your hands off me." He grabbed her by the wrists, twisting. Roxanne's cry of pain had both detectives moving quickly to intervene.

"Take it easy, Wyatt."

"Sweetheart."

That was her cue. In a blind rush of tears, Roxanne stumbled toward Luke and knocked the briefcase from the desk. The locks sprang. An icy glimmer of diamonds spilled out, chased by the fire of rubies.

"Oh." Roxanne pressed her hands to her mouth. "My God, it's the Queen's lace necklace from the Clideburg collection. You." She lifted her arm, pointing an accusing finger. "You stole them. Just like you stole from Madame all those years ago."

"You're crazy. He planted them." Sam looked around wildly, unable to believe his carefully structured world could fall apart so quickly. "The bastard planted them. He set me up." He lunged. Luke braced. Even as Lorenzo moved to intercept, Roxanne shifted her body. It burned her that it would appear she was scrambling out of harm's way. But then, the end justifies everything. Her foot hooked nimbly under Sam's leg and sent him sprawling on the open briefcase.

"You didn't run far enough." Sam sat up, breath heaving. "You won't pull off this little magic trick, Callahan. I've still got you. In the safe." He wiped a hand across the back of his mouth as he rose. His eyes were too wide, his face gray, his lips peeled back in a mockery of a grin. "I have evidence in the safe against this man. He's a thief and a murderer. This woman's a thief as well. They all are. I can prove it. I can prove it." Limping toward the safe, he continued to mutter under his breath.

"Mr. Wyatt." Sapperstein put a restraining hand on his shoulder. "I advise you to wait for your attorney."

"I've waited long enough. I've waited years. You wanted to search, didn't you? Well, search this." He spun the dial on the safe, twisting it back and forward until the last number of the combination. He yanked it open and reached in. Then he stared, goggle-eyed, as a file folder spilled out, scattering garishly colored photographs.

"Interesting snapshots, Mr. Wyatt." Lorenzo scooped up a handful, pursing his lips as he shuffled through them. "You're real photogenic—and agile." He grinned, passing the photos to his partner.

"That's not me." Still staring, Sam wiped his mouth with the back of his hand. "It's Gunner. It's supposed to be Gunner. They're faked. Anyone can see that. I've never been with any of those people. I've never seen them before."

"None of them seem to consider you a stranger," Sapperstein murmured. He'd done a turn in Vice, but never seen anything quite so . . . creative. "You know, looks like these should come with a disclaimer. 'Don't try these tricks at home.' "

"Yeah." Getting into the spirit, Lorenzo tapped one snapshot depicting a particularly lewd and unusual position. "How do you suppose he twisted himself into that move? My wife would love it."

"Never mind." Sapperstein cleared his throat. There was, he remembered belatedly, a lady present. "Mr. Wyatt, if you would sit down until we—"

"They're faked!" Sam shouted. "He did it. He lied and cheated." Breathing hard, he pointed at Luke. "But he'll pay. All of them will. I've got proof." He was chuckling as he reached into the safe. His nerve cracked completely when he pulled out a diamond tiara.

"It's a trick," he said—blubbered. "A trick." He backed up, staring at the jeweled crown in his hands while a giggle escaped through his terrible grin. "It'll disappear."

Sapperstein nodded to Lorenzo, who removed the tiara. "You have the right to remain silent," he began, slipping on the cuffs while Sapperstein emptied the safe of jewels.

"I'm going to be president." Spittle flew as Sam raged. "Eight more years, I only need eight more years."

"Oh, I think you're going to get more than that," Luke murmured. He snapped his fingers and offered Roxanne the rose that appeared between them. "Alacazam, Rox."

"Yeah." She pressed her face to his chest to hide a mile-wide grin. "But what are we going to do for an encore?"

35

Fall in New Orleans was warm and bright and blissfully dry. The days grew shorter, but night after night the sunsets were a spectacular symphony of color and hue that seared the throat and dazzled the eye.

Max died during one of those brilliant light shows, in his own bed, with a ruby-red sun as his final curtain. His family was with him, and as LeClerc said over one of the innumerable cups of coffee consumed during that night, it was the best way to die.

Roxanne had to be content with that, and with the fact that Luke had placed the philosophers' stone in their father's frail hand so that he slipped from one world to the next holding it.

It wasn't a brilliant gem or a glittery jewel. The stone was a simple gray rock, worn smooth by time and questing fingers. In size, it had fit neatly into the cup of her palm, resting there as it had rested in other palms in other centuries.

If it had held power, she hadn't felt it. She hoped Max had.

They buried it with him on a bright November morning, with a blue sky overhead and a faint breeze rustling in the wild grass that sprang up between the raised tombs of the city he'd loved. There was perfume on the air, and the strains of Chopin stroked from a dozen violins.

Max would have detested black crape and organ music.

Hundreds had crowded into the cemetery, people he'd touched somehow during his life. Young magicians eager to make their marks, old ones whose hands and eyes were failing them even as Max's mind had failed him. Someone released a dozen white doves that fluttered and cooed overhead, giving the illusion of angels come to bear Max's soul away.

Roxanne found the gesture incredibly lovely.

Max's farewell performance, as he would have expected, was a class act.

Over the next few days, Roxanne drifted, never quite able to break free of the drag of grief. Her father had been the single most important influence in her life. While he had been ill, she'd had no choice but to take charge of the family. But as long as he'd been there in body, she'd had the illusion—again illusion—of having him.

She wished she could have shared their latest triumph with him. The headlines still shouted the scandal of Samuel Wyatt, former senatorial candidate, now indicted for grand larceny, among a variety of lesser charges.

They'd found other evidence in his Maryland home. A small device that resembled something between a remote control unit and a calculator, a fine set of burglar's tools in stainless steel polished to a gleam, a glass cutter, a motorized crossbow that propelled a grappling hook, a single gold cuff link, etched with the initials SW, and most damning, a diary, painstakingly detailing thefts committed over a span of fifteen years.

It had taken Jake a month to complete it, forging Sam's hand. But it had been a job well done.

Swiss accounts, in excess of a quarter of a million, had been unearthed. Luke considered it an investment that had already paid off—in spades.

Roxanne had been prepared to feel sympathy for Justine, but was amused when she read that Sam's devoted wife, cleared of all implication, had already filed for divorce and was living in a chalet in the Swiss Alps.

As for Sam, he no longer insisted he wanted to be president. He claimed he was president. The psychiatrists continued their deliberate tests while Sam ran his private government from a padded cell.

It was, Roxanne supposed, a kind of justice.

But that was behind her. The corner it had taken her five years to turn was at her back. A dozen long paths spread out before her, and she simply didn't know which she wanted to take.

"It's getting chilly out here." In the shadowy dusk, Lily crossed the courtyard to where Roxanne sat on the iron bench watching the fountain. "You should have a jacket."

"I'm fine." To show company was welcome, she held up a hand, slipping an arm around Lily's shoulder when the older woman joined her on the bench. "I love this spot. I can't remember a time when I haven't been able to feel better after sitting here."

"Some places are magic." Lily glanced up to the window of the room she'd shared with Max for so many years. "This one's always been magic for me."

They sat in silence for a few minutes, listening to the splash and tinkle of the fountain. The shadows lengthened and became the dark.

"Don't miss him too much, honey." Lily knew she'd put it badly, wished she had Max's flair for words. "He wouldn't want you to hurt for too long."

"I know. I was afraid at first if I let it stop hurting it meant I'd stopped loving him. But I know that's wrong. I was sitting here, remembering the day we all left for D.C." She tilted her head, resting it on Lily's shoulder. "He was in his chair, looking out of the French doors. Just looking out. He wanted to go, Lily. I knew it. I felt it. He needed to go."

She laughed, a low genuine sound Lily hadn't heard in too many days.

"But he was stubborn," Roxanne continued. "Leave it to Max to die on Halloween. Like Houdini." Her arm tightened around Lily's shoulders. "I swear he must have planned it. And I was thinking now that if there's a heaven for magicians, he's there, doing pocket tricks with Robert-Houdin, trying to outdo the Herrmanns and conjuring with Harry Kellar. Oh, he'd like that, wouldn't he, Lily?"

"Yes." Damp-eyed but smiling, Lily shifted into a hug. "And he'd fight tooth and nail for top billing."

"Appearing tonight and for eternity, Maximillian Nouvelle, Conjurer Extraordinaire." Laughing again, she kissed both of Lily's cheeks. "I'm not hurting anymore. I'll always miss him, but it doesn't hurt."

"Then I'm going to say something else." She cupped Roxanne's face in her hands. "Make your own. You've always been good at that, Roxy, always bold and strong and smart. Don't stop now."

"I don't know what you mean."

Lily heard a door open and looked over her shoulder to see Luke under the pool of light by the kitchen door. "Make your own," Lily repeated and rose. "I'm going inside to put my two cents' worth in on those wallpaper samples Alice is mooning over. I swear that girl'll pick nothing but pastels and flowers if someone doesn't give her a goose."

"You're just the one to do it."

"You come in if you get cold," Lily ordered.

"I will."

Lily passed Luke on the courtyard. "And if you can't keep her warm," she said under her breath, "I wash my hands of you."

Luke sat on the bench, drew Roxanne close and kissed her until her bones went limp.

With her head tilted back on his arm she opened her eyes again. "What was that for?"

"Just following orders. But this one's for me." He kissed her again, lingering over it. With a satisfied sigh, he sat back, stretched out his long legs and crossed them at the ankles. "Nice night, huh?"

"Mmm. Moon's coming up. How many times did Nate con you into reading *Green Eggs and Ham*?"

"Enough so I can recite it by memory. Who the hell wants to eat green eggs anyway? It's disgusting."

"You miss the not so subtle metaphor, Callahan. It's about not judging things by their appearance, and testing new ground."

"Really? Funny, I've been thinking about testing new ground." But he wanted to be sure it was the time. The first silver fingers of moonlight slipped out of the sky as he turned his head to study her. "How are you, Rox?"

"I'm good." She felt his eyes on her, that old, familiar intensity. "I'm good, Luke," she repeated and smiled at him. "I know I couldn't keep him forever, no matter how much magic I tucked up my sleeve. It helps, knowing you loved him as much as I did. And maybe, in some strange way, the five years you were gone gave me the time to concentrate so closely on him when he needed me most. He hung on until you came back, and I could go on without him."

"Fate?"

"Life's a good enough word. Things are changing now." She huddled closer, not because she was cold. Because it felt right. "Mouse and Alice will be moving out before too long. And doesn't it fit neatly now that they're starting their own family you just happen to have a house that's perfect for them up for sale?"

"With a nice third-floor apartment, suitable for a bachelor. Now Jake can drive them crazy."

"You know you love him."

"Love's a strong word, Rox." But he smiled. "What I feel for Jake is more of a mild tolerance punctuated with periods of extreme annoyance."

"Lily's going to work on finding him a wife."

"She hides that sadistic streak so well. At least he's useful backstage." Because he enjoyed it, and it was a handy misdirection, Luke picked up her hand to toy with her fingers. "You know, Rox, I've been thinking about the act."

She gave a sleepy sigh. "Think it's ready to take on the road?"

"Yeah, it's ready. But I was thinking about something closer to home."

"Such as."

"Such as this building for sale on the south edge of the Quarter. Good size. Needs a lot of work, but it has potential."

"Possibilities? What kind?"

"The magic kind. The Nouvelle Magic Shop, New Orleans. A theater to break in new acts, to amaze the masses. Maybe with a little magic store tucked in it to sell tricks. A first-class operation."

"A business." Intrigued but wary, she eased back so that she could see his face. In it she saw barely restrained excitement. "You want to start a business?"

"Not just a business. A possibility. You and me, partners. We'd perform there, draw some of the big names and give a few new ones a shot. A carnival, Rox, but this one would stay in one place. It could be just as magical."

"You've been giving this a lot of thought. Since when?"

"Since Nate. I want to be able to give him what Max gave me. A base." To give the idea a chance to simmer, he lifted her fingers to his lips, kissing them one by one. "We'd still go on the road. That's what we do. But we wouldn't be traveling nine out of twelve months. He'll be starting school full-time soon."

"I know. I've thought of that. I was planning to cut back once he did. Work around his schedule."

"If we did this, you wouldn't have to cut back, and you'd accomplish the same thing." He saw the interest light in her eyes and dove in for the kill. "There's just one hitch."

"There's always a trap door. What is it?"

"You have to marry me."

She couldn't say she was surprised. It was more like a quick, powerful electric shock. "Excuse me?"

"You're going to have to marry me. That's it."

"That's it?" She would have laughed, but she didn't think she had the strength for it. She did manage to gain her feet. "You're telling me I have to marry you. As in 'I do' and 'till death do us part'?"

"I'd ask you, but I figure you'd waste time weighing the odds. So I'm telling."

Her chin came up. "And I'm telling you—"

"Hold it." He held up a hand, standing so they'd be face to face. "I was going to ask you the night I came back from Sam's with my pockets full of sapphires."

That not only stopped her temper but muddled her head. "You were?"

"I had it pretty well planned. I was going to go for the romantic route. I even had a ring in my pocket. But I had to hock it in Brazil."

"In Brazil. I see."

"What would you have done if I had asked you then?"

"I don't know." That was the pure, sterling truth. "We'd never talked about it. I guess I thought things would keep going the way they were going."

"They didn't."

"No, they didn't." Baffled, she blew out a breath. "I would have thought about it. I would have thought about it hard."

"And if I ask you now you'll do the same thing. So I'm bypassing that. We're getting married or the rest of the deal's off."

"You can't bully me into marriage."

"If bullying doesn't work, I'll seduce you." He ran his hands up and down her arms, an old habit that still thrilled her. "And I'll start by telling you I love you. That you're the only woman I've ever loved. Ever will love." Smooth as silk, he drew her close to let his lips play over hers. "I want to make promises to you, and for you to make them to me. I want more children with you. I want to be here when they grow inside you."

"Oh, Luke." If she hadn't known better, she would have sworn she smelled orange blossoms. Marriage, she thought. It was so ordinary, so commonplace. So exciting. "Promise you'll never, ever call me the little woman."

"I'll swear it in blood."

"Okay." She pressed a hand to her mouth, as if shocked the word had escaped. Then she laughed and said it again. "Okay. You're on."

"No pulling back," he warned, lifting her up to spin her in a circle.

"I never welch."

"Then the next time we're onstage, it'll be introducing Callahan, and his beautiful wife, Roxanne Nouvelle."

"Not on your life." She punched his shoulder when he dropped her to the ground.

"All right. Just Callahan and Nouvelle." He arched a brow. "It's alphabetical, Rox."

"Nouvelle and Callahan. I'm the one who taught you your first card trick, remember?"

"You never let me forget. Deal." He shook her hand formally. "Nate's going to have himself two legally married parents and a dog. What more could a kid want?"

"It's so conventional, it's scary." She combed a hand through her hair. "And about that dog—"

"Jake's out walking him. Don't worry. Mike hasn't chewed up anything worth talking about for an hour. And don't bother with that hard-ass line, Roxy. I saw you feeding him chocolate chip cookies this morning."

"It was a plan. I figured if I fed him until he got fat, he wouldn't be able to waddle upstairs and pee on the bedroom rug."

"You scratched his ears, made kissy noises and let him lick your face."

"It was a moment of insanity. But I'm feeling much better now."

"Good, because there's just one more thing."

"Just one more."

"Yeah. We're giving up stealing."

"We're—" She really had no choice but to sit down. "Giving up?"

"Cold turkey." He sat beside her. "I've given this a lot of thought, too. We're parents now, and I'd like to make another baby as soon as possible. I don't think you should be doing second-story work with a baby on board."

"But—it's what we do."

"It's what we did," he corrected. "And we were the best. Let's go out on top, Roxy. With Max, it was the end of an era. We've got to start our own. And Christ, what do we do if Nate does grow up to be a cop?" He was kissing her fingers again, and laughing. "He might arrest us. What kind of guilt is that to lay on a kid, sending up his own parents?"

"You're being ridiculous. Children go through stages."

"What did you want to be when you were four?"

"A magician," she said on a sigh. "But to give it up, Callahan. Couldn't we just . . . cut back?"

"It's cleaner this way, Rox." He patted her hand. "You know it is."

"We'll only steal from really rich men with red hair."

"Bite the bullet, babe."

Letting out a groan she sat back. "Married, starting a business and going straight all at once. I don't know, Callahan. I may explode."

"We'll take it one day at a time."

She knew he had her. The image of Nate, all three feet of him, wearing a badge and tearfully locking her behind bars was too much. "The next thing you'll be telling me we should start doing kids' birthday parties." When he made no response, she sat bolt upright. "Oh God, Luke."

"It's not that bad. It's just . . . well, the other day when I took Nate to nursery school, I sort of got into this conversation with his teacher. I guess I promised we'd do this little act for the Christmas party."

There was silence for a full minute, then she began to laugh. She laughed until she had to hold her sides to keep her ribs intact. He was perfect, she realized. Absolutely perfect. And absolutely hers.

"I love you." She surprised him by throwing her arms around his neck and kissing him hard and long. "I love who you turned out to be."

"Same goes. Want to neck in the moonlight?"

"You bet I do." She pressed a finger to his lips before they met hers. "One warning, Callahan. If you go out and buy a station wagon, I'm turning you into a frog."

He kissed her finger, then her mouth, deciding he'd wait for a more opportune moment to mention the Buick he'd put a deposit on that morning.

As Max would have said, timing was everything.

Private Scandals

To Pop

Part One

"'The time has come,' the Walrus said,
'to talk of many things.'"
—Lewis Carroll

Chicago, 1994

It was a moonless midnight in Chicago, but to Deanna, the moment had all the makings of *High Noon.* It was easy to see herself in the quietly dignified, stalwart Gary Cooper role, preparing to face down the canny, vengeance-seeking gunslinger.

But damn it, Deanna thought, Chicago was *her* town. Angela was the outsider.

It suited Angela's sense of the dramatic, Deanna supposed, to demand a showdown in the very studio where they both had climbed ambition's slippery ladder. But it was Deanna's studio now, and it was *her* show that garnered the lion's share of the ratings points. There was nothing Angela could do to change that, short of conjuring up Elvis from the grave and asking him to sing "Heartbreak Hotel" to the studio audience.

A ghost of a smile flitted around Deanna's lips at the image, but there wasn't much humor in it. Angela was nothing if not a worthy opponent. Over the years she had used gruesome tactics to keep her daily talk show on top.

But whatever Angela had up her sleeve this time wasn't going to work. She had underestimated Deanna Reynolds. Angela could whisper secrets and threaten scandal all she wanted, but nothing she could say would change Deanna's plans.

She would, however, hear Angela out. Deanna thought she would even attempt, one last time, to compromise. To offer, if not friendship, at least a cautious truce. There was little hope the breach could be spanned after all this time and all the hostility, but hope, to Deanna's mind, sprang eternal.

At least until it dried up.

Focusing on the matter at hand, Deanna pulled into the CBC Building's parking lot. During the day, the lot would be crammed with cars—technicians, editors, producers, talent, secretaries, interns. Deanna would be dropped off and picked up by her driver, avoiding the hassle. Inside the great white building, people would be rushing to put out the news—at seven A.M., noon and five and ten P.M.—and *Let's Cook!* with Bobby Marks, the weekly *In Depth* with Finn Riley, and the top-rated talk show in the country, *Deanna's Hour.*

But now, just after midnight, the lot was nearly empty. There were half a dozen cars belonging to the skeleton crew who were loitering in the newsroom, waiting for something to happen somewhere in the world. Probably hoping any new wars would wait to erupt until the lonely night shift ended.

Wishing she were somewhere else, anywhere else, Deanna pulled into an empty space and shut off the engine. For a moment she simply sat, listening to the night, the swish of cars on the street to the left, the rumble of the huge air-conditioning system that kept the building and the expensive equipment cool. She had to get a handle on her mixed emotions and her nerves before she faced Angela.

Nerves were second nature in the profession she'd chosen. She would work with them, or through them. Her temper was something she could and would control, particularly if losing it would accomplish nothing. But those emotions, the ones that ran so strong and so contradictory, were another matter. Even after all this time, it was difficult to forget that the woman she was about to face was one she had once admired and respected.

From bitter experience Deanna knew that Angela was an expert in emotional manipulation. Deanna's problem—and many said her talent—was an inability to hide her feelings. They were there, up front, shouting to anyone who cared to listen. Whatever she felt was mirrored in her gray eyes, broadcast in the tilt of her head or the expression of her mouth. Some said that's what made her irresistible, and dangerous. With a flick of her wrist, she turned the rearview mirror toward her. Yes, she mused, she could see the sparks of temper in her own eyes, and the simmering resentment, the dragging regret. After all, she and Angela had been friends once. Or almost friends.

But she could also see the pleasure of anticipation. That was a matter of pride. This bout had been a long time coming.

Smiling a little, Deanna took out a tube of lipstick and carefully painted her mouth. You didn't go one-on-one with your arch rival without the most basic of shields. Pleased that her hand was rock steady, she dropped the lipstick back in her purse, climbed out of the car. She stood a moment, breathing in the balmy night while she asked herself one question.

Calm, Deanna?

Nope, she thought. What she was, was revved. If the energy was fueled by nerves, it didn't matter. Slamming the car door behind her, she strode across the lot. She slipped her plastic ID out of her pocket and punched it into the security slot beside the rear door. Seconds later, a little green light blipped, allowing her to depress the handle and pull the heavy door open.

She flicked the switch to light the stairway, and let the door ease shut behind her.

She found it interesting that Angela hadn't arrived before her. She'd have taken a car service, Deanna thought. Now that Angela was settled in New York, she no longer had a regular driver in Chicago. It surprised Deanna that she hadn't seen a limo waiting in the lot.

Angela was always, always on time.

It was one of the many things Deanna respected about her.

The click of Deanna's heels on the stairs echoed hollowly as she descended a level. As she slipped her card in the next security slot, she wondered briefly who Angela had bribed, threatened or seduced to gain entry to the studio.

Not so many years before, Deanna had rushed down that same route, wide-eyed and enthusiastic, running errands at the snap of Angela's demanding fingers. She'd been ready to preen like an eager puppy for any sign of approval. But, like any smart pup, she'd learned.

And when betrayal had come, with its keen-edged disillusionment, she might have whimpered, but she'd licked her wounds and had used everything she'd learned—until the student became the master.

It shouldn't have surprised her to discover how quickly old resentments, long cooled, could come rolling to a boil. And this time, Deanna thought, this time when she faced Angela, it would be on her own turf, under her own rules. The naive kid from Kansas was more than ready to flex the muscles of realized ambition.

And perhaps once she did, they would finally clear the air. Meet on equal terms. If it wasn't possible to forget what had happened between them in the past, it was always possible to accept and move on.

Deanna slipped her card into the slot beside the studio doors. The light blinked green. She pushed inside, into darkness.

The studio was empty.

That pleased her. Arriving first gave her one more advantage, as a hostess escorting an unwelcome guest into her home. And if home was where you grew from girl to woman, where you learned and squabbled, the studio was home.

Smiling a little, Deanna reached out in the dark for the switch that controlled a bank of overhead lights. She thought she heard something, some whisper that barely disturbed the air. And a feeling stabbed through that fine sense of anticipation. A feeling that she was not alone.

Angela, she thought, and flicked the switch.

But as the overhead lights flashed on, brighter ones, blinding ones, exploded inside her head. As the pain ripped through them, she plunged back into the dark.

She crawled back into consciousness, moaning. Her head heavy with pain, lolled back against a chair. Groggy, disoriented, she lifted a hand to the worst of the ache. Her fingers came away lightly smeared with blood.

She struggled to focus, baffled to find herself sitting in her own chair, on her own set. Had she missed a cue? she wondered, dizzy, staring back at the camera where the red light gleamed.

But there was no studio audience beyond the camera, no technicians working busily out of range. Though the lights flooded down with the familiar heat, there was no show in progress.

She'd come to meet Angela, Deanna remembered.

Her vision wavered again, like water disturbed by a pebble, and she blinked to clear it. It was then her gaze latched on to the two images on the monitor. She saw herself, pale and glazed-eyed. Then she saw, with horror, the guest sitting in the chair beside hers.

Angela, her pink silk suit decorated with pearl buttons. Matching strands of pearls around her throat, clustered at her ears. Angela, her golden hair softly coiffed, her legs crossed, her hands folded together over the right arm of the chair.

It was Angela. Oh yes, there was no mistaking it. Even though her face had been destroyed.

Blood was splattered over the pink silk and joined by more that ran almost leisurely down from where that lovely, canny face should be.

It was then Deanna began to scream.

1

Chicago, 1990

In five, four, three...

Deanna smiled at the camera from her corner of the set of *Midday News.* "Our guest this afternoon is Jonathan Monroe, a local author who has just published a book titled *I Want Mine.*" She lifted the slim volume from the small round table between the chairs, angling it toward Camera Two. "Jonathan, you've subtitled this book *Healthy Selfishness.* What inspired you to write about a trait most people consider a character flaw?"

"Well, Deanna." He chuckled, a small man with a sunny smile who was sweating profusely under the lights. "I wanted mine."

Good answer, she thought, but it was obvious he wasn't going to elaborate without a little prompting. "And who doesn't, if we're honest?" she said, trying to loosen him up with a sense of comradeship. "Jonathan, you state in your book that this healthy selfishness is quashed by parents and cargivers, right from the nursery."

"Exactly." His frozen, brilliant smile remained fixed while his eyes darted in panic.

Deanna shifted subtly, laying her hand over his rigid fingers just under camera range. Her eyes radiated interest, her touch communicated support. "You believe the demand of adults that children share toys sets an unnatural precedent." She gave his hand an encouraging squeeze. "Don't you feel that sharing is a basic form of courtesy?"

"Not at all." And he began to tell her why. Though his explanations were delivered in fits and starts, she was able to smooth over the awkwardness, guiding him through the three-minute-fifteen-second spot.

"That's *I Want Mine,* by Jonathan Monroe," she said to the camera, winding up. "Available in your bookstores now. Thank you so much for joining us today, Jonathan."

"It was a pleasure. As a side note, I'm currently working on my second book, *Get Out of My Way, I Was Here First.* It's about healthy aggression."

"Best of luck with it. We'll be back in a moment with the rest of the *Midday News.*" Once they were into commercial, she smiled at Jonathan. "You were great. I appreciate your coming in."

"I hope I did okay." The minute his mike was removed, Jonathan whipped out a handkerchief to mop his brow. "First time on TV."

"You did fine. I think this will generate a lot of local interest in your book."

"Really?"

"Absolutely. Would you mind signing this for me?"

Beaming again, he took the book and pen she offered. "You sure made it easy, Deanna. I did a radio interview this morning. The DJ hadn't even read the back blurb."

She took the autographed book, rising. Part of her mind, most of her energy, was already at the news desk across the studio. "That makes it hard on everyone. Thanks again," she said, offering her hand. "I hope you'll come back with your next book."

"I'd love to." But she'd already walked away, maneuvering nimbly over snaking piles of cable to take her place behind the counter on the news set. After slipping the book under the counter, she hooked her mike to the lapel of her red suit.

"Another screwball." The comment from her co-anchor, Roger Crowell, was typical.

"He was very nice."

"You think everyone's very nice." Grinning, Roger checked his hand mirror, gave his tie a minute adjustment. He had a good face for the camera—mature, trustworthy, with distinguished flecks of gray at the temples of his rust-colored hair. "Especially the screwballs."

"That's why I love you, Rog."

This caused snickering among the camera crew. Whatever response Roger might have made was cut off by the floor director signaling time. While the TelePrompTer rolled, Roger smiled into the camera, setting the tone for a soft segment on the birth of twin tigers at the zoo.

"That's all for *Midday*. Stay tuned for *Let's Cook*! This is Roger Crowell."

"And Deanna Reynolds. See you tomorrow."

As the closing music tinkled in her earpiece, Deanna turned to smile at Roger.

"You're a softy, pal. You wrote that piece on the baby tigers yourself. It had your fingerprints all over it."

He flushed a little, but winked. "Just giving them what they want, babe."

"And we're clear." The floor director stretched his shoulders. "Nice show, people."

"Thanks, Jack." Deanna was already unhooking her mike.

"Hey, want to get some lunch?" Roger was always ready to eat, and countered his love affair with food with his personal trainer. There was no disguising pounds from the merciless eye of the camera.

"Can't. I've got an assignment."

Roger rose. Beneath his impeccable blue serge jacket, he wore a pair of eye-popping Bermuda shorts. "Don't tell me it's for the terror of Studio B."

The faintest flicker of annoyance clouded her eyes. "Okay, I won't."

"Hey, Dee." Roger caught up with her on the edge of the set. "Don't get mad."

"I didn't say I was mad."

"You don't have to." They walked down the single wide step from the glossy set to the scarred wood floor, skirting around camera and cable. They pushed through the studio doors together. "You are mad. It shows. You you get that line between your eyebrows. Look." He pulled her by the arm into the makeup room. After flicking on the lights, he stood behind her, his hands on her shoulders as they faced the mirror. "See, it's still there."

Deliberately, she eased it away with a smile. "I don't see anything."

"Then let me tell you what I see. Every man's dream of the girl next door. Subtle, wholesome sex." When she scowled, he only grinned. "That's the visual, kid. Those big, trust-me eyes and peaches and cream. Not bad qualities for a television reporter."

"How about intelligence?" she countered. "Writing ability, guts."

"We're talking visuals." His smile flashed, deepening the character lines around his eyes. No one in television would dare refer to them as wrinkles. "Look, my last co-anchor was a Twinkie. All blow-dried hair and bonded teeth. She was more worried about her eyelashes than she was punching the lead."

"And now she's reading the news at the number-two station in LA." She knew how the business worked. Oh yes, she did. But she didn't have to like it. "Rumors are, she's being groomed for network."

"That's the game. Personally, I appreciate having someone at the desk with a brain, but let's not forget what we are."

"I thought we were journalists."

"*Television* journalists. You've got a face that was made for the camera, and it tells everything you're thinking, everything you're feeling. Only problem is, it's the same off camera, and that makes you vulnerable. A woman like Angela eats little farm girls like you for breakfast."

"I didn't grow up on a farm." Her voice was dry as a Midwest dust bowl.

"Might as well have." He gave her shoulders a friendly squeeze. "Who's your pal, Dee?"

She sighed, rolled her eyes. "You are, Roger."

"Watch your back with Angela."

"Look, I know she has a reputation for being temperamental—"

"She has a reputation for being a stone bitch."

Stepping away from Roger, Deanna uncapped a pot of cold cream to remove her heavy makeup. She didn't like having her coworkers pined against one another, competing for her time, and she didn't like feeling pressured into choosing between them. It had been difficult enough juggling her responsibilities in the newsroom and on set with the favors she did for Angela. And they were only favors, after all. Done primarily on her own time.

"All I know is that she's been nothing but kind to me. She liked my work on *Midday* and the 'Deanna's Corner' segment and offered to help me refine my style."

"She's using you."

"She's teaching me," Deanna corrected, tossing used makeup pads aside. Her movements were quick and practiced. She hit the center of the wastebasket as consistently as a veteran free-throw shooter. "There's a reason Angela has the top-rated talk show in the market. It would have taken me years to learn the ins and outs of the business I've picked up from her in a matter of months."

"And do you really think she's going to share a piece of that pie?"

She pouted a moment because, of course, she wanted a piece. A nice big one. *Healthy selfishness,* she thought, and chuckled to herself. "It's not as though I'm competing with her."

"Not yet." But she would be, he knew. It surprised him that Angela didn't detect the ambition glinting just behind Deanna's eyes. But then, he mused, ego was often blinding. He had reason to know. "Just some friendly advice. Don't give her any ammunition." He took one last study as Deanna briskly redid her makeup for the street. She might have been naive, he mused, but she was also stubborn. He could see it in the way her mouth was set, the angle of her chin. "I've got a couple of bumpers to tape." He tugged on her hair. "See you tomorrow."

"Yeah." Once she was alone, Deanna tapped her eye pencil against the makeup table. She didn't discount everything Roger said. Because she was a perfectionist, because she demanded, and received, the best for her show, Angela Perkins had a reputation for being hard. And it certainly paid off. After six years in syndication, *Angela's* had been in the number-one spot for more than three.

Since both *Angela's* and *Midday News* were taped at the CBC studios, Angela had been able to exert a little pressure to free up some of Deanna's time.

It was also true that Angela had been nothing but kind to Deanna. She had shown Deanna a friendship and a willingness to share that were rare in the highly competitive world of television.

Was it naive to trust kindness? Deanna didn't think so. Nor was she foolish enough to believe that kindness was always rewarded.

Thoughtfully, she picked up the brush marked with her name and pulled it through her shoulder-length black hair. Without the cover of heavy theatrical makeup necessary for the lights and camera, her skin was as elegantly pale as porcelain, a dramatic contrast to the inky mane of hair and the smoky, slightly slanted eyes. To add another touch of drama, she'd painted her lips a deep rose.

Satisfied, she pulled her hair back in a ponytail with two quick flicks of her wrist.

She never planned to compete with Angela. Although she hoped to use what she learned to boost her own career, what she wanted was a network spot, someday. Maybe a job on 20/20. And it wasn't beyond the realm of possibility that she could expand the weekly "Deanna's Corner" segment on the noon news into a full-fledged syndicated talk show of her own. Even that would hardly be competing with Angela, the queen of the market.

The nineties were wide open for all manner of styles and shows. If she succeeded, it would be because she'd learned from the master. She would always be grateful to Angela for that.

"If the son of a bitch thinks I'm going to roll over, he's in for an unpleasant surprise." Angela Perkins glared at the reflection of her producer in her dressing room mirror. "He agreed to come on the show to hype his new album. Tit for tat, Lew. We're giving him national exposure, so he's damn well going to answer some questions about his tax evasion charges."

"He didn't say he wouldn't answer them, Angela." The headache behind Lew McNeil's eyes was still dull enough to keep him hoping it would pass. "He just said he won't be able to be specific as long as the case is pending. He'd like it if you would concentrate on his career."

"I wouldn't be where I am if I let a guest dictate my show, would I?" She swore again, ripely, then wheeled in the chair to snarl at the hairdresser. "Pull my hair again, sweetie, and you'll be picking up curlers with your teeth."

"I'm sorry, Miss Perkins, but your hair is really too short..."

"Just get it done." Angela faced her own reflection again, and deliberately relaxed her features. She knew how important it was to relax the facial muscles before a show, no matter how high the adrenaline. The camera picked up every line and wrinkle, like an old friend a woman meets for lunch. So she breathed deeply, closing her eyes a moment in a signal to her producer to hold his tongue. When she opened them again, they were clear, a diamond bright blue surrounded by silky lashes.

And she smiled as the hairdresser swept her hair back and up into a wavy blond halo. It was a good look for her, Angela decided. Sophisticated but not threatening. Chic but not studied. She checked the style from every angle before giving the go-ahead nod.

"It looks great, Marcie." She flashed the high-powered smile that made the hairdresser forget the earlier threat. "I feel ten years younger."

"You look wonderful, Miss Perkins."

"Thanks to you." Relaxed and satisfied, she toyed with the trademark pearls around her throat. "And how's that new man in your life, Marcie? Is he treating you well?"

"He's terrific." Marcie grinned as she gave Angela's hair a large dose of spray to hold the style. "I think he might be the one."

"Good for you. If he gives you any trouble, you let me know." She winked. "I'll straighten him out."

With a laugh, Marcie backed away. "Thanks, Miss Perkins. Good luck this morning."

"Mmm-hmmm. Now, Lew." She smiled and lifted a hand for his. The squeeze was encouraging, feminine, friendly. "Don't worry about a thing. You just keep our guest happy until airtime. I'll take care of the rest."

"He wants your word, Angela."

"Honey, you give him whatever he wants." She laughed; Lew's headache sprang into full-blown agony. "Don't be such a worrier." She leaned forward to pluck a cigarette from the pack of Virginia Slims on the dressing table. She flicked on a gold monogrammed lighter, a gift from her second husband. She blew out one thin stream of smoke.

Lew was getting soft, she mused, personally as well as professionally. Though he wore a suit and tie, as dictated by her dress code, his shoulders were slumped as if pulled down by the weight of his expanding belly. His hair was thinning out, too, she realized, and was heavily streaked with gray. Her show was known for its energy and speed. She didn't enjoy having her producer look like a pudgy old man.

"After all these years, Lew, you should trust me."

"Angela, if you attack Deke Barrow, you're going to make it tough for us to book other celebrities."

"Bull. They're six deep waiting for a chance to do my show." She jabbed her cigarette in the air like a lance. "They want me to hype their movies and their TV specials and their books and their records, and they damn well want me to hype their love lives. They need me, Lew, because they know that every day millions of people tune in." She smiled into the mirror, and the face that smiled back was lovely, composed, polished. "And they tune in for me."

Lew had worked with Angela for more than five years and knew exactly how to handle a dispute. He wheeled. "Nobody's denying that, Angela. You are the show. I just think you should tread lightly with Deke. He's been around the country-music scene a long time, and this comeback of his has a lot of sentiment behind him."

"Just leave Deke to me." She smiled behind a mist of smoke. "I'll be very sentimental."

She picked up the note cards that Deanna had finished organizing at seven that morning. It was a gesture of dismissal that had Lew shaking his head. Angela's smile widened as she skimmed through the notes. The girl was good, she mused. Very good, very thorough.

Very useful.

Angela took one last contemplative drag on her cigarette before crushing it out in the heavy crystal ashtray on her dressing table. As always, every pot, every brush, every tube was aligned in meticulous order. There was a vase of two dozen red roses, which were brought in fresh every morning, and a small dish of multicolored coated mints that Angela loved.

She thrived on routine, at being able to control her environment, including the people around her. Everyone had their place. She was enjoying making one for Deanna Reynolds.

Some might have thought it odd that a woman approaching forty, a vain woman, would have taken on a younger, lovely woman as a favored apprentice. But Angela had been a pretty woman who with time, experience and illusion had become a beautiful one. And she had no fear of age. Not in a world where it could be so easily combated.

She wanted Deanna behind her because of her looks, because of her talent, because of her youth. Most of all, because power scented power.

And for the very simple reason that she liked the girl.

Oh, she would offer Deanna tidbits of advice, friendly criticism, dollops of praise—and perhaps, in time, a position of some merit. But she had no intention of allowing someone she already sensed as a potential competitor to break free. No one broke free from Angela Perkins.

She had two ex-husbands who had learned that. They hadn't broken free. They had been dispatched.

"Angela?"

"Deanna." Angela flung out a hand in welcome. "I was just thinking about you. Your notes are wonderful. They'll add so much to the show."

"Glad I could help." Deanna lifted a hand to toy with her left earring, a sign of hesitation she'd yet to master. "Angela, I feel awkward asking you this, but my mother is a huge fan of Deke Barrow's."

"And you'd like an autograph."

After a quick, embarrassed smile, Deanna brought out the CD she was holding behind her back. "She'd love it if he could sign this for her."

"You just leave it to me." Angela tapped one perfect, French-manicured nail along the edge of the CD. "And what is your mother's name again, Dee?"

"It's Marilyn. I really appreciate it, Angela."

"Anything I can do for you, sweetie." She waited a beat. Her timing had always been excellent. "Oh, and there is a little favor you could do for me."

"Of course."

"Would you make reservations for dinner for me tonight, at La Fontaine, seven-thirty, for two? I simply don't have time to deal with it myself, and I forgot to tell my secretary to handle it."

"No problem." Deanna pulled a pad out of her pocket to make a note.

"You're a treasure, Deanna." Angela stood then to take a final check of her pale blue suit in a cheval glass. "What do you think of this color? It's not too washed-out, is it?"

Because she knew that Angela fretted over every detail of the show, from research to the proper footwear, Deanna took time for a serious study. The soft drape of the fabric suited Angela's compact, curvy figure beautifully. "Coolly feminine."

The tension in Angela's shoulders unknotted. "Perfect, then. Are you staying for the taping?"

"I can't. I still have copy to write for *Midday.*"

"Oh." The annoyance surfaced, but only briefly. "I hope helping me out hasn't put you behind."

"There are twenty-four hours in the day," Deanna said. "I like to use all of them. Now, I'd better get out of your way."

" 'Bye, honey."

Deanna shut the door behind her. Everyone in the building knew that Angela insisted on having the last ten minutes before she took the stage to herself. Everyone assumed she used that time to go over her notes. That was nonsense, of course. She was completely prepared. But she preferred that they think of her brushing up on her information. Or even that they imagine her taking a quick nip from the bottle of brandy she kept in her dressing table.

Not that she would touch the brandy. The need to keep it there, just within reach, terrified as much as it comforted.

She preferred they believe anything, as long as they didn't know the truth.

Angela Perkins spent those last solitary moments before each taping in a trembling cycle of panic. She, a woman who exuded an image of supreme self-confidence; she, a woman who had interviewed presidents, royalty, murderers and millionaires, succumbed, as she always did, to a vicious, violent attack of stage fright.

Hundreds of hours of therapy had done nothing to alleviate the shuddering, the sweating, the nausea. Helpless against it, she collapsed in her chair, drawing herself in. The mirror reflected her in triplicate, the polished woman, perfectly groomed, immaculately presented. Eyes glazed with the terror of self-discovery.

Angela pressed her hands to her temples and rode out the screaming roller coaster of fear. Today she would slip, and they would hear the backwoods of Arkansas in her voice. They would see the girl who had been unloved and unwanted by a mother who had preferred the flickering images on the pitted screen of the tiny Philco to her own flesh and blood. The girl who had wanted attention so badly, so desperately, she had imagined herself inside that television so that her mother would focus those vague, drunken eyes just once, and look at her.

They would see the girl in the secondhand clothes and ill-fitting shoes who had studied so hard to make average grades.

They would see that she was nothing, no one, a fraud who had bluffed her way into television the same way her father had bluffed his way into an inside straight.

And they would laugh at her.

Or worse, turn her off.

The knock on the door made her flinch.

"We're set, Angela."

She took a deep breath, then another. "On my way." Her voice was perfectly normal. She was a master at pretense. For a few seconds longer, she stared at her reflection, watching the panic fade from her own eyes.

She wouldn't fail. She would never be laughed at. She would never be ignored again. And no one would see anything she didn't allow them to see. She rose, walked out of her dressing room, down the corridor.

She had yet to see her guest and continued past the green room without a blink. She never spoke to a guest before the tape was rolling.

Her producer was warming up the studio audience. There was a hum of excitement from those fortunate enough to have secured tickets to the taping. Marcie, tottering in four-inch heels, rushed up for a last-minute check on hair and makeup. A researcher passed Angela a few more cards. Angela spoke to neither of them.

When she walked onstage, the hum burst open into a full-throttle cheer.

"Good morning." Angela took her chair and let the applause wash over her while she was miked. "I hope everyone's ready for a great show." She scanned the audience as she spoke and was pleased with the demographics. It was a good mix of age, sex and race—an important visual for the camera pans. "Anyone here a Deke Barrow fan?"

She laughed heartily at the next round of applause. "Me too," she said, though she detested country music in any form. "I'd say we're all in for a treat."

She nodded, settled back, legs crossed, hands folded over the arm of her chair. The red light on the camera blinked on. The intro music swung jazzily through the air.

" 'Lost Tomorrows,' 'That Green-Eyed Girl,' 'One Wild Heart.' Those are just a few of the hits that made today's guest a legend. He's been a part of country-music history for more than twenty-five years, and his current album, *Lost in Nashville,* is zooming up the charts. Please join me in welcoming, to Chicago, Deke Barrow."

The applause thundered out again as Deke strode out onstage. Barrel-chested, with graying temples peeking out from beneath his black felt Stetson, Deke grinned at the audience before accepting Angela's warm handshake. She stood back, letting him milk the moment by tipping his hat.

With every appearance of delight, she joined in the audience's standing ovation. By the end of the hour, she thought, Deke would stagger offstage. And he wouldn't even know what had hit him.

Angela waited until the second half of the show to strike. Like a good host, she had flattered her guest, listened attentively to his anecdotes, chuckled at his jokes. Now Deke was basking in the admiration as Angela held the mike for excited fans as they stood to ask questions. She waited, canny as a cobra.

"Deke, I wondered if you're going by Danville, Kentucky, on your tour. That's my hometown," a blushing redhead asked.

"Well now, I can't say as we are. But we'll be in Louisville on the seventeenth of June. You be sure to tell your friends to come on by and see me."

"Your *Lost in Nashville* tour's going to keep you on the road for several months," Angela began. "That's rough on you, isn't it?"

"Rougher than it used to be," he answered with a wink. "I ain't twenty anymore." His broad, guitar-plucking hands lifted and spread. "But I gotta say I love it. Singing in a recording studio can't come close to what it's like to sing for people."

"And the tour's certainly been a success so far. There's no truth, then, to the rumor that you may have to cut it short because of your difficulties with the IRS?"

Deke's congenial grin slipped several notches. "No, ma'am. We'll finish it out."

"I feel safe in speaking for everyone here when I say you have our support in this. Tax evasion." She rolled her eyes in disbelief. "They make you sound like Al Capone."

"I really can't talk about it." Deke shuffled his booted feet, tugged at his bola tie. "But nobody's calling it tax evasion."

"Oh." She widened her eyes. "I'm sorry. What are they calling it?"

He shifted uncomfortably on his chair. "It's a disagreement on back taxes."

" 'Disagreement' is a mild word for it. I realize you can't really discuss this while the matter's under investigation, but I think it's an outrage. A man like you, who's brought pleasure to millions, for two generations, to be faced with potential financial ruin because his books weren't in perfect order."

"It's not as bad as all that—"

"But you've had to put your home in Nashville on the market." Her voice dripped sympathy. Her eyes gleamed with it. "I think the country you've celebrated in your music should show more compassion, more gratitude. Don't you?"

She hit the right button.

"Seems like the tax man doesn't have much to do with the country I've been singing about for twenty-five years." Deke's mouth thinned, his eyes hardened like agates. "They look at dollar signs. They don't think about how hard a man's worked. How much he sweats to make something of himself. They just keep slicing at you till most of what's yours is theirs. They turn honest folk into liars and cheaters."

"You're not saying you cheated on your taxes, are you, Deke?" She smiled guilelessly when he froze. "We'll be back in a moment," she said to the camera, and waited until the red light blinked off. "I'm sure most of us here have been squeezed by the IRS, Deke." Turning her back on him, she held up her hands. "We're behind him, aren't we, audience?"

There was an explosion of applause and cheers that did nothing to erase the look of sickly shock from Deke's face.

"I can't talk about it," he managed. "Can I get some water?"

"We'll put the matter to rest, don't you worry. We'll have time for a few more questions." Angela turned to her audience again as an assistant rushed out with a glass of water for Deke. "I'm sure Deke would appreciate it if we avoided any more discussion on this sensitive subject. Let's be sure to give him plenty of applause when we get back from commercial, and give Deke some time to compose himself."

With this outpouring of support and empathy, she swung back toward the camera. "You're back with *Angela's*. We have time for just a couple more questions, but at Deke's request, we'll close the door on any discussion of his tax situation, as he isn't free to defend himself while the case is still pending."

And of course, when she closed the show moments later, that was exactly the subject on every viewer's mind.

2

Deanna hated covering tragedies. Intellectually she knew it was her job as a journalist to report the news, and to interview those who had been wounded by it. She believed, unwaveringly, in the public's right to know. But emotionally, whenever she pointed a microphone toward grief she felt like the worst kind of voyeur.

"The quiet suburb of Wood Dale was the scene of sudden and violent tragedy this morning. Police suspect that a domestic dispute resulted in the shooting death of Lois Dossier, thirty-two, an elementary school teacher and Chicago native. Her husband, Dr. Charles Dossier, has been taken into custody. The couple's two children, ages five and seven, are in the care of their maternal grandparents. At shortly after eight A.M. this morning, this quiet, affluent home erupted with gunfire."

Deanna steadied herself as the camera panned the trim two-story dwelling behind her. She continued her report, staring straight at the lens, ignoring the crowd that gathered, the other news teams doing their stand-ups, the sweet spring breeze that carried the poignant scent of hyacinth.

Her voice was steady, suitably detached. But her eyes were filled with swirling emotion.

"At eight-fifteen A.M., police responded to reports of gunfire, and Lois Dossier was pronounced dead on the scene. According to neighbors, Mrs. Dossier was a devoted mother who took an active interest in community projects. She was well liked and well respected. Among her closest friends was her next-door neighbor, Bess Pierson, who reported the disturbance to the police." Deanna turned to the woman at her side, who was dressed in purple sweats. "Mrs. Pierson, to your knowledge, was there any violence in the Dossier household before this morning?"

"Yes—no. I never thought he would hurt her. I still can't believe it." The camera zoomed in on the swollen, tear-streaked face of a woman pale with shock. "She was my closest friend. We've lived next door to each other for six years. Our children play together."

Tears began to spill over. Despising herself, Deanna clutched the woman's hand with her free one, and continued. "Knowing both Lois and Charles Dossier, do you agree with the police that this tragedy was a result of a domestic dispute that spiraled out of control?"

"I don't know what to think. I know they were having marital problems. There were fights, shouting matches." The woman stared into the void, shell-shocked. "Lois told me she wanted to get Chuck to go into counseling with her, but he wouldn't." She began to sob now, one hand covering her eyes. "He wouldn't, and now she's gone. Oh God, she was like my sister."

"Cut," Deanna snapped, then wrapped her arm around Mrs. Pierson's shoulders. "I'm sorry. I'm so sorry. You shouldn't be out here now."

"I keep thinking this is a dream. That it can't be real."

"Is there somewhere you can go? A friend or a relative?" Deanna scanned the trim yard, crowded with curious neighbors and determined reporters. A few feet to the left another crew was rolling tape. The reporter kept blowing the takes, laughing at his own twisting tongue. "Things aren't going to quiet down here for a while."

"Yes." After a last, sobbing breath, Mrs. Pierson wiped at her eyes. "We were going to the movies tonight," she said, then turned and dashed away.

"God." Deanna watched as other reporters stabbed their microphones toward the fleeing woman.

"Your heart bleeds too much," her cameraman commented.

"Shut up, Joe." She pulled herself in, drew a breath. Her heart might have been bleeding, but she couldn't let it affect her judgment. Her job was to give a clear, concise report, to inform and to give the viewer a visual that would make an impact.

"Let's finish it. We want it for *Midday*. Zoom up to the bedroom window, then come back to me. Make sure you get the hyacinths and daffodils in frame, and the kid's red wagon. Got it?"

Joe studied the scene, the White Sox fielder's cap perched on his wiry brown hair tipped down to shade his eyes. He could already see the pictures, cut, framed, edited. He squinted, nodded. Muscles bunched under his sweatshirt as he hefted the camera. "Ready when you are."

"Then in three, two, one." She waited a beat while the camera zoomed in, panned down. "Lois Dossier's violent death has left this quiet community rocked. While her friends and family ask why, Dr. Charles Dossier is being held pending bond. This is Deanna Reynolds in Wood Dale, reporting for CBC."

"Nice job, Deanna." Joe shut down the camera.

"Yeah, dandy." On her way to the van, she put two Rolaids in her mouth.

CBC used the tape again on the local portion of the evening news, with an update from the precinct where Dossier was being held on charges of second-degree murder. Curled in a chair in her apartment, Deanna watched objectively as the anchor segued from the top story into a piece on a fire in a South Side apartment building.

"Good piece, Dee." Sprawled on the couch was Fran Myers. Her curly red hair was lopsidedly anchored on top of her head. She had a sharp, foxy face accented by eyes the color of chestnuts. Her voice was pure New Jersey brass. Unlike Deanna, she hadn't grown up in a quiet suburban home in a tree-lined neighborhood, but in a noisy apartment in Atlantic City, New Jersey, with a twice-divorced mother and a changing array of step-siblings.

She sipped ginger ale, then gestured with her glass toward the screen. The movement was as lazy as a yawn. "You always look so great on camera. Video makes me look like a pudgy gnome."

"I had to try to interview the victim's mother." Jamming her hands in the pockets of her jeans, Deanna sprang up to pace the room, wiry energy in every step. "She wouldn't answer the phone, and like a good reporter, I tracked down the address. They wouldn't answer the door, either. Kept the curtains drawn. I stayed outside with a bunch of other members of the press for nearly an hour. I felt like a ghoul."

"You ought to know by now that the terms 'ghoul' and 'reporter' are interchangeable." But Deanna didn't smile. Fran recognized the guilt beneath the restless movements. After setting down her glass, Fran pointed to the chair. "Okay. Sit down and listen to advice from Auntie Fran."

"I can't take advice standing up?"

"Nope." Fran snagged Deanna's hand and yanked her down onto the sofa. Despite the contrasts in backgrounds and styles, they'd been friends since freshman orientation in college. Fran had seen Deanna wage this war between intellect and emotion dozens of times. "Okay. Question number one: Why did you go to Yale?"

"Because I got a scholarship."

"Don't rub your brains in my face, Einstein. What did you and I go to college for?"

"You went to meet men."

Fran narrowed her eyes. "That was just a side benefit. Stop stalling and answer the question."

Defeated, Deanna let out a sigh. "We went to study, to become journalists, to get high-paying, high-profile jobs on television."

"Absolutely correct. And have we succeeded?"

"Sort of. We have our degrees. I'm a reporter for CBC and you're associate producer of *Woman Talk* on cable."

"Excellent launching points. Now, have you forgotten the famous Deanna Reynolds's Five-Year Plan? If so, I'm sure there's a typed copy of it in that desk."

Deanna glanced over at her pride and joy, the single fine piece of furniture she'd acquired since moving to Chicago. She'd picked up the beautifully patinated Queen Anne desk at an auction. And Fran was right. There was a typed copy of Deanna's career plan in the top drawer. In duplicate.

Since college, she had modified her plans somewhat. Fran had married and settled in Chicago and had urged her former roommate to come out and try her luck.

"Year One," Deanna remembered. "An on-camera job in Kansas City."

"Done."

"Year Two, a position at CBC, Chicago."

"Accomplished."

"Year Three, a small, tasteful segment of my own."

"The current 'Deanna's Corner,' " Fran said, and toasted the segment with her ginger ale.

"Year Four, anchoring the evening news. Local."

"Which you've already done, several times, as substitute."

"Year Five, audition tapes and résumés to the holy ground: New York."

"Which will never be able to resist your combination of style, on-camera appeal and sincerity—unless, of course, you continue to second-guess yourself."

"You're right, but—"

"No buts." On this Fran was firm. She expended some of the energy she preferred to hoard by propping her feet on the coffee table. "You do good work, Dee. People talk to you because you have compassion. That's an advantage in a journalist, not a flaw."

"It doesn't help me sleep at night." Restless and suddenly tired, Deanna scooped a hand through her hair. After curling her legs up, she studied the room, brooding.

There was the rickety dinette she'd yet to find a suitable replacement for, the frayed rug, the single solid armchair she'd had recovered in a soft gray. Only the desk stood out, gleaming, a testimony to partial success. Yet everything was in its place; the few trinkets she'd collected were arranged precisely.

This tidy apartment wasn't the home of her dreams, but as Fran had pointed out, it was an excellent launching point. And she fully intended to launch herself, both personally and professionally.

"Do you remember, back at college, how exciting we thought it would be to sprint after ambulances, interview mass murderers, to write incisive copy that would rivet the viewers' attention? Well, it is." Letting out a sigh, Deanna rose to pace again. "But you really pay for the kick." She paused a moment, picked up a little china box, set it down again. "Angela's hinted that I could have the job as head researcher on her show for the asking—on-air credit with a significant raise in salary."

Because she didn't want to influence her friend, Fran pursed her lips and kept her voice neutral. "And you're considering it?"

"Every time I do, I remember I'd be giving up the camera." With a half laugh, Deanna shook her head. "I'd miss that little red light. See, here's the thing." She plopped down on the arm of the couch. Her eyes were glowing again, darkened to smoke with suppressed excitement. "I don't want to be Angela's head researcher. I'm not even sure I want New York anymore. I think I want my own show. To be syndicated in a hundred and twenty markets. I want a twenty-percent share. I want to be on the cover of *TV Guide.*"

Fran grinned. "So, what's stopping you?"

"Nothing." More confident now that she'd said it aloud, Deanna shifted, resting her bare feet on the cushion of the sofa. "Maybe that's Year Seven or Eight, I haven't figured it out yet. But I want it, and I can do it. But—" She blew out a breath. "It means covering tears and torment until I've earned my stripes."

"The Deanna Reynolds's Extended Career Plan."

"Exactly." She was glad Fran understood.

"You don't think I'm crazy?"

"Sweet pea, I think that anyone with your meticulous mind, your camera presence and your polite yet strong ambition will get exactly what she wants." Fran reached into the bowl of sugared almonds on the coffee table, popped three in her mouth. "Just don't forget the little people when you do."

"What was your name again?"

Fran threw a pillow at her. "Okay, now that we have your life settled, I'd like to announce an addition to the Fran Myers's My Life Is Never What I Thought It Would Be Saga."

"You got a promotion?"

"Nope."

"Richard got one?"

"No, though a junior partnership at Dowell, Dowell and Fritz may be in the offing." She drew a deep breath. Her redhead's complexion flushed like a blooming rose. "I'm pregnant."

"What?" Deanna blinked. "Pregnant? Really?" Laughing, she slid down on the couch to grasp Fran's hands. "A baby? This is wonderful. This is incredible." Deanna threw her arms around Fran to squeeze, then pulled back sharply to study her friend's face. "Isn't it?"

"You bet it is. We weren't planning on it for another year or two, but hell, it takes nine months, right?"

"Last I heard. You're happy. I can see it. I just can't believe—" She stopped, jerked back again. "Jesus, Fran. You've been here nearly an hour, and you're just getting around to telling me. Talk about burying the lead."

Feeling smug, Fran patted her flat belly. "I wanted everything else out of the way so you could concentrate on me. Us."

"No problem there. Are you sick in the mornings or anything?"

"Me?" Fran quirked a brow. "With my cast-iron stomach?"

"Right. What did Richard say?"

"Before or after he stopped dancing on the ceiling?"

Deanna laughed again, then sprang up to do a quick spin of her own. A baby, she thought. She had to plan a shower, shop for stuffed animals, buy savings bonds. "We have to celebrate."

"What did we do in college when we had something to celebrate?"

"Chinese and cheap white wine," Deanna said with a grin. "Perfect, with the adjustment of Grade A milk."

Fran winced, then shrugged. "I guess I'll have to get used to it. I do have a favor to ask."

"Name it."

"Work on that career plan, Dee. I think I'd like my kid to have a star for a godmommy."

When the phone rang at six A.M., Deanna pulled herself out of sleep and into a hangover. Clutching her head with one hand, she fumbled for the receiver with the other.

"Reynolds."

"Deanna, darling, I'm so sorry to wake you."

"Angela?"

"Who else would be rude enough to call you at this hour?" Angela's light laugh came through the phone as Deanna blearily looked at the clock. "I have an enormous favor to ask. We're taping today, and Lew's down with a virus."

"I'm sorry." Valiantly, Deanna cleared her throat and managed to sit up.

"These things happen. It's just that we're dealing with a sensitive issue today, and when I considered it, I realized you would really be the perfect one to handle the guests offstage. That's Lew's area, you know, so I'm really in a bind."

"What about Simon, or Maureen?" Her brain might have been cloudy, but Deanna remembered the chain of command.

"Neither one of them are suited for this. Simon does excellent pre-interviews over the phone, and God knows Maureen's a jewel at handling transportation and lodging arrangements. But these guests require a very special touch. Your touch."

"I'd be glad to help, Angela, but I'm due in to the station at nine."

"I'll clear it with your producer, dear. He owes me. Simon can handle the second taping, but if you could just see your way clear to helping me out this morning, I'd be so grateful."

"Sure." Deanna shoved her tousled hair back and resigned herself to a quick cup of coffee and a bottle of aspirin. "As long as there's no conflict."

"Don't worry about that. I still have clout with the news department. I'll need you here by eight, sharp. Thanks, honey."

"All right, but—"

Still dazed, Deanna stared at the phone as the dial tone hummed. A couple of details had been overlooked, she mused. What the hell was this morning's topic, and who were the guests that needed such special care?

Deanna stepped into the green room with an uneasy smile on her face and a fresh pot of coffee in her hand. She knew the topic now, and scanned the seven scheduled guests cautiously, like a veteran soldier surveying a mine field.

Marital triangles. Deanna took a bracing breath. Two couples and the other women who had almost destroyed their marriages. A mine field might have been safer.

"Good morning." The room remained ominously silent except for the murmur of the morning news from the television. "I'm Deanna Reynolds. Welcome to *Angela's*. Can I freshen anyone's coffee?"

"Thank you." The man seated in a chair in the corner shifted the open briefcase on his lap, then held out his cup. He gave Deanna a quick smile that was heightened by the amusement glittering out of soft brown eyes. "I'm Dr. Pike. Marshall Pike." He lowered his voice as Deanna topped off his cup. "Don't worry, they're unarmed."

Deanna's eyes lifted to his, held. "They still have teeth and nails," she murmured.

She knew who he was, the segment expert, a psychologist who would attempt to cap this particular can of worms before the roll of ending credits. Mid-thirties, she gauged, with the quick expertise of a cop or a reporter. Confident, relaxed, attractive. Conservative, judging by his carefully trimmed blond hair and well-tailored chalk-striped suit. His wing tips were polished to a high gleam, his nails were manicured and his smile was easy.

"I'll watch your flank," he offered, "if you watch mine."

She smiled back. "Deal. Mr. and Mrs. Forrester?" Deanna paused as the couple glanced toward her. The woman's face was set in a resentful scowl, the man's in miserable embarrassment. "You'll be on first . . . with Miss Draper."

Lori Draper, the last segment of the triangle, beamed with excitement. She looked more like a bouncy cheerleader ready to execute a flashy C jump than a sultry vamp. "Is my outfit okay for TV?"

Over Mrs. Forrester's snort, Deanna assured her it was. "I know the basic procedure was explained to all of you in the pre-interview. The Forresters and Miss Draper will go out first—"

"I don't want to sit next to her." Mrs. Forrester's hiss squeezed through her tightly primmed mouth.

"That won't be a problem—"

"I don't want Jim sitting next to her, either."

Lori Draper rolled her eyes. "Jeez, Shelly, we broke it off months ago. Do you think I'm going to jump him on national TV, or what?"

"I wouldn't put anything past you." Shelly snatched her hand away as her husband tried to pat it. "We're not sitting next to her," she said to Deanna. "And Jim's not going to talk to her, either. Ever."

This statement set the match to the smoldering embers in triangle number two. Before Deanna could open her mouth, everyone was talking at once. Accusations and bitterness flew through the room. Deanna glanced toward Marshall Pike and was greeted with that same easy smile and a lift of one elegant shoulder.

"All right." Deanna pitched her voice over the din as she stepped into the fray. "I'm sure you all have valid points, and quite a bit to say. Why don't we save it for the show? All of you agreed to come on this morning to tell your sides of the story, and to look for some possible resolutions. I'm sure we can arrange the seating to suit everyone."

She ran briskly through the rest of the instructions, controlling the guests in the same way a kindergarten teacher controls recalcitrant five-year-olds. With determined cheerfulness and a firm hand.

"Now, Mrs. Forrester—Shelly—Jim, Lori, if you'll all come with me, we'll get you settled and miked."

Ten minutes later, Deanna stepped back into the green room, grateful that no blood had been spilled. While the remaining triangle sat stonily, staring at the television screen, Marshall was up, perusing a tray of pastries.

"Nicely done, Ms. Reynolds."

"Thank you, Dr. Pike."

"Marshall." He chose a cinnamon danish. "It's a tricky situation. Though the triangle was technically broken when the affair ended, emotionally, morally, even intellectually, it remains."

Damn right, she thought. If anyone she loved cheated on her, it would be he who would be broken—in every way. "I suppose you deal with similar situations in your practice."

"Often. I decided to focus on the area after my own divorce." His smile was sweet and sheepish. "For obvious reasons." He glanced down at her hands, noting that she wore a single ring, a garnet in an antique gold seeing on her right hand. "You're not in the market for my particular skill?"

"Not at the moment." Marshall Pike was enormously attractive, she mused—the charming smile, the long, slender build that had even Deanna, who hit five-ten in her heels, tilt her head up to meet the flattering interest in the deep brown eyes. But at this moment she needed to focus the lion's share of her attention on the sullen group behind him.

"The program will start right after this commercial." Deanna gestured toward the set. "Marshall, you won't be going on until the final twenty minutes, but it would help if you'd watch the show to formulate specific advice."

"Naturally." He enjoyed watching her, the way she revved in neutral. He could almost hear the engine gun of her energy. "Don't worry. I've done *Angela's* three times."

"Ah, a vet. Is there anything I can get you?"

His eyes slid toward the trio behind him, then came back to Deanna's. "A flak jacket?"

She chuckled, gave his arm a squeeze. He'd be just fine, she decided. "I'll see what I can do."

The show proved to be emotional, and though bitter accusations flew, no one was seriously wounded. Off camera, Deanna admired the way Angela kept a light hand on the reins, allowing her guests to go their own way, then easing them back when tempers threatened to boil over.

She pulled the audience in as well. With an unerring instinct, she offered the mike to just the right person at just the right time, then segued smoothly back to a question or comment of her own.

As for Dr. Pike, Deanna mused, they couldn't have chosen a more skilled mediator. He exuded the perfect combination of intellect and compassion, mixed with the concise, teaspoon-size advice so necessary for the medium.

When the show was over, the Forresters were clutching hands. The other couple had stopped speaking to each other, and the two *other women* were chatting like old friends.

Angela had hit the mark again.

"Decide to join us, Deanna?" Roger pinched her arm as he swung up beside her.

"I know you guys can't get through the day without me." Deanna wove her way through the noisy newsroom toward her desk. Phones were ringing, keyboards clattering On one wall, current shows from CBC and the other three networks were flashing on monitors. From the smell of things, someone had recently spilled coffee.

"What's our lead?" she asked Roger.

"Last night's fire on the South Side."

With a nod, Deanna sat at her desk. Unlike most of the other reporters, she kept hers meticulously neat. Sharpened pencils stood points down in a flowered ceramic cup, a notepad aligned beside them. Her Filofax was opened to today's date.

"Arson?"

"That's the general consensus. I've got the copy. We've got a taped interview with the fire marshal, and a live remote at the scene." Roger offered her his bag of licorice. "And being a nice guy, I picked up your mail."

"So I see. Thanks."

"Caught a few minutes of A*ngela's* this morning." He chewed thoughtfully on his candy. "Doesn't discussing adultery so early in the day make people nervous?"

"It gives them something to talk about over lunch." She picked up an ebony letter opener and slit the first envelope.

"Venting on national television?"

She lifted a brow. "Venting on national television seemed to have helped the Forresters' relationship."

"Looked to me like the other couple was heading for divorce court."

"Sometimes divorce is the answer."

"Is that what you think?" He kept the question light. "If your spouse was cheating, would you forgive and forget, or would you file papers?"

"Well, I'd listen, I'd discuss it, try to find out the reason it happened. Then I'd shoot the adulterous swine full of holes." She grinned at him. "But, that's just me. And see, hasn't it given us something to talk about?" She glanced down at the single sheet in her hand. "Hey, look at this."

She angled the sheet so they could both see it. In the center of the paper, typed in dark red ink, was a single sentence.

"The old secret admirer, hmm?" Roger spoke carelessly, but there was a frown in his eyes.

"Looks that way." Curious, she turned the envelope over. "No return address. No stamp, either."

"I just pulled the mail out of your box." Roger shook his head. "Somebody must have slipped it in."

"It's kind of sweet, I guess." She rubbed a quick chill from her arms and laughed. "And creepy."

"You might want to ask around, see if anybody noticed somebody sneaking around your mail slot."

"It's not important." She tossed both letter and envelope in the trash and picked up the next.

"Excuse me."

"Oh, Dr. Pike." Deanna set down her mail and smiled at the man standing behind Roger. "Did you get lost on your way out?"

"No, actually, I was told I'd find you here."

"Dr. Marshall Pike, Roger Crowell."

"Yes, I recognized you." Marshall offered a hand. "I watch you both often."

"I just caught part of your act myself." Roger slipped his bag of candy into his pocket. His thoughts were still focused on the letter, and he promised himself he'd slip it back out of her trash at the first possible moment. "We need copy on the dog show, Dee."

"No problem."

"Nice to have met you, Dr. Pike."

"Same here." Marshall turned back to Deanna when Roger walked away. "I wanted to thank you for keeping things sane this morning."

"It's one of the things I do best."

"I'd have to agree. I've always thought you report the news with clearheaded compassion. It's a remarkable combination."

"And a remarkable compliment. Thanks."

He took a survey of the newsroom. Two reporters were arguing bitterly over baseball, phones were shrilling, an intern wheeled a cart heaped with files through the narrow spaces between desks. "Interesting place."

"It is that. I'd be glad to give you a tour, but I do have copy to write for *Midday*."

"Then I'll take a rain check." He looked back at her, that sweet, easy smile at the corners of his mouth. "Deanna, I was hoping, since we've been through the trenches together, so to speak, you'd be willing to have dinner with me."

"Dinner." She studied him more carefully now, as a woman does when a man stops being simply a man and becomes a possible relationship. It would have been foolish to pretend he didn't appeal to her. "Yes, I suppose I'd be willing to do that."

"Tonight? Say, seven-thirty?"

She hesitated. She was rarely impulsive. He was a professional, she mused, well mannered, easy on the eyes. And more important, he had exhibited both intelligence and heart under pressure. "Sure." She took a square of notepaper from a smoked-glass holder and wrote down her address.

3

"Coming up on *Midday*, the story of a woman who opens her home and heart to Chicago's underprivileged children. Also the latest sports report with Les Ryder, and the forecast for the weekend with Dan Block. Join us at noon."

The minute the red light blinked out, Deanna unhooked her mike and scrambled up from the news desk. She had copy to finish and a phone interview scheduled, and she needed to review her notes for the upcoming "Deanna's Corner." In the two weeks since she had pinch-hit for Lew, she'd put in more than a hundred hours on the job without breaking stride.

She whipped through the studio doors and was halfway down the hall toward the newsroom when Angela stopped her.

"Honey, you only have two speeds. Stop and go."

Deanna paused only because Angela blocked the way.

"Right now it's go. I'm swamped."

"I've never known you not to get everything done, and at exactly the proper time." To keep her in place, Angela laid a hand on her arm. "And this will only take a minute."

Deanna struggled with impatience. "You can have two, if we talk on the move."

"Fine." Angela turned and matched her stride to Deanna's. "I've got a business lunch in an hour, so I'm a little strapped myself. I need a tiny favor."

"All right." With her mind already on her work, Deanna swung into the newsroom and headed for her desk. Her papers were stacked according to priority: the precise notes to be transcribed and expanded into copy, the list of questions for the phoner and her cards for "Deanna's Corner." She turned on her machine and typed her password while she waited for Angela to explain.

Angela took her time. She hadn't been in the newsroom for months, she mused, possibly longer, since her offices and studio were in what CBC employees called "the Tower," a slim white spear that shot up from the building. It was a not-so-subtle way to separate the national and non-news programs from the local ones.

"I'm giving a little party tomorrow night. Finn Riley's due back from London this evening, and I thought I'd give a little welcome-home thing for him."

"Mmm-hmm." Deanna was already working on her lead.

"He's been gone so long this time, and after that nasty business in Panama before he went back to his London post, I thought he deserved some R and R."

Deanna wasn't sure a small, bloody war should be called "that nasty business," but she nodded.

"Since it's all so impulsive, I really need some help putting everything together. The caterers, the flowers, the music—and of course, the party itself. Making sure everything runs smoothly. My secretary just can't handle it all, and I really want it to be perfect. If you could give me a couple of hours later today—and tomorrow, of course."

Deanna battled back the sense of resentment, and obligation. "Angela, I'd love to help you out, but I'm booked."

Angela's persuasive smile never altered, but her eyes chilled. "You're not scheduled for Saturday."

"No, not here—though I am on call. But I have plans." Deanna began to tap a finger on her notes. "A date."

"I see." Angela's hand went to her pearls, where her fingers rubbed one smooth, glowing sphere. "Rumor has it that you've been seeing a lot of Dr. Marshall Pike."

The evening news might run on facts and verified information, but Deanna understood that newsrooms and television studios ran on gossip. "We've been out a few times in the last couple of weeks."

"Well, I wouldn't want to interfere—and I hope you won't take this the wrong way, Dee." To add intimacy to the statement, Angela rested a hip on Deanna's desk. "Do you really think he's your type?"

Torn between manners and her own schedule, Deanna chose manners. "I don't really have one. A type, I mean."

"Of course you do." With a light laugh, Angela tilted her head. "Young, well built, the outdoorsy type. Athletic," she continued. "You need someone who can keep up with the vicious pace you set for yourself. And a good intellect, naturally, but not overly cerebral. You need someone who can make his point in quick, fifteen-second bites."

She really didn't have time for any of this. Deanna picked up one of her sharpened pencils and ran it through her fingers. "That makes me sound sort of shallow."

"Not at all." Angela's eyes widened in protest even as she chuckled. "Darling, I only want the very best for you. I'd hate to see a passing interest interfere with the momentum of your career, and as for Marshall... He's a bit slick, isn't he?"

Temper glinted in Deanna's eyes, and was quickly suppressed. "I don't know what you mean. I enjoy his company."

"Of course you do." Angela patted Deanna's shoulder. "What young woman wouldn't? An older man, experienced, smooth. But to let him interfere with your work—"

"He's not interfering with anything. We've gone out a few times in the last couple of weeks, that's all. I'm sorry, Angela, but I really have to get back on schedule here."

"Sorry," she said coolly. "I thought we were friends. I didn't think a little constructive advice would offend you."

"It hasn't." Deanna fought back a sigh. "But I'm on deadline. Listen, if I can squeeze out some time later today, I'll do what I can to help you with the party."

As if a switch had been thrown, the icy stare melted into the warmest of smiles. "You're a jewel. Tell you what, just to prove there's no hard feelings, you bring Marshall tomorrow night."

"Angela—"

"Now, I won't take no for an answer." She slid off the desk. "And if you could get there just an hour or two early, I'd be so grateful. No one organizes like you, Dee. We'll talk about all of this later."

Deanna leaned back in her chair when Angela strolled away. She felt as though she'd been steamrolled with velvet.

With a shake of her head, she looked down at her notes, her fingers poised over her keyboard. Frowning, she relaxed them again. Angela was wrong, she thought. Marshall wasn't interfering with her work. Being interested in someone didn't have to clash with ambition.

She enjoyed going out with him. She liked his mind—the way he could open it to see both sides of a situation. And the way he laughed when she dug in on an opinion and refused to budge.

She appreciated the fact that he was letting the physical end of their relationship develop slowly, at her pace. Though she had to admit it was becoming tempting to speed things up. It had been a long time since she'd felt safe enough, and strong enough, with a man to invite intimacy.

Once she did, Deanna thought, she would have to tell him everything.

She shook the memory away quickly, before it could dig its claws into her heart. She knew from experience it was best to cross one bridge at a time, then to prepare to span the next.

The first bridge was to analyze her relationship with Marshall, if there was a relationship, and to decide where she wanted it to go.

A glance at the clock made her moan.

She would have to cross that personal bridge on her own time. Setting her fingers on the keyboard, she got to work.

Angela's staff privately called her suite of offices "the citadel." She reigned like a feudal lord from her French provincial desk, handing out commands and meting out reward and punishment in equal measures. Anyone who remained on staff after a six-month probationary period was loyal and diligent and kept his or her complaints private.

She was, admittedly, exacting, impatient with excuses and demanding of certain personal luxuries. She had, after all, earned such requirements.

Angela stepped into the outer office, where her executive secretary was busily handling details for Monday's taping. There were other offices—producers, researchers, assistants—down the quiet hallway. Angela had long since left the boisterous bustle of newsrooms behind. She had used reporting not merely as a stepping-stone, but as a catapult for her ambitions. There was only one thing she wanted, and she had wanted it for as long as she could remember: to be the center of attention.

In news, the story was king. The bearer of the tale would be noticed, certainly, if she was good enough. Angela had been very good. Six years in the pressure cooker of on-air reporting had cost her one husband, netted her a second and paved the way for *Angela's*.

She much preferred, and insisted on, the church-like silence of thick carpets and insulated walls.

"You have some messages, Miss Perkins."

"Later." Angela yanked open one of the double doors leading to her private office. "I need you inside, Cassie."

She began to pace immediately. Even when she heard the quiet click of the door closing behind her secretary, she continued to move restlessly, over the Aubusson, past the elegant desk, away from the wide ribbon of windows, toward the antique curio cabinet that held her collection of awards.

Mine, she thought. She had earned them, she possessed them. Now that she did, no one would ever ignore her again.

She paused by the framed photos and prints that adorned a wall. Pictures of Angela with celebrities at charity events and award ceremonies. Her covers of TV *Guide* and *Time* and *People*. She stared at them, drawing deep breaths.

"Does she realize who I am?" she murmured. "Does she realize who she's dealing with?"

With a shake of her head, she turned away again. It was a small mistake, she reminded herself. One that could be easily corrected. After all, she was fond of the girl.

As she grew calmer, she circled her desk, settled into the custom-made pink leather chair the CEO of her syndicate—her former husband—had given her when her show hit number one in the ratings.

Cassie remained standing. She knew better than to approach one of the mahogany chairs with their fussy needlepoint cushions until invited.

"You contacted the caterer?"

"Yes, Miss Perkins. The menu's on your desk."

Angela glanced at it, nodded absently. "The florist."

"They confirmed everything but the calla lilies," Cassie told her. "They're trying to find the supply you want, but suggested several substitutes."

"If I'd wanted a substitute, I'd have asked for one." She waved her hand. "It's not your fault, Cassie. Sit down." Angela closed her eyes. She was getting one of her headaches, one of those pile-driving thumpers that came on in a rush of pain. Gently, she massaged the center of her forehead with two fingers. Her mother had gotten headaches, she remembered. And had doused them with liquor. "Get me some water, will you? I've got a migraine brewing."

Cassie got up from the chair she'd just taken and walked across the room to the gleaming bar. She was a quiet woman, in looks, in speech. And was ambitious enough to ignore Angela's faults in her desire for advancement. Saying nothing, she chose the crystal decanter that was filled with fresh spring water daily and poured a tumblerful.

"Thanks." Angela downed a Percodan with water, and prayed for it to kick in. She couldn't afford to be distracted during her luncheon meeting. "Do you have a list of acceptances for the party?"

"On your desk."

"Fine." Angela kept her eyes closed. "Give a copy of it, and everything else, to Deanna. She'll be taking care of the details from here."

"Yes, ma'am." Aware of her duties, Cassie walked behind Angela's chair and gently massaged her temples. Minutes clicked by, counted off by the quiet tick of the long case clock across the room. Musically, it announced the quarter-hour.

"You checked on the weather forecast?" Angela murmured.

"It's projected to be clear and cool, a low in the mid-forties."

"Then we'll need to use the heaters on the terrace. I want dancing."

Dutifully, Cassie stepped away to note the instructions down. There was no word of thanks for her attentiveness; none required. "Your hairdresser is scheduled to arrive at your home at two. Your dress will be delivered by three at the latest."

"All right, then, let's put all that aside for the moment. I want you to contact Beeker. I want to know everything there is to know about Dr. Marshall Pike. He's a psychologist with a private practice here in Chicago. I want the information as Beeker collects it, rather than waiting for a full report."

She opened her eyes again. The headache wasn't in full retreat, but the pill was beating it back. "Tell Beeker it isn't an emergency, but it is a priority. Understood?"

"Yes, Miss Perkins."

By six that evening, Deanna was still going full steam ahead. While she juggled three calls, she beefed up copy that would be read on the late news. "Yes, I understand your position. But an interview, particularly a televised interview, would help show your side." Deanna pursed her lips, sighed. "If you feel that way, of course. I believe your neighbor is more than willing to tell me her story on the air." She smiled when the receiver squawked in indignation. "Yes, we'd prefer to have both sides represented. Thank you, Mrs. Wilson. I'll be there at ten tomorrow."

She spotted Marshall coming toward her and lifted a hand in a wave as she punched down the next blinking light on her phone. "Sorry, Mrs. Carter. Yes, as I was saying, I understand your position. It is a shame about your tulips. A televised interview would help show your side of the dispute." Deanna smiled as Marshall stroked a hand down her hair in greeting. "If you're sure. Mrs. Wilson has agreed to tell me her story on the air." Tipping the receiver a safe inch from her ear, Deanna rolled her eyes at Marshall. "Yes, that would be fine. I'll be there at ten. 'Bye."

"Hot breaking story?"

"Hot tempers in suburbia," Deanna corrected as she disconnected. "I have to put in an hour or two tomorrow after all. A couple of neighbors are engaged in a pitched battle over a bed of tulips, an old, incorrect survey and a cocker spaniel."

"Sounds fascinating."

"I'll give you the scoop over dinner." She didn't object when he lowered his head, and met his lips willingly. The kiss was friendly, without the pressure of intimacy. "You're all wet," she murmured, tasting rain and cool skin.

"It's pouring out there. All I need is a nice warm restaurant and a dry wine."

"I've got one more call waiting."

"Take your time. Want anything?"

"I could use a cold drink. My vocal cords are raw."

Deanna cleared her mental decks and punched in the next button. "Mr. Van Damme, I'm terribly sorry for the interruption. There seems to be a mix-up with Miss Perkins's wine order for tomorrow night. She'll need three cases of Taittinger's, not two. Yes, that's right. And the white wine?" Deanna checked off her list as the caterer recited from his. "Yes, that's right. And can I ease her mind about the ice sculpture?" She sent Marshall another smile when he returned with a cold can of 7-Up. "That's wonderful, Mr. Van Damme. And you do have the change from tarts to petits fours? Terrific. I think we've got it under control. I'll see you tomorrow, then. 'Bye."

With a long exhale, Deanna dropped the phone on its hook. "Done," she told Marshall. "I hope."

"Long day for you?"

"Long, and productive." Automatically she began to tidy her desk. "I appreciate your meeting me here, Marshall."

"My schedule was lighter than yours."

"Mmm." She took a deep drink, then set the can aside before shutting down her workstation. "And I owe you one for changing plans for tomorrow to accommodate Angela."

"A good psychologist should be flexible." He watched her as she straightened papers and organized notes. "Besides, it sounds like a hell of a party."

"It's turning out that way. She's not a woman to do anything halfway."

"And you admire that."

"Absolutely. Give me five minutes to freshen up, then I promise to focus all my energy on relaxing with you over dinner."

When she stood, he shifted so that his body just brushed hers. It was a subtle move, a subtle suggestion. "You look very fresh to me."

She felt the trickle of excitement run down her spine, the warmth of awareness bloom in her stomach. Tilting her head to meet his eyes, she saw the desire, the need and the patience, a combination that sent her pulse skipping.

She had only to say yes, she knew, and they would forget all about dinner, and all about relaxing. And for one moment, one very long, very quiet moment, she wished it could be that simple.

"I won't be long," she murmured.

"I'll wait."

He would, she thought when he moved aside to let her by. And she would have to make up her mind, soon, whether she wanted to continue along the comfortable, companionable road of this relationship, or shift gears.

"Having your head shrunk, Dee?"

She spotted the cameraman by the door, biting into a Milky Way. "That's so lame, Joe."

"I know." He grinned around the chocolate. There was a button that said AVAILABLE pinned to his tattered denim vest. He had holes in the knees of his jeans. Techs didn't have to worry about appearance. That was just the way Joe liked it. "But somebody's got to say it. Did you set up those two interviews for the morning? The tulip wars?"

"Yeah. Sure you don't mind giving up your Saturday morning?"

"Not for overtime pay."

"Good. Delaney's still at the desk, isn't he?"

"I'm waiting for him." Joe bit off more candy. "We've got a poker game tonight. I'm going to hose him for the double shift he stuck me with last week."

"Do me a favor, then, and tell him we're set, both women, ten o'clock."

"Will do."

"Thanks." Deanna hurried away to do quick repairs on her hair and makeup. She was applying fresh lipstick when Joe burst into the ladies' room. The door slammed back against the wall, echoing as he lunged at her.

"Jesus, Joe, are you nuts?"

"Get your butt in gear, Dee. We've got an assignment, and we've got to move fast." He grabbed her purse from the sink with one hand and her arm with the other.

"What, for God's sake?" She tripped over the threshold as he hauled her out the door. "Did somebody start a war?"

"Almost as hot. We've got to get out to O'Hare."

"O'Hare? Damn it, Marshall's waiting."

Fighting impatience, Joe let Deanna tug her arm free. If he had any complaints about her, it was that her vision wasn't quite narrow enough. She always saw the peripheral when the camera needed a tight shot.

"Go tell the boyfriend you've got to go be a reporter. Delaney just got word there's a plane coming in, and it's in trouble. Big time."

"Oh, God." She made the dash back into the newsroom with Joe on her heels. Bursting through the pandemonium, she snatched a fresh notebook from her desk. "Marshall, I'm sorry. I have to go."

"I've already gathered that. Do you want me to wait?"

"No." She dragged a hand through her hair, grabbed her jacket. "I don't know how long I'll be. I'll call you. Delaney!" she called out.

The stout assignment editor waved the stub of his unlit cigar in her direction. "Take off, Reynolds. Keep in touch on the two-way. We'll be patching you in live. Get me a goddamn scoop."

"Sorry," she called to Marshall. "Where's the plane coming in from?" she shouted to Joe as they raced up the stairs. His motorcycle boots clattered on the metal like gunfire.

"London. They'll be feeding us the rest of the information as we go." He shoved open the outside door and then plunged out into a torrent of rain. His Chicago Bulls sweatshirt was immediately plastered to his chest. He shouted over the storm while he unlocked the van. "It's a 747. More than two hundred passengers. Left engine failure, some problem with the radar. Might have taken a hit of lightning." To punctuate his words, a spear of lightning cracked the black sky, shattering the dark.

Already drenched, Deanna climbed into the van. "What's the ETA?" Out of habit, she switched on the police scanner under the dash.

"Don't know. Let's just hope we get there before they do." He'd hate to miss getting a shot of the crash. He gunned the engine, glanced at her. The gleam in his eyes promised a wild ride. "Here's the kicker, Dee. Finn Riley's on board. The crazy son of a bitch called in the story himself."

4

Sitting in the forward cabin of the beleaguered 747 was like riding in the belly of a dyspeptic bronco. The plane bucked, kicked, shuddered and shook as if it were struggling mightily to disgorge its complement of passengers. Some of the people on board were praying, some were weeping, still others had their faces buried in airsickness bags, too weak to do anything but moan.

Finn Riley didn't give much thought to prayer. In his own way he was religious. He could, if the need arose in him, recite the Act of Contrition just as he had through all those shadowy sessions in the confessional as a child. At the moment, atonement wasn't on the top of his list.

Time was running out—on his battery pack on his laptop computer. He'd have to switch to his tape recorder soon. Finn much preferred writing copy as the words flowed from his mind to his fingers.

He glanced out the window. The black sky exploded again and again with spears of lightning. Like lances of the gods—nope, he decided, deleting the phrase. Too corny. A battleground, nature against man's technology. The sounds were definitely warlike, he mused. The prayers, the weeping, the groans, the occasionally hysterical laugh. He'd heard them in trenches before. And the echoing boom of thunder that shook the plane like a toy.

He used the last moments of his dying battery playing that angle.

Once he'd shut down, he secured the disk and the computer in his heavy metal case. He'd have to hope for the best there, Finn mused, as he slipped his mini-recorder from his briefcase. He'd seen the aftermath of plane crashes often enough to know what survived was pure luck.

"It's May fifth, seven-oh-two Central time," Finn recited into the recorder. "We're aboard flight 1129 approaching O'Hare, though it's impossible to see any lights through the storm. Lightning struck the port engine about twenty minutes ago. And from what I could squeeze out of the first-class flight attendant, there's some problem with the radar, possibly storm-related. There are two hundred and fifty-two passengers on board, and twelve crew."

"You're crazy." The man sitting next to Finn finally lifted his head from between his knees. His face, under its sheen of sweat, was pale green. His upper-class British voice was slurred more than a little with a combination of scotch and terror. "We could be dead in a few minutes and you're talking into some bloody machine."

"We could be alive in a few minutes, too. Either way, it's news." Sympathetic, Finn dragged a handkerchief out of the back pocket of his jeans. "Here."

"Thanks." Mumbling, the man dabbed at his face. As the plane shuddered again, he laid his head weakly against the seat and closed his eyes. "You must have ice water for blood."

Finn only smiled. His blood wasn't icy, it was hot, pumping hot, but there was no use in trying to explain that to a layman. It wasn't that he wasn't afraid, or that he was particularly fatalistic. But he did have the reporter's unique sense of tunnel vision. He had his recorder, his notebook, his laptop. These were shields that gave the illusion of indestructibility.

Why else did a cameraman continue to roll tape when bullets were flying? Why did a reporter jab a mike into the face of a psychopath, or run in instead of out of a building during a bomb threat? Because he was blinded by the shields of the Fourth Estate.

Or maybe, Finn mused with a grin, they were just crazy.

"Hey." He shifted in his seat and aimed the recorder. "Want to be my last interview?"

His companion opened red-rimmed eyes. What he saw was a man only a few years younger than himself, with clear, pale skin shadowed by a hint of a beard shades darker than the tousled mane of wavy bronze hair that swept the collar of a leather bomber's jacket. Sharp, angular features were softened by a mouth spread in an engaging grin that featured a crooked eyetooth. The grin brought out dimples that should have softened the face, yet only made it tougher. Like dents in rock.

But it was the eyes that held the onlooker's attention. Just now they were a deep, misty blue, like a lake dappled in fog, and they were filled with amusement, self-deprecation and recklessness.

The man heard a sound bubble in his own throat and was stunned to realize it was a laugh. "Fuck you," he said, grinning back.

"Even if we buy it on this run, I don't think they'll air that. Network standards. Is this your first trip to the States?"

"Jesus, you are crazy." But some of his fear was ebbing. "No, I make the trip about twice a year."

"What's the first thing you want to do if we land in one piece?"

"Call my wife. We had a row before I left. Silly business." He mopped his clammy face again. "I want to talk to my wife and kids."

The plane lost altitude. The PA crackled under the sounds of screams and sobs.

"Ladies and gentlemen, please remain in your seats, with your seat belts fastened. We will be landing momentarily. For your own safety, please put your head between your knees, grasp your ankles firmly. Once we land, we'll begin emergency evacuation procedures."

Or they'll scrape us up with shovels, Finn mused. The vision of the wreck of Pan Am flight 103 spread over Scotland played uneasily in his mind. He remembered too well what he'd seen, what he'd smelled, what he'd felt when he'd broadcast that report.

He wondered, fatalistically, who would stand in front of twisted, smoking metal and tell the world about the fate of flight 1129.

"What's your wife's name?" Finn asked as he leaned forward.

"Anna."

"Kids?"

"Brad and Susan. Oh God, oh God, I don't want to die."

"Think about Anna and Brad and Susan," Finn told him. "Pull them right into your head. It'll help." Cool-eyed, he studied the Celtic cross that had worked its way out from under his sweater to dangle on its chain. He had people to think about, as well. He closed his hand over the cross, held it warm in his hand.

"It's seven-oh-nine, Central time. The pilot's taking us in."

"Can you see it yet? Joe, can you see it?"

"Can't see a goddamn thing through this goddamn rain." He squinted, hefting his camera. Rain ran off the bill of his fielder's cap and waterfalled in front of his face. "Can't believe there's no other crews here yet. It's just like Finn to call the son-of-a-bitching story in so we'd get an exclusive."

"They'll have heard about it by now." Straining to see through the gloom, Deanna shoved sopping hair from her eyes. In the lights of the runway, the rain looked like a hail of silver bullets. "We won't be alone out here for long. I hope we're right about them using this runway."

"We're right. Wait. Did you hear that? I don't think that was thunder."

"No, it sounded like—there!" She stabbed a finger toward the sky. "Look. That's got to be it."

The lights were barely visible through the slashing rain. Faintly, she heard the mutter of an engine, then the answering wail of emergency vehicles. Her stomach flipped over.

"Benny? Are you copying this?" She lifted her voice over the storm, satisfied when she heard her producer's voice come through her earpiece. "It's coming down now. Yes?" She nodded to Joe. "We're set. We're going live," she told Joe, and stood with her back to the runway. "Go from me, then follow the plane in. Keep on the plane. They've got us," she murmured, listening to the madhouse of the control room through her earpiece. "In five, Joe."

She listened to the lead-in from the anchor, and her cue. "We've just spotted the lights from flight 1129. As you can see, the storm has become very violent, rain is washing over the runways in sheets. Airport officials have refused to comment on the exact nature of the problem with flight 1129, but emergency vehicles are standing ready."

"What can you see, Deanna?" This from the anchor desk back in the studio.

"The lights, and we can hear the engine as the plane descends." She turned as Joe angled the camera skyward. "There!" In the lightning flash, the plane was visible, a bright silver missile hurtling groundward. "There are two-hundred and sixty-four passengers and crew aboard flight 1129." She shouted over the scream of storm, engines and sirens. "Including Finn Riley, CBC's foreign correspondent returning to Chicago from his post in London. Please God," she murmured, then fell silent, letting the pictures tell the story as the plane came into clear view.

It was laboring. She imagined herself inside as the pilot fought to keep the nose up and level. The sound must have been deafening.

"Almost," she whispered, forgetting the camera, the mike, the viewers as she kept her gaze riveted on the plane. She saw the landing gear, then the bright red, white and blue logo of the airline slashed on the side of the plane. There was only static in her earpiece.

"I can't hear you, Martin. Stand by."

She held her breath as the wheels hit, skidded, bounced off the tarmac. Held it still as the plane slid and swayed, chased down the runway by the flashing lights of emergency vehicles.

"It's skidding," she called out. "There's smoke. I can see what looks like smoke under the left wing. I can hear the brakes screaming, and it's slowing. It's definitely slowing, but there's a problem with control."

The wing dipped, skimming the tarmac and shooting up a shower of sparks. Deanna watched them sizzle and die in the wet as the plane swerved. Then, with a shuddering bump, it stopped, diagonally across the runway.

"It's down. Flight 1129 is on the ground."

"Deanna, is it possible for you to assess the damage?"

"Not from here. Just the smoke I spotted at the left wing, which corroborates our unofficial reports of left-engine failure. Emergency crews are soaking down the area with foam. Ambulances are standing by. The door's opening, Martin. The chute's coming out. I can see—yes, the first passengers being evacuated."

"Get closer," the producer ordered. "We're cutting back to Martin to give you time to get closer."

"We'll move closer to the scene, and bring you more on flight 1129, which has just landed at O'Hare. This is Deanna Reynolds for CBC."

"You're clear," her producer shouted. "Go."

"Goddamn!" Excitement pitched Joe's voice up an octave. "What pictures. What pictures. It's fucking Emmy time."

She shot him a look, but was too used to the cameraman's style to comment. "Come on, Joe. Let's see if we can get some interviews."

They dashed toward the runway as more passengers slid down the emergency chute into the arms of waiting rescue workers. By the time they reached the huddle of vehicles, and reset for broadcast, there were half a dozen people safely out. One woman sat on the ground, weeping into her folded arms. With the singlemindedness of a newsman, Joe rolled tape.

"Benny, we're at the scene. Are you getting this?"

"Absolutely. It's good film. We'll be putting you back live. Get me one of the passengers. Get me—"

"Riley," Joe shouted. "Hey, Finn Riley."

Deanna glanced back toward the chute in time to see Finn make his slide to earth. On hearing his name called, he turned his head. Eyes narrowed against the driving rain, he focused on the camera. And grinned.

He landed easily, despite the metal case he clutched. Rain dripped from his hair, skimmed down his leather jacket and soaked his boots.

In an easy lope he covered the ground from chute to camera.

"You lucky son of a bitch." Joe beamed and punched Finn on the shoulder.

"Good to see you, Joe. Excuse me a minute." Without warning, he grabbed Deanna and planted a hard kiss on her mouth. She had time to feel the heat radiating from his body, to register the shock of electricity from his mouth to hers, a quick burst of power, before he released her.

"Hope you don't mind." He gave her a charming smile. "I thought about kissing the ground, but you look a hell of a lot better. Can I borrow these a minute?"

He was already tugging her earpiece free. "Hey."

"Who's producing?"

"Benny. And I—"

"Benny?" He snagged her mike. "Yeah, it's me. So, you got my call." He chuckled. "My pleasure. Anything I can do for the news department." He listened a moment, nodded. "No problem. We're going live in ten," he told Joe. "Keep an eye on that for me," he asked Deanna, and set his case down at her feet. He dragged the hair out of his face and looked into the camera.

"This is Finn Riley, reporting live from O'Hare. At six thirty-two this evening, flight 1129 from London was struck by lightning."

Deanna wondered why the rain running off her clothes didn't sizzle as she watched Finn make his report. Her report, she corrected. Two minutes after hitting the ground and the sneaky bastard had usurped her, stolen her piece and delegated her to gofer.

So he was good, Deanna fumed as she watched him leading the viewers on the odyssey of flight 1129 from London. That was no surprise. She'd seen his reports before—from London, yes, and from Haiti, Central America, the Middle East.

She'd even intro'd a few of them.

But that wasn't the point.

The point was that he'd snatched her piece away from her. Well, Deanna decided, he might have upstaged her, but he was going to discover that stealing her newspiece wasn't a snap.

Interviews were her strong point, she reminded herself. That was her job, she told herself, struggling to cool off. And that's what she would do. Brilliantly.

Turning her back on Finn, she hunched her shoulders against the downpour and went to look for passengers.

Moments later, there was a tap on her back. She turned, lifted a brow. "Did you need something?"

"Brandy and a roaring fire." Finn wiped rain from his face. He was in gear, fueled by the chaos and the immediacy of the report. And the simple fact that he wasn't a dead man. "Meantime, I figured we'd round out the piece with some interviews. Some passengers, a few of the emergency crew—some of the flight crew, if we're lucky. We should be able to get it in for a special report before the late news."

"I've already lined up a couple of passengers who are willing to talk to me on air."

"Good. Take Joe and do it, while I see if I can finagle an interview with the pilot."

She snagged his arm before he could pivot away. "I need my mike."

"Oh. Sure." He handed it over, then offered the earpiece. She looked like a wet dog, he mused. Not a mongrel, no indeed. One of those classy Afghan hounds that manage to maintain dignity and style under the worst of circumstances. His pleasure at being alive went up another notch. It was a pure delight to watch her glaring at him. "I know you, don't I? Aren't you on the *Sunrise News?*"

"Not for the past several months. I'm on *Midday.*"

"Congratulations." He focused on her more intently, the misty blue of his eyes turning sharp and clear. "Diana—no, Deanna, Right?"

"You have a good memory. I don't believe we've spoken before."

"No, but I've caught your work. Pretty good." But he was already looking beyond her. "There were some kids on the flight. If you can't get them on mike, at least get them on camera. The competition's here now." He gestured to where other newsmen were milling among the passengers. "Let's work fast."

"I know my job," she said, but he was already moving away.

"He doesn't seem to have a problem with self-esteem."

Beside her, Joe snorted. "He's got an ego the size of the Sears Tower. And it isn't fragile. The thing is, when you do a piece with him, you know he's going to do it right. And he doesn't treat his crew like mentally deficient slaves."

"Too bad he doesn't treat other reporters with the same courtesy." She spun on her heel. "Let's get pictures."

It was after nine when they returned to CBC, where Finn was greeted with a hero's welcome. Someone handed him a bottle of Jameson, seal intact. Shivering, Deanna headed straight for her desk, turned on her machine and started writing copy.

This, she knew, would go national. It was a chance she didn't intend to miss.

She tuned out the shouting and laughing and back-slapping and wrote furiously, referring now and then to the sketchy notes she'd scribbled in the back of the van.

"Here." She looked down and saw a hand, wide-palmed, long-fingered, scarred at the base of the thumb, set down a glass on her desk. The glass held about an inch of deep amber liquid.

"I don't drink on the job." She hoped she sounded cool, not prim.

"I don't think a swallow of whiskey's going to impair your judgment. And," he said, drifting easily into a rich Pat O'Brien brogue, "it'll put some heat in your belly. You don't plan on operating heavy machinery, do you?" Finn skirted her chair and sat on the edge of her desk. "You're cold." He handed her a towel. "Knock it back. Dry your hair. We've got work to do."

"That's what I'm doing." But she took the towel. And after a moment's hesitation, the whiskey. It might have been only a swallow, but he was right, it put a nice cozy fire in her stomach.

"We've got thirty minutes for copy. Benny's already editing the tape." Finn craned his head around to scan her screen. "That's good stuff," he commented.

"It'll be better if you'd get out of my way."

He was used to hostility, but he liked to know its source. "You're ticked because I kissed you? No offense, Deanna, but it wasn't personal. It was more like primal instinct."

"I'm not ticked because you kissed me." She spoke between her teeth and began to type again. "I'm ticked because you stole my story."

Hooking his hands around his knee, Finn thought about it and decided she had a small, if not particularly salient point. "Let me ask you a question. Which makes better film? You doing a stand-up, or me giving a play-by-play of the flight minutes after evacuation?"

She spared him one heated glance, and said nothing.

"Okay, while you're thinking it over, we'll print out my copy and see how it reads with yours."

She stopped. "What do you mean, your copy?"

"I wrote it on the plane. Got a quick interview with my seatmate, too." The reckless amusement was back in his eyes. "Should be good for human interest."

Despite her annoyance, she nearly laughed. "You wrote copy while your plane was going down?"

"Those portable computers will work anywhere. You've got about five minutes before Benny comes along and starts tearing his hair out."

Deanna stared after him when Finn walked off to commandeer a desk.

The man was obviously a lunatic.

And a damned talented one, she decided thirty minutes later.

The edited tape was completed, the graphics set less than three minutes before airtime. The copy, reworked, rewritten and timed, was plugged into the TelePrompTer. And Finn Riley, still in his sweater and jeans, was seated behind the anchor desk, going national with his report.

"Good evening. This is a special report on flight 1129. I'm Finn Riley."

Deanna knew he was reading the news, since she had written the first thirty seconds herself. Yet it felt as though he were telling a story. He knew exactly which word to punch, when to pause. He knew exactly how to go through the camera and into the home.

It wasn't an intimacy, she mused, worrying her earring. He wasn't settling in for a cozy chat. He was . . . bringing tidings, she decided. Carrying the message. And somehow staying aloof from it.

Neat trick, she thought, since he had been on the very plane he was describing.

Even when he read his own words, words he had written while plunging through the sky in a crippled plane with its port engine smoking, he was removed. The storyteller, not the story.

Admiration snuck past her defenses.

She turned to the monitor when they switched to film, and saw herself. Hair dripping, eyes huge, face pale as the water that rained over her. Her voice was steady. Yes, she had that, Deanna thought. But she wasn't detached. The fear and terror were there, transmitted as clearly as her words.

And when the camera shifted to capture the plane skidding on the runway, she heard her own whispered prayer.

Too involved, she realized, and sighed.

It was worse when she saw Finn on the monitor, taking over the story minutes after escaping the damaged plane. He had the look of a warrior fresh from battle—a veteran warrior who could discuss each blow and thrust concisely, emotionlessly.

And he had been right. It made better film.

At commercial, Deanna went up into the control booth to watch. Benny was grinning like a fool even as sweat popped onto his wide, furrowed brow. He was fat and permanently red-faced and made a habit of tugging on tufts of his lank brown hair. But he was, Deanna knew, a hell of a producer.

"We beat every other station in town," he was telling Finn through the earpiece. "None of them have any tape of the landing, or the initial stages of evacuation." He blew Deanna a kiss. "This is great stuff. You're back in ten, Finn. We'll be going to the tape of passenger interviews. And cue."

Through the last three and a half minutes, Benny continued to murmur to himself, pulling at his hair.

"Maybe we should have put him in a jacket," he said at one point. "Maybe we should have found him a jacket."

"No." There was no use being resentful. Deanna put a hand on Benny's shoulder. "He looks great."

"And in those last moments in the air, some, like Harry Lyle, thought of family. Others, like Marcia DeWitt and Kenneth Morgenstern, thought of dreams unfulfilled. For them, and all the others aboard flight 1129, the long night ended at seven-sixteen, when the plane landed safely on runway three.

"This is Finn Riley for CBC. Good night."

"Up graphics. Music. And we're clear!"

A cheer erupted in the control booth. Benny leaned back in his swivel chair and lifted his arms in triumph. Phones started to shrill.

"Benny, it's Barlow James on two."

A hush fell over control, and Benny stared at the receiver as though it were a snake. Barlow James, the president of the news division, rarely phoned.

Every eye was on Benny as he swallowed and took the phone. "Mr. James?" Benny listened a moment, his ruddy face going ghostly, then flushing hot candy pink. "Thank you, sir." Opening his mouth wide, Benny flashed a thumb's up and set the cheering off again. "Yes, sir, Finn's one in a million. We're glad to have him back. Deanna Reynolds?" He swiveled in his chair and rolled his eyes at Deanna. "Yes, sir, Mr. James, we're proud to have her on our team. Thank you very much. I'll let them know."

Benny replaced the receiver, stood and did a fast boogie that sent his belly swaying over his belt. "He loved it," Benny sang. "He loved it all. They want the whole eight minutes for the affiliates. He loved you." Benny grabbed Deanna's hands and spun her around. "He liked your fresh, intimate style—that's a quote. And the fact that you looked good soaking wet."

With a choked laugh, Deanna stepped back and rammed straight into Finn.

"Two pretty good qualities in a reporter," Finn decided. He caught a whiff of her hair as he steadied her, rain and apple blossoms. "Nice job, guys." He released Deanna to shake hands with the control crew. "Really terrific."

"Mr. James said welcome back, Finn," Benny said. As he relaxed again, the pudge of his belly sagged comfortably at his belt. "And he's looking forward to beating your butt at tennis next week."

"In his dreams." Out of the corner of his eye, he saw Deanna descending the stairs. "Thanks again."

He caught up with her in the newsroom just as she was shrugging into her coat.

"It was a good piece," he said.

"Yes, it was."

"Reading copy isn't one of my priorities, but reading yours was a pleasure."

"It's certainly a night for compliments." She swung her purse over her arm. "Thanks, and welcome back to Chicago."

"Need a lift?"

"No, I've got my car."

"I don't." He flashed her a smile. Dimples winked out, charmingly. "Probably hell getting a cab in this weather."

She studied him. In her heels, she was about the same height he was, and she got a good, close look at those innocent blue eyes. Too innocent, she thought, especially in combination with that quick, dashing grin and the wink of dimples. He *wanted* to look innocent, she decided. Therefore he did. Neat trick.

"I suppose, as a professional courtesy, I could give you a ride you home."

Her hair was still wet, he noted, and she hadn't bothered to repair her makeup. "Are you still ticked at me?"

"No, actually, I'm down to mildly miffed."

"I could buy you a burger." He reached out to toy with one of the buttons on her jacket. "Maybe I could talk you down to slightly steamed."

"These things generally run their course. In any case, I think your homecoming's been exciting enough. I've got a call to make."

She was involved with someone, Finn realized. It was too bad. Really too bad. "Just the lift, then. I appreciate it."

5

For some, organizing a party was a casual affair. Food, drink, music and good company were tossed together and left to mix in their own way.

For Deanna, it was a campaign. From the moment Cassie had passed the torch to her barely twenty-four hours earlier, no detail was left unattended to, no list unfulfilled. Like a general rousing troops, she inspected the caterer, the florist, the bartender, the housekeeping staff. She arranged, rearranged and approved. She counted stemware, discussed the playlist with the band and personally tasted Van Damme's chicken kabobs in peanut butter sauce.

"Incredible," she murmured, her eyes closed, her lips just parted as she savored the flavor. "Really, really incredible."

When she opened her eyes, she and the slim young caterer beamed at each other.

"Thank God." Van Damme offered her a glass of wine as they stood in the center of Angela's enormous kitchen. "Miss Perkins wanted cuisine from around the world as her theme. It took a great deal of thought and preparation, in a short amount of time, to come up with flavors that would complement one another. The ratatouille, the deep-fried mushrooms à la Berlin, the tiny spanakopita . . ." The list went on.

Deanna didn't know ratatouille from tuna fish, but made appropriate noises. "You've done a wonderful job, Mr. Van Damme." Deanna toasted him and drank. "Miss Perkins and all of her guests will be delighted. Now I know I can leave all of this in your hands."

She hoped. There were half a dozen people in the kitchen, rattling pans, arranging trays, bickering. "We have thirty minutes." She took one last glance around. Every inch of Angela's rose-colored counters was filled with trays and pots. The air was thick with delicious smells. Van Damme's assistants rushed about. Marveling that anyone could function amid the confusion, Deanna escaped.

She hurried toward the front of the house. Angela's lofty living room was all pastels and flowers. Delicate calla lilies streamed out of crystal vases. Fairy roses swam in fragile bowls. The floral theme was continued with the tiny violets dotting the silk wallpaper and the pale pattern of the Oriental carpets spread over the floor.

The room, like all of Angela's trim two-story home, was a celebration of feminine decorating, with soft colors and deep cushions. Deanna's practiced eye scanned over the sherbet-colored pillows on the curved-back sofa, the arrangement of slender tapers, the presentation of pale pink and green mints in crystal candy dishes. She could hear the faint sounds of the band tuning up through the closed terrace doors.

For a moment, she imagined the house as hers. More color, she thought. Fewer frills. But she would definitely enjoy the lofty ceilings and curved windows, the cozy fireplace set with apple wood.

She'd want some art on the walls. Bold prints, sinuous sculptures. And a few well-chosen antiques to mix with edgy modern pieces.

One day, she mused, and shifted a vase an inch on a tabletop.

Satisfied, she took a final tour of the main level. She had just started across the foyer to the staircase when the door chimes pealed. Too early for guests, she thought as she turned to answer. She sincerely hoped it wasn't a last-minute delivery she'd have to deal with.

Finn stood on the porch with dusk gathering behind him. A breeze wafted up, played with his hair and brought Deanna the scent of man and nightfall. He grinned at her, letting his gaze roam up from the toes of her sneakers to her tousled hair.

"Well, hi. Are you covering tonight's event?"

"So to speak." He'd shaved, she noted. And though he hadn't bothered with a tie, the slate-gray jacket and trousers made the casual look elegant. "You're early."

"By request." He stepped inside and shut the door at his back. "I like your party dress."

"I was just going up to change." And he was blowing a hole in her schedule. She caught herself playing with her earring and dropped her hand hastily. "Why don't you come in and sit down. I'll tell Angela you're here."

"What's your hurry?" he asked as he followed her into the living room.

"No hurry. Do you want a drink? The bartender's in the kitchen, but I can handle something simple."

"Don't bother."

He sat on the arm of the sofa as he glanced around speculatively. Deanna was no more suited to the ornate femininity of the room than he was, Finn decided. She made him think of Titania. And, though he couldn't say why, Titania made him think of wild sex on a damp forest floor.

"Nothing's changed around here in the last six months. I always feel as though I'm walking into the royal gardens."

Deanna's lips twitched. She quashed the disloyal urge to laugh and agree. "Angela's fond of flowers. I'll go get her."

"Let her primp." Finn snagged Deanna's hand before she could walk out. "She's fond of that, too. Do you ever sit down?"

"Of course I sit down."

"I mean when you're not driving a car or writing copy."

She didn't bother to tug her hand free. "Occasionally I sit down to eat."

"That's interesting, so do I. Maybe we could do it together sometime."

Deanna lifted a brow, tilted her head. "Mr. Riley, are you coming on to me?"

He sighed, but the laughter stayed in his eyes. "Miss Reynolds, I thought I was being so subtle."

"No."

"No, I'm not being subtle?"

"No, you're not. And no." Now she did slide her hand from his. "It's a nice offer, but I'm involved with someone." *Maybe,* she added to herself. "And if I weren't, I don't think it's wise to mix personal and professional relationships."

"That sounds very definite. Are you always very definite?"

"Yes." But she smiled. "Definitely."

Angela paused in the doorway, set her teeth against temper. The picture of her protégée and her lover smiling intimately at each other in her living room had her gorge rising. Though the taste of fury was familiar, even pleasant, she took a deep breath, fixed a smile on her lips.

"Finn, darling!" She flew across the room, a curvy golden blossom stemmed in pale blue silk. Even as Finn rose from the sofa, she threw herself into his arms and fastened her mouth possessively on his. "Oh, I've missed you," she murmured, sliding her fingers up into the thick tangle of his hair. "So much."

She had an impact, Finn thought. She always did. The offer of unapologetic sex was there in the press of her body, the heat of her mouth. His body responded even as his mind took a wary step in retreat.

"It's good to see you, too." He untangled himself, holding her at arm's length to study her. "You look wonderful."

"Oh, so do you. Shame on you, Deanna." But she didn't take her eyes off Finn. "For not telling me the guest of honor was here."

"I'm sorry." Deanna resisted the urge to clear the huskiness from her throat. She wished now she had left the room the moment Angela had entered, but the greedy, knowing look on the woman's face as she raced to Finn had rooted Deanna to the spot. "I was just about to."

"She was going to mix me a drink first." Finn looked over Angela's shoulder to Deanna. There was still amusement there, Deanna noticed. And if she wasn't mistaken, a faint touch of embarrassment.

"I don't know what I'd do without her." Turning, Angela slid one arm around Finn's waist, cuddling her body back into the curve of his in a way only small, soft women could manage easily. "I can depend on Deanna for absolutely everything. And do. Oh, I forgot." Laughing, she held out a hand for Deanna, as if to invite her into the charmed circle. "With all this confusion, I completely forgot about the excitement last night. I was nearly sick with worry when I heard about the plane." She shuddered, and squeezed Deanna's hand. "And I meant to tell you what a terrific job you did on the remote. Isn't it just like Finn to hop right out of the center of a near disaster and do a report?"

Deanna's eyes flicked up to Finn's, then back to Angela's. There was so much sexual heat in the room she could barely breathe. "I wouldn't know. I'm sure the two of you would like some time alone before the guests arrive, and I really need to change."

"Oh, of course, we're keeping you. Deanna's a tiger for timetables," Angela added, tilting her head up to Finn's. "Run along, dear." Her voice was a purr as she released Deanna's hand. "I'll handle things from here."

"Why don't I fix that drink?" Finn shifted away from Angela when Deanna's quick footsteps rapped up the stairs.

"I'm sure there's champagne back there," Angela told him as he walked behind the rosewood bar. "I want to toast your homecoming with the best."

Obliging, Finn took a bottle from the small refrigerator built into the back of the bar. He considered several different ways to handle the situation with Angela as he removed the foil and twisted the wire.

"I tried to phone you several times last night," she began.

"When I got in, I let the machine pick up. I was pretty wiped out." The first lie—but not the last, he decided with a grimace as he popped the cork. Bubbling wine fizzed up to the lip, then retreated.

"I understand." She crossed to the bar, laid a hand on his. "And you're here now. It's been a long six months."

Saying nothing, he poured her wine and opened a bottle of club soda for himself.

"Aren't you joining me?"

"I'll stick with this for now." He had a feeling he'd need a clear head tonight. "Angela, you went to an awful lot of trouble. It wasn't necessary."

"Nothing is too much trouble for you." She sipped the wine, watching him over the rim.

Perhaps it was the coward's way to keep the bar between them. But his eyes were direct, steady and cool. "We had some good times, Angela, but we can't go back."

"We'll be moving forward," she agreed. She brought his hand to her lips, drew the tip of his finger into her mouth. "We were so good together, Finn. You remember, don't you?"

"I remember." And his blood pounded in response. He cursed himself for being as mindless as one of Pavlov's dogs. "It's just not going to work."

Her teeth nipped sharply into his flesh, surprising, and arousing, him. "You're wrong," she murmured. "I'll show you." The doorbell chimed again, and she smiled. "Later."

He felt like a man locked behind bars of velvet. The house was crowded with people, friends, coworkers, network brass, associates, all happily celebrating his return. The food was fabulous and exotic, the music low and bluesy. He wanted to escape.

He didn't mind being rude, but understood if he attempted to leave, Angela would create a scene that would reverberate from coast to coast. There were too many people in the business here for an altercation to go unreported. And he much preferred reporting news, rather than being reported on. With that in mind, he opted to tough it out, even with the inevitable messy showdown with her at the end of the interminable party.

At least the air was clear and fresh on the terrace. He was a man who could appreciate the scent of spring blossoms and newly cut grass, of mingling women's perfumes and spicy food. Perhaps he would have enjoyed being alone to absorb the night, but he'd learned to be flexible when there was no choice.

And he had the talent for listening and exchanging conversation while his mind wandered. For now he let it trail to his cabin, where he would sit by the fire with a book and a brandy, or hunch over his bait box making new lures. Alone. The fantasy of being alone kept him sane through discussions of ratings and programming.

"I tell you, Riley, if they don't beef up Tuesday nights, we're going to face another cutback in the news division. Makes me sick to think about it."

"I know what you mean. Nobody's forgotten the body count from two years ago." He spotted Deanna. "Excuse me a minute, there's something I have to do." He squeezed through the crowd on the terrace and slipped his arms around her. When she stiffened, he shook his head. "This isn't a come-on, it's a diversion."

"Oh?" Automatically, she matched her steps to his as he danced. "From what?"

"From a diatribe on network politics. Tuesday night's schedule."

"Ah." She ran her tongue around her teeth. "We're a little weak there, as I'm sure you know. Our lead-in for the late news is—"

"Shut up." He smiled at her when she laughed, and enjoyed the fact that they were eye to eye. "You're a long one, aren't you?"

"So I've been told. You know, of course, that as the guest of honor, you're required to mingle."

"I hate rules."

"I live for them."

"Then consider this dance mingling. We'll even make small talk. I like your dress." It was true. The Adolfo gown's simple lines and bold red color were a welcome change from Angela's overly fussy pastels and lace.

"Thank you." Curiously she studied his face. She could almost see the pain rapping at his temples. "Headache?"

"No, thanks, I have one already."

"Let me get you some aspirin."

"It's all right. It'll pass." He drew her closer, laid his cheek against hers. "Better already. Where are you from?"

"Topeka." She'd nearly sighed, nearly closed her eyes before she snapped back to attention. He was entirely too smooth, she decided, though the adjective seemed odd when she was pressed tight to a body that was tough as iron.

"Why Chicago?"

"My roommate from college settled here after she got married. She talked me into relocating. The position with CBC made the move easy."

She smelled fabulous, he mused. The scent of her hair and skin made him think of spiced wine and quiet smoke. He thought of his lake, dappled in starlight, and the musical call of crickets in high grass. "Do you like to fish?"

"Excuse me?"

"Fish. Do you like to fish?"

She drew back to look at his face. "I have no idea. What sort of fishing?"

He smiled. It wasn't just the puzzlement in her eyes that caused his lips to curve. It was the fact that she was so obviously considering his question as seriously as one on world politics.

"You made the right move, Kansas. Curiosity like that should take you right to the top in this business. God knows you've got the face for it."

"I prefer to think I've got the brains for it."

"If you do, then you know that looks matter in television news. The public likes their death, destruction and dirty politics delivered by an attractive medium. And why the hell not?"

"How long did it take you to get that cynical?"

"About five minutes after I landed my first on-the-air job at the number-three station in Tulsa." Finn's thoughts veered forward; it would take only an inch to taste her ripe, sexy and serious mouth. "I beat out two other candidates because I looked better on tape."

"And your work had nothing to do with it?"

"It does now." He toyed with the ends of the hair that rained over her shoulders.

His fingers felt entirely too good against her skin, Deanna realized, and shifted gears. "Where did you get the scar?"

"Which one?"

"This one." She moved his hand between them, tilted the scar up.

"Oh. Bar fight. In . . ." His eyes narrowed as he tried to place the incident. "Belfast. A charming little pub that caters to the IRA."

"Mmm." As a precaution she kept his hand in hers. However intimate the gesture looked, it prevented him from touching her. "Don't you think it's undignified for a well-known television correspondent to brawl in bars?"

"I'm entitled to some entertainment, but it was a long time ago." The scared thumb brushed gently up the side of hers, down again, toward the wrist, where her pulse began to stutter. "I'm much more dignified now." And he smiled, drawing her closer.

Every muscle in her body turned to water. "I don't think so."

"Try me." It was a low, murmured challenge she had no answer for. "Someone's looking for you."

Shaking off the mood, she glanced over her shoulder and spotted Marshall. When their eyes met, he smiled and held up two glasses of champagne.

"I guess that's my cue to let you go." Finn did, then captured her hand for one last moment. "Just how seriously involved are you?"

She hesitated, looking down at their joined hands. The desire to link fingers was very strong. "I don't know." She met his eyes squarely. "I haven't decided."

"Let me know when you do." He released her hand, and watched her walk away.

"I'm sorry I'm late." Marshall kissed her briefly before he offered Deanna a flute of champagne.

"It's all right." She sipped, surprised that her throat felt so dry.

"It's a little chilly out here, isn't it?" Concerned, he touched her hand. "You're cold. Come inside."

"All right." She glanced back toward Finn as Marshall led her away. "I'm sorry the evening was spoiled yesterday."

"Don't worry about it." After a quick scan of the room, Marshall guided her toward a quiet corner. "We both face emergencies in our work."

"I did call you after I got in."

"Yes, I got the message from my service." His eyes flicked down to his glass before he drank. "I decided to make it an early night."

"Then you didn't see the report."

"Last night? No. But I did catch pieces of it on the morning news. Wasn't that Finn Riley you were dancing with just now?"

"Yes."

"He's had quite a homecoming all in all. I can't imagine being that concise and detached after being so close to death. I suppose he's hardened to it."

Deanna frowned. "I'd say it's more a matter of instinct and training."

"I'm glad your instinct and training haven't made you so cold. Your report from the airport was very passionate, very genuine."

She smiled weakly. "It was supposed to be objective and informative."

"It was very informative." He kissed her again. "And you looked beautiful in the rain." Lingering over the kiss, he missed her wince of annoyance. "Barring news bulletins," he said quietly, "can we plan on slipping away early, having some time alone?"

Twenty-four hours before, she would have said yes, she realized. Now, with the murmur of conversation around them, the music drifting in through the terrace doors, the fizz of champagne on her tongue, she hesitated. Marshall tipped a finger under her chin, a gesture she'd once found endearing.

"Problem?" he asked.

"No. Yes." She let out a breath, impatient with her own wavering. It was time to step back, she thought, and take stock. "I'm sorry, Marshall, Angela's counting on me to see this party through. And to be honest, things are moving a little fast for me."

He didn't remove his hand, but she sensed him drawing in. "I didn't mean to push."

"You weren't. You haven't." She curled her fingers over his wrist in a gesture that was both apologetic and affectionate. "I tend to be cautious—maybe overcautious—in relationships. There are reasons, and I'll explain them to you, when I can."

"No need to rush." He let his hand drop away from her chin. "You know how much I want to be with you, and it's not simply sexual."

"I know that." Rising to her toes, she laid her cheek against his. And remembered, very clearly, the feel of her cheek resting against Finn's as they'd danced.

• • •

He was tired, and he didn't tire easily. Years of snatching sleep on trains and planes and buses, of camping out in jungles and deserts and behind enemy lines had toughened him. He enjoyed the fine linens and mint-bedecked pillows of luxury hotels, but Finn could sleep just as soundly with his head on a bedroll and the echoes of artillery fire as a lullaby.

Tonight he pined for bed and oblivion. Unfortunately, there was unfinished business. He might have been a man to ignore rules, but he never ignored problems.

"That was the last of them." Angela swept back into the living room looking as fresh and lovely as she had hours earlier. "Everyone was so glad to see you again." She wrapped her arms around him, nestling her head beneath his shoulder.

His hand lifted to stroke her hair in a habitual gesture. She felt soft, and somehow pink, he thought. It was like being tangled in a fragrant, climbing vine. If he didn't nip off the feelers, it would certainly choke him.

"Let's sit down. We need to talk."

"I know it's hard to believe, but I'm about talked out." She skimmed a hand down his shirt, then back up to toy with his top button. "And I've been waiting all evening to be alone with you, to give you your real homecoming." She leaned forward for a kiss. Her eyes flashed like jagged cobalt when he held her off.

"Angela, I'm sorry. I'm not interested in picking up where we left off six months ago." He kept his hands firm on her shoulders. "We ended it badly, and I regret that, but we did end it."

"You're not going to punish me for being overly emotional, for saying things in the heat of the moment. Finn, we meant too much to each other."

"We had an affair," he corrected. "We had sex. It was great sex. And we had a kind of odd friendship. We might be able to salvage the friendship if we put the rest out of the picture."

"You're being cruel."

"I'm being honest."

"You don't want me?" She tossed back her head and laughed. The sound, like her eyes, was glassy. "I know you do. I can feel it." Her skin was glowing as she stepped toward him again. Her lips parted, curved, as she watched his eyes drop to them and linger. "You know what I can do for you, Finn. What I'll let you do to me. You want as much as I want."

"I don't take everything I want."

"But you took me. Right here, on this floor the first time. Remember?" With her eyes locked on his, she slid her hands up his chest, shivering with triumph when she felt the unsteady thud of his heart under her palm. "I drove you crazy; you tore my clothes off of me. Remember what it was like?" Her voice lowered, sliding through his system like tainted honey.

He remembered, and the memory made him sick with desire. The bite of her fingernails on his back, her teeth at his shoulder. She'd drawn blood and he hadn't given a damn.

"I want you to take me again, Finn." She watched his face as her hand crept downward.

His fingers curled at her back, digging into the silk. He knew what it would be like and, for a moment, desperately craved that moment of violent pleasure. But he remembered much more than the urgent sex and the dazzling fantasies.

"It isn't going to happen again, Angela." He let his hands drop away from her back. She was quick. He should have been prepared, but her vicious backhanded blow knocked him back two steps.

His eyes heated like suns, but he lifted a hand and coolly wiped the blood from his lip. "More than this room hasn't changed, I see."

"It's because I'm older than you, isn't it?" She hurled the words at him as her fury contorted the careful beauty of her face. "You think you can find someone younger, someone you can mold and train and teach to grovel."

"We've played that tune before. I'd say we've played them all." He turned heading for the door. He was nearly across the foyer when she threw herself at his feet.

"Don't. Don't leave me!" She clung to his legs, sobbing. Rejection sliced at her, bringing as much fear as pain. As it always did. As it always would. "I'm sorry." And she meant it, completely, utterly, at that moment. It only made it worse. "I'm sorry. Please, don't leave me."

"For God's sake, Angela." Pummeled by pity and disgust, he dragged her to her feet. "Don't do this."

"I love you. I love you so much." With her arms twined around his neck, she wept against his shoulder. The love was as true as her earlier fury, as volatile, and as capricious.

"If I thought you meant that, I'd feel sorry for both of us." He jerked her back, gave her a quick shake. Tears. He'd always considered them a woman's most potent and most underhanded weapon. "Turn it off, damn it. Do you think I could have slept with you on and off for three months and not know when you're manipulating me? You don't love me, and you only want me because I walked away."

"That's not true." She lifted her tear-ravaged face. There was such innocent hurt in it, such wretched sincerity, that he nearly faltered. "I do love you, Finn. And I can make you happy."

Furious, with her as well as with his own weakness for her, he pried her arms away. "Do you think I didn't know that you put pressure on James to have me fired just because you didn't want me to take the London assignment?"

"I was desperate." She covered her face with her hands and let the tears leak through her fingers. "I was afraid of losing you."

"You wanted to prove you were in control. And if James hadn't been so solidly behind me, you could have fucked up my career."

"He didn't listen to me." She lowered her hands, and her face was cold. "Neither did you."

"No. I came here tonight because I'd hoped we'd both had enough time to let things settle. Looks like I was wrong."

"Do you think you can walk out on me?" She spoke quietly and with utter calm as Finn moved toward the door. The tears were forgotten. "Do you think it's simple to just turn your back and walk away? I'll ruin you. It may take years, but I swear, I'll ruin you."

Finn paused at the door. She stood in the center of the foyer, her face blotched and puffy with weeping, her eyes swollen and hard as stone. "Thanks for the party, Angela. It was a hell of a show."

• • •

Deanna would have agreed. As Finn strode toward his car, she was yawning in the elevator as it climbed toward her apartment. She was grateful she had the entire next day off. It would give her time to recover, and time to think through her situation with Marshall.

But the only thing on her schedule now was a long, soothing bath and a good night's sleep.

She had her keys out of her purse before the elevator doors opened. Humming to herself, she unlocked both the standard lock and the dead bolt. Out of habit, she hit the light switch beside the door as she crossed the threshold.

Quiet, she thought. Wonderful, blessed silence. With the door locked again behind her, she crossed automatically to her phone machine to check messages. As she played them back, she slipped out of her black satin pumps and wriggled her cramped toes. She was smiling at the recording of Fran's voice reciting possible baby names when she spotted the envelope near the door.

Odd, she mused. Had that been there when she'd come in? She crossed the room, glancing through the security peephole before bending to scoop up the note.

There was nothing written on the sealed envelope. Puzzled, and fighting off another yawn, she tore it open, unfolded the single sheet of plain white stationery.

There was only one sentence, typed in bold red ink.

Deanna, I adore you.

6

"We've got thirty seconds to air."

"We'll make it." Deanna slipped into her chair beside Roger on the news set. Through her earpiece she heard the frantic overlapping voices in the control room. A few feet away, the floor director was shouting demands for information and dancing in place. One of the camera crew was smoking lazily and chatting with a grip.

"Twenty seconds. Jesus." Roger wiped his damp palms on his knees. "Where did Benny get the bright idea to add music to the tape?"

"From me." Deanna gave Roger a brief apologetic smile. "It was just a toss-off idea when I was previewing it. It really will make the piece perfect." Someone was shouting obscenities through her earpiece, and her smile turned a little sickly. Why did she always want perfection? "Honestly, I didn't know he'd grab onto it this way."

"Ten fucking seconds." Roger took a last glimpse in his hand mirror. "If we have to fill, I'm dumping on you, babe."

"We're going to be fine." Her jaw was set stubbornly. She'd make it fine, by God. She'd make it the best damn one-minute-ten the station had ever aired. The swearing in the control room turned to a pandemonium of cheers as the floor director began his countdown. "Got it." She glanced smugly in Roger's direction, then faced the camera.

"Good afternoon, this is *Midday*. I'm Roger Crowell."

"And I'm Deanna Reynolds. The passenger count on flight 1129 from London last

Friday was two hundred and sixty-four. Early this morning, that number rose by one. Matthew John Carlyse, son of passengers Alice and Eugene Carlyse, made his first appearance at five-fifteen this morning. Though six weeks premature, Matthew weighed in at a healthy five pounds."

As the tape rolled, to the accompaniment of the crooning "Baby, Baby," Deanna let out a relieved breath and grinned at the monitor. Her idea, she reminded herself. And it *was* perfect. "Great pictures."

"Not bad," Roger agreed, and was forced to smile when the monitor focused on the tiny form squirming and squawling in the incubator. There was a small set of wings pinned to his blanket. "Almost worth the ulcer."

"The Carlyses named their son after Matthew Kirkland, the pilot who landed flight 1129 safely at O'Hare Friday night despite engine failure. Mr. Carlyse said that neither he nor his wife were concerned about making the return flight to London at the end of the month. Young Matthew had no comment."

"In other news . . ." Roger segued into the next segment.

Deanna glanced down at her copy, reviewing her pacing. When she looked up again, she spotted Finn in the rear of the studio. He rocked back on his heels, his thumbs hooked in his front pockets, but he gave her a nod of congratulations.

What the hell was he doing there, watching, evaluating? The man had a full week's free time coming to him. Why wasn't he at the beach, the mountains, somewhere? Even as she turned to the camera again and picked up her cue, she could feel his eyes on her, coolly blue and objective.

By the time they broke for the last commercial before "Deanna's Corner," her nerves had evolved into bubbling temper.

Deanna pushed back from the news desk, descended the step and marched across the snaking cables. Before she could greet her guest for the day, Finn stepped in front of her.

"You're better than I remember."

"Really?" She gave the hem of her jacket a quick tug. "Well, with a compliment like that, I can die happy."

"Just an observation." Curious, he wrapped his fingers around her arm to hold her in place. "I can't make up my mind about you. Am I still on the blacklist because I bumped you off the story the other night?"

"You're not on any list. I just don't like being watched."

He had to grin. "Then you're in the wrong business, Kansas."

He let her go. Impulsively he took one of the folding chairs out of camera range. He hadn't intended to stay, and knew he did so simply to irritate her. He'd come in that afternoon, as he'd come in the evening before, because he enjoyed being back in the Chicago studios.

He didn't have much in his life at the moment other than his career. He preferred it that way. He watched Deanna ease her guest's nerves with off-camera chitchat, and considered. Would she be relieved or annoyed to know he hadn't given her a thought over the remainder of the weekend? Years in the business had made him an expert at compartmentalizing his life. Women didn't interfere with his work, the sculpting of a story or his ambitions.

The months in London had added to his reputation and his credibility, but he was happy to be back.

His thoughts swung back to Deanna as he heard her laugh. A good, smoky sound, he thought. Subtle sex. It suited her looks, he decided. And those eyes. They were warm now, and filled with lively interest as her guest hyped a one-woman art show scheduled for that evening.

At that moment, Finn didn't give a damn about art. But he was interested, very interested in Deanna. The way she leaned forward, just a little, to add a sense of intimacy to the interview. Not once did he catch her looking at her notes and scrambling for the next question.

Even when they broke, Deanna continued to give her guest her attention. As a result, the artist left the studio with her ego fully pumped. Deanna slipped back behind the news desk with Roger for the close.

"She's good, isn't she?"

Finn glanced behind him. Simon Grimsley was standing just inside the studio doors. He was a thin-shouldered man, with a long, narrow face set in perpetual lines of worry and doubt. Even when he smiled, as he did now, there was a look in his eyes that spoke of inescapable doom. He was losing his hair, though Finn knew him to be on the shy side of thirty. He was dressed, as always, in a dark suit and snugly knotted tie. And, as always, the attire accented his bony frame.

"How's it going, Simon?"

"Don't ask." Simon rolled his dark, pessimistic eyes. "Angela's in one of her moods today. Big time."

"That's not exactly a breaking story, Simon."

"Don't I know it." He lowered his voice as the red light blinked on. "Threw a paperweight at me," he whispered. "Baccarat. Lucky she doesn't have much of an arm."

"Maybe she could get a job with the Cubs."

Simon gave what passed for a chuckle, then guiltily stifled it. "She's under a lot of pressure."

"Yeah, right."

"It isn't easy staying number one." Simon let out a sigh of relief when the "on the air" sign blinked off. Live television kept him in a constant state of turmoil. "Deanna." He signaled to her and nearly hooked his foot in a coil of cable in his hurry to catch up. "Nice show. Really nice."

"Thanks." She looked from him to Finn, then back. "How'd this morning's taping go?"

"It went." He grimaced. "Angela asked me to get this message to you." He offered a pale pink envelope. "It seemed important."

"Okay." She resisted the urge to bury the note in her pocket. "Don't worry, I'll get back to her."

"Well, I'd better get upstairs. Come by this afternoon's taping if you get a chance."

"I will."

Finn watched the door swing shut behind Simon. "I'll never understand how anyone so nervous and depressed can deal with the characters *Angela's* books."

"He's organized. I don't know anyone better at sorting things out than Simon."

"That wasn't a criticism," Finn said as he matched her stride out of the studio. "It was a comment."

"You seem to be full of comments today." Out of habit, she turned into the dressing room to redo her makeup.

"Then I've got another one. Your interview with the artist—Myra, was it?—was solid."

Pleasure snuck through her guard. "Thanks. It was an interesting subject."

"It didn't have to be. You kept her grounded when she started to run on about technique and symbolism. You kept it light and friendly."

"I prefer light and friendly." Her eyes met his in the mirror and sizzled. "I'll leave Gorbachev and Hussein to you."

"I appreciate it." He shook his head as she freshened her lipstick. "You're touchy. The observation was meant as a compliment."

He was right, she thought. She was being touchy. "Do you know what I think, Finn?" She smoothed back her hair and turned. "I think there's too much energy in this room. Conflicting energy."

He had felt electricity since the moment he'd scooped her against him on a rainy runway. "And how does all that conflicting energy make you feel?"

"Crowded." She smiled, in direct response to the amusement in his eyes. "I suppose that's why it always seems you're in my way."

"I guess I'd better move aside then, and give you some room."

"Why don't you?" She picked up the pink envelope she'd set on the counter, but before she could open it, Finn took her hand.

"Question. How do you justify your job as a reporter for CBC with your job with Angela?"

"I don't have a job with Angela. I work the news." In quick, competent moves, she ran a brush through her hair and tied it back. "I occasionally do favors for Angela. She doesn't pay me."

"Just a couple of pals helping each other out?"

She didn't care for the edge in his voice. "I wouldn't say Angela and I were pals. We are friends, and she's been very generous with me. The news division doesn't have a problem with my personal association with Angela, or with the time I give her."

"So I hear. But then the entertainment division wouldn't step back from applying a little pressure when they've got the clout of a top-rated show." He rocked back on his heels, studying her. "It makes me wonder why Angela would go to the trouble just to use you."

Her hackles rose. "She isn't using me. I'm learning from her. And learning is something I find useful."

"Learning what, exactly?"

How to be the best, she thought, but cautiously kept that thought to herself. "She has incredible interviewing skills."

"That she does, but yours seem sharp enough to me." He paused. "At least on soft news."

She nearly snarled, delighting him. "I enjoy what I do, and if I didn't, it still wouldn't be any of your business."

"An accurate statement." He should have dropped the subject, but he knew too well what Angela could do with her claws once they were dug in. Unless he missed his guess, Deanna would bleed fast and copiously. "Would you listen to a friendly warning about Angela?"

"No. I make up my mind about people on my own."

"Suit yourself. I wonder," he continued, searching her face. "Are you as tough as you think you are?"

"I can be tougher."

"You'll need to be." He released her hand and walked away.

Alone, Deanna let out a long, steadying breath. Why was it every time she spent five minutes with Finn, she felt as though she'd run a marathon? Exhausted and exhilarated. Pushing him firmly out of her mind, she tore open Angela's note. The handwriting was a series of loops and flourishes drawn with a fountain pen.

Deanna darling,
I have something vitally important to discuss with you. My schedule today is maddening, but I can slip away about four. Meet me for tea at the Ritz. Lobby lounge. Believe me, it's urgent.

Love,
Angela

Angela hated to be kept waiting. By four-fifteen, she'd ordered a second champagne cocktail and begun to steam. She was about to offer Deanna the chance of a lifetime, and rather than gratitude, she was greeted with rudeness. As a result, she snapped at the waitress when her drink was served, and scowled around the sumptuous lounge.

The fountain behind her tinkled musically. It soothed her a bit, like the frothy sip of champagne. It wasn't really drinking, she thought, pleasing herself. It was like tasting success.

The gilt and glory of the Ritz was a long way from Arkansas, she reminded herself. And she was about to go further yet.

The reminder of her plans softened the frown on her face. The smile bolstered the courage of a matron with blue-tinted hair who approached for an autograph. Angela was all gracious affability. When Deanna hurried in at twenty after four, she saw Angela chatting amiably with a fan.

"Excuse me." Deanna took the seat across from Angela. "I'm sorry I'm late."

"Don't give it a thought." Waving away the apology, Angela smiled. "So nice to have met you, Mrs. Hopkins. I'm glad you enjoy the show."

"I wouldn't miss it. And you're even lovelier in person than you are on TV."

"Isn't that sweet?" Angela said to Deanna when they were alone. "She watches the show every morning. Now she'll be able to brag to her bridge club that she met me in person. Let's get you a drink."

"We'd better make it tea. I'm driving."

"Nonsense." Angela caught the waitress's attention, tapped her glass, then held up two fingers. "I refuse to celebrate with something as passive as tea."

"Then I'd better know what we're celebrating." Deanna slipped out of her jacket. One drink, she estimated, could easily last the entire thirty minutes she'd allowed for the meeting.

"Not until you have your champagne." Angela smiled coyly before sipping her own.

"I really need to thank you again for being such a trouper the other night. It turned out to be a wonderful party."

"There wasn't much to do."

"Easy for you to say. You're able to keep a handle on all those little details." With a flutter of her fingers, Angela dismissed them. "They just annoy me." Setting her drink aside again, she took out a cigarette. "And what do you think of Finn?"

"I'd have to say he's one of the best reporters on CBC or any of the networks. Powerful. He has a way of cutting to the heart of an issue, and letting just enough of himself sneak through to intrigue the audience."

"No, no, not professionally." Angela blew out an impatient stream of smoke. "As a man."

"I don't know him as a man."

"Impressions, Deanna." Angela's voice sharpened, putting Deanna on alert. "You're a reporter, aren't you? You're trained to observe. What are your observations?"

Boggy ground, Deanna decided. The station had been ripe with rumors of past history, and the speculation of a current affair between the two stars. "Objectively? He's very attractive, charismatic, and I suppose I'd have to use the word 'powerful' again. He's certainly well liked by the techs, and by the brass."

"Especially the women." Angela began to jiggle her foot, a sign of agitation. Her father had been charismatic, too, hadn't he? she remembered bitterly. And attractive, and certainly powerful—when he was on a winning streak. And he'd left her as well, her and her pathetic, drunken mother for another woman and the siren call of a royal flush. But she'd learned since then, learned a lot about payback. "He can be very charming," she continued. "And very devious. He isn't above using people to get what he wants." She drew deeply on the cigarette, smiled thinly through a mist of smoke. "I noticed him seek you out at the party, and thought I'd give you a friendly warning."

Deanna lifted a brow, wondering how Angela would feel if she knew Finn had used the same phrase just a few hours earlier. "No need."

"I know that you're involved with Marshall at the moment, but Finn can be very persuasive." She tapped out her cigarette, leaning closer. Girl to girl. "I know how news travels at the studio, so there's no need to pretend you don't know about what was between Finn and me before he went to London. I'm afraid since I broke things off, he might try to salve his ego and strike back at me, by making a play for someone I care about. I wouldn't want to see you hurt."

"I won't be." Uncomfortable, Deanna shifted back. "Angela, I really am running thin on time. If this is what you wanted to talk to me about—"

"No, no. Just making small talk. And here we go." She beamed as their drinks were served. "Now we have the proper tools for a toast." She lifted her glass, waited until Deanna had lifted hers. "To New York." The flutes clinked joyfully together.

"New York?"

"All my life I've been working toward it." After a hasty sip, Angela set her glass down. Excitement was shimmering around her in restless waves. Nothing, not even champagne could compete with it. "Now it's reality. What I'm telling you now is in the strictest confidence. Understood?"

"Of course."

"I had an offer from Starmedia, Deanna, an incredible offer." Her voice bubbled like the wine. "I'll be leaving Chicago and CBC in August, when my contract's up. The show will be moving to New York, with the addition of four prime-time specials a year." Her eyes were like blue glass, her fingers running up and down the flute like excited birds searching for a place to land.

"That's wonderful. But I thought you'd already agreed to renew with CBC and the Delacort syndicate."

"Verbally." She shrugged it off. "Starmedia is a much more imaginative syndicate. Delacort's been taking me for granted. I'm going where I'm most appreciated—and most rewarded. I'll be forming my own production company. And we won't just produce *Angela's.* We'll do specials, TV movies, documentaries. I'm going to have access to the best in the business." She paused, always a showman. "That's why I want you to come with me as my executive producer."

"You want me?" Deanna shook her head as if to clear jumbled thoughts. "I'm not a producer. And Lew—"

"Lew." Angela dismissed her longtime associate with a toss of her head. "I want someone young, fresh, imaginative. No, when I make this move, I won't be taking Lew with me. The job's yours, Deanna. All you have to do is take it."

Deanna took a long, slow sip of champagne. She'd been expecting the offer of head researcher, and because ambition pointed elsewhere, she was prepared to decline. But this, this was out of nowhere. And it was far more tempting.

"I'm flattered," she began. Flabbergasted, she corrected. "I don't know what to say."

"Then I'll cue you. Say yes."

With a quick laugh, Deanna sat back and studied the woman across from her. Eager, impulsive and, yes, ruthless. Not bad qualities all in all. There was also talent and brains and those edgy nerves Angela thought no one noticed. It was the combination that had pushed her to the top, and was keeping her there.

A top spot on the top show in the market, Deanna calculated. "I wish I could jump at it, Angela. But I need to think this through."

"What is there to think about?" The wine was fizzing in Angela's head. Deanna was just quick enough to save a flute from upending when Angela reached carelessly across the table. "You don't get offers like this every day in this business, Deanna. Take what there is when you can. Do you know the kind of money I'm talking about? The prestige, the power?"

"I have some idea."

"A quarter of a million a year, to start. And all the benefits."

It took Deanna a moment to close her mouth. "No," she said slowly. "Apparently I didn't have any idea."

"Your own office, your own staff, a car and driver at your disposal. Opportunities to travel, to socialize with the cream."

"Why?"

Pleased, Angela sat back. "Because I can trust you. Because I can depend on you, and because I see something of myself when I look at you."

A quick chill danced up Deanna's spine. "It's a very big step."

"Small ones are a waste of time."

"That may be, but I need to think this through. I don't know if I'm suited."

"I think you're suited." Angela's impatience was simmering again. "Why would you doubt it?"

"Angela, one of the reasons I imagine you're offering me this job is because I'm a good detail person. Because I'm thorough and obsessively organized. I wouldn't be any of those things if I didn't take the time to sort this out."

With a nod, Angela took out another cigarette. "You're right. I shouldn't be pushing, but I want you with me on this. How much time do you need?"

"A couple of days. Can I let you know by the end of the week?"

"All right." She flicked on her lighter and studied the flame briefly. "I'll just say one more thing. You don't belong behind a desk on some local noon show reading the news. You were made for bigger things, Deanna. I saw it in you right from the beginning."

"I hope you're right." Deanna let out a long breath. "I really do."

The little gallery off Michigan Avenue was crammed with people. Hardly larger than the average suburban garage, the showroom was brightly lit to suit the bold, splashy paintings arranged nearly frame to frame along the walls. The moment Deanna stepped inside, she was glad she'd followed the impulse to stop in. Not only did it take her mind off Angela's stunning offer that afternoon, but it allowed her to follow up firsthand on her own interview.

The air was ripe with sounds and scents. Cheap champagne and clashing voices. And color, she mused. The blacks and grays of the crowd were a stark contrast to the vibrancy of the paintings. She regretted she hadn't wrangled a camera crew to do a brief update.

"Quite an event," Marshall murmured in her ear.

Deanna turned, smiled. "We won't stay long. I know this isn't exactly your style."

He glanced around at the frantic colors slashed over canvas. "Not exactly."

"Wild stuff." Fran edged her way through, her husband Richard's hand firmly gripped in hers. "Your spot this afternoon had some impact."

"I don't know about that."

"Well, it didn't hurt." Tilting her head up, Fran sniffed the air. "I smell food."

"It's gotten so she can smell a hot dog boiling from three blocks away." Richard shifted in to drape an arm around Fran. He had a pretty, boyish face that smiled easily. His pale blond hair was conservatively cut, but the tiny hole in his left earlobe had once sported a variety of earrings.

"It's heightened sensory awareness," Fran claimed. "And mine tells me there are pigs-in-a-blanket at three o'clock. Catch you later." She dragged Richard away.

"Hungry?" Bumped from behind, Deanna moved comfortably into Marshall's protective arm.

"Not really." Using the advantage of height, he scouted the area and led her away from the heart of the crowd. "You're being a good sport about this."

"Coming here? It's interesting."

She laughed and kissed him again. "A very good sport. I'd just like to make a quick pass through, and congratulate Myra." Deanna looked around. "If I can find her."

"Take your time. Why don't I see if I can find us some canapés."

"Thanks."

Deanna threaded her way through the crowd. She enjoyed the press of bodies, the undertones of excitement, the snippets of overheard conversations. She'd made it halfway around the room when a bold painting stopped her. Sinuous lines and bold splashes against a textured background of midnight blue, it turned the canvas into an explosion of emotion and energy. Fascinated, Deanna moved closer. The label beneath the sleek ebony frame read AWAKENINGS. Perfect, Deanna thought. Absolutely perfect.

The colors were alive and seemed to be fighting their way free of the canvas, away from the night. Even as she studied the work, she felt her pleasure turn to desire, and desire to determination. With a little juggling of her budget...

"Like it?"

She felt jolted into awareness. But she didn't bother to turn around to face Finn.

"Yes, very much. Do you spend much time in galleries?"

"Now and then." He stepped up beside her, amused at the way she stared at the painting. Every thought in her head was reflected in her eyes. "Actually, your spot this afternoon convinced me to drop in."

"Really?" She looked at him then. He was dressed much as he'd been when he'd crossed the runway. His expensive leather jacket unsnapped, his jeans comfortably worn, boots well broken in.

"Yes, really. And I owe you one, Kansas."

"Why is that?"

"This." He nodded toward the painting. "I just bought it."

"You—" She looked from him to the painting and back again. Her teeth locked together. "I see."

"It really caught me." He dropped a hand on her shoulder and faced the painting. If he continued to look at her, Finn knew he'd break out in a grin. It was all there in her eyes—the disappointment, the desire, the irritation. "And the price was right. I think they're going to find out very soon that they're underselling her."

It was hers, damn it. She'd already imagined it hanging above her desk at home. She couldn't believe he'd snapped it out from under her. "Why this one?"

"Because it was perfect for me." With the lightest of pressure on her shoulder, he turned her to face him. "I knew the moment I saw it. And when I see something I want..." He trailed a finger up the side of her throat, feather light, while his eyes stayed on hers. "I do what I can to have it."

Her pulse jumped like a rabbit, surprising her, annoying her. They were standing toe to toe now, their eyes and mouths lined up. And too close, just an inch too close, so that she could see herself reflected in the dreamy blue of his eyes.

"Sometimes what we want is unavailable."

"Sometimes." He smiled, and she forgot the crowd pressing them together, the coveted painting at her back, the voice in her head telling her to back away. "A good reporter has to know when to move fast and when to be patient. Don't you think?"

"Yes." But she was having a hard time thinking at all. It was his eyes, she realized, the way they focused as if there were nothing and no one else. And she knew, somehow, that he would continue to look at her just that way, even if the ground suddenly fell away beneath her.

"Want me to be patient, Deanna?" His finger roamed over her jawline, lingered.

"I—" The air backed up in her lungs. And for a moment, one startled moment, she felt herself swaying toward him.

"Oh, I see you found refreshments already," Marshall said.

She saw the wry amusement on Finn's face. "Yes, Marshall." Her voice was unsteady. Fighting to level it, she gripped his arm as though he were a rock in the stormy sea. "I ran into Finn. I don't think you've met. Dr. Marshall Pike, Finn Riley."

"Of course. I know your work." Marshall offered a hand. "Welcome back to Chicago."

"Thanks. You're a psychologist, right?"

"Yes. I specialize in domestic counseling."

"Interesting work. The statistics seem to point to the end of the traditional family, yet the overall trend, if you look at advertising, entertainment, seems to be making a move back to just that."

Deanna looked for a barb, but found nothing but genuine interest as Finn drew Marshall into a discussion on American family culture. It was the reporter in him, she imagined, that made it possible for him to talk to anyone at any time on any subject. At the moment, she was grateful.

It comforted her to have her hand tucked into Marshall's, to feel that she could be, if she chose, part of a couple. She preferred, overwhelmingly, Marshall's gentle romancing to Finn's direct assault on the nervous system. If she had to compare the two men, which she assured herself she certainly didn't, she would have given Marshall top points for courtesy, respect and stability.

She smiled up at him even as her eyes were drawn back to the dramatic and passionate painting.

When Fran and Richard joined them, Deanna made introductions. A few minutes of small talk, and they said their goodbyes. Deanna tried to pretend she didn't feel Finn's eyes on her as they nudged their way to the door.

"Be still my heart," Fran muttered in Deanna's ear. "He's even sexier in person than he is on the tube."

"You think so?"

"Honey, if I was unmarried and unpregnant, I'd do a lot more than think." Fran shot one last look over her shoulder. "Yum-yum."

Chuckling, Deanna gave her a light shove out the door. "Get a hold of yourself, Myers."

"Fantasies are harmless, Dee, I keep telling you. And if he'd been looking at me the way he was looking at you, I'd have been a puddle of hormones at his feet."

Deanna combated the jitters in her stomach with a brisk gulp of spring air. "I don't melt that easily."

Not melting easily, Deanna thought later, was part of the problem. When Marshall pulled his car to the curb in front of her building, she knew that he would walk her up. And when he walked her up, he would expect to be invited inside. And then...

She simply wasn't ready for the "and then."

The flaw was in her, undoubtedly. She could easily blame her hesitation toward intimacy on the past. And it would be true enough. She didn't want to admit another part of her hesitation was attributable to Finn.

"You don't need to walk me up."

He lifted a hand to toy with her hair. "It's early yet."

"I know. But I have an early call in the morning. I appreciate your going by the gallery with me."

"I enjoyed it. More than I anticipated."

"Good." Smiling, she touched her lips to his. When he deepened the kiss, drawing her in, she yielded. There was warmth there, passion just restrained. A quiet moan of pleasure sounded in her throat as he changed the angle of the kiss. The thud of his heart raced against hers.

"Deanna." He took his mouth on a slow journey of her face. "I want to be with you."

"I know." She turned her lips to his again. Almost, she thought dreamily. She was almost sure. "I need a little more time, Marshall. I'm sorry."

"You know how I feel about you?" He cupped her face in his hand, studying her. "But I understand, it has to be right. Why don't we get away for a few days?"

"Away?"

"From Chicago. We could take a weekend." He tipped her face back and kissed the side of her mouth. "Cancún, St. Thomas, Maui. Wherever you like." And the other side. "Just the two of us. It would let us see how we are together, away from work, all the pressures."

"I'd like that." Her eyes drifted closed. "I'd like to think about that."

"Then think about it." There was a look of dark triumph in his eyes. "Check your schedule, and leave the rest to me."

7

Deanna hadn't expected the pricks of disloyalty. Television was, after all, a business. And part of the business was to get ahead, to make the best deal. But while the May sweeps consumed the CBC Building, with nightly ratings discussed and analyzed by everyone from top brass to the maintenance crews, she felt like a traitor.

Next year's budgets were being forecasted off the sweeps, and the forecasts were being made on faulty assumptions.

She knew *Angela's* would be gone before the start of the fall season. And with the deal Angela had made, she would compete with CBC's daytime lineup as well as with prime-time specials.

The more celebratory the mood in the newsroom, the more guilt jabbed at Deanna's conscience.

"Got a problem, Kansas?"

Deanna glanced up as Finn made himself comfortable on the corner of her desk. "Why do you ask?"

"You've been staring at that screen for the past five minutes. I'm used to seeing you move."

"I'm thinking."

"That doesn't usually stop you." Leaning forward, he rubbed his thumb between her eyebrows. "Tension."

In defense, she shifted back in her chair to break the contact. "We're in the middle of the May sweeps. Who isn't tense?"

"*Midday's* holding its own."

"It's doing better than that," she snapped back. Pride and loyalty welled together. "We've got a twenty-eight-percent share. We're up three full ratings points since the last sweeps."

"That's better. I'd rather see you fired up than unhappy."

"I wasn't unhappy," she said between her teeth. "I was thinking."

"Whatever." He rose then, and hauled up the garment bag he'd set on the floor.

"Where are you going?"

"New York." In an easy, practiced move, Finn slung the bag over his shoulder. "I'm putting in a few days as substitute host on *Wake Up Call.* Kirk Brooks's allergies are acting up."

Deanna arched a brow. She knew that CBC's *Wake Up Call* was performing poorly, lagging well behind *Good Morning America* and *Today.* "You mean the ratings are acting up."

Finn shrugged and took one of the candy-coated almonds from the bowl on her desk. "That's the bottom line. The brass figures the viewers will think somebody who's been through a few firefights and earthquakes is glamorous." Disgust crossed his face as he swallowed. "So, I'll get up early for a few days and wear a tie."

"It's a little more than that. It's a complicated show. Interviews, breaking stories—"

"Chitchat." The phrase was ripe with contempt.

"There's nothing wrong with chitchat. It involves the viewer, brings them into the picture. And it opens doors."

His lips curved into something between a smile and a sneer. "Right. The next time I interview Qaddafi I'll be sure to ask how he feels about Madonna's new video."

Intrigued, she tilted her head back to study him. She thought she'd pegged him as the reckless rebel who did precisely as he chose and kept the executives groping for the Maalox. "If you hate it so much, why are you doing it?"

"I work here," he said simply, and helped himself to a handful of candy.

Deanna lowered her eyes, toyed with papers on her desk. So did she, she thought miserably. So did she. "Then it's a matter of loyalty."

"First." What was going on inside that head of hers? he wondered. It was a pity he didn't have time to hang around and dig it out. "Then you can expand it. If *Wake Up Call* goes in the sewer, the revenue suffers. What's the first place that feels it?"

"The news department."

"Damn right. You've got the morning show scraping the bottom of the ratings barrel, and the fact that a couple of fatheaded idiots can't seem to program a decent Tuesday night, and before you can say Nielsen, we've got cutbacks."

"Monday and Friday are strong," she murmured. "And we've got *Angela's.*"

"It's a little tough knowing that Angela and a handful of sitcoms are saving our ass." Then he smiled, shrugged. "Screwy business. I don't suppose you'd kiss me goodbye."

"I don't suppose I would."

"But you'll miss me." There was enough laughter in his eyes to make her grin back at him.

"You're not going off to war, Finn."

"Easy for you to say. Stay tuned." He sauntered off. Deanna watched him walk up to another woman reporter. The woman laughed, then planted an exaggerated kiss on his mouth. As applause erupted, he turned, grinned at Deanna. With a final salute to the newsroom, he swung through the doors.

Deanna was still chuckling when she returned to her copy. The man might have his flaws, she mused, but at least he could make her laugh.

And, she admitted, he could make her think.

Mentally, she pulled out her list. Two columns, neatly typed, specifying her reasons to accept and decline Angela's offer. There was a hard copy in the top drawer of her desk at home. It was a simple matter to visualize it. With a sigh, she added one word to the "decline" column.

Loyalty.

"Miss Reynolds?"

She blinked and focused. Behind a porcelain pot of lush red hibiscus was a round, cheerful face. It took her a moment to click it in. But when he shoved a pair of wire-rimmed glasses up his pug nose, she remembered.

"Jeff, hi. What's all this?"

"For you." He set it on her desk, then immediately shoved his hands in his pockets. As an editorial assistant, Jeff Hyatt was more comfortable with equipment than with people. He gave Deanna a fleeting smile, then stared at the flowers. "Nice. I ran into the delivery boy, and since I was on my way in . . ."

"Thanks, Jeff."

"No problem."

Deanna had already forgotten him as she reached for the card tucked among the blooms.

How about Hawaii?

Smiling, she reached out to stroke a blossom. One more on the "decline" list, she mused. Marshall.

"Miss Reynolds to see you, Miss Perkins."

"Ask her to wait." With a cigarette smoldering between her fingers, Angela frowned over Beeker's report on Marshall Pike. It was certainly interesting reading, and demanded her full attention. His credentials were well earned—the doctorate from Georgetown, the year studying abroad. And financially, the psychologist did well for himself counseling socialites and politicians on their floundering marriages and dysfunctional families. He offset his lucrative practice by donating three afternoons a week to social services.

Overall, a nice, upstanding profile of a man who had studied well and worked hard and was devoted to preserving family life.

Angela knew all about profiles, and the illusions they fostered.

His own marriage had failed. A quiet, civilized divorce hadn't caused much of a ripple in Chicago society, and certainly hadn't harmed his practice. Still, it was interesting. Interesting because Beeker had discovered that the size of Marshall's settlement with his ex-wife was a whopper, as were the alimony payments. Much more than a brief, childless marriage warranted.

He hadn't contested it, Angela mused. A smile lifted the corners of her mouth as she continued to read. Perhaps he hadn't dared. When a thirty-five-year-old man was caught entertaining his secretary's very lovely, very naked and very young daughter at two A.M., he didn't have a lot of room for negotiations. A minor, however willing, was still a minor. And adultery, particularly with a sixteen-year-old, carried a hefty price tag.

He'd been clever in covering himself, Angela mused, scanning Beeker's file. The secretary had taken a fat lump sum and a glowing reference and moved her family to San Antonio. The wife had taken a great deal more, but barely a whisper about the good doctor had escaped. And when it had—and Angela admired him for his boldness—rumor tied him obliquely with the secretary, not her nubile daughter. . . .

So, the elegant Dr. Pike continued his practice as one of Chicago's most eligible bachelors.

The eminent family counselor with a weakness for teenagers. An interesting topic for a show, she decided, and laughed out loud. No, no, they would keep this one private. Some information was worth a great deal more than ratings. Angela closed the file and slipped it into a drawer. She wondered how much Deanna knew.

"Send her in, Cassie."

Angela was all smiles when Deanna walked in. "Sorry I kept you waiting. I had a little something to finish up."

"I know you're busy." Deanna briefly tugged on her earring. "Do you have a few minutes?"

"Of course." She rose, gesturing to a chair. "How about some coffee?"

"No, don't bother." Deanna sat, made herself fold her hands quietly in her lap.

"No trouble. Something cold instead?" Delighted, for the moment, to serve, Angela crossed to the bar and poured them both a mineral water. "If I didn't have a dinner tonight, I'd have Cassie bring in some of those fudge cookies I know she's got in her desk." She laughed lightly. "She doesn't think I know about them. But then, I make it a policy to know everything about my people." After handing Deanna a glass, she dropped into a chair and stretched out her legs. "It's been quite a day so far. And I'm off at dawn for California."

"California? I didn't know you were going on location."

"No, I'm speaking at the commencement exercises at Berkeley." Not bad, Angela thought, for someone who waited tables to get through Arkansas State. "I'll be back for Monday's tapings. You know, Dee, since you stopped by, you might take a look at my speech. You know how I value your input."

"Sure." Miserable, Deanna sipped at the water. "I can't do it until after five, but—"

"No problem. You can fax it back to me at home. I'll give you a copy."

"All right. Angela—" The only way to handle this was straightforwardly. "I'm here to talk to you about your offer."

"I was hoping you were." Relaxed, satisfied, Angela slipped off her shoes and reached for a cigarette. "I can't tell you how much I'm looking forward to the move to New York, Deanna. That's where the pulse of this business is, you know." She snapped on her lighter, took a quick drag. "That's where the power is. I've already got my agent looking for an apartment."

Her eyes lost their calculating edge and turned dreamy. Inside she was still the girl from Arkansas who wanted to be a princess. "I want something with a view, lots of windows and light, lots of room. A place where I can feel at home, where I can entertain. If I find the right place, we may even shoot some of the specials there. The viewing audience likes to get a peek at our personal lives."

She smiled as she tapped her cigarette. The soft look in her eyes sharpened. "We're going places, Dee. Women have finally gained a solid foothold in broadcasting, and we're going right to the top. You and me." She reached over and gave Deanna's hand a quick squeeze. "You know, your brains, your creativity are only part of the reason I want you with me." Her voice was persuasive and ringing with sincerity. "I can trust you, Dee. I can relax around you. I don't have to tell you what that means to me."

Deanna closed her eyes a moment while guilt churned in her stomach.

"I don't think there's ever been another woman I've felt so close to," Angela concluded.

"Angela, I want—"

"You're going to be more than my executive producer; you're going to be my right hand. In fact, I should have my agent looking for a place for you, too. Nearby," she murmured, envisioning the late-night girl talks she'd never been permitted during her youth. "It's going to be wonderful, for both of us."

"Angela, slow down." With a half laugh, Deanna held up a hand. "I think I understand how much this deal with Starmedia means to you, and I'm thrilled for you. You've been wonderful to me, your help, your friendship, and I wish you all the success in the world." Leaning over, Deanna took Angela's hand. "But I can't take the job."

The gleam in Angela's eyes dimmed. Her mouth tightened. The unexpected rejection nearly stopped her breath. "Are you certain you understand just what I'm offering you?"

"Oh yes, I do. I do," she repeated, squeezing Angela's hand between both of hers before she got up to pace. "And believe me, I've thought about this carefully. I've had a hard time thinking of anything else." She turned back, gesturing with her hands. "And I just can't do it."

Very slowly, Angela straightened in her chair. She crossed her legs. The simple gesture eradicated all the softness. "Why?"

"A lot of reasons. First, I have a contract."

With a sound caught between disgust and amusement, Angela waved it aside. "You've been around long enough to know how easily that's dealt with."

"That may be, but when I signed I gave my word."

Taking another contemplative drag, Angela narrowed her eyes. "Are you that naive?"

Deanna understood it was meant as an insult. But she merely lifted a shoulder. "There are other factors. Even knowing you don't plan to take Lew, I'd feel guilty stepping into his shoes—particularly since I don't have his experience. I'm not a producer, Angela. And though it's awfully tempting to forget that and jump at the offer—the money, the position, the power. Christ, New York." She blew out a breath that fluttered her bangs. She hadn't fully understood how much she wanted all those things until they had been within reach and she'd had to let them go. "And the chance to work with you. Really work with you, that isn't easy for me to turn my back on."

"But you are." Angela's tone was cool. "That's precisely what you're doing."

"It's just not for me. Other factors just got in the way, no matter how hard I tried to reposition them. My ambitions run in front of the camera. And I'm happy in Chicago. My job, my home, friends are here."

Angela tapped out the cigarette in quick, short bursts, like machine-gun fire. "And Marshall? Did he factor into this decision?"

Deanna thought of the pot of red hibiscus on her desk. "Somewhat. I do have feelings for him. I'd like to give them a chance."

"I have to tell you, you're making a mistake. You're letting details and personal feelings cloud your professional judgment."

"I don't think so." Deanna crossed the room to sit again, leaned forward. It was a tricky business, she thought, turning down an offer without seeming ungrateful. Particularly when the offer had taken on all the connotations of a favor to a friend. "I've looked at this from every angle. That's what I do—occasionally what I overdo. Your offer wasn't easy to turn down, and I don't do it lightly. I'll always be grateful and incredibly flattered that you had enough faith in me to ask."

"So you're going to sit back and read copy?" Now it was Angela who rose. Fury was bubbling so hot within her she could feel it searing under her skin. She'd offered the girl a feast, and she was settling for crumbs. Where was the gratitude? Where was the fucking loyalty? "Your choice," she said coolly as she sat behind her desk. "Why don't you take a few more days—the weekend, while I'm away—in case you have any second thoughts." She shook her head to cut off any comment from Deanna. "We'll talk again Monday," Angela said in dismissal. "Between tapings. Pencil it in for, oh . . ." Her mind was working frantically as she flipped through her appointment book. "Eleven-fifteen." Her smile was warm, friendly again when she glanced up. "If you're of the same mind then, I won't give you an argument. Fair enough?"

"All right." It seemed more gracious, and certainly easier to agree. "I'll see you Monday, then. Have a nice trip."

"I will." Deliberately she waited until Deanna was at the door. "Oh, Dee." She smiled and held up a manila envelope. "My speech?"

"Right." Deanna crossed the room again, to take the package.

"Try to get it back to me before nine. I need my beauty sleep."

Angela waited until the door closed before she folded her hands on the desk. Her fingers turned bone-white with the pressure. She took a long moment, staring at the closed door, breathing shallowly. It wouldn't do to rage, she told herself. No, not this time. For Deanna she had to be cool and calm and concise to review the facts.

She'd offered Deanna a position of power, her own unqualified friendship, her trust. And she preferred to read the news at noon because she had a contract, a lease on an apartment and a man.

Could she actually be that artless? Angela wondered. That guileless? That stupid?

She relaxed her hands, forced herself to lean back in her chair and even her breathing. Whatever the answer, Deanna would learn that no one ever turned Angela down.

Calmer now, Angela opened a drawer and took out Marshall's file. The look on her face wasn't hard, nor was it glittery with anger. Her lips trembled into a pout, a child's expression on being denied. Deanna wasn't going to go with her to New York, she mused. And she was going to be very, very sorry.

• • •

Deanna had taken one step into the outer office when her guilty mood vanished into a flood of surprised pleasure.

"Kate. Kate Lowell."

The leggy, doe-eyed woman turned, brushing her glorious mane of flaming hair aside. Her face—the ivory complexion, the delicate bones, the melting eyes and generous mouth—was as stunning as it was famous. The quick, flashing smile was automatic. She was, first and last, an actress.

"Hello."

"Those braces sure as hell did the job." Now Deanna laughed. "Kate, it's Dee. Deanna Reynolds."

"Deanna." The furious nervous tension beneath the smile dissolved. "Oh, God, Deanna." The infectious giggle that turned men to putty rang out. "I can't believe it."

"Imagine how I feel. It has to be fourteen, fifteen years."

For Kate, for one beautiful moment, it felt like yesterday. She could remember all the long talks—the innocence of girlish confidences.

Under Cassie's fascinated eye, the two women crossed the room and embraced. They hung on to each other a moment, tight.

"You look wonderful," they said simultaneously, then laughed.

"It's true." Kate drew back, but kept Deanna's hand in hers. "We do. It's a long way from Topeka."

"Longer for you. What's Hollywood's newest star doing in Chicago?"

"A little business." Kate's smile dimmed. "A little hype. What about you?"

"I work here."

"Here?" The remnants of the warm smile vanished. "For Angela?"

"No, downstairs. In the newsroom. *Midday,* with Roger Crowell and Deanna Reynolds."

"Don't tell me two of my favorite people know each other." Angela stepped out, the gracious hostess. "Kate, dear, I'm sorry you had to wait. Cassie didn't tell me you were here."

"I just got in." The hand still gripping Deanna's stiffened, then relaxed. "My plane was delayed this morning, so I've been running behind all day."

"Awful, isn't it? Even a woman with your talents is subject to the whims of technology. Now tell me . . ." She strolled over to lay a proprietary hand on Deanna's shoulder. "How do you know our Dee?"

"My aunt lived across the street from Deanna's family. I spent a couple of summers in Kansas as a child."

"And you were playmates." Angela's laugh was delighted. "That's charming. And Deanna's been keeping her brush with fame all to herself. Shame on you."

In a subtle move, no less potent for its polish, Kate shifted. The gesture eased Angela out of the circle. "How's your family?"

"They're fine." Baffled by the tension snapping in the air, Deanna tried to find the source of it in Kate's eyes. All she could see—was allowed to see—was the soft, tawny gold. "They never miss one of your movies. Neither do I. I remember how you'd put on plays in your aunt's backyard."

"And you'd write them. Now you're reporting the news."

"And you're making it. You were incredible in *Deception,* Kate. I cried buckets."

"There's Oscar talk." Smoothly, Angela moved forward to drape an arm around Kate's shoulders. "How could there not be when Kate so effectively played the heroic young mother fighting to keep her child." A look passed between them, sharp as a razor. "I attended the premiere. There wasn't a dry eye in the house."

"Oh, I imagine there was one." Kate's smile was brilliant, and curiously feline. "Or two."

"I'd love to give you girls time to catch up." Angela pressed her fingers warningly on Kate's shoulder. "But we're running late."

"I'll let you go." Tucking Angela's speech under her arm, Deanna stepped back. "How long will you be in Chicago?"

"I'm leaving tomorrow." Kate stepped back as well. "It was good to see you."

"And you." Oddly hurt, Deanna turned and walked away.

"Isn't that sweet?" Angela gestured Kate into her office, shut the door. "You running into a childhood friend—who just happens to be my protégée—right in my office. Tell me, Kate, have you kept in touch with Dee? Shared all your secrets with her?"

"Only a fool shares secrets willingly, Angela. Now let's not waste time on small talk. Let's get down to business."

Satisfied, Angela sat behind her desk. "Yes, let's."

To Finn Riley, New York was like a woman: A long-legged, slick-skinned siren who knew her way around the block. She was sexy; she was by turns tacky and chic. And God knew she was dangerous.

Perhaps that was why he preferred Chicago. Finn loved women, and had a weakness for the long-legged, dangerous type. But Chicago was a big, burly man, with sweat on his shirt and a cold brew in his fist. Chicago was a brawler.

Finn trusted an honest fight more than he ever would a seduction.

He knew his way around Manhattan. He'd lived there briefly with his mother during one of his parents' trial separations. He'd lost track of how many trial separations there had been before the inevitable divorce.

He remembered how reasonable they both had been. How bloodless and civilized. And he remembered being shuffled off to housekeepers, secretaries, prep schools, to spare him, supposedly, from that well-choreographed discord. In reality, he knew neither of his parents had been comfortable with a young boy who had asked direct questions and hadn't been satisfied with logical, gutless answers.

So he had lived in Manhattan, and on Long Island, and in Connecticut and Vermont. He'd summered in Bar Harbor and on Martha's Vineyard. He'd done time in the hallowed halls of three of New England's top prep schools.

Perhaps that was why he still had such restless feet. The minute roots started to dig in, he felt honor-bound to rip them out and move on.

Now he was back in New York. Temporarily. Where he knew the underbelly as well as he knew his mother's elegant penthouse on Central Park West.

He couldn't even say if he preferred one to the other. Any more than he could say that he minded putting in a few days on *Wake Up Call.*

At the moment, Finn put New York out of his mind and concentrated on the ball whizzing toward his nose. It wasn't self-defense nearly as much as it was the spirit of competition. And God knew the exertion of the court was a welcome change from the hours he'd spent sitting on a sofa on the set the last four days.

He sliced out with his racket, letting out a grunt of effort that was lost as the ball caromed off the wall. The power sang up his arm, the echo of the smash reverberated in his head. Adrenaline raced through him as his opponent cracked the ball back.

He met it with a solid backhand. The sweat dribbled satisfactorily down his back, dampening his ragged CBC T-shirt. For the next five minutes, there was only the smash and echo of the ball, the smell of sweat and the sound of labored breathing.

"Son of a bitch." Barlow James sagged against the wall as Finn blew one by him. "You're killing me."

"Shit." Finn didn't bother with the wall. He slid straight down to the floor of the Vertical Club. Every muscle in his body was weeping. "Next time I'll bring a gun. It'll be easier on both of us." He groped for a towel, mopped his soaking face. "When the hell are you going to get old?"

Barlow's laugh barked off the walls of the racquetball court. He was a brawny six-foot-four, flat of stomach, broad of chest, with shoulders like concrete blocks. At sixty-three, he was showing no signs of slowing down. As he crossed toward Finn, he pulled an orange neon sweatband away from his silver mane of hair. Finn had always thought Barlow had a face that belonged on Mount Rushmore. Craggy, huge and powerful.

"Getting soft, kid." Barlow pulled a bottle of Evian out of his gym bag and tossed it underhand to Finn. The second one he kept himself, drinking in deep, greedy gulps. "Almost took you that time."

"I've been playing with Brits." Since he nearly had his breath back, Finn grinned up at him. "They're not as mean as you."

"Well, welcome back to the States." Barlow offered a hand, hauling Finn to his feet. It was like being gripped by a friendly grizzly. "You know, most people would have considered the post in London a promotion, even a coup."

"It's a nice town."

Barlow let out a sigh. "Let's hit the showers."

Twenty minutes later, they were stretched out on massage tables being pummeled.

"Damn good show this morning," Barlow commented.

"You've got a good crew, solid writers. Give it a little time and you'll be competitive."

"Time is shorter than it used to be in this business. I used to hate the goddamn bean counters." He bared his teeth in a grimace. "Now *I'm* a goddamn bean counter."

"At least you're a bean counter with imagination."

Barlow said nothing. Finn held his silence, knowing there was a purpose to this informal meeting.

"Give me an opinion on the Chicago bureau."

"It's tight," Finn said cautiously. "Hell, Barlow, you were bureau chief there for more than ten years, you know what we're working with. You've got a solid combination of experience and fresh blood. It's a good place to work."

"Ratings for the local evening news are weak. What we need is a stronger lead-in. I'd like to see them shift *Angela's* to four, pull her audience along."

Finn shrugged. He didn't ignore ratings, but he did detest their importance. "She's been at nine in Chicago and most of the Midwest for years. You might have a tough time pulling it off."

"Tougher than you think," Barlow murmured. "You and Angela . . . ah, there's nothing going on there anymore?"

Finn opened his eyes, cocked a brow. "Are we going to have a father-son chat, Pop?"

"Wiseass." Barlow chuckled, but his eyes were keen. Finn knew the look. "I wondered if you two had picked up where you left off."

"Where we left off was in the toilet," Finn said dryly. "And no."

"Hmmm. So are relations friendly or strained?"

"Publicly, friendly. Realistically, she hates my guts."

Barlow grunted again. It was good news, he thought, because he was fond of the boy. It was bad news because it meant he might not be able to use him. Making up his mind, he shifted on the table, wrapping the sheet around him and dismissing both masseuses.

"I've got a problem, Finn. A nasty little rumor that came buzzing in my ear a couple of days ago."

Finn pushed himself up. At any other time he would have made a crack about two grown men having an intense conversation while they were half naked and smelling of ginseng. "You want it to buzz in my ear?"

"And stop there."

"All right."

"Word is Angela Perkins is pulling up stakes—in Chicago and with CBC and Delacort."

"I haven't caught wind of that." Considering, Finn pushed the hair away from his face. Like any reporter, he hated getting news secondhand. Even if the news was only a rumor. "Look, it's contract time, right? She probably started the hum herself to get the brass to offer another truckload of money."

"No. Fact is, she's keeping it quiet. Real quiet. What I hear is that her agent's making negotiating noises, but they don't ring true. The leak came from Starmedia. If she leaves, Finn, it'll be a big hole."

"That's the entertainment division's problem."

"Their problem's our problem. You know that."

"Fuck."

"Well said. I only mention it because I thought if you and Angela were still . . ."

"We're not." Finn frowned. "I'll see what I can find out when I get back."

"Appreciate it. Now, let's get some lunch. We'll talk about news magazines."

"I'm not doing a news magazine." It was an old argument, one they continued with perfect amiability as they trailed sheets into the locker room.

"Hawaii sounds perfect," Deanna said into the phone.

"I'm glad you think so. How about the second week in June?"

Pleased with the idea, Deanna poured a mug of coffee. She carried it and her portable phone to the table where she'd set up her laptop. "I'll put in for it. I haven't taken any time since I started at the station, so I don't think it'll be a problem."

"Why don't I stop by? We can talk about it, look at some brochures."

She closed her eyes, knowing she couldn't ignore the insistent blip on her computer screen. "I wish we could. I've got work. I had something come in at the last minute that held me up." She didn't mention the hour she'd spent punching up Angela's speech. "Pulling the anchor desk this weekend's really tied me up. How about brunch on Sunday?"

"Say about ten? I could meet you at the Drake. We can look over the brochures and decide on what suits us."

"Perfect. I'll be looking forward to it."

"So will I."

"I'm sorry about tonight."

"Don't be. I've got some work myself. Good night, Deanna."

"Good night."

Marshall hung up. Mozart was playing on the stereo, a quiet fire was burning in the hearth and the scent of lemon oil and fragrant smoke hung in the air.

After polishing off his brandy, he walked up the stairs to his bedroom. There, with the sound of violins lilting through the recessed speakers, he stripped out of his tailored suit. Beneath, he wore silk.

It was a small affectation. He liked soft, expensive things. He liked, admittedly and without shame, women. His wife had often joked about it, he remembered, had even appreciated his admiration for the opposite sex. Until, of course, she'd found him intimately admiring young Annie Gilby.

He winced at the memory of his wife arriving home a full day early from a business trip. The look on her face when she'd walked into the bedroom and discovered him making loud, boisterous love to Annie. It had been a horrible mistake. A tragic one. His argument, perfectly justified, that his wife's preoccupation with her career and her lack of occupation in their bedroom had made him easy game, had fallen on deaf ears.

It hadn't mattered to her that the girl had utterly and deliberately seduced him, had played on his weaknesses, his frustrations. There had been other women, yes. But they had been momentary diversions, discreet sexual releases when his wife was away or involved with her own decorating business. And not worth mentioning.

He would never have hurt Patricia, Marshall assured himself now as he chose dark slacks and a shirt. He had loved her completely, and he missed her miserably.

He was a man who needed to be married, who needed a woman to talk to, to share his life and home with. A bright, intelligent woman, like Patricia. True, he needed the stimulation of beauty. That wasn't a flaw. Patricia had been beautiful, and ambitious; she had a sense of style and taste that was faultless.

In short, she'd been perfect for him. Except for her inability to understand a few very human flaws.

When she had discovered them, she'd been unforgiving as stone. And he had lost her.

Though he still missed her, he understood life continued.

Now he had found someone else. Deanna was beautiful, ambitious, intelligent. She was as perfect a companion as he could want. And he wanted her—had wanted her since he had first seen her face on the television screen. Now she was more than an image, she was reality. He was going to be very careful with her.

Sexually, she was a bit repressed, but he could be patient. The idea of taking her away from Chicago, away from the pressures and distractions, had been brilliant. Once she was relaxed, secure, she would belong to him. Until that time he would harness his needs, his frustrations.

But he hoped it wouldn't be much longer.

8

"Maui," Fran said over a mouthful of cheeseburger. "For the weekend. That's so un-Deanna."

"Is it?" Deanna paused over her own meal and considered. "Maybe it is, and I'm going to enjoy every minute of it. We're getting a suite in a hotel right on the beach where the brochure says you can see whales. Binoculars," she said suddenly, and dug in her purse for a pad. "I need a good pair."

Fran craned her neck and read the neat list Deanna had started. "Now, that's our Deanna. Are you going to eat all those fries?"

"No, help yourself." Already engrossed in her list, Deanna pushed her plate toward Fran.

"A weekend in Hawaii sounds pretty serious." Fran doused the fries with ketchup. "Is it?"

"It could be." She glanced up again, and the bloom in her cheeks spoke volumes. "I really think it could be. I feel comfortable with Marshall."

Fran grimaced. "Sweet pea, you feel *comfortable* with an old pair of bunny slippers."

"Not that kind of comfortable. I can relax around him. I know he's not going to pressure me, so that I can . . . just let things happen. When it feels right. I can talk to him about anything."

The words came quickly. Too quickly, Fran mused. If she knew Deanna, and she did, she'd have bet a month's pay her best friend was going out of her way to convince herself.

"He has this incredible sense of fairness," Deanna continued. "We're interested in so many of the same things. And he's romantic. I didn't realize how wonderful it would be to have someone send me flowers and arrange candlelight dinners."

"That's because you were always looking for the trapdoor."

"Yeah." Deanna let out a little breath, closed her notebook. "I'm going to tell him about Jamie Thomas."

In an automatic gesture of support, Fran reached out and covered Deanna's hand with hers. "Good. That means you trust him."

"I do." Her eyes darkened with determination. "And I want a normal, healthy relationship with a man. By God, I'm going to have one. I won't be able to do that until I tell him what happened to me. He's coming over for dinner tomorrow."

Fran abandoned the fries to fold her arms on the table between them. "If you need any moral support, you only have to call."

"I'll be fine. I've got to get back," she said after a glance at her watch. "I've got to do a news break at eight-thirty."

"You've got the ten o'clock tonight, too, don't you?" Fran stuffed a last fry in her mouth. "Richard and I'll watch you, while we're all snuggled up in bed. I'll make sure he's naked."

"Thanks." Deanna counted out bills for the tab. "That'll give me a nice visual while I'm reading the news."

It was nearly midnight when Deanna climbed into bed. As always, she checked her alarm, then made certain there was a pencil and pad on the nightstand beside the phone. The phone rang just as she was reaching for the light. Instinctively, she picked up the receiver with one hand, the pencil with the other.

"Reynolds."

"You were wonderful tonight."

The flutter of pleasure made her smile as she eased back against the pillows. "Marshall. Thanks."

"I just wanted you to know I was watching. It's the next best thing to being with you."

"It's nice to know." It felt glorious, snuggling back in bed, pleasantly sleepy, with the voice of the man she thought she might love in her ear. "I've been thinking about Hawaii all day."

"So have I. And about you." He had her taped image freeze-framed on his set, quietly arousing himself with her image and her voice. "I'm very indebted to Angela Perkins for bringing us together."

"Me too. Sleep well, Marshall."

"I will. Good night, Deanna."

Warm and content, Deanna replaced the receiver. Hugging herself, she laughed and indulged in a dreamy fantasy. She and Marshall walking along the beach while the sun dripped color into the water. Soft breezes. Soft words. The gentle tug low in her stomach pleased her. Normal, she told herself. Certainly that proved she was a normal woman with normal needs. She was ready to take the next step toward fulfilling them. She was eager to.

Only seconds after she switched off the lamp and snuggled down, the phone rang again. Chuckling to herself, she lifted the receiver in the dark.

"Hi," she murmured. "Did you forget something?"

There was only echoing silence in response.

"Marshall?" Her sleepy voice shifted into puzzlement. "Hello? Who's there?" Then into unease as the dull silence continued. "Hello? Is anyone there?" The quiet click brought on a quick shudder.

Wrong number, Deanna assured herself as she hung up. But she was cold. And it was a long time before she warmed again and slept.

Someone else lay awake in the dark. The ghostly light from the television screen was the only relief. Deanna smiled there, looking out into the room, looking directly into the eyes of her audience of one. Her voice, so smooth, so sweet, so seductive, played over and over on the recorder as it was rewound.

"I'm Deanna Reynolds. Good night. I'm Deanna Reynolds. Good night. I'm Deanna Reynolds. Good night."

"Good night." The answering whisper was soft, no more than a purr of pleasure.

• • •

Angela had planned every detail meticulously. Standing in the center of her office, she turned a slow circle. Everything was ready. There was a faint fragrance of jasmine in the air from the vase of flowers on the table by the love seat. The television set, for once, was blank. The quiet strains of Chopin eased through the speakers of the stereo. Beeker had been very thorough in his report. Marshall Pike preferred classical music, romantic settings and a woman with style. She wore the same trim designer suit she'd worn for that morning's taping, but she'd removed the blouse. The jacket fit with a snug "V," and there was a cunning hint of black lace teasing the cleavage.

At precisely eleven o'clock, she answered the buzzer on her desk. "Yes, Cassie."

"Dr. Pike is here, Miss Perkins."

"Ah, good." A feline smile crossed her face as she walked toward the office door. She liked a man to be prompt. "Marshall." She held out both hands to grip his, easing forward and tilting her head to offer her cheek. And to give him an interesting glimpse of black lace. "I really appreciate your making time for me today."

"You said it was important."

"Oh, and it is. Cassie, would you mind taking those letters right to the post office? Then you can go ahead and take your lunch. I won't need you back here until one." Turning, Angela led Marshall into her office, being certain to leave the door open a few inches. "What can I get you, Marshall? Something cold?" She trailed a fingertip down her jacket. "Something hot?"

"I'm fine."

"Well then, let's sit down." She took his hand again, steered him toward the love seat. "It's awfully good to see you again."

"It's good to see you, too." Puzzled, he watched her settle back, her skirt riding up on her thigh as she crossed her legs.

"You know how pleased I am with the help you've given me on the show, but I asked you here today to discuss something more personal."

"Oh?"

"You've been seeing a lot of Deanna."

He relaxed and struggled to keep his eyes from roaming down from her face. "Yes, I have. In fact, I've been meaning to call you and thank you for indirectly bringing us together."

"I'm very fond of her. As I'm sure you are," she added, laying a hand lightly on his thigh. "All that energy, that youthful enthusiasm. A beautiful girl."

"Yes, she is."

"And so sweet. Wholesome, really." Angela's fingers stroked lightly along his leg. "Not your usual type."

"I don't know what you mean."

"You're a man who's attracted to experience, to a certain sophistication. Except in one illuminating case."

He stiffened, drew back. "I don't know what you're talking about."

"Yes, you do." Her voice remained pleasant, easy. But her eyes had sharpened like two blue blades. "You see, I know all about you, Marshall. I know about your foolish slip with one Annie Gilby, age sixteen. And all about your previous, I should say pre-

Deanna, arrangement with a certain woman who lives on Lake Shore. In fact, I made it my business to know everything there is to know about you."

"You've had me followed?" He *struggled* for outrage, but panic had already outdistanced everything else. She could ruin him, with one careless announcement on her show. "What right do you have to pry into my personal life?"

"None at all. That's what makes it so exciting. And it *is* exciting." She toyed with the top button of her jacket. When his eyes flicked down to the movement, she glanced at the antique clock behind him. Eleven-ten, she thought, coolheaded, cold-blooded. Perfect.

"If you think you can use some sort of blackmail to ruin my relationship with Deanna, it isn't going to happen." His palms were wet, from fear, and from a terrible arousal. He would resist it. He had to resist it. "She's not a child. She'll understand."

"She may, or she may not. But I do." With her eyes on his, Angela flicked open the first button on her jacket. "I understand. I sent my secretary away, Marshall." Her voice lowered, thickened. "So I could be alone with you. Why do you think I went to all the trouble to find out about you?" She released the second button, toyed with the third and last.

He wasn't sure he could speak. When he forced the words out, they were like grains of sand in his throat. "What kind of game is this, Angela?"

"Any kind you want." She shot forward, quick as a snake, and caught his bottom lip between her teeth. "I want you," she whispered. "I've wanted you for a long time." Straddling him, she pressed his face against the breasts that strained against the hint of black lace. "You want me, don't you?" She felt his mouth open, grope blindly for flesh. There was a flash, razor-edged and hot, that was power. She'd won. "Don't you?" she demanded, gripping his head in both hands.

"Yes." He was already dragging her skirt up to her waist.

Deanna waited impatiently for the elevator to climb to sixteen. She really didn't have time to keep the appointment with Angela. But she was obligated by that invincible combination of manners and affection. She glanced at her watch again as people shuffled on and off on seven.

Angela was going to be upset, she mused. And there was no preventing it. Deanna hoped the dozen roses she'd brought along would soften the refusal.

She owed Angela much more than a few flowers, she thought. So many people didn't see what a generous and giving person Angela Perkins was, or how vulnerable. All they saw was the power, the ambition, the need for perfection. If Angela had been a man, those traits would have been celebrated. But because she was a woman, they were considered flaws.

As she stepped off the elevator on sixteen, Deanna promised herself that she would follow Angela's example, and the hell with the critics.

"Hi, Simon."

"Dee." He moved past her, double time, then stopped short and rushed back. "It's not her birthday. Tell me it's not her birthday."

"What? Oh." Seeing the horror on his face as he stared at the armload of flowers, she laughed. "No. These are a thank-you gift."

He let out a sigh, pressing his fingers to his eyes. "Thank God. She'd have killed me if I'd forgotten. She was already chewing off heads this morning because her flight was delayed getting in last night."

Deanna's friendly smile faded. "I'm sure she was just tired."

Simon rolled his eyes. "Right, right. And who wouldn't be? I get jet-lagged on the el." To show his complete sympathy with his boss's mood swings, he sniffed deeply at the flowers. "Well, those should brighten her mood."

"I hope so." Deanna continued down the corridor, wondering if Angela was taking Simon to New York. If she wasn't taking Lew . . . just how much of her staff would be laid off? Simon, the perennial bachelor and fussbudget, might be a bit twitchy, but he was loyal.

The twinge of guilt at knowing, when he didn't, that his career was on the line made her wince.

She found the outer office deserted. Puzzled, she looked at her watch again. Cassie must have had an early errand. With a shrug, she approached Angela's door.

She heard the music first, quiet, lovely. The fact that the door was open several inches was rare. Deanna knew that Angela was obsessive about keeping it firmly shut whether she was in or out. Shrugging, she crossed over, knocked lightly.

She heard other sounds now, not as quiet, not as lovely as the music. She knocked again, easing the door open wider.

"Angela?"

The name stuck in her throat as she saw the two forms wrestling on the love seat. She would have stepped back immediately, with embarrassment flaming in her cheeks, but she recognized the man, and the heat drained away into cold shock.

Marshall's hands were on Angela's breasts, his face buried in the valley between them. Even as she watched, those hands, ones she'd admired for their elegance, slid down to tug at the stylish linen skirt.

And as he did, Angela turned her head, slowly, even while her body arched forward. Her eyes met Deanna's.

Even in her haze of shock, Deanna saw the quick smile, the cagey delight before the distress clicked in. "Oh my God." Angela shoved against Marshall's shoulder. "Deanna." Her voice held the horror she couldn't quite bring to her eyes.

He turned his head. His eyes, dark and glassy, fixed on Deanna's. All movement froze, hideously, as if a switch had freeze-framed them. Deanna broke the tableau with a strangled cry. She turned and ran, trampling the roses she'd dropped at her feet.

Her breath was heaving by the time she reached the elevator. There was pain, a terrible pain radiating out from her chest. She stabbed the Down button again and again. Driven, she whirled away and ran for the stairs. She couldn't stand still, couldn't think. She stumbled down, saving herself from a fall by instinct rather than design. Knowing only that she had to get away, she plunged down, floor after floor, her sobbing breaths echoing behind her.

At street level, she rammed blindly against the door. She battered against it, weeping, until she found the control to depress the handle. Shoving through, she ran straight into Finn.

"Hey." Amusement came and went in a heartbeat. The moment he saw her face, his laughter fled. She was pale as a sheet, her eyes wild and wet. "Are you hurt?" He gripped her by the shoulders, drawing her out into the sunlight. "What happened?"

"Let me go." She twisted, shoving against him. "Goddamn it, leave me alone."

"I don't think so." Instinctively, he wrapped his arms around her. "Okay, baby. I'll just hold on, and you can cut loose."

He rocked, stroking her hair while she wept against his shoulder. She didn't hold back, but let all the shock and hurt pour out with the tears. The surging pressure in her chest eased with them, like a swelling soothed with cool water. When he sensed her calming, Finn shifted his hold. With his arm around her shoulders, he led her across the lot to a low stone wall.

"Let's sit." He dragged a handkerchief out of his pocket and pressed it into her hands. Though he hated a woman's tears, escaping Deanna's would brand him as the worst sort of coward. "You can pull yourself together and tell Uncle Finn all about it."

"Go to hell," she muttered, and blew her nose.

"That's a good start." Gently, he brushed the hair away from her damp cheeks. "What happened, Deanna?"

She looked away from him. There was too much concern, too much willingness to understand in his eyes. "I just found out I'm an idiot. That I have no sense of judgment, and that no one can be trusted."

"Sounds like a résumé for a television news anchor." When she didn't smile, he took her hand. "I haven't got any whiskey on me, and I gave up smoking last year. The best I can offer you is a shoulder."

"I seem to have used that already."

"I have another one."

Instead of leaning on it, she sat up straighter, squeezed her eyes tight a moment. Maybe she was an idiot, but she still had pride. "I just walked in on a woman I considered a friend, and a man I was considering as a lover."

"That's a big one." And he didn't have any clever words to smooth it over. "The psychologist?"

"Marshall, yes." Her lips trembled. With an effort, she firmed them. The tears she'd shed didn't shame her, but they were over. She meant to keep it that way. "And Angela. In her office."

Muttering an oath, he glanced up to the windows on the sixteenth floor. "I don't suppose you could have mistaken the situation."

Her laugh was as dry as dust. "I'm a trained observer. When I see two people, one half naked, pawing each other, I know what they're up to. I don't need corroboration to make the report."

"I guess not." He was silent a moment. The breeze whispered through the plot of grass behind them and waved through the bank of tulips that spelled out CBC in sunny yellow. "I could round up a crew," Finn considered, "go up to sixteen with a camera, lights and a mike, and make his life a living hell."

This time her laugh was less strained. "Interview him at the scene of the crime? It's a nice offer."

"No, really, I'd enjoy it." The more he thought about it the more he believed it was the perfect solution. "Dr. Pike, as a respected family counselor, how do you explain being caught with your pants down in a place of business before noon? Was this a professional call? A new form of therapy you'd like to share with the public?"

"They weren't down—yet," she said with a sigh. "I interrupted them. And while your offer's tempting, I'd just as soon handle the situation myself." She pushed the used handkerchief back in his hand. "Goddamn it, they made a fool out of me." Springing off the wall, Deanna wrapped her arms tightly around her body. "She planned it. I don't know why, I don't even know how, but she planned it. I saw it in her eyes."

This news didn't surprise him. Nothing about Angela did. "Have you pissed her off lately?"

"No." She lifted her hand to push back her hair and then stopped. New York, she thought, and nearly laughed again. "Maybe I did," she said softly. "And this is some twisted form of payback for what she sees as ingratitude." Furious now, Deanna turned back toward him. "She knew how I felt about him, and she used it. And what timing. Less than an hour before I have to go on." She looked at her watch, then covered her face with her hands. "Oh God. I've only got twenty minutes."

"Take it easy. I'll go down and tell Benny you're sick. They'll get a sub."

For one indulgent moment, she considered his offer. Then she remembered Angela's crafty, satisfied smile. "No. She'd enjoy that too much. I can do my job."

Finn studied her. Her face was tracked with tears and her eyes were puffy and red-rimmed, but she was determined. "They grow them tough in Kansas," he said with approval.

Her chin rose another notch. "Damn right they do."

"Let's get you into makeup."

She said nothing until they'd crossed the lot, walked through the door. "Thanks."

"You're welcome. Got any Visine?"

She grimaced as they started up the steps. "That bad?"

"Oh, it's worse."

He kept their conversation light as he steered her into makeup. He brought her ice for her eyes, water for her throat, then stayed to chat while she concealed the worst of the damage with cosmetics. But he was thinking, and his thoughts were anything but light. Anything but kind.

"That's not half bad," he commented. "Try a little more blusher."

He was right. Deanna stroked the brush over her cheek. And saw Marshall's reflection in the mirror. Her hand trembled once before she set the brush aside.

"Deanna, I've been looking for you."

"Oh?" She felt Finn coil beside her, like a big, mean cat about to spring, and laid a hand on his arm. With a jolt she realized the slightest signal from her would have him tearing in. It wasn't as unattractive an image as she wanted to think. "I've been right here," she said coolly. "I have a show to do."

"I know. I..." His eyes clung to hers, soft and brown and pleading. "I'll wait."

"There's no need for that." Odd, she thought. She felt powerful. Invincible. There seemed to be no relation between the woman she was at this moment and the one who had run sobbing from Angela's office. "I have a couple minutes to spare." Calmly, she leaned back against the counter and smiled at Finn. There was blood in her eye that had nothing to do with tears. "Would you mind leaving us alone?"

"Sure." He reached over and tipped her chin up another inch with his fingertip.

"That's a good look for you, Kansas." With a last, ice-edged stare at Marshall, he strolled out.

"Was it necessary to bring him into our private business?"

Deanna cut him off with a look. "Can you really have the gall to criticize me at a time like this?"

"No." Marshall's shoulders drooped. "No, of course not. You're right. It's just that I find this difficult, and embarrassing enough without the gossip spreading through the newsroom."

"Finn has more interesting things to discuss than your sex life, Marshall. I promise you. Now if you have something to say, you'd better say it. I only have a few minutes."

"Deanna." He stepped forward and would have reached for her, but the flash in her eyes warned him. "I have no excuse for what happened—or nearly happened. But I want you to know there's nothing between me and Angela. It was an impulse," he continued, speaking quickly when Deanna remained silent. "Purely physical and meaningless. It had nothing to do with what I feel for you."

"I'm sure it didn't," she said after a moment. "And I believe you. I believe it was impulsive, meaningless sex."

Relief flooded through him. He hadn't lost her. His eyes brightened as he reached out to her. "I knew you'd understand. I knew the minute I saw you that you were a woman generous enough to accept me, to understand me. That's why I knew we were meant to be together."

Rigid as stone, she stared up at him. "Take your hands off me," she said quietly. "Right now."

"Deanna." When he only tightened his hold, she fought back a bubble of panic, a quick, ugly sensory memory, and shoved.

"I said now." Free, she stepped back and took a deep, steadying breath. "I said I believed you, Marshall, and I do. What you did with Angela had nothing to do with your feelings for me. However, it had everything to do with mine for you. I trusted you, and you betrayed that trust. That makes it impossible for us to part friends. So, we'll just part."

"You're hurt now." A muscle twitched in his cheek. "So you're not being reasonable." It was like Patricia, he thought. So much like Patricia.

"Yes, I'm hurt," she agreed. "But I'm being very reasonable." A ghost of a smile flitted around her mouth, as insulting as a slap. "I make a habit out of being reasonable. I'm not calling you any of the names that occur to me."

"You see this as my fault. As a weakness." Confident in his skills as a mediator, he shifted gears. "What you haven't yet been able to see is your part in it. Your responsibility. I'm sure you'll agree that no successful relationship is the result of one person's efforts. All the weeks we've been together I've been patient, waiting for you to allow our relationship to move to the natural and very human phase of physical pleasure."

She didn't think he could shock her again. But she'd been wrong. "You're saying because I wouldn't go to bed with you, I forced you to turn to Angela?"

"You're not seeing the grays, Deanna," he said patiently. "I respected your wishes, your need to progress slowly. At the same time, it's necessary for me to satisfy my own needs. Angela was certainly a mistake—"

She nodded slowly. "I see. I'm glad we straightened this out, Marshall, before it went any further. Now I'm going to very reasonably tell you to go to hell."

She started out, her eyes going to smoke when he blocked the doorway. "We haven't finished, Deanna."

"I've finished, and that's all that counts. We both made a mistake, Marshall, a big one. Now get out of my way, and stay out of it before I make another one and embarrass us both by tearing the skin off your face."

Stiffly, he stepped aside. "I'll be ready to discuss this when you've calmed down."

"Oh, I'm calm," she muttered as she headed for the studio. "I'm dead calm, you bastard."

She shoved through the studio doors, strode across the floor and took her place behind the anchor desk.

Finn watched her through the first break. Once he was satisfied she was under control, he slipped out and walked to the elevator.

Over a celebratory glass of champagne, Angela watched the noon report in her office. She didn't give a damn about the words or images, but she was interested, even fascinated, by Deanna. The girl looked as cool and sweet as an ice-cream soda, Angela thought. Except for the eyes. Angela would have been bitterly disappointed if she hadn't seen the banked fury in Deanna's gaze.

"Direct hit," she murmured, delighted.

I win, she thought again, but couldn't prevent a twinge of admiration.

Curled in the leather chair behind her desk, she sipped and smiled, and finally raised her glass in silent toast to Deanna.

"She's got style, doesn't she?" Finn said from the doorway.

To her credit, Angela didn't jolt. She continued to sip and study the screen. "Absolutely. She could go a long way in the business with the right teacher."

"Is that the role you've carved out for yourself here?" Finn crossed the room, skirted the desk to stand behind Angela's chair. "Going to teach her your way, Angela?"

"My way works. Dee would be the first to tell you how generous I've been with her."

"She scares you, doesn't she?" Finn lowered his hands to Angela's shoulders, holding her firm so that they both faced Deanna's image.

"Why should she?"

"Because she's got more than style. You've got plenty of that yourself. She's got brains, but you have those, too. And guts, and drive. But then she tops you, Angela. Because she's got class. Bred-in-the-bone class." His fingers dug in when she started to shift. He couldn't know just how deeply he'd hit the mark. "That's something you'll never have. You can wear your pearls and your thousand-dollar suits; it doesn't mean a damn. Because you can't wear class. You can't buy it and you can't fake it." He spun her chair around, leaning over her so they were face to face. "And you'll never have it. So she scares the hell out of you, and you had to find a way to show her who was on top."

"Did she come running to you, Finn?" She was shaken, much more than she cared to admit, but she lifted her glass and sipped delicately, even though the drink now seemed a little more like a crutch. "Was she shocked and devastated and crying out for comfort?"

"You're such a bitch, Angela."

"You always liked that about me." Her eyes laughed over the rim of her glass. Then she shrugged. "The truth is, I'm sorry she was hurt that way. There's no denying that Marshall wasn't right for her, but I know she cared for him. The simple fact was he was attracted to me, and I to him." Because she wanted to believe her excuse, she did. Her voice rang with sincerity. "Things got out of hand, and I blame myself entirely. It was thoughtless."

"The hell it was. You don't take a breath without thinking it through."

She smiled again, looking up under her lashes. "Don't be jealous, Finn."

"You're pathetic. Did you think this stunt was going to break her?"

"If she had loved him, it would have." Pursing her lips, she examined her nails. "So, perhaps I did her a favor."

He laughed. "Maybe you did at that. You sure as hell did me one." He turned back to her and grinned. "I want her, and you just cleared the path."

He didn't have to dodge the glass she hurled. It struck the window a full six inches from his head. The crystal shattered. Delighted, Finn stuck his hands in his pockets.

"Your aim still stinks."

There was no laughter now, nor any of the regret she'd convinced herself she felt. There was only rage. "Do you think she'll want you after she hears what I can tell her?"

"Do you think she'll listen to anything you say after this stunt?" There was reckless humor in his eyes. "You overshot your mark this time. She's not going to come whimpering to you. She's going to tough it out. And she's going to get better. And you're going to start looking over your shoulder."

"Do you think I'm worried about some fluffy little news reader?" she demanded. "All I have to do is make a phone call and she'd be gone. Like that." She snapped her fingers. "Who do you think's been keeping this station out of the basement for the last two years? And where do you think it'll go when I pull up stakes?"

"So you *are* leaving." He nodded, rocked back on his heels. "Well congratulations and bon voyage."

"That's right. When the new season opens I'll be in New York, and *Angela's* will be produced by my own company. CBC's affiliates will come crawling to pay my price to air my show. Within two years, I'll be the most powerful woman in television."

"You might pull it off," he agreed. "For a while."

"I'll still be on top when you're scrounging around for a two-minute spot on the late news." She was trembling now, her temper pricked and pecked by needles of insecurity. "People want me. They admire me. They respect me."

"I certainly did."

Both Finn and Angela turned to the doorway, where Deanna stood, pale under her camera makeup. She noted, with no surprise, that Angela had salvaged most of the rose blooms and had set them prominently on her desk.

"Deanna." Tears swimming in her eyes, Angela started across the room. "I don't know how I can ever apologize."

"Please don't. I think, since it's only the three of us here, we can be honest. I know you planned the whole episode, that you arranged to have me walk in just when I did."

"How could you say such a thing?"

"I saw your face." Her voice hitched, but she steadied herself. She would not lose control. "I saw your face," she repeated. "I'm not sure whether it was because you wanted to prove that I was wrong about Marshall, or if it was because I couldn't accept your offer. Maybe it was a combination of both."

Hurt, every bit as genuine as the pearls at her throat, shuddered through Angela's voice. "You should know me better."

"Yes, I should have known you better. But I wanted to believe in you. I wanted to be flattered that you befriended me, that you saw something in me. So I didn't look past the surface."

"So." Blinking at tears, Angela turned away. "You're going to toss our friendship aside because of a man."

"No, I'm tossing it aside because of me. I wanted you to know that."

"I gave you my time, my help, my affection." Whirling, Angela pounced. "No one turns me down."

"Then I guess I'm the first. Good luck in New York." Good copy, Deanna told herself as she walked out. Damn good copy.

"Don't forget to look over your shoulder," Finn said as he closed the door quietly behind him.

9

ANGELA TRADES WINDY CITY FOR BIG APPLE
TALK SHOW QUEEN TO REIGN IN NEW YORK
MULTIMILLION-DOLLAR DEAL FOR CHICAGO'S FAVORITE BLONDE

The headlines gloated over the news. Even staunch vehicles like the *Chicago Tribune, The New York Times, The Washington Post* carried the banner. For one sunny day in June, stories of Angela's record-breaking deal overshadowed the troubled economy and unrest in the Middle East.

She was in her element.

With the graciousness of royalty, she granted interviews, welcomed a team from *People* into her home, chatted with Liz Smith over the phone. She had a quote for *Variety* and agreed to a layout in *McCall's*.

Finally, through hard work, blind ambition and sheer guts, she had attained what she'd always craved. Undivided attention.

She was canny enough to have nothing but the highest praise for CBC, for Delacort and for Chicago. She even worked up a few tears on *Entertainment Tonight*.

And her clipping service captured every word, every inch of print that revolved around her.

Then, amidst the uproar, she delivered the coup de grace. She would be taking the last six weeks on her contract as vacation.

"She knows how to turn the screws, doesn't she?" Fran rolled a pair of mismatched socks into a ball and tossed them into a laundry basket.

"That's not the worst of it." Deanna paced the tiny living room of Fran's downtown apartment. "Half her staff got pink-slipped. The others have the choice of pulling up stakes and moving to New York or looking for a new job." She hissed through her teeth. "There aren't any damn jobs."

"Obviously you don't read the papers. The administration says we're not in a recession. It's all in our minds."

Unamused, Deanna picked up a book of baby names and slapped it against her palm as she roamed the room. "I saw Lew McNeil's face when he left the building yesterday. God, Fran, he's been with her almost six years, and she cuts him loose without a thought."

Fran chose another pair of socks, one navy, one black. Close enough, she decided, and bundled them together. The heat made her purple tank top stick to her skin. "I'm sorry, Dee, for all of them. Everybody in television knows the game usually stinks. But I'm more concerned about you. Is Marshall still calling?"

"He stopped leaving messages on my machine." She shrugged. "I think he finally figured out I wasn't going to call back. He still sends flowers." With a bitter laugh, she tossed the baby book back onto the coffee table. "Can you believe it? He really thinks if he blankets me in enough posies, I'll forget everything."

"Want to have a men-are-scum session? Richard's playing golf, so he can't be offended."

"No, thanks." For the first time, she focused on her friend. "Fran, you just rolled up a gray sock with a blue one."

"I know. It adds a little excitement to the mornings. I gotta tell you, Dee, Richard's getting staid. You know, Saturday golf dates, three-piece suits. The house in the 'burbs we're buying. Jesus, we used to be rebels. Now we're . . ." She shuddered, lowered her voice. "Mainstream."

Laughing, Deanna sat cross-legged on the floor. "I'll believe that when you buy a Volvo and an espresso machine."

"I almost bought one of those 'Baby On Board' signs the other day. I came to my senses just in time."

"Then you're okay. I haven't even asked how you're feeling."

"Fabulous, really." Fran jabbed a loose pin back into her messy topknot. "All these women at work who've had kids look at me with scorn and envy. They have all these horror stories about pregnancy—morning sickness, fainting, water retention. And I feel like Rocky." She lifted an arm, flexed her muscle and managed to make a couple of freckles ripple. "Like I could go the distance without breaking a sweat." Lips pursed, she held up a checked argyle and a white sweat sock. "What do you think?"

"Why be subtle?" For the next few minutes they worked silently, folding laundry. "Fran, I've been thinking."

"I wondered when you'd get around to it. I could practically see the idea hopping around in your brain."

"It could be impractical," Deanna mused. "Hell, it could be impossible. After I run it by you, I want you to be completely honest."

"All right." Fran shoved the laundry basket away with one bare foot. "Shoot."

"Delacort, Angela's old syndicate, is going to have a big hole in their line-up and in their revenue. I'm sure they can fill it adequately enough, but . . . Did you know Delacort's CEO was Angela's second husband?"

"Sure. Loren Bach." Aside from the occasional grisly mystery, Fran's favorite reading was gossip rags, and she wasn't ashamed of it. If you wanted to know what celebrity was doing what with whom, and where, she was your girl. "They hooked up right after she ditched her first one—the real estate tycoon. Anyway, Loren Bach put a lot of money and muscle behind our girl. Made her a star."

"And though there were a few rumors, and some items in gossip columns to the contrary, they supposedly parted amicably." That much, Deanna had read. "Knowing Angela the way I do now, I really doubt that."

Fran's eyebrows wiggled. Not only did she love gossip, she loved dirty gossip best. "Word was she cost him a cool two million in the settlement, plus the house and furnishings, so I'd make it four mil. I wouldn't think Bach would have too much residual affection for our heroine."

"Exactly. And Bach has a long-standing relationship with Barlow James, the president of CBC's news division." Deanna rubbed her nervous hands on her knees. "And Mr. James likes my work."

Fran cocked her head, her eyes bright as a bird's. "So?"

"So I've got some money saved, I've got some connections." The idea had her heart jittering so that she pressed the heel of her hand against it as if to slow its pace. She wanted this very much, maybe too much. Enough, she realized, to skip several steps of her carefully calculated career plan. "I want to rent a studio, put together a tape. I want to pitch it to Loren Bach."

"Jesus." Fran leaned back against the cushions of the couch and goggled. "Is this you talking?"

"I know how it sounds, but I've thought it through. Bach moved Angela from a small, local show to a national hit. He could do it again. I'm hoping he wants to do it again, not only for his company, but personally. I can put together a series of clips from 'Deanna's Corner' and my news reports. I think I can get Barlow James to back me. And if I had a pilot, something simple and slick, I might have a shot." She rose again, too excited to sit. "The timing's perfect. The syndicate's still reeling from Angela's defection, and they haven't groomed a successor. If I could convince them to give me a chance locally, a handful of markets in the Midwest, I know I could make it work."

Fran blew out a breath, tapped her fingers on her flat belly. "It's off the wall, all right. And I love it." Letting her head fall back, she laughed at the ceiling. "It's just screwy enough to fly."

"I'll make it fly." Deanna came back to crouch in front of Fran and grip her hands. "Especially if I have an experienced producer."

"You can count on me. But the cost of the studio, the techs, even a trimmed-down production staff. It's a lot to risk."

"I'm willing to risk it."

"Richard and I have some put away."

"No." Touched, grateful, Deanna shook her head. "Absolutely not. Not with my godchild on the way. I'll take your brain, your back and your time, but not your money." After patting Fran's belly, she stood again. "Believe me, the first three are more important."

"Okay. So what's your format, what's your topic, where's your audience?"

"I want something simple, comfortable. Nothing issue-oriented. I want to do what I do best, Fran. Talk to people. Get them to talk to me. We get a couple of deep, cozy chairs. God knows I need new furniture anyway. Keep it chummy, intimate."

"Fun," Fran said. "If you're not going for the tears and angst, go for the fun. Something the audience can get involved in."

Deanna pulled at her earlobe. "I thought I might draw on some of the guests I've had on 'Deanna's Corner.' Sort of a woman-in-the-arts thing."

"It's not bad, but it's tame. And it's lofty. I don't think you want talking heads for a demo, especially arty ones." Fran thought over the possibilities. "We did this makeover thing on *Woman Talk* last year. Went over big."

"You mean a before-and-after sort of thing?"

"Yeah. Makeup, hair. It's fun. It's satisfying. But you know what I'd like?" She curled her legs up, leaned forward. "A fashion show sort of thing. What's new for summer? What's hot? What's now? You get, say, Marshall Field's involved. They get to show off some of the summer styles. Career stuff, evening stuff, casual wear."

Eyes half closed, Deanna tried to visualize it. "Right down to shoes and accessories, with a fashion coordinator. Then we choose women out of the audience."

"Exactly. Real women, no perfect bodies."

Warming to the idea, Deanna reached for her purse and took out a notebook. "We'll have to have chosen them earlier. So the fashion coordinator has time to find the right look, the right outfit."

"Then they get, say, a hundred-dollar gift certificate from the department store."

"How to look like a million for a hundred dollars or less."

"Oh, I like it." Fran rocked back. "I really like it."

"I've got to get home." Deanna scrambled up. "Make some calls. We've got to move fast."

"Sweet pea, I've never known you to move any other way."

It required eighteen-hour days, the bulk of Deanna's savings and a surplus of frustration. Because she was able to wrangle only a week off from her duties at CBC, she did without sleep. Fueled on coffee and ambition, she pushed the project forward. Meetings with the promotion people at Marshall Field's, phone calls to union reps, hours of searching for the right set accessories.

The first *Deanna's Hour* might need to be produced on a shoestring, but she didn't intend for it to look that way. Deanna oversaw every step and stage. A loss or a victory, she was determined that it carry her mark.

She bargained. A set of chairs for on-screen credit. She promised. A few hours' labor for a full-time position if the pilot was picked up. She begged and she borrowed. Fifty folding chairs from a local women's group. Floral arrangements, equipment, bodies.

On the morning of the taping, the small studio she had rented was in chaos. Lighting technicians shouted orders and suggestions as they made last-minute adjustments. The models were crammed into a bread box-size dressing room, jockeying for enough space to dress. Deanna's mike shorted out, and the florist delivered a funeral wreath instead of the baskets of summer blossoms.

" 'In loving memory of Milo.' " Deanna read the card and let loose with a quick, hysterical laugh. "Oh, Christ, what else?"

"We'll fix it." Firmly, and perhaps frantically, in control, Fran gave her a brisk shove. "I've already sent Richard's nephew Vinnie out for baskets. We'll just pull the flowers out and toss them in. It'll look great," she said desperately. "Natural."

"You bet. We've got less than an hour." She winced at the sound of a crashing folding chair. "If anyone actually shows up for the audience, we're going to look like idiots."

"They're going to show up." Fran attacked the gladiolas. Her hair stood out in corkscrew spikes, like an electric halo. "And we'll be fine. Between the two of us we contacted every women's organization in Cook County. Every one of the fifty tickets is spoken for. We could have managed twice that if we'd had a bigger studio. Don't worry."

"You're worried."

"That's a producer's job. Go change, do your hair. Pretend you're a star."

"Oh, Miss Reynolds? Deanna?" The fashion consultant, a petite, perky woman with a permanent smile, waved from offstage.

"I want to kill her," Deanna said under her breath. "I want it bad."

"Stand in line," Fran suggested. "If she's changed her mind about the running order again, I get first shot."

"Oh, Deanna?"

"Yes, Karyn." Deanna fixed a smile on her face and turned. "What can I do for you?"

"I just have a teeny little problem? The walking shorts in pumpkin?"

"Yes?" Deanna gritted her teeth. Why did the woman have to make a question out of every statement?

"They just don't suit Monica. I don't know what I was thinking of. Do you think we could have someone dash over to the store and pick up the same outfit in eggplant?"

Before Deanna could open her mouth, Fran eased forward. "I'll tell you what, Karyn. Why don't you call the store, have someone dash over here with the outfit."

"Oh." Karyn blinked. "I suppose I could, couldn't I? Goodness, I'd better hurry. It's almost show time."

"Whose idea was it to do a fashion show?"

Fran went back to dismantling the funeral wreath. "It must have been yours. I would never have thought up something this complicated. Go put yourself together. You won't make much of a fashion statement in sweats and with curlers in your hair."

"Right. If I'm going to bomb, I might as well look my best doing it."

Deanna's dressing room was the size of a closet, but it boasted a sink, a john and a mirror. She grinned when she saw the big gold star Fran had taped to the door.

Maybe it was just a symbol, she mused as she ran a fingertip over the foil, but it was her symbol. Now she was going to have to earn it.

Even if everything fell apart, she'd have three weeks' worth of incredible memories. The rush and thrill of putting the show together, the fascination and strain of handling all the details. And the knowledge, the absolute certainty that this was exactly what she wanted to do with her life. Added to that, astoundingly, was the fact that so many people believed she could.

There had been tips from the floor director at CBC, advice from Benny and several others on the production end. Joe had agreed to head up the camera crew and had persuaded a few of his pals to help with the sound and lighting end. Jeff Hyatt had arranged for editing and graphics.

Now she would either earn their faith in her—or blow it.

She was fastening on an earring and giving herself a final pep talk when the knock sounded on the door.

"Don't tell me," she called out. "The eggplant won't do either, and we have to dash back for tomato."

"Sorry." Finn pushed open the door. "I didn't bring any food."

"Oh." She dropped the back of her earring and swore. "I thought you were in Moscow."

"I was." He leaned against the jamb as she retrieved the little gold clasp. "And look what happens when I go away for a couple of weeks. You're the top story in the newsroom gossip pool."

"Great." Her stomach sank as she fought the earring into place. "I must have been out of my mind to start this."

"I imagine you were thinking clearly." She looked fabulous, he realized. Nervous, but revved and ready. "You saw an open door and decided you could walk through first."

"It feels like an open window. On the top floor."

"Just land on your feet. So what's your topic?"

"It's a fashion show, with audience participation."

His grin broke out, dimples winking. "A fashion show? That kind of fluff, with your news background?"

"This isn't news." She elbowed past him. "It's entertainment. I hope. Don't you have a war to cover or something?"

"Not at the moment. I figured I'd stick around awhile. Then I could head back to the newsroom with the scoop. Tell me." He put a hand on her shoulder to slow her down. "Are you doing this for yourself, or to irritate Angela?"

"Both." She pressed a fist to her stomach to try to quiet it. "But for me first."

"Okay." He could feel the energy, and the nerves vibrating against his palm. He wondered what it would be like to tap it, when they were alone. "And what's the next step?"

She sent him a sidelong look, hesitated. "Off the record?"

"Off the record," he agreed.

"A meeting with Barlow James. And if I manage to get his endorsement, I'm going to Bach."

"So, you don't intend to pitch in the minors."

"Not for long." She let out a long breath. "A minute ago I was sure I was going to be sick." She tossed her hair back. "Now I feel great. Really great."

"Dee!" Holding her headset in place, Fran rushed down the narrow corridor. "We've got a full house." She snatched Deanna's hand and squeezed. "Every seat. The three women we picked out from the Cook County Historical Society are psyched. They can't wait to start."

"Then let's not."

"Okay." Fran looked sick. "Okay," she said again. "We can go whenever you're ready."

She left the warm-up to Fran, standing just off set and listening to the laughter and applause. The nerves were gone. In their place was a burst of energy so huge she could barely hold still. Pushed by it, she made her entrance, settled into her chair under the lights, in front of the camera.

The theme music, compliments of Vinnie, Richard's nephew and an aspiring musician, danced out. Off camera, Fran signaled for applause. The red light shone steadily.

"Good morning, I'm Deanna Reynolds."

She knew there was chaos off set—the scrambling wardrobe changes, the barking of orders, the inevitable glitches. But she felt completely in control, chatting amiably with the perky, detestable Karyn, then roaming the audience for comments as the models strutted their stuff.

She could almost forget it was a career move instead of a lark as she giggled with an audience member over a pair of polka-dot micro shorts.

She looked like a woman entertaining friends, Finn mused as he loitered at She back of the studio. It was an interesting angle, because it wasn't an angle at all. As a hard newsman with a natural disdain for fluff, he couldn't say he was particularly interested in the topic. But his tastes aside, the audience was enchanted. They cheered and applauded, let out the occasional "ooh" and "aah," then balanced it with cheerful groans over an outfit that didn't hit the mark.

Most of all, they related to Deanna. And she to them, in the way she slipped an arm around an audience member, made eye contact or stepped back to let her guests take the spotlight.

She'd walked through the door, he decided, and smiled to himself. He slipped out thinking it wouldn't hurt to put in a call to Barlow James, and hold that door open a little wider.

Angela swept through the lofty living room of her new penthouse apartment. Her heels clicked over parquet floors, muffled on carpet, clicked over tile as she stalked from airy window seat to gleaming breakfront. As she paced, she smoked in quick, ragged jerks, struggling with temper, fighting for control.

"All right, Lew." Calmer, she stopped beside a pedestal table, stabbing out the cigarette in a crystal ashtray and tainting the scent of roses with smoke. "Tell me why you think I'd be interested in some little homemade tape of a second-rate news reader?"

Lew shifted uncomfortably on the velvet settee. "I thought you'd want to know." He heard the whine in his own voice and lowered his eyes. He detested what he was doing: crawling, belly-rolling for scraps. But he had two kids in college, a high-dollar mortgage and the threat of unemployment urging him on. "She rented a studio, hired techs, called in favors. She got some time off from the newsroom and put together a fifty-minute show, plus an audition tape of some of her old stuff." Lew tried to ignore the ulcer burning in his gut. "I hear it's pretty good."

"Pretty good?" Angela's sneer was as sharp as a scalpel. "Why would I have any interest in 'pretty good'? Why would anyone? Amateurs try to push their way into the market all the time. They don't worry me."

"I know—I mean there's talk around the job how the two of you had words."

"Oh?" She smiled frostily. "Did you fly all the way from Chicago to feed me the latest CBC gossip, Lew? Not that I don't appreciate it, but it seems a little extreme."

"I figured..." He took a steadying breath, ran a hand through his thinning hair. "I know you offered Deanna my job, Angela."

"Really? Did she tell you that?"

"No." Whatever pride he had left surfaced. He met her eyes squarely. "But it leaked. Just like it leaked that she turned you down." He saw the familiar flash in her eyes. "And I know," he hurried on, "after working with you for so many years, I know you wouldn't like to see her benefit from your generosity."

"How could she?"

"By turning it into a matter of loyalty to the station. By soliciting Barlow James."

He had her interest now. To conceal it, she turned, flipping open an enamel box and taking out a cigarette. Her eyes flicked over toward the bar, where champagne was always chilling. Frightened by the depth of longing for one small swallow, she moistened her lips and looked away again.

"Why should Barlow get involved?"

"He likes her work. He's made a point of calling the station a few times to say so. And when he came to visit the Chicago bureau last week, he made time for a meeting with her."

Angela snapped on her lighter.

"Word is he took a look at the tape. He liked it."

"So he wants to flatter one of his young female reporters?" Angela tossed her head back, but her throat tightened against the smoke. Just one swallow, she thought. One cool, frothy sip.

"She sent the tape to Loren Bach."

Very slowly, Angela lowered the cigarette and left it to smolder in the ashtray. "Why, that little bitch," she said softly. "Does she really think she can begin to compete with me?"

"I don't know if she's aiming that high. Yet." He let that idea simmer. "I do know that some of the Midwest affiliates are concerned about the cost of your new show. They might be willing to plug into something cheaper, and closer to home."

"Then let them. I'll bury whatever they put up against me." Giving a bark of a laugh, she strode over to survey her view of New York. She had everything she'd wanted. Needed. At last, at long last, she was the queen overlooking her subjects from her high, impregnable tower. No one could touch her now. Certainly not Deanna. "I'm on top here, Lew, and I'm damn well going to stay there. Whatever it takes."

"I can use my connections, find out what Loren Bach decides."

"That's fine, Lew," she murmured, staring over the tops of the trees of Central Park. "You do that."

"But I want my job back." His voice quavered with emotion, with self-disgust. "I'm fifty-four years old, Angela. At my age, and the way things are out there right now, I can't afford to be sending out résumés. I want a firm, two-year contract. By that time both my kids'll be out of college. I can sell the house in Chicago. Barbara and I can buy a smaller one out here. We don't need the room now. I just need a couple of years to make sure I have something to fall back on. That's not too much to ask."

"You've certainly thought this through." Angela sat on the window seat, lifting her arms and laying them atop the flowered cushion. Her throat had opened again, all on its own. That pleased her. She didn't need a drink when she had the taste of power.

"I've done good work for you," he reminded her. "I can still do good work. Plus, I have plenty of contacts back in Chicago. People who'll pass on inside information, if there's a need for it."

"I can't see that there will be, but..." She smiled to herself, considering. "I don't like to ignore possibilities. And I always reward loyalty." She studied him. A drone, she decided. One who would work tirelessly, and one who was afraid enough to bury ethics under necessity. "I'll tell you what, Lew. I can't offer you executive producer. That slot's already filled." She watched him pale. "Assistant producer. I know that technically it's a demotion, but we don't have to look at it that way."

Her smile was bolstering. As easily as a child, she forgot her earlier disgust with him, and her careless betrayal. Now, once again, they were teammates.

"I've always depended on you, and I'm glad I can continue to do so. It's a negligible cut in salary, and it is New York. That makes up for a lot, doesn't it?" She beamed at him, pleased with her own generosity. "And to show you how much I value you, I'll want you on board for the first special. We'll have legal draw up a contract, make it official. In the meantime..." She rose, crossed to him to take his hand between both of hers in the warm, affectionate gesture of old friends. "You go back and tidy up your affairs in Chicago. I'll have my real estate agent look for a cozy little place for you and Barbara. Maybe Brooklyn Heights." She rose on her toes to kiss his cheek. "And you keep your ears open, won't you, dear?"

"Sure, Angela," he said dully. "Whatever you say."

10

Loren Bach's office capped the lofty silver tower that was home for Delacort's Chicago base. Its glass walls offered a view that stretched beyond the Monopoly board of downtown. On a clear day, he could see into misted plains of Michigan. Loren liked to say he could stand guard over hundreds of the stations that carried Delacort's programming, and thousands of homes that watched.

The suite of offices reflected his personality. Its main area was a streamlined, masculine room designed for serious work. The deep green walls and dark walnut trim were pleasant to the eye, an uncluttered backdrop for the sleek, modern furnishings and recessed television screens. He knew that it was sometimes necessary to entertain in an office, as well as do business. As a concession and a convenience, there was a semicircular sofa in burgundy leather, a pair of padded chrome chairs and a wide smoked-glass table. The contents of a fully stocked refrigerator catered to his addiction to Classic Coke.

One of his walls was lined with photographs of himself with celebrities. Stars whose sitcoms and dramas had moved into syndication, politicians running for office, network bigwigs. The one telling omission was Angela Perkins.

Adjoining the office was a washroom in dramatic black and white, complete with a whirlpool and sauna. Beyond that was a smaller room that held a Hollywood bed, a big-screen TV and a closet. Loren had never broken the habit of his lean years, and continued to work long hours, often catching a few hours' sleep and a change of clothing right in the workplace.

But his sanctuary was an area that had been converted from office space. It was cluttered with colorful arcade games where he could save worlds or video damsels in distress, electronic pinball machines that whirled with light and sound, a talking Coke machine.

Every morning he allowed an hour to indulge himself with the bells and whistles and often challenged network executives to beat his top scores. No one did.

Loren Bach was a video wizard, and the love affair had begun in childhood in the bowling alleys his father had owned. Loren had never had any interest in tenpins, but he'd had an interest in business, and in the flash of the silver ball.

In his twenties, with his degree from MIT still hot, he'd expanded the family business into arcades. Then he'd begun to dabble in the king of video: television.

Thirty years later, his work was his play, and his play was his work.

Though he had allowed a few decorative touches in the office area—a Zorach sculpture, a Gris collage—the core of the room was the desk. So it was more of a console than a traditional desk. Loren had designed it himself. He enjoyed the fantasy of sitting in a cockpit, controlling destinies.

Simple and functional, its base was fitted with dozens of cubbyholes rather than drawers. Its work surface was wide and curved, so that when Loren sat behind it, he was surrounded by phones, computer keyboards, monitors.

An adept hacker, Loren could summon up any desired information skillfully and swiftly, from advertising rates for any of Delacort's—or its competitors'—programs, to the current exchange rate of dollar to yen.

As a hobby, he designed and programmed computer games for a subsidiary of his syndicate's.

At fifty-two, he had the quiet, aesthetic looks of a monk, with a long, bony face and a thin build. His mind was as sharp as a scalpel.

Seated behind his desk, he tapped a button on his remote. One of the four television screens blinked on. Eyes mild and thoughtful, he sipped from a sixteen-ounce bottle of Coke and watched Deanna Reynolds.

He would have viewed the tape without the call from Barlow James—Loren took at least a cursory study of anything that crossed his desk—but it was doubtful that he would have slotted time for it so quickly without the endorsement.

"Attractive," he said into his mini-recorder, in a voice as soft and cool as morning snow. "Good throat. Excellent camera presence. Energy and enthusiasm. Sexy but non-threatening. Relates well to audience. Scripted questions don't appear scripted. Who does her writing? Let's find out. Production values need improvement, particularly the lighting."

He watched the full fifty minutes, reversing the tape occasionally, freeze-framing, all the while making his brief comments into the recorder.

He took another long sip from the bottle, and he was smiling. He'd lifted Angela from minor local celebrity into a national phenomenon.

And he could do it again.

With one hand he froze Deanna's face on the screen; with the other, he punched his intercom. "Shelly, contact Deanna Reynolds at CBC, Chicago news division. Set up an appointment. I'd like to have her come in as soon as possible."

• • •

Deanna was used to worrying about her appearance. Working in front of the camera meant that part of the job dealt with looking good. She would often discard a perfectly lovely suit that appealed to her because the cut or the color wasn't quite right for TV.

But she couldn't remember agonizing over the image she projected more than she did when preparing to meet Loren Bach.

She continued to second-guess herself as she sat in the reception area outside his office.

The navy suit she'd chosen was too severe. Leaving her hair down was too frivolous. She should have worn bolder jewelry. Or worn none at all.

It helped somehow to focus on clothes and hairstyles. Twinkie habits, she knew. But it meant she didn't obsess about what this meeting could mean to her future.

Everything, she thought as her stomach clutched. Or nothing.

"Mr. Bach will see you now."

Deanna only nodded. Her throat tightened up like a vise. She was afraid any word that fought its way free would come out as a squeak.

She stepped through the doors the receptionist opened, and into Loren Bach's office.

He was behind his desk, a sloped-shouldered, skinny man with a face that reminded Deanna of an apostle. She'd seen photographs and television clips, and had thought he'd be bigger somehow. Stupid, she thought. She of all people knew how different a media image could be from reality.

"Ms. Reynolds." He rose, extending a hand over the curved Lucite. "It's nice to meet you."

"Thank you." His grip was firm, friendly and brief. "I appreciate your taking the time."

"Time's my business. Want a Coke?"

"I..." He was already up and striding across the room to a full-sized, built-in refrigerator. "Sure, thanks."

"Your tape was interesting." With his back to her, Loren popped the caps on two bottles. "A little rough on some of the production values, but interesting."

Interesting? What did that mean? Smiling stiffly, Deanna accepted the bottle he handed her. "I'm glad you think so. We didn't have a great deal of time to put it together."

"You didn't think it necessary to take the time?"

"No. I didn't think I had the time."

"I see." Loren sat behind his desk again, took a long swig from the bottle. His hands were white and spidery, the long, thin fingers rarely still. "Why not?"

Deanna followed his lead and drank. "Because there are plenty of others who'd like to slip into *Angela's* slot, at least locally. I felt it was important to get out of the gate quickly."

He was more interested in how she'd do coming down the stretch. "Just what is it you'd like to do with *Deanna's Hour*?"

"Entertain and inform." Too glib, she thought immediately. Slow down, Dee, she warned herself. Honesty's fine, but put a little thought into it. "Mr. Bach, I've wanted to work in television since I was a child. Since I'm not an actress, I concentrated on journalism. I'm a good reporter. But in the last couple of years, I've realized that doing the news doesn't really satisfy my ambitions. I like to talk to people. I like to listen to them—and I'm good at both."

"It takes more than conversational skills to carry an hour show."

"It takes a knowledge of how television works, how it communicates. How intimate, and how powerful, it can be. And making the subject forget, while the light's on, that he or she is talking to anyone but me. That's my strong point." She shifted, her body edging forward. "I did some summer-interning at a local station in Topeka while I was in high school, and I interned for four years at a station in New Haven during college. I worked as a news writer in Kansas City before my first on-air job. Technically, I've been working in television for ten years."

"I'm aware of that." He was aware of every detail of her professional life, but he preferred getting his own impressions, face to face. He appreciated the fact that she kept her eyes and her voice level. He remembered his first meeting with Angela. All those sexual spikes, that manic energy, that overpowering femininity. Deanna Reynolds was a different matter altogether.

Not weaker, he mused. Certainly not less potent. Simply . . . different.

"Tell me, other than fashion shows, what sort of topics did you plan to do?"

"I'd like to concentrate on personal issues rather than front-page ones. And I'd like to avoid shock television."

"No redheaded lesbians and the men who love them?"

She relaxed enough to smile. "No, I'll leave those to someone else. My idea is to balance shows like the demo with more serious ones, but to keep it very personal, involving the audience—studio and the home audience. Topics like step-families, sexual harassment in the workplace, how men and women cope with middle-age dating. Issues that target in on what the average viewer might be experiencing."

"And you see yourself as a spokesperson for the average viewer?"

She smiled again. Here, at least, she could be confident. "I *am* the average viewer. I'm certainly going to watch a special on PBS that interests me, but I'm more than happy to pull up a bar stool with the gang at *Cheers.* I share my first cup of coffee in the morning with the *Chicago Tribune* and Kirk Brooks on *Wake Up Call.* And unless I have an early call, I go to bed with *The Tonight Show*—unless Arsenio looks better that night." Now she grinned and sipped again. "And I'm not ashamed of it."

Loren laughed, then drained his Coke. She'd very nearly described his own viewing habits. "I'm told you moonlighted for Angela."

"Not moonlighting exactly. It wasn't as structured or formal as that. And I was never on her payroll. It was more of an . . . apprenticeship." Deanna screened the emotion from her voice. "I learned quite a bit."

"I imagine you did." After a moment, Loren steepled his hands. "It's no secret that Delacort is unhappy about losing *Angela's.* And anyone involved in the business would know that we don't wish her well." His eyes were dark as onyx against his Byronically pale skin. Yes, an apostle, Deanna thought again, but not one who would have gone cheerfully to the Roman lions. "However," he continued, "given her track record, she should continue to dominate the market. We're not ready to go head to head with her, nationally, with another talk-show format."

"You'll counter-program," Deanna said, making Loren stop, raise a brow. "Go against her with game shows, high-rated reruns, soaps, depending on the demographics."

"That would be the idea. I had considered spot-testing a talk-show format, in a handful of CBC affiliates."

"I only need a handful," she said evenly, but gripped the soft-drink bottle with both hands to hold it steady. Sink or swim, she decided. "To start."

Perhaps it was personal, Loren mused. But what of it? If he could use Deanna Reynolds to take a small slice out of Angela, he could afford the cost. If the project failed, he would write it off as experience. But if he could make it work, if he could make Deanna work, the satisfaction would be worth more, much more than advertising revenue.

"Do you have an agent, Ms. Reynolds?"

"No."

"Get one." His dark, mild eyes sharpened. "I'd like to welcome you to Delacort."

"Tell me again," Fran insisted.

"A six-month contract." No matter how many times she said it aloud, the words still echoed gleefully in Deanna's ears. "We'll tape right here at CBC, one show a day, five days a week."

Still dazed even after two weeks of negotiations, she wandered Angela's office. All that was left were the pastel walls and carpet and the steely view of Chicago. "I'll be able to use this office, and two others in accordance with CBC's end of the deal, during the probationary period. We'll be carried by ten affiliates in the Midwest—live in Chicago, Dayton and Indianapolis. We have six weeks to put it together before we premiere in August."

"You're really doing it."

With a half laugh, Deanna turned back. She wasn't smiling like Fran, but her eyes were glowing. "I'm really doing it." She took a deep breath, grateful that none of Angela's signature scent remained in the air. "My agent said the money they're paying me is a slap in the face." Now she grinned. "I told him to turn the other cheek."

"An agent." Fran shook her head and sent her cowbell earrings dancing. "You've got an agent."

Deanna turned toward the window and grinned out at Chicago. She'd chosen a small, local firm, one that could focus on her needs, her goals.

"I've got an agent," she agreed. "And a syndicate—at least for six months. I hope I've got a producer."

"Sweet pea, you know—"

"Before you say anything, let me finish." Deanna turned back. Behind her, the spears and towers of the city shot up into the dull gray sky. "It's a risk, Fran, a big one. If things don't work out, we could be out on our butts in a few months. You've got a solid job at *Woman Talk,* and a baby on the way. I don't want you to jeopardize that for friendship."

"Okay, I won't." Fran shrugged, and because there was no place to sit, settled on the floor, grateful for the give of elastic over her expanding waist. "I'll do it for ego. Fran Myers, Executive Producer. Has a nice ring." She circled her knees with her arms. "When do we start?"

"Yesterday." Laughing, Deanna sat beside her, slung an arm over her shoulders. "We need staff. I might be able to lure in some of Angela's who got pink-slipped or didn't want to relocate. We need story ideas and people to research them. The budget I have to work with is slim, so we'll have to keep it simple." She stared at the bare, pastel walls. "Next contract, it'll be a hell of a lot bigger."

"The first thing you need is a couple of chairs, a desk and a phone. As producer, I'll see what I can beg, borrow or steal." She scrambled to her feet. "But first, I have to go tender my resignation."

Deanna caught her hand. "You're sure?"

"Damn right. I already discussed the possibility with Richard. We looked at it this way: If things go belly-up in six months, I'd be ready for maternity leave anyway." She patted her stomach and grinned. "I'll call you." She paused at the doorway. "Oh, one more thing. Let's paint these damn walls."

Alone, Deanna pulled her knees up to her chest and lowered her head. It was all happening so fast. All the meetings, the negotiations, the paperwork. She didn't mind the long hours; she thrived on them. And the realization of an ambition brought with it a burst of energy that was all but manic. But beneath the excitement was a small, very cold ball of terror.

It was all going in the right direction. Once she adjusted to the new pace, she'd get her bearings. And if she failed, she would simply go back a few steps and start again.

But she wouldn't regret.

"Ms. Reynolds?"

Thoughts scattering, Deanna looked up and saw Angela's secretary in the doorway. "Cassie." With a rueful smile, she glanced around. "Things look a little different these days."

"Yeah." Cassie's own smile came and went. "I was just getting some things out of the outer office. I thought I should let you know."

"That's all right. It won't be my territory officially until next week." She rose and smoothed down her skirt. "I heard you'd decided not to make the move to New York."

"My family's here. And I guess I'm Midwest through and through."

"It's rough." Deanna studied her, the short, tidy curls, the sad eyes. "Do you have something else?"

"Not yet. I've got some interviews lined up, though. Miss Perkins made the announcement, and a week later she's gone. I haven't gotten used to it."

"I'm sure you're not alone there."

"I'll get out of your way. I just had some plants to take home. Good luck with your new show."

"Thanks. Cassie." Deanna stepped forward, hesitated. "Could I ask you something?"

"Sure."

"You worked for Angela for about four years, right?"

"It would have been four years in September. I started as a secretarial assistant straight out of business college."

"Even down in the newsroom we'd hear occasional grumbling from her staff. Some complaints, some gossip. I don't recall ever hearing anything from your direction. I wondered why that was."

"I worked for her," Cassie said simply. "I don't gossip about people I work for."

Deanna lifted a brow, kept her eyes steady. "You don't work for her anymore."

"No." Cassie's voice cooled. "Ms. Reynolds, I know that the two of you had . . . a disagreement before she left. And I understand that you'd feel some hostility. But I'd rather you didn't draw me into a discussion about Miss Perkins, personally or professionally."

"Loyalty or discretion?"

"I'd like to think it's both," Cassie said stiffly.

"Good. You know I'm going to be doing a similar type of program. You may not repeat gossip, but you certainly can't help but hear it around here, so you'd know that my contract is of short term. I may not get beyond the initial six months or ten affiliates."

Cassie thawed a bit. "I've got some friends downstairs. The newsroom pool's running in your favor about three to one."

"That's nice to know, but I imagine that's a matter of loyalty as well. I need a secretary, Cassie. I'd like to hire someone who understands that kind of loyalty, one who knows how to be discreet as well as efficient."

Cassie's expression altered from polite interest to surprise. "Are you offering me a job?"

"I'm sure I won't be able to pay you what Angela did, unless—no, damn it, *until*—we can make this thing fly. And you'll probably have to put in some very long, tedious hours initially, but the job's yours if you want it. I hope you'll think about it."

"Ms. Reynolds, you don't know if I was in on what she did to you. If I helped set it up."

"No, I don't," Deanna said calmly. "I don't need to know. And I think, whether we work together or not, you should call me Deanna. I don't intend to run a less efficient organization than Angela did, but I hope to run a more personal one."

"I don't have to think about it. I'll take the job."

"Good." Deanna held out a hand. "We'll start Monday morning. I hope I can get you a desk by then. Your first assignment's going to be to get me a list of who Angela laid off, and who on it we can use."

"Simon Grimsley would be on top of it. And Margaret Wilson from Research. And Denny Sprite, the assistant production manager."

"I've got Simon's number," Deanna muttered, dragging out her address book to note down the other names.

"I can give you the others."

When Deanna saw Cassie take out a thick book and flip it open, she laughed. "We're going to be fine, Cassie. We're going to be just fine."

It was difficult for Deanna to believe that she was leaving the newsroom behind. Particularly since she was huddled in Editing reviewing a tape.

"How long is it now?" she asked.

Jeff Hyatt, in the editor's chair, glanced at the digital clock on the console. "Minute fifty-five."

"Hell, we're still long. We need to slice another ten seconds. Run it back, Jeff."

She leaned forward in her swivel chair, like a runner off the mark, and waited for him to cue it up. The report of a missing teenager reunited with her parents had to fit into its allotted time. Intellectually, Deanna knew it. Emotionally, she didn't want to cut a second.

"Here." Jeff tapped the monitor with one blunt, competent finger. "This bit of them walking around the backyard. You could lose it."

"But it shows the emotion of the reunion. The way her parents have her between them, their arms linked."

"It's not news." He shoved up his glasses and smiled apologetically. "It's nice, though."

"Nice," she muttered under her breath.

"Anyway, you've got that together-again business in the interview portion. When they're all sitting on the couch."

"It's good film," Deanna muttered.

"All you need's a rainbow arching around them."

Deanna turned at Finn's voice and scowled. "I didn't have one handy."

Despite her obvious annoyance, he stepped over, dropped his hands on her shoulders and finished watching the tape. "It has more impact without it, Deanna. You soften the interview and the emotion you're after by having them take a stroll together. Besides, it's news, not a movie-of-the-week."

He was right, but it only made it harder to swallow. "Take it out, Jeff."

While he ran tape, editing and marking time, she sat with her arms folded. It was going to be one of the last pieces she did for CBC News. It was a matter of ego, as well as pride, that made her want it perfect.

"I need to do the voice-over," she said with a telling look at Finn.

"Pretend I'm not here," he suggested.

When Jeff was set, she took a moment to study the script. Holding a stopwatch in one hand, she nodded, then began to read.

"A parent's worst nightmare was resolved early this morning when sixteen-year-old Ruthanne Thompson, missing for eight days, returned home to her family in Dayton. . . ."

For the next several minutes, she forgot Finn as she and Jeff worked on perfecting the segment. At last, satisfied, she murmured a thanks to the editor and rose.

"Good piece," Finn commented as he walked out of Editing with her. "Spare, solid and touching."

"Touching?" She stopped to angle a look at him. "I didn't think that counted with you."

"It does if it's news. I heard you're moving upstairs next week."

"You heard right." She turned into the newsroom.

"Congratulations."

"Thanks—but you might want to hold off on that until after the first show."

"I've got a feeling you'll pull it off."

"Funny, so do I. Up here." She tapped her head. "It's my stomach that doubts."

"Maybe you're just hungry." Casually, he twined a lock of her hair around his finger. "How about dinner?"

"Dinner?"

"You're off the schedule at six. I looked. I'm clear until eight A.M., when I have to catch a plane for Kuwait."

"Kuwait? What's up there?"

"Rumblings." He gave her hair a little tug. "Always rumblings. So how about a date, Kansas? Some spaghetti, some red wine. A little conversation?"

"I've sort of given up dating for a while."

"Are you going to let that shrink control your life?"

"It has nothing to do with Marshall," she said coolly. But, of course, it did. And because it did, she executed a quick about-face. "Listen, I like to eat, and I like Italian. Why don't we just call it dinner?"

"I won't argue over semantics. Why don't I pick you up at seven? That'll give you time to go home and change. The place I have in mind is casual."

She was glad she'd taken him at his word. She'd been tempted to fuss, at least a little, then had settled on a roomy blouse and slacks that suited the midsummer mugginess. Comfort seemed to be the tone of the evening.

The place he'd chosen was a small, smoky café that smelled of garlic and toasting bread. There were cigarette burns in the checkered tablecloths and hacks in the wooden booth that would have played hell with panty hose.

A stubby candle stuck out of the mouth of the obligatory Chianti bottle. Finn shoved it to the side as they slid into a booth. "Trust me. It's better than it looks."

"It looks fine." The place looked comforting. A woman didn't have to be on her guard in a restaurant that looked like someone's family kitchen.

He could see her relaxing, degree by degree. Perhaps that was why he'd brought her here, he thought. To a place where there was no hovering maître d', no leather-bound wine list.

"Lambrusco okay with you?" he asked as a T-shirt-clad waitress approached their booth.

"That's fine."

"Bring us a bottle, Janey, and some antipasto."

"Sure thing, Finn."

Amused, Deanna rested her chin on her cupped hand. "Come here often?"

"About once a week when I'm in town. Their lasagna's almost as good as mine."

"You cook?"

"When you get tired of eating in restaurants, you learn to cook." His lips curved just a little as he reached across the table to play with her fingers. "I thought about cooking for you tonight, but I didn't think you'd go for it."

"Oh, why?" She moved her hands out of reach.

"Because cooking for a woman, if you do it right, is a surefire seduction, and it's clear you like to take things one cautious, careful step at a time." He tilted his head when the waitress returned with the bottle, filled their glasses. "Am I right?"

"I suppose you are."

He leaned forward, lifting his glass. "So, here's to the first step."

"I'm not sure what I'm drinking to."

Watching her, his eyes dark and focused, he reached out, rubbed his thumb over her cheekbone. "Yes, you do."

Her heart stuttered. Annoyed at herself, she exhaled slowly. "Finn, I should make it clear that I'm not interested in getting involved, with anyone. I have to put all my energies, all my emotions into making the show work."

"You look like a woman with enough emotion to go around to me." He sipped, studying her over the rim. "Why don't we just see what develops?"

The waitress slid the platter of antipasto on the table. "Ready to order?"

"I'm ready." Finn smiled again. "How about you?"

Flustered, Deanna picked up the plastic-coated menu. Odd, she thought, she couldn't seem to comprehend a thing written there. It might as well have been in Greek. "I'll go for the spaghetti."

"Make it two."

"Gotcha." The waitress winked at Finn. "White Sox are up by two in the third."

"White Sox?" Deanna arched a brow as the waitress toddled off. "You're a White Sox fan?"

"Yeah. You into baseball?"

"I played first base in Little League, batted three thirty-nine my best season."

"No shit." Impressed, and pleased, he tapped a thumb to his chest. "Short-stop. Went all-state in high school. Three-fifty my top season."

With deliberate care, she chose an olive. "And you like the Sox. Too bad."

"Why?"

"Seeing as we're in the same profession, I'll overlook it. But if we go out again, I'm wearing my Cubs hat."

"Cubs." He shut his eyes and groaned. "And I was nearly in love. Deanna, I thought you were a practical woman."

"Their day's coming."

"Yeah, right. In the next millennium. Tell you what. When I get back in town, we'll take in a game."

Her eyes narrowed. "At Comiskey or Wrigley?"

"We'll flip for it."

"You're on." She nibbled on a pepperoncini, enjoying the bite. "I'm still ticked about them putting lights in at Wrigley."

"They should have done it years ago."

"It was tradition."

"It was sentiment," he corrected. "And you put sentiment up against ticket sales, sales win every time."

"Cynic." Her smile froze suddenly. "Maybe I could get baseball wives on the show. Cubs and Sox. You'd have viewer interest right off, people taking sides. God knows all you have to do is mention sports or politics in this town to get people going. And we could talk about being married to someone who's on the road weeks at a time during the season. How they deal with slumps, injuries, Baseball Annies."

"Hey." Finn snapped his fingers in front of her face and made her blink.

"Oh, sorry."

"No problem. It's an education to watch you think." It was also, to his surprise, arousing. It made a man wonder—hope—that she would concentrate as fiercely on sex. "And it's a good idea."

Her smile spread inch by inch until her face glowed with it. "It's be a hell of a kickoff, wouldn't it?"

"Yeah, but you're mixing your sports metaphors."

"I'm going to love this." With her wine in one hand, she settled back against the booth. "I'm really going to love this. The whole process is so fascinating."

"And news wasn't?"

"It was, but this is more—I don't know. Personal and exciting. It's an adventure. Is that how you feel about flying off to one country after another?"

"Most of the time. Different place, different people, different stories. It's hard to get into a rut."

"I can't imagine you worrying about that."

"It happens. You get cozy, lose the edge."

Cozy? In war zones, disaster areas, international summits? She didn't see how. "Is that why you didn't stay in London?"

"Part of it. When I stop feeling like a foreigner, I know it's time to come home. Have you ever been to London?"

"No. What's it like?"

It was easy to tell her, easy for her to listen. They talked over pasta and red wine, over cappuccino and cannoli until the candle in the bottle beside them began to gutter, and the juke fell silent. It was the lack of noise that made Deanna glance around. The restaurant was almost empty.

"It's late," she said, surprised when she glanced at her watch. "You have a plane to catch in less than eight hours."

"I'll manage." But he slid out of the booth as she did.

"You were right about the food. It was fabulous." But her smile faded when he reached out and cupped the nape of her neck in his hand. He held her there, his eyes on hers as he closed the distance between them.

The kiss was slow, deliberate and devastating. She'd expected more of a one-two punch from a man whose eyes could bore a hole in the brain. Perhaps that was why the soft, lazy romance of the kiss disarmed her so completely.

She lifted a hand to his shoulder, but rather than easing him away, as she had intended, her fingers dug in. Held on. Her heart took a long, seamless somersault before it thudded against her ribs.

When her mouth yielded under his, he deepened the kiss. Slowly still, teasing a response from her until her hand slid from his shoulder to cling at his waist.

Dozens of thoughts struggled to form in her head, then skittered away. For here was heat, and pleasure and the undeniable promise, or threat, of much more.

More was what he wanted. Much more desperately than he had anticipated. However simple he'd intended the kiss to be, he was almost undone by it. He eased her away. The small, baffled sound she made as her eyes blinked open had him gritting his teeth against a quick, vicious ache.

It was important to keep steady—though at the moment she couldn't have said why. Instinct alone had her stepping back an inch.

"What was that for?"

"Other than obvious reasons?" He should be amused by the question. "I figured if we got that done here, you wouldn't project what could, should or might happen when I took you home."

"I see." She realized her purse had dropped to the floor, and bent to retrieve it. "I don't plan every aspect of my life out like a feature story."

"Sure you do." He ran a finger down her cheek. It was hot and flushed and made him long for another taste. "But that's okay with me. Just consider that your lead. We'll pick up the rest of the copy when I get back."

11

By the end of July, Deanna had what could loosely be called a staff. In addition to Fran and Simon, she had a single researcher and a booker, overseen by Cassie. They were still in dire need of bodies and brains—and a budget to pay for them.

The technical end was solid. At one of the endless meetings Deanna attended, it was agreed that Studio B would be fully staffed and carefully lit. Production values would be top-notch.

All she had to do was give them something to produce.

She'd temporarily moved two desks into Angela's old office. One for herself, one for Fran: they divided the work, and brainstormed ideas.

"We've got the first eight shows booked." Fran paced the office, a clipboard in one hand. "Cassie's handling travel and lodging. She's doing a good job, Dee, but she's ridiculously overworked."

"I know." Deanna rubbed her gritty eyes and struggled to clear her brain. "We need an assistant producer, and another researcher. And a general dogsbody. If we can get the first dozen shows under our belt, we might be able to swing it."

"Meantime, you're not getting enough sleep."

"Even if I had the time, I couldn't." She reached out for the ringing phone. "My stomach's in a constant state of turmoil, and my mind just won't shut off. Reynolds," she said into the receiver. "No, I haven't forgotten." She glanced at her watch. "I have an hour." She blew out a breath as she listened. "All right, tell them to send the wardrobe up. I'll pick what suits and be down for makeup in thirty minutes. Thanks."

"Photo shoot?" Fran remembered.

"And the promos. I can't accuse Delacort of chintzing on the advertising. But damn, I don't have time. We need a staff meeting, and we still have to go through those responses to the eight-hundred number and the write-in."

"I'll schedule it for four." Fran grinned. "Wait until you read some of the stuff from the write-in. Margaret's idea on why ex-husbands should be shot down like a dog is a hoot."

Deanna's smile was strained. "We did tone that down, didn't we?"

"Yeah. It went out 'Why Your Ex-Husband Is Your Ex.' Tame enough, but the responses weren't. We've got everything from serious abuse cases to guys who cleaned engine parts in the kitchen sink. We'll need an expert. I thought a lawyer instead of a counselor. Divorce lawyers have terrific stories, and Richard has plenty of contacts."

"Okay, but—" She broke off as a clothes rack wheeled through the doorway. "Come on, Fran, help me play closet." A head peeked around the suits and dresses. "Oh, hi, Jeff. They've got you making deliveries?"

"I wanted a chance to come up and see the operation." With a shy smile he glanced around. "We're rooting for you downstairs."

"Thanks. How's everybody in the newsroom? I haven't had a chance to stop down for days."

"Pretty good. The heat brings out the loonies, you know? Lots of hot stories breaking." He rocked the rack, loitering as Deanna began to go through the wardrobe. "Deanna, I was kind of wondering, if you—you know—get an opening up here. For somebody to pick up loose ends, answer the phone. You know."

Deanna stopped with her hand on a crimson blazer. "Are you kidding?"

"I know you've got people who've worked this end of things before. But I always wanted to do this kind of television. I just thought . . . you know."

"When can you start?"

He looked startled. "I . . ."

"I mean it. We're desperate. We need someone who can do a little of everything. I know you can from your work downstairs. And your editing skills would be invaluable. The pay's lousy and the hours are miserable. But if you want a shot as an assistant producer—with on-screen credit and all the coffee you can drink—you're hired."

"I'll give my notice," Jeff said through a grin that all but split his face. "I may have to work another week or two, but I can give you all my extra time."

"God, Fran, we've found a hero." Deanna took him by the shoulders and kissed his cheek. "Welcome to bedlam, Jeff. Tell Cassie to fit you for a straitjacket."

"Okay." Flushing, laughing, he backed out of the room. "Okay. Great."

Fran pulled out a plum-colored suit and held it up in front of Deanna. "General dogsbody?"

"One of the best. Jeff can mow down a mountain of paperwork like a beaver taking out a tree. He carries all this stuff in his head. Ask him what won for best picture in 1956, and he knows. What was the lead story on the ten o'clock on Tuesday of last week? He knows. I like the red."

"For the promos," Fran agreed. "Not the stills. What does he do downstairs?"

"Editorial assistant. He also does some writing." She pulled out a sunny yellow dress with turquoise sleeves and round fuchsia buttons. "He's good. Dependable as a sunrise."

"As long as he works long and cheap."

"That's going to change." Her eyes darkened as she held Fran's next selection up in front of her. "I know how much everyone's putting into this. Not just timewise. I'm going to make it work."

To give their chances a boost, Deanna granted interviews—print, radio, television. She appeared on a segment of *Midday* and was interviewed by Roger. She took two days and visited all the affiliates within driving distance, and put in personal phone calls to the rest.

She personally oversaw every detail of her set design, pored over press clippings for program ideas and spent hours reviewing responses to the ads for topic guests.

It left little time for a social life. And it certainly provided a good excuse to avoid Finn. She'd meant what she'd said when she'd told him she didn't want to get involved. She couldn't afford to, she'd decided. Emotionally or professionally. How could she trust her own judgment when she'd been so willing to believe in Marshall?

But Finn Riley wasn't easily avoided. He dropped into her office, stopped by her apartment. Often he carried take-out pizza or white cartons filled with Chinese food. It was hard to argue with his casual comment that she had to eat sometime. In a weak moment, she agreed to go out to the movies with him. And found herself just as charmed, and just as uneasy, as before.

"Loren Bach on one," Cassie told her.

It was still shy of nine o'clock, but Deanna was already at her desk. "Good morning, Loren."

"Countdown, five days," he said cheerfully. "How are you holding up?"

"By my knuckles. The publicity's generated a lot of local interest. I don't think we'll have any problem filling the studio."

"You're getting some interest on the East Coast as well. There's a nice juicy article in the *National Enquirer* about the 'All About Eve' of talk shows. Guess who's playing Margo Channing?"

"Oh hell. How bad is it?"

"I'll fax you the article. They spelled your name right, Eve—ah, Deanna." He chuckled, tickled with his own humor. "From one who knows our heroine well, I can tell you she leaked this little tidbit. Makes it sound as though she all but picked you up out of the street, played big sister and mentor, then was stabbed in the back for her generosity."

"At least they didn't claim I'd been dropped from a spaceship into her front yard."

"Maybe next time. In the meantime, you got some national press. And whether she knows it or not, linked your name with hers in such a way that'll make people curious. I think we can get some play out of this. A tag in *Entertainment Weekly*, maybe another squib in *Variety*."

"Great. I guess."

"Deanna, you can buck the tabloids when you've built the muscle. For now, just consider it free press."

"Courtesy of Angela."

"Word is she's negotiating a contract to write her autobiography. You might be worth a chapter."

"Now I'm excited." Her chair squeaked as she leaned back, reminding her she'd forgotten to oil the springs. That made her lean forward again and add the chore to her growing list on the corner of her desk. "I hope you don't mind if I just concentrate on pulling off the first show. I'll worry about repaying Angela for her generosity later."

"Deanna, you make the show work, that'll be payment enough. Now, let's talk business."

Twenty minutes later, with a headache just beginning to brew behind her eyes, she hung up. What had ever made her think she was good with details? Deanna wondered. What had ever made her think she wanted the responsibility of helming a talk show?

"Deanna?" Cassie entered with a tray. "I thought you'd like some coffee."

"You read my mind." Deanna set aside papers to make room for the pot. "Do you have time for any? We might want to tank up before the rest of the day's schedule hits."

"I brought two cups." She poured both before she took a chair. "Do you want to go over your agenda for today?"

"I don't think so." The first sip of hot black coffee punched its caffeine-laced fist straight into her bloodstream. "It's engraved on my forehead. Have we set up a lunch for the baseball wives after the show?"

"Simon and Fran will play host. Reservations are confirmed. And Jeff thought it might be nice to have roses in the green room when they arrive. I wanted to run it by you."

"Good old Jeff. Very classy idea. Let's put cards on each bunch with a personal thank-you from the staff." After another sip, she pressed a hand to her jittery stomach. "Christ, Cassie, I'm scared to death." Setting the cup aside, she took a deep, calming breath and leaned forward. "I want to ask you something, and I really want you to be brutally honest, okay? No sparing feelings, no false pep talk."

"All right." Cassie laid her steno pad on her lap. "Shoot."

"You worked for Angela a long time. You probably know as much about the ins and outs of this sort of a show as any producer or director. I imagine you have an opinion of why *Angela's* works. And I want to know, candidly, if you believe we have a shot at this."

"You want to know if we can make *Deanna's Hour* competitive?"

"Not even that," Deanna said, shaking her head. "If we can get through the first half a dozen shows without being laughed out of the business."

"That's easy. After next week, people are going to do a lot of talking about *Deanna's Hour.* And more people are going to tune in to see what the deal is. They're going to like it, because they're going to like you." She chuckled at Deanna's expression. "That's not sucking up. The thing is, the average viewer won't see or appreciate the work that's gone into making it all look good and run smoothly. They won't know about the long hours or the sweat. But you know, so you'll work harder. The harder you work, the harder everyone else will. Because you do something Angela didn't. Something I guess she just couldn't. You make us feel important. That makes all the difference. Maybe it won't put you on top of the ratings heap right away, but it puts you on top with us. That counts."

"It counts a lot," Deanna said after a moment. "Thanks."

"In a couple of months, when the show's cruising and the budget opens up, I'm going to come back in here. That's when I'm going to suck up." She grinned. "And hit you for a raise."

"If the damn budget ever opens up, everyone's getting a raise." Deanna blew at her bangs. "In the meantime, I need to see the tapes on the promos for the affiliates."

"You need a promotion manager."

"And a unit manager, and a publicity director, a permanent director and a few production assistants. Until that happy day, I'm wearing those hats, too. Have the newspapers come in yet?"

"I passed them on to Margaret. She's going to screen them for ideas and make clippings."

"Fine. Try to get me the clippings before lunch. We're going to want something really hot for the second week in September. Bach just told me we'll be going up against a new game show in three cities during fall premiere week."

"Will do—oh, and your three o'clock with Captain Queeg is rescheduled for three-thirty."

"Captain—oh, Ryce." Not bothering to hide the smile, Deanna noted it down on her calendar. "I know he's a little eccentric, Cassie."

"And overbearing."

"And overbearing," Deanna agreed. "But he's a good director. We're lucky to have him for the few opening weeks."

"If you say so." She started out, then hesitated and turned back. "Deanna, I didn't know if I should mention it, then I figured it wouldn't be right to start censoring your calls."

"What?"

"Dr. Pike. He called when you were on with Mr. Bach."

Thoughtfully, Deanna set aside her pen. "If he calls back, put him through. I'll take care of it."

"Okay. Oops." She grinned and stepped back to avoid running into Finn. "Morning, Mr. Riley."

"Hey, Cassie. I need a minute with the boss."

"She's all yours." Cassie closed the door behind her.

"Finn, I'm sorry, I'm swamped." But she wasn't quite quick enough to avoid the kiss when he skirted the desk. She wasn't sure she wanted to.

"I know, I've only got a minute myself."

"What is it?" She could see the excitement in his eyes, feel it in the air sparking around him. "It's big."

"I'm on my way to the airport. Iraq just invaded Kuwait."

"What?" Her reporter's adrenaline made her spring up. "Oh, Jesus."

"Blitzkrieg style. An armored thrust, helicopter-supported. I have a couple of contacts at Green Ramp in North Carolina, a couple of guys I got to know during the fighting at Tocumen airfield in Panama a few months ago. Odds are we'll go with diplomatic and economic pressure first, but there's a damn good chance we'll deploy troops. If my instincts are worth anything, it's going to be big."

"There are blowups over there all the time." Weakly she sat on the arm of her chair.

"It's land, Kansas. And it's oil, and it's honor." He lifted her to her feet, caught her hair in his hand to draw it away from her face. He wanted—needed, he admitted—a long look at her. A good long look. "I may be gone for a while, especially if we send troops."

She was pale, struggling to be calm. "They think he has nuclear capabilities, don't they? And certainly access to chemical weapons."

Dimples flashed recklessly. "Worried about me?"

"I was just wondering if you were taking a gas mask as well as a camera crew." Feeling foolish, she stepped back. "I'll watch for your reports."

"Do that. I'm sorry I'll miss your premiere."

"That's okay." She managed a smile. "I'll send you a tape."

"You know." He toyed with a strand of her hair. "Technically, I'm going off to war. The old 'I'm shipping out, babe, and who knows what tomorrow might bring.'" He smiled into her dark, serious eyes. "I don't suppose I could convince you to lock that door over there and give me a memorable send-off."

She was afraid he could. "I don't fall for tired old lines. Besides, everyone knows Finn Riley always brings back the story alive."

"It was worth a shot." But he slipped his arms around her waist. "At least give me something to take into the desert with me. I hear it gets pretty cold at night."

There was a part of her that feared. And a part that yearned. Listening to both, she wrapped her arms around his neck. "All right, Riley. Remember this."

For the first time, she pressed her lips to his without hesitation. There was more than the quick, familiar thrill when her mouth opened to his, more than the slow, grinding ache she'd tried so hard to deny. There was need, yes, to taste, to absorb and, curiously, to comfort.

When the kiss deepened, she let herself forget everything else, and just feel.

She could smell him—soap and light, clean sweat. His hair was soft and full, and seemed to beckon her fingers to comb through and hold on. When his mouth became less patient, when she heard his quiet groan of pleasure, she responded heedlessly, mating her tongue with his, nipping at his lip to add the dark excitement of pain to the pleasure.

She thought he trembled, but could no longer find the will to soothe.

"Deanna." Desperately, he took his mouth over her face, along her throat, where her pulse beat like wings. "Again."

His lips crushed down on hers again, absorbing the flavor, the warmth. Shaken, he drew back just enough to rest his brow against hers, to hold her another moment where he felt so oddly centered, so curiously right.

"Goddamn," he whispered. "I'm going to miss you."

"This wasn't supposed to happen."

"Too late." He lifted his head, brushed his lips over her forehead. "I'll call when I can." As soon as he'd said it, Finn realized he'd never made that promise before. It was the kind of unstated commitment that had him stepping back, tucking his hands safely in his pockets. "Good luck next week."

"Thanks." She took a step back herself so that they took each other's measure like two boxers after a blood-pumping round in the ring. "I know it's a useless thing to say, but be careful."

"I'll be good." His grin was quick and reckless. "That's more important." He walked to the door, then stopped, his hand on the knob. "Listen, Deanna, if that asshole shrink does happen to call back—"

"You were eavesdropping."

"Of course I was, I'm a reporter. Anyway, if he does call back, brush him off, will you? I don't want to have to kill him."

She smiled, but the smile faded quickly. Something in Finn's eyes told her he was serious. "That's a ridiculous thing to say. It happens that I'm not interested in Marshall, but—"

"Lucky for him." He touched a finger to his brow in salute. "Stay tuned, Kansas. I'll be back."

"Arrogant idiot," Deanna muttered. When her eyes began to sting, she turned to stare out at Chicago. There might be a war on the other side of the world, she thought as the first tear spilled over. And a show to produce right here.

So what in the hell was she doing falling in love?

"Okay, Dee, we're nearly ready for you." Fran scooted back into the dressing room. "The studio audience is all in."

"Great." Deanna continued to stare blindly at the mirror as Marcie put the finishing touches on her hair. "Just great."

"They're wearing Cubs hats and White Sox T-shirts. Some people even brought banners, and they're waving them around. I'm telling you, they're revved."

"Great. Just great."

Smiling to herself, Fran glanced down at her clipboard. "All six of the wives are in the green room. They're really chummy. Simon's in there now, going over the setup with them."

"I went in to introduce myself to them earlier." Her voice was a monotone. She could feel the nausea building like a tidal wave. "Oh God, Fran, I really think I'm going to be sick."

"No, you're not. You don't have time. Marcie, her hair looks fabulous. Maybe you can give me some tips on mine later. Come on, champ." Fran gave Deanna a tug that brought her out of the chair. "You need to go out and give the audience a pep talk, get them on your side."

"I should have worn the navy suit," Deanna said as Fran dragged her along. "The orange and kiwi is too much."

"It's gorgeous—and it's bright and young. Just the right combo. You look hip, but not trendy, friendly but not homespun. Now look." Making a little island of intimacy in the midst of backstage chaos, Fran took Deanna by the shoulders. "This is what we've all been slaving for over the last couple of months—what you've been aiming toward for years. Now go out there and make them love you."

"I keep thinking about all this stuff. What if a fight breaks out? You know how rabid Sox and Cubs fans can be. What if I run out of questions? Or can't control the crowd? What if someone asks why the hell I'm doing a silly show about baseball when we're sending troops to the Middle East?"

"Number one, nobody's going to fight because they're going to be having too much fun. Number two, you never run out of questions, and you can control any crowd. And finally, you're doing this show on baseball because people need to be entertained, especially during times like these. Now pull it together, Reynolds, and go do your job."

"Right." She took a deep breath. "You're sure I look okay?"

"Go."

"I'm going."

"Deanna."

She turned, surprised, then infuriated to see Marshall standing an arm's length behind her. Fran's snarl had her stepping forward. "What are you doing here?"

His smile was easy, though his eyes held regret. "I wanted to wish you luck. In person." He held out a bouquet of candy pink roses. "I'm very proud of you."

She didn't reach for the flowers, but she kept her eyes level with his. "I'll accept the wish for luck. Your pride is your business. Now, I'm afraid only staff is allowed back here."

Very slowly, he lowered the flowers. "I didn't know you had it in you to be cruel."

"It seems we were misled. I have a show to do, Marshall, but I'll take a moment to tell you once again that I have no desire to resume any sort of relationship with you. Simon?" She called out without taking her eyes from Marshall's. "Show Dr. Pike out, will you? He seems to have made a wrong turn."

"I know the way," he said between clenched teeth. He let the roses fall to the floor, reminding her how she had dropped a similar bouquet. The scent of them turned her stomach. "I won't always be turned away so easily."

He stalked off with Simon nervously dogging his heels. Deanna allowed herself one long, calming breath.

"Creep," Fran muttered, lifting a hand automatically to soothe the tension in Deanna's shoulders. "Bastard. To come here like this right before a live show. Are you going to be all right?"

"I'm going to be fine." She shook off the fury. There was too much riding on the next hour for her to indulge herself. "I am fine." She headed out, taking the hand mike from Jeff as she passed.

Jeff smiled broadly as he watched her. "Break a leg, Deanna."

She straightened her shoulders. "Hell, I'm going to break two." She stepped onto the set, smiled at the sea of faces. "Hi, everyone, thanks for coming. I'm Deanna. In about five minutes we're going to get this show rolling. I hope you're going to help me out. It's my first day on the job."

"Put in the damn tape." In her towering New York office, Angela stubbed out one cigarette and immediately lit another.

"I went out on a limb to get a copy of this," Lew told her as he slipped the tape into the VCR.

"You told me, you told me." And she was sick of hearing it. Sick, too, with fear of what she might see on the monitor in the next few minutes. "Cue it up, damn it."

He hit the Play button and stepped back. Eyes narrowed, Angela listened to the intro music. Too close to rock, she decided with a smirk. The average viewer wouldn't like it. The pan of the audience—people in baseball caps, applauding and waving banners. Middle-class, she decided, and leaned back comfortably.

It was going to be all right after all, she assured herself.

"Welcome to *Deanna's Hour*." The camera did a close-up of Deanna's face. The slow, warm smile, the hint of nerves in the eyes. "Our guests today, here in Chicago, are six women who know all there is to know about baseball—and not just about squeeze plays and Texas Leaguers."

She's jittery, Angela thought, pleased. She'd be lucky to make it through to commercial. Anticipating the humiliation, Angela allowed herself to feel sorry for Deanna. After all, she thought with a soft, sympathetic sigh, who knew better than she what it was like to face that merciless glass eye?

She'd taken on too much, too soon, Angela realized. It would be a hard lesson, but a good one. And when she failed, as she certainly would, and came knocking on the door looking for help. Angela decided she would be gracious enough, forgiving enough to give her a second chance.

But Deanna made it to commercial, segueing into the break over applause. After the first fifteen minutes, the pleasant flavor of gloating sympathy had turned bitter in her throat.

She watched the show through to the closing credits, saying nothing.

"Turn it off," she snapped, then rose to go to the wet bar. Rather than her usual mineral water, she reached for a split of champagne, spilling it into a flute. "It's nothing," she said, half to herself. "A mediocre show with minimal demographic appeal."

"The response from the affiliates was solid." With his back to her, Lew ejected the tape.

"A handful of stations in the dust bowl of the Midwest?" She drank quickly, her lips tightening on the gulp. "Do you think that worries me? Do you think she could play that in New York? It's what works here that matters. Do you know what my share was last week?"

"Yes." Lew set the tape aside and played the game. "You've got nothing to worry about, Angela. You're the best, and everyone knows it."

"Damn right I'm the best. And when my first prime-time special hits during the November sweeps, I'll start getting the respect I deserve." Grimacing, she drained the champagne. It no longer tasted celebratory, but it thawed all the little ice pockets of fear. "I've already got the money." She turned around, steadier. She could afford to be generous, couldn't she? "We'll let Deanna have her moment, and why not? She won't last. Leave the tape, Lew." Angela went back to her desk, settled down and smiled. "And ask my secretary to come in. I have a job for her."

Alone, Angela swiveled in her chair to study the view of her new home. New York was going to do more than make her a star, she mused. It was going to make her an empire.

"Yes, Miss Perkins."

"Cassie—damn it, Lorraine." Spinning around, she glared at her new secretary. She hated breaking in new employees, being expected to remember their names, their faces. Everyone always expected too much from her. "Get me Beeker on the phone. If he can't be reached, leave a message with his service. I want a call-back ASAP."

"Yes, ma'am."

"That's all." Angela glanced toward the champagne, then shook her head. Oh no, she wasn't going to fall into that trap. She wasn't her mother. She didn't need liquor to get through the day. Never had. What she needed was action. Once she lit a fire under Beeker and had him digging deeper and harder for dirt on Deanna Reynolds, she'd have all the action she could handle.

Part Two

"All fame is dangerous."
—Thomas Fuller

12

"Cooked beneath a blazing sun, an enemy of rainfall, of plant life, of human beings, are the shifting sands of the Saudi desert." Finn did his best not to squint into the camera as that merciless sun beat down on him. He wore an olive-drab T-shirt, khakis and a faded bush hat. "Sandstorms, unrelenting heat and mirages are common in this hostile environment. Into this world the forces of the United States have come to draw their line in the sand.

"It has been three months since the first men and women of the armed forces were deployed under Desert Shield. With the efficiency and ingenuity of the Yankee, these soldiers are adjusting to their new environment, or in some cases, adjusting their environment to suit them. A wooden box, a liner of Styrofoam and an air-conditioner blower." Finn rested his hand on a wooden crate. "And a few industrious GIs have created a makeshift refrigerator to help combat the one-hundred-and-twenty-degree heat. And with boredom as canny an enemy as the climate, off-duty soldiers spend their time reading mail from home, trading the precious few newspapers that get through the censors and setting up lizard races. But the mails are slow, and the days are long. While parades and picnics back home celebrate Veterans Day, the men and women of Desert Shield work, and wait.

"For CBC this is Finn Riley, in Saudi Arabia."

When the red light blinked off, Finn unhooked his sunglasses from his belt loop and slipped them on. Behind him was an F-15C Eagle and men and women in desert fatigues. "I could go for some potato salad and a brass band, Curt. How about you?"

His cameraman, whose ebony skin gleamed like polished marble with his coat of sweat and sun block, rolled his eyes to heaven. "My mama's homemade lemonade. A gallon of it."

"Cold beer."

"Peach ice cream—and a long, slow kiss from Whitney Houston."

"Stop, you're killing me." Finn took a deep drink of bottled water. It tasted metallic and overwarm, but it washed the grit out of his throat. "Let's see what they'll let us take pictures of, and we'll try for some interviews."

"They ain't going to give us much," Curt grumbled.

"We'll take what we can."

Hours later, in the relative comfort of a Saudi hotel, Finn stripped to the skin. The shower washed away the layers of sand and sweat and grit of two days and nights in the desert. He felt a sweet, almost romantic longing for the yeasty tang of an American brew. He settled for orange juice and stretched out on the bed, coolly naked, quietly exhausted. Eyes closed, he groped for the phone to begin the complicated and often frustrating process of calling the States.

The phone woke Deanna out of a dead sleep. Her first jumbled thought was that it was a wrong number again, probably the same idiot who had dragged her out of a soothing bath earlier, only to hang up without apology. Already cranky, she jiggled the phone off the hook.

"Reynolds."

"Must be, what? Five-thirty in the morning there." Finn kept his eyes closed and smiled at the husky sound of her voice. "Sorry."

"Finn?" Shaking off sleep, Deanna pushed herself up in bed and reached for the light. "Where are you?"

"Enjoying the hospitality of our Saudi hosts. Did you have any watermelon today?"

"Excuse me?"

"Watermelon. The sun's a bitch here, especially about ten in the morning. That's when I started to have this fantasy about watermelon. Curt got me going, then the crew started torturing themselves. Snow cones, mint juleps, cold fried chicken."

"Finn," Deanna said slowly. "Are you all right?"

"Just tired." He rubbed a hand over his face to pull himself back. "We spent a couple of days out in the desert. The food sucks, the heat's worse and the fucking flies . . . I don't want to think about the flies. I've been up for about thirty hours, Kansas. I'm a little punchy."

"You should get some sleep."

"Talk to me."

"I've seen some of your reports," she began. "The one on the hostages Hussein's calling 'guests' was gripping. And the one from the air base in Saudi."

"No, tell me what you've been doing."

"We did a show today on obsessive shoppers. One guest stays up every night watching one of the shopping channels and ordering everything on the screen. His wife finally cut the cable when he bought a dozen electronic flea collars. They don't have a dog."

It made Finn laugh, as she'd hoped it would. "I got the tape you sent. It bounced around a little first, so it took a while. The crew and I watched it. You looked good."

"I felt good. We're getting picked up by another couple of stations in Indiana. Late afternoon. We'll be going up against a monster soap, but who knows?"

"Now tell me you miss me."

She didn't answer right away, and caught herself wrapping the phone cord around and around her hand. "I suppose I do. Now and then."

"How about now?"

"Yes."

"When I get home, I want you to come with me up to my cabin."

"Finn—"

"I want to teach you how to fish."

"Oh?" A smile tugged at her mouth. "Really?"

"I don't think I should get serious about a woman who doesn't know one end of a rod from the other. Keep it in mind. I'll be in touch."

"All right. Finn?"

"Hmmm?"

She could tell he was nearly asleep. "I'll, ah, send you another tape."

" 'Kay. See you."

He managed to get the phone back on the hook before he started to snore.

The reports continued to come. The escalation of hostilities, the negotiations for the release of the hostages many feared would be used as human shields. The Paris summit, and the president's Thanksgiving visit to U.S. troops. By the end of November, the UN had voted on Resolution 678. The use of force to expel Iraq from Kuwait was approved, with a deadline for Saddam of January fifteenth.

On the homefront there were yellow ribbons flying—from the tips of car antennae and porch banisters. They were mixed with holly and ivy as America prepared for Christmas, and for war.

"This toy piece will show not only what's hot for kids for Christmas, but what's safe." Deanna looked up from her notes and narrowed her eyes at Fran. "Are you okay?"

"Sure." With a grimace, Fran shifted her now-considerable bulk. "For someone who's got what feels like a small pick-up truck sitting on her bladder, I'm dandy."

"You should go home, put your feet up. You're due in less than two months."

"I'd go crazy at home. Besides, you're the one who should be exhausted, schmoozing half the night at the charity dinner-dance."

"It's part of the job," Deanna said absently. "And, as Loren pointed out, I made a number of contacts, and got some press."

"Mmm. And about five hours' sleep." Fran fiddled with a toy rabbit that wiggled its ears and squeaked when she pressed its belly. "Do you think Big Ed would like this?"

Brow lifted, Deanna studied Fran's belly, where "Big Ed," as the baby was called, seemed to be growing by leaps and bounds. "You already have two dozen stuffed animals in the nursery."

"You started it with that two-foot teddy bear." Setting the bunny aside, Fran reached among the toys scattered on the office floor and chose a combat-fatigued GI Joe. "Why the hell do they always want to play soldier?"

"That's one of the questions we'll ask our expert. Have you heard from Dave?"

Fran tried not to worry about her stepbrother, a National Guard officer who was in the Gulf. "Yeah. He got the box we sent over. The comic books were a big hit. Wow!" With a sound between a gasp and a laugh, she pressed a hand to her stomach. "Big Ed just kicked one through the posts."

"Is Richard really going to buy the baby a Bears helmet?"

"Already has. Which reminds me, I want to make sure we get gender molding into this segment. How society, and parents, continue stereotypes by buying this kind of thing for boys"—she waved the GI Joe—"and this sort of thing for girls." She nudged a Fisher-Price oven with her foot.

"Ballet shoes for girls, football cleats for boys."

"Which leads to girls shaking pom-poms on the sidelines while boys make touchdowns."

"Which," Deanna continued, "leads to men making corporate decisions and women serving coffee."

"God, am I going to screw this kid up?" Fran levered herself out of the chair. The fact that she waddled made her nervous pacing both comic and sweet. "I shouldn't have done this. We should have practiced on a puppy first. I'm going to be responsible for another human being, and I haven't even started a college fund."

Over the past few weeks, Deanna had become used to Fran's outbursts. She sat back and smiled. "Hormones bouncing again?"

"You bet. I'm going to go find Simon and check on last week's ratings—and pretend I'm a normal, sane human being."

"Then go home," Deanna insisted. "Eat a bag of cookies and watch an old movie on cable."

"Okay. I'll send Jeff in to pick up the toys and move them down to the set."

Alone, Deanna sat back and closed her eyes. It wasn't only Fran who was on edge these days. The entire staff was running on nerves. In six weeks, *Deanna's Hour* would either be re-signed with Delacort, or they would all be out of a job.

The ratings had been inching up, but was it enough? She knew she was putting everything she had into the show itself, and everything she could squeeze out into the public relations and press events Loren insisted on. But was that enough?

The trial run was almost over, and if Delacort decided to dump them . . .

Restless, she rose and turned to face the window. She wondered if Angela had ever stood there and worried, agonized over something as basic as a single ratings point. Had she felt the responsibility weigh so heavily on her shoulders—for the show, for the staff, for the advertisers? Is that why she'd become so hard?

Deanna rolled her tensed shoulders. It wouldn't simply be her career crumbling if the show was axed, she thought. There were six other people who had their time and energy and, yes, their egos, invested. Six other people who had families, mortgages, car payments, dentist bills.

"Deanna?"

"Yes, Jeff. We need to get these toys down to the . . ." She trailed off as she turned and spotted a seven-foot plastic spruce. "Where in the world did you get that?"

"I, ah, liberated it from a storeroom." Jeff stepped out from behind the tree. His cheeks were flushed from both nerves and exertion. His glasses slid slowly down the bridge of his nose. His boyishness was endearing. "I thought you might like it."

Laughing, she examined the tree. It was pretty pathetic, with its bent plastic boughs and virulent green color no one would mistake for natural. She looked at Jeff's grinning face, and laughed again. "It's exactly what I need. Let's put it in front of the window."

"It looked kind of lonely down there." Jeff centered it carefully in front of the wide pane. "I figured with some decorations..."

"Liberated."

He shrugged. "There's stuff in this building nobody's used—or seen—for years. Some lights, some balls, it'll look fine."

"And plenty of yellow ribbons," she said, thinking of Finn. "Thanks, Jeff."

"Everything's going to be okay, Deanna." He put a hand on her shoulder, gave it a quick, shy squeeze. "Don't worry so much."

"You're right." She pressed her hand on top of his. "Absolutely right. Let's get the rest of the crew in here and decorate this baby."

Deanna worked throughout the holidays with the plastic tree glowing behind her. By juggling appointments and putting in three eighteen-hour days, she made time for a frantic, twenty-four-hour trip home over Christmas. She returned to Chicago's bitter cold on the last plane on Boxing Day.

Loaded down with luggage, gifts and tins of cookies from Topeka, she unlocked her apartment. The first thing she saw was the plain white envelope on the rug, just inside. Uneasy, she set her bags aside. It didn't surprise her to find a single sheet in the envelope or to see the bold red type.

Merry Christmas, Deanna.
I love watching you every day.
I love watching you.
I love you.

Weird, she mused, but harmless considering some of the bizarre mail that had come her way since August. She stuffed the note in her pocket, and she'd barely flipped the lock back in place when a knock sounded on the other side of the door. She tugged off her wool cap with one hand, opened the door with the other.

"Marshall."

His Burberry coat was neatly folded over his arm. "Deanna, hasn't this gone on long enough? You haven't answered any of my calls."

"There's nothing going on at all. Marshall, I just this minute got back into town. I'm tired, I'm hungry, and I'm not in the mood for a civilized discussion."

"If I can swallow my pride enough to come here, the least you can do is ask me in."

"Your pride?" She felt her temper rise. A bad sign, she knew, when only a few words had been exchanged. "Fine. Come in."

He glanced at her bags as he stepped through the door. "You went home for Christmas, then?"

"That's right."

He laid his coat over the back of a chair. "And your family's well?"

"Hale and hearty, Marshall, and I'm not in the mood for small talk. If you have something to say, say it."

"I don't believe this is something we can resolve until we sit down and talk it through." He gestured to the sofa. "Please."

She shrugged out of her coat and took a chair instead. She linked her hands firmly in her lap and waited.

"The fact that you're still angry with me proves that there's an emotional investment between us." He sat, resting his hands on his knees. "I realized that trying to resolve things right after the incident was a mistake."

"The incident? Is that what we're calling it?"

"Because," he continued, calmly, "emotions, on both sides, were running too close to the surface, making it difficult to compromise and vent constructively."

"I rarely vent constructively." She smiled then, but her eyes were hot. "I don't suppose we got to know each other well enough for you to realize that under certain circumstances, I have a nasty temper."

"I understand." He was pleased, very pleased that they were communicating again. "You see, Deanna, I believe part of our difficulties stemmed from the fact that we didn't know each other as well as we should have. We share the blame there, but it's a very human, very natural inclination to show only your best sides when developing a relationship."

She had to take a deep breath, had to school herself to remain seated when the urge to spring up and strike out was churning inside her. "You want to share the blame for that, fine—particularly since I have no intention of ever moving beyond that stage with you."

"Deanna. If you'll be honest, you'll admit that we were creating something special between us." As a good therapist, he kept his eyes steady on hers, his voice mild and soothing. "A meeting of intellects, of tastes."

"Oh, I think our meeting of intellects and tastes took a sharp division when I walked in and found you and Angela groping each other. Tell me, Marshall, did you have the brochures for our proposed Hawaiian tryst in your jacket pocket at the time?"

His color rose. "I have apologized repeatedly for that lapse."

"Now it's a lapse. Before it was an incident. Let me give you my term for it, Marshall. I call it a betrayal, a betrayal by two people I admired and cared for. Deliberate on Angela's side, and pathetic on yours."

The muscle in his jaw began to twitch. "You and I had not fully committed to each other, sexually or emotionally."

"You're saying that if I'd gone to bed with you, it wouldn't have happened? I'm not buying it." She sprang to her feet. "I'm not sharing the blame for this one, pal. You're the one who thought with your glands. So take my advice, doctor, and get the hell out of my house. I want you to stay away from me. I don't want you knocking at my door. I don't want to hear your voice on the phone. And I don't want any more calls in the middle of the damn night where you can't even drum up the guts to speak."

He stood, standing stiffly. "I don't know what you're talking about."

"Don't you?" Her cheeks were flaming.

"I only know that I want to make things right. My eyes have been opened during these months since you cut me out of your life, Deanna. I know you're the only woman who can make me happy."

"Then you're in for a sad life. I'm not available, and I'm not interested."

"There's someone else." He stepped forward, gripping her forearms before she could jerk away. "You can speak of betrayal when you so casually, so easily move from me to someone else."

"Yes, there's someone else, Marshall. There's me. Now take your hands off me."

"Let me remind you what we had," he murmured, pulling her against him. "Let me show you the way it could be."

The old fear returned, making her tremble as she fought free of his grip. Struggling for air, she braced herself against the chair. Cornered, she was cruel. "You know what would make an interesting topic for my show, Marshall? Try this on. Respected family counselors who harass women they've dated as well as seducing underage girls." She wrapped her arms tight around her body as his color drained. "Yes, I know all about it. A child, Marshall? Can you imagine how that revolts me? The woman you were seeing while you were supposedly developing our relationship is small change compared to that. Angela sent me a little package before she left for New York."

Cold sweat pearled on his brow. "You have no right to publicize my private life."

"And no intention of doing so. Unless you continue to harass me. And if you do—" She trailed off.

"I expected better than threats from you, Deanna."

"Well, looks like you were wrong again." She strode to the door, yanked it open. "Now get out."

Shaken, he picked up his coat. "You owe me the courtesy of giving me the information you have."

"I owe you nothing. And if you're not out this door in five seconds, I'm going to let out a scream that'll raise the roof on this building and bring the neighbors running."

"You're making a mistake," he said as he walked to the door. "A very big mistake."

"Happy holidays," she told him, then slammed the door and turned the bolt.

"Great show, Deanna." Marcie wiped at her eyes as Deanna walked back into the dressing room. "It was great to have all those families of soldiers over in the Gulf on together. And those tapes from over there."

"Thanks, Marcie." Deanna walked over to the lighted makeup mirror and removed her earrings. "You know, Marcie, it's New Year's Eve."

"I've heard rumors."

"It's that time for 'Out with the old, in with the new.'" Pushing a hand through her hair, Deanna turned in front of the mirror, critically studying left profile, right, full face. "And Marcie, my friend, I'm feeling reckless."

"Oh yeah?" Marcie stopped arranging her makeup case in preparation for Bobby Marks. "What kind of reckless? Like going-out-and-picking-up-strange-men-at-cheap-bars reckless?"

"I didn't say I was insane, I said I was reckless. How much time do you have free before Bobby comes in?"

"About twenty minutes."

"Okay, that should do it." Deanna boosted herself into the swivel chair, then spun it away from the mirror. "Change me."

Marcie nearly gave in to the urge to rub her hands together. "You're serious?"

"Deadly. I had a nasty scene with a former relationship a few days ago. I don't know if I'm going to have a job much less a career this time next month. I may just be falling in love with a man who spends more time out of the country than in, and in two weeks we could be at war. Tonight, New Year's Eve, I will not be with the man I think I may be falling in love with, but at a crowded party socializing with strangers because socializing with strangers is now part of my job. So I'm feeling reckless, Marcie, reckless enough to do something drastic."

Marcie clipped the knee-length bib around Deanna's neck. "Maybe you'd better define 'drastic' before I get started."

"Nope." Deanna inhaled deeply, exhaled slowly. "I don't want to know. Surprise me."

"You got it." Marcie picked up her spray bottle and dampened Deanna's hair. "You know, I've been wanting to do this for weeks."

"Now's your chance. Make me a new woman."

Little tangles of nerves formed in Deanna's stomach as Marcie snipped. And snipped. She watched with a faltering heart as tresses of ebony hair hit the tiled floor at her feet.

"You know what you're doing, right?"

"Trust me," Marcie told her, as she snipped some more. "You're going to look fabulous. Distinctive."

"Ah, distinctive?" Wary, Deanna tried to turn toward the mirror.

"No peeking." Marcie laid a firm hand on her shoulder. "It's like going into a cold pool," she explained. "If you try to ease it a little at a time, it's a hard, miserable experience. And sometimes you chicken out and back off before you get under. If you do it all at once, you have that one nifty shock, then you love it." She pursed her lips as she wielded the scissors. "You know, maybe it's more like losing your virginity."

"Holy shit!"

Marcie glanced up and grinned at CBC's resident television chef. "Hiya, Bobby. Almost done here."

"Holy shit," he said again, and stepped inside to stare at Deanna. "What'd you do, Dee?"

"I wanted a change." Her voice was weak as she started to lift a hand to her hair. Marcie pushed it away.

"A cold pool," she said darkly.

"It's a change, all right." Bobby stepped back, and shook his head. "Hey, can I have some of this hair?" Stooping, he picked up a handful. "I can have a toupee made. Hell, I could have half a dozen.

"Oh, God, what have I done?" Deanna squeezed her eyes tight.

"Dee? What's keeping you? We need to—oh, Jesus!" Fran stopped in the doorway, one hand covering her gaping mouth, the other pressed to her belly.

"Fran." Desperate, Deanna reached out. "Fran. Fran, I think I had a nervous breakdown. It's New Year's Eve," she babbled. "Bobby's making toupees. I think my life is flashing in front of my eyes."

"You cut it," Fran managed after a moment. "You really cut it."

"But it'll grow back, right?" Deanna snatched a lock of hair from her bib. "Right?"

"In five or ten years," Bobby predicted cheerfully, and arranged some of Deanna's shorn locks atop his bald dome. "Not quite soon enough to honor the clause I imagine you have in your contract restricting appearance changes."

"Oh God." Deanna's already pale cheek went dead white. "I forgot. I just didn't think. I went a little crazy."

"Be sure to have your lawyer use that one with Delacort," Bobby suggested.

"They'll love it," Marcie said grimly. "She'll see for herself in a minute." Marcie fluffed and combed. Unsatisfied, she added a dab of gel, working it in, then styling with the concentration of a woman cutting diamonds. "Now you just take a deep breath, and hold it," Marcie advised, unhooking the bib. "And don't say anything until you take a really good look."

No one spoke as Marcie turned Deanna slowly toward the mirror. Deanna stared at the reflection, her lips parted in shock, her eyes huge. The long mane of hair was gone, replaced by a short, sleek cap with a saucy fringe of bangs. In a daze, she watched the woman in the mirror lift a hand, touch the nape of her neck, where the hair stopped.

"It follows the shape of your face," Marcie said nervously when Deanna only continued to stare. "And it shows off your eyes and eyebrows. You've got these great dark eyebrows with this terrific natural arch. Your eyes are a little almond-shaped and dramatic, but they kind of got lost with all that hair."

"I . . ." Deanna let out a breath, took another. "I love it."

"You do?" As her knees buckled in relief, Marcie dropped into the chair beside her. "Really?"

Deanna watched her own smile bloom. "I love it. Do you realize how many hours a week I had to devote to my hair? Why didn't I think of this before?" She grabbed a hand mirror to view the back. "This is going to save me almost eight hours a week—an entire workday." She picked up the earrings she'd discarded and put them back on. "What do you think?" she asked Fran.

"Not to diminish your time-saving priorities, you look incredible. The hip girl-next-door."

"Bobby?"

"It's sexy. A cross between an Amazon and a pixie. And I'm sure Delacort won't mind reshooting all the promos."

"Oh my God." As the idea took root, Deanna turned to Fran. "Oh my God."

"Don't worry, you'll dazzle Loren with it tonight. Then we'll work it into the next show."

"Post-holiday blues?"

"Sure, sure." Thinking frantically, Fran gnawed on her lip. "Ah—something as simple and frivolous as a new hairstyle can give you that quick lift after the party's over."

"I'll buy it," Bobby decided. "Now, if you ladies don't mind, I need to get into makeup. I have a trout to sauté."

Early in the first light of the new year, with a video of *Deanna's Hour* playing on the TV, a single, lonely figure wandered a small, dark room. On the table where framed pictures of Deanna beamed into the shadowy light, a new treasure was laid: a thick tress of ebony hair wrapped in gold cord.

It was soft to the touch, soft as silk. After a last caress, the fingers wandered away, toward the phone. They dialed slowly, so that the joy could be drawn out. Moments later, Deanna's voice drifted through the receiver, sleepy, a bit uneasy, bringing with it a silver spear of pleasure that lasted long after the receiver was replaced again.

13

It was after two A.M. in Baghdad when Finn reviewed his notes for the scheduled live broadcast on CBC's *Evening News.* He sat on the single chair that wasn't heaped with tapes or cable, dragging on a fresh shirt while his mind honed ideas and observations into a report.

He tuned out his surroundings, the noise of preparation, the smell of cold food and the chatter.

His crew was spread around the suite, checking equipment and tossing jokes. A sense of humor, particularly if it was dark, helped cut the tension. For the past two days, they had hoarded food and bottled water.

It was January sixteenth.

"Maybe we should tie some sheets together," Curt suggested. "Hang them outside the window like a big white flag."

"No, we'll send up my Bears cap." The engineer flicked a finger at its brim. "What red-blooded American boy's going to bomb a football fan?"

"I heard the Pentagon told them to hit the hotels first." Finn glanced up from his notes and grinned. "You know how fed up Cheney is with the press." Finn picked up the phone that connected him with Chicago and caught the byplay at the news desk between commercials. "Hey, Martin. How'd the Bulls do last night?" As he spoke he moved in front of the window so that Curt could get a video test of him against the night sky. "Yeah, it's quiet here. Nerves are pretty high—so's the anti-American sentiment."

When the director cut in, Finn nodded. "Got it. They're picking up the feed," he told Curt as he moved out onto the balcony. "We'll go on in the next segment. In four minutes."

"Bring up the lights," Curt demanded. "I got a bad shadow here."

Before anyone could move, there was a rattling boom in the distance.

"What the hell was that?" The engineer went pale and swallowed his gum. "Thunder? Was that thunder?"

"Oh, Jesus." Finn turned in time to see the searing glow of tracer rounds split the night sky. "Martin. You still there? Haversham?" He called to the director even as Curt shifted the camera to the sky. "We've got explosions here. The air raid's started. Yes, I'm sure. Get me on the air for God's sake. Get me on the goddamn air."

He heard the curses and cheers from the Chicago control room, then nothing but a statical hiss.

"Lost it. Fuck." Coolly, he eyed the violent light show. He didn't give a thought, at the moment, to one of those deadly lights striking the building. Every thought in his head was focused on transmitting the story. "Keep running that tape."

"You don't have to tell me twice." Curt was all but hanging over the railing. "Look at that!" he shouted in a voice that was tight with nerves and excitement. Air-raid sirens screamed over the crash of exploding shells. "We got ourselves a front-row seat."

In frustration, Finn held his microphone out to record the sounds of battle. "Get Chicago back."

"I'm trying." The engineer worked controls with trembling hands. "I'm trying, goddamn it."

Eyes narrowed, Finn stalked to the balcony rail, then turned to the camera. If they couldn't go live, at least they'd have tape. "Baghdad's night sky erupted at approximately two thirty-five this morning. There are flashes and the answering spears from antiaircraft. Flames shoot up from the horizon sporadically." When he turned, he saw, with both awe and dull disbelief, the searing comet trail of a tracer flash by at eye level. Its deadly, eerie beauty made his blood pump. What a visual. "Oh, Christ, did you get that? Did you get it?"

He heard his engineer swear thinly as the building shook. Finn shoved his blowing hair out of his face and shouted into his mike. "The city is being rattled by the air raid. The waiting is over. It's started."

He turned back to the engineer. "Any luck?"

"No." Though his color was still gone, he managed a wobbly grin. "I think our friendly hosts are going to be coming along pretty soon to evict us."

Now Finn grinned, a quick, reckless flash as deadly as rifle fire. "They have to find us first." While Finn taped his war report, Deanna sat, numbed with boredom, through another interminable dinner. Strains of monotonous piano music wafted through the ballroom of the hotel in Indianapolis. In addition to after-dinner speeches, mediocre wine and rubber chicken, all she had to look forward to was the long trip back to Chicago.

At least, she thought, selfishly, she wasn't suffering alone. She'd dragged Jeff Hyatt with her.

"It's not too bad," he murmured, as he swallowed a bite. "If you put enough salt on it."

She sent him a look that was nearly as bland as the meal. "That's what I love about you, Jeff. Always the optimist. Let's just see if you can smile about the fact that after we finish not eating this, the station manager, the head of sales and two of our advertisers are going to give speeches."

He thought about it a moment, opted for water rather than wine. "Well, it could be worse."

"I'm waiting."

"We could be snowed in."

She shuddered. "Please, don't even joke about that."

"I like these trips, really." Head ducked, he glanced at her, then back to his plate. "Going through the station, meeting everyone, watching them roll out the red carpet for you."

"I like that part myself. Spending time at one of the affiliates and seeing all that enthusiasm for the show. And most of the people are terrific." She sighed and toyed with the lump of rice next to her chicken. She was just tired, she thought. All of her life, she'd had a surplus of energy, and now it seemed she was running on empty. All those demands on time, on her brain, on her body.

Celebrity, she'd discovered, was not all glamour and limos. For every perk there was a price. For every rich-and-famous elbow she rubbed, there were half a dozen corporate dinners or late-night meetings. For every magazine cover, there were canceled social plans. Helming a daily show didn't simply mean having camera presence and good interviewing skills. It meant being on call twenty-four hours a day.

You got what you asked for, Dee, she reminded herself. Now stop whining and get to work. With a determined smile, she turned to the man beside her. Fred Banks, she remembered, station owner, golf enthusiast and hometown boy.

"I can't tell you how much I enjoyed seeing your operation today," she began. "You have a wonderful team."

He puffed up with pride. "I like to think so. We're number two now, but we intend to be number one within the year. Your show's going to help us accomplish that."

"I hope so." She ignored the little ball of tension in her stomach. Her six months was almost up. "I'm told you were born right here in Indianapolis."

"That's right. Born and bred."

While he expounded on the delights of his hometown, Deanna made appropriate comments while her eyes scanned the room. Every table was circled by people who were in some way depending on her to make it. And doing a good show wasn't enough. She'd done so that morning, she thought. Nearly ten hours before—if you didn't count time for makeup, hair, wardrobe and preproduction. Then there'd been an interview, a staff meeting, phone calls to return, mail to screen.

Mail that had included another odd letter from what she was coming to think of as her most persistent fan.

You look like a sexy angel with your hair short.
I love the way you look.
I love you.

She'd tucked the note away and had answered three dozen others. All that before she'd hopped a plane with Jeff for Indianapolis and the tour of the affiliate, the meetings and handshakes with the local staff, the business lunch, the spot on the news and now this never-ending banquet.

No, a good show wasn't enough. She had to be diplomat, ambassador, boss, business partner and celebrity. And she had to wear each and every hat correctly—while pretending she wasn't lonely, or worried about Finn, or missing those quiet hours when she could curl up with a book for pleasure rather than because she'd be interviewing the author.

This was what she wanted, Deanna told herself, and beamed at the waiter as he served the peach melba.

"You can sleep on the plane going home," Jeff whispered in her ear.

"It shows?"

"Just a little."

She excused herself and pushed back from the table. If she couldn't fix the fatigue, at least she could fix its signs.

She was nearly at the doors when she heard someone tap on the podium mike.

Automatically, she looked back and saw Fred Banks standing under the lights. "If I can have your attention. I've just received word that Baghdad is under attack by UN forces."

There was a buzzing in Deanna's ears. Dimly she heard the noise level rise in the ballroom, like a sea at high tide. From somewhere nearby a waiter raised a triumphant fist.

"I hope they kick that bastard's sorry butt."

Slowly, all fatigue washing away, she walked back to the table. She had a job to finish.

Finn sat on the floor of a hotel bedroom, his laptop on his knees. He hammered out copy as fast as it could pass from his mind to his fingers. It was nearly dawn now, and though his eyes were gritty, he felt no sense of fatigue. Outside, the fire-fight continued. Inside, a game of cat and mouse was under way.

During the past three hours, they had moved twice, hauling equipment and provisions. While Iraqi soldiers swept the building, moving guests and international news crews to the basement of the hotel, Finn and his crew had slipped from room to room. The successful intrigue had his blood pumping.

While he took his round at sentry duty, his two companions sprawled on the bed and snatched sleep.

Satisfied with the copy he'd finished thus far, Finn turned off the computer. He rose, working out the kinks in his back, in his neck, and thinking wistfully of breakfast: blueberry pancakes and gallons of hot coffee. He made do with a handful of Curt's trail mix, then hefted the camera.

At the window he recorded the final images of the first day of war, the lightning flashes of cruise missiles and smart bombs, the streaks of tracers. He speculated on how much devastation they would see when dawn broke. And how much they would get on tape.

"I'm gonna have to report you to the union, pal."

Finn lowered the camera and glanced back at Curt. The cameraman was standing beside the bed, rubbing his tired eyes.

"You're just pissed because I can handle this baby as well as you."

"Shit." Challenged, Curt walked over to take the camera. "You can't do nothing but look pretty on tape."

"Then get ready to prove it. I've got some copy to read."

"You're the boss." He rolled tape in silence as bombs exploded. "Are we going to work on a way to get out of here?"

"I've got some contacts in Baghdad." Finn watched the fires leaping from the horizon. "Maybe."

The moment the last after-dinner speech was finished, the last hand shaken, the last cheek kissed, Deanna headed for a phone. While Deanna called Fran and Richard, Jeff used the phone beside her to contact the Chicago newsroom.

"What?" Richard answered with a snarl. "What is it?"

"Richard? Richard, it's Deanna. I'm on my way to the airport in Indianapolis. I heard about the air strike, and—"

"Yeah, right. We heard. But we've got our own little crisis right here. Fran's in labor. We're just about to head out to the hospital."

"Now?" Because it felt like her circuits were about to overload, Deanna pressed her fingers hard against her temple. "I thought we had another ten days."

"Tell that to Big Ed. Breathe, Fran, don't forget to breathe."

"Look, I won't hold you up. Just tell me if she's okay."

"She just finished half a pizza—that's why she didn't tell me she was in labor. She already contacted Bach. Looks like you're going to be preempted tomorrow. No, damn it, you're not going to talk to her, Fran, you're going to breathe."

"I'll be there as soon as I can. Tell her . . . Oh, Jesus, just tell her I'll be there."

"I'm counting on it. Hey, we're going to have a baby! See you."

With the line buzzing in her ear, Deanna rested her brow against the wall. "What a day."

"Finn Riley reported the air strike."

"What?" Alert again, she spun around to Jeff. "Finn? He's all right, then?"

"He was on the line with the studio when it hit. He got about five seconds of pictures across before they lost the feed."

"So we don't know," she said slowly.

"Hey, he's been through stuff like this before, right?" He put a hesitant arm around her shoulders as he led her out to their waiting car.

"Yes, of course. Of course he has."

"And look at it this way. We're getting out of here at least an hour early, because everybody wanted to get home and turn on the tube."

She nearly laughed. "You're good for me, Jeff."

He beamed back at her. "Same goes."

It was six A.M. when Deanna finally unlocked the door to her apartment and staggered inside. She'd been up for a full twenty-four hours and was long past fatigue. But, she reminded herself, she'd fulfilled her professional obligations, and she'd seen her goddaughter born.

Aubrey Deanna Myers, she mused, and smiled blearily as she walked to the bedroom. An eight-pound miracle with red hair. After watching that incredibly beautiful life slide into the world, it was hard to believe there was a war raging on the other side of the world.

But as she tugged off her clothes, unspeakably grateful that her show was preempted that morning, she switched on the television and brought that war into her home.

What time was it in Baghdad? she wondered, but her mind simply wouldn't cope with the math. Wearily she sat on the edge of the bed in her underwear and tried to concentrate on the images and reports.

"Be careful, damn you."

It was her last thought as she slid down over the bedspread and tumbled into sleep.

Late during the second night of the Gulf War, Finn set up at a Saudi base. He was tired and hungry and longed for a bath. He could hear the roar of jets taking off from the airfield to make their way to Iraq. Other news teams, he knew, would be broadcasting reports.

His mood was foul. As a result of the Pentagon's restrictions on the press, he would have to wait his turn in the pool before he could travel to the front—and then he could go only where military officials instructed. For the first time since World War II, all reports would be subject to censorship.

It was one of the few words Finn considered an obscenity.

"Don't you want to take time to shave that pretty face?"

"Cram it, Curt. We're on in ten." He listened to the countdown in his earpiece. "In the predawn hours of day two of Desert Storm..." he began.

On her couch in Chicago, Deanna leaned forward and studied Finn's image on-screen. Tired, she thought. He looked terribly tired. But tough and ready. And alive.

She toasted him with her diet soda as she ate the peanut butter sandwich she'd fixed for dinner.

She wondered what he was thinking, what he was feeling, as he spoke of sorties and statistics or answered the scripted questions of the news anchor. The Arabian sky spread at his back, and occasionally he had to raise his voice over the sound of jet engines.

"We're glad that you're safely out of Baghdad, Finn. And we'll stay tuned for further reports."

"Thanks, Martin. For CBC, this is Finn Riley in Saudi Arabia."

"Good seeing you, Finn," Deanna murmured, then sighed and rose to take her dishes into the kitchen. It wasn't until she passed her answering machine that she noticed the rapid blink of the message light.

"Oh, hell, how could I have forgotten?"

Setting the dishes aside, she pushed Rewind. She'd slept a blissful six hours, then had rushed out again. A stop by the hospital, a few hours at the office, where chaos had reigned. That chaos, and the war talk, had driven her out again with a thick file of clippings and a bag of mail. She'd worked the rest of the evening, ignoring the phone. Without checking her messages.

Having a baby and a war was certainly distracting, she thought as she hit Play.

There was a call from her mother. One from Simon. Dutifully, she scribbled the messages on a pad. There were two hang-ups, each with a long pause before the click of the receiver.

"Kansas?" Deanna dropped her pencil as Finn's voice filled the room. "Where the hell are you? It must be five A.M. there. I've only got this line for a minute. We're out of Baghdad. Christ, the place is a mess. I don't know when I'll be able to get through again, so catch me on the news. I'll be thinking about you, Deanna. God, it's hard to think about anything else. Buy yourself a couple of flannel shirts, will you? And some wading boots. It can get cold at the cabin. Write, okay? Send a tape, a smoke signal. And let me know why the hell you're not answering your phone. Later."

And he was gone.

Deanna was reaching down to press Rewind and listen to the message again when Loren Bach's voice flowed out. "Jesus H. Christ, you're a hard woman to get in touch with. I called your office, and your secretary said you were at the hospital. Scared the life out of me until she explained it was Fran having her baby. Heard it's a girl. Don't know why the hell you're not home yet, but here's the deal: Delacort would like to renew your contract for two years. Our people will be contacting your agent, but I wanted to be the first to tell you. Congratulations, Deanna."

She couldn't have said why, but she sat down on the floor, covered her face with her hands and wept.

Things moved quickly over the next five weeks, at home and away. With the new contract with Delacort signed and sealed, Deanna found both her budget and her hopes expanding. She was able to add to her staff, and furnish a separate office for Fran when she returned from maternity leave.

Best of all, the ratings began a slow, steady climb during the first weeks of the new year.

She had ten cities now, and though she still fell behind *Angela's* whenever the shows were scheduled head to head, the margin had slimmed.

To celebrate the success, she bought a softly patterned Aubusson carpet to replace the flea-market rug in her living room. It went, she thought, perfectly with the desk.

She had a cover on *Woman's Day* scheduled for April, a feature in *People* and, for old time's sake, agreed to appear on a segment of *Woman Talk*. The *Chicago Tribune* did a Sunday spread, calling her a star on the rise.

She turned down, with a combination of amusement and horror, an offer to pose for *Playboy*.

When the red light blinked on, Deanna was seated on set. She smiled, slipping easily, comfortably into thousands of homes.

"Do you remember your first love? That first kiss that made your heart beat faster? The long talks, the secret glances?" She sighed and had the audience sighing with her. "Today, we're going to reunite three couples who remember very well. Janet Hornesby was sweet sixteen when she had her first romance. That was fifty years ago, but she hasn't forgotten the young boy who stole her heart that spring."

The camera began to pan the panel, focusing on giddy, nervous smiles as Deanna continued to speak.

"Robert Seinfield was just eighteen when he left his high school sweetheart and moved two thousand miles away with his family. Though a decade has passed, he still thinks of Rose, the girl who wrote him his first love letter. And twenty-three years ago, college plans and family pressures separated Theresa Jamison from the man she'd thought she'd marry. I think our guests today are wondering, What if? I know I am. We'll find out, after this."

"God, great show." Fran, Aubrey snug in a baby saque at her torso, marched out on the set. "I think Mrs. Hornesby and her fellow might have a second chance."

"What are you doing here?"

"I wanted Aubrey to see where her mother works." Nestling the baby, she looked longingly around the set. "I've missed this place."

"Fran, you've just had a baby."

"Yeah, I heard about that. You know, Dee, you should think about a follow-up show. People love the sentimental stuff. If any of those three couples get together, you could do a kind of anniversary thing."

"I've already thought of that." Deanna stepped back, hands on hips. "Well," she said after a minute. "You look good. Really."

"I feel good. Really. But as much as I love being a mom, I hate being a homebody. I need work or I'm liable to do something drastic. Like take up needlepoint."

"We couldn't let that happen. Let's go up and talk about it."

"I want to say hi to the crew first."

"I'll be up in the office when you're finished." Smiling smugly, Deanna headed to the elevator. She'd won her fifty-dollar bet with Richard. He'd been positive she'd last two full months. On the ride up to the sixteenth floor, she glanced at her watch and calculated time. "Cassie," she began, the minute she stepped into the outer office. "See if you can reschedule my lunch meeting for one-thirty."

"No problem. Great show, by the way. Word is the phones were going crazy."

"We aim to please." With her schedule in mind, she dropped down behind her desk to study the mail Cassie had stacked for her. "Fran stopped by downstairs. She'll be up in a few minutes—with the baby."

"She brought the baby? Oh, I can't wait to see her." She stopped, disturbed by the expression on Deanna's face. "Is something wrong?"

"Wrong?" Baffled, Deanna shook her head. "I don't know. Cassie, do you know how this got here?" She held up a plain white envelope that carried only her name.

"It was already on your desk when I brought the other mail in. Why?"

"It's just weird. I've been getting these notes on and off since last spring." She turned the paper around so Cassie could read it.

" 'Deanna, you're so beautiful. Your eyes look into my soul. I'll love you forever." ' Cassie pursed her lips. "I guess it's flattering. And pretty tame compared to some of the letters you get. Are you worried about it?"

"Not worried. Maybe a little uneasy. It doesn't seem quite healthy for someone to keep this up for so long."

"Are you sure they've all been from the same person?"

"Same type of envelope, same type of message in the same type of red print." Distress curled loosely in her stomach. "Maybe it's someone who works in the building."

Someone she saw every day. Spoke with. Worked with.

"Anyone been asking you out, or coming on to you?"

"What? No." With an effort, Deanna shook off the eerie mood, then shrugged. "It's stupid. Harmless," she said, as if to convince herself, then deliberately tore the page in two and tossed it in the trash. "Let's see what business we can clear up before noon, Cassie."

"Okay. Did you happen to catch Angela's special last night?"

"Of course." Deanna grinned. "You didn't think I'd miss my toughest competition's first prime-time program, did you? She did a nice job."

"Not all the reviewers thought so." Cassie tapped the clippings on Deanna's desk. "The one from the *Times* was a killer."

Automatically Deanna reached into the stack and read the first clipped review.

" 'Pompous and shallow.' " She winced. " 'By turns simpering and sniping.' "

"The ratings weren't what they expected, either," Cassie told her. "They weren't embarrassing, but they were hardly stellar. The *Post* called her self-aggrandizing."

"That's just her style."

"It was a little much, doing that tour of her penthouse for the camera and cooing about New York. And there were more shots of her than her guests." Cassie shrugged, grinned. "I counted."

"I imagine this will be tough for her to take." Deanna set the reviews aside again. "But she'll bounce back." She shot Cassie a warning look. "I've had my problems with her, but I don't wish hatchet reviews on anyone."

"I wouldn't either. I just don't want you to be hurt by her."

"Bullets bounce off me," Deanna said dryly. "Now let's forget about Angela. I'm sure I'm the last thing on her mind this morning."

Angela's initial tantrum over the reviews had resulted in a snowstorm of shredded newspaper. It littered the floor of her office. She ground newsprint into the pink pile as she paced.

"Those bastards aren't getting away with taking a slice at me."

Dan Gardner, the new executive producer of *Angela's*, wisely waited until the worst of the storm had passed. He was thirty, built like a middleweight with a compact, muscular body. His conservatively styled brown hair suited his boyish face, accented by dark blue eyes and subtly clefted chin.

He had a shrewd mind and a simple goal: to ride to the top on whatever vehicle could get him there the fastest.

"Angela, everyone knows reviews are crap." He poured her a soothing cup of tea. It was a pity, he thought, that their strategy of allowing no previews of the first show had failed. "Those jerks always take cheap shots at whoever's on top. And that's just where you are." He handed her the delicate china cup. "On top."

"Damn right I am." Tea slopped over into the saucer as she whirled away. Fury was better than tears, she knew. No one, absolutely no one would have the satisfaction of seeing how hurt she was. She'd been so proud, showing off her new home, sharing her life with her audience.

They had called it "simpering."

"And the ratings would have proved it," she snapped back, "if it hadn't been for this damn war. The goddamn viewers just can't get enough of the fucking thing. Day and night, night and day, we're bombarded. Why don't we just blow the damn country off the map and be done with it?"

Tears were close, perilously close. She battled them back and sipped the tea like medicine.

She wanted a drink.

"It's not hurting us. Your lead-in to the six o'clock news has come up in five markets. And the viewers loved your remote at Andrews Air Force Base last week."

"Well, I'm sick of it." She hurled the teacup at the wall, sending shards flying and drops splattering over the silk wallpaper. "And I'm sick of that little bitch in Chicago trying to undermine my ratings."

"She's a flash in the pan." He hadn't even jolted at the explosion. He'd been expecting it. Now that it was done, he knew she could begin to calm. And when she'd calmed, she'd be needy.

He'd been seeing to Angela's needs for several months.

"In a year she'll be old news, and you'll still be number one."

She sat behind her desk, leaning back, eyes shut. She was slipping. Nothing seemed to be going the way she'd planned when she'd formed her production company. She was in charge, yes, but there was so much to do. So many demands, so many, many ways to fail.

But she couldn't fail, could never face that. She calmed herself by taking long, slow breaths, just as she did during bouts of stage fright. It was much more productive, she reminded herself, to focus on someone else's failure.

"You're right. Once Deanna bottoms out, she'll be lucky to get a gig on public access." And she had something that might hurry that fine day along.

As the smile curved Angela's lips, Dan walked behind the chair to massage the tension from her shoulders. "You just relax. Let me do all the worrying."

She liked the feel of his hands on her—gentle, competent, sure. They made her feel protected, safe. She so desperately needed that now.

"They love me, don't they, Dan?"

"Of course they do." His hands trailed up to her neck, then brushed down over her breasts. They were soft and heavy and never failed to arouse him. His voice thickened as he felt her nipples harden between the light pinch of his thumb and forefinger. "Everybody loves Angela."

"And they'll keep watching." She sighed, relaxing as his hands molded her.

"Every day. Coast to coast."

"Every day," she murmured, and her smile widened. "Go lock the door, Dan. Tell Lorraine to hold my calls."

"I'd love to."

14

During the frigid nights in the desert, it was hard to remember the blazing heat of day. Just as after the first bombs exploded it was difficult to remember the deadly tedium of the long weeks of Desert Shield.

Finn had been through other wars, though he'd never been so hamstrung by military regulations. There were ways, however, for the enterprising reporter to stretch them. He would never have denied that certain sensitive intelligence data couldn't be broadcast without endangering troops. But he wasn't a fool, nor was he blindly ambitious. He saw his job, and his duty, as finding out what was happening, not just what the official reports claimed was happening.

Twice he and Curt climbed into his rented truck with a portable satellite dish bracketed in the bed, and headed out. Over the poorly marked roads and the shifting sand, they managed to link up with U.S. troops. Finn listened to complaints and to hopes, and returned to base to report both.

He watched Scuds fly and Patriots intercept them. He slept in snatches and lived with the possibility of a chemical assault.

When the ground war began, he was ready, eager, to follow it into Kuwait City.

It would be called the Mother of Battles, the hundred hours of fierce fighting to liberate Kuwait. While allied troops took up positions along the Euphrates River, along the highways linking Kuwait to other cities, Iraqis fled. Hustling, as one trooper told Finn, "to get out of Dodge."

There were massive traffic jams, trapped tanks, abandoned possessions. From a dusty truck heading toward the city, Finn observed the wreckage. Mile after mile of shattered vehicles lined the road. Cars, stripped for parts, tilted on crates. Personal possessions littered the roadway, mattresses, blankets, frying pans and ammo clips. Incredibly, a chandelier, its crystals gleaming in the sun, lay on the sand like scattered jewels. And worse, much worse, was the occasional corpse.

"Let's get some tape of this." Finn stepped out of the truck, his boots crunching down on one of the cassette tapes that were blowing across the highway.

"Looks like the garage sale from hell," Curt commented. "Crazy bastards must have been looting on their way out."

"It always comes down to getting your own, doesn't it?" Finn pointed toward a swatch of hot pink flapping from beneath an overturned truck. The evening gown shimmered with sequins. "Where the hell did she expect to wear that?"

Finn prepared for a stand-up as Curt set up his equipment. He hadn't thought anything else could surprise him. Not after seeing the pathetically gaunt Iraqi soldiers wearily surrendering to allied troops. Seeing the fear and fatigue, and the relief, on their faces as they emerged from their foxholes in the desert. He hadn't thought anything else about war could affect him, not the torn bodies, the atrocities of scavengers or the stink of death cooking under the merciless sun.

But that flap of pink silk, rustling seductively in the desert wind, turned his stomach.

It was worse inside the city. The raw nerves, the anger, the devastation, all coated in a layer of oily soot from the fires that depleted Kuwait's lifeblood of oil.

When the wind blew toward the city, the sky would darken with smoke. Midday would become midnight. The seaside was dotted with mines, and explosions rocked the city several times a day. Gunfire continued, not only in celebratory bursts, but in savage drive-by attacks on Kuwaiti soldiers. Survivors searched the cemetery for the remains of loved ones, many of whom had suffered torture and worse.

Through all he observed, through all he reported, Finn continued to think of a sequined evening gown billowing out of the sand.

Like the rest of the world, Deanna watched the end of the war on television. She listened to the reports on the liberation of Kuwait, the official cease-fire, the statistics of victory. It became a habit to drop into the newsroom before she left the CBC Building, hoping for a few scraps of information that hadn't yet been aired.

But the reality of day-to-day responsibilities kept her grounded. Whenever she had a free night, she watched the late news, then slipped in a tape of that morning's show. In the privacy of her apartment, she could watch herself critically, searching for ways to improve her on-air skills or to tighten the overall format.

She sat cross-legged on the floor, comfortable in sweatshirt and jeans, a notepad open across her knees. The earrings were wrong, she noted. Every time she moved her head they swung—a distraction for the viewer, she thought, and wrote: No more dangling earrings.

And the hand gestures were too broad. If she didn't watch it, she'd end up being parodied on *Saturday Night Live.* She should be so lucky, she thought with a grin, and scribbled on her pad.

Did she touch people too much? Nibbling her lips, Deanna watched. She always seemed to be laying a hand on a guest's arm or circling an audience member's shoulder. Maybe she should—

The knock on the door had her swearing. Her schedule didn't allow for unexpected visitors after ten. Grudgingly, she switched off the VCR. She glimpsed through the peephole. Then she was tugging at locks, dragging at the chain.

"Finn! I didn't know you were back!"

She didn't know who moved first. In a heartbeat, they were wrapped together, his mouth hard on hers, her hands fisted in his hair. The explosion of need rattled them both, the swell of heat, the blast of power. The bomb detonated inside her, leaving emotions shattered, needs raw. Then he was kicking the door closed as they tumbled to the floor.

She didn't think. Couldn't think. Not with his mouth burning on hers and his hands already urgently possessing. Like tussling children, they rolled over the rug, the only sounds incoherent murmurs and strained breathing.

It wasn't dreamlike, but stark reality. The only reality that mattered. His hands were rough, streaking under the fleece of her shirt to take, digging into her hips to press her fiercely against him.

She seemed to be erupting beneath him, with short, static bursts of energy. Her skin was hot, smooth, unbearably soft. He wanted to taste it, to devour it, to consume the flavor of her flesh and blood and bone. Her mouth wasn't enough—her throat, her shoulder, where he dragged the shirt down. He felt like an animal, rabid and starving, and wanted to glory in it. Yet he knew he could hurt her, would hurt her, if he didn't harness the worst of the need.

"Deanna." He wished he could find some spark of tenderness within the furnace that roared inside him. "Let me . . ." He lifted his head, struggling to clear his vision. He'd barely looked at her, he realized. The moment she'd opened the door and said his name, his control had snapped.

Now she was vibrating like a plucked string beneath him, her eyes huge and dark, her mouth swollen. And her skin . . . He brought his fingertips to her cheek, stroking over the flushed, damp flesh.

Tears. He'd always considered them a woman's greatest weapon. Shaken, he brushed them away and cleared his throat. "Did I knock you down?"

"I don't know." She felt like a jumble of nerve ends and sparks. "I don't care." Slowly, beautifully, her smile bloomed. She framed his face in her hands. "Welcome home." She let their slow, quiet kiss soothe them both.

"I've been told I have considerable finesse with women." Taking her hand, he closed it into a loose fist and pressed it to his lips. "Though it might be hard for you to believe at the moment."

"I'd rather not ask for corroboration."

His grin flashed. "Look, why don't we . . ." He trailed off as he stroked a hand over her hair. Confused, he pulled back, eyes narrowed, and studied her. "What in the hell did you do to your hair?"

In automatic defense, she combed her fingers through it. "I cut it. New Year's Eve." Her smile wavered. "The viewers like it—three to one. We did a poll."

"It's shorter than mine." With a half laugh, he moved back to squat on his haunches. "Come here, let me get a good look." Without waiting for assent, he hauled her to a sitting position.

She sat, pouting a little, her eyes daring him, and the lamplight glowing over the glistening cap. "I was tired of dealing with it," she muttered when he only continued his silent study. "This saves me hours a week, and it suits the shape of my face. It looks good on camera."

"Um-hmm." Fascinated, he reached out to toy with her earlobe, then skimmed his finger down the side of her throat. "Either several months of celibacy is playing hell with my libido, or you're the sexiest woman alive."

Delighted, flustered, she hugged her knees. "You look pretty good yourself. You know they're calling you the Desert Hunk."

He winced. After the ribbing he'd taken from his associates, he was hardpressed to find the humor in it. "It'll pass."

"I don't know. There's already a fan club here in Chicago." Seeing that he could be embarrassed only amused her. "You did look pretty hunky with Scuds flying in the sky behind you, or with tanks rolling across the sand at your back. Especially since you didn't shave for a couple of days."

"Once the ground war started, water was at a premium."

Her amusement faded. "Was it bad?"

"Bad enough." He took her hand, gently now, remembering to appreciate the elegance. That was what he needed, the warm reality of her. Maybe, in a day or two, the things he'd seen, the things he'd heard would fade a little.

"Do you want to talk about it?"

"No."

"You look tired." She could see now how drawn he was beneath the desert tan. "When did you get back?"

"About an hour ago. I came straight here."

Even as her heart picked up rhythm, she responded to the weariness in his eyes. "Why don't I fix you something to eat? You can get your bearings."

He kept her hand in his, wishing he could explain to her, to himself, how much steadier he felt being here. Being close. "I wouldn't turn down a sandwich, especially if it came with a beer."

"I can probably handle that." She got to her feet, gave his hand a tug. "Come on, stretch out on the couch, relax with Carson. While you're eating, I'll fill you in on all the news and gossip from CBC."

He rose, waiting until she'd punched the remote. "Are you going to let me stay tonight, Deanna?"

She looked back at him, her eyes huge, but steady. "Yes."

Turning quickly, she walked into the kitchen. Her hands were trembling, she realized. And it was wonderful. Her whole body was quivering in response to that long, last look he'd given her before she'd rushed away. She didn't know what it would be like, but she knew that she'd never wanted anyone more. The months of separation hadn't stunted the emotions that had begun growing inside her.

And that first greedy kiss as they'd tumbled heedless to the floor had been more stunning, more erotic than any fantasy she'd woven while she'd waited for him to come back.

He'd come to her. She pressed a hand to her stomach. Nerves were jittering, she thought. But they were good nerves, hot and strong, not cold, cowardly ones.

Tonight, she would take the step. She would reclaim herself. Because she wanted, Deanna thought. Because she chose.

Putting a sandwich of cold ham and cheese on a platter, she added a pilsner of beer. She lifted the tray and smiled to herself. Desire was as basic and human as hunger. Once they had satisfied the latter, she would take him to her bed, into her body.

"I could put together something hot," she said as she carried the tray back into the living room. "There's a can of soup in the—" Deanna broke off and stared.

Carnac the Magnificent was on a roll. Ed was hooting in response. And Finn Riley, the Desert Hunk, was sleeping like a baby.

He'd pried off his battered hightops, but hadn't bothered to remove his jacket. Unrelenting work, travel and jet lag had finally taken their toll. He lay flat on his stomach, his face smashed into one of Deanna's satin pillows, his arm dangling limply over the edge of the couch.

"Finn?" Deanna set the tray aside and put a hand on his shoulder. When she shook him, he didn't stir, a hundred and sixty pounds of exhausted male.

Resigned, she went for a spare blanket and tucked it around him. She locked the front door, secured the chain. Switching the lamp to low, she sat down on the floor in front of him. "Our timing," she said quietly and kissed his cheek, "continues to suck." With a sigh, she picked up the sandwich and tried to fill the void of sexual frustration with food and television.

Finn pulled out of the dream, chilled with sweat. The fading vision behind his eyes was horrid—the body riddled with bullets at his feet, blood and gore staining the pilk silk and sequins of the tattered evening gown. In the quiet light of morning, he struggled to sit up, rubbing his hands over his face.

Disoriented, he tried to get his bearings. Hotel room? What city? What country? A plane? A taxi?

Deanna. Remembering, Finn let his head fall back against the cushions and moaned. First he'd tossed her to the floor, then he'd passed out. A rousing segment in the frustrating journal of their romance.

He was surprised she hadn't dragged him out of the apartment by the feet and left him snoring in the hall. Fighting free of the blanket, he staggered up. He swayed a moment, his body still floating with fatigue. He'd have killed for coffee. He supposed that was why he thought he smelled some brewing. After months in the desert, he knew that mirages weren't only the result of heat, but of desperate human desires.

He rolled his stiff shoulders and swore. Christ, he didn't want to think about desires.

But maybe it wasn't too late. A quick injection of instant coffee, and he could slip into bed with Deanna and make up for his neglect the night before.

Bleary-eyed, he stumbled toward the kitchen.

She was no mirage, standing there in a beam of sunlight, looking fresh and lovely in slacks and a sweater, pouring gloriously scented coffee into a red ceramic mug.

"Deanna."

"Oh!" She jolted, nearly upending the mug. "You startled me. I was concentrating on some mental notes for the show." She set the pot down, brushed suddenly damp hands down her hips. "How'd you sleep?"

"Like a rock. I don't know whether to be embarrassed or apologetic, but if you share that coffee, I'll be anything you want."

"There's nothing to be embarrassed or apologetic about." But she couldn't meet his eyes as she reached for the mug. "You were exhausted."

He lightly stroked a hand over her hair. "How angry are you?"

"I'm not." But her gaze cut away from his when she pushed the mug into his hand. "Do you want cream or sugar?"

"No. If not angry, what?"

"It's hard to explain." There wasn't enough room in the kitchen, she realized. And he was blocking the way out. "I've really got to go, Finn. My driver will be here in a few minutes."

He stood his ground. "Try to explain."

"This isn't easy for me." Unnerved, she snapped out the words and turned away. "I'm not experienced in morning-after conversation."

"Nothing happened."

"That's not the point, not really. I wasn't thinking last night. I couldn't. When I saw you, I was overwhelmed by what was happening, what I was feeling. No one's ever wanted me the way you did last night."

"And I blew it." No longer interested in coffee, he set the mug carefully on the counter. "I'm sorry. Maybe I shouldn't have stopped that first mad rush, but I was afraid I'd hurt you."

She turned slowly, her eyes reflecting her confusion. "You weren't hurting me."

"I would have. Christ, Deanna, I could have eaten you alive. And tearing into you on the floor, it was . . ." He thought bitterly of Angela. "It was too careless."

"That's my point. Not on your side, Finn, on mine. I was careless, and that's not like me." There seemed to be nothing she could do with her hands. She lifted them, let them fall as he continued to stand and study her. "The feelings you've stirred up aren't like me. And the way things turned out . . ." She tugged at her earlobe. "It gave me time to think."

"Great." He snatched up the mug again and took a long drink. "Terrific."

"I haven't changed my mind," she said as she watched his eyes darken. "But we need to talk, before this goes any further. Once I explain, once you understand, I hope we can keep going."

There was a plea in her eyes, something she needed from him. He didn't have to know what it was to respond. Crossing to her, he cupped her chin in his hands and kissed her lightly. "Okay. We'll talk. Tonight?"

Nerves vanished in relief. "Yes, tonight. Fate must be looking out for me. It's the first free weekend I've had in two months."

"Come to my place." As her body softened beautifully against his, he kissed her again, lingering, persuasive. "There's something I very much want to do." He nipped at her lip until her eyes fluttered closed.

"Yes."

"I very, mmm, very much..." He traced her lips with his tongue, dipped slowly inside to savor. "Want to cook for you."

"So, what's he going to cook?"

"I didn't ask." Briskly, Deanna checked over her wardrobe list, noting the dates that certain skirts, blazers, blouses and accessories had been worn. She had a production assistant who dated and tagged each piece, listing not only when it had been worn, but in combination with what other items.

"It's pretty serious when a man cooks for you—especially on a Friday night." Fran kept one eye on Aubrey, who was taking a peaceful nap in the Portacrib. "Very high-powered wooing."

"Maybe." Deanna smiled at the idea. Meticulously, she began to arrange her choices for the following week's line-up of shows. "I plan on enjoying it."

"My instincts tell me he's good for you. I'd like a little more time to check him out personally, but the look on your face when you came in this morning was almost enough."

"What kind of look?"

"Happiness. Strictly feminine happiness. Different from the gleam in your eye when Delacort renewed us, or when we got picked up by six new stations."

"How about when we moved into first place in Columbus?"

"Even different from that. This is all-important. The show, what you're able to do with it. The way you've shifted things around so I can bring Aubrey to work."

"I want her here, too," Deanna reminded her. "Nobody on staff is going to have to make the choice between parenthood and career. Which brings up a topic idea I had."

Fran picked up her clipboard. "Shoot."

"Finding ways to incorporate day care into the workplace. Right in office buildings and factories. I read an article about this restaurant, family-run. They have what amounts to a preschool right off the kitchen. I've already given Margaret the clipping."

"I'll check it out."

"Good. Now let me tell you my idea about Jeff."

"Jeff? What about him?"

"He's doing a good job, wouldn't you say?"

"I'd say he's doing a great one." Fran glanced over as Aubrey sighed in her sleep. "He's totally devoted to you and the show, and he's a wizard at cutting through the fat."

"He wants to direct." Pleased that she'd been able to surprise Fran, Deanna sat back. "He hasn't said anything to me, to anyone. He wouldn't. But I've watched him. You can see it by the way he hangs around the studio, talking to the camera-men, the techs. Every time we get a new director, Jeff all but interrogates him."

"He's an editor."

"I was a reporter," Deanna pointed out. "I want to give him a shot. God knows we need a permanent director, somebody who can slide into the groove, who understands my rhythm. I think he'll fit the bill. What, as executive producer, do you think?"

"I'll talk to him," Fran said after a moment. "If he's interested, we've got a show scheduled for next week on video dating. It's light. We could test him out on it."

"Good."

"Deanna." Cassie stood in the doorway, a newspaper rolled tight in her hand.

"Don't tell me. I've only got twenty minutes before shooting the new promo, and after that I've got to get across town and charm the Chicago chapter of NOW. I swear, warden, I wasn't trying to make a break for it."

"Deanna," Cassie repeated. There was no humor in her eyes. Only distress. "I think you should see this."

"What is it? Oh, not the tabloids again." Prepared to be mildly irked, she took the paper from Cassie, unfolded it and glanced at the screaming headline. "Oh my God." Her knees went to jelly as she groped behind her for a chair. "Oh, Fran."

"Take it easy, honey. Let me see." Fran eased Deanna down into a chair and took the paper.

SECRET LIFE OF AMERICA'S GIRL NEXT DOOR
Midwest's Darling a Party-Hardy College Girl
Deanna's Former Lover Tells All!

There was a big red EXCLUSIVE! bannering the corner, and a sidebar hinting at WILD NIGHTS! DRUNKEN ORGIES! SEX ON THE FIFTY-YARD LINE! beneath a recent photo of Deanna. Beside her was a grainy photograph of a man she'd tried to forget.

"That son of a bitch!" Fran exploded. "That lying bastard. Why the hell did he go to the tabs with this? He's dripping with money."

"Who knows why anyone does anything." Sickened, Deanna stared at the bold headlines. The frightened, broken girl she had been resurfaced. "He got his picture in the paper, didn't he?"

"Honey." Fran quickly turned the paper over. "Nobody's going to believe that trash."

"Of course they are, Fran." Her eyes were bright and hard. "They'll believe it because it makes titillating copy. And most people won't get past the headlines anyway. They'll scan them when they're checking out in the supermarket. Maybe they'll read the copy on the front page, even flip through to the inside. Then they'll go home and chat about the story with their neighbors."

"It's crap. Exploitive crap, and anybody with a working brain knows it."

"I just thought you should know." Cassie handed Deanna a cup of water. "I didn't want you finding out from someone else."

"You were right."

Cassie pressed her lips together. "You've gotten some calls on it." Including one, which she would not pass on, from Marshall Pike.

"I'll handle them later. Let me see, Fran."

"I'm going to fucking burn this rag."

"Let me see," Deanna repeated. "I can't deal with it if I don't know what it says."

Fran reluctantly handed the paper to her. As with the worst of tabloid press, there was just enough truth mixed in with the lies to have impact. She had indeed gone to Yale. And she had dated Jamie Thomas, a star tackle. Yes, she had attended a postgame party with him in the autumn of her junior year. She'd danced, she'd flirted. She'd consumed more alcohol than might have been wise.

She certainly had taken a walk to the playing field with him on that cool, clear night. And she had laughed as he'd rushed over the grass, tackling invisible opponents. She'd even laughed when he'd tackled her. But the story didn't say that she'd stopped laughing very quickly. There was no mention of fear, of outrage, of sobbing.

In Jamie's recollection she hadn't fought. She hadn't screamed. In his version he hadn't left her alone, her clothes torn, her body bruised. He didn't say how she'd wept on that chilly grass, her spirit shattered and her innocence violently stolen.

"Well." Deanna brushed a tear from her cheek. "He hasn't changed his story over the years. Maybe he's embellished it a little more, but that's to be expected."

"I think we should contact Legal." It took all of Fran's control to speak calmly. "You should sue Jamie Thomas and the paper for libel, Dee. You're not going to let him get away with it."

"I let him get away with a lot worse, didn't I?" Very neatly, very deliberately, she folded the paper, then tucked it into her purse. "Cassie, please clear my schedule after the NOW meeting. I know it may cause some problems."

"No problem," Cassie said instantly. "I'll take care of it."

"Cancel everything," Fran told her.

"No, I can do what I have to do." Deanna picked up her sweater. However steady her voice, her movements, her eyes were devastated.

"Then I'll go with you. You're not going home alone."

"I'm not going home at all. There's someone I need to talk to. I'll be fine." She squeezed Fran's arm. "Really. I'll see you Monday."

"Damn it, Dee, let me help."

"You always have. I really have to do this one thing alone. I'll call you."

She didn't expect the explanation to be easy. But she hadn't known she would find herself sitting in the driveway beside Finn's beautiful old house, fighting for the courage to walk up and knock on the door.

She sat watching the bare limbs of the spreading maples tremble in the high March wind. She wanted to watch the strong, white sunlight flash and gleam off the tall, graceful windows, and glint off the tiny flecks of mica in the weathered stone.

Such a sturdy old house, she thought, with its curving gables and arrow-straight chimneys. It looked like a dependable place, a haven against storms and wind. She wondered if he'd chosen to give himself some personal calm away from the chaos of his work.

She wondered if it would offer her any.

Bracing herself, she stepped from the car, walked along the walkway of stones and stepped up onto the covered porch he'd had painted a deep, glossy blue.

There was a brass knocker in the shape of an Irish harp. She stared at it a long time before she knocked.

"Deanna." He smiled, holding out a hand in welcome. "It's a little early for dinner, but I can fix you a late lunch."

"I need to talk to you."

"So you said." He let his hand drop when she didn't take it, then closed the door. "You look pale." Hell, he thought, she looked as fragile as glass. "Why don't you sit down?"

"I'd like to sit." She followed him into the first room off the hallway.

Her first distracted glimpse of the room simply registered man. No frills, no flounces, just sturdy, dignified old pieces that murmured of easy wealth and masculine taste. She chose a high-backed chair in front of the fire that burned low. The warmth was comforting.

Without asking, he walked to a curved cabinet and chose a decanter of brandy. Whatever was preying on her mind went deep enough to make her withdraw.

"Drink this first, then tell me what's on your mind."

She sipped, then started to speak.

"Finish it," he interrupted impatiently. "I've seen wounded soldiers with more color than you have right now."

She sipped again, more deeply, and felt the heat fight with the ice shivering in her stomach. "There's something I want to show you." She opened her bag, took out the paper. "You should read this first."

He glanced down. "I've already seen it." In a gesture of disdain, he tossed it aside. "You've got more sense than to let that kind of tripe get to you."

"Did you read it?"

"I stopped reading poorly written fiction when I was ten."

"Read it now," Deanna insisted. "Please."

He studied her another minute, concerned and confused. "All right."

She couldn't sit after all. While he read, Deanna got up to wander around the room, her hands reaching nervously for mementos and knickknacks. She heard the paper rattle in his hands, heard him swear quietly, viciously under his breath, but she didn't look back.

"You know," Finn said at length, "at least they could hire people who can write a decent sentence." A glance at her rigid back made him sigh. He tossed the paper aside again. He rose, crossing to lay his hands on her shoulders. "Deanna—"

"Don't." She stepped away quickly, shaking her head.

"For Christ's sake, you've got too much sense to let some sloppy journalism turn you inside out." He couldn't stem the impatience, or the vague disappointment in her reaction. "You're in the spotlight. You chose to be. Toughen up, Kansas, or go back and stick with the noon news."

"Did you believe it?" She whirled around, her arms folded tight across her chest.

For the life of him he couldn't figure out how to handle her. He tried for mild amusement. "That you were some sort of nubile nymphomaniac? If you were, how could you have resisted me for so long?"

He was hoping for a laugh, and would have settled for an angry retort. He got nothing but frozen silence. "It's not all a lie," she said at length.

"You mean you actually went to a couple of parties in college? You popped the top on a few beers and had a fling with a jock?" He shook his head. "Well, I'm shocked and disillusioned. I'm glad I found this out before I asked you to marry me and have my children."

Again, his joke didn't make her laugh. Her eyes went from blank to devastated. And she burst into terrible tears.

"Oh, Christ. Don't, baby. Come on, Deanna, don't do this." Nothing could have unmanned him more. Awkward, cursing himself, he gathered her close, determined to hold her tight, even when she resisted. "I'm sorry." For what, he couldn't say. "I'm sorry, baby."

"He raped me!" she shouted, jerking away when his arms went limp. "He raped me," she repeated, covering her face with her hands as the tears fell hot and burning. "And I didn't do anything about it. I won't do anything now. Because it hurts." Her voice broke on a sob as she rocked back and forth. "It never, never stops hurting."

He couldn't have been more shocked, more horrified. For a moment, everything in him froze and he could only stand and stare as she wept uncontrollably into her hands with the sun at her back and the fire crackling cheerfully beside her.

Then the ice inside him broke, exploded with a burst of fury so ripe, so raw that his vision hazed. His hands curled into fists, as if there were something tangible he could pummel.

But there was nothing but Deanna, weeping.

His arms dropped to his sides again, leaving him feeling helpless and miserable. Relying on instinct, he scooped her up, carried her to the couch, where he could sit, cradled her in his lap until the worst of the tears were spent.

"I was going to tell you," she managed. "I spent last night thinking about it. I wanted you to know before we tried—to be together."

He had to get past the anger, somehow. But his jaw was clenched and his words sharp. "Did you think it would change anything I feel for you?"

"I don't know. But I know it scars you, and no matter how many ways you're able to go on with your life, it's always in there. Since it happened..." She took the handkerchief he offered and mopped at her face. "I haven't been able to put it aside far enough, or deep enough, to feel able to make love with a man."

The hand that was stroking her hair faltered only a moment. He remembered vividly the way he had plunged in the night before. And the way he would have initiated the physical end of their relationship if something hadn't restrained him.

"I'm not cold," she said in a tight, bitter voice. "I'm not."

"Deanna." He eased her head back so that she would meet his eyes. "You're the warmest woman I know."

"Last night there was nothing there but you; I had no time to think. This morning it didn't seem fair for you not to know first. Because if things didn't work, physically, it would be my fault. Not yours."

"I think that's the first really stupid thing I've ever heard you say. But we'll put it aside for now. If you want to talk this through, I'll listen."

"I do." But she shifted away so that she could sit on her own. "Everyone on campus knew Jamie Thomas. He was a year ahead of me, and like most of the other women in college, I had a crush on him. So when he made a move in my direction at the beginning of my junior year, I was flattered and dazzled. He was a football star, and a track star, and he had a three-point-oh average. I admired that, and his plans to go into the family firm. He had brains and ambition, a good sense of humor. Everybody liked him. So did I."

She took a steadying breath, let herself remember. "We saw a lot of each other during the first couple months of that semester. We studied together, and went for long walks and had all those deep, philosophical discussions college students can be so smug about. I sat in the stands at football games and cheered him on."

She paused. "We went to a party after the biggest game of the season. He'd had a terrific game. Everybody was celebrating, and we got a little drunk. We went back to the field, just he and I, and he started to run through all these football moves. Clowning around. Then he stopped clowning, and he was on top of me. It seemed all right at first. But he got really rough, and he frightened me. I told him to stop. But he wouldn't stop.

Cut the act, Dee. You know you want it. You've been begging for it all night.

She shuddered, gripping her hands tight. "And I started crying, begging him. And he was so strong, and I couldn't get away. He was tearing my clothes. He was hurting me."

Goddamn tease.

"I called for help, but there was no one. I screamed. He put his hand over my mouth when I screamed. He had big hands. And I could only see his face."

You're going to love it, babe.

"His eyes were glazed—like glass. And he was inside me. It hurt so much I thought he would kill me. But he didn't stop. He didn't stop until he'd finished. After a while—it seemed like such a long time—he rolled off me, and he laughed.

Come on, Dee, you know you had fun. Ask around. Nobody makes the women happy like good old Jamie.

"Then he stopped laughing, and he got angry because I was crying. I couldn't stop crying."

Don't pull that shit with me. We both wanted it. You say anything different and half the football team will say you made it with them, right here. Right on the fucking fifty-yard line.

"He yanked me up, stuck his face in mine. And he warned me that if I tried to pretend I hadn't been willing, no one would believe me. Because he was Jamie Thomas. And everyone liked Jamie. So he left me there, and I didn't do anything. Because I was ashamed."

The grainy newspaper photo swam into Finn's mind, and he struggled against the violence that rose in him. But he kept his tone even. "Didn't you have anyone to go to?"

"I told Fran." Her nails were biting into her palm and slowly, deliberately she relaxed her hand. "After a couple of weeks, I couldn't hide it from her. She wanted to go to the dean, but I wouldn't." She stared down at her own hands and felt the hot shame wash over her again. "She finally bullied me into counseling. After a while, I got over the worst of it. I don't want it to control my life, Finn." She looked at him then, eyes swollen and full of grief. "I don't want it to spoil what we may be able to have."

He was afraid any words he tried might be the wrong ones. "Deanna, I can't tell you it doesn't matter, because it does." When she dropped her gaze, he touched her cheek, urging her eyes back up to his. "Because I can't stand the thought of you being hurt that way. And because you may not be able to trust me."

"It isn't that," she said quickly. "It's me."

"Then let me do something for you." Gently, he kissed her forehead. "Come to the cabin with me. Now, Today. Just a weekend alone where we can relax."

"Finn, I don't know if I can give you what you want."

"I don't care about what you can give me. I'm more interested in what we can give each other."

15

She supposed he called the place a cabin because it was built of wood. Far from the primitive box she'd imagined, the trim, two-story structure had upper and lower covered decks joined by open stairs. Outside, the cedar shingles had silvered with weather and time and were accented by deep blue shutters. Tall, spreading yews tucked the house into its own private reserve.

Instead of a lawn, rocks, low evergreens, flowering bushes, herbs and hardy perennials covered the ground. A few brave crocuses were already peeking through.

"You garden. How did you learn?"

"I read a lot of books." Finn hauled their suitcases from the trunk while Deanna stood at the head of the gravel drive and looked around. "I never know how long I'll be away, so grass wasn't practical. I didn't like the idea of hiring a lawn service. It's mine." Faintly embarrassed by the statement, he shrugged. "So I spent a few weeks putting in stuff that wouldn't need a lot of attention."

"It's beautiful."

He'd wanted her to think so, he realized. "It'll look better in another month or two. Let's go inside. I'll start a fire, then show you around."

She followed him up to the porch, ran her hand along the arm of a rocking chair. "It's hard to picture you sitting here, looking out over a rockery and doing nothing."

"It'll get easier," he promised, and led her inside.

The cabin opened up into a large room, topped by a loft and a quartet of skylights. One wall was dominated by a fireplace fashioned of river rock; another was crowded with books on built-in shelves. The paneling was the color of honey, as was the flooring, over which he'd scattered rugs—Orientals, French, English, Indian. And, incredibly, the lush black sheen of a bear rug, complete with snarling head and claws.

Catching her eye, Finn grinned. "It was a gift—some of the guys from the station."

"Is it real?"

"Afraid so." He crossed to the hearth, where the bear spread like a wide black pool. "I call him Bruno. Since I'm not the one who shot him, we get along pretty well."

"I guess he's . . . good company."

"And he doesn't eat much." He sensed her nerves, shivering along the chilled air. And he understood them. He'd rushed her out of Chicago before she'd been able to think things through. Now she was alone with him. "Colder in here than it is outside."

"Yes." She rubbed her hands as she wandered to one of the windows to study his view. There was no other house to disturb the panorama, only those lush yews and trees not yet greening. "It doesn't seem that we could be only an hour or so out of the city."

"I wanted somewhere I could get away." He built a fire competently, quickly. "And where I could get back quickly if a story broke. There's a TV, radio and fax machine in the other room."

"Oh, I see. You can take the boy out of the newsroom . . . That's nice," she said, and walked over to where the wood was beginning to crackle and spark.

"There's another fireplace upstairs." He took her bag and gestured toward the steps that led to the loft.

The second floor held one large bedroom that echoed the simple furnishings of the main room. A sitting area in front of a window contained a love seat in deep hunter green, another rocker, a low pine table and a three-footed stool. The gleaming brass bed was covered with burgundy corduroy and faced a small stone fireplace. There was a pine dresser and a roomy armoire.

"Bath's through there." Finn indicated the door with a nod of his head as he crouched to set the fire.

Curious, Deanna nudged the door open. Staring, she stood on the threshold unsure whether to laugh or applaud. Although the rest of the cabin might have reflected rustic elegance, in the bathroom, Finn had gone for dramatic.

The ebony, oversized tub was fitted with jets and surrounded by a ledge that snugged against a wide window. The separate shower was constructed of glass block and white tile. The wall over the sink was mirrored and hugged by a long counter of black-and-white tiles, as neat as a chessboard. A portable television sat on it, facing the tub.

"Some bathroom."

"If you're going to relax," Finn commented as he rose, "you might as well relax."

"No TV in the bedroom?"

Finn opened one door of the armoire. There, atop a trio of drawers, was the blank eye of a television screen. "There's a shortwave in the drawer of the nightstand." When she laughed, he held out a hand. "Come down and keep me company while I cook dinner."

"You, ah, didn't bring your bags up," she said as they started down.

"There's another bedroom downstairs."

"Oh." She felt the tension dissolve, even as she was pricked by regret.

He stopped at the base of the steps, turned, put his hands on her shoulders and kissed her lightly. "Okay?"

She rested her brow against his a moment. "Yes," she said. "Okay."

And it was, sitting at the breakfast bar putting a salad together while Finn sliced potatoes into thin strips for frying, listening to the high March wind blow through the evergreens and tap at the windows. It was easy, relaxing in the country kitchen while potatoes fried and chicken grilled and laughing at his stories of adventures in the marketplaces in Casablanca.

All the while the kitchen TV murmured, keeping the world in the background, and somehow making the atmosphere they shared more intimate.

The room was warm and cozy, with dark curtaining the windows and candles flickering on the kitchen table. "It's wonderful," she told him after another bite of chicken. "You're as good as Bobby Marks."

"And I'm cuter."

"Well, you've got more hair. I suppose I should offer to cook tomorrow."

"That depends." He curled his fingers around hers, grazed his teeth over her knuckles. "How are you at broiling fresh fish?"

"Is that what's on the menu?"

"If our luck holds. We should be able to pull a couple out of the lake in the morning."

"In the morning?" She blinked. "We're going fishing in the morning?"

"Sure. What do you think I brought you up here for?" When she laughed he shook his head. "Kansas, you don't understand the master plan. After we've dropped line together for a couple of hours, pulled in trout together, cleaned them—"

"Cleaned them?"

"Sure. After all that, you won't be able to resist me. The excitement, the passion, the elemental sexuality of fishing will have overwhelmed you."

"Or will have bored me senseless."

"Have a little faith. There's nothing like man—or woman—against nature to stir up the juices."

"That's quite a plan." She tipped back in her chair, amazingly relaxed. "Have you had much success with it?"

He only grinned and topped off their wine. "Want to look at my lures?"

"I don't think so. You can surprise me tomorrow."

"I'll wake you up at five."

The glass froze an inch from her lips. "At five? A.M.?"

"Dress warm," he warned her.

Deanna had been certain she'd be restless, had been sure her nerves would resurface the moment the house was quiet around her. But the instant she'd snuggled under the blankets, she'd dropped into a deep, dreamless sleep. A sleep that was rudely disturbed by a hand shaking her shoulder.

She opened her eyes, blinked into the dark and closed them again.

"Come on, Kansas, rise and shine."

"Is there a war?" she mumbled into the pillow.

"There's a fish with your name on it," Finn told her. "Coffee'll be ready in ten minutes."

She sat up, blinked again and was able to make out his silhouette beside the bed. And she could smell him—soap and damp skin. "How come you have to catch fish at dawn?"

"Some traditions are sacred." He leaned down, unerringly finding her warm, sleepy mouth with his. Her sigh of response had his muscles tightening, and his mind skidding toward an entirely different morning activity. "You'll want that long underwear I told you to pack." He cleared his throat, forced himself to step back before he gave up and crawled under the blankets with her. "It'll be cold out on the lake."

He left her huddled in bed. He hadn't slept well. Big surprise, Finn thought wryly. She needed time, he reminded himself. And care. And patience. What she didn't need was for him to unstrap the desire that was clawing inside of him. It would frighten her, he was sure, if she understood just how much he wanted.

It very nearly frightened him.

There was fog on the lake. Light fingers of it tore like cotton in the breeze and muffled the sound of the boat's motor. In the east the sky was struggling to light, and the silver sun glanced off the mist, hinting at rainbows. She could smell water and pine, and the soap from Finn's shower. Deanna sat at the bow of the small boat, her hands resting on her knees, the collar of her jacket turned up against the chill.

"It's beautiful." Her breath puffed out in smoke. "Like we're the only ones around for miles."

"The Senachwine gets plenty of campers and hikers." He cut the engine and let the boat drift on water as calm as glass. "We've probably got company on the lake already."

"It's so quiet." But she did hear, in the distance, the putt of another engine, the call of a bird and the faint lap of water against the hull.

"That's the best thing about fishing." After dropping anchor, he handed her a rod. "You can't rush it. You can't crowd it. All you have to do is sit in one spot and let your mind rest."

"Let your mind rest," she repeated.

"What we're doing here is float fishing," he began. "It takes more finesse than bait fishing."

"Right."

"No sarcasm, please. It's an art."

"Art? Really."

"The art," Finn continued, "is to lay the float gently on the surface so that it entices the fish as you skillfully reel it back."

Deanna glanced up from her study of the pretty lures and looked out over the water. "I don't see any fish."

"You will. Trust me. Now you're going to cast the line out. It's all in the wrist."

"That's what my father always says about horseshoes."

"This is every bit as serious." He moved surefootedly to her end of the boat.

"Horseshoes are serious?"

"Christ, Deanna, don't you know anything? When a man needs to relax, to unwind, it doesn't mean he doesn't want competition."

She grinned when he shifted her hands on the rod. "My father would like you."

"Sounds like a sensible man. Now keep your hands firm, wrists supple." He steadied her, casting the line out so that it landed with a quiet plop in the still waters. Ripples ringed magically around the lure, spreading, delighting her.

"I did it!" Beaming, she looked over her shoulder at Finn. "Okay, you did it, but I helped."

"Not bad. You have potential." He took up his own rod, chose a lure. He cast off soundlessly, with barely a ripple on the lake. Through Deanna's pleasure came the hot spirit of competition.

"I want to do it again."

"You're supposed to do it again. But you have to reel it in first."

Her brow arched. "I knew that."

"Slow," he said, with a hint of a smile as he demonstrated. "Smooth. Patience is as much an art as casting."

"So we just sit here, and keep tossing the line out and bringing it back in?"

"That's the idea. I get to sit here and look at you. Which is a pretty good way to spend the morning. Now if you were a man, we'd liven things up by telling lies—about fish and women."

Her brow was knitted in concentration as she cast off again. Her lure did not land soundlessly, but she enjoyed its celebratory plop. "In that order, I imagine."

"Generally, you mix it up. Barlow James and I once spent six hours out here. I don't think we told each other a single truth."

"I can lie."

"Nope. Not with those eyes. I'll make it easy for you; tell me about your family."

"I've got three brothers." She stared at the lure, looking for action. "Two older and one younger. The older two are married, and the youngest is still in college. Should I, like, move this around or anything?"

"No, just relax. Are they all still in Kansas?"

"Yeah. My father owns a hardware business, and my oldest brother went in with him. My mother keeps the books. What are you doing?"

"Playing this one out," he said calmly as he reeled in. "He's hooked."

"You've got one." She leaned forward in the boat, jerking her line. "Already?"

"Did you grow up in the city or the suburbs?"

"The 'burbs," she said impatiently. "How come you've got one already? Oh, look!" She stared, fascinated, as he drew the fish out of the lake. It wriggled, the strengthening sun flashing off its fins. The fascination remained as he netted it and plopped it onto the bottom of the boat. "You must have used a better lure than mine," she said as Finn removed it and laid the fish on ice.

"Want to trade?"

The stubborn line creased her brow. "No." She studied him as he cast off again. Determined, she reeled in, shifted positions, then cast off the opposite side of the boat with more enthusiasm than style.

When Finn only grinned at her, she put her nose in the air. "What about your family?"

"I don't have any to speak of. My parents divorced when I was fifteen. I was the only child. They're both lawyers." He braced his rod so that he could uncap the thermos of coffee and pour for both of them. "They buried each other under a very civilized mountain of papers, and agreed to split everything fifty-fifty. Including me."

"I'm sorry."

"What for?" It wasn't a bitter question, but a simple one. "Family ties don't run strong in the Rileys. We each have our own life, and prefer it that way."

"I don't mean to criticize, but that sounds awfully cold."

"It is cold." He sipped coffee and absorbed the quiet pleasure of the chilly morning with the sun breaking over the water. "It's also practical. We don't have anything in common but blood. Why pretend otherwise?"

She didn't know how to respond. She was far away from her family, but the connection was there, always there. "They must be proud of you."

"I'm sure they're pleased that the money they spent on my education wasn't wasted. Don't look like that." He reached out and patted her ankle. "I wasn't traumatized or scarred. The fact is, it's been a plus careerwise. If you don't have roots, you don't have to keep ripping them out every time you get an assignment."

Perhaps there was no need to feel sympathy for the man, but she couldn't prevent it spreading in her for the boy he'd been. "Roots don't have to hold you back," she said quietly. "Not if you know how to transplant them."

"Kansas?"

"Yes?"

"You've got a bite."

"I've got—oh!" Her line tugged again. If Finn hadn't reached out and held her still, she would have leaped up and capsized them. "What do I do? I forgot. Wait, wait," she said, before he could reply. "I want to do it myself."

Brow puckered in concentration, she turned the reel, feeling the resistance as the fish fought back. There was a moment when she felt an urge to release it. Then the line went taut, and the spirit of competition overwhelmed everything else.

When she finally dropped the catch awkwardly in the bottom of the boat, she shouted with laughter. "He's bigger than yours."

"Maybe."

She slapped Finn's hand aside before he could remove the lure. "I'll do it."

With the sun rising higher in the east, they grinned at each other over a five-pound trout.

They carried four fish back to the cabin with them. Two apiece. Deanna had argued hotly for a tie breaker, but Finn had started the motor. You didn't catch more than you could eat, he'd told her as he cleaned them.

"That was great." Still revved, Deanna spun around the kitchen. "Really great. I feel like a pioneer. Are we going to have fish for lunch?"

"Sure. We'll fry some up. Let me beef up the fire in the living room first."

"I really thought it would be boring," she said, following him in. "I mean that in a good way." Laughing, she combed a hand through her hair. "But it was exciting, too. I don't know. Satisfying." She laughed again.

"You've got a knack for it." Finn added another log, sat back on his heels. "We can go out for a couple hours tomorrow morning before we head back."

"I'd like that." She watched the firelight dance over his forearm as he prodded the quiet flames into a roar. His profile was to her, relaxed, his eyes dark as they stared into the fire. His hair fell over his brow, curled above the collar of his shirt. "I'm glad you brought me here."

He looked over his shoulder, smiled. "So am I."

"Not just for the fishing lesson."

His smile faded, but his eyes stayed on hers. "I know."

"You brought me here to get me away from the papers, and the talk, and the ugliness." She looked past him, into the fire, where the flames were rising. "You haven't asked me any more questions."

He laid down the poker and turned to face her. "Did you want me to?"

"I don't know." She tried for a smile. "What question would you ask?"

He asked the one that had kept him restless through the night. "Are you afraid of me?"

She hesitated. "A little," she heard herself say. "More afraid of what you can make me feel."

He glanced back at the fire. "I won't pressure you, Deanna. Nothing happens between us that you don't want." He looked back at her now, his eyes dark, intense. "I promise."

Rather than relaxing, the tension coiled in her stomach; his words, and her certainty that he would keep them, balled it tighter. "It's not that kind of fear, Finn. It's... seductive."

The look in his eyes made her body yearn. She turned away quickly so that she could say it all, say it quickly. "Because of what happened, I've never been able to get back what I lost. Until you." She turned back slowly. The nerves were vicious. She could feel her heart pounding strong and hard in her breast. "I think, until you. And I'm afraid of that. And afraid that I might spoil it."

Though he stood, he didn't approach her. "Whatever happens between us happens to and because of both of us. It'll wait until you're ready."

She looked down at her hands, linked tight in front of her. "I'd like to ask you a question."

"All right."

"Are you afraid of me?"

She stood there, lashes concealing her eyes, slim and fragile-looking in the oversized shirt. A log shifted lazily behind him and sent out a short, small burst of sparks.

"Deanna, I've never been so afraid of anything in my life as I am of you, and what you can make me feel."

Her lashes lifted then. And she was no longer so fragile, not with her eyes huge and smoky, her lips softly curved. The first step toward him was the hardest. Then it was easy, to walk to him, to slip her arms around him, to rest her head on his shoulder.

"I couldn't have asked for a better answer. Finn, I don't want to lose what I'm feeling right now." When he didn't move, she looked up, lifted her hands to his chest. "I don't think I will if you make love with me."

Of all the emotions he'd expected to feel, alarm was the last. Yet it was alarm that came first, swiftly, overpoweringly, as she looked up at him with trust and doubt warring in her eyes. "There's no pressure here, Deanna."

"There is. Not from you. In me." Was that his heart racing under her palm? she wondered. How could it be beating so fast when he was watching her so calmly, when his hands were so light on her shoulders. "I need you."

It wasn't merely desire that stabbed through him at the words. There was something sharper and hotter fused with it. His hands slid from her shoulders to her face, cupping it as he lowered his mouth to hers.

"I won't hurt you."

"I know," she said, but trembled nonetheless. "I'm not afraid of that."

"Yes, you are." And he regretted that, bitterly. "But you won't be." He promised that, fiercely. "You only have to tell me to stop."

"I won't." There was determination in her eyes again. He swore to himself he would change it to pleasure.

Her mouth went dry when he unbuttoned her shirt. Slowly, his eyes on hers, he peeled away the first layer, cast it aside. Then smiled. "This is going to take a while."

Her laugh bubbled out, nervous and shaky. "I've got plenty of time."

Her eyes closed, her mouth lifted to his. It was right, so simply, so easily right to press her body to his, to lift her arms and take him to her. She shivered again when he tugged the turtleneck away. But it wasn't from cold. Nor was it from fear. Still her breath caught when he lifted her into his arms and laid her on the thick pelt of the hearthrug.

"I don't want you to think of anything but me." He kissed her again, lingered over it before sitting back to tug off her boots. "No one but me."

"No, I'm not. I can't."

Sun and firelight danced over her closed lids. She listened to it hiss and spark, heard the rustle as he removed his own shirt, pried off his boots. Then he was beside her, gently stroking her face until she opened her eyes and looked at him.

"I wanted you from the first moment I saw you."

She smiled, willing herself to relax, to beat back those little frissons of doubt. "Almost a year ago."

"Longer." His lips toyed with hers, warmed them, waited for hers to respond. "You came running into the newsroom. You headed straight for your desk, then you pulled back your hair with this red ribbon and started beating out copy. It was a few days before I left for London." He skimmed a hand over the insulating silk covering her torso, barely touching her, hinting only of what could be. "I watched you for a while. It was like someone had hit me with a hammer. All those months later, I saw you standing on the tarmac in the rain."

"And you kissed me."

"I'd saved it up for six months."

"Then you stole my story."

"Yeah." He grinned, then lowered his mouth to her curved lips. "And now I've got you."

She stiffened instinctively when his hand slipped under the silk. But he didn't grope, didn't rush. In moments, the easy caress of his fingers on her skin had her muscles loosening. When they slid up to circle her breast, her body curved to welcome them.

Like warm rain, this pleasure was soft and quiet and soothing. She accepted it, absorbed it, then ached for it, as he slowly undressed her.

The heat from the fire radiated out, but she felt only his hands, molding gently, exploring, arousing. His touch lingered, then moved on, lighting flames in which those tiny raindrops of pleasure began to sizzle. When she trembled now, she trembled from the heat. And her breath strangled in her throat.

He no longer felt the beast clawing at him. There was a sweetness here, and a power. He knew as his lips roamed from hers down to the swell of her breasts that she was his, as completely, as absolutely as if they had been lovers for years.

Her body was like water in his hands, rising and falling with the tide of pleasure they brought to each other. He heard the wind scraping at the windows, the spit of the fire in the hearth. And the sound of his name whispering from her lips.

He knew he could make her float, as she was floating now, her eyes like smoke and her muscles like warmed wax. And he knew he had only to inch her higher, just a bit higher, to watch her break through those clouds into the storm.

She felt his teeth scrape over her hip, and the hand she was stroking through his hair went taut. Heat coiled hot in her belly as his tongue streaked over her. She shook her head to refuse it, to will away the sudden, uncontrollable quivering. Then the furnace of pressure built so quickly. She writhed, struggling toward it, struggling away. She tried to call out, to tell him to wait, to give her a moment to prepare. But the pleasure geysered through her, spurting molten through her system.

He watched the instant of frantic denial, the stunned panic, the mindless pleasure.

Everything she felt echoed inside him. As breathless as she, he levered himself over her, raining kisses over her glowing face until she was wrapped around him, until her movements grew frantic and his own churning need demanded release.

"Look at me." He fought the words out of his burning throat. "Look at me."

And when she did, when their eyes met, held, he slipped inside her. Slowly, his hands fisted in the rug as if he could grip control there, he lowered to her, felt her rise to meet him until they moved together silkily.

When her lips curved, he pressed his face to her throat and took them both over the edge.

16

Still dreaming, she turned to him, and he was there. Arms moving to enfold her, body ready to possess her. As the warm light of dawn slid lazily into the room, they joined again. Rhythm fluid, flesh warm, passions met. It was so easy, so effortless, to glide together, without hurry, without thought, while the air throbbed as steady as a pulse.

The ebb and flow of their bodies, the movement of sex as simple as breathing, had her lips curving before they met his in a long, deep, dusky kiss.

When their needs peaked, as gentle as the morning, she sighed out his name and drifted from dream to reality to find him still pulsing inside her, a second heartbeat.

"Finn." She spoke again, smiling into the quiet morning light. The cross he wore pressed against her skin, just below her heart.

"Hmmm?"

"This is an even better way to start the day than fishing."

He chuckled, nuzzling at her neck. "Yesterday morning all I could think about was crawling into this bed with you."

Her smile spread. "Well, you're here now'."

"It seems I am." He lifted his head, studying her as he toyed with the hair at her temple. Her eyes were big and sleepy, her skin glowing with that translucent polish that was the afterflush of good sex. "We overslept."

"No." Delighted with how easy it was, she ran her hands down his back to the taut skin of his buttocks. "We slept perfect. Absolutely perfect."

"You know . . ." He cupped her breast, rubbing his thumb over the nipple and watching her lips part on an unsteady breath. "I was going to teach you how to fly-fish this morning."

At his gentle tug, fresh arousal settled in her belly. "Were you?"

"A dry fly-fisherman is the aristocrat of angling. It takes . . . a master's touch."

She turned her head when he lowered his mouth to her throat. "I could learn."

"I think you could." He scraped his teeth over the pulse that fluttered like bird wings. There was nothing, he decided, more erotic than feeling a woman open herself to pleasure. "I believe you have unlimited potential."

She sighed, tightening in response as he hardened inside her. "I always want to be the best. It's probably a flaw."

"I don't think so," he murmured. She arched to meet him, already shuddering over the first peak. "It's definitely a virtue."

"Deanna, why would a sharp woman like you continue this sentimental attachment to a loser?"

"It's not sentimental." Deanna sniffed as she unlocked the door to her apartment. "It's a very practical, very logical loyalty. The Cubs are going to surprise everyone this year."

"Yeah, right." After indulging in a snort, Finn followed her inside. "It would be a surprise if they managed to crawl out of the basement. When's the last time the Cubs came close?"

That stung. "That's not the point." Her voice, despite her best intentions, was very prim. "They have heart."

"Too bad they don't have bats."

She stuck her nose in the air and turned to her answering machine. "Excuse me. I have to check my messages."

"No problem." Grinning, he dropped down on the couch. "We can finish this later. I probably didn't mention that I was captain of the debate team in college. And this is one I can't lose."

To show her disdain, she stabbed the Play button.

"Deanna, Cassie. Sorry to bother you at home—even if you're not there. We've got a couple of changes in Monday's schedule. I'll just fax them to you. If you have any questions, you know where to reach me. And, oh hell, we've had a lot of calls on the tabloid article. I've screened a lot of them out, but if you want to respond, I have a list of reporters you may want to agree to speak with. I'll be in most of the weekend. Call if you want me to set something up."

"She never asked any questions," Deanna murmured. "No one at the office asked any questions at all."

"They know you."

She nodded, switching off the machine for a moment. "You know, Finn, as hard as the job can be, as much energy as it demands, I wake up some mornings with the feeling that I've fallen into clover."

"If you ask me, making a living out of chatting for an hour a day smells more like gravy."

That made her smile a little. "You handle the earthquakes. I'll handle the heartaches."

He tugged off his jacket. "It's a shame to waste all those brains."

"I'm not wasting them," she began hotly. "I'm—" But she caught the glint in his eye and stopped. He was only trying to draw her in again. "No thanks, captain. I'm not going to debate you." She turned back to the answering machine, stopped again. "Do you ever worry that someone's going to take it all away from you? Tell you one day that it's over, that there'll be no more cameras?"

"No." His confidence, the easy arrogance of it, made her smile widen. "And neither should you." He tipped her chin up, kissed her. "You're terrific at fluff."

"Shut up, Finn." She stabbed the Play button again, then scribbled down the brief message from Simon on a potential hitch on tomorrow's show, another from Fran telling her the hitch had been diverted. She waited through the blank tape on a delayed hang-up, then gritted her teeth over three calls from reporters who'd managed to wangle her unlisted number.

"You all right?" Finn came up behind her to rub the tension from her shoulders.

"Yes." She indulged herself a moment by leaning back against him. "I'm fine. I have to decide whether to refuse to comment or to draft a statement. I guess I don't want to think about it yet."

"Then don't."

"Playing ostrich won't make it go away." She straightened, stepped aside to stand on her own. "I want to make the right decision. I hate making mistakes."

"Then you've got two choices. You react emotionally, or you react like a reporter."

Her brow creased as she thought it through. "Or I combine the two," she said softly. "I've been thinking about doing a show on date rape. I kept pulling back because I thought I was too close. But maybe I'm just close enough."

"Why would you put yourself through that, Deanna?"

"Because I've *been* through it. Because men like Jamie walk away from it. And because..." She let out a long breath that threatened to catch in her throat. "I'm tired of being ashamed that I didn't do anything about it. I've got a chance to make up for that now."

"It'll hurt you."

"Not the way it once did." She reached for him then. "Not anymore."

His grip on her tightened. Damn it, he needed to protect her. And she needed to stand on her own. The one thing he could do was track down Jamie Thomas and have a nice, long... chat. "If you decide to do the show, let me know. I want to be there if I can."

"Okay." She tilted her head back to kiss him before drawing away. "Why don't I open some wine? Let's forget about all this for a while."

She needed to. He could see the tension creeping back, like a thief, into her eyes. "As long as you're going to let me stay. And this time I won't fall asleep on the couch."

"I won't give you the chance," she told him, and walked into the kitchen.

Out of habit, he moved to the television first, switching it on just as the late news began. He turned toward the couch, intending to take his boots off and put his feet up. He spotted the envelope lying on the rug just inside the door.

"I've got some chips." Deanna carried out a tray and set it on the coffee table. "The drive gave me an appetite." Her smile froze when she spotted the envelope in his hand. "Where did you get that?"

"It was inside the door." He'd started to hold it out to her, but drew it back now. She'd gone pale. "What's the problem?"

"It's nothing." Annoyed with herself, she shook off the vague, niggling fear. "It's silly, that's all." Trying to convince them both she was unconcerned, she took the envelope and split it open.

Deanna,
nothing they say would ever change my feelings.
I know it's all a lie.
I'll always believe you.
I'll always love you.

"A shy fan," she said with a shrug that came off as more of a defensive jerk. "Who needs to get a life."

Finn took the sheet from her, scanned it. "Response to the tabloids, I'd say."

"Looks like." But the anonymous faith didn't cheer her.

"I take it you've gotten one of these before."

"I'd have a whole collection if I'd kept them." She picked up her glass of wine. "They've been coming on and off for a year."

"A year?" He looked at her, his eyes intense. "Like this?"

"Here, at the newsroom, at my office." She moved her shoulders again, restless. "Always the same format and same type of message."

"Have you reported it?"

"To whom? The police?" Whatever unease she'd felt vanished in a laugh. "Why? What could I tell them? Officer, I've been receiving anonymous love letters. Call out the dogs?"

"A year makes it more than harmless love letters. It makes it obsession. Obsessions are not healthy."

"I don't think a dozen or so sappy notes over a year constitutes an obsession. It's just someone who watches me on TV, Finn, or who works in the building. Someone who's attracted to the image but too shy to approach me in person for an autograph." She thought about the calls, those silent messages in the middle of the night. And that he had been able to slip a note under her door. "It's a little spooky, but it's not threatening."

"I don't like it."

She took his hand to draw him down on the couch with her. "It's just your reporter's instinct working on overdrive." Because his mouth was much more intoxicating, she set the wine aside. "Of course, if you want to be a little jealous . . ."

Her eyes were laughing at him. Finn smiled back, letting her set the mood. But he thought about the single sheet of paper lying open on the coffee table, its message of devotion as red as blood.

"Not one statement." Angela chuckled to herself and stretched on her stomach over the pink satin sheets of her big bed. The television was on, and newspapers and magazines littered the floor around her.

It was a beautiful room, majestic and museum-like with its curved and gilded antiques and fussy, feminine flounces. One of the maids had griped to a friend that she was surprised there wasn't a velvet rope across the door and a charge for admission.

There were mirrors on every wall, oval and square and oblong, reflecting both the taste she'd purchased and her own image.

The only colors other than the gold and wood tones were pink and white, a candy cane she could savor in long, greedy licks.

There were banks of roses, dewy fresh, so that she never had to breathe without drawing in the rich, satisfying scent she equated with success. At the head of the giltwood bed was a mountain of pillows, all slick silks and frothy lace. She tapped her pink-tipped toes against them, and gloated.

Near the bed was a fauteuil, where she had carelessly tossed one of her many negligees.

Once, long ago, she had envied others their beautiful possessions. She had, as a child, as a young woman, stared through shop windows and wished. Now she owned, or could own, whatever she desired.

Whomever.

Naked, his subtle muscles gleaming, Dan Gardner straddled her hips and rubbed fragrant oil into her back and shoulders.

"It's been over a week," she reminded him, "and she hasn't made a peep."

"Do you want me to contact Jamie Thomas?"

"Hmmm." Angela stretched luxuriously under his hands. She was feeling pampered and victorious. And calm, beautifully calm. "Go ahead, and tell him to keep talking to reporters, maybe expand on the story a bit. Remind him that if he doesn't make enough trouble for our little Dee, we'll have to leak the story about his love affair with China White."

"That should do it." Dan admired the body under his as much, or nearly as much, as he admired Angela's mind. "If it comes out he's earmarking business funds for cocaine, his career will bottom out. Even if it is in Daddy firm."

"Remind him of that if he balks. Rich boy's going to pay," she murmured. She would have hated him for being born into wealth and privilege and squandering it all on a weakness like drugs. But the pathetic way he'd folded after her first threat made her despise him.

"Oh, and send a case of Dom Perignon to Beeker." Angela examined her nails, scowling at a minute flaw in the candy-pink polish. "He did a good job. But keep him on the case. If we find enough of the dirt our little Dee's brushed under the rug, we can bury her in it."

"I love your mind, Angela." And aroused by it, he bit her sharply on the shoulder. "It's so beautifully twisted."

"I don't give a damn what you think of my mind." With a low chuckle, she levered herself so that he could slip his oil-slicked hands over her breasts. "And in this case it's focused straight and true. However it happened, she's sneaking up in the ratings. I'm not going to allow that, Dan, not after she betrayed my friendship. So you just keep—" She scrambled suddenly to her knees, letting out a howl of protest as a clip of Deanna and Finn rolled over the screen.

"In other entertainment news," the announcer continued, "talk-show star Deanna Reynolds accompanied CBC foreign correspondent Finn Riley to a National Press Club banquet in Chicago, where Riley was honored for his work during the Gulf War. The inside word is that Riley, America's Desert Hunk, is considering an offer to head a weekly news magazine for CBC. Riley had no comment about the project, or his personal relationship with Chicago's darling Deanna."

"No!" Angela exploded from the bed, a compact, golden missile detonating. "I took her in. I offered her opportunities, gave her my affection. And she moves in on me."

She stalked naked to an open bottle of champagne and poured lavishly. There were tears, as genuine and as painful as her bitterness, stinging her eyes.

"And that son of a bitch turned on me, too." In one violent gesture, she tossed the sparkling wine back. Its heat burst into her stomach like love. "He turned on me, and he turned to her. To *her*. Because she's younger." Enraged, and suddenly frightened when she saw the glass was empty, she hurled it toward the television. It slapped the corner of the cabinet and sliced delicately in two. "She's nothing. Less than nothing. A pretty face and a tight body. Anybody can have those. She won't keep Finn. He'll shake her off, and so will the viewers." She dashed the tears aside with a vicious hand, but her mouth continued to tremble. "They'll want me. They always want me."

"She can't come close to you, Angela." Dan approached her slowly, making sure his eyes were filled with understanding and desire. "You're the best there is. In public." Gently, he turned her so that they faced the full-length mirror. "In private," he murmured, watching her watching his hands caress. "You're so beautiful. She's built like a boy, but you . . . You're a woman."

Desperate for reassurance, she clasped her hands over his, tightening her grip until he squeezed her breasts painfully. "I need to be wanted, Dan. I need to know people want me. I can't survive without that."

"They do. I do." He was used to her outbursts, accustomed to her neediness. And he knew how to use both to his advantage. "When I see you on the set, so cool, so controlled, you dazzle me." He slipped his hand between her thighs, patiently stroking until she was damp, until she quivered. Until he did. "And I can hardly wait until I can get you alone, like this."

Her breath grew shallow, but her vision was clear, focused hard on the glass as his busy hands worked over her. The flavor of champagne was still on her tongue, making her yearn for more. Crave more. She swallowed it and concentrated on what she saw in the glass.

"You'd do anything for me."

"Anything."

"And to me."

He laughed. He knew where the power was. The more she needed, the more she plotted, the more she placed in his hands. And the truth was, sex with Angela was like a dark, violent ride into an irresistible hell.

"What do you want me to do, Angela?"

"Take me here, right here, so I can watch."

He laughed again. She was quivering like a bitch in heat, her eyes riveted on her own body. Her vanity, the pathetic insecurity of it, was one more hold he had on her. But when he started to shift, she shoved him back.

"No." She could barely breathe now. Her full white breasts still carried the angry red marks from his hands. She wanted them there, wanted them as proof that she was desired. "From behind. Like an animal."

His mouth watered at the image. His erection ached like a wound. Desperate to take, he shoved her roughly to her knees. Eyes feral, teeth bared, she watched him crouch over her. He jerked her head back by the hair, hissing when she growled low in her throat.

"I won't stop. Even if you beg."

"Fuck me." Her smile glinted like a sword already bloodied. "And when you're done, we're going to find a new way to make her pay."

"Watch." He held her head still with one hand. "I want you to watch."

He drove himself into her viciously, the blood all but bursting in his veins when she cried out in pain and shock and greedy pleasure. His fingers dug hard into her hips while he rammed inside her again and again until the sweat ran off both of them like rain, and his vision dimmed.

But hers stayed clear. She saw the blood on her lip where her teeth had dug in, the sheen of sweat and tears on her face. And as the horrible, loveless orgasm slammed through the agony and need, Dan's face dissolved into Finn's. And she smiled as he cried out her name and shuddered, shuddered, shuddered.

She was wanted. She was desired. She was the best.

"Deanna, are you sure you want to do this?" Fran nibbled on her thumbnail, a habit she'd broken years before, as she stood beside Deanna's desk.

"Absolutely sure." She continued to sign the outgoing mail. Her signature was quick and neat and automatic. "It's a show I want to do. How many carts did we get back?"

Fran frowned down at the forms in her hand, the carts they passed to the audience after each program. These had been typed simply: Do you know of anyone who has experienced date rape? Is this a topic you would be willing to discuss on *Deanna's Hour*?

There was room for comments, for names and phone numbers. Out of the two hundred carts Fran had surveyed, she had chosen only two.

"These are the ones I thought you should see." Reluctantly, Fran laid them on the desk. "It's going to be painful for you, Deanna."

"I can handle it."

She skimmed the first cart, then went back and read each word again.

He said I asked for it. I didn't. He said it was my own fault. I'm not sure. I'd like to try to talk about it, but I don't know if I can.

Setting the cart aside, she reached for the second.

It was my first date after my divorce. It was three years ago, and I haven't been with a man since. I'm still afraid, but I trust you.

"Two women," Deanna murmured. Yes, it was painful. There was a tight, angry fist lodged in her chest. "Right out of the studio audience. How many more, Fran? How many more are out there wondering if it was their fault? How many more are afraid?"

"I can't stand to see you hurt this way. You know if you do this, you're going to have to bring up Jamie Thomas."

"I know that. I've already run it by Legal."

"And if he sues?"

Deanna sighed, barely refrained from rubbing her eyes and smearing makeup. She hadn't slept well—and with Finn in Moscow, she'd slept alone. But it hadn't been doubt keeping her wakeful. It had been anticipation.

"Then he sues. To encapsulate what I got from Legal, he's already gone public with his version. Since it's a matter of his word against mine, I'm going public with my version. I could have done so in a dozen interviews since the tabloids hit. Two dozen," she corrected, with a grim smile. "I prefer to do it this way, my way, on my own show."

"You know the press will jump all over it."

"I know." She was calm now, dead calm. "That's why we're going to schedule it during the May sweeps."

"Jesus, Dee—"

"I'm going public with this, Fran, and I hope to God even one woman who watches is helped by what I'm doing." She used the heels of her hands to rub the dampness from her cheek. "And by Christ, I'm going to kill the competition in the ratings while I'm at it."

• • •

Deanna's nerves were steady as stone before the show. In her precise manner, she had gone over her scripted question cards while Marcie put the finishing touches on her makeup. Prepared, even eager, she swiveled in her chair toward Loren Bach.

"Now, are you here to observe, Loren, or to offer advice?"

"Some of both." He folded his long, white fingers together. "As you know, I don't make it a habit to interfere with the content of the show."

"I do know that, and I appreciate it."

"But I do make a habit out of protecting my people." He sat silently a moment, gathering his thoughts while he studied the orderly room filled with stacks of newspapers, magazines, all current, a shelf of neatly marked videos that could be slipped into the VCR for viewing. The room smelled lightly of cosmetics and lotions. Feminine, yes, he mused, but also tools of the trade. The dressing room was as much a work space as her office.

"It's possible for you to do this show, and do an excellent job, without bringing your personal experience into it."

"Possible, yes." She rose then to close the door Marcie had left open. "Are you asking me to do that, Loren?"

"No. I'm reminding you of it."

"Then I'll remind you that I'm part of the show, not just a host. An intimate part; that's what makes it work for me and, I think, for the viewing audience."

He smiled, and his eyes remained keen. She looked polished and poised, he mused. "I wouldn't argue with that. But Deanna, if you have any doubts about what you're doing, there is no need to go ahead."

"I don't have doubts, Loren. I have fears. I think, at least I hope, that facing them is the answer. You may have concerns that Jamie Thomas will try some sort of legal retribution, but—"

Loren waved that away. "I have lawyers to deal with that. In any case, it seems the brunt of the publicity backfired on him. He is, at the moment, on an extended vacation in Europe."

"Oh, I see." She took a deep breath. "Well then."

"You don't mind if I stay to watch the show?" He rose as she did.

"I'd appreciate it." On impulse she leaned forward and kissed his cheek. When he blinked in surprise, she smiled. "That wasn't for my business associate. It was for your support."

When she opened the door, she found herself instantly scooped up into Finn's arms.

"You're supposed to be in Moscow."

"I'm back." He'd pulled every string he could grab to arrive in Chicago in time for the show. "You look good, Kansas. How do you feel?"

"Shaky." She pressed a hand to her stomach. "Ready."

"You'll be fine." He kept an arm around her shoulders and nodded to Loren. "Good to see you."

"And you. You can keep me company while Deanna goes to work."

"Fine." Finn walked Deanna toward the set. "Working tonight?"

"I have a network dinner at seven. But I think I can get out by ten."

"Want to come by my place?"

"Yes." She gripped his hand, hard. The closer she got to the set, the more her stomach twisted. She shot one look at Fran, braced herself. "Like diving into a cold pool."

"What?"

She forced a smile as she glanced up at Finn. "Just some advice I got once. See you in an hour, huh?"

"I'll be here."

Deanna took her place with the three women already fidgeting onstage. She spoke quietly to each one of them, then miked, waited for her cue.

Music. Applause. The objective red eye of the camera.

"Welcome to *Deanna's Hour.* Our show today deals with a painful subject. Rape in any form is tragic and horrible. It takes on a different dimension when the victim knows and trusts her attacker. Every woman on this stage has been a victim of what is called date, or acquaintance, rape. And we all have a story to tell. When it happened to me nearly ten years ago, I did nothing. I hope I'm doing something now."

17

To celebrate Deanna's first year on the air, Loren Bach threw a party in his penthouse overlooking Lake Michigan. Over the low music and chink of glasses, voices buzzed. Faintly, from the adjoining game room, came the beeps and bells of video games.

In addition to the staff of the show and CBC and Delacort executives, he had invited a handful of carefully selected columnists and reporters. The publicity on Deanna since the May sweeps showed no sign of abating. Loren had no intention of allowing it to.

While the ratings climbed, so did the advertising revenue. As Chicago's darling rapidly became America's darling, Deanna's growing celebrity opened the doors to booking stellar names who breezed on the show to hype their hot summer movies and concert tours. She continued to mix the famous with segments on dealing with jealous spouses, choosing the right swimwear and computer dating.

The result was a carefully crafted show with an appealing, casual, homey look. Deanna was at the core, as awestruck as her audience by the appearance of a glamorous movie star, as amused as they by the notion of choosing a mate with a machine, as wary and unnerved as any woman of stripping down to a bikini on a public beach.

The girl-next-door image drew the audience. The sharp, practical mind behind it structured the vision.

"Looks like you made it, kid."

Deanna smiled at Roger as she kissed his cheek. "Through the first year, anyway."

"Hey, in this business that's a minor miracle." He chose a baby carrot from his buffet plate and bit in with a sigh. He'd put on a few pounds over the past months. The camera gleefully advertised every ounce. "Too bad Finn couldn't be here."

"The Soviets would pick my anniversary to stage a coup." She tried not to worry about Finn, back in Moscow.

"Have you heard from him?"

"Not for a couple of days. I saw him on the news. Speaking of which, I caught your new promo. Very sharp."

"Our news team is your news team," Roger said in his announcer's voice. "Keeping Chicago informed."

"You and your new partner have a nice rhythm."

"She's all right." He switched to celery, found it just as bland. "Good voice, good face. But she doesn't get my jokes."

"Rog, nobody gets your jokes."

"You did."

"No." She patted his cheek. "I pretended I did, because I love you you."

There was a quick pinch around his heart. "We still miss you around the newsroom."

"I miss you too, Roger. I'm sorry about you and Debbie."

He shrugged, but the wounds of his recent divorce were still tender. "You know what they say, Dee. Shit happens. Maybe I'll be looking into that computer dating."

She gave a snort of laughter and squeezed his hand. "I have one word of advice on that. Don't."

"Well, since Finn's busy hopping all over the globe, maybe you'd be interested in a stable, slightly older man."

She would have laughed again, but she wasn't entirely sure he was joking. "There happens to be this stable, slightly older man whose friendship means a lot to me."

"Hi, Dee."

"Jeff."

"I saw you didn't have a glass, and thought you might like some champagne."

"Thanks. You never miss a detail. I pulled a coup of my own when I stole Jeff away from the news department," she told Roger. "We'd never get *Deanna's Hour* on the air without him."

He beamed with pleasure. "I just pick up the loose ends."

"And tie them up in a bow."

"Excuse me." Barlow James slipped behind Deanna and circled her waist with his arm. "I need to steal the star for a moment, gentlemen. You're looking fit, Roger."

"Thanks, Mr. James." With a wan smile, Roger held up another carrot. "I'm working on it."

"I won't keep her long," Barlow promised, and led Deanna toward the open terrace doors. "You look more than fit," he commented. "You look luminous."

She laughed. "I'm working on it."

"I believe I have something that might add to the glow. Finn contacted me this morning."

Relief came one heartbeat before pleasure. "How is he?"

"In his element."

"Yes." She looked out at the lake, where pale fingers of moonlight nudged past clouds to brush the water. The silhouettes of boats rocked gently in the current. "I suppose he is."

"You know, between the two of us, we might be able to apply enough pressure to convince him to do that news magazine and keep his butt in Chicago."

"I can't." Though she wished she could. "He has to do what suits him best."

"Don't we all," Barlow said with a sigh. "Now, I've dulled some of that glow. This should bring it back." He took a long slim box from his inside jacket pocket. "Finn asked me to pick this up for you. Something he had made before he was called away. I'm to tell you he's sorry he can't give it to you himself."

She said nothing as she stared at its contents. The bracelet was delicately fashioned of oval gold links, cut to catch the light and joined together by the rainbow hue of multicolored gems. Emerald, sapphire, ruby, tourmaline fired and flashed in the moonlight. At the center a filigreed *D* and *R* flanked a brilliant array of sizzling diamonds that shaped a star.

"The star's self-explanatory, I believe," Barlow told her. "It's to commemorate your first year. We're confident there'll be many more."

"It's beautiful."

"Like the woman it was made for," Barlow said, slipping it from the box to clasp it around her wrist. " 'The boy certainly has taste. You know, Deanna, we need a strong hour on Tuesday nights. You may not feel comfortable using your influence to persuade him to fill it. But I do." He winked and, patting her shoulder, left her alone.

"You're too damn far away," she said quietly, rubbing a fingertip over the bracelet.

She had so much that she wanted, she reminded herself. So much that she'd worked toward. So why was she still so unsettled? Very much like the boats on the water below, she mused. Anchored, yes, but still shifting, still tugging against the tide.

Her show was rapidly becoming national. But she had yet to select a new apartment. She was enjoying national exposure in the media, most of it flattering. And she was standing alone at a party thrown in her honor, feeling lost and discontented.

For the first time in her life her professional goals and personal ones seemed out of balance. She knew exactly what she wanted for her career, and could see the steps toward achieving it so clearly. She felt capable and confident when she thought of pushing *Deanna's Hour* to the top of the market. And whenever she stood in front of the audience, the camera on and focused, she felt incredibly alive, completely in control, with just enough giddy pleasure thrown in to make it all a continual thrill.

She wasn't taking success for granted, for she knew too well the caprices of television. But she knew that if the show was canceled tomorrow, she would pick up, go on and start over.

Her personal needs weren't so clear-cut, nor was the route she wanted to take. Did she want the traditional home and marriage and family? If it was possible to mix that kind of ideal with a high-powered and demanding career, she would find a way.

Or did she want what she had now? A place of her own, a satisfying yet strangely independent relationship with a fascinating man. A man she was madly in love with, she admitted. And who, though the words hadn't been said, she was certain loved her as deeply.

If they changed what they had, she might lose this breathless, stirring excitement. Or she might discover something more soothing and equally thrilling to replace it.

And because she couldn't see the answer, because the confusion in her heart blinded her vision, she struggled all the harder to separate intellect from emotion.

"There you are." Loren Bach strode out on the balcony, a bottle of champagne in one hand, a glass in the other. "The guest of honor shouldn't be hiding in the shadows." He topped off her glass before setting the bottle aside on the glass table beside him. "Particularly when the media is in attendance."

"I was just admiring your view," she countered. "And giving that media a chance to miss me."

"You're a sharp woman, Deanna." He clicked his glass against hers. "I'm taking this evening to feel very smug about going with my instincts and signing you."

"I'm feeling pretty smug about that myself."

"As long as you don't let it show. That wide-eyed enthusiasm is what sells, Dee. That's what the audience relates to."

She grimaced. "I am wide-eyed and enthusiastic, Loren. It's not an act."

"I know." He couldn't have been happier. "That's why it's so perfect. What did I read about you recently—" He tapped a finger against his temple as if to shake the memory loose. " 'Midwest sensibilities, an ivy-league brain, a face that makes a man yearn for his high school sweetheart, all coated with a quiet sheen of class.' "

"You left out my quick, sexy laugh," she said dryly.

"Complaining, Deanna?"

"No." She leaned comfortably against the railing to face him. The scent of hibiscus from the bold red blooms in the patio pots mixed exotically with the fragrance of champagne and lake water. "Not for a minute. I love every bit of it. The spread in *Premiere,* the cover on *McCall's,* the People's Choice nomination—"

"You should have won that," he muttered.

"I'll beat Angela next time." She smiled at him, her bangs fluttering in the light breeze, the diamonds at her wrist glinting in the starlight. "I wanted that Chicago Emmy, and I've got it. I intend to win a national one, when the time comes. I'm not in a hurry, Loren, because I'm enjoying the ride. A lot."

"You make it look easy, Dee, and fun." He winked. "That's the way I sell computer games. And that's the way you slip right through the television screen into the viewer's living room. That's the way you up the ratings." His smile hardened, glinted in the shadowy light. "And that's the way you're going to knock Angela out of first place."

Because the gleam in Loren's eye made her uneasy, Deanna chose her response carefully. "That's not my primary goal. As naive as it may sound, Loren, all I want is to do a good job and provide a good show."

"You keep doing that, and I'll handle the rest." It was odd, he thought, that he hadn't realized just how much revenge against Angela burned in him. Until Deanna. "I'm not going to claim that I made Angela number one, because it's more complex than that. But I speeded the process along. My mistake was to be deluded enough by the screen image and marry someone who didn't exist off camera."

"Loren, you don't have to tell me this."

"No, no one has to tell you anything, but they do. That's part of your charm, Deanna. I can tell you that Angela shed me as carelessly as a snake sheds its skin when she'd decided she'd outgrown me. It's going to give me a lot of satisfaction to help you gun her down, Deanna." He drank again, with relish. "A great deal of deep satisfaction."

"Loren, I don't want to go to war with Angela."

"That's all right." He touched his glass to hers again. "I do."

Lew McNeil was as obsessed with Angela's success as Loren Bach was with her failure. His future depended on it. He had hopes to retire in another decade, with his nest egg securely in place. He had no hopes of remaining with *Angela's* for that long. His best chance was to work out his contract while the show remained a number-one hit, then slide gently into another producing slot.

He had some reason to worry. While *Angela's* was still in command of the top rung, and the show had added another Emmy to its collection, its star was fraying at the edges. In Chicago she had managed to command her staff using her iron will and her penchant for perfection, and leavening them with doses of considerable charm.

Since the move to New York, a great deal of the charm had been shaken by stress, and the stress was doused with French champagne.

He knew—had made it his business to know—that she had poured a great deal of her own money into the fledgling A. P. Productions. The veteran show kept the company out of the red, but Angela's dabbling in television movies had been disastrous thus far. Her last special had received lukewarm reviews, but the ratings had put the show into the top ten of the week.

That was fortunate, but her daily ratings had plummeted in August, when she had insisted on running repeats while she took an extended vacation in the Caribbean.

No one could deny that she deserved the break. Just as no one could deny that the timing had been poor with *Deanna's Hour* steadily closing the distance in points.

There were other mistakes, other errors in judgment, the largest being Dan Gardner. As the power shifted gradually from Angela's hands to those of her lover and executive producer, the tone of the show altered subtly.

"More complaints, Lew?"

"It's not a complaint, Angela." He wondered how many hours of his life he'd spent standing beside her chair in her dressing room. "I only wanted to say again that I think it's a mistake to have a homeless family on the program with a man like Trent Walker. He's a shark, Angela."

"Really?" She took a slow drag on her cigarette. "I found him quite charming."

"Sure, he's charming. He was real charming when he bought that shelter then turned the building into high-priced condos."

"It's called urban renewal, Lew. In any case, it should be fascinating to see him debate with a family of four who are currently living in their station wagon. Not only topical"—she crushed out the cigarette—"but excellent TV. I hope he wears the gold cuff links."

"If it goes the wrong way, it may look as though you're unsympathetic to the plight of the homeless."

"And what if I am?" Her voice cracked like a whip. "There are jobs out there. Too many of these people would rather take a handout than earn an honest living." She thought of the way she'd waited tables and cleaned up slop to pay for her education. The humiliation of it. "Not all of us were born to the good life, Lew. When my book comes out next month, you can read along with everyone else how I overcame my modest beginnings and worked my way to the top." With a sigh, she dismissed the hairdresser. "That's fine, dear, run along. Lew, let me say first that I don't appreciate your second-guessing me in front of members of my staff."

"Angela, I wasn't—"

"And second," she interrupted, still frigidly pleasant. "There's no need for concern. I have no intention of letting anything go wrong, or of giving the soft-hearted public an unflattering opinion on my stand. Dan's already seeing to it that it leaks that I, personally, will sponsor the family we're highlighting on the show. I will at first modestly decline to comment, then, reluctantly, will agree that I have found employment for both parents, along with six months' rent and a stipend for food and clothing. Now . . ." She gave her hair one last fluff as she rose. "I'd like to look them over before we go on the air."

"They're in the green room," Lew murmured. "I decided to put Walker elsewhere for the time being."

"Fine." She swept by him and into the corridor. All graciousness and warm support, she greeted the family of four who sat nervously huddled together on the sofa in front of the television. Waving away their thanks, she pressed food and drink on them, patted the little boy on the head and tickled the toddler under the chin.

Her smile snapped off like a light when she started back to her dressing room. "They don't look like they've been living on the street for six weeks to me. Why are their clothes so neat? Why are they so clean?"

"I—they knew they were going on national TV, Angela. They put themselves together as best they could. They've got pride."

"Well, dirty them up," she snapped. She had a headache coming on like a freight train and wanted her pills. "I want them to look destitute, for Christ's sake, not like some middle-class family down on their luck."

"But that's what they are," Lew began.

She stopped, turned, freezing him with eyes as cold as a doll's. "I don't care if the four of them have fucking MBA's from Harvard. Do you understand me? Television is a visual medium. Perhaps you've forgotten that. I want them to look like they just got swept off the street. Put some dirt on those kids. I want to see holes in their clothes."

"Angela, we can't do that. It's staging. It crosses the line."

"Don't tell me what you can't do." She jabbed one frosty pink nail into his chest. "I'm telling you what's going to be done. It's my show, remember. *Mine.* You've got ten minutes. Now get out of here and do something to earn your salary." She shoved him out, slamming the door behind him.

The panic attack had nearly overtaken her in the hall. Chills raced over her skin; she leaned back against the door shuddering. She would have to go out there soon. Go out and face the audience. They would be waiting for her to make the wrong move, to say the wrong words. If she did, if she made one mistake, they would leap at her like wild dogs.

And she would lose everything. Everything.

On wobbly legs, she lunged across the room. Her hands shook as she poured the champagne. It would help, she knew. She'd discovered after years of denial that just one small glass before a show could chase away those cold, clammy chills. Two could ease all those gnawing fears.

She swallowed greedily, draining the glass, then poured the second with a steadier hand. A third glass wouldn't hurt, she assured herself. Just smoothing out the rough edges. Where had she heard that before? she wondered as she brought the crystal to her lips.

Her mother. Good God, her mother.

Just smoothing out the rough edges, Angie. A couple sips of gin smooths them all right out.

Horrified, she dropped the full glass, spilling bubbling wine over the rug. She watched it spread, like blood, and turned away shivering.

She didn't need it. She wasn't like her mother. She was Angela Perkins. And she was the best.

There would be no mistakes. She promised herself that as she turned to the mirror so that her image, glossy and elegant, could calm her. She would go out and do what she did best. And she would keep those wild dogs at bay yet again. She would tame them, and make them love her.

"Satisfied, Lew?" Still riding on the echoes of applause, Angela dropped into the chair behind her desk. "I told you it would work."

"You were great, Angela." He said it because it was expected.

"No, she was fabulous." Dan sat on the edge of her desk and leaned over to kiss her. "Having that kid sit on your lap was inspired."

"I like kids," she lied. "And that one seemed to have some brains. We'll see to it that he gets in school. Now..." She sat back, letting the family slip from her mind as casually as she slipped out of her shoes. "Let's get down to business. Who is *she* looking to book next month?"

Resigned, Lew passed Angela a list. He didn't have to be told they were discussing Deanna. "The names with the asterisks have already booked."

"She's going after some heavy hitters, isn't she?" Angela mused. "Movies, fashion. Still steering clear of politics."

"Fluff over substance," Dan said, knowing that comment would please her.

"Fluff or not, we wouldn't want her to get lucky. She's already snagged too much press. That damn Jamie Thomas affair." Her mouth tightened into a thin line of disgust as she thought of him hiding out in Rome.

"We still have the data on him," Dan reminded her. "Easy enough to leak his drug problem to the press."

"Leaking that gains us nothing, and would only drum up more sympathetic press for Deanna. Let it go." She scanned the sheet of paper. "Let's see who we know well enough on here to persuade to give Deanna a pass." She glanced up and gave Lew a bland smile. "You can go. I won't need you."

When Lew closed the door quietly behind him, Dan lighted Angela's cigarette. "That hangdog face of his gets old fast," he commented.

"But he has his uses." Pleased, she tapped the list with one lacquered nail. "It's very satisfying to know what our little Dee is planning almost before she does." Angela checked two names on the list. "I can take care of both of these with a casual phone call. It's so gratifying to have important people owe you. Ah, now, look here. Kate Lowell."

"Very hot." Dan rose to pour them both a Perrier. "One of those rarities that makes the term 'actress-model' a compliment."

"Yes, she's very beautiful, very talented. And very hot right now with her new movie burning up the box office." Angela's smile was slow and surprisingly sweet. "It so happens Deanna knows Kate. They summered in Topeka together. And it so happens I know an interesting little secret of Kate's. A little secret that will make certain she won't be chatting to her old pal on the air. In fact, I think we'll just book her ourselves. I'll take care of this one. Personally."

• • •

"I just don't understand it, Finn." Deanna snuggled down on the couch beside him, resting her head against his chest. "One minute we were making the travel arrangements, the next we get a line from her publicist about unexpected scheduling conflicts."

"It happens." He was more interested in nibbling on her fingers than talking shop.

"Not like this. We tried to reschedule, gave them an open date, and got the same response. I really wanted her on in November, but I didn't contact her personally because I didn't want it to seem like calling in a favor from a friend." She shook her head, remembering how warm, then how distant Kate had been when they'd seen each other in Angela's office. "Damn it, we used to be friends."

"Friendships are often one of the first casualties of this business. Don't let it get you down, Kansas."

"I'm trying not to. I know we'll get someone else. I guess I feel snubbed, personally and professionally." She made an effort to push it out of her mind. Their time was too precious to waste. "This is nice."

"What is?"

"Just sitting here, doing nothing. With you."

"I like it myself. Kind of habit-forming." He stroked a finger over the bracelet she wore. Since his return from Moscow, he hadn't seen her without it. "Barlow James is in town."

"Mmm. I heard. Do you want something to eat?"

"No."

"Good." She sighed lustily. "Neither do I. I don't want to move all day. All wonderful Sunday."

An absolutely free Sunday for both of them, she mused. And she didn't want to spoil it by mentioning the latest note she'd found mixed with her viewer mail.

I know you don't really love him, Deanna.
Finn Riley can't mean as much to you as I will.
I can wait for you.
I'll wait forever.

Of course, that note had been nothing compared to the one from the Alabamian truck driver who wanted her to see the country from the bed in his sixteen-wheeler. Or the self-ordained minister who claimed to have had a vision of her naked—a sign from God that she, and her checkbook, were meant to join him in his work.

So it was nothing to worry about. Really, nothing at all.

"I had a meeting with him yesterday."

She blinked. "Who?"

"Barlow James." Because he could see she was clicking into her think mode, Finn tugged at her ear. "Keep up, will you?"

"Sorry. Where's he sending you now?"

"I have to leave for Paris in a few days. I thought you might like to fly out there next weekend."

"Fly out to Paris?" She turned to look at him. "For the weekend?"

"You take the Concorde. We eat French food, see French sights and make love in a French hotel. I might even be able to fly back with you."

The idea made her sit upright. "I can't imagine flying off to Paris for a weekend."

"You're a celebrity," he reminded her. "You're supposed to do things like that. Don't you ever read fan magazines?"

Her eyes were alight with the possibilities. "I've never been to Europe."

"You've got a passport, don't you?"

"Sure. I even renewed it recently, a habit from my reporting days, when I nursed the vague hope of copping some exciting foreign assignment."

"So, I'll be your exciting foreign assignment."

"If I could clear my schedule . . . I *will* clear my schedule." She twisted around to throw her arms around him.

"Where are you going?" he demanded, tightening his grip when she started to wriggle away.

"I have to make a list. I have to get a Berlitz tape and a guidebook, and—"

"Later." He laughed his way into the kiss. "God, you're predictable, Kansas. Whatever I toss at you, you make a list."

"I'm organized." She thumped a fist against his chest. "That doesn't mean I'm predictable."

"You can write up six lists later. I haven't told you about my meeting with Barlow."

But she wasn't listening. She'd need one of those mini video recorders, she decided. Like Cassie had. And a phrase book. "What?" She blinked when Finn tugged on her hair. " 'The meeting with Barlow," she said, tucking her mental list aside. "You just said he was sending you to Paris."

"That's not what the meeting was about. It was a continuation of discussions we've been having on and off for about a year."

"The news magazine." She grinned. "He won't give up, will he?"

"I'm going to do it."

"I think it's—you're what!" She jerked upright again. "You're going to do it?"

He'd expected her to be surprised. Now he was hoping she'd be pleased. "It's taken us a while to agree on terms and format."

"But I didn't think you were interested at all. You like being able to plug into any story that comes along. Toss your garment bag over your shoulder, pick up your laptop and go."

"The paladin of newscasters." He toyed with her earring. "I'd still do that, to an extent. When something breaks, I'd go, but I'd be covering it for the show. We'd do remotes whenever they were called for, but we'd base here in Chicago." That had been a sticking point, since Barlow had wanted him in New York. "I'd be able to take a story and explore all the angles instead of fitting it into a three-minute piece on the news. And I'd spend more time here. With you."

"I don't want you to do this for me." She got to her feet quickly. "I won't deny that it's hard for me to say goodbye so often, but—"

"You've never said so."

"It wouldn't have been fair. God, Finn." She dragged both hands through her hair. "What could I have said? Don't go. I know there are world-altering events taking place, but I'd rather you stay home with me?"

He rose as well, brushed a knuckle down her check. "It wouldn't have hurt my ego to hear it."

His quiet words shivered through her. "It wouldn't have been fair to either of us. And you changing the thrust of your career because of me won't be fair either."

"I'm not just doing this for you. I'm doing it for myself, too."

"You said you didn't want to put down roots." She was distressed, because she realized she was near tears. She wouldn't have been able to explain them to him, or to herself. "I remember that. Finn, we're professionals, and we both understand the demands of the career. I don't want to make you feel pressured."

"You don't get it, do you?" His impatience was back. "There's nothing I wouldn't do for you, Deanna. Things have changed for me in this past year. It's not as easy for me to pick up and go. It's not a snap for me to fall asleep in some hotel halfway around the world. I miss you."

"I miss you too," she said. "Does that make you happy?"

"Damn straight it does." He eased her forward, kissed her softly, gently, until her mouth grew greedy and hot under his. "I want you to miss me. I want it to kill you every time I go away. And I want you to feel as baffled and uncomfortable and as frustrated as I am with this whole mess we've gotten ourselves into."

"Well, I do, so that's just fine for both of us."

"Fine and dandy." He released her. If she wanted to fight with reason, he'd give her plenty of it. Objective words were, after all, his stock-in-trade. "I'll still have to go. I'll have more control over where and when, but I'll have to go. And I want you to suffer whenever I do."

"You," she said precisely, "can go to hell."

"Not without you." He caught her face in his hand, holding tight when she would have jerked away. "Goddamn it, Deanna. I love you."

When his hand went limp, she stepped back on shaky legs. Her eyes were huge and fixed on his face. It took her a moment before she could breathe again. Another moment before she could form coherent words. "You've never said that before."

Her reaction wasn't precisely what he'd hoped for. Then again, he had to admit that his declaration hadn't been exactly polished. "I'm saying it now. You have a problem with it?"

"Do you?"

"I asked you first."

She only shook her head. "I don't suppose I do. It makes it kind of handy, because I love you too." She let out a quick, catchy sigh. "I didn't realize how much I needed the words."

"You're not the only one who has to take things in stages." He reached out, touched her cheek. "Pretty scary, huh?"

"Yeah." She took his wrist, held tight while the first flood of pleasure poured through her. "I don't mind being scared. In fact, I like it, so if you'd like to tell me again, it's okay."

"I love you." He scooped her up, making her laugh as they tumbled onto the couch. "You'd better hold on to me," he warned her, and tugged her sweater over her head. "I'm about to scare you to death."

18

In Depth with Finn Riley premiered in January, a mid-season replacement for a disastrous hospital drama. The network had high hopes that a weekly news magazine featuring a recognizable face could drag the time slot out of the ratings basement. Finn had experience and credibility, and most important, he was wildly popular with women, particularly in the coveted eighteen-to-forty category.

CBC ushered the show onto the air with plenty of hype. Promos were run, ads were designed, theme music was composed. By the time the set, with its three-dimensional world map and sleek glass counter, was constructed, Finn and the three reporters on his team were already hard at work.

His vision of the project was much simpler than jazzy promotion spots or expensive props. He was, as he told Deanna, doing something he'd always fantasized about. He was coming in as relief pitcher after the seventh-inning stretch. All he had to do was throw strikes.

With his first program, he managed to strike out the competition with a thirty-percent share. Around water coolers the next morning, Americans chatted about the U.S. chances for Olympic gold, and Finn Riley's cagey interview with Boris Yeltsin.

In the spirit of friendly competition, Deanna scheduled a program featuring Rob Winters, a veteran film actor whose directorial debut was winning critical and popular acclaim.

Charming, handsome and cozily at home in front of the camera, Rob kept both the studio and viewing audiences entertained. His final anecdote, involving the filming of a steamy love scene and an unexpected invasion of sea gulls, closed the show with a roar of laughter.

"I can't thank you enough for doing the show." Deanna clasped his hand-warmly after he'd finished signing autographs for lingering members of the audience.

"I nearly didn't." While security ushered the last of the audience from the studio, he studied Deanna carefully. "To be frank, the only reason I agreed to come on was because I was pressured not to." He flashed his famous grin. "That's why I have a reputation for being difficult."

"I'm not sure I understand. Your agent advised you against doing this?"

"Among others." Deanna studied him, confused. "Got a minute?" he asked.

"Of course. Would you like to go upstairs to my office?"

"Fine. I could use a drink." His quick smile was back. "You'd last about twenty minutes in Hollywood with eyes like that." He put a friendly hand on her arm as they walked on set toward the elevator. "If you let enough people see what you're thinking, you'll be gobbled up and swallowed whole."

Deanna stepped inside the elevator, pushed the button for the sixteenth floor. "And what am I thinking?"

"That it's barely ten o'clock in the morning and I'm going to start knocking back doubles." His grin was as fast and potent as a jigger of whiskey. "You're thinking I should have stayed at Betty Ford a little longer."

"You did tell me during the show that you didn't drink any longer."

"I don't—alcohol. My newest addiction is Diet Pepsi with a twist of lime. A little embarrassing, but I'm man enough to handle it."

"Deanna—" Cassie turned from her workstation. When she saw the man beside Deanna, her eyes popped wide open.

"Did you need me for something, Cassie?"

"What?" She blinked, flushed, but didn't take her eyes off Rob's face. "No—no, it's nothing."

"Rob, this is Cassie, my secretary and sergeant at arms."

"Nice to meet you." Rob took her limp hand in both of his.

"I enjoy your work, Mr. Winters. We're all thrilled you could do the show today."

"My pleasure."

"Cassie, hold my calls, please. I'll fix you that drink," she told Rob as she led him into her office.

The room had changed considerably from the early days. The walls were painted a bold teal, and the carpet had been replaced by oak flooring and geometric rugs. The furniture was streamlined and built for comfort. Gesturing Rob to a chair, she opened a compact refrigerator.

"I haven't been up here in four or five years, I guess." He stretched out his long legs and glanced around. "It's an improvement." He looked back at Deanna. "But then, pastel pinks probably aren't your style."

"I suppose not." She sliced lime and added it to two iced soft drinks. "I'm curious why your agent advised you against doing the show." Curious wasn't the word, but she kept her voice mild. "We do our best to make our guests comfortable."

"It probably had something to do with a call from New York." He accepted the glass, waited until Deanna took a seat. "From Angela Perkins."

"Angela?" Baffled, she shook her head. "Angela called your agent about your coming on my show?"

"The day after your people contacted him." Rob took a long sip. "She said a little bird had told her that I was considering a stop in Chicago."

"Sounds like her," Deanna muttered. "But I don't know how she could have found out so quickly."

"She didn't say." Watching Deanna's face, he rattled the ice in his glass. "And she didn't bring it up when she spoke to me, either. Two days later. With my agent she used charm, reminding him that she'd booked me on *Angela's* when my career was floundering, and that if I agreed to go on with you, she wouldn't be able to welcome me to New York as she'd hoped to. She wanted me for her next special, and guaranteed that she would use her influence to add weight to my Oscar nomination. Which meant talking the film up in public and in private and contributing to the ad campaign."

"Some not-so-subtle bribery." Her voice tightened with anger held under strict control. "But you're here."

"I might not have been if she'd stayed with bribery. I want that award, Deanna. A lot of people, including me, thought I was washed up when I went into rehab. I had to beg for money to make this film. I made deals and promises, told lies. Whatever it took. Halfway through production, the press was saying that the public was going to stay away in droves because nobody gave a shit about an epic love story. I want that award."

He paused, drank again. "I'd just about made up my mind to take my agent's advice and give you a pass. Then Angela called me. She didn't use charm, she threatened me. And that was her mistake."

Deanna rose to refill his glass. "She threatened not to support the film if you came on my show?"

"She did better than that." He took out a cigarette, shrugged. "Do you mind? I haven't kicked this vice yet."

"Go ahead."

"I came here because I was pissed." He struck a match, blew out smoke. "My little way of telling Angela to get fucked. I wasn't going to bring any of it up, but there's something about the way you handle yourself." He narrowed his eyes. "You've just got to trust that face of yours."

"So I'm told." She managed a smile, though bitterness was bubbling in her throat. "Whatever the reason you came on, I'm glad you did."

"You're not going to ask me what else she threatened me with?"

Her smile fluttered again, more easily. "I'm trying not to."

He gave a short laugh and set the Pepsi aside. "She told me you were a manipulative, scheming monster who'd use any means necessary to stay in the spotlight. That you'd abused her friendship and trust, and that the only reason you were on the air was that you were screwing Loren Bach."

Deanna merely lifted a brow. "I'm sure Loren would be surprised to hear it."

"It sounded more like a self-portrait to me." He took another drag, tapped his cigarette restlessly in the ashtray. "I know what it is to have enemies, Deanna, and since it seems we now have a mutual one, I'm going to tell you what Angela held over my head. I'll need you to keep it to yourself for twenty-four hours, until I get back to the coast and arrange a press conference."

Something cold skittered up her spine. "All right."

"About six months ago I went in for a routine exam. I was worn out, but then I'd been working pretty much around the clock for more than a year, doing the film, overseeing the editing, gearing up for promotion. I'd been a pretty regular customer of the medical profession during my drinking days, and my doctor is very discreet. Discretion aside, Angela managed to get wind of the test results." He took one last drag on the cigarette, crushed it out. "I'm HIV-positive."

"Oh, I'm sorry." Instantly she reached out and gripped his hand hard in hers. "I'm so sorry."

"I always figured the booze would get me. Never figured it would be sex."

He lifted the glass. The ice rattled musically when his hand shook. "Then again, I spent enough time drunk that I didn't know how many women there were, much less who they were."

"We're finding out more every day—" She cut herself off. It was so trite, she thought, so pathetically useless. "You're entitled to your privacy, Rob."

"An odd statement from an ex-reporter."

"Even if Angela leaks this, you don't have to confirm."

He sat back again, looking amused. "Now you're pissed."

"Of course I am. She used me to get to you. It's just television, for God's sake. It's *television.* We're talking about ratings points here, not world-altering events. What kind of business is this that someone would use your tragedy to shake down the competition?"

In a lighter mood, he sipped at his drink. "It's show business, babe. Nothing's closer to life and death than life and death." He smiled wryly. "I ought to know."

"I'm sorry." She closed her eyes and fought for control. "A temper tantrum isn't going to help you. What can I do?"

"Got any friends who are voting members of the Academy?"

She smiled back. "Maybe a couple."

"You might give them a call, use that sexy, persuasive voice to influence their vote. And after that, you can go back in front of the camera and beat the pants off *Angela's*."

Her eyes kindled. "You're damn right I will."

She called a staff meeting that afternoon in her own office and sat behind her desk to project the image of authority. The anger was still with her, simmering deep. As a result, her voice was clipped, cool and formal.

"We have a problem, a serious one, that just recently came to my attention." She scanned the room as she spoke, noting the puzzled faces. Staff meetings were often tiresome, sometimes heated, but always informal and essentially good-natured.

"Margaret," she continued. "You contacted Kate Lowell's people, didn't you?"

"That's right." Unnerved by the chill in the air, Margaret nibbled on the earpiece of her reading glasses. "They were very interested in having her come on. We had the hook that she'd lived in Chicago for a few years when she was a teenager. Then they switched off. Scheduling conflicts."

"How many other times has that happened in the last six months?"

Margaret blinked. "It's hard to say right off. A lot of the topic ideas don't pan out."

"I mean specifically celebrity-oriented shows."

"Oh, well." Margaret shifted in her seat. "We don't do a lot of those because the format generally runs to civilian guests, the everyday people you do so well. But I'd guess that five or six times in the last six months we've had somebody wiggle off the hook."

"And how do we handle the projected guest list. Simon?"

He flushed. "Same as always, Dee. We toss around ideas, brainstorm. When we come up with some workable topics and guests, we do the research and make some calls."

"And the guest list is confidential until it's confirmed?"

"Sure it is." He nervously slicked a hand over his hair. "Standard operating procedure. We don't want any of the competitors to horn in on our work."

Deanna picked up a pencil from the glass surface of her counter, tapped it idly. "I learned today that Angela Perkins knew we were interested in booking Rob Winters within hours of our contacting his agent." There was a general murmuring among the staff. "And I suspect," Deanna continued, "from what I learned, that she was also aware of several others. Kate Lowell appeared on *Angela's* two weeks after her people claimed a scheduling conflict. She wasn't the only one. I have a list here of people we tried to book who guested on *Angela's* within two weeks of our initial contact."

"We've got a leak." The muscles in Fran's jaw twitched. "Son of a bitch."

"Come on, Fran." Jeff cast worried glances around the room. He shoved at his glasses. "Most of us have been here from the first day. We're like family." He tugged at the collar of his T-shirt, cutting his eyes back to Deanna. "Man, Dee, you can't believe any of us would do anything to hurt you or the show."

"No, I can't." She pushed a hand through her hair. "So I need ideas, suggestions."

"Jesus. Jesus Christ," Simon mumbled under his breath as he pressed his fingers to his eyes. "It's my fault." Dropping his hands, he gave Deanna a shattered look. "Lew McNeil. We've kept in touch all along. Hell, we've been friends for ten years. I never thought . . . I'm sick," he said. "I swear to God it makes me sick."

"What are you talking about?" Deanna asked quietly, but she thought she knew.

"We talk once, twice a month." He shoved back from the table, crossing the room to pour a glass of water. "Usual stuff—shop talk." Taking out a bottle, he shook two pills into his hand. "He'd bitch about Angela. He knew he could to me, that it wouldn't go any further. He'd tell me some of the wilder ideas her team had come up with for segments. Maybe he'd ask who we were lining up. And I'd tell him." He swallowed the pills audibly. "I'd tell him, because we were just two old friends talking shop. I never put it together until this minute, Dee. I swear to Christ."

"All right, Simon. So we know how, we know why. What are we going to do about it?"

"Hire somebody to go to New York and break all of Lew McNeil's fingers," Fran suggested as she rose to go stand beside the clearly distressed Simon.

"I'll give that some thought. In the meantime, the new policy is not to discuss any guests, any topic ideas or *any* of the developmental stages of the show outside of the office. Agreed?"

There was a general murmuring. No one made eye contact.

"And we have a new goal. One we're all going to concentrate on." She paused, waiting until she could skim her gaze over each face. "We're going to knock *Angela's* out of the number-one spot within a year." She held up a hand to stop the spontaneous applause. "I want everyone to start thinking about ideas for remotes. We need to start taking this show on the road. I want sexy locations, funny locations. I want the exotic, and I want Main Street, USA."

"Disney World," Fran suggested.

"New Orleans, for Mardi Gras," Cassie put in, and lifted her shoulders. "I always wanted to go."

"Check it out," Deanna ordered. "I want six doable locations. I want all the topic ideas we have cooking on my desk by the end of the day. Cassie, make a list of all the personal appearance requests I've got and accept them."

"How many?"

"All of them. Fit them into my schedule. And put in a call to Loren Bach." She sat back and rested her palms on the surface of the desk. "Let's get to work."

"Deanna." Simon stepped forward as the others filed out. "Can I have a minute?"

"Just," she said, and smiled. "I want to get started on this campaign."

He stood stiffly in front of her desk. "I know it might take you a little time to replace me, and that you'd like a smooth transition. I'll hand in my resignation whenever you want."

Deanna was already drawing a list on a legal pad in front of her. "I don't want your resignation. Simon. I want you to use that wily brain of yours to put me on top."

"I screwed up, Dee. Big time."

"You trusted a friend."

"A competitor," he corrected. "God knows how many shows I sabotaged by opening my big mouth. Shit, Dee, I was bragging, playing 'My job's bigger than your job.' I wanted to needle him because it was the only way I could stick it to Angela."

"I'm giving you another way." She leaned forward, eyes keen. She felt the power in her now, and she would use it, she knew, to finish what Angela had begun. "Help me knock her out of the top slot, Simon. You can't do that if you resign."

"I can't figure why you'd trust me."

"I had a pretty good idea where the leak had come from. Simon, I spent enough time around here to know you and Lew were tight." She spread her fingers. "If you hadn't told me, you wouldn't have had to offer to resign. I'd have fired you."

He rubbed a hand over his face. "So I admit to being a jerk and I keep my job."

"That about sums it up. And I expect, because you're feeling like one, you'll work even harder to put me on top."

More than a little dazed, he shook his head. "You picked up a few things from Angela after all."

"I got what I needed," she said shortly. She snatched up her phone when it buzzed. "Yes, Cassie?"

"Loren Bach on one, Deanna."

"Thanks." She let her finger hover over the button as she glanced back at Simon. "Are we straight on this?"

"As an arrow."

She waited until the door shut behind Simon, then drew in a deep breath. "Loren," she said when she made the connection. "I'm ready to go to war."

In the cold, gloomy hours of a February morning, Lew kissed his wife goodbye. She stirred sleepily, and gave his cheek a pat before snuggling under the down quilt for another thirty-minute nap.

"Chicken stew tonight," she mumbled. "I'll be home by three to put it on."

Since their children had grown, each had fallen into a comfortable morning routine. Lew left his wife sleeping and went downstairs alone to eat breakfast with the early news. He winced over the weather report, though a glance out the window had already told him it wasn't promising. The drive from Brooklyn Heights to the studio in Manhattan was going to be a study in frustration. He bundled into a coat, pulled on gloves, put on the Russian-style fur hat his youngest son had given him for Christmas.

The wind was up, tossing the nasty wet snow into his face, letting it sneak under the collar of his coat. It was still shy of seven, dreary enough that the streetlights still glowed. The snow muffled sound and seemed to smother the air.

He saw no one out in the tidy neighborhood but an unhappy cat scratching pitifully on his owner's front door.

Too used to Chicago winters to complain about a February storm, Lew trudged to his car and began to clean the windshield.

He paid no attention to the fairy-tale world forming behind him. The low evergreens with their frosting of white, the pristine carpet that coated winter grass and pavement, the dancing flakes that swirled in the dull glow of the streetlamps.

He thought only of the drudgery of scraping his windshield clean, of the discomfort of snow on his collar, of the nip of the wind at his ears. Of the traffic he had yet to face.

He heard his name called, softly, and turned to peer through the driving snow.

For a moment he saw nothing but white and the snow-smothered beam of light from the streetlamp.

And then he saw. For just an instant, he saw.

The shotgun blast struck him full in the face, cartwheeling his body over the hood of his car. From down the block a dog began to bark in high, excited yips. The cat streaked away to hide in a snow-coated juniper.

The echo of the shot died quickly, almost as quickly as Lew McNeil.

"That was for Deanna," the killer whispered, and drove slowly away.

When Deanna heard the news a few hours later, the shock of it overshadowed the envelope she'd found on her desk. It said simply:

Deanna, I'll always be there for you.

19

Deanna lounged in Finn's big tub with steaming water whirling and pulsing around her, her eyes half closed and a frothy mimosa in her hand. It was the middle of a Saturday morning, and she had more than an hour before Tim O'Malley, her driver, would be by to pick her up for an appearance in Merrillville, Indiana.

She felt as lazy and smug as a cat curled in a sunbeam.

"What are we celebrating?"

"You're in town; I'm in town. And not counting your afternoon across the state line today, it looks like it could stay that way for a week."

From the opposite end of the tub, Finn watched her tension ease, degree by degree. She'd been wound tight as a spring for weeks. Longer, he thought, sipping the icy drink. Even before Lew McNeil's random and senseless murder, she'd been a bundle of nerves. In the weeks following Lew's death her feelings had shifted from remorse to anger to guilt to frustration over a man who had done his best to sabotage her show for his own ends.

Or Angela's ends, Finn theorized.

But now she smiled, and her eyes were heavy with pleasure. "Things have been a little chaotic lately."

"You flying off to Florida, me chasing presidential candidates from state to state. Both of us trying to put together a show with press and paparazzi dogging our heels." He shrugged, rubbing his foot up and down her slick, slippery leg.

It hadn't been easy for anyone on her staff, or his, to work with the continued and pesky attention the media had focused on their relationship. For reasons neither of them could fathom, they had become the couple of the year. Just that morning, Deanna had read about her wedding plans in a tabloid some helpful soul had tucked under the front doormat.

All in all it made her uneasy, unsure and far too distracted.

"Do you call that chaotic?" Finn asked, and drew her attention back.

"You're right, just another day in the simple life." Her sigh was long and sumptuous. "And at least we're getting things done. I really liked your show on Chicago's decaying infrastructure, even if it did make me start to worry that the streets are going to crumble under my car."

"Everything was there—panic, comedy, half-crazed city officials. Still, it wasn't as gripping as your interview with Mickey and Minnie Mouse."

One eye opened. "Watch it, pal."

"No, really." His grin was wicked. "You've got America talking. What kind of relationship do they have, and what part does Goofy play in it? These burning questions need to be answered—and who knows, it might help take some of the heat off us?"

"We were dealing with American traditions," she shot back. "On the need for entertainment and fantasy, and the enormous industry that fuels it. Which is every bit as relevant as watching politicians sling insults at each other. More," she said, gesturing with her glass. "People need some mode of escape, particularly during a recession. You do your shows on global warming and the socioeconomic troubles in the former Soviet Union. Riley. I'll stick with the everyday issues that affect the average person."

He was still grinning at her. Deanna took a sip of her mimosa and scowled at him. "You're riding me on purpose."

"I like the way your eyes get dark and edgy." He set his glass aside so that he could slide forward and lay his body over hers. Water sloshed lazily over the lip of the tub. "And you get this line right here"—he rubbed his thumb between her brows—"that I get to smooth away."

His free hand was busy smoothing something else. "Some might say you're a sneaky bastard, Finn."

"Some have." He nipped at her lips. "Others will. And speaking of Mickey and Minnie." His hands cruised over her hot, soft skin.

"Were we?"

"I was wondering if we can compare our relationship to theirs. Undefined and long-term."

While the jets of water frothed around them and between them, she stroked a hand through his damp hair. It felt so good to be here, to know that at any moment the comforting heat could erupt into explosive heat. "I can define it: We're two people who love each other, who enjoy each other, who want to be with each other."

"We could be with each other more if you'd move in with me."

It was a subject they'd discussed before. And one they had been unable to resolve. Deanna pressed her lips to his shoulder. "It's easier for me to have my own place when you're away."

"I'm here more than I'm gone these days."

"I know." Her lips slid up his throat as she tried to distract him. "Give me some time to work it out in my head."

"Sometimes you've got to trust your impulses, Deanna, your instincts." His mouth met hers, tasting of frustration and desire. He knew if he pushed, she'd agree, but his instinct warned him not to rush her. "I can wait. Just don't make me wait too long."

"We can give it a trial run." Her blood was pulsing as frantically as the bubbling water. "I'll move some things in, stay here through next week."

"I'll make it hard for you to leave again."

"I bet you will." She smiled, pushing his hair back, framing his face. "I'm so in love with you, Finn. You can believe that. And I swear, the rumors about me and Goofy are all lies. We're just friends."

He tipped her head back so that her body slipped farther into the water. "I don't trust the long-eared son of a bitch."

"I just used him to make you jealous—though he does have a certain guileless charm I find strangely appealing."

"You want charm? Why don't I—damn." Finn tossed his wet hair back and reached for the tubside phone. "Hold that thought," he told her. "Yeah, Riley."

Deanna was considering several interesting ways to distract him when she saw the change in his face. The water shifted and slopped over as he climbed from the tub to reach for a towel.

"Get Curt," he said, dripping as he slung the towel around his waist. "And contact Barlow James. I want a full crew, a mobile unit on the spot five minutes ago. I'll be at the site in twenty minutes." He swore, not so lightly, under his breath. "You can if I tell you that you can."

"What is it?" Deanna turned off the tub and rose. Water streamed from her as she shook out a towel. She already knew he was leaving.

"There's a hostage situation over in Greektown." With a quick flick of the wrist, he turned on the television even as he headed into the bedroom to drag on clothes. "It's bad. Three people are already dead."

She shivered once. Then as quick, as brisk as he, she reached for her robe. She wanted to tell him she'd go with him. But of course she couldn't. There were several hundred people waiting for her in the ballroom of an Indiana hotel.

Why was she so cold? she wondered as she bundled hurriedly into her robe. He was already tucking a shirt into his slacks, as calmly as a man going to his office to work on tax forms. He'd survived air raids and earthquakes. Surely a skirmish in Greektown was nothing to worry about.

"You'll be careful."

He grabbed a tie, a jacket. "I'll be good." As she reached into the closet for the suit she'd chosen for her afternoon appearance, he spun her around for a kiss. "I'll probably be back before you."

The worst kind of war was one with no front lines or battle plans. It was fueled on anger and fear and the blind need to destroy. The once-tidy restaurant with its pretty, striped awning and sidewalk tables was destroyed. Shards from the broken window sparkled like scattered gems over the sidewalk. The flap of the awning in the raw spring wind was smothered by the static-filled drone of police radios. Reporters held back by barricades swarmed like hungry wolves.

There was another volley of gunshots from inside. And a long, terrified scream.

"Jesus." Sweat popped out on Curt's brow as he held the camera steady. "He's killing them."

"Get a shot of that cop there," Finn ordered. "The one with the bullhorn."

"You're the boss." Curt focused in on a cop in a neon orange trench coat with a hangdog face and graying hair. Amid the screams and shouts, the weeping, the bitter threats and curses from inside the restaurant, the steely-eyed cop continued to talk in a soothing monotone.

"Pretty cool customer," Curt observed, then at a signal from Finn shifted, crouched to get a shot of the SWAT team taking position.

"Cool enough," Finn agreed. "If he keeps at it, they might not need the sharpshooters. Keep rolling. I'm going to see if I can work my way over and find out who he is."

The ballroom was filled to capacity. From where Deanna sat on the raised dais, she could see all three hundred and fifty people who had come to hear her talk about women in broadcasting. She was going to give them their money's worth. She'd gone over her notes thoroughly once again on the drive from Chicago, letting her concentration lapse only when she caught a glimpse of Finn on the limo's television.

He was, as Barlow James would say, in his element. And, it seemed, she was in hers.

She waited through the flattering introduction, through the applause that followed it, then rose and walked to the podium. She scanned the room, smiled.

"Good afternoon. One of the first things we learn in broadcasting is that we work weekends. Since we are, I hope to make the next hour as entertaining as it is informative. That, to me, is television, and I've found it a very satisfying way to make a living. It occurred to me that as you are professionals, you wouldn't have much opportunity to watch daytime TV, so I'm hoping to convince you to set your VCRs Monday morning. We're on at nine here in Merrillville."

That earned Deanna her first chuckle, and set the tone for the next twenty minutes, until her speech segued into a question-and-answer period.

One of the first questioners asked if Finn Riley had accompanied her.

"I'm afraid not. As we all know, one of the boons, and the curses, of this business is the breaking story. Finn's reporting on one right now, but you can catch him on *In Depth* Tuesday nights. I always do."

"Miss Reynolds, how do you feel about the fact that looks have become as much a part of the criteria for on-air jobs as credentials?"

"I would certainly agree with network executives that television is a visual medium. To a point. I can tell you this: If in thirty years Finn Riley is still reporting, and considered a statesman, I'd not only expect but demand, as a woman, to be given the same respect."

Finn wasn't thinking about the future. He was too involved in the present. Using wile, guile and arrogance, he'd managed to gain a position beside the hostage negotiator, Lieutenant Arnold Jenner. Jenner still held the bullhorn but had taken a short break in his appeal to his quarry to release the hostages.

"Lieutenant, the word I've gotten here is that Johnson—that's his name, isn't it, Elmer Johnson?"

"It's the one he answers to," Jenner said mildly.

"He has a history of depression. His VA records—"

"You wouldn't have access to his medical records, Mr. Riley."

"Not directly." But he had contacts, and he'd used them. "My take on this is that Johnson served in the military and has been troubled since his discharge in March of last year. Last week he lost his wife and his job."

"You're well informed."

"I get paid to be. He went into this restaurant at just past ten this morning—that's about three hours ago—armed with a forty-four Magnum, a Bushmaster, a gas mask and a carbine. He shot and killed two waiters and a bystander, then took five hostages, including two women and a twelve-year-old girl, the owner's daughter."

"Ten," Jenner said wearily. "The kid's ten. Mr. Riley, you do good work, and usually I enjoy it. But my job right now is to get those people out of there alive."

Finn glanced over, noting the position of the sharpshooters. They wouldn't wait much longer. "What are his demands? Can you tell me that?"

It hardly mattered, Jenner decided. There had been only one, and he hadn't been able to meet it. "He wants his wife, Mr. Riley. She left Chicago four days ago. We're trying to locate her, but we haven't had any luck."

"I can get it on the air. If she catches a bulletin, she may make contact. Let me talk to him. I might be able to get him to bargain if I tell him I'll put all my people on it."

"You that desperate for a story?"

Insults were too common in his line of work for Finn to take offense. "I'm always ready to bargain for a story, Lieutenant." His eyes narrowed as he measured the man beside him. "Look, the kid's ten. Let me try."

Jenner believed in instinct, and he also knew, without a doubt, that he couldn't hold the situation from flash point much longer. After a moment, he handed Finn the bullhorn. "Don't promise what you can't deliver."

"Mr. Johnson. Elmer. This is Finn Riley. I'm a reporter."

"I know who you are." The voice came out, a high-pitched shriek through the broken glass. "Do you think I'm stupid?"

"You were in the Gulf, right? I was too."

"Shit. You figure that makes us buddies?"

"I figure anybody who did time over there's already been to hell." The awning flapped, reminding him of the road to Kuwait, and the sparkle of pink sequins. "I thought maybe we could make a deal."

"There ain't no deal. My wife gets here, I let them go. She doesn't, we're all going to hell. For real."

"The cops have been trying to reach her, but I thought we could put a new spin on it. I've got a lot of contacts. I can get your story national, put your wife's picture on television screens from coast to coast. Even if she isn't watching, someone who knows her is bound to be. We'll put a number on, a special number where she can call in. You can talk to her, Elmer."

That was good, Jenner decided, even as he braced to rip the bullhorn from Finn's hands if the need arose. Using his first name, offering him not only hope but a few minutes of fame. His superiors might not approve, but Jenner thought it could work.

"Then do it!" Johnson shouted out. "Just fucking do it."

"I'll be glad to, but I can't unless you give something back. Just let the little girl come out, Elmer, and I'll plug your story across the country within ten minutes. I can even fix it so you can get a message to your wife. In your own words."

"I'm not letting anybody out, except in a body bag."

"She's just a kid, Elmer. Your wife probably likes kids." Christ, he hoped so. "If you let her go, she'll hear about it, and she'll want to talk to you."

"It's a trick."

"I've got a camera right here." He glanced toward Curt. "Is there a TV in the bar in there?" he called out.

"What if there is?"

"You can watch everything I do. Everything I say. I'll have them put me on live."

"Then do it. Do it in five minutes, fucking five minutes, or you're going to have another body in here."

"Call the desk," Finn shouted. "Patch me in. Set up for live now." Then he turned back to Jenner.

"You'd make a pretty good cop—for a reporter."

"Thanks." He handed Jenner the bullhorn. "Tell him to send her out while I'm on the air, or I go to black."

In precisely five minutes, Finn faced the camera. Whatever his inner turmoil, his delivery was calm and well paced, his eyes cool. Behind him was the shattered exterior of the restaurant.

"This morning in Chicago's Greektown, this family-run restaurant erupted with violence. Three people are known dead in the standoff between police and Elmer Johnson, a former mechanic who chose this spot to take his stand. Johnson's only demand is contact with his estranged wife, Arlene."

Though he sensed activity behind him, Finn's eyes stayed fixed on the camera's light.

"Johnson, well armed, is holding five hostages. In his appeal to—"

There was a scream from behind him. Finn shifted instantly to give Curt room to tape.

It happened quickly, as if all the waiting hours had been focused on this one moment. The child, trembling and weeping, stepped outside. Even as the shadow of the awning fell over her face, a wild-eyed man sprinted out, screaming as he hurtled toward escape. The rash of gunfire from the restaurant propelled the man forward, off his feet. It was Jenner, Finn saw, who scooped the child aside even as Johnson stumbled to the door.

The sniper's bullet plowed through Johnson's forehead.

"Oh man." Curt kept repeating the words over and over under his breath as he held the camera steady. "Man, oh man, oh man."

Finn only shook his head. The burning in his left arm made him glance down curiously. Brows knit, he touched the hole in his sleeve. His fingers came away sticky with blood.

"Well, hell," he murmured. "I got this coat in Milan."

"Shit, Riley." Curt's eyes bulged. "Shit. You're hit."

"Yeah." He didn't feel any pain yet, only dull annoyance. "You just can't patch leather, either."

• • •

On Monday, as soon as the morning show was taped, Deanna stood in the center of her office, her eyes glued to the TV screen. It seemed unbelievable that she could hear Finn's voice supplying the details over the special report.

She saw the scene as he had, the shattered glass, the bloodied body. The camera bobbled and swung as the sniper fired. Her heart jerked as she heard the pop and ping of bullets.

Through it all, Finn's voice remained calm, cool, with an underpinning of fury she doubted any of his viewers were aware of. She stood, a fist pressed to her heart as the camera zoomed in on the child, weeping in the arms of a rumpled man with graying hair.

"Deanna." Jeff hesitated in the doorway, then crossed the room to stand beside her.

"It's horrible," she murmured. "Unbelievable. If that man hadn't panicked and run out that way, if he hadn't done that, it might have turned out differently. That little girl, she could have been caught in the cross fire. And Finn..."

"He's okay. Hey, he's right downstairs. Back on the job."

"Back on the job."

"Deanna," he said again, and laid a hand on her shoulder. "I know it must be tough for you. Not only knowing it happened, but actually watching it." He walked over and switched off the set. "But he's okay."

"He was shot." She whirled away from the blank screen and struggled for composure. "And I was in Indiana. You can't imagine how horrible it was to have Tim come into the ballroom and tell me he'd seen it on the limo's set. And to be helpless. Not to be there when they took him to the hospital."

"If it upsets you this much, and you asked him, he could get a desk job."

For the first time all morning she gave him a genuine smile. "Things don't work that way. I wouldn't want them to. We'd better get back to work." She gave his hand a quick squeeze before rounding her desk. "Thanks for listening."

"Hey. That's what I'm here for."

"Everybody stays late tonight," Angela announced at an emergency staff meeting. "Nobody leaves until we lock in this show. I want a panel, and I want it hard-line. Three from this white supremacist group, three from the NAACP. I want radicals." She sat behind her desk, her fingers drumming on the surface. "Make sure each side gets at least a dozen tickets, so they can seed the audience. I want to blow the roof off."

She stabbed a finger at her head researcher. "We've got some statistics here in New York. Get me some of the relatives."

"Some of them might not be easy to persuade."

"Then pay them," she snapped. "Money always turns the tide. And I want some tape, as graphic as possible, from rallies. Some witnesses to racially motivated crimes, perpetrators would be better. Promise that we'll protect their identities. Promise them anything, just get them."

When she fell into silence, Dan gave a nod that signaled the end of the meeting. He waited until the door was closed again.

"You know, Angela, you could be walking on thin ice here."

Her head snapped up. "You sound like Lew."

"I'm not advising you against doing it. I'm just suggesting that you watch out for the cross fire."

"I know what I'm doing." She'd seen Finn's report, as had nearly every other American with a television set. Now she was going to outdo him as well as Deanna. "We need something hot, and the timing couldn't be better. The country's in an uproar about race, and the city's a mess."

"You're not worried about Deanna Reynolds." He smiled, knowing he had to defuse the tantrum he saw building in her eyes.

"She's climbing up my back, isn't she?"

"She'll slip off." He took her rigid hands in his. "What you need now is a boost in publicity. Something that will focus the public's attention on you." He lifted her hand, admiring the way the sun dashed off the diamonds in her watch. "And I've got an idea how to do it."

"It better be good."

"It's more than good, it's inspired." He kissed her hand, watching her over her knuckles. "The American public loves one thing more than they love hearing about graft and sex and violence. Weddings," he said as he drew her gently to her feet. "Big, splashy weddings—private weddings dotted with celebrities. Marry me, Angela." His eyes were soft. "I'll not only make you happy, I'll see to it that your picture's on every major newspaper and magazine in the country."

The flutter of her heart was quick. "And what would you get out of it, Dan?"

"You." Reading her clearly, he lowered his head to kiss her. "All I want is you."

On the second Saturday in June, Angela donned a Vera Wang shell-pink gown of silk, encrusted with tiny pearls. Its sweetheart neckline framed a flattering hint of her rounded breasts, its full, elaborate skirt accented her tiny waist. She wore a wide-brimmed hat with a fingertip veil and carried a bouquet of white orchids.

The ceremony took place in the country home she'd purchased in Connecticut, and was attended by a stellar guest list. Some were pleased to be there, drawn either by sentiment or the notion of having their name and photo included in the press releases. Others came because it was easier to accept than to face Angela's fury later.

Elaborate gifts crowded the large parlor and, under uniformed guard, were on display for the select members of the press. No one seeing all this, Angela thought, would doubt how much she was loved.

The reception spilled out into the rose garden, where a champagne fountain bubbled and white doves cooed.

When the event was buzzed incessantly by helicopters crammed with paparazzi, she knew it was a success.

Like any new bride, she glowed. The sun glinted off the five-carat diamond gracing her left hand as she posed with Dan for photos.

She told the reporters, regretfully, that her mother, her only living relative, was too ill to attend. In reality she was tucked in a private clinic, drying out.

Kate Lowell, looking young and fresh in a billowing sundress, kissed Angela's cheek for the benefit of the cameras. Her long red-gold hair flowed down her bare back, melted copper over sun-kissed peaches. She had a face the camera worshiped, ice-edged cheekbones, full lips, huge gold eyes. The image was completed by a sinuous body, killer legs and a rich infectious giggle.

Kate Lowell could have become a star on the sole basis of her glorious physical attributes. She certainly had done her share of commercial endorsements. But she had something more: talent and charm that burned every bit as hot as her box-office appeal. And ambition that seared through both.

She enchanted the photographer by shooting him a dazzling smile, then turned the other cheek for Angela. "I hate your guts," she said softly.

"I know, darling." Beaming, Angela slipped her arm around Kate's waist, fingers digging ruthlessly into flesh as she turned her best side to the camera. "Smile pretty now, show why you're the number-one female box-office draw."

Kate did, with a smile that could have melted steel at five paces. "I wish you were dead."

"You and so many others." She hooked her arm through Kate's and strolled off, two bosom friends stealing a private moment. "Now, is it true that you and Rob Winters are considering scripts for a TV movie?"

"No comment."

"Now, now, darling." Angela's voice was a purr, deadly feline. "Didn't we agree to scratch each other's backs?"

"I'd like to scratch your eyes." But she knew she couldn't. There was much too much at stake for her to indulge herself quite that blatantly. Still, there were other weapons. Tilting her head, Kate studied Angela's face. "That's an excellent tuck, by the way. Barely noticeable." Her smile was quick and sincere when Angela bristled. "Don't worry, *darling*, it'll be our secret. After all, a girl's got to do everything necessary to maintain the illusion of youth. Especially when she's married to a younger man."

Behind the flirty little veil, Angela's eyes were as hard as marbles. It was her day, by God. Hers. And nothing and no one would spoil it. "A script's come my way, Katie dear. I think you'll find it fascinating. And I think you'll be able to pique Rob's interest as well. The two of you have been pals for years, and it would be a friendly boost if you persuaded him to do it. After all, he doesn't have a great deal of time left to pick and choose, does he?"

"You bitch."

Angela gave a trilling laugh. Nothing could have pleased her more than seeing Kate's smug smile fade. "The trouble with actors is they need someone to write that clever dialogue. You'll have the script by Monday, darling. I really would consider it a favor if you'd read it quickly."

"I'm getting tired of your favors, Angela. Other people might call it blackmail."

"I'm not other people. It's simply a matter of my having certain information that I'm more than happy to keep to myself. A favor to you, dear. In return, you do one for me. That's called cooperation."

"One day you're going to cooperate yourself right into hell."

"It's just business." With a sigh, Angela patted Kate's flushed cheeks. "You've been around long enough to know better than to take everything so personally. We'll discuss terms when I get back from my honeymoon. Now, you'll have to excuse me. I can't ignore my guests."

Although Kate's imagination didn't run to dialogue, she had no trouble with visuals. As Angela glided away, Kate saw the frothy silk splattered with blood.

"One day," she whispered, yanking a rose from a bush and crushing it in her hand. "One day, someone's finally going to get the guts and do it."

"She looks wonderful." Lolling on the couch in the cabin, Deanna studied the front cover of *People.* "Radiant."

Finn drummed up the energy to glance over. They had finally been able to synchronize a full three days off, together. If the phone didn't ring, the fax didn't shrill and the world didn't collapse within the next twenty-four hours, they would have made it through.

"She looks like one of those prop wedding cakes. All fancy fake icing over the inedible."

"Your vision's skewed by malice."

"Yours should be, too."

She only sighed and flipped through to the cover story. "I don't have to like her to admit she's lovely. And she looks happy, really happy. Maybe marriage will mellow her."

He only snorted. "Since this is her third time at bat, that's doubtful."

"Not if this is the right one. I don't wish her bad luck, personally or professionally." She peered over the top of the magazine. "I want to whip her butt on merit."

"You are whipping her butt."

"In Chicago, and a few other markets. But this wedding's bound to shift the tide at least for a time."

He stretched his arms over his head, muscles rippling. Deanna could see the faint scar where the bullet had sliced through.

"Why do you think she did it?"

"Oh come on, Finn, give her some credit. A woman doesn't get married so that she can get her picture on a few covers."

"Kansas." Amazed that she could still be so naive, he took the magazine from her. "When you're slipping down the ladder, you grab hold of any handy rope."

"I think that's a mixed metaphor."

"You think this is for love?" Laughing, he sent the magazine sailing. Angela, the happy bride, landed facedown. "She's had six weeks of free publicity since the day her secret engagement mysteriously leaked."

"It could have leaked." She gave him a friendly shove with her stockinged foot. "And even if she planted it, it doesn't change the bottom line. She's a beautiful, vibrant woman who fell for a gorgeous, magnetic man."

"Gorgeous?" Finn snagged her foot by the ankle. "You think he's gorgeous?"

"Yes, he's—" She shrieked, twisting as he tickled her foot. "Stop that."

"And magnetic?"

"Sexy." Giggling helplessly, she reared up to try to free herself. "Sinfully attractive." She tried biting when he wrestled her down.

"You fight like a girl."

She blew her hair out of her eyes and tried to buck him off. "So what?"

"I like it. And I'm now honor-bound to erase Dan What's-his-name from your mind."

"Dan Gardner," she said primly. "And I don't know if you can. I mean, he's so elegant, so polished, so . . ." She gave a mock shiver. "So romantic."

"We'll shoot for a contrast."

With one swipe, he dragged his hand down her breezy cotton blouse and sent buttons flying.

"Finn!" Caught between shock and amusement, she started to shove him back. The laughing protest ended on a strangled gasp as he fastened his mouth to her breast.

Instant heat. Instant need. It burst through her like light, blindingly bright. The hands that had playfully pressed against his shoulders tightened like vises, short, neat nails digging crescents into his flesh. Her heart stuttered beneath his greedy mouth, losing its pace, then racing ahead in a wild sprint.

His hands were already tugging aside the remains of her blouse, then streaking over bared skin to arouse and demand. The strong summer sun streamed through the windows, fell over her in hot white light. Her skin was moist from it, from his rough, impatient touch. With his mouth still feasting on her, he slid his hand under the baggy leg of her shorts and drove her ruthlessly to a fast, violent climax.

"Again." Driven himself, he fixed his mouth on hers, swallowing her cry as he pushed her higher.

He wanted her like this. So often he was content to let them take each other slowly, savoring each touch, each taste on the long, lazy journey toward fulfillment. He loved the way her body grew sinuous and soft, the way his own pleasures built layer by layer.

But now he wanted only the fast, molten ride, the mindlessness of hurried, urgent sex. He wanted to possess her, to brand her, to feel her body rock fitfully under his, until he was sunk deep.

He tore at her clothes even as she tugged and yanked at his. Her breath was hot on his flesh, her mouth streaking hungrily over him, sounds of desperate excitement humming in her throat.

He shifted, gripping her hips and lifting her up so that the muscles in his arms quivered. Then he was sheathed in her. Their twin cries of triumph shivered on the sultry air.

With her head thrown back, her long, slim body glistening with sweat, she took him deeper, drove him as he had driven her. Ruthlessly, relentlessly. She gripped his hands, guiding them over her damp body, urging him to claim more while her heart galloped in a mad race of its own.

The orgasm struck, a sweaty fist that pummeled and pummeled and left her body a mass of indescribably exquisite aches. The air was clogged and burning in her lungs. She sobbed to release it, sobbed to gulp it back in.

She felt his body lunge, vaulting her over that final, keen edge. Like wax melted in the sun, she slid down to him and lay limp.

His own mind cleared gradually, the static from the storm dying to a steady quiet that was her breathing. The dark haze that had covered his vision lifted so that he closed his eyes against the hard sunlight.

"I guess I protected my honor," he murmured. She gave a strangled laugh.

"I didn't know—God, I can't breathe." She tried again. "I didn't know tweaking your ego would be so . . . rewarding."

"Relaxed?"

She sighed. "Very."

"Happy?"

"Completely."

"Then this is probably a good time to ask you to think about something."

"Hmmm. I don't think I *can* think just now."

"Put this in the back of your mind." His hand gently massaged her back. "Let it stew there for a while."

"What am I supposed to stew about?"

"Marrying me."

She jerked back. "Marrying you?"

"Is looking shocked another way to tweak my ego?"

"No." Staggered, she pressed a hand to her cheek. "God, Finn, you know how to toss one in from left field."

"We'll talk baseball later—since the Cubs are in the basement." Goddamn nerves, he thought, while his stomach clenched. It was ridiculous for him to feel these tugs of panic, but all he could imagine was her saying no. Absolutely not.

For the first time in his life he wanted something and someone he wasn't sure he could have.

He levered himself up so that they sat, naked, facing each other, both still achy and sated with sex. The plan was, he reminded himself, to keep it light, natural.

"It shouldn't be such a surprise, Deanna. We've been lovers for more than a year."

"Yes, but . . . we haven't even resolved living together yet—"

"One of my points. My strategy in getting you to live with me; then easing you into marriage just isn't panning out."

"Your strategy?"

He didn't mind the edge in her voice. It matched the one in his own. "Kansas, the only way to handle you is like a chess game. A man has to think a half dozen moves ahead and outflank you."

"I don't think I care for that analogy."

"It's an accurate one." He pinched her chin lightly between his fingers. "You spend so much time thinking things through, trying to avoid making the wrong move. I have to give you a shove."

"Is that what this proposal is?" She batted his hand away. "A shove?"

"We'll call it more of a nudge, since I'm willing to let you think it over."

"That's generous of you," she said between her clenched teeth.

"Actually," he continued, "I'm giving us both time. I can't say I'm completely sold on the idea myself."

She blinked. "Excuse me?"

It was inspired, he realized. Absolutely inspired. Two could play tweak-the-ego. "We're coming from opposite fields here on this subject. You from a big, happy family, all those traditional trappings, where 'till death do us part' means something. For me, marriage has always meant 'till divorce do us part.' "

Incensed, she snatched up her blouse, swore, then tossed it aside. "For someone so cynical, I'm surprised you'd consider it."

His mouth quivered as she dragged on his T-shirt. "I'm not cynical, I'm realistic.

Marriage has become like newspapers. You toss them out when you're through, and not a hell of a lot of people bother to recycle."

"Then what's the point?" She yanked on her shorts.

"I'm in love with you." He said it quietly, simply, and stopped her from storming out of the room. "I'd like to think about the idea of starting a life with you, having children, giving some of those traditional trappings a shot."

His words deflated her anger. "Damn you, Finn," she said helplessly.

He grinned up at her. "Then you'll think about it."

20

Dan Gardner didn't marry Angela for her money. Not entirely. Some people were unkind enough to think he had—even to say he had. During the first few weeks of their marriage there was considerable speculation in the tabloid press about the matter, as well as the disparity in their ages: ten years almost to the day. A firm believer in publicity, Dan had planted the articles himself.

But there were other reasons he had married her. He admired her skills. He understood her flaws and, most important to him, how to exploit them. It was he, recognizing her insecurities and her suspicions, who had insisted on signing a prenuptial agreement. Divorce would not benefit him. But Dan wasn't planning on divorce—unless it benefited him. It was he—knowing her weakness for romance and her need to be the center of love—who arranged for candlelit dinners for two, quiet weekends in the country. When she needed attention beyond what he could provide, he arranged for that as well. As Angela became more and more obsessed with eroding ratings, he picked up the threads of several A. P. Production projects and deftly increased the profits.

He might not have married her for her money, but he intended to enjoy it.

"Look at this!" Angela heaved a copy of *TV Guide* across the room. It landed with Deanna's picture faceup. "Just look! 'Daytime's new princess,' my ass." Her silk robe billowed out like a sail as she paced the snowy carpet of her penthouse. " 'Warm and accessible, sexy and sharp.' They fawned over her, Dan. Goddamn it, they gave her the cover and two full pages."

"Don't let it spook you." Because they were staying in for the evening, Dan poured her a full flute of champagne. She was easier to handle when she was drunk and weepy. And when she was needy, the sex was simply stupendous. "She's just got a longer way to fall now, that's all."

"That's not all." Angela snatched the glass away from him. She didn't want to need a drink, but she did and she was in no mood to fight the longing. "You saw the ratings. She's had a twenty-percent share for the last three weeks."

"And you ended up the year as number one," he reminded her.

"It's a new year," she snapped back. "Yesterday doesn't count." She drank deeply, then planted the dainty heel of her feathered mule in Deanna's left eye. "Not so pretty now, are you?" Fueled on envy, she kicked the magazine aside. "No matter what I do she keeps moving up. Now she's getting my press." After draining the glass, she thrust it back at Dan.

"*Angela's* isn't your only interest." Dutifully he refilled the glass for her. "You have the specials, the projects A. P. Productions is involved with. Your interests and your impact are more diverse than hers." He watched her eyes consider as she drank. "She's got one note, Angela. She plays it well, but it's just one note."

The description steadied her quaking heart. "She was always limited, with her little timetables and note cards." But as her fury drained, despair crept into the void. "I don't want her cutting me out, Dan." Her eyes filled, swimming with hot tears as she gulped down champagne. "I don't think I could stand it. Not from her of all people."

"You're making it too personal." Sympathetically, he filled her glass again, knowing that after the third drink she'd be as pliant as a baby with a full tummy.

"It is personal." The tears spilled over, but she let Dan lead her to the couch. She cuddled there on his lap with tangled threads of contentment and unease working through her. It had been the same cuddling on her father's lap on the rare occasions when he had been home and sober. "She wants to hurt me, Dan. She and that bastard Loren Bach. They'd do anything to hurt me."

"No one's going to hurt you." He tipped the glass to her lips the way a mother might urge medicine on a whiny child.

"They know I'm the best."

"Of course they do." Her neediness aroused him. As long as her neuroses bloomed, he was in charge. Setting her glass aside, he parted her robe to nuzzle her breasts. "Just leave everything to me," he murmured. "I'll take care of it."

"Do arguments with your mate end up as war zones, with flying accusations and flying dishes? 'How to Fight Fair,' tomorrow on *Deanna's Hour*."

"Okay, Dee, we need some bumpers for the affiliates."

She rolled her eyes at the assistant director, but dutifully scanned the cue cards. "View the best on Tulsa's best. KJAB-TV, channel nine. Okay, let's run through them."

For the next hour she taped promos for affiliates across the country, tedious chore at best, but one she always agreed to.

When it was done, Fran walked on set with a chilled sixteen-ounce bottle of Pepsi. She waddled a little, heavily pregnant with her second child. "The price of fame," she said.

"I can pay it." Grateful, Deanna took a long, cool drink. "Didn't I tell you to go home early?"

"Didn't I tell you I'm fine? I've got three weeks yet."

"Three more weeks and you won't fit through the doorway."

"What was that?"

"Nothing." Deanna drank again before heading off set. She paused by the large mirror, hooking an arm through Fran's so that they stood side by side. "Don't you think you're a bit bigger than you were when you were carrying Aubrey?"

Fran snuck an M&M into her mouth. "Water weight."

Deanna caught the whiff of candy and lifted a brow. "Sure it couldn't have anything to do with all those chocolate doughnuts you've been scarfing down?"

"The kid has a yen for them. What am I supposed to do? The cravings have to be filtered through me first." Tilting her head, Fran studied her reflection. The new chin-length hair bob might have been flattering, she thought. If her face hadn't looked like an inflated balloon. "Jeez, why did I buy this brown suit? I look like a woolly mammoth."

"You said it, I didn't." Deanna turned toward the elevators, eyeing Fran owlishly as she pressed the button.

"No cracks about weight restrictions, pal." With what dignity she could muster, Fran waddled in and stabbed sixteen. "I can't wait until it's your turn. If you'd just give in and marry Finn, you could start a family. You, too, could experience the joys of motherhood. Swollen feet, indigestion, stretch marks and the ever-popular weak bladder."

"You're making it so appealing."

"The trouble—and the reason I am once again approaching the size of a small planet—is that it is appealing." She pressed a hand to her side as the baby—once again dubbed Big Ed—tried out a one-two punch. "There's nothing quite like it," she murmured. The doors opened. "So, are you going to marry the guy or what?"

"I'm thinking about it."

"You've been thinking about it for weeks." Fran braced a hand on her spine as they walked to Deanna's office.

"He's thinking, too." She knew it sounded defensive. Annoyed, she sailed through the empty outer office into her own. "And things are complicated right now."

"Things are always complicated. People who wait for the perfect moment usually die first."

"That's comforting."

"I wouldn't want to push you."

"Wouldn't you?" Deanna smiled again.

"Nudge, sweetie pie, not push. What's this?" Fran picked up the single white rose that lay across Deanna's desk. "Classy," she said, giving it a sniff. "Romantic. Sweet." She glanced at the plain white envelope still resting on the blotter. "Finn?"

No, Deanna thought, her skin chilled. Not Finn. She struggled for casualness and picked up a pile of correspondence Cassie had typed. "Could be."

"Aren't you going to open the note?"

"Later. I want to make sure Cassie gets these letters out before the end of the day."

"God, you're a tough sell, Dee. If a guy sent me a single rose, I'd be putty."

"I'm busy."

Fran's head jerked up at the change in her tone. "I can see that. I'll get out of your way."

"I'm sorry." Instantly contrite, Deanna reached out. "Really, Fran. I didn't mean to bite your head off. I guess I'm a little wired. The Daytime Emmy business is coming up. That stupid tabloid story about my secret affair with Loren Bach hit last week."

"Oh, honey, you're not letting that get to you. Come on. I think Loren got a kick out of it."

"He can afford to. It didn't make him sound as though he was sleeping his way to a thirty-percent share."

"Nobody believes those things." She huffed at Deanna's expression. "Well, nobody with an IQ in the triple digits. As far as the Emmys go, you've got nothing to worry about there either. You're going to win."

"That's what they keep telling Susan Lucci." But she laughed and waved Fran away. "Get out of here—and go home this time. It's nearly five anyway."

"Talked me into it." Fran laid the rose back on the desk, not noticing Deanna's instinctive recoil. "See you tomorrow."

"Yeah." Alone, Deanna reached cautiously for the envelope She took the ebonny-handled letter opener from her desk set and slit it cleanly open.

DEANNA, I'D DO ANYTHING FOR YOU.
IF ONLY YOU'D LOOK AT ME, REALLY LOOK.
I'D GIVE YOU ANYTHING. EVERYTHING.
I'VE BEEN WAITING SO LONG.

She was beginning to believe the writer meant every word. She slipped the note neatly back into the envelope, opened her bottom desk drawer to place it on the mounting stack of similar messages. Determined to handle the matter practically, she picked up the rose, studying its pale, fragile petals as if they held a clue to the identity of the sender.

Obsession. A frightening word, she thought, yet surely some forms of obsession were harmless enough. Still, the flower was a change in habit. There'd been no tokens before, only the messages in deep red. Surely a rose was a sign of affection, esteem, fragrant and sweet. Yet the thorns marching up the slender stem could draw blood.

Now she was being foolish, she told herself. Rising, she filled a water glass and stuck the rose inside. She couldn't stand to see a beautiful flower wither and die. Still, she set it on a table across the room before she went back to her desk.

For the next twenty minutes, she signed correspondence. She still had the pen in her hand when her intercom buzzed.

"Yes, Cassie."

"It's Finn Riley on two."

"Thanks. I've finished these letters. Can you mail them on your way home?"

"Sure thing."

"Finn? Are you downstairs? I'm sorry, we had a couple of glitches here and I'm running behind." She glanced at her watch, grimaced. "I'll never make dinner at seven."

"Just as well. I'm across town, stuck at a meeting. Looks like I won't make it either."

"I'll cancel, then. We'll eat later." She glanced up at Cassie as the woman slipped the signed correspondence from Deanna's desk. "Cassie, cancel my seven o'clock, will you?"

"All right. Is there anything else you need before I go? You know I can stay to go over those tapes with you."

"No, thanks. See you tomorrow. Finn?"

"Still here."

"I've got some tapes I need to review. Why don't you swing by here and pick me up on the way home? I'll cancel my driver."

"Looks like it'll be about eight, maybe later."

"Later's better. I'll need at least three hours to finish here. I get more done when everyone's gone home anyway. I'll raid Fran's food stash and burrow in until I hear from you."

"If I can't make it, I'll let you know."

"I'll be here. 'Bye."

Deanna replaced the receiver, then swiveled in her chair to face the window.

The sun was already setting, dimming the sky, making the skyline gloomy. She could see lights blinking on, pinpoints against the encroaching dusk.

She imagined buildings emptying out, the freeway filling. At home, people would be switching on the evening news and thinking about dinner.

If she married Finn, they would go home. To their home, not his, not hers.

If she married Finn . . . Deanna toyed with the bracelet she always wore, as much a talisman to her as the cross Finn wore was to him. She would be making a promise of forever if she married him.

She believed in keeping promises.

They would begin to plan a family.

She believed, deeply, in family.

And she would have to find ways, good, solid, clever ways to make it all work. To make all the elements balance.

That was what stopped her.

No matter how often she tried to stop and reason everything out, or how often she struggled to list her priorities and plan of attack, she skittered back like a spooked doe.

She wasn't sure she could make it work.

There wasn't any hurry, she reminded herself. And right now her priority had to be managing that next rung on the ladder.

She glanced at her watch, calculating the time she needed against the time she had. Long enough, she thought, to let herself relax briefly before getting back to work.

Trying one of the stress-reduction techniques she'd learned from a guest on her show, she shut her eyes, drawing long, easy breaths. She was supposed to imagine a door, closed and blank. When she was ready, she was to open that door and step into a scene she found relaxing, peaceful, pleasant.

As always, she opened the door quickly, too quickly, impatient to see what was on the other side.

The porch of Finn's cabin. Spring. Butterflies flitted around the blooming herbs and flowering ground cover of his rock garden. She could hear the sleepy droning of bees hovering around the salmon-colored azalea-she had helped him plant. The sky was a clear, dazzling blue so perfect for dreams.

She sighed, beautifully content. There was music, all strings. A flood of weeping violins flowing through the open windows behind her.

Then she was lying on that soft, blooming lawn, lifting her arms to Finn. The sun haloed around his hair, casting shadows over his face, deepening his eyes until they were so blue she might have drowned in them. Wanted to. And he was in her arms, his body warm and hard, his mouth sure and clever. She could feel her body tighten with need, her skin hum with it. They were moving together, slowly, fluidly, as graceful as dancers, with the blue bowl of the sky above them and the drone of bees throbbing like a pulse.

She heard her name, a whisper twining through the music of the dream. And she smiled and opened her eyes to look at him.

But it wasn't Finn. Clouds had crept over the sun, darkening the sky to ink so that she couldn't see his face. But it wasn't Finn. Even as her body recoiled, he said her name again.

"I'm thinking of you. Always."

She jerked awake, skin clammy, heart thumping. In automatic defense, she wrapped her arms tight around herself to ward off a sudden, violent chill. The hell with meditation, she thought, struggling to shake off the last vestige of the dream. She'd take work-related stress any day. She tried to laugh at herself, but the sound came out more like a sob.

Just groggy, she thought. A little groggy from an unscheduled catnap. But her eyes widened as she stared at her watch. She'd been asleep for nearly an hour.

A ridiculous waste of time, she told herself, and rose from the chair to work out kinks. Work, she told herself firmly, and started to shrug out of her suit jacket as she turned back to her desk.

And there were roses. Two perfectly matched blooms speared up from the water glass in the center of her desk. In instant denial, she stepped forward, her eyes cutting across the room to where she had set the single flower earlier. It was no longer there. No longer there, she thought dully, because it was now on her desk, joined by its mate.

She rubbed the heel of her hand against her breastbone as she stared at the roses. Cassie might have done it, she thought. Or Simon or Jeff or Margaret. Anyone who'd been working late. One of them had found the second rose somewhere and had brought it in, slipped it in with the first. And seeing her sleeping, had simply left them on her desk.

Seeing her sleeping. A shudder ran through her, weakening her legs. She'd been asleep. Alone, defenseless. As she sagged against the arm of the chair, she saw the tape resting on her blotter. She could tell from the manufacturer's label it wasn't the type they used on the show.

No note this time. Perhaps a note wasn't necessary. She thought about running, rushing pell-mell out of the office. There would be people in the newsroom. Plenty of people working the swing between the evening and the late news.

She wasn't alone.

A telephone call would summon security. An elevator ride would take her into the bustle of activity a few floors below.

No, she wasn't alone, and there was no reason to be afraid. There was every reason to play the tape.

She wiped her damp palms on her hips before taking the tape from its sleeve and sliding it into the VCR slot.

The first few seconds after she hit Play were a blank, blue screen. When Deanna watched the picture flicker on, her forehead creased in concentration. She recognized her building, heard the whoosh of traffic through the audio. A few people breezed by on the sidewalk, in shirtsleeves, indicating warm weather.

She watched herself come through the outside door, her hair flowing around her shoulders. Dazed, she lifted a hand, combing her fingers through the short cap. She watched herself check her watch. The camera zoomed in on her face, her eyes smoky with impatience. She could hear, hideously, the sound of the camera operator's unsteady breathing.

A CBC van streaked up to the curb. The picture faded out.

And faded in. She was strolling along Michigan with Fran. Her arms were loaded with shopping bags. She wore a thick sweater and a suede jacket. As she turned her head to laugh at Fran, the picture froze, holding steady on her laughing face until dissolve.

There were more than a dozen clips, snippets of her life. A trip to the market, her arrival at a charity function, a stroll through Water Tower Place, playing with Aubrey in the park, signing autographs at a mall. Her hair short now, her wardrobe indicating the change of seasons.

Through it all, the mood-setting soundtrack of quiet breathing.

The last clip was of her sleeping, curled in her office chair.

She continued to stare after the screen sizzled with snow. Fear had crept back, chilling her blood so that she stood shivering in the slanted light of the desk lamp.

For years he'd been watching her, she thought. Stalking her. Invading small personal moments of her life and making them his. And she'd never noticed.

Now he wanted her to know. He wanted her to understand how close he was. How much closer he could be.

Leaping forward, she fumbled with the Eject button, finally pounded it with her fist. She grabbed her bag, stuffing the tape inside as she dashed from the office. The corridor was dark, shadowy from the backwash of light from her office. A pulse beat in the base of her neck as she dashed to the elevator.

Her breath was sobbing when she pushed the button. She whirled around and pressed her back to the wall, scanning the shadows wildly for movement.

"Hurry, hurry." She pressed a hand to her mouth as her voice echoed mockingly down the empty corridor.

The rumble of the elevator made her jump. Nearly crying out in relief, she spun toward the doors, then fell back when she saw a form move away from the corner of the car and step toward her.

"Hey, Dee. Did I give you a jolt?" Roger stepped closer as the doors slithered closed at his back. "Hey, kid, you're white as a sheet."

"Don't." She cringed back; her eyes flashed toward the fire door leading to the stairs. She would have to get past him. She would get past him.

"Hey, what's going on?" The concern in Roger's voice had her gaze sliding cautiously back to him. "You're shaking. Maybe you'd better sit down."

"I'm fine. I'm leaving now."

"You'd better catch your breath first. Come on. Let's—"

She jerked back, avoiding his hand. "What do you want?"

"Cassie stopped downstairs on her way out." He spoke slowly, letting his hand fall back to his side. "She said you were working late, so I thought I'd come up and see if you wanted to catch some dinner."

"Finn's coming." She moistened her lips. "He'll be here any minute."

"It was just a thought. Dee, is everything okay? Your folks all right?"

A new fear gripped her throat, digging in like talons. "Why? Why do you ask that?"

"You're rattled. I thought you'd gotten some bad news."

"No." Giddy with panic, she edged away. "I've got a lot on my mind." She barely muffled a scream as the elevator rumbled again.

"Jesus, Dee, take it easy." In reflex, he grabbed her arm as she started to race by him toward the stairs. She swung back to fight, and the elevator doors opened.

"What the hell's going on?"

"Oh, God." Tearing free from Roger, Deanna fell into Finn's arms. "Thank God you're here."

His grip tightened protectively as his eyes bored into Roger's. "I said, what the hell's going on?"

"You tell me." Shaken, Roger dragged a hand through his hair. "I came up a minute ago, and she was ready to jump out of her skin. I was trying to find out what happened."

"Did he hurt you?" Finn demanded of Deanna and earned a curse of outrage from Roger.

"No." She kept her face buried against his shoulder. The shaking, the horrible shaking wouldn't stop. She thought she could hear her own bones rattling together. "I was so scared. I can't think. Just take me home."

Finn managed to pry a disjointed explanation from her on the drive home, then, pushing a brandy on her, had watched the tape himself.

She offered no protest when he strode to the phone and called the police. She was calmer when she related the story again. She understood the value of details, of timetables, of clear-cut facts. The detective who interviewed her in Finn's living room sat patiently, jotting in his notepad.

She recognized the gray-haired man from the tape from Greektown—he had snatched the little girl out of the line of fire.

Arnold Jenner was a quiet, meticulous cop. His square face was offset by a nose that had been broken, not on the job but by a line drive during a precinct softball game. He wore a dark brown suit that strained only slightly over the beginnings of a paunch. His hair was caught somewhere between brown and gray and trimmed ruthlessly short. There were lines around his mouth and eyes that indicated he either laughed or frowned easily. His eyes, a pale, sleepy green, should have been as nondescript as the rest of him. But as Deanna stared into them, she was comforted by a sense of trust.

"I'd like to have the letters."

"I didn't save all of them," she told him, and felt ashamed by the tired acceptance in his eyes. "The first few—well, it seemed harmless. On-air reporters get a lot of mail, some of it on the odd side."

"Whatever you have, then."

"I have some at the office, some at my apartment."

"You don't live here?"

"No." She shot a look at Finn. "Not exactly."

"Mmm-hmmm." Jenner made another note. "Miss Reynolds, you said that last portion of tape would have been taken this evening, between five-thirty and six-twenty."

"Yes. I told you, I'd fallen asleep. I was tense, so I thought I'd try this routine a guest on the show had suggested. An imagery, meditation thing." She shrugged, feeling foolish. "I guess it's not my style. I'm either awake or I'm asleep. When I woke up, I saw the second rose on the desk. And the tape."

He made noises in his throat. Like a doctor, Deanna thought.

"Who would have access to your offices at that hour?"

"All manner of people. My own staff, anyone working downstairs."

"So the building would be closed to all but CBC personnel?"

"Not necessarily. The rear door wouldn't be locked at that hour. You'd have people going off shift, others coming on, people picking them up or dropping them off. Sometimes even tours."

"Busy place."

"Yes."

His eyes lifted to hers again, and she realized why they weren't nondescript. He wasn't simply looking at her: he was looking in. Finn had that ability, that same quick, scalpel gaze that cut right through into your thoughts. Perhaps that was why she found him reassuring.

"Is there anyone you can think of? Someone you've rebuffed? Someone who's shown a more than casual or friendly interest in you?"

"No. Really, there's no one I know who would keep doing something like this. I'm sure it's a stranger—a viewer, probably. Otherwise I'd probably have noticed them taping me."

"Well, the way your show's been going, that doesn't narrow the possible suspects." In an old habit, he doodled on his pad. The doodle became Deanna's face, the frightened eyes and the mouth that struggled to curve up. "You do a lot of public appearances. Have you noticed any particular face that keeps showing up?"

"No. I thought of that."

"I'll take the tape with me." He rose then, tucking his notebook neatly in his pocket. "Someone will come by for the notes."

"There's nothing else, is there?" She rose as well. "There's really nothing else."

"You never know what we might pick up from the tape. Sophistication of equipment or some small identifying sound. In the meantime, try not to worry. This kind of thing happens more often than you think." And because she kept trying to smile, he wanted to reassure her. "You hear about the big ones, like that woman who keeps breaking into Letterman's house, but the truth is, it's not just celebrities who have to deal with obsessions. Not too long ago we had this woman focused on this stockbroker. Nice-looking guy, but no Adonis. Anyhow, she called him at work, at home, sent telegrams, left love notes under the windshield wiper of his car. She even had pictures of herself in a wedding dress that she had doctored with one of him in a tux. Showed it to his neighbors to prove they were married."

"What happened?"

"He took out a peace bond on her, and she broke it by camping on his doorstep. She went in for a psychiatric evaluation. When she got out, she decided she wasn't in love with the stockbroker anymore. Claims she divorced him."

"So the moral is, sometimes these things run their course."

"Could be. Thing is, some people don't have as firm a grip on reality as they might. You'd probably feel better if you tightened up your security a little."

"I'll do that. Thank you, Detective Jenner."

"I'll be in touch. A real pleasure meeting you, Miss Reynolds, and you, Mr. Riley. I've spent a lot of time with the two of you in my living room."

"So, that's that," she said as she closed the door behind Jenner.

"Not by a long shot." Finn took her firmly by the shoulders. He hadn't interrupted her interview with Jenner. But now it was his turn. "You're not working late alone anymore."

"Really, Finn—"

"That's not negotiable, so don't give me grief on this. Do you know what went through me when I saw you standing in the hall, terrified, fighting off Crowell?"

"He was trying to help," she began, then closed her eyes and sighed. "Yes, yes, I think I do know. I'm sorry. I'll bring work home when I have to."

"Until this thing is resolved, you need twenty-four-hour protection."

"A bodyguard?" She would have laughed if she wasn't afraid he'd take a chunk out of her. "Finn, I won't work late in the building. I'll even make sure I have a buddy when I go on any remotes or appearances. But I'm not hiring some thug named Reno to lurk over me."

"It's not unusual for a woman in your position to hire private security."

"Whatever my position, I'm still Deanna Reynolds from Topeka, and I refuse to have some big-shouldered hulk frighten off the people I'm trying to reach. I couldn't stand it, Finn. That's just too Hollywood for me. I'm not taking this lightly," she continued. "Believe me, I'm going to take very serious care of myself. But I haven't been threatened."

"You've been spied on, followed, taped, harassed by anonymous notes and phone calls."

"And it frightens me, I admit it. You were right about the police. I should have called them before. Now that you have, I feel like the whole situation has been put in the right compartment. Let's give them a chance to do what we pay them for."

Frustrated, he stalked down the hall and back. "A compromise," he said at length. "Christ, I'm always digging up compromises for you."

Judging the storm was blowing over, she moved in to wrap her arms around him. "That's why our relationship is so healthy. What's the compromise—a bodyguard named Sheila?"

"You move in here. I'm not budging on this, Deanna. Keep your place; I don't care. But you live here, with me."

"Funny." In a subtle peace treaty, she pressed a kiss to his cheek. "I was going to suggest the same solution."

He tipped her face up to his. He wanted to ask, badly, if she was agreeing because she was frightened or because she needed him. But he didn't ask. "What about when I'm out of town?"

"I've been thinking about asking you how you felt about dogs." Her lips curved against his. "We could go by the pound this weekend. With so many abandoned animals, it seems the right route."

21

Awards were not important. Quality work and the satisfaction of a job well done were their own reward. Statues and speeches were nothing more than industry hype.

Deanna didn't believe any of it.

For a girl from Kansas whose first on-the-air job had been reporting on a dog show, alighting from a limo in Los Angeles as an Emmy nominee was a thrill. And she didn't mind admitting it.

The day was perfect. There was bound to be smog, but she didn't see it. The sky was the deep, dreamy blue of a watercolor painting, dazzled by the brilliant white sun. A balmy breeze teased the elegant gowns and carefully coiffed hair of the attendees and wafted the scents of perfume and flowers over the enthusiastic crowd.

"I can't believe I'm here." It took all of her willpower not to bounce on the seat of the limo like a kid at the circus. Then she gave up and bounced anyway.

"You've earned it." Charmed by her, Finn took her hand and brought it to his lips.

"I know that, up here." She tapped her temple. "But in here"—she laid her hand on her heart—"I'm afraid someone's going to pinch me and I'll wake up and realize it's only a dream. Ouch."

"See, you're awake." He grinned as she rubbed her forearm. "And you're still here."

However giddy she felt, she slid gracefully from the limo, tossing her head up as she straightened and scanned the crowd. The sun glinted off her short, beaded gown and scattered light.

Finn thought she'd chosen well; the strapless column of glittery scarlet made her look young and fresh and every inch the star. Several people in the crowd recognized her instantly and shouted her name.

Their reaction obviously surprised her, he realized with a hint of a smile. She looked dazed, then dazzled, then delighted. She waved back, not with the careless insouciance of a seasoned veteran, but with genuine pleasure and enthusiasm.

"I feel like I'm walking into a movie." She chuckled as she linked hands with Finn. "No, like I'm walking out of the last reel, and I've got the hero."

He pleased her, and the crowd, by kissing her. Not just a friendly peek but a deep, lingering embrace that gave the paparazzi plenty of fuel. They stood a moment in the flashing sun, a picture-perfect couple in evening dress. "That was because you're beautiful." He kissed her again to the eruption of cheers. "And that's for luck."

"Thanks. On both counts."

They started toward the building, where fans and onlookers had been parted like the Red Sea by police barricades. Celebrities and press were mingling, creating quick bites that would be shown on the evening news segments.

She knew some of these people, Deanna thought. Some had come on her show, had sat beside her and chatted like old friends. Others she had met during the benefits and events that became part of the job. She exchanged greetings and good wishes, cheek busses and handclasps as they wandered toward the lobby.

Mikes slashed out at them, cameras wheeled in their direction, impeding progress.

"Deanna, how does it feel to be here tonight?"

"Who designed your dress?"

"Finn, what's it like to have a hit show when so many news magazines have failed?"

"Any marriage plans?"

"Christ, it's like an obstacle course," Finn muttered as they worked their way through the gaggle of reporters.

"I'm loving every minute of it." She eased closer, eyes dancing. "Don't you know when they ask about your dress designer, you've made it?"

"They didn't ask me."

She turned, fussing with his tie. "And you look so nice, too. Very GQ."

He grimaced. "Please. I can't believe I got talked into doing that photo layout."

"It was smashing."

"I'm a newscaster, not a model."

"But you have such cute dimples."

They didn't flash. They didn't so much as wink as he cornered her with one steely-eyed glare. "Keep that up and I'll leak the news that you changed your underwear three times before getting into that dress tonight."

"Okay, they're not cute. No matter what Mary Hart said last week on *ET*."

"She said—never mind." No way was he going to get pulled into that one. "Let's get a drink before we go in."

"Considering the occasion, it'll have to be champagne. Just one," she added, pressing a hand to her middle. "I don't think my system can handle any more."

"Wait here. I'll fight the horde."

"I told you you were my hero."

She turned, and would have scooted off into a corner, where she could stand and observe, but she found herself face to face with Kate Lowell.

"Hello, Dee."

"Hello, Kate." Deanna offered a hand and they shook like strangers. "It's good to see you."

"It doesn't feel as though you mean it," she said as she straightened her shoulders. "You look terrific, ready to win."

"I hope so."

"I'd like to wish you luck. Really excellent luck, considering your competition."

"Thanks."

"Don't. It's purely selfish on my part. By the way, Rob Winters said to send his best if I ran into you."

Deanna's stiff smile softened. "How is he?"

"Dying," Kate said shortly, then let out a breath between her teeth. "Sorry. We've been friends for a long time, and it's hard to watch."

"You don't have to apologize. I understand about friendships and loyalties."

Kate dropped her gaze. "Direct hit, Dee."

"Cheap shot," she corrected. Instinctively she took Kate's hand again. There was none of the mannered politeness this time. Just support, basic and unstudied. "I can't even imagine what it must be like for you."

Kate studied their joined hands, remembered how easy it had once been. "Dee, why didn't you announce Rob's condition when he told you about it?"

"Because he asked me not to."

Kate shook her head. "That was always enough for you. I'd wondered if you'd changed."

"I have, but that hasn't."

"I really hope you win tonight. I hope you cut her off at the knees." With this, she turned and walked away.

As Deanna watched the other woman walk through the crowd, she thought she understood the tears she'd seen in Kate's eyes, but not the venom in her voice.

"Well, we have come up in the world." Angela glided into Deanna's line of vision, a frothy dream of candy-pink silk and icy diamonds. "Smile for the camera, dear," she whispered as she leaned forward to air-kiss both of Deanna's cheeks. "Surely you haven't forgotten everything I taught you."

"I haven't forgotten a thing." Deanna let her lips curve up. She hated the fact that her stomach jittered with nerves. Hated more the fact that they were bound to show. "It's been a long time."

"It certainly has. I don't believe you've met my husband. Dan, this is Deanna Reynolds."

"A pleasure." As polished as a fine gem, Dan took Deanna's hand in his. "You're every bit as charming as Angela told me."

"I'm sure she told you nothing of the kind, but thanks. I saw your pre-Emmy special last night, Angela. I enjoyed it."

"Did you?" Angela held up a cigarette for Dan to light. "I have so little time to watch television myself these days."

"That's interesting. I'd think that would insulate you from your audience. I love to watch. I suppose I'm really the average viewer."

"Average isn't something I'd settle for." Angela's gaze shifted over Deanna's shoulder, smoldered. "Hello, Finn. Isn't it interesting that we'd all have to come to Los Angeles to have a reunion?"

"Angela." Smoothly, he passed Deanna her glass of champagne, then slipped an arm around her waist. "You're looking well."

"He used to be much more clever with his compliments," Angela told Dan. She made the rest of the introductions and, spotting a camera out of the corner of her eye, angled herself into a prominent position. "I really must powder my nose before we go in. Deanna, come along with me. No woman goes to the ladies' room alone."

Though Finn tightened his grip, Deanna eased away. "Sure." Better to face whatever unpleasantness Angela had in mind now, she decided, than wait for it to be played out in public. "Finn, I'll meet you inside in a minute."

To offer the camera a friendly tableau, Angela hooked her arm through Deanna's. "We haven't had one of our private talks for ages, have we?"

"It would be a little tough, since we haven't seen each other in two years."

"Always so literal." With a light laugh, Angela swung into the ladies' lounge. It was nearly empty, as she'd hoped. Later it would be full, but now people were eager to be seated. She walked to the mirrored counter, pulled out a chair and did exactly what she'd said she would do. She powdered her nose. "You've chewed off most of your lipstick," she said dryly. "Nervous?"

"Excited." Deanna remained standing, but set her glass aside to dig a lipstick out of her evening bag. "I imagine that's a natural reaction to being nominated."

"It becomes routine after a while. I have several awards, you know. Interesting that you've been nominated for that show on date rape. I'd considered that more of a self-confessional hour, not a mix of views." Angela patted her hair, searching for any out-of-place strands as she turned her face side to side. "I imagine Finn will cop one of the prime-time statues himself when they come out. He's well liked in the industry, and he's been able to create a show that appeals to the news buffs as well as the viewer looking for entertainment."

"I thought you didn't watch television."

Angela's eyes sharpened. It surprised Deanna that their reflection didn't leave slices on the glass. "I glance at something now and then, if I think it might interest me. Of course, Finn has always interested me." Slowly, with relish, she glided her tongue over her lips. "Tell me, do his eyes still go that wicked cobalt shade when he's aroused?" She dabbed perfume at her wrists. "You do manage to arouse him occasionally, don't you?"

"Why don't you ask him?"

"I may do that—if I get him alone. Then again, if I get him alone, he might forget all about you." Smiling, she twirled up a spiral of hot pink lipstick. "So what would be the point?"

Deanna wasn't nervous any longer, she was simply irked. "The point might be that you're married, and that Finn stopped being interested in you a long time ago."

"Do you really believe that?" Angela's laugh was as brisk and chilly as a puff of December air. "Darling, if I decided to have an affair with Finn—and Dan's a very understanding man, so my marriage is no obstacle—he'd not only be willing, he'd be grateful."

Moving beyond irked, Deanna felt little knots of tension twine in her stomach, but her smile came easily. "Angela." There was a laugh in her voice. "Trying to make me jealous is a waste of time. You had sex with Finn. I know that. And I'm not naive enough to imagine he didn't find you tremendously attractive and alluring. But what I have with him now is on an entirely different level. You're only embarrassing yourself by trying to convince me he's like some trained mutt who'll come running if you snap your fingers."

Angela slapped the lid on the lipstick. "You're very cool, aren't you?"

"No, not really. I'm just happy." She sat then, hoping they could bury at least the sharpest edge of the hatchet. "Angela, we were friends once—or at least friendly. I'm grateful for the opportunity you gave me to learn and observe. Maybe the time's passed where we can be friendly, but I don't see why we have to snipe at each other. We're competitors, but there's more than enough room for both of us."

"Do you think you can compete with me?" Angela began to shake, from her shoulders down to her spine. "Do you really think you can come close to what I've achieved, to what I have, to what I'm going to have?"

"Yes," Deanna said, and rose. "Yes, I do. And I don't have to resort to planting lies in the tabloids or low-level espionage to do it. You've been in the business long enough to tolerate a little heat, Angela."

"You cocky bitch. I'll bury you."

"No, you won't." Her pulse was drumming now, a primitive tom-tom rhythm that pumped through her blood in anticipation of a fight. "You're going to have a hell of a time keeping up with me."

On a cry of outrage, Angela snatched the champagne flute and tossed the contents in Deanna's face. Two women who entered the room froze like statues as Angela followed up with a vicious slap.

"You're nothing," Angela shrieked, her face as pink as the silk she wore. "Less than nothing. I'm the best. The fucking best."

She lunged, fingers curled and extended like claws. With a haze of fury misting her vision, Deanna struck out, her open palm cracking Angela's flushed cheek. In an instant all movement froze. For once at least, they were both on equal terms. Horrified, the two women in the doorway gasped in unison and stared.

"Ladies, excuse us." Kate Lowell stepped out from the stalls to the lounge, and motioned to the women. They flew out again, obviously in a hurry to bear tidings. "Well, well, and I thought all the competition was going to be out there."

Dazed, Deanna stared down at her hand, which was still burning from the blow it had delivered. She blinked against the champagne stinging her eyes. "Oh hell."

Kate nodded to the outside door, still swinging from the exit of the other women. "It's going to make an interesting sidebar in tomorrow's Daytime Emmy coverage." She smiled suddenly, a brilliant flash of perfect teeth. "Would you like me to referee?"

"Stay out of this." Teeth clenched, Angela took a step toward Deanna. She'd been humiliated now, publicly. That, above all, was intolerable. "And you stay out of my way. You've crossed the line."

"I didn't turn the other cheek," Deanna returned, "and I don't intend to. So why don't we try to stay out of each other's way?"

"You won't win tonight." With a hand that continued to tremble, Angela picked up her bag. "Or ever."

"Lousy exit line," Kate mused as the door swung shut behind Angela.

"I don't know. It had potential." Deanna closed her stinging eyes. "What now?"

"Clean yourself up." Kate moved forward briskly to run cold water on a snowy washcloth. "Put yourself back together and get out there."

"I lost my temper," she began, then caught sight of herself in the mirror. "Oh Jesus." Her cheeks were suffused with heat, dripping with wine. Her eyes were smoldering and smudged with mascara.

"Put the image back on," Kate advised, handing her the damp cloth. "And when you walk out, walk out with a smile."

"I think I should—" Braced for the worst, she spun toward the door as it swung open. Her already hot cheeks fired further as Finn strolled in.

"I beg your pardon, ladies, but as a reporter it's my duty to ask what the hell's going on in here. Somebody said—" He broke off, taking in the scene with one pithy glance. "Christ, Kansas, I can't leave you alone for a minute." He sighed, picked up one of the dry, fluffy hand towels on the counter and offered it. "I didn't think that was a maidenly blush I noticed on Angela's cheek. Which one of you slugged her?"

"The pleasure was Deanna's."

He leaned over to kiss her damp cheek. "Nice going, champ." He touched his tongue to her lip. "You're supposed to drink the champagne, baby, not wear it."

Deanna set her shoulders and turned back to the mirror to deal with the damage. She would not be cowed, she promised herself. She simply would not be. "Just keep everyone out for five minutes, will you?"

"Your category's coming up," he said casually as he headed for the door.

"I'll be there."

She was, makeup freshened, hair fluffed, nerves raw. She sat beside Finn, her hand clenched spasmodically over his. Out of camera range, she hoped.

Her mind was as keen as a sword as she watched the presenters breeze or fumble their way through scripted jokes and into lists of nominees. She applauded politely, or occasionally with enthusiasm, as winners were announced and made their way to the stage.

She filed every instant, every gesture, every word in her memory. Because it mattered now, horribly. She'd lost a good deal of the sweet excitement she'd felt when they'd rolled up in the limo. No, she thought, she wasn't just the kid from Kansas now, dazzled by the lights and the luminaries. She was Deanna Reynolds, and she belonged.

It wasn't simply an award any longer, a pat on the back for a job well done.

Now it was a symbol. The culmination of what had started so long ago. It was a symbol of triumph over the deceit, the manipulations, the ugly intrigue that had flashed into pathetic spite in a ladies' washroom.

The camera was on her. She could feel that cool, objective eye focus in. She could only hope that for once her emotions weren't so clearly mirrored on her face. She heard Angela's name announced, then her own.

She couldn't catch her breath. Then Finn lifted their joined hands to his lips and the sharpest edge of tension smoothed.

"And the Emmy goes to . . ."

God, how could it take so long to open one envelope?

"Deanna Reynolds, for *Deanna's Hour*, 'When You Know Him.' "

"Oh." All the breath that had backed up in her lungs came out in that one long sound. Before she could take another, Finn's mouth was over hers.

"I never had a doubt."

"Me neither," she lied, and was laughing as she rose out of the chair to walk through the applause to the stage.

The award was cool and smooth in her hands. And solid as stone. She was afraid if she looked at it, she'd weep. Instead she looked out into the lights.

"I want to thank my team, every one of them. They're the best. And I want to thank the women who appeared on the show, who battled back their fears to bring a painful subject out of the dark. I can't think of any show I've done, or will do, that could be as difficult or as rewarding for me. Thank you for giving me something to remind me. Now I'm going backstage to stare at this beautiful lady."

After the speeches, the applause, the interviews and the parties, Deanna lay propped up in bed, resting in the curve of Finn's shoulder. Casually, she crossed her feet at the ankles.

"I think mine's prettier than your National Press Award," she said.

"Mine's more professional."

She pursed her lips, studying the gold statue standing on the bureau. "Mine's shinier."

"Deanna." He turned his head to kiss her temple. "You're gloating."

"Yep. And I'm going to keep right on gloating. You've won all sorts of awards, Overseas Press Club, the George Polk. You can afford to be jaded."

"Who says I'm jaded? And when I win my Emmy it'll be every bit as shiny as your Emmy."

With a delighted laugh, she rolled over to lie on top of him. "I won. I didn't want to admit how badly I wanted that statue. After that scene with Angela, I felt I had to win. For me, yes, but also for everybody who works with me. When they called my name, I was flying. Really flying. It was great."

"An interesting evening all around." He ran a hand down her spine, enjoying the way her body curved to his touch. "Tell me again how you demolished her."

Deanna's lashes fluttered down. "I did not demolish her. It was a particularly effective but ladylike slap."

"Like hell." Grinning, he tipped her face up, then laughed out loud at the unholy glee in her eyes.

"I shouldn't be proud of it." She chuckled and sat up to straddle him, her body pale and naked. "But for just an instant, before I was horrified, I felt wonderful. Then I was numb, then I was furious all over again." She linked her fingers, lifting her arms up high. "Besides, she started it."

"And you finished it. You can count on her coming after you with both barrels now."

"Let her. I feel invulnerable. Impervious." She stretched high. "Incredible. It just can't get any better than this."

"Yes, it can." To prove it, he reared up, running a line of kisses up her torso. Her soft sigh glided through him. Her hands fluttered down to cradle his head.

"You might be right."

The sky was pearling with dawn, chasing the shadows from the room. Her body arched back, already fluid and ready for his. They had loved once in delirious haste, and now moved together slowly, letting the needs smolder and the air spark.

Gliding fingertips, whispering sighs, quiet urgings for more. Torso to torso they pressed together, tangled sheets pooled around them and morning sliding softly into the room. A touch, a taste, a subtle shift in rhythm. They lowered together to roll lazily over the bed, length to length.

No rush, no hurry. Quiet explosions shuddered through her blood, then streamed away like silk until others built. Her mouth sought his, sighs merging, tongues dancing. Even when he slipped into her, filling her, the flash of heat was as comforting as a sunbeam.

Across town there was another hotel room bed that hadn't been slept in, or loved in. Angela sat on the edge of it, her robe held protectively over her breasts. The dress she had worn was a tattered heap of silk on the floor, a victim of her temper.

Most of that temper was spent now, and she huddled like a child on the big bed, fighting back tears.

"It doesn't mean anything, honey." Dan urged champagne on her, the equivalent to a kiss where it hurt. "Everybody knows the fucking awards are a sham."

"People watch." She stared straight ahead, sipping the wine she'd ordered chilled for celebration and now served as commiseration. "Thousands of people, Dan. They saw her walk up there, when it should have been me. They saw her pick up my award. My award, goddamn her."

"And they'll forget about it tomorrow." He stifled both impatience and disgust. The only way to handle Angela, and to keep them both riding high, was to cajole, flatter and lie. "Nobody remembers who got what when the glitter fades."

"I remember." She tossed up her head, and her face was icy again, eerily controlled.

"I remember. She's not getting away with it. With any of it. I'm going to do whatever it takes to make her pay. For the slap, for the award. Everything."

"We'll talk about it later." He'd already gotten word on the incident in the lounge. Too many people—people who couldn't be easily bought off—had heard that Angela struck first. "Now you've got to relax. You have to look your best when we fly home later today."

"Relax?" she spat at him. "Relax? Deanna Reynolds is getting my press, my ratings, now my awards." And there was Finn. Oh, no, she wouldn't forget Finn. "How the hell can you tell me to relax?"

"Because you can't win if you look like a resentful has-been." He watched her eyes flare with fury, then chill to an icy gleam.

"How dare you speak to me that way? And tonight of all nights."

"I'm telling you this for your own good," he continued, assured he had the upper hand when her lips trembled. "You need to project dignity, maturity, confidence."

"She's ruining my life. It's just like when I was a kid. Someone was always taking what I wanted."

"You're not a kid anymore, Angela. And there'll be other awards."

She wanted *this* award. But she held the words back. He'd only become more remote and disgusted. She needed him beside her, supporting her, believing in her. "You're right. Absolutely right. Tomorrow, in public, I will be gracious, humble and dignified. And believe me, Deanna Reynolds is not going to win another award that should be mine." Forcing a smile, she reached out a hand and drew him down beside her. "I'm just so disappointed, Dan. For both of us. You worked just as hard as I did for that Emmy."

"We'll work harder for the next one." Relieved, he kissed the top of her head.

"Sometimes it takes more than work. God knows I've had plenty of experience there." She sighed and drank again. She'd drink all she wanted tonight, she promised herself. At least she deserved that much. "When I was a kid I did all the chores around the house. Otherwise we would have lived in a pigsty. I've always liked things to look right, to look pretty. To look the best they can. I started doing cleaning for other people. Did I ever tell you that?"

"No." Surprised that she had now, he rose to fetch the bottle. He topped off her glass. "You don't like to talk about your childhood. I understand that."

"I'm in the mood for it." She sipped again, gesturing toward her cigarettes. Obligingly, Dan picked them up, lighted one for her. "I earned extra money that way, so I could buy things. My own things. But I earned more than money. You know . . ." She took a contemplative drag. "It's amazing what people leave lying around their homes, tucked into drawers, closed in boxes. I was always curious about people. That's why I ended up in this business, I suppose. And I found out a lot about the people I worked for. Things they preferred to be kept private. I might mention to a certain married woman the name of a man not her husband. Then I might admire some earrings, or a bracelet, or a dress." Through the haze of smoke, she smiled at the memory. "It was magical how quickly what I admired became mine. Just for doing the small favor of keeping information to myself."

"You started young," Dan observed. Her voice was only a little slurred, so he added more wine to her glass.

"I had to. Nobody was going to fight for me. Nobody was going to lift me out of that hellhole I lived in but me. Mama drunk; Daddy off gambling or whoring."

"It was tough on you."

"It made me tough," she corrected. "I watched the way people lived, and I saw what I wanted. I found ways to get what I wanted. I improved myself and I broke my back to be the best. No one's going to take me off the top of the heap, Dan. Certainly not Deanna Reynolds."

He tipped her face back for a kiss. "That's the Angela I know and love."

She smiled. Her head felt light, dizzy, her body free. Why, she wondered, had she been so afraid of relaxing with a bottle or two? "Prove it," she invited, and slipped the robe off her shoulders.

22

The snow outside the cabin was fairy-tale white. Rocks and shrubs caused the white covering to heave into mounds and bumps so that it resembled a blanket under which dozens of elves might burrow, waiting for spring. No cloud marred the eerie, icy blue of the sky, and the sun glinted off the glossy bark of trees.

From the window, Deanna watched Finn and Richard help Aubrey build a snowman. In her bright blue snowsuit, the toddler looked like a little exotic bird who'd lost her way going south. Curling tendrils of hair, as red as a cardinal's wing, escaped from her cap.

Beside her the men were giants, bulky in their heavy coats and boots. She watched as Richard showed Aubrey how to pat and mold a snowball. He pointed at Finn, and with a giggle that carried through the glass, Aubrey bounced it lightly off Finn's knee, but he crumpled convincingly to the ground as if hit by a boulder.

The dog, the mop-haired mongrel Finn and Deanna had dubbed Cronkite, sent up a din of barks and a shower of snow in his desperation to join the game.

"Sounds like quite a snowman." Fran shifted her infant daughter from her right to her left breast. Kelsey latched on, suckling happily.

"They've started a small war," Deanna reported. "Casualties are light, but it looks to be an extended battle."

"You can go out and spend some of that nervous energy. You don't have to stay in here with me."

"No, I like watching. I'm so glad all of you could come up for the weekend."

"Since it's the first free one you've had in six weeks, I'm amazed you'd share it."

"Getting away with friends is one of those luxuries I've had to do without too much." She sighed a little. There was no use thinking about all the weekends, the holidays, the quiet evenings at home she'd missed. She had what she'd asked for. "I've discovered I need things like this to keep me centered."

"Glad to help. Richard found the idea of fishing in this weather just primitive and macho enough to pique his interest. As for me"—she stroked her daughter's cheek as she rocked gently in the chair Finn had hauled in from the porch and scrubbed down for just that purpose—"I was ready to go anywhere. When we get snow this early in November, it's going to be a long winter."

"And not a particularly pleasant one." Fran was right about the nervous energy, Deanna realized. She could feel it swirling inside—white water in the bloodstream. Deanna turned away from the window to sit on the hearth, where the fire crackled hot and brightly behind her. "I feel like I've been under siege, Fran. All this—this tabloid crap about Angela and me brawling in the ladies' lounge at the Emmys."

"Honey, most of that's died down, and everyone knew it was crap to begin with."

"Most everyone." Restless, she rose again, prowling. "All those sly allegations in the press about her bearing up stoically after I supposedly refused her offer of friendship. Friendship, my butt." She shoved her hands in her pockets, dragged them out again to gesture. "And that nasty undertone of glee in some of the stories. 'Talk show divas in cat fight.' 'Claws bared in ladies' room.' And it was just close enough to the truth to make us both look like idiots. Of course, Loren couldn't be happier. The ratings have skyrocketed since the Emmys, and there's no sign of a downswing. People who couldn't care less about the content of the show are tuning in to see if I lose it and punch out a guest."

Fran snickered, then caught Deanna's quick glare. "Sorry."

"I wish I could think it was funny." Grabbing the poker, she stabbed viciously at the flaming logs. "I did think it was funny, until I started getting letters."

"Oh, Dee, the majority of the mail has been supportive, even flattering."

"So I'm perverse." Her shoulders jerked. Oh, she hated the fact that she was being a fool. Hated more that she couldn't seem to stop thinking about the whole ugly incident. "I keep remembering the ones that weren't. The ones that ranged from 'You should be ashamed of yourself,' to 'You should be horsewhipped for your lack of gratitude to a fragile little flower like Angela Perkins.' " Her narrowed eyes were as hot as the flames. "Belladonna probably looks like a fragile little flower."

"I wouldn't know." Fran shifted the baby to her shoulder. "Most of that's blown over. Why don't you tell me what's really eating at you?"

Deanna gave the fire one last poke. "I'm scared." She said it quietly, as a fresh frisson of ice skated up her spine. "I got another note."

"Oh God. When?"

"Friday, right after I spoke to the literacy group at the Drake."

"Cassie was with you."

"Yes." Deanna rubbed at the dull ache at the back of her neck. "I don't seem to go anywhere alone anymore. Always an entourage."

"Cassie's hardly an entourage." But Fran recognized the twist of topic as avoidance. "Tell me about the note, Dee."

"We ran a little long with the photo session afterward. Cassie left—she had a few things she wanted to finish up at the office before the weekend."

She flashed back to it, the scene as clear in her mind as a film loop. Another handshake, another snick of the camera shutter. People crowding around for a word, for a look.

"Just one more picture, Deanna, please. You and the mayor's wife."

"*Just* one more." Cassie spoke up, her smile amiable, her voice firm. "Miss Reynolds is already running late for her next appointment."

Deanna remembered feeling amusement. Her next appointment, thankfully, was throwing a few sweaters into her suitcase and heading out of the city.

She posed again, with the mayor's wife and the plaque for her work for literacy, then eased her way along, with Cassie running interference.

"Good job, Dee. Here, let me take that." Cassie slipped the plaque into her briefcase while Deanna bundled into her coat.

"It didn't feel like a job. They were great."

"They were—you were." Cassie cast a leery eye over her shoulder. The elegant lobby of the Drake was still crowded with people. "But take my word on this. Just keep walking and don't look back or you won't get out of here until midnight." To hurry her along, Cassie took her arm and led Deanna out of the lobby and onto the sidewalk. "Listen, I'm going to take a cab back to the office."

"Don't be silly. Tim can drop you off."

"Then you'll think of something you just have to do while you're there. Go home," Cassie ordered. "Pack, leave. Don't show your face in this town until Sunday night."

It sounded too good to argue. "Yes, ma'am."

Laughing, Cassie kissed her cheek. "Have a great weekend."

"You too."

They parted there, heading in opposite directions through the snapping wind and swirling snow.

"Sorry I'm late, Tim."

"No problem, Miss Reynolds." With his long black coat flapping around his knees, Tim opened the door of the limo. "How'd it go?"

"Fine. Really fine, thanks."

Still glowing with the energy of a job well done, she slipped inside the cushy warmth.

And there it was. Just that plain envelope, a square of white against the burgundy leather seat. . . .

"I asked Tim if someone had come up to the car," Deanna continued, "but he hadn't seen anyone. It was cold and he'd gone inside the building for a while. He said the car was locked, and I know how conscientious Tim is, so I'm sure it was."

Too many notes, Fran thought, as her stomach muscles juggled. And they were coming too often in the last couple of months. "Did you call the police?"

"I called Lieutenant Jenner from the car phone. I don't have any control over this." Her voice rose as much in frustration as fear. And it helped, she realized, to have something, anything other than fear coursing through her. "I can't analyze it and put it in a slot. I can't tidy it up or toss it away." Determined to calm herself, she rubbed her hands over her face as if she could massage away the panic. "I can't even discuss this rationally. Every time I remind myself that I haven't been threatened, I haven't been hurt, I feel this little bubble of hysteria building up. He finds me everywhere. I want to beg him to leave me alone. To just leave me alone. Fran," she said helplessly, "I'm a mess."

Fran got up to lay Kelsey in the playpen. She crossed to take Deanna's hands in hers. There was more than comfort in the contact—anger simmered just beneath. "Why haven't you told me this before? Why haven't you let me know how much this is upsetting you?"

"You've got enough to handle. Aubrey, the new baby."

"So you took pity on the new mother and pretended that you were shrugging this whole business off as a by-product of fame?" Suddenly furious, Fran slapped both hands on her hips. "That's crap, Dee. Insulting crap."

"I didn't see the point in worrying you," Deanna shot back. "There's so much stuff going on right now—the show, the backlash from Angela; Margaret's teenager wrecked the car, Simon's mother died." Despising the need to defend herself, she turned back to the window. "Finn's going off to Haiti next week." Outside the dog leaped at flying snowballs. Deanna wanted to weep. Resting her head on the cool glass, she waited until her system leveled. "I thought I could handle it myself. I wanted to handle it myself."

"What about Finn?" Fran walked over to rub her hand over Deanna's stiff back. "Does he have a clue what's going on inside you right now?"

"He has a lot on his mind."

Fran didn't bother to repress a disgusted snort. "Which means you've been playing the same game with him. Did you tell him about this last note?"

"It seemed best to wait until he got back from this next trip."

"It's selfish."

"Selfish?" Her voice cracked in surprised hurt. "How can you say that? I don't want him worried about me when he's thousands of miles away."

"He *wants* to worry about you. Jesus, Dee, how can anyone so sensitive, so compassionate, be so obstinate? You've got a man out there who loves you. Who wants to share everything with you, good and bad. He deserves to know what you're feeling. If you love him half as much as he loves you, you've got no right to keep things from him."

"That wasn't what I meant to do."

"It's what you are doing. It's unfair to him, Dee. Just like—" She cut herself off, swearing. "I'm sorry." But her voice was stiff and cool. "It's none of my business how you and Finn deal with your relationship."

"No, don't stop now," Deanna said, equally cool. "Finish it. Just like what?"

"All right, then." Fran took a deep breath. Their friendship had lasted more than ten years. She hoped it would weather one more storm. "It's unfair for you to ask him to put his own needs on hold."

"I don't know what you mean."

"For God's sake, look at him, Dee. Look at him with Aubrey." She clamped her hand on Deanna's arm and pushed her back to the window. "Take a good look."

She did, watching Finn spin Aubrey around and around, snow spewing up at his feet. The child's delighted shrieks echoed like a song.

"That man wants a family. He wants you. You're denying him both because you haven't got everything neatly stacked in place. That's not just selfish, Dee. It's not just unfair. It's sad." When Deanna said nothing, she turned away. "I've got to change the baby." Gathering Kelsey up, she left the room.

Deanna stood where she was for a long time. She could see Finn wrestling with the dog as Aubrey leaped into her father's arms to slide a ragged cap onto the top of the big-bellied snowman.

But she could see more. Finn crossing the tarmac in a torrent of rain, a cocky grin on his face and a swagger in his step. Finn exhausted and asleep on her couch, or laughing as she reeled in her first fat fish. Gentle and sweet as he took her to bed. Gritty-eyed and grim as he returned from observing some fresh disaster.

He was always there, she realized. Always.

She went through the motions that evening, serving up big bowls of beef stew, laughing at Richard's jokes. If someone had peeked in the kitchen window, they would have seen a jolly group of friends sharing a meal. Attractive people, comfortable with one other. It would have been difficult to spot any tension, any discord.

But Finn was a trained observer. Even had that not been the case, he could judge Deanna's moods by the flick of an eyelash.

He hadn't questioned her about the tension he sensed, hoping she would tell him on her own. As the evening wore on, he accepted, impatiently, that he would have to push. Perhaps he would always have to push.

He watched her settle down in the living room, a smile on her face. Unhappiness in her eyes.

God, the woman frustrated him. Fascinated him. For almost two years they had been lovers, as physically intimate as it was possible to be. Yet no matter how open she was, how honest, she managed to tuck away little pieces. Closing them off from him, locking them tight and hoarding them.

She was doing it now, he realized.

Her hand might reach for his, holding it with comfortable familiarity. But her mind was elsewhere, methodically working through a problem she refused to share.

Her problem, she would say in that reasonable tone that by turns infuriated and amused him. Nothing she couldn't handle on her own. Nothing she needed him to deal with.

Hurt, Finn set his glass aside and slipped upstairs.

He built up the fire in the bedroom, brooding over it. He wondered how long he could wait for Deanna to take the next step. Forever, he thought, with an oath. She was as much a part of him as his muscle and bone.

The need that had been growing in him for family, for a steady, rooted life, was nothing compared with his need for her.

What was much worse, as well as totally unexpected, was that he wanted, quite desperately, for her to need him.

A new one for Riley, he mused, and wished he could see the humor in this realization. The need to be needed, to be tied down, to be . . . settled, he realized, wasn't a particularly comfortable sensation, and after several months, he understood it wasn't going to go away.

And he was beginning to hate the status quo.

She found him crouched at the hearth, staring into the flames. After closing the door quietly at her back, she crossed over, brushed a hand through his hair.

"What the hell is going on, Deanna?" He continued to stare into the fire. "You've been edgy since we got here last night, and pretending not to be. When I came in before dinner, you'd been crying. And you and Fran are circling each other like a couple of boxers in the tenth round."

"Fran's angry with me." She sat on the hassock and folded her hands in her lap. She could feel his tension in the air. "I guess you will be, too." Lowering her eyes, she told him about the note, answering his terse questions and waiting for his reaction.

She didn't wait long.

He stood where he was, with the fire snapping at his back. His gaze never left her face and was calm, entirely too calm.

"Why didn't you tell me right away?"

"I thought it was best to wait until I'd sorted through it a bit."

"You thought." He nodded, slipped his hands into his pockets. "You thought it was none of my concern."

"No, of course not." She hated the fact that his cool interviewing skills always put her on the defensive. "I just didn't want to spoil the weekend. There's nothing you can do anyway."

His eyes darkened at that—the wicked cobalt Angela had described. It was a sure sign of passion. Yet his voice, when he responded, didn't alter so much as a degree in tone. That was control.

"Goddamn you, Deanna, you sit there and make me treat this like a hostile interview where I have to drag the facts out of you." Fear and fury burned through him. "I'm not tolerating this. I'm fed up with your tucking things away and filing them under 'For Deanna Only.' " He stepped forward then and, with a speed that had her blinking, pulled her to her feet. She'd expected him to be angry, but she hadn't expected the rage she saw on his face.

"Finn," she said carefully. "You're hurting me."

"What do you think you're doing to me?" He released her so quickly she staggered back a step. He spun away, shoving fisted hands in his pockets. "You don't have a clue. Don't you know how badly I want to get my hands on this creep? That I want to break him in half for causing you one minute of fear? How useless I feel when you get one of those goddamn notes and the color drains out of your face? And how much worse it is, how much harder it is, because after all this time you don't trust me?"

"It isn't a matter of trust." The violence in his eyes had her heart jumping into her throat. In all the time they'd been together, she'd never seen him so close to the edge. "It's not, Finn. It's pride. I didn't want to admit that I couldn't handle it alone."

He was silent for a long time, the only sound the spit of flames eating steadily at dry logs. "Damn your pride, Deanna," he said quietly. "I'm tired of beating my head against it."

Panic welled up inside her like a geyser. His words were a closing statement, a segment ender. With an involuntary cry of alarm, she grabbed his arm before he could stalk out. "Finn, please."

"I'm going for a walk." He stepped back, holding palms up, afraid he might cause them both irreparable damage if he touched her. "There are ways of working off this kind of mad. The most constructive one is to walk it off."

"I didn't mean to hurt you. I love you."

"That's handy, because I love you, too." And at the moment, his love felt as though it were killing him. "It just doesn't seem to be enough."

"I don't care if you're mad." She reached out again and clung. "You should be mad. You should shout and rage."

Gently, while he could still manage it, he loosened her grip. "You're the shouter, Deanna. It's in the genes, I'd say. And I come from a long line of negotiators. It just so happens I'm out of compromises."

"I'm not asking you to compromise. I only want you to listen to what else I have to say."

"Fine." But he moved away from her, to the window seat in the shadows. "Talk's your forte, after all. Go ahead, Deanna, be reasonable, objective, sympathetic. I'll be the audience."

Rather than rise to the bait, she sat again. "I had no idea you were this angry with me. It's not just about me not telling you about this last note, is it?"

"What do you think?"

She'd interviewed dozens of hostile guests over the years. She doubted if any would be tougher than Finn Riley with his Irish up. "I've taken you for granted, and I've been unfair. And you've let me."

"That's good," he said dryly. "Start out with a self-deprecating statement, then circle around. It's no wonder you're on top."

"Don't." She threw her head back, the firelight glinting in her eyes. "Let me finish. At least let me finish before you tell me it's over."

There was silence again. Though she couldn't see his face when he spoke, she heard the weariness in his voice. "Do you think I could?"

"I don't know." A tear spilled over, glimmering in the shifting light. "I haven't let myself think about it until recently."

"Christ, don't cry."

She heard him shift, but he didn't move toward her.

"I won't." She brushed the tear away, swallowed the others that threatened. She knew she could weaken him with tears. And that she would despise herself for it. "I've always thought that I could make everything come out in order, if I just worked at it diligently enough. If I planned it all carefully enough. So I wrote lists, adhered to timetables. I've cheated us both by treating our relationship as if it were a task—a wonderful task—but a task to be handled." She was talking too fast, but couldn't stop, the words tumbling over each other in their hurry to be said. "And I suppose I was feeling pretty smug about the job I was doing. We fit so well together, and I loved being your lover. And then today, I watched you outside, and I realized for the first time how badly I've botched it all." God, she wished she could see his face, his eyes. "You know how I hate to make mistakes."

"Yes, I do." He had to take a moment. It wasn't only her pride on the line. "It sounds as though you're the one doing the ending, Deanna."

"No." She sprang up. "No, I'm trying to ask you to marry me."

A log collapsed in the grate, shooting sparks and hissing fire. When it settled again, the only sound she heard was her own unsteady breathing. He rose, crossed from shadow into light. His eyes were as guarded and enigmatic as an ace gambler calling a bluff. "Are you afraid I'll walk if you don't do this?"

"I imagine the hole there would be in my life if you did, and I'm terrified. And because I'm terrified I wonder why I've waited so long. Maybe I'm wrong and you don't want marriage anymore. If that's the way you feel, I'll wait." She thought if he continued to stare at her with that mild curiosity, she'd scream. "Say something, damn it. Yes, no, go to hell. Something."

"Why? Why now, Deanna?"

"Don't make this an interview."

"Why?" he repeated. When he grabbed her arms she realized there was nothing mild about his mood.

"Because everything's so complicated now." Her voice rose, trembled, broke. "Because life doesn't fit into any of my neat scheduling plans, and I don't want being married to you to be neat and orderly. Because with the November sweeps raging, and all this crazy publicity with Angela, and you going off to Haiti, it's probably the worst possible time to think about getting married. So that makes it the best time."

Despite his tangled emotions, he laughed. "For once your logic totally eludes me."

"I don't need life to be perfect, Finn. For once, I don't need that. It just has to be right. And we're so absolutely right." She blinked back more tears, then gave up and let them fall. "Will you marry me?"

He tipped her head back so that he could study her face. And he smiled, slowly, as all those tangled emotions smoothed out into one silky sheet. "Well, you know, Kansas, this is awfully sudden."

News of the engagement spread quickly. Within twenty-four hours of the official announcement, Deanna's office was deluged with calls. Requests for interviews, offers from designers, caterers, chefs, congratulatory calls from friends. Curiosity calls from other reporters.

Cassie fielded them, batting the few back to Deanna that required the personal touch.

Oddly there had been no calls, no notes, no contact at all from the one person who had been hounding her for years. No matter how often Deanna told herself she should be relieved at the respite, it frightened her more than seeing one of those neat, white envelopes on her desk or tucked under her door.

But none came, because none were written. In the shadowy little room where pictures of Deanna beamed contentedly from walls and tabletops, there was little sound but weeping. Hot, bitter tears fell on the newspaper print that announced the engagement of two of television's most popular stars.

Alone, alone for so long. Waiting, waiting so patiently. So sure that Finn would never settle down. That Deanna could still be had. Now the hope that fueled patience was smashed, a delicate cup of fragile glass tossed aside and discovered to have been empty all along.

There was no sweet wine of triumph to be shared. And no Deanna to fill those empty hours.

But even as the tears dried, the planning began. She merely had to be shown—surely that was all—that no one could love her more completely. She needed to be shown, to be shocked into awareness. And, she needed to be punished. Just a little.

There was a way to arrange it all.

Deanna had voted for a small, simple wedding. A private ceremony, she told Finn as he'd finished up the last of his packing for Haiti. Just family and close friends.

And it had been he who'd tossed her the curve.

"Nope. We're shooting the works on this one, Kansas." He'd zipped up his garment bag and slung it over his shoulder. "A church wedding, organ music, acres of flowers and several weeping relatives neither one of us remembers. Followed by a reception of mammoth proportions where some of those same relatives will drink too much and embarrass their respective spouses."

She chased down the steps after him. "Do you know how long it would take to plan something like that?"

"Yeah. You've got five months." He dragged her close for a hard, deep kiss. "You've got an April deadline, Deanna. We'll look over your list when I get back."

"But, Finn." She was forced to scoot down and grab the dog by the collar before he joyfully rushed out of the door Finn opened.

"This time *I* want it perfect. I'll call as soon as I can." He started down to where his driver waited, swinging around and walking backward with a grin teasing his dimples. "Stay tuned."

So she was now planning a full-scale wedding. Which, of course, prompted the topic idea of wedding preparations and related stress.

"We could book couples who'd broken up because the fighting and spats during the wedding plans undermined their relationship."

From her seat at the head of the conference table, Deanna eyed Simon owlishly. "Thanks, I needed that."

"No, really." He turned his chuckle into a cough. "I have this niece..."

Margaret groaned and pushed her purple-framed glasses up her pug nose. "He's always got a niece, or a nephew, or a cousin."

"Can I help it if I've got a big family?"

"Children, children." Hoping to restore order, Fran shook Kelsey's rattle. "Let's try to pretend we're a dignified, organized group with a number-one show."

"We're number one," Jeff chanted, grinning as others picked up the rhythm. "We're number one."

"And we want to stay there." Laughing, Deanna held up both hands. "Okay, though it doesn't do anything for my peace of mind, Simon's got a good idea. How many couples do you figure break up sometime between the *Will you* and the *I do*?"

"Plenty," Simon said with relish. "Take my niece—" He ignored the paper airplane Margaret sailed in his direction. "Really, they'd booked the church, the hall, found the caterer. All this time, according to my sister, they fought like tigers. The big blowup came over the bridesmaids' dresses. They couldn't agree on the color."

"They called off the wedding because of the bridesmaids' dresses?" Deanna narrowed her eyes. "You're making this up."

"Swear to God." To prove it, Simon placed a hand on his heart. "She wanted seafoam, he wanted lavender. Of course, the flowers were a contributing cause. If you can't agree on that, how can you agree on where to send your kids to college? Hey." He brightened. "Maybe we can get them."

"We'll keep it in mind." Deanna jotted down notes. Among them was a warning to be flexible over colors. "I think the point here is that wedding preparations are stressful, and there are ways of lessening the tension. We'll want an expert. Not a psychologist," she said quickly, thinking of Marshall.

"A wedding coordinator," Jeff suggested, watching Deanna's face for signs of approval or dismissal. "Somebody who orchestrates the whole business professionally. It is like a business," he said, glancing around for confirmation. "Marriage."

"You betcha." Fran tapped the rattle against the table. "A coordinator's good. We could talk about staying within your means and expectations. How not to let your fantasies about perfection cloud the real issue."

"Cheap shot," Deanna tossed back. "We could use the mother and father of the bride. Traditionally they're in charge of the checkbook. What kind of strain is it personally and financially? And how do we decide, reasonably and happily, on invitations, the reception, the music, the flowers, the photographer? Do we have a buffet or a sit-down meal? What about centerpieces? The wedding party, decorations, the guest list?" The faintest hint of desperation crept into her voice. "Where the hell do you put out-of-town guests, and how is anyone supposed to pull all this together in five months?"

She lowered her head on her arms. "I think," she said slowly, "we should elope."

"Hey, that's good," Simon piped up. "Alternatives to wedding stress. I had this cousin . . ."

This time Margaret's airplane hit him right between the eyes.

Within weeks, Deanna's organized desk was jumbled with sketches of bridal gowns, from the elaborately traditional to the funkily futuristic.

Behind her, the same homely plastic tree Jeff had hauled into her office that first Christmas leaned precariously to starboard, overweighted by balls and garlands.

Someone—Cassie, she assumed—had spritzed some pine-scented air freshener around. The cheery aroma made the fading dyed plastic boughs even more pathetic. And Deanna loved it.

It was a tradition now, a superstition. She wouldn't have replaced the ugly tree with the richest blue spruce in the city.

"I can't quite see saying 'I do' in something like this." She held up a sketch for Fran's perusal. The short, skinny dress was topped with a headpiece that resembled helicopter blades.

"Well, after, Finn could give you a spin and the two of you could glide down the aisle. Now this one's hot." She held up a drawing; the elongated model was spread-legged in a bare-midriff mini with spike-heeled boots.

"Only if I carry a whip instead of a bouquet."

"You'd get great press." She tossed it aside. "You don't have a lot of time to decide before April comes busting out all over."

"Don't remind me." She shuffled another sketch on top, her twin-diamond engagement ring flashing. A diamond for each year it had taken him to wear her down, he'd told her as he'd slipped it on her finger. "This one's nice."

Fran peeked over her shoulder. "That one's gorgeous." She oohed a bit over the billowing skirts and full sleeves. The bodice was snug, trimmed in pearls and lace with the design repeating on the flowing train. The headpiece was a simple circlet from which the frothy veil flowed.

"It's really stunning. Almost medieval. A real once-in-a-lifetime dress."

"You think so?"

Recognizing her interest, Fran narrowed her eyes. "You've already decided on it."

"I want a completely unbiased opinion. And yes," she admitted with a laugh. "I knew the minute I saw it." She tidied the pile, laying her choice on top. "I wish the rest of it were so simple. The photographer—"

"I'm in charge of that."

"The caterer."

"Cassie's department."

"Music, napkins, flowers, invitations," she said before Fran could interrupt her again. "Let me at least pretend this is driving me crazy."

"Tough, when you've never looked happier in your life."

"I really have you to thank for it. You gave me the kick in the butt I needed."

"Glad to oblige. Now, we're going to get out of here while you've got a free evening and go down to Michigan Avenue for some trousseau shopping. With Finn on a shoot across town, this is the only chance I've got. There's not a minute to waste."

"I'm ready." She grabbed her purse as the phone rang. "Almost." Because Cassie was already gone for the day, Deanna answered herself. "Reynolds," she said out of habit, and her brilliant smile withered. "Angela." She glanced up and caught the interest in Fran's eye. "That's very nice of you. I'm sure Finn and I will be very happy."

"Of course you are," Angela cooed into the receiver as she continued to slice through a cover photo of Finn and Deanna with a letter opener. "You always were the confident one, Deanna."

To keep herself calm, Deanna shifted to study the teetering Christmas tree. "Is there something I can do for you?"

"No, not at all. There's something I want to do for you, dear. Let's call it an engagement gift. A little tidbit of information you might be interested in, about your fiancé."

"There's nothing you can tell me about Finn I'd be interested in, Angela. I appreciate your best wishes, and now I'm afraid I'm just on my way out."

"Don't be in such a rush. I recall your having a healthy sense of curiosity. I doubt you've changed so much. It really would be very wise, for you and for Finn, if you listened to what I have to say."

"All right." Setting her teeth, Deanna sat down again. "I'm listening."

"Oh, no, dear, not over the phone. It so happens I'm in Chicago. A little business, a little pleasure."

"Yes, your luncheon with the League of Women Voters tomorrow. I read about it."

"There's that, and another little matter. But I'll be free for a chat, say, at midnight."

"The witching hour? Angela, that's so obvious, even for you."

"Watch your tone, or I won't give you the opportunity of hearing what I have to say before I go to the press. You can consider my generosity a combination engagement and Christmas gift, darling. Midnight," she repeated. "At the studio. My old studio."

"I don't—damn it." Echoing Angela's response, Deanna slammed down the phone.

"What's she up to?"

"I'm not sure." With her celebratory mood in tatters, Deanna stared into space. "She wants to meet with me. Claims she has some information I need to hear."

"She only wants to cause trouble, Dee." The worry was in Fran's voice, in her eyes. "*She's* in trouble. In the past six months, her show's gone dramatically downhill with rumors about her drinking, about her staging shows, bribing guests. It's hardly a surprise that she'd want to fly out on her broomstick and hand you a poisoned apple."

"I'm not worried about it." Deanna shook off the mood and rose again. "I'm not. It's time the two of us had it out once and for all. In private. There's nothing she can say or do that can hurt me."

Part Three

"All power of fancy over reason
is a degree of insanity."
—Samuel Johnson

23

But someone had hurt Angela.

Someone had killed her.

Deanna continued to scream, high, piercing cries that burned her throat like acid. Even when her vision grayed, Deanna couldn't take her eyes off the horror beside her. And she could smell the blood, hot and coppery and thick.

She had to escape before Angela reached out with that delicate, dead hand and squeezed it around her throat.

With little mewling sounds of panic, she crawled out of the chair, afraid to move too fast, afraid to take her eyes off of what had been Angela Perkins. Every move, every sound was echoed by the monitor while the camera objectively recorded, its round, dark eye staring. Something tugged her back. On a soundless gasping scream, Deanna lifted her hands to fight what she couldn't see, and tangled her fingers in the wires of a lapel mike.

"Oh God. Oh God." She tore herself free, hurling the mike aside and fleeing the set in a blind panic.

She stumbled, caught a horrified glimpse of herself in the wide wall mirror. A hot laugh bubbled in her throat. She looked insane, she thought wildly. And she bit down on her hysteria, afraid it would slide from her throat in a mad chuckle. She nearly fell, tripping over her own feet as she ran down the dark corridor. Someone was breathing down her neck. She could feel it, she knew it, hot, greedy breath whispering behind her.

Sobbing, she hurtled into her dressing room, slammed the door, threw the lock, then stood in the dark with her heart pounding like a rabbit's.

She fumbled for the light, then screamed again when her own reflection jumped at her. A glittery gold garland ringed the mirror. Like a noose, she thought. Like a spangled noose. Boneless with terror, she slid down against the door. Everything was spinning, spinning, and her stomach heaved in response. Clammy with nausea, she crawled to the phone. The sound of her own whimpering iced her skin as she punched the number for emergency.

"Please, please help." Dizzy and sick, she lay on the floor, cradling the receiver. "Her face is gone. I need help. The CBC Building, Studio B. Please hurry," she said, and let the darkness swallow her.

It was just past one A.M. when Finn arrived home. His first thoughts were for a hot shower and a warm brandy. He expected Deanna home within the hour, after whatever emergency meeting she had. She'd been vague about the details when she'd caught him between shoots, and he hadn't had the time or the inclination to press. They'd both been in the business too long to question midnight meetings.

He sent his driver off and started up the walk, both amused and embarrassed that the dog was setting up a din that would wake the neighbors for blocks.

"Okay, okay, Cronkite. Try for a little dignity." He reached for his keys as he climbed onto the porch, wondering why Deanna had forgotten to leave on the porch light. Little details like that never escaped her.

Wedding plans were rattling her brain, he thought, pleased at the idea.

Something crunched under his foot. He glanced down and saw the faint glitter of broken glass. His initial puzzlement turned to fury when he saw the jagged shards of the beveled glass panels beside the door.

Then his mouth went dry. What if her meeting had been canceled? What if she'd come home? He burst through the door in thoughtless fear, shouting her name.

Something crashed at the back of the house, and the dog's frantic barking turned into a desperate howl. Thinking only of Deanna, Finn hit the lights before he sprinted toward the source of the crash.

He found nothing but destruction, a mindless and brutal attack on their possessions. Lamps and tables were overturned, glassware shattered. When he reached the kitchen, his mind was cold as ice. He thought he saw a form running across the lawn. Even as he tore aside the shattered door to give chase, the dog howled again, scratching pitifully against the locked utility room door.

He wanted to give chase. It burned in him to hunt down whoever had done this and throttle him. But the possibility that Deanna was somewhere in the house, hurt, stopped him.

"Okay, Cronkite." He unlocked the door and staggered back as the dog leaped joyously at him. His thick body was shivering. "Scared you, did he? Me too. Let's find Deanna."

He searched every room, growing colder with every moment. The devastation was as total as tornado damage, both the priceless and the trivial capriciously destroyed.

But the worst, the most terrifying, was the message scrawled in Deanna's lipstick on the wall above the bed they shared.

I loved you
I killed for you
I hate you

"Thank God she wasn't here. Thank God." Grimly he picked up the phone and called the police.

"Take it easy." Lieutenant Jenner helped Deanna steady a glass of water.

"I'm all right now." But her teeth chattered on the rim of the glass. "I'm sorry. I know I was incoherent before."

"Understandable." He'd had a good long look at Angela Perkins's body and found Deanna's condition understandable indeed. He didn't blame her for huddling inside the locked room, needing to be gently persuaded to open the door to admit him. "You're going to want to have a doctor take a look at you."

"I'm fine, really."

Shock, he imagined. It was nature's way of closing down the system and offering the illusion of comfort. But her eyes were still glassy, and even though he'd thrown his overcoat over her shoulders, she was shivering.

"Can you tell me what happened?"

"I found her. I came in and found her."

"What were you doing at the studio after midnight?"

"She asked me to meet her. She called—she . . ." She sipped again. "She called."

"So you arranged to meet her here."

"She wanted to—to talk to me. She said she had information about . . ." Defenses clicked in. "About something I needed to know. I wasn't going to come, then I thought it might be best if we had it out."

"What time did you get here?"

"It was midnight. I looked at my watch in the parking lot." The colored lights in the distance, the haze of Christmas cheer. "It was midnight. I thought maybe she hadn't arrived yet, but she could have had her driver drop her off. So I let myself into the studio. And it was dark, so I thought she wasn't here, and that was good. I wanted to be first. Then, when I started to turn on the lights, something hit me. When I woke up I was on the set, and I couldn't think. The camera was on. Oh, God, the camera was on, and I saw, in the monitor, I saw her." She pressed a hand to her mouth to hold back the whimpers.

"Take a minute." Jenner leaned back.

"I don't know anything else. I ran in here and locked the door. I called the police, and I passed out."

"Did you see anybody on your way to the studio?"

"No. No one. The cleaning crews would have gone by now. There would be a few people in the newsroom, manning the desk overnight, but after the last broadcast, the building clears out."

"You need a card to get into the building, don't you?"

"Yes. They put in a new security system about a year ago."

"Is this your purse, Miss Reynolds?" He held out a generous shoulder bag in smooth black leather.

"Yes, that's mine. I must have dropped it when I—when I came in."

"And this card." He held up a clear plastic bag. Inside was a slim, laminated card with her initials in the corner.

"Yes, that's mine."

He set the bag aside and continued to take notes. "What time did Miss Perkins contact you about this meeting?"

"About five. She called my office."

"Your secretary took the call?"

"No, she'd already gone home. I took it myself." Something trembled through the shield of shock. "You think I killed her? You think I did that to her? Why?" She lurched to her feet, swaying like a drunk as the overcoat slid to the floor. "How could I? Why would I? Do you think I lured her here, and murdered her, then taped it all so I could show it to all my loyal viewers in the morning?"

"Calm down, Miss Reynolds." Jenner got cautiously to his feet. She looked as though she might dissolve if he touched her. "No one's accusing you of anything. I'm just trying to get the facts."

"I'll give the facts. Someone killed her. Someone blew her face away and propped her up on the set. Oh God." She pressed a hand to her head. "This can't be real."

"Sit down and catch your breath." Jenner took her by the arm. There was a commotion in the corridor behind him and he turned to the door.

"Goddamn it, I want to see her." Finn shoved his way clear of the cop trying to detain him and burst through the doorway. "Deanna." He sprinted forward as she swayed toward him. "You're all right." He vised his arms around her, burying his face in her hair. "You're all right."

"Finn." She pressed against him, desperate for the feel of his flesh, his warmth, his comfort. "Someone killed Angela. I found her. Finn, I found her."

But he was already drawing her away, appalled by the swelling and matted blood on the back of her head. Relief twisted into a dark, keen thirst for revenge. "Who hurt you?"

"I don't know." She burrowed back into his arms. "I didn't see. They think I did it. Finn, they think I killed her."

Over her trembling shoulder he stared stonily at Jenner. "Are you out of your mind?"

"Miss Reynolds is mistaken. We have no intention of charging her at this time. Nor, in my opinion, in the future."

"Then she's free to go."

Jenner rubbed his chin. "Yes. We'll need her to sign a statement, but we can do it tomorrow. Miss Reynolds, I know you've had a shock, and I apologize for having to put you through the questioning. I advise you to go by the hospital, have someone take a look at you."

"I'll take her. Deanna." Gently Finn eased her back to the chair. "I want you to wait here a minute. I need to talk to Lieutenant Jenner."

She clung to his hand. "Don't leave."

"No, just outside the door. Just for a minute. Detective."

Jenner followed Finn into the corridor, nodding to a uniform to back off. "She's had a rough night, Mr. Riley."

"I'm aware of that. I don't want you to add to it."

"Neither do I. But certain wheels have to turn. I've got a nasty murder, and as far as I can tell, she's the only witness. You wouldn't mind telling me where you were tonight?"

Finn's eyes cooled. "No, I wouldn't. I was taping a segment on the South Side. I'd guess I'd have about a dozen witnesses to place me there until about midnight. My driver took me home, dropped me off just after one. I put in a call to 911 at one-twenty."

"Why?"

"Because my house had been trashed. You want to verify that, contact your superior."

"I don't doubt your word, Mr. Riley." Jenner rubbed his chin again, toying with the timetable. "You said one-twenty?"

"Give or take a minute. Whoever broke in left a message for Deanna on the bedroom wall. You can check with your associates for details. I'm getting Deanna out of here."

"I'll do that." Jenner made another note. "Mr. Riley, I'd take her out another way. I wouldn't want her going through the studio."

"Hey, Arnie!" Another plainclothes cop signaled from the studio end of the corridor. "M. E.'s finished here."

"Tell him to hang on a minute. We'll be in touch, Mr. Riley."

Saying nothing, Finn turned back into the dressing room. He took off his own coat, pushing Deanna's limp arms through the sleeves. He didn't want to waste time looking for hers. "Come on, baby, let's get out of here."

"I want to go home." She leaned heavily against him as he led her out.

"No way. I'm taking you to E.R."

"Don't leave me there."

"I'm not leaving you."

He took the long way around, circumventing the studio, choosing the angled stairs that led to the parking lot. Because he knew what to expect before he opened the door, he kissed her brow, held her by the shoulders.

"The place is going to be swarming with reporters and Minicams."

She squeezed her eyes tight, shivered. "I know. It's okay."

"Just hold on tight to me."

"I already am."

When he shoved the door open, the flash of klieg lights blinded her. She shielded her eyes and saw nothing but eager bodies rushing toward her, microphones stabbing out like lances and the wide, demanding eye of the camera.

Questions hurtled at her, making her hunch her shoulders in defense as Finn propelled her through the surging sea of reporters.

She knew most of them, she realized. Liked most of those she knew. Once upon a time they had competed for stories. Once upon a time she would have been among them, pressing forward, scurrying for that one telling picture, that one mumbled comment.

Then flying to the news desk to get the item—she was an item now—on the air minutes, even seconds, before the competition.

But she was no longer the observer. She was the observed. How could she tell them how she felt? How could she tell them what she knew? Her mind was like glass, throbbing from some deadly, high-pitched whine. She thought if she couldn't have silence, she would explode and shatter.

"Christ, Dee."

A hand reached for her, hesitating as she cringed away. And she saw Joe, the Minicam on his shoulder, his baseball cap askew.

"I'm sorry," he said, and swore again. "I'm really sorry."

"It's all right. I've been there, remember? It's just the job." She climbed gratefully into Finn's car and closed her eyes. Tuned out.

Jenner turned the studio over to the forensic team. Since he'd already had two men question the occupants of the building, he decided to wait until morning before doing a follow-up there. Instead, he left the CBC Building and drove to Finn Riley's home.

He wasn't surprised, or displeased, when Finn pulled into the driveway behind him.

"How's Miss Reynolds?"

"She's got a concussion," Finn said tersely. "They're keeping her overnight for observation. I had a feeling I'd find you here."

Jenner nodded as they started up the walk. "Chilly night," he said conversationally. "Dispatch showed your call came in at one twenty-three. First unit arrived at one twenty-eight."

"It was a quick response." Though it hadn't seemed quick as he'd spent that endless five minutes looking over the destruction of his home. "Are you handling B and Es, too, Lieutenant?"

"I like to diversify. And the truth is"—he paused just outside the door—"I figure I've got an interest in this. Between the business in Greektown and the investigation on those letters Miss Reynolds has been getting, I figure I've got an interest. Does that bother you?"

Finn studied Jenner in the starlight. The man looked tired, yet completely alert. It was a combination Finn understood perfectly. "No."

"Well then." Jenner sliced through the police tape over the damaged door. "Maybe you'll take me on the grand tour."

Riley was a pretty snappy dresser, Jenner mused as they moved inside. The kind who leaned toward leather jackets and faded jeans. Jenner had tried on a leather jacket once. He'd looked like a cop. He always did.

"Did you mention the trouble here to Miss Reynolds?"

"No."

"Can't blame you. She's had a rough night." He glanced around. The place looked as if it had been bombed. "So have you."

"You could say that. Almost every room was trashed." Finn gestured toward the living area off the main hall. "I didn't take a lot of time going through it."

Jenner grunted. Word was the minute Finn had learned of the trouble at CBC, he'd sprinted out, leaving the destruction behind.

"You must be pretty steamed." That was putting it mildly, Jenner mused. What he saw on Finn's face was cold rage. If he'd run across the perp, he'd have sliced him into little pieces. Though it was unprofessional, Jenner would have given a great deal to see it.

"I can replace the things," Finn said as they started upstairs.

"Yeah." Jenner stepped inside the bedroom, nodded toward the wall. "So our friend's taken to writing on walls." Taking out his pad, Jenner copied the writing style onto a blank page. This was the first time the writer had exposed himself this way. "Makes a statement." One quick scan and he'd taken in the devastation of the room. "Forensics are going to have a hell of a time sorting through this mess." He toed a broken perfume bottle with his foot. "Tiffany," he commented. "A hundred fifty an ounce. My wife, she likes that scent. I bought her the cologne for her birthday. And those sheets. Irish linen. My grandmother had a tablecloth. I used to rub my face over it when I was a kid."

Nearly amused, Finn leaned on the doorjamb and studied Jenner. "Is this how you conduct an investigation, Lieutenant? Or do you moonlight for an insurance company?"

"Always was a sucker for quality." He slipped his pad back in his pocket, just above the snug weight of his weapon. "So, Mr. Riley, I'd have to say we have a connection."

"So, Lieutenant, I'd have to agree with you."

"Murder happened by midnight." He scratched the back of his neck. "The drive from CBC to here takes fourteen minutes, at the speed limit. He spends, say, ten minutes setting the stage, turning on the equipment. Another ten to get over here. You get home about twenty after one. Yeah, I'd say that's enough time."

"You're not telling me anything I don't know, Lieutenant. What's next?"

"We'll canvass the neighborhood tomorrow. Somebody might have seen something."

"You haven't had time to interview Dan Gardner."

"No." A ghost of a smile moved Jenner's lips. "My next stop."

"Mine too."

"Mr. Riley, you'd be better off going back to the hospital, watching over your lady. Leave this to me."

"I'll watch out for Deanna," Finn returned. "And I'm going to talk to Gardner. I'm going to use everything and everyone I know to get to the root of this. I can go with you, Lieutenant, or I can go around you."

"That's not friendly, Mr. Riley."

"I'm not feeling friendly, Lieutenant Jenner."

"Don't imagine you are, but this is police business."

"So was Greektown."

Jenner's brows lifted as he studied Finn. The man knew which buttons to push, he mused.

"I like you," Jenner said after a moment. "I liked the way you handled yourself in Greektown. Saw you take that hit." He scratched his chin, considered. "You just kept right on reporting."

"That's my job."

"Yeah, and I got mine. I'm willing to bend the rules a bit, Mr. Riley, for a couple reasons. One, I really admire your lady, and two... I figure there's a ten-year-old girl out there who just might owe you her life. I might not have mentioned, I have a granddaughter that age."

"No, you didn't mention it."

"Well." Jenner simply nodded again. "You can follow me in your car."

• • •

When Deanna surfaced, it was midmorning. Yet it wasn't necessary to orient herself; she remembered everything too clearly. She was in the hospital under observation. She wished she could laugh at the term. She understood that she would remain under all manner of observation for a long time.

She turned her head, mindful of the dull ache swimming inside, and studied Finn. He was dozing in the chair beside the bed, his hand covering hers. Unshaven, exhausted and pale, he was the most comforting sight she could imagine.

Not wanting to disturb him, she shifted slowly. But her slight movement woke him.

"Are you hurting?"

"No." Her voice was weak; she put an effort into strengthening it. "You shouldn't have sat up all night. They'd have found somewhere for you to stretch out."

"I can sleep anywhere. I'm a reporter, remember?" He scrubbed his hands over his face, then stretched out the kinks in his back. "You should try to get some more sleep."

"I want to go home. A mild concussion isn't enough to keep me in the hospital." She sat up, but cautiously, knowing if she so much as sneezed he'd run for a nurse. "No double vision, no memory lapses, no nausea."

"You're pale as wax, Deanna."

"You're not looking so hale and hearty yourself. Want to crawl in here with me?"

"Later." He scooted over to sit on the side of the bed and touched his hand to her cheek. "I love you."

"I know. I don't think I could have gotten through last night without you."

"You don't have to get through anything without me."

She smiled, but her eyes strayed from his to the television bracketed to the wall at the foot of the bed. "I don't suppose you've heard the morning news?"

"No." He turned, looked at her intently. "No," he repeated. "We'll deal with it later."

Yes, she thought. Later was better. "It was horrible the way she died. Horrible the way it was all so perfectly staged. I need to think about it, but I can't seem to."

"Then don't. Don't push it, Deanna." He looked over as he heard Fran's voice, lifted high in indignant rage as she argued with the guard outside the door. "I'll tell her you're resting."

"No, please. I want to see her."

Finn had just gone to the door to have a word with the guard when Fran burst in. She bulleted toward the bed and snatched Deanna into her arms. "Oh God, I've been sick ever since I heard. Are you all right? How bad are you hurt?"

"Just a bump on the head." She returned the embrace, squeezing hard. "I was just about to get up and get dressed."

"Are you sure?" Fran drew her back; she might have been examining one of her children for symptoms. "You're so pale. Finn, go get the doctor. I think he should take another look at her."

"No." She took Fran's hands firmly in hers. "They just wanted me overnight for observation. I've been observed. The office? What's going on?"

Something flickered in Fran's eyes, then she shrugged. "Chaos. What else? The cops are taking statements from everyone."

"I should go in, do something."

"No." The protest came quickly, fiercely. "I mean it, Dee. There's nothing you can do, and if you came in at this point, you'd only add to the confusion. As soon as I go back and tell everyone you're okay, it should calm down a little." Her lips trembled before she wrapped her arms around Deanna again. "You really are okay? It must have been horrible for you. Every time I think of what could have happened—"

"I know." Comforted, Deanna cradled her head on Fran's shoulder. "Angela. God, Fran, I still can't believe it. Who could have hated her that much?"

Pick a number, Fran thought. "I don't want you to worry about the show or the office. We ran a re-broadcast today. Cassie's canceling and rescheduling guests we'd booked for the next week."

"That's not necessary."

"I'm the producer, and I say it is." After a last squeeze, Fran pulled back and turned to Finn for support. "Are you going to throw your weight in with me?"

"It doesn't appear to be necessary, but sure. I'm taking her up to the cabin for a while."

"I can't just leave. Jenner's bound to want to talk to me again. And I have to talk to Loren, to my staff."

Finn studied her a moment. There was pain in her eyes as well as the dregs of terror and shock. "Here's the way I see it," he said mildly. "I can spring you out of here later today and take you to the cabin. Or I can arrange for them to keep you in that bed for another couple of days."

"That's absurd." Deanna wanted to be angry, but she was too tired. "Just because we're getting married doesn't mean you can arrange my life."

"It does when you're too stubborn to do what's best for you."

"Well." Fran gave a satisfied nod and kissed Finn's cheek. "Now that I know she's in capable hands, I'm going to go find that doctor. I need to talk to you," she said under her breath, then turned back to Deanna. It was a relief to see the sulky turn of her friend's mouth. "Don't worry about the details," she told her. "The gang and I can handle everything. I'll be back in a few minutes."

"Fine. Great." Deanna plopped back on the pillows, wincing when the sudden movement made her head pound. "Just tell everyone I decided to go fishing."

"Good idea." Finn walked to the door to open it for Fran. "I'll see if I can round up someone to put through the release papers. Stay in bed," he ordered, and walked outside. "What is it you don't want her to know?"

"There are cops swarming all over the sixteenth floor." Fran cast one last, worried glance over her shoulder as they walked to the elevators. "Her office has been torn apart, like someone went through it in an insane rage. Chairs hurled around, broken glass. All the lists she'd put together for the wedding and the sketches of the dresses were ripped up. Somebody had written all over the walls in red ink." As Finn watched, her cheeks drained of color so that her freckles stood out in stark relief. "It just said 'I love you,' again and again and again. I don't want her to see it, Finn."

"She won't. I'm going to take care of her."

"I know that." Fran pressed her fingers to her eyes. "But I'm scared. Whoever killed Angela is so focused on Dee. I don't think he'll ever leave her alone."

Finn's eyes were sharp as a sword. "He won't get near her. There's someone I have to meet. You stay with her until I get back."

• • •

After a two-hour catnap, Jenner rapped on the door of Dan Gardner's hotel suite. Beside him Finn was running through a mental list of questions he wanted answered.

"He'd better be in the mood to talk this time."

Jenner only shrugged. He didn't mind taking the long route, as long as it ended in the right place. "Hard to talk when you're sedated."

"Conveniently," Finn murmured.

"Guy's wife gets snuffed, he's entitled to break down."

"Wouldn't you think he'd want some details before he went under, Lieutenant? The way I see it, the longer he delays talking to you, the longer he has to formulate an alibi. Angela Perkins was a wealthy woman. Care to guess who's the chief beneficiary?"

"Then if he killed her, he'd have been stupid not to have an alibi to begin with. I've got a feeling you're a man used to being in charge of things."

"And?"

"You're going to have to take a backseat here. I've got an instinct about you, Mr. Riley, so I'm letting you tag along—that way I can pick your brain. But you're going to have to remember who's running this investigation."

"Cops and reporters have a lot in common, Lieutenant. We won't be the first who've used each other."

"Nope." Jenner heard the rattle of the chain. "But that doesn't change the pecking order."

Finn nodded grudgingly as the door opened. Dan Gardner looked like a man who'd been on a wild, two-day bender. His face was gray, his eyes sunken, and his hair stood out in tufts. His black silk robe and pajamas added an elegance that only accented his unkempt appearance, like fresh gilt on a tattered painting.

"Mr. Gardner?"

"Yeah." Dan brought a cigarette to his lips, gulping in smoke like water.

"I'm Detective Jenner." He held up his badge.

Dan glanced at it, then spotted Finn. "Hold it. What's he doing here?"

"Research," Finn said.

"I'm not talking to any reporters, especially this one."

"That's funny, coming from someone who woos the press like a lovesick suitor." Finn put a hand on the door before Dan could shut it. "I'll keep it off the record. But I can tell you, you're better off speaking with me when you've got a cop around. I'm in a real bad mood."

"I'm not well."

"I sympathize, Mr. Gardner," Jenner put in before Finn could comment. "You're certainly not obliged to speak in Mr. Riley's presence, but I have a feeling he'll just come back. Why don't we try it this way, and keep this as short as possible? It would be easier on you to do this here than to come to the station."

Dan stared at them both a moment, then with a shrug, he turned around, leaving the door open.

The drapes were still drawn, giving the parlor of the suite a gloomy air. The smell of cigarettes was strong, mixing uneasily with the fragrance from the two huge vases of roses flanking the sofa.

Dan sat between them, blinking when Jenner switched on a lamp.

"I'm sorry to have to disturb you at this time, Mr. Gardner," Jenner began. "But I need your cooperation."

Dan said nothing, only took another greedy drag from the cigarette. Angela's brand, he thought, and felt the smoke sting bitterly in his throat.

"Can you tell us what you know about your wife's activities yesterday?"

"Besides getting murdered?" With a humorless laugh, he roused himself to go to the bar and pour a generous portion of whiskey.

Finn only lifted a brow as Dan drank it down, poured again. It was barely ten A.M.

"It would help," Jenner continued, "if we had a clear sense of her movements throughout the day. Where she went, who she had contact with."

"She got up about ten." Dan came back to the sofa. The whiskey helped, he realized. He felt as though he were gliding an inch above the floor. "She had a massage, had her hair and makeup done, a manicure. All here in the suite." He drank with one hand, smoked with the other, his movements mechanical and strangely rhythmic. "She did a print interview, *Chicago Tribune,* then went downstairs to the ballroom for the luncheon. She had several other appointments through the day—interviews, meetings. Most of them here in the suite."

He crushed out the cigarette, sat back with the blue haze of smoke hovering over his head like a dirty halo.

"Were you with her?" Finn demanded.

Dan shot him one resentful glance, then shrugged. "I was in and out. Mostly out. Angela didn't like distractions when she was dealing with the press. She had a dinner interview with *Premiere* magazine to hype her next special." In a jerky movement, he reached over to yank another cigarette from the pack on the coffee table. "She told me she didn't know how long it would run, and that she had a later meeting afterward, that I should go out to a blues bar and amuse myself."

"And did you?" Jenner asked.

"I had a steak, a couple of drinks, listened to some piano at the Pump Room."

Jenner noted it down. "Did you have any company?"

"I wasn't in the mood for company. We haven't had a lot of time to relax in the past few months, so I took advantage of it." His bloodshot eyes narrowed. "Are you looking for Angela's schedule, or mine?"

"Both," Jenner said pleasantly. He doodled a bit, a quick sketch of the room, of Dan Gardner's face. "It helps if we have a clear sense of things. When did you last see your wife, Mr. Gardner?"

"Just before seven, when she was getting ready for dinner."

"And did she tell you she planned to meet Deanna Reynolds at CBC later that night?"

"No." He bit the word off. "If she had, I would have discouraged it." He leaned forward now, enough of a showman to know which lines to punch. "He knows it, too," he added, jerking his head toward Finn. "That's why he wants in on the investigation, to try to head it off. It's no secret Deanna Reynolds hated my wife, was envious and driven to destroy her. I have no doubt that she killed Angela, or had her killed."

"That's an interesting theory," Finn mused. "Is that the line you're going to feed through your publicist?"

Jenner cleared his throat. "Did Miss Reynolds make any threats against your wife that you're aware of?"

Dan's eyes cut back to Jenner, bored in. "I told you, she attacked her physically once before. Christ knows she attacked her emotionally dozens of times over the years. She wanted Angela out of the way. Now she is. That should be clear enough. What are you doing about it?"

"We're looking into it," Jenner said mildly. "Mr. Gardner, what time did you return to the hotel last night?"

"Twelve-thirty, one o'clock."

"Did you meet anyone, speak with anyone who could verify that?"

"I resent the implication, Lieutenant. My wife is dead." He stabbed out the cigarette, breaking it in two. "And from what I've been told, there was only one person with her." He stared at Finn, secure that he could say whatever he chose with impunity. "A person who had every reason to hurt her. I don't appreciate being asked to supply an alibi."

"But can you?" Finn countered.

His teeth snapped together. "You're really reaching, aren't you, Riley? Do you really think you can throw the police off Deanna and onto me?"

Finn lifted a brow. "I don't believe you answered the question."

"It's possible one of the night clerks saw me come in. It's also possible that the waitress at the club would remember serving me, and what time I left. What kind of alibi does Deanna Reynolds have?"

Was it rage? Jenner wondered. Or was it fear that simmered in Gardner's voice? "I'm afraid I can't discuss that at this time. Do you have any idea how your wife might have gained access to the CBC Building and Studio B?"

"She worked there for some time," Dan said dryly. "I imagine she walked in. She'd know the way."

"There's a security system that wasn't in operation during the time your wife was based in the building."

"Then I'd imagine Deanna let her in. Then she killed her." He shifted forward, resting one hand on the black silk covering his knee. "Imagine what this will do for her ratings, Lieutenant Jenner. He knows." Dan jabbed a finger toward Finn. "How many Nielsen homes will tune in to watch a cold-blooded killer, Riley? She'll murder the competition." He laughed, rubbing a hand over and over his face. "Just like she murdered Angela."

"Whoever killed your wife won't benefit from it." Jenner glanced at Finn, pleased to see he was maintaining an outward calm. Jenner decided he liked the pattern of their work together. Not something as clichéd as good cop—bad cop. Just teamwork. "Did Miss Perkins have an appointment book, a calendar?"

"Her secretary kept her calendar, but Angela always carried a small date book in her purse."

"Would you mind if we took a look in her room?"

Dan pressed the heels of his hands to his eyes. "Fuck, do what you want."

"You ought to order up some breakfast, Mr. Gardner," Jenner said as he rose.

"Yeah. I ought to do that."

Jenner took out a card and left it on the coffee table beside the ashtray of smoldering butts. "I'd appreciate it if you'd contact me if you think of anything else. We'll be out of your way in just a few minutes."

The first thing Finn did in the bedroom of the suite was open the drapes. Light spilled relentlessly into the room. The bureau top was crowded with bottles and pots, the expensive toys of a vain woman who could afford the best. A champagne flute with a pale pink outline of lipstick at the rim stood in the center. A floral silk robe flowed gracefully over the arm of a chair, its hem brushing matching ballet-style slippers.

The only evidence that a man shared the room was the suit hung on the valet.

"You didn't mention an appointment book in her purse, Lieutenant."

"There wasn't one." He glanced around the room like a hound sniffing the air. "Cosmetics, hotel key, cigarettes, lighter, a silk hankie, a roll of Certs, an eelskin wallet with ID, credit cards and better than three hundred cash. But no date book."

"Interesting." Finn nodded toward the champagne flute. "I'd say that was hers, wouldn't you, sitting there with her perfumes and skin creams."

"More than likely."

"There's another out in the parlor, over by the wet bar. Lipstick on that, too. Dark, hot-red lipstick."

"Good eye, Mr. Riley. Why don't we see if room service knows who Angela's drinking partner was?"

Carla Mendez had never had much excitement in her life. She'd been the oldest of five children born to a shoe salesman and a waitress and had lived a simple, uninspired life. At thirty-three, she had three children and a husband who was slavishly faithful and usually out of work.

Carla didn't mind her job as a hotel maid. She didn't like it particularly, but she did her job well if mechanically and tucked away tiny bottles of shampoo and skin cream as religiously as she tucked away her tips.

She was a small, sturdy woman, built like a fireplug, with tightly permed black hair and tiny dark eyes that were nearly lost in a network of worry lines. But her eyes were bright now, flitting from cop to reporter.

She didn't like cops. If Jenner had approached her alone, she would have closed up like a clam, on principle. But she couldn't resist Finn Riley. The way his dimples deepened when he smiled at her, the gentlemanly way he'd taken her hand.

And he wanted to interview her.

It was, for Carla, the biggest moment of her life.

Sensing her mood, Jenner hung back and let Finn take the ball.

"What time did you come into Miss Perkins's room to turn down the bed, Mrs. Mendez?"

"Ten o'clock. Usually I'd turn down much earlier, but she told me not to come in, not to disturb her before ten. She had appointments." Primly, she tugged on the hem of her uniform. "I don't like to work so late, but she was very nice." The twenty-dollar tip had been even nicer. "I've seen her on TV, too. But she wasn't stuck-up or anything. She was real polite. Messy, though," she added. "She and her husband used about six bath towels between them every day. And she had cigarette butts in every single ashtray. Dishes everywhere." She glanced around the parlor. "Cleaning up after people gives you insight," she said, and left it at that.

"I'm sure it does." Finn gave her an encouraging smile. "Was Miss Perkins with her husband when you were turning down the bed in their suite?"

"Can't say. Didn't see him. Didn't hear him. But I heard her, and the other one."

"The other one?"

"The other woman. They were scratching at each other like cats." Carla tugged on her hem again, examined her shoes. "Not that I listened. I mind my own business. I've been working in this hotel for seven years. You can't do that if you poke into people's private lives. But when I heard how she'd been murdered—Miss Perkins—I said to Gino, that's my husband, I said to Gino that I'd heard Miss Perkins going at it with this woman in her suite only a couple hours before she was dead. He said I should maybe tell my supervisor, but I thought it might cause trouble."

"So you haven't told anyone about it?" Finn prompted.

"No. And when you came in and said you wanted to talk to me about the people in 2403, I figured you already knew." Her eyes flashed back up. "Maybe you didn't."

"What can you tell us about the woman who was with Miss Perkins, Mrs. Mendez?"

"I didn't see her, but I heard her all right. Heard both of them. The woman said, 'I'm sick and tired of playing your games, Angela. And one way or the other they're going to stop.' Then Miss Perkins laughed. I knew it was her 'cause like I said, I've seen her on TV. And she laughed the way people do when they're feeling mean. And she said something like, 'Oh, you'll keep playing, darling. The stakes . . .' " Carla screwed up her nose as she concentrated. " 'The stakes are too high,' she said, 'for you to do anything else.' They called each other names for a while. Then the other woman said, 'I could kill you, Angela. But maybe I'll do something even better than that.' Then I heard the door slam, and Miss Perkins was laughing again. I finished up real quick and went out in the hall."

"You know, Mrs. Mendez, I think you should try my line of work." She preened and tugged on her hem again. "You're very observant," he added.

"It comes natural, I guess. You see a lot of funny things working in a hotel."

"I'm sure you do. I wonder . . . Did you see the woman who'd left?"

"No. There wasn't anybody out there, but it took me a couple of minutes to finish stacking fresh towels, so she could have gotten on the elevator. That was my last room, so I went home after that. The next morning I heard that Miss Perkins had been killed. At first I thought maybe that woman had come back and killed her right there in my suite. But I found out it didn't happen in the hotel at all. It happened at the TV station where Deanna Reynolds has her show. I like her show better," she added guilelessly. "She has such a nice smile."

Deanna tried to use that smile as Finn hesitated at the front door of the cabin. "I'm fine," she told him. She'd told him that repeatedly since she'd been released from the hospital three days before. "Finn, you're going to pick up a few things at the store; you're not leaving me to defend the fort against marauding hostiles. Besides"—she bent down to scratch the dog's ears—"I have a champion."

"Champion wimp." He cupped Deanna's face in his hands. "Let me worry, okay? It's still a new experience for me to fret." He grinned. "I like fretting over you, Deanna."

"As long as you're not fretting so much you forget to buy me that candy bar."

"Hershey's Big Block, no almonds." He kissed her, relieved when her lips curved gently, sweetly under his. The day he'd had her to himself at the cabin had dulled the edge of her horror, he knew, but she still slept poorly and jolted at unexpected sounds. "Why don't you take a nap, Kansas?"

"Why don't you go get me that candy bar?" She drew back, her smile securely in place. "Then you can take a nap with me."

"Sounds like a pretty good deal. I won't be long."

No, she thought as she watched him walk to the car. He wouldn't be long. He hated leaving her alone. Though what he expected her to do was beyond her. Collapse in a hysterical heap? she wondered, lifting her hand in a wave as he headed down the lane. Run screaming from the house?

With a sigh, she crouched down again to rub the dog while he whined and scratched at the door. He loved to go for rides, she thought now. But Finn had left him behind, a canine sentry.

Not that she could blame Finn for being overprotective at this point. She'd been alone with a murderer, after all. A murderer who could have taken her life as quickly, as cruelly as he had taken Angela's. Everyone was worried about poor Deanna, she thought. Her parents, Fran. Simon, Jeff, Margaret, Cassie. Roger and Joe and plenty of others from the newsroom. Even Loren and Barlow had called to express concern, to offer help.

"Take all the time you need," Loren had told her, without a single mention of ratings or expenses. "Don't even think about coming back until you're stronger."

But she wasn't weak. Deanna decided. She was alive.

No one had tried to kill her. Surely everyone must understand that one simple point. Yes, she had been alone with a murderer, but she was alive.

Straightening, she wandered around the cabin, tidying what was already competently neat. She brewed some tea she didn't want, then wandered more with the cup warming her hands. She poked at the cheerfully blazing fire.

She stared out the window. She sat on the couch.

She needed, desperately needed, to work.

This wasn't one of their stolen weekends filled to the brim with laughter and lovemaking and arguments over newspaper editorials. There wasn't a newspaper in the house, she thought in frustration. And Finn said there was some trouble with the cable, so television was out as well.

He was doing his best to keep the outside world at bay, she knew. To put her in a protective bubble, where nothing and no one could cause her distress.

And she'd let him, because what had happened in Chicago had seemed too horrible to think about; she'd let Finn push it all to the side for her.

But now she needed to take some action.

"We're going back to Chicago," she told the dog, who responded with a thud of his tail on the floor. She turned to the steps, intending to pack, when she heard the sound of a car on the drive. "He couldn't even have gotten to the store yet," she muttered, heading to the door behind the happily barking dog. "Look, Cronkite, I love him, too, but he hasn't been gone ten minutes." Deanna pushed open the screen, laughing as the dog bulleted through. But when she looked up and saw the car, the laughter died.

She didn't recognize the car, a dull brown sedan with dings in both fenders. But she recognized Jenner and found herself tugging the collar of her flannel shirt around her throat. She should have felt relieved to see him, to know he was trying to solve the case. Instead she felt only a tightening of the nerves that trapped her somewhere between fear and resignation.

Jenner grinned, obviously charmed by Cronkite's yapping and dancing around his legs. He bent down, unerringly finding the spot between Cronkite's ears that sent the dog into spasms of pleasure.

"Hey there, boy. There's a good dog." He chuckled when Cronkite plopped down on his rump and extended a paw to shake. "Know your manners, do you?" With the dog's dusty paw in his hand, he glanced up when Deanna stepped out on the porch. "This is quite a watchdog you've got here, Miss Reynolds."

"I'm afraid that's as fierce as he gets." The brisk December breeze invaded her bones. "You're a long way from Chicago, Lieutenant."

"Nice drive." Leaving his hand extended for the dog to sniff, he glanced around. The snow had melted, and the evergreens were glossily green. The breeze hummed through denuded trees and threatened to pick up and get mean. "Pretty place. Must feel good to get out of the city now and then."

"Yes, it does."

"Miss Reynolds, I'm sorry to disturb you, but I have some questions on the Perkins homicide."

"Please, come in. I've just made tea, but I can put on coffee if you'd prefer." How could they talk about murder without a nice, sociable cup? Deanna thought as her stomach turned.

"Tea's fine." Jenner walked toward the door with the dog prancing behind him.

"Sit down." She gestured him inside, toward the great room. "I'll just be a minute."

"Mr. Riley's not with you?" Jenner took a turn around the room, interested in the getaway lives of the rich.

"He went to the store. He'll be back shortly."

Hepplewhite. Jenner noted a side table and ladder-back chair. The rug was Native American. Navajo, he imagined. The glassware was Irish. Waterford.

"You have a good eye, Lieutenant." Her face bland, Deanna carried the tea tray into the room.

He didn't realize he'd spoken aloud, and smiled a little. It didn't bother him to be caught snooping. He got paid for it. "I like quality stuff. Even when I can't afford it." He nodded to the vase on the mantel, stuffed with early spring blooms. "Staffordshire?"

"Dresden." Annoyed, Deanna set the tray down with a snap. "I'm sure you didn't drive all the way out here to admire the bric-a-brac. Have you found out who killed Angela?"

"No." Jenner settled himself on the sofa with the dog at his feet. "We're beginning to put things together."

"That's comforting. Sugar, lemon?"

She was playing it tough, Jenner thought. "Black, thanks." He might have believed Deanna's act, if it hadn't been for the shadows under her eyes. "With sugar. Lots of it."

His grin apologetic, Jenner began to spoon sugar into the cup Deanna poured for him. "Sweet tooth. Miss Reynolds, I don't want to make you go through your whole statement again—"

"And I appreciate it." Deanna caught herself snapping the words, and sighed. "I want to cooperate, Lieutenant. I just don't see what more I can tell you. I had an appointment with Angela. I kept it. Someone killed her."

"Didn't it strike you as odd that she'd want to meet so late?"

Deanna eyed Jenner over the rim of her cup. "Angela was fond of making odd demands."

"And were you fond of going along with them?"

"No, I wasn't. I didn't want to meet her at all. It's no secret that we weren't on friendly terms, and I knew we'd quarrel. The fact that we would made me nervous." Deanna set down her cup, curled up her legs. "I don't like confrontations, Lieutenant, but I don't run away from them, as a rule. Angela and I had a history that I'm sure you're aware of."

"You were competitors." Jenner inclined his head a fraction. "You didn't like each other."

"No, we didn't like each other, and it was very personal on both sides. I was ready to have it out with her, and a part of me hoped that we could settle things amicably. Another part was looking forward to yanking out a few handfuls of her hair. I won't deny I wanted her out of my way, but I didn't want her dead." She looked back at Jenner, calmer now, steadier. "Is that why you're here? Am I a suspect?"

Jenner rubbed a hand over his chin. "The victim's husband, Dan Gardner, seems to think you hated her enough to kill her. Or have her killed."

"Have her killed?" Deanna blinked at that and nearly laughed. "So now I hired a convenient hit man, paid him to murder Angela, knock me unconscious and roll tape. Very inventive of me." She sprang up, color washing back into her cheeks. "I don't even know Dan Gardner. It's flattering that he should consider me so clever. And what was my motive? Ratings points? It seems to me I should have arranged it so that I didn't miss the November sweeps."

The bruised, helpless look was gone, Jenner noted. She was fired up, burning on indignation and disgust. "Miss Reynolds, I didn't say we agreed with Mr. Gardner."

She stared for a moment, eyes kindling. "Just wanted a reaction? I hope I satisfied you."

Jenner cocked a brow. "Miss Reynolds, did you visit Miss Perkins at her hotel on the night she was murdered?"

"No." Frustrated, Deanna raked a hand through her hair. "Why should I have? We were meeting at the studio."

"You might have gotten impatient." Jenner knew he was reaching. Deanna's fingerprints hadn't been found in the suite, certainly they weren't on the extra champagne flute.

"Even if I had, Angela told me that she'd be busy until midnight. She had meetings."

"Did she mention with whom?"

"We weren't chatting, Detective, and I had no interest in her personal or her business plans."

"You knew she had enemies?"

"I knew she wasn't particularly well liked. Part of that might have been her personality, and part of it was because she was a woman with a great deal of power. She could be hard and vindictive. She could also be charming and generous."

"I don't imagine you found it charming when she arranged for you to walk in on her and Dr. Pike, in compromising circumstances."

"That's old news."

"But you were in love with him?"

"I was almost in love with him," Deanna corrected. "A very large difference." Oh, what was the point of all this? she wondered, and rubbed at the headache brewing dead center of her forehead. "I won't deny it hurt me, and it infuriated me, and it changed my feelings about both of them irrevocably."

"Dr. Pike tried to continue your relationship."

"He didn't look on the incident in the same way I did. I wasn't interested in continuing anything with him, and I made that clear."

"But he did persist for quite a while."

"Yes."

Jenner recognized the emotion behind the clipped response. "And the notes, the ones you've been receiving with some regularity for several years. Did you ever consider that he was sending them?"

"Marshall?" She shook her head. "No. They're not his style."

"What is?"

Deanna's eyes shut. She remembered the photographs, the detective's report. "Perhaps you should ask him."

"We will. Have you been involved with anyone other than Dr. Pike? Anyone who might have been so disturbed by the announcement of your engagement to Mr. Riley that they would break into your office, or Mr. Riley's home?"

"No, there's been—what do you mean, break in?" She gripped the wing of the chair she stood beside.

"It seems logical that whoever sent the notes is also responsible for the destruction of your office and the house you share with Mr. Riley," Jenner began. And, he believed, for Angela's murder.

"When?" Deanna could barely whisper the word. "When did this happen?"

Intrigued, Jenner stopped tapping his pencil on his pad. The rosy glow anger had brought to Deanna's cheeks had drained, leaving her face white as bone. Riley hadn't told her yet, he realized. And the man wasn't going to be pleased to have been scooped. "The night Angela Perkins was shot, Finn Riley's house was broken into."

"No." Still gripping the chair, she shifted, lowered herself before her legs buckled. "Finn didn't—no one told me." She squeezed her eyes shut, fighting the kick of nerves in her stomach. When she opened them again, they were dark as pitch and burning dry. "But you will. I want to know what happened. Exactly what happened."

There was going to be more than a little tiff when Finn Riley returned, Jenner decided. As he related the facts, he watched her take them in. She winced once, as though the words were darts, then went very still. Her eyes remained level, and curiously blank until he had finished.

She said nothing for a moment, leaning forward to pour more tea. Her hand was steady. Jenner admired her poise and control, particularly since he'd seen the ripple of horror cross her face.

"You think that whoever's been sending the notes, whoever broke into my office and my home, killed Angela."

It was a reporter's voice, Jenner noted. Cool and calm and without inflection. But her eyes weren't blank any longer. They were terrified. For some reason he remembered a report she'd done years before, a woman in the suburbs who'd been shot to death by her husband. Her eyes hadn't been blank then, either.

"It's a theory," he said at length. "It makes more sense for only one person to be involved."

"Then why not me?" Her voice broke, and she shook her head impatiently. "Why Angela and not me? If he was so angry, so violently angry with me, why did he kill her and leave me alive?"

"She was in your way," Jenner said briskly, and watched as the full impact struck Deanna like a blow.

"He killed her for me? Oh Jesus, he did it for me."

"We can't be sure of that." Jenner began, but Deanna was already shoving out of her chair.

"Finn. Good God, he could come after Finn. He broke into the house. If Finn had been there, he would have..." She pressed a hand to her stomach. "You have to do something."

"Miss Reynolds—"

But she heard the sound of tires on gravel. She whirled, racing the dog to the door, shouting for him.

Finn was already cursing the other car in the drive when he heard her call his name. His annoyance at the intrusion faded as he saw her sprint out of the house. She leaped trembling into his arms, choking back sobs.

Finn gathered her close, his eyes hot and lethal as they skimmed over her shoulder to where Jenner stood on the porch. "What the hell have you done?"

"I'm sorry." It was the best Finn could think of to say as he faced Deanna across the living room. Jenner had left them alone. After, Finn thought bitterly, he'd dropped his bomb.

"What for? Because I found out from Jenner? Or because you didn't trust me enough to tell me in the first place?"

"That it happened at all," he said carefully. "And it wasn't a matter of trust, Deanna. You're barely out of the hospital."

"And you didn't want to upset my delicate mental balance. That's why the television is conveniently on the blink. That's why you wanted to go to the store alone, and didn't bring back the paper. We wouldn't want poor little Deanna to hear any news that might upset her."

"Close enough." He plunged his hands into his pockets. "I thought you needed some time."

"You thought. Well, you thought wrong." She spun around, headed for the stairs. "You had no right to keep this from me."

"I did keep it from you. Damn it, if we're going to fight, at least do it face to face." He stopped her on the landing, grabbing her arm, turning her around.

"I can fight when I'm packing." She shook him off and stalked into the bedroom.

"You want to go back, fine. We'll go back after we've settled this."

She dragged an overnight case out of the closet. "We don't have to go anywhere. I'm going." She tossed the case onto the bed, threw open the lid. "Alone." In quick, jerky moves, she plucked bottles and jars from the dresser. "I'm going back to my apartment. I can get whatever I've left at your house later."

"No," he said, very calmly, "you're not."

She heaved a perfume bottle toward the open case. It bounced merrily on the bed.

"That's exactly what I'm doing." With her eyes on his, she pried his fingers loose. "You lied to me, Finn. If Jenner hadn't come out here for some follow-up questions, I wouldn't have known about the break-in, or that you'd interviewed Dan Gardner and that hotel maid. I wouldn't have known anything."

"No, and you might have gotten a few nights' sleep."

"You lied," she repeated, refusing to see past that. "And don't tell me keeping the truth from me is different than lying. It's the same. I won't continue in a relationship that isn't honest."

"You want honest. That's fine." He turned, shut the door with a quiet click. A final click. "I'll do anything and everything in my power to protect you. That's a fact." Eyes steady, he walked back to her. "You're not walking out on me, Deanna. That's a fact. And you're not using some bullshit about rights and trust as your escape hatch. If you want out, then at least be honest."

"All right." She shifted so that he couldn't see the way her hands shook as she packed. "I made a mistake when I agreed to marry you, and I've had time to think it through. I need to concentrate on my career, on my own life. I can't do that if I'm trying to make a marriage work, if I'm starting a family. I talked myself into thinking I could do it all, but I was wrong." The diamonds on her finger winked mockingly at her. She couldn't quite bring herself to take the ring off. Not yet. "I don't want to marry you, Finn, and it's not fair to either of us to continue this way. My priority right now is my work, and getting it back on track."

"Look at me, Deanna. I said look at me." With his hands Finn on her shoulders, he turned her to face him. The sensation of panic faded into steely confidence. "You're lying."

"I know you don't want to believe—"

"Jesus Christ, Deanna, don't you know that I can see it in your face. You could never lie worth a damn. Why are you doing this?"

"I don't want to hurt you any more than necessary, Finn." She held herself rigid in his arms, stared over his shoulder. "Let me go."

"Not a chance in hell."

"I don't want you." Her voice cracked. "I don't want this. Is that clear enough?"

"No." He jerked her forward, covered her mouth with his. She trembled immediately, her body shuddering against his, her lips heating. "But that is."

"It's not the answer." But her body yearned for his, for the warmth, the strength.

"You want me to apologize again?" Gently now, he stroked a hand over her hair. "Fine. I'm sorry, and I'd do exactly the same thing. If you want to call it lying to you, then I'd lie. I'd do whatever I had to do to keep you safe."

"I don't want to be protected." She broke away, curled her hands into impotent fists. "I don't need to be protected. Can't you see? Don't you understand? He used *me* to kill her. He used *me*. He isn't going to hurt *me*; I don't need to be protected. But God knows who else he might hurt because of me."

"Me," he said quietly, furiously. "That's what this is all about. You think he might try for me. The best way to prevent that is to dump me, right? To make sure everyone knows you've broken it off."

Her lips trembled before she pressed them together. "I'm not going to argue with you, Finn."

"You're absolutely right about that." He picked up her case and upended the contents. "Don't ever try that with me again. Don't ever use my feelings on me like that again."

"He'll try to kill you," she said dully. "I know he will."

"So you lied, to try to protect me." When she opened her mouth, shut it again, he smiled. "Quid pro quo, Deanna. We'll call it even. So you don't want to be protected—neither do I. What do you want?"

She lifted her fisted hands to her cheeks, then let them fall. "I want you to stop watching me as though I were going to fall apart."

"Done. What else?"

"I want you to swear you won't keep anything from me, no matter how much you think it'll upset me."

"Deal, and same goes."

She nodded slowly, watching him. "You're still angry."

"Yeah. I'm still angry. It's a residual effect when the woman I love cuts me in half."

"You still want me."

"God, yes, I still want you."

"You haven't made love with me since this happened. Whenever I'd turn to you, you'd soothe and you'd cuddle, but you haven't touched me."

"No, I haven't." He felt the blood begin to swim in his veins. "I wanted to give you time."

"I don't want time!" she shouted at him, felt the first sweet snap of release. "I'm not fragile or weak or delicate. I want you to stop looking at me as though I were, as though I'd crumble. I'm alive. I want to feel alive. Make me feel alive."

He reached out, brushed his knuckle down her cheek. "You should have asked for something more difficult."

He kissed her. She could feel the sparks of fury he was struggling to bank, taste the hot frustration, the searing need.

"Don't," she murmured. "Don't be gentle. Not now."

He wanted to be. But she was pulling him down on the bed, her hands already frantic as they tugged at his clothes. He couldn't be gentle, couldn't tap the well of tenderness when her mouth was driving him beyond caution into madness.

Her body vibrated against his as she arched and strained and writhed. More was all she could think. More of him. More of that simmering violence she had watched him fight to chain for days. She wanted him to release it now, inside her.

She could hear her own heart drum heavily in her ears, feel each separate pulse throb. Her muffled cry was one of triumph as he ripped her shirt aside, seeking flesh.

The wind kicked against the windows, rattling glass. It hooted down the chimney, struggling to puff smoke into the room. But the fire blazed in the hearth and burned brighter with the threat of the storm.

On the bed they rolled like thunder.

His mouth was on her, ravenous, teeth scraping skin already damp with passion. His breath was hot and quick, his hands bruising in their hurry to possess. She reared up to meet him, her head falling back, her moan long and feral.

Faster. Faster. The desperation peaked as he yanked at her jeans, his hungry mouth racing down her shuddering torso toward the violent heat. Her hands dived into his hair, pressed him closer, closer. Her nails scraped unfelt down his back as the first orgasm pummeled her.

"Now." She nearly wept it, dragging him up, frantic for him to fill her. Her hands clutched at his hips, her legs wrapped around his waist. "Now," she said again, then cried out when he drove himself into her.

"More." He yanked her body up, plunged deeper, thrusting hard, still harder while the ferocity of pleasure racked through him. His body felt like an engine, tireless, primed to run. He mated it with hers, steel cased in velvet, pumping faster each time he felt her muscles contract like a moist fist around him.

When she arched, straining, he pulled her to him until they were torso to torso. Her teeth sank into his shoulder even as her body moved like wet silk against his. Again she went rigid, her body stiffening, then breaking into shudders. Her eyes sprang open, staring glazed into his while she went limp.

"I can't."

He shoved her back, grasping her hands and dragging them over her head. "I can."

He devoured her, letting the animal take over, ripping each new response from her with impatient teeth, enticing new fires with tongue and lips.

His breath was burning in his throat, his blood pounding in his head, in his loins. The final wave of sensation swamped him, flooded through his system like light—white and blinding. He thought she cried out again, just his name, as he emptied himself into her.

24

Marshall Pike's office looked like an elegant living room. But no one lived there. It reminded Finn of an ambitious model home, decorated for prospective buyers who would never slouch on the brocade sofa or wrestle on the Aubusson rug. There would certainly never be a careless ring left by a careless glass set on the Chippendale coffee table. No child would ever play hide-and-seek behind the formal silk draperies or cuddle up to read in one of the deep-cushioned chairs.

Even Marshall's desk seemed more of a prop than a usable fixture. The oak was highly polished, the brass fittings gleamed. The desk set of burgundy leather fit seamlessly into the color scheme of wines and ferns. The ficus tree by the window wasn't plastic, but it was so perfect, its leaves so radically dust-free, it might as well have been.

Finn had lived with easy wealth all of his life, and the material trappings it could buy, but he found Marshall Pike's pristine office, with its low hum of an air filter discreetly sucking impurities, soulless.

"I would, naturally, be happy to cooperate with the police." Piously, Marshall tugged the sleeves of his jacket over the monogrammed cuffs of his crisp white shirt. "As I explained to you, they haven't found it necessary to question me. Why would they? I have nothing to say to the press."

"As I explained to you, I'm not here as a member of the press. You're not obligated to talk to me, Pike, but if you don't..." Finn spread his hands. Jenner was going to be pissed, he thought, that he hadn't cleared this interview with the police. But this particular contact was personal. "Some of my associates might appreciate having their memory jogged about a certain incident between you and Angela. One that slipped through the cracks a couple of years ago?"

"I can't imagine that something so trivial would be of interest to anyone."

"It's amazing, isn't it, what grabs the viewer's attention? And what, if presented with a certain angle, will intrigue the police."

The man was reaching, of course, Marshall assured himself. There was nothing, absolutely nothing to connect him with Angela but a momentary lapse of judgment. And yet... a word to the wrong person could result in publicity his practice couldn't afford.

A few questions, he decided, a few answers wouldn't matter. He was, after all, an expert at communication. If he couldn't handle an overexposed reporter, he didn't deserve the degrees hanging prominently on the wall behind him.

More, he would enjoy outwitting the man Deanna had chosen over him.

"My last appointment for the day canceled." He shook his head as if in pity for the unhappy couple who wouldn't benefit from his skills. "I don't have another engagement until seven. I can spare you a few moments."

"That's all I'll need. When did you hear about Angela's death?"

"On the news, the morning after the murder. I was shocked. I understand that Deanna was with her in the studio. As you know, Deanna and I had a relationship. Naturally, I'm concerned about her."

"I'm sure that will help her sleep easy at night."

"I have tried to contact her, to offer my support."

"She doesn't need it."

"Territorial, Mr. Riley?" Marshall asked with a curve of the lips.

"Absolutely, Dr. Pike," Finn answered.

"In my profession, it's essential to be fair-minded." He continued to smile. "Deanna meant a great deal to me at one time."

With some interviews you prodded, with others you planted. In Marshall's case, Finn noted that the shorter the question, the more expansive the answer.

"Did she?"

"A great deal of time has passed. And Deanna is engaged to you. Regardless, I would still offer whatever support or help I could to someone I was fond of, particularly under such shocking circumstances."

"And Angela Perkins?" Finn leaned back in his chair. However relaxed his pose, he was alert, watching every flick of Marshall's eye. "Were you fond of her?"

"No," he said shortly. "I was not."

"Yet it was your affair with Miss Perkins which ended your relationship with Deanna."

"There was no affair." Marshall linked his hands on the desktop. "There was a momentary lapse of control and common sense. I came to understand rather quickly that Angela had orchestrated the entire incident for her own reasons."

"Which were?"

"In my opinion? To manipulate Deanna and to cause her distress. She was successful." His smile was thin and humorless. "Although Deanna did not accept the position Angela had offered her in New York, she did sever ties with me."

"You resent that?"

"I resent, Mr. Riley, that Deanna refused to see the incident for what it was. Less than nothing. A mere physical reaction to deliberate stimuli. There was no emotion involved, none at all."

"Some people are more emotional about sex than others." Finn smiled wider, deliberately baiting him. "Deanna's very emotional."

"Indeed," he said, and left it at that. When Finn remained silent, annoyance pushed him on. "I don't understand how my unfortunate misstep could be related to the investigation."

"I didn't say it was," Finn said pleasantly. "But, just to clear up that matter, why don't you tell me where you were on the night of the murder? Between the hours of eleven and two?"

"I was home."

"Alone?"

"Yes, alone." Confident now, Marshall relaxed. His eyes were mild. "I'm sure you'd agree, if I'd been planning on murder I would have had the simple intelligence to provide myself with an alibi. However, I had dinner, alone, spent a few hours working on case studies, then went to bed."

"Did you speak with anyone? Receive any phone calls?"

"I let the service take my calls. I don't like to be interrupted when I'm working—barring emergencies." He smiled cockily. "Do you advise me to contact my lawyer, Mr. Riley?"

"If you think you need one." If he was lying, Finn mused, he was cool about it. "When was the last time you saw Angela?"

For the first time in the interview there was a flash of genuine pleasure in Marshall's eyes. "I haven't seen Angela since she made the move to New York. That would be over two years ago."

"Have you had any contact with her since that time?"

"Why would I? We did not have a love affair, as I explained."

"You didn't have one with Deanna, either," Finn commented, and had the satisfaction of wiping the smile from Marshall's face. "But you've continued to contact her."

"Not for nearly a year. She is not forgiving."

"But you have sent notes. Made calls."

"No, I haven't. Not until I heard about this. She hasn't returned my calls, so I must assume she neither wants nor needs my help." Assured he'd been more than reasonable, he tapped his cuff again, rose. "As I said, I do have an appointment at seven, and I need to go home and change for the evening. I must say, this was an interesting interlude. Be sure to give Deanna my best."

"I don't think so." Finn rose as well, but made no move to leave. "I've got another question. You can call this one from reporter to psychologist."

Marshall's lips jerked into a sneer. "How could I refuse?"

"It's about obsession." Finn let the word hang a moment, watching for any sign: an avoidance of eye contact, a tic, a change in tone. "If a man, or a woman, was fixed on someone, long-term, say, two or three years, and he had fantasies but he couldn't bring himself to approach this person, face to face, and in these fantasies he felt he'd been betrayed, what would he be feeling? Love? Or hate?"

"A difficult question, Mr. Riley, with such little information. I can say that love and hate are as intricately entwined as the poets claim. Either one can take control, and either one, depending on circumstances, can be dangerous. Obsessions are rarely constructive, for either party. Tell me, are you planning a show on the topic?"

"Could be." Finn reached for his coat. "As a layman, I wonder if someone who was dealing with that kind of obsession might be able to hide it. Go through the day-to-day motions without letting the mask slip." He studied Marshall's face now. "The old John Smith who mows down half a dozen people in a Kmart. The neighbors say what a nice, quiet guy he was."

"It happens, doesn't it? Most people are very clever at allowing others to see only what they wish to be seen. And most people only see what they choose in any case. If the human race were simpler, both of us would be looking for other means of employment."

"You have a point. Thanks for your time."

As Finn walked out of the office, through the reception area and to the bank of elevators, he wondered if Marshall Pike was the type who could calmly blow a woman's face off and walk away. There was cold blood there. That much he was sure of.

Smarm under the polish, Finn mused. It could have been pure animal reaction, he supposed, a territorial instinct. No, Finn concluded, that unease came from the reporter in him. The man was hiding something, and it was up to him to ferret it out.

It wouldn't hurt to take a run by the hotel and see if anyone had spotted Marshall in the area on the night of Angela's death.

In his office, Marshall sat behind his desk. He waited, and waited until he heard the faint rumble of the elevator. And he waited again until he heard nothing at all. Snatching up the phone, he punched in numbers, wiped his damp palm over his face.

He heard Finn's voice relay the information he already knew: Deanna wasn't there. Marshall slammed down the phone and buried his head in his hands.

Goddamn Finn Riley. Goddamn Angela. And goddamn Deanna. He had to see her. And he had to see her now.

"You shouldn't have come back yet." Jeff stood in Deanna's office, his pleasant, homely face set in stubborn lines of worry. The smell of paint was still fresh.

They both knew why the walls had been painted, the rug replaced. There were long, jagged scratch marks marring the surface of Deanna's desk. The police had unsealed the room only forty-eight hours before and there hadn't been time to repair or replace everything.

"I was hoping you'd be glad to see me."

"I am glad to see you, but not here." Since it was just past eight in the morning, they were alone. Jeff felt obligated to convince her to give herself more time. When the rest of the staff arrived, he had no doubt they would add their weight. But now it was up to him to watch out for her. "You've been through a nightmare, Dee, and it hasn't even been a week."

Yes it had, she thought. One week tonight. But she didn't correct him. "Jeff, I've already been through this with Finn—"

"He shouldn't have let you come in."

Her hackles rose, but she bit back the first furious retort. Perhaps her nerves were still raw, she decided, if she was ready to snarl at poor Jeff. "Finn doesn't *let* me anything. If it makes you feel better, he agrees with you completely about my taking more time. I don't." She eased a hip down on the wide sill of the plate-glass window. Behind her, wet snow fell in thick, listless sheets. "I need to work, Jeff. Angela's death was horrible, but hiding my head under the covers isn't going to make it, or my part in it, go away. And I need my pals." She held out a hand. "I really do."

She heard him sigh, but he crossed to her and took her hand. "We wanted to be there for you, Dee. All of us."

"I know you did." She squeezed his hand, urging him down on the sill with her. "I guess this hasn't been easy on anyone. Did you have to talk to the police?"

"Yeah." He grimaced, shoving at his glasses. "That Detective Jenner. 'Where were you on the night in question?' " Jeff demanded in such a perfect mimic of Jenner that Deanna laughed. "We all got the treatment. Simon was sweating bullets. You know how he is under pressure. Wringing his hands, gulping audibly. He got so worked up that Fran made him lie down, then tore into the cop for harassment."

"Sorry I missed it." She leaned her head against Jeff's shoulder, content to be back with friends. "What else did I miss?" She could feel his body tense and she squeezed his hand in reassurance. "I'd feel better if I knew, Jeff. I've only gotten some sketchy details about how the office was torn up. I miss our Christmas tree." Her smile was brief and sad. "Silly, isn't it? When you think of everything that was destroyed in here, I miss that stupid tree."

"I'll get you another one. Just as ugly."

"Impossible." But she let it go. "Tell me."

He hesitated a moment. "The office was pretty messed up, Dee. But it was mostly cosmetic damage. Once the cops let us in, Loren had it cleaned out, repainted, recarpeted. He was royally pissed. Not at you," he said quickly. "It was the whole deal, you know. The fact that somebody got in and . . . did what they did."

"I'll call him."

"Deanna . . . I'm sorry. I don't know what else to say. I'm so damn sorry you had to go through all that. I wish I could say I'm sorry about Angela, but I'm not."

"Jeff—"

"I'm not," he repeated, and tightened his grip on her hand. "She wanted to hurt you. She did everything she could to ruin your career. Using Lew, making up lies, dragging that whole business with that creep football player into the public. I can't be sorry she won't be around to try something else." He let out a long breath. "I guess that makes me pretty cold."

"No, it doesn't. Angela didn't inspire great love and devotion."

"You do."

She lifted her head and turned to smile at him, when a sound in the doorway made them both jump.

"Oh, God." Cassie stood, a paperweight in one hand, a brass sculpture in the other. "I thought someone had broken in again." She pressed the hefty glass paperweight to her heart.

On watery legs, Deanna managed the two steps to a chair. "I came in early," she said, trying desperately to sound calm and in control. "I thought I might start catching up."

"I guess that makes three of us." With her eyes on Deanna, Cassie set the sculpture and paperweight aside. "Are you sure you're okay?"

"No." Deanna closed her eyes for a moment. "But I need to be here."

Perhaps her nerves were raw and her temper short, but by midmorning Deanna found some comfort in the basic office routine. Bookings had to be rearranged and rescheduled, others fell through completely due to the time lapse. New story ideas were devised and discussed. Once word spread that Deanna was back in harness, the phones began to shrill. People from the newsroom popped upstairs, out of both genuine concern and pure curiosity.

"Benny's hoping you'll do an interview," Roger told her. "An exclusive for old times' sake."

Deanna passed him half the sandwich she was nibbling at her now overburdened desk. "Benny thinks a lot of old times' sake."

"It's news, Dee. And pretty hot when you consider it happened right here at CBC and involved two major stars."

A *major star,* she thought. What was the difference between a major star and a minor one? She knew what Loren would have said: A minor star sought airtime. A major star sold it.

"Give me some time, will you?" She rubbed at the tension in the back of her neck. "Tell him I'm thinking about it."

"Sure." His gaze wandered from hers to his own hands. "I'd appreciate it, if you decide to do it, if you let me do the interview." His eyes cut back to her, then away again. "I could use the boost. There are rumors of cutbacks in the newsroom again."

"There are always rumors of cutbacks in the newsroom." She resented the favor he was asking, and wished she didn't. "All right, Roger, for old times' sake. Just give me a couple of days."

"You're a peach, Dee." And he felt like sludge. "I'd better get down. I've got some bumpers to tape." He rose, leaving the sandwich untouched. "It's good to have you back. You know if you need a friendly ear, I've got two."

"Off the record?"

He had the grace to flush. "Sure. Off the record."

She held up both hands as if to gesture the words back. "Sorry. I'm touchy, I guess. I'll have Cassie set up an interview in a day or two, all right?"

"Whenever you're ready." He walked to the door. "This really sucks," he murmured as he shut the door behind him.

"You bet." Deanna leaned back in her chair, closing her eyes, letting herself hear only the impersonal murmur of the television across the room. Angela was dead, she thought, and that made her a hotter news item than she had ever been when she was alive.

The really horrid bottom line, Deanna knew, was that she was now hot news as well. And hot news made for hot ratings. Since the murder, *Deanna's Hour*—reruns of *Deanna's Hour,* she corrected—had spurted up in points, pummeling the competition. No game show or daytime drama could hope to withstand the mighty weight of murder and scandal.

Angela had given her greatest rival the success she'd hoped to take away. She'd only had to die to do it.

"Deanna?"

Her heart flew to her throat, her eyes sprang open. On the other side of her desk, Simon jumped as violently as she. "Sorry," he said quickly. "I guess you didn't hear me knock."

"That's okay." Disgusted with her reaction, she chuckled weakly. "My nerves don't seem to be as strong as I thought. You look exhausted."

He tried to smile, but couldn't bring it off. "Having trouble sleeping." He fumbled out a cigarette.

"I thought you'd quit."

"Me too." Embarrassed, he moved his shoulders. "I know you said you wanted to start taping on Monday."

"That's right. Is there a problem?"

"It's just that . . ." He trailed off, puffing hard on the cigarette. "I thought, under the circumstances—but maybe it doesn't matter to you. It just seemed to me . . ."

Deanna wondered if she grabbed onto his tongue and pulled, if the words would spill out. "What?"

"The set," he blurted out, and passed a nervous hand over his thinning hair. "I thought you might want to change the set. The chairs . . . you know."

"Oh God." She pressed a fist to her mouth as the vision of Angela, sitting cozily, sitting dead in the spacious white chair, flashed into her mind. "Oh God, I haven't thought."

"I'm sorry, Deanna." For lack of something better he patted her shoulder. "I shouldn't have said anything. I'm an idiot."

"No. No. Thank God you did. I don't think I could have handled . . ." She imagined herself striding out on the set, then freezing in shock and horror. Would she have run screaming, as she had done before? "Oh, Simon. Oh, sweet Jesus."

"Dee." Helplessly he patted her shoulder again. "I didn't mean to upset you."

"I think you just saved my sanity. Put the set decorator on it, Simon, please? Have him change everything. The color scheme, the chairs, tables, the plants. Everything. Tell him—"

Simon had already taken out a notebook to scribble down her instructions. The simple, habitual gesture somehow cheered Deanna.

"Thanks, Simon."

"I'm the detail man, remember?" He tapped out the half-smoked cigarette. "Don't worry about it. We'll have a whole new look."

"But keep it comfortable. And why don't you knock off early? Go get yourself a massage."

"I'd rather work."

"I know what you mean."

"I didn't know it would affect me like this." He tucked the pad away. "I worked with her for years. I can't say I liked her much, but I knew her. I stood right here, in this spot, when she was sitting there." He glanced up again, meeting Deanna's eyes. "Now, she's dead. I can't stop thinking about it."

"Neither can I."

"Whoever did it was in here, too." Warily, he scanned the room, as if he expected someone to lunge out of a corner wielding a gun. "Jesus, I'm sorry. All I'm doing is scaring the shit out of both of us. I guess it's eating on me because her memorial service is tonight."

"Tonight? In New York?"

"No, here. I guess she wanted to be buried in Chicago, where she got her big break. There's not going to be a viewing or anything, because . . ." He remembered why and swallowed hard. "Well, there's just going to be a service at the funeral parlor. I think I should go."

"Give the details to Cassie, will you? I think I should go, too."

"This isn't just stupid," Finn said with barely controlled fury. "It's insane."

Deanna watched the windshield wipers sweep at the ugly, icy sleet. The snow that had fallen throughout the day had turned to oily gray slop against the curbs. The sleet that replaced it battered down, cold and mean.

It was a good night for a funeral.

Her chin came up and her jaw tightened. "I told you that you didn't have to come with me."

"Yeah, right." He spotted the crowd of reporters huddled outside the funeral parlor and drove straight down the block. "Goddamn press."

She nearly smiled at that, felt a giddy urge to laugh out loud. But she was afraid it would sound hysterical. "I won't mention anything about pots and kettles."

"I'm going to park down the block," he said between his teeth. "We'll see if we can find a side or a back entrance."

"I'm sorry," she repeated when he'd parked. "Sorry to have dragged you out to this tonight." She had a headache she didn't dare mention. And a raw sick feeling in her stomach that promised to worsen.

"I don't recall being dragged."

"I knew you wouldn't let me come alone. So it amounts to the same thing. I can't even explain to myself why I feel I have to do this. But I have to do it."

Suddenly, she twisted toward him, gripping his hand hard. "Whoever killed her could be in there. I keep wondering if I'll know him. If I look him in the face, if I'll know. I'm terrified I will."

"But you still want to go inside."

"I have to."

The sleet helped, she thought. Not only was it cold, but it demanded the use of long, disguising coats and shielding umbrellas. They walked in silence, against the wind. She caught sight of the CBC van before Finn ducked around the side of the building. He hustled her inside, drenching them both as he snapped the umbrella closed.

"I hate goddamned funerals."

Surprised, she studied his face as she tugged off her gloves, shed her coat. She could see it now. More than annoyance with her for insisting on attending, more than concern or even fear, there was dread in his eyes. "I'm sorry. I didn't realize."

"I haven't been to one since . . . in years. What's the point? Dead's dead. Flowers and organ music don't change it."

"It's supposed to comfort the living."

"Not so I've noticed."

"We won't stay long." She took his hand, surprised that it would be he rather than she who needed comfort.

He seemed to shudder, once. "Let's get it over with."

They walked out of the alcove. They could already hear the murmur of voices, the muted notes of a dirge. Not organ music, he realized, horribly relieved, but piano and cello in somber duet. The air smelled of lemon oil, perfume, flowers. He would have sworn he smelled whiskey as well, sharp as a blade cutting through the overly sweetened air.

The thick carpet was a riot of deep red roses and muffled their footsteps as they walked down a wide hall. On both sides heavy oak doors were discreetly shut. At the end they were flung open. Cigarette smoke added to the miasma of scent.

When he felt her tremble, Finn tucked his arm more firmly around her waist. "We can turn around and leave, Deanna. There's no shame in it."

She only shook her head. Then she saw the first video camera. The press, it seemed, wasn't merely huddled outside. Several had been allowed in, complete with camera crews, microphones and lights. Cables were strewn over the garden of carpet in the main viewing room.

In silence, they slipped inside.

The cathedral ceiling with its painted mural of cherubim and seraphim tossed the murmuring voices and chinking glasses everywhere.

The room was crowded with people. As Deanna looked from face to face, she wondered if she would see grief or fear or simply resignation. Would Angela feel she was being mourned properly? And would her killer be here, to observe?

No one wept, Finn noted. He did see shock and sober eyes. Voices were muted respectfully. And the cameras recorded it all. Would they, he wondered, inadvertently record one face, one that couldn't quite hide the knowledge, and the triumph? He kept Deanna close to his side, knowing that the murderer could be in the room, watching.

There was a photograph of Angela in a gold frame. The flattering publicity shot sat atop a gleaming mahogany coffin.

It reminded Finn, much too vividly, of what lay inside the discreetly closed lid. Feeling Deanna shudder beside him, he instinctively drew her closer.

"Let's get the hell out of here."

"No."

"Kansas—" But when he looked at her he saw more than the shock and fear. He saw what was missing on so many of the other faces that crowded the room: grief.

"Whatever her motives," Deanna said quietly, "she helped me once. And whoever did this to her used me." Her voice broke. "I can't forget that."

Neither could he. That was what terrified him. "It would be better if Dan Gardner doesn't spot either one of us."

Deanna nodded, spotting him at the front of the room, accepting condolences. "He's using her too, even though she's dead. It's horrible."

"He'll ride her press for a while. She'd have understood that."

"I suppose."

"An interesting scene, isn't it?" Loren commented when he joined them. He gave Deanna a hard, searching look, then nodded. "You're looking well."

"No I'm not." Grateful for the lie, she kissed his cheek. "I didn't think you'd come."

"I could say the same." He warmed her chilled hands between his. "It seemed necessary somehow, but I'm already regretting it." His expression changed to one of disgust as he looked over his shoulder at Dan Gardner. "Rumor is he plans to air clips from this viewing along with the special Angela taped for next May. And he's demanding another five thousand a minute from sponsors. The son of a bitch will get it, too."

"Bad taste often costs more than good," Deanna murmured. "There must be five hundred people in here."

"Easily. A handful are even sorry she's dead."

"Oh, Loren," Deanna's stomach clenched like a fist.

"I hate to admit I'm one of them." Then he sighed and shrugged off the mood. "She'd have gotten an ego boost out of that piece of news." To clear the emotion from his voice, Loren coughed gently into his hand. "You know, I can't decide if Angela deserved Dan Gardner or not. It's a tough call."

"I'm sure she didn't deserve you." The tears burning in her eyes made Deanna feel like a hypocrite since they weren't for Angela. "We're not staying, Loren. Why don't you come with us?"

"No, I'm going to see this through. But I think you should avoid any publicity here tonight. Slip out quietly."

When they were back in the alcove, Deanna turned into Finn's arms. "I had no idea he still loved her."

"I don't think he did, either." He tipped her face up until their eyes were level. "Are you all right?"

"Actually, I'm better." She turned her head until her cheek rested on his shoulder. Most of the fear had ebbed, she realized. That jittering panic she'd nearly grown accustomed to feeling in her stomach had quieted. "I'm glad we came."

"Excuse me." Kate Lowell's sultry voice had Deanna turning her head. She stood in the doorway, sleek and somber in black silk, her hair waves of flame over her shoulders. "I'm sorry to interrupt."

"You haven't," Deanna responded. "We were just leaving."

"So am I." She glanced over her shoulder toward the sounds of voices and music. "It's not my kind of party." She smiled slightly. "She was a bitch," Kate said. "And I hated her guts. But I'm not sure even Angela deserved to be used quite so blatantly." She sighed once, moving her shoulders as if to shrug it all away. "I'd like a drink. And I need to talk to you." She looked at Finn and frowned. "I suppose it'll have to be both of you, and it hardly matters at this point." She watched Finn's brow rise, and smiled again, with more feeling. "Really gracious, aren't I? Listen, why don't you find us a bar? I'll buy us all a drink and tell you a little story you might find interesting."

25

"To Hollywood," Kate said as she raised her glass of scotch. "Land of illusions."

Puzzled, Deanna nursed her wine while Finn stuck with coffee.

It wasn't the sort of bar where one would expect to find one of Hollywood's major stars. The piano player was glumly noodling out the blues so that the notes rose sluggishly on air thick with smoke. Their corner was dim, as Kate had requested. On the table scarred with nicks their drinks rested near a chipped amber glass ashtray.

"You came a long way for the funeral of someone you didn't like." Deanna watched Kate's elegant nails tap the table in time with the piano.

"I was in town. But if I hadn't been, I'd have made the trip. For the pleasure of making sure she was dead." Kate sipped her scotch again, then set the glass aside. "I don't imagine you cared for her any more than I did, but this might be rougher on you, since you found her." Kate's eyes softened as she stared into Deanna's. "As the story goes, it wasn't a pretty sight."

"No, it wasn't."

"I wish it had been me," Kate said under her breath. "You're a softer touch, always were. Even after everything she did, and tried to do, to you. I know a lot more about that than you might imagine," she added when Deanna studied her. "Things that didn't make it into the press. Angela liked to brag. She hated you." She inclined the glass toward Finn. "Because you didn't come to heel when she snapped her fingers. And she wanted you for exactly the same reason. She figured Deanna was in her way, from all manner of angles. She'd have done anything to remove you."

"This isn't news." Noting that Kate's glass was dry, Finn signaled for another. The lady, he concluded, was stalling.

"No, it's just my little prelude." She stretched back, but the sinuous gesture was all nerves. "I don't suppose you'd be surprised to know that Angela went to some trouble and expense to dig up that business from your past, Deanna. The date rape. It backfired, of course." Her lips curved into a lovely smile. "Some of her projects did. That's what she called them. Not blackmail." She sulked a moment, fingers tapping, tapping, tapping "Rob Winters was one of her projects. So was Marshall Pike." She didn't glance at the waitress, but nudged the glass aside even as it was set in front of her. "There are plenty more. Names that would astonish you. She used a P.I. named Beeker. He's in Chicago. Angela kept him very busy documenting data for her projects. It cost me five thousand dollars to shoehorn his name out of Angela's secretary. But then, everybody has a price. I had mine," she added quietly.

"You're saying Angela blackmailed people?" Deanna leaned forward. "She traded secrets for money?"

Occasionally. She preferred trading secrets for favors. Her terms again. Absently, she reached into the plastic bowl of mixed nuts. "Do me a little favor, darling, and I'll keep this tidbit of information all to myself.' 'Your wife has a drug problem, Senator. Don't worry, I won't breathe a word if you just do me a favor. What multi-Grammy winner was a victim of incest? What popular television star has ties to the KKK? Ask Angela. She made it her business to know what skeleton was in what closet. And if she was confident she had her hooks in you deeply enough, she might tell you what closet. It was a way of flexing her power. She was confident she had her hooks in me."

"And now she's dead."

Kate acknowledged Finn's comment with a nod. "Funny, now that she's no longer a threat to me, I feel compelled to do what she always threatened to do. I'm going public. Actually, I'd decided to do so on the very night she was murdered. The police might find that convenient, don't you think? Like a bad script. I saw her that night." She read the horror in Deanna's eyes. "Not at the studio. At her hotel. We argued. Since there was a maid in the next room, I imagine the police already know about it."

She lifted a brow at Finn. "Yes, I can see at least you knew about it. Well then. I'm going to go in and make a statement before they come to me. I believe I even threatened to kill her." Kate closed her eyes. "There's that bad script again. I didn't kill her, but you'll have to decide whether to believe me when I'm finished."

"Why are you telling us?" Deanna demanded. "Why don't you go directly to the police?"

"I'm an actress. I like the chance to choose my audience. You were always a good one, Dee." She reached out then in a quick, fleeting gesture of friendship. "And, in any case, I think you're entitled to know the whole story. Didn't you ever wonder why I backed out of coming on your show? Why I've never been available to appear on it?"

"Yes. But I think you've answered that. Angela was blackmailing you. And the favor was for you to boycott my program."

"That was one of them. I was in a precarious and fascinating position a couple of years ago, when you approached me. I had two whopping box-office successes. And the critics loved me. The wholesomely sexy girl-next-door. Don't believe that hype about stars not reading their reviews. I pored over mine. Every word," she said with a long, dreamy smile. "I could probably still quote a few of the best ones. All I ever wanted was to be an actor. A star," she corrected with an easy shrug. "And that's what they called me. The first movie star of the new generation. A throwback to Bacall and Bergman and Davis. And it didn't take me years. One supporting role in a film that took off like a rocket, and an Academy nomination. Then I costarred with Rob and we burned up the screen, we broke hearts. The next movie, my name was over the title. My image was locked in. A woman who charms with a smile." She laughed at that, drank again. "The good girl, the heroine, the woman you'd like your son to bring home for dinner. That's the image. That's what Hollywood wants from me, that's what the public expects. And that's what I've delivered. They've given me plenty of credit for talent, but the image is every bit as important."

Her eyes slitted. "Do you think the top producers and directors, the players, the men who decide what project flies and what project gets buried would flood my agent with offers if they knew their perfect heroine, the woman who won an Oscar for playing the desperately devoted mother, had gotten pregnant at seventeen, and had given up the child without a second thought?"

She laughed when Deanna's mouth opened. But it wasn't a merry sound. "Doesn't fit, does it? Even in these enlightened times, how many of those ticket buyers would shell out seven bucks to watch me play the long-suffering or feisty heroine?"

"I don't . . ." Deanna stopped, waiting for her thoughts to settle. "I don't see why it should matter. You made a choice, one I'm sure was anything but easy for you. And you were a child yourself."

Amused, Kate glanced at Finn. "Is she really that naive?"

"About some things." He was, despite his pride in being a sharp judge of character, doing some rapid mental shuffling. "I can see why an announcement like that would have shaken things up. You'd have taken some knocks in the press. But you'd have pulled out of it."

"Maybe. I was afraid. Angela knew that. And I was ashamed. She knew that, too. She was very sympathetic at first. 'How hard it must have been on you, dear. A young girl, with her whole life in flux because of one tiny mistake. How difficult it must have been for you to do what you thought was best for the child.' "

Annoyed with herself, Kate flicked a tear away. "And you see, since it had been difficult, even horrible, and because she was sympathetic, I broke down. Then she had me. She reminded me that it wouldn't do for certain Hollywood brass to discover that I'd made this tiny mistake. Oh, she understood, she sympathized completely. But would they? Would the ticket-buying public who'd crowned me their valiant princess understand?"

"Kate, you were seventeen."

Very slowly, Kate lifted her gaze to Deanna's. "I was old enough to make a child, old enough to give her away. Old enough to pay for it. I hope I'm strong enough now to face the consequences." She frowned at her glass. If she didn't survive, if she crashed and burned, it would kill her. Angela had known that. "A few years ago, I wasn't. It's as simple as that. I don't think I could have survived the hate mail then, or the tabloids, or the bad jokes." She smiled again, but Deanna saw her pain. "I can't say I'm looking forward to it now. But the simple fact is, the cops are bound to track me down. Sooner or later they'll dig up Beeker and all of Angela's nasty files. I'm going to choose my own time and place for my public announcement. I'd like to do it on your show."

Deanna blinked. "Excuse me?"

"I said I'd like to do it on your show."

"Why?"

"Two reasons. First, for me it would be the ultimate payback to Angela. You don't like that one," she murmured, seeing the disapproval in Deanna's eyes. "You'll like this better. I trust you. You've got class, and compassion. This isn't going to be easy for me, and I'm going to need both. I'm scared." She set her drink down. "I hate that reason, but I might as well admit it. I lost the child through my ambition," she said quietly. "That's gone," she said fiercely. "I don't want to lose what I've got, Deanna. What I've worked for. Angela's just as dangerous to me dead as she was alive. At least I can pick my time and place this way. I've got a lot of respect for you. I always have. I'm going to have to talk about my private life, my personal griefs. I'd like to start off talking with someone I respect."

"We'll juggle the schedule," Deanna said simply. "And do it Monday morning."

Kate closed her eyes a moment, gathered what resources she had left. "Thanks."

The sleet had stopped by the time they arrived home, leaving the air chill and damp and gloomy. Clouds hovered, thick and black. There was a light on in one of the front windows, streaming gold through the glass in cozy welcome. The dog began to bark the moment Finn slipped the key into the lock.

It should have been a homecoming. But there was the ever-present smell of paint reminding them their home had been violated. Drop cloths were spread in the hallway, and the dog's barking echoed emptily. So many of the rooms had been cleared out of broken crockery, damaged furniture. It was like being greeted by a mortally ill friend.

"We can still go to a hotel."

Deanna shook her head. "No, that's only another way of hiding. I can't help feeling responsible for this."

"Then work on it."

She recognized the impatience in his voice. She stooped to pet the dog as Finn peeled off his coat. "They were your things, Finn."

"Things." He shoved his coat on the hall rack. In the mirrored surface he saw her head bent over the dog's. "Just things, Deanna. Insured, replaceable."

She stayed where she was but lifted her head. Her eyes were wide and weary. "I love you so much. I hate knowing he was here, that he touched anything that was yours."

He crouched beside her, causing the dog to roll belly up in anticipation. But Finn took Deanna by the shoulders, his eyes suddenly fierce. "You are the only thing I have that's irreplaceable. The first time I met you, the first time, I knew that nothing that had happened to me before, or that would happen after, would mean as much. Can you understand that?" His hand moved roughly into her hair. "It's overwhelming what I feel for you. It's terrifying. And it's everything."

"Yes." She brought her hands to his face, guided his mouth to hers. "I can understand that." Emotions welled up, pouring into the kiss so that her lips were urgent and edgy. Even as Finn tugged at her coat, the dog wriggled between them, whining.

"We're embarrassing Cronkite," he murmured, drawing Deanna to her feet.

"We should find him a wife."

"You just want to go to the pound again and liberate another mutt."

"Now that you mention it . . ." But her smile faded quickly. "Finn, I have to talk to you about something."

"Sounds serious."

"Can we go upstairs?"

She wanted the bedroom, since it was almost fully restored. He'd seen that the work there had been completed first. The things that hadn't been destroyed had been placed there. Above the bed, where she knew a desperate message had been scrawled, the paint was fresh and clean. He'd hung the painting there—the one he had bought out from under her in the gallery so long ago.

Awakenings. All those vivid splashes of color. That energy and verve. He'd known she'd needed it there, a reminder of life. And so the room had become a haven.

"Are you upset about Kate?"

"Yes." She kept her hand in his as they climbed the stairs. "But this is about something else." She walked into the bedroom, moved to the fireplace, the window, then back. "I love you, Finn."

The tone put him on guard. "We've established that."

"Loving you doesn't mean I have the right to intrude in every area of your life."

Curious, he tilted his head. He could read her like a book. She was worried. "Which areas do you consider off limits?"

"You're annoyed." Baffled, she tossed up her hands. "I can never quite understand how easily I can set you off, especially when I'm trying to be reasonable."

"I hate it when you think you're being reasonable. Just spill it, Deanna."

"Fine. What did Angela have on you?"

His expression altered subtly, from impatience to utter confusion. "Huh?"

"Don't do that." She ripped off her coat and tossed it aside. In her tasteful black suit and damp shoes, she paced the room. "If you don't want to tell me, just say so. I'll agree that anything you've done in the past isn't necessarily connected to our relationship."

"Slow down, and stop stalking around the room. What do you think I've done?"

"I don't know." Her voice sounded shrill to herself. "I don't know," she said more calmly. "And if you think I don't need to know, I'll try to accept it. But once the police question this Beeker character, your secret is bound to come out anyway."

"Hold on." He held up both hands as she unbuttoned her suit jacket. "If I'm reading this correctly—and stop me anytime if I veer off—you think that Angela was blackmailing me. Have I got that part?"

Marching to the closet, she yanked out a padded hanger. "I said I wouldn't intrude if you didn't want me to. I was being reasonable."

"You certainly were." He came over, clamped his hands on her shoulders and steered her rigid body to a chair. "Now sit down. And tell me why you think I was being blackmailed."

"I went to meet Angela that night because she said she knew something about you. Something that could hurt you."

He sat himself then, on the edge of the bed, as a new kind of fury ate at him. "She lured you to the studio by threatening me?"

"Not directly. Not exactly." She dragged a hand through her hair. "There was nothing she could tell me that would change my feelings for you. I wanted to make sure she understood that. That she left us both alone."

"Deanna, why didn't you come to me?"

She winced from the simple, rational question. "Because I wanted to handle her myself," she shot back. "Because I don't need you or anyone running interference for me."

"Isn't that precisely what you misguidedly tried to do for me?"

That shut her up, but again, only for a moment. It was, she knew, master interviewer against master interviewer. And it was a competition she didn't mean to lose. "You're evading the issue. What would she have told me, Finn?"

"I don't have a clue. I'm not gay; I don't use drugs; I've never stolen anything. Except a couple of comic books when I was twelve—and nobody could prove it."

"I don't think this is funny."

"She wasn't blackmailing me, Deanna. I had an affair with her, but that was no secret. She wasn't the first woman I'd been involved with, but there haven't been any deviant sexual encounters I'd want to hide. I don't have any ties to organized crime, never embezzled. I'm not hiding any illegitimate children. I never killed anyone."

He broke off abruptly, and the impatient amusement drained out of his face. "Oh Jesus." He brought both hands to his face, pressing the heels to his eyes. "Jesus Christ."

"I'm sorry." Competition forgotten, she sprang up to go to him. "Finn, I'm sorry. I should never have brought it up."

"Could she have done that?" he said to himself. "Could even she have done that? And for what?" He let his hands drop, and his eyes were haunted. "For what?"

"Done what?" Deanna asked quietly, her arms still around him.

Finn drew back, just a little, as if what was working inside him might damage her. "My best friend in college. Pete Whitney. We got hooked on the same girl. We got drunk one night, really plowed, and tried to beat the crap out of each other. Did a pretty good job. Made sure it was off campus. Then we decided, hell, she wasn't worth it, and we drank some more."

His voice was cool, detached. His newscaster's voice. "That's the last time I've been drunk. Pete used to joke that it was the Irish in me. That I could drink or fight or talk my way out of anything." He remembered the way he'd been then—angry, rebellious, belligerent. Determined to be absolutely nothing like his chilly and civilized parents. "I'm not much of a drinker anymore, and I've figured out that words are generally a better weapon than fists. He gave me this." Finn tugged the Celtic cross out from under his shirt, closed his hand around it. "He was my closet friend, the closest thing to family I ever had."

Was, Deanna thought, and ached for him.

"We forgot about the girl. She wasn't as important to either of us as we were to each other. We killed off another bottle. My eye was swollen up like a rotten tomato, so I tossed him the keys, climbed into the passenger seat, passed out. We were twenty, and we were stupid. The idea of getting into a car filthy drunk didn't mean anything to us. When you're twenty, you're going to live forever. But Pete didn't.

"I woke up when I heard him scream. That's it. I heard him scream and the next thing I remember is waking up with all these lights and all these people and feeling as if I'd been run over by a truck. He'd taken a turn too fast, hit a utility pole. We'd both been thrown from the car. I had a concussion, a broken collarbone, broken arm, lots of cuts and bruises. Pete was dead."

"Oh, Finn." She wrapped her arms around him again, held on.

"It was my car, so they figured I'd been driving. They were going to charge me with vehicular manslaughter. My father came down, but by the time he got there they'd already found several witnesses who had seen Pete take the wheel. He wasn't any more or any less dead, of course. It didn't change that, or the fact that I'd been drunk and stupid, criminally careless."

He tightened his fingers around the silver cross. "I wasn't hiding it, Deanna. It's just not something I like to remember. Funny, I thought about Pete tonight, when we walked into Angela's funeral. I haven't been to one since Pete's. His mother always blamed me. I could see her point."

"You weren't driving, Finn."

"Does it really matter?" He looked at her then, though he already knew the answer. "I could have been. My father gave the Whitneys a settlement, and that was pretty much the end of it. I wasn't charged with anything. I wasn't held responsible."

He turned his face into Deanna's hair. "But I was. I was just as responsible as Pete. The only difference is I'm alive and he's not."

"The difference is, you were given a second chance and he wasn't." She closed her hand over his, so that they both held the cross. "I'm so sorry, Finn."

So was he. He'd spent his adult life making himself into the man he was, as much for Pete as for himself. He wore the cross every day as a talisman, yes, and as a reminder.

"Angela could have dug up the facts easily enough," Finn said. "She could even have made it appear that the Riley money and power influenced the outcome. But she would have blackmailed you not me. She'd have known if she'd come to me, I'd have told her to take out an ad."

"I want to tell the police."

He eased her back on the bed so that they were curled together, wrapped close. "We'll tell them a lot of things. Tomorrow." Gently, he tipped her face toward his. "Would you have protected me, Deanna?"

She started to deny it, but caught the gleam in his eye. She knew he'd recognize a lie. "Yes. So?"

"So, thanks."

She smiled as she lifted her mouth toward his.

Not so far away someone was weeping. The tears were hot and bitter, scalding the throat, the eyes, the skin. Photographs of Deanna looked on, smiling benignly at the sobbing form. Three candles tossed the only light, their flames, straight and true, highlighting the pictures, the single earring, the lock of hair bound in gold thread. All of the treasures on the altar of frustrated desire.

There were stacks of videotapes, but the television screen was silent and dark tonight.

Angela was dead, but still that wasn't enough. Love, deep, dark and demented, had triggered the gun, but it wasn't enough. There had to be more.

The candleglow shot the shadow of a form hunched into a ball, racked with despair. Deanna would see, had to see that she was loved, cherished, adored.

There was a way to prove it.

Finn would have preferred to handle the interview alone. Jenner would have preferred to do the same. Since neither of them could manage to shake the other loose, they drove to Beeker's office together.

"Might as well make the best of it," Jenner said. "I'm doing you a favor, Mr. Riley, letting you tag along."

That statement earned Jenner a frigid stare. "I don't tag along, Lieutenant. And let me remind you that you wouldn't know about Kate Lowell or Beeker if we hadn't come to you with the information."

Jenner grinned and rubbed his chin, which he'd nicked shaving. "And I get the feeling you wouldn't have come to me if Miss Reynolds hadn't insisted."

"She feels easier knowing the police are on top of things."

"And how does she feel about your being involved in the investigation?" Silence. "Doesn't know," Jenner concluded. "As a man married thirty-two years last July, let me mention that you're skating on thin ice."

"She's terrified. And she's going to continue to be terrified until you have Angela's killer under wraps."

"Can't argue with that. Now, this Kate Lowell business. Being a reporter, you might not agree, but I think she's entitled to her privacy."

"It's tough to argue for privacy when you make your living in the public eye. I believe in the right to know, Lieutenant. But I don't believe in blackmail, or in poking telescopic lenses into someone's bedroom window."

"Got your dander up." Pleased, Jenner scooted through a yellow light. "Me, I feel sorry for her. She was a kid, probably scared."

"You're a soft touch, Lieutenant."

"Like hell. You can't be a cop and be a soft touch." But he was, damn it. And since it embarrassed the hell out of him, he took the aggressive route. "She still could've killed Angela Perkins."

Finn waited as Jenner doubled-parked, then flipped the officer-on-duty sign over on the dash. "Entertain me."

"She argues with Angela at the hotel. She's fed up with Angela, enraged at being made to suffer for something that happened when she was still wet behind the ears."

"There's that soft touch again. Keep going," Finn prompted as he climbed out of the car.

"She's tired of Angela holding it over her head and threatens her. She hears the maid in the bedroom so she leaves. But she follows Angela to CBC, confronts her in the studio, murders her. Then Deanna comes in, and she gets creative. She's been in films for years. She knows how to set up a camera."

"Yes." There was a quick, nippy breeze that smelled of the lake. Finn drew it in, the easy freshness of it as they crossed the street. "Then she decides to disguise her motive by going public with exactly what she killed Angela over. Better the world knows she's an unwed mother than a murderer."

"It doesn't play," Jenner concluded.

"Not for me. If Beeker has half the dirt Kate thinks, we'll have a dozen more scenarios by dinnertime." They walked into the office building, Jenner flashing his badge at the security guard in the lobby.

Upstairs, Jenner scanned the wide corridor. The oil paintings were originals and very good. The carpet was thick. Tall, leafy plants were tucked into niches every few feet.

The doors of Beeker Investigations were glass and whispered open into an airy reception area complete with a tidy miniature spruce for the holiday season.

A trim, thirtyish brunette piloted a circular reception desk fashioned from glass blocks. "May I help you?"

"Beeker." Jenner offered the receptionist his ID for inspection.

"Mr. Beeker is in conference. Lieutenant. Will one of his associates be able to help you?"

"Beeker," he said again. "We'll wait, but I'd buzz him if I were you."

"Very well." Her friendly smile chilled a few degrees. "May I ask what this is in reference to?"

"Murder."

"Nice touch," Finn murmured when they wandered over to the deep-cushioned chairs in the waiting area. "Real Joe Friday stuff." He took another look around. "Very elegant surroundings, for a P.I."

"A couple of clients like Angela Perkins means this guy nets in a month what I do in a year."

"Lieutenant Jenner?" The receptionist, obviously miffed, stood in the center of the room. "Mr. Beeker will see you now." She guided them through another set of glass doors, past several offices. She knocked lightly on the door at the end of the hall, and opened it.

Clarence Beeker was like his office, trim, subtly elegant and serviceable. He stood, a man of average height and slim build, behind his Belker desk. The hand he extended was fine-boned.

His hair was graying dashingly at the temples, and he had a finely drawn face that was more handsome with the lines and crevices etched by time. His body was obviously trim beneath his Savile Row suit.

"Might I see some identification?" His voice was smooth, like cool cream over rich coffee.

Jenner was disappointed. He'd expected Beeker to be sleazy.

He examined the shield after slipping on silver-framed reading glasses. "I recognize you, Mr. Riley. I often watch your show on Tuesday nights. Since you've brought a reporter along, Detective Jenner, I assume this is an unofficial visit."

"It's official enough," Jenner corrected. "Mr. Riley's here as a special liaison of the mayor's." Not by a flicker did Jenner or Finn react to the glib lie.

"I'm honored. Please sit. Tell me what I can do for you."

"I'm investigating Angela Perkins's murder," Jenner began. "She was a client of yours."

"She was." Beeker settled behind his desk. "I was shocked and distressed to read about her death."

"We have information leading us to believe that the deceased was blackmailing a number of people."

"Blackmail." Beeker's graying brows rose. "It seems a very unattractive term to be connected to a very attractive woman."

"It's also an attractive motive for murder," Finn put in. "You investigated people for Miss Perkins."

"I handled a number of cases for Miss Perkins over our ten-year association. Given the nature of her profession, it was advantageous for her to be privy to details, backgrounds, the personal habits of those she would interview."

"Her interest, and her use of those personal habits, might have led to her death."

"Mr. Riley, I investigated and reported for Miss Perkins. I'm sure you understand both those functions. I had no more control over her use of the information I provided than you do over the public's use of the information you provide to them."

"And no responsibility."

"None," Beeker agreed pleasantly. "We provide a service. Beeker Investigations has an excellent reputation because we are skilled, discreet and dependable. We abide by the law, Detective, and a code of ethics. Whether or not our clients do so is their business, not ours."

"One of your clients got her face shot off," Jenner said shortly. "We'd like to see copies of the reports you wrote for Miss Perkins."

"I'm afraid, as much as I prefer to cooperate with the police, that would be impossible. Unless you have a warrant," he said pleasantly.

"You don't have a client to protect, Mr. Beeker." Jenner leaned forward. "What's left of her is in a coffin."

"I'm aware of that. However, I do have a client. Mr. Gardner has this company under retainer. As the deceased's husband and beneficiary, I am morally bound to accede to his wishes."

"Which are?"

"To investigate his wife's murder. To be frank, gentlemen, he's dissatisfied with the police investigation to date. And as he was my client during his wife's life, and continues to be after her death, I can't ethically turn over my files without the proper warrant. I'm sure you understand my position."

"And you'll understand mine," Finn said pleasantly. "Liaison or not, I am a reporter. As such, I have an obligation to inform the public. It would be interesting to inform the public of the kind of work you did for Angela. I wonder how many of your other clients would appreciate that connection."

Beeker had stiffened. "Threats, Mr. Riley, aren't appreciated."

"I'm sure they're not. But that doesn't make them any less viable." Finn glanced at his watch. "I think I have enough time to squeeze in a quick feature on the evening news. We'd be able to do an in-depth version tomorrow."

Jaw clenched, Beeker lifted his phone, buzzed his secretary. "I'll need copies of Angela Perkins's files. All of them." He cradled the phone again, linked his fingers. "It will take a little time."

"We've got plenty," Jenner assured him. "While we're waiting, why don't you tell us where you were on the night Angela Perkins was shot?"

"I'd be happy to. I was at home, with my wife and my mother. As I recall, we played three-handed bridge until about midnight."

"Then you won't object to us questioning your wife and your mother?"

"Of course not." Though he wasn't pleased at being outmaneuvered, Beeker was a practical man. "Perhaps I can offer you gentlemen coffee while we wait for the files?"

26

Marshall Pike had been waiting in his car in the CBC parking lot for more than an hour when Deanna finally walked out. He felt the quick, unbidden tightening of his muscles in response at the sight of her: part anger, part lust. For the past two years, he had been forced to content himself with images of her on the TV screen. Seeing her now in the gloom of dusk, short-skirted, her legs flashing as she hurried toward a dark sedan, exceeded his memories.

"Deanna," he called to her, climbing quickly out of his own car.

She stopped, glanced toward him, peering through the rapidly deepening night. The quick, friendly smile of greeting faded. "Marshall, what do you want?"

"You never returned any of my calls." He cursed himself for sounding petulant. He wanted to appear strong, dynamic.

"I wasn't interested in speaking with you."

"You're going to speak with me." He clamped his hand over her arm. His gesture made Deanna's driver spring out of the car.

"Call off your dog, Deanna. Surely you can spare five minutes?"

"It's all right, Tim." But she removed Marshall's hand before turning to her driver. "I won't keep you waiting long."

"No problem, Miss Reynolds." He gave Marshall a measured look, then tipped his cap. "No problem at all."

"If we could be private." Marshall gestured across the lot. "Your guard will be able to see you, Deanna. I'm sure he'll leap to your rescue should I try to manhandle you."

"I think I can handle you alone." She crossed the lot with him, hoping the metting would be brief. The wind was bitterly cold and she didn't relish speaking with him. "Since I can't think of anything we'd have to discuss on a personal level. I assume you wanted to talk to me about Angela."

"It would have been difficult for you. Finding her."

"Yes, it was."

"I could help you."

"Professionally?" Her brow quirked. The wind, and anger, brought color to her cheeks, a snap to her eyes. "No thanks. Tell me what you want."

For the moment, he stared at her. She was still perfect. Fresh, seductive. All luminous eyes and moist lips. "Have dinner with me," he said at last. "The French place you always liked so much."

"Marshall, please." There was no anger in her voice, only pity. It scraped like rusty blades over his ego.

"Oh yes, I seem to have forgotten to congratulate you on your engagement to our dashing correspondent."

"Thank you. Is that all?"

"I want the file." At her blank look he tightened his grip. "Don't pretend you don't understand. I know Angela gave you a copy of her investigator's report on me. She told me. She gloated over it. I didn't ask for it before because I'd hoped that you'd come to realize what I could offer you. Now, under the circumstances, I need it."

"I don't have it."

Rage darkened his face. "You're lying. She gave it to you."

"Yes, she did." Her arm was throbbing now, but she refused to struggle. "Do you really think I would have kept it all this time? I destroyed it ages ago."

He gripped both her arms now, nearly lifting her off her feet. "I don't believe you."

"I don't give a damn what you believe. I don't have it." More furious than frightened, she struggled against him. "Can't you understand I didn't care enough to keep it? You weren't important enough."

"Bitch." Too incensed to think clearly, he dragged her toward his car. "You won't hold that file over my head." He grunted, his wing tips skittering on the pavement as he was yanked from behind. He went down painfully, bruising his hip and his dignity.

"No, Tim, don't." Though she was shaking, Deanna grabbed her driver's arm before he could haul Marshall to his feet and knock him down all over again.

Tim adjusted his bulky coat, seeing Marshall was quelled. "You okay, Miss Reynolds?"

"Yes, I'm fine."

"Hey!" A baseball cap shielding his eyes, a camera on his shoulder, Joe raced across the lot. "Dee? You okay?"

"Yes." She pressed a hand to her temple as Marshall got to his feet. Perfect, she thought. Pictures at ten. "Yes, I'm okay."

"I was just pulling into the lot when I saw this guy hassling you." Joe's eyes narrowed. "The shrink, right?" He slapped a hand on Marshall's chest before Marshall could step toward his car. "Hold on, pal. Dee, you want me to call the cops, or should Tim and I just show this creep what happens to men who push women around?"

"Just let him go."

"Sure?"

She looked into Marshall's eyes. There was something dead in them now, but she couldn't find any pity. "Yes. Let him go."

"The lady's giving you a break," Joe muttered. "If I catch you bothering her again, I won't be so nice."

Silently, Marshall got into his car. He locked the doors, fastened his seat belt before driving out of the lot.

"Are you sure he didn't hurt you, Miss Reynolds?"

"No, he didn't. Thank you, Tim."

"No problem." Tim sauntered proudly back to the car.

"I wish you'd let me punch him." Joe gave a regretful sigh before looking back at Deanna. "Spooked you, huh?" He glanced at the camera on his shoulder, grimaced. "I got so pissed I didn't get any tape of it."

That, at least, was something. "I guess there's no point in my asking you not to mention this in the newsroom."

He grinned as he walked her to her car. "No point at all. News is news."

She didn't want to tell Finn, but they'd made a deal. No holding back. She'd hoped Finn would have to work late, but as luck would have it, he opened the door and greeted her with a long, sloppy kiss.

"Hiya."

"Hi yourself." She rocked back on her heels and gave Cronkite the caress he was whining for.

"We had a change in schedule, so I got home a little early." The change in schedule had been canceling all of his appointments and spending his afternoon with Jenner reading through Beeker's files. "Made dinner."

Cooperating, Deanna sniffed the air. "Smells great."

"New recipe." With one brow cocked, he tipped a finger under her chin. "What?"

"What, what?"

"You're upset."

She scowled and pushed his hand away. "Damn it, Finn, that's irritating. Don't you know a woman likes to think she has some mystery?" Still hoping to stall, she peeled out of her coat and hung it on the hall rack.

"What happened, Kansas?"

"We'll talk about it later. I'm starving."

He merely shifted and blocked her path. "Spill it."

She could argue, but since an argument was precisely what she was hoping to avoid, what was the point?

"Will you promise to hear me out and not overreact?"

"Sure." He smiled at her as he swung an arm around her shoulders and led her to the steps. They sat together near the bottom landing, with the dog happily at their feet. "Is it about Angela?"

"Not directly." She blew out a long breath. "It was Marshall. He sort of ambushed me in the parking lot."

"Ambushed?"

His icy tone alerted her. But when she looked up at Finn, his eyes seemed calm enough. Curious, a little annoyed, but calm. "Just a figure of speech. He was upset. You know I haven't returned his calls." When Finn said nothing, she let the rest tumble out. "He was just angry and upset, that's all. About that. And about the files Angela had sent to me. I told you about them. Marshall has it in his head that I kept them. Of course, with the investigation going on he's worried. Naturally."

"Naturally," Finn said pleasantly.

He'd hear about the rest anyway, Deanna reminded herself. From Joe, or someone else in the newsroom. That would be worse. "We had a little scuffle."

There was a dangerous light in Finn's eyes. "Did he put his hands on you?"

Deanna shrugged, hoping to lighten the mood. "In a manner of speaking. It was really just one of those push-shove sort of things. But Tim was there," she added quickly. "And Joe. So it was nothing. It was really nothing."

"He put his hands on you," Finn repeated. "And he threatened you?"

"I don't know that I'd call it a threat. It was just—Finn!" He was already up, removing his coat from the rack. "Finn, damn it, you said you'd be reasonable."

He shot her one look, one stunningly frigid look that had her heart stopping. "I lied."

Her knees were knocking together, but she was on his heels as he strode out of the house. The cold and the look in Finn's eye had her teeth chattering as she struggled into her coat. "Stop this now. Right now! What are you going to do?"

"I'm going to go explain to Pike why he should keep his hands off my woman."

"Your woman?" That tore it. She bounded ahead of him, slapping both hands onto his chest. "Don't you pull that macho bullshit on me, Finn Riley. I'm not going to . . ."

Her voice slid back down her throat when he propped his hands under her elbows and lifted her off the ground. His eyes were blazing.

"You are my woman, Deanna. That's not an insult, that's a fact. Anybody who manhandles you, anybody who threatens you has to deal with me. That's another fact. Got a problem with it?"

"No. Yes." Her feet hit the ground with a thump and she ground her teeth. "I don't know." How was she supposed to think when all she could see were those furious, deadly eyes boring into her. "Let's go back inside and talk this through reasonably."

"We'll talk when I get back."

She raced to the car after him. "I'm going with you." There was still a chance, a slim one, that she could talk him down.

"Go inside, Deanna."

"I'm going with you." She opened the door, climbed in and slammed it shut. He wasn't the only one who could slice flesh with a look. "If *my man's* going to go make a fool of himself, I'm going to be there. Got a problem with that?"

Finn slammed the door and turned the key. "Hell no."

The best Deanna could hope for now was that Marshall wouldn't be home.

The wind had picked up and held a fresh threat of snow. It raced through Finn's hair, sent it flying around his face as he stalked up to Marshall's door. He had only one thing on his mind and, like a skilled reporter, easily blocked out all distractions: Deanna's mumbled curses, the occasional swish of tires on the street, the numbing chill in the air.

"He's not worth it," Deanna said for the hundredth time. "He's just not worth your making a scene."

"I have no intention of making a scene. I'm going to talk to him, and he's going to listen. And then, unless I'm very much mistaken, you'll never see or hear from him again."

He had been wanting a confrontation since the day Deanna had rushed out of the CBC Building in tears, and into his arms. Finn could already feel the grim satisfaction of pleasure postponed.

Deanna saw his eyes slit like a predator's as the door opened. Her stomach clenched and she had one wild thought: to jump between them.

But Finn didn't lunge, as she'd been half terrified he would. He simply strolled across the threshold and into the foyer.

"I don't believe I invited you in." Marshall ran a finger over the black tie of his tuxedo. "And I'm afraid I'm on my way out."

"We'll make this as quick as possible, since I don't believe Deanna's comfortable being here."

"Deanna's always welcome in my home," Marshall said stiffly. "You are not."

"What you don't seem to understand is that we're a team. When you threaten her, you threaten me. I don't react well to threats, Dr. Pike."

"My conversation with Deanna was personal."

"Wrong again." Finn stepped closer. The feral gleam in his eyes had Marshall stepping back. "If you come near her again, if you ever put your hands on her again, I'll bury you, in every way you can imagine."

"There are laws to protect a man against a physical attack in his own home."

"I have better ways of dealing with you. Angela's file on you made very interesting reading, Pike."

Marshall's eyes slid to Deanna. "She doesn't have the file. She destroyed it."

"No, Deanna doesn't have it. But you don't know what I have, do you?"

Marshall's attention snapped back to Finn. "You have no right—"

"I've got the First Amendment. Steer clear, Pike, way clear. Or I'll break you in half with it."

"You bastard." Fear of exposure propelled Marshall forward. He swung out, more in panic than design. Finn easily avoided the blow and followed it by one punishing fist to the midsection.

It was over in seconds. Deanna had done no more than squeak in response. Marshall had done no more than moan. And Finn she realized as she gaped, had made no sound at all.

Then he crouched down, impossibly graceful and smooth. "Listen carefully. Don't ever come near Deanna again. Don't call, don't write, don't send a telegram. Are you getting this?" He was satisfied when Marshall blinked. "That should conclude our little interview. He stepped back to where Deanna still stood, openmouthed on the stoop. Quietly, he shut the door. "Let's go."

Her legs were jelly. She had to lock her knees to keep from swaying. "Good God, Finn. Good God."

"We're going to have to reheat dinner," he said as he guided her to the car.

"You just—I mean you—" She didn't know what she meant. "We can't just leave him there."

"Of course we can. He doesn't need paramedics, Deanna. I only wrinkled his tux and bruised his ego."

"You hit him." Once she was scated, strapped in, she pressed both hands to her mouth.

His black mood had passed. He felt almost sunny as he drove fast through the windswept night. "Not exactly my style, but since he swung first, it worked for me."

She turned her head away. She couldn't explain, couldn't *believe* what she was feeling. The way he'd sliced Marshall with words. Sharp and cold as a sword. Then he'd shifted his body aside, graceful as a dancer. She hadn't seen the blow coming any more than Marshall had. He'd moved so fast, so stunningly. She pressed a hand to her stomach and bit back a little moan.

"Pull over," she said in a muffled voice. "Right now."

He did, terrified she was about to be sick, disgusted because he hadn't reined in his temper long enough to make her stay home. "Take it easy, Deanna. I'm sorry you had to see that, but—"

Whatever else he'd intended to say was lost as she lunged at him. In one fluid move, she tore off her seat belt and whipped toward him. Her mouth was hot and wet and hungry. Through his shock, and instant arousal, he felt the violent thud of her heart.

And her hands. Jesus. Her hands.

Cars sped by them. He could only groan as she dived deeper into his mouth, her tongue greedy, her teeth vicious.

Both of them were panting for air when she leaned back.

"Well," he managed, but his mind was wiped as clean as glass. "Well."

"I'm not proud of it." She flopped back in her seat, face flushed, eyes bright. "I don't approve of intimidation or fighting. I absolutely don't. Oh God." With a half laugh, she squeezed her eyes shut. Her body was vibrating like an overheated engine. Intellect, she discovered, could be completely overpowered by glands. "I'm going to explode. Drive fast, will you?"

"Yeah." His aching hand trembled a bit as he turned the key again. Then, as he punched the accelerator, he started to grin. The grin became a hard, deep-throated laugh. "Deanna, I'm crazy about you."

She had to curl her fingers into fists to keep herself from tearing at his clothes. "We're both crazy," she decided. "Drive faster."

Marshall comforted himself as best he could, pampering his bruised stomach muscles, taking a painkiller. Shame and fury had driven him out of the house. He opted for a drink first, then two, before keeping his date at the opera.

He hadn't thought he'd enjoy the music, or the company. But both had soothed him. He was a civilized man, he reminded himself. A respected man. He would not be intimidated by some grandstanding reporter like Finn Riley. He would simply bide his time, calmly.

Enchanted by the diva's final aria, he still felt peaceful when he pulled in to his driveway, even though his stomach ached dully. Another dose of painkiller would take the edge off, he knew. Fury and frustration had been eased by Mozart's music. Humming lightly, Marshall set the security on his car. If Deanna had the file, and he could no longer be sure, he would convince her to return it to him. But he'd wait until Riley was away on assignment.

They would talk, he promised himself, and finally set the past behind them. As Angela was behind them.

His eyes gleamed as he reached for his keys. He thought he sensed a movement to his left. He had time to turn, time to understand. He didn't have time to scream.

Finn was watching Deanna sleep when the phone rang. They'd started on each other in the foyer, worked their way up the steps. Halfway up they'd decided, tactically, that they'd made it far enough.

It made him grin to remember how she'd torn at his clothes. Attacked him, he thought smugly. Of course, he'd been a willing victim, but she'd shown surprising energy, and amazing resilience. He almost thought it a shame he hadn't dealt so satisfactorily with Pike before.

He dismissed all thoughts of Pike as he settled back, pleasantly aroused when Deanna curled her body against his.

He wouldn't wake her, though it was very tempting to do so. He was too relieved that she no longer tossed and turned or awakened quaking as she had for several nights after Angela's murder. Instead, he simply enjoyed the way her body fit to his.

He swore when the phone rang and she woke.

"Take it easy." Like Deanna, he expected to hear nothing but breathing when he lifted the receiver.

"Finn? It's Joe."

"Joe." He saw the tension dissolve from Deanna's shoulders. "I guess it would be pointless to mention it's after one A.M."

"Got a tip for you, pal. I was whiling away some time with Leno and monitoring my police scanner. We had us a murder over at Lincoln Park."

"I'm not on the crime beat."

"I checked it out, Finn. Figured you'd want to know right way, instead of catching it on the early news. It was Pike. You know, the shrink who hassled Dee today. Somebody did him."

Finn's gaze cut to Deanna's. "How?"

"The same way as Angela. In the face. My police connection wouldn't give me much. But he bought it right on his own doorstep. A neighbor reported hearing gunshots around midnight. A black-and-white checked it out and found him. I'm calling from the cop shop. We've got a unit on it. Story'll break top of the hour on *Sunrise.*"

"Thanks."

"I figured Dee would take it better from you."

"Yeah. Keep me posted?"

"You bet."

He hung up, dispirited.

"Something's wrong." She could see it in his face, in the way the air had seemed to thicken around him. "Just tell me straight out, Finn."

"Okay." He covered her hands with his. "Marshall Pike's been murdered."

Her hands jerked once, then went still. "How?"

"He was shot."

She already knew, but had to ask. "The same as Angela? It was the same as Angela, wasn't it?"

"It looks that way."

She made a strangled sound in her throat, but eased back when he reached for her. "I'm all right. We need to tell the police about what happened after work today. It has to be connected."

"It's possible."

"Don't circle around it," she snapped out, and pushed off the bed. "Marshall harassed me today, and we went over there. Hours later, he's shot. We can't pretend that one had nothing to do with the other."

"And if it is connected, what can you do?"

"Whatever I can." She dragged a sweater over her head, snatched trousers from the closet. "Even though I didn't pull the trigger, I am the cause, and there has to be something I can do."

She didn't resist when he put his arms around her, but clung to him, pressing her face to his shoulder.

"I have to do something, Finn. I can't bear it otherwise."

"We'll go see Jenner." He cupped her face in his hands, kissed her. "We'll figure something out."

"Okay." She finished dressing in silence. She was sure he wouldn't feel guilty about facing down Marshall only hours before, because he would see what he had done as pure and simple justice. And perhaps he was right.

Is that what whoever had leveled a gun at Marshall's face had thought as well?

The idea sickened her. "I'll wait downstairs," she said as he pulled out his boots.

She saw the envelope before she reached the bottom landing. It lay crisp and white against the glossy floor of the foyer, inches inside the door. There was a quick pain, a twist in the gut like a fist punching muscle. Then she went numb, crossing the polished wood, bending down.

She opened the envelope as Finn came down behind her.

"Goddamn it." He took it from her limp fingers, and read.

He'll never hurt you again.

When they left the house, someone was watching, a heart bursting with love and need and terrible grief. Killing for her had been nothing. It had been done before, and needed to be done again.

Perhaps she would see, at last.

27

Jeff stood in the control booth overlooking the studio, biting his lip in agitation. Deanna was about to film her first show since Angela's death.

"Camera Three, on Dee." He barked out orders. "Take Two, zoom out. Wider on One, pan. Give me Dee tight, Three, music in. Great, great applause. Start the playback tape."

He applauded himself, as did the others in the booth. From their perch overlooking the stage they could see the audience surge to its feet and cheer.

"Ride it," Jeff ordered. Oh yeah, he thought, sharing the triumph. She's back. "Ride the applause."

Down below Deanna stood on the new set with its jewel tones and banks of cheery holly bushes and let the waves of applause wash over her. It was, she knew, a show of support, a welcoming home. When her eyes filled she didn't bother to blink back the tears. She didn't think about it.

"Thanks." She let out a long, unsteady breath. "It's really good to be back. I..." She trailed off while she scanned the crowd. There were familiar faces dotted among the strangers. Faces from the newsroom, from production. Pleasure glowed on her face. "It's really good to see you. Before we get rolling, I'd like to thank you all for your letters and phone calls over the past week. Your support has helped me, and everyone involved with the show, through a difficult time."

And that, she thought, was all the space she could give, would give, to the past.

"Now I'd like to bring out a woman who's given us all so many hours of entertainment. She's incandescent. Luminous. With a talent as golden as her eyes. According to *Newsweek,* Kate Lowell can 'ignite the screen with a sweep of the eyelash, by the flash of her signature smile.' She's proven both her popular and her critical appeal by holding the number-one box-office position for two straight years, and by winning an Oscar for her portrayal of the heroic, unforgettable Tess in *Deception.* Ladies and gentlemen, Kate Lowell."

Again, the applause erupted. Kate swept into it, looking confident and fresh and every bit the star. But when Deanna took her hand, she found it cold and trembling. Deliberately Deanna wrapped her in an embrace.

"Don't do anything you're not ready to do," she murmured in Kate's ear. "I'm not going to push you into any revelations."

Kate hesitated a moment. "Oh God, I'm glad you're here, Dee. Let's sit down, okay? My knees are shaking."

It wasn't an easy show, from any angle. Deanna was able to guide the first ten minutes through juicy Hollywood chitchat, keeping the audience amused to the point where she assumed Kate had changed her mind about the announcement.

"I like playing women of strength, and character." In a fluid movement that rustled silk, Kate crossed her long, million-dollar legs. "And there do seem to be more scripts being written for strong women, women who are not just bystanders but who have beliefs and standards they're willing to fight for. I'm grateful for the chance to play those women, because I didn't always fight for what I wanted."

"So you feel as though you're able to do that now, through your work?"

"I relate to many of the characters I've played. Tess in particular. Because she was a woman who sacrificed everything, risked everything for the sake of her child. In an odd sort of way, I mirrored Tess. Mirror images are opposites. And I sacrificed my child, my chance with my child, when I gave it up for adoption ten years ago."

"Damn." In the control booth, Jeff's eyes popped wide. The audience had dropped into stunned silence. "Damn," he said again. "Camera Two, tight on Kate. Man, oh man."

But even as he worriedly bit his lip again, he focused on Deanna's face. She'd known, he realized, and let out a long, calming breath. She'd known. . . .

"An unplanned pregnancy at any time, under any circumstances, is frightening." Deanna wanted her audience to remember that. "How old were you?"

"I was seventeen. I had, as you know, Dee, a supportive family, a good home. I'd just begun my modeling career, and I thought the world was at my feet. Then I discovered I was pregnant."

"The father? Do you want to talk about him?"

"Was a nice, sweet boy who was every bit as terrified as I. He was my first." She smiled a little now, remembering him. "I was his. We were dazzled by each other, by what we felt for each other. When I told him, we just sat there, numb. We were in LA, and we'd gone to the beach. We sat there and watched the surf. He offered to marry me."

"Some people might feel that would have been the answer. You didn't?"

"Not for me, or the boy, or the child." Kate continued, using all of her skill to keep her voice level. "Do you remember the way we used to talk about what we wanted to do when we grew up?"

"Yes. I do." Deanna linked her fingers with Kate's. "You never had any doubts."

"I'd always wanted to be an actress. I'd made some progress modeling, and I was going to conquer Hollywood come hell or high water. Then I was pregnant."

"Did you consider abortion? Discuss the option with the father, with your family?"

"Yes, I did. As difficult as it was, Dee, I remember how supportive my parents were. I'd hurt them, disappointed them. I didn't realize how much until I was older and had some perspective. But they never wavered. I can't explain to you why I decided the way I did. It was a purely emotional decision, but I think my parents' unflagging support helped me make it. I decided to have the baby and give it away. And I didn't know, not until it came time to do just that, how hard it would be."

"Do you know who adopted the baby?"

"No." Kate dashed a tear away. "No. I didn't want to know. I'd made a deal. I had chosen to give the child to people who would love and care for it. And it wasn't my baby any longer, but theirs. She would be ten years old now, nearly eleven." Eyes swimming, she looked toward the camera. "I hope she's happy. I hope she doesn't hate me."

"Thousands of women face what you faced. Each choice they make is theirs to make, however difficult it is. I think one of the reasons you play admirable, accessible women so well is that you've been through the hardest test a woman can face."

"When I played Tess, I wondered how everything would have worked out if I'd chosen differently. I'll never know."

"Do you regret your choice?"

"A part of me always will regret I couldn't be a mother to that child. But I think I've finally realized, after all these years, that it really was the right one. For everybody."

"We'll be back in a moment," Deanna said to the camera, then turned to Kate. "Are you all right?"

"Barely. I didn't think it would be so hard." She took two deep breaths, but kept her eyes on Deanna rather than look out at the audience. "The questions are going to come fast and furious. And God, the press tomorrow."

"You'll get through it."

"Yes, I will. Dee." She leaned forward and gripped Deanna's hand. "It meant a lot to me, to be able to do this here, with you. It seemed, for a minute or two, as if I were just talking to you. The way we used to."

"Then maybe this time you'll keep in touch."

"Yeah, I will. You know, I realized while I was talking why I hated Angela so much. I thought it was because she was using me. But it was because she was using my baby. It helps knowing that."

"Hell of a show." Fran fisted her hands on her hips as Deanna walked into the dressing room. "You knew. I could tell you knew. Why the hell didn't you tell me? Me, your producer and your best friend."

"Because I wasn't sure she'd go through with it." The strain of the past hour had Deanna's shoulders aching. Rolling them in slow circles, she went directly to the lighted mirror to change makeup. Fran was miffed. She understood that, expected it. Just as she understood and expected it would wear off quickly. "And I didn't feel it was right to talk about it until she did. Give me a gauge on audience reaction, Fran."

"After the shock waves died off? I'd say about sixty-five percent were in her corner, maybe ten percent never got past the stunned stage, and the remaining twenty-five were ticked off that their princess stumbled."

"That's about how I figured it. Not bad." Deanna slathered her face with moisturizer. "She'll be all right." She lifted a brow at Fran's reflection. "Where do you stand?"

After a moment of stilted silence, Fran exhaled hard, fluttering her choppy bangs. "In her corner, one hundred percent. It must have been hell for her, poor kid. God, Dee, what made her decide to go public that way?"

"It all has to do with Angela," Deanna began, and told her.

"Blackmail." Too intrigued now for even mild annoyance, Fran let out a low whistle. "I knew she was a bitch, but I never thought she'd sunk that low. I guess the list of suspects just expanded by several dozen." Her eyes widened. "You don't think Kate—"

"No, I don't." Not that she hadn't considered it, thoroughly, Deanna thought, logically, and she hoped objectively. "Even if I thought she killed Angela, which I don't, she doesn't have any reason to have killed Marshall. She didn't even know him."

"I guess not. I wish the cops would figure it out and lock this lunatic up. It worries me sick that you're still getting those notes." Now that all was forgiven, she moved over, automatically massaging Deanna's stiff shoulders. "At least I can rest easier knowing Finn won't be going out of town until this is over."

"How do you know that?"

"Because—" Fran caught herself, looked quickly at her watch. "Gosh, what am I doing sitting around here talking? I've got a hundred things—"

"Fran." Deanna stood and stepped in front of her. "How do you know that Finn's not going out of town until this is over? The last I heard he was scheduled to go to Rome right after Christmas."

"I, ah, I must have gotten mixed up."

"Like hell."

"Damn it, Dee, don't get that warrior look on your face."

"How do you know?"

"Because he told me, okay?" She tossed up her hands in disgust. "And I was supposed to keep my big mouth shut about the fact that he's canceled the Rome shoot and anything else that takes him out of Chicago."

"I see." Deanna lowered her eyes, brushed a speck of lint from her teal silk skirt.

"No, you don't see because you've got your blinders on. Do you really expect the man to fly gleefully across the Atlantic while this is going on? For Christ's sake, he loves you."

"I'm aware of that." But her spine was rigid. "I have things to do myself," she said, and stormed out.

"Good going, Myers." Muttering oaths, Fran snatched up the dressing room phone and called up to Finn's office. If she'd inadvertently started a war, the least she could do was tell him to be fully armed.

In his office above the newsroom, Finn replaced the receiver and sent a scowl at Barlow James. "You're about to get some reinforcements. Deanna's on her way up."

"Fine." Pleased, Barlow settled back in his chair, stretched his burly arms. "We'll get all this settled once and for all."

"It is settled, Barlow. I'm not traveling more than an hour away from home until the police make an arrest."

"Finn, I understand your concerns for Deanna. I have them as well. But you're short-sheeting the show. You're overreacting."

"Really?" Finn's voice was cool, deceptively so. "And I thought I was taking two murders and the harassment of the woman I love so well."

Sarcasm didn't deflate Barlow. "My point is that she can obtain round-the-clock protection. Professionals. God knows a woman in her financial position can afford the very best. Not to slight your manhood, Finn, but you're a reporter, not a bodyguard. And," he continued before Finn could respond, "as skilled a reporter as you are, you are not a detective. Let the police do their job and you do yours. You have a responsibility to the show, to the people who work with you. To the network, to the sponsors. You have a contract, Finn. You're legally bound to travel whenever and wherever news is breaking. You agreed to those terms. Hell, you demanded them."

"Sue me," Finn invited, eyes gleaming in anticipation of a bout. He glanced up as the door slammed open.

She stood there in her snazzy silk suit, eyes flashing, chin angled. Each stride a challenge, she marched to his desk, slapped her palms on the surface.

"I won't have it."

He didn't bother to pretend he didn't understand. "You don't have any say in this, Deanna. It's my choice."

"You weren't even going to tell me. You were just going to make some lame excuse about why the trip was canceled. You'd have lied to me."

He'd have killed for her, he thought, and shrugged. "Now that's not necessary." He leaned back in the chair, steepled his fingers. Though he was wearing a sweater and jeans, he looked every inch the star. "How did the show go this morning?"

"Stop it. Just stop it." She whirled, jabbing a finger at Barlow. "You can order him to go, can't you?"

"I thought I could." He lifted his hands, let them fall. "I came from New York hoping to make him see reason. I should have known better." With a sigh, he rose. "I'll be in the newsroom for the next hour or so. If you fare any better than I did, let me know."

Finn waited until the door clicked shut. The sound was as definitive as that of the bell in a boxing ring. "You won't, Deanna, so you might as well accept it."

"I want you to go," she said, spacing each word carefully. "I don't want our lives to be interfered with. It's important to me."

"You're important to me."

"Then do this for me."

He picked up a pencil, ran it through his fingers once, twice, then snapped it neatly in two. "No."

"Your career could be on the line."

He tilted his head as if considering it. And damn him, his dimples winked at her. "I don't think so."

He was, she thought, as sturdy, as unshakable and as unmovable as granite. "They could cancel your show."

"Throw out the baby with the bathwater?" Though he wasn't feeling particularly calm, he levered back, propped his feet on the desk. "I've known network execs to do dumber things, so let's say they decide to cancel a highly rated, profitable and award-winning show because I'm not going on the road for a while." He stared up at her, his eyes darkly amused. "I guess you'd have to support me while I'm unemployed. I might get to like it and retire completely. Take up gardening or golf. No, I know. I'll be your business manager. You'd be the star—you know, like a country-western singer."

"This isn't a joke, Finn."

"It isn't a tragedy, either." His phone rang. Finn picked up the receiver, said, "Later," and hung up again. "I'm sticking, Deanna. I can't keep up with the investigation if I'm off in Europe."

"Why do you need to keep up with it?" Her eyes narrowed. "Is that what you've been doing? Why there was a rerun last Tuesday night? All those calls from Jenner. You're not working on *In Depth,* you're working with him."

"He doesn't have a problem with it. Why should you?"

She spun away. "I hate this. I hate that our private and professional lives are becoming mixed and unbalanced. I hate being scared this way. Jumping every time there's a noise in the hall, or bracing whenever the elevator door opens."

"That's my point. That's exactly how I feel. Come here." He held out a hand, gripping hers when she walked around the desk. With his eyes on hers, he drew her into his lap. "I'm scared, Deanna, right down to the bone."

Her lips parted in surprise. "You never said so."

"Maybe I should have. Male pride's a twitchy business. The fact is, I need to be here, I need to be involved, to know what's happening. It's the only way I've got to fight back the fear."

"Just promise me you won't take any chances, any risks."

"He's not going after me, Deanna."

"I want to be sure of that." She closed her eyes. But she wasn't sure.

After Deanna left, Finn went down to the video vault. An idea had been niggling at him since Marshall's murder, the notion that he'd forgotten something. Or overlooked it.

All Barlow's talk about responsibilities, loyalties, had triggered a memory. Finn skimmed through the black forest of video cases until he found February 1992.

He slipped the cassette into the machine, fast-forwarding through news reports, local, world, weather, sports. He wasn't sure of the precise date, or how much coverage there had been. But he was certain Lew McNeil's previous Chicago connection would have warranted at least one full report on his murder.

He got more than he'd hoped for.

Finn slowed the tape to normal, eyes narrowing as he focused in on the CBC reporter standing on the snowy suburban sidewalk.

"Violence struck in the early morning hours in this affluent New York neighborhood. Lewis McNeil, senior producer of the popular talk show *Angela's*, was gunned down outside his home in Brooklyn Heights this morning. According to a police source, McNeil, a Chicago native, was apparently leaving for work when he was shot at close range. McNeil's wife was in the house. . . ." The camera did its slow pan. "She was awakened shortly after seven A.M. by the sound of a gunshot."

Finn listened to the rest of the report, eyes fixed. Grimly, he zipped through another week of news, gathering snippets on the McNeil murder investigation.

He tucked his notes away and headed into the newsroom. He found Joe as the cameraman was heading out on assignment.

"Question."

"Make it a quick one. I'm, on the clock."

"February ninety-two. Lew McNeil's murder. That was your camerawork on the New York stand-up, wasn't it?"

"What can I say?" Joe polished his nails on his sweatshirt. "My art is distinctive."

"Right. Where was he shot?"

"As I recall, right outside his house." As he thought back, Joe reached into his hip pocket for a Baby Ruth. "Yeah, they said it looked like he was cleaning off his car."

"No, I mean anatomically. Chest, gut, head? None of the reports I reviewed said."

"Oh." Joe frowned, shutting his eyes as if to bring the scene back to mind. "They'd cleaned up pretty good by the time we got there. Never saw the stiff." He opened his eyes. "Did you know Lew?"

"Some."

"Yeah, me too. Tough." He bit off a hefty section of chocolate. "Why the interest?"

"Something I'm working on. Didn't your reporter ask the cops for details?"

"Who was that—Clemente, right? Didn't last around here very long. Sloppy, you know? I can't say if he did or not. Look, I've got to split." He headed for the stairs, then rapped his knuckles on the side of his head. "Yeah, yeah." He headed up the steps backward, watching Finn. "Seems to me I heard one of the other reporters talking. He said Lew caught the bullet in the face. Nasty, huh?"

"Yeah." A grim satisfaction swam through Finn's blood. "Very nasty."

Jenner munched a midmorning danish, washing down the cherry filling with sweetened coffee. As he ate and sipped, he studied the grisly photos tacked to the corkboard. The conference room was quiet now, but he'd left the blinds open on the glass door that separated it from the bull pen of the precinct.

Angela Perkins. Marshall Pike. He stared at what had been done to them. If he stared long enough, he knew he could go into a kind of trance—a state of mind that left the brain clear for ideas, for possibilities.

He was just annoyed enough at Finn for emotion to interfere with intellect. The man should have told him the details of his conversation with Pike. However slight it had been, it had been police business. The idea of Finn interviewing Pike alone burned Jenner more bitterly than the station house coffee.

He remembered their last meeting, in the early hours of the morning that Pike had been murdered.

"We're clear that the shooter knows Miss Reynolds." Jenner ticked the fact off on a finger. "Was aware of her relationship, or at least her argument, with Pike." He held up a second finger. "He or she knows Deanna's address, knew Pike's and had enough knowledge of the studio to set up the camera after killing Angela Perkins."

"Agreed."

"The notes have shown up under Deanna's door, on her desk, in her car, in the apartment she still keeps in Old Town." Jenner had lifted a brow, hoping that Finn would offer some explanation for that interesting fact. But he hadn't. Finn knew how to keep information to himself. It was one of the things Jenner admired about him. "It has to be someone who works at CBC," Jenner concluded.

"Agreed. In theory." Finn smiled when Jenner let out a huff of breath. "It could be someone who *worked* there. It's possible it's a fan of Deanna's who's been in the studio. A regular audience member. Lots of people have enough rudimentary knowledge of television to work a camera for a still shot."

"I think that's stretching it."

"So let's stretch it. He sees her every day on TV."

"Could be a woman."

Finn let that cook a moment, then shook his head. "A remote possibility. Let's shuffle that aside for a minute and try out this theory: It's a man, a lonely, frustrated man. He lives alone, but every day Deanna slips through the television screen right into his living room. She's sitting right there with him, talking to him, smiling at him. He's not lonely when she's there. And he wants her there all the time. He doesn't do well with women. He's a little afraid of them. He's a good planner, probably holds down a decent job, a responsible one, because he knows how to think things through. He's thorough, meticulous."

Impressed, Jenner pursed his lips. "Sounds like you've done your homework."

"I have. Because I'm in love with Deanna I think I understand him. Thing is, he's got this temper, this rage. He didn't kill in a rage. I think he did that coolly." And that was what chilled Finn's blood. "But he trashes my house, Deanna's office. He writes his feelings of betrayal on the wall. All but splatters them there. How did she betray him? What changed from the time she got the first note to Angela's murder?"

"She hooked up with you?"

"She'd been involved with me for two years." Finn leaned forward. "We got engaged, Jenner. The official announcement had barely hit the streets when we had Angela's murder and the break-ins."

"So he killed Angela because he was ticked at Deanna Reynolds?"

"He killed Angela, and Pike, because he loves Deanna Reynolds. What better way to show his devotion than to remove people who upset or annoy her? He trashed her things, taking special care with the wedding-gown sketches, the newspaper reports of the engagement, photographs of Deanna and me. He was enraged because she'd announced, publicly, that she preferred another man to him. That she was willing to take vows to prove it."

Nodding slowly, Jenner doodled on a sheet of paper. "Maybe you didn't get your psychiatrist's degree at Sears. Why hasn't he gone after you?"

Instinctively, Finn reached up to run his fingers over his sleeve. Beneath it was a scar from a bullet. A bullet that hadn't come from the sniper or the SWAT team. But he couldn't be sure. "Because I haven't done anything to *hurt* Deanna. Marshall did, on the day he was killed, and a couple of years ago, when he fell into Angela's trap."

"I should have talked to him." Jenner tapped a fist lightly on his files. "He could have known something, seen something. It's possible he'd received threats."

"I doubt that. He was the type who'd have come running to the cops. Or he would have told me when I talked with him."

"You were too busy beating him up."

"I didn't beat him up." Finn folded his arms across his chest. "He swung, I swung. Once. In any case, I meant he would have told me when I talked to him at his office a few days ago."

Jenner stopped doodling. "You went to see him about Angela Perkins's murder?"

"It was a theory."

"One you didn't feel necessary to share?"

"It was personal."

"Nothing's personal on this, nothing." Jenner edged forward, eyes narrowed. "I've let you in on this investigation because I think you're a smart man, and I sympathize with your position. But you cross me and you're out."

"I'll do what I have to do, Lieutenant, with or without you."

"Reporters aren't the only ones who can harass. Keep that in mind." Jenner closed his file, rose. "Now I have work to do."

No, Jenner thought now, sympathy and admiration aside, he wasn't about to let Finn go off on his own. He might be wearing blinders to the fact that his life was in danger, but Jenner knew better.

He rose to refill his coffee cup, and glanced through the glass door. "Speak of the devil," he murmured. Jenner pulled open the door. "Looking for me?" he asked Finn, and waved away the uniform who was blocking Finn's path. "It's all right, officer. I'll see Mr. Riley." He nodded briefly at Finn. "You've got five minutes."

"It's going to take a little longer." Finn studied the police photos on the board dispassionately. There were snapshots of both victims taken prior to and after death. Side by side, they were like before-and-after shots gone desperately wrong. "You're going to need to put one more set up there."

Twenty minutes later, Jenner completed his conversation with the detective in Brooklyn Heights. "They're faxing us the file," he told Finn. "Okay, Mr. Riley, who knew that McNeil was passing information on to Angela?"

"Deanna's staff. I'd be certain of that. I'd also give odds that it would have leaked downstairs." There was an excitement brewing in him now. The kind he recognized as energy from a puzzle nearly solved. "There's always been a lot of interaction between Deanna's people and the newsroom. Are we on the same wavelength here? Three people are dead because they threatened Deanna in some way."

"I can't comment about that, Mr. Riley."

Finn shoved back from the table. "Damn it, I'm not here as a reporter. I'm not looking for a scoop, the latest tidbit from an unnamed police source. You want to frisk me for a mike?"

"I don't think you're after a story, Mr. Riley," Jenner said calmly. "If I'd ever thought that, you never would have gotten your foot in the door. But maybe I think you're too used to doing things your own way, to running your own show to handle the delicate matter of cooperation."

Finn slammed his hands down on the table. "If you think you're going to brush me off, you're wrong. You're right about the harassment, Lieutenant. One phone call and I can have a dozen cameras dogging your every move. I can put so much pressure on you that you won't be able to sneeze without someone sticking a mike up your nose. Before you catch your next breath Chicago will be buzzing about a serial killer. The commissioner and the mayor will love that, won't they?" He waited half a beat. "You use me, or I'll use you. It's your choice."

Jenner folded his arms on the table, leaned forward against them. "I don't like threats."

"Neither do I. But I'll do a lot more than threaten if you try to block me out now." He looked at the victims on the board. "He could lose it." He spoke quietly now, carefully. "He could lose it anytime and try to put her up there. You're pissed because I did some tracking on my own, fine. Be pissed. But use me. Or by God I'll use you."

Objectively, Jenner buried his irritation, calculating how much damage would be done by a media war. Too much, he mused. It was always too much.

"Let's do this, Mr. Riley. Let's say we theorize that McNeil was the first victim of three—and we'll want to keep that under our hat."

"I told you I'm not interested in a story."

"Just laying down the ground rules. We'll theorize that, and that only a limited number of people had the knowledge that would lead to motive for his murder." He gestured to a chair, waiting for Finn to sit again. "Tell me about those people. Start with Loren Bach." In the spirit of compromise, Jenner opened the file on Loren that Angela had commissioned from Beeker.

Cassie walked into Deanna's office, then let out a long, long sigh. Deanna stood on a stool in the center of the room, the seamstress at her feet. Yards of shimmering white silk billowed.

"It's gorgeous."

"It's barely started." But Deanna was almost sighing herself as she brushed a hand over the sweeping skirt neatly pinned to the lacy bodice. Irish lace, she mused. For Finn. "But you're right."

"I've got to get my camera." Inspired, Cassie bolted for the door. "Don't move."

"I'm not going anywhere."

"You must be still," the seamstress complained over a mouthful of pins. Her voice was raspy, as if she'd already swallowed more than her share.

Deanna used all her willpower not to shift from foot to foot. "I am being still."

"You're vibrating like a spring."

"Sorry." Deanna took a long, steadying breath. "I guess I'm nervous."

"The bride-to-be," Cassie recited as she walked back in with a Palmcorder blocking her face. "Deanna Reynolds, the reigning queen of daytime TV, has chosen an elegant gown of..."

"Italian silk," the seamstress prompted. "With touches of Irish lace and a sea of freshwater pearls."

"Exquisite," Cassie said soberly. "And tell us, Miss Reynolds"—with an expert's touch, she zoomed in on Deanna's face—"how do you feel on this exciting occasion?"

"Terrified." She crossed her eyes. If the fitting took five minutes over the allotted hour, she'd be making up time all week. "And partially insane. Other than that I'm enjoying every minute of it."

"If you'll just stand perfectly still, I'll do a little circle around so that our viewers can get the full effect." Cassie sidestepped, panned back. "This'll go in my growing library of life behind *Deanna's Hour*."

Deanna felt her smile stiffen. "Do you have a lot of tape?"

"Oh, a little of this, a little of that. Simon pulling what's left of his hair out. Margaret tossing spitballs. You racing for the elevator."

Beneath the sparkling bodice, Deanna's heart thudded thickly. "I guess I've never paid much attention. So many cameras around. You always keep that at hand, don't you?"

"You never know what historical, or humiliating, moment you might capture."

Someone had captured her, Deanna remembered, while she'd slept at her desk. Coming to work, going from, shopping, playing with Fran's baby in the park.

They'd captured her unconscious in the studio beside Angela's body.

Cassie, who was in and out of the office dozens of times a day. Cassie, who knew every detail of Deanna's schedule. Cassie, who had dated one of the studio camera operators.

"Turn it off, Cassie."

"One more second."

"Turn it off." Her voice sharpened, and Deanna set her teeth to steady it.

"Sorry." Obviously baffled, Cassie lowered the camera. "I guess I got carried away."

"It's all right. I'm just edgy." Deanna managed to smile again. It was ridiculous, she told herself. It was insane even to speculate that Cassie would be capable of murder.

"It's your first day back." Cassie touched her hand and Deanna had to force herself not to jerk away. "God knows it was a madhouse around here after the show with all those calls coming in about Kate Lowell. Why don't you give yourself a break after you've finished the fitting, and go home? I can reschedule the rest of the afternoon's business."

"I think that's a good idea." She spoke slowly over the erratic thud of her heart. "I've got a lot of things to deal with at home."

Cassie's mouth thinned. "I didn't mean you should jump out of one madhouse into another. You're not going to get any work done there, with all those painters and carpenters slogging away. I think—" She saw that Deanna's eyes had focused behind her and turned. "Jeff." Her mouth softened at the admiration on his face. "She looks fabulous, doesn't she?"

"Yeah. Really." He glanced at the camera Cassie held. "You got pictures?"

"Sure. Capture the moment. Listen, unless it's a crisis, hold it off, will you? This is a momentous occasion. Dee's going home early."

"Oh, good idea. Finn called, Deanna. He said to tell you he had a meeting and he'd see you at home. He thought he might get there by four."

"Well, that's lucky. Maybe I'll beat him there."

"Not if you don't hold still," the seamstress muttered.

But it was barely three-thirty when Deanna slipped into her shoes and grabbed her briefcase. "Cassie, can you call Tim?"

"Already done. He should be waiting downstairs."

"Thanks." She stopped by the desk, feeling ashamed and foolish about her earlier thoughts. "I'm sorry about before, Cassie. The camera business."

"Don't worry about it." Cassie zipped open one of the daily letters that heaped on her desk. "I know I'm a nuisance." She chuckled. "I like being a nuisance with it. See you tomorrow."

"Okay. Don't stay late."

More at ease, Deanna walked to the elevator, checking her watch as she punched the Down button. With any luck, she could surprise Finn by arriving first. It wouldn't take much effort, she knew, to persuade him to fix some blackened chicken and pasta. She was in the mood for something spicy to cap off her first day back in harness.

She could deal with a mountain of paperwork and phone calls there. Then, if she scheduled a break, she could slink into something designed to drive Finn crazy.

They'd have dinner late. Very late, she decided, and swung out of the elevator.

Maybe she'd wrap a few last-minute Christmas gifts, or talk Finn into baking some cookies. She could run a couple of the new segment ideas by him.

The flash of sunlight had her reaching automatically for her tinted glasses. Slipping them on, she climbed into the back of the waiting limo.

"Hi, Tim." She closed her eyes and stretched. The limo was beautifully warm.

"Hi, Miss Reynolds."

"Turned out to be a beautiful day." Out of habit, she reached for the bottle of chilled juice that was always stocked for her. She looked up idly at the back of her driver. Despite the car's warmth, he was huddled inside his coat, his cap tipped low.

"Sure did."

Sipping the juice, she flipped open her briefcase. She set the file neatly labeled "Wedding Plans" aside and reached for the daily correspondence Cassie had culled for her to read. She'd always considered the drive to and from the office part of the workday. In this case, she had to make up the time she'd taken with the fitting, and for knocking off early.

But by the third letter, the words were blurring. There was no excuse for being so tired so early in the day. Annoyed, she slid her fingers under her glasses to rub her eyes clear. But they blurred all the more, as if she'd swabbed them with oil. Her head spun once, sickly, and her arm fell heavily to the seat beside her.

So tired, she thought. So hot. As if in slow motion, she tried to shrug out of her coat. The papers fluttered to the floor, and the effort of reaching for them only increased the dizziness.

"Tim." She leaned forward, pressed a hand against the back of the front seat. He didn't answer, but the word had sounded dim and far away to her own ears. As she struggled to focus on him the half-empty bottle of juice slipped from her numbed fingers.

"Something's wrong," she tried to tell him as she slid bonelessly to the plushly carpeted floor of the car. "Something's very wrong."

But he didn't answer. She imagined herself falling through the floor of the limo and into a dark, bottomless pit.

28

Deanna dreamed she was swimming up through red-tinted clouds, slowly, sluggishly pulling herself toward the surface, where a faint, white light glowed through the misty layers. She moaned as she struggled. Not from pain but nausea that rolled up, burning in her throat.

In defense, she kept her eyes closed, taking long, deep breaths and willing the sickness back. Drops of clammy sweat pearled on her skin so that her thin silk blouse clung nastily to her arms and back.

When the worst had passed, she opened her eyes cautiously.

She had been in the car, she remembered. Tim had been driving her home and she'd become ill. But she wasn't home now. Hospital? she wondered dully when she let her eyes cautiously open. The room was softly lit with delicate violets trailing up the wallpaper. A white ceiling fan gently stirred the air with a whispering sound of blades. A glossy mahogany bureau held a collection of pretty, colored bottles and pots. A magnificent poinsettia and a miniature blue spruce decorated with silver bells added seasonal flair.

Hospital? she thought again. Groggily, she tried to sit up. Her head spun again, hideously, shooting that fist of nausea back into her stomach. Her vision doubled. When she tried to bring her hand to her face, it felt weighted down. For a moment she could only lie still, fighting back the sickness. She saw that the room was a box, a closed, windowless box. Like a coffin.

A spear of panic sliced through the shock. She reared up, shouting, stumbling drunkenly from the bed. Staggering to a wall, she ran her fingers over the delicate floral wallpaper in a dizzy search for an opening. Trapped. She wheeled around, eyes wide. Trapped.

She saw then what was on the wall over the bed. It was enough to crush the bubbling hysteria. A huge photograph smiled sassily down at her. For several stunned moments Deanna stared at Deanna. Slowly, with the sound of her own heartbeat thudding in her ears, she scanned the rest of the room.

No, there were no doors, no windows, just flowers, bowers of them, wall to wall. But there were other photographs. Dozens of pictures of her were lined on the side walls. Candid shots, magazine covers, press photos stood cheek by jowl against the dainty wallpaper.

"Oh God. Oh God." She heard the whimpering panic in her own voice and bit down fiercely on her lip.

Looking away from her own images, her eyes glassy with shock, she stared at the refectory table, its snowy white runner stiff with starch as a backdrop for silver candle holders, glossy white tapers. Dozens of little treasures had been arranged there: an earring she'd lost months before, a tube of lipstick, a silk scarf Simon had given her one Christmas, a glove of supple red leather—one of a pair that had disappeared the winter before.

There was more. She eased closer, straining against the tidal wave of fear as she studied the collection. A memo she'd handwritten to Jeff, a lock of ebony hair wrapped in gold cord, other photographs of her, always of her, in elegant and ornate frames. The shoes she'd been wearing in the limo were there as well, along with her jacket, neatly folded.

The place was like a shrine, she realized with a shudder. The sound in her throat was feral and frightened. There was a television in the corner, a shelf of leather-bound albums. And most terrifying, cameras bracketed the upper corners of the room. The pinpoints of their red lights beamed like tiny eyes.

She stumbled back, fear soaring like a slickly coated bird. Her gaze sliced from one camera to the other.

"You're watching me." She fought back the terror in her voice. "I know you are. You can't keep me here. They'll look. You know they'll find me. They're probably looking already."

She looked down at her wrist to check the time, but saw that her watch was gone. How long? she wondered frantically. It might have been minutes, or days, since she'd passed out in the car.

The car. Her breath began to hitch. "Tim." She pressed her lips together until the ache snapped through the need to weep. "Tim, you have to let me go. I'll try to help you. I promise that. I'll do whatever I can. Please, come in here, talk to me."

As though only her invitation had been required, a section of the wall slid open. In reflex, Deanna surged forward, only to bite back a moan of despair as her head spun in sickening circles from the drug. Still, she straightened her shoulders and hoped that she hid the worst of her fear.

"Tim," she began, then only stared in confusion.

"Welcome home, Deanna."

His face flushed with shy pleasure, Jeff stepped into the room. He carried a silver tray on which rode a wineglass, a china plate of herbed pasta and a single red rosebud.

"I hope you like the room." In his unhurried and efficient way, he set the tray on the bureau. "It took a long time for me to get it just right. I didn't want you to be just comfortable. I wanted you to be happy. I know there's no view." He turned toward her, eyes too bright though apology quavered in his voice. "But it's safer this way. No one will bother us when we're in here."

"Jeff." Calm, she ordered herself. She had to stay calm. "You can't keep me here."

"Yes I can. I've planned it all carefully. I've had years to work it out. Why don't you sit down, Dee? You're probably feeling a little groggy, and I want you to be comfortable while you eat."

He stepped forward, and though she braced, he didn't touch her.

"Later," he continued, "after you understand everything, you'll feel a lot better. You just need time." He lifted a hand as if to touch her cheek, but drew it away again as if he didn't want to frighten her.

"Please try to relax. You never let yourself relax. I know you might be a little afraid right now, but it's going to be all right. If you fight me, I'll have to . . ." Because he couldn't bear to say the words, he slipped a hypo out of his pocket. "I don't want to." Her instant recoil had him pushing the needle out of sight again. "Really, I don't. And you wouldn't be able to get away."

Smiling again, he moved a table and chair closer to the bed. "You need to eat," he said pleasantly. "You always worried me when it came to taking care of yourself. All those hurried or skipped meals. But I'll take good care of you. Sit down, Deanna."

She could refuse, she thought. She could scream and rant and threaten. And for what? She'd known Jeff, or thought she'd known him, for years. He could be stubborn, she reminded herself. But she'd always been able to reason with him.

"I am hungry," she told him, and hoped her stomach wouldn't rebel. "You'll talk to me while I eat? Explain things to me?" She gave him her best interviewer's smile.

"Yes." The smile burned across his face like a fever. "I thought you might be angry at first."

"I'm not angry. I'm afraid."

"I'd never hurt you." He took one of her limp hands in his and squeezed lightly. "I won't let anyone hurt you. I know you might be thinking about getting past me, Deanna. Getting through the panel. But you can't. I'm really very strong, and you're still weak from the drug. No matter what you do, you'll still be locked in. Sit down."

As if in a dream, she did as he told her. She wanted to run, but even as the thought communicated from brain to body, her legs folded. How could she run when she could barely stand? The drug was still in charge of her system. It was precisely the kind of detail he would have thought of. Precisely the kind of detail that had made him such an invaluable part of her team.

"It's wrong to keep me here, Jeff."

"No, it's not." He set the tray on the table in front of her. "I've thought about it for a long, long time. And this is for the best. For you. I'm always thinking of you. Later on, we can travel together. I've been looking into villas in the south of France. I think you'd like it there." He touched her then, just a brushing caress on her shoulder. Beneath her blouse her skin crawled. "I love you so much."

"Why didn't you ever tell me? You could have talked to me about the way you felt."

"I couldn't. At first I thought it was just because I was shy, but then I realized that it was all like a plan. A life plan. Yours and mine."

Anxious to explain, he pulled up another chair. As he leaned forward, his glasses slid down his nose. While her vision blurred, then cleared, she watched him shove them up again—an old habit, once an endearing one, that now chilled her blood.

"There were things you needed to do, experiences—and men—you had to get out of your system before we could be together. I understood that, Dee. I never blamed you for Finn. It hurt me." Resting his hands on his knees, he let out a sigh. "But I didn't blame you. And I couldn't blame him." His face brightened again. "How could I when I knew how perfect you were? The first time I saw you on TV, I couldn't get my breath. It scared me a little. You were looking right at me, into me. I'll never forget it. You see, I was so lonely before. An only child. I grew up in this house. You're not eating, Deanna. I wish you would."

Obediently, she picked up her fork. He wanted to talk. Seemed eager to. The best way to escape, she calculated, was to understand. "You told me you grew up in Iowa."

"That's where my mother took me later. My mother was wild." The apology crept back into his voice. "She would never listen to anyone, never obey the rules. So naturally, Uncle Matthew had to punish her. He was older, you see. He was head of the family. He'd keep her in this room, trying to make her see that there were proper ways to do things, and improper ways." His face changed as he spoke, tightening around the mouth and eyes, growing somehow older, sterner. "But my mother never learned, no matter how hard my uncle tried to teach her. She ran away and got pregnant. When I was six, they took her away. She had a breakdown, and I came to live with Uncle Matthew. There was no one else to take me in, you see. And it was his family duty."

Deanna choked down a bite of pasta. It stuck like paste in her throat, but she was afraid to try the wine. He could have drugged it, she thought, like the bottle of juice. "I'm sorry, Jeff, about your mother."

"It's okay." He shrugged it off like a snake shedding skin. His face smoothed out again like a sheet stroked with careful hands. "She didn't love me. No one's ever loved me but Uncle Matthew. And you. It's just wine, Dee. Your favorite kind." Grinning at the joke, he picked up the glass and sipped to show her. "I didn't put anything in it. I didn't have to, because you're here now. With me."

Drugged or not, she avoided the wine, unsure how it would mix with the drugs in her system. "What happened to your mother?"

"She had dementia. She died. Is your dinner all right? I know pasta's your favorite."

"It's fine." Deanna slipped another bite through her stiff lips. "How old were you when she died?"

"I don't know. Doesn't matter, I was happy here, with my uncle." It made him nervous to talk about his mother, so he didn't. "He was a great man. Strong and good. He hardly ever had to punish me, because I was good, too. I wasn't a trial to him, like my mother was. We took care of each other." He spoke quickly now, fresh excitement blooming. "He was proud of me. I studied hard and I didn't hang out with other kids. I didn't need them. I mean, all they wanted to do was ride in fast cars and listen to loud music and fight with their parents. I had respect. And I never forgot things like cleaning my room or brushing my teeth. Uncle Matthew always told me I didn't need anybody but family. And he was the only family I had. Then, when he died, there was you. So I knew it was right."

"Jeff." Deanna used all her skills to keep the conversation flowing, to steer it in the direction she wanted. "Do you think your uncle would approve of what you're doing now?"

"Oh, absolutely." He beamed, his face sunny and innocent and terrifying. "He talks to me all the time, up here." He tapped his head, winked. "He told me to be patient, to wait until the time was right. You know when I first started sending you letters?"

"Yes, I remember."

"I dreamed about Uncle Matthew for the first time then. Only it wasn't like a dream. It was so real. He told me I had to court you, the way a gentleman would. That I had to be patient. He always said that good things take time. He told me that I would have to wait, and that I had to look out for you. Men are supposed to cherish their women, to protect them. People have forgotten that. No one seems to cherish anyone anymore."

"Is that why you killed Angela, Jeff? To protect me?"

"I planned that for months." He leaned back again, rested one bent leg across his knee. Conversations with Deanna had always been a high point of his life. And this, he thought, was the very best. "You didn't know that I let her think I was taking Lew's place."

"Lew's? Lew McNeil's?"

"After I killed him—"

"Lew." Her fork rattled against the china when it slipped through her fingers. "You killed Lew."

"He betrayed you. I had to punish him. And he used Simon. Until I started to work with you, I never really had friends. Simon's my friend. I was going to kill him, too, but I realized he'd been used. It wasn't really his fault, was it?"

"No." She said it quickly, punctuating the word by laying her hand over Jeff's. "No, Jeff, it wasn't Simon's fault. I care very much about Simon. I wouldn't want you to hurt him."

"That's what I thought." He grinned, a child praised by an indulgent adult. "You see, I know you so well, Deanna. I know everything about you. Your family, your friends. Your favorite foods and colors. Where you like to shop. I know everything you're thinking. It's as though I were right inside your head. Or you're inside mine," he added slowly. "Sometimes I'd think you were inside mine. I knew you wanted Angela to go away. And I knew you'd never hurt her yourself. You're too gentle, too kind." He turned his hand over to squeeze hers. "So I did it for you. I arranged to meet her in the parking lot at CBC. She sent her driver away, just like I'd told her to. I let her in, took her down to the studio. I'd told her that I had copied papers from the office. Story ideas, guests, plans for remotes. She was going to buy them from me. Only she didn't tell me you were coming." Incredibly, his bottom lip poked out in a pout. "She lied to me about that."

"You killed her. And you turned the cameras on."

"I was angry with you." His mouth quivered, his eyes lowered. Deanna gripped her fork again with some idea of using it as a weapon. The effects of the drug were wearing off, and she felt stronger. She thought she could thank fear for that. But his eyes lifted to hers and the searing light in them had her fingers going numb.

"I knew it was wrong, but I wanted to hurt you. I nearly wanted to kill you. You were going to marry him, Dee. I could understand your sleeping with him. Weak flesh. Uncle Matthew explained all about how sex can pervert, and how weak people can be. Even you." The hand that covered hers tightened, tightened, until bone rubbed bone. "So I understood, and I was patient, because I always knew you'd come to me. But you couldn't marry him, you couldn't take vows. I knew it was you when you opened the door. I always know when it's you. I hit you. I wanted to hit you again, but I couldn't. So I carried you to the chair, and I put Angela in the other one and turned on the camera. I wanted you to see what I'd done for you. I'd already been upstairs, in your office." He compressed his lips, sighed and gently released her throbbing hand. "It was wrong of me to wreck your office. I shouldn't have gone to Finn's house, either. I'm sorry."

He said it as though he'd neglected to keep a luncheon appointment.

"Jeff, have you ever told anyone about your feelings?"

"Just my uncle, when we talk in my head. He was sure you'd understand soon, and come home with me. And after I heard what that creep did to you in the parking lot, I knew it was nearly time."

"Marshall?"

"He tried to hurt you. Joe told me how he'd acted, so I waited for him. I killed him the same way I'd killed the others. It was symbolic, Deanna. My vision destroyed their vision. It's almost holy, don't you think?"

"It's not holy to kill, Jeff."

"You're too forgiving." His eyes scanned her face, adoringly. "If you forgive people who've hurt you, they'll only hurt you again. You have to protect what's yours."

He remembered the dog that had come into their yard time after time, digging up Uncle Matthew's flowers, spoiling the grass. He'd cried when his uncle had poisoned the dog. Cried until Uncle Matthew had explained to him why it was right and honorable to defend your own against any intruder. With that in mind, he got up and went to the bureau. He opened the top drawer and took out a list.

"I've planned it," he told her. "You and I always make lists and plan things out. We're not the type who run off without thinking, are we?" Beaming again, he offered the list to her.

LEW MCNEIL

ANGELA PERKINS

MARSHALL PIKE

DAN GARDNER
JAMIE THOMAS
FINN RILEY?

"Finn," was all she could say.

"He's not for sure. I put him down in case he hurt you. I nearly did it once before. Nearly. But at the last minute I realized I was only going to kill him because I was jealous. It was like Uncle Matthew was there, and he jerked the rifle at the last minute. I was really glad I didn't kill him when I saw how upset you were that he'd been shot."

"In Greektown," Deanna said through trembling lips. "That day in Greektown. You shot him?"

"It was a mistake. I'm really sorry."

"Oh God." Horrified, she cringed back. "Oh my God."

"It was a mistake." His voice was sulky, dangerously so. Jeff looked away from her. "I said I was sorry. I won't do anything to him unless he hurts you."

"He hasn't. He won't."

"Then I won't have to do anything about him."

Her palm dampened against the paper, and her heart began to beat heavily in her throat. "Promise me you won't, Jeff. It's important to me that Finn's safe. He's been very good to me."

"I'm better for you."

There was a child's petulance on his face now. Deanna exploited the moment. "Promise me, Jeff, or I'll be very unhappy. You don't want that, do you?"

"No." He struggled between her needs and his own. "I guess it doesn't matter now. Not now that you're here."

"You have to promise." She clamped her teeth together to keep the desperation from her voice. Reason, she told herself. Calm reason. "I know you wouldn't break your word to me."

"All right. If it makes you happy." To show his sincerity, he took out a pen and scratched Finn's name off the list. "See?"

"Thank you. And Dan Gardner—"

"No." His voice sharp, he folded the page. "He's already hurt you, Dee. He's said terrible things about you; he helped Angela try to ruin you. He has to be punished."

"But he doesn't matter, Jeff. He's nothing." Calm, she reminded herself. Calm but firm. Adult to child. "And Jamie Thomas, that was years and years ago. I don't care about them."

"I do. I care. I'd have killed him first, right away, but he was in Europe. Hiding out," he said scornfully. "It's not easy to get a weapon through customs, so I was patient." Now he beamed. "He's back now, you know. He's in New Hampshire. I'll be going there soon."

The drug was no longer making her ill, but the nausea rolled greasily in her stomach. "I don't care about him. About any of them, Jeff. I don't want you to hurt them for me."

He turned his face away, sulking. "I don't want to talk about this anymore."

"I want—"

"You have to think about what I want, too." He shoved the list back in the drawer, slammed it hard enough to rattle bottles. "I'm only thinking of you."

"Yes, I know. I know you are. But if you go to New York to kill Gardner, or New Hampshire for Jamie, I'll be all alone here. I don't want to be locked up alone, Jeff."

"Don't worry." His tone gentled. "I've got plenty of time, and I'll be very careful. I'm so glad you're here."

"Would you let me go outside please? I need some air."

"I can't. Not yet. It isn't part of the plan." He sat again, leaning forward. "You need three months."

Horror drained her blood. "You can't keep me locked up like this for three months."

"It's all right. You'll have everything you need. Books, TV, company. I'll rent movies for you, cook your meals. I've bought clothes for you." He sprang up to slide open another panel. "See? I spent weeks choosing just the right things." He gestured inside to the closet full of slacks and dresses and jackets. "And there's shirts and sweaters, nightclothes and underthings in the bureau. Over here..." He pushed open another hidden door. "The bathroom."

He flushed, stared at his shoes. "There aren't any cameras in there. I swear. I wouldn't spy on you in the bathroom. I stocked your favorite bath oils and soaps, your cosmetics. You'll have everything you need."

Everything you need. Everything you need. The words spun around and around in her head. She couldn't keep the hitch out of her voice. "I don't want to be locked up."

"I'm sorry. That's the only thing I can't give you right now. Soon, when you've really come to understand, it'll be different. But anything else you want, I'll get for you. Whenever I have to leave, you'll be all right here. The room's secure, soundproofed. Even if someone came into the house, they wouldn't find you. Outside the door is a bookcase. It's really cool. I designed it myself. No one would ever guess there was a room in here, so you'll be safe and sound whenever I'm gone. And when I'm busy around the house, I can watch you." He pointed toward the cameras. "So if you need me, I'll know."

"They'll come and find me, Jeff. Sooner or later. They won't understand. You have to let me go."

"No, I have to keep you. Do you want to watch TV?" He crossed over, picked up the remote from the nightstand. "We have full cable."

Fighting back a hysterical laugh, she pressed her fingers to her eyes. "No, no, not now."

"You can watch whenever you want. And the shelf is full of videos. Movies, and tapes I've taken of you. And the scrapbooks." He bustled around the room, an energetic host anxious to entertain. "I've kept them for you. Everything that's ever been written up on you is in here. Or there's the stereo. I have all your favorite music. There's a little refrigerator in the bathroom that I stocked with drinks and snacks."

"Jeff." She could feel that bubble of panic swelling. Her hands shook as she stood. "You've gone to a lot of trouble. I understand that. And I understand that you've done what you thought you had to do. But this is wrong. You're keeping me prisoner."

"No, no, no." He came to her quickly, grabbing her hands when she jerked back. "You're like the princess in the fairy tale, and I'm protecting you. I'm cherishing you.

It's like you're under a spell, Dee. One day you'll wake up and I'll be here. And we'll be happy."

"I'm not under a spell." She yanked away, fury simmering under fear like an exotic stew. "And I'm not a goddamn princess. I'm a human being, with the right to make my own choices. You can't lock me up and expect me to be grateful because I've got bathroom privileges."

"I knew you'd be angry at first." Disappointment sighed through his voice as he reached down for her dinner dishes. "But you'll calm down."

"The hell I will." She leaped at him, striking out with her free hand. The first blow glanced off his cheekbone. China shattered on the floor and flew like bullets. Snarling, she scrambled after a shard.

She screamed, fighting like a madwoman as he wrestled her to the floor. He was strong, so much stronger than he looked with those long, gangly arms. He made no sound, no sound at all, simply clamped a hand painfully on her wrist until her fingers opened to release the makeshift weapon.

He dragged her to the bed, stoically suffering her flailing feet and fists. When she was pressed under him, his erection hard against her thigh, her terror doubled.

There were worse things than being locked in. "No!" She tried to buck him off, her fingers fisting and unfisting while he clamped her hands over her head.

"I want you, Deanna. God, I want you." His fumbling kiss dampened her jaw. The sensation of her body writhing beneath his had a red haze of need cloaking his vision. Her heart was chugging like a piston against his, and her skin was soft as water, hot as fire. "Please, please." He was almost weeping as his mouth covered hers. "Just let me touch you."

"No." Sickened, she turned her head. Control. She grasped onto her only hope. "You'd be no better than Jamie. You're hurting me, Jeff. You have to stop hurting me."

Tears tracked down his cheeks when he lifted his head. "I'm sorry. Deanna, I'm so sorry. It's just that I've waited so long. We won't make love until you're ready. I swear it. Don't be afraid of me."

"I am afraid." He wouldn't rape her, she realized, and was almost ashamed that she was willing to settle for that. "You have me locked up. You've told me no one can find me. What if something happened to you? I could die here."

"Nothing's going to happen. I've planned everything, every detail. I love you, Deanna, and I know under it all, you love me too. You've shown me in hundreds of ways. The way you smile at me. The way you touch me, or laugh. The way you'll catch my eye across the room. You made me your director. I can't begin to explain what that meant to me. You trusted me to guide you. You believed in me. In us."

"It's not love. I don't love you."

"You're just not ready yet. Now you need to rest." He braceleted her wrists in one hand, fought the hypo free with the other.

"No. Don't." She twisted, wrenched, begged. "Please don't. I can't go anywhere. You've said I can't get away."

"You need to rest," he said quietly, and slid the needle under her skin. "I'll watch out for you, Deanna."

Her head lolled back, and his tears fell to mix with hers. He waited, miserably, until her struggles to fight off the drug ceased. When her body went limp, he clamped down on the urge to stroke his hands over it.

Not until she's ready, he reminded himself, content to brush the dampness from her cheeks. Gently, he shifted her onto the pillows and placed a chaste kiss on her brow.

His princess, he thought, studying her as she slept. He'd built her an ivory tower. They'd live there together. Forever.

"Isn't she perfect, Uncle Matthew? Isn't she beautiful? You'd have loved her too. You'd have known she was the one, the only one."

He sighed. Uncle Matthew wasn't speaking to him. He'd been wrong to allow sex to twist his plans. He'd have to be punished. Bread and water only for two days. That's what his uncle would have done. Meekly he crouched down to clean up the broken dishes. He tidied the room, turned the lights down. With one last, longing glance at Deanna, he slipped out of the room, shutting the panel silently.

"I think it would be best if you'd take Miss Reynolds home." Jenner rode up in the elevator with Finn. He still resented Finn's earlier pressuring but he covered it with quiet dignity. "I'd prefer that she was out of the office when we re-interrogate her staff."

"The minute she finds out that's what you intend to do, she won't budge." Pleased that matters seemed to be moving forward, Finn leaned against the wall. "I'll do what I can to convince her to stay out of the way, but that's the best I can offer. Deanna's fiercely loyal. She won't want to accept that one of her own people is involved."

"She may have to." Jenner headed out of the car the moment the doors opened. "If she kicks up too much of a fuss, we can take her people in to the station. She'll like that less."

"You can try. You don't know her the way I do, Lieutenant. Cassie," he said as he walked into the reception area. "She in?"

"No." Baffled, she stopped gathering the stacks of mail she'd intended to post on the way home. "What are you doing here?"

"Cassie Drew?" Jenner inclined his head. "We'd like to ask you some more questions. I wonder if you could get the rest of Miss Reynolds's staff together?"

"I—I don't know who's still in the building. Finn?"

"Why don't you buzz everyone," he suggested. "And find Deanna for me, will you?" He wanted to get her out, and quickly. Some instinct told him to hurry. He intended to heed it. "Tell her I'm in the mood to cook."

"She's gone home. She left right after you called."

"I called?" He felt uneasy. "Did Deanna tell you I called?"

"No, you left a message about a meeting, and getting home early. It came in during her fitting, and she left as soon as she was done."

Finn shoved open the door to Deanna's office, took one quick scan. "Did you take the message?"

"No, I was in with her when it came in. Jeff took it."

His eyes were like blue ice when he turned back. "Did he say he spoke to me?"

"Yes—I guess. Is something wrong?" Fear began to gnaw through confusion. Cassie's gaze darted from Jenner to Finn and back again. "Is something wrong with Deanna?"

Rather than answer, Finn grabbed the phone and punched in his home number. Two rings later, he heard the answering machine click on. With his teeth set, he waited through the message. "Deanna? Pick up if you're there. Pick up the phone, damn it."

"She'd have to be home by now. She left more than an hour ago. Finn, what's going on?"

"What did Jeff tell her?"

"That you'd called, just as I said."

"Why didn't you answer the phone?"

"I—" Frightened, and not knowing why, she put a hand on the desk to keep her balance. "I didn't hear the phone. I didn't hear it."

"Where's Jeff?"

"I don't know. He—"

But Finn was already racing down the hall. He burst into one room, found Simon in consultation with Margaret. "Hey, Finn. Don't bother to knock."

"Where's Jeff?"

"He wasn't feeling well. He went home." Simon was rising from the desk as he spoke. "What's the problem?"

"Finn." Though her hands were stiff with cold, Cassie tugged on Finn's sleeve. "I called for Tim myself. I talked to him. He met her downstairs."

"Get him on the line. Now."

"Mr. Riley." Jenner spoke calmly as Cassie rushed off to obey. "I've got a black-and-white on its way to your house right now. Odds are Miss Reynolds wasn't answering the phone. That's all."

"What the hell's going on?" Simon demanded. "What's happened now?"

"Tim doesn't answer his page." Cassie stood in the hallway, a hand at her throat. "I got his machine on his home phone."

"Give me the address," Jenner said briskly.

29

"Mr. Riley, I know you're upset, but you're going to have to let me handle this."

Jenner stood on the sidewalk in front of Jeff's suburban home, aware he was only temporarily blocking Finn from storming the door. "She's in there. I know it."

"Not to belittle your instincts, but we can't know that. We only know that Jeff Hyatt delivered a message. We're going to check everything out," Jenner reminded him. "The same way we checked out the driver, Tim O'Malley."

"Who wasn't home," Finn ground out, staring at the windows behind Jenner. "And the company car wasn't in the lot. And no one's seen O'Malley since sometime in the afternoon." His gaze, icy still, cut like a blade back to Jenner. "So where the hell is he? Where the hell is Deanna?"

"That's what we're going to try to find out. I'm not going to waste my time telling you to get back in your car and go home, but I am telling you to let me handle this with Hyatt."

"So handle it."

His voice might have been cold, his eyes frosty, but Jenner recognized a powder keg ready to explode. The melodious sound of church bells rang out when Jenner pressed the doorbell. Beneath his feet was a mat with the word WELCOME woven in black. In the center of the door was a glossy Christmas wreath topped by a bright red bow. Colored lights had been neatly strung around the frame. Jeff Hyatt appeared ready for the holidays.

He'd known they would come, and he was ready. Clad comfortably in a tattered sweater and baggy sweats, Jeff descended the stairs. He'd watched them arrive from his bedroom window. He smiled to himself as he paused before the door. This, he knew, was the next step toward freeing Deanna. Toward binding her.

He pulled open the door. "Hey, Finn." Confusion clouded his eyes as he looked at his visitors. "What's up?"

"Where is she?" Finn spaced each word precisely. Yes, there was a powder keg inside him, and only the knowledge that it could explode over Deanna kept it tapped. "I want to know where she is."

"Hey." His grin tilted into confusion. Jeff stared blankly at Finn, then at Jenner. "What's going on? Is something wrong?"

"Mr. Hyatt." Jenner stepped neatly between the two men. "I need to ask you some questions."

"Okay." Jeff rubbed his fingertips against his temple. "No problem. Do you want to come in?"

"Thank you. Mr. Hyatt," Jenner began, "did you relay a message to Miss Reynolds at approximately three o'clock this afternoon?"

"Yeah. Why?" Wincing, Jeff continued to massage his temple. "Jesus. Can we sit down? I've got this monster headache." He turned into the living area. The furnishings were straight out of a catalogue. Matching tables, matching chairs, twin lamps, a soulless, practical suite favored by uninspired bachelors or newlyweds on a strict budget. Only Jeff sat.

"You told her I called?"

"Sure I did." Jeff's smile was cautious. His eyes were wary. "Your assistant said to tell Dee you had this meeting and were planning on getting home early."

"You didn't talk to Mr. Riley?" Jenner demanded.

"No. I thought it was kind of weird that the call came through my office, but when I went to tell Dee, I saw that she and Cassie were all involved. Dee was getting her wedding dress fitted. She looked incredible."

"Why did you leave the office early?"

"This headache. I haven't been able to ditch it all day. It makes it hard to concentrate. Listen." He stood again, obviously impatient and bewildered. "What's this all about? Is it some kind of crime to deliver a phone message?"

"What time did you leave the office?"

"Right after I talked to Dee. I came home—well, I went to the store first, picked up some more heavy-duty aspirin. I thought if I laid down awhile..." His voice trailed off. "Something's happened to Dee." As if his legs wouldn't support him, he lowered slowly to the couch again. "Oh my God. Is she hurt?"

"She hasn't been seen since she left the office," Jenner told him.

"Oh God. Jesus. Have you talked to Tim? Didn't he drive her home?"

"We're unable to locate Mr. O'Malley."

On a shaking breath, Jeff rubbed his hands over his face. "It wasn't a message from your assistant, was it, Finn? I didn't ask any questions. I wasn't paying attention." His jaw quivered when he dropped his hands again. His eyes were dark with an emotion disguising itself as fear. "All I could think about was getting home and going to bed. I just said, sure, I'll tell her. And I did."

"I don't believe you." Finn didn't move a muscle, but the words cracked toward Jeff like a slap. "You're a meticulous man, Jeff. That's how Deanna describes you." And the minutes were ticking away. "Why would you, with everything that's been going on, pass along a half-baked message like that?"

"It was supposed to be from you," Jeff shot back. The way Finn studied him, as if he could see all the secrets swimming in his brain, put Jeff on edge. "Why wouldn't I pass it along?"

"Then you won't mind if we go through the house." Finn turned to Jenner. "Through every inch of it."

"You think I—" Jeff snapped his mouth shut, pushed himself from the couch. "Go ahead," he said to both men. "Search it. Go through every room. I want you to."

"We appreciate your cooperation, Mr. Hyatt. It would be best if you came with us while we do."

"Fine." Jeff stood for a moment, staring at Finn. "I know how you feel about her, and I guess I can't really blame you for this."

They went through every room, searching through closets, cupboards, through the garage, where Jeff's undistinguished sedan was parked. It took less than twenty minutes.

Finn noted the tidy, practical furnishings, the well-pressed, practical clothes. As a director for a number-one show, he'd be well compensated financially. And Finn could see that he sure as hell wasn't spending any money on himself.

Just what, he wondered, was Jeff Hyatt saving his pennies for?

"I wish she was here." Jeff felt a quick, gleeful surge as they walked past the bookcase. "At least she'd be safe. I want to help. I want to do something. We can start with the press. We can get national coverage. By morning we'll have everyone in the country looking for her. Everybody knows her face." He looked beseechingly at Finn. "Someone will see her. He can't keep her locked in a tower somewhere."

"Wherever he has her"—Finn never took his eyes off Jeff's—"I'll find her."

Without a backward glance, Finn strode out of the house. Seconds later, the sound of his engine roared.

"I can't blame him," Jeff muttered. He looked toward Jenner. "No one could."

He locked up carefully behind the policeman. His smile grew wider, wider, wider as he climbed the stairs. They might come back. A small, grinning part of him hoped they would. Because he would lead them right through the house, right by the hidden room where his princess slept.

They would never find her. And eventually they would go away. He and Deanna would be alone. Always.

He turned on the television in his room. The evening news didn't interest him. He flipped a switch on the splitter behind the set and settled down to watch Deanna.

She slept on, still as a doll behind the glass of the screen. The tears he wept now were of simple joy.

• • •

Jenner caught up with Finn at home. He made no mention of the speed limits Finn had ignored. "We'll be checking out Hyatt and O'Malley thoroughly. Why don't you be a reporter and get the story on the air?"

"It'll be on the air." Standing in the chill December wind, Finn struggled to stave off panic. "Hyatt looked as innocent as a newborn lamb, didn't he?"

"Yes, he did." Jenner blew out a smoky breath. Three days until Christmas, he thought. He would do everything in his power to be certain it was a day of celebration.

"I had some trouble with that house," Finn said after a moment.

"What kind?"

"Nothing out of place. Not a crooked picture, not a dustball. Books and magazines lined up like soldiers, furniture all but geometrically arranged. Everything centered, squared and bandbox clean."

"I noticed. Obsessive."

"That's how it strikes me. He fits the pattern."

Jenner acknowledged that with a slight nod. "A man can be obsessively neat without being obsessively homicidal."

"Where was the Christmas tree?" Finn muttered.

"The Christmas tree?"

"He's got the wreath, he's got the lights. But no tree. You'd think he'd have a tree somewhere."

"Maybe he's one of those traditionalists who don't put it up until Christmas Eve." But the omission was interesting.

"One more thing, Lieutenant. He claims he came home early to lie down. The bed in his room was the only thing mussed up. Pillow scrunched a bit, bedspread wrinkled. We got him up from his nap."

"So he says."

"Why did he have his shoes on?" Finn's eyes gleamed in the lowering light. "The laces were tied in double knots. Someone that neat doesn't lie down on his bed with his shoes on."

He'd missed that clue, damn it, Jenner thought. "I believe I mentioned this before, Mr. Riley, you have a good eye."

He couldn't stay at home. Not without her. Finn did the only thing that seemed possible. He went back to the station, avoiding the newsroom. He couldn't bear to answer questions, to be asked questions. He went to his office, brewed a pot of strong coffee. He added a healthy dose of whiskey to the first cup.

He booted up his computer.

"Finn." Fran stood in the doorway, her face splotchy, her eyes swollen and red. Before he'd risen completely, she took a stumbling step forward. "Oh God, Finn."

He stroked her shaking shoulders, though he felt no well of comfort that he could offer. It was just the routine, the show of comfort that meant nothing to anyone.

"I had to take Kelsey to the pediatrician for her checkup. I wasn't here. I wasn't even here."

"You couldn't have changed anything."

"I might have." She shoved away, eyes fierce now. "How did he get to her? I've heard a dozen different stories."

"This is the place for them. Truth or accuracy, which do you want?"

"Both."

"One's not the same as the other, Fran. You've been in the game long enough. Accurately, we don't know. She left early, went out to the lot where her car and driver were supposed to be waiting. Now she's gone. Her driver seems to have vanished into thin air."

She didn't like the cool control of his voice or the workaday hum of his computer. "Then what's the truth, Finn? Why don't you tell me what the truth is?"

"The truth is that whoever has been sending her those notes, whoever killed Lew McNeil, Angela and Pike, has Deanna. They've got an APB out on her, and one on O'Malley and the car."

"Tim wouldn't. He couldn't."

"Why?" The single word was like a bullet. "Because you know him? Because he's part of Deanna's extended family? Fuck that. He could have." Finn sat down, drained half his coffee. The shock of caffeine and whiskey spread through him like velvet lightning. "But I don't think he did. I can't be sure until he turns up. If he turns up."

"Why wouldn't he?" Fran demanded. "He's worked for Dee for two years. He's never missed a single day."

"He's never been dead before, has he?" He swore at her, at himself when her color faded to paste. Rising, he poured her whiskey, straight. "I'm sorry, Fran. I'm half out of my mind."

"How can you sit in here and say things like that? How can you work, think about work, when Dee's out there somewhere? This isn't some international disaster you're covering, goddamn it, where you're the steady, unflappable journalist. This is Dee."

He jammed useless hands in his pockets. "When something's important, vital, when the answer means everything, you sit, you work, you think it through, you take all the facts and create a scenario that plays. Something that's accurate. I think Jeff's got her."

"Jeff." Fran choked on whiskey. "You're crazy. Jeff's devoted to Dee, and he's harmless as a baby. He'd never hurt her."

"I'm counting on that," he said dully. "I'm betting my life on it. I need everything you've got on him, Fran. Personnel records, memos, files. I need your impressions, your observations. I need you to help me."

She said nothing, only studied his face. No, his eyes weren't cold, she realized. They were burning up. And there was terror behind them. "Give me ten minutes," she said, and left him alone.

She came back in less than her allotted time with a stack of files and a box of computer disks. "His employment record, résumé, application for employment. Tax info." Fran smiled weakly. "I lifted his desk calendars. He keeps them from year to year. They were all filed."

Meticulous. Obsessive. Though his blood iced, Finn accessed the first disk.

"That's his personnel file from CBC. I hope you don't mind breaking the law."

"Not a bit. This application is from April eighty-nine. When did Dee go on air at CBC?"

"About a month before that." Fran reached for the whiskey to unclog her throat. "It doesn't prove anything."

"No, but it's a fact." The first he could build on. "Same address he's got now. How'd he afford a house like that when he'd been working as a radio gofer?"

"He inherited it. His uncle left it to him. Finn, I had to call Dee's family." She pressed a hand to her mouth. "They're getting the first flight out in the morning."

"I'm sorry." He stared hard at the screen. Families. He'd never had one to worry about before. "I should have done it."

"No, I didn't mean that. I just—I don't know what to say to them."

"Tell them we're going to get her back. That's the truth. Fran, see if you can find the date in his calendar when Lew McNeil was killed. It was February ninety-two."

"Yeah, I remember." She opened the book, flipped through the pages, skimming Jeff's neat, precise notations. "We had a show that day. Jeff was directing. I remember because we had snow and everybody was worried that the audience would be thin."

"Do you remember if he came in?"

"Sure, he was here. He never missed. Looks like he had a ten o'clock meeting with Simon."

"He'd have had time," Finn murmured.

"Christ Almighty, do you really think he could have gone to New York, shot Lew, come back and waltzed into the studio to direct a show, all before lunch?"

Yes, Finn thought coldly. Oh yes, he did. "Fact: Lew was killed about seven—that's Central time. There's an hour's time difference between Chicago and New York. Speculation: He flies in and out, maybe he charters a plane. I need his receipts."

"He doesn't keep his personal stuff here."

"Then I'll have to get back in his house. You make sure he comes in tomorrow morning. And you make sure he stays."

She got up, poured coffee into her whiskey. "All right. What else?"

"Let's see what else we can find."

She'd lost track of time. Day or night, there was no difference in the claustrophobic world Jeff had created for her. Her head was cotton from the drug, her stomach raw, but she ate the breakfast he'd left for her. She didn't open the plain white envelope he'd left on her tray.

For a timeless, sweaty interlude, she tried to find an opening in the wall, had pried and poked with a spoon until her fingers had cramped uselessly. All she'd accomplished was to mar the pristine wallpaper.

She couldn't be sure if he was gone, or how long she'd been alone. Then she remembered the television and jumped like a cat on the remote.

Still morning, she thought, her eyes filming with tears as she scanned the channels. How easy it was to time your life around the familiar schedule of daytime TV. The bright laughter of a familiar game show was both mocking and soothing.

She'd slept through her own show, she realized, and choked back a bitter laugh.

Where was Finn? What was he doing? Where was he looking for her?

She rose mechanically, walked into the bathroom. Though she'd already checked once, she repeated the routine of standing on the lip of the tub, climbing onto the lid of the toilet and searching for hidden cameras.

She had no choice but to trust Jeff that he wouldn't pry in this room. She slid the door closed, tried not to think about the lack of a lock. And she stripped.

She had to bite back the fear that he would come in when she was most vulnerable. She needed the cold, bracing spray to help clear her mind. She scrubbed hard, letting her thoughts focus as she soaped and rinsed, soaped and rinsed.

He hadn't missed a detail, she thought. Her brand of shampoo, of powder, creams. She used them all, finding some comfort in the daily routine. Wrapped in a bath sheet, she walked back into the bedroom to go through the drawers.

She chose a sweater, trousers. Just the sort of outfit she would pick for a day of relaxing at home. Ignoring the fresh shudder, she carried the outfit, and the lacy underwear he'd provided, into the bathroom.

Dressed, she began to pace. Pacing, she began to plan.

Finn parked his car half a block down, then backtracked on foot. He walked straight to Jeff Hyatt's front door. He didn't bother to knock. Since he'd just hung up his car phone with Fran, he knew Jeff was in the office.

Finn had the extra set of keys Fran had taken from Jeff's bottom desk drawer. There were three locks. A lot of security, he mused, for a quiet neighborhood. He unbolted all three and, once inside, took the precaution of locking up again.

He started upstairs first, clamping down on the urge to dive wildly into desk and files. Instead he searched meticulously, going through each drawer, each paper with his reporter's eye keen for any tiny detail. He wanted a receipt, some proof that Jeff had traveled to New York and back on the day of Lew's murder.

The police might overlook his reporter's instinct, but they wouldn't overlook facts. Once they had Jeff in custody, they would sweat out of him Deanna's whereabouts. He kept his eyes open, too, for some proof that Jeff had another house, a room, an apartment. He might be holding her there.

He wouldn't believe she was dead.

The pattern so far was to kill people in public places.

He shut the last drawer of the desk and moved to the files.

By the time he'd finished, his palms were damp. Biting back the taste of despair, he strode from the office into Jeff's bedroom. He'd found nothing, absolutely nothing except proof that Jeff Hyatt was an organized, dedicated employee who lived quietly and well, almost too well, within his means.

While Finn searched the bedroom, Deanna paced the floor beneath him. She knew she would have only one chance, and that failure would be more than risky. It might be fatal.

In the room above, Finn scanned row after row of videotapes. The man was beyond a buff, Finn mused. He was fanatical. The neat labels indicated television series, movies, news events. Over a hundred black cases lined the wall beside the television. Finn juggled the remote in his hand, deciding if he had time after searching the house, he'd screen a few to see if there was anything more personal on tape.

He set the remote down, only a push of a button away from bringing Deanna to life on screen. He turned to the closet.

The scent of mothballs, an old woman's odor, tickled his nostrils. Slacks hung straight and true, jackets graced padded hangers. The shoes were stretched on trees. The photo album he found on the shelf revealed nothing but snapshots of an elderly man, sometimes alone, sometimes with Jeff beside him. His jaw seemed permanently clenched, his lips withered to a scowl. Beneath each shot was a careful notation.

Uncle Matthew on 75th birthday. June 1983. Uncle Matthew and Jeff, Easter 1977. Uncle Matthew, November 1988.

There was no one else in the book. Just a man, young, a little thin, and his hard-faced uncle. Never a young girl or a laughing child, a romping pet.

The book felt unhealthy, diseased, in his hand. Finn slid it back on the shelf, careful to align the edges.

Details, he thought grimly. Two could play.

Underwear was tucked into the top dresser drawer. All snowy white boxers, pressed and folded. There was nothing beneath them but plain white paper, lightly scented with lilac.

It was almost worse than the mothballs, Finn thought, and moved down to the next drawer.

None of the usual hiding places was utilized. He found no papers, no packets taped to the undersides or backs of drawers, no valuables tucked into the toes of shoes. The nightstand drawer held a current *TV Guide* with selected programs highlighted in yellow. A pad and a sharpened pencil and an extra handkerchief joined it.

He'd been in the house for nearly an hour when he hit pay dirt. The diary was under the pillow. It was leather-bound, glossy and locked. Finn was reaching in his pocket for his penknife when he heard the rattle of a key in the lock.

"Goddamn it, Fran." He glanced back at the closet, rejecting it instantly not only as a cliché, but also as a humiliating one. He'd rather face a foe than hide from one. He stepped forward toward the bedroom door just as Jeff walked down the hallway, whistling on his way to the kitchen.

"Don't seem too devastated, do you? You son of a bitch." Muttering under his breath, Finn slipped toward the stairs.

He couldn't wait to see her. Jeff knew he was taking a chance leaving the office when Fran was so insistent that he stay. But he'd slipped out, antsy to get home. To get to Deanna. The office was in an uproar, he thought. No one could work, and he could always claim to have needed to be alone. Nobody would blame him.

He poured a glass of milk, arranged fancy tea cookies on a china plate and put them all on a tray with another single rose.

She'd be rested now, he was certain. She'd be feeling better, more at home. And soon, very soon, she would see how well he could care for her.

Finn waited at the top of the stairs. He heard Jeff whistling and the sound of dishes ringing together. He heard the footsteps, a quiet click, followed moments later by another.

Then he heard nothing at all.

Where did the bastard go? he wondered. Moving quietly, he descended the stairs. He slipped like a shadow from room to room. By the time he reached the kitchen, he was baffled. He saw the bakery box of cookies, caught the candy scent of icing. But the man had vanished like smoke.

• • •

"You look wonderful." Secure in the soundproofed room, Jeff smiled shyly at Deanna. "Do you like the clothes?"

"They're very nice." She willed herself to smile back. "I took a shower. I can't believe you went to all the trouble to pick out all my favorite brands."

"You saw the towels? I had them monogrammed with your initials."

"I know." Her stomach rolled. "It was very sweet of you, Jeff. Cookies?"

"They're the ones you like best."

"Yes, they are." Watching him, she walked over, fighting not to grit her teeth. She kept her eyes on his as she chose a cookie, bit in delicately. "Wonderful." She saw his gaze lower to her mouth as she licked at a crumb. "You were gone a long time."

"I came back as soon as I could. I'm going to turn in my resignation next week. I have plenty of money put away, and my uncle invested. I won't have to leave you again."

"It's lonely here. By myself." She sat on the edge of the bed. "You'll stay with me now, won't you?"

"As long as you want."

"Sit with me." In a subtle invitation, she touched the bed beside her. "I think if you explain things to me now, I'd be ready to understand."

His hands trembled as he set the tray down. "You're not angry?"

"No. I'm still a little scared. It frightens me to be locked in here."

"I'm sorry." He eased down beside her, careful to keep an inch of space between them. "One day it'll be different."

"Jeff." She made contact by laying her hand over his. "Why did you decide to do this? How did you know this was the time?"

"I knew it had to be soon, before the wedding. When I came in yesterday and saw you in your wedding dress—I couldn't wait any longer. It was like a sign. You were so beautiful, Dee."

"But it was a terrible risk. Tim was downstairs waiting."

"It was me. I was waiting. I used his hat and his coat, the sunglasses. I had to get Tim out of the way."

"How?" When he looked down, staring at their joined hands, her heart dropped. "Jeff. Is Tim dead?"

"I didn't do it the way I did the others." Eager, anxious, he looked back at her, his eyes as hopeful as a child's. "I wouldn't have done that. Tim didn't hurt you. But I had to get him out of the way, and fast. I liked him, too, really. So I was real quick. He didn't suffer. I put him in the trunk of the car after—and then when I'd brought you here, I drove the car to a parking lot downtown. I left it there and I came home. To be with you." His face crumbled when she turned hers away. "You've got to understand, Deanna."

"I'm trying to." *Oh, God. Tim.* "You haven't hurt Finn?"

"I promised I wouldn't. He's had you all this time, and I've been waiting."

"I know. I know." Instinctively she soothed. "They're looking for me, aren't they?"

"They won't find you."

"But they're looking."

"Yes!" His voice rose as he pushed off the bed. Everything had gone perfectly up till now, he reminded himself. Perfectly. But he felt as though he were standing on the edge of a cliff, and couldn't see the bottom. "And they'll look and look. And then they'll stop. And nobody will bother us. Nobody."

"It's all right." She rose, too, though her legs trembled. "You know how curious I am about everything. Always asking questions."

"You won't miss being on television. Dee." He used his sleeve to wipe a tear away. "I'm your best audience. I could listen to you for hours and hours. I do. But now I won't have to watch a tape. Now it can be real."

"You want it to be real, don't you?"

"More than anything."

Her heart slammed against her ribs as she reached out to stroke his cheek. "And you want me."

"You're all I've ever wanted." His face twitched under her palm. "All these years, you're all I've wanted. I've never been with another woman. Not like Pike. Not like Riley. I was waiting for you."

She wished she could harden her heart, but part of her wept for him. "You want to touch me." She steeled herself and lifted his hand, placed it on her breast. "Like this."

"You're soft. So soft." There was something pathetic and terrifying about the way his hand shook against her, even as his fingers moved to caress.

"If I let you touch me, the way you want, will you let me go outside?"

He jerked back as though she'd burned him. Bitter betrayal welled in his throat. "You're trying to trick me."

"No, Jeff." It was all right for her desperation to show, she told herself. Let him see her weakness. "I don't like being closed in. It frightens me. I only want to go outside for a few minutes, get some air. You want me to be happy, don't you?"

"It's going to take time." His mouth set in a stubborn line. "You're not ready."

"You know how I have to keep busy, Jeff." She stepped toward him, careful to keep her eyes fixed on his. When she slid her arms up his chest, his eyes clouded, darkened. "Sitting here like this, hour after hour, is upsetting me. I know how much you've done for me." And she felt the outline of the syringe in his pocket. "I know you want us to be together."

"We are together." He brought his unsteady hand back to her breast. When she didn't flinch, he smiled. "We'll always be together."

He lowered his head to kiss her. She slipped the needle from his pocket.

"Deanna," he murmured.

Her sharp indrawn breath betrayed her. She twisted, fighting to plunge the needle into him as they grappled to the floor.

Searching for Jeff finally brought Finn back to the bookcase. He had seen what he and Jenner had missed on their first search. The dimensions, he thought, as the spit in his mouth dried to dust. The dimensions were wrong. The bookcase couldn't be an end wall. Couldn't be.

She was in there, he realized. Deanna was in there. And she wasn't alone. He had one panicked notion of hurling himself bodily against the shelves. His body quivered with the effort of holding back. It wasn't the way. God knew what Jeff would do to her in the time it took him to break through.

Struggling for calm, he began to search methodically for a mechanism.

• • •

She was losing. The hypo squirted out of her fingers when he rolled over her. She screamed as her head rapped hard against the floor. Though her vision blurred, she could see him above her, his face distorted, his tears running. And she knew he could kill. Not only others, but her.

"You lied," he cried out in an agony of despair. "You lied. I have to punish you. I have to." And sobbing, he closed his hands around her throat.

She used her nails to rake his face. The blood surged to the surface and ran like his tears. When he howled in pain, she squirmed free. Her fingers brushed over the syringe as he snagged her ankle.

"I loved you. I loved you. Now I have to hurt you. It's the only way you'll understand. It's for your own good. That's what Uncle Matthew says. It's for your own good. You'll have to stay in here. You'll have to stay and have bread and water until you're ready to behave." He chanted the words as he dragged her back toward the bed. "I'm doing my best for you, aren't I? I gave you a roof over your head. I put clothes on your back. And this is the way you thank me? You'll just have to learn. I know best."

He snagged her hand, yanked up her arm.

She plunged the needle into him.

Finn heard the sound of sirens in the distance, but they meant nothing. Every ounce of concentration was focused on the puzzle at hand. There was a way in. There was always a way. And he would find it.

"It's here," he murmured to himself. "Right here. The son of a bitch didn't walk through the wall." His finger hit a nub. He twisted. The panel opened in well-oiled silence.

Deanna stood beside the bed, the syringe gripped in one hand. Eyes glazed, murmuring her name, Jeff crawled across the mattress toward her.

"I love you, Deanna." His hand brushed hers before he went limp.

"Oh, Jesus. Deanna." In one leap, Finn had her in his arms.

She swayed, the needle dropping from her loose fingers. "Finn." His name burned her bruised throat and felt like heaven. From what seemed like a long, long distance, she heard him swear when her body jerked with a shudder.

"Did he hurt you? Tell me if you're hurt."

"No. No, he wanted to take care of me." She buried her face in Finn's shoulder. "He only wanted to take care of me."

"Let's get out of here." He carried her through the opening, down the hall, where he dragged at the locks.

"I kept asking him to let me go outside." She breathed in the raw air like wine. "He shot you, Finn. He was the one who shot you. And he killed Tim."

She jolted at the sound of screeching brakes.

"Well." Jenner climbed out of his car, moments ahead of two black-and-whites. The picture of Finn carrying Deanna down the front steps wasn't what he'd expected to see after he'd gotten the frantic call from Fran Myers. But it was an image that satisfied. "Went off on your own again, Mr. Riley."

"You can't trust a reporter, Lieutenant."

"Guess not. Good to see you, Miss Reynolds. Merry Christmas."

• • •

Deanna studied her reflection in the dressing room mirror. The bruises had faded from her throat, and the haunted look had ebbed from her eyes.

But her heart was still sore.

As Joe had often told her during her reporting days, she had one that bled too easily. She couldn't afford for it to bleed now. She had a show to do in thirty minutes.

"Hey."

She glanced over, saw Finn. Smiled. "Hey back."

"Can you spare a minute?"

"I've got several for you." She swiveled in her chair, held out her hands. "Don't you have a plane to catch?"

"I called the airport. My flight is delayed two hours. I've got time on my hands."

Suspicion gleamed in her eyes. "You're not going to miss that plane."

"I know, I know. You've already laid down the law. I've got a job to do, and you're not going to support me if I screw it up. I'm going to Rome. Only a week off schedule." He bent down, kissed her. "I figured I had time to give one more shot at talking you into coming with me."

"I've got a job to do, too."

"The press is going to be all over you."

She arched her brows. "Promises, promises." She stepped off the chair, turned a circle. "How do I look?"

"Like something I don't want to be several thousand miles away from." He tipped up her chin, looked deep into her eyes. "You're hurting."

"I'm better. Finn, we've been through this." She saw his face change, harden. "Don't."

"I don't know how long it's going to take before I close my eyes and stop seeing you in that room. Knowing you were there all those hours, and I'd walked right by you." He pulled her roughly against him. "I still want to kill him."

"He's sick, Finn. All those years of emotional abuse. He needed to escape, and he used television. And one day, the day he found his uncle dead, I walked out of the screen and into his life."

"I don't give a damn how sick he is, how warped or how pathetic." He drew her back. "I can't, Deanna. I don't have it in me to care. And I can't stand hearing you blame yourself."

"I'm not. Really, I'm not. I know it wasn't my fault. Nothing he did was my fault." Still, she thought of Tim, whose body had been found in the trunk of her company car in a downtown parking lot. "I was never real to him, Finn. Even all the time we worked together, I was never anything but an image, a vision. Everything he did he did because he'd twisted that image. I can't blame myself for that. But I can still be sorry."

"Dee." Fran stepped into the doorway, winked at Finn. "We need the star in five."

"The star's ready."

"I can postpone the flight, stick around for the press conference after the show."

"I can handle reporters." She kissed Finn firmly, on the mouth. "I've had plenty of experience."

"Want to get married, Kansas?" With his arm around her, he walked her into the corridor, down toward the set.

"You bet I do. April third. Be there."

"I never miss a deadline." He turned her around to face him. "I'm crazy about you." And winced. "Bad choice of words."

She wasn't surprised that she could laugh. Nothing surprised her now. "Call me from Rome." Marcie leaped forward to repair Deanna's lipstick. "And don't forget, you have to handle the flowers for the church and reception. You have the list I made you?"

Behind her back, he rolled his eyes. "Which one?"

"All of them."

"No you don't." Marcie threw up a hand before Deanna could lean into another kiss. "You've got thirty seconds, and I don't want my work smeared."

"Stay tuned, Kansas. I'll be back."

Deanna took another step toward stage. "The hell with it." She whirled around, flew into Finn's arms. Over Marcie's groan, she clamped her lips to his. "Hurry back," she told him, and rushed toward the stage, nailing her cue.

The floor director stabbed a finger toward her. Over the sound of applause, she smiled into the camera's glass eye and slipped seamlessly into millions of lives.

"Good morning. It's good to be home."

Hidden Riches

To Mom, because she loves trinkets, and a good bargain

Prologue

He didn't want to be there. No, he hated being trapped in the elegant old house, prodded and pinched by restless ghosts. It was no longer enough to shroud the furniture in dustcovers, lock the doors and walk away. He had to empty it and, by emptying it, purge himself of some of the nightmares.

"Captain Skimmerhorn?"

Jed tensed at the title. As of last week he was no longer captain. He'd resigned from the force, turned in his shield, but he was already weary of explaining it. He shifted aside as two of the movers carried a rosewood armoire down the staircase, through the grand foyer and out into the chilly morning.

"Yes?"

"You might want to check upstairs, make sure we got everything you wanted put in storage. Otherwise, looks like we're all done here."

"Fine."

But he didn't want to go up those stairs, walk through those rooms. Even empty they would hold too much. Responsibility, he mused as he reluctantly started up. His life had been too crowded with responsibility to ignore one now.

Something nudged him along the hallway toward his old room. The room where he had grown up, the room he had continued to inhabit long after he'd lived here alone. But he stopped in the doorway just short of crossing the threshold. Hands jammed into tight fists in his pockets, he waited for memories to assault him like sniper fire.

He'd cried in that room—in secret and in shame, of course. No Skimmerhorn male ever revealed a weakness in public. Then, when tears had dried, he'd plotted in that room. Small, useless childish revenges that had always boomeranged back on him.

He'd learned to hate in that room.

Yet it was only a room. It was only a house. He'd convinced himself of that years before when he had come back to live there as a man. And hadn't he been content? he asked himself now. Hadn't it been simple?

Until Elaine.

"Jedidiah."

He flinched. He'd nearly brought his right hand out of his pocket to touch a weapon that was no longer there before he caught himself. The gesture, and the fact that he'd been so lost in his own morbid thoughts that someone could have come up behind him, reminded him why the weapon no longer hung at his side.

He relaxed and glanced back at his grandmother. Honoria Skimmerhorn Rodgers was neatly wrapped in mink, discreet daytime diamonds winking at her ears, her snowy hair beautifully coiffed. She looked like a successful matron on her way out for lunch at her favorite club. But her eyes, as vivid a blue as his own, were filled with concern.

"I'd hoped I'd convinced you to wait," she said quietly, and reached out to lay a hand on his arm.

He flinched automatically. The Skimmerhorns simply weren't touchers. "There was no reason to wait."

"But there's a reason for this?" She gestured toward the empty room. "There's a reason to empty out your home, to put aside all of your belongings?"

"Nothing in this house belongs to me."

"That's absurd." The faint whisper of her native Boston crept into her tone.

"By default?" He turned his back on the room to face her. "Because I happen to still be alive? No, thanks."

If she hadn't been so worried about him, the curt answer would have earned him a ringing reprimand. "My dear, there's no question of default. Or any kind of fault." She watched him close in, shut off, and would have shaken him if it would have helped. Instead, she touched his cheek. "You only need some time."

The gesture left his muscles taut. It took all of his willpower not to jerk away from the gentle fingers. "And this is my way of taking it."

"By moving out of the family home—"

"Family?" He laughed at that, and the sound of it echoed nastily down the hall. "We were never a family here, or anywhere."

Her eyes, previously soft with sympathy, hardened. "Pretending the past doesn't exist is as bad as living in it. What are you doing here? Tossing away everything you've earned, everything you've made of yourself? Perhaps I was less than enthusiastic about your choice of profession, but it was your choice and you succeeded. It appears to me that you made more of the Skimmerhorn name when you were promoted to captain than all your ancestors did with their money and social power."

"I didn't become a cop to promote my damn name."

"No," she said quietly. "You did it for yourself against tremendous family pressure—including my own." She moved away from him to walk down the hall. She had lived here once, years before as a bride. An unhappy one. "I saw you turn your life around, and it awed me. Because I knew you did it for no one but yourself. I often wondered how you were strong enough to do that."

Turning back, she studied him, this son of her son. He had inherited the bold good looks of the Skimmerhorns. Bronzed hair, tousled by the wind, swept around a lean, rawboned face that was taut with stress. She worried, woman-like, because he had lost weight, though the fining down of his features only heightened their power. There was strength in the tall, broad-shouldered build that both accented and defied the romantic masculine beauty of pale gold skin and sensitive mouth. The eyes, a deep striking blue, had come from her. They were as haunted and defiant now as they had been in the young, troubled boy she remembered so well.

But he was no longer a boy, and she was afraid there was little she could do to help the man.

"I don't want to see you turn your life around again, for the wrong reasons." She shook her head, walking back toward him before he could speak. "And I might have had reservations when you moved back in here alone after your parents died, but that, too, was your choice. And for some time, it seemed you'd made the right one again. But this time your solution to a tragedy is to sell your home, throw away your career?"

He waited a beat. "Yes."

"You disappoint me, Jedidiah."

That stung. It was a phrase she rarely used, and had more bite than a dozen of his father's raging insults. "I'd rather disappoint you than be responsible for the life of a single cop. I'm in no shape to command." He looked down at his hands, flexed them. "I may never be. And as for the house, it should have been sold years ago. After the accident. It would have been sold if Elaine had agreed to it." Something backed up in his throat. Guilt was as bitter as bile. "Now she's gone too, and it's my decision."

"Yes, it's yours," she agreed. "But it's the wrong one."

Rage sizzled in his blood. He wanted to hit something, someone, pound his fists into flesh. It was a feeling that came over him all too often. And because of it, he was no longer Captain J. T. Skimmerhorn of the Philadelphia Police Department, but a civilian.

"Can't you understand? I can't live here. I can't sleep here. I need to get the hell out. I'm smothering here."

"Then come home with me. For the holidays. At least until after the first of the year. Give yourself a little more time before you do something irreversible." Her voice was gentle again as she took his rigid hands in hers. "Jedidiah, it's been months since Elaine—since Elaine was killed."

"I know how long it's been." Yes, he knew the exact moment of his sister's death. After all, he'd killed her. "I appreciate the invitation, but I've got plans. I'm looking at an apartment later today. Over on South Street."

"An apartment." Honoria's sigh was ripe with annoyance. "Really, Jedidiah, there's no need for that kind of nonsense. Buy yourself another house if you must, take a long vacation, but don't bury yourself in some miserable room."

He was surprised he could smile. "The ad said it was quiet, attractive and well located. That doesn't sound miserable. Grandmother"—he squeezed her hands before she could argue—"let it be."

She sighed again, tasting defeat. "I only want what's best for you."

"You always did." He suppressed a shudder, feeling the walls closing in on him. "Let's get out of here."

1

A theater without an audience has its own peculiar magic. The magic of possibilities. The echoing voices of actors running lines, the light cues, the costumes, the nervous energy and vaulting egos that bound from center stage to the empty back row.

Isadora Conroy absorbed the theater's magic as she stood in the wings of the Liberty Theater, watching a dress rehearsal for *A Christmas Carol*. As always, she enjoyed the drama, not only Dickens, but also the drama of edgy nerves, of creative lighting, of the well-delivered line. After all, the theater was in her blood.

There was a vibrancy that pulsed from her even in repose. Her large brown eyes glinted with excitement and seemed to dominate the face framed by a swing of golden-brown hair. That excitement brought a flush to ivory skin, a smile to her wide mouth. It was a face of subtle angles and smooth curves, caught between wholesome and lovely. The energy inside her small, compact body shimmered out.

She was a woman interested in everything around her, who believed in illusions. Watching her father rattling Marley's chains and intoning dire predictions to the fear-struck Scrooge, she believed in ghosts. And because she believed, he was no longer her father, but the doomed miser wrapped for eternity in the heavy chains of his own greed.

Then Marley became Quentin Conroy again, veteran actor, director and theater buff, calling for a minute change in the blocking.

"Dora." Hurrying up from behind, Dora's sister, Ophelia, said, "We're already twenty minutes behind schedule."

"We don't have a schedule," Dora murmured, nodding because the blocking change was perfect. "I never have a schedule on a buying trip. Isn't he wonderful, Lea?"

Though her sense of organization was hampered, Lea glanced out onstage and studied their father. "Yes. Though God knows how he can stand to put on this same production year after year."

"Tradition." Dora beamed. "The theater's rooted in it." Leaving the stage hadn't diminished her love of it, or her admiration for the man who had taught her how to milk a line. She'd watched him become hundreds of men onstage. Macbeth, Willie Loman, Nathan Detroit. She'd seen him triumph and seen him bomb. But he always entertained.

"Remember Mom and Dad as Titania and Oberon?"

Lea rolled her eyes, but she was smiling. "Who could forget? Mom stayed in character for weeks. It wasn't easy living with the queen of the fairies. And if we don't get out of here soon, the queen's going to come out and run through her list of what might happen to two women traveling alone to Virginia."

Sensing her sister's nerves and impatience, Dora swung an arm around Lea's shoulders. "Relax, honey, I've got her covered, and he's going to take five in a minute."

Which he did, on cue. When the actors scattered, Dora stepped out to center stage. "Dad." She took a long look, skimming down from the top of his head to his feet. "You were great."

"Thank you, my sweet." He lifted an arm so that his tattered shroud floated. "I think the makeup is an improvement over last year."

"Absolutely." In fact, the greasepaint and charcoal were alarmingly realistic; his handsome face appeared just short of decay. "Absolutely gruesome." She kissed him lightly on the lips, careful not to smudge. "Sorry we'll miss opening night."

"Can't be helped." Though he did pout just a little. Although he had a son to carry on the Conroy tradition, he'd lost his two daughters, one to marriage, one to free enterprise. Then again, he did occasionally shanghai them into a minor role. "So, my two little girls are off on their adventure."

"It's a buying trip, Dad, not a trip to the Amazon."

"Just the same." He winked and kissed Lea in turn. "Watch out for snakes."

"Oh, Lea!" Trixie Conroy, resplendent in her costume complete with bustle and feathered hat, rushed out onstage. The Liberty's excellent acoustics carried her throaty voice to the rear balcony. "John's on the phone, dear. He couldn't remember if Missy had a scout meeting tonight at five, or a piano lesson at six."

"I left a list," Lea muttered. "How's he going to manage the kids for three days if he can't read a list?"

"Such a sweet man," Trixie commented when Lea dashed off. "The perfect son-in-law. Now, Dora, you will drive carefully?"

"Yes, Mom."

"Of course you will. You're always careful. You won't pick up any hitchhikers?"

"Not even if they beg."

"And you'll stop every two hours to rest your eyes?"

"Like clockwork."

An inveterate worrier, Trixie gnawed on her bottom lip. "Still, it's an awfully long way to Virginia. And it might snow."

"I have snow tires." To forestall more speculation, Dora gave her mother another kiss. "There's a phone in the van, Mom. I'll check in every time we cross a state line."

"Won't that be fun?" The idea cheered Trixie enormously. "Oh, and Quentin, darling, I've just come from the box office." She gave her husband a deep curtsy. "We're sold out for the week."

"Naturally." Quentin lifted his wife to her feet and twirled her in a graceful spin that ended in a deep dip. "A Conroy expects nothing less than standing room only."

"Break a leg." Dora kissed her mother one last time. "You too," she said to Quentin. "And Dad, don't forget you're showing the apartment later today."

"I never forget an engagement. Places!" he called out, then winked at his daughter. "Bon voyage, my sweet."

Dora could hear his chains clanging when she hit the wings. She couldn't imagine a better send-off.

To Dora's way of thinking, an auction house was very like a theater. You had the stage, the props, the characters. As she had explained to her baffled parents years before, she wasn't really retiring from the stage. She was merely exploring another medium. She certainly put her actor's blood to good use whenever it was time to buy or sell.

She'd already taken the time to study the arena for today's performance. The building where Sherman Porter held his auctions and ran a daily flea market had originally been a slaughterhouse and was still as drafty as a barn. Merchandise was displayed on an icy concrete floor where cows and pigs had once mooed and squealed on their way to becoming pot roasts and pork chops. Now humans, huddled in coats and mufflers, wandered through, poking at glassware, grunting over paintings and debating over china cabinets and carved headboards.

The ambience was a bit thin, but she'd played in less auspicious surroundings. And, of course, there was the bottom line.

Isadora Conroy loved a bargain. The words "On Sale" sent a silvery tingle through her blood. She'd always loved to buy, finding the basic transaction of money for objects deeply satisfying. So satisfying that she had all too often exchanged money for objects she had no use for. But it was that love of a bargain that had guided Dora into opening her own shop, and the subsequent discovery that selling was as pleasurable as buying.

"Lea, look at this." Dora turned to her sister, offering a gilded cream dispenser shaped like a woman's evening shoe. "Isn't it fabulous?"

Ophelia Conroy Bradshaw took one look, lifted a single honey-brown eyebrow. Despite the dreamy name, this was a woman rooted in reality. "I think you mean frivolous, right?"

"Come on, look beyond the obvious aesthetics." Beaming, Dora ran a fingertip over the arch of the shoe. "There's a place for ridiculous in the world."

"I know. Your shop."

Dora chuckled, unoffended. Though she replaced the creamer, she'd already decided to bid on that lot. She took out a notebook and a pen that boasted a guitar-wielding Elvis to note down the number. "I'm really glad you came along with me on this trip, Lea. You keep me centered."

"Somebody has to." Lea's attention was caught by a colorful display of Depression glass. There were two or three pieces in amber that would add nicely to her own collection. "Still, I feel guilty being away from home this close to Christmas. Leaving John with the kids that way."

"You were dying to get away from the kids," Dora reminded her as she inspected a lady's cherrywood vanity.

"I know. That's why I'm guilty."

"Guilt's a good thing." Tossing one end of her red muffler over her shoulder, Dora crouched down to check the work on the vanity's brass handles. "Honey, it's only been three days. We're practically on our way back. You'll get home tonight and smother the kids with attention, seduce John, and everybody'll be happy."

Lea rolled her eyes and smiled weakly at the couple standing beside her. "Trust you to take everything down to the lowest common denominator."

With a satisfied grunt, Dora straightened, shook her chin-length sweep of hair away from her face and nodded. "I think I've seen enough for now."

When she checked her watch, she realized it was curtain time for the matinee performance back home. Well, she mused, there was show business, and there was show business. She all but rubbed her hands together in anticipation of the auction opening.

"We'd better get some seats before they—oh wait!" Her brown eyes brightened. "Look at that."

Even as Lea turned, Dora was scurrying across the concrete floor.

It was the painting that had caught her attention. It wasn't large, perhaps eighteen by twenty-four inches with a simple, streamlined ebony frame. The canvas itself was a wash of color, streaks and streams of crimson and sapphire, a dollop of citrine, a bold dash of emerald. What Dora saw was energy and verve, as irresistible to her as a red-tag special.

Dora smiled at the boy who was propping the painting against the wall. "You've got it upside down."

"Huh?" The stock boy turned and flushed. He was seventeen, and the sight of Dora smiling at him reduced him to a puddle of hormones. "Ah, no, ma'am." His Adam's apple bobbed frantically as he turned the canvas around to show Dora the hook at the back.

"Mmm." When she owned it—and she certainly would by the end of the afternoon—she would fix that.

"This, ah, shipment just came in."

"I see." She stepped closer. "Some interesting pieces," she said, and picked up a statue of a sad-eyed basset hound curled up in a resting pose. It was heavier than she'd expected, and pursing her lips, she turned it over and over for a closer inspection. No craftsman's mark or date, she mused. But still, the workmanship was excellent.

"Frivolous enough for you?" Lea asked.

"Just. Make a terrific doorstop." After setting it down she reached for a tall figurine of a man and woman in antebellum dress caught in the swirl of a waltz. Dora's hand closed over thick, gnarled fingers. "Sorry." She glanced up at an elderly, bespeckled man who gave her a creaky bow.

"Pretty, isn't it?" he asked her. "My wife had one just like it. Got busted when the kids were wrestling in the parlor." He grinned, showing teeth too white and straight to be God-given. He wore a red bow tie and smelled like a peppermint stick. Dora smiled back.

"Do you collect?"

"In a manner of speaking." He set the figurine down and his old, shrewd eyes swept the display, pricing, cataloguing, dismissing. "I'm Tom Ashworth. Got a shop here in Front Royal." He took a business card from his breast pocket and offered it to Dora. "Accumulated so much stuff over the years, it was open a shop or buy a bigger house."

"I know what you mean. I'm Dora Conroy." She held out a hand and had it enveloped in a brief arthritic grip. "I have a shop in Philadelphia."

"Thought you were a pro." Pleased, he winked. "Noticed you right off. Don't believe I've seen you at one of Porter's auctions before."

"No, I've never been able to make it. Actually, this trip was an impulse. I dragged my sister along. Lea, Tom Ashworth."

"Nice to meet you."

"My pleasure." Ashworth patted Lea's chilled hand. "Never does warm up in here this time of year. Guess Porter figures the bidding'll heat things up some."

"I hope he's right." Lea's toes felt frozen inside her suede boots. "Have you been in business long, Mr. Ashworth?"

"Nigh onto forty years. The wife got us started, crocheting doilies and scarves and what-all and selling them. Added some trinkets and worked out of the garage." He took a corncob pipe from his pocket and clamped it between his teeth. "Nineteen sixty-three we had more stock than we could handle and rented us a shop in town. Worked side by side till she passed on in the spring of eighty-six. Now I got me a grandson working with me. Got a lot of fancy ideas, but he's a good boy."

"Family businesses are the best," Dora said. "Lea's just started working part-time at the shop."

"Lord knows why." Lea dipped her chilly hands into her coat pockets. "I don't know anything about antiques or collectibles."

"You just have to figure out what people want," Ashworth told her, and flicked a thumbnail over a wooden match to light it. "And how much they'll pay for it," he added before he puffed the pipe into life.

"Exactly." Delighted with him, Dora hooked a hand through his arm. "It looks like we're getting started. Why don't we go find some seats?"

Ashworth offered Lea his other arm and, feeling like the cock of the walk, escorted the women to chairs near the front row.

Dora pulled out her notebook and prepared to play her favorite role.

The bidding was low, but certainly energetic. Voices bounced off the high ceiling as the lots were announced. But it was the murmuring crowd that fired Dora's blood. There were bargains to be had here, and she was determined to grab her share.

She outbid a thin, waiflike woman with a pinched mouth for the cherrywood vanity, snapped up the lot that included the creamer/slipper for a song and competed briskly with Ashworth for a set of crystal saltcellars.

"Got me," he said when Dora topped his bid yet again. "You're liable to get a bit more for them up north."

"I've got a customer who collects," Dora told him. And who would pay double the purchase price, she thought.

"That so?" Ashworth leaned closer as the bidding began on the next lot. "I've got a set of six at the shop. Cobalt and silver."

"Really?"

"You got time, you drop on by after this and take a look."

"I might just do that. Lea, you bid on the Depression glass."

"Me?" Horror in her eyes, Lea gaped at her sister.

"Sure. Get your feet wet." Grinning, Dora tilted her head toward Ashworth's. "Watch this."

As Dora expected, Lea started out with hesitant bids that barely carried to the auctioneer. Then she began to inch forward in her seat. Her eyes glazed over. By the time the lot was sold, she was snapping out her bid like a drill sergeant commanding recruits.

"Isn't she great?" All pride, Dora swung an arm over Lea's shoulders to squeeze. "She was always a quick study. It's the Conroy blood."

"I bought all of it." Lea pressed a hand to her speeding heart. "Oh God, I bought all of it. Why didn't you stop me?"

"When you were having such a good time?"

"But—but—" As the adrenaline drained, Lea slumped in her chair. "That was hundreds of dollars. Hundreds."

"Well spent, too. Now, here we go." Spotting the abstract painting, Dora rubbed her hands together. "Mine," she said softly.

• • •

By three o'clock Dora was adding half a dozen cobalt saltcellars to the treasures in her van. The wind had kicked up, stinging color into her cheeks and sneaking down the collar of her coat.

"Smells like snow," Ashworth commented. He stood on the curb in front of his shop and, with his pipe clenched in his hand, sniffed the air. "Could be you'll run into some before you get home."

"I hope so." Pushing back her flying hair, she smiled at him. "What's Christmas without it? It was great meeting you, Mr. Ashworth." She offered her hand again. "If you get up to Philadelphia, I'll expect you to drop by."

"You can count on it." He patted his pocket where he'd slipped her business card. "You two ladies take care of yourselves. Drive safely."

"We will. Merry Christmas."

"Same to you," Ashworth added as Dora climbed in the van.

With a last wave she started the van and pulled away from the curb. Her eyes flicked up to the rearview mirror and she smiled as she saw Ashworth standing on the sidewalk with his pipe in his teeth and his hand lifted in a farewell salute. "What a sweetheart. I'm glad he got that figurine."

Lea shivered and waited impatiently for the van to heat. "I hope he didn't overcharge you for those saltcellars."

"Mmm. He made a profit, I'll make a profit and Mrs. O'Malley will add to her collection. Everybody gets what they want."

"I guess. I still can't believe you bought that hideous painting. You'll never be able to sell it."

"Oh, eventually."

"At least you only paid fifty dollars for it."

"Fifty-two seventy-five," Dora corrected.

"Right." Twisting in her seat, Lea looked at the boxes packed into the rear of the van. "You know, of course, that you don't have room for all this junk."

"I'll make room. Don't you think Missy would like that carousel?"

Lea imagined the outsize mechanical toy in her daughter's pink-and-white bedroom and shuddered. "Please, no."

"Okay." Dora shrugged. Once she'd cleaned up the carousel, she might let it spin in her own living room for a while. "But I think she'd go for it. You want to call John and tell him we're on our way back?"

"In a little while." With a sigh, Lea settled back. "This time tomorrow, I'll be baking cookies and rolling out pie dough."

"You asked for it," Dora reminded her. "You had to get married, have kids, buy a house. Where else is the family going to have Christmas dinner?"

"I wouldn't mind if Mom didn't insist on helping me cook it. I mean, the woman never cooked a real meal in her life, right?"

"Not that I remember."

"And there she is, every Christmas, underfoot in my kitchen and waving around some recipe for alfalfa and chestnut dressing."

"That one was bad," Dora recalled. "But it was better than her curried potatoes and succotash casserole."

"Don't remind me. And Dad's no help, wearing his Santa hat and hitting the eggnog before noon."

"Maybe Will can distract her. Is he coming alone or with one of his sweeties?" Dora asked, referring to their brother's list of glamorous dates.

"Alone, last I heard. Dora, watch that truck, will you?"

"I am." In the spirit of competition, Dora gunned the engine and passed the sixteen-wheeler with inches to spare. "So when's Will getting in?"

"He's taking a late train out of New York on Christmas Eve."

"Late enough to make a grand entrance," Dora predicted. "Look, if he gets in your hair, I can always—oh, hell."

"What?" Lea's eyes sprang open.

"I just remembered, that new tenant Dad signed up is moving in across the hall today."

"So?"

"I hope Dad remembers to be there with the keys. He was great about showing the apartment the last couple of weeks while I was tied up in the shop, but you know how absentminded he is when he's in the middle of a production."

"I know exactly how he is, which is why I can't understand how you could let him interview a tenant for your building."

"I didn't have time," Dora muttered, trying to calculate if she'd have an opportunity to call her father between performances. "Besides, Dad wanted to."

"Just don't be surprised if you end up across the hall from a psychopath, or a woman with three kids and a string of tattooed boyfriends."

Dora's lips curved. "I specifically told Dad no psychopaths or tattoos. I'm hoping it's someone who cooks, and hopes to suck up to the landlord by bringing me baked goods on a regular basis. Speaking of which, do you want to eat?"

"Yeah. I might as well get in one last meal where I don't have to cut up anyone's food but my own."

Dora swung toward the exit ramp, cutting off a Chevy. She ignored the angry blast of horns. There was a smile on her face as she imagined unpacking her new possessions. The very first thing she would do, she promised herself, was find the perfect spot for the painting.

High in the glittery tower of a silver building overlooking the cramped streets of LA, Edmund Finley enjoyed his weekly manicure. The wall directly across from his massive rosewood desk flickered with a dozen television screens. CNN, Headline News and one of the home-shopping networks all flashed silently across the wall. Other screens were tuned in to various offices in his organization so that he could observe his employees.

But unless he chose to listen in, the only sounds in the vast sweep of his office were the strains of a Mozart opera and the steady scrape of the manicurist's nail file.

Finley liked to watch.

He'd chosen the top floor of this building so that his office would overlook the panorama of Los Angeles. It gave him the feeling of power, of omnipotence, and he would often stand for an hour at the wide window behind his desk and simply study the comings and goings of strangers far below.

In his home far up in the hills above the city, there were television screens and monitors in every room. And windows, again windows where he could look down on the lights of the LA basin. Every evening he would stand on the balcony outside his bedroom and imagine owning everything, everyone, for as far as his eye could see.

He was a man with an appetite for possessions. His office reflected his taste for the fine and the exclusive. Both walls and carpet were white, pure white to serve as a virgin backdrop for his treasures. A Ming vase graced a marble pedestal. Sculptures by Rodin and Denécheau filled niches carved into the walls. A Renoir hung in a gold frame above a Louis Quatorze commode. A velvet settee reputed to have been Marie Antoinette's was flanked by gleaming mahogany tables from Victorian England.

Two high glass cabinets held a stunning and esoteric display of objets d'art: carved snuff bottles of lapis and aquamarine, ivory netsukes, Dresden figurines, Limoges ring boxes, a fifteenth-century dagger with a jeweled handle, African masks.

Edmund Finley acquired. And once he acquired, he hoarded.

His import-export business was enormously successful. His smuggling sideline more so. After all, smuggling was more of a challenge. It required a certain finesse, a ruthless ingenuity and impeccable taste.

Finley, a tall, spare, distinguished-looking man in his early fifties, had begun to "acquire" merchandise as a youth working the docks in San Francisco. It had been a simple matter to misplace a crate, to open a trunk and to sell what he took. By his thirtieth year he had amassed enough capital to start his own company, enough savvy to play heavily on the dark side and win and enough contacts to ensure a steady flow of merchandise.

Now he was a wealthy man who preferred Italian suits, French women and Swiss francs. He could, after decades of transactions, afford to keep what appealed most to him. What appealed most was the old, the priceless.

"You're all done, Mr. Finley." The manicurist placed Finley's hand gently on the spotless blotter on his desk. She knew he would check her work carefully while she packed up her tools and lotions. Once he had raged at her for ten minutes for missing a minute speck of cuticle on his thumb. But this time, when she dared to glance up, he was smiling down at his buffed nails.

"Excellent work." Pleased, he rubbed his thumbs and fingertips together. Taking a gold money clip from his pocket, Finley peeled off a fifty. Then with one of his rare and disarming smiles, he added another hundred. "Merry Christmas, dear."

"Oh—thank you. Thank you very much, Mr. Finley. Merry Christmas to you, too."

Still smiling, he dismissed her with a wave of his buffed fingertips. His sporadic generosity came as naturally as his constant greed. He relished both. Before the door had closed behind her, he had swiveled in his chair, folded his hands over his silk vest. Through the stream of sunlight he studied his view of Los Angeles.

Christmas, he thought. What a lovely time of year. One of goodwill toward men, ringing bells and colored lights. Of course, it was also the time of desperate loneliness, despair and suicide. But those small human tragedies didn't touch or concern him. Money had catapulted him above those fragile needs for companionship and family. He could buy companionship. He had chosen one of the richest cities in the world, where anything could be bought, sold, possessed. Here youth, wealth and power were admired above all else. During this brightest of holiday seasons, he had wealth, and he had power. As for youth, money could buy the illusion.

Finley scanned the buildings and sun-glinted windows with his bright green eyes. He realized with a vague sense of surprise that he was happy.

The knock on his office door made him turn as he called out, "Enter."

"Sir." Abel Winesap, a small, stoop-shouldered man with the heavy title of "Executive Assistant to the President," cleared his throat. "Mr. Finley."

"Do you know the true meaning of Christmas, Abel?" Finley's voice was warm, like mulled brandy poured over cream.

"Ah..." Winesap fiddled with the knot of his tie. "Sir?"

"Acquisition. A lovely word, Abel. And the truest meaning of this delightful holiday, don't you agree?"

"Yes, sir." Winesap felt a shiver whisper down his spine. What he had come to report was difficult enough. Finley's happy mood made the difficult more dangerous. "I'm afraid we have a problem, Mr. Finley."

"Oh?" Finley's smile remained, but his eyes frosted. "And what might that be?"

Winesap gulped in fear. He knew that Finley's frigid anger was more lethal than another man's rage. It had been Winesap who had been chosen to witness Finley's termination of an employee who had been embezzling. And he remembered how calmly Finley had slit the man's throat with a sixteenth-century jeweled dagger.

Betrayal, Finley believed, deserved quick punishment, and some ceremony.

Winesap also remembered, to his dismay, that it had been he who had been delegated to dispose of the body.

Nervously, he continued with his story. "The shipment from New York. The merchandise you were expecting."

"Has there been a delay?"

"No—that is, in a manner of speaking. The shipment arrived today as expected, but the merchandise..." He moistened his thin, nervous lips. "It isn't what you ordered, sir."

Finley placed his pampered hands on the edge of the desk and the knuckles turned bone white. "I beg your pardon?"

"The merchandise, sir. It isn't what was ordered. Apparently there was a mix-up somewhere." Winesap's voice petered out to a whimper. "I thought it best to report it to you at once."

"Where is it?" Finley's voice had lost its jovial warmth. It was a chilly hiss.

"In Receiving, sir. I thought—"

"Bring it up. Immediately."

"Yes, sir. Right away." Winesap escaped, grateful for the reprieve.

Finley had paid a great deal of money for the merchandise, and a great deal more to have that merchandise concealed and smuggled. Having each piece stolen, then disguised, transported from various locations to his factory in New York. Why, the bribes alone had run close to six figures.

To calm himself, he paused by a decanter of guava juice and poured generously.

And if there had been a mistake, he thought, steadier, it would be rectified. Whoever had erred would be punished.

Carefully, he set the Baccarat low-ball glass aside and studied himself in the oval

George III mirror above the bar. He brushed a fussy hand over his thick mane of dark hair, admiring the glint and gleam of silver that threaded through it. His last face-lift had smoothed away the sags under his eyes, firmed his chin and erased the lines that had dug deeply around his mouth.

He looked no more than forty, Finley decided, turning his face from side to side to study and approve his profile.

What fool had said that money couldn't buy happiness?

The knock on his door shattered his mood. "Come," he snapped out, and waited as one of his receiving clerks wheeled in a crate. "Leave it there." He jabbed a finger toward the center of the room. "And go. Abel, remain. The door," he said, and Winesap scurried to shut it behind the departing clerk.

When Finley said nothing more, Winesap blanched and walked back to the crate. "I opened it as you instructed, Mr. Finley. As I began to inspect the merchandise, I realized there had been an error." Gingerly he reached into the crate, dipping his hand into a sea of shredded paper. His fingers trembled as he pulled out a china teapot decorated with tiny violets.

Finley took the teapot, turning it over in his hands. It was English, a lovely piece, worth perhaps $200 on the open market. But it was mass-produced. Thousands of teapots exactly like this one were on sale across the world. So to him it was completely worthless. He smashed it against the edge of the crate and sent shards flying.

"What else?"

Quaking, Winesap plunged his hand deep into the crate and drew out a swirling glass vase.

Italian, Finley deduced as he inspected it. Handmade. A value of $100, perhaps $150. He hurled it, barely missing Winesap's head, and sent it crashing against the wall.

"There's—there's teacups." Winesap's eyes darted to the crate and back to his employer's stony face. "And some silver—two platters, a candy dish. A p-pair of crystal goblets etched with wedding bells."

"Where is my merchandise?" Finley demanded, biting off each word.

"Sir, I can't—that is, I believe there's been . . ." His voice drained out to a whisper. "An error."

"An error." Finley's eyes were like jade as he clenched his fists at his sides. DiCarlo, he thought, conjuring up an image of his man in New York. Young, bright, ambitious. But not stupid, Finley reminded himself. Not stupid enough to attempt a double cross. Still, he would have to pay, and pay dearly for this error.

"Get DiCarlo on the phone."

"Yes, sir." Relieved that Finley's wrath was about to find a new target, Winesap darted to the desk to place the call.

As Winesap dialed, Finley crunched shards of china into the carpet. Reaching into the crate, he systematically destroyed the rest of the contents.

2

Jed Skimmerhorn wanted a drink. He wasn't particular about the type. Whiskey that would burn a line down his throat, the seductive warmth of brandy, the familiar tang of a beer. But he wasn't going to get one until he'd finished carting boxes up these damn rickety back steps and into his new apartment.

Not that he had a hell of a lot of possessions. His old partner, Brent, had given him a hand with the sofa, the mattress and the heavier pieces of furniture. All that remained were a few cardboard boxes filled with books and cooking utensils and other assorted junk. He wasn't sure why he'd kept even that much when it would have been easier to put it all in storage.

Then again, he wasn't sure of a lot of things these days. He couldn't explain to Brent, or to himself, why he'd found it so necessary to move across town, out of the huge old Colonial and into an apartment. It was something about fresh starts. But you couldn't start fresh until you'd ended.

Jed had been doing a lot of ending lately.

Turning in his resignation had been the first step—perhaps the hardest. The police commissioner had argued, refusing to accept the resignation and putting Jed on extended leave. It didn't matter what it was called, Jed mused. He wasn't a cop anymore. Couldn't be a cop anymore. Whatever part of him had wanted to serve and protect was hollowed out.

He wasn't depressed, as he'd explained to the department shrink. He was finished. He didn't need to find himself. He just needed to be left alone. He'd given fourteen years of his life to the force. It had to be enough.

Jed elbowed open the door to the apartment and braced it with one of the boxes he carried. He slid the second box across the wooden floor before heading back down the narrow hallway toward the outside steps that served as his entrance.

He hadn't heard a peep from his neighbor across the hall. The eccentric old man who had rented him the place had said that the second apartment was occupied but the tenant was as quiet as a mouse.

It certainly seemed that way.

Jed started down the steps, noting with annoyance that the banister wouldn't hold the weight of a malnourished three-year-old. The steps themselves were slick with the sleet that continued to spit out of the colorless sky. It was almost quiet in the back of the building. Though it fronted on busy South Street, Jed didn't think he'd mind the noise and Bohemian atmosphere, the tourists or the shops. He was close enough to the river that he could take solitary walks when he chose.

In any case, it would be a dramatic change from the manicured lawns of Chestnut Hill, where the Skimmerhorn family home had stood for two centuries.

Through the gloom he could see the glow of colored lights strung on the windows of neighboring buildings. Someone had wired a large plastic Santa and his eight tiny reindeer to a roof, where they were caught in the pretense of flying day and night.

It reminded him that Brent had invited him to Christmas dinner. A big, noisy family event that Jed might have enjoyed in the past. There had never been big, noisy family events in his life—or none that could have been called fun.

And now there was no family. No family at all.

He pressed his fingertips to the ache at his temple and willed himself not to think of Elaine. But old memories, like the ghost of past sins, snuck through and knotted his stomach.

He hauled the last of the boxes out of the trunk and slammed it with a force that rattled the reconditioned Thunderbird down to its tires. He wasn't going to think of Elaine, or Donny Speck or responsibilities or regrets. He was going to go inside, pour a drink and try to think of nothing at all.

With his eyes narrowed against the stinging sleet, he climbed the steep steps one last time. The temperature inside was dramatically higher than the wind-punched air outside. The landlord was generous with the heat. Overly generous. But then, it wasn't Jed's problem how the old guy spent his money.

Funny old guy, Jed thought now, with his rich voice, operatic gestures and silver flask. He'd been more interested in Jed's opinion on twentieth-century playwrights than in his references and rent check.

Still, you couldn't be a cop for nearly half your life and not understand that the world was made up of a lot of odd characters.

Once inside, Jed dumped the last box onto the oak table in the dining area. He dug through crumpled newspaper in search of that drink. Unlike the crates in storage, these boxes weren't marked, nor had they been packed with any sort of system. If there had been any practical genes in the Skimmerhorn blood, he figured Elaine had gotten his share as well as her own.

The fresh thought of his sister made him swear again, softly through his teeth. He knew better than to let the thought dig roots, for if it did it would bloom with guilt. Over the past month he'd become all too aware that guilt could give you night sweats and a dull, skittering sense of panic.

Sweaty hands and panic weren't desirable qualities in a cop. Nor was the tendency to uncontrollable rage. But he wasn't a cop anymore, Jed reminded himself. His time and his choices, as he'd told his grandmother, were his own.

The apartment was echoingly empty, which only served to satisfy him that he was alone. One of the reasons he'd chosen it was because he'd have only one neighbor to ignore. The other reason was just as simple, and just as basic: It was fabulous.

He supposed he'd lived with the finer things for too long not to be drawn to them. However much he claimed that his surroundings didn't matter, he would have been quietly miserable in some glossy condo or soulless apartment complex.

He imagined the old building had been converted into shop and apartments sometime in the thirties. It had retained its lofty ceilings and spacious rooms, the working fireplace and slim, tall windows. The floors, a random-width oak, had been highly polished for the new tenant.

The trim was walnut and uncarved, the walls a creamy ivory. The old man had assured Jed they could be painted to suit his tastes, but home decorating was the last thing on Jed's mind. He would take the rooms precisely as they were.

He unearthed a bottle of Jameson, three-quarters full. He studied it a moment, then set it on the table. He was shoving packing paper aside in search of a glass when he heard noises. His hands froze, his body braced.

Tilting his head, he turned, trying to locate the source of the sound. He'd thought he'd heard bells, a tingling echo. And now laughter, a smoky drift of it, seductive and female.

His eyes turned to the brass, open-work floor vent near the fireplace. The sounds floated up through it, some vague, some clear enough that he could hear individual words if he chose to listen.

There was some sort of antique or curio shop beneath the apartment. It had been closed for the last couple of days, but it was apparently open for business now.

Jed went back to his search for a glass and tuned out the sounds from below.

"I really do appreciate your meeting us here, John." Dora set a newly acquired globe lamp beside the antique cash register.

"No problem." He huffed a bit as he carted another crate into the overflowing storeroom. He was a tall man with a skinny frame that refused to fill out, an honest face that might have been homely but for the pale, shy eyes that peered at the world from behind thick lenses.

He sold Oldsmobiles in Landsdowne and had been named Salesman of the Year two years running using a low-key, almost apologetic approach that came naturally to him and charmed the customers.

Now he smiled at Dora and shoved his dark-framed glasses back up his nose. "How did you manage to buy so much in such a short time?"

"Experience." She had to rise on her toes to kiss John's cheek, then she bent and scooped up her younger nephew, Michael. "Hey, frog face, did you miss me?"

"Nuh-uh." But he grinned and wrapped his pudgy arms around her neck.

Lea turned to keep an eagle eye on her two other children. "Richie, hands in your pockets. Missy, no pirouetting in the shop."

"But, Mom..."

"Ah." Lea sighed, smiled. "I'm home." She held out her arms for Michael. "Dora, do you need any more help?"

"No, I can handle it from here. Thanks again."

"If you're sure." Dubiously, Lea glanced around the shop. It was a mystery to her how her sister could function in the clutter she constantly surrounded herself with. They had grown up in chaos, with every day dawning with a new drama or comedy. For Lea, the only way to remain sane as an adult was structure. "I really could come in tomorrow."

"No. It's your day off, and I'm counting on scarfing down my share of those cookies you'll be baking." As she herded her family toward the door, Dora slipped a pound bag of M&M's to her niece. "Share," she ordered under her breath. "And don't tell your mom where you got them." She ruffled Richie's hair. "Scram, creep."

He grinned, showing the wide gap of his missing two front teeth. "Burglars might come tonight and rob you blind." Reaching out, he toyed with the long dangle of citrine and amethyst that swung at her ear. "If I spent the night, I'd shoot them for you."

"Why, thank you, Richie," Dora said in serious tones. "I can't tell you how much I appreciate that. But I'll just have to shoot my own burglars tonight." She nudged her family outside, then began to lock up immediately, knowing that Lea would wait until she had turned every lock and engaged the security alarm.

Alone, she turned and took a deep breath. There was the scent of apple and pine from the potpourri set all around the shop. It was good to be home, she thought, and lifted the box that contained the new acquisitions she'd decided to take to her apartment upstairs.

She moved through the storeroom to unlock the door that led to the inside stairway. She had to juggle the box, her purse and her overnight bag, as well as the coat she'd stripped off on entering the shop. Muttering to herself, she managed to hit the light switch in the stairway with her shoulder.

She was halfway down the hall when she saw the light spilling out of the neighboring apartment. The new tenant. Shifting her grip, she walked to the door that was braced open with a box and peered in.

She saw him standing by an old table, a bottle in one hand, a glass in the other. The room itself was sparsely furnished with a sofa and an overstuffed chair.

But she was more interested in the man who stood in profile to her and downed a long swallow of whiskey.

He was tall with a tough, athletic build that made her think of a boxer. He wore a navy sweatshirt with sleeves pushed up to the elbows—no visible tattoos—and Levis worn white at the stress points. His hair was a bit unkempt, falling carelessly over his collar in a rich shade of ripening wheat.

In contrast, the watch at his wrist was either an amazingly good knockoff, or a genuine Rolex.

Though her appraisal took only seconds, Dora sensed her neighbor was not celebrating his new home. His face, shadowed by the high slash of cheekbones and the stubble of a beard, seemed grim.

Before she had made a sound, she saw his body tense. His head whipped around. Dora found herself fighting the instinct to step back in defense as he pinned her with eyes that were hard, expressionless and shockingly blue. "Your door was open," she said apologetically, and was immediately annoyed that she'd excused herself from standing in her own hallway.

"Yeah." He set the bottle down, carrying the glass with him as he crossed to her. Jed took his own survey. Most of her body was obscured by the large cardboard box she carried. A pretty oval face, slightly pointed at the chin, with an old-fashioned roses-and-cream complexion, a wide, unpainted mouth that was just curving up in a smile, big brown eyes that were filled with friendly curiosity, a swing of sable-colored hair.

"I'm Dora," she explained when he only continued to stare. "From across the hall? Need any help getting organized?"

"No." Jed booted the box away with his foot and closed the door in her face.

Her mouth fell open before she deliberately snapped it shut. "Well, welcome to the neighborhood," she muttered as she turned away to her own door. After an initial fumble for her keys, she unlocked her door and slammed it behind her. "Thanks a lot, Dad," she said to the empty room. "Looks like you found me a real prize."

Dora dumped her things on a settee blooming with cabbage roses, brushed her hair back with impatient fingers. The guy might have been a pleasure to look at, she mused, but she preferred a neighbor with a modicum of personality. Marching to her candlestick phone, she decided to call her father and give him an earful.

Before she'd dialed the second number, she spotted the sheet of paper with its big heart-shaped happy face drawn at the bottom. Quentin Conroy always added some little drawing—a barometer of his mood—on his notes and letters. Dora hung up the phone and began to read.

Izzy, my darling daughter.

Dora winced. Her father was the only living soul who called her by that derivative of her name.

> *The deed is done. Well done, if I say so myself. Your new tenant is a strapping young man who should be able to help you with any menial work. His name, as you see on the copies of the lease awaiting your signature, is Jed Shimmerhorn. A full-bodied name that brings lusty sea captains or hearty pioneers to my mind. I found him fascinatingly taciturn, and sensed a whirlpool bubbling under those still waters. I couldn't think of anything nicer to give my adored daughter than an intriguing neighbor.*
>
> *Welcome home, my firstborn babe.*
> *Your devoted father.*

Dora didn't want to be amused, but she couldn't help smiling. The move was so obvious. Put her within elbow-rubbing space of an attractive man, and maybe, just maybe, she would fall in love, get married and give her greedy father more grandchildren to spoil.

"Sorry, Dad," she murmured. "You're in for another disappointment."

Setting the note aside, she skimmed a finger down the lease until she came to Jed's signature. It was a bold scrawl, and she dashed her own name on the line next to it on both copies. Lifting one, she strode to her door and across the hall and knocked.

When the door opened, Dora thrust the lease out, crushing the corner against Jed's chest. "You'll need this for your records."

He took it. His gaze lowered, scanned, then lifted again. Her eyes weren't friendly now, but cool. Which suited him. "Why'd the old man leave this with you?"

Her chin tilted up. "The old man," she said in mild tones, "is my father. I own the building, which makes me, Mr. Skimmerhorn, your landlord." She turned on her heel and was across the hall in two strides. With her hand on the knob, she paused, turned. Her hair swung out, curved, settled. "The rent's due on the twenty-first of each month. You can slip the check under my door and save yourself a stamp, as well as any contact with other humans."

She slipped inside and closed the door with a satisfied snick of the lock.

3

When Jed jogged to the base of the steps leading up to his apartment, he'd sweated out most of the physical consequences of a half bottle of whiskey. One of the reasons he'd chosen this location was the gym around the corner. He'd spent a very satisfying ninety minutes that morning lifting weights, punching the hell out of the heavy bag and burning away most of his morning-after headache in the steam room.

Now, feeling almost human, he craved a pot of black coffee and one of the microwave breakfasts he'd loaded into his freezer. He pulled his key out of the pocket of his sweats and let himself into the hallway. He heard the music immediately. Not Christmas carols, thankfully, but the rich-throated wail of gospel according to Aretha Franklin.

At least his landlord's taste in music wouldn't irritate him, he mused, and would have turned directly into his own rooms except he'd noted her open door.

An even trade, Jed figured, and, dipping his hands into his pockets, wandered over. He knew he'd been deliberately rude the night before. And because it had been deliberate, he saw no reason to apologize. Still, he thought it wise to make some sort of cautious peace with the woman who owned his building.

He nudged the door open a bit wider, and stared.

Like his, her apartment was spacious, high ceilinged and full of light from a trio of front windows. That was where the similarity ended.

Even after growing up in a house adorned with possessions, he was amazed. He'd never seen so much stuff crammed into one single space before. Glass shelves covered one wall and were loaded with old bottles, tins, figurines, painted boxes and various knickknacks that were beyond his power to recognize. There were a number of tables, and each of them was topped by more glassware and china. A brightly floral couch was loaded with colored pillows that picked up the faded tones of a large area rug. A Multan, he recognized. There'd been a similar rug in his family's front parlor for as long as he could remember.

To complement the season, there was a tree by the window, every branch laden with colored balls and lights. A wooden sleigh overflowed with pinecones. A ceramic snowman with a top hat grinned back at him.

It should have been crowded, Jed thought. It certainly should have been messy. But somehow it was neither. Instead he had the impression of having opened some magic treasure chest.

In the midst of it all was his landlord. She wore a scarlet suit with a short straight skirt and a snugly fitted jacket. While her back was to him, he pursed his lips and wondered what sort of mood he'd been in the evening before not to have noticed that nifty little body.

Under Aretha's rich tones, he heard Dora muttering to herself. Jed leaned against the doorjamb as she propped the painting she'd been holding on the sofa and turned. To her credit, she managed to muffle most of the squeal when she spotted him.

"Your door was open," he told her.

"Yeah." Then, because it wasn't in her nature to be monosyllabic like her tenant, she shrugged. "I've been recirculating some inventory this morning—from up here to downstairs." She brushed at her bangs. "Is there a problem, Mr. Skimmerhorn? Leaky plumbing? Mice?"

"Not so I've noticed."

"Fine." She crossed the room and moved out of his view until he shifted inside the door. She stood beside a pedestal dining room table pouring what smelled gloriously like strong coffee from a china pot into a delicate matching cup. Dora set the pot back down and lifted a brow. Her unsmiling lips were as boldly red as her suit. "Is there something you need?"

"Some of that wouldn't hurt." He nodded toward the pot.

So now he wanted to be neighborly, Dora thought. Saying nothing, she went to a curved glass cabinet and took out another cup and saucer. "Cream? Sugar?"

"No."

When he didn't come any farther into the room, she took the coffee to him. He smelled like soap, she realized. Appealingly so. But her father had been right about the eyes. They were hard and inscrutable.

"Thanks." He downed the contents of the fragile cup in two swallows and handed it back. His mother had had the same china, he recalled. And had broken several pieces heaving them at servants. "The old—your father," he corrected, "said it was okay for me to set up my equipment next door. But since he's not in charge I figured I should check with you."

"Equipment?" Dora set his empty cup back on the table and picked up her own. "What sort?"

"A bench press, some weights."

"Oh." Instinctively, she took her gaze over his arms, his chest. "I don't think that's a problem—unless you do a lot of thudding when the shop's open."

"I'll watch the thudding." He looked back at the painting, studied it for a moment. Again, bold, he thought, like her color scheme, like the punch-in-the-gut scent she wore. "You know, that's upside down."

Her smile came quickly, brilliantly. She had indeed set it on the sofa the way it had been displayed at auction. "I think so, too. I'm going to hang it the other way."

To demonstrate, she went over and flipped it. Jed narrowed his eyes. "That's right side up," he agreed. "It's still ugly, but it's right side up."

"The appreciation of art is as individual as art itself."

"If you say so. Thanks for the coffee."

"You're welcome. Oh, Skimmerhorn?"

He stopped, glanced back over his shoulder. The faint glint of impatience in his eyes intrigued her more than any friendly smile would have.

"If you're thinking of redecorating or sprucing up your new place, come on down to the shop. Dora's Parlor has something for everybody."

"I don't need anything. Thanks for the coffee."

Dora was still smiling when she heard his door close. "Wrong, Skimmerhorn," she murmured. "Everybody needs something."

Cooling his heels in a dusty office and listening to the Beach Boys harmonize on "Little St. Nick" wasn't how Anthony DiCarlo had pictured spending this morning. He wanted answers, and he wanted them now.

More to the point, Finley wanted answers, and wanted them yesterday. DiCarlo tugged on his silk tie. He didn't have answers yet, but he would. The phone call from Los Angeles the day before had been crystal clear. Find the merchandise, within twenty-four hours, or pay the consequences.

DiCarlo had no intention of discovering what those consequences were.

He looked up at the big white-faced clock overhead and watched the minute hand click from 9:04 to 9:05. He had less than fifteen hours left. His palms were sweaty.

Through the wide glass panel stenciled with an overweight Santa and his industrious elves, he could see more than a dozen shipping clerks busily stamping and hauling.

DiCarlo sneered as the enormously fat shipping supervisor with the incredibly bad toupee approached the door.

"Mr. DiCarlo, so sorry to keep you waiting." Bill Tarkington had a weary smile on his doughy face. "As you can imagine, we're pretty frantic around here these days. Can't complain, though, no sir, can't complain. Business is booming."

"I've been waiting fifteen minutes, Mr. Tarkington," DiCarlo said, his fury clear. "I don't have time to waste."

"Who does, this time of year?" Unflaggingly pleasant, Tarkington waddled around his desk to his Mr. Coffee machine. "Have a seat. Can I get you some of this coffee? Put hair on your chest."

"No. There's been an error, Mr. Tarkington. An error that must be corrected immediately."

"Well, we'll just see what we can do about that. Can you give me the specifics?"

"The merchandise I directed to Abel Winesap in Los Angeles was not the merchandise which arrived in Los Angeles. Is that specific enough for you?"

Tarkington pulled on his pudgy bottom lip. "That's a real puzzler. You got your copy of the shipping invoice with you?"

"Of course." DiCarlo took the folded paper from the inside breast pocket of his jacket.

"Let's have a look-see." His fat, sausage fingers moved with a quick, uncanny grace as he booted up his computer. "Let's see now." He rattled a few more keys. "That was to ship out on December seventeenth. . . . Yep, yep, there she is. She went out just fine. Should have arrived yesterday, today at the latest."

DiCarlo ran a hand through his wavy black hair. Idiots, he thought. He was surrounded by idiots. "The shipment did arrive. It was incorrect."

"You're saying the package that plopped down in L.A. was addressed to another location?"

"No. I'm saying what was *in* the package was incorrect."

"That's an odd one." Tarkington sipped some coffee. "Was the package packed here? Oh, wait, wait, I remember." He waved DiCarlo's answer away. "We provided the crate and the packing, and you supervised. So how in the wide, wide world did the merchandise get switched?"

"That is my question," DiCarlo hissed, his hand slamming the desk.

"Now, now, let's stay calm." Determinedly affable, Tarkington hit a few more keys. "That shipment went out of section three. Let's see who was on the belt that day. Ah, here we go. Looks like Opal." He swiveled around to beam at DiCarlo. "Good worker, Opal. Nice lady, too. Had a rough time of it lately."

"I'm not interested in her personal life. I want to speak to her."

Tarkington leaned forward and flicked a switch on his desk. "Opal Johnson, please report to Mr. Tarkington's office." He flicked the switch off, then patted his toupee to make sure it was still in place. "Sure I can't get you some coffee? A doughnut, maybe?" He tossed open the lid on a cardboard box. "Got us some nice raspberry-jelly-filled today. Some tractor wheels, too."

DiCarlo let out a sound like steam escaping a kettle and turned away. With a shrug, Tarkington helped himself to a doughnut.

DiCarlo clenched his fists as a tall, striking black woman strode across the warehouse. She was wearing snug jeans and a bright green sweater with a Nike hip pouch. Her hair was pulled back in a curly ponytail. The yellowing smudges of old bruises puffed around her left eye.

She opened the door and poked her head in. The room was immediately filled with the noise of conveyor belts and the scent of nerves. "You call for me, Mr. Tarkington?"

"Yeah, Opal. Come on in a minute. Have some coffee?"

"Sure, okay." As she closed the door, Opal took a quick scan of DiCarlo as possibilities raced through her mind.

They were laying her off. They were firing her outright because she'd fallen behind her quota last week after Curtis had knocked her around. The stranger was one of the owners come to tell her. She took a cigarette out of her pouch and lit it with shaky hands.

"We got ourselves a little problem here, Opal."

Her throat seemed to fill with sand. "Yes, sir?"

"This is Mr. DiCarlo. He had a shipment go out last week, on your line."

The quick surge of fear had Opal choking on smoke. "We had a lot of shipments going out last week, Mr. Tarkington."

"Yes, but when the shipment arrived, the merchandise was incorrect." Tarkington sighed.

With her heart hammering in her throat, Opal stared at the floor. "It got sent to the wrong place?"

"No, it got to the right place, but what was inside it was wrong, and since Mr. DiCarlo oversaw the packing himself, we're baffled. I thought you might remember something."

There was a burning in her gut, around her heart, behind her eyes. The nightmare that had plagued her for nearly a week was coming true. "I'm sorry, Mr. Tarkington," she forced herself to say. "It's hard to recall any one shipment. All I remember about last week is working three double shifts and going home to soak my feet every night."

She was lying, DiCarlo decided. He could see it in her eyes, in her body stance—and bided his time.

"Well, it was worth a shot." Tarkington gestured expansively. "Anything pops into your mind, you let me know. Okee-doke?"

"Yes, sir, I will." She crushed the cigarette out in the dented metal ashtray on Tarkington's desk and hurried back to her belt.

"We'll start a trace on this, Mr. DiCarlo. With a red flag. Premium prides itself on customer satisfaction. From our hands to your hands, with a smile," he said, quoting the company motto.

"Right." He was no longer interested in Tarkington, though he would have found some satisfaction in plowing his fists into the man's bulging belly. "And if you want to continue to enjoy the patronage of E. F., Incorporated, you'll find the answers."

DiCarlo circled the noisy shipping room and headed for Opal's station. She watched his progress with nervous eyes. Her heart was thudding painfully against her ribs by the time he stopped beside her.

"What time's your lunch break?"

Surprised, she nearly bobbled a box of cookware. "Eleven-thirty."

"Meet me outside, front entrance."

"I eat in the cafeteria."

"Not today," DiCarlo said softly. "Not if you want to keep this job. Eleven-thirty," he added, and walked away.

She was afraid to ignore him, afraid to oblige him. At 11:30, Opal donned her olive-green parka and headed for the employees' entrance. She could only hope that by the time she'd circled the building, she'd have herself under control.

She would have liked to skip lunch altogether. The Egg McMuffin she'd eaten that morning kept threatening to come back for a return visit.

Don't admit anything, she coached herself as she walked. They can't prove you made a mistake if you don't admit it. If she lost the job, she'd have to go back on welfare again. Even if her pride could stand it, she wasn't sure her kids could.

Opal spotted DiCarlo leaning against the hood of a red Porsche. The car was dazzling enough, but the man—tall, dark, glossily handsome and wrapped in a cashmere coat of pale gray—made her think of movie stars. Terrified, awed, intimidated, she walked toward him, head lowered.

DiCarlo said nothing, simply opened the passenger door. His mouth twitched when he caught her instinctive sigh on sliding over the leather seat. He climbed behind the wheel, turned the key.

"Mr. DiCarlo, I really wish I could help you about that shipment. I—"

"You're going to help me." He shoved the gear shift into first, and the car shot away from Premium like a slick red bullet. He'd already decided how to play her, and gave Opal two full minutes of silence to stretch her nerves. He fought back a satisfied smile when she spoke first.

"Where are we going?"

"No place in particular."

Despite the thrill of riding in a first-class car, she moistened dry lips. "I got to be back in a half hour."

He said nothing to that, only continued to drive fast.

"What's this all about?"

"Well, I'll tell you, Opal. I figured we could deal better together away from the work atmosphere. Things have been pretty harried for you the last few weeks, I imagine."

"I guess so. The Christmas rush."

"And I figure you know just what happened to my shipment."

Her stomach did a quick jig. "Look, mister, I already told you I didn't know what happened. I'm just doing my job the best I can."

He swung the car into a hard right turn that had her eyes popping wide. "We both know it wasn't my screwup, honey. We can do this hard, or we can do this easy."

"I—I don't know what you mean."

"Oh yeah." His voice held the same dangerous purr as the Porsche's engine. "You know just what I mean. What happened, Opal? Did you take a liking to what was in the crate and decide to help yourself? An early Christmas bonus?"

She stiffened, and some of her fear drained away in fury. "I ain't no thief. I ain't never stolen so much as a pencil in my whole life. Now you turn this car around, Mr. Big Shot."

It was just that kind of sass—as Curtis was fond of telling her—that earned her bruises and broken bones. Remembering that, she cringed against the door as the final word faded away.

"Maybe you didn't steal anything," he agreed after she'd started to tremble again. "That's going to make me really sorry to bring charges against you."

Her throat snapped shut. "Charges? What do you mean, charges?"

"Merchandise, which my employer considers valuable, has vanished. The police will be interested to learn what happened to that shipment once it got into your hands. And even if you're innocent, it's going to leave a big question mark on your work record."

Panic was pounding like an anvil at the base of her skull. "I don't even know what was in the crate. All I did was ship it. That's all I did."

"We both know that's a lie." DiCarlo pulled into the parking lot of a convenience store. He could see that her eyes were filled with tears, her hands twisting and twisting the strap of her shoulder bag. Almost there, he thought, and shifted in his seat to offer her a cold merciless stare.

"You want to protect your job, don't you, Opal? You don't want to get fired, and arrested, do you?"

"I got kids," she sobbed as the first tears spilled over. "I got kids."

"Then you'd better think about them, about what could happen to them if you got into this kind of trouble. My employer is a hard man." His eyes flicked over her fading facial bruises. "You know about hard men, don't you?"

Defensively, she lifted a hand to her cheek. "I—I fell down."

"Sure you did. Tripped on somebody's fist, right?" When she didn't answer he continued to press, lightly now. "If my boss doesn't get back what belongs to him, he's not just going to take it out on me. He'll work his way through Premium until he gets down to you."

They'd find out, she thought, panicking. They always found out. "I didn't take his stuff, I didn't. I just—"

"Just what?" DiCarlo leaped on the word and had to force himself not to wrap a hand around her throat and squeeze out the rest.

"I got three years in with Premium." Sniffing, she dug in her bag for a Kleenex. "I could make floor supervisor in another year."

DiCarlo bit back a stream of abuse and forced himself to stay cool. "Listen, I know what it's like to climb up that ladder. You help me out here, and I'll do the same for you. I don't see any reason that what you tell me has to go beyond you and me. That's why I didn't do this in Tarkington's office."

Opal fumbled for a cigarette. Automatically, DiCarlo let the windows down a crack. "You won't go back to Mr. Tarkington?"

"Not if you play straight with me. Otherwise . . ." To add impact, he slid his fingers under her chin, pinching as he turned her face to his.

"I'm sorry. I'm really sorry it happened. I thought I got it right afterward, but I wasn't sure. And I was afraid. I had to miss a couple of days last month 'cause my youngest was sick, and last week I was late one day when I fell and . . . and I was so rushed I mixed up the invoices." She turned away, braced for a blow. "I dropped them. I was dizzy and I dropped them. I thought I had everything put back right, but I wasn't real sure. But I checked on a bunch of deliveries yesterday, and they were okay. So I thought I was clear, and nobody'd have to know."

"You mixed up the invoices," he repeated. "Some idiot clerk gets a dizzy spell and screws up the paperwork and puts my butt in a sling."

"I'm sorry." She sobbed. Maybe he wasn't going to beat her, but he was going to make her pay. Opal knew someone always made her pay. "I'm really sorry."

"You're going to be a lot sorrier if you don't find out where the shipment went."

"I went through all the paperwork yesterday. There was only one other oversized crate that came through that lot in the morning." Still weeping, she reached in her bag again. "I wrote down the address, Mr. DiCarlo." She fished it from her purse and he snatched it.

"Sherman Porter, Front Royal, Virginia."

"Please, Mr. DiCarlo, I got kids." She wiped at her eyes. "I know I made a mistake, but I've done real good work at Premium. I can't afford to get fired."

He slipped the paper into his pocket. "I'll check this out, then we'll see."

Her jaw dropped with the weight of hope. "Then you won't tell Mr. Tarkington?"

"I said we'll see." DiCarlo started the engine as he plotted out his next steps. If things didn't go his way, he'd come back for Opal and it wouldn't just be her face that he'd leave black and blue.

At the main counter in her shop, Dora put the finishing touch of a big red bow on a gift-wrapped purchase. "She's going to love them, Mr. O'Malley." Pleased with the transaction, Dora patted the brightly wrapped box containing the cobalt saltcellars. "And it'll be an even bigger surprise, since she hasn't seen them in the shop."

"Well, I appreciate your calling me, Miss Conroy. Can't say I know what my Hester sees in these things, but she sure does set store by them."

"You're going to be her hero," Dora assured him as he tucked the purchase under his arm. "And I'll be happy to hold the other set for you until your anniversary in February."

"That's nice of you. You sure you don't want a deposit on them?"

"Not necessary. Happy Christmas, Mr. O'Malley."

"Same to you and yours." He walked out, a satisfied customer, with a spring in his step.

There were another half a dozen customers in the shop, two being helped by Dora's assistant, Terri. The prospect of another big day before the after-holiday lull made Dora's heart swell. Skirting the counter, she wandered the main room of the shop, knowing the trick was to be helpful but not intrusive.

"Please let me know if you have any questions."

"Oh, miss?"

Dora turned, smiling. There was something vaguely familiar about the stout matron with lacquered black hair.

"Yes, ma'am. May I help you?"

"Oh, I hope so." She gestured a bit helplessly toward one of the display tables. "These are doorstops, aren't they?"

"Yes, they are. Of course, they can be used for whatever you like, but that's the primary function." Automatically, Dora glanced over as the bells jingled on her door. She merely lifted a brow when Jed walked in. "Several of these are from the Victorian period," she went on. "The most common material was cast iron." She lifted a sturdy one in the shape of a basket of fruit. "This one was probably used for a drawing room. We do have one rather nice example of nailsea glass."

It was currently in her bedroom upstairs, but could be whisked down in a moment.

The woman studied a highly polished brass snail. "My niece and her husband just moved into their first house. I've got them both individual gifts for Christmas, but I'd like to get them something for the house as well. Sharon, my niece, shops here quite a lot."

"Oh. Does she collect anything in particular?"

"No, she likes the old and the unusual."

"So do I. Was there a reason you had a doorstop in mind?"

"Yes, actually. My niece does a lot of sewing. She's put together this really charming room. It's an old house, you see, that they've been refurbishing. The door to her sewing room won't stay open. Since they have a baby on the way, I know she'd want to be able to keep an ear out, and that this would be an amusing way to do it." Still, she hesitated. "I bought Sharon a chamber pot here a few months ago, for her birthday. She loved it."

That clicked. "The Sunderland, with the frog painted on the inside bottom."

The woman's eyes brightened. "Why, yes. How clever of you to have remembered."

"I was very fond of that piece, Mrs. . . ."

"Lyle. Alice Lyle."

"Mrs. Lyle, yes. I'm glad it found a good home." Pausing, Dora tapped a finger to her lips. "If she liked that, maybe she'd appreciate something along these lines." She chose a brass figure of an elephant. "It's Jumbo," she explained. "P. T. Barnum's?"

"Yes." The woman held out her hands and chuckled as Dora passed Jumbo to her. "My, hefty, isn't he?"

"He's one of my favorites."

"I think he's perfect." She took a quick, discreet glance at the tag dangling from Jumbo's front foot. "Yes, definitely."

"Would you like him gift-boxed?"

"Yes, thank you. And . . ." She picked up the sleeping hound Dora had purchased at auction only the day before. "Do you think this would be suitable for the nursery?"

"I think he's charming. A nice, cozy watchdog."

"I believe I'll take him along, too—an early welcoming gift for my newest grandniece or-nephew. You do take Visa?"

"Of course. This will just take a few minutes. Why don't you help yourself to some coffee while you wait?" Dora gestured to the table that was always set with tea and coffeepots and trays of pretty cookies before she carried both doorstops back to the counter. "Christmas shopping, Skimmerhorn?" she asked as she passed him.

"I need a—what do you call it? Hostess thing."

"Browse around. I'll be right with you."

Jed wasn't completely sure what he was browsing around in. The packed apartment was only a small taste of the amazing array of merchandise offered in Dora's Parlor.

There were delicate figurines that made him feel big and awkward, the way he'd once felt in his mother's sitting room. Still, there was no sense of the formal or untouchable here. Bottles of varying sizes and colors caught the glitter of sunlight and begged to be handled. There were signs advertising everything from stomach pills to boot polish. Tin soldiers arranged in battle lines fought beside old war posters.

He wandered through a doorway and found the next room equally packed. Teddy bears and teapots. Cuckoo clocks and corkscrews. A junk shop, he mused. People might stick a fancy name on it, like "curio shop," but what it was, was junk.

Idly, he picked up a small enameled box decorated with painted roses. Mary Pat would probably like this, he decided.

"Well, Skimmerhorn, you surprise me." Framed by the doorway, Dora smiled. She gestured toward the box he held as she walked to him. "You show excellent taste. That's a lovely piece."

"You could probably put bobby pins or rings into it, right?"

"You probably could. Originally it was used to hold patches. The well-to-do wore them in the eighteenth century, at first to cover smallpox scars, and then just for fashion. That particular one is a Staffordshire, circa 1770." She looked up from the box, and there was a laugh in her eyes. "It goes for twenty-five hundred."

"This?" It didn't fill the cup of his palm.

"Well, it is a George the Third."

"Yeah, right." He put it back on the table with the same care he would have used on an explosive device. The fact that he could afford it didn't make it any less intimidating. "Not quite what I had in mind."

"That's no problem. We have something for everyone's mind. A hostess gift, you said?"

He grunted and scanned the room. Now he was afraid to touch anything. He was back again, painfully back in childhood, in the front parlor of the Skimmerhorn house.

Don't touch, Jedidiah. You're so clumsy. You don't appreciate anything.

He blocked off the memory with its accompanying sensory illusion of the mingled scents of Chanel and sherry.

He didn't quite block off the scowl. "Maybe I should just pick up some flowers."

"That's nice, too. Of course, they don't last." Dora was enjoying his look of pure masculine discomfort. "A bottle of wine's acceptable as well. Not very innovative, but acceptable. Why don't you tell me a little about our hostess?"

"Why?"

Dora's smile widened at the suspicion in his voice. "So that I can get a picture of her and help you select something. Is she the athletic, outdoors type, or a quiet homebody who bakes her own bread?"

Maybe she wasn't trying to make him feel stupid, Jed thought, but she was succeeding just the same. "Look, she's my partner—ex-partner's wife. She's a trauma nurse. She's got a couple of kids and likes to read books."

"What sort of books?"

"I don't know." Why the hell hadn't he just gone by the florist?

"All right, then." Taking pity on him, she patted his arm. "It sounds to me as though we have a busy, dedicated woman. A compassionate and a romantic one. A hostess gift," she mused, tapping her finger to her lip. "It shouldn't be too personal. Something for the house." With a nod, she turned away and walked to a corner that was fashioned to resemble an old-fashioned pantry. "I think this would do nicely." Dora took down a footed wooden jar trimmed in brass.

Jed frowned over it. His parents hadn't gone for novelty antiques. "What's it—like for cookies?"

"How clever of you." Dora beamed at him. "It's a biscuit jar. Victorian. This one's oak from about 1870. A practical and ornamental gift, and at forty dollars, it won't cost you more than a dozen long-stem roses or a good French wine."

"Okay. I guess she'd get a kick out of it."

"See? That wasn't so painful. Can I help you with anything else? A last-minute Christmas gift?"

"No, that's it." He followed her back into the main room. The place smelled—cozy, he decided. Like apples. There was music playing softly. He recognized a movement from *The Nutcracker* and was surprised that he suddenly felt relaxed. "Where do you get all this stuff?"

"Oh, here and there," she said over her shoulder. "Auctions, flea markets, estate sales."

"And you actually make a living out of this."

Amused, she took a box from behind the counter and unfolded it. "People collect, Skimmerhorn. Often they don't even realize it. Didn't you ever have marbles as a boy, or comic books, baseball cards?"

"Sure." He'd had to hide them, but he'd had them.

She lined the box with tissue, working quickly, competently. "And didn't you ever trade your cards?" She glanced up to find him staring down at her hands.

"Sure I did," he murmured. His gaze lifted, locked on hers. He'd felt something watching her work that had gone straight to the gut like a hot arrow. "Just like you played with dolls."

"Actually, I didn't." She couldn't quite manage a smile. For a moment there, he'd looked as though he could've taken her in one quick bite. "I never liked them much. I preferred imaginary playmates, because you could change them into any character you wanted at the time." With more care than necessary she fit the lid with its gold-embossed DORA'S PARLOR onto the box. "What I was getting at is that most children collect and trade. Some people never grow out of it. Shall I gift-wrap this for you? There's no extra charge."

"Yeah, go ahead."

He shifted, then moved down the counter. Not that he was interested in what was displayed there, but to give himself some breathing room. The sexual tug he'd felt wasn't new, but it was the first time he'd experienced it because a woman had pretty hands.

And huge brown eyes, he added. Then there was that smile, he thought. She always looked as though she was laughing at some secret joke.

Obviously he'd been celibate too long if he was attracted to a woman who laughed at him.

To pass the time he picked up a baseball-shaped item with a hole in the top. The words "Mountain Dew" were painted on the side. Curious, Jed turned it over in his hand. He didn't think it could be some sort of odd drinking cup for the soft drink.

"Interesting, isn't it?" Dora set the gaily wrapped package in front of him.

"I was wondering what it was."

"A match striker." She put her hands over his on the bowl and guided his thumb to the rough edge. "You put the matches in the top, then light them on the side. Mountain Dew was a whiskey. This is from the late nineteenth century." She caught the glimmer of a smile on his face. "Do you like it?"

"It's different."

"I'm very fond of the different." She kept her hands warm over his for another moment. "Take it. Consider it a housewarming gift."

The inexplicable charm the object had for him dimmed considerably. "Hey, I don't think—"

"It's not valuable, monetarily. A neighborly gesture, Skimmerhorn. Don't be snotty."

"Well, when you're so sweet about it."

She laughed then and gave his hand a quick squeeze. "I hope your friend likes her gift." She walked away then to help another customer, but she watched out of the corner of her eye as Jed left the shop.

An unusual man, she mused. And, of course, the unusual was her stock-in-trade.

DiCarlo raced along the Van Wyck toward the airport, dialing his car phone with one hand and steering with the other. "DiCarlo," he stated, flipping the phone to speaker. "Get me Mr. Finley." With his nerves bubbling, he checked his watch. He'd make it, he assured himself. He had to make it.

"Mr. DiCarlo." Finley's voice filled the car. "You have good news, I assume."

"I tracked it all down, Mr. Finley." DiCarlo forced his words into a calm, businesslike tone. "I found out just what happened. Some idiot clerk at Premium switched the shipments. Sent ours to Virginia. I'll have it straightened out in no time."

"I see." There was a long pause. DiCarlo's bowels turned to ice water. "And what is your definition of 'no time'?"

"Mr. Finley, I'm on my way to the airport right now. I've got a flight booked into Dulles and a rental car waiting. I'll be in Front Royal before five east coast time. I have the name and address where the shipment was misdirected." His voice weakened. "I'm handling all of this at my own expense, Mr. Finley."

"That's wise of you, Mr. DiCarlo, as I don't wish for your mistake to cost me more than it already has."

"No, sir. And you have my word that this mistake will be corrected expediently."

"Very well. I'll expect you to contact me when you reach your destination. Naturally, I'll want the clerk fired."

"Naturally."

"And, Mr. DiCarlo? You do know how important that merchandise is to me, don't you? You will use any means necessary to recover it. Any means at all."

"Understood." When the connection broke, DiCarlo smiled grimly. The way this mess was screwing up his holiday, he was more than ready to use any means. Any means at all.

4

"This is quite a mix-up, isn't it?" While he asked this rhetorical—and to DiCarlo, unamusing—question, Sherman Porter rummaged through his dented file cabinet.

"Guess we'd have caught it here, but we had ourselves an auction going on," Porter continued as he carelessly destroyed the filing system. "Hell of a turnout, too. Moved a lot of inventory. Shitfire, where does that woman put things?"

Porter opened another file drawer. "Don't know how I'm supposed to find anything with Helen off for a week visiting her daughter in D.C. You just did catch me. We'll be closing till New Year's."

DiCarlo looked at his watch. Six-fifteen. His time was running out. As for patience, even the dregs of that had vanished. "Maybe I didn't make myself clear, Mr. Porter. The return of this merchandise is vitally important to my employer."

"Oh, you made that clear. A man wants what's his, after all. Here now, this looks promising." Porter unearthed a short stack of neatly typed sheets. "See, Helen's listed all the merchandise we auctioned, the lot numbers, selling price. Woman's a jewel."

"May I see that?"

"Sure, sure." After handing over the papers, Porter pulled open the bottom drawer of his desk. He took out a bottle of Four Roses and a couple of dusty jelly glasses. He offered DiCarlo a sheepish grin. "Join me in a drink? It's after hours now, and it keeps the cold away."

DiCarlo eyed the bottle with distaste. "No."

"Well, I'll just help myself then."

DiCarlo took out his own list and compared. It was all there, he noted, torn between relief and despair. All sold. The china hound, the porcelain figurine, the abstract painting, the bronze eagle and the stuffed parrot. The enormous and ugly plaster replica of the Statue of Liberty was gone, as well as a pair of mermaid bookends.

Inside his pocket, DiCarlo had another list. On it were descriptions of what had been carefully and expensively hidden in each piece of merchandise. An engraved Gallé vase valued at nearly $100,000, a pair of netsukes stolen from a private collection in Austria and easily worth six figures. An antique sapphire brooch, reputed to have been worn by Mary, Queen of Scots.

And the list went on. Despite the chill of the room, DiCarlo's skin grew clammy. Not one single item remained in Porter's possession. Sold, DiCarlo thought, all sold.

"There's nothing left," he said weakly.

"Said we had a good turnout." Pleased with the memory, Porter poured another drink.

"I need this merchandise."

"So you said, but that shipment came in just minutes before we started the auction, and there wasn't time to do an inventory. Way I figure it, your boss and I could sue the pants right off Premium." Because the idea held appeal, Porter smiled and drank again. "Bet they'd settle on a nice tidy sum, too."

"Mr. Finley wants his property, not a lawsuit."

"Up to him, I guess." With a shrug, Porter finished off his liquor. "Helen keeps a mailing list of our customers. Pays to send out notices when we're having an auction. Best I can say is you go through it, match up the names and addresses with the names she's got there next to the stuff we sold. You can get in touch, explain things. Of course, you'll return *my* merchandise. I paid for it, right?"

It would take days to round up Finley's stock, DiCarlo thought, sickened. Weeks. "Naturally," he lied.

Porter grinned. The way he figured it, he'd already sold one lot. Now he'd sell another—all for the price of one.

"The mailing list?"

"Oh, sure, sure." Comfortably buzzed on Four Roses, Porter shuffled through a drawer and came up with a metal box full of index cards. "Go ahead, take your time. I'm not in any hurry."

Twenty minutes later, DiCarlo left Porter comfortably drunk. He had one bright pinpoint of hope. The porcelain figurine was still in Front Royal, the property of a Thomas Ashworth, antique dealer. DiCarlo grasped hold of the possibility that regaining possession of one piece quickly would placate Finley and buy time.

As he drove through light traffic to Ashworth's shop, DiCarlo worked out his strategy. He would go in, explain the mishap, keeping it light, friendly. Since Ashworth had paid only $45 for the figure, DiCarlo was prepared to buy it back and include a reasonable profit for the dealer.

It could all be handled quickly, painlessly. Once he had the figurine, he would phone Finley and tell him that everything was under control. With any luck, Finley would be satisfied to have Winesap contact the rest of the list, and DiCarlo would be back in New York to enjoy Christmas.

The scenario brightened his mood to the extent that DiCarlo was humming as he parked his car by the curb in front of Ashworth's shop. It wasn't until he was out of the car and across the sidewalk that his easy smile faded.

CLOSED

The large cardboard sign on the glass-fronted door glared back at him.

DiCarlo was at the door in two strides, rattling the knob, pounding on the glass. It couldn't be closed. With his breath coming quickly, he raced to the wide display window, cupping his hands beside his face as he pressed it to the glass. He could see nothing but shadows and his own misery.

Finley would accept no excuses, he knew. Would tolerate nothing so vague as simple bad luck.

Then, as his lips peeled back in a snarl, DiCarlo saw the porcelain figure of a man and woman in ball dress, embracing lightly.

DiCarlo clenched his gloved hands into fists. He wasn't about to let a lock and a sheet of glass stop him.

The first step was to move his car. DiCarlo circled the block slowly, instincts humming as he kept an eye out for cruising patrol cars. He parked two blocks away. From his glove compartment he took what he thought he'd need. A flashlight, a screwdriver, his revolver. He slipped them all into the pockets of his cashmere coat.

This time he didn't approach the shop from the front, but headed up a side street with the firm, unhurried steps of a man who knew where he was headed. But as he walked, his eyes darted from side to side, watchful, wary.

It was a small town, and on a cold, blustery night most of its citizens were home enjoying the evening meal. DiCarlo passed no one as he walked toward the rear entrance of Ashworth's shop.

Nor did he spot any evidence of a security system. Moving quickly, he used the screwdriver to jimmy the door. The sound of splintering wood made him smile. He'd nearly forgotten the simple pleasure of breaking and entering during his years of corporate thievery. DiCarlo slipped inside, shut the door behind him. He flicked on his flashlight, shielding the beam with his hand as he swung it right and left. He'd entered through what appeared to be a small, cramped office. Because he would need to cover his tracks, DiCarlo had decided to make the break-in appear to be a random burglary. Impatient with the time he needed to waste, he pulled open drawers, upended contents.

He chuckled to himself as he spotted a plastic bank envelope. It looked as though his luck had changed. A quick flip through the small bills inside and he estimated the take to be about $500. Satisfied, he stuffed the money into his pocket and used the light to guide him into the main shop.

It seemed to DiCarlo that a little vandalism was just the touch he needed. He smashed a milk-glass lamp and a Capo di Monte vase at random. Then, because it felt so good, he kicked over a table that held a collection of demitasses. On impulse, and because it had been years since he'd had the thrill of stealing, he dropped a few cloisonné boxes into his pockets.

He was grinning when he snatched up the figurine. "Gotcha, baby," he murmured, then froze as light flooded into the shop from a stairway to his right. Swearing under his breath, DiCarlo squeezed himself between a rosewood armoire and a brass pole lamp.

"I've called the police." An elderly man wearing a gray flannel robe and carrying a nine-iron inched down the steps. "They're on their way, so you'd best stay right where you are."

DiCarlo could hear the age in the voice, and the fear. For a moment he was baffled as he smelled roasted chicken. The old man had an apartment upstairs, DiCarlo realized, and cursed himself for crashing through the shop like an amateur.

But there wasn't time for regrets. Tucking the figurine under his arm like a football, he hurtled toward Ashworth, as he had once hurtled down midtown Fifth Avenue with elderly matrons' Gucci bags stuffed in his jacket.

The old man grunted on impact, teetered on the steps, his worn bathrobe flapping over fish-white legs as thin and sharp as pencils. Breath wheezing, Ashworth swung awkwardly with the golf club as he fought to save his balance. More in reaction than intent, DiCarlo grabbed at the club as it whooshed by his ear. Ashworth pitched forward. His head hit a cast-iron coal shuttle with an ominous crack.

"Ah, Christ." Disgusted, DiCarlo shoved Ashworth over with the toe of his shoe. In the spill of the upstairs light, he could see the flow of blood, the open staring eyes. Fury had him kicking the body twice before he pulled himself back.

He was out the rear door and half a block away when he heard the sound of sirens.

Finley was switching channels on several of his television screens when the call came through.

"DiCarlo on line two, Mr. Finley."

"Put him through." After he'd switched the phone to speaker, Finley said, "You have news for me?"

"Yes. Yes, sir. I have the porcelain figurine with me, Mr. Finley, as well as a list locating all the other merchandise." DiCarlo spoke from his car phone, and kept his speed to a law-abiding fifty-five on his way back to Dulles International.

Finley waited a beat. "Explain."

DiCarlo began with Porter, pausing every few sentences to be certain Finley wanted him to continue. "I'd be happy to fax the list to you as soon as I reach the airport, Mr. Finley."

"Yes, do that. You sound a bit . . . uneasy, Mr. DiCarlo."

"Well, actually, sir, there was a bit of a problem in recovering the figurine. An antique dealer in Front Royal had purchased it. His shop was closed when I arrived, and knowing that you wanted results quickly, I broke in to retrieve it. The dealer was upstairs. There was an accident, Mr. Finley. He's dead."

"I see." Finley examined his nails. "So I assume you took care of this Porter."

"Took care of?"

"He can link you to the . . . accident, correct? And a link to you, Mr. DiCarlo, is a link to me. I suggest you snap the link quickly, finally."

"I'm—I'm on my way to the airport."

"Then you'll have to turn around and go back, won't you? Don't bother with that fax. After you've finished tidying up in Virginia, I'll expect you here, with the figurine. We'll discuss the next steps."

"You want me in California? Mr. Finley—"

"By noon, Mr. DiCarlo. We'll be closing early tomorrow. The holidays, you know. Contact Winesap with your flight information. You'll be met."

"Yes, sir." DiCarlo broke the connection and headed for the first exit ramp. He hoped to God Porter was still in his office and well drunk so that he could put a bullet in the man's brain with little fuss.

If he didn't get this whole mess straightened out soon, he'd never make it home for Christmas dinner.

"Really, Andrew, *really*, there's no need for you to walk me up." With the self-defense only a woman who'd been bored beyond redemption could possibly understand, Dora body-blocked the stairway. *Just let me get inside,* she thought, behind a locked door. Then she could beat her head against the wall in private.

Andrew Dawd, a CPA who considered bundling funds into tax shelters the height of intrigue, gave one of his hearty laughs and pinched her cheek. "Now, Dora, my mother taught me to always see the girl to her door."

"Well, Mama's not here," Dora pointed out, and inched up the steps. "And it's late."

"Late? It's not even eleven. You're not going to send me off without a cup of coffee, are you?" He flashed the white teeth that his doting mama had spent thousands to have straightened. "You know you make the best coffee in Philadelphia."

"It's a gift." She was searching for some polite way to refuse when the outside door slammed open, slammed shut.

Jed strode down the hall, his hands balled into the pockets of his scarred leather bomber jacket. It was left unsnapped to the wind over a sweatshirt and torn jeans. His hair was windblown, his face unshaven—which suited the surly look in his eye.

Dora had to wonder why, at that moment, she preferred Jed's dangerous look to the three-piece-suited, buffed and polished accountant beside her. The lack, she decided, was most certainly in her.

"Skimmerhorn."

Jed summed up Dora's date with one brief glance as he fit his key into his lock. "Conroy," he said. With that as greeting and farewell, he slipped inside and closed the door.

"Your new tenant?" Andrew's dark, well-groomed eyebrows rose into the high forehead his mother assured him was a sign of intelligence, and not male-pattern baldness.

"Yes." Dora sighed and caught a whiff of Andrew's Halston for Men, and the clashing, wild-animal scent Jed had left stirring in the air. Since she'd missed her chance to make excuses, she unlocked her own door and let Andrew in.

"He seems remarkably . . . physical." Frowning, Andrew shed his London Fog overcoat, folding it neatly over the back of a chair. "Does he live alone?"

"Yep." Too frustrated for tidiness, Dora tossed her mink, circa 1925, toward the couch on her way to the kitchen.

"Of course, I know how important it is to keep an apartment tenanted, Dora, but don't you think it would have been wiser—certainly safer—to rent to another female?"

"A female what?" Dora muttered, then paused as she poured beans into her old, hand-cranked coffee grinder. "No." While she ground beans, she glanced over her shoulder where Andrew was standing behind her, lips pursed in disapproval. "Do you?"

"Certainly. I mean the two of you do live here, alone."

"No, I live here, alone. He lives there." Because it annoyed her to have him breathing down her neck while she worked, Dora said, "Why don't you go put on some music, Andrew?"

"Music?" His blandly handsome face cleared. "Of course. Mood."

Moments later she heard the quiet strains of an old Johnny Mathis recording. She thought, Uh-oh, then shrugged. If she couldn't handle an accountant who wore Brooks Brothers suits and Halston cologne, she deserved to pay the price. "The coffee'll be a few minutes," she said as she walked back into the living room. Andrew was standing, hands on his narrow hips, studying her new painting. "That's something, isn't it?"

He tilted his head right, then left. "It's certainly bold." Then he turned to her to take a moment to admire how she looked in the short black dress covered with fiery bugle beads. "And it suits you."

"I picked it up at an auction in Virginia just a couple of days ago." She sat on the arm of a chair, automatically crossing her legs without giving a thought to the way the movement urged her skirt higher on her thighs.

Andrew gave it considerable thought.

"I thought I'd enjoy living with it awhile before I put it in the shop." She smiled, then catching the predatory look in his eye, popped off the chair like a spring. "I'll go check the coffee."

But he caught her hand and swung her, in what she imagined he considered a stylish move, into his arms. She barely avoided colliding her head with his chin. "We should take advantage of the music," he told her as he glided over the rug. His mother had paid good money for dance lessons and he didn't want to waste it.

Dora forced herself to relax. He did dance well, she mused as she matched her steps to his. She smiled and let her eyes close. She let the music and the movement take her, laughing softly when he lowered her into a stylish dip.

He wasn't such a bad guy, she mused. He looked good, he moved well. He took care of his mother and had a solid portfolio. Just because he'd bored her silly on a couple of dates didn't mean . . .

Suddenly he clamped her hard against him, shattering her mellow mood. That she could understand and certainly overlook. But, as she pressed a hand against his chest, she felt the unmistakable outline of a toothbrush he'd slipped into the inside pocket of his jacket.

As conscientious as she knew Andrew to be, she sincerely doubted he carried it with him to brush after every meal.

Before she could comment, his hands had streaked under the hem of her dress to grab her silk-covered bottom.

"Hey!" Furious, she reared back, but even as she managed to free her mouth, he was slobbering kisses over her neck and shoulder.

"Oh, Dora, Dora, I want you."

"I get the picture, Andrew." While she squirmed, one of his hands snuck up to tug her zipper. "But you're not going to have me. Now pull yourself together."

"You're so beautiful, so irresistible."

He had her pressed against the side of a chair. Dora felt her balance going and swore. "Well, resist, or I'll have to hurt you."

He only continued to mumble seductive phrases as he tumbled with her to the floor. It wasn't the indignity of being sprawled under a crazed accountant that bothered her so much. It was the fact that they'd rammed against the coffee table and sent several of her treasures crashing to the floor.

Enough was enough. Dora brought her knee up between Andrew's thighs. Even as he grunted, she popped him hard in the eye.

"Off!" she shouted, shoving at him. Groaning, he rolled, curling up like a boiled shrimp. Dora scrambled to her feet. "If you don't get up right now, I'll hit you again. I mean it."

Afraid, he heaved himself to his hands and knees. "You're crazy," he managed, and took out a snowy-white handkerchief to check his face for blood.

"You're right. Absolutely." She picked up his coat and held it out. "You're better off without me. Now run along home, Andrew. And put some ice on that eye."

"My eye." He probed at it, winced. "What am I supposed to tell Mother?"

"That you walked into a door." Impatience snapping around her, Dora helped him to his feet. "Go away, Andrew."

Struggling for dignity, he snatched his coat away from her. "I took you out to dinner. Twice."

"Consider it a bad investment. I'm sure you can find a way to deduct it." She yanked open her door just as Jed opened his across the hall. "Out! And if you ever try anything like that again, I'll blacken both your eyes."

"Crazy." Andrew scurried toward the door. "You're out of your mind."

"Come back and I'll show you crazy." She pulled off a spiked heel and hurled it like a discus. "And you're fired." The shoe hit the back of the door with a satisfying thump. Dora stood, one shoe off, one shoe on, catching her breath. The quiet sound of Jed clearing his throat had her spinning back. He was grinning. It was the first time she'd seen him grin, but she wasn't in the mood to be pleased with the way it made his usually surly face approachable.

"See something funny, Skimmerhorn?"

He thought about it. "Yeah." Because it had been a long time since he'd been quite so amused, he leaned against the doorjamb and continued to grin. "Interesting date, Conroy?"

"Fascinating." She hobbled down the hall to retrieve her shoe. Slapping it against her palm, she hobbled back. "You still here?"

"Looks like."

Dora let out a long breath, dragged a hand through her tumbled hair. "Want a drink?"

"Sure."

As she crossed the threshold into her apartment, she pulled off the other shoe and tossed them both aside. "Brandy?"

"Fine." He glanced at the broken china on the floor. That must have been the crash he'd heard. Between that and the shouting, he'd had a bad moment deciding whether or not to intervene. Even when he'd carried a badge, he'd worried more about answering a domestic dispute than collaring a pro.

He looked over at Dora while she poured brandy into snifters. Her face was still flushed, her eyes still narrowed. He had to be grateful his Seventh Cavalry routine hadn't been necessary.

"So, who was the jerk?"

"My former accountant." Dora handed Jed a snifter. "He spends the evening boring me into a coma talking about Schedule Cs and long-term capital gains, then figures he can come back here and rip my clothes off."

Jed skimmed his gaze down her glittery black dress. "Nice clothes," he decided. "Don't know why he'd waste his time with capital gains."

Dora drank again, tilted her head. "Give me a minute. I think there was supposed to be a compliment buried in there."

Jed shrugged. "Looks like he got the worst of it."

"I should have broken his nose." Pouting, she walked over and crouched to pick up broken bric-a-brac. "Look at this!" Temper began to simmer again. She held up a broken cup. "This was Derby. Eighteen-fifteen. And this ashtray was Manhattan."

Jed crouched beside her. "Expensive?"

"That's not the point. This used to be a Hazel Ware candy dish—Moroccan amethyst, with lid."

"It's trash now. Leave it be; you're going to cut yourself. Get a broom or something."

Muttering, she rose and went out to rummage in the kitchen. "He even had a toothbrush in his pocket." She came out, waving a whisk broom and dustpan like a shield and spear. "A damn toothbrush. I bet the son of a bitch was an Eagle Scout."

"Probably had a change of underwear in his overcoat pocket." Gently, Jed took the broom from her.

"I wouldn't be surprised." Dora stalked back to the kitchen for the trash can. She winced as Jed dumped a load of broken glass into the trash can. "And a couple of condoms."

"Any self-respecting Eagle Scout would have those in his wallet."

Resigned, she sat on the arm of the chair again. The theatrics, it seemed, were over. "Were you?"

"Was I what?"

"An Eagle Scout."

He dumped the last load of glass, then sent her a long look. "No. I was a delinquent. Better watch your feet over here. I might have missed some splinters."

"Thanks." Too wired to sit, Dora rose to replenish both snifters. "So what do you do now?"

"You ought to know." Jed took out a pack of cigarettes, lighted one. "I filled out an application."

"I didn't have a chance to read it. Can I have one of those?" She nodded to his cigarette. "I like to smoke in times of stress or great annoyance."

He passed her the one he'd already lighted and took out another. "Feeling better?"

"I guess." She took a quick drag, blew it out as quickly. She didn't like the taste, only the effect. "You didn't answer my question."

"What question?"

"What do you do?"

"Nothing." He smiled, but there was nothing humorous about it. "I'm independently wealthy."

"Oh. I guess it pays to be a delinquent." She took another pull on the cigarette. The smoke and the brandy were making her pleasantly dizzy. "So what do you do with yourself all day?"

"Nothing much."

"I could keep you busy."

His brow lifted. "Is that so?"

"Honest labor, Skimmerhorn. That is, if you're any good with your hands."

"I've been told I'm good enough." His fingers hovered at her back, over the zipper that had been pulled nearly to her waist. After a moment's hesitation, he zipped it neatly into place. Dora jolted, blinked.

"Ah . . . thanks. What I meant was, I need some new shelves in the storeroom. And this place always needs a little this or that."

"Your outside banister's a joke."

"Oh." Her lips moved into a pout, as though the insult had been personal. To Dora, it very nearly was. "Can you fix it?"

"Probably."

"We could work it off the rent, or I could pay you by the hour."

"I'll think about it." He was thinking about something else at the moment—about how badly he wanted to touch her. Just a brush of his thumb along the curve of her throat. He couldn't say why, but he wanted to do that, only that, and to see if the pulse at the base of that long, slender throat would throb in response.

Annoyed with himself, Jed set aside his empty snifter and moved past her to pick up the trash can. "I'll take this back for you."

"Thanks." She had to swallow. It wasn't as simple as it might have been, not with the obstruction in her throat. There was something about the way the man looked at her that sent all sorts of weird jangles through her system.

Stupid, she told herself. It had simply been a long and exhausting day. She started toward the kitchen.

"Really, thanks," she said again. "If you hadn't come in, I'd have spent an hour kicking things."

"That's all right. I liked watching you kick him."

She smiled. "Why?"

"I didn't like his suit." He stopped in the doorway to look down at her. "Pinstripes put me off."

"I'll keep that in mind." With the smile still curving her lips, she glanced up. Jed followed her gaze and studied the sprig of mistletoe over his head.

"Cute," he said, and because he was a man who'd decided to stop taking chances, started to move by her.

"Hey." Amused by the situation, and his reaction, Dora caught his arm. "Bad luck," she told him. Hiking up to her toes, she brushed her mouth lightly over his. "I don't like to risk bad luck."

He reacted instinctively, in much the same way he would have to a gunshot or a knife at the back. Thought came after action. He caught her chin in his hand to hold her still. "You're risking more than bad luck, Isadora."

And he brought his mouth down on hers in a kiss tasting of smoke and brandy and an underlying violence that had the blood draining out of her head.

Oh God, my God, was all she had a chance to think. Or perhaps she groaned it as her lips parted helplessly under his.

It was quick, seconds only, but when he released her, she rocked back down on her heels, eyes wide.

He stared down at her for another moment, cursing himself and fighting a vicious urge to do exactly what the idiot accountant had tried.

"I wouldn't try kicking me on the way out," he said softly. "Lock your door, Conroy."

He walked out, across the hall, and locked his own.

5

"What are you so cranky about?" Lea demanded. She'd popped back into the storeroom to announce a $500 sale, and had been greeted, for the third time that morning, by a short snarl.

"I'm not cranky," Dora snapped. "I'm busy." She was currently boxing up a four-piece place setting of Fire-King Dinnerware, honeysuckle pattern. "People ought to be shot for trying to cram their shopping into the last two days before Christmas. Do you realize I have to take Terri off the floor and have her deliver this across town this afternoon?"

"You could have told the customer to come back in for it."

"And I might have lost the sale," Dora tossed back. "I've had these damn dishes for three years. I'm lucky to have palmed them off on anyone."

"Now I know something's wrong." Lea crossed her arms. "Spill it."

"Nothing's wrong." Except that she hadn't been able to sleep. And there was no way, absolutely no way she was going to admit that she'd let one quick kiss tie her up into knots. "I've just got too much to do and not enough time to do it."

"But you like that, Dora," Lea pointed out.

"I've changed." Dora wrapped the last cup in newspaper. "Where's that stupid packing tape?" She turned, then stumbled back against the desk when she spotted Jed at the base of the stairs.

"Sorry." But he didn't look it. "I came down to see if you still wanted me to fix that banister."

"Banister? Oh . . . oh, well." She hated being flustered. The only thing she hated more was being wrong. "You have to get wood or something?"

"Or something." He looked over when Lea firmly cleared her throat.

"Oh, Lea, this is Jed Skimmerhorn, the new tenant. Jed, my sister, Lea."

"Nice to meet you." Lea extended a hand. "I hope you're settling in all right."

"Not much to settle. Do you want the banister fixed or not?"

"Yes, I suppose. If you're not too busy." Dora found the packing tape and kept herself occupied by sealing the carton. When the idea dawned, she went with it. "Actually, you could help me out. You've got a car, right? The Thunderbird?"

"So?"

"I have a delivery—in fact, I have three of them. I really can't spare my assistant."

Jed hooked his thumbs in his front pockets. "You want me to make deliveries?"

"If it wouldn't be a problem. You'd keep track of your gas and mileage." She offered him a sunny smile. "You might even cop a couple of tips."

He could have told her to go to hell. He wasn't sure why he didn't. "How can I resist?" He eyed, with vague dislike, the box she was sealing. "Where to?"

"It's all written down. Those are the other two right there." She nodded toward the corner of the room. "You can carry them out through the side door to your car."

Saying nothing, Jed hefted the first box and disappeared outside.

"*That's* the new tenant?" Lea whispered. Possibilities were already racing through her mind as she hurried to the door to peek through. "Who is he? What does he do?"

"I just told you who he is. His name's Skimmerhorn."

"You know what I mean." She watched Jed muscle the box into the backseat of the T-Bird, then quickly stepped back across the room. "He's coming back."

"I hope so," Dora said dryly. "He's only got one of the boxes." She lifted the second one herself and passed it to Jed when he came to the door. "They're fragile," she told him, and got a grunt in response.

"Did you see his shoulders?" Lea hissed. "John doesn't have shoulders like that in my wildest fantasies."

"Ophelia Conroy Bradshaw, shame on you. John's a wonderful guy."

"I know that. I'm nuts about him, but he doesn't have any shoulders. I mean, he's got them, of course, but they're just kind of bone and . . . God!" After studying the way Jed's Levis stretched when he leaned over the trunk of his car, she patted her heart and grinned. "It's always reassuring to know the attraction cells still operate. So what's he do?"

"About what?"

"About . . . the invoices," she said quickly. "Don't forget to give Mr. Skimmerhorn the invoices, Dora." She picked them up herself and handed them over to Jed as he stepped in to pick up the last box.

"Thanks." He gave Lea an odd look, wary of the gleam in her eye. "You want me to pick up that lumber, or what?"

"Lumber? Oh, the banister," Dora remembered. "Sure, go ahead. You can slip the bill under my door if I'm not around."

He couldn't resist. He knew he should, but he couldn't. "Another hot date?"

She smiled sweetly and yanked open the door. "Kiss my ass, Skimmerhorn."

"I've thought of it," he murmured. "I have thought of it." With that, he sauntered out.

"Tell," Lea demanded. "Tell all. Don't leave out any detail, however small or insignificant."

"There's nothing to tell. I went out with Andrew last night, and Jed met him when I was kicking him out."

"You kicked Jed out?"

"Andrew—he made a pass," Dora said with the last of her patience. "And I kicked him out. Now, if we've finished our little gossip session—"

"Almost. What does he do? Jed, I mean. He must lift weights or something to have shoulders like that."

"I never knew you had such a shoulder fixation."

"I do when they're attached to a body like that one. Let's see, he's a longshoreman."

"Nope."

"A construction worker."

"You lose the trip for two to Maui. Would you like to try for the Samsonite luggage?"

"Just tell me."

Dora had spent part of her sleepless night digging up Jed's application. One of his references had been Commissioner James L. Riker of the Philadelphia Police Department. Which made sense, she mused, since Jed's last place of employment had been the Philadelphia PD.

"He's an ex-cop."

"Ex?" Lea's eyes went wide. "Christ, he was fired from the force for taking bribes? Dealing drugs? For killing someone?"

"Put your imagination on hold, sweetie." Dora patted her sister's shoulder. "I swear, you should have been the one to take after Mom and Dad on the stage. He resigned," she said. "A few months back. According to the copious notes Dad took when he called the commissioner of police, Jed's got a pot full of commendations, and they're keeping his service revolver warm for him in hopes that he'll come back."

"Well, then why did he quit?"

"That didn't seem to be anyone's business," she said primly, but she was just as curious, and just as annoyed as Lea that their father hadn't asked. "Game over." She held up her hand to ward off another spate of questions. "If we don't get back inside to help Terri, she'll make my life a living hell."

"All right, but I feel good knowing you've got a cop right across the hall. That should keep you out of trouble." She stopped dead, goggle-eyed. "Oh God, Dory, do you think he was carrying a gun?"

"I don't think he'll need one to deliver dinnerware." With this, Dora shoved her sister through the door.

Under any other circumstances, DiCarlo would have felt foolish sitting in an elegant reception area holding a cheap statue in his lap. In this particular reception area, decorated with muted Impressionist prints and Erté sculptures, he didn't feel foolish at all. He felt scared, bone scared.

He hadn't really minded the murder. Not that he enjoyed killing like his cousin Guido, but he hadn't minded it. DiCarlo looked at putting a small-caliber bullet between Porter's eyes as self-defense.

But he'd had a lot to worry about on the long flight from east to west coast. Considering his string of bad luck, he wondered whether by some twisted hook of fate he had the wrong statue warming in his lap. It certainly looked like the one he'd seen packed into the crate at Premium. In a just world, there couldn't be two such ugly porcelain creations in the same small town.

"Mr. DiCarlo?" The receptionist said. "Mr. Finley will see you now."

"Ah, right. Sure." DiCarlo rose, hooking the statue under his arm and straightening the knot of his tie with his free hand. He followed the blonde to the double mahogany doors and worked on fixing a pleasant smile on his face.

Finley didn't rise from behind his desk. He enjoyed watching DiCarlo nervously cross the ocean of white carpet. He smiled, coldly, noting the faint beading of sweat over DiCarlo's upper lip.

"Mr. DiCarlo, you have tidied up in the great state of Virginia?"

"Everything there is taken care of."

"Excellent." He gestured to his desk so that DiCarlo set the statue down. "And this is all you've brought me?"

"I also have a list of the other merchandise. And all the locations." At the wave of Finley's fingers, DiCarlo dived into his pocket for the list. "As you see, there were only four other buyers, and two of them are also dealers. I think it should be simple enough to go right into those shops and buy back that merchandise."

"You think?" Finley said softly. "If you could think, Mr. DiCarlo, my merchandise would already be in my possession. However," he continued when DiCarlo remained silent, "I'm willing to give you the opportunity to redeem yourself."

He rose then and ran a fingertip over the overly sweet female face of the statue. "An unfortunate piece of work. Quite hideous, don't you agree?"

"Yes, sir."

"And this man, this Ashworth, paid in good coin for it. Amazing, isn't it, what people will find appealing. One has only to look to see the lines are awkward, the color poor, the material inferior. Ah well. 'Beauty's but skin deep.' " He picked up an unused marble white ashtray from his desk and decapitated the woman.

DiCarlo, who had only hours before cold-bloodedly murdered two men, jolted when the ashtray smashed the second head away. He watched, his nerves jumping, as Finley systematically broke away limbs.

"An ugly cocoon," Finley murmured, "to protect sheer beauty." From inside the torso of the figurine he pulled a small object wrapped in layers of heavy bubble plastic. Delicately, he unwrapped it, and the sound he made was like that of a man undressing a lover.

What DiCarlo saw looked like a gold cigarette lighter, heavily ornate and studded with some sort of stones. To him it was hardly more attractive than the statue that had hidden it.

"Do you know what this is, Mr. DiCarlo?"

"Ah, no, sir."

"It is an etui." Finley laughed then, caressing the gold. For that moment, he was supremely happy—a child with a new toy, a man with a new lover. "Which tells you nothing, of course. This small, ornamental case was used to hold manicure sets, or sewing implements, perhaps a buttonhook or a snuff spoon. A pretty little fancy that went out of fashion toward the end of the nineteenth century. This one is more intricate than most, as it's gold, and these stones, Mr. DiCarlo, are rubies. There are initials etched into the base." Smiling dreamily he turned it over. "It was a gift from Napoleon to his Josephine. And now it belongs to me."

"That's great, Mr. Finley." DiCarlo was relieved that he'd brought the right figurine, and that his employer seemed so pleased.

"You think so?" Finley's emerald eyes glittered. "This bauble is only a portion of what is mine, Mr. DiCarlo. Oh, I'm pleased to have it, but it reminds me that my shipment is incomplete. A shipment, I might add, that has taken me more than eight months to accumulate, another two months to have transported. That's nearly a year of my time, which is quite valuable to me, not to mention the expense." He hefted the ashtray again and swung it through the delicate folds of milady's gown. Thin shards of porcelain shot like tiny missiles through the air. "You can understand my distress, can you not?"

"Yes, sir." Cool sweat slipped clammily down DiCarlo's back. "Naturally."

"Then we'll have to see about getting it back. Sit down, Mr. DiCarlo."

With an unsteady hand, DiCarlo brushed porcelain splinters off the buttery leather of a chair. He sat cautiously on the edge of his seat.

"The holidays make me magnanimous, Mr. DiCarlo." Finley took his own seat and continued to caress the etui in intimate little circles. "Tomorrow is Christmas Eve. You have plans, I imagine."

"Well, actually, yes. My family, you see..."

"Families." Finley's face lit up with a smile. "There is nothing like family around the holidays. I have none myself, but that is unimportant. Since you've managed to bring me one small portion of my property, so quickly, I hate to take you away from your family at Christmas." Keeping the etui trapped between his palms, he folded his hands. "I'll give you until the first of the year. Generous, I know, but as I said, the holidays. They make me sentimental. I'll want everything that is mine by January one—no, no, make it the second." His smile spread and widened. "I trust you won't disappoint me."

"No, sir."

"Naturally, I'll expect progress reports, holiday or no. You can reach me here, or on my private number. Do stay in touch, Mr. DiCarlo. If I don't hear from you at regular intervals, I'd have to come looking for you myself. We wouldn't want that."

"No, sir." DiCarlo had an uncomfortable image of being hunted by a rabid wolf. "I'll get right on it."

"Excellent. Oh, and have Barbara make a copy of this list for me before you go, will you?"

Jed couldn't say why he was doing it. He'd had no business going down to the shop that morning in the first place. He was perfectly content to spend his days working out in the gym, lifting weights in his own apartment, catching up on his reading. God knew what crazy impulse had had him wandering downstairs and somehow volunteering to make Dora's deliveries.

Of course, he remembered with what was almost a smile, he had gotten tipped pretty well at that. A few bucks, and in one memorable case a brightly colored tin filled with homemade Christmas cookies.

It hadn't been such a big deal, and it had been interesting to see how much more enthusiastically you were greeted when you knocked on someone's door carrying a box rather than a badge.

He could have crossed the whole experience off as a kind of experiment, but now he was standing out in the cold replacing a banister. The fact that he was enjoying it on some deep, elemental level made him feel like an idiot.

He was forced to work outside because Dora didn't have ten feet of unoccupied space anywhere in her building. Since her idea of tools had run to a single screwdriver and a ball peen hammer with a taped handle, he'd had to drop by Brent's to borrow some. Of course, Mary Pat had grilled him on everything from his eating habits to his love life while plying him with Snickerdoodles. It had taken him nearly an hour to escape with his sanity and a power saw.

The events of the day had taught Jed one important lesson: He would keep to himself from this point on, just as he had planned. When a man didn't like people to begin with, there was no rational reason to mix with them.

At least there was no one to bother him in the rear of the building, and he enjoyed working with his hands, liked the feel of wood under them. Once, he'd considered adding a small workshop onto the back of the house in Chestnut Hill. A place where he could have tinkered and built when the job gave him time. But that had been before Donny Speck. Before the investigation that had become an obsession.

And, of course, it had been before Elaine had paid the price.

Before Jed could switch off his mind, he saw it again. The silver Mercedes sedan sitting sedately under the carport. He saw the dull gleam of pearls around Elaine's neck and remembered inanely that they had been a birthday gift from the first of her three husbands. He saw her eyes, the same brilliant blue as his own—perhaps the only family trait they had shared—lift and look curiously in his direction. He saw the faint annoyance in those eyes and saw himself racing across the manicured lawn, between the well-tended rosebushes that had smelled almost violently of summer.

The sun had glinted off the chrome, speared into his eyes. A bird high up in one of the trio of apple trees had trilled insanely.

Then the explosion had ripped through the air with a hot fist that had punched Jed back, sent him flying away toward the roses, where the petals were sheared off by the force of the blast.

The silver Mercedes was a ball of flame with a belch of black smoke stinking upward into the summer sky. He thought he heard her scream. It could have been the screech of rending metal. He hoped it had been. He hoped she'd felt nothing after her fingers had twisted the key in the ignition and triggered the bomb.

Swearing, Jed attacked the new banister with Brent's power sander. It was over. Elaine was dead and couldn't be brought back. Donny Speck was dead, thank Christ. And however much Jed might have wished it, he couldn't kill the man again.

And he was exactly where he wanted to be. Alone.

"Ho, ho, ho."

Distracted by the hearty voice behind him, Jed switched off the sander. He turned, his eyes narrowed behind his tinted aviator glasses as he studied, with equal parts annoyance and curiosity, the pink-cheeked Santa.

"You're a couple days early, aren't you?"

"Ho, ho, ho," Santa said again, and patted his comfortable belly. "Looks like you could use a little Christmas cheer, son."

Resigned to the interruption, Jed took out a cigarette. "Mr. Conroy, right?" He watched Santa's face fall. "It's the eyes," Jed told him, and struck a match. They were Dora's eyes, Jed thought. Big and brown and full of secret jokes.

"Oh." Quentin considered, then brightened. "I suppose a policeman is trained to see past disguises, the same way an actor is trained to assume them. I have, of course, played many upholders of law and order in my career."

"Right."

"In keeping with the season, I've been entertaining the children at Tidy Tots Day Care." He stroked his silky white beard. "A small engagement, but a satisfying one, as it gives me the opportunity to play one of the world's most beloved characters to an audience of true believers. Children are actors, you see, and actors, children."

Amused despite himself, Jed nodded. "I'll take your word for it."

"I see Izzy's put you to work."

"Izzy?"

"My darling daughter." Quentin wiggled his eyebrows and winked. "Pretty thing, isn't she?"

"She's all right."

"Cooks, too. Don't know where she gets it from. Not her mother." Conspiratorily, Quentin leaned closer. "Not to complain, but boiling an egg is a culinary triumph for her. Of course, she has other talents."

"I'm sure she does. Dora's inside."

"Naturally. A dedicated businesswoman, my firstborn, not at all like the rest of us in that aspect—though, of course, she could have had a brilliant career on the stage. Truly brilliant," he said with some regret. "But she chose the world of retail. Genes are a peculiar thing, don't you think?"

"I haven't given it a lot of thought." A lie, he thought. A basic one. He'd spent a great deal of his life thinking about inherited traits. "Listen, I need to finish this before I lose the light."

"Why don't I give you a hand?" Quentin said with the unexpected streak of practicality that made him a good director as well as an actor.

Jed studied the padded belly, the red suit and flowing white cotton beard. "Don't you have elves to handle this kind of thing?"

Quentin laughed merrily, his booming baritone echoing on the windy air. "Everything's unionized these days, boy. Can't get the little buggers to do anything not in the contract."

Jed's lips quirked as he turned on the sander again. "Once I finish here, you can help me put it up."

"Delighted."

A patient man, Quentin sat on the bottom step. He'd always liked to watch manual labor. "Watch" being the key word. Fortunately, a modest inheritance had kept him from starving while pursuing his acting career. He'd met his wife of thirty years during a production of *The Tempest,* he as Sebastian and she as Miranda. They had entered the brave new world of matrimony and had traveled from stage to stage, with considerable success, until settling in Philadelphia and founding the Liberty Players.

Now, at the comfortable age of fifty-three—forty-nine on his résumé—he had whipped the Liberty Players into a respected troupe who performed everything from Ibsen to Neil Simon at a steady profit.

Perhaps because his life had been easy, Quentin believed in happily ever after. He'd seen his younger daughter tidily wed, was watching his son staunchly carrying the family name onto the stage. That left only Dora.

Quentin had decided that this healthy young man with the unreadable eyes was the perfect solution. Smiling to himself, he pulled a flask out of Santa's pillow belly, took a quick nip. Then another.

"Well done, boy," Quentin said half an hour later as he heaved himself up to pat the banister. "Smooth as a lady's cheek. And it was a pleasure to watch you work. How does one secure it in place?"

"Take a hold," Jed suggested. "Carry your end up to the top."

"This is fascinating." The silver bells on Quentin's boots jangled as he climbed the stairs. "Not that I'm a complete novice, you see. I have assisted in the building of sets. We once constructed a rather spiffy Jolly Roger for a production of *Peter Pan*." Quentin twirled his white moustache, and a look of menace gleamed in his eye. "I played Hook, naturally."

"I'd have bet on it. Watch yourself." Making use of Brent's electric drill, Jed secured banister to post. Throughout the procedure, Quentin kept up a running conversation. Jed realized it was as easy to tune him out as it was to tune out the background music in a dentist's office.

"As easy as that." Back at the base of the steps, Quentin shook the rail and beamed. "Steady as a rock, too. I hope my Izzy appreciates you." He gave Jed a friendly slap on the back. "Why don't you join us for Christmas dinner? My Ophelia puts on an impressive production."

"I've got plans."

"Ah, of course." Quentin's easy smile didn't reveal his thoughts. He'd done his research on Jed Skimmerhorn much more thoroughly than anyone knew. He was well aware that Jed had no family other than a grandmother. "Perhaps New Year's, then. We always throw a party at the theater. The Liberty. You'd be welcome."

"Thanks. I'll think about it."

"In the meantime, I think we both deserve a little reward for our labors."

He pulled out the flask again, winking at Jed as he poured whiskey into the silver top. He handed the makeshift cup to Jed.

Since he couldn't think of any reason not to, Jed tossed back the whiskey. He managed to choke back a gasp. The stuff was atomic.

"By God!" Quentin slapped Jed's back again. "I like seeing a man drink like a man. Have another. Here's to full white breasts that give a man's head sweet rest."

Jed drank again and let the whiskey work up a nice buffer against the cold. "Are you sure Santa should be drinking?"

"Dear boy, how do you think we get through those long, cold nights at the North Pole?

"We'll be doing *South Pacific* next. Nice change, all those palm trees. We try to fit a couple of musicals into our schedule each year. Crowd pleasers. Have to have Izzy bring you by."

He tipped more into Jed's cup and began a rousing rendition of "There Is Nothin' Like a Dame."

It must be the whiskey, Jed decided. That would explain why he was sitting outside in the cold at dusk, finding nothing particularly odd about watching Santa belt out a show tune.

As he downed another capful, he heard the door open behind him and looked around lazily to see Dora standing at the top of the steps, her hands fisted on her hips.

Christ, she had great legs, he thought.

She spared Jed one withering glance. "I should have known you'd encourage him."

"I was minding my own business."

"Sitting on the back steps drinking whiskey with a man in a Santa suit? Some business."

Because his tongue had thickened considerably, Jed enunciated with care. "I fixed the banister."

"Bully for you." Dora strode down the steps and caught her father's arm just as Quentin was executing a fancy spin. "Show's over."

"Izzy!" Delighted, Quentin kissed her lustily and gave her a bear hug. "Your young man and I were seeing to carpentry repairs."

"I can see that. You both look very busy at the moment. Let's go inside, Dad." She took the flask and shoved it into Jed's hand. "I'll come back for you," she said under her breath, and dragged her father upstairs.

"I was minding my own business," Jed said again, and meticulously capped the flask before slipping it into his back pocket. By the time Dora returned, he was loading up Brent's tools with the care of a man packing fine china.

"So." He slammed the trunk, leaned heavily against it. "Where's Santa?"

"Sleeping. We have one rule around here, Skimmerhorn. No drinking on the job."

Jed straightened, then wisely braced himself against the car again. "I was finished." Blearily, he gestured toward the banister. "See?"

"Yeah." She sighed, shook her head. "I shouldn't blame you. He's irresistible. Come on, I'll take you upstairs."

"I'm not drunk."

"You're plowed, Skimmerhorn. Your body knows it, it just hasn't gotten through to your brain yet."

"I'm not drunk," he said again, but didn't object when she slipped an arm around his waist to lead him up the steps. "I made fifteen bucks and two dozen cookies on the deliveries."

"That's nice."

"Pretty good cookies." He bumped into her as they passed through the doorway. "Christ, you smell good."

"I bet you say that to all your landlords. Got your keys?"

"Yeah." He fumbled for them, gave up and leaned against the wall. Served him right, he thought, for drinking that hard with only a few Snickerdoodles in his system.

Sighing, Dora slid her hand into his front pocket. She encountered a hard thigh and loose change.

"Try the other one," he suggested.

She looked up, caught the easy and surprisingly charming smile. "Nope. If you enjoyed that, you're not as drunk as I thought. Fish them out yourself."

"I told you I wasn't drunk." He found them, then wondered how he was supposed to fit the key into the lock when the floor was weaving. Dora guided his hand. "Thanks."

"It's the least I can do. Can you get yourself to bed?"

He braced a hand on the doorjamb. "Let's get this straight, Conroy. I don't want to sleep with you."

"Well, that certainly puts me in my place."

"You got complication all over you, baby. Those big, brown eyes and that tough little body. I just want to be alone."

"I guess that kills any hope I've been harboring that I'll bear your children. But don't worry, I'll get over it." She steered him toward the couch, shoved him down, then propped up his feet.

"I don't want you," he told her as she pried off his boots. "I don't want anyone."

"Okay." She looked around for a blanket, and settled on a couple of towels he'd hung over his bench press. "Here you go, nice and cozy." She tucked them neatly around him. He looked awfully cute, she thought, all drunk and surly and heavy-eyed. Going with impulse, she leaned over and kissed the end of his nose.

"Go to sleep, Skimmerhorn. You're going to feel like hell tomorrow."

"Go away," he muttered, closed his eyes and tuned out.

6

She was right. He felt terrible. The last thing Jed wanted was someone pounding on his door while he was trying to drown himself in the shower. Cursing, he twisted off the taps, wrapped a towel around his waist and dripped his way to the door. He yanked it open.

"What the hell do you want?"

"Good morning, Skimmerhorn." Dora breezed in with a wicker basket over her arm. "I see you're your usual bright and cheerful self."

She was wearing some sort of short-skirted outfit in vivid blues and gold that made his eyes throb. "Get lost."

"My, we are feeling nasty this morning." Unoffended, she unpacked the basket. Inside was a red plaid thermos, a mason jar filled with some sort of vile-looking orange liquid and a snowy-white napkin folded around two flaky croissants. "Since my father instigated this little affair, I thought I should see to your welfare this morning. We'll need a glass, a cup and saucer, a plate." When he didn't move, she tilted her head. "Fine, I'll get them. Why don't you go put some clothes on? You made it clear that you're not interested in me on a physical level, and the sight of your damp, half-naked body might send me into an unbridled sexual frenzy."

A muscle in his jaw twitched as he ground his teeth. "Cute, Conroy. Real cute." But he turned and strode off into the bedroom. When he came back wearing gray sweats torn at the knee, she'd set a neat breakfast on his picnic table.

"Had any aspirin yet?"

"I was working on it."

"These first, then." She offered him three pills. "Take them with this. Just gulp it down."

He scowled at the sickly orange liquid she'd poured into a tumbler. "What the hell is it?"

"Salvation. Trust me."

Because he doubted he could feel much worse, he swallowed the pills with two big gulps of Dora's remedy. "Christ. It tastes like embalming fluid."

"Oh, I imagine it's the same principle. Still, I can guarantee the results. Dad swears by it, and believe me, he's the expert. Try the coffee—it won't do much for the hangover, but you'll be fully awake to enjoy it."

Because his eyes were threatening to fall out, he pressed the heels of his hands against them. "What was in that flask?"

"Quentin Conroy's secret weapon. He has a still in the basement where he experiments like a mad scientist. Dad likes to drink."

"Now there's news."

"I know I should disapprove, but it's hard to. He doesn't hurt anyone. I'm not even sure he hurts himself." She broke off a corner of one of the croissants and nibbled. "He doesn't get surly or arrogant or nasty with it. He'd never consider getting behind the wheel of a car—or operating heavy machinery." She shrugged. "Some men hunt or collect stamps. Dad drinks. Feeling better?"

"I'll live."

"That's fine, then. I've got to go open up. You'd be amazed at how many people shop on Christmas Eve." She started out, paused with her hand on the knob. "Oh, and the banister looks good. Thanks. Let me know when you feel up to hammering together some shelves. And don't worry." She flashed him a smile. "I don't want to sleep with you either."

Dora closed the door quietly and hummed her way down the hall.

DiCarlo was feeling fine. His luck was back; the rented Porsche was tearing up 95. Neatly boxed on the seat beside him rode a bronze eagle and a reproduction of the Statue of Liberty, both easily purchased from a novelty shop just outside of Washington, D.C.

It had gone slick as spit, DiCarlo thought now. He had walked into the shop, done some nominal browsing, then had walked out again, the proud owner of two pieces of American kitsch. After a quick detour into Philadelphia to pick up the next two items on his list, he would head into New York. All things being equal, he would make it home by nine o'clock, with plenty of time for holiday celebrations.

The day after Christmas he would take up his schedule again. At this pace, he figured he would have all of Mr. Finley's merchandise in hand well before deadline.

He might even earn a bonus out of it.

Tapping his fingers along with the dance track, he dialed Finley's private number on the car phone.

"Yes."

"Mr. Finley. DiCarlo."

"And do you have something of interest to tell me?"

"Yes, sir." He all but sang it. "I've recovered two more items from D.C."

"The transactions went smoothly?"

"Smooth as silk. I'm on my way to Philadelphia now. Two more items are in a shop there. I should arrive by three at the latest."

"Then I'll wish you Merry Christmas now, Mr. DiCarlo. I'll be difficult to reach until the twenty-sixth. Naturally, if you have something to report, you'll leave a message with Winesap."

"I'll keep in touch, Mr. Finley. Enjoy your holiday."

Finley hung up the phone but continued to stand on his balcony, watching the smog clog the air over LA. The etui hung around his neck on a fine gold chain.

DiCarlo did arrive in Philadelphia by three. His luck was holding steady as he walked into Dora's Parlor fifteen minutes before closing. The first thing he noticed was a statuesque redhead wearing a green elf's cap.

Terri Starr, Dora's assistant, and a devoted member of the Liberty Players, beamed at DiCarlo.

"Merry Christmas," she said in a voice as clear as holiday bells. "You've just caught us. We're closing early today."

DiCarlo tried out a sheepish smile. "I bet you hate us eleventh-hour shoppers."

"Are you kidding? I love them." She'd already spotted the Porsche at the curb and was calculating ending the business day with a last whopping sale. "Are you looking for anything in particular?"

"Actually, yes." He took a look around the shop, hoping he'd spot either the painting or the china hound quickly. "I'm on my way home, and I have an aunt who collects statues of animals. Dogs in particular."

"I might be able to help you out." Topping six foot in her spiked heels, Terri moved through the shop like a staff sergeant inspecting troops. She'd sized up DiCarlo's suit and overcoat as well as his car, and led him toward the jade.

"This is one of my favorite pieces." She opened a curved glass cabinet and took out an apple-green carved Foo dog, one of their most expensive objects. "Gorgeous, isn't he?"

"Yes, but I'm afraid my aunt's tastes aren't quite so sophisticated." He let amusement play around his eyes. "You know how these little ladies are."

"Are you kidding? You can't run a curio shop and not know. Let's see, then." With some regret Terri replaced the jade. "We've got a couple of nice cocker spaniels in plaster."

"I'll take a look. Would it be all right if I just browsed around? I know you'd like to get out of here, and I might see something that strikes me as being Aunt Maria."

"You go right ahead. Take your time."

DiCarlo saw the plaster cockers. He saw cloisonné poodles and blown-glass retrievers. There were plastic dalmations and brass Chihuahuas. But nowhere did he see the china hound.

He kept his eye peeled for the painting as well. There were dozens of framed prints, faded portraits, advertising posters. There was no abstract in an ebony frame.

"I think I've found the perfect—" Terri backed up two steps when DiCarlo whirled around. She was a woman who prided herself on reading expressions. For a moment there, she'd thought she'd read murder in his. "I—sorry. Did I startle you?"

His smile came so quickly, wiping out the icy gleam in his eyes, she decided she'd imagined it. "Yes, you did. Guess my mind was wandering. And what have we here?"

"It's Staffordshire pottery, a mama English sheepdog and her puppy. It's kind of sweet, isn't it?"

"Right up Aunt Maria's alley." DiCarlo kept the pleasant smile in place even after he'd spotted the four-figure price tag. "I think she'd love it," he said, hoping to buy time by having it wrapped. "I had something a little different in my mind, but this is Aunt Maria all over."

"Cash or charge?"

"Charge." He pulled out a credit card. "She used to have this mutt, you see," he continued as he followed Terri to the counter. "A brown-and-white spotted dog who curled up on the rug and slept twenty hours out of twenty-four. Aunt Maria adored that dog. I was hoping to find something that looked like him."

"That's so sweet." Terri nestled the Staffordshire in tissue paper. "You must be a very considerate nephew."

"Well, Aunt Maria helped raise me."

"It's too bad you weren't in a few days ago. We had a piece very much like you're talking about. In china, a spotted hound, curled up asleep. It was only in the shop a day before we sold it."

"Sold it?" DiCarlo said between smiling teeth. "That's too bad."

"It wasn't nearly as fine a piece as the one you've just bought, Mr.... DiCarlo," she added after a glance at his credit card. "Believe me, your aunt's going to love you come Christmas morning."

"I'm sure you're right. I notice you also carry art."

"Some. Mostly posters and old family portraits from estate sales."

"Nothing modern, then? I'm doing some redecorating."

"Afraid not. We've got some stuff piled in the storeroom in back, but I haven't noticed any paintings."

While she wrote up his bill, DiCarlo drummed his fingers on the counter and considered. He had to find out who had bought the dog. If it hadn't been broad daylight, with a wide display window at his back, he might have stuck his gun under the clerk's pretty chin and forced her to look up the information for him.

Of course, then he'd have to kill her.

He glanced at the window behind him. There wasn't much traffic, vehicular or pedestrian. But he shook his head. A young girl wrapped in a parka zoomed by on Rollerblades. It wasn't worth the risk.

"Just sign here." Terri passed him the sales slip and his card. "You're all set, Mr. DiCarlo. I hope you and your aunt have a terrific Christmas."

Because she watched him through the window, DiCarlo set the box carefully in the trunk of the car, then waved cheerfully before climbing in. He slid smoothly away from the curb.

He'd go somewhere for a late lunch. When it was dark, when the shop was empty, he'd be back.

Dora gave Jed's door her best businesslike rap. She knew he was going to growl at her—it couldn't be helped. The fact was, she'd gotten used to the way he snarled and spat. She didn't look forward to it, but she'd gotten used to it.

He didn't disappoint her.

His short-sleeved sweatshirt was damp with sweat. His forearms glistened with it. She might have taken a moment to admire the basic masculinity, but she was too busy studying the scowl on his face.

Jed gripped the ends of the towel he'd hooked around his neck. "What do you want now?"

"Sorry to disturb you." She peeked over his shoulder and spotted his weight equipment scattered over the living area. "When you're so involved with building muscles, but my phone's out of order. I need to make a call."

"There's a phone booth on the corner."

"You're such a sweet guy, Skimmerhorn. Why hasn't some lucky woman snapped you up?"

"I beat them off with a stick."

"Oh, I bet you do. Be a pal. It's a local call."

For a minute, she thought he was going to shut the door in her face. Again. But he swung the door wider and stepped back. "Make it fast," he told her, and stalked into the kitchen.

To give her privacy? Dora wondered. Hardly. Her judgment proved correct when he came back in glugging Gatorade from the bottle. Dora juggled the phone, swore softly, then dropped the receiver back on the hook.

"Yours is out, too."

"Not so surprising, since we're in the same building." He'd left his door open, as she had. From her apartment he could hear the strains of music. Christmas music this time. But it was something that sounded like a medieval choir, and intrigued rather than annoyed.

Unfortunately, Dora had exactly the same effect on him.

"You always dress like that to talk on the phone?"

She was wearing a slithery jumpsuit in silver with strappy spiked heels. A chain of stars hung at each ear. "I have a couple of parties to drop in on. How about you? Are you spending Christmas Eve lifting weights?"

"I don't like parties."

"No?" She shrugged and the silver silk whispered invitingly at the movement. "I love them. The noise and the food and the gossip. Of course, I enjoy having conversations with other human beings, so that helps."

"Since I haven't got any wassail handy to offer you, why don't you run along?" He tossed the towel aside and picked up a barbell. "Make sure your date doesn't hit the Christmas punch."

"I'm not going with anyone, and since I don't want to have to worry about how often I dip into the Christmas punch, I was calling a cab." She sat on the arm of the couch, frowning as she watched Jed lift his weights. She shouldn't have felt sorry for him, she mused. He was the last person on earth that inspired sympathy. And yet she hated to imagine him spending the evening alone, with barbells. "Why don't you come with me?"

The long, silent look he sent her had her hurrying on.

"It's not a proposition, Skimmerhorn. Just a couple of parties where you hang out and make nice."

"I don't make nice."

"I can see you're rusty, but it is Christmas Eve. A time of fellowship. Good will among men. You might have heard of it."

"I heard rumors."

Dora waited a beat. "You forgot bah-humbug."

"Take off, Conroy."

"Well, that's a step up from this morning. People will say we're in love." She sighed, rose. "Enjoy your sweat, Skimmerhorn, and the coal I'm sure Santa's going to leave in your stocking." She stopped, tilted her head. "What's that noise?"

"What noise?"

"That." Her eyes narrowed in concentration. "Oh boy. Don't tell me we *do* have mice."

He lowered the barbell and listened. "Someone down in the shop."

"What?"

"In the shop," he repeated. "The sound carries up through the vent. Don't you know your own building, Conroy?"

"I'm not over here that much, and not when the shop's open." She started to dismiss it, then froze. "But the shop's not open." Her voice had lowered to a stage whisper. "There's no one down there."

"Somebody is."

"No." Her hand slid up to rub at the nerves in her throat. "We closed hours ago. Terri left by three-thirty."

"So she came back."

"On Christmas Eve? She's giving one of the parties I'm going to." Dora's heels clicked smartly on the floor as she crossed to the door.

"Where are you going?"

"Downstairs, of course. Somebody must have cut the alarm and broken in. If they think they can gather up a sack of goodies from my shop, they're in for a surprise."

He swore, ripely, then took her arm, pushed her into a chair. "Stay there." He strode into the bedroom. Dora was still working out what name to call him when he walked back in, carrying a .38.

Her eyes rounded. "What's that?"

"It's a parasol. Stay in here. Lock the door."

"But—but—"

"Stay." Jed closed the door behind him. It was probably her assistant, he thought as he moved quickly, silently down the hall. Or her sister, who'd forgotten some package she'd hidden. Or the old man, looking for a bottle.

But there was too much cop in him to take chances. And too much cop to dismiss the fact that the phones were out, and that the sounds coming through the vent had been stealthy, rather than careless.

He reached the door that led down to the storeroom, eased it open. There was no generous spill of light from below. He heard a sound—a drawer closing.

Did she keep cash down there? he wondered, and swore under his breath. Probably. In some old-time canister or cookie jar.

A movement behind him had him braced and pivoting. And swearing again. Dora was three steps back, her eyes swallowing her face, and a barbell hefted in one hand.

Jed jerked a thumb. She shook her head. He curled his hand into a fist. She lifted her chin.

"Idiot," he muttered.

"Same goes."

"Stay back, for Christ's sake."

He started down, jerking still when the third step groaned under his foot. There was a rapid series of pops, and the wall inches away from his face spat plaster.

Jed crouched, took the rest of the steps in a sprint, rolling when he hit bottom and coming up, weapon drawn in time to see the rear door slam shut. He heard Dora clattering down after him, shouted for her to stay put.

He hit the door at a run, went through low. The cold air bit into his lungs like slivers of ice. But his blood was hot. The sound of running footsteps echoed off to the right. Ignoring Dora's frantic demands to stop, he raced after them.

It was instinct and half a lifetime of training. After he'd run about two blocks, he heard the roar of an engine, the squeal of tires. He knew he'd lost his quarry.

He ran on for another half a block, on the off chance that he could catch a glimpse of the car. When he returned to Dora he found her standing in the center of the small gravel lot, shivering.

"Get inside."

Her fear had already turned to anger. "Your face is bleeding," she snapped.

Her hands slid away from his arm. The color the cold had slapped into her cheeks drained away. Jed watched her pupils dilate.

"If you faint on me, I'm really going to get pissed off." He grabbed her chin, gave her head a little shake. "It's over now. He's gone. Okay?"

"Your face is bleeding," she said dully.

"You already told me that."

"He could have shot you."

"I could have been spending the night with an exotic dancer. Shows you how far 'could have' is from reality. How about that quarter?"

"I don't . . ." Automatically, she checked her pockets. "I have a phone in my van."

"Of course you do." He strode over to her van, shaking his head when he found it unlocked.

"There's nothing in it," she began, huffing. It pleased him to see her color was back.

"Except a phone, a stereo tape deck." He lifted a brow. "A Fuzzbuster."

"It was a gift." She folded her arms.

"Right." He punched in Brent's number and waited two rings.

"Merry Christmas!"

"Hi, Mary Pat." He could hear children yelling in the background over a forceful recording of "Jingle Bells." "I need to talk to Brent for a minute."

"Jed. You're not calling to make some lame excuse about tomorrow? I swear I'll come drag you out here myself."

"No, I'll be there."

"Two o'clock sharp."

"I'll set my watch. MP, is Brent around?"

"Right here making his world-famous sausage stuffing. Hang on."

There was a clatter. "Jingle Bells" gave way to "Rudolf." "Hey, Captain. Merry, merry."

"Sorry to bust in on your cooking, but we had a little problem over here."

"Jody, let go of that cat! What sort of problem?"

"Break-in. The shop below the apartment."

"They get anything?"

"I have to have her check." He brushed wind-tossed hair from his face and watched Dora shiver. "Took a couple of pops at me. Used a silencer."

"Shit. You hit?"

"No." He checked his cheek again. The bleeding was nearly stopped. "He had a car close. From the sound of the engine, it wasn't an economy."

"Sit tight, Kimo Sabe. I'll call it in and be on my way."

"Thanks." He hung up and looked at Dora, who was dancing from foot to foot in a fruitless effort to keep warm. "Maybe you'd better break out that brandy again. Come on." Because her hands were frozen, he took them, warming them automatically as they walked back to the shop. "You can take a look around, see if anything is missing."

"I'm not supposed to touch anything, right?"

"You keep up with the cop shows."

"Can we close the door?"

"Sure." He took a brief glance at the jimmied lock, then closed out the cold. After he'd switched on the lights, he simply stood and absorbed.

The storeroom was crammed. On one wall, boxes were stacked from floor to ceiling. Shelves held uncrated merchandise in no sort of order he could discern. There were two four-drawer file cabinets shoved into a corner. The top of each was piled with more boxes.

There was a desk, which seemed to be an island of sanity. It held a phone, a lamp, a porcelain pitcher stuffed with pencils and pens, and a bust of Beethoven, which served as a paperweight.

"Nothing's gone," she said.

"How can you tell?"

"I know my inventory. You must have scared him off." She walked over to the shelves and tapped what looked to Jed to be an old perfume or lotion bottle. "This Daum Nancy is worth well over a thousand. This Castelli plate nearly that much. And this." She took down a box with a picture of a child's toy on it.

"Nando? A kid's robot?"

"Boxed, it's worth easily two thousand to a collector." She sniffed and replaced it.

"And you just leave this stuff out?"

"I have a security system. Had one," she muttered. "I can hardly drag all my stock into a vault every night."

"What about cash?"

"We deposit everything but about a hundred in small bills and change every night." She walked over to the desk, opened the top drawer. She took out an envelope, flipped through the bills inside. "Here it is. Like I said, you must have scared him off." She stepped away and heard a paper rustle under her foot. Bending down, she scooped it up. "Charge ticket," she told Jed. "Funny, this would have been filed."

"Let's see." He snatched it out of her hand. "Timothy O'Malley. Five-fifty and tax on December twenty-first. For saltcellars?"

"His wife collects."

"Five hundred for salt shakers?"

"Cellars," Dora corrected, and snatched the receipt back. "Peasant."

"Bloodsucker."

Unamused, she turned to replace the receipt in its file. "Look at this!" she demanded. "These drawers are a mess."

He came to peer over her shoulder. "They're not supposed to be?"

"Of course not. I keep very careful records. The IRS terrifies me the same as they terrify all good Americans. And Lea spent a week purging and updating these files last month."

"So he was after something in your files. What do you keep in here?"

"Nothing of value. Receipts, invoices, mailing lists, inventory printout, delivery sheets. Business stuff." Baffled, she ran a hand through her hair. The stars dangling from her ears sparkled in the light. "There's no reason for anyone to break in here for paperwork. A crazed IRS agent? A psychopathic accountant?"

As soon as she'd said it, Dora bit her tongue.

"What was that jerk's name the other night?"

"Don't be ridiculous. Andrew would never do anything like this."

"Didn't you say he was an accountant?"

"Well, yes, but—"

"And you fired him?"

"That's hardly any reason to—"

"Andrew what?"

She blew out a long breath, fluttering her bangs. "I'll give you his name, his address, his phone number, then you can go do cop things like harass him for his alibi on the night in question."

"I'm not a cop."

"If it looks like a cop, sounds like a cop"—she sniffed at him—"smells like a cop . . ."

"How would you know what a cop smells like?"

She angled her chin. "Gun oil and sweat. Come to think of it, you even taste like a cop."

"How's that?"

"I don't know." Very deliberately she dropped her gaze to his mouth, then lifted it slowly. "Tough, authoritative, just a little bit mean."

"I can be meaner." He edged closer so that she was trapped between him and the file cabinet.

"I figured that. Did I tell you that I've always had this problem with authority? Goes all the way back to my elementary-school days when I bucked Miss Teesworthy over quiet time."

He pressed her back. "You didn't mention it." No gun oil and sweat here, he realized. It seemed the whole room smelled like Dora, that hot, spicy scent that made a man's mouth water.

"I do," she continued. "That's one of the reasons I started my own business. I hate taking orders."

"You're lousy at taking them. I told you to stay put."

"I had this driving need to stay close to the man with the gun." She lifted her hand, rubbed her thumb over the cut on his cheek. "You scared me."

"You didn't get scared until it was over."

"No, I was scared all along. Were you?"

"No. I love having people shoot at me."

"Then this is probably just a reaction we're having." She slid her arms around his neck, found the fit to her liking. "You know, from the shock."

"I told you to back off."

"So push me away." Her lips curved. "I dare you."

They were still curved when his mouth came down. She expected him to be rough, and she was ready for it. His body slammed hers back into the file cabinet. The handles dug into her back, but she was too busy gasping with pleasure to notice the discomfort.

He knew it was a mistake. Even as he steeped himself with her, he knew. Somehow she'd already dug a hook into his mind he'd been unable to shake loose. Now she was trembling against him, making soft little sounds of shocked arousal deep in her throat. And she tasted—God she tasted every bit as hot and sweet as she smelled.

It had been so long, so very long since he'd allowed himself to tumble into that dark, soft oblivion of woman.

He drew back, wanting to clear his head, but she fisted both of her hands in his hair and pulled him against her. "More," she murmured as her mouth ravaged his. "I always want more."

With him she could have more. She knew it. With him there would be no vague sense of the incomplete. She could feast and be filled, and still have more.

For one wild moment he considered taking her there, on the floor of the cramped, dusty storeroom with gun smoke still fading from the air. Perhaps he would have, perhaps he would have had no choice, but he was still sane enough to hear the rattle at the door upstairs, and the spit of gravel under tires outside.

"The troops are here." He took Dora by the shoulders and set her firmly aside. She saw in his eyes what he would continue to deny. He was a cop again. "Why don't you go put on some coffee, Conroy? It doesn't look like you're going to make your parties after all."

She stared up the stairs, keeping her back to him when she spoke. "And that's it?"

"Yeah." He wished violently for the cigarettes he'd left upstairs. "That's it."

7

Dora had brandy. Jed drank coffee. Cop, she thought nastily. After all, they didn't drink on duty—at least on TV. Wanting to ignore him as completely as he was ignoring her, she curled herself onto the couch and studied the cheerful lights of her Christmas tree.

She liked Jed's pal, though. Lieutenant Brent Chapman, with his wrinkled slacks, stained tie and easy grin. He'd come in smelling of sausage and cinnamon, his heavy horn-rims magnifying mild brown eyes. His manner was so reassuring that Dora found herself making coffee and setting out cookies as though she were entertaining unexpected guests rather than being involved in a police investigation of shots fired.

Brent's questions were slow and thoughtful and very nearly relaxing.

No, there was nothing missing as far as she could tell.

No, there was nothing in the files of any monetary value.

Yes, the shop had been crowded the past couple of weeks, but no, she couldn't remember anyone acting suspicious or asking unusual questions.

Enemies? This brought on a quick laugh. No, not unless you counted Marjorie Bowers.

"Bowers?" Brent's ears perked up. He kept his pencil hovering over his dog-eared notepad.

"We were both up for the lead in the school play. Junior year. It was a production of *West Side Story*. I creamed her in the auditions, so she started this rumor that I was pregnant."

"I don't really think—"

"With my reputation at stake, I had no choice," Dora went on. "I ambushed her after school." She flicked a glance over to Jed, who was busy frowning at the bull's-head cheese dish on her breakfront.

"That's very interesting. But I don't think it applies here."

"Well, she really hated me." Dora picked up her snifter again, shrugged. "Then again, that was in Toledo. No, I'm wrong. Junior year must have been in Milwaukee. We moved around a lot in those days."

Brent smiled. He'd taken a liking to Jed's landlord. A great many people who'd been through a break-in and gunfire didn't retain any sense of humor. "We're looking for something a bit more recent."

"Tell him about the bean counter," Jed ordered.

"For heaven's sake. Andrew wouldn't—"

"Dawd," Jed interrupted. "Andrew Dawd. He was Dora's accountant until a couple of days ago. He put some moves on her, so she gave him a black eye and his walking papers." He smiled nastily in Dora's direction. "And kicked his ass."

"I see." Brent tucked his tongue in his cheek as he scribbled the name in his book. He would have liked to have smiled, but the gleam in Dora's eye warned him to keep a sober countenance. "Did he, ah, threaten any reprisals?"

"Certainly not. Give me a cigarette, Skimmerhorn."

He lighted one for her. "Annoyed or stressed?" he asked when he offered it.

"You be the judge." She snatched it from him, took a quick puff. "The most violent thing Andrew would have done was to go home and whine to his mother."

"It wouldn't hurt to talk with him," Brent pointed out gently. "Where can we reach him?"

Dora shot Jed a look of intense dislike. "Dawd, Dawd and Goldstein, an accounting firm on Sixth and Market."

Brent nodded and picked up one of the cookies she'd spread on a pretty fluted dish at his elbow. "Hell of a way to spend Christmas Eve, huh?"

"I did have other plans." Dora drummed up a smile. "I'm sorry you had to leave your family."

"Just part of the job. Great cookies."

"Thanks. Why don't I give you some to take home? You've got kids, don't you?"

"Three." In a knee-jerk reaction, Brent reached for his wallet to show off pictures. While Jed rolled his eyes and paced away, Dora rose to admire the children's snapshots. There were two girls and a boy, all spit and polish for school pictures.

"The oldest girl looks like you," Dora commented.

"Yeah, she does. That's Carly. She's ten."

"I have a niece who just turned ten. Fifth grade."

"Carly's in the fifth, too. Over at Bester Elementary in Landsdowne."

"Missy goes to Bester." While Jed looked on, his partner and his landlord beamed at each other. "I bet they know each other."

"That wouldn't be Missy Bradshaw, would it? She has a younger brother named Richie, who's a real . . ."

"Terror, yes, that's right."

"She's been over to the house a dozen times. They only live a block over. Missy's parents and my wife and I are in the same car pool."

"Would you two like to be alone?" Jed asked.

They both spared Jed a pitying glance. "Tell me, Brent, is he always so crabby?"

"Pretty much." He tucked his wallet away and rose. There were cookie crumbs dusting his shirt and finger smudges on his glasses. Dora found him charming. "But he was the best cop I ever worked with, so you can feel safe having him across the hall."

"Thanks. I'm going to get you those cookies." Pointedly ignoring Jed, she walked into the kitchen.

"Some landlord," Brent commented, and wiggled his eyebrows.

"Get a grip. How soon will you have anything on the slugs you dug out of the plaster?"

"Jesus, Jed, it's Christmas. Give the lab boys a few days. We'll check out the prints, too, but that's pretty much a waste of time."

"If he's pro enough to use a silencer, he's pro enough to wear gloves."

"You got it."

"What do you figure—" Jed broke off when Dora walked back, carrying a paper plate covered with aluminum foil.

"Thanks, Miss Conroy."

"Dora. You will let me know if you find out anything?"

"Count on it. You just relax. Jed'll keep an eye on things."

"Well." She sent Jed a long, cool glance. "I can sleep easy now."

"There you go. Merry Christmas."

"I'll walk you out." Jed nodded to Dora. "I'll be back."

As they walked down the hall, Brent snuck another cookie from under the foil. "You've been here what, about a week?"

"Almost."

"How'd you piss her off already?"

"It's a gift. Look, why do you figure a pro would break into a junk shop and rifle a bunch of paperwork?"

"That's the sixty-four-dollar question." Brent walked through the rear door, sucking in his breath at the slap of wind. "There's a lot of valuable stuff in there."

"But he didn't go for the valuable stuff, did he?"

"Hadn't gotten around to it. You interrupted him."

"He sees lights on upstairs, he cuts the phone wires. He whacks the security system. But he doesn't go for the Daum Nancy."

"The what?"

"Never mind," Jed snapped, annoyed with himself. "He goes right for the files."

"Because he's looking for something."

"Yeah." Jed pulled out a cigarette. "But did he get it? And what would anyone look for in the files of a junk shop?"

"Receipts?" Brent offered as he opened his car door.

"Inventory lists, names, addresses."

"You can take the boy off the force, but you can't take the force out of the boy."

"I take a personal interest when somebody shoots at me."

"Can't blame you for that. We miss you downtown, Captain."

Something flickered in Jed's eyes that might have been grief, then was quickly gone. "The city seems to be hobbling along without me."

"Listen, Jed—"

"Save it." He wasn't in the mood for a lecture, or a pep talk, or a guilt trip. "Let me know what comes through."

"You'll be the first." Brent climbed into the car, rolled down the window. "Oh, and watch your butt, pal. I believe that lady could kick it."

Jed's response was a snort. He headed back inside. He wanted to make certain Dora was locked up for the night before he went back downstairs for another look.

Just as an interested civilian, he told himself.

"They've cleared out," he told her when he breezed through her open door. "You can count on Brent. He's a good detail man."

"Terrific. Sit down."

"I've got stuff to do. Lock your door."

"Sit down," she repeated, and pointed to a chair. "I'm going to clean up that cut."

"I can do it myself."

"Don't you know anything, Skimmerhorn? When you're wounded defending a woman, she's honor bound to whip out the antiseptic. If I was wearing a petticoat, I'd have to rip it into bandages."

Jed skimmed one more look over the glitter of her jumpsuit. "What are you wearing under that?"

"Excellent muscle tone." Because she was looking forward to it, Dora dragged him over to the chair. "Now you're supposed to say, 'Shucks, ma'am, it's only a scratch.' "

"It is." He smiled thinly. "But it could have been worse."

"Undoubtedly." With a whisper of silk, she knelt beside the chair and dabbed at the cut with one of the cotton balls she'd set out. "My sister would say you could have put out your eye. With Lea, everything's a potential eye poker. She inherited our mother's worry genes." Dora soaked another cotton ball and said brightly, "This may sting a bit."

As the shallow scratch erupted with fire, Jed snagged her wrist. "Goddamn it, what is that?"

"Alcohol." She fluttered her lashes. "It'll clean out any grit."

"Right down to the bone," Jed muttered.

"Don't be a baby, Skimmerhorn. Hold still."

He grimaced as she dabbed again. "You called me by my first name when you were clattering down the steps, screaming hysterically."

"I never scream hysterically."

"You did this time." He grinned wickedly. " 'Jed! Jed! Oh, Jed!' "

Dora dropped the cotton ball into a shallow enamel bowl. "At the time I thought you were about to be murdered. Unfortunately, I was wrong." She put a thumb to his chin to push his head to the side, examining the cut. "Do you want a Band-Aid?"

"No." His eyes gleamed. "Aren't you going to kiss it?"

"No." She rose then, started to pick up the bowl, set it down again. "Listen, I've got to ask. I know what you'll say. You'll say not to worry, that it was just one of those freak things that happen. But I have to ask anyway. Do you think he'll be back?"

Jed studied her face. There was a strain in her eyes she'd done a good job of hiding up until now. There was little he could, or would, do to alleviate it.

"I don't know," he said flatly.

"Great." Dora closed her eyes, drew a deep breath. "I should have known better than to ask. If you can't figure out what he was doing here in the first place, how can you tell if he'll be back or not?"

"Something like that." He could have lied, Jed told himself, uneasy that her cheeks were pale again. It wouldn't have been so hard to offer a phony reassurance to give her a peaceful night. Her eyes, when she opened them, were very dark, very tired.

"Look." He rose, and surprised them both by reaching out to tuck her hair behind her ear before snatching his hand back and stuffing it in his pocket. "Look," he said again. "I don't think you've got anything to worry about tonight. What you need to do is go to bed, tune out. Let the cops do their job."

"Yeah." It was on the tip of her tongue to ask him to stay, and only part of the reason was fear of being alone. She shook her head, rubbed her hands up and down her arms to warm them. "I'll be out most of tomorrow—at my sister's. I'll leave you the number in case . . . Just in case," she finished.

"Fine. Lock up behind me. Okay?"

"You bet." She had her hand on the knob when he stepped into the hall. "You too. Lock up, I mean."

"Sure." He waited until she'd closed the door, turned the bolts. His lips quirked when he heard the unmistakable sound of a chair scraping across the floor, the rattle of the knob as it was wedged under it. Good thinking, Conroy, he decided, then went down to take another look at the storeroom.

In a pretty Federal townhouse shaded by stately oaks, a well-to-do matron was enjoying a glass of sherry and a showing of Bing Crosby's *White Christmas* on her big-screen TV.

At the sound of a quiet footstep behind her, Mrs. Lyle smiled and held up a hand. "Come watch, Muriel," she invited, addressing her longtime housekeeper. "This is my favorite number."

She didn't cry out when the blow came. The delicate crystal shattered against the edge of the coffee table, splattering the Aubusson rug with blood-red sherry.

Somewhere through the haze of pain that left her paralyzed, she heard the crashing of glass and a furious male voice demanding over and over, "Where is the dog? Where is the fucking dog?"

Then she heard nothing at all.

It was midnight when DiCarlo rode the elevator up to his apartment in Manhattan. His arms were laden with boxes he'd copped from the back of a liquor store.

He'd been lucky to find the receipt for the stupid dog, he told himself, and wondered idly if the bullets he'd sprayed up the stairs of the antique shop had hit anything. Or anyone.

Not to worry, he thought. The gun was untraceable. And he was making progress.

He hefted the boxes more comfortably as he walked out of the elevator into the hallway. He had the bronze eagle, the plaster Statue of Liberty, the china dog.

And a partridge in a pear tree, he thought, and chuckled to himself.

"So . . ." Dora snacked on a raw carrot while Lea checked the Christmas goose. "Jed goes racing out after the guy, waving this big gun while I stand there like your typical

Hollywood heroine, with my hands clutched at my breasts. You got any dip for these veggies?"

"In the fridge. Thank God you weren't hurt." Harassed by the number of pots simmering on the stove, the sound of her children wreaking havoc in the family room and the very real fear that her mother would invade the kitchen at any moment, Lea shuddered. "I've been worried for years about your shop being burglarized. I'm the one who convinced you to put in that security system, remember?"

"A lot of good it did me, too." Dora dunked a spear of broccoli into sour-cream-and-chive dip, then leaned on Lea's cheery breakfast bar as she nibbled. "Jed said it was Mickey Mouse."

"Well, really." Lea paused in her stirring to be indignant. "John's cousin Ned said it was state-of-the-art."

"John's cousin Ned is a jerk. Great dip." She tried it with cauliflower. "Anyway, the cops came and did all this cop stuff—Dad would have loved the staging—and asked all these questions." Dora had purposely left out the part about the bullets. It didn't seem like Christmas conversation. "And it turns out that Jed's ex-partner is a neighbor of yours."

"Oh?" Lea chewed her knuckle as she basted her candied yams.

"Carly Chapman's father. She goes to school with Missy."

"Carly?" While she ran through her daughter's friends, Lea lifted a lid and sniffed. "Oh, yeah. Brent and Mary Pat. We carpool."

"So I hear." Dora helped herself to a glass of the wine Lea had breathing on the counter. "Here's the good part. They're going to question Andrew."

"You're kidding! Andrew?"

"Jilted accountant seeks revenge by destroying woman's tax files." Dora shrugged and passed a glass of wine to her sister. "Makes as much sense as anything. When's dinner?"

"Twenty minutes. Why don't we take what you've left of my crudités out. If we can keep Mom busy for—" She broke off, swore lightly under her breath as Trixie Conroy made her entrance.

Trixie always made an entrance, whether it was onto a stage or into the corner market. She'd dressed for the simple family dinner in a flowing caftan of bleeding colors that trailed fringe from its sweeping hem and draping sleeves. The material billowed theatrically around her willowy form. Her hair, cropped gamine short, was a bold, fire-engine red. Her face, milk-pale and unlined, thanks to religious pampering and one discreet lift, was striking. The soft blue eyes Lea had inherited were lavishly lashed, the full, sensuous mouth lushly red.

She breezed into the kitchen, trailing silks and her signature scent—one ripe with woodsy undertones.

"Darlings!" Her voice was as dramatic as the rest of her, a husky whisper that could easily carry to the last row in any theater. "It's so lovely to see my two girls together." She took a deep sniff of the air. "Oh, and those glorious aromas. I do hope you're not overheating my meatballs, Ophelia."

"Ah..." Lea sent Dora a desperate look and was met by a shrug. "No, of course not." Lea hadn't heated them at all, but had stuck them under the sink with hopes of palming them off on the dog later. "Mom, did you know... they're green."

"Naturally." Trixie buzzed around the stove, clanging lids. "I dyed them myself in honor of the season. Perhaps we should put them out now, as an appetizer."

"No. I think we should..." Since she couldn't think of a good ruse, Lea sacrificed her sister. "Mom, did you know someone broke into Dora's shop?"

"Damn it, Lea."

Lea ignored the muttered curse and barreled ahead. "Last night."

"Oh, my baby. Oh, my lamb." Trixie rushed across the kitchen to clasp Dora's face between her heavily ringed hands. "Are you hurt?"

"Of course not."

"Why don't you take Mom in the other room, Dora? Sit down and tell her all about it."

"Yes, yes, you must." Trixie gripped Dora's hand and dragged her toward the doorway. "You should have called me the minute it happened. I would have been there in the blink of an eye. My poor little darling. Quentin! Quentin, our daughter was robbed."

Dora had time for one speedy glare over her shoulder before she was yanked into the fray.

The Bradshaw family room was in chaos. Toys were strewn everywhere, making the practical buff-colored carpet an obstacle course. There were shouts and yips as a remote control police cruiser, operated by a steely-eyed Michael, terrorized the family dog, Mutsy. Will, looking very New York in a dark silk shirt and paisley tie, entertained Missy with bawdy numbers on the spinet. John and Richie were glassy-eyed over a Nintendo game, and Quentin, well plied with eggnog, boisterously kibitzed.

"Quentin." Trixie's stage voice froze all action. "Our child has been threatened."

Unable to resist, Will played a melodramatic riff on the piano. Dora wrinkled her nose at him.

"I wasn't threatened, Mom." Dora gave her mother a comforting pat, eased her into a chair and handed over her glass of wine. "The shop was broken into," she explained. "It didn't amount to much, really. They didn't get anything. Jed scared them off."

"I had a feeling about him." Quentin tapped the side of his nose. "A sixth sense, if you will. Were there fisticuffs?"

"No, Jed chased him away."

"I'd've shot him dead." Richie leaped onto the couch and fired an imaginary automatic weapon. "I told you."

"So you did."

"Richie, don't stand on the furniture," John ordered automatically. "Dora, you called the police?"

"Yes. And it's all in the hands of Philadelphia's finest." She scooped up Richie herself. "And the investigating officer is the father of a really, really good friend of yours, frog face. Jody Chapman."

"Jody Chapman!" Richie made gagging noises and clutched his throat.

"She sends her love." Dora fluttered her lashes and smacked her lips. The resulting din of groans and shrieks had her convinced the crisis had passed.

"Willowby!" Trixie cut through the noise with one word and a raised hand. "You'll stay at Isadora's tonight. I won't feel safe unless I know a man's keeping watch."

"Mother." It was enough to make Dora take back her wine. "I, on behalf of all feminists, am ashamed of you."

"Social and political ideals pale when it comes to the welfare of my child." Trixie gave a regal nod. "Will, you'll stay with your sister."

"No problem."

"Well, I have a problem," Dora cut in. "He leaves shaving gunk in the sink, and he makes long, obscene phone calls to his women in New York."

"I use my calling card." Will grinned. "And you wouldn't know they were obscene if you didn't listen."

"Your mother knows best." Quentin rose to help himself to more eggnog. Tonight he looked trim and dapper in a starched collar and a derby. He detoured to kiss his wife's hand. "I'll go by the shop myself tomorrow and take stock of the situation. Don't worry your pretty head, my sweet."

"Talk about obscene," Will mumbled, then grimaced. "What is that stench?"

"Dinner," Lea announced, swinging through the kitchen door. She smiled grimly at her mother. "Sorry, darling, I seem to have burned your meatballs."

A block away, Jed was trying to ease himself out the door. He'd enjoyed Christmas dinner at the Chapmans' more than he'd anticipated. It was hard not to get a kick out of the kids, who were still wide-eyed and enthusiastic over their Christmas loot. Impossible not to relax with the scents of pine and turkey and apple pie sweetening the air. And there was the simple fact that he liked Brent and Mary Pat as people, as a couple.

And the longer he stayed in their comfortable home, the more awkward he felt. There was no way to avoid comparing the homey family scene—a fire crackling in the hearth, kids playing on the rug—with his own miserable childhood memories of the holiday.

The shouting matches. Or worse, far worse, the frigid, smothering silences. The year his mother had smashed all the china against the dining room wall. The year his father had shot out the crystal drops on the foyer chandelier with his .25.

Then there had been the Christmas Elaine hadn't come home at all, only to turn up two days later with a split lip and a black eye. Had that been the year he'd been arrested for shoplifting in Wanamakers? No, Jed remembered. That had been a year later—when he'd been fourteen.

Those were the good old days.

"At least you can take some of this food home with you," Mary Pat insisted. "I don't know what I'll do with it all."

"Be a pal," Brent put in, patting his wife's bottom as he moved past her to pop the top on a beer. "You don't take it, I'll be eating turkey surprise for a month. Want another?"

Jed shook his head at the beer. "No, I'm driving."

"You really don't have to go so soon," Mary Pat complained.

"I've been here all day," he reminded her, and because she was one of the few people he felt relaxed with, kissed her cheek. "Now I'm going home to see if I can work off some of those mashed potatoes and gravy."

"You never put on an ounce. It makes me sick." She heaped leftovers into a Tupperware container. "Why don't you tell me more about this gorgeous landlord of yours?"

"She's not gorgeous. She's okay."

"Brent said gorgeous." Mary Pat sent her husband a narrow look. He only lifted his shoulders. "Sexy, too."

"That's because she gave him cookies."

"If she's Lea Bradshaw's sister, she must be more than okay." Mary Pat filled another container with generous slices of pie. "Lea's stunning—even first thing in the morning with a bunch of squalling kids in the car. The parents are actors, you know. Theater," Mary Pat added, giving the word a dramatic punch. "I've seen the mother, too." She rolled her eyes. "I'd like to look like that when I grow up."

"You look fine, hon," Brent assured her.

"Fine." Shaking her head, Mary Pat sealed the containers. "Does he say gorgeous? Does he say sexy?"

"I'll say it."

"Thank you, Jed. Why don't you bring the landlord over sometime? For dinner, or drinks?"

"I pay her rent; I don't socialize with her."

"You chased a bad guy for her," Mary Pat pointed out.

"That was reflex. I gotta go." He gathered up the food she'd pressed on him. "Thanks for dinner."

With her arm hooked around Brent's waist, Mary Pat waved goodbye to Jed's retreating headlights. "You know, I might just drop by that shop."

"You mean snoop around, don't you?"

"Whatever it takes." She leaned her head against his shoulder. "I'd like to get a look at this gorgeous, sexy, single landlord of his."

"He won't appreciate it."

"We'll see. He needs someone in his life."

"He needs to come back to work."

"So we'll double-team him." She turned, lifting her mouth for a kiss. "He won't have a chance."

In LA Finley dined on pressed duck and quail eggs. Joining him in his mammoth dining room was a stunning blonde, green-eyed, slenderly built. She spoke three languages and had an excellent knowledge of art and literature. In addition to her beauty and intelligence, she was nearly as wealthy as Finley. His ego demanded all three attributes in a companion.

As she sipped her champagne, he opened the small, elegantly wrapped box she'd brought.

"So thoughtful of you, my dear." He set the lid aside, pausing in anticipation.

"I know how you enjoy beautiful things, Edmund."

"Indeed I do." He flattered her with a warm look before reaching into the tissue paper. He lifted out a small ivory carving of a kirin, cradling it gently, lovingly in his palm. His deep, appreciative sigh whispered on the air.

"You admire it every time you dine with me, so I thought it would be the perfect Christmas gift." Pleased with his reaction, she laid her hand over his. "It seemed more personal to give you something from my own collection."

"It's exquisite." His eyes gleamed as he studied it. "And, as you told me, one of a kind."

"Actually, it seems I was mistaken about that." She picked up her glass again and missed the sudden spasm in his fingers. "I was able to obtain its twin a few weeks ago." She laughed lightly. "Don't ask me how, as it came from a museum."

"It's not unique." His pleasure vanished like smoke, replaced by the bitter fire of disappointment. "Why would you assume I would wish for something common?"

The change in tone had her blinking in surprise. "Edmund, it's still what it is. A beautiful piece of exceptional workmanship. And extremely valuable."

"Value is relative, my dear." As he watched her, cool-eyed, his fingers curled around the delicate sculpture. Tighter, tighter, until the carving snapped with a sound like a gunshot. When she cried out in distress, he smiled again. "It seems to be damaged. What a pity." He set the broken pieces aside, picked up his wine. "Of course, if you were to give me the piece from your collection, I would truly value it. It is, after all, one of a kind."

8

When Jed knocked on Dora's door a little after nine on the day after Christmas, the last thing he expected was to hear a man's voice saying wait a damn minute.

There was a thud, a curse.

Will, a flowered sheet wrapped around his thin frame like a toga, and favoring the toe he'd smashed against the Pembroke table, opened the door to an unfriendly sneer.

"If you're selling anything," he said, "I hope it's coffee."

She sure could pick them, Jed thought nastily. First a pin-striped accountant with overactive glands, now a skinny kid barely out of college.

"Isadora," Jed said, and showed his teeth.

"Sure." Mindful of the trailing sheet, Will moved back so that Jed could step inside. "Where the hell is she?" he muttered. "Dora!" His voice echoed richly off the walls and ceiling.

The kid had lungs, Jed decided, then noticed, intrigued, the tangle of pillows and blankets on the sofa.

"You're not getting in here until I dry my hair." Dora stepped out of the bathroom, dressed in a terrycloth robe and armed with a hand-held hair dryer. "You can just—oh." She stopped, spotting Jed. "Good morning."

"I need to talk to you for a minute."

"All right." She combed her fingers through her damp hair. "You met my brother?"

Brother, Jed thought, annoyed with himself for the quick, unquashable sense of relief. "No."

"The guy in the sheet is Will. Will, the guy who needs a shave is Jed, from across the hall."

"The ex-cop who chased off the burglar." Will's sleep-glazed eyes cleared. "Nice to meet you. I played a drug dealer once, in a Sly Stallone film? Got killed in the first reel, but it was a great experience."

"I bet."

"Here." Dora passed Will the hair dryer. "You can use the shower. I'll make the coffee, but you have to make breakfast."

"Deal." He headed off, trailing flowered sheets.

"My mother thought I needed a man in the house after the break-in," Dora explained. "Will was the only one available. We can talk in the kitchen."

It was the same efficient galley setup as his own, but was obviously more well used, and certainly more organized. She chose what Jed now recognized as a biscuit tin and scooped coffee beans out and into a grinder before she spoke again.

"So how was your Christmas?"

"Fine. I've got a guy coming by around noon to hook up a new security system. One that works."

Dora paused. The scent of ground coffee and her shower filled the room and made Jed's juices swim. "Excuse me?"

"He's a friend of mine. He knows what he's doing."

"A friend," she repeated, going back to her grinding. "First, I must say I'm amazed you have any. Second, I suppose you expect me to be grateful for your incredible gall."

"I live here, too. I don't like being shot at."

"You might have discussed it with me."

"You weren't around." He waited while she put a kettle on to boil. "You need a couple of real locks on the doors. I can pick them up at the hardware."

With her lips pursed in thought, Dora measured coffee into a filtered cone. "I'm debating whether to be amused, annoyed or impressed."

"I'll bill you for the locks."

That decided her. Her lips curved up, then the smile turned into a quick, throaty laugh. "Okay, Skimmerhorn. You go ahead and make our little world safe and sound. Anything else?"

"I figured I might measure for those shelves you want."

She ran her tongue around her teeth, reached around him for the wicker basket of oranges. "Getting tired of being a man of leisure?" When he said nothing, she sliced through an orange with a wicked-looking knife. "I'll show you what I have in mind after breakfast. As it happens, we're not opening until noon today." After slicing half a dozen oranges, she put the halves into a clunky-looking device that squeezed out the juice. "Why don't you set the table?"

"For what?"

"Breakfast. Will makes terrific crepes." Before he could answer, the kettle shrilled. Dora poured boiling water over the coffee. The smell was all it took.

"Where do you keep your plates?"

"First cupboard."

"One thing," he said as he opened the cabinet door. "You might want to put some clothes on." He sent her a slow smile that had her throat clicking shut. "The sight of your damp, half-naked body might send me into a sexual frenzy."

It didn't amuse her at all to have her own words tossed back in her face. Dora poured herself a cup of coffee and walked away.

"Smells good," Will decided, strolling in now wearing black jeans and a sweater. His hair, a few shades lighter than Dora's, had been blow-dried into artful disarray. He looked like an ad for Ralph Lauren. "Dora makes great coffee. Hey, would you mind switching on the tube? CNN, maybe. I haven't heard what's happening out there for a couple of days." Will poured both himself and Jed a cup before rolling up his sleeves.

"Damn you, Will!"

Dora's voice made her brother wince, grin. "I forgot to wash out the sink," he explained to Jed. "She really hates to find shaving cream glopped in it."

"I'll keep that in mind if it ever becomes an issue."

"It's all right for her to hang underwear everyplace though." He pitched his voice to carry out of the kitchen and through the bathroom door, adding just a dollop of sarcasm for flavor. "Growing up with two sisters, I never went into the bathroom without fighting my way through a jungle of panty hose."

While he spoke, Will measured ingredients and stirred with careless finesse. He caught Jed's eye and grinned again. "We're all great cooks," he said. "Lea, Dora and me. It was self-defense against years of takeout and TV dinners. So about this burglary thing." Will went on without breaking stride. "Do you think it's anything to worry about?"

"I always worry when somebody shoots at me. I'm funny that way."

"Shoot?" Will's hand hovered an inch above the edge of the bowl, the egg he'd just cracked dripping inside. "What do you mean 'shoot'?"

"A gun. Bullets." Jed sipped his coffee. "Bang."

"Jesus, Jesus. She didn't say anything about shooting." Still carrying the dripping eggshell, he dashed into the living room and down the short hall and jerked open the bathroom door.

Dora nearly poked her eye out with her eyeliner. "Damn it, Will."

"You didn't say anything about shooting. Christ, Dory, you made it sound like a joke."

She sighed, tapped the eye pencil on the lip of the pedestal sink and gave Jed a hard stare over Will's shoulder. She should have looked silly with one eye lined and the other naked. Instead she looked sulky, sexy and steamed.

"Thanks loads, Skimmerhorn."

"Anytime, Conroy."

"Don't blame him." Incensed, Will took Dora by the shoulders and shook. "I want to know exactly what happened. And I want to know now."

"Then ask the big-nosed cop." She gave Will a shove. "I'm busy," she said, and shut the bathroom door, deliberately turned the lock.

"Isadora, I want answers." Will hammered on the door. "Or I'm calling Mom."

"You do, and I'll tell her about your weekend on Long Island with the stripper."

"Performance artist," he muttered, but turned toward Jed. "You," he said, "you fill me in while I finish making breakfast."

"There's not that much to tell." There was a sick feeling in Jed's gut. It didn't come from running over the events of Christmas Eve while Will whipped up apple crepes. It came from watching the brother and sister together, in seeing the concern and anger on Will's face—emotions that came from a deeply rooted love, not simply from family loyalty.

"And that's it?" Will demanded.

"What?" Jed forced himself back to the present.

"That's it? Some joker breaks in, messes with the files, takes a couple of potshots at you and runs away."

"More or less."

"Why?"

"That's what the police are paid to find out." Jed helped himself to a second cup of coffee. "Look, there's a new security system going in this afternoon. And new locks. She'll be safe enough."

"What kind of a cop were you?" Will asked. "A beat type, a narc, what?"

"That's irrelevant, isn't it? I'm not a cop now."

"Yeah, but..." Will trailed off, frowning down at the crepes he scooped onto a flower-blue platter. "Skimmerhorn? That's what she called you, right? Kind of name sticks in the mind. I remember something from a few months ago. I'm a news junkie." Will rattled it around in his mind, as he might lines long ago memorized. "Captain, right? Captain Jedidiah Skimmerhorn. You're the one who blew away Donny Speck, the drug lord. 'Millionaire cop in shoot-out with drug baron,'" Will remembered. "You made a lot of headlines."

"And headlines end up lining bird cages."

Will would have pressed, but he remembered more. The assassination of Captain Skimmerhorn's sister with a car bomb. "I guess anyone who could take out a top-level creep like Speck ought to be able to look out for my big sister."

"She can look out for herself," Dora announced. With a juice pitcher in one hand, Dora answered the ringing kitchen phone. "Hello? Yes, Will's right here. Just a minute." Dora fluttered her lashes. "Marlene."

"Oh." Will scooped two crepes onto his plate and gathered up his fork. "This might take a while." After taking the phone from his sister, he leaned against the wall. "Hello, gorgeous." His voice had dropped in pitch and was as smooth as new cream. "Baby, you know I missed you. I haven't thought of anything else. When I get back tonight I'll show you just how much."

"Sick," Dora muttered.

"Why didn't you tell him the whole story?"

Dora shrugged, kept her voice low. "I didn't see any need to worry my family. They tend to be dramatic under the best of circumstances. If my mother finds out I've got a stomach virus, she immediately diagnoses malaria and starts calling specialists. Can you imagine what she'd have done if I'd told her someone shot holes in my wall?"

Jed shook his head, savoring the crepes.

"She'd have called the CIA, hired two bulky bodyguards named Bubba and Frank. As it was, she stuck me with Will."

"He's all right," Jed said just as Will made kissy noises into the phone and hung up. Before he'd taken two steps, the phone rang again.

"Hello." Will's eyes gleamed. "Heather, darling. Of course I missed you, baby. I haven't been able to think of anything else. I'll get everything straightened out by tomorrow night and show you just how much."

"Nice touch," Jed said, and grinned into his coffee.

"You would think so. Since he's busy making love through AT&T, I'm turning off the television." She rose and had nearly tapped the Off button when a bulletin stopped her.

"There are still no leads in the Christmas tragedy in Society Hill," the reporter announced. "Prominent socialite Alice Lyle remains in a coma this morning as a result of an attack during an apparent burglary in her home sometime December twenty-fourth. Mrs. Lyle was found unconscious. Muriel Doyle, Lyle's housekeeper, was pronounced dead at the scene. Both Mrs. Lyle and her housekeeper were discovered by Mrs. Lyle's niece Christmas morning. Alice Lyle, the widow of Harold T. Lyle of Lyle Enterprises, remains in critical condition. A Philadelphia police spokesperson states that a full investigation is under way."

"Oh God." Hugging her elbows, Dora turned back to Jed. "I know her. She was in the shop before Christmas, buying a gift for her niece."

"It's a wealthy neighborhood," Jed said carefully. "Lyle's a prominent name. Burglaries can turn ugly."

"She bought a couple of doorstops," Dora remembered. "And she was telling me how her niece was expecting a baby." She shuddered. "How awful."

"You can't take it inside." Jed got up to turn off the television himself.

"Is that what they teach you in cop school?" she snapped, then immediately shook her head. "Sorry. That's why I never listen to the damn news. The only thing I read in the paper are the classified section and the comics." She pushed her hair back and struggled to shake off the mood. "I think I'll go down and open up early, leave Will to clean up the mess before he goes back to New York."

This time he didn't resist the urge to brush his knuckles along her jawline. The skin there was as soft as rose petals. "It's tough when they're not strangers."

"It's tough when they are." She lifted a hand, touched his wrist. "Is that why you quit?"

He dropped his hand. "No. I'll head out to the hardware. Thanks for breakfast."

Dora merely sighed when the door closed behind him. "Will, when you finish your obscene call, do the dishes. I'm going down to the shop."

"I'm finished." He popped out of the kitchen and snagged the juice. "You're full of secrets, aren't you, Dory? How come you didn't tell me that your tenant was the big bad cop who took down Donny Speck?"

"Who's Donny Speck?"

"Jeez, what world do you live in?" He nibbled on little bits of crepe while he cleared the table. "Speck ran one of the biggest drug cartels on the east coast—probably the biggest. He was crazy, too; liked to blow people up if they messed with him. Always the same MO—a pipe bomb triggered by the ignition."

"Jed arrested him?"

"Arrested, hell. He whacked him in a real, old-fashioned gunfight."

"Killed him?" Dora asked through dry lips. "Is that—is that why he had to leave the force?"

"Shit, I think he got a medal for it. It was all over the news last summer. The fact that he's the grandson of L. T. Bester, Incorporated, got him a lot of press, too."

"Bester, Inc.? As in large quantities of money?"

"None other. Real estate, Dora. Shopping malls. Philadelphia doesn't have too many loaded cops."

"That's ridiculous. If he was loaded, why would he be renting a one bedroom apartment over a curio shop?"

Will shook his head. "You're a Conroy and you're questioning eccentricity?"

"I lost my head a minute."

"Anyway." Will filled the sink with hot soapy water. "The way I see the script here, I figure our hero, the wealthy police captain, is taking some downtime. Last summer was pretty hairy. The Speck investigation kept him in the news for months, then when his sister was killed in the car explosion—"

"Wait." She gripped Will's arm. "His sister?"

"They figured it was Speck, but I don't think they ever proved it."

"Oh, that's horrible." Paling, she pressed a hand to her grinding stomach. "Horrible."

"Worse—he saw it happen. The headlines said: 'Police captain watches sister's fiery death.' Pretty tough."

"Poor Jed," Dora murmured.

"The tabloids got a lot of play out of it, too. Can't remember it all, but there were lots of hints of scandal in the Skimmerhorn-Bester clan. The sister'd been divorced three or four times. The parents used to have public brawls. I think there was some stuff about Jed getting in scrapes as a juvenile. You know how people like to read about wealthy families suffering."

"No wonder he wants to be left alone. But," she continued after a moment, "that's not the answer." Leaning over, she kissed Will's cheek. "Lock up when you leave. See you New Year's?"

"Wouldn't miss it. Dora?"

"Hmm?"

"Do what he tells you. I like having you around."

"I like being around." She grabbed her keys and headed downstairs.

Customer traffic was light through the morning, which gave Dora time to think. What she didn't know about Jed Skimmerhorn could apparently fill a football stadium. The fascinating tidbits Will had dropped only made her lack of knowledge seem more acute.

"Good morning, Izzy, my darling daughter." Quentin swept into the shop with mink earmuffs clamped over his mane of striking pewter-colored hair. He was wearing an ankle-length shearling coat, a Christmas gift from his wife.

"Dad. Just the man I want to see."

"It's rewarding to be wanted by your children. Proves a man's worth in his middle years. Ah, Terri, a vision as always." He strode over to the redhead, took her hand and bowed theatrically over it. "A credit to the Liberty Players, to your humble director as well as to Dora's Parlor. What, no clientele this morning?"

"A couple of browsers, one exchange and a brisk sale of a twenty-dollar door knocker in the shape of a roaring hippo," Dora reported. "I imagine the malls are packed. Terri, you can handle things out here, can't you?"

"Blindfolded and hog-tied."

"Dad." Dora took her father's arm and drew him out of the main shop into one of the smaller display rooms. "What do you know about Jed Skimmerhorn?"

"Know?" To stall for time, Quentin took out a roll of spearmint Certs. "Let's see. He's about six-one, I'd say. A hundred seventy-five pounds, athletically proportioned. Mid-thirties. Anglo-Saxon lineage from his coloring."

"Cut it out. I know you, Quentin D. Conroy. Lea might think you'd rent the apartment to some chain-wielding biker with 'Born to Raise Hell' tattooed on his chest, but I know better."

Quentin blinked, clearly shocked. "Lea said such a thing? A serpent's tongue, by God." He slapped his fist into his palm.

"Don't change the subject. Whatever there is to know about Skimmerhorn, you know or he wouldn't be living here. So spill it. What's this business about his being from some wealthy family?"

"The Bester-Skimmerhorn clan," Quentin confirmed. Wearily, he slipped out of his coat and folded it lovingly over a balloon-back chair. "Most of the money is from his mother's side, though the Skimmerhorn branch aren't exactly pikers. Jed is the heir, if you will, as there is only himself and a couple of distant cousins remaining on the dwindling family tree."

"So he really is independently wealthy," Dora murmured. "I'll be damned."

"Independence was apparently more important." Quentin coughed gently into his hand. His cheeks pinked. "You know I dislike repeating gossip, Izzy."

"You'll only have to say it once."

He chuckled, patted her cheek. "My girl is quick. Very quick. Well then, rumor is that young Jed joined the police force against his family's wishes. They disapproved of his choice of career and threatened to cut him off." His voice had dropped into its story-telling mode, rich and perfectly paced. "In any case, the parents were notorious socialites. I say 'notorious' literally. They were given to public displays of bickering. It was no secret that they detested each other, but neither would divorce the other due to the convoluted financial connection between Bester and Skimmerhorn."

"Heartwarming," Dora murmured.

"Oh, indeed. Jed made a name for himself on the police force. He gained a reputation for being part bloodhound, part terrier. Sniffing out clues and getting his teeth into a case." Quentin smiled, enjoying his own analogy. "A bit over a year ago he was made captain, a position many feel would have been a stepping-stone leading to chief of police. Then there was Donny Speck."

"Will told me. Speck killed Jed's sister."

"That's the general assumption. As to why Jed left his position, I can only speculate. I would suggest that you ask him yourself."

"He wouldn't tell me."

"Is your interest personal or professional?"

She thought it through, then accepted the mint her father thumbed out of the roll. "I haven't decided. Thanks for the details." She kissed his cheek. "Which I shouldn't have had to ask for in the first place."

"You're quite welcome."

"Jed's back in the storeroom. You can go bother him while he puts in the new lock."

"It would be a pleasure." He picked up his coat, draped it over his arm.

"You can leave that here."

"Here . . . ah, no, no." Avoiding Dora's eye, he stroked the coat lovingly. "I'll just take it along. I might get chilly."

Might need the flask in the inside pocket, Dora corrected, and returned to work.

• • •

Back in the storeroom, Jed was putting Brent's drill to use again. He had a nice thick dead bolt nearly installed when Quentin toddled in.

"And happy Boxing Day to you. It seems you're our man of the hour. May I extend my deepest and most sincere gratitude."

"Mr. Conroy."

"Quentin, please. After all, according to Will you've protected my little girl at the risk of your own life and limb." Quentin settled into a ladder-back chair. "Tell me, do we have any clues?"

"Call headquarters and ask Lieutenant Brent Chapman. He's in charge."

"But, my dear boy, you were on the scene, weapon drawn. Where are the bullet holes? Will told me shots were exchanged."

"In the plaster, by the stairway." Amused, Jed watched Quentin stride over to peer at the wall. He wouldn't have been surprised if the man had pulled a magnifying glass and a deerstalker out of his pocket.

"Curious, isn't it? You know, I once played Poirot in a little theater production of *Orient Express*."

"And Will played a drug dealer with Stallone. Quite a family."

"One must play the villain as well as the hero to fully develop one's art. We have theater in our blood, you know. Although Izzy's seems to lean more toward props." He came back and settled himself again. He stretched back, crossed his legs at the ankles and folded his hands on his trim belly. "Do you have the time?"

Jed twisted his wrist to read his watch. "Couple minutes shy of noon."

"That's fine then." Satisfied, Quentin reached in his coat for his flask.

"Don't bring that near me."

Quentin smiled genially. "I'm afraid I'd filled it with what we might call my high-test the other day. We have a much lower octane today."

"I'll pass just the same."

"Well, here's to all the girls I've loved." Quentin took a slow drink, sighed, then tucked the flask away again. Dora might pop in at any time. "I had another reason for dropping by this morning. I'd like to renew the invitation to our annual New Year's Eve party, at the theater. My wife would like to thank you personally for looking out for our Izzy."

"I'm not big on parties."

"I'd consider it a personal favor if you'd at least drop in. After this incident, I'm concerned about Izzy driving there alone." Having planted the seed, Quentin snuck one more nip before making his exit.

With business slowed to a crawl, Dora left Terri in charge and spent most of the afternoon reorganizing her files. It was nearly dusk when Jed came downstairs and, without a word to her, began measuring the wall where she'd told him to put the shelves.

Dora ignored him, too, for nearly five minutes. "This security system you've dumped on me is complicated enough for Fort Knox."

Jed scribbled down figures on a pad. "All you do is cue in a six-digit code."

"And if I forget the code, bells and buzzers go off, lights flash—and some guy with a bullhorn shouts for me to come out with my hands up."

"So don't forget the code."

"I'm not good with numbers. That's why I have an accountant."

"Had an accountant. He's clean, by the way."

"Clean? Andrew? Of course he is. His mother checks every night to see if he's washed behind his ears."

Jed's measuring tape rewound with a snap. "Why the hell did you ever go out with him in the first place?"

"He was talking about paragraph twenty-five of the new tax law. I was terrified not to." Then she smiled because at least they were having a conversation. "Actually, I felt kind of sorry for him. His mother really is a smothering old witch."

"On the night in question, Andrew was with the smothering old witch and about two dozen other people at the Dawd, Dawd and Goldstein Christmas party. He's alibied tight until ten-thirty."

"I never thought it was him anyway." She spent another few moments separating receipts from invoices. "I called the hospital."

"What?"

"Mrs. Lyle, on the news this morning? I couldn't get it out of my mind." Dora refiled a Federal Express receipt. "She's still in a coma. I sent flowers. I guess that was stupid."

"Yeah." Christ, why was he letting her get to him this way? "But people usually appreciate stupid gestures."

"I do." Dora let out a long breath and shoved back from her desk. "Skimmerhorn, you want to get out of here?"

"I'm almost finished with the measurements. Then I'll get out of your way."

"No, I mean out." Restlessly, she pulled her hand through her hair. "Do you want to go get a pizza, see a movie? I don't want to face this pile of paperwork right now."

"It's a little early for a movie."

"It won't be after the pizza." She put on her best persuasive voice. "Be a pal, Skimmerhorn. The only thing worse than going to the movies alone is going to a drive-in movie alone."

He shouldn't, he knew. After what had nearly happened between them the night before, he should be avoiding her. "What's your security code?"

"Why?"

"Because we'll have to lock up if we're going out."

The tension cleared out of her eyes. "It's twelve twenty-four ninety-hree. Christmas Eve, ninety-three?" She smiled and grabbed her coat. "I figured it was a date that would stay with me."

"Good thinking." He shrugged into his jacket. After a brief hesitation he took the hand she held out. "We'll check the locks."

9

Mary Pat believed in the direct approach. The best way to satisfy her curiosity about Jed's landlord was to do a little shopping. She entered Dora's Parlor, as pleased with the ambience as she was to see her car-pool partner.

"Lea, hi."

"Well, hello." Lea set down the blown-glass cuspidor she'd been dusting. "What brings you to this part of town?"

"My mother's birthday." It hardly mattered that it wasn't for three months. "I loved the biscuit barrel Jed bought me from here, and thought I might find something unique."

"Unique we have. How are the kids?"

"Oh, driving us crazy. I'm counting the days until school starts up again."

"Who isn't?" Lea's mind worked fast. Mary Pat would be the perfect source to pump about Jed. "So, you and Jed are friends."

"For years." Mary Pat examined a collection of Goss china and looked for an opening to casually grill Lea about her sister. "He and Brent were partners before Jed made captain, were on the same squad for six years. Your sister has a charming place here. How long has she been in business?"

"Since the first grade," Lea said dryly. "She always liked to wheel and deal. But officially, for about three years."

A hard-edged businesswoman? Mary Pat wondered. A profit hound? "She certainly has some beautiful things." She edged over a price tag on a Deco cocktail shaker, let out a soundless whistle. "I hope she hasn't had any more trouble since the break-in."

"No, thank God." Lea walked over to the silver coffee service and poured two cups. "Cream, right? No sugar?"

"Mmmm. Thanks."

"We're awfully grateful Jed was here. It eases the mind knowing that Dora's got a policeman right across the hall."

"And one of the best, too. Brent thinks if Jed pulls out of this and comes back on the job he could be chief in another ten years."

"Really?" Guiltily thinking of diets, Lea added a miserly half teaspoon of sugar to her own cup.

Mary Pat turned back the topic of conversation.

"I was surprised when he moved in here. Your sister's quite the entrepreneur—a shop owner, a landlord."

"Oh, Dora loves to run things."

Pushy, Mary Pat decided. Arrogant. She was glad, for Jed's sake, that she'd come by to snoop. She turned when she heard voices drifting in through the doorway.

"I think I know where to find just what you're looking for, Mrs. Hendershot." Dora helped an elderly woman leaning heavily on a birchwood cane through the shop.

"You'll call me," she demanded in a voice that boomed shockingly from the frail body. "My great-granddaughter's wedding is in two months. Young people, always hurrying."

"Don't worry." Dora held the woman's arm as they came to the door and, despite the thin protection of her silk suit, walked her out to the classic DeSoto waiting at the curb. "We're going to find her the perfect gift."

"Don't disappoint me." Mrs. Hendershot propped her cane on the passenger seat as she took the wheel. "Get inside, girl, you'll catch your death."

"Yes, ma'am." Dora made it to the curb before Mrs. Hendershot roared off into traffic. Dora hurried back inside, rubbing her chilled hands. "If she had the pole position at Indy, nobody would beat her."

"A woman that age shouldn't be driving," Lea stated, and poured her sister a cup of coffee.

"Why not? She handles that old tank like a pro. Good morning," she said to Mary Pat. "Is Lea helping you?"

Mary Pat had had ample time to study her quarry. She approved, with a tinge of envy, the stylishness of Dora's floral jacket, and the straight, snug skirt the color of apricots. As a woman who stood on her feet for hours on end, she marveled at Dora's choice of high-heeled pumps, and wondered if the sapphire clusters at her ears were real or paste.

"I came in looking for a birthday gift. Lea and I are neighbors."

"This is Mary Pat Chapman," Lea told her.

All of Mary Pat's preformed opinions shattered when Dora smiled and took her hand. There was instant warmth, quick friendliness. "I'm so glad you came by. I was hoping I'd get a chance to meet you. Brent was terrific the other night, keeping me calm. By the way, did you like the biscuit barrel?"

"Yes, I did." Mary Pat relaxed. "In fact, I liked it so much I came by to look for a gift for my mother." She hesitated, then set her cup down. "That's only part of the reason I came in. Mostly I'm here to check you out."

Dora's eyes laughed over the rim of her cup. "Who could blame you? Well, while you're checking me out, why don't we find Mom a present? Did you have anything in mind?"

"Not a thing. Have you ever been married?"

Dora almost giggled at the unambiguous interrogation. "Nope. I was almost engaged once. Remember Scott, Lea?"

"Unfortunately."

"He moved to LA, and our romance faded quietly away. How about something in a perfume bottle? We have several nice pieces in crystal, porcelain, blown glass."

"Maybe. She does have a vanity table. Oh, this one's lovely." She picked up a heart-shaped bottle with cut flowers decorating both front and back. "You consider your shop successful? Ah, financially?"

Dora grinned. "I'm not interested in a man's bank account, even one as nicely padded as Jed's. I'm much more interested in his body. That bottle runs seventy-five, but if you like it, I'll give you ten percent off. An introductory special."

"Sold." Mary Pat grinned back. "He is easy on the eyes, isn't he?"

"Very. Would you like this gift-wrapped?"

"Yeah." Mary Pat followed Dora to the counter. "I'm not usually so pushy, but Jed's like family."

"I understand. If I hadn't, I'd have been pushy back."

More than pleased with the results of her visit, Mary Pat laughed. "Good. You know, Dora, all Jed needs is—" She broke off when the man in question came through from the storeroom.

"Conroy, do you want these—" He stopped, narrowed his eyes. "MP."

"Hey." Her smile was quick and a little forced. "Fancy meeting you here."

He knew her well, too well. He hooked his thumbs in his pockets with forced casualness. "What are you doing?"

"I'm buying a present." She took out her credit card to prove it. "For my mother."

"And I certainly hope she likes it." With her back to Jed, Dora sent Mary Pat a slow wink. "She has thirty days to exchange it." She turned toward Jed. "Did you want something?"

Annoyance tightened his mouth. "Do you want these damn shelves fixed or adjustable?"

"You can make them adjustable? Terrific. Jed's been such a help around here." Beaming, Dora turned to Mary Pat. "I don't know what I did without him."

"There's nothing like having a handyman around," Mary Pat agreed. "Jed helped Brent finish off the family room last year. You'll have to see it sometime."

"You're about as subtle as nuclear waste, Mary Pat." Jed scowled at both of them and slammed the storeroom door behind him.

"He's such a friendly, low-key sort of guy," Dora stated.

"That's why we love him."

Mary Pat left a few minutes later, satisfied with her morning's work.

The woman was asking for trouble, Jed thought grimly as he sent the power saw ripping through a board. She figured she could handle herself. It was tempting to prove her wrong. He would have done it, too, he decided, if she hadn't been so close to the truth on one single point.

He wasn't scared of her. Damned if he was. But . . . He set the saw aside and took out a cigarette. She sure as hell made him nervous.

He liked listening to her laugh. He'd even gotten a strange sort of kick at the way she'd talked back to the movie screen the evening before in the darkened theater. She didn't have any problem with conversation, he mused. Hell, he imagined he could sit alone with her for an hour without saying a word and there wouldn't be any holes in the conversation.

He'd be stupid not to admit he liked the way she looked. Big eyes and short skirts. She wasn't any wilty pushover either. He admired the way she'd taken on the accountant, her fists raised and fire in her eye.

Jed caught himself grinning and crushed the cigarette under his boot.

He wasn't going to let her get to him. He didn't need the headache. Didn't want the complication. Didn't care for the feeling of being sucked into a situation by his hormones.

Maybe he'd spent some time—too much time—imagining peeling Isadora Conroy out of one of those trim suits she wore. That didn't mean he was going to act on it.

After all, he mused, he'd been raised to be suspicious, cynical and aloof, in the best Skimmerhorn tradition. His years on the force had only heightened the tendency. As long as he didn't trust the lady, he could keep his hands to himself.

Ten minutes of standing out in the cold cooled his blood. Jed gathered up lumber and headed back inside.

She was still there, sitting at her desk. Before he could come up with an appropriately sarcastic comment, he saw her face. Her cheeks were dead white, her eyes dark and gleaming.

"Bad news?" he said, and carefully deleted any interest from his voice. When she didn't answer, he set the lumber aside. "Dora?" He stepped in front of the desk, said her name again.

She lifted her face. One of the tears swimming in her eyes spilled over and slipped down her cheek. He'd seen hundreds of women cry, some with callous expertise, some with the abandon of wild grief. He couldn't remember any affecting him more than that single, silent tear.

She blinked, spilling another, and with a strangled sound pushed back from the desk. His intellect ordered him to let her go, but he caught up to her in two strides. Firmly, he turned her around until she faced him.

"What is it? Is it your father?"

Battling fiercely for control, she shook her head. She wanted to lay her head on Jed's shoulder. Perhaps because he offered it, she refused.

"Sit down." Though she held herself stiff, he guided her back to her seat. "Do you want me to get your sister?"

"No." Dora pressed her lips together, took a deep breath. "Go away."

He'd have been relieved to oblige her, but he already had enough guilt on his shoulders. He went into the tiny adjoining bath and poured a glass of tepid water into a Dixie cup. "Here. Drink this. Then sit back, close your eyes and take some deep breaths."

"What's that? Skimmerhorn's all-purpose cure?"

Uneasy with the urge to stroke and soothe, he jammed his hands into his pockets. "Something like that."

Since her throat felt raw, she drank the water.

With her eyes closed, Jed thought she looked fragile, not at all like the vital woman who'd tweaked his libido only moments before. He sat on the edge of her desk and waited.

"Okay," she said after a moment. "It works." She sighed, opened her eyes again. "Thanks."

"What set you off?"

"The call." She sniffled, then reached in a desk drawer for a pack of tissues. "I met this other dealer on a buying trip right before Christmas. I just called down there to see if he had this piece my last customer wanted." She had to take another long breath. "He's dead. He was killed during a burglary last week."

"I'm sorry." They were two words Jed hated because they always seemed useless.

"I only met him once. I outbid him for a couple of lots. Lea and I went by his shop after the auction and he made hot chocolate." Her voice broke and she took a moment to strengthen it. "That was his son on the phone. He was killed the next night."

"Did they catch the guy?"

"No." She looked back at Jed. Both of them were relieved that her eyes were dry again. "I don't know any of the details. I didn't want to ask. How do you handle it?"

she demanded, gripping Jed's hand with an urgency that surprised them both. "How do you handle being close to the horrible day in and day out?"

"You don't look at things the same way on the job as you do as a civilian. You can't."

"Did you leave because you stopped looking at things like a cop?"

"That's part of it." He pulled his hand away, distanced himself.

"I don't think that's a good reason."

"I did."

"Interesting choice of tense, Skimmerhorn." She rose, wishing her stomach wasn't still so shaky. "You should have said 'I do'—unless you've changed your mind. We could go into that, but I'm not feeling up to a debate right now. I've got to go talk to Lea."

Gregg and Renee Demosky arrived home to their Baltimore split-level at 6 P.M. sharp. They were, as usual, bickering. They had sniped at each other all during the twenty-minute drive from Gregg's dental practice, where Renee was his dental hygienist, and continued the bout in the garage, where Gregg parked their bronze BMW beside their spiffy Toyota Supra, and as they reached the door to the house.

"We could have gone out to dinner," Renee said as she slammed open the front door. She was a statuesque blonde just beginning to thicken in the middle.

"Once in a while I'd like to see people, when they don't have their mouths wide open," she complained. "We're in a rut, Gregg."

"I like being in a rut," he muttered. "Come on, Renee, ease off. All I want is to relax in my own home. Is that too much to ask?"

"And I want to have a nice night out, maybe down at the Inner Harbor." Renee yanked open the refrigerator and took out a tuna casserole. "But no, I come home, after standing on my feet all day flossing other people's teeth, and have to fix dinner."

Gregg headed straight for the scotch in the living room.

"Don't you walk away from me when I'm talking to you." Renee shoved the casserole into the oven and hurried out on his heels.

She stopped, as her husband already had, to stare at the destruction of their living room. What wasn't missing was broken or jumbled in the center of the room, where the Persian rug had been. The entertainment corner across from the conversation pit was depressingly empty of their twenty-five-inch stereo TV, VCR and multiple-CD player.

"Oh, Gregg!" Resentments were forgotten as Renee grabbed her husband. "We've been robbed."

"Don't cry, baby. I'll take care of everything. Go in the kitchen and call the police."

"All our things. All our pretty things."

"Just things." He gathered her close and kissed the top of her head. "We can get more things. We've still got each other."

"Oh." Renee blinked tears out of her eyes as she looked up at him. "Do you mean that?"

"Sure I do." He ran an unsteady hand over her hair. "And after the cops finish up, and we figure out what the hell happened, we're going out. Just you and me."

• • •

DiCarlo was whistling along with Tina Turner on his car stereo. He had the mermaid bookends—as well as $600 in cash the Demoskys had hidden in the freezer, a fine ruby-and-diamond ring Renee had left carelessly on her dresser and the profit he'd made by fencing all the electronic equipment to an old connection of his in Columbia, Maryland.

All in all, he considered it an excellent day. Making it look like a random burglary had helped pay his traveling expenses. He was going to treat himself to a first-class hotel after he'd picked up the parrot in Virginia.

That would leave only another quick trip to Philly for the painting.

In another day or two, Finley would have to admit just how reliable and how creative Anthony DiCarlo could be. And, DiCarlo mused, he was bound to earn a substantial reward for services rendered.

10

A well-mannered fire simmered in the grate of the Adam fireplace. It threw pretty, dancing lights over the Oriental carpet and silk-papered walls. A distinguished vermouth picked up the subtle lighting and sparkled in the heavy, faceted Baccarat glass. Van Cliburn played an elegant Chopin étude. Tasteful hors d'oeuvres had been offered on Georgian silver by the aged and discreet butler.

It was exactly the sort of room Jed had skulked through during his childhood, with the carefully placed bric-a-brac whispering of old money. But there was a subtle difference here. In this room, in this house, he had known some transient happiness. In this room he hadn't been threatened or berated or ignored.

Yet it still reminded him, painfully, of the boy he had been.

Jed rose from the miserably uncomfortable Louis XIV side chair to pace his grandmother's front parlor.

In evening clothes he looked the part of the Bester-Skimmerhorn heir. It was only his eyes, as he stared down at the flickering fire, that reflected the other paths he'd chosen, and the internal struggle to find his true place.

He wouldn't have minded a visit. Of all of his relatives, Honoria was the only one he'd had generous feelings for during his youth. As fate would have it, she was the only relative he had left. But the command performance grated.

He'd refused to take Honoria to the Winter Ball, twice—directly and concisely. She had simply ignored his refusal and, using a combination of guile, guilt, and tenacity had wheedled him into dragging out his tux.

"Well, Jedidiah, you're still prompt."

Honoria stood in the parlor doorway. She had sharp, New England cheekbones and brilliant blue eyes that missed little. Her snowy hair was softly coiffed around her narrow face. Her lips, still full and oddly sensuous, were curved. Smugly. Honoria knew when she'd won a match, whether it be a rousing game of bridge or a battle of wills.

"Grandmother." Because it was expected, and because he enjoyed it, Jed crossed over to take her hand and lift it to his lips. "You look beautiful."

It was quite true, and she knew it. Her Adolpho gown of royal blue set off both her eyes and her stately figure. Diamonds glittered at her throat, at her ears, at her wrists. She enjoyed the gems because she had earned them, and because she was vain enough to know they would turn heads.

"Pour me a drink," she ordered, in a voice that still carried a hint of Boston from her youth. "That will give you time to tell me what you're doing with your life."

"We won't need much time for that." But he walked obediently to the liquor cabinet.

He remembered when she had caught him filching from that same cabinet nearly twenty years before. How she had insisted that he drink from the decanter of whiskey—and keep drinking while she watched, steely-eyed. And after, when he'd been miserably sick, she had held his head for him.

"When you're old enough to drink like a man, Jedidiah, you and I will share a civilized cocktail. Until then, don't take what you can't handle."

"Sherry, Grandmother?" he asked, and grinned.

"Now, why would I want an old woman's drink when there's good whiskey around?" Silks rustling, she sat near the fire. "When am I going to see this hovel you've moved yourself into?"

"Anytime you like, and it's not a hovel."

She snorted and sipped at the whiskey in a heavy crystal tumbler. "A drafty apartment above some seamy little shop."

"I haven't noticed any drafts."

"You had a perfectly adequate home."

"I had a twenty-room mausoleum that I hated." He'd known this was coming. After all, it was from her he'd inherited the tenacity that had made him a good cop. Rather than face the chair again, he leaned against the mantel. "I've always hated it."

"It's wood and brick," she said dismissively. "It's a foolish waste of energy to hate the inanimate. In any case, you would have been welcome here. As you always were."

"I know." They'd been through it all before. But because he wanted to erase the concern from her eyes, he grinned. "But I didn't want to interfere with your sex life."

She didn't miss a beat. "You'd hardly have done so from the east wing. However, I have always respected your independence." And because she sensed some subtle lightening in him since the last time she'd made the offer, she let that part of the argument rest. "When do you intend to go back to your badge, and your work?"

His hesitation was brief. "I have no intention of going back."

"You disappoint me, Jedidiah. And, I think, you disappoint yourself." She rose, regally. "Fetch my wrap. It's time we left."

Dora loved a party. One of her favorite ways to reward herself for a hard day was to primp, dress up and spend an evening in a crowd. It didn't matter if she knew a single soul, as long as there were plenty of people, chilled champagne, music and interesting food.

As it happened, she knew a great many people attending the Winter Ball. Some were friends, some were customers, some were patrons of her family's theater. She was able to entertain herself by mingling, moving from group to group to exchange pecks on the cheek and fresh gossip. Though she'd taken a chance wearing the strapless white gown, the press of bodies heated the room and kept her comfortable.

"Dora, darling, you look fabulous." Ashley Draper, a social climber of the first order who had recently shed her second husband, swooped down on Dora in a cloud of Opium.

Because Ashley fell slightly below the borders of friendship, Dora was amused by the quick air kiss. "You look radiant, Ashley."

"You're a dear to say so, even though I know I'm a bit washed out. Right after the first of the year, I'm going to spend a week at the Green Door. The holidays are so fatiguing, aren't they?"

"God knows how we get through them." Dora popped a stuffed olive into her mouth. "I thought you'd be in Aspen."

"Next week." Ashley waved a fuchsia-tipped hand toward another couple. "What a ghastly dress," she murmured through her smiling lips. "It makes her look like a stuffed eggplant."

Because it was a killingly accurate statement, Dora laughed and remembered why she tolerated Ashley. "Are you here stag?"

"Lord no." Ashley scanned the crowd. "My escort's that amazing hunk of beefcake with the Samson locks."

Once again Ashley's description was on the money. Dora picked him out quickly. "My, my."

"An artist," Ashley purred. "I've decided to be a patron. Speaking of the men in our lives, I heard that Andrew broke off your business association."

"Did you?" It only amused Dora that Andrew, or more likely his mother, had twisted the facts. "Let's just say I'm looking for someone a bit more substantial to stand between me and the IRS."

"And how is your little shop doing?"

"Oh, we manage to sell a trinket now and again."

"Mmm, yes." Finances didn't interest Ashley, as long as the alimony check came on time. "We missed you the other night at the Bergermans'. Christmas Eve?"

"I was . . . unexpectedly detained."

"I hope he was worth it," Ashley purred, then grabbed Dora's hand in a crushing grip. "Look, here." She lowered her voice to confidential tones. "It's the grand dame herself. She rarely puts in an appearance here."

"Who?" Curiosity piqued, Dora craned her neck. She lost the rest of Ashley's hissed explanation the minute she saw Jed. "Surprise, surprise," she murmured. "Excuse me, Ashley, I have to go see a man about a tux."

And he did look fabulous in it, she mused as she circled the ballroom to come up behind him. She waited until he'd procured two glasses of champagne.

"I know," she said at his shoulder. "You went back on the force, and now you're undercover." She caught his soft oath as he turned. "What is it, an international jewel thief? A ring of insidious pâté burglars?"

"Conroy. Do you have to be everywhere?"

"I have an invitation." She tapped her beaded evening bag. "How about you, copper?"

"Christ. It's bad enough I have to be here at all without—"

"Jedidiah!" Honoria's authoritative voice halted any complaints. "Have you lost whatever slight degree of manners I managed to teach you? Introduce your friend to your grandmother."

"Grandmother?" On a quick laugh, Dora took Honoria's narrow-boned hand. "Really? I'm delighted to meet you, Mrs. Skimmerhorn, even though it destroys my theory that Jed was hatched from a very hard-shelled, very stale egg."

"His social graces are lacking." Honoria studied Dora with growing interest. "And it's Mrs. Rodgers, my dear. I was briefly married to Walter Skimmerhorn, but rectified the matter as soon as humanly possible."

"I'm Dora Conroy, Jed's landlord."

"Ah." There was a world of expression in the single syllable. "And how do you find my grandson as a tenant?"

"His temperament's a bit unreliable." Dora shot a look at Jed, pleased by the fire in his eyes. "But he appears to be neat enough, and he's certainly not rowdy."

"I'm relieved to hear it. There were times, you know, during his youth, that I feared his landlord would be a warden."

"Then you must be pleased he chose the right side of the law."

"I'm very proud of him. He's the first and only Skimmerhorn to amount to anything."

"Grandmother." Very deliberately, Jed took her arm. "Let me get you some hors d'oeuvres."

"I'm capable of getting my own." Just as deliberately, she shook him off. "And there are several people I must speak to. Dance with the girl, Jedidiah."

"Yeah, Jedidiah," Dora said as Honoria swept off. "Dance with the girl."

"Go find somebody else to harass," he suggested, and turned toward the bar. He was going to need something stronger than champagne.

"Your grandma's watching, pal." Dora tugged on his sleeve. "Five will get you ten she'll lecture you if you don't escort me onto the dance floor and exude some charm."

Setting the champagne aside, Jed took her arm. If his fingers dug in a bit hard, she was determined not to grimace. "Don't you have a boyfriend around here?"

"I don't see boys," Dora said, grateful when Jed had to shift his grip into dance position. "If you mean do I have a date, then no. I don't usually like to bring a date to a party."

"Why?"

"Then I'd have to worry if he was having a good time, and what I prefer doing is having one myself." The orchestra was playing a silky version of "Twilight Time." "You're a nice dancer, Skimmerhorn. Better than Andrew."

"Thanks a lot."

"Of course, it would be a nice touch if you looked at me, instead of glaring at the other dancers." When his gaze lowered, she tilted her head and smiled. "What about you? Are you having a good time?"

"I hate these things." It was a shame, a damn shame, he thought, that she felt so incredibly good in his arms. "You probably love them."

"Oh, I do. You'd like them more if you accepted them for what they are."

"Which is?"

"A chance to show off." She lifted a finger from his shoulder to tease his hair. "I'm terrific at showing off."

"I'd already figured that out."

"Astonishing deductive powers. Comes from being a police captain."

He slid a hand up her back, encountered bare skin. "Do you ever go out at night in anything that doesn't glitter?"

"Not if I can help it. Don't you like the dress?"

"What there is of it." The song ended and another began, but he'd forgotten he didn't want to dance with her. Honoria glided by in the arms of a distinguished-looking man with a silver moustache. "You look okay, Conroy."

"My." She widened her eyes. "Feel my heart pound."

"If I feel your heart, I'll do it in private."

"Are you exuding charm for your grandmother's sake?"

He looked down at her again. Something in her smile encouraged one of his own. "She liked you."

"I'm a likable person."

"No, you're not. You're a pain in the ass." He stroked his hand up and down her bare back where the silk of the gown gave way to the silk of her flesh. "A very sexy pain in the ass."

"I'm getting to you, Jed." And her heart was pounding, just a little, as she trailed her fingers along his neck.

"Maybe." Testing them both, he dipped his head, brushed her mouth with his.

"Absolutely," she corrected. She felt the quickening in her stomach spread to a fluttering. She ignored the curious heads turned their way and kept her mouth an inch away from his. "We could go home tonight and tear each other's clothes off, jump into bed and relieve some of this tension."

"An interesting image, Conroy, but it sounds like there's an 'or' coming."

"Or," she said, and tried to smile, "we could get to be friends first."

"Who said I wanted to be your friend?"

"You won't be able to help yourself." She touched a hand to his cheek, as much in compassion as arousal. "I can be a pretty good friend. And I figure you need one."

She moved something in him, no matter how hard he tried to stand against it. "How do you figure that?"

"Because everyone does. Because it's hard to be alone in a room full of people, but you are."

After a violent inner struggle, he rested his brow against hers. "Goddamn it, Dora. I don't want to care about you. I don't want to care about—"

"Anything?" she finished for him. When she looked up into his eyes this time, her heart broke. "You're not dead," she murmured.

"Close enough." He pulled himself back. "I want a drink."

She went with him to the bar, ordered champagne while he chose scotch. "Tell you what." Her voice was light again. "We'll try something new. I won't give you a hard time—and vice versa. I won't make suggestive comments or clever insults."

He rattled the ice in his glass while he studied her. "What's left?"

"We'll both be agreeable and have a good time." At his lifted brow she laughed, hooked her arm through his. "Okay, I'll have a good time, and you'll make the best of the situation. Hungry?"

"I could be."

"Let's go check out the buffet. If you have a plate in your hand, none of the women who are ogling you will expect you to dance."

"Nobody's ogling me." But he went with her.

"Sure they are. I'd ogle you myself if I didn't know you." She debated between the salmon mousse and the stuffed mushrooms, settled on both. "I don't believe I've seen you at the Winter Ball before, and I've attended the last three years."

He'd always been able to use work as an excuse, Jed remembered. He plucked a cube of cheese from her plate and said nothing.

"This conversation thing is tough for you, isn't it?" She kept a smile on her face as she heaped more food on her plate, then generously held it out to share. "I'll give you a hand. I say something, then, depending on the content, you laugh, look bemused, annoyed, intrigued, and say something back. Ready?"

"You've got an awfully smart mouth, Conroy."

"Good. Good start." She sampled a thumb-sized spinach pastry. "Tell me, is your grandmother the Honoria Rodgers who purchased the Qing dynasty cloisonné enamel candle holder, in the form of an elephant, at Christie's a few months ago?"

"I don't know about elephants, but she's the only Honoria Rodgers I'm aware of."

"Gorgeous piece—at least it looked terrific in the catalogue. I couldn't get up to New York, but I put in a couple of telephone bids during that auction. Not on the Qing, though. Out of my range. I'd love to see it sometime."

"If you're wrangling for an invitation, you should talk to her."

"Just making chitchat, Skimmerhorn. Try one of these," she invited with her mouth full, and picked up another pastry. "Incredible."

Before he could accept or refuse, she had it up to his mouth and in. "Great, huh?"

"I don't like spinach." Grimacing, he washed it down with scotch.

"I used to be the same way, but my father got me hooked on it by singing 'Popeye the Sailorman.' I was twenty," she said earnestly. "And naive." When his lips quirked, she lifted her glass in toast. "There now. And you look so pretty when you smile."

"Dora, darling." With her young artist in tow, Ashley glided up to the buffet. "How do you manage to eat like that and stay so slim?"

"Just a little agreement I have with Satan."

Ashley laughed gaily and gave Jed one long sweeping glance—what Dora would definitely term an ogle. "Isadora Conroy, Heathcliff." She presented her date as though he were the prize stud at a thoroughbred farm. "I discovered him in this marvelous little gallery on South Street."

"Oh?" Dora didn't bother to remind Ashley that her shop was on South. "I've always wanted to discover something—like Christopher Columbus. Or Indiana Jones." Because Heathcliff only looked baffled, she took pity on him. After passing her plate to Jed, she offered a hand. "Ashley tells me you're an artist."

"I am. I—"

"He does the most sensual life studies." Ashley stroked Heathcliff's arm, as a woman might a favored pet. "You simply must see them sometime."

"Top of my list."

"I don't believe you've introduced us to your escort."

"I don't have one. That's an odd term, don't you think? It sounds as though you'd need someone along because you couldn't find where you were going yourself. Personally, I have an excellent sense of direction."

"Dora." Ashley gave another quick, tinkling laugh. "You're such a wit."

"Only half," Jed said under his breath.

Dora spared him even the mildest of glances. "Jed Skimmerhorn, Ashley Draper and Heathcliff."

"Oh, I recognized Captain Skimmerhorn." Ashley held out a hand, waiting until Jed had juggled the plate back to Dora. "I should say, the elusive Captain Skimmerhorn." Her fingers glided over his. "It's so rare that we're able to tempt you to one of our little affairs."

"I don't find little affairs tempting."

This time Ashley's laugh was low and throaty. "I prefer long, steamy ones myself. And how do you two know each other?"

Dora picked up the ball to save Ashley from one of Jed's nastier comments. "Jed and I share a passion," she said, and took a slow, deliberate sip of champagne. "For pincushions."

Ashley's avid eyes went blank. "For—"

"Jed has the most incredible collection. We met at a flea market, when we both reached for the Victorian blue-satin-and-lace heart-shaped—pins included." She gave a fluttery, romantic sigh.

"You collect . . . pincushions?" Ashley asked Jed.

"Since I was a child. It's an obsession."

"And he's such a tease." Dora gave him an intimate look over the rim of her glass. "He keeps dangling his horse's hoof with plated mounts under my nose. And he knows perfectly well I'd do anything—*anything*—to have it."

"Negotiations . . ." He trailed a fingertip down the line of her throat. "Are open."

"How fascinating," Ashley murmured.

"Oh, it is," Dora agreed. "Oh, there's Magda and Carl. Excuse us, won't you? I simply have to catch up."

"Pincushions?" Jed muttered against her ear as they lost themselves in the crowd.

"I thought about sardine dishes, but they seemed so pretentious."

"You could have told her the truth."

"Why?"

He thought about it. "Simplicity?"

"Too boring. Besides, if she knew you lived across the hall from me, she'd start hanging around my apartment, hoping to seduce you. We wouldn't want that, would we?"

Lips pursed in consideration, Jed glanced over his shoulder to give Ashley a thorough study. "Well . . ."

"She'd only use you and toss you aside," Dora assured him. "I see your grandmother over there. Should you join her?"

"Not if you're going to grill her about candle holders."

That hadn't been her intention—exactly. "You're just afraid she'll make you dance with me again. Tell you what, I really will go talk to Magda and Carl, and you can catch up with me later, if you like."

He took her arm, frowned down at his own hand and removed it. "Stick around."

"What a charming invitation. Why?"

"Because if I'm going to be trapped in here for a couple more hours, it might as well be with you."

"Poetry, sheer poetry. How can I resist? Let's go see if your grandmother wants some nibbles. I promise not to bring up candle holders unless it seems appropriate."

"Jed."

A hand clamped on his shoulder. Jed braced, turned. "Commissioner," Jed said, both his face and voice neutral.

"Good to see you." Police Commissioner James Riker gave Jed a quick but thorough study. What he saw obviously pleased him as his thin, dark face creased in a smile. "You're keeping fit, I see."

"Yes, sir."

"Well, you were overdue for a vacation, God knows. How was your Christmas?"

"Fine." Because he couldn't ignore Riker's pointed look toward Dora, Jed did his duty. "Commissioner Riker, Dora Conroy."

"Hello." As both her hands were full, Dora beamed him a smile instead of a handshake. "So, you're in charge of keeping the law and order in Philadelphia."

"I'm in charge of keeping men like Jed on the job."

If Riker couldn't feel the tension shimmering off Jed, she could. The need to protect clicked in. Dora smoothly changed the course. "I suppose most of your work now is administrative."

"Yes, it is."

"Do you miss the action?" She smiled, handing Jed her empty glass. "In fiction cops always miss the action."

"As a matter of fact, I do. From time to time."

"I have to ask. I have this bloodthirsty nephew who'll want to know. Were you ever shot?"

If the question surprised him, Riker covered it well. "No. Sorry."

"That's all right. I'll lie."

"I hope you'll forgive me, Miss Conroy, but I need to steal Jed for a minute. The mayor would like a word with him."

Dora gave way graciously. "Nice to have met you, Commissioner Riker."

"My pleasure. I'll only keep Jed a moment."

Trapped, Jed handed her back her empty glass. "Excuse me."

Oh, he really hated this, she mused as she watched him walk away. It hadn't shown, not in his face, not in his eyes, but he hated it. A man faced a firing squad with more enthusiasm.

When he returned he'd be simmering with fury or tight-lipped with guilt or simply miserable. Feeling for him, Dora wondered if she could find some way to distract him, to turn whatever emotions the commissioner and the mayor managed to stir up into a different channel.

Joke him out of it? she mused as she wandered over to get a refill on her champagne. Irritate it out of him would probably be easier. It wouldn't even take much effort.

"I would think they would take more care as to who attends these affairs."

The gravelly voice was instantly recognizable. Dora turned with a bright smile on her face. "Mrs. Dawd, Andrew. How . . . interesting."

Mrs. Dawd drew air fiercely through her nostrils. "Andrew, fetch my club soda."

"Yes, Mother."

Mrs. Dawd, with her bulky frame draped in black satin, leaned forward, close enough that Dora saw the few gray hairs stabbing out of her chin that her tweezers had missed. "I knew what you were, Miss Conroy. I warned him, of course, but Andrew is as susceptible as any man to a woman's wiles."

"I had all my wiles surgically removed. I could show you the scars."

The woman ignored her. "But what would you expect, bred from a family of actors?"

Dora took a careful breath, a careful sip. She would not, absolutely not, let this idiotic old woman make her lose her temper.

"Those acting families," Dora said lightly. "The Fondas, the Redgraves, the Bridges. God knows how they can be permitted to taint society."

"You think you're clever."

"Mother, here's your drink."

Mrs. Dawd swept Andrew and the club soda back with a violent gesture. "You think you're clever," she said again, her voice lifting enough to have several onlookers murmuring. "But your little tricks didn't work."

"Mother—"

"Be still, Andrew." There was fire in her eyes now. She was the mama bear protecting her cub.

"Yes, Andrew, be still." Dora's smile was tiger sharp. "Mother Dawd was about to tell me about my little tricks. Do you mean the one when I told your slimy son to get his hand out from under my skirt?"

The woman hissed in anger. "You *lured* him into your apartment, and when your pathetic seduction failed, you attacked him. Because he recognized you for exactly what you are."

There was a laser gleam in Dora's eye now. "Which is?"

"Whore," she hissed. "Slut. Floozy."

Dora set down her glass to free her hand. She balled it into a fist and gave serious consideration to using it. She settled for upending her plate on Mrs. Dawd's heavily lacquered hair.

The resulting screech should have shattered crystal. With salmon mousse dripping into her eyes, Mrs. Dawd lunged. Dora braced for the attack, then gave out a howl of her own as she was snatched from behind.

"Jesus Christ, Conroy," Jed muttered as he dragged her toward the ballroom doors. "Can't I leave you alone for five minutes?"

"Let me go!" She might have taken a swing at him, but he locked her arms at her sides. "She had it coming."

"I don't feel like bailing you out of jail." He strode toward a sitting area with cushy chairs and potted plants. He heard the orchestra strike up "Stormy Weather."

Perfect.

"Sit." He punctuated the order with a shove that had her tumbling into a chair. "Pull yourself together."

"Look, Skimmerhorn, that was my own personal business."

"You want me to have the commissioner haul you in for disturbing the peace?" he asked mildly. "A couple hours in the tank would cool you off."

He would, too, she thought viciously. Dora huffed, tapped her foot, folded her arms. "Give me a—"

He already had a cigarette lit and was handing it to her.

"Thanks." She fell into silence.

He knew her routine. She would take three, maybe four quick shallow puffs, then stab it out.

One, he counted. Two. She shot him a furious glare. Three.

"I didn't start it." Her lips moved into a pout as she crushed out the cigarette.

Jed decided it was safe to sit. "I didn't say you did."

"You didn't threaten to have *her* arrested."

"I figured she was going to have enough problems picking pimentos out of her hair. Want a drink?"

"No." She preferred to sulk. "Look, Skimmerhorn, she was insulting me, my family, women in general. And I took it," she said righteously. "I took it even when she called me a tramp, a slut, a whore."

A great deal of his amusement faded. "She said that to you?"

"And I took it," Dora barreled on, "because I kept telling myself she was just a crazy old lunatic. I was not going to cause a scene. I was not going to lower myself to her level. Then she went too far, she went one step too far."

"What did she do?"

"She called me a—a floozy."

Jed blinked, gamely struggled to swallow the tickle at the back of his neck. "A what?"

"A floozy," she repeated, slapping her fist on the chair.

"Let's go take her down."

Dora's chin came up, her eyes narrowed. "Don't you dare laugh."

"I'm not. Who's laughing?"

"You are, damn it. You're biting your tongue right now to hold it back."

"I am not."

"You are too. You're slurring your words."

"It's the scotch."

"Like hell." She turned her head away, but he'd caught the quiver of her lips. When he brought her face back to his, they grinned foolishly at each other.

"You made it an interesting evening, Conroy."

"Well." Her temper spent, she giggled, then leaned back to rest her head on his shoulder. "I was trying to think of some way to distract you so you wouldn't be upset from the mayor and Riker."

"Why should I be upset?"

"They were pressuring you, weren't they?" Though he didn't move, she felt a part of him shift away. "Lucky for me, Mrs. Dawd came along so I didn't have to invent something."

"So you dumped food on her head to lift my spirits."

"No, it was strictly a selfish act, but it did have a nice side benefit." She turned her head. "Give me a kiss, will you?"

"Why?"

"Because I'd like one. Just a friendly one."

He put a finger under her chin to tip it up, touched his lips to hers. "Friendly enough?"

"Yeah, thanks."

She started to smile, but he shifted his hand, cupped it around her throat. With his eyes open, he lowered his mouth to hers again, teased her lips apart with his tongue and tasted the arousal on her first shaky breath.

It was like water, pure, sweet water after an agonizing thirst. He sipped easily.

She felt the rush of need, the hard, sharp-edged wave of it that left her limp. He didn't bring her closer, nor did he deepen the kiss. Instead it was slow, cool, devastatingly controlled.

When he drew back, she kept her eyes closed, absorbing the flood of sensation. Her heart was still pounding in her ears when she opened her eyes. "God," was all she managed to say.

"Problem?"

"I think so." She pressed her lips together. She could have sworn they were vibrating. "I think . . . I think I'll go." Her knees wobbled when she stood. It was very difficult, she thought, to be in charge of a situation when your knees wobbled. She pressed a hand to her stomach where the hard ball of need had hotly lodged. "God," she said again, and walked away.

11

The new security system on Dora's building brought DiCarlo a great deal of irritation. The extra time needed to bypass it, and to get through the sturdier locks, completely wrecked his schedule. He'd hoped to get in and out of the storeroom by midnight. For surely if the Conroy woman had bought the damn painting, the damn painting was inside, regardless of what the idiot redheaded clerk had told him on Christmas Eve.

Now he'd be lucky to be inside by midnight. And worse, a nasty sleet was beginning to fall. His surgeon's gloves were hardly adequate protection against the cold.

At least there was no moon, he thought as he worked and shivered. And there were no vehicles in the graveled lot, which meant no one was home. Despite the complications, he could still be in New York by morning. He'd sleep the entire day, then catch a late flight to the coast. Once he'd handed over Finley's toys, accepted the gratitude and a generous bonus, he'd fly back to New York for a rollicking New Year's Eve.

DiCarlo shivered as the cold snuck under his collar like frigid little ants.

When the final tumbler fell, he gave a little grunt of satisfaction.

In less than fifteen minutes he was certain that the painting was not in the storeroom. Using self-control, he curbed the urge to wreck the place. If the painting was going to cause a problem, it would be best if no one knew there'd been a break-in.

He did another, thorough tour of the shop, automatically picking up a few small trinkets as he went, including the jade Foo dog Terri had tried to sell him.

Resigned, DiCarlo headed upstairs. He cursed, but without much heat when he encountered the lock on the door at the top of the steps. This one was basically for looks, and he was through it quickly.

He listened, heard nothing. No radio, television, conversation. Still, he moved silently down the hall, peering out the door to be certain the parking lot was still empty.

Three minutes later he was inside Jed's apartment. That search was over almost before it had begun. There were no paintings on the wall, none tucked into the closets. He found nothing under the bed but a dog-eared paperback copy of Shirley Jackson's *The Haunting of Hill House* and a balled-up sock.

He did find the .38 in the nightstand of some interest, but after a brief examination, replaced it. Until he'd found the painting, he couldn't afford to steal anything noticeable. He gave the bench press and weights in the living room a quick glance on his way out.

He was in Dora's apartment in a matter of seconds. She hadn't bothered to lock it.

The search here was a different matter. Where Jed's apartment had held a minimum of furniture, Dora's was packed. The clutter in Jed's came from carelessness. In Dora's it was a life-style.

There were several paintings. A watercolor still life, two oval portraits, one of a stern-faced man in starched collar, one of an equally stern-faced woman. Other art ranged from signed lithographs, advertising posters, and pen-and-ink sketches to the finger paintings stuck to the refrigerator. But the abstract wasn't on the wall.

He moved into the bedroom to search the closet. Because he, too, had left the door unlocked, he barely had time to react when he heard it open. By the time it slammed, DiCarlo was deep in the closet hidden behind a colorful assortment of outfits that smelled erotically of woman.

"I have to be crazy," Dora told herself. "Absolutely crazy." She peeled out of her coat, laid it over the back of a chair and yawned hugely. How did she let her parents talk her into it? Why had she let them talk her into it?

Still muttering to herself, she walked straight to the bedroom. Her plans for the evening had been so simple, she thought. A nice, solitary meal of grilled chicken and wild rice; a long, fragrant bath with a glass of chardonnay as a companion. She'd intended to top it all off with a good book by the bedroom fire.

But no, she thought, and switched on the Tiffany lamp beside the bed. Oh, no, she had to fall into that old family trap of the show must go on.

Was it her fault that three stagehands had come down with the flu? Was it her fault she'd let her father badger her into joining the union?

"Absolutely not," she decided, tugging her tight-fitting black cashmere sweater over her head. "I didn't give them the damn flu. I didn't have to feel obligated to jump into the void just because I have an IATSE card."

Sighing, she bent over to unlace her black Chucks. Instead of a quiet, relaxing evening at home, she'd answered her mother's frantic call for help and had spent hours handling props and hauling scenery.

She'd even reluctantly enjoyed it. Standing backstage and listening to the voices echo, rushing out when the lights dimmed to make a scenery change, feeling a vicarious pride when the cast took their curtain calls.

After all, Dora thought with a yawn, what's bred in the bone . . .

Through the two-inch crack in the closet door, DiCarlo had an excellent view. The more he saw, the more his annoyance at being interrupted faded. The situation had possibilities, previously unexplored ones.

The woman who was bending and stretching at the foot of the bed had performed a very intriguing striptease and was now wearing only a couple of very tiny, very lacy black swatches. DiCarlo studied the smooth curve of her bottom as Dora bent to touch her toes.

She was beautifully built, in a firm, compact style. And from the way she was moving, it appeared she'd be very, very agile.

She'd changed his plans, but DiCarlo prided himself on creative thinking. He'd simply wait until the very pretty, very alone lady had gotten into bed.

Dora turned, and he took the opportunity to admire the thrust of lace-trimmed breasts.

Very nice, he thought, and smiled in the dark. Very nice indeed.

And once she was in bed, DiCarlo figured it would be a simple matter, using his considerable charms—and his .22 automatic—to convince her to tell him where the painting was.

And after business, pleasure. He might not even have to kill her afterward.

Dora shook back her hair, rolled her shoulders. It was as if she were posing, DiCarlo thought. The blood surged into his loins and throbbed impatiently. With her eyes closed and the beginnings of a smile on her face, she circled her head gently.

She lifted her hands to the front hook of the bra.

The pounding on her door had Dora jolting. In the closet, DiCarlo's breath hissed out in a combination of rage and frustration.

"Hold on!" Dora shouted, grabbing a white terrycloth robe from the foot of the bed. She struggled into it as the pounding continued. Switching on lights as she went, she hurried out to the living room. She hesitated with her hand on the knob. "Jed?"

"Open up, Conroy."

"You gave me a start," she said as she opened the door. "I was just—" The look on his face stopped her. She'd seen fury before, but never quite so intense, and never aimed so fiercely in her direction. Instinctively, she lifted a hand to her throat and stepped back. "What?"

"What the hell did you think you were doing?"

"Ah . . . going to bed," she said carefully.

"Do you think because I pay you rent you can use your fucking key and poke through my things anytime you want?"

She lowered her hand again, gripped the knob firmly. "I don't know what you're talking about."

"Cut the crap." Jed snagged her wrist and yanked her into the hall. "I know when my place has been tossed."

"You're hurting me." Her attempt at sternness failed miserably. She was afraid, really afraid he could do a lot worse.

"You took that risk when you messed with my privacy." Enraged, he shoved her up against the opposite wall. Her muffled cry of surprised pain only added to his fury. "What were you looking for?" he demanded. "What the hell did you think you'd find?"

"Let go of me." She twisted, too terrified for denials. "Take your hands off me."

"You want to go through my things?" His eyes burned into hers.

The animal was out of the cage, was all she could think.

"You figure because you've got me churned up inside you can paw through what I keep in my drawers, in my closet, and I'll let it go?" He jerked her away from the wall and, pushed by his own demons, dragged her stumbling after him. "Fine." He slammed his door open, shoved her inside. "Take a look now. Take a good one."

Even her lips had lost color. Her breath shuddered in and out through them. He was between her and the door. There was no possible hope of getting past him toward escape. As her heart drummed hard against her ribs, she saw by his face there was no chance of reason.

"You're out of your mind."

Neither of them heard DiCarlo slip down the hall and away. They stood two feet apart with Dora tugging with a shaking hand at the robe that had fallen off her shoulder.

"Did you think I wouldn't notice?" He moved too quickly for her to evade, grabbing her robe by the lapels and yanking her to her toes. Seams gave way with quick pops. "I was a cop for fourteen Goddamn years. I know the signs."

"Stop it!" She shoved against him. The sound of her robe ripping at the shoulder was like a scream. Tears of terror and rage sprang to her eyes, drenching them, clouding her vision. "I haven't been in here. I haven't touched anything."

"Don't lie to me." But the first seed of doubt squeezed through his fury.

"Let me go." She tore free, falling back and ramming hard into the table. Slowly, like a woman waiting for the tiger to spring again, she backed away. "I haven't been in here. I just got home ten minutes ago. Go feel the hood of my car, for Christ's sake. It's probably still warm." Her voice hitched and sputtered in time with her heart. "I've been at the theater all night. You can call, check."

He said nothing, only watched her edge for the door. Her robe had fallen open. He could see her muscles quiver and the sheen of panic sweat. She was crying now, fast, choking sobs as she fumbled with the doorknob.

"Stay away from me," she whispered. "I want you to stay away from me." She fled, leaving his door swinging open and slamming her own.

He stood exactly where he was, waiting for his own heartbeat to slow, waiting for some grip on control, however slippery.

He hadn't been wrong. Goddamn it, he hadn't been wrong. Someone had been inside. He knew it. His books had been moved, his clothes run through, his gun examined.

But it hadn't been Dora.

Sickened, he pressed the heels of his hands to his eyes. He'd snapped. No surprise there, he thought, dropping his hands. He'd been waiting to snap for months. Wasn't that why he'd turned in his badge?

He'd come home after a miserable day of dealing with lawyers and accountants and bankers, and he'd snapped like a twig.

And if that wasn't bad enough, he'd terrorized a woman. Why had he picked on her? Because she'd gotten to him. She'd gotten to him and he'd found the perfect way to make her pay the price. Nice going, Skimmerhorn, he berated himself, and headed for the kitchen. And the whiskey.

He stopped himself before he poured the first glass. That was the easy way. He dragged a hand through his hair, took a long breath and walked over to Dora's to take the hard way.

At the knock, she stopped rocking on the arm of the chair. Her head jerked up. She scrambled to her feet.

"Dora, I'm sorry." On the other side of the door, Jed shut his eyes. "Damn," he whispered, and knocked again. "Let me come in a minute, will you? I want to make sure you're all right." The silence dragged on, tightening his chest. "Just give me a minute. I swear I won't touch you. I want to see if you're okay, that's all."

In frustration he turned the knob.

Her eyes widened as she watched it rotate. Oh God, oh God, she thought in panic, she hadn't locked it. A little sound caught in her throat. She lunged for the door just as Jed opened it.

When she froze, he saw the wild fear on her face, something he'd seen on too many faces over too many years. He hoped he remembered how to defuse fear as skillfully as he'd remembered how to incite it. Very slowly, he lifted his hands, palms out.

"I'll stay right here. I won't come any closer." She was shaking like a leaf. "I won't touch you, Dora. I want to apologize."

"Just leave me alone."

Her cheeks were still wet, but her eyes were dry now, dry and terrified. He couldn't walk away until he'd eased that fear. "Did I hurt you?" He swore at the stupidity of the question. He could already see the bruises. "Of course I hurt you." The way she'd cried out when he'd shoved her against the wall played back in his head and made his stomach clench.

"Why?"

The fact that she would ask surprised him. "Does it matter? I don't have any excuses. Even an apology's pretty lame after what I did. I'd like to—" He took a step forward, stopping when she flinched. He'd have preferred a fist to the gut. "I'd like to say it was justified, but it wasn't."

"I want to know why." Her hand clenched and unclenched on the neck of her robe. "You owe me why."

It was a hot ball in his throat. He couldn't be sure which would be more painful, holding it there or spitting it out. But she was right. He owed her why.

"Speck tossed my house a week after he killed my sister." Neither his face nor his voice gave away what it cost him to tell her. "He left a snapshot of her, and a couple of newspaper clippings about the explosion on my dresser." The nausea surged, almost as violently as it had all those months ago. He paled as he fought it back. "He just wanted me to know he could get to me, anytime. He wanted to make sure I knew who was responsible for Elaine. When I came home tonight, and I thought you'd been in, it brought it back."

She had a beautifully expressive face. He could read every emotion perfectly. The fear, and the anger that had been building to combat it, faded away. In their stead were flickers of sorrow, understanding and, like salt to his wounds, sympathy.

"Don't look at me like that." His tone was curt and, she thought, defensive. "It doesn't change what I did, or the fact that I was capable of doing worse."

She lowered her eyes. "You're right. It doesn't. When you kissed me last night, I thought something was happening with us. Really happening." She lifted her gaze again, and her eyes were cool. "But it can't be, or else this wouldn't have happened. Because you'd have trusted me. That hurts too, Jed, but that's my mistake."

He knew what it was to feel helpless, but had never expected to feel it with her. "I can move out if you want," he said stiffly. "I can leave tonight and pick up my stuff later."

"It isn't necessary, but you do what you want."

Nodding, he stepped backward into the hallway. "Are you going to be all right?"

For an answer, she walked to the door, closed it quietly and turned the lock.

• • •

She found the flowers on her desk in the morning. Daisies, a little wilted and smelling of far-off spring, were stuffed into a Minton vase. Sternly, Dora quashed the first surge of pleasure and ignored them.

He hadn't moved out. That much had been clear from the monotonous thud of weights bumping the floor when she'd passed his door earlier.

She wasn't about to let that please her either. As far as she was concerned now, Jed Skimmerhorn was a paying tenant. Nothing more. No one was going to terrify her, threaten her and break her heart, then lure her back with a straggling bunch of daisies. She would cash his monthly check, nod to him politely if they happened to pass in the hall and get on with her own life.

It was a matter of pride.

Since Terri and Lea were handling the shop, she took out her accounts payable, opened the checkbook for Dora's Parlor and prepared to work.

A few minutes later she snuck a peek at the daisies and caught herself smiling. Then the sound of boots coming down the stairs had her firming her lips and staring at her electric bill.

Jed hesitated at the base of the stairs, searching for something reasonable to say. He would have sworn the temperature had dropped ten degrees since he'd come into the storeroom. Not that he could blame her for giving him the chill, he decided. But it only made him feel more foolish for buying flowers on the way back from the gym.

"If you're going to be working in here, I can finish up those shelves later."

"I'll be doing paperwork for a couple of hours," she said. She didn't glance up.

"I've got some stuff to do downtown." He waited for a response, got nothing. "Do you need anything while I'm out?"

"No."

"Fine. Great." He started back upstairs. "Then I'll finish them up this afternoon. After I go out and buy myself a hair shirt."

Dora lifted a brow, listened to the top door slam. "Probably thought I'd throw myself in his arms because he bought me flowers. Jerk." She looked over as Terri walked through from the shop. "Men are all jerks."

Normally Terri would have grinned, agreed and added her own examples. Instead she stood in the doorway, wringing her hands.

"Dora, did you take the jade dog upstairs? The little Chinese piece? I know you like to shift things around."

"The Foo dog?" Lips pursed, Dora tapped her pen on the desk. "No. I haven't circulated any inventory since before Christmas. Why?"

Terri gave a breathless laugh, a sickly smile. "I can't find it. I just can't find it anywhere."

"It probably just got moved. Lea might have—"

"I've already asked her," Terri interrupted. Her voice sounded weak. "I showed it to a customer the other day. Now it's gone."

"Don't panic." Dora pushed away from her desk. "Let me take a look around. I might have moved it myself."

But she knew she hadn't. Dora's Parlor might have looked like a homey, cluttered space where treasure and trash were carelessly arranged side by side. But there had always been a method to the arrangement. Dora's method.

She knew her stock, and its place, down to the last silk postcard.

Lea was busy with a customer and only sent her sister a quick, concerned look, then continued to show tobacco jars.

"It was in this cabinet," Terri said quietly. "I showed it Christmas Eve, right before closing. And I'm positive I saw it here yesterday when I sold the Doulton figure. They were side by side; I would have noticed if it had been missing then."

"All right." Dora patted Terri's shoulder soothingly. "Let's look around."

Even the first glance was alarming. Dora homed in on a satinwood bonheur. She made sure to keep her voice calm and low. "Terri, have you sold anything this morning?"

"A tea set—the Meissen—and a couple of cigarette cards. Lea sold the mahogany cradle and a pair of brass candlesticks."

"You didn't sell anything else?"

"No." Terri's already pale cheeks went whiter. "What is it? Something else is gone."

"The vinaigrette, the enamel one that was there." Dora controlled a curse. "And the inkwell that was beside it."

"The pewter?" Terri turned to the bonheur, groaned. "Oh God, Dora."

Dora shook her head to ward off any more comment and did a swift tour of the entire shop.

"The Chelton paperweight," she said a few moments later. "The Baccarat perfume bottle, the Fabergé desk seal—" That one, priced at $5,200, was tough to swallow. "And the Bakelite cigarette case." Which, at roughly $3, infuriated her almost as much as the Fabergé. "All small enough to fit into a purse or a pocket."

"We haven't had more than eight or nine people in all morning," Terri began. "I don't see how—Oh, Dora, I should have watched more carefully."

"It's not your fault."

"But—"

"It's not." Though she felt sick with anger, she slipped an arm around Terri's waist. "We can't treat everyone who walks through the doorlike a shoplifter. We'd end up putting in those damn security mirrors and shoving all our stock behind locked glass. It's the first time we've been hit this hard."

"Dora, the Fabergé."

"I know. I'll report it to the insurance company. That's what they're for. Terri, I want you to take your lunch break now."

"I couldn't eat."

"Then go for a walk. Go buy a dress. It'll make you feel better."

Terri blew her nose. "Aren't you mad?"

"Mad? I'm furious." Her eyes narrowed and snapped. "I'm hoping they come back and try to lift something else so I can break all their sticky little fingers. Now go, clear your head."

"Okay." She blew her nose again and left Dora alone in the small side parlor.

"Bad?" Lea asked when she stuck her head in.

"Bad enough."

"Honey, I'm sorry."

"No 'I told you to lock things up'?"

Lea sighed. "I figure this should prove I was right, but after working here these past few weeks, I understand why you don't. It would spoil the atmosphere."

"Yeah." Defeated, Dora rubbed at the beginning of a headache between her eyes. "You can buy a lot of atmosphere for ten thousand."

"Ten thousand," Lea repeated. Her eyes widened. "Ten thousand *dollars?* Oh my God, Dory."

"Don't worry, I'm insured. Goddamn it. Look, put up the Closed sign for an hour. Go out and get some lunch or something. I want to go in the back and have a tantrum, and I'd like privacy."

"Are you sure?" Lea took one look at the glint in her sister's eyes. "You're sure. I'll lock up."

"Thanks."

12

Jed wondered if going back to the cop shop for the first time since his resignation was just another way to punish himself. He could have set up a meeting with Brent elsewhere and avoided the wrenching reminder that he was now a civilian.

But Jed walked into his old precinct, the place where he'd spent eight of his fourteen years on the force, because he knew he had to face it. After the way he'd spun out of control the night before, he admitted there were plenty of things he was going to have to face.

Everything was the same. The air still smelled of spilled coffee, underwashed bodies and stale smoke—all with a much nastier undertone of disinfectant. The walls had been painted recently, but the color was the same institutional beige. The sounds—all familiar. Ringing phones, clattering keyboards, raised voices.

The fact that he walked in this time without the weight of his weapon strapped to his side made him feel more than awkward. This time he felt naked.

He nearly walked out again, but two uniforms turned toward the doors on their way to patrol. Recognition flickered on both of their faces. The one on the left—Snyder, Jed remembered—jerked to attention.

"Captain, sir."

They were getting younger every year, Jed mused. This one was hardly old enough to shave. The only way through it was ahead. Jed nodded to both of them as he passed. "Officers."

He stopped at the desk, waited until the bull-shouldered sergeant turned. "Ryan." The man might have had shoulders like a bull, but he had the face of a teddy bear. When he spotted Jed, that face creased into a smile so big his eyes seemed to disappear into the soft folds of ruddy Irish skin.

"Captain. Son of a bitch." He reached over the desk to grasp Jed's hand like a vise gripping steel. "Good to see you. Really good."

"How's it going?"

"Oh, you know. Same old same old." He leaned companionably on the counter that separated them. "Lorenzo got winged in a liquor store hit last week."

"I heard about that. How's he doing?"

"Milking it," Ryan said with a wink. "Time was, a guy took a pop, he mopped up the blood and got back on the street."

"After he chewed the bullet out with his teeth."

"That's the way." Someone shouted for Ryan, and he shouted back that they should hold on. "We miss you around here, Captain," he said, leaning on the desk again. "Goldman's okay as an acting captain. I mean he pushes paper with the best of them, but let's face it. The man's an asshole."

"You'll break him in."

"No, sir." Ryan shook his head. "Some you do, some you don't. The men knew they could talk to you, straight. Knew they'd find you on the street as often as you'd be riding the desk. With Goldman you gotta climb up the chain of command and tippytoe through regulations and procedure." His genial face wrinkled into a sneer. "You won't catch him going through the door, not unless there's a camera and three reporters on the other side."

Whatever Jed felt about Ryan's easy flow of information, he kept to himself. "Good press doesn't hurt the department. Is Lieutenant Chapman in? I need to talk to him."

"Sure, I think he's in his office. You can track him down."

Jed waited, then lifted his brow. "Give me a visitor's badge, Ryan."

Ryan turned pink with embarrassed dismay. "Shit, Captain."

"I need a visitor's badge, Sergeant."

"Makes me sick," Ryan muttered as he pulled one out. "I gotta tell you, it makes me sick."

"You told me." Jed clamped the badge onto his shirt.

To get to Brent, he had to walk through the bull pen. He would have preferred a nice slow waltz on hot coals. His stomach clenched each time his name was called, each time he was forced to stop and exchange a word. Each time he forced himself to ignore the speculation, the unasked questions.

By the time he reached Brent's door, the tension was rapping at the base of his neck like a dull spike.

He knocked once, then pushed the door open. Brent was sitting at his overburdened desk, the phone at his ear. "Tell me something I don't know." He glanced up. Instantly the irritation in his eyes cleared. "Yeah, yeah, and when you're ready to shoot straight, we'll deal. I'll get back to you." He hung up and leaned back in his chair. "I thought the noise level out there rose a few degrees. You were in the neighborhood, thought you'd drop by, right?"

"No." Jed sat down, took out a cigarette.

"I know, you needed a fix of cop coffee."

"When I get that bad, I'll have myself committed." Jed struck a match. He didn't want to ask, didn't want to get involved. But he had to. "Is Goldman being as big an asshole as Ryan claims?"

Grimacing, Brent rose to pour two cups of coffee from the pot on his hot plate. "Well, he's not exactly Mr. Popularity around here. I caught Thomas down in the locker room sticking pins in a Goldman doll. I recognized it because it had those little beady eyes and big teeth."

Jed took the coffee. "What did you do about the doll?"

"I stuck a couple pins in it myself. So far, Goldman doesn't seem to be in any particular discomfort."

Jed grinned. The first sip of coffee wiped that off his face. "You know, I could put in your name with the chief. I figure he'd listen to my recommendation."

"Not interested." Brent took off his glasses to wipe ineffectively at the smudges. "I'm lousy at delegating. Thomas might end up sticking pins in an incredibly handsome doll wearing horn-rims." He leaned against the edge of his desk. "Come back, Jed."

Jed lowered his eyes to his coffee, slowly lifted them again. "I can't. Christ, Brent, I'm a mess. Give me a badge right now and I don't know what I'd do, or who'd pay for it. Last night." He had to stop. He took a deep drag on his cigarette. "Somebody'd been in my place, in my things."

"You had another break-in over there?"

Jed shook his head. "This was slick. A couple things out of place, a drawer shut when I'd left it partway open, that kind of thing. I'd been out most of the day. Elaine's estate, the settlement on her house." Weary, he kneaded the back of his neck. "After all that, I went and had a drink, I went to a movie. I came home, took one look around and went after Dora."

He picked up his coffee again. It was no more bitter than the taste already lodged in his throat. "I mean I went after her, Brent. Saw the crime, made the collar." In disgust, he crushed out his cigarette and rose. "I pushed her around."

"Christ, Jed." Stunned, he watched Jed pace the office. "You didn't—you didn't hit her?"

"No." How could he be offended by the question? Jed wondered. "I scared the hell out of her, though. Scared myself after I pulled it in. I didn't think it through. I didn't keep it chilled. I just snapped. I'm not going to take the chance of doing something like that from behind a badge, Brent." He turned back. "That badge used to mean something to me."

"I've known you almost ten years. I never once saw you misuse it."

"And I don't intend to. Anyway, that's not why I'm here. Dora didn't go into my apartment. So who did?"

"Might have been a return from whoever broke in the other night. Looking for something to lift."

"I don't have a lot in there with me, but there was a couple hundred in cash in the drawer. My thirty-eight. A Sony Walkman. Dora's place across the hall's loaded."

"What about the security?"

"I looked it over, couldn't find anything. This guy's good, Brent. A pro. It could be a connection to Speck, somebody who wants revenge."

"Speck wasn't the kind to inspire loyalty after death." But, like Jed, Brent wasn't willing to dismiss the possibility. "I'm going to do some checking. Why don't I put a couple of eyes on the building?"

Normally Jed would have cringed at the thought of protection. Now he merely nodded. "I'd appreciate it. If somebody wants me, I wouldn't like to have Dora caught in the middle."

"Consider it done. So tell me, how are you handling things with Dora?"

"I apologized." He snorted, turned to study Brent's poster of Eastwood's Dirty Harry. "Big fucking deal. I offered to move out, but she didn't seem to care one way or the other." He muttered under his breath, but Brent's ears were keen.

"What was that? Did you say something about flowers?"

"I bought her some damn flowers," Jed snapped. "She won't even look at them. She sure as hell won't look at me. Which would be just fine and dandy, except..."

"Except?"

Jed whirled back, a bleak expression on his face. "Goddamn it, Brent, she's got me. I don't know how she did it, but she's got me. If I don't have her soon, I'm going to start drooling."

"Bad sign," Brent said with a slow nod. "Drooling's a very bad sign."

"You getting a kick out of this?"

"Well... yeah." Brent grinned and pushed up his glasses. "A big one, actually. I mean, as I recall, you've always been smooth and on top of things—no pun intended—with women. Always figured it was all that high-class breeding. Now you're standing there with this hook in your mouth. It looks good on you."

Jed just glared.

"So she's pissed," Brent continued. "She'll make you sweat for a little while, beg a little."

"I'm not begging. Screw begging." He jammed his hands in his pockets. "I'd rather she be angry than frightened." No, he realized, he didn't think he could handle having her look at him with fear in her eyes again. "I thought I might pick up some more flowers on the way back."

"Maybe you'd better think sparkles, pal. The kind you hang around your neck."

"Jewelry? I'm not going to bribe her to forgive me."

"What are the flowers for?"

"Flowers aren't a bribe." Amazed that a married man could know so little, Jed headed for the door. "Flowers are sentimental. Jewelry's mercenary."

"Yeah, and there's nobody more mercenary than an angry woman. Just ask my wife," Brent shouted when Jed kept going. "Hey, Skimmerhorn! I'll be in touch."

Chuckling to himself, Brent went back to his desk. He called up the Speck file on the computer.

Jed was surprised to find Dora still at her desk when he returned. He'd been gone more than three hours, and in the short time he'd known her, he'd never seen her huddled with paperwork for more than half that time. Dora seemed to prefer the contact with customers, or perhaps it was the satisfaction of collecting money.

Probably both.

It didn't surprise him that she ignored him every bit as completely as she had that morning, but this time he thought he was prepared.

"I got you something."

Jed set the large box on the desk in front of her. When she glanced at it, he had the small satisfaction of spotting the flicker of curiosity in her eyes.

"It's, ah, just a robe. To replace the one that got torn last night."

"I see."

He moved his shoulders restlessly. He wasn't getting much of a reaction from her, and he figured he'd paid big time. Poking around a woman's lingerie department with the salesclerk beaming at him had made him feel like a pervert. At least he'd been able to settle for practical terrycloth.

"I think I got the size right, but you might want to check."

Carefully, she closed her checkbook and folded her hands on top of it. When she looked up at him, the curiosity had been replaced by glittering anger. "Let me get this straight, Skimmerhorn. Do you think that a bunch of pathetic flowers and a robe are what it's going to take to clear the path?"

"I—"

She didn't give him a chance. "You figure a handful of daisies will charm me into sighs and smiles? Is that what you think? I don't know how you've played it before, pal, but it doesn't work that way with me." She rose from the desk, slapped her palms down on the department-store box and leaned forward. If eyes were weapons, he'd have already bled to death. "Inexcusable behavior isn't reconciled by a couple of lame gifts and a hangdog expression."

She caught herself on the edge of a shout and paused to fight for control.

"You should keep going," Jed said quietly. "Get the rest of it out."

"All right, fine. You muscle your way into my apartment flinging accusations. Why? Because I was handy, and because you didn't like the way things were moving between us. You didn't even consider that you might be wrong, you just attacked. You scared the bloody hell out of me, and worse . . ." She pressed her lips together and turned away. "You humiliated me, because I just took it. I just stood there trembling and crying. I didn't even fight back." Now that she'd admitted it, she felt calmer and faced him again. "I hate that most of all."

He understood that all too well. "You'd have been crazy to take me on in the mood I was in."

"That's not the point."

"It is the point." He felt anger stirring again, viciously self-directed. "For Christ's sake, Dora, you were facing a maniac who had you by better than fifty pounds. What were you going to do, wrestle me to the ground?"

"I know self-defense," she said, lifting her chin. "I could have done something."

"You did." He remembered the way her terrified tears had defused him. "You're crazy if you let yourself be embarrassed because you were afraid."

"I don't think insulting me is going to smooth the waters, Skimmerhorn." She lifted a hand to push back her hair. It wasn't her usual casual gesture, Jed noted. It was a weary one. "Look, I've had a rough day—"

She broke off when he took her hand. Even as she stiffened, he gently straightened her arm. She'd pushed up the sleeves of her jacket to work. There was a light trail of bruises on her forearms, marks he knew would match the press of his fingers.

"I can keep saying I'm sorry." His eyes were eloquent. "That doesn't mean a hell of a Lot." He released her, tucked his hands away in his pockets. "I can't tell you I've never put bruises on a woman before, because I have. But it was always in the line of duty, never personal. I hurt you. And I don't know how to make it up to you."

He started for the steps.

"Jed." There was a sigh in her voice. "Wait a minute." Sucker, she admitted, and flipped open the top of the box. The robe was nearly identical to hers, but for the color. She smoothed a finger down the deep-green terrycloth lapel.

"They didn't have a white one." He wasn't sure if he'd ever felt more foolish in his life. "You wear a lot of bright colors, so . . ."

"It's nice. I didn't say I was forgiving you."

"Okay."

"I'd just prefer if we could put things back on some reasonable level. I'm not comfortable feuding with the neighbors."

"You've got a right to set the rules."

She smiled a little. "You must really be suffering to hand over that kind of power."

"You've never been a man buying women's lingerie. You don't know about suffering." He wanted to touch her, but knew better. "I am sorry, Dora."

"I know. Really, I do. I was nearly as mad at myself as I was at you this morning. Before I could cool off we had some trouble in the shop. So when you came back, I was ready for blood."

"What kind of trouble?"

"Shoplifting." Her eyes hardened again. "This morning, not long after you left to buy a hair shirt."

He didn't smile. "Are you sure it was all there last night when you closed up?"

That stiffened her spine. "I know my stock, Skimmerhorn."

"You said you got in a few minutes before I did last night."

"Yes, what does—"

"You were upset when I left you. You were still upset this morning. I don't suppose you'd have noticed."

"Noticed what?"

"If anything was missing from upstairs. Let's go take a look now."

"What are you talking about?"

"Somebody was in my place last night."

She caught herself before she spoke, but he saw the doubt on her face.

"I'm not saying that to excuse my behavior, but somebody was in my place," he said again, struggling to keep his voice calm. "Cops see things civilians don't. I had an idea that it might have been some of Speck's men, dropping around to hassle me, but it could have been something else. Somebody looking for some trinkets."

"What about the alarm system. Those burglary-proof locks you put in?"

"Nothing's burglary-proof."

"Oh." She closed her eyes briefly as he took her hand and pulled her up the stairs. "Well, that certainly makes me feel better. A minute ago I was happy being furious at a shoplifter. Now you've got me worried that I had some cat burglar prowling around my apartment."

"Let's just check it out. Got your keys?"

"It's not locked." His look made her bristle. "Look, ace, the outside door's locked, and I was right downstairs. Besides . . ." She shoved open the door. "Nobody's been in here."

"Mmm-hmm." He bent down to examine the lock, saw no obvious signs of tampering. "Did you leave this unlocked when you went out last night?"

"Maybe." She was beginning to sulk. "I don't remember."

"Keep any cash in the house?"

"Some." She crossed to the kneehole desk and opened a drawer. "It's right where it's supposed to be. And so is everything else."

"You haven't looked."

"I know what's in here, Jed."

He scanned the room himself, skimming, identifying knickknacks as skillfully as he would faces in a mugbook. "What happened to the painting? The one over the couch?"

"The abstract? My mother thought she liked it, so I took it over so she could live with it awhile." She gestured to the two portraits that replaced it. "I thought I'd like having those two for company. But I was wrong. They're entirely too somber and disapproving, but I haven't had the chance to—"

"Jewelry?"

"Sure, I have jewelry. Okay, okay." She rolled her eyes and headed back to the bedroom. She opened a camphorwood-and-ebony chest that sat on a lowboy. "It looks like it's all here. It's a little tougher to remember, because I lend Lea pieces, and she lends me . . ." She took out a velvet pouch and shook out a pair of emerald earrings. "If anybody was going to riffle through here, they'd go for these. They're the real thing."

"Nice," he said after a cursory glance. It didn't surprise him that she had enough jewelry to adorn a dozen women. Dora enjoyed quantity. Nor did it surprise him that her bedroom was as crowded and homey as her living room. Or as subtly feminine. "Some bed."

"I like it. It's a Louis the Fifteenth reproduction. I bought it from a hotel in San Francisco. I couldn't resist that headboard."

It was high, covered with deep blue brocade and gently curved at the top. She'd added a lushly quilted satin spread and an army of fussy pillows.

"I like to sit up late and read with a fire going." She closed the jewelry box. "One of the things that sold me on this building was the size of the rooms, and that I could have a fireplace in my bedroom. It's—as my father would say—the cat's meow." She grinned. "Sorry, Captain, it doesn't look like I have a crime to report."

He should have been relieved. But he couldn't ignore the tickle at the back of his neck. "Why don't you give me a list of the stolen goods? We—Brent can have some men check out the pawnshops."

"I've already reported it."

"Let me help." This time he went with the urge to touch her, to see if she'd back away. But when he ran a hand down her arm, she only smiled.

So he was forgiven, he thought. Just that simply.

"All right. It wouldn't be smart to turn down the services of a police captain over a simple shoplifting. Let me—" She started forward, but he didn't move with her or aside. All she accomplished was to come a step closer. Her heart stuttered in her chest with an emotion that had nothing to do with fear. Nothing at all. "The list's downstairs."

"I think you should know, you were right."

"That's always good to know. What was I right about this time?"

"I was tangled up about what was happening between us."

"Oh." It came out shaky; she couldn't help it. "What was happening between us?"

His eyes darkened. She thought of the cobalt glass on display in the shop. "I was wanting you. I was wondering what it would be like to undress you, and to touch you, and to feel you under me. I was wondering if your skin tasted like it smelled."

She stared at him while her stomach muscles danced. "Is that what was happening?"

"On my end. It was making me a little crazy."

"And it's better now?"

He shook his head. "Worse. Now I can imagine doing all those things in that bed. If you want to pay me back solid for last night, all you have to do is tell me you're not interested."

She let out the air that had backed up in her lungs. "Interested" wasn't precisely the word she would have chosen. "I think..." On a weak laugh, she pushed both hands through her hair. "I think I'm going to say I'm going to consider your offer carefully, and get back to you on it."

"You know where to find me."

"Yeah, I do."

He hadn't expected to fluster her, but he was enjoying it. "You want to have dinner? We could... discuss the terms."

The quick, wild fluttering of her heart made her feel very young, and very foolish. "I can't. I have a date—with my nephew." She picked up a silver-backed brush from her bureau, set it down again. "He's at that stage where he detests girls, so every now and again I take him out to the movies or the arcade. A kind of guys' night out."

"You're a girl."

"Not to Richie." She picked up the brush again, twisting the handle through her hands. "I don't mind sitting through ninety minutes of *Zombie Mercenaries from Hell*—that makes me one of the guys."

"If you say so." He flicked a glance down to her nervous hands and grinned. "We'll try guys' night out later, then."

"Sure. Maybe tomorrow."

"I think I can work it into my schedule." Gently, he took the brush from her restless fingers and laid it aside. "Why don't we go get that list?"

When they'd passed safely out of the bedroom, Dora let out a small, relieved breath. She was definitely going to think this over—as soon as some of the blood returned to her head.

"Got your keys downstairs?" Jed asked her when they stepped into the hall.

"What—oh, yeah."

"Good." He turned the lock before shutting the door.

DiCarlo might have enjoyed his luxurious suite at the Ritz-Carlton, with its soft, king-sized bed, a fully stocked honor bar, excellent room service and masseuse on call.

He might have enjoyed it—if he'd had the painting in his possession.

Instead he fumed.

Without the man in apartment two's ill-timed arrival, DiCarlo figured he would have had the painting—or known its whereabouts.

He hesitated to call Finley. There was nothing to report for the night's work but failure, and he still had until January the second. Coming up empty for one night played hell with his schedule, but in reality it was only a delay, not a disaster.

He chewed another nut and washed it down with the Beaujolais left over from his lunch. It baffled him that the man knew his apartment had been searched. Leaning back, DiCarlo went over his moves of the night before step by step. He hadn't disturbed anything. He'd resisted taking even easily fenceable merchandise from the two apartments. What he'd taken from the store below would be attributed to simple shoplifting.

Since the man suspected the woman next door had entered his apartment, his plans didn't change.

All he had to do was go back in, DiCarlo decided. He'd do exactly what he had planned to do the night before—exactly. Only this time he would go in knowing he'd kill the woman when he'd finished.

13

The temperature had dipped to a brisk fourteen degrees under a dazzling night sky splattered with icy stars and sliced by a thin, frosty moon. The shops along South Street were locked up tightly, and traffic was light. Occasionally someone stepped out of one of the restaurants, huddled inside a warm coat, and made a dash for a car or the subway. Then the street would be quiet again, with only the splash from the streetlamps to light the way.

DiCarlo spotted the police cruiser on his first circle of the block. His hands tightened on the wheel as he turned the corner to ride along the river. He hadn't counted on outside interference. Cops were usually too busy to stake out a building because of a possible minor break-in and a little shoplifting.

So, maybe the lady was boffing the chief of police, DiCarlo mused. Or maybe it was just bad luck. Either way, it was only one more detail. And one more reason to take the shapely Miss Conroy out when he was finished with her.

To calm himself, he tooled around aimlessly for ten minutes, switching the radio off and running through various scenarios in his head. By the time he'd circled around to South again, DiCarlo had his plan formulated. He pulled to the curb in front of the black-and-white. Taking his Philadelphia street map out of the glove box, he climbed out of the car. DiCarlo knew the cop would see only a well-dressed man in a rental car, obviously lost.

"Got a problem there, buddy?" The uniform rolled down his window. The air inside smelled of coffee and pastrami.

"I sure do." Playing his part, DiCarlo grinned sheepishly. "I was glad to see you pulled over here, Officer. I don't know where I made the wrong turn, but I feel like I've been driving around in circles."

"Thought I saw you drive by before. We'll see if we can set you straight. Where you trying to get to?"

"Fifteenth and Walnut?" DiCarlo pushed the map inside the window. "I found it on here, fine. Finding it in the car's been something else."

"No problem. You just want to go down here to Fifth and make a left. You'll run right into Walnut at Independence Square, make another left." He reached for a pen. "Let me show you."

"I appreciate it, Officer." Smiling, DiCarlo pressed his silenced pistol against the uniform's breast. Their eyes met for less than a heartbeat. There were two muffled pops. The cop's body jerked, slumped. Meticulously, DiCarlo checked the pulse, and when he found none, quietly opened the driver's door with his gloved hands, straightened the body into a sitting position. He rolled up the window, locked the door, then strolled back to his own car.

He was beginning to understand why his cousin Guido got such a kick out of murder.

Dora was disappointed that Richie hadn't taken her up on her invitation to sleep over. It seemed he'd had a better offer, so she'd dropped him off at a friend's after the movies.

She wished now that she'd swung back by Lea and John's and picked up the other kids for the night. A nice noisy pajama party would have calmed her nerves. The simple fact was, she didn't want to be alone.

No, she corrected, the complicated fact was, she didn't want to be alone and a few easy steps away from Jed Skimmerhorn. No matter how attractive and charming he'd been that afternoon, she couldn't let herself forget that he was a man capable of wild bursts of temper.

She believed—and accepted—his apology absolutely. She even understood a portion of his motivation. That didn't negate the fact that he was a crate of dynamite set with a very short fuse. She didn't want to be in harm's way when and if he exploded again.

Then again, she had a temper of her own. She might have had a longer fuse, but pound for pound she'd gauge her explosive quality equal to his.

Maybe that was just what he needed, she reflected. A woman who would stand up to him, fight back, win as often as she lost. If he had someone who understood the need to kick inanimate objects now and again, it might help him open up. It might help him squeeze out the poison in the wounds that troubled him. It might—

"Hold it, Dora," she mumbled. "You're getting this backwards. It's not what he needs, it's what *you* need." And what she didn't need was to take on a lover with more problems than a Eugene O'Neill play. She turned into the little gravel lot behind the shop. No matter how cute he was when he smiled.

The T-Bird was gone. Dora frowned a moment, then shook her head. For the best, she thought. If he wasn't around, she couldn't think about knocking on his door and inviting trouble.

Her boots crunched over the gravel, clattered up the back stairs that she usually took in a run. After entering the code into the alarm system, she unlocked the door, then secured it behind her.

She wouldn't tempt fate and listen for Jed's return, she decided, but make an early night of it. A pot of tea, a fire and that book she'd been trying to read: the perfect remedies for a troubled mind. And with any luck, they would also erase the effects of *Scream, If You Dare*—the horror movie she'd treated Richie to that evening.

She let herself into her apartment and turned on the Christmas tree. The cozy, colored lights never failed to cheer her. Once she had the stereo on low, she pried off her boots, peeled off her coat. Everything went neatly into her hall closet while she hummed along with Billie Holiday.

In her stocking feet, she padded into the kitchen to heat the kettle. Her hand on the tap jerked as a board creaked in the other room. Her heart made a beeline for her throat so that she stood frozen—water splashing into the sink—listening to the sound of her own racing heart.

"Get a grip, Conroy," she whispered. Imagine, letting a silly film give her the willies. There wasn't any seven-foot superhuman psychopath in her living room, waiting with a butcher knife. The building was settling, that was all.

Amused with herself, she put the kettle on to boil, adjusted the heat. She walked back into the living room, and stopped dead.

It was pitch dark, dark as a cave, with only the thin backwash of light from the kitchen illuminating the silhouettes of furniture. Which, of course, made the dark worse.

But she'd turned the tree on, hadn't she? Of course she had, she assured herself as her hand crept up to her throat to soothe a jittery pulse. A fuse? No, no, the stereo was still playing and they were on the same plug. She reasoned it out slowly, waiting for her heart rate to settle. The tree lights had probably shorted. Shaking her head at her overactive imagination, she started across the room to fix it.

And the kitchen light went out behind her.

Her breath sucked in on a gasp that she forced back out with a slow shudder. Slippery little fingers of fear slid over her skin. For a full minute she didn't move, listening to every sound. There was nothing but her own drumming heartbeat and shallow breathing. Lifting a hand to her head, she laughed. Of course there was nothing. A bulb blew, that was all.

Creative imagination was a killer, she mused. All she had to do was—

A hand clamped over her mouth, an arm snaked around her waist. Before she could think to struggle, she was yanked back against a hard body.

"You don't mind the dark, do you, honey?" DiCarlo kept his voice at a whisper, for practical purposes, and to add another element to her fear. "Now you stay real still and keep real quiet. You know what this is?" He loosened his grip enough to slip his gun under her sweater, run the side of it up over her breast. "It's a big, mean gun. You don't want me to have to use it, do you?"

She shook her head, squeezing her eyes tight when he stroked her flesh with steel. All capacity for thought vanished.

"Good girl. Now I'm going to take my hand away. If you scream, I'll have to kill you."

When he removed the hand from her mouth, Dora pressed her lips together to stop them from trembling. She didn't ask what he wanted. She was afraid she knew.

"I watched you the other night, in the bedroom, when you took off your clothes." His breath quickened as he slipped his free hand between her legs. "You had on black underwear. Lacy. I liked it."

She groaned, turning her head away as he rubbed through the wool of her slacks. Watched her. He'd watched her, was all she could think, repulsed.

"You're going to do that little striptease for me again, right after we take care of a little business.

"I—I have money," she managed. She kept her teeth clenched, her eyes straight ahead as she fought to distance her mind from what he was doing to her body. "A few hundred in cash. I'll give it to you."

"You're going to give me all sorts of things. Does this one fasten in the front, too."

He toyed with her bra as she whimpered. "Oh, yeah, that's just fine. What color is it?" When she didn't answer, he pressed the barrel of the gun against her heart. "You want to answer me when I ask you a question."

"R-red."

"Panties, too?"

A flush of shame rose up on her clammy skin. "Yes, yes, they're red."

"You are a hot one." He laughed, finding himself amazingly aroused by her trembling plea to stop. It was a bonus he hadn't expected.

"We're going to have a real good time, baby, and nobody'll get hurt. As long as you give me what I want. Say you understand."

"Yes."

"Yes, what?"

She bit down on the terror. "Yes, I understand."

"Good. Real good. First, I want you to tell me where it is, then we'll get down to the party."

Tears were shimmering in her eyes, burning them. She thought she'd been scared the night before with Jed. But that was nothing, nothing compared to the ice-edged horror that clawed through her now.

And she was doing nothing but whimpering, shaking and waiting to be victimized. She forced her trembling chin to firm. She wasn't helpless—wouldn't be helpless. He might rape her, but she wouldn't make it easy.

"I don't know what you're talking about." She didn't have to fake the shudders, and hoped he thought she was completely beaten when she went limp against him. "Please, please don't hurt me. I'll give you whatever you want if you don't hurt me."

"I don't want to have to." God, he felt hard as iron. Every time he slid the gun over her flesh, she quivered, and his blood sizzled. Those bleeding hearts who called rape a crime of violence were full of shit, he realized. It was about power. All about power.

"You cooperate, and we'll get on fine." He slipped the barrel of the gun under the front hook of her bra, sliding it slowly up and down the valley between her breasts. "Now, I looked all through the place and couldn't find it. You tell me where the picture is, and I'll take the gun away."

"The picture?" Her frantic mind whirled. Cooperate, he'd said, and he'd take the gun away. So she'd cooperate. But she wouldn't be powerless. "I'll give you the picture, any picture you want. Please, move the gun. I can't think when I'm so scared."

"Okay, baby." DiCarlo nipped at her earlobe and lowered the gun. "That feel better?"

"Yes."

"You didn't say thank you," he said, and teased her by bringing the gun back up her torso again.

She shut her eyes. "Yes, thank you."

Satisfied that she recognized who was in charge, he moved the gun again. "Much better. Just tell me where it is, and I won't hurt you."

"All right." She cupped her left fist with her right hand. "I'll tell you." Using the force of both arms, she rammed her elbow into his stomach. He grunted with pain as he stumbled back. Dora heard a clatter behind her as she raced for the door.

But her legs felt numb with fear. She fell into the hall, nearly lost her footing. She'd reached the rear door and was dragging at the locks when he caught her. She screamed then and, with survival her only thought, turned to claw at his face.

Swearing, DiCarlo hooked an arm around her throat. "We're not going to be able to be so nice now, are we?" Deliberately he cut off her air and began to pull her backward toward the dark apartment.

They both heard footsteps pounding up the stairs. With one desperate swipe, DiCarlo smashed the fluted hall sconce and waited in the shadows.

Jed came in low, weapon drawn.

"Toss it down," DiCarlo hissed, jerking on his arm to make Dora choke. "I've got a gun at her back. Make the wrong move and the lady won't have a spine left."

Jed couldn't see a weapon, but he could see the pale outline of Dora's face and hear her desperate struggle for air. "Ease off." With his eyes fixed on DiCarlo, he crouched, set his gun on the floor. "She won't be much of a shield if you strangle her."

"Stand up, hands behind your head. Kick the gun over here."

Jed straightened, linked his fingers behind his head. He knew Dora's eyes were on him, but he didn't look at her. "How far do you think you'll get?"

"Far enough. Kick the gun over here."

Jed nudged it halfway between himself and Dora, knowing the man who held her would have to come closer if he wanted it. Close enough, Jed figured, and they'd have a chance.

"Sorry," Jed said. "Looks like I missed the extra point."

"Back. Back against the wall, Goddamn it." DiCarlo was beginning to sweat now. Things weren't going the way they were supposed to. But he had the woman. And if he had the woman, he'd get Finley's painting.

Shifting, he began to sidestep down the hall toward the open door, with Dora between him and Jed. When he reached for Jed's gun, he pulled her down with him as he crouched to retrieve it. The movement loosened his hold around her throat.

Even as Jed prepared his move, she sucked in her breath. "He doesn't have a gun," she gasped out, and threw her body back.

Her foot hit the .38, sent it skidding out the door. Jed dragged her aside and braced for DiCarlo's attack. But rather than attack, DiCarlo ran.

Jed tackled him at the door. They went through together in a violent tangle of limbs and curses. With a report like a bullet, the banister cracked in two jagged pieces under the weight. By the time they'd hit the ground, Dora was scrambling through the door and down the steps in search of the gun.

A blow glanced off Jed's kidneys. Another caught him low in the gut. He plowed his fist into the other man's face and had the satisfaction of seeing blood splatter.

"I can't find it!" Dora shouted.

"Get the hell out of here." Jed blocked the foot DiCarlo kicked toward his head and heaved his opponent backward.

Instead she let out an outraged howl when DiCarlo grabbed part of the broken banister, taking a vicious swing that missed Jed's face by inches. Teeth bared, she took three running steps and leaped on DiCarlo's back.

She bit down enthusiastically on his neck and drew blood before he flung her aside.

Pain exploded as her head hit the edge of a step. Dora reared up, managed to gain her feet again. But her vision doubled, tripled, then blacked out completely as she crumpled to the ground.

When she opened her eyes again, everything swam in and out of focus. And it hurt. Dora let her eyes shut and tried to slip back into the void.

"No, you don't. Come on, baby, open up." Jed tapped Dora's cheeks with the back of his hand until the annoyance had her moaning and opening her eyes again.

"Cut it out." She shoved his hand aside and started to sit up. The room revolved like a carousel.

"Not so fast." Very much afraid her eyes were going to do that slow roll to the back of her head again, Jed eased her back down. "Try staying awake, but do it horizontal."

"My head." She touched a tentative hand to the back of her head and hissed in reaction. "What hit me?"

"It was what you hit. Just relax. How many fingers?" He held a hand in front of her face.

"Two. Are we playing doctor?"

Though he worried about a concussion, at least her vision and speech were clear. "I think you're okay." The flood of relief was instantly dammed by temper. "Not that you deserve to be after that idiotic move of yours. What were you doing, Conroy? Riding piggyback?"

"I was trying to help." It all came rushing back, much too quickly, much too clearly. Her fingers gripped his, reminding him that he was still holding her hand. "Where is he?" This time, despite the flash of pain, she pushed herself up. "Did he get away?"

"Yeah, he got away. Damn it. I'd have had him if you..."

Her eyes narrowed, dared him. "If I what?"

"You went down like a tree. I thought you'd been wrong about the gun." The memory brought on a fast, greasy wave of nausea. "The idea that he'd shot you kind of took my mind off bashing his face in. It turned out all you'd done was crack that amazingly hard head of yours."

"Well, why didn't you go after him?" She tried to shift, noticed she was wrapped in a crocheted afghan like a moth in a cocoon.

"I guess I could have left you there, unconscious, freezing, bleeding—"

"Bleeding?" Gingerly, she checked her head again. "Am I bleeding?"

"You didn't lose much." But he began to shift into his professional mode. "You want to tell me what that was about? I don't suppose it was another of your dates gone wrong."

She stared at him, then looked away. "Should we call the cops?"

"I did. Brent's on his way."

"Oh." She glanced around the apartment. "He did have a gun, before. I don't know what happened to it."

"It was under the table. I've got it."

Her smile was weak and didn't last. "You've been busy."

"You took your sweet time coming around. Another couple of minutes and I'd have called an ambulance."

"Lucky me."

"Enough stalling." He sat beside her, took her hand again, too gently for her to refuse the contact. "Tell me what happened. Exactly what happened."

"I guess you were right about somebody breaking in here yesterday. It seems he was in here, too. I really didn't notice anything moved or taken, but he said he'd seen me undressing." She hesitated. "And since he described my style of underwear, I have to believe him."

He recognized the signs, humiliation rushing through the fear, shame jockeying with anger. "Dora, I can have Brent call in a woman officer if it would be easier for you."

"No." She took a deep breath. "He must have been hiding in here somewhere—the bedroom again maybe. I went right into the kitchen, to make tea . . . I left the water on."

"I took care of it."

"Oh, good. I'm fond of that kettle." She began to toy with the fringe of the afghan. "Anyway, when I came back in here, the tree was off. I'd just turned it on, so I figured the plug had come out of the socket or something. I started to go over and fix it, and the light in the kitchen went off. He grabbed me from behind."

Her voice had started to shake. Dora cleared her throat. "I would have fought back. I like to think I'd have fought back, but he put the gun under my sweater and started to, um, started to rub it over me." She gave a weak laugh. "I guess some guys really do look at a gun as a phallic symbol."

"Come here." He gathered her close, easing her throbbing head onto his shoulder. While his own rage ate through him he stroked her hair. "It's all right now."

"I knew he was going to rape me." She closed her eyes and burrowed in "A bunch of us took this self-defense course last year, but I couldn't remember a thing. It was like this sheet of ice slipped over my brain and I couldn't get through it. He kept saying what a good time we were going to have, and I got so angry. He was slobbering on my neck and telling me I just had to be good, I just had to cooperate. I got so mad because he thought I wasn't going to do anything to protect myself. I guess you could say I broke through the ice, because I rammed my elbow into his stomach, and I ran. That's where you came in."

"Okay." He didn't want to think of what might have happened if he hadn't come in. "Did you know him?"

"I don't think so. I didn't recognize his voice. It was too dark in here to see, and he was behind me. I think I got a pretty good look at him outside, but he didn't seem familiar." She let out a cleansing breath. "Your brand new banister's busted."

"I guess I'll have to fix it again. Got some aspirin?"

"Bathroom medicine chest." She smiled when she felt his lips brush against her temple. That helped, too. "Bring me a couple dozen, will you?" Calmer, she leaned back when he stood up. The crumpled towel on the coffee table caught her eye. It was her satin-edged, hand-embroidered fingertip towel. And it was dotted with blood.

"Damn, Skimmerhorn, did you have to use the good linen?" Disgusted, she leaned forward to pluck it up. "And it's wet, too! Do you know what wet cloth does when it's left on wood?"

"I wasn't thinking about the furniture." He rattled around in the medicine chest. "I can't find any aspirin."

"Let me." She'd been rather pleased to be able to stand and walk on her own, until she caught a glimpse of her reflection in the mirrored cabinet above the bathroom sink. "Oh my God."

"Dizzy?" Sharp-eyed for signs of fainting, he took her arms, prepared to sweep her up.

"No, revolted. The only makeup left on my face is what's smeared under my eyes. I look like something out of the Addams family." Reaching up, she took a small blue apothecary bottle from the top shelf. "Aspirin."

"Why isn't it in the right bottle?"

"Because plastic aspirin bottles are ugly and offend my impeccable sense of style." She shook out four, handed the bottle back to Jed.

"How do you know they aren't antihistamines?"

"Because antihistamines are in the amber bottle, aspirin is in the blue one." She ran water into a porcelain cup and downed the pills in one swallow. She winced at the sound of the knock on her door. The grandmother of all headaches was setting up residence just under her skull. "Is that the cavalry?"

"I imagine. Stay here."

She watched him, eyes widening as she saw the gun hooked in the back of his jeans. He reached for it and stood at the side of the door. "Yeah?"

"It's Brent."

"It's about damn time." He yanked open the door and a portion of his bottled-up fury descended onto his former partner. "What the hell kind of cops are you putting on these days when an armed rapist can stroll right by them and break into a locked building?"

"Trainor was a good man." Brent's mouth was tight and grim. He looked over Jed's shoulder to where Dora was standing in the bathroom doorway. "Is she all right?"

"No thanks to Philadelphia's finest. If I hadn't—" He broke off because the look in Brent's eyes had finally penetrated his temper. "Was?"

"Dead. Twice in the chest, close range. So close there are fucking powder burns on his shirt."

Dora's steps slowed as she saw the look they exchanged. "What is it? What else happened?"

"I asked Brent to put a man on the building, in case whoever broke in came back." Jed took out a cigarette. "He came back." He struck a match. "And the cop's dead."

"Dead?" The color that had come back into her cheeks washed away.

"I want you to sit down," Jed said flatly. "And run through the whole thing again, step by step."

"How was he killed?" But she already knew. "He was shot, wasn't he?"

"Let's sit down, Dora." Brent started to take her arm, but she shook him away and stepped back.

"Was he married?"

"That's not—"

"Don't tell me it's not my concern." She slapped a hand onto Jed's chest before he could finish the sentence. "A man was outside, trying to protect me. Now he's dead. I want to know if he had a family."

"He had a wife," Brent said quietly while guilt gnawed at him with small, dull teeth. "Two kids, both in high school."

Hugging her arms, she turned away.

"Dora." Jed started to reach out, to touch her, but let his hand fall back to his side again. "When a man or woman joins the force, they know what the risks are."

"Shut up, Skimmerhorn. Just shut up. I'm going to make coffee." She pushed back her tousled hair. "We'll go over it again."

Later, they sat at Dora's dining room table, going over her statement point by point.

"Funny he'd come back—we've got to figure three times." Brent checked his notes. "And taking out a cop to get inside. Not the pattern of your usual rapist."

"I wouldn't know. The more frightened I was, the better he liked it." She recited the lines as if rehearsing for a play. "I could tell he was excited, that he didn't want it to happen too quickly. Because he kept talking. He said..." She opened her eyes. "I forgot. He said something about a picture."

"He wanted pictures?" Brent asked.

"I—no. No, I don't think that was it. He wanted a specific picture, wanted me to tell him where it was. I wasn't really listening then, because I knew I had to do something or he was going to rape me."

"What kind of pictures do you have?"

"All sorts, I suppose. Family pictures, snapshots of vacations and birthday parties. Nothing anyone would be interested in."

"When's the last time you took any?" Jed questioned. "What did you take them of?"

"I took some at Christmas, at Lea's. I haven't even had them developed yet. Before that..." She pulled a hand through her hair, holding it back from her face before she let it go. "Christ, I don't know for certain. Weeks, probably months."

"I'd like to have that film developed, if you don't mind." Brent smiled. "It never hurts to check."

"I'll go get it."

"It doesn't fit," Jed said when she left the room. "A guy doesn't kill a cop, then walk across the street to rape a woman and raid her photo album."

"We have to start somewhere. He wanted a picture, we'll look at her pictures. Maybe she took a shot of something she shouldn't have."

"Maybe." But he couldn't make the piece fit into the puzzle.

"Did you get a good enough look at him for a make?"

"Six foot, a hundred seventy. Dark hair, dark eyes, slim build. He had on a cashmere coat, gray, and a navy or black suit with a red tie. Funny a guy wearing a suit and tie for a rape."

"It's a funny world."

"Here's the film." She set the container on the table. "There were a couple shots left, but I don't think I'll be using them."

"Thanks." Brent pocketed it. "I'd like you and Jed to work with the Identi-Kit. It's a little toy we have to help put together a composite."

"Sure." The show must go on, she thought miserably. "I'll get my coat."

"Not tonight." Brent adjusted his glasses and rose. "You need some rest. You'd do a better job of it tomorrow. If you think of anything else, you call, anytime."

"I will. Thanks."

When they were alone, Dora stacked the cups and saucers. It was still too difficult to look Jed in the eye. "I haven't gotten around to thanking you."

"You're welcome." He put his hands over hers. "Leave them. I should probably take you to the hospital. Let them examine that hard head of yours."

"I don't want doctors poking at me." She pressed her lips together to keep her voice from quavering. "I don't want anybody poking at me. The aspirin's taking the edge off the headache."

"It doesn't do much for a concussion."

"Neither does anything else." She turned her hands under his, linked fingers in a plea for understanding. "Don't push, okay?"

"Who's pushing?" He slipped his hands from hers to tip her head back and examine her eyes. What he saw was simple exhaustion. "Go to bed."

"I'm not tired. All this coffee will probably keep me awake for . . . I nearly brought Richie back here with me tonight." That thought churned in her stomach. "If he . . ." That was one train of thought she couldn't afford to indulge. "It should have been safe here."

"It will be." Gently he laid his hands on her shoulders and kneaded the tight muscles. "The next time I go out for cigarettes and milk, I'll take you with me."

"Is that where you were?" Because she wanted to lean back against him, a little too much, she picked up the cups and carried them into the kitchen. "I didn't see any bag."

"I left it in the car when I heard you scream."

The cups rattled when she set them down on the counter. "Good thinking. Do you always take a gun to the market?"

"They really hose you for milk in those convenience stores." He touched her hair when she managed a choked laugh.

"Don't worry, I'm not falling apart."

"I'm not worried." But he left his hand on her hair, lightly. "Do you want me to call your sister? Your father or your mother?"

"No." Dora plugged the sink, flipped on the water. "I guess I'll have to tell them something tomorrow, and that'll be bad enough."

She wasn't fooling with dishes out of a sense of neatness, he knew, but because she was postponing that moment of being alone again. At least that was something he could take care of.

"Tell you what, why don't I bunk out on the couch for tonight? I promise not to leave shaving gunk in the bathroom sink."

With one indulgent sigh, she shut off the tap and turned to bury her face against his chest. "Thanks."

He hesitated, then slipped his arms around her. "Don't thank me yet. I might snore."

"I'll risk it." She rubbed her cheek against his. "I'd tell you that you could share the bed, but—"

"Bad timing," he finished.

"Yeah. The worst." She eased away. "I'll get you a pillow."

14

She looked good. Really good. Jed hadn't spent much time observing sleeping women, and certainly not unless they'd shared the bed with him, but none had looked better than Dora in the morning.

She slept sprawled on her stomach, her hair, tousled from the night, was swept back from her cheek, leaving her face unframed but for the fringe of bangs. She looked enormously appealing.

He'd thought it was because of those big, dark eyes, and the way they dominated her expressive face. But the eyes were closed now, the face at rest.

And she still looked damn good.

Maybe it was her skin. Dora's skin was like silk, smooth white silk faintly blushed with rose.

He shook himself, both embarrassed and appalled by his train of thought. When a man started thinking up metaphors about a woman's skin, he was in deep.

Jed walked over, set his mug on the nightstand, then sat on the edge of the bed.

He could smell her—that carelessly sexy scent that always made his mouth go dry. Another problem, he decided, when a man fell into the obvious perfume trap.

"Isadora." He touched her shoulder over the thick quilt, shook lightly, as he had every two hours through the night to be certain she was lucid.

She made a sound that was caught somewhere between pouty and annoyed, and turned over. The movement slithered the quilt down past her shoulders. Thoughtfully, Jed studied the flannel gown she'd chosen. It looked thick as a suit of armor and was an eye-popping blue. He made out two little pink appliqués that looked like pigs' ears. Curious, he lifted the quilt. Sure enough, a fat pink pig face grinned back at him.

He imagined she'd selected it because she thought it would be warm, and completely sexless.

She'd been half right, he decided, and dropped the quilt.

"Isadora." He shook her shoulder again, then took hold of it to prevent her from turning aside. "Izzy," he whispered close to her ear. "Wake up."

"Go away, Dad."

Grinning, he leaned closer and caught the lobe of her ear between his teeth. That had her eyes springing open. It also kindled a ball of heat in the direct center of her body.

She blinked, focused, but before she could orient herself found her mouth thoroughly captured. Dazed, she lifted a hand to his shoulder, fingers digging in as the ball of heat erupted.

"You awake now?" Jed murmured, and pleased himself by nipping lightly at her lower lip.

"Oh yeah. Wide." She cleared her throat, but her voice remained sleepily husky.

"Who am I?"

"Kevin Costner." She smiled and stretched her shoulders. "Just a little harmless fantasy of mine, Skimmerhorn."

"Isn't he married?"

"Not in my fantasies."

Only a little miffed, Jed leaned back. "How many fingers?"

"Three. I thought we established I was all right last night."

"We're reestablishing it this morning." Her eyes were heavy—sexily so, he noted. But the pupils were normal. "How's the head?"

She lay still a minute, taking inventory. Besides the tingling going on, there were aches. Entirely too many of them. "It hurts. My shoulder's sore, too."

"Try these."

Dora looked down at the aspirin in his hand. "Two? Skimmerhorn, I take two when I break a nail."

"Don't be such a wimp." He knew that would do it. She scowled, took the pills, then the mug of coffee he offered.

Irritation turned to surprise at the first sip. "Pretty good coffee. Almost tastes like mine."

"It is yours—your beans, anyway. I watched you do it once."

"Quick study." Wanting to enjoy the moment, she plumped a pillow at her back and snuggled into it. "Did you sleep okay on the couch?"

"No, but I slept. I used the shower. Don't you have any soap that isn't shaped like little flowers or swans?"

"I had some sea horses, but I used them up." She leaned forward, sniffed at him as she toyed with the dark blond hair curled damply over his collar. "Mmmm. Gardenia."

He covered her face with his hand and gently shoved her back.

"Tell you what," she offered. "The next time I'm out shopping, I'll see if I can find some shaped like a little weight lifter. With that appealing masculine aroma of sweaty gym socks."

With the mug cupped in both hands, she sipped again, sighed. "I can't remember the last time anyone brought me coffee in bed." Smiling, she tilted her head and studied him. With his hair damp from her shower, his chin shadowed with stubble and his eyes nearly as annoyed as they were beautiful, he made a very appealing picture.

"You're a tough one to figure, Skimmerhorn. You had to know with minimal effort you could have been in here with me last night. You knew what buttons to push, but you didn't push them."

"You were hurt and you were tired." But he'd thought about it. Oh yeah, he'd thought about it. "I'm not an animal."

"Oh, yes you are. You're this big, restless, ill-tempered animal—and that's part of the allure." She ran her fingers along the cheek he hadn't bothered to shave. "All those hard muscles and that bad attitude. There's something irresistible about knowing you have an equal capacity for mean as you do for kindness. I'm a sucker for bad boys with soft hearts."

He took the hand she pressed to his cheek, intended to push it away. But she linked her fingers with his and sat up to kiss him. Very softly, very sweetly, so that every muscle in his body throbbed in reaction.

"You're pressing your luck, Dora."

"I don't think so."

He could have proven her wrong, would have if he hadn't been able to see the headache so clearly in her eyes. He could have pushed her back on the bed, purging that feral need she'd built inside him.

But he didn't, because there was no way to take what he wanted without hurting her.

"Listen to me." He spoke carefully, keeping his eyes on hers. "You don't know me. You don't know what I'm capable of, or what I'm not capable of. The only thing you can be sure of is that I want you, and when I'm certain you're a hundred percent, I'm going to have you. I won't ask."

"There's no need for that, since I've already answered yes."

"And I won't be kind." He looked down at their joined hands and deliberately let hers go. "It won't matter a damn to me if you're sorry after."

"When I make a choice, I don't play the hindsight game. I also know you're not warning me, you're warning yourself."

He dropped his hands and rose. "We've got other things to deal with today. What are you doing about the shop?"

"We're closed today."

"Good. We've got to get down to the station house. Get yourself together, and I'll make some breakfast."

"Can you?"

"I can pour milk on cold cereal."

"Yummy."

She tossed the quilt aside as he started out. "Oh, Conroy," he said over his shoulder, "I like your pig."

While Jed and Dora were sharing a box of cornflakes, DiCarlo paced his New York apartment. He hadn't slept. He'd worked his way through half a bottle of Cutty Sark during the long night, but the effects couldn't dull his fevered mind or give him peace.

He couldn't go back to Philadelphia. The dead cop was one thing, but he'd left behind two witnesses. Two who had certainly seen his face well enough for an ID.

They'd make him, DiCarlo thought grimly, and poured another glass. And they'd tie him to the dead patrol. If there was one thing DiCarlo knew about cops, it was that they were relentless in pursuing anyone who'd killed one of their own.

So not only couldn't he return, but he'd need to go underground, at least until the weather chilled. A couple of months, he mused. Six at the most. That was no problem. He had plenty of contacts, plenty of liquid cash. He could spend a nice warm winter in Mexico, swilling margaritas. Once the cops finished chasing their tails, he would return.

The only hitch was Edmund J. Finley.

DiCarlo studied the merchandise he'd stacked against the wall beside his Christmas tree. They looked like sad, neglected presents, unwrapped and unwanted.

The bookends, the parrot, the eagle, Lady Liberty, the china dog. Counting the figurine he'd already delivered, that made six out of seven. Anyone but Finley would consider that a success.

It was only one lousy painting, he thought. Christ knew he'd given it his best shot. He had a black eye, a split lip and sore kidneys. His cashmere coat was ruined.

He'd done more than his share to correct a mistake that hadn't been his in the first place. As soon as he had time, he was going to pay back Opal Johnson for that. In spades.

In the meantime, he just had to figure out the best way to approach Finley. After all, Finley was a businessman and knew one had to take losses along with profit. So he would approach Finley just that way. Businessman to businessman. It wouldn't hurt to put Finley in a cheery mood by personally presenting him with the five newly recovered items first, then elicit sympathy and admiration by detailing the specifics.

He'd explain about the cop, too. Surely a man like Finley would understand the great personal risk taken by icing a badge.

Not enough, DiCarlo admitted, and picked up his ice pack to press it against his bruised cheekbone. He crossed to his foyer mirror to examine himself. It was just as well he was too busy to celebrate New Year's Eve. He could hardly go out in a crowd of people, since his face looked as though it had gone through a meat grinder.

He was going to have to get back to the Conroy woman, and the man across the hall as well. It would take some time. DiCarlo prodded gently beside his swollen eye, winced. He could be patient. Six months, a year. They'd have forgotten about him by then. But he wouldn't forget.

There would be no plans to kill her humanely this time. No indeed. This was one vendetta that would be executed slowly and with great pleasure.

The idea made him smile, then swear as the movement opened his split lip. DiCarlo staunched the blood with the back of his hand, turned away from the mirror. She would pay, there was no question. But his first order of business was Finley.

He knew he could run from the cops, but he wasn't certain he could escape his employer. He would use reason, practicality and flattery. And . . . DiCarlo pressed the ice bag against his mouth and smiled with his eyes only. Good faith. He would offer to put another man on the job, at his own expense.

Surely that was an offer that would appeal to Finley's business sense. And his greed.

Satisfied, DiCarlo went to the phone. The sooner he was finished in California, the sooner he could hit the beaches in Mexico.

"I want to book a flight, first class, New York to LA. First available. Not until six-fifteen?" He drummed his fingers on his desk, calculating. "Yes, yes, that will be fine. No, one way. I'll want to book another flight from LA to Cancún, on the first of January." He opened a desk drawer, took out his passport. "Yes, I'm sure the weather will be an improvement."

"I think his face was a little longer." Dora watched the computer-generated image change on the monitor to the quick rattle of the operator's fingers on the keyboard. "Yeah, that's it. And thinner, too." Unsure, Dora shook her head and looked over at Jed. "Did he have more eyebrows? I think I'm making him look like Al Pacino."

"You're doing fine. Finish going through your impressions, then we'll add mine."

"Okay." She closed her eyes and let the dark image come back, but the quiver of panic came with it, and she opened her eyes again. "I only got a quick look. He . . ." She reached for the ice water she'd requested. "I think he had more hair than that—and it might have had some curl to it."

"Okay." The operator tried on a different hairstyle. "How's that?"

"It's closer. Maybe his eyes were heavier—you know, more lid."

"Like this?"

"Yes, I think . . ." She let out a sigh. "I don't know."

Jed moved behind her chair, laid his hands on her shoulders and automatically began to knead out the tension. "Thin out the lips and nose," he ordered. "The eyes were deeper set. Yeah, that's it. She was right about the eyebrows, a little heavier. More. Square off the chin some."

"How do you do that?" Dora whispered.

"I got a better look at him than you, that's all."

No, that wasn't all, she thought. Not nearly all. He'd seen what she'd seen, but he'd absorbed and filed and retained. Now she was watching the image of her attacker taking shape on the monitor.

"Now deepen the complexion," Jed suggested, narrowing his eyes, focusing in. "Bingo."

"That's him." Shaken, Dora reached up to lay a hand over Jed's. "That *is* him. That's incredible."

Like a proud papa, Brent patted the monitor. "It's a hell of a tool. Jed had to do some fast shuffling to get it in the budget."

Dora smiled weakly and forced herself to stare into the computerized eyes. "Better than Nintendo."

"Give us a printout," Brent told the operator. "We'll see if we can come up with a match."

"I'd like a copy." Relieved to have it behind her, Dora got to her feet. "I want to make sure Lea and Terri see it, in case they notice him hanging around near the shop."

"We'll get you one." Brent nodded to the operator. "Why don't you come back to my office for a few minutes?" He took her arm, guiding her out of the conference room and down the hall. She glanced at a door, read CAPTAIN J.T. SKIMMERHORN on the glass.

It looked as though the department was keeping a light in the window.

She looked up at Jed. "T for testosterone?"

"You're a laugh a minute, Conroy."

"Oh, I forgot to mention it last night." Brent opened his office door and ushered Dora inside. "I got a call from your mother the other day."

"My mother?" Dora lifted a brow and chose a chair.

"An invitation to their New Year's Eve bash at the theater."

"Oh." Tomorrow, Dora remembered. She'd all but put it out of her mind. "I hope you can make it."

"We're looking forward to it. The Liberty Theater New Year's Eve bash has quite a rep." Brent reached in a drawer and took out an envelope. "Your pictures. We're keeping copies, but there doesn't seem to be anything unusual about them."

She slipped them out and chuckled. The first shot was of Richie's wide open mouth, taken at super-close range. Self-portrait, Dora imagined. She'd have recognized that crooked eyetooth anywhere. Obviously, the little brat had gotten hold of her camera.

"Disgusting, but not unusual." She put the envelope inside her purse. "So, where do we go from here?"

"You don't," Jed snapped. "The police do."

"Oh, are you back in command, Captain?" She only smiled at the killing look he aimed at her. "Who exactly is in charge?" she asked Brent.

He cleared his throat, pushed up his glasses. "Well, it's my case."

"Well then." Dora folded her hands in her lap and waited.

"Until we run this guy down," Brent began, watching from the corner of his eye as Jed paced, "we'll put a couple of guards on your building."

She thought of the cop, of the wife, of the children. "I don't want anyone else put at risk."

"Dora, there isn't a man in this precinct who wouldn't volunteer for the duty. Not after Trainor. This guy's a cop killer." He glanced over at Jed. "Which is why it was easy for me to put a rush on Ballistics. The bullet they took out of Trainor matched the ones we dug out of the wall in your building."

"Surprise, surprise," Jed muttered.

"I've got a case to build." Brent took off his glasses to polish them on his wrinkled shirt. "If we bring this bastard in alive, I want stacks of evidence. I'm sending out the ballistic report to other precincts throughout the city and the state. Something might match."

It was a good move. Jed only wished he didn't feel so bitter at not being able to instigate it. "Where's Goldman?"

"In Vail," Brent said under his breath. "Skiing. He took a week's vacation."

If Jed hadn't been so angry, he'd have been stupefied. "Son of a bitch. He's got a dead cop at his feet—one of his own men. He's got no business taking vacation during the holidays when his men are working double shifts."

"He had the time coming." Brent snatched up his shrilling phone. "Call back," he barked into it, and slammed it down again. "Look, I hope he breaks his candy ass. Maybe then you'll get off yours and come back where you belong. We got a dead cop, and the morale level around here's about butt high on a dwarf because we've got a commanding officer who's more worried about having his pretty teeth bonded than seeing to his men." He stabbed a finger at Jed. "What the hell are you going to do about it?"

Jed drew slowly on his cigarette, exhaled, drew again. He didn't speak, didn't dare. Instead he turned on his heel and walked out.

"Screw it." Brent looked at Dora, grimaced. "Sorry."

"Don't worry about it." Actually, she'd found the entire incident illuminating. "Do you think it did any good?"

"No." It embarrassed him to lose his temper in public. It always did. A dull flush was already working up his neck. "Once Jed's made up his mind, you couldn't change it with mortar fire." He dropped down into his chair. "Made me feel better, though."

"Well, that's something. I'd better go after him."

"I wouldn't."

She only smiled and picked up her coat. "See you tomorrow night."

She caught up with him half a block away. Dora didn't bother to shout his name and ask him to wait. She was quite sure it would have been a waste of breath. Instead she trotted up beside him, matched her stride to his.

"Nice day," she said conversationally. "The temperature's up a bit, I think."

"You'd be smart to stay away from me right now."

"Yeah, I know." She tucked her hand through his arm. "I like walking in the cold. Gets the blood moving. If we turn this way, we'll end up in Chinatown. Some great little shops."

Jed deliberately turned the other way.

"Mmm, perverse," Dora commented. "You're not really mad at him, you know."

"Don't tell me what I am." He tried to shake her off, but she hung on like a silk-covered burr. "Will you get lost, Conroy?"

"Impossible. I know my way around this neighborhood too well." She studied his profile, but resisted the urge to stroke the tension out of his jaw. "You can yell at me if you think it'll make you feel better. It usually works when I'm mad at myself."

"Do I have to have you arrested for harassment?"

She batted her lashes. "Do you think it would work, a little thing like me molesting a big, tough guy like you?"

He shot her one brief, nasty look. "At least you could shut up."

"I'd rather annoy you. You know, if you keep your jaw clenched like that, you're going to break a tooth. Lea used to grind her teeth at night, and now she has to wear this plastic thing in her mouth whenever she goes to bed. It's stress. Lea's always been a worrier. Not me. When I sleep, I tune everything out. I mean, that's the point of sleep, isn't it?"

Before they could round the next corner, Jed stopped, turned toward her. "You're not going to quit, are you?"

"Nope. I can keep this up indefinitely." Reaching down, she tugged up the zipper of his jacket, smoothed the collar. "He's frustrated because he cares about you. It's tough being cared about, because it loads all this responsibility on. You've had a potful of responsibility, I imagine. It must be a relief to toss it out for a while."

It was tough to hold on to temper with someone who understood so perfectly. But if he let go of temper, despair might creep in. "I had reasons for resigning. They still hold."

"Why don't you tell me what they were?"

"They're my reasons."

"Okay. Want to hear my reasons for leaving the stage?"

"No."

"Good, I'll tell you." She began to walk again, leading him back around the block to where he'd parked his car. "I liked acting. That's hardly surprising with all those hammy genes swimming around in my blood. I was good, too. Once I graduated from the kid parts, I took on stuff like *Our Town* and *The Glass Menagerie*. The reviews were terrific. But..." She glanced up under her lashes. "Piqued your interest yet?"

"No."

"But," she continued, undaunted, "it wasn't really what I wanted to do. Then, about five years ago, I got an inheritance, from my godmother. Anna Logan. Maybe you've heard of her? She made a big splash in B movies back in the thirties and forties, then went into agenting."

"I never heard of her."

"Well, she was loaded." A car zoomed by, too fast, and sent up a breeze that fluttered Dora's hair. It was still flying when she turned her head to smile up at Jed. "I was fond of her, too. But she was about a hundred years old and had had a hell of a life. Anyway, I took the money and a couple of courses in business management. Not that I needed them—the courses, I mean. Some things are innate."

"Is there a point to this, Conroy?"

"I'm getting to it. When I told my family what I was going to do, they were upset. It really hurt them that I wasn't going to use what they considered my gifts and carry on in the Conroy tradition. They loved me, but they wanted me to be something I couldn't. I wouldn't have been happy in the theater. I wanted my own shop, my own business. So even though it disappointed them, I went ahead and did what was right for me. It took a long time before I adjusted to the responsibility of being cared for, worried over and loved."

For a moment he said nothing. It surprised him that he wasn't angry any longer. Sometime during her monologue his temper had dissipated, broken up like a nasty storm and blown away on the wind of Dora's persistence.

"So the moral of your incredibly long, convoluted story is that since I don't want to be a cop, I shouldn't get pissed because a friend wants to guilt me back onto the force."

With a sigh, Dora stepped in front of him, put her hands lightly on his shoulders. "No, Skimmerhorn, you missed it entirely." Her eyes held his now, very sober and sympathetic. "I wasn't cut out to be an actor, so I made a choice that my family didn't agree with, but that I knew, inside, was right for me. You're a cop right down to the bone. You just need to wait until you're ready to admit you made the right choice in the first place."

He snagged her arm before she could walk again. "Do you know why I left?" His eyes weren't angry now, but dark and blank and, to Dora, frightening because of the emptiness of emotion. "I didn't have to kill Speck. There were other ways to bring him down, but I ignored them. I pushed the situation to the point where I knew one of us would die. It turned out to be him. I got a fucking commendation for it, even though I could have brought him in without firing a shot. If I had it to do over again, I'd do it exactly the same way."

"You made a choice," she said carefully. "I imagine most people would consider it the right one—your superiors obviously did."

Impatience vibrated from him. "It's what I consider that counts. I used my badge for personal revenge. Not for the law, not for justice. For myself."

"A human frailty," she murmured. "I bet you've had a hell of a time adjusting to the fact that you're not perfect. Now that you have, you'll probably be a better cop when you put that badge back on."

He tightened his grip on her arm, yanked her forward an inch. When her chin angled up, he eased off but kept her still. "Why are you doing this?"

For an answer, the very simplest answer, she grabbed a handful of his hair and pulled his mouth down to hers. She tasted that impatience in the kiss, but there was something else twined with it. The something else was need—deep and human.

"There's that," she said after a moment. "And I guess we'd have to say that despite what I've always considered my good common sense, I care about you, too." She watched him open his mouth, close it again. "Take responsibility for that, Skimmerhorn."

Turning away, she walked the few steps to the car, then pulled out his keys. "I'm driving."

He waited until she'd unlocked the passenger door and had scooted over to the wheel. "Conroy?"

"Yeah."

"Same goes."

Her lips curved as she gunned the engine. "That's good. What do you say, Skimmerhorn? Let's go for a ride."

15

Finley's home was a museum to his ambitions, small and large. Originally built by a director of action films whose love of elaborate construction had soon outreached both his means and his skills, it was tucked high in the hills over Los Angeles.

Finley had purchased it during a flat period in the market, and had immediately set about installing a more elaborate security system, an indoor lap pool for those rare rainy days and a high stone wall that surrounded the property like a moat around a castle.

Finley was a voyeur, but he objected to being watched.

In the third-floor tower, he revamped the director's lofty screening room, adding a bank of television monitors and a high-powered telescope. Gone were the wide, reclining chairs. In their place, Finley had chosen a large, plush conversation pit in maroon velvet. He often entertained there, while home movies, starring himself, flickered on the screen.

Naturally he had hired decorators. He had gone through three companies during the six months it had taken him to furnish the house to his satisfaction.

The walls in every room were white. Some were painted, some lacquered, some papered, but all were in pure, virginal white, as were the carpet, the tiles, the bleached wood flooring. All the color came from his treasures—the figurines, the sculptures, the trinkets he had accumulated.

In room after room there were acres of glass—in windows, in mirrors, in cabinets, in breakfronts—and miles of silks in the drapes and upholstery, pillows, tapestries.

Every table, every shelf, every niche, held some masterpiece he had hungered for. When one began to bore him, as they always did, Finley shifted it to a less prominent position and set about acquiring more.

He was never satisfied.

In his closet, rows of suits were three deep. Wool and silk, linen and gabardine. All conservatively tailored, all in deep colors: navy, black, grays and a few more frivolous medium blues. There were no casual clothes, no sport jackets, no natty shirts with little polo players on the breast.

Fifty pairs of black leather shoes, all highly glossed, waited on glass shelves to be chosen.

There was a single pair of white Nikes to go along with his exercise clothes. It was one of his butler's responsibilities to dispose of these every two weeks and replace them with another spotless white pair.

His ties were arranged meticulously according to shade, the blacks giving way to the grays, the grays to the blues.

His formal attire was kept in a stunning rococo armoire.

In his bureau were neatly folded stacks of crisp white shirts, monogrammed at the cuffs, black argyle socks, white silk boxer shorts and Irish linen handkerchiefs. All were lightly scented with the lavender sachet his housekeeper replaced weekly.

The master suite included the dressing room, two walls mirrored from floor to ceiling. There was a small wet bar in case the gentleman grew thirsty while preparing for an evening out. There was a balloon-back chair and a gilded console table with a Tiffany butterfly lamp, in the event he needed to sit and contemplate his choice of attire.

To the right of the dressing room was the master bedroom. Paintings by Pissarro, Morisot and Manet graced the white silk walls, each with its own complimentary lighting. The furnishings here were lushly ornate, from the Louis XVI boulle bureau to the cabriole nightstands to the gilded settee flanked by Venetian blackamoor torchères. Overhead a trio of Waterford chandeliers sprinkled light.

But the bed was his pride, his joy. It was a massive affair, designed in the sixteenth century by Vredeman de Vries. It had four posters complete with tester, headboard and footboard, constructed of oak and deeply carved and painted with cherubs' heads, flowers and fruit.

His vanity had tempted him to install a mirror in the tester, but the devaluation that would have caused brought him to his senses.

Instead he had a camera, discreetly hidden by the carved lintel near the ceiling, that aimed directly at the bed, operated by a remote control gun kept in the top drawer of his nightstand. He paused and flicked on the monitor.

They were preparing lunch in the kitchen, the pheasant salad he'd requested. He watched the cook and the kitchen maid work in the sunny white-and-stainless-steel room.

Finley switched the monitor to the drawing room. He watched DiCarlo sip at the club soda and lime, rattle the ice, tug at his tie.

That was good. The man was worried. Overconfidence displeased Finley. Efficiency was vital. Overconfidence bred mistakes. He supposed he should let the poor boy off the hook soon. After all, he had brought the merchandise two days ahead of deadline.

Initiative was worth something. Perhaps he wouldn't have the boy's arm broken after all.

DiCarlo tugged at his tie again. He couldn't shake the feeling that he was being watched. The sensation had him checking his hair, the line of his suit, his fly.

He took another swallow and laughed at himself. Anybody would feel as though they were being watched, he decided, if they were stuck in a room with a hundred statues and paintings. All those eyes. Painted eyes, glass eyes, marble eyes. He didn't know how Finley stood it.

He must have an army of servants to dust all this junk, DiCarlo thought. Setting his glass aside, he rose to wander the room. He knew better than to touch. Well aware of how fanatic Finley was about his acquisitions, DiCarlo kept his arms at his sides and his hands to himself.

It was a good sign, he concluded, that Finley had invited him to the house rather than demanding an office meeting. It made it friendlier, more personal. Over the phone, Finley's voice had sounded pleasant and pleased.

With enough charm, DiCarlo figured he could smooth over the missing painting, convince Finley that it was simply a matter of a little more time. All in all, DiCarlo was certain that they would part amicably and he could return to the Beverly Hills Hotel to find some willing woman to toast in the new year with him.

And tomorrow, he thought, smiling, Mexico.

"Mr. DiCarlo, I trust I haven't kept you waiting overlong."

"No, sir. I've been admiring your home."

"Ah." Finley crossed to a japanned liquor cabinet. "I'll have to give you the grand tour after lunch. Would you like some claret?" He held up a Victorian jug in the shape of a cockatoo. "I have an excellent Chateau Latour."

"Thank you." DiCarlo's confidence began to soar.

"Dear me." Finley lifted a brow and let his eyes scan DiCarlo's bruised face. "Did you have an accident of some sort?"

"Yes." DiCarlo touched the bandage at the back of his neck. The memory of Dora's teeth sinking in had him steaming all over again. "Nothing serious."

"I'm glad to hear it. It would be a pity if there was any scarring." He finished pouring the claret. "I hope your plans for the holiday haven't been upset by this trip. I didn't expect you for another day or two."

"I wanted to bring you the results as soon as possible."

"I like a man with a sense of responsibility. Cheers." Well satisfied, he tapped his glass against DiCarlo's. He smiled as the door chimes echoed down the hallway. "Ah, that will be Mr. Winesap. He'll be joining us to inspect the merchandise. Mr. Winesap is quite excellent with his lists, as you know. Now, I hope you'll both forgive me, but I can't stem my impatience any longer," he said as Winesap entered. "I must see my treasures. I believe they were taken into the library." He gestured toward the door. "Gentlemen?"

The hallway was tiled in white marble, and wide enough to accommodate a huge box settle and hall rack while leaving room for three to pass abreast.

The library smelled of leather and lemon and roses. The roses were arranged in two tall Dresden vases set atop the mantel. There were hundreds of books, perhaps thousands, in the split-level room, not on wall shelves but in cases and cabinets, some open, some glass-fronted. There was a charming four-tier revolving bookcase from the Regency period, as well as an Edwardian model Finley had arranged to have stolen from a castle in Devon.

He'd wanted the room to have the feel of a country squire's library, and had succeeded very well, adding deep leather chairs, a collection of antique pipes and a hunting portrait by Gainsborough.

In keeping with the cozy theme, the ubiquitous monitors were hidden behind a trompe l'oeil panel of a bookcase.

"And here we are." With a spring in his step, Finley walked to the library table and picked up a mermaid bookend.

As instructed, the butler had left a small hammer, a knife and a large wastebasket. Finley picked up the hammer and neatly decapitated a blue-eyed mermaid.

"Mustn't move too swiftly on these," he said softly, and continued to chip away, delicately, at the cheap plaster.

"This was made in Taiwan," he told his guests. "At a busy little plant I have an interest in. We ship merchandise primarily to North and South America, and make a tidy, if uninteresting, profit. These, however, are what we might call one of a kind. Some are excellent reproductions of valuable pieces, excellent enough to fool even an expert."

He took out a small square of bubbled plastic, tossing the rest of the bookend aside, then using the knife to slit the packing material open. Inside the plastic was a chamois cloth, and in that a small, very old netsuke.

He examined it, minutely, delighted. A woman crouched on hands and knees with a round-bellied man behind her, his hand clasped possessively over her breast. Her ivory head was turned slightly toward her left shoulder and up so that it appeared she was trying to see his face as he prepared to enter her from the rear.

"Excellent, excellent." After setting it aside, he carefully destroyed the second bookend.

The next piece continued the theme, with a woman kneeling at a man's feet, her head tilting back and a smile on her face as she clutched his erect penis.

"Such craftsmanship." Finley's voice shook with emotion. "Over two hundred years old, and no amount of technology can improve on it. The Japanese understood and appreciated eroticism in art while Europeans were covering their piano legs and pretending children hatched under cabbage leaves."

He took the knife and disemboweled the parrot.

"And here," he said, opening a velvet pouch. "Ah, and here." The lightest of tremors passed deliciously through him when he let the sapphire brooch drop into his waiting palm.

It was set in an intricate gold filigree encrusted with diamonds, a stone of more than eight carats, in a deep cornflower blue, square cut and majestic.

"Worn by Mary, Queen of Scots." Finley stroked the stone, the setting, turned it over to admire the back. "While she was plotting intrigue and her clandestine love affairs. It was part of the booty good Queen Bess took after she'd had her pretty cousin executed."

He could all but smell the blood and betrayal on the stones. And it pleased him.

"Oh, the trouble and expense it's taken me to acquire this bauble. It shall have a place of honor," he said, and set it gently aside.

Like a spoiled child on Christmas morning, he wanted more.

The engraved Gallé vase in the bowels of the Statue of Liberty thrilled him. Momentarily he forgot his guests as he cooed over it, stroking its long sides, admiring the lithe female forms decorating the Art Nouveau glass.

His eyes had taken on a glassy sheen that had Winesap averting his in faint embarrassment.

From within the hollowed base of the bronze eagle, Finley released a padded box. Saliva pooled in his mouth as he tore the padding aside. The box itself was a smooth rosewood, lovingly oiled and polished. But the lid was the treasure, a micro mosaic panel commissioned in Imperial Russia for Catherine the Great—perhaps by her canny lover Orlov after he'd murdered her husband and lifted Catherine onto the throne.

More blood, Finley mused. More betrayal.

Signed by the artist, it was a wonderfully delicate reproduction of the Imperial Palace fused onto glass.

"Have you ever seen anything more exquisite? The pride of czars and emperors and kings. Once this sat behind glass in a museum where unwashed tourists could come and gawk. Now it's mine. Mine alone."

"It's a beauty, all right." DiCarlo hated to interrupt, but it was nearly time to make his pitch. "You know the value of art, Mr. Finley. What's the point in having something priceless if any jerk can walk in off the street and see it?"

"Exactly, exactly. True art must be possessed, it must be hoarded. Museums buy for posterity. The soulless rich for investment. Both processes are abhorrent to me." His eyes were very green now, very bright and a little mad. "To own, Mr. DiCarlo, is everything."

I get your point there, and I'm happy to have played a part in bringing you your merchandise. Of course, there was some difficulty—"

"I'm sure." Finley waved him off before the mood was spoiled. "But we must finish here before we discuss your trials and tribulations." He used the hammer on the dog, bursting its belly open. The hound gave birth to a gold cat. "It's quite solid," Finley explained as he unwound the heavy wrapping. "A beautiful piece, of course, but all the more because of its background. It's said to have been a gift from Caesar to Cleopatra. Impossible to prove the validity of that, though it has been dated correctly. Still, the myth is enough," he said softly, lovingly. "Quite enough."

His hands shook with excitement as he set it down. "And now, the painting."

"I, ah . . ." It seemed a good time to stand. "There was a little trouble with the painting, Mr. Finley."

"Trouble?" Finley's smile remained fixed. He scanned the room, saw no sign of his final possession. "I don't believe you mentioned any trouble, Mr. DiCarlo."

"I wanted to get you this merchandise without any more delay. These pieces represent a great deal of time and money on your part, and I knew you'd want them in your hands at the earliest possible moment."

"We are speaking now of the painting." And now the painting was all that mattered to Finley. Cleopatra, Catherine and Mary of Scotland were all forgotten. "I don't see it here. Perhaps it's eyestrain. An optical illusion."

The sarcasm brought a dull flush to DiCarlo's cheeks. "I wasn't able to bring it on this trip, Mr. Finley. As I started to tell you, there was a problem."

"A problem?" He continued to smile, pleasantly, though the acids in his stomach had begun to churn. "Of what nature?"

Encouraged, DiCarlo resumed his seat. He explained briefly about the three break-ins, reminding Finley that the first had resulted in the recovery of the china hound. He made sure he highlighted his search for the painting, at great personal risk.

"So I'm sure you'll agree, sir," he concluded, as though wrapping up a sales meeting, "that it would be dangerous for all of us for me to return to Philadelphia at this time. I do have a contact who I can put on the matter, at my own expense, of course. Since you've recovered six of the seven pieces, I'm sure you'll be patient. I see no reason why the painting can't be in your hands within, say, six weeks."

"Six weeks." Finley nodded, tapped his forefinger to his lip. "You say you shot a police officer."

"It was necessary. He was watching the building."

"Mmm. And why do you suppose he was doing that?"

"I can't be sure." Sincerity in every pore, DiCarlo leaned forward. "I left absolutely no sign of forced entry. I did overhear an argument between the Conroy woman and her tenant. He was violent. It might be that she asked for police protection."

"Interesting that she simply didn't have him evicted," Finley commented—very, very pleasantly. "You did say the tenant was the one who battered your face."

DiCarlo stiffened with wounded pride. "It was probably a lovers' quarrel. I figure the guy was getting more than a roof over his head out of her."

"Do you?" Finley let the crudeness of the remark pass. "We will have to discuss this further, Mr. DiCarlo. After lunch, perhaps."

"Sure." Relieved, DiCarlo settled back. "I'll run through all the details with you."

"That will be fine. Well, shall we dine, gentlemen?"

They enjoyed the pheasant salad along with a chilled Pouilly-Fumé in the formal dining room with its Victorian furniture and sun-swept garden view. Throughout, Finley kept the conversation away from business. It interfered with the palate, as he explained to DiCarlo. He spent an hour playing jovial host, generously refilling DiCarlo's glass himself.

When the last drop of wine and the final morsel of trifle had been consumed, Finley pushed back from the table.

"I hope you'll forgive us, Abel, but as much as I regret it, Mr. DiCarlo and I should conclude our business. Perhaps a walk around the grounds, through the garden?" he said to DiCarlo.

Pleasantly buzzed on wine, rich food and success, DiCarlo patted his stomach. "I could use a walk after that meal."

"Good, good. I'm a bit of a fanatic about exercise. I'd enjoy the company. We won't be long, Abel."

Finley led DiCarlo out into a solarium complete with potted palms and a musical fountain, through the atrium doors and into the garden.

"I want to tell you how much I admire you, Mr. Finley," DiCarlo began. "Running your business, having a home like this. You sure cut a wide path for yourself."

"I like to think so." Finley's shoes crunched lightly over the smooth white stones on the garden path. "Do you know flowers, Mr. DiCarlo?"

"Just that women are usually suckers for them."

Laughing appreciatively, Finley led him through the garden, finally stopped to admire the view. Finley stood looking out over the Los Angeles basin, drawing deeply of the fragrances around him. Flowers—early roses, jasmine. The tang of freshly watered mulch and clipped grass.

"Your plans, Mr. DiCarlo?" Finley said abruptly.

"What? Oh. It's all simple. I put my man on it. He'll take care of the Conroy woman. Believe me, after he gets through with her, she'll tell him anything." His lips thinned a moment as he grudgingly accepted he wouldn't have the pleasure of beating the painting's location out of her. "Like I said, he might have to wait a week or two, until things cool off. But he'll snatch her, put on the pressure until she leads him to the painting."

"And then."

"He'll whack her, don't worry." DiCarlo smiled a little, professional man to professional man. "He won't leave any loose ends."

"Ah, yes, loose ends. Most inconvenient. And yourself?"

"Me, I figured I'd take a few months in Mexico. Odds are they got a look at me. It was dark, sure, but I don't like to take those kind of chances. If they manage to make me, I'd rather be across the border."

"Wise, I'm sure." Finley bent over a rosebush, sniffed delicately at a pale pink bud just beginning to part its tender petals. "It occurs to me, Mr. DiCarlo, that if they make you, they may involve me—however indirectly."

"No way. No possible way. Rest easy, Mr. Finley, they'd never tie a man like you with a couple of break-ins in a Philadelphia junk shop."

"Loose ends," Finley said with a sigh. When he straightened, he held a pearl-handled revolver in his hand. And he was smiling again, charmingly. "It's best to snip them off."

He fired, aiming just above DiCarlo's belt buckle. The sound echoed over the hills and sent terrified birds screaming skyward.

DiCarlo's eyes widened with surprise, then glazed with pain. The unbelievable fire of the pain. Dully, he looked down at his belly, pressing a hand against the spreading stain before his knees crumpled beneath him.

"You disappoint me, Mr. DiCarlo." Finley didn't raise his voice but bent low to let the words carry. "Did you take me for a fool? Did you think so much of yourself that you believed I would take your pathetic excuses and wish you bon voyage?"

He straightened and, while DiCarlo writhed in pain from the gunshot, kicked him viciously in the ribs.

"You failed!" he shouted, and kicked again, again, screaming over DiCarlo's groaning pleas for mercy. "I want my painting. I want what's mine. It's your fault, your fault I don't have it."

Spittle ran from Finley's mouth as he shot DiCarlo's left kneecap, then his right. DiCarlo's thin scream of pain faded away into animal whimpers.

"I would have killed you quickly if you hadn't insulted my intelligence. Now it may take you hours, hours of agony. And it's not enough."

He had to force himself to replace the revolver in his pocket. He took out a handkerchief and gently dabbed the perspiration from his brow.

"Not enough," he repeated. He bent down close again, pressing his face into DiCarlo's. "You had your orders. Did you forget who was in charge?"

"Please," DiCarlo moaned, too deep in shock to realize his pleas were useless, and that he was already dead. "Help me. Please."

In a fussy gesture, Finley replaced the handkerchief in his breast pocket. "I gave you plenty of time, more than enough to redeem yourself. I'd even considered giving you absolution. I can be a generous man, but you, you failed me. Failure, Mr. DiCarlo, is unforgivable."

Still shaking with rage, he straightened again. He knew he would need an hour of meditation at the very least before he would manage to compose himself for the formal affair he was attending that night.

Ineptitude, he fumed. Inefficiency in employees. He brushed dust from his sleeve as he walked back toward the solarium. Intolerable.

"Winesap!" he snapped.

"Sir." Winesap tiptoed in, folded his nervous hands. He'd heard the shots, and was very much afraid of what was coming next.

"Dispose of Mr. DiCarlo."

Winesap's shoulders slumped. "Of course, Mr. Finley. Right away."

"Not now." Finley took out a genuine tortoiseshell comb to straighten his windblown hair. "Let him bleed to death first."

Winesap glanced through the glass wall to where DiCarlo was lying on his back, babbling piteously at the sky. "Should I wait in here?"

"Of course. How else will you know when he's dead?" Finley sighed, replaced his comb. "I realize that tomorrow's a holiday, Abel, and I wouldn't dream of interfering with whatever plans you might have. So I'll ask that you focus your attention the following day on gathering all the information you can on this Isadora Conroy in Philadelphia." He sniffed his hand, wrinkled his nose at the scent of gunpowder. "I'm afraid I'm going to have to take care of this matter myself."

16

"Happy New Year!"

Jed was greeted at the lobby doors of the Liberty Theater by a bald bean pole of a man dressed in a red leather jumpsuit studded with silver stars. Caught by surprise, Jed found himself bear-hugged and back-patted.

His new friend smelled strongly of wine and Giorgio for Men.

"I'm Indigo."

Since the man's skin approximated the color, Jed nodded. "I can see that."

"Marvelous party." Indigo took out a slim black cigarette, tucked the end into a gold cigarette holder and posed with one hand on his narrow hip. "The band's hot, the champagne's cold and the women . . ." He jiggled his brows up and down. "Are plentiful."

"Thanks for the update."

Cautious, Jed started to ease by, but Indigo was the friendly sort and draped an arm over Jed's shoulders. "Do you need some introductions? I know everyone."

"You don't know me."

"But I'm dying to." He steered Jed through the lobby crowd toward the concession stand, where drinks were being poured by two quick-handed bartenders. "Let me guess." He stepped back half an inch, cocked his head, drew once on the European cigarette. "You're a dancer."

"No."

"No?" Indigo's mobile face creased in thought. "Well, with that body, you should be. Gene Kelly had the most marvelous athletic build, you know. Champagne here." He waved his cigarette toward a bartender. "And one for my friend."

"Scotch," Jed corrected. "Rocks."

"Scotch, rocks?" Indigo's almond-shaped eyes danced. "Of course, I should have seen it instantly. An actor—dramatic, naturally—down from New York."

Jed took his drink and dug out a buck for the tip jar. Sometimes, he decided, it was best simply to cooperate. "Yeah. I'm between parts," he said, and escaped with his drink.

The lobby of the Liberty Theater was fashioned in Gothic style, with yards of ornate plasterwork, pounds of curlicues and gremlins decorating the gilded molding. Over the doors that led into the theater itself were bronze masks of Comedy and Tragedy.

Tonight the area was packed with people who all seemed determined to be heard above the din. The space smelled of perfumes and smoke and the popcorn that erupted cheerfully in a machine beside the concession stand.

Dora would have told Jed that it quite simply smelled of theater.

Guests were milling around, and the attire ranged from white tie to torn Levis. A group of three in somber black sat wedged on the floor in a corner and read aloud from a collection of Emily Dickinson. Through the open doors he could hear the band tear into a blistering rendition of the Stones' "Brown Sugar."

The Winter Ball, Jed mused, it wasn't.

The house lights were up. He could see people crowded in the aisles, dancing or standing, talking and eating, while onstage the band pumped out rock.

In the box seats and mezzanine and into the second balcony were still more partygoers, shooting the noise level toward sonic with the help of the Liberty Theater's excellent acoustics.

An instinct in Jed gave a fleeting thought to maximum capacities and fire codes before he set about trying to find Dora in what seemed to be the population of Pennsylvania.

Mingling had never been his forte. There had been too many enforced social occasions during his childhood, and too many humiliating public displays by his parents. He would have preferred a quiet evening at home, but since he'd dragged himself out for this, the least she could do was be available.

If she hadn't left for the party so early, with the excuse of being needed to help set up and keep her mother away from the caterers, he could have come with her, kept an eye on her.

He didn't like the idea of her being alone when her attacker was still loose. Though he could hardly call a gathering of this size being alone, he was uneasy about her nonetheless. Otherwise, he wouldn't be there.

Two parties in one week. Jed sipped scotch and worked his way toward the front of the theater. That was more than he'd chosen to attend in a year.

He squeezed between two women, was offered—and refused—a spangled party hat and gave serious consideration to squeezing his way back again and escaping.

Then he saw her. And wondered how he could have missed her. She was sitting on the edge of the stage, dead center, in what had to be an avalanche of sound, holding what appeared to be an intimate conversation with two other women.

She'd done something to her hair, Jed noted. Piled it up on her head in a tangle of dark, wild curls that looked just on the edge of control. And her eyes, he thought, watching as she gripped one of her companions' hands and laughed. She'd painted them up so that they looked bigger, deeper, sultry as a gypsy's. Her lips, which continued to curve as they moved to form words he couldn't hear, were a bold, daring red.

She'd worn a black-and-silver jumpsuit with a high neck, long sleeves and sleek legs that fit like a second skin and should have been illegal. The silver beads splattered over it caught the stage lights every time she moved, and flashed like lightning.

As she'd known they would, he mused. She might have left the stage, but she still knew how to lure the spotlight.

He wanted his hands on her. For a moment that thought and the accompanying slap of desire blocked out everything else.

Setting his glass on the armrest of an aisle seat, he pushed his way forward against the current of people.

"But he's a method actor, after all," Dora said, grinning. "Naturally if he's going to pitch the product, he'd want to catch the flu. What I want to know is what happened after he—" She broke off when hands hooked under her armpits and lifted her from the stage.

She got a quick glimpse of Jed's face before he covered her mouth with his. Fierce, hungry, urgent need rammed into her, cartwheeling from her stomach to her chest so that her heart was stuttering when he released her.

"Well, hi." Staggered, she put a hand on his arm for balance. In her spike-heeled boots she was nearly eye level with him, and the intensity of his look had every pulse point jumping in time with the band's backbeat. "Glad you could make it. I—ah—this is . . ."

She turned to her two friends and went blank.

"Excuse us." Jed pulled her away until he found a corner. He couldn't call it quiet, but at least they didn't have to shout at each other. "What do you call that thing you're wearing?"

"This?" She glanced down at the spangled cat suit, then back up at his face. "Sexy. Do you like it?"

"I'll let you know as soon as I manage to roll my tongue back into my mouth."

"You have such a way with words, Skimmerhorn. Do you want a drink, some food?"

"I had a drink. I was met at the door by a seven-foot black man in red leather. He hugged me."

"Indigo." Her eyes sparkled. "He's a very sociable sort."

"He's got me pegged as an out-of-work actor from New York." Experimentally, he touched a fingertip to one of her curls, wondering what it would take to have them all tumbling down toward her shoulders.

"Indigo's a bit flamboyant, but he's an excellent director, and he has a very good eye. It's a good thing you didn't tell him you're a cop." She took Jed's hand and led him backstage, where another bar and a buffet were set up. "He doesn't like them."

"I'm not a cop." He started to order another scotch, then opted for club soda while Dora chose champagne. "Why doesn't he like them?"

"Oh, he used to work part-time at this club—as a bouncer. The cops raided this crap game in the back room and hauled him in." She angled her head, shifted her shoulders and did a dead-on imitation of Indigo. "Darling, it was a frightful experience. Do you have any idea what kind of people they put in those cells?"

"Yeah. Criminals."

"Don't say that to him. I'm the one who bailed him out, and let me tell you, the man was wrecked." In an automatic gesture, she straightened the collar of Jed's shirt. "It would be difficult for you to sympathize, I imagine, as you've only been on the outside of the bars."

"I've seen them from both sides."

"Oh, well then." With a brisk, practical movement, she brushed the windswept hair from his forehead. "You'll have to tell me about that sometime."

"Maybe I will. Have you finished grooming me?"

"Yes. You look very nice in black—a bit of the rebel, maybe. Sort of James Deanish."

"He's dead."

"Yes, of course. I meant if he'd lived to see thirty." Her smile was thoughtful and amused. "Are all cops so literal-minded, or is it just you?"

"It's a matter of fact and fantasy. I'm more comfortable with fact."

"Too bad. I spent most of my life steeped in fantasy. You could say laboring over it." She chose a radish rose from the buffet, crunched. "I prefer it to straight reality."

"When you were an actress."

Her laugh bubbled out, frothy as the wine. "Need I remind you, I'm a Conroy. I may not be on the legitimate stages these days, but I'm still an actress." Leaning closer, she nipped teasingly at his earlobe. "If you ever decided to try the stage, I might be tempted to come out of retirement."

The lance of heat arrowed straight down the center of his body. "Why don't we just stick with who we are?"

"The world will never know what they missed." She glanced down at his drink. "You don't have to play designated driver, you know. We can cab back."

"I'll stay with this." He reached out, cupped a hand under her chin. "I want a very clear head when I make love with you tonight."

"Oh." She lifted her own glass with an unsteady hand. "Well."

He grinned. "Run out of lines, Conroy?"

"I... Ah..."

"Isadora!"

Jed saw a statuesque redhead poured into a glitter of green that slicked down a regal body, then frothed out in stiff fans from the knees to the ankles. As she bore down on them, she looked exotically like a ferocious mermaid.

Blessing Trixie's timing, Dora let out a pent-up breath and turned to her mother. "Problem?"

"That caterer is a beast. God knows why I continue to hire him." She aimed a look over her shoulder that could have melted steel. "He refused, absolutely refused, to listen to a word I said about the anchovy paste."

Since it had been Will's shift to keep their mother separated from the caterer, Dora took a quick glimpse around. Her little brother was, she decided, a dead man. "Where's Will?"

"Oh, off with that pretty girl he brought with him from New York." Trixie tossed up her hands. The movement sent the colored beads that dripped from her ears dancing. A catering crisis left her no time for remembering names. "The model."

"Miss January," Dora said under her breath.

"Now, the anchovy paste," Trixie began. She drew in a deep breath, preparing to launch into an indignant speech.

"Mom, you haven't met Jed."

"Jed?" Distracted, Trixie patted her hair. Her face transformed when she took her first good look. Subtly, she angled her chin, swept her mink lashes and peered at Jed from under them. Flirting, in Trixie's opinion, was an art. "I'm thrilled to meet you."

Jed understood what was expected when he took her offered hand. He kissed her knuckles. "The pleasure's mine, Mrs. Conroy."

"Oh, Trixie, please." She nearly crooned it. "Otherwise I'll feel old, and staid."

"I'm sure that would be impossible. I saw you perform *Hello Dolly* last year. You were magnificent."

Trixie's smooth cheeks pinked with pleasure. "Oh, how very kind of you to say so. I do adore Dolly Levi, such a full, richly textured character."

"You captured her perfectly."

"Yes." She sighed at the memory. "I like him, Dora. Tell me, Jed—my, you have very *large* hands, don't you?"

"Mom." Since he'd behaved so nicely, Dora took pity on him. "Jed's the tenant Dad found for me."

"The tenant—the tenant!" Instantly, maternal instincts outweighed flirtations. "Oh, my dear, dear boy!" Overcome with gratitude, Trixie threw her arms around Jed's neck. She had a grip like a linebacker. "I am so completely, so irrevocably in your debt."

Dora simply ran her tongue around her teeth when Jed shot her a helpless look.

"It was nothing," he said, awkwardly patting Trixie's back. "I just answered an ad."

"You saved my darling Isadora from that horrible burglar." Rearing back, Trixie kissed both of his cheeks. "We'll never be able to repay you for chasing him away and keeping our little girl from being robbed."

He narrowed his eyes at Dora over her mother's heaving shoulders. Dora looked aside.

"I keep an eye on her," Jed said meaningfully. "Don't worry."

"Worry is a mother's lot, dear." With a sad smile, Trixie sighed.

"There you are, passion flower." In white tie and tails, Quentin swaggered up, still steady after keeping two bartenders hopping. He gave his wife a long, lingering kiss that had Jed's brow raising. "I've come to claim my bride for a dance."

"Of course, dear." Trixie slipped her arms around him and they began to glide, tango style.

"Have you met the young man I picked out for Izzy?"

"Yes, just now." On the turn, Trixie tossed back her head and beamed at Jed. He wouldn't have been surprised if a rose had suddenly appeared between her teeth. "You have such excellent taste."

"Izzy, show Jed around the theater. There's more to our humble abode than a simple stage." Quentin winked, dipped his wife, then tangoed her away.

"Passion flower?" Jed asked after a moment.

"It works for them."

"Obviously." He couldn't remember ever seeing his parents exchange the most impersonal of embraces, much less a smoldering kiss. The only passion he had ever witnessed between them had been hurled insults and crockery.

"You never mentioned you'd been here before."

"What?"

"To the theater," she said, drawing his attention back to her. *"Hello Dolly?"*

"You didn't ask." He guided Dora away from the crowd near the bar. "You didn't tell her, did you?"

"I don't want to upset her. Don't give me that look," she snapped. "You saw how she acted when she thought about the break-in. Can you imagine what would happen if I told her some maniac held a gun on me?" When he didn't respond, she tapped her foot. "I'm going to tell her, in my own way."

"Your business," Jed said, and took out a cigarette. "But if she catches wind of it from someone else, it'll be worse."

"I don't want to think about it right now." She snatched Jed's cigarette, took one brisk puff, then handed it back. "I'll show you around. The building's mid-nineteenth-century. It used to be a popular music hall." She headed away from the stage, down one of the narrow corridors. "It started getting run-down after vaudeville died, barely escaped the wrecking ball a couple of times. After—" She pushed open the door to a dressing room. Putting her hands on her hips, she watched Will untangle himself from a torrid embrace. "Desertion," she said, "is a hanging offense."

Will grinned and slipped his arm around a curvy woman in a tiny red dress. "Lorraine was helping me run lines. I'm up for a mouthwash commercial."

"You were on duty, Will. I've had my shift and Lea doesn't come on until after midnight."

"Okay, okay." With his date in tow, Will squeezed through the door. "Catch you later."

Jed didn't bother to disguise his admiration of Lorraine's hips, which were swinging like a pendulum.

"Pop your eyes back in your head, Skimmerhorn," Dora advised. "Someone might step on them."

"In a minute." He turned back to Dora when Lorraine had swiveled out of view. "His shift for what?" Jed asked.

"For keeping Mom out of the caterer's hair. Come on, I'll take you up to the fly floor. There's a wicked view of the stage from there."

As the evening wore on, Jed stopped questioning the fact that he was enjoying himself. Although he didn't like crowds, had no use for parties and making conversation with strangers, he didn't feel any impatient urges to leave early. When he ran into the Chapmans in the first balcony, he concluded that they were also enjoying themselves.

"Hey, Jed. Happy new year." Mary Pat kissed him, then leaned on the rail again to watch the action below. "What a party. I've never seen anything like this."

Jed checked out her view. A swarm of people, streams of color, blasts of noise. "The Conroys are—unique."

"You're telling me. I met Lea's father. We jitterbugged." Her face flushed with laughter. "I didn't know I *could* jitterbug."

"She didn't have to do much more than hang on," Brent commented. "That old guy can move."

"He's probably got enough fuel in him." Jed caught a glimpse of Quentin below, with a party hat jauntily tilted on his head.

"Where's Dora?" Brent asked. "I haven't seen her since we got here."

"She moves around. Indigo wanted to dance with her."

"Indigo?" Mary Pat leaned farther over the balcony to wave back at strangers and toss confetti.

"Can't miss him. He's a giant, bald black guy in red leather."

"Oh. *Oh,*" she repeated after her quick scan located him. "God, I wish I could dance like that." She propped her elbows on the rail and moved her hips gently to the beat.

"Anything turn up yet?" Jed asked Brent.

"It's early." Brent nursed a beer. "We're sending the picture around. If he's got a sheet, we'll have something after the holiday. I did some legwork myself, looking for a matchup on known sex offenders or B and E men. Nothing yet." Brent looked down in his empty glass, adjusted his hornrims. "Let's go get a beer."

"Oh, no you don't." Mary Pat popped up from the rail and grabbed Brent's arm. "You're going to dance with me, Lieutenant. It's almost midnight."

"Couldn't we stay up here and neck?" Brent dragged his feet as his wife pulled him along. "Listen, Jed'll dance with you."

"I'm getting my own woman."

By the time the three had managed to elbow and squeeze their way down to the orchestra level, the lead singer was shouting into the mike, holding up his hands for silence.

"Come on, everybody, listen up! We got one minute until zero hour, so find your significant other—or a handy pair of lips—and get ready to pucker up for the new year."

Jed ignored the din and a couple of interesting proposals from solo women and cut through the crowd.

He saw her, stage right, laughing with her brother as they poured champagne into dozens of outstretched glasses.

She set down an empty and picked up another, turning to see that the band had full glasses to toast. And she saw him.

"Will." With her eyes on Jed's, she pushed the bottle at her brother. "You're on your own."

"There'll be a stampede!" he shouted, but she was already walking to the edge of the stage.

"Get ready, people!" The singer's voice boomed out over the theater. "Count with me now. Ten, nine . . ."

It felt as though she were moving in slow motion, through water, warm, silky water. Her heart beat hard and high in her chest.

"Eight, seven . . ."

She leaned down, put her hands on Jed's shoulders. He gripped her waist.

"Six, five . . ."

The walls shook. She stepped off into the air, into the colorful rain of confetti, felt his muscles ripple against her as she combed a hand through his hair and hooked her legs around him.

"Four, three . . ."

Inch by inch she slid down his body, her eyes locked on his, her breath already quickened.

"Two, one . . ."

Her mouth opened to his, hot and hungry. Their twin sounds of pleasure were drowned out in an explosion of cheers. On an incoherent murmur, she changed the angle of the kiss and dived deeper, both hands fisted in his hair.

He continued to lower her from the stage to the ground, certain that something in him would explode—head, heart, loins. Even when she stood, her body remained molded to his in a way that gave him painful knowledge of every curve and valley.

She tasted more dangerous than whiskey, more effervescent than champagne. He understood that a man could be drunk when he had a woman in his system.

He took his mouth from hers but kept her firmly against him. Her eyes were half closed, her lips just parted. As he watched, her tongue slipped out to skim lightly over her lips, as if she wanted to absorb the lingering taste of him.

"Give me another," she murmured.

But before he could, Quentin bounded up and swung an arm around each of them. "Happy new year, *mes enfants.*" With a tilt of his head, he pitched his voice so that it flowed like wine over the din. " 'Ring out the old, ring in the new, Ring, happy bells, across the snow: The year is going, let him go; Ring out the false, ring in the true.' "

"Tennyson," Jed murmured, obscurely touched, and Quentin beamed at him.

"Quite right." He kissed Dora, then Jed, with equal enthusiasm. Before Jed could adjust to the shock, Trixie descended on them.

"I love celebrations." There were more kisses, lavishly given. "Will, come here and kiss your mother."

Will obliged, leaping dramatically off the stage and catching his mother up in a theatrical dip. He kissed his father, then he turned to Jed.

Braced, Jed held his ground. "I don't want to have to punch you."

Will only grinned. "Sorry, we're a demonstrative bunch." Despite the warning, he gave Jed a hard, tipsy hug. "Here's Lea and John."

Thinking of survival, Jed stepped back, but found himself blocked by the stage. He gave up, accepting it philosophically when he was kissed by Lea and embraced by John—whom he'd yet to meet.

Watching it all, and the various reactions that flickered over his face, Dora laughed and found a full glass of champagne.

Here's to you, Skimmerhorn. You ain't seen nothing yet.

It took DiCarlo a long, agonizing time to die. Winesap had waited patiently, while doing his best to block out the thin calls for help, the delirious prayers and the babbling sobs.

He didn't know how Finley had handled the servants. He didn't want to know. But he had wished, several times during the interminable three-hour wait, that DiCarlo would do the decent thing and simply die.

Then, when dusk began to fall and there were no more sounds from outside the solarium, Winesap wished DiCarlo had taken longer, much longer.

He didn't relish the task at hand.

Sighing, he went out of the house, past the sprawled body and across the south lawn toward a stone-sided toolshed. He had inquired, meekly, if a drop cloth or sheet of plastic might be available.

Following Finley's instructions, Winesap located a large painter's cloth, splattered with white. His back creaking from the weight, he shouldered the roll, returned to the garden and his grisly task.

It was easy to block the routine from his mind. He had only to imagine it was he who lay staring sightlessly at the deepening sky, and the entire process didn't bother him overmuch.

He spread the cloth over the white stones. They were stained liberally with blood, sticky with it. And the flies ... Well, all in all, Winesap mused, it was a gruesome bit of business.

Crouching, breath whistling through his teeth, Winesap rolled DiCarlo's limp body over and over until it was nicely centered on the cloth.

He took a rest then. Physical labor always made him sweat profusely. He unfolded a handkerchief and mopped his dripping face and neck. Wrinkling his nose, he tossed the handkerchief down and rolled it under the body.

He sat again, careful to avoid bloodstains, and carefully removed DiCarlo's wallet. He held it gingerly between his thumb and forefinger and decided to burn it, money and all, at the first opportunity.

With the resignation of the overburdened, he meticulously checked the rest of DiCarlo's pockets to be certain he'd removed any and all forms of identification.

Faintly, from a second-floor window, he heard the strains of some Italian opera. Finley was preparing for his evening out, Winesap mused.

After all, tomorrow was a holiday.

17

The night was clear as glass, the air brittle. A thin layer of frost on the T-Bird's side window sparkled like an icy spiderweb in the beam of streetlamps. Inside, the heater hummed efficiently, adding another bass note to B. B. King's "Blue Monday" from the radio.

The warmth, the blues and the slow smooth ride might have lulled Dora to sleep. If her nerves hadn't been snapping. To combat the tension, she kept up a nonstop commentary on the party, the people and the music that required little or no response from Jed.

When they pulled up behind her building, she'd nearly run dry.

"It's all right, isn't it?" she asked.

"Is what all right?"

Her fingers vised over her evening bag. "The guards Brent put on."

"Is that what's got you so wound up?"

She studied the building, the stream from the back-door light, the glow in the window from the lamp she'd left burning. "I did a pretty good job of blocking it out for most of the night."

"It's all right." Leaning over, he unsnapped her seat belt himself. "They were both there."

"Good. That's good." But her nerves didn't settle. In silence they climbed out of opposite sides of the car, started to the stairs, up.

She didn't like being jumpy, she thought as Jed unlocked the outside door. At the moment it had nothing to do with intruders and guards. It had everything to do with what was going to happen once they were inside, and alone.

Which made absolutely no sense at all, she decided. She stepped into the hallway and dug out her keys on the way to her door. She wanted him, wanted very much to finish what had started between them.

And yet...

Jed took the keys from her rigid fingers and unlocked the door himself.

It was a matter of control, she realized as she slipped out of her coat, laid it over a chair. Always before she'd made certain that she held the wheel in a relationship, that she steered it in the direction of her choice.

But she wasn't in the driver's seat with Jed, and they both knew it.

She heard the door close at her back, lock. Fresh nerves scrambled into her throat.

"Do you want a drink?" She didn't turn, but headed straight for the brandy.

"No."

"No?" Her fingers hovered over the decanter, fell away. "I don't either." She crossed to the stereo, switched on the CD changer without any idea what music she'd left inside. Bessie Smith picked up where B. B. had left off.

"I'll have to take the tree down in a few days." She reached out and touched a bough. "On Twelfth Night. Pack everything away, burn a few sprigs of pine in the fire. It always makes me a little sad." She jolted when Jed's hands cupped her shoulders.

"You're nervous."

"Me?" She laughed and wished she'd poured something, anything that would wash away the dry heat in her throat.

"I like it."

Feeling foolish, she turned and managed a small smile. "You would. It makes you feel superior."

"There is that." He lowered his head and kissed the corner of her mouth. "It also lets me know you'll remember this, for a long time. Come with me."

He kept her hand in his on the short walk to the bedroom.

He wanted to move slowly, discovering her inch by fascinating inch, savoring those nerves even as he was exploiting them. Until she was helpless, and his.

He switched on the bedside lamp, and looked at her.

Her breath shuddered out when he touched his lips to hers. Tenderness was the last thing she'd expected from him, and the most devastating gift he could give. Her lips parted beneath his, accepting, even as her heart jammed like a fist in her throat.

Her head fell back, a gesture of surrender that had need twisting sharp in his gut. But he continued to play her lips delicately, letting the moment spin out.

"You're shaking," he murmured, trailing his lips down her jawline, sliding his tongue over warm, smooth skin, wallowing in the flavor of flesh.

"That's you."

"You could be right." He brought his mouth back to hers, deepening the kiss until pleasure swam giddily in her head. Now there were sighs, and breathless murmurs, the hard thud of racing hearts.

"Let me turn down the bed," she whispered. But when she turned, shifted aside, he drew her back against him, nuzzling his lips at the nape of her neck.

"That can wait."

His hands were spread over her midsection where the pressure was coiled taut as a rattler. "I don't think I can."

"It's not going to be quick." He slid his hands up her sides, down again. "It's not going to be easy."

"Jed—" His name ended on a moan. His hands were over her breasts now, caressing, thumbs skimming, circling lightly over the peaks while his tongue did outrageous things to the back of her ear. Eyes closed, she relinquished any thought of control and arched back against him.

He used his teeth now, satisfying his own primitive need for the taste of flesh while he undid the tiny buttons that ranged from her throat to the juncture of her thighs. Her breathing slowed, deepened, like a woman in a trance. The side of his thumb barely brushed her skin as he moved with tormenting laziness from button to button.

"I've had all night to wonder." He spoke softly, close to her ear, and fought to keep his hands from taking too greedily. "All night to imagine what was under here."

Slowly, he spread the material open, skimmed his fingers down her center. There was nothing but woman.

"Sweet Christ." He buried his face in her hair as desire ripped through him. Her skin was hot and soft, the muscles quivering helplessly under his hands. Each tremor rippled from her into him as they stood pressed close in the lamplight.

He hadn't known a need could be so outrageous, or the desire to give and take so brutally keen, like a blade honed and waiting for its mark. He only knew he wanted every inch of her and the satisfaction of having her crave every bit as desperately as he.

Dreamlike, she lifted an arm, hooked it around his neck. It was almost like floating, she thought. And the air was polished like silver. Then he would touch again, and that softly glowing air took on an edge, like a sword turned in the sun.

Her eyes half closed, she leaned back against him, absorbing both the pride and the wonder as his hands roamed over her skin. She turned her head so that her mouth could find his again. Her lips clung, wet and hungry, urging him to take more. She could no longer pinpoint the focus of pleasure. There were too many sensations sprinting and careening through her. His mouth, yes, there was pleasure in that, the firm pressure of lips, the scrape of teeth, the tangle of tongues.

There was more in the rock-hard press of his body against hers, the faint tremors that whispered of a violence held rigidly under control. The heat that shimmered around him that spoke of dark and desperate needs.

And there were his hands. God, his hands that stroked and molded and possessed, just a few degrees shy of rough until she was afraid she would lose all sense of self and beg for more.

Her breath came in whimpers, in low, throaty groans, and her body pressed back against his, rocking in a quickening rhythm that demanded. To please her, and himself, he ran his hand down the center of her body until he cupped her. She was already damp and heated. With fingertips only he sent her hurtling over the edge. Her body went rigid, arched back against him. She cried out as the fast, hard orgasm rammed her. When her legs buckled, he slipped deeper into her, groaning as she gasped out in stunned delight.

"More?"

Her head reeled. To keep her balance she locked her other arm around him. "Yes."

He drove her up again, arousal spurting inside him each time she moaned out his name. He understood a man could be drunk and on the edge of control without sampling a swallow of liquor. And that a woman could slip into the blood like a drug. As the greed welled inside him, he spun her around to drag the snug material over her shoulders.

There was a fierceness on his face, a violence in his eyes that should have frightened her. Though her heart gave a wild leap, it had nothing to do with fear.

"I want you." Her voice was low and thick, like honey poured over flame. The hands that tugged the shirt over his head were far from steady. But her eyes, nearly level with his, were strong and sure. She unsnapped his jeans, tossing back her head as she moved closer. "I want you inside me. Now."

In response he gripped her hips and tumbled with her onto the bed.

They rolled twice, tearing impatiently at each other's clothes until damp flesh pressed to damp flesh. But when she would have locked herself around him and taken him into her, he shifted, sliding down her body. While she writhed and moaned beneath him, he feasted on her, suckling her breasts so that the answering contractions low in her belly were all but unbearable.

Panting, she gripped his hair, her body curved in desperate invitation. "Now. For God's sake, now."

He caught her nipple between his teeth, tugging until her nails dug into his shoulders. "This time I want more."

But the more he took, the more he needed. She gave, completely, unrestrictedly, abandoning herself to the flood of sensations. Still, it wasn't enough.

As he had promised himself, he explored every inch of her, tasting, touching, possessing. Whatever he asked, she gave. Whatever she offered, he took.

He could watch her. The light sheened over her damp skin, making it gleam like one of her porcelain figurines. But she was flesh and blood, her hands as curious as his, her mouth as avid.

Beneath them the spread was as slick and smooth as water. The music drifted in, all crying sax and throbbing bass.

When he slipped inside her, her low throaty moan shuddered from her lips into his. Slowly, savoring, he slid deeper, deeper, swallowing her frantic gasps, inciting more with the play of his tongue over hers.

He braced himself over her, desperate to see her face, to watch those flickers of mindless pleasure. She came again, tightening convulsively around him so that he sucked in his breath at the storm of sensation.

Her eyes flew open, glazed and huge, to fix on his face. Her lips trembled as she tried to speak, but there was only another shuddering moan. He was all she could see, all she could feel, and all she wanted. Each slow stroke shivered through her so that her body was a mass of sparking nerves and tearing needs. He ignited them again and again until she could do nothing but wrap herself around him and let him take her where and how he chose.

She cried out again. Jed buried his face in her hair and let himself follow.

The music had changed. Elton John was singing his ode to Marilyn. Dora lay sprawled crosswise on the bed, her numbed body barely aware of Jed's weight. She did feel his lips pressed lightly to the side of her breast, and his heartbeat, still raging. She found the strength to lift her hand, to run it over his hair and down to his shoulder.

Her touch, somehow both maternal and loverlike, caused him to stir. He felt as though he'd just tumbled down a very tall mountain without skis and had landed in a deep, warm spring. Going with the urge, he kissed the curve of her breast and watched her smile.

"You okay?" he asked her.

"No. I can't see anything."

It was his turn to smile. "Your eyes are closed."

"Oh." She opened them and sighed. "Thank God. I thought I'd been struck blind." Turning her head on the rumpled spread, she looked down at him. "I don't think I'll ask how you're doing. You look entirely too pleased with yourself."

He levered himself up to kiss her. Her hair had tumbled down, as he'd imagined it would, and was a riot of curls around her face. Her lips were swollen, her eyes sleepy.

He felt something stir—not the rekindled desire he'd expected, but something else. Something he didn't recognize as contentment. "Ask anyway."

"Okay." She brushed the hair away from his forehead. "How's it going, Skimmerhorn?"

"It's going good."

"Your gift for words stuns me."

He laughed, kissed her again, then rolled over, gathering her close to his side. "It's too bad I can't think of any Tennyson."

The idea of him quoting poetry made her smile grow misty. "How about Shelley? 'I arise from dreams of thee in the first sweet sleep of night, when the winds are breathing low, and the stars are shining bright.' "

She humbled him. "That's nice." He tipped her face up for a kiss that was both sweet and dreamy. "Really nice."

Content with that, she nuzzled closer. "As a Conroy I was raised on bards and playwrights."

"They did a good job with you." She only smiled as he continued to study her, his hand still cupped under her chin, his eyes dark and intent as they scanned her face. "I want you again."

"I was hoping you would."

"Dora, you look terrible."

"Lea, what would I do without you around to boost my ego?"

Unfazed, Lea fisted her hands on her hips as she studied her sister's pale face and shadowed eyes. "Maybe you're coming down with something. That flu's still going around, you know. I think you should close the shop for the day."

Dora walked around the counter as a customer came in. "That kind of thinking is why you're the employee and I'm the boss." She put on a sunny smile. "Good morning. May I help you?"

"Are you Dora Conroy?"

"That's right." Dora held out a hand. She knew she looked pale and wan from lack of sleep, but the woman who was currently clutching her hand looked near collapse. "Would you like some coffee? Some tea?"

"I . . ." The woman shut her eyes and pulled off her blue ski cap. "I'd love some coffee, but I'm not supposed to drink it." She laid a hand on the gentle mound of her belly. "Tea would be nice."

"Cream? Lemon?"

"No, just black."

"Why don't you sit down?" Taking charge, Dora guided the woman to a chair. "We're all starting a little slow this morning. After-holiday fatigue." When a young couple strolled in, Dora gestured for Lea to see to them. She poured two cups of tea.

"Thanks. I'm Sharon Rohman," she told Dora as she accepted her cup.

"I'm afraid I'm a little vague on details today. Oh!" It hit her all at once. Immediately she sat down and reached for Sharon's hand. "You're Mrs. Lyle's niece. I'm so sorry about what happened. The last time I called the hospital, I was told she was still in a coma."

Sharon pressed her lips together. "She came out of it last night."

"Oh, I'm so glad to hear that."

"She's still critical." Sharon lifted her cup, then rattled it back in the saucer without drinking. "The doctors can't say if or when she'll recover. She's—she's very fragile."

Dora's eyes stung in response. "It's a dreadful time for you. I don't suppose there's anything worse than waiting."

"No, there isn't." But the easy, undemanding sympathy helped her relax.

"We've always been close. Really like girlfriends. The first person I told about the baby after my husband was my aunt."

"You look so tired," Dora said gently. "Why don't you come upstairs to my apartment? You can stretch out for a few minutes in private."

The kindness had Sharon's eyes welling. "I can't stay. I need to get back to the hospital."

"Sharon, this strain can't be good for you or your baby."

"I'm being as careful as I can." She brushed at a tear with the back of her hand. "Believe me, I'm doing everything the doctor tells me." She took a deep breath, then, more relaxed, Sharon said, "Miss Conroy—"

"Dora."

"Dora." Sharon took a soothing breath. "I came by this morning to thank you for the flowers you sent to the hospital. They were lovely. Aunt Alice loves flowers. Her garden is a showplace. The nurses have told me you've called several times to check on my aunt's condition."

"I'm relieved it's improving."

"Thank you. But you see, I thought I knew all of her friends. I don't know how you're connected."

"The truth is, we only met briefly. Here. She came into the shop right before Christmas."

Sharon gave a puzzled shake of her head. "She bought something from you?"

"A couple of things." Dora didn't have the heart to tell Sharon they had been gifts for her and her baby. "She mentioned she'd come in because you'd shopped here a few times."

"Yes." Baffled, Sharon smiled as Dora refilled her cup. "You always have such interesting things. I hope you're not offended, but I find it a bit strange that you'd be so concerned over a woman you'd met only once, as a customer."

"I liked her," Dora said simply. "And it bothered me a great deal that she'd been hurt so soon after she'd been here."

"She was shopping for me, wasn't she?"

"She's very fond of you."

"Yes." With an effort, Sharon drew herself in. She had to be strong, she knew, for her baby, for her aunt. "Whoever killed Muriel and hurt my aunt destroyed a lot of her things as well. It seems so senseless."

"Do the police have any leads?"

"No." Sharon blew out a helpless little sigh. "Nothing. They've been very kind, right from the beginning. I was hysterical by the time they got to her. I found her lying there on Christmas morning, and—and poor Muriel. I was really calm when I called for an ambulance and the police. And then I just went to pieces. It's helped to talk to them. The police can be so detached and analytical."

Dora thought of Jed. "I know." After a moment's hesitation, Dora made a decision. "Would you like to know what she bought for you?"

"Yes, I would, very much."

"She said that you sewed. She bought you a Victorian doorstop so you could keep the door open and hear the baby in the nursery."

"A doorstop?" A soft smile played around Sharon's mouth. "A brass elephant—like Jumbo?"

"Exactly."

"We found it in the corner of the living room." Tears threatened again, but they didn't feel so hot and desperate. "It's just the sort of thing she'd buy for me."

"She picked up a doorstop for the nursery, too. A china dog, curled up and sleeping."

"Oh, I didn't see that. It must have been broken. He shattered most of the gifts she'd wrapped, and a great deal of her things as well." She curled her fingers around Dora's. "It looked as though he'd gone crazy. I suppose he had to be crazy, didn't he, to kill one old woman and leave another for dead." But she shook the question away. "I'd like to take her something when I go to see her this morning. Could you help me pick something out?"

"I'd love to."

Twenty minutes later, Dora watched Sharon get in her car and drive away.

"What was that all about?" Lea asked. "The poor thing looked so unhappy."

"That was Mrs. Lyle's niece—the woman who was attacked on Christmas Eve."

"Society Hill? She's in a coma, isn't she?"

"She's come out of it."

Lea shook her head. "It's awful to think that someone could break into your home that way."

A quick shiver raced up Dora's spine as she remembered her own experience. "Awful," she agreed. "I hope they find him."

"In the meantime." Firmly, Lea turned Dora to face her. "Back to you. Why do you look so exhausted when you had the entire day off yesterday?"

"I haven't a clue. I spent the entire day in bed." With a smile playing around her mouth, Dora drew away to rearrange a collection of music boxes.

"Wait a minute." Eagle-eyed, Lea shifted to get another look at Dora's face. "Oh," she said, drawing the word out into three ascending syllables. "The light dawns. Jed."

Dora opened the lid on an enameled box that played the "Moonlight Sonata." "What about him?"

"Don't play that game with me, Isadora. Just whose bed did you spend the day in?"

"My own." Then she grinned and closed the box. "And it was incredible."

"Really?" Lea was all ears. "Okay, spill it."

"Well, he's . . . I can't," she realized, baffled. "This is different."

"Uh-oh," Lea said, and grinned, ear to dainty ear. "Do you remember what I did the first time John kissed me?"

"You came home, crawled into bed and cried for an hour."

"That's right. Because I was scared and thrilled and absolutely sure I'd just met the man I was going to be with for the rest of my life." The memory made her smile now, sweetly. Smugly.

"You were eighteen years old," Dora pointed out. "Overly dramatic and a virgin."

"So you're twenty-nine, overly dramatic and you've never been in love before."

A windy sigh. "Of course I have."

"No, you haven't."

Dora picked up a dust cloth. "I haven't said I'm in love with Jed."

"Are you?"

"I don't know."

"There," Lea said triumphantly. "My point exactly. If you weren't, you'd say so. Since you are, you're confused. Where is he, anyway?"

"Out." Because she felt she'd been outmaneuvered, Dora scowled. "I don't keep him on a leash."

"Testy," Lea said with a wise nod. "Another sure sign."

"Look, I'll analyze my own feelings when I have the time." She snatched up the cloth again and began to polish the already spotless countertop. "Ever since he came around, things have been upside down. The shop's broken into, the apartment's searched. I'm nearly raped and you—"

"What?" Lea was around the counter in two strides, gripping Dora's hands. "What did you say?"

"Damn." Though she tried to tug her hands away, Dora knew she'd already gone too far. "It wasn't really as bad as that. I exaggerated because you made me mad."

"Just hold on." Lea strode to the door, locked it and slapped the Closed sign up. "You're going to tell me everything, Dory, right now."

"All right." Resigned, Dora rubbed her hands over her face. "You'd better sit down."

It took some time, given that Lea interrupted frequently, but it was eventually told, beginning to end.

"I want you to promise not to tell Mom or Dad about this until I have a chance to."

"You go up and pack." Lea sprang to her feet. With her eyes glittering blue, she looked to Dora like a slim blonde angel ready to hurl her harp and halo. "You're moving in with John and me."

"I am not. Honey, I'm perfectly safe here."

"Oh, perfectly," Lea tossed back.

"I am. The police are looking for him, and they've even put guards on the building." She laughed then, adoring Lea. "Jesus, honey, I'm sleeping with a cop."

That mollified, a little. "I don't want you left alone. Not for five minutes."

"For heaven's sake—"

"I mean it." The gleam in Lea's eyes left no room for argument. "If you don't promise, I'll get John and we'll haul you home with us. And I want to talk to Jed myself."

"Help yourself." Dora tossed up her hands in surrender. It was impossible to play big sister with a woman who was the dictatorial mother of three. "He won't tell you anything I haven't. I'm absolutely, completely safe. Guaranteed."

They both shrieked when the door rattled.

"Hey!" Terri shouted and banged. "What are we doing locked up in the middle of the day?"

"Not a word," Dora muttered, and crossed over to unlock the door. "Sorry, we were taking a break."

Terri pursed her lips as she studied the two women. The air smelled suspiciously of a family fight. "Looks like you both could use one. Busy morning?"

"You could say so. Listen, there's a new shipment in the back. Why don't you unpack it? I'll price it when you're done."

"Sure." Obliging, Terri shrugged out of her coat as she strode to the storeroom. She could always listen through the door if things got interesting.

"We're not finished, Isadora."

"We are for now, Ophelia." Dora kissed Lea's cheek. "You can grill Jed when he gets back."

"I intend to."

"And nag him, too, will you? I'd like to see how he handles it."

Lea puffed up with indignation. "I don't nag."

"World's champ," Dora muttered in her best subliminal voice.

"And if you think this is a joke, you're—"

"Hey, Dora." Terri poked her head out of the storeroom. There was a puzzled smile on her face, and the copy of the computer-generated picture of DiCarlo in her hand. "Why do you have a picture of the guy who came in Christmas Eve?"

"What?" Dora struggled to keep her voice even. "Do you know him?"

"He was our last customer Christmas Eve. I sold him the Staffordshire—the mama dog with pup?" She glanced down at the picture, wiggled her brows. "Believe me, he looks better in person than he does here. He a pal of yours?"

"Not exactly." Her heart had begun to dance in her chest. "Terri, did he pay cash?"

"For the Staffordshire? Not likely. He charged it."

Excitement rippled into Dora's heart, but she was actress enough to void it from her voice. "Would you mind digging up the receipt for me?"

"Sure." Terri's face fell. "Don't tell me the guy's a deadbeat. I got approval on the card."

"No, I'm sure it's all right. I just need the receipt."

"Okay. He had some Italian name," she added. "Delano, Demarco, something." Shrugging, she closed the door behind her.

"DiCarlo," Brent said, handing Jed a rap sheet. "Anthony DiCarlo, New York. Mostly small-time stuff: larceny, confidence games, a couple of B and Es. Did a short stretch for extortion, but he's been clean as a whistle for nearly six years."

"Not being caught doesn't make you clean," Jed murmured.

"NYPD faxed this to me this morning. There's a cooperative detective up there who's going to do some legwork for me. Shouldn't be too hard to find out if our boy has an alibi for the other night."

"If he has one, it's fantasy. This is him." Jed tossed the file photo onto Brent's desk. "Maybe I should take a trip to New York."

"Maybe you should give our friends in the Big Apple a little time."

"I'll think about it."

"You look pretty relaxed for a man who's thinking about kicking ass."

Jed's lips twitched. "Do I?"

"Yep." Leaning back, Brent nodded. Lea would have commended him on his romantic radar. "That's what I thought," he murmured, and grinned. "Dora's quite a woman. Nice going, Captain."

"Shut up, Chapman," Jed said mildly on his way out. "Keep me posted, will you?"

"Sure." Brent waited until the door closed before he picked up the phone to report to Mary Pat.

18

He did think about it. Jed knew Dora would be down in the shop, so he went straight up to his own apartment. He stripped down to gym shorts and a T-shirt before settling on the bench press. He'd think better after he'd worked up a sweat.

He had to decide how much to tell her. She had a right to know it all—but there was a matter of rights, and a matter of what was best for her. If he knew Dora, and he was beginning to think he knew her very well, she'd want to do something about it. One of a cop's biggest headaches was civilian interference.

Not that he was a cop, he reminded himself, and kept up a steady rhythm with the weights. But when a man had spent nearly half his life on the force, he couldn't be considered a civilian either.

New York could handle it. But they didn't have a vested interest. All Jed had to do was let the image of Dora's pale, unconscious face swim into his mind to remind him just how vested his interest was.

A trip to New York, some poking around wouldn't infringe overmuch on the official investigation. And if he could do something tangible, something real, he might not feel so . . .

He paused with the barbell fully extended and scowled at the ceiling. Just how did he feel? Puffing out air, he lowered the bar again, lifted, lowered.

Useless, he realized. Unsettled. Unfinished.

Nothing in his life had ever really had a closure because nothing had ever really been open to begin with. It had been easier to keep himself shut off, removed. Easier, hell, Jed thought. It had been necessary for survival.

So why had he joined the force? He supposed he had finally recognized his own need for order, for discipline and, yes, even for family. The job had given him all of that. And more. A sense of purpose, of satisfaction and of pride.

Donny Speck had cost him that; but this wasn't about Speck, he reminded himself. It wasn't about Elaine. This was about protecting the woman across the hall. The woman he'd begun to feel something for.

That was something else to think about.

He didn't stop lifting when he heard the knock, but his lips curved when she called his name.

"Come on, Skimmerhorn, I know you're in there. I need to talk to you."

"It's open."

"How come you make me lock mine?" she demanded. She walked in looking all business in a hunter-green suit, and smelling of sin. "Oh." Her eyebrows lifted as she took a long slow scan of his body stretched out on the bench, muscles oiled with sweat and rippling. Her heart did a fast somersault. "Sorry to interrupt your male ritual. Shouldn't there be drums pounding or some sort of pagan chant in the background?"

"Did you want something, Conroy?"

"I want a lot of things. Red suede shoes, a couple of weeks in Jamaica, this Böttger teapot I saw over on Antique Row." She walked over to kiss his upside down lips, tasted salt. "How soon will you be finished—I might get excited watching you sweat."

"Looks like I'm finished now." Jed rattled the bar back in the brace.

"You won't be so cranky after I tell you what I found out." She paused, dramatic timing. "Terri recognized the picture."

"What picture?" Jed slid off the bench, reached for a towel.

"*The* picture. The magic picture we put together on the computer. Jed, he was in the shop on Christmas Eve." Excitement had her pacing the room, heels clicking on bare wood, her hands gesturing. "His name is—"

"DiCarlo, Anthony," Jed interrupted, amused when Dora's jaw dropped. "Last known address East Eighty-third Street, New York."

"But how did you . . . Damn." Sulking, she shoved the receipt back in her pocket. "You could have at least pretended to be impressed with my skills as a detective."

"You're a real Nancy Drew, Conroy." He went to the kitchen, took a jug of Gatorade from the fridge and gulped it straight from the bottle. When he lowered it, she was standing in the doorway with a dangerous glint in her eye. "You did okay. The cops just work faster. Did you call it in?"

"No." Her lip poked out. "I wanted to tell you."

"Brent's in charge of the investigation," Jed reminded her. He reached out and flicked a finger over her bottom lip. "Stop pouting."

"I'm not. I never pout."

"With that mouth, baby, you're the world champ. What did Terri say about DiCarlo?"

"Brent's in charge of the case," she said, primly. "I'll go back to my own apartment and call him. He might appreciate it."

Jed caught her face in his hand, gave it a little squeeze. "Spill it, Nancy."

"Well, since you put it that way. She said he was very smooth, very polite." Moving around Jed, she opened the fridge herself, gave an involuntary and very feminine sound of disgust. "God, Skimmerhorn, what is that thing in the bowl?"

"Dinner. What else did she say?"

"You can't eat this. I'll fix dinner."

"DiCarlo," Jed said flatly, and took her by the shoulders before she could poke into his cupboards.

"He said he had this aunt he wanted to buy a special gift for. Terri said she showed him the Foo dog—which I'm now sure he helped himself to when he broke in." She scowled over that a minute. "She said he was a snappy dresser and drove a Porsche."

He wanted more than that. "Is she downstairs?"

"No, she's gone for the day. We're closed."

"I want to talk to her."

"Now?"

"Now."

"Well, sorry, I don't know where she is now. She had an early dinner date with some new guy she's seeing." Dora let out a huff when Jed walked out of the kitchen. "If it's important, you could catch her at the theater later. Curtain's at eight. We can grab her for a few minutes backstage between scenes."

"Fine."

"But I don't see what good it would do." Dora followed him toward the bedroom. "I've already talked to her, and we have the name and address."

"You don't know the questions to ask." After stripping off his T-shirt, Jed tossed it into a corner. "He might have said something. The more we know, the easier it'll be to break him down in interrogation. We've got a couple hours if you really want to cook..."

But she wasn't listening. When he turned back, she was standing very still, a hand pressed against her heart and a look of utter shock on her face.

"What?" Instinct had him spinning around, scanning the room through narrowed eyes.

"The bed," she managed. "Oh..."

His tensed muscles relaxed. The quick flutter of embarrassment annoyed the hell out of him. First she criticized his cooking, now his housekeeping. "It's the maid's year off." He frowned at the rumpled sheets and blankets. "I don't see the point in making it when I'm just going to mess it up again."

"The bed," she repeated, reverently. "French Art Nouveau, about nineteen hundred. Oh, look at the inlay." She knelt by the footboard to run her fingertips gently over the image of a slender woman in a flowing gown holding a pitcher. The sound that came from her throat was one a woman makes in the heat of passion. "It's rosewood," she said, and sighed.

Amused, Jed watched her climb onto the bed and examine the headboard on her hands and knees. "Oh, the workmanship here," she murmured. "Look at this carving." Lovingly, she caressed the curves. "The delicacy."

"I think I've got a magnifying glass around here," Jed told her when she all but pressed her nose to the wood.

"You don't even know what you have here, do you?"

"I know it was one of the few pieces in that mausoleum I grew up in that I liked. Most of the rest's in storage."

"Storage." She closed her eyes and shuddered at the thought. "You have to let me go through what you have." She sat back on her heels, all but clasped her hands in prayer. "I'll give you fair market value for whatever I can afford. Just promise me, swear that you won't go to another dealer until I can make an offer."

"Pull yourself together, Conroy."

"Please." She scrambled to the edge of the bed. "I mean it. I don't expect favors because of a personal relationship. But if there are things you don't want." She looked back at the headboard, rolled her eyes. "God, I can't stand it. Come here."

"Uh-oh." A grin tugged at his mouth. "You're going to try to seduce me so I'll lower my price."

"Seduce, hell." Her breath had already quickened when she unbuttoned her jacket, peeled it off to reveal a flimsy camisole in the same deep green. "I'm going to give you the ride of your life, buddy."

"Ah..." He wasn't sure which emotion was uppermost. Shock or arousal. "That's quite an offer, Conroy."

"It's not an offer, pal, it's a fact." She rose to her knees to unzip her skirt, wiggled out of it. When she'd finished, she knelt on the bed wearing the camisole, a matching garter belt, sheer black hose and spiked heels. "If I don't have you on this bed, right now, I'll die."

"I don't want to be responsible for that." God, his knees were weak. "Conroy, I'm covered with sweat."

She smiled. "I know." She made a grab, caught him by the waistband of his shorts. He didn't put up much of a fight. "You're about to get a lot sweatier."

She tugged. Jed let himself be taken down. When she rolled over on top of him, he caught at her hands. "Be gentle with me."

She laughed. "Not a chance."

She crushed her mouth to his, nipping his lips apart and plunging in a kiss that erased every rational thought from his mind. Even as he released her hands to hold her, she was pressing down on him, mercilessly rubbing heat to heat.

He pulled in air that did nothing more than clog thickly in his chest. "Dora, let me—"

"Not this time." Fisting her hands in his hair, she ravished his mouth.

She was rough, relentless, reckless, tormenting him to within an inch of sanity until he didn't know whether to curse her, or to beg. Sensation after staggering sensation whipped through him leaving his system churning and edgy and desperate for more. His hands streaked under her camisole and he tortured himself with the firm, ripe swell of her breasts.

She arched back at his touch. A low, feline sound of approval purred in her throat as she stripped the material over her head. With her head thrown back, she covered his hands with hers, riding them down over her torso, over her flat belly. Her fingers tightened on his when he drove her over the first, shuddering peak. But when he tried to roll her over, she locked her legs tight around him, laughing huskily at his oath.

She slid down, dug her teeth into his shoulder. He tasted of salt and sweat and hot-blooded male. The combination whirled in her head like a heady wind. He was strong. The muscles under her urgent hands were like rippled iron. But she could draw a breathless, vulnerable moan from him with the dance of her fingers. She could feel his heart thundering under her lips.

He clutched at the smooth flesh over the top of her stockings, too frantic now to think of bruises. Now, at last now, she let him lift her. His vision grayed when she lowered herself onto him, taking steel deep, deep into velvet. Dazed, he watched her body bow back, her eyes closed, her hands sliding up her own sweat-slicked body in an uninhibited caress as she tightened urgently around him.

Then she began to move, slowly at first, steeped in her own pleasure, absorbing shock after delirious shock. Then faster, still faster, the muscles in her thighs taut as wire, her hips rocking like pistons. Each time her body stiffened, the force of it ripped through him like a flame-tipped arrow.

He reared up, his mouth seeking her breast, her shoulder, her lips. Crazed, he dragged her head back by the hair, ravaging her throat while he made hoarse promises neither of them understood. All he understood was at that moment he would have died for her. He certainly would have killed for her.

The climax pummeled him, a violent and welcome fist that stole his breath and left him staggered. Jed banded his arms around her, pressed his face between her breasts and let it shatter him.

"Dora." He turned her head so that his lips could cruise gently over her skin. And again. "Dora." He held her close until her body had ceased to shudder. When he leaned back, his eyes narrowed. Lifting a finger to her cheek, he caught a tear on the tip. "What's this?"

She could only shake her head and gather him against her. She rested her cheek on his hair. "I thought after yesterday, it wouldn't get any better. That it couldn't."

It worried him, that tremor in her voice. "If I'd known an old bed would turn you into a maniac, I'd have brought you in here days ago."

She smiled, but her eyes were still troubled. "It's a terrific bed."

"I've got about six more in storage."

She laughed. "We'll kill ourselves."

"I'll risk it."

So would she, Dora thought. So would she. Because Lea had been absolutely right. She was in love with him.

Two hours later they arrived at the Liberty Theater in time to hear Nurse Nellie demonstrate how to wash a man out of her hair. Dora had taken Jed through the stage door and up into the wings. Her father was there, mouthing the lyrics and pantomiming the moves.

"Hey." Dora pinched his cheek. "Where's Mom?"

"In Wardrobe. A little problem with Bloody Mary's sarong. Jed, my boy." He pumped Jed's hand while keeping an eye onstage. "Glad you came by. We have an appreciative audience tonight, barely an empty seat in the house. Light cue," he muttered under his breath, then beamed at the glow of a spot. "A smooth cue is as exhilarating as a waltz."

"We just dropped by to see how things were," Dora said, and shot a warning look at Jed. "And I need a minute with Terri at intermission. Shop business."

"I don't want you pulling her out of character."

"Don't worry." She slipped an arm around his shoulders and, despite the fact that she'd seen the production countless times, was soon as absorbed in the staging as he.

Jed hung back, more intrigued by Dora and Quentin than the dialogue onstage. Their heads were tilted together as they discussed some minor bit of business that had been added to the scene. Quentin's arm came up to wrap around her waist; Dora's body angled toward his.

Jed experienced a sensation that shocked him more than a blow to the neck. It was envy.

Had he ever felt that easy affection, that simple sense of companionship with his own father? he wondered. The answer was very simple and very bleak. No. Never. He couldn't remember a single conversation that hadn't been fraught with undercurrents of tension, disillusionment, resentment. Now, even had he wanted to, it was much too late to make peace. It was certainly useless to try to understand why.

When the old bitterness threatened, he walked quietly back toward the dressing rooms. He'd have a cigarette and wait to question Terri.

Dora looked over her shoulder. Her smile faded when she saw he was no longer there.

"Dad?"

"And music," he whispered. "Good, good. Hmmm?"

"I'm in love with Jed."

"Yes, my sweet, I know."

"No, Dad. I'm really in love with him."

"I know." For no one else would he have broken his concentration. But he turned to Dora with a twinkling grin. "I picked him for you, didn't I?"

"I don't think he's going to want me to be. Sometimes I can almost see where he's bleeding inside."

"You'll fix that, given time. 'What wound did ever heal but by degrees?' "

"Othello." She wrinkled her nose. "I didn't care for the ending in that one."

"You'll write your own. Conroys are excellent improvisers." A thought popped into his brain and made his eyes gleam. "Perhaps you'd like me to give him a little nudge. I could arrange a quiet man-to-man talk, with some of my special brew."

"No." She tapped a finger on his nose. "No," she repeated. "I'll handle this myself." Lowering her hand, she pressed it to her jittery stomach. "I'm scared," she confessed. "It's happened so fast."

"In the blood," Quentin said sagely. "The minute I saw your mother, I broke out in a vicious sweat. Most embarrassing. It took me nearly two weeks to get up the nerve to ask her to marry me. I kept going up on the lines."

"You never blew a line in your life." She kissed him as the applause broke out. "I love you."

"That's exactly what you should tell him." He gave her a squeeze. "Listen, Izzy, we're bringing the house down."

Responding to the applause, and the sudden chaos backstage, Jed went back to the wings just as Dora caught Terri.

"Hey, you working props tonight?"

"No." Dora got a good grip on Terri's arm. "I need to talk to you for a minute."

"Sure. How about that dance number? Those lessons I've been taking are paying off."

"You were great." With a nod to Jed, Dora steered Terri briskly through the stage-hands and technicians. "We'll just need a corner of the dressing room."

Several other members of the chorus were already inside, repairing hair and makeup.

Though some were stripped down to their underwear for costume changes, no one gave Jed more than a brief glance.

"Can I borrow this?" Dora asked, and commandeered a stool before anyone would refuse. "Sit down, Terri, get off your feet."

"You don't know how good that feels." She shifted toward the mirrors, choosing a makeup sponge to dab at the greasepaint moistened by sweat.

"About DiCarlo," Dora began.

"Who?" Terri stopped running lines in her head. "Oh, the guy from Christmas Eve." She smiled at Jed. "Dora's been real mysterious about him."

"What did he buy?" Jed asked.

"Oh, a Staffordshire figure. Never even winked at the price. He looked like he could afford it without any trouble though. And it was for his aunt. His favorite aunt. He said how she'd practically raised him, and she was getting really old. You know, a lot of people don't think that old people like getting nice things, but you could tell he really loved her."

Jed let her run down. "Did he show any interest in anything else?"

"Well, he looked all around, took his time. I thought he might bite on the Foo dog because he was looking for an animal."

"An animal?" Jed's eyes sharpened, but his voice remained cool and flat.

"You know, a statue of one. His aunt collects statues. Dogs," she added, relining her eyes with quick, deft movements. "See, she had this dog that died, and—"

"Was he specific?" Jed interrupted.

"Uh . . ." Terri pursed her lips and tried to think back. "Seems to me he really wanted a dog like the one his aunt had had who died—said he hadn't been able to find exactly what he'd been looking for." She freshened her lipstick, checked the results. "I remember he talked about the dog his aunt had—the dead one. I thought how we'd had that china piece that would have been perfect. It sounded like the dead dog had modeled for it. While he was alive, you know." She picked up a brush to fuss with her hair. "You know, Dora, the one you picked up at that auction. We'd already sold it, though."

Dora felt her blood drain. "To Mrs. Lyle."

"I don't know. You handled that sale, I think."

"Yes." Light-headed, Dora twisted her fingers together. "Yes, I did."

"Hey!" Alarmed, Terri turned on the stool. "Are you okay?"

"I'm fine." She forced a smile. She needed to get out. Needed air. "Thanks, Terri."

"No problem. Are you staying for the rest of the show?"

"Not tonight." Sickened, Dora fumbled for the door. "I'll see you tomorrow."

"Maybe you'd better go after her," Terri said to Jed. "She looked a little faint."

"Did you tell him about the china piece?"

"Yeah, I think so." Baffled, Terri slid off the stool and went to the door to see if Dora was in the corridor. "It seemed like such a coincidence, you know. I told him how we'd had something, but we'd sold it. I'm going to see what's wrong with Dora."

"I'll do it."

He caught up to her at the stage door, just as she was pushing through and drawing in deep breaths of air.

"Shake it off, Conroy." He held her by the shoulders at arm's length. He was afraid if he did more, she'd snap like a twig.

"I sold it to her." When she tried to jerk away, he merely tightened his hold. "For God's sake, Jed, I sold it to her. I don't know what he wanted it for, why he would have killed for it, but I sold it to her and the day after he found out—"

"I said shake it off." He all but lifted her off her feet, his face close to hers. "You sell lots of things—that's what you do. You're not responsible for what happens to the people who buy them."

"I can't be like that!" she shouted at him, and struck out. "I can't close myself off that way. That's your trick, Skimmerhorn. Make sure you don't give a damn, make sure nothing slips through and actually makes you feel. That's you. Not me."

That got through, and twisted in his gut. "You want to blame yourself, fine." Gripping her arm, he pulled her away from the door. "I'll take you home and you can spend the night beating yourself up over it."

"I don't have to apologize for having feelings. And I can get myself home."

"You wouldn't get two blocks before that bleeding heart of yours splashed on the sidewalk."

The buzzing in her ears came first. It always did when her temper snapped. Quick as a snake she rounded on him, leading with her left. He dodged that, but it was only a fake. Her sneaky right caught him in the jaw and snapped his head back.

"Son of a bitch." He saw stars. Later, he might take a moment to admire the fact that she'd all but knocked him on his ass. But now, eyes slitted with fury, he clenched his fists. She tossed her chin up in challenge.

"Try it," she invited. "Just try it."

It could have been funny—if there had been only temper in her eyes. If there hadn't been the quiver of tears beneath the dare. "Fuck this," he muttered. Ducking under her raised fists, he caught her around the waist and scooped her up over his shoulder.

She exploded with a volley of oaths, furious at the indignity of having to hammer at his back. "Put me down, you chicken-hearted bastard. You want to fight?"

"I've never coldcocked a woman in my life, Conroy, but you can be the first."

"Goddamn you, put me down and try it. They'll have to scrape you up off the pavement. When I'm finished, they'll have to pick you up with tweezers. They'll..." It drained out of her, as it always did, quickly, completely. She went limp, shut her eyes. "I'm sorry."

He wasn't finished being angry. "Shut up." He yanked out his keys, punched them into the door lock. In a smooth, economic move, he pulled her down, protected her head with his hand and shoved her into the car.

She kept her eyes closed, listening to him stalk around the car, open the door, slam it again. "I am sorry, Jed. I apologize for hitting you. Does it hurt?"

He wiggled his throbbing jaw. "No." He wouldn't have admitted it if it had been broken. "You hit like a girl."

"The hell I do." Insulted, she snapped up in her seat. The cool look in his eyes made her slump back again. "I wasn't angry with you," she murmured as he drove out of the lot. "I needed to vent at someone, and you were handy."

"Glad I could help."

If he was trying to chastise her with that frigid tone, she thought, he was doing a first-rate job. "You deserve to be mad." She kept her eyes lowered.

It was more difficult to take her sincerity, and her misery, than it had been to take the punch. "Just let it go. And Conroy? Don't mention to anybody that you got past my guard."

She turned back and, seeing the worst had passed, mustered up a smile. "I'll take it to my grave. If it's any consolation, I might have broken several fingers."

"It's not." But he took her hand, lifted it to touch to his lips. The stunned expression on her face had him scowling again. "What's the problem now?"

Since he'd released her hand she brought it up to her own cheek. "You threw me off a minute, that's all. The sweet routine hasn't exactly been your style with me."

Uncomfortable, he shifted in his seat. "Don't make me regret it."

"I probably shouldn't tell you, but bits of business like that—hand kissing and similar romantic gestures—make me all squishy inside."

"Define 'similar romantic gestures.' "

"Oh, like flowers, and long smoldering looks. Now that I think of it, you've done pretty well in the long-smoldering-look department. Then there's the big guns. Sweeping me up into your arms and carrying me up a curving staircase."

"You don't have a curving staircase."

"I could imagine I did." On impulse, she leaned over and kissed his cheek. "I'm glad you're not mad at me anymore."

"Who said I wasn't? I just don't want to fight when I'm driving." He lapsed into silence a moment. "About Mrs. Lyle," he began. "I'm going to need to check on her condition. If she comes out of it, she might put some pieces together for me."

"Us," Dora corrected quietly. "She's awake. Her niece came by the shop this morning." She linked her fingers again, tightly, and concentrated on keeping her voice calm and even. "She told me that Mrs. Lyle had come out of the coma, but that the doctors weren't committing themselves about her recovery."

"It's too late to try to get in to see her tonight," Jed said after a moment. "I can probably pull some strings tomorrow."

"I don't think you'd have to. I'd only have to ask Sharon—the niece." Dora kept her eyes straight ahead and tried not to resent the absence of concern in his voice. "But I won't do it unless I'm sure she's up to it. I won't let her be interrogated after what she's been through."

Tires spat out gravel when he turned into the lot. "Do I look like the gestapo, Conroy? You figure I'll shine a light in her eyes and find ways of making her talk?"

Saying nothing, she snapped down the door handle and climbed out. He reached the steps before her and blocked the way.

"Dora." Searching for patience, he took her hands. They were icy and stiff. "I know what I'm doing, and I'm not in the habit of badgering hospitalized old ladies for information." He looked down at her face. He didn't like to ask. He didn't like to need. But he found he had no choice. "Trust me."

"I do." Watching his face, she linked her fingers with his. "Completely. This whole thing has shaken me up some, that's all. I'll get in touch with Sharon first thing in the morning."

"Good." A bit shaken himself, he lowered his head to kiss her. No, he didn't like to ask. He didn't like to need. But he did. "Stay with me tonight."

The worry cleared from her eyes. "I was hoping you'd ask."

19

Dora had never considered herself phobic about hospitals. She was young and healthy and hadn't spent a great deal of time in one, and never as a patient. When she thought of hospitals at all, she thought of babies in the nursery, bouquets of flowers and the brisk efficiency of the nursing staff striding down the corridors in crepe-soled shoes.

Yet standing outside the Critical Care Unit waiting to speak with Mrs. Lyle, she felt as if a stone were lodged in her chest. Too quiet, she thought. It was much too quiet, with death patiently lurking behind glass doors and thin curtains, waiting to choose. She could hear the muffled beats and hums from machines and monitors, like grumbling old women complaining about aches and pains. From somewhere down the corridor came the pathetic sound of low and steady weeping.

All at once she wanted a cigarette, with a razor-sharp craving.

Sharon stepped through the swinging doors. Though she looked strained, her lips curved into a smile when she saw Dora. "She's lucid. I can't tell you how good it felt to talk to her, really talk to her."

"I'm glad." Battered with both guilt and relief, Dora took Sharon's hand in both of hers. "Sharon, this is Captain Skimmerhorn and Lieutenant Chapman."

"Hello. Dora told me you want to talk to Aunt Alice."

"We've cleared it with her doctor," Brent said. "And we appreciate your cooperation."

Sharon's mouth thinned into a hard, bloodless line. "Whatever I can do to help you find the person who did this to my aunt. She's expecting you."

Jed read the concern in the way Sharon looked back toward the doors. "We won't tire her."

"I know." Her hand fluttered up, then came to rest on the child in her womb. There was family to protect. And there was family to avenge. "Dora said you'd be careful. You'll let me know, won't you, if you learn anything?"

"Of course they will." Dora steered her toward a bench. "In the meantime, you sit down. Get off your feet. Try to relax."

"We've only got fifteen minutes with her," Jed said quietly when Dora returned. "Let's make it count. You," he added with a nod toward Dora. "Do nothing, say nothing unless you get the go-ahead."

"Yes, Captain."

Ignoring her, he turned to Brent. "She shouldn't be going in at all."

"She's seen the statue, we haven't. Let's see if it means anything." He led the way through the doors, past the nurses' station and into one of the small, curtained rooms.

Dora was grateful she'd been ordered to silence. She couldn't trust her voice. The woman she remembered as elegant and enthusiastic lay on the narrow bed, her eyes closed and shadowed with dingy bruises. The formerly deeply black hair was dulled, and gray was beginning to show at the roots, and her skin was sallow against the startlingly white bandages. Her face was drawn, the cheekbones jutting up sharply against skin that looked thin enough to tear at a touch.

"Mrs. Lyle." Brent stood at the bedside, spoke quietly.

Dora could see the pale blue veins in the eyelids when they fluttered. The monitor continued its monotonous beep as Mrs. Lyle struggled to focus.

"Yes?" Her voice was weak, and rough, as if her vocal cords had been sandpapered while she slept.

"I'm Lieutenant Chapman. Do you feel able to answer a few questions?"

"Yes."

Dora watched Mrs. Lyle try to swallow. Automatically she moved forward to pick up the cup of water and slip the straw between the dry lips.

"Thank you." Her voice was a shade stronger. She focused on Dora and smiled. "Miss Conroy. How nice of you to visit."

Jed's order was easily forgotten. "I'm glad you're feeling better." She reached down to close her fingers gently over Mrs. Lyle's frail hand. "I'm sorry you were hurt."

"They told me Muriel is dead." The tired eyes filled slowly, the aftermath of a storm already spent. "She was very dear to me."

Guilt was like a wave battering against the wall of Dora's composure. She could stand against it, but she couldn't ignore it. "I'm so sorry. The police hope you'll be able to help them find the man who did this." She pulled a Kleenex out of the box beside the bed and gently dried Mrs. Lyle's cheeks.

"I want to help." Firming her lips, she looked back at Brent. "I didn't see him, Lieutenant. I didn't see anyone. I was . . . watching a movie on television, and I thought I heard Muriel—" She broke off then and her fingers shifted in Dora's for comfort. "I thought I heard her come in behind me. Then there was this horrible pain, as if something had exploded in my head."

"Mrs. Lyle," Brent began, "do you remember buying a china dog from Miss Conroy the day before you were attacked?"

"Yes, for Sharon's baby. A doorstop," she said, and turned her head toward Dora again. "I'm worried that Sharon's not getting enough rest. This stress—"

"She's fine." Dora assured her.

"Mrs. Lyle." Jed stepped forward. "Do you remember anything else about the statue?"

"No." Though she tried to concentrate, memories drifted through like clouds. "It was rather sweet. A watchdog, I thought, for the baby. Is that what he wanted?" Her hand moved restlessly again. "Is that what he wanted? The little dog? I thought—I thought I heard him shouting for the dog. But that couldn't be."

Jed leaned forward so that her eyes would focus on his. There was panic in hers, but he had to press, just a little further. "What did you think you heard him shouting, Mrs. Lyle?"

" 'Where's the dog?' And he swore. I was lying there, and I couldn't move. I thought I'd had a stroke and was dreaming. There was crashing and shouting, shouting over and over about a dog. And then there was nothing." She closed her eyes again, exhausted. "Surely he didn't murder Muriel for a little china dog."

"But he did, didn't he?" Dora asked when they stood together at the elevators.

"Not much doubt of it." Brent worried his glasses, stuck his hands in his pockets. "But that's not the end of it. The bullet that killed Muriel came from the same gun that killed Trainor." He looked at Jed. "Matched the ones we dug out of the plaster at the shop."

"So he came back for something else." Calculating, Jed stepped into the elevator. "The dog wasn't it—or wasn't all of it. Whatever *it* is."

"But the piece wasn't valuable or unique," Dora murmured. "It wasn't even marked. I only bid on it because it was cute."

"You bought it at an auction." Slowly, Jed turned the possibilities over in his mind. "Where?"

"In Virginia. Lea and I went on a buying trip. You remember. I got back the day you moved in."

"And the next day you sold the dog." He took her arm to pull her out of the elevator when they reached the lobby. "There was a break-in at the shop, Mrs. Lyle was attacked, then another break-in. What else did you buy, Dora?"

"At the auction. A lot of things." She dragged her hand through her hair, leaving her coat unbuttoned to the cold as she stepped outside between the two men. The brisk air helped blow away some of the sickly scent of hospital. "I have a list at the shop."

"Don't they have lots at auctions?" Brent asked. "Or groups of merchandise that come from the same place or the same seller?"

"Sure. Sometimes you buy a trunk full of junk just to get one piece. This wasn't Sotheby's; it was more of a flea market, but there were several good buys."

"What did you buy right before the dog, and right after?"

She was tired, down to the bone. The vague throb in her temple warned of a titanic headache in progress. "Christ, Skimmerhorn, how am I supposed to remember? Life hasn't been exactly uneventful since then."

"That's bull, Conroy." His voice took on an edge that had Brent's brows raising. He'd heard it before—when Jed had been interrogating an uncooperative suspect. "You know everything you buy, everything you sell, and the exact price, tax included. Now what did you buy before the dog?"

"A shaving mug, swan-shaped." She snapped the words out. "Circa nineteen hundred. Forty-six dollars and seventy-five cents. You don't pay tax when you buy for resale."

"And after the dog?"

"An abstract painting in an ebony frame. Primary colors on white canvas, signed E. Billingsly. Final bid fifty-two seventy-five—" She broke off, pressed a hand to her mouth. "Oh my God."

"Right on target," Jed muttered.

"A picture," she whispered, horrified. "Not a photograph, a painting. He wanted the painting."

"Let's go find out why."

Dora's cheeks were the color of paste as she groped for Jed's hand. "I gave it to my mother." Nausea rolled greasily in her stomach. "I gave it to my mother."

"I adore unexpected company." Trixie batted her luxuriant lashes as she hooked her arms through Jed's and Brent's. "I'm delighted you were able to find time in your busy day to drop in."

"Mom, we only have a few minutes," Dora began.

"Nonsense." Trixie was already towing the two men out of the postage-stamp foyer and into what she preferred to call the drawing room. "You must stay for lunch. I'm sure Carlotta can whip up something wonderful for us."

"That's nice of you, Mrs. Conroy, but—"

"Trixie." Her laugh was a light trill as she tapped a teasing finger against Brent's chest. "I'm only Mrs. Conroy to strangers and bill collectors."

"Trixie." A dull flush crept up Brent's neck. He didn't think he'd ever been flirted with by a woman old enough to be his mother before. "We're really a little pressed for time."

"Pressing time is what causes ulcers. No one in my family ever had stomach problems—except dear Uncle Will, who spent his whole life making money and none of it enjoying it. Then what could he do but leave it all to me? And of course, we enjoyed it very much. Please, please, sit."

She gestured toward two sturdy wing chairs in front of a crackling fire. She arranged herself on a red velvet settee, much like a queen taking the throne.

"And how is your charming wife?"

"She's fine. We enjoyed your party the other night."

"It was fun, wasn't it?" Her eyes sparkled. She draped an arm casually over the back of the settee—a mature Scarlett entertaining her beaux at Tara. "I adore parties. Isadora, dear, ring for Carlotta, won't you?"

Resigned, Dora pulled an old-fashioned needlepoint bell rope hanging on the left of the mantel. "Mom, I just dropped by to pick up the painting. There's . . . some interest in it."

"Painting?" Trixie crossed her legs. Her blue silk lounging pants whispered with the movement. "Which painting is that, darling?"

"The abstract."

"Oh, yes." She shifted her body toward Jed. "Normally, I prefer more traditional styles, but there was something so bold and high-handed about that work. I can see that you'd be interested. It would suit you."

"Thanks." He assumed it was a compliment. In any case, it seemed easier to play along. "I enjoy abstract expressionism—Pollock, for example, with his complicated linear rhythms, his way of attacking the canvas. Also the energy and verve of say, de Kooning."

"Yes, of course," Trixie enthused, bright-eyed, though she hadn't a clue.

Jed had the satisfaction of seeing sheer astonishment on Dora's face. He only smiled, smugly, and folded his hands. "And of course, there's Motherwell. Those austere colors and amorphous shapes."

"Genius," Trixie agreed. "Absolute genius." Dazzled, she glanced toward the hall at the sound of familiar stomping.

Carlotta entered, hands on the hips of the black sweatpants she wore in lieu of a uniform. She was a small, stubby woman, resembling a tree stump with arms. Her sallow face was set in permanent annoyance.

"What you want?"

"We'll have tea, Carlotta," Trixie instructed, her voice suddenly very grande dame. "Oolong, I believe."

Carlotta's beady black eyes scanned the group. "They staying for lunch?" she demanded in her harsh and somehow exotic voice.

"No," Dora said.

"Yes," her mother said simultaneously. "Set for four, if you please."

Carlotta lifted her squared-off chin. "Then they eat tuna fish. That's what I fixed; that's what they eat."

"I'm sure that will be delightful." Trixie waggled her fingers in dismissal.

"She's just plain ornery," Dora muttered as she sat on the arm of Jed's chair. It was unlikely they would escape without tea and tuna fish, but at least she could focus her mother on the matter at hand. "The painting? I thought you were going to hang it in here."

"I did, but it simply didn't work. Too frenzied," she explained to Jed, whom she now considered an expert on the subject. "One does like to let the mind rest in one's drawing room. We put it in Quentin's den. He thought it might energize him."

"I'll get it."

"An extraordinary girl, our Isadora," Trixie said when Dora was out of earshot. She smiled at Jed, but didn't quite disguise the gleam of calculation in her eyes. "So bright and ambitious. Strong-minded, of course, which only means she requires an equally strong-minded man to compliment her. I believe a woman who can run her own business will run a home and family with equal success. Don't you, dear?"

Any response could spring the trap. "I imagine she could do whatever she set out to do."

"No doubt about it. Your wife is a professional woman, isn't she, Brent? And a mother of three."

"That's right." Since Jed was clearly on the hot seat, Brent grinned. "It takes a team effort to keep all the balls in the air, but we like it."

"And a single man, after a certain age..." Trixie aimed a telling look at Jed, who barely resisted the urge to squirm. "He benefits from that teamwork. The companionship of a woman, the solace of family. Have you ever been married, Jed?"

"No." Jed's eyes sharpened when Dora walked back in, carrying the painting.

"Mom, I'm sorry, I'm afraid you'll have to eat lunch alone. I called in to the shop to let them know I'd be delayed getting back. There's a little problem I need to see to. I'll have to leave right away."

"Oh, but darling..."

"We'll do lunch soon." She bent to kiss Trixie's cheek. "I think I have something Dad might like better for his den. One of you drop by and we'll see."

"Very well." With a resigned sigh, Trixie set down her cup and rose. "If you must go, you must. But I'll have Carlotta pack up lunch for you."

"You don't—"

Trixie patted Dora's cheek. "I insist. It'll just take a moment."

She hurried off, leaving Dora sighing.

"Very smooth, Conroy." Jed took the painting from her to examine it himself.

"Speaking of smooth." She turned back, smiling curiously. "Amorphous shapes?"

"I dated an artist for a while. You pick stuff up."

"It should be interesting to see what you've picked up from me."

"I don't even like tuna fish." But Dora bit into the sandwich nonetheless while Jed finished removing the frame from the canvas.

"I like the way she chopped up hardboiled eggs and pickles." Brent polished off his second sandwich with a sigh of satisfaction.

They'd chosen to work in Dora's apartment rather than the storeroom because there was both room and privacy. No one had mentioned the fact that Brent hadn't insisted on taking the painting or the information he'd gathered to his superior.

It was an unspoken fact that Brent still considered Jed his captain.

"Nothing in the frame." Still, Jed set it carefully aside. "Nothing to the frame, for that matter. We'll let the lab boys take a look."

"Can't be the painting itself." Dora washed down tuna with Diet Pepsi. "The artist is an unknown—I checked the day after I bought it in case I'd happened across some overlooked masterpiece."

Thoughtfully, Jed turned the painting over. "The canvas is stretched over plywood. Get me something to pry this off with, Conroy."

"You think there might be something inside?" She spoke from the kitchen, rummaging through drawers. "A cache of drugs—no, better. Diamonds." She brought out a screwdriver. "Rubies, maybe. They're more valuable these days."

"Try reality," Jed suggested, and went to work on the backing.

"It could be," she insisted, peering over his shoulder. "It has to be something worth killing for, and that's usually money."

"Quit breathing down my neck." Jed elbowed her away before prying at the plywood.

"It's my painting," she reminded him. "I have a bill of sale."

"Nothing," Jed muttered as he examined the backing he'd removed. "No secret compartments."

Dora glared at him. "There might have been."

"Right." Ignoring her, he tapped a hand on the back of the exposed canvas.

"That's odd. The back of that canvas has a lot of age to it." Dora pushed her way in for a closer look. "Although I suppose Billingsly could have painted over an old canvas to save money."

"Yeah. And sometimes people paint over paintings to smuggle them through customs."

"You think there's an old master behind there?" Amused, Dora shook her head. "Now who's dreaming?"

But he was paying no more attention to her than he would to a fly buzzing around the ceiling. "We need to get this paint off, see what's under it."

"Hold it, Skimmerhorn. I paid for this. I'm not going to have you screw it up over some cop's 'hinkey feeling.' "

"How much?" Impatience and disgust warred as he turned to her.

Pleased that he understood, she folded her arms over her chest. "Fifty-two dollars and seventy-five cents."

Muttering, he pulled out his wallet, counted out bills.

Dora tucked her tongue in her cheek and accepted them. Only her strong feelings for Jed kept her from recounting them. "Overhead," she said primly. "And a reasonable profit. Make it an even eighty and we'll call it square."

"For Christ's sake." He slapped more bills into her palm. "Greedy."

"Practical," she corrected, and kissed him to close the deal. "I have some stuff in the storeroom that should work. Give me a minute." Dora slipped the money into her pocket and went downstairs.

"She made you pay for it." Filled with admiration, Brent leaned back in his chair. "And made twenty-seven bucks and change on the deal. I thought she was kidding."

"I doubt Dora ever kids when it comes to money." Jed stepped back, lighted a cigarette and studied the painting as if he could see through the splashes of red and blue. "She might have a soft heart, but she's got a mind like a corporate raider."

"Hey!" Dora kicked at the door with her shoe. "Open up. My hands're full." When Jed opened the door, she came in loaded down with a drop cloth, a bottle and several rags. "You know, it might be better if we called in some expert. We could have it X-rayed or something."

"For now, we're keeping this to ourselves." He dropped the rags on the floor, then took the bottle. "What's in here?"

"A solution I use when some idiot has painted over stenciling." She knelt on the floor to roll back the rug. "We need a very careful touch. Give me a hand with this."

Brent was already beside her, grinning at the way Jed scowled when Jed noted where his eyes had focused. He crouched and spread the cloth.

"Trust me, I've done this before," she explained. "Some philistine painted over this gorgeous old credenza so it would match the dining room color scheme. It took forever to get it back in shape, but it was worth it." She sat back on her heels, blew the hair out of her eyes. "Want me to give it a try?"

"I paid for it," Jed reminded her. "It's mine now."

"Just offering to help." She handed him a rag. "I'd start on a corner if I were you. In case you mess up."

"I'm not going to mess up." But after he knelt beside her, he did indeed start on a corner. He dampened the rag and, working in slow, delicate circles, removed the end of the signature.

"Bye-bye, Billingsly," Dora murmured.

"Put a lid on it, Conroy." He dampened the rag again then gently removed the stark white paint, the primer. "Something's under here."

"You're kidding." Excitement bubbled into her voice as she leaned closer. "What is it? I can't see." She tried to crane her neck over his shoulder and got an elbow in the ribs for her trouble. "Damn, Skimmerhorn, I just want a look."

"Back off." His muscles tensed as he delicately removed more of the primer. "Pay dirt," he murmured. "Son of a bitch."

"What?" Refusing to be put off, Dora nudged him until she could crouch close to the corner. "Monet." She whispered the name, as though in church. "Claude Monet. Oh my God, I bought a Monet for fifty-two dollars and seventy-five cents."

"I bought a Monet," Jed reminded her. "For eighty."

"Children." Brent laid a hand on each of their backs. "I'm not much of an art buff, but even I know who this guy is, and I don't think anybody would have painted that abstract crap over the real thing."

"Unless it was being smuggled," Jed finished.

"Exactly. I'll run a check, see if there've been any art thefts in the last few months that included our friend here."

"It might have been in a private collection." Dora let her fingers hover over Monet's signature, but didn't touch. "Don't take off any more, Jed. You could damage it."

She was right. Jed stemmed his impatience and set the rag aside. "I know somebody who does some restoration work. She could probably handle this, and she'd keep quiet about it."

"The old girlfriend?" Dora asked.

"She isn't old." In an unconscious move he skimmed a hand over Dora's hair, resting his fingers on the nape of her neck as he looked over at Brent.

"You're going to have to take this to Goldman."

"That's the next step."

Jed looked down at the artist's signature against a deep misty green. "I shouldn't ask you, but I'm going to."

"How much time do you want?" Brent asked, anticipating him.

"Time enough to check out this auction house in Virginia and find the trail." He kept his voice even.

Brent nodded and picked up his coat. "I've got enough on my plate checking out DiCarlo. NYPD reports that he hasn't been seen at his apartment for a few days. Between that and trying to keep Philadelphia safe for women and children, I could let certain details slip my mind. You'd be doing me a favor if you could pull together what a china statue of a dog and a painting have in common. Keep in touch."

"I will."

"And watch your back. See you, Dora."

"Bye, Brent." She stayed where she was a moment. "How high a limb did he just go out on for you?"

"High enough."

"Then we'd better be sure we can pull a net under him."

"We?" He grabbed her hand as she got to her feet. "I don't remember anything about we."

"Then your memory's faulty. Why don't you call your friend the artist, then book us a flight for Virginia? I'll be packed in ten minutes."

"There's not a woman alive who can pack for a trip in ten minutes."

"Skimmerhorn." She spoke over her shoulder as she headed for the bedroom. "I was born on the road. Nobody packs faster than an actor ducking an opening-night bomb."

"I don't want you with me. It could be dangerous."

"Fine, I'll book my own flight."

"Goddamn, you're a pain in the ass."

"So I've been told. Oh, and make sure it's first-class, will you? I never travel coach."

Winesap knocked lightly on Finley's office door. He knew his employer had just completed a forty-five-minute conference call, and wasn't sure of his mood. Gingerly, he poked his head inside. Finley was standing at the window, his hands clasped behind his back.

"Sir?"

"Abel. It's a fine day, isn't it? A fine day."

The trepidation curdling Winesap's stomach smoothed out like lake water. "Yes, sir, it is."

"I'm a fortunate man, Abel. Of course, I've made my own fortune, which makes it all the sweeter. How many of those people down there enjoy their work, do you suppose? How many go home at the end of the business day fulfilled? Yes, Abel, I am a fortunate man." He turned back, his face wreathed in smiles. "And what can I do for you?"

"I have a dossier on Isadora Conroy."

"Excellent work. Excellent." He beckoned Winesap forward. "You are of great value to me, Abel." As he reached for the file, Finley squeezed Winesap's bony shoulder with his free hand. "Of great value. I would like to demonstrate my appreciation." Opening his top desk drawer, Finley took out a velvet box.

"Thank you, sir." Humbled and touched, Winesap opened the box. "Oh, Mr. Finley," he said in a choked voice. Choked because he didn't have a clue what he was looking at.

It seemed to be a spoon of some sort with a large bowl and a short handle shaped like an eagle.

"I'm delighted you're pleased. I chose it from my own collection of caddy spoons. The pewter, I thought, suited you best. A strong, durable material often underrated."

"Thank you, sir. Thank you. I don't know what to say."

"It's nothing." Finley brushed away the gratitude. "A token only of my appreciation." He sat now, tapping his finger to his top lip. "You serve me well, Abel. I reward loyalty just as I punish betrayal. Quickly, precisely and thoroughly. Hold my calls for the next hour."

"Yes, sir. Thank you again."

But Finley had already quickly, precisely and thoroughly blocked Winesap from his reality. He opened the file and concentrated on Isadora Conroy.

20

It was raining in thin chilly sheets when Jed drove into Front Royal. The weather had been miserable throughout the plane ride from Philadelphia International to Dulles, and promised to remain so. The defroster on the rental car worked at two speeds: blast and trickle. Each time Jed was forced to crank it up, the interior turned into a small, efficient sauna.

Dora chatted away on the drive, her easy voice and casual observations relaxing him. He wasn't required to respond, or even to listen. She had a way of making him absorb her mood even while his mind was working out the details of the next steps to be taken.

"If you ever went into the subliminal tape business," Jed commented, "you could make a fortune."

"Do you think so?" Dora flipped down the visor and used the attached mirror to freshen her lipstick. "Make the next two rights," she told him, and recapped her lipstick. "There's a parking lot in back of the building."

"Since there's a sign and an arrow, I probably could have figured that out."

"I was not ticked off."

"Of course you were." With a bright smile on her face, Dora patted his arm. "It's a man thing. The way you insisted on doing the driving even though I knew the way was a man thing. I don't mind. I think it's cute."

"I did the driving because I didn't trust you not to end up in a five-car pileup because you were so busy talking about the ozone layer or Z Z Top."

"Ah." She leaned over and kissed his cheek. "You were listening."

"My ears are still ringing." Jed pulled up into a slot beside a battered Ford pickup. "Remember, Conroy, you're not here on a buying jaunt."

"I know, I know." She rolled her eyes as he climbed out of the car. "And you'll ask the questions," she continued. "I'll stand two paces behind like a good little girl and keep my mouth shut."

He waited until she'd shut her door. "That's right." He studied her while the rain dampened her hair. "It's a nice mouth—even if it runs most of the time."

"Well, that set my heart fluttering." She hooked her arm through his and started for the rear door. "It won't be warm inside," she told him as he pulled open the metal door with a screech of hinges. "But it'll be dry. Mr. Porter has a rep for extreme frugality. No frills, no shiny displays, but some pretty good bargains." She took a deep gulp of the air and her eyes kindled. "God, just look at this stuff."

He was. But what he saw was row after row of dusty furniture and smeared glass crowded with junk. There were tangles of jewelry, most of it outrageously tacky and all of it dull from disuse. An entire cabinet was stuffed with salt and pepper shakers, another with a variety of bottles that were none too clean. There was a Shriner's cap set jauntily atop a cracked gumball machine and several cardboard boxes filled with paperback books at ten cents apiece.

"I think that's a Maxfield Parrish print."

Before Dora could make a beeline, Jed snagged her arm. From the gleam in her eyes, he knew that getting her through would be similar to walking over hot coals. It would have to be done fast, and without any looking back.

"Where are the offices?"

"In the front, to the right. Jed, I only want to see—"

But he was already hauling her along while she tugged on his arm like a puppy straining at the leash. "Toughen up, Conroy. Your palms are sweating."

"This is really cruel," she muttered. But she lifted her chin. "Are you sure you don't want me to talk to Porter? Dealer to dealer?"

"I said I'd do the talking."

"Testosterone surge," Dora said under her breath.

The office was open but empty when they reached it. It looked to Jed to be the only space in the building that had seen a dust rag or scrub brush within the last decade. In contrast to the helter-skelter arrangement of the market, the desk was shining and neat, the file cabinets clean and tidily shut. The air carried the vague scent of some lemony spray wax.

"There's been some reorganizing since the last time I was here." Curious, Dora poked her head inside. The desk blotter was spotless, and on the left corner stood a good porcelain vase with fresh hothouse roses. "Last time there was a girlie calendar on the wall—from nineteen fifty-six—and the rest of it looked as though there had been a small bomb detonation. I remember thinking I didn't see how anyone could work in that kind of chaos." She caught Jed's bland stare and shrugged. "My kind of chaos is organized." She paused to look around and tried not to yearn too much toward the bargain table. "Maybe Porter's roaming through somewhere. He's easy enough to spot. He sort of looks like a ferret."

"May I help you?"

Jed put a hand on Dora's shoulder to keep her quiet and turned to the tidily dressed woman with glasses hanging from a gold chain. "We'd like to speak to Mr. Porter."

Helen Owings's eyes clouded and filled alarmingly fast with hot tears. "Oh," she said, and dug in her pocket for a tissue. And again, "Oh," as she mopped her streaming eyes.

"I'm sorry." Before Jed could react, Dora had her by the arm and was leading her into the office, into a chair. "Can I get you some water?"

"No, no." Helen sniffled, then began to tear the damp tissue into tiny pieces. "It was just such a shock, your asking for him. You couldn't have known, I suppose."

"Have known what?" Jed shut the door quietly and waited.

"Sherman—Mr. Porter's dead. Murdered." Though the word came out fruity with drama, Helen's lips trembled.

"Oh God." Dora groped for a chair herself while her brain did a slow, sickening spin.

"Right before Christmas." Helen blew her nose on what was left of her tissue. "I found him myself. There." She lifted a hand, pointed at the desk.

"How was he killed?" Jed demanded.

"Shot." Helen covered her face with her hands, then dropped them into her lap to twist them together. "Shot through the head. Poor, poor Sherman."

"Do the police have any suspects?" Jed asked.

"No." Helen sighed and began to draw on what was left of her rattled composure. "There doesn't seem to have been a motive. Nothing was taken that we can determine. There were no—signs of struggle. I'm sorry, Mr. . . . ?"

"Skimmerhorn."

"Mr. Skimmerhorn. Did you know Sherman?"

"No." He debated for a moment how much to tell her. As usual, he decided less was best. "Miss Conroy is a dealer in Philadelphia. We're here about some items that were auctioned on December twenty-first."

"Our last auction." Her voice broke. After taking a deep breath, she straightened her shoulders in an obvious effort to compose herself. "You'll excuse me for being so upset, I hope. We've just reopened today, and I'm still a little shaky. Was there a problem?"

"A question." Jed smiled with charm and sympathy. "Miss Conroy bought two pieces. We're interested in where and how you acquired them."

"May I ask why? We usually don't reveal our sources. After all, another dealer could come in and outbid us."

"We're interested in more background on the items," he said reassuringly. "We're not going to try to cut off your supply."

"Well . . ." It wasn't entirely regular, but Helen couldn't find any harm in it. "I may be able to help you. Do you remember the lot number?"

"F fifteen and F eighteen," Dora said dully. She'd remembered something else, something that made her stomach roll. But when Jed murmured her name, she shook her head.

"F fifteen and eighteen," Helen repeated, grateful for something practical to do. She rose and went to the file cabinets. "Oh yes, the F lots were from the New York shipment. A small estate sale." She smiled, taking the folder to the desk. "To be frank, Mr. Skimmerhorn, I believe most of the items were picked up at yard sales. I remember that the quality was not what I'd expected. Conroy... yes, you purchased both pieces. I'm afraid I can't tell you very much about them. I—"

The knock on the door interrupted her. "Miz Owings?"

"Yes, Richie?"

"We got a question out here about that Early American dry sink. People are in a hurry."

"All right, tell them I'll be right there." Helen rose, smoothed down her hair, her skirt. "Will you excuse me just a minute?"

Jed waited until she'd walked out before picking up the file himself. He scanned the lists, the inventories, the prices, then simply pocketed what he felt was relevant.

"What are you doing?" Dora demanded. "You can't do that."

"It'll save time. Come on."

"She knows my name."

"So, we'll make copies then send the originals back." He took a firm grip on her hand, but this time it wasn't necessary. She didn't try to linger or dig in her heels to study any of the dusty treasures. Once they were outside and in the car, Jed took her chin in his hand. "Okay, spill it. You went white as a sheet in there."

"I remembered Mr. Ashworth. I told you about him. He was the dealer I met at the auction that day. He bought a piece from that shipment."

"The guy who was killed during a burglary," Jed murmured. "You said his shop was around here."

"Yes, just a couple miles away."

"Then that's where we're going next." He switched on the engine. "Can you handle it?"

"Yes. But I want to stop and call the shop first."

"You've only been away a couple hours, Conroy. It should run well enough without you."

"I don't want Terri or Lea anywhere near the place." She set her jaw and stared straight ahead. "I want it closed."

"Okay." He closed his hand over hers and found it cold and rigid. "Okay."

Although he'd taken the precaution of packing an overnight bag, Jed had hoped to make the trip to Virginia and back in one day. There was no question of doing so after visiting Ashworth's shop.

Dora needed some downtime, and he was going to see that she got it.

She said nothing when he checked into a hotel near the airport. The fact that she'd said little throughout the rainy ride from Front Royal concerned him nearly as much as the information they'd gleaned from Tom Ashworth's grandson. In addition to Ashworth's death and the damage done during the break-in, the figurine had apparently been taken.

Jed unlocked the door of the hotel room, set the overnight bags aside, then pointed Dora toward a chair. "Sit down. You need to eat."

"I'm not hungry."

"Yes, you are." He picked up the phone and ordered two steaks, coffee and a bottle of brandy without consulting her. "Thirty minutes," he said when he hung up. "Which probably means forty. You've got time to stretch out."

"I..." Numb, she looked toward the bed. "I think I'll have a bath."

"Fine. Take your time."

She rose, picked up her bag. She didn't look at him. "Don't you feel anything?" she asked in a voice that cracked with fatigue. "Three people are dead—at least three. There might be more. People I care about might be in danger simply because they work for me. And you order dinner. Doesn't it make you scared? Doesn't it make you sick? Doesn't it make you anything?"

The last question lashed out like a whip as she clutched the bag to her chest and forced herself to look at his face. Jed met her eyes levelly. "Yeah, it makes me something. It makes me pissed off. Go take your bath, Dora. Tune it out for a while."

Wearily, she turned away. "It doesn't work like that." She closed the door quietly behind her. In a moment, he heard the water running in the tub.

He lighted a cigarette, swearing under his breath as he fought with the matches. She was disappointed in him—that's what had been in her eyes when she'd finally looked at him. And it mattered, maybe too much, what she thought of him, what she felt for him, how she looked at him.

She mattered too much.

He crossed to the bathroom door, lifted his hand to knock. Then dropped it again. There was nothing to be said, he thought. Actions were necessary. He went back to the phone and called Brent.

"Lieutenant Chapman."

"It's Jed."

"What have you got?"

"A couple of dead guys." Jed blew out smoke and automatically kept his voice low. "Sherman Porter, owned the auction house where Dora picked up the painting and the dog. Shot in his office right before Christmas. You might want to call the locals here for details."

"I've got it."

"Ashworth, Thomas, local antique dealer, killed during a burglary about the same time Porter bought it. He'd been at the auction with Dora, bought a porcelain figurine." Jed consulted his list. "A man and a woman, about two feet high, in period dress. Antebellum. He didn't keep it long."

"Value?"

"Negligible. I've got a rundown here of what else was in the shipment, and who bought what."

"You've been busy, Captain. Read it off, but take it slow. My shorthand's rusty."

When he'd finished the list, Jed crushed out his cigarette. "I'd appreciate it if you'd put a rush on running these people down."

"You don't have to ask."

"The shipment came down from New York, supposed to be from some estate sale, but the woman in charge seemed to think the stuff was yard-sale junk—not exactly what she'd been expecting. I've got the name of the guy who sent it down. I'm going to check him out tomorrow, in person."

"Let me have the name. We'll run a make on him just in case."

"Franklin Flowers, Brooklyn address. Any more on Mrs. Lyle?"

"Her condition seems to be stabilizing. She doesn't remember any more than what she told us."

"The painting?"

"Your old girlfriend's still working on it. Nice thought to have her working in your grandmother's place." A hint of amusement lightened Brent's voice. "Your grandmother told me, in no uncertain terms, that the process wouldn't be rushed."

"You've got a man on her?"

"Twenty-four hours. I've had to blow a little smoke in Goldman's direction, call in a few favors. Reports are the duty includes petits fours and café au lait. I wouldn't mind pulling it myself. Give me your number in case I come up with anything tonight."

Jed read it off the phone. "Are you taking any heat on this?"

"Nothing I can't handle. Goldman decided to take an interest in Trainor's shooter. Did a standup in front of the courthouse. You know: 'When one of my men is killed, I won't rest until the perpetrator is brought to justice.' Film at eleven."

"We'll dump DiCarlo right in his lap."

The disgust in Jed's voice gave Brent hope. "If we can find him. Our boy seems to have gone underground."

"Then we'll dig him up. I'll call you from New York."

He hung up, leaned back against the headboard and smoked another cigarette. The water had stopped running. He hoped she was lying back in the tub, her eyes closed and her mind blank.

Dora was lying back. She did have her eyes closed while the hot water and bath salts slowly relaxed her body. It was more difficult to relax her mind. She kept seeing the way Helen Owings's eyes had filled and overflowed. She kept hearing the way Thomas Ashworth III's voice had thickened when he'd spoken of his grandfather. She kept remembering how pale and fragile Mrs. Lyle had looked lying in a hospital bed surrounded by machines.

Even in the warmth of the bath she could feel the memory of the cool barrel of a gun pressed against her breast.

Worse, she could still hear Jed's flat, dispassionate voice questioning the victims, and see his eyes, so gorgeously blue, blank out all emotion. No heat, no ice, no sympathy.

Wasn't that its own kind of death? she wondered. Not to feel—no, she corrected, not to *allow* yourself to feel. And that was so much worse. To have the capacity to permit yourself to stand to the side and observe and dissect without any of the grief touching you.

Perhaps she'd been wrong about him all along. Perhaps nothing really touched him, nothing got through all those carefully constructed layers of disinterest and frigid objectivity.

He was simply doing a job, putting together a puzzle, yet none of the pieces meant any more than a step taken toward a solution.

She stayed in the water until it began to cool. Postponing the moment when she would have to face him again, Dora dried off carefully, soothed herself by slowly creaming her skin. She let the towel drop, then reached for her robe.

Her hand hesitated, then brushed over the vivid green terrycloth. She'd let herself forget that side of him, she realized. The gentle side, the perhaps reluctantly-kind-but-kind-nonetheless side.

Sighing a little, she slipped into the robe. It was her own fault, she decided. She always seemed to look for more, and was always disappointed if more wasn't available. But it was so hard to settle, she thought, and secured the belt. So Goddamn hard to settle.

She opened the door, letting out a flow of steam and scent. He was standing at the window, looking out at the rain. The room-service cart was beside him, set for two. He'd already poured himself a cup of coffee from the pot and was lifting the cup to his lips as he turned to her.

It was like a fist in the solar plexus, watching her come into the room. The bath had brought color back to her cheeks, yet her skin had that soft, fragile glow brought on by exhaustion. The hair she'd pinned carelessly up was damp from the steam. And quite suddenly, the air smelled only of her.

He'd dimmed the lights, not for romance but because he'd thought the softer light would comfort her. In it she looked fragile and lovely, like a flower under glass.

He forced himself to bring the cup the rest of the way to his lips and drank deeply. "Dinner's here," he said as he set the cup aside. "You'd better eat while it's hot."

His eyes weren't blank now, she noted. Nor were they disinterested. It was more than desire she saw in them, more basic, more needy than lust. It was hunger for woman. For her.

"You're trying to make things easier for me." Why hadn't she realized that before? she wondered.

"I got you some fuel, that's all." He started to pull out a chair, but she was crossing to him. Her arms went around him, her body pressed close, she buried her face against his neck. She made it impossible for him not to offer whatever he had in comfort. He held her like that, his hands stroking her back, and watched the rain stream down the window.

"I was scared," she murmured.

"You don't need to be." His grip on her tightened fractionally, then relaxed again. "Nothing's going to happen to you."

"I was scared of more than that. I was scared that you wouldn't be here to hold me like this when I needed you to. Or that if you were, it would be because it was a part of the job you couldn't graciously avoid."

"You're being stupid. I don't worry about doing anything graciously."

She laughed a little, surprised that she could. "I know. I know that. But you see, I got in your way." She tilted her head back so that she could watch his face, so that she could see what she needed to see there. "Pushing you to feel things you can't afford to feel if you're going to do what you have to do. Wanting you to have feelings for me you don't want to have."

"I don't know what I feel for you."

"I know that, too." She lifted a hand to his cheek, smoothing away the tension. "Right now you want me, so we'll make that enough." She touched her lips to his, gently, gently deepening the kiss. "Make love with me."

Need coiled in his gut. "That isn't what you need now."

"Yes, it is." She drew him toward the bed. "Yes, it is."

Later, she curled against him, steeped and sleepy. He'd been so gentle, she thought. He'd been so patient. And, she knew, he'd been absorbed. It hadn't been only she who had forgotten, for that one stretch of time, why they were there. He'd given everything she'd asked for, and had taken everything she'd needed to offer. Now she listened to the rain and let her consciousness hang suspended just above sleep.

"The food might be cold," Jed said. "But you still need to eat. You looked ready to keel over when we walked in here."

"I'm feeling better." She smiled when he linked his hand with hers. He was doing things like that more often, she thought. She wondered if he realized it. "Tell me what we do next."

"We go to New York in the morning."

"You said 'we.' " She cuddled closer. "You're making progress, Skimmerhorn."

"Just saving myself an argument."

"Uh-uh. You like having me around. You might as well admit it."

"I like having you in bed. Most other times you're a pain in the neck."

"That may be, but you still like it." Dora pushed herself up, ran a hand through her tangled hair. "You did make me feel better."

He skimmed a fingertip over her nipple. "My pleasure."

She laughed and shook back her hair. "Not just that—though it was exceptional." Smiling gently, she rubbed her knuckles over his chin. "I like having you around, too."

He caught her wrist, held it. "Maybe you shouldn't. Maybe you should be running hard in the other direction."

"I don't think so."

"You don't know me, Dora. You don't have any idea where I come from, and you wouldn't understand it if you did."

"Try me."

He shook his head, started to get up.

"Try me," she said again, and made it a dare.

"I want dinner." He tugged his jeans on again and turned his back on her to uncover their cold steaks.

"Fine. We can talk while we eat." It wasn't an opportunity she was going to let slip by. Pulling on her robe, she took a seat at the room-service cart. He'd gotten only one cup for coffee. Obviously, she mused, he'd figured it would keep her awake when he wanted her to sleep. She poured some into the brandy snifter and drank it black and cool. "Where do you come from, Skimmerhorn?"

He was already regretting his words and the position they put him in. "Philadelphia," he said simply, and cut into his steak.

"Moneyed Philadelphia," she corrected. "I know that." So, she would prime the pump. "I also know that the money came from both sides, and that your parents' marriage had the scope of a high-powered merger." She shook salt onto her steak. "And that they indulged in a number of public spats."

"They hated each other, for as long as I can remember." He shrugged, but the movement was stiff. "You got the merger right. Neither of them was willing to let go of any of the joint assets, so they lived together in mutual disgust and animosity for twenty-seven years. And ironically—or maybe suitably—died together when their driver lost control of the limo and crashed."

"It was hard for you, losing them both that way."

"No." He lifted his eyes, met hers. "It wasn't. I didn't feel anything for them when they were alive but a kind of mild contempt. I told you, you wouldn't understand."

She waited a moment, eating because the food was there and filled a hole. "You're wrong. I think I do. You didn't respect them, and somewhere along the line you'd given up loving them."

"I never loved them."

"Of course you did. A child always loves until the love is abused badly enough—and often long after. But if you stopped, it was because you needed to. So when they died, if you felt anything, it would have been guilt because you couldn't feel more." She paused again, measuring him. "Close enough?"

It was a bull's-eye, but he wasn't ready to say so. "They had two children they didn't particularly want," he continued. "Elaine, and then me, because it was important to carry on the name. I was reminded of that over and over while I was growing up."

You're a Skimmerhorn. You're the heir. The least you can do is—not be so stupid. Show some gratitude. Be less of a nuisance.

"My responsibilities," Jed continued tightly, fighting back the ghosts of resentment. "And their expectations. Your parents wanted you to go into the theater; mine wanted me to make more money from the family fortune."

"And in our own ways, we let them down."

"It's not the same, Dora. Your parents' ambitions for you came out of pride. Mine came out of greed. There was no affection in my house."

He hated saying it, hated remembering it, but she'd spun the wheel and he couldn't stop it until it had completed the circle.

"Your sister—"

"Meant no more to me than I meant to her." He said it flatly, without passion, because it was pathetically true. "An accident of fate made us both prisoners in the same cell, but inmates don't always develop a fondness for each other. The four of us spent most of our time avoiding one another." He smiled a little at that, humorlessly. "Even in a house that size it wasn't always easy."

Though she knew he hadn't intended it, her sympathy was stirred. "Wasn't there anyone you could talk to?"

"About what?" He gave a short laugh. "It wasn't any secret that my parents hated each other. The fights they had in public were only the preliminaries. They'd always finish them up at home. If they weren't at each other's throats, they were at mine or at Elaine's. I turned to petty larceny, malicious mischief and short cons. She turned to men. She'd had two abortions before she was twenty. They managed to keep them quiet, just as they managed to keep my trouble with the law quiet. Shipping us off to boarding school didn't help. I got kicked out of mine, and Elaine had an affair with one of her teachers.

"In the end, they threw up their hands—it was one of the few things they agreed on. They made a deal with Elaine, settled a tidy sum of money on her if she married a handpicked candidate. I went to live with my grandmother. Elaine's first marriage lasted just shy of two years. I went into the police academy about the same time she was divorced. That really pissed them off." He picked up the brandy and poured generously. "They threatened to cut both of us out of the will, but they didn't want to let all those holdings fall out of the family. So Elaine went through another husband, I got my badge. And they died."

She felt too much—much more, she knew, than he would want her to offer. The pity for the child, the outrage on his behalf, the sorrow for a family that had had nothing to bind them together.

"Maybe you're right," she said slowly. "I can't understand how people could stay together when there was no love. Or how they could be incapable of giving it to their children. That doesn't mean I don't understand you."

"What you need to understand is that I may not be able to give you what you want."

"Then that's my problem, isn't it?" She took the brandy and poured. "It occurs to me, Skimmerhorn, that you're more worried I might be able to give you exactly what you want."

21

Dora had always loved New York. Years before, she had imagined herself living there. A loft in the Village, a favorite ethnic restaurant, a circle of Bohemian friends who always dressed in black and quoted from the latest esoteric literature. And a wacky neighbor, of course, who was always falling in and out of love with the wrong man.

But she'd been fourteen at the time, and her vision had changed.

Yet she still loved New York, for its unrelenting pace, its energy, its arrogance. She loved the people hurrying down the sidewalks careful not to make eye contact with anyone else, the shoppers burdened with bags from Saks and Macy's and Bendel's, the electronics shops that were perpetually having going-out-of-business sales, the sidewalk vendors with their roasted chestnuts and bad attitudes, and the blatant rudeness of the cabdrivers.

"Son of a bitch," Jed muttered as a cab cut him off with little more than a coat of paint to spare.

Dora beamed. "Great, isn't it?"

"Yeah. Right. I doubt a cop's written a moving violation in this hellhole since the turn of the century."

"It wouldn't be very productive. After all—oh, look!" Dora rolled down her window, craned her neck.

"You breathe out there, you're going to die."

"Did you see that outfit?" Dora narrowed her eyes, not against exhaust fumes, but to try to make out the name and address of the shop. "It was fabulous. It would just take me five minutes if you could find a place to park."

He snorted. "Get real, Conroy."

She huffed and plopped back in her seat. "Maybe after we're done, we could come back by. All you'd have to do is circle the block."

"Forget it. Aren't there enough shops in Philadelphia?"

"Of course there are. That's not the point. Shoes," she said with a long sigh and studied another storefront while Jed fought Madison Avenue traffic uptown. "They're having their after-Christmas sale."

"I should have known better. Goddamn it, get out of my lane!" he shouted, and took the aggressive route by gunning it past another cab. "I should have known better," he repeated, "than to have driven you through Manhattan. It's like offering a steak to a starving dog."

"You should have let me drive," she corrected. "I'd be more good-natured about it, and I wouldn't have been able to look at the shops. Besides, you're the one who wanted to check out DiCarlo's apartment."

"And we may get there alive yet."

"Or we could have taken a cab from the airport."

"I stress the word *alive*."

Dora was feeling very much alive. "You know, we could stay over tonight, book into some hideously expensive midtown hotel. Catch Will's play." She looked longingly at a boutique. "Shop."

"This isn't a sight-seeing trip, Conroy."

"I'm just trying to make the best of the situation."

Ignoring her, Jed made the turn onto Eighty-third. After a quick scan for a spot big enough to slip the rental car into, he did the sensible thing and double-parked. "I'm going to have to trust you."

"All right." She prepared to be trustworthy. "About what?"

"I want you to sit behind the wheel while I go in and check out DiCarlo—run down the super, maybe a couple of neighbors."

Her mouth moved dangerously close to a pout. "How come I can't come in?"

"Because I want the car to be here when I get back. If you have to move it, you drive around the block, making no stops whatsoever for outfits or shoes, and park it right back here. Got it?"

"I'm not an idiot," she began, but he kissed her and got out.

"Lock your doors, Conroy."

When five minutes passed into ten, and ten into twenty, Dora began to consider leaving Jed a note telling him to pick her up at the boutique, then hailing a cab to get her there. She was just reaching into her purse for a notepad when Jed jogged back to the car.

He switched on the engine and waited for a chance to jump back into traffic. "Now, how the hell do we get to Brooklyn?"

"Is that all you have to say? You leave me sitting here for nearly half an hour, now you want a map to Brooklyn?"

"The super let me into DiCarlo's apartment."

"That's hardly an excuse." She fumed a moment in silence, but curiosity prevailed. "So? What did you find?"

"A couple dozen Italian shoes. Several Armani suits. A few bottles of Dom Perignon and silk underwear in a rainbow of colors."

"So, DiCarlo likes the finer things."

"I also found a checkbook with a balance of a little over seven thousand, a porcelain Madonna and several dozen framed family photos."

"He saves his money, hasn't forgotten his religious roots and appreciates his family. So far he doesn't sound like a cold-blooded murderer."

"And Ted Bundy had a pretty face and a nice smile." He turned on Lexington and headed downtown. "I also found some letterhead from E. F., Incorporated, based in LA with a branch here in Manhattan, a lot of paperwork from the same and about a dozen messages on his phone machine from Mama, cousin Alphonso, Aunt Sophia and some bimbo named Bambi."

"Why, because a woman is named Bambi, do you assume she's a bimbo?"

"My mistake." He snuck through an amber light. "Just because she called DiCarlo Tony-kins, giggled and left a message in squealing baby talk is no reason for me to assume she's a bimbo."

"That's better."

"What I didn't find was an address book, a passport or any cash. Given that, and the fact that his messages were unanswered, no one in the building has seen him for more than a week and his mail hasn't been picked up, leads me to believe he hasn't been around in a while."

"That's a reasonable deduction. Do you think he's still in Philadelphia?"

She said it lightly, but he caught the undertone of worry. "It's a possibility. No one's going to bother your family, Dora. There's no reason to."

"I think you're right. If he's there, he's waiting for me to come back." She grimaced. "Cheerful thought."

"He won't get near you. That's a promise."

Jed fought his way from Manhattan to Brooklyn Heights, fueled on cigarettes and the not entirely unpleasant sensation of jousting in traffic. By the time he found Franklin Flowers's address, he had fit together the pieces he had so far, jumbled them and let them reassemble. He slipped smoothly into a parking spot.

"Looks like you're in on this one, Conroy." He leaned toward her, ducking his head to get a better look at the storefront through her window.

F. FLOWERS

WE BUY AND SELL

"Who doesn't?" he wondered. "Don't forget, Conroy—"

"I know. You'll do the talking."

They entered the shop. It was hardly bigger than the average living room and crammed with merchandise ranging from ratty teddy bears to pole lamps. Though it was deserted, Jed heard a voice coming from the back room behind a beaded curtain. As the sign on the counter instructed, he rang a brass bell that had once graced the front desk of a small-time bawdy house in the Bronx.

"One moment, please." The voice was male, the words delivered like a song.

Flowers was as good as his word. Before Dora could finish her survey of a group of Avon bottles, he came through the curtain with a rattle of beads and a puff of fragrant smoke.

He was a big man, perhaps six-four, gone soft in the middle. Like his teddy bears, he had a round, homely face that radiated sweetness. His hair was parted nearly at his ear to allow him to comb strands of thin blond hair over a wide bald spot. Between two thick fingers he held a slim brown cigarette.

"Good morning!" Again he sang, like a kindergarten teacher reciting the ABCs. "No, no." Clucking his tongue, he glanced toward a row of ticking clocks. "It's afternoon already. Where does the time go? I never seem to be able to keep up. The world seems to move too quickly for me. And what may I do for you?"

Since Dora was busy admiring the jovial giant, she had no trouble letting Jed take the lead.

"Mr. Flowers?"

"Yes, I'm Frank Flowers, and this is my own little place." He drew delicately on his cigarette, exhaled through lips pursed as if for a kiss. "As you can see, we buy and sell almost anything. What can I interest you in today?"

"Do you know Sherman Porter?"

Flowers's jolly expression disintegrated. "Poor Sherman. I received word just two days ago. Tragic. The world we live in so often appalls me. Shot down like a dog at his own desk." He shuddered. "Hideous. Simply hideous."

"You sent a shipment to him," Jed continued when Flowers took time to sigh and smoke. "It arrived in Virginia on the twenty-first of December."

"Oh yes." Flowers smiled sadly. "Who would have guessed it would be the last time Sherman and I would do business together? Fate is such a cruel and capricious mistress. Nearly six years. We were associates and, I like to think, friends."

Jed pulled out the papers he'd taken from Helen's file. "There seems to be a question about the shipment."

"Really?" Flowers shuffled grief aside and frowned over the idea. "I find that odd. Helen never mentioned it—of course, it's understandable under the tragic circumstances, I suppose. But she certainly could have phoned me with any problem rather than sending you to New York."

"We had other business here," Jed said smoothly. "You purchased the merchandise from an estate sale?"

"A small one, yes, in the Catskills. Such air, such scenery. I picked up several minor gems. Several of the larger pieces I sold to other clients. It was impractical to ship heavy furniture to Virginia when I have outlets much closer to home."

He blew two neat smoke rings. "You see, I most often act as an agent for dealers. This little place"—he gazed fondly around his shop, a doting parent at a slow-witted child—"it's very dear to me, you see, but can hardly keep the wolf from the door. As I recall, I chose some very nice pieces for Sherman." Flowers put out his cigarette in a marble ashtray. "I can't imagine what problem there might be."

"The painting," Jed began.

"Painting?" Flowers frowned, set a fist on his hip. "I didn't send a painting."

"The abstract, signed E. Billingsly."

"Abstract?" Tilting his head, Flowers giggled like a girl. "Oh, my dear, no. I would *never* touch an abstract. Too bizarre for my tastes. And they're so hard to sell. No, I'm afraid there's been some mistake."

"Do you have a list of the inventory you shipped?"

"Naturally. I'm a bear for organization. An abstract painting, you say? No wonder Helen has a problem. I'll be back in a jiff."

He disappeared behind the curtains.

"Maybe he has a partner," Dora whispered. "And his partner put the painting in the shipment. Or maybe—" She broke off when Flowers stepped back in, carrying two files, one in sunny yellow, the other in bright red.

"I color-code, you see." Smiling, he set the files on the counter. "The yellow will be exactly what I purchased at the sale. He flipped open the folder. Inside were meticulously typed sheets listing merchandise, with descriptions. "Now that would have been . . . December twelve, I believe." He flipped briskly through. "And here we are, in January already. The time passes too quickly. Here now." Carefully placing the top pages face-down, he tapped a finger on the file. "Woodlow Estate, Catskills, December twelve. You can see this is the entire list, with the receipt attached. There's no painting."

Nor was there a china dog, Jed observed. Or a figurine matching the description of the one Tom Ashworth had died for.

"And this is one of my shipping files, specifically dealing with Sherman—God rest him. As you can see," he said as he opened it, "the top shipment was the last shipment—packing slip attached. Not a painting in sight." He grinned cheerfully. "It must have gotten mixed up with my things after uncrating. Sherman, bless him, was a teensy bit careless."

"Yes," Jed said. "I'm sure you're right."

"He's wrong," Dora stated as she pulled open the car door. "I saw the stockboy setting up that entire lot. It had just arrived."

"Yeah." Jed took out his keys, but he didn't start the car. His eyes were opaque as he jiggled them restlessly in his hand.

"There was a painting. I bought the damn thing."

"There was a painting," Jed agreed. "There was a china dog and a lot of other things. None of which are listed on Flowers's file. Not one item matches."

"Maybe he was lying." She looked back across the street and shook her head. "But I don't think he was lying."

"No, he wasn't lying." Shifting in his seat, Jed turned to her. "Tell me this, Conroy. If you were smuggling a Monet and several other illegal valuables, for your own use or for someone else's, and you'd taken the time to conceal them, to make them look ordinary—"

"I wouldn't have them shipped to auction," she interrupted, her eyes darkening with inspiration. "I wouldn't let them be purchased by people scattered all over the east coast."

"Because then you'd have to go to the trouble, and take the risk, of getting them back again—when you'd had them in the first place."

"So somebody messed up. DiCarlo?"

"Might be."

"What else?" she demanded. "There's a 'what else' in your eyes."

"The packing slips. The one in Flowers's file, and the one I lifted from Porter's. They were both from Premium Shipping." He started the car. "I've got some calls to make."

• • •

Dora drank endless cups of coffee and toyed with a club sandwich, using her time in the small Brooklyn restaurant while Jed made his calls from the pay phone to think the puzzle through. Taking out her pad, she began to make notes and diagrams.

"Looks like the Monet's genuine." Jed sat down and pulled Dora's plate to his side of the booth. "They'll need to run tests to be a hundred percent, but my grandmother and her pal gave it thumbs up."

"Who's her pal?"

"A guy she knows. Used to be a curator at the Met." He wolfed down a triangle of sandwich and signaled for coffee. "It also turns out that every name on the list, everybody who bought from the shipment, was hit during the period between the twenty-second of December and New Year's."

"Hit?" The blood drained out of her face. "You mean, they're dead?"

"No." Jed took her hand and gave it a solid squeeze. "Robbed. In each case, the piece they'd bought at the auction was taken. Sloppy jobs. From what Brent tells me they look like deliberately sloppy jobs. And there's still no sign of DiCarlo. He's some sort of vice president of the New York branch of E.F., Incorporated. He hasn't shown for work since before Christmas. He did call in a few times, but not since the end of the year. His secretary and his staff claim not to know his whereabouts. His mother filed a missing-person's report with the NYPD this morning."

"So, he's on the run." Dora picked up her coffee and missed the flicker in Jed's eyes. "Good. I hope he keeps running until he falls off a cliff. What do we do now?"

Jed moved his shoulders and chose another section of the sandwich. "If we can put enough evidence together to tie him to the murders in Philly and in Virginia, we can call in the Feds."

"You don't have to tell me you don't want to do that. I'm beginning to read you, Captain."

"I like to finish what I start." Idly, he turned her notebook around so he could read it. A smile tugged at his mouth. "Playing Nancy Drew again?"

"You're not wearing a badge, Skimmerhorn. I guess that makes you Joe Hardy."

He let that pass. Her diagrams interested him. At the top she had Premium Shipping, with lines leading off right and left. At the end of one she'd written Porter. The tail of the other ended in a question mark. Below it was a list of the inventory Flowers claimed to have shipped. Shooting down from Porter were all the names of buyers from the auction and their purchases. Another line connected her name with Mrs. Lyle's.

"What are you getting at here, Nancy?"

"It's a theory." Her spine stiffened at his tone. "I have two, actually. The first is that DiCarlo was double-crossed. Whoever he had handling the valuables pulled a fast one and shipped them to Virginia."

"Motive?"

"I don't know." She huffed and snatched up her coffee. "Some disgruntled underling he hadn't promoted, a woman scorned—or maybe just some hapless clerk who screwed up."

"That might work if the disgruntled underling or the scorned woman had kept some of the loot. And even a hapless clerk would be hard-pressed to screw up by sending a shipment of merchandise to some dinky auction house in Virginia where it's unlikely DiCarlo had any ties."

"For all you know, DiCarlo might have been using Porter's as a clearing-house for smuggled merchandise for years." She tossed her hair back and scowled at him. "I suppose you have a better theory?"

"Yeah, I got one. But let's look behind door number two." He was grinning now, enjoying himself. He tapped her diagram. "What have you got here?"

"I don't have to take your superior amusement, Skimmerhorn."

"Indulge me." He lifted her hand, nipped at her knuckles. "Just for a minute."

"Well, it's obvious to me there were two shipments. The one from the estate sale, and the one with the smuggled goods. Since we agree that it would have been impossibly stupid for DiCarlo to have purposely shipped off his loot to Virginia where it would be offered for sale to the highest bidder, the logical conclusion is that the two shipments were mixed up."

"Keep going," he encouraged. "You're about to earn a merit badge."

"And since both packing slips originated from Premium, one could deduce that the mix-up happened there."

"Nice going, Nancy." Pleased with her, he pulled out his wallet and tossed bills on the table. "Let's go check out Queens."

"Wait a minute." She caught up with him at the door. "Are you saying you think I'm right?"

"I'm saying we should check it out."

"Nope, not good enough." She shifted her body to block the door. "Look me in the eye, Skimmerhorn, and say you think I'm right."

"I think you're right."

She let out a whoop of triumph and yanked open the door herself. "Then what are we waiting for?"

"You know," Dora said after they'd cooled their heels in Bill Tarkington's office for fifteen minutes, "most of police work is really boring."

"Thinking about giving it up, Conroy?"

She braced her elbow on the arm of her chair, cupped her chin in her hand. "Is this the sort of thing you did every day for all those years?"

He kept his back to her, watching the belts and the shipping clerks. "I couldn't calculate the number of hours I spent waiting."

She yawned, hugely. "I suppose it teaches you patience."

"No. Not necessarily. You juggle enough hours of tedium with enough moments of terror, and it teaches you not to relax your guard."

She could see his profile from where she sat. Only a part of him was in the room with her, she realized. Another part was somewhere he wouldn't let her follow. "How do you handle the terror?"

"By recognizing it, by accepting it."

"I can't imagine you being afraid," she murmured.

"I told you that you didn't know me. I think this is our man now."

Tarkington bounced up to the door, beaming his cheery smile. "Mr. Skimmerhorn?"

He pumped Jed's hand enthusiastically. "And Miss Conroy. I apologize for making you wait. How about some coffee? A doughnut. Maybe a nice danish."

Before Jed could decline, Dora was beaming at Tarkington. "I'd love some coffee."

"Just let me pour you a cup." Happy to serve, Tarkington turned to fill three cups. Dora sent Jed a smug look.

"We know you're busy, Mr. Tarkington. I hope we won't keep you long."

"Don't you worry about it. Always got time for a customer, yes sir. Cream? Sugar?"

"Black," Jed told him, and watched, slightly appalled, when Tarkington dropped a flood of sugar into one of the cups.

"Now then." He passed out the coffee, took a sip from his own heavily sweetened cup. "You had some question about a shipment, didn't you?"

"That's right." Jed reached in his pocket to read off the numbers of the shipping invoice he'd copied from Flowers. "A package shipped out of this building on December seventeenth from a Franklin Flowers, destination Sherman Porter, Front Royal, Virginia. Number ASB-54467."

"That's fine." Tarkington settled himself behind his desk. "We'll just call that right on up. What was the problem, exactly?"

"The merchandise shipped was not the merchandise received."

Tarkington's fingers dropped away from the keys of his computer. His face took on a pained look, as though he were suffering from intestinal gas. "Oh Lordy, Lordy, not again."

"You had this happen before?" Jed demanded.

Recovering, Tarkington punched keys. "I assure you, Mr. Skimmerhorn, Premium has a top-notch reputation. I can only say that the Christmas rush this year was unusually bad. December seventeenth, you said." His little eyes brightened. "That could be it!"

"What?"

"There was another complaint about a shipment that went out that very same day. The client was very upset, let me tell you. Not nearly as patient as you and Miss Conroy."

"DiCarlo," Dora said involuntarily.

Before Jed could snarl at her, Tarkington was beaming again. "Righto. Do you know him?"

"We've met." Dora kept an easy smile on her face.

"Isn't that a coincidence?" Shaking his head at the way of the world, Tarkington happily tapped keys. "This takes a weight off these old shoulders, let me tell you. I've done everything possible to locate Mr. DiCarlo's merchandise, and now it seems likely that the two shipments were mismarked and misdirected. I can't come up with a ready answer as to how that could have happened, but the solution seems simple as apple pie. I'll contact Mr. DiCarlo immediately."

"We'll take care of that." Jed scanned the computer screen over Tarkington's shoulder and noted the shipping clerk's name.

"That would save me an embarrassing moment." He slurped at his coffee and winked, showing Jed and Dora that they were, indeed, happy campers. "We will, of course, reimburse both you and Mr. DiCarlo for all shipping charges."

"Fine."

"I was right," Dora said under her breath as they walked away.

"Pat yourself on the back later." Jed walked up to the nearest clerk. "Where's Johnson?"

"Opal?" The clerk jerked his head toward another conveyor belt. "Over there. Line six."

"What are we doing now?" Dora asked.

"Checking tedious details."

Dora didn't find it tedious at all. Not when they'd sat with Opal in the employee lunchroom and listened to her story. Because she was obviously fascinated and sympathetic, Jed sat back, lighted a cigarette and let Dora play good cop.

He wasn't about to tell her, but he'd have said she'd been born for it.

"Can you believe it?" The excitement was drumming again as they made their way across the parking lot. "She drops a handful of invoices, and we end up with a smuggled Monet." She grinned as Jed unlocked the car door. "Maybe I like police work after all."

"Stick with selling knickknacks," Jed advised.

"At least you could say I did a good job."

"You did a good job. Don't get cocky."

"I'm not cocky." She slipped out of her shoes. "But now we know how, we know why and we know who. All we have to do now is find DiCarlo."

"Leave that one to the big boys, baby."

"You're going to turn it over?" Astonishment shimmered out of every pore. "You're going to turn it over now?"

"I didn't say that. I said it's time for you to step back."

"You're not making one move without me, Skimmerhorn. If I hadn't bought smuggled goods and ended up in the middle of this mess, you'd still be sulking and lifting weights."

"You want me to thank you for that?"

"You will. When you come to your senses." Relaxed, she sighed and smiled. "Sure you don't want to take me up on that expensive hotel?"

"I've seen enough of New York, thanks."

And he had something else to check out now. Bill Tarkington's computer screen had been a fount of information, including the intended recipient of DiCarlo's illicit shipment. Abel Winesap of E.F., Incorporated, Los Angeles.

22

The chill in the air didn't prevent Finley from his morning ritual. Every day, regardless of the weather, he swam fifty laps in his hourglass-shaped pool while Vivaldi poured out of the speakers hidden in the jasmine plants. It was, to him, a matter of discipline. Of course, the water was heated to a pleasant eighty-three degrees—exactly.

As he cut through the warm water with strong, sure strokes, thin fingers of steam curled up into the cool winter air. He counted the laps himself, gaining arrogance and satisfaction with each turn.

The pool was his, and his alone. Finley allowed no servant, no companion, no guest, to sully his waters.

Once, when he had been entertaining, a tipsy acquaintance had tumbled in. The following day Finley had had the pool drained, scrubbed out and refilled. Needless to say, his hapless guest had never been invited back.

Now, he rose in the water, enjoying the sensation of having the water slice off his skin. Gooseflesh popped out over his body as he strode up the wide, curving steps, onto the terra-cotta skirt and into the snowy-white robe his butler held for him.

"Time?" he said, rubbing down briskly.

"Twelve minutes, eighteen seconds, sir."

The butler always stopped the clock at precisely that time. Once, he made the mistake of timing Finley at a bit over thirteen minutes. An ugly scene had followed, during which the man had nearly lost his well-paying job. Finley never went over twelve-eighteen again.

"Excellent." Smugly satisfied, Finley accepted his vitamin drink, a concoction created especially for him by his personal trainer. Even served in a Waterford tumbler, the thick, nasty-looking mixture of herbs, vegetables and Chinese roots tasted foul. Finley drank it quickly, as though it were the fresh, clear water of the Fountain of Youth. He'd convinced himself it was exactly that.

Finley dismissed the butler by handing him back both the damp towel and the empty glass.

Now that the first part of his morning ritual was behind him, Finley allowed himself to consider the problem of Isadora Conroy. It was not an altogether unpleasant problem, he mused. One couldn't become overly disgruntled at the prospect of dealing with a young, beautiful woman. He strode in through the French doors of the parlor as he reflected on the possibilities.

Secure in his power, Finley showered and groomed and dressed. He enjoyed a pleasant breakfast of fresh fruit, whole-wheat toast and herbal tea on the patio a few feet from where he had gut-shot DiCarlo. All the while he considered Isadora. When the solution came to him, he smiled, even chuckled softly, and blotted his lips.

It would work, he decided. And if it didn't—well then, he would simply kill her.

Dora was trying not to be annoyed. It was too predictable a reaction, she told herself, much too typical. Any woman would be annoyed if she awakened alone in bed without a clue as to where her lover had gone, or when he might be returning.

She wasn't *any* woman, Dora reminded herself. And she wasn't going to be annoyed—she wasn't even going to be mildly miffed. They were each free to come and go as they pleased. She wouldn't even ask him where the hell he'd been.

But when she heard the knock on the door, she tugged down the hem of her oversized sweatshirt, lifted her chin and marched into the living room.

"Okay, Skimmerhorn, you pig," she muttered. "This better be good."

She yanked open the door, searing words ready to leap off her tongue. She had to swallow them back when she stood face-to-face with Honoria Skimmerhorn Rodgers.

"Oh." Dora pushed at the hair she'd bundled untidily on top of her head. "Mrs. Rodgers. Hello."

"Good morning, Dora." Not by the flicker of an eyelash did Honoria reveal her amusement in watching the changes in Dora's expressive face. The fury, the shock, the embarrassment. "Have I caught you at an awkward time?"

"No. No. I was just..." Dora swallowed a nervous giggle and smiled. "If you're looking for Jed, he doesn't seem to be around."

"Actually, I was hoping for a word with you. May I come in?"

"Of course." Dora stepped back, miserably regretting that she hadn't opened the shop that day and therefore hadn't dressed for work. She felt like a used dust rag in her Steelers sweatshirt and bare feet while Honoria swept in smelling of Paris and wrapped in a luxurious fur jacket.

"How charming!" The sincerity in Honoria's voice did a great deal to put Dora back on keel. "How utterly charming." Her appreciative gaze roamed the room while she tugged off her gloves. "I must confess, I often wondered about these apartments over shops on South Street. It's quite large, isn't it?"

"I need a lot of room. May I take your coat?"

"Yes, thank you."

As Dora hung up the mink, Honoria continued to wander the room. "I peeked in your shop window downstairs. I was disappointed to find it closed. But this"—she ran a fingertip along the sinuous, female lines of a Deco lamp—"is every bit as delightful."

"One of the best things about selling is that I can live with my stock as long as I like. Would you like some coffee, tea?"

"I'd love some coffee, if it's not too much trouble."

"Not at all. Please, sit down, make yourself at home."

"Thank you. I believe I'll do just that."

Honoria didn't consider herself nosy—simply interested. She was interested enough to study and approve Dora's view of bustling and artsy South Street from the tall living room windows. She also enjoyed and approved the decor of the apartment—warm and cozy, she decided, while remaining eclectic and a tad theatrical. Yes, she liked the room very much—a perfect mirror of Dora's personality.

The girl would do, she thought, and lifted up a tortoiseshell tea caddy to admire it. The girl would do very, very well.

"Here we are." Dora carried out a tray laden with a Fiesta ware pot and cups. She wished she could find some tactful way to dash into the bathroom and put on her lipstick. "Shall we take it in here?"

"That would be fine. Let me make room on the table for you. What a marvelous aroma. Scones?" Her eyes brightened. "How delightful."

"I always keep some around." Honoria's simple pleasure had Dora relaxing again. "There's something so civilized about scones."

With a laugh, Honoria settled herself. "You're very polite not to ask me what I'm doing knocking on your door at nine in the morning." Honoria sipped her coffee, paused, sipped again. "This is quite exceptional."

"I'm glad you like it." Dora waited as Honoria added a dab of blackberry jelly to a scone. "Actually, it's harder for me not to ask you about the painting."

"Good." Honoria let the scone lay on her tongue, sighing a little as she swallowed. "My dear, my mother would have been delighted with you. I haven't tasted better since she died."

"I'd be happy to give you the recipe for your cook."

"I'd appreciate it. Now." She sat back, balancing her cup and saucer with the uncanny skill only women of a certain class seem to acquire. "I believe you and I can trade information."

"Oh? I don't think I understand."

"My grandson asks me to keep a certain painting in my home, and to allow an old friend to work on this painting. I'm to do this in the strictest confidence, and with police protection." She smiled, inclined her head. "There is no explanation accompanying the request, of course."

"Of course." Returning the smile, Dora leaned forward. "Tell me, Mrs. Rodgers, why do we go along with him?"

"Call me Ria—my husband always did. We go along with him, dear child, because we care too much not to." A delicate pause. "Am I right?"

"Yes. Yes, you are. That doesn't make *him* right." Dora's earlier irritation returned in full force. "I'll tell you everything I know, Ria, then you can tell me the results."

"Precisely what I had in mind."

Dora started at the beginning. Jed would have several logical reasons, she assumed, why his grandmother should be spared the knowledge and the concern that accompanied it. Yet she rationalized that he had already involved Honoria, completely voluntarily. She was only providing the background as a matter of courtesy.

Honoria listened without interruption. She sipped her coffee, her reaction showing only in the darkening of her eyes, a thinning of her mouth, the occasional lift of a well-shaped eyebrow. There was temper, but there was also breeding.

And here, Dora thought, was where Jed had inherited his control.

"This has been terrible for you," Honoria said at length.

"Mrs. Lyle's the worst. No matter what Jed says, I feel responsible."

"Of course you do." This was said staunchly, and made Dora feel more comforted than a dozen polite denials. "You wouldn't be the woman you are if you didn't. This DiCarlo . . ." The name came through Honoria's lips ripe with cultured distaste. "Do the authorities have any idea where he might be hiding?"

"I don't think so." In a frustrated gesture, Dora lifted her hands, let them fall. "If they do, they haven't found it necessary to mention it to me."

"So like men. Do you know, I believe it goes back to when they had to crawl out of the cave and hunt for meat with rocks and clubs. The hunter." She smiled when she said it, with a kind of cool indulgence Dora admired. "Women, of course, were left in the cave to give birth in the dirt and the dark, to cook the meat on a dung fire and tan the hides. But men still thought they knew best."

"Jed hasn't even told me what's going to be done with the painting."

"There, you see?" Her point proven, Honoria refilled her coffee cup, then Dora's. "I wish I could tell you what his plans are, but he hasn't deemed it necessary to share them with me either. I can, however, tell you about the painting itself. It's brilliant."

Her face shone with emotion. "Though there are tests to be run, there's no doubt as to its authenticity. Not to me. It's one of his water lily studies, no doubt painted at Giverny." Her eyes went misty with dreams. Her voice softened like a woman speaking of a lover. "Ah, the light—ethereal and lyrical. That soft, seductive power that pulls you into the painting, makes you believe you can smell the damp flowers and still water." Her eyes cleared again. "He painted more than seventeen in that series."

"I know. Coincidentally, he's my favorite impressionist painter. I never thought I'd own one, even indirectly."

"I have one—a gift from my husband on our tenth anniversary. One of Monet's garden studies. Side by side, those paintings are breathtaking. Before the police took it away, I stood in my bedroom, looking at them, and weeping. I wish I could believe this DiCarlo had stolen it because of its beauty and not for its monetary value. That would make it almost understandable."

"You'd think they'd have let me see it," Dora complained. "I did buy it. But no, I wake up this morning and the bed's empty. Jed's gone off somewhere—and does he let me know where, or what he's up to? No. Not even a note under a refrigerator magnet. It seems to me—" She broke off, appalled. This was Jed's grandmother. His *grandmother*. "I beg your pardon," she managed.

"Not at all." To prove it, Honoria tossed back her head and laughed. "Oh no, not at all. I'm delighted. I do hope, my dear, that you'll give him hell when he returns. He's always needed it from someone who loved him. God knows he took enough of it from those who didn't. It's not at all the same thing, you know."

"No, I suppose not." Most of her embarrassment faded, but the flush remained. "Mrs. Rodgers—Ria, I wouldn't want you to think that I usually . . . develop intimate relationships with my tenants."

"You still expect me to be shocked." Thoroughly enjoying Dora's reaction, Honoria smiled and helped herself to a second scone. "I'll tell you why I married Jed's grandfather, shall I? He was an incredibly handsome man—very strong and blond and physically exciting. In other words, I was hot for him."

She nibbled delicately at the scone, her eyes alive with amusement. "Fortunately, Jed has inherited many of his grandfather's physical traits and none of his emotional ones. Walter Skimmerhorn was a cold, often cruel and incessantly boring man. All of which are unforgivable flaws in a husband. It took me less than a year of marriage to realize my mistake. To my regret, it required a considerably longer amount of time to correct it."

And the bitter dregs of that resentment still festered.

"You, on the other hand," Honoria continued, "have already discovered there is much, much more to my grandson than an excellent physique. If I were to give any advice to the young people of today in such matters, it would be that they live together—as you and Jed are essentially doing now—before marriage."

"We're not—" Dora's heart gave a quick and, to her embarrassment, decisively female flutter. "I hope I haven't given you the impression that we're thinking of marriage."

"Not at all," Honoria said lightly. Giving in to sentiment, she imagined the beautiful great-grandchildren Jed and Dora would make for her. "Now, Jed tells me your parents are Liberty Theater. I've enjoyed many productions there. I hope I'll be able to meet them."

"Ah . . ." Before Dora could answer, they were interrupted by another knock on the door. "Excuse me a minute."

More than a little frazzled by the mention of marriage, and the neat segue into her family, Dora opened the door. Jed stood on the other side of the threshold. He took one long look, running his gaze from her bare feet to the top of her tousled hair. She looked rumpled and sexy and deliciously flushed.

"Conroy." He snatched her to him and before she could speak had engaged her mouth in a hot, steamy kiss. "You got anything on under there?"

"Skimmerhorn." If she'd been flushed before, she was now painfully pink. "Your—"

"I'll find out for myself." He scooped her up and, covering her mouth again, stepped inside with her.

Desperately embarrassed, she shoved against his chest. "Skimmerhorn." After tearing her mouth from his, she sucked in a deep breath. "I think you'd better put me down and say hello to your grandmother."

"What?"

"Good morning, Jedidiah." Honoria brushed her fingers over her linen napkin. "Dora and I were just having some coffee. Perhaps you'd like to join us."

"Grandmother." To his credit, he said it easily, even if he did set Dora on the floor rather abruptly. "Were you waiting to see me?"

"Not at all, I paid a friendly call." She glanced over as Dora walked in with an extra cup and saucer. "Dora and I were exchanging views on Monet. It happens he's a favorite with both of us."

"It's police business now."

"Then where's your shield, Skimmerhorn?" Dora asked sweetly, and poured him a cup of coffee.

"Shut up, Conroy."

"His manners are my failing," Honoria explained. "I hope you'll forgive me."

"Think nothing of it," Dora told her. "I don't. Jedidiah," she said, delighted when he bared his teeth at her, "your grandmother and I would like to know what's being done with the Monet."

It seemed easier to give them something than to fight them both. "We—Brent," he corrected, "took the whole business to Commissioner Riker this morning. It's being kept under wraps for the time being."

"So," Honoria mused. "He went over that detestable Goldman's head. Wise. The man is a horse's ass and has no business being in command."

"Is that your *professional* opinion, Grandmother?" Jed asked, and earned the mild stare that had caused him to flush in his youth.

"You know, Dora," Honoria continued, "I made the mistake of never completely approving of Jedidiah's decision to become a police officer, until he resigned. I'm afraid I didn't tell him I was proud of him soon enough."

"It's always soon enough," Dora said.

"You have a very fluid sense of compassion." Well pleased with her morning's work, Honoria rose. "He'll need that. Thank you so much for the coffee. I hope I'll be welcome back."

"Anytime." Dora took Honoria's hand and did what Jed had yet to do. She kissed the woman's cheek. "I'll get your coat."

"I have an appointment shortly." Honoria tugged on her gloves. "So I don't have time to see your apartment."

"There's nothing to see," Jed told her flatly. But he took the coat from Dora and helped his grandmother into it. "I appreciate your help in this." He bent down and kissed her, despite the discomfort of having Dora looking on. "I'd appreciate it more if you'd forget it now."

She only smiled. "I'd like you to bring Dora for dinner soon. Call me and we'll arrange it. Thank you again, dear," she said to Dora. "I'll come back when the shop's open. There was a piece in the window—the bronze huntress."

"Yes, I know the one."

"I'm very interested." With a quick wink at Dora, she sailed out.

"What a terrific lady."

"What did she want?"

"The basic courtesy of information." Dora started to lift the tray, then set it down with a rattle when Jed took her shoulder.

"If I'd wanted her to have information," he began with barely controlled fury, "I'd have given it to her."

"You opened Ria up when you took the painting to her. I'm sorry, Jed, if you're angry, but when she asked me directly, I answered."

"Damn it." Her calm sincerity was the pin that burst the balloon of his temper. "Do you know the tap dancing we're doing to keep this quiet?"

"I have some idea." She lifted a brow. "Do you think your granny's going to take out a full-page ad?"

His mouth twitched at the idea of the elegant Honoria being called his granny. "The fewer people who have the details, the better."

"Including me." Now she did lift the tray and walked stiffly into the kitchen with it. "That's why I woke up alone in bed this morning, without any explanation from you as to where you were going, what you were doing."

"Hold it. What the hell are you talking about?"

"Nothing." Her voice low and furious, she began to load the coffee things into the sink for rinsing. "Nothing at all. Go kill a bear with your bare hands, why don't you?"

"Conroy." Caught between amusement and exasperation, he leaned against the doorjamb. "You're ticked because I went out this morning?"

"Why should I be?" She rounded on him with hurt anger in her eyes. "I'm used to waking up in bed alone."

"Damn." Baffled, he scrubbed his hands over his face. "Look, I got up early. I didn't want to wake you. . . ." He remembered exactly the way she'd looked, curled in the bed, her hair spread on the pillow. Yes, he'd wanted to wake her up, he thought. But it hadn't been to tell her he was going out. "I went to the gym for an hour, caught breakfast with Brent. We had some things to go over."

"Did I ask you for an explanation?" Her voice was cold, but her temper was not as she shoved by him.

"Yeah." Cautious, he followed her back into the living room. "You did."

"Oh, forget it!" Disgusted with herself, she pinched the bridge of her nose between her thumb and forefinger.

"I really need to satisfy my curiosity. What does a woman wear under baggy football sweats?" He scooped her up again, nuzzled her neck on the way to the bedroom.

"Nothing important. In fact . . ." She laughed as they tumbled like wrestling children onto the bed. "Nothing at all."

"There's a hole in the shoulder."

"I know. I was mortified when your grandmother caught me in it."

"And a stain." He ran his finger between her breasts. "Right here."

"A nice full-bodied burgundy. It splashed on me when I was making lasagna." She sighed and slid her fingers into his hair. "I've been meaning to cut it up for rags, but—" She gasped, stunned when he ripped the shirt down the center.

"That ought to take care of it." Before she could decide whether to laugh or swear at him, he took her breast into his mouth and sent a quick and urgent greed swimming in her blood. "I've wanted to rip your clothes off since the first time I saw you."

"You—" Staggered, and aroused, she gulped in air as his hands stroked possessively down to her waist. "You shut the door in my face the first time you saw me."

"It seemed a more rational reaction at the time." He tore the sweatpants with one powerful twist of his hands. "I could have been wrong."

He leaned back, his hands over hers on the spread. The sun was bright through the open curtain, spilling generously over her face, her skin, her hair. The ruined clothes lay in tatters beneath her. It made him feel, however fancifully, like a warrior about to reap the spoils of war.

Her body, aware, aroused, alluring, quivered as though it were his hands rather than his eyes that skimmed over it. Her breasts were small, firm, milk-white, the nipples temptingly erect.

Lowering his head, he circled each rose-colored peak with his tongue until her breath was short and shallow and her body taut as a bowstring. The pulse at her wrists pounded like gunshots under his fingers.

"I want to watch you." His voice was thick as he took a hand from hers to slide between her thighs. From silk to velvet to damp satin.

The orgasm curled inside her like a snake, striking quickly, violently, so that her body reared up in shock when she cried out.

"It never seems to be enough," he whispered. He was surprised he could breathe. Watching Dora in pleasure was unspeakably erotic, uncannily seductive. She greedily consumed it, and she generously released it. Her capacity for giving and for taking passion was unstintingly honest and impossible to resist.

So he watched as she absorbed the aftershocks of sensation as he pulled off his clothes.

He needed to see her, to see every flicker and flash of emotion on her face. Kneeling, he lifted her hips, slid her slowly toward him, slipped slowly into her.

The sound she made at the mating was feline and throaty. He never took his eyes from her face, even when his vision dimmed and his control shattered.

"I owe you a sweatshirt." In a friendly gesture, Jed tugged his own over her head.

Dora examined it. "This is even rattier than the one you tore up." And she wouldn't have parted with it for diamonds. "Besides, you owe me sweatpants, too."

"Mine wouldn't fit you." He pulled them on, then stood looking at her as she sat on the edge of the bed. Reaching down, he twined a lock of her hair around his finger. "We could start a fire, and spend the rest of the morning in bed watching game shows."

She tilted her head. "That sounds incredibly tempting, Skimmerhorn. Why do you suppose I have this odd feeling that you're trying to keep me out of the way?"

"Out of whose way?"

"Yours."

"How can you be out of my way when I'm planning on spending as much time as possible on top of you?"

"You and Brent are working on something and you don't want me to know what it is." It was disappointing, and enormously frustrating, that he showed no reaction at all to her accusation. "That's all right." She shrugged it off and smoothed a hand over the rumpled spread. "I'll find out anyway."

"How?"

She smiled. "When I'm on top of *you*, I'll vamp it out of you."

"Vamp?" But he fought back a laugh as he worked a flattened cigarette out of his pack. "You can't expect me to concentrate on Bob Barker or Vanna White after a statement like that."

"Bob Barker?" She laughed, so thoroughly delighted with him she gave in to the need to leap up and into his arms. "Bob Barker? God, Skimmerhorn, I love you."

She started to lean back and kiss him senseless when she felt him stiffen. Very slowly, very quietly, her heart sank to her knees.

"Whoops." She fought for a light tone as she untangled herself from him. "Wasn't supposed to let that one out, was I? Sorry." Because the hurt was still swelling, she turned away, avoiding his eyes. "Chalk it up to the heat of the moment, or whatever works for you."

He wasn't sure he could get his tongue around a word, but finally managed her name. "Dora—"

"No, really." Oh God, oh God, she thought, panicked. She was going to cry if she didn't do something quickly. "It was just a slip of the tongue, nothing to get worried about."

Forcing a smile, she turned back. It was as bad as she'd feared. His face was set, his eyes absolutely blank.

"Listen, Skimmerhorn, the 'L' word comes real easy to me. My family boots it around like a football—you know us theatrical types."

She lifted her hand again, running it through her hair in that restless and lovely feminine gesture he'd grown so fond of.

"So look." Her voice was bright again, excessively cheerful. "Why don't you start that fire? I'll make us something appropriate to snack on while watching game shows."

She took a step forward, stopped. He hadn't moved, but had blocked her retreat through simple will.

"You meant it, didn't you?" He said it quietly, and the eyes that had fastened on her face made it impossible for her to hedge.

"Yes, I meant it." The defense came automatically. He watched as her shoulders straightened, her chin firmed. "They're my feelings, Jed, and I know how to deal with them. I'm not asking you to match them, or even to accept them if that's difficult for you." The first licks of temper glinted in her eyes. "And since it obviously bothers you so much to hear them, I'll be careful not to mention them again. Ever. All right?"

No, it was far from all right. He couldn't pinpoint the moment when things had changed between them any more than he could pinpoint his own feelings. But he could do something to stabilize what was becoming a dangerous situation.

"Get dressed," he told her. "I've got something I want to show you."

23

The weather, at least, was promising. The sun beat hard against the T-Bird's windshield, giving Dora an excuse to slip on tinted glasses. However thin the defense, she felt better shielded.

As Jed drove north on Germantown Avenue under a vividly blue sky, she passed the time watching the pedestrian traffic. The temperature had risen to nearly fifty, allowing people to walk with a more cheerful step. They drove through the center of the city, far from the rivers with their frisky breezes, toward Chestnut Hill.

Not such a long way from South Street mile for mile, just vast distances of ambience and income.

He hadn't spoken since they'd started the drive. She didn't ask where they were going. She was almost sure she knew. His reasons for making the trip would soon become apparent—just as the consequences of her rash and impulsive declaration of love.

Rather than dwell on what was to come, Dora sat back and tried to enjoy the scenery, the beautifully restored homes and storefronts, the glitter of crystal and gold in the shops, the charm of the cobblestones beneath the T-Bird's monster tires.

Far up the hill the trees were old and stately, the homes trim and elegant. It was a neighborhood of minks and diamonds, of heirlooms and fat portfolios, of country club memberships and well-behaved lapdogs. She wondered fleetingly how it had appeared to a small boy growing up.

Jed pulled up in a narrow driveway beside a lovely old Colonial. The brick had mellowed to a soft dusky rose and the trim was an elegant and unfaded Wedgwood blue. Tall windows glinted and winked in the strong sunlight, tossing back reflections while preventing the curious from seeing the secrets within.

It was a fine house, Dora mused. Beautifully maintained, perfect in its setting and somehow strongly feminine, with its neat lines and dignity. If she had picked it herself, she realized, for herself, it couldn't have been more perfect. The age, the tradition, the setting all clicked quietly into place with her image of the ideal family home.

She imagined it in the summer when the roses planted beneath those tall windows would be sumptuously blooming, carrying bold color and womanly scent. And in the fall when the big, leafy trees would burst into golds and scarlets. The picture was completed with lace at the windows and a dog in the yard.

And because she imagined so well, her heart broke a little. She doubted very much that Jed saw the house as she did.

Saying nothing, she alighted from the car to stand and study. Only a discreet portion of the city noise traveled up here, on the hill. There would be no camera-snapping tourists here searching for monuments, no bold flash of a blade skater careering down the sidewalk, no tempting scents of pizza and hoagies from a corner deli.

And wasn't that what she wanted? she asked herself. The noise, the smells and the freedom of being in the center of it?

"This is where you grew up?" she asked.

"That's right." He led the way to the door flanked with lovely beveled glass inserts. When he'd unlocked it, he stepped back and waited for Dora to go in ahead.

The foyer was two stories, tipped with a many-tiered chandelier that would graciously light the way up the grand oak staircase. The floor was tiled with large black-and-white squares of marble. Her soft suede half boots barely made a sound as she crossed it.

There is something richly fascinating about empty houses. There is the thin, echoing air and the sense of vastness. There is the curious wonder of who had lived there, and what they had lived with, and the automatic projection of self into the rooms. There I would put my favorite lamp, and here my little table.

Dora felt that fascination now, but it was tinged with a deeper curiosity for where Jed had fit into the architecture and design.

She couldn't feel him here. Though she knew he stood beside her, it was as though the part of him that mattered most had stepped back at the threshold, and left her to enter alone.

The wallpaper with its tiny tea roses had faintly lighter rectangular sections where paintings had hung. The bare foyer cried out for flowers, she thought. Tall urns with freesia spilling out, bold stalks of lilies lancing up and some pretty, welcoming rug over that cold marble to soften the rigid formality of the entrance.

She ran her hand over the gleaming newel post at the base of the banister—a banister, she thought, fashioned for a child's bottom or a woman's trailing fingers.

"You're planning to sell it."

He was watching her, carefully, as she wandered from the foyer into the front parlor. Already, by simply entering, his muscles had tensed. Dora was right, Jed wasn't seeing pretty flowers or welcoming rugs.

"It's on the market. Elaine and I inherited it fifty-fifty, and she wasn't happy with any of the offers we received. I didn't really give a damn one way or the other." Because they wanted to fist, he tucked his hands into the pockets of his jacket. "So since she had a house of her own, I lived here awhile." He stayed where he was when Dora walked over to study the scrubbed and empty hearth. "It's mine now, and the realtor's starting over."

"I see." There should be family photos framed on the mantel, she thought. Crowds of them jockeying for position, celebrating the births and passage of generations. There should be an old Seth Thomas deep in their center, gently ticking off the time.

Where were the heavy candlesticks with their tapers burned low? she wondered, almost desperately. Where were the deep-cushioned chairs with petit point footstools tilted toward the fire?

A fire would take away the chill, she thought, rubbing her arms absently as she wandered out again and down the hall. It was much colder than it needed to be.

She found a library, stripped of books; another parlor with a view of a cobbled patio that begged for flower boxes; the dining room, vast and empty but for another chandelier, and finally the kitchen, with its charming hearth and brick oven.

Here's where the warmth should center, she thought, with the sun streaming through the window over the sink and bread baking fragrantly. But she found no warmth there, only the cold, echoing silence of a house untenanted and unwanted.

"It's a pretty view from here," she said for no other reason than to fill the void. There should be a sandbox in the yard, she thought, linking her tensed fingers together. A swing hanging from the thick bough of the big maple.

"We weren't allowed in here."

"Excuse me?" She turned back from the window, certain she'd misunderstood.

"We weren't allowed in here," he repeated, and his eyes were on her as if the pecan cupboards and rosy countertops didn't exist. "Only the servants. Their wing was through there." He gestured but didn't look toward a side door. "Along with the laundry and utility rooms. The kitchen was off limits."

She wanted to laugh and accuse him of making it up. But she could see quite clearly that he was telling the truth. "What if you had a desperate craving for some cookies?"

"One didn't eat between meals. The cook, after all, was paid to produce them, and we were expected to do them justice—at eight A.M., one P.M. and seven in the evening. I used to come in here at night, just for the principle of it." Now he did look around, his eyes flat and blank. "I still feel like a trespasser in here."

"Jed—"

"You should see the rest of it." He turned and walked out.

Yes, he wanted her to see it, he thought grimly. Every stone, every curve of molding, every inch of paint. And once she had, once he had walked through with her, he hoped never to walk through the door again.

She caught up with him at the base of the stairs, where he was waiting for her. "Jed, this isn't necessary."

"Let's go upstairs." He took her arm, ignoring her hesitation.

He remembered how it had smelled here—the air heavy with beeswax and funereal flowers, the expensive clashes of his mother's and sister's perfumes, the sting of cigar smoke from one of his father's Havanas.

He remembered, too, when it hadn't been silent. When there were voices raised forever in anger and accusation, or lowered in disgust. How the servants had kept their eyes downcast, their ears closed and their hands busy.

He remembered being sixteen, and being innocently attracted to one of the new maids. When his mother had come across them harmlessly flirting in the upstairs hall—right here, he thought—she had dismissed the girl on the spot.

"My mother's room." Jed inclined his head toward a doorway. "My father's was down the hall. As you can see, there were several rooms between."

She wanted to sigh and tell him she'd had enough, but knew it wasn't enough for him. "Where was yours?"

"There."

Dora moved down the hall and peeked into the room. It was large and airy, bright with afternoon light. The windows overlooked the rear lawn and the tidy privet hedge that marched along the verge of the property. Dora sat on the narrow window seat and looked out.

She knew there were always ghosts in old houses. A building couldn't stand for two hundred years and not carry some memories of those who had walked in it. These ghosts were Jed's, and he was violently possessive about them. What good would it do, she wondered, to tell him how easy it would be to exorcise them?

It only needed people. Someone to run laughing down the steps or to curl up dreaming by a fire. It only needed children slamming doors and racing in the halls.

"There used to be a chestnut tree out there. I'd go out that way at night, hitch a ride and go down to Market Street to raise hell. One night, one of the servants spotted me and reported it to my father. He had the tree cut down the next day. Then he came up here, locked the door and beat the hell out of me. I was fourteen." He said it without emotion, took out a cigarette, lighted it. "That's when I started lifting weights." His eyes flashed through the smoke. "He wasn't going to beat me again. If he tried, I was damn well going to be strong enough to take him. A couple of years later, I did. And that's how I earned boarding school."

Something sour rose up in her throat. She forced herself to swallow it. "You expect that to be hard for me to understand," she said quietly. "Because my father never raised a hand to us. Not even when we deserved it."

Jed considered the tip of his cigarette before tapping the ash on the floor. "My father had big hands. He didn't use them often, but when he did, it was without control."

"And your mother?"

"She preferred throwing things, expensive things. She knocked me unconscious once with a Meissen vase, and then took the two thousand in damages out of my college fund."

Dora nodded, continued to stare out the window while she struggled not to be sick. "Your sister?"

"They vacillated between treating her like a Dresden doll and an inmate. Tea parties one day, locked doors the next." He shrugged. "They wanted her to be the perfect lady, the virginal debutante who would follow the Skimmerhorn rules and marry well. Whenever she didn't conform, they put her in solitary."

"Excuse me?"

"Locked her in her room, a couple of days, maybe a week. Then they'd bribe her with shopping sprees or parties until she did what they wanted." To combat the bitterness in his mouth, he took another drag. "You'd have thought sharing the misery would have made us close, but somehow it never did. We didn't give a damn about each other."

Slowly, she turned her head, looked at him over her shoulder. "You don't need to apologize to me for your feelings."

"I'm not apologizing." He snapped the words out. "I'm explaining them." And he refused to let her unquestioning compassion soothe him.

"I got the call to go see Elaine—supposedly from one of her staff, but it was one of Speck's men. They wanted me on the scene when it happened. They knew she went out every Wednesday at eleven to have her hair done. I didn't." His gaze lifted again, latched onto Dora's. "I knew nothing about her, wanted to know nothing about her. I was minutes away from her house, and royally pissed at being summoned, when the dispatch came through with the bomb threat. You could say Speck had a good sense of timing."

He paused a moment, walked over to the small hearth and crushed out the cigarette on the stone. "I was first on the scene, just as Speck planned. I could see her in the car when I was running. The roses were blooming," he said softly, seeing it all perfectly again, not like a film, not like a dream, but stark reality. "She looked toward me. I could see the surprise on her face—and the irritation. Elaine didn't like to have her routine interrupted, and I imagine she was ticked off at the idea of the neighbors seeing me run across the lawn with my weapon out. Then she turned the key, and the car went up. The blast knocked me back into the roses."

"You tried to save her, Jed."

"I didn't save her," he said flatly. "That's for me to live with, and the guilt of it because she meant no more to me than a stranger. Less, because she wasn't a stranger. We lived in this house together for nearly eighteen years, and we shared nothing."

She turned back then, and sat quietly. Jed felt a quick jolt of surprise at how lovely, how perfect she looked there with the sun pouring liquidly around her, her eyes calm and watchful, her mouth solemn. Odd, he thought, there had never been anything in this house he'd considered beautiful. Until now.

"I understand why you brought me here," she began. "Why you felt you had to—but you didn't have to. I'm glad you did, but it wasn't necessary." She sighed then and let her hands rest in her lap. "You wanted me to see a cold, empty house where very little is left but the unhappiness that used to live here. And you wanted me to understand that, like the house, you have nothing to offer."

He had a need, an almost desperate one, to step forward and rest his head in her lap. "I don't have anything to offer."

"You don't want to," she corrected. "And considering the role models in your life, it's certainly logical. The problem is, Skimmerhorn, emotions just aren't logical. Mine aren't." She tilted her head and the sun creamed over her skin, warming it, as her voice was warm, as the room was warm with her in it. "I told you I love you, and you'd probably have preferred a slap in the face, but there it is. I didn't mean to say it—or maybe I did."

In a vulnerable and weary gesture, she brushed a hand through her hair. "Maybe I did," she repeated softly. "Because even though I understood how you might react, I'm just not used to bottling my feelings inside. But they are my feelings, Jed. They don't ask you for anything."

"When a woman tells a man she loves him, she's asking for everything."

"Is that how you see it?" She smiled a little, but her eyes were dulled with sadness. "Let me tell you how I see it. Love's a gift, and can certainly be refused. Refusing doesn't destroy the gift, it simply puts it aside. You're free to do that. I'm not asking for a gift in return. It's not that I don't want it, but I don't expect it."

She rose then and, crossing the room, took his face gently in her hands. Her eyes were still sad, but there was a bottomless compassion in them that humbled him. "Take what's offered, Jed, especially when it's offered generously and without expectations. I won't keep throwing it in your face. That would only embarrass us both."

"You're leaving yourself open, Dora."

"I know. It feels right to me." She kissed him, one cheek, the other, then his mouth. "Relax and enjoy, Skimmerhorn. I intend to."

"I'm not what you need." But he gathered her close and held on. Because she was what he needed. She was so exactly what he needed.

"You're wrong." She closed her eyes and willed the threatening tears away. "You're wrong about the house, too. You're both just waiting."

He kept losing his train of thought. Jed knew the details he and Brent discussed were vital, but he kept seeing Dora sitting on the window seat of his old, hated room, with sunlight pooling around her.

And he kept remembering the way her hands had felt against his face when she'd smiled and asked him to accept love.

"Jed, you're making me feel like a boring history teacher."

Jed blinked, focused. "What?"

"Exactly." Blowing out a breath, Brent leaned back in his desk chair. "You want to tell me what's on your mind?"

"It's nothing." He washed the mood away with some of the station house's atomic coffee. "What you've picked up on Winesap makes it look like he's another underling. I still think the best way to handle this is to approach the top man, Finley. Not directly. The longer we can keep the smuggled painting under wraps, the better."

"What I can gather on the guy wouldn't fill a teacup," Brent complained. "He's rich—rich enough to make you look like a piker, pal—successful, single, obsessively private."

"And as the head of a large import-export firm, would be the perfect warehouse for smuggled goods."

"If wishing only made it so," Brent murmured. "We've got no hard evidence on Finley. Sure, the shipment was addressed to his assistant, and DiCarlo works for him."

"DiCarlo's small-time, a hustler. You've only got to look at his rap sheet."

"And Finley has no rap sheet. He's the American ideal, a modest self-made man and a solid citizen."

"Then a little digging shouldn't hurt him," Jed pointed out. "I want to take a trip to LA."

"I thought that was where this was leading." Uncomfortable, Brent shifted. "Listen, Jed, I know you've got a personal investment in this. The department wouldn't have diddly without you."

"But," Jed interrupted, "I'm not with the department."

Feeling miserable, Brent pushed at his glasses, fiddled with papers on his desk. "Goldman's asking questions."

"Maybe it's time you answered them."

"The commissioner thinks so."

"I'm a civilian, Brent. There's nothing to stop me from taking a trip to the coast—at my own expense, on my own time."

"Why don't you cut the crap?" Brent blurted out. "I know you've got a meeting with the commissioner in an hour, and we both know what he's going to say. You can't keep straddling this. Make my life easier and tell me you're coming back on the job."

"I can't tell you that. I *can* tell you I'm thinking about it."

The oath dried up on Brent's tongue. "Seriously?"

"More seriously than I ever thought I would." Jed rose and paced to the frosted glass door, to the scarred file cabinets, to the coffeepot thick with dregs. "Goddamn, I miss this place." Nearly amused at himself, Jed turned back. "Isn't that some shit? I miss it—every minute of the tedium, the fucking reports, the candy-assed rookies. Nine mornings out of ten I reach for my shoulder harness before I remember it's not there. I even thought about buying one of those frigging police scanners so I'd know what the hell's going on."

"Hallelujah." Brent folded his hands, prayerlike. "Let me tell Goldman. Please, let me be the one."

"I didn't say I was coming back."

"Yeah, you did." On impulse Brent leaped up, grabbed Jed by the shoulders and kissed him.

"Christ, Chapman. Get a grip."

"The men are going to welcome you back like a god. What does Dora think about it?"

Jed's foolish grin faded. "She doesn't think anything. We haven't talked about it. It doesn't concern her."

"Oh." Brent tucked his tongue in his cheek. "Uh-huh. Mary Pat and I have a bet. She says I'll be renting a tux as best man by the end of the school year. I say Easter vacation. We tend to mark time by the school calendar."

The quick flutter of panic in Jed's stomach staggered him. "You're off base."

"Come on, Captain, you're crazy about her. Ten minutes ago you were staring into space daydreaming. And if she wasn't the star of the show, I'll kiss Goldman on the mouth."

"You're awful free with your affections these days. Drop it, will you?"

He knew that tone of voice—the verbal equivalent of a brick wall. "Okay, but I've got dinner for two at the Chart House riding on you." Brent leaned back on the edge of his desk. "I'd appreciate a rundown of what you and the commissioner come up with. Whether you go to LA officially or not, I can arrange some backup."

"We'll touch base tomorrow."

"And, Captain," Brent added before Jed made it to the door. "Do me a favor and let them bribe you back, okay? I can make you a list of the things we could use around here."

Brent grinned and settled down to fantasize about breaking the news to Goldman.

It was nearly midnight when Dora gave up the attempt to sleep and bundled into her robe. An ordinary case of insomnia. It wasn't because Jed hadn't come home, or called.

And things were really bad, she admitted, when she started lying to herself.

She switched on the stereo, but Bonnie Raitt's sultry blues seemed entirely too appropriate, so she turned it off again. Wandering into the kitchen, she put the kettle on to boil.

How could she have blown it like this? she wondered as she debated without interest between Lemon Lift and chamomile. Hadn't she known that a man would head for the hills when he heard those three fateful words? Nope. She tossed a tea bag into a cup. She hadn't known because she'd never said them before. And now that she was in the real show, she'd rushed her cue.

Well, it couldn't be taken back, she decided. And she was sorry she and Jed hadn't read the same script.

He hadn't echoed the words back, or swept her up in delight. He had systematically and subtly withdrawn, inch by inch, since that fateful moment some thirty-six hours earlier. And she was very much afraid he would continue to withdraw until he had faded completely away.

Couldn't be helped. She poured the hot water into the cup and let the tea steep while she rummaged for cookies. She couldn't force him to let her show him what it could be like to give and take love. She could only keep her promise and not throw it in his face again. However much that hurt.

And she had some pride left—Bonnie Raitt was wrong about that, she thought. Love *did* have pride. She was going to pull herself together and get on with her life—with him, she hoped. Without him, if necessary. She figured she could start now by going downstairs and putting her wide-awake brain to work.

Carrying her tea, she headed out, remembering at the last minute to slip her keys into her robe pocket and lock the door behind her. She hated that, that sensation of not being completely safe in her own home. Because of it, she felt compelled to switch on lights as she went.

Once settled in the storeroom, she picked up the tedious task of continuing the reorganization of the files DiCarlo had upended.

As always, the steady work and the quiet relaxed and absorbed her. She enjoyed putting the proper thing in the proper place, and pausing occasionally to study a receipt and remember the thrill of the sale.

A paperweight commemorating the New York World's Fair, at $40. A marquetry toilet mirror, at $3,000. Three advertising signs, Brasso, Olympic ale and Players cigarettes, at $190, $27 and $185, respectively.

Jed stood midway down the stairs watching her. She'd set all the lights burning, like a child left home alone at night. She was wearing the green robe and an enormous pair of purple socks. Each time she leaned down to read a piece of paper, her hair fell softly over her cheek and curtained her face. Then she would push it back, the movement fluid and unstudied, before she filed the paper away and reached for another.

His heart rate, which had spiked when he'd seen the hallway door open, settled comfortably. Even with the desire that seemed to nag him whenever she was close, he was always comfortable looking at her.

He'd already settled his weapon back under his jacket when she turned.

She caught a glimpse of a figure and stumbled back. Papers went flying as she choked on a scream.

"What are you doing?" she said furiously. "Trying to scare me to death?"

"No." He came down to the base of the steps. "What the hell are you doing, Conroy? It's after midnight."

"What does it look like I'm doing? I'm practicing the minuet." Humiliated by her reaction, she crouched down to pick up scattered papers.

"You were very graceful." He bent down, placed a hand over hers. "I'm sorry I scared you. I guess you were too involved to hear me."

"Never mind."

"You should be in bed." He tilted her face up toward the light. "You look tired."

"Thanks so much."

"And you're bitchy, too."

"I am not bitchy." She sucked in an insulted breath. "I resent that term both as a feminist and as a dog lover."

Patiently, he tucked her hair behind her ear. She'd managed to cover it remarkably quickly, he mused. But her eyes had been worried and wary after the first fright had faded. He'd hurt her already, and was very likely to do so again.

"Come on upstairs, baby."

"I haven't finished yet."

He lifted a brow. There was the faintest edge of resentment in her tone. It made him feel small and incredibly stupid.

"You're pissed at me."

"I'm not." She straightened, drew a deep breath and, with an effort of will, made the statement the truth. "I am not," she repeated, calm again. "If I'm out of sorts it's because I feel useless having to keep the shop closed, and deceitful because I'm lying to my family."

"You don't have to do either of those things. There's no reason not to open tomorrow, and you'd feel better if you came clean with your family."

She considered it. "I will open," she decided, "but I'm not telling my family. Not yet. It's for me to deal with."

He started to argue and found he couldn't. Wasn't that the same rationale he was using to ease his conscience? He wasn't going to tell her about his meeting with the commissioner or his decision to pick up his badge. Not yet.

"Come upstairs," he repeated. "I'll give you a back rub."

"Why?"

"Because you're tense," he said between his teeth. "Damn, Conroy, why do you care why? All you have to do is lie there and enjoy it."

Eyes narrowed, she stepped back. "You're being nice to me. Why? You're setting me up for something, Skimmerhorn. You're planning on doing something you know I won't like." She raced up the steps after him.

"Don't keep things from me." She laid a hand on his arm as he unlocked his door. "Please. It's something about DiCarlo, isn't it? About the painting, the whole mess."

It was more than that. And less. He wondered if it was the coward's way out to give her that one part.

"I'm going to LA to have a talk with DiCarlo's boss."

"Winesap?" Her brow creased as she concentrated. "That's who the shipment was supposed to go to, wasn't it?"

"The top man's name is Finley, Edmund G.," Jed told her. "I'll start with him."

"And you think he—Finley—was expecting the shipment, that he arranged for the smuggling?"

"Yeah." He poured whiskey, for both of them. "That's what I think."

"What do you know about him?"

"Enough to buy a ticket for LA." He handed her the glass, then offered a brief rundown.

"Import-export," she mused when he'd finished. "Then he's probably a collector. They almost always are. It's possible that he was unaware of DiCarlo's sideline—after all, you said it was a big company. But if he isn't..."

He caught the gleam in her eye and bit back a sigh. "Don't think, Conroy. You can be dangerous when you think."

"But I am thinking." She lifted the whiskey, tossed it back in one burning swallow. "And what I think is, you aren't the one who should talk to Finley." She held out the glass for a refill. "I am."

24

"You're out of your mind."

"That is a perfectly sane, rational statement." Since Jed made no move to share, Dora took the bottle and refilled her glass herself. "And if you'd put that male ego on hold a minute, you'd see why."

"It has nothing to do with ego." Although it did, however slightly, and that fact burned the hell out of him. "It has to do with simple common sense. You're in no position to tackle something like this."

"On the contrary." She was warming up to the idea now, and began moving around the room, swirling her whiskey, relishing the part to be played. "I'm in the perfect position. I, after all, was the victim of his employee. I, the baffled innocent, will appeal to Finley's sympathies if he, in turn, is innocent and, since I too am a collector, to his imagination if he's guilty. In short, Skimmerhorn—" She circled back and tapped her glass to his. "This part is tailor-made for me."

"It's not a damn audition, Conroy."

"But it is, essentially. Lord, when are you going to get some furniture in here?" In lieu of a decent chair, she scooted up to sit on the table. "What was your plan, Captain, to barge into his offices, gun blasting?"

"Don't be any more ridiculous than necessary."

"I thought not. You would, if I may interpret the scene, request a meeting to discuss the ugly situation informally, possibly soliciting his help to locate DiCarlo?"

She lifted a brow, waiting for his denial or assent, and got neither. Undaunted, she plowed ahead. "Meanwhile, you'd be looking for a chink in his armor, if indeed he has any armor or chinks. While doing so, you'd get a firsthand view of his operation, his style, and develop an informed opinion as to his culpability."

"You sound like a freaking lawyer," he muttered. "I hate lawyers."

"That's the cop talking. I have some very good friends who are lawyers—and my father was an excellent Clarence Darrow in a production of *Inherit the Wind*. Now, let's see." She crossed her legs; the robe shifted open over long smooth thighs. "How would I play this?"

"You're not, Conroy." Because he felt something essential slipping neatly out of his fingers, he spoke with a snap and caught her chin in his hand. "You are not going."

"Yes, I am," she said, unperturbed. "Because we both know it's the perfect solution." Smiling, she took his hand off her chin then kissed it. "You can come with me. Keep me away from Rodeo Drive."

There was only one way to deal with her, Jed thought, and that was calmly. "Dora, I don't have a handle on this guy. We can't get any hard data. He might be some nice, grandfatherly type who collects stamps in his spare time, and has nothing to do with smuggling. Or DiCarlo might just have been the trigger on his gun. Walking onto his turf is risky, and I'm not taking risks with you."

"Why?" She said it softly. "One would almost think you care."

He jammed his frustrated hands in his pockets. "Damn it, you know I care."

"I know you want, but caring is entirely different. Still, it's nice to hear."

"Don't circle around me on this." She wasn't going to lure him into a dangerous discussion of feelings again. "The point is Finley. If he's involved, he's going to take one look at you and see through that pretty face of yours like plate glass."

"My, my, you tell me you care and that I'm pretty in one night. My heart swells."

"I ought to smack you," he said through clenched teeth.

"But you won't." She smiled and held out a hand. "Lots of bark and little bite, that's you, Skimmerhorn. Let's get some sleep. We can hash this out in the morning."

"There's nothing to hash. I'm going. You're not."

She let her hand fall away. "You don't trust me. That's it, isn't it?" She clamped her teeth over her bottom lip to still the trembling, but her voice thickened and shook even as her eyes filled.

"It's not a matter of trust." He dragged a hand out of his pocket, through his hair. "Don't take it so personally."

"How else can I take it?" The first tear spilled over, ran a lonely trail down her cheek. Her eyes were glistening with more, combined with fragile hurt. "Don't you understand that I need to do something? That I can't just sit in the background after me and my home have been violated this way? I can't bear it, Jed. I can't bear having you think of me as some helpless victim who only gets in your way."

"Stop it." Her tears weakened him, unmanned him. "Come on, baby, don't." He awkwardly lifted a hand to her hair. "I can't stand that." Gently he kissed her quivering lips. "I don't think of you as helpless."

"Useless, then," she said on a hitching sob.

"No." He brushed her tears away with his thumbs and was nearly ready to beg. "You're not trained to do this. If he suspects anything, the whole sting could fall apart before it gets started."

She sniffled, pressed her face to his throat. "Do you suspect—?"

"What?"

"Do you suspect?" she demanded in a perfectly controlled voice. Leaning back, she grinned at him without a trace of remorse. "Fell for it, didn't you?" Laughing, she patted his cheek while he stared at her through slitted and infuriated eyes. "Don't feel too stupid, Skimmerhorn. I told you once I was good." She lifted her glass again to toast herself. "And I am very, very good. And that was just an impromptu performance."

"Maybe I will smack you. You ever turn on tears again like that, I swear I will."

"Made you feel like a heel, didn't I?" She sighed, lustily. "Sometimes I do miss the stage." Then she shrugged. "But not very often. Be assured, Captain, that our Mr. Finley will see exactly what I want him to see. I'll play him like an accordion."

She could do it. He hated the fact that he was certain she could do it perfectly. "And if I lose my mind enough to consider agreeing to this harebrained idea, you'd do exactly as you were told?"

"No—but I'd try to do exactly as I was told. It's just a fishing expedition, Jed."

He'd thought so, but he preferred to know his water, and bait his own hook. "I don't want you hurt."

She softened all over, eyes, mouth, heart. "That's one of the nicest things you've ever said to me."

"If he hurts you, I'd kill him."

Her easy smile vanished. "Don't put that weight on my shoulders. Okay? It scares me."

He lifted her off the table, set her on her feet. "Conroy, I said I didn't think you were helpless, and that I didn't think you were useless, but I never told you what I think you are."

"No, you didn't." She grimaced, braced.

"Important," he said simply, and melted her heart. "Very important."

By noon the next day, Dora felt at least one part of her life was shifting back into normal gear. The shop was open for business. The first sale warmed her soul so that she gave her customer an impulsive ten percent off. When Lea walked in to help with the afternoon flow, Dora greeted her with a fierce hug.

Laughing, Lea untangled herself. "What's all this? Did you win the lottery?"

"Better. We're open."

Lea peeled off her coat and fluffed her hair. "You never explained why we were closed."

"Too complicated," Dora said breezily. "I needed a day or two of downtime."

"That break-in bothered you more than you let on." Lea's nod was self-satisfied. "I knew it."

"I guess it did. Anyway, we've got a couple of browsers, and I just bought those tea cookies from the bakery again—the ones with the chocolate filling."

Lea took a deep breath. "How am I supposed to lose the four pounds I gained during the holidays?"

"Willpower."

"Right. Oh, Mom said to ask you about the painting."

The cookie box nearly slipped out of Dora's fingers. "Painting?"

"Something about you lent her a painting and had to take it back." Lea gave up on willpower and chose a frosted cookie. "She's thinking about buying it for Dad for Valentine's Day. Seems he really took a shine to it."

"Oh . . . I, ah, sold it." At least that was true, she reminded herself. She still had Jed's $80 tucked in her jewelry box like love letters.

"Are you okay?" Lea's keen eyes scanned Dora's face. "You look a little flustered."

"Hmm? No, I'm fine. Just getting back in the swing. Actually, I'm a little scattered. I may have to go to LA for a couple of days."

"What for?"

"There's an import business out there that I may want to cultivate. I don't want to close the shop again." No reason to, she assured herself. Since Brent was still pulling strings to ensure police protection.

"Don't worry about it. Terri and I can keep things going." The phone on the counter rang twice. Lea raised a brow. "Want me to get that?"

"No." Dora shook off the guilt and lifted the receiver that was an inch away from her hand. "Good afternoon, Dora's Parlor."

"I'd like to speak to Miss Isadora Conroy, please."

"Speaking."

"Miss Conroy." From his desk in Los Angeles, Winesap turned to his meticulously rehearsed notes. "This is, ah, Francis Petroy."

"Yes, Mr. Petroy," Dora said as Lea turned to greet a customer.

"I hope I'm not disturbing you, but I was given your name and number by a Mrs. Helen Owings of Front Royal, Virginia."

"Yes." Dora's fingers tightened on the receiver. "What can I do for you?"

"I hope it's what we can do for each other." Winesap read the words "genial chuckle" in his notes and did his best imitation of one. "It concerns a painting you bought at auction in December. A Billingsly."

All moisture evaporated in her mouth. "Yes, I know the piece. An abstract."

"Exactly. As it happens, I'm a collector of abstract work. I specialize in unknown and emerging artists—in a regretfully small way, you understand."

"Of course."

"I was unable to attend that particular auction—a family emergency. It gave me some hope when Mrs. Owings informed me that the painting had been sold to a dealer, rather than an art collector."

"Actually," Dora said, playing for time. "I'm a little of both."

"Oh dear." He shuffled through his papers. Nothing in his copious notes addressed that particular response. "Oh dear."

"But I'm always interested in a legitimate offer, Mr. Petroy. Perhaps you'd like to come in and see the painting. It would have to be sometime late next week, I'm afraid." She paused and mimed flipping through an appointment book. "My schedule's rather hectic until then."

"That would be excellent. Really excellent." Relieved, Winesap mopped his sweaty neck with a handkerchief. "What day would be good for you, Miss Conroy?"

"I could fit you in on Thursday, say at two?"

"Perfect." Hurried, Winesap scribbled down the date. "I hope you'll hold the painting until then. I'd hate to miss the opportunity."

"Oh, I'd hate you to miss it, too." She smiled grimly at the wall. "I promise, it won't go anywhere until we have the chance to discuss terms. Do you have a number where I can reach you in case something comes up?"

"Certainly." As his notes instructed, Winesap recited the number for one of Finley's fronts in New Jersey. "During business hours," he said. "I'm afraid I keep my private number unlisted."

"I understand perfectly. Next Thursday then, Mr. Petroy."

She hung up, almost too furious to enjoy the sense of elation. He thought she was an idiot, Dora fumed. Well, DiCarlo or Finley or Petroy or whoever the hell you are, you're in for a rude surprise.

"Lea! I have to go out for an hour. If Jed comes in, tell him I have to talk to him."

"Okay, but where—" Lea broke off, fisting her hands on her hips as she stared at the closing door.

She should have called ahead. Dora turned back into the parking lot after a fruitless trip to the police station. Lieutenant Chapman was in the field. Sounded as though he were out hunting pheasant, she thought grumpily.

How was she supposed to tell anyone she'd made contact if there wasn't anyone around to tell? Then she spotted Jed's car and allowed herself a smug smile. He was about to learn that he wasn't the only one who could think on his feet.

She found him in the storeroom, calmly painting shelves.

"There you are. I hate to use a cliché, but where's a cop when you need one?"

He continued to paint. "If you'd needed a cop, you should have called nine-one-one."

"I went to the source instead." Wanting to prolong the excitement, she peeled off her coat. "But Brent was out. How come they call it a field? I don't recall passing through any fields in Philadelphia."

"Just our little way of impressing civilians. Why did you need Brent?"

"Because." She paused for drama. "I made contact."

"With what?"

"With whom, Skimmerhorn. Don't be dense. I got a call from Mr. Petroy—only I don't think it was Mr. Petroy. It could have been DiCarlo, but the voice didn't really jibe. Maybe he disguised it, but I'm pretty good with voices. He could have had someone else make the call," she said, considering. "Or it could have been Finley, but—"

"Sit down, Conroy." Jed laid the brush across the top of the paint can. "Try a Jack Webb."

"A Jack Webb? Oh." Her eyes brightened. "Just the facts. I get it."

"You're a real whip. Sit."

"Okay." She settled and imagined herself filing a report. As a result, she related the entire phone conversation precisely, thoroughly and without embellishments. "How's that?" she asked when she was done.

"What the hell were you thinking of, making an appointment to meet him without checking with me?"

She'd expected him to be impressed, not irritated. "I had to do something, didn't I? Wouldn't he have been suspicious if a dealer had seemed reluctant to meet with him?" Her back stiffened defensively. "But it's definitely fishy. An art collector inquiring about a painting from an artist who probably doesn't even exist. I checked on Billingsly. There isn't any Billingsly, so why should anyone go to the trouble to track down a Billingsly painting? Because," she said, and lifted a finger for emphasis, "he wants a Monet."

"That's brilliant, Conroy. Just Goddamn brilliant. And it's not the point."

"Of course it is." She blew out a breath, stirring her bangs. "He thought I was stupid. He thought I was some money-grubbing junk dealer who doesn't know her butt from a delft vase, but he's going to find out differently."

"That's also beside the point. You should have put him off until I got back."

"I did very well on my own, thank you. I'm not an idiot."

"Do you have star sixty-nine on your phone system?"

Her face went blank. "Excuse me?"

"Return call. You press a couple of buttons and your phone rings back whoever called you last."

"Oh." As the wind leaked out of her sails, she examined her nails. "Yeah. I guess I do."

He studied her bowed head. "I don't suppose you thought to try it?"

"I can't think of everything," she mumbled. Hopefully, she looked up. "We can try it now."

"The phone's rung three times since I got back."

"Oh." She pushed up from the chair. "Go ahead, tell me I blew it."

"I don't have to, you just did." He gave her hair a tug. "Don't take it too hard, Nancy Drew, even amateur sleuths screw up now and again."

She knocked his hand away. "Take a leap, Skimmerhorn."

"Brent and I will work out how to handle Petroy on Thursday. We'll be back by then."

"Back? Are you and Brent going somewhere?"

"No, you and I are." He tucked his thumbs in his pockets. He still wasn't happy about it, but she'd made an odd sort of sense. "We're leaving for LA tomorrow."

"I'm going to do it?" She pressed a hand to her heart, then tossed her arms wide and vaulted into his. "I'm actually going to do it." Thrilled with the prospect, she raced kisses over his face. "I knew you'd see it my way."

"I didn't. I was outvoted." He wasn't going to admit he'd seen the simple beauty of her idea and had recommended it to Brent.

"Whatever." She kissed him again, hard. "Tomorrow?" she said, rearing back. "God, that's so quick. I have to decide what I'm going to wear."

"That's the least of your worries."

"No, no, no, the proper presentation is essential to character. My navy pinstripe," she considered. "It's very polite and businesslike. Or maybe the red double-breasted—more power and sex. I could distract him with my legs."

"Go for the businesslike."

Because she enjoyed the faint trace of annoyance in the tone, she smiled. "Definitely the red."

"For all you know, he won't even see you."

"Of course he'll see me." She stopped, frowned. "How are we going to make him want to see me?"

"Because you're going to call him, and you're going to say exactly what I tell you to say."

"I see." She tilted her head, lifted a brow. "Have you written me a script, Skimmerhorn? I'm a quick study. I can be off book in no time."

"Just do what you're told."

In Los Angeles, Winesap entered Finley's office with a worried frown creasing his face. "Mr. Finley, sir. Miss Conroy, she's on line two. She's waiting to speak with you."

"Is that so?" Finley closed the file he'd been studying, folded his hands on top of it. "An interesting development."

Winesap's hands twisted together like nervous cats. "Mr. Finley, when I spoke with her earlier today, she was quite cooperative. And I certainly never mentioned my connection with you. I don't know what this might mean."

"Then we'll find out, won't we? Sit, Abel." He lifted the receiver and, smiling, leaned back in his chair. "Miss Conroy? Edmund Finley here."

He listened, his smile growing wider and more feral. "I'm afraid I don't follow you, Miss Conroy. You're inquiring about one of my employees—Anthony DiCarlo? I see. I see." He picked up a letter opener from his desk and tested the honed point with the pad of his thumb. "Of course, I understand if you feel a personal meeting is important. I don't know if I'll be able to help. We've told the police all we know about Mr. DiCarlo's unexplained disappearance, which is, unfortunately, nothing. Very well," he added after a moment. "If you feel you can't discuss it over the telephone, I'd be happy to see you. Tomorrow?" His brows raised. Gently he scraped the point of the letter opener over the Conroy file. "That is rather short notice. Life and death?" He barely suppressed a chuckle. "I'll see if it can be arranged. Will you hold? I'll give you to my assistant. He'll check my calendar. I'll look forward to meeting you."

With a flourish of wrist, Finley punched the Hold button. "Give her four o'clock."

"You have a meeting at three-thirty, sir."

"Give her four o'clock," Finley repeated, and held out the phone.

"Yes, sir." Winesap took the receiver in his damp hand, engaged the line. "Miss Conroy? This is Abel Winesap, Mr. Finley's assistant. You'd like an appointment for tomorrow? I'm afraid the only time Mr. Finley has open is at four. Yes? You have the address? Excellent. We'll be expecting you."

"Delightful." Finley nodded approval when Winesap replaced the receiver. "Simply delightful. 'Fools walk in,' Abel." He opened Dora's file again and smiled genially at her dossier. "I'm certainly looking forward to this. Clear my calendar for tomorrow afternoon. I want no distractions when I see Miss Isadora Conroy. She will have all my attention."

"Tomorrow, four o'clock," Dora said, and turned to Jed. "He sounded puzzled but cooperative, pleasant but reserved."

"And you sounded on the verge of hysteria but controlled." Impressed despite himself, he tipped her face up with his finger and kissed her. "Not bad, Conroy. Not bad at all."

"There's something else." Though she wanted to, she didn't take his hand. If she had, he'd have seen that hers was chilled. "I think I just spoke with Mr. Petroy."

"Finley?"

"No." She forced a thin smile. "His assistant, Winesap."

25

Dora was pleased, and impressed, when the cab pulled up in front of the pink stucco villa that was the Beverly Hills Hotel. "Well, well, Skimmerhorn, you surprise me. This makes up for not springing for a night at the Plaza in New York."

"The room's booked in your name." Jed watched Dora gracefully offer her hand to the doorman. The gesture was one of a woman who'd been sliding out of limos all her life. "You have to put it on your credit card."

She cast a withering look at him over her shoulder. "Thanks a bunch, big spender."

"You want to advertise the fact that you're traveling out here with a companion?" he asked when she sailed through the doors and into the lobby. "A cop?"

"You left out the 'ex.' "

"So I did," he murmured, and waited while Dora checked in. The tony lobby of the BHH didn't seem exactly the right setting to tell her that the "ex" wouldn't apply much longer.

Dora covertly scanned the lobby for passing movie stars when she handed the desk clerk her card for imprint. "I'm going to bill you for this, Skimmerhorn."

"It was your idea to come."

True enough. "Then I'll only bill you for half." She accepted her card, and two keys, passed one to the waiting bellman. "Some of us are not independently wealthy."

"Some of us," he said as he slipped an arm around her waist, "paid for the airfare."

She was touched by the easy way he'd linked them together as they trailed the luggage to the elevator and up to the room.

Dora quickly slipped out of her shoes and padded over to the window to check out the view. There was nothing quite so Californian, she mused, as lush lawns, regal palms and cozy stucco cottages.

"I haven't been in LA since I was fifteen. We stayed in an incredibly bad hotel in Burbank while my father did a part in a small, forgettable film with Jon Voight. It did not distinguish either of their careers."

She stretched her back, rolled her shoulders. "I guess I'm a snob. An east coast snob, because LA doesn't do it for me. It makes me think of unnecessary eye tucks and designer yogurt. Or maybe it's designer eye tucks and unnecessary yogurt. After all, who really needs yogurt in their lives?"

She turned back, her smile becoming puzzled when he only continued to stare at her. "What is it?"

"I just like looking at you sometimes, that's all."

"Oh."

When he saw that the statement had both pleased and flustered her, he smiled back. "You're okay, Conroy. Even with the pointy chin."

"It's not pointy." She rubbed it defensively. "It's delicately sculptured. You know, maybe we should have booked a suite. This room's hardly bigger than a closet. Or maybe we can just go out for a while, get something to eat, soak up some smog."

"You're nervous."

"Of course I'm not nervous." She tossed her bag onto the bed and undid the straps.

"You're nervous," Jed repeated. "You talk too much when you're nervous. Actually, you talk too much all the time but there's a different quality to the babble when you're nervous. And you can't keep your hands still." He laid his gently over hers.

"Obviously I've already become too predictable. The first death knell in any relationship."

He simply turned her around, keeping her hands in his. "You've got a right to be nervous. I'd be more worried about you if you weren't."

"I don't want you to worry." Because she didn't, she willed her hands to relax in his. "I'm going to be fine. Classic opening-night jitters, that's all it is."

"You don't have to do this. I can keep the appointment for you."

"I never give the understudy a chance to steal my thunder." She inhaled and exhaled twice, deeply. "I'm okay. Wait till you read the reviews."

Since she so obviously needed him to, he played along. "What did you used to do before opening night?"

Thinking back, she sat on the edge of the bed. "Well, you'd pace a lot. Pacing's good. And you'd keep running lines in your head and going over the blocking. I'd get out of my street clothes and into a robe—sort of like a snake shedding. And vocalize. I used to do a lot of tongue twisters."

"Such as?"

"Moses supposes his toeses are roses, that kind of thing." Grinning, she waggled her tongue between her teeth. "You've got to limber the tongue."

"Yours has always seemed pretty limber to me."

"Thanks." She laughed and looked back at him. "Good job, Skimmerhorn. I feel better."

"Good." He gave her hair a brotherly tousle, then turned to the phone. "I'll order up some room service, then we'll go over the routine again."

Dora groaned and flopped back on the bed. "I hate heavy-handed directors."

But he didn't let up. Two hours later they had eaten, argued, discussed every possible contingency, and he was still unsatisfied. He listened to her reciting tongue twisters in the bathroom and frowned at the door. He'd have felt better if she'd been wearing a wire. Foolish, he supposed, as she'd be walking into a fully staffed office building in broad daylight, but it would have eased his mind. If he hadn't been concerned that Finley's security might have picked up on it, he'd have insisted.

It was a simple job, he reminded himself. One with little to no risk. And he'd already taken the precaution of seeing that the minimal degree of risk was all but eliminated.

It was the *all but* that nagged at him.

The door opened, and Dora stepped out wearing the red suit that showed off every glorious curve in that sexy body, highlighting her legs in a way that would make any man this side of the grave salivate.

"What do you think?" She was holding two different pairs of earrings up to each lobe. "The drops or the knots?"

"How the hell should I know?"

"The knots," she decided. "More discreet." She fastened them on. "I'd forgotten how much better you feel once you're in costume. There's just those little ripples of nerves that keep the adrenaline up." She reached for her bottle of perfume.

He frowned as she spritzed on scent—the throat, the back of the neck, the wrists, the backs of her knees. Something about the female ritual made his stomach jitter. When she picked up her antique silver brush and pulled it slowly through her hair, he knew what that something was. It made him feel like a voyeur.

"You look fine." He had to clear his throat. "You can stop primping now."

"Brushing your hair isn't primping. It's basic grooming." While she gave it another sweep, she caught his gaze in the mirror. "I'd swear you're more nervous than I am."

"Just stick to the plan and try to remember everything you see. Don't bring up the painting. You haven't got a clue about the painting. Try to go through Winesap. We're running him down, but I want your impressions—not your speculations, your impressions."

"I know." Patiently she set the brush aside. "Jed, I know exactly what to do and how to do it. It's simple. Simpler because I might have done just this if I hadn't known about the painting. It's a very logical step."

"Just watch your ass."

"Darling, I'm counting on you to do that for me."

• • •

Dora was impressed with the decor of Finley's outer office, trying to pick up helpful clues. As she'd suspected, he was a collector, and their mutual interest would give them a firm foundation. Her hands were chilled. That was good, too. The honest nerves she projected were just what she needed to set the tone for her visit.

It was difficult to hang on to those nerves, and character, when she really wanted to walk over and examine some of Finley's treasures firsthand. She felt favorably toward anyone who put malachite vases and Chiparus figures in his waiting area. And the settee she was using was no reproduction. Early Chippendale, Dora thought reverently, high-style rococo.

She sincerely hoped Finley would prove himself to be in the clear. She'd love to develop a business relationship.

But if he wasn't...

The thought of that had the nerves creeping back. She fiddled with the calla lily pin at her lapel, brushed at her skirt, looked at her watch.

Damn, it was four-ten, she thought. How long was he going to keep her waiting?

"Excellent. Excellent," Finley murmured to Dora's video image. She was every bit as lovely as he'd expected from the faded newspaper photos Winesap had unearthed from old Show and Style sections. Her wardrobe showed a flair for color and line as well as an affection for the feminine. He respected a woman who knew how to present herself to her best advantage.

He enjoyed the way her hands moved restlessly through her hair, over her body. Nerves, he thought, pleased. A spider gained more thrill from a panicky fly than a resigned one. And despite the nerves, he noted, her eyes were drawn again and again to pieces in his collection. That flattered him.

They would do very well together, he decided. Very well indeed.

He buzzed his receptionist. It was time to begin.

"Mr. Finley will see you now."

"Thank you." Dora rose, tucked her envelope bag under her arm and followed the woman to the double doors.

When she entered, Finley smiled and stood. "Miss Conroy, I'm so sorry to have kept you waiting."

"I'm just happy you could see me at all." She crossed the rug, that pool of white, and took his extended hand. Her first impression was one of vitality and health and of well-channeled power.

"It seemed important to you. What can we offer you? Some coffee, tea or perhaps some wine."

"Wine would be lovely." And would give her the prop of a glass to twist in her hands as she told her story.

"The Pouilly-Fumé, Barbara. Please sit, Miss Conroy. Be comfortable." In a move calculated to disarm her, he rounded the desk and took the chair beside her. "And how was your flight?"

"Long." Dora's smile was fleeting. "But I shouldn't complain. The weather was turning nasty at home. But of course, I'll go back tomorrow."

"So soon?" His bright eyes glinted with just the right touch of curiosity. "I'm flattered to have such a pretty young woman travel all this way just to see me."

His receptionist had uncorked the bottle. Obviously, Dora mused, her duties included those of a wine steward. She passed Finley the cork and tipped an inch of wine in his glass for approval.

"Yes," he said after rolling the wine on his tongue and swallowing. "That will do nicely." When the wine was poured in both glasses, the secretary slipped soundlessly out of the room. Finley raised his glass. "To your health, Miss Conroy, and a safe journey home."

"Thank you." It was beautiful wine, silk on the tongue, with just a hint of smoke. "I know it might sound foolish, coming all this way just to see you, Mr. Finley. But I honestly felt compelled." As if overcome, she looked down into the pale gold wine in her glass, let her fingers tighten on the stem. "Now that I'm here, I don't know where to start."

"I can see you're upset," Finley said kindly. "Take your time. You told me on the phone this had to do with Anthony DiCarlo. Are you . . ." He paused delicately. "A friend?"

"Oh no." There was horror in her voice, in her eyes as she dragged them back to Finley's. She imagined DiCarlo's voice whispering in her ear to bring the rusty edge of revulsion into her voice. "No. He—Mr. Finley, I need to ask how much you know about him."

"Personally?" Thinking, he pursed his lips. "I'm afraid I don't know many of my branch employees as well as I might. The company is very large now, and unfortunately that depersonalizes matters. We had a meeting here just before Christmas. I noticed nothing out of the ordinary. He seemed as competent as always."

"Then he's worked for you for some time?"

"Six years, I believe. More or less." He sipped more wine. "I have studied his file since this odd disappearance, to refresh my memory. He has an excellent record with the company. Mr. DiCarlo worked his way up the corporate ladder rather quickly. He showed initiative and ambition. Both of which I believe in rewarding. He came from a poor background, you know."

When she only shook her head, he smiled and continued. "As I did myself. The desire to better oneself—this is something I respect in an employee, and also tend to reward. As one of my top executives on the east coast, he's proven himself to be reliable and cunning." He smiled again. "In my business, one must be cunning. I'm very much afraid of foul play. As Mr. DiCarlo's work record would indicate, he isn't a man to neglect his responsibilities this way."

"I think—I think I might know where he is."

"Really?" There was a flash in Finley's eyes.

"I think he's in Philadelphia." As if to bolster her courage, Dora took another quick sip, and her hand shook lightly. "I think he's . . . watching me."

"My dear." Finley reached for her hand. "Watching you? What do you mean?"

"I'm sorry. It's not making sense. Let me try to start at the beginning."

She told the story well, with several pauses for composure, and one significant break in which she described the attack.

"And I don't understand," she finished, with her eyes wet and shimmering. "I don't understand why."

"My dear, how horrible for you." Finley was all baffled sympathy while his mind performed rapid calculations. It appeared DiCarlo had left out a few significant details, he mused. There had been no mention in his report of an attempted rape, nor of a knightly neighbor coming to the rescue. It explained the bruises on his face during his last, and final, visit, however.

"You're telling me," Finley began, his tone lightly shocked, "that the man who broke into your shop, the man who attacked you, was Anthony DiCarlo."

"I saw his face." As if overcome, Dora covered her own with her hand. "I'll never forget it. And I identified him to the police. He's killed a police officer, Mr. Finley, and a woman. He left another woman for dead, one of my customers." The thought of Mrs. Lyle urged the first tear down her cheek. "I'm sorry. I've been so upset, so frightened. Thank you," she managed when Finley gallantly offered his handkerchief. "None of it makes any sense, you see. He only stole a few trinkets, and as for Mrs. Lyle, my customer, he took nothing of any real value. Just a china dog, a statue she'd bought from me the day before. I think he must be crazy," she murmured, lowering her hand again. "I think he must be mad."

"I hope you understand this is difficult for me to take in. Mr. DiCarlo has worked for me for years. The idea of one of my own staff attacking women, murdering police officers. Miss Conroy—Isadora." He took her hand again, gently, a father comforting a child after a bad dream. "Are you absolutely certain it was Anthony DiCarlo?"

"I saw his face," she said again. "The police said he had a record. Nothing like—like this, and nothing for several years, but—"

"I knew he'd had some trouble." With a sigh, Finley sat back. "Just as I felt I understood the need to overcome the past mistakes. But I would never have believed... It seems I misjudged him, badly. What can I do to help you?"

"I don't know." Dora twisted the handkerchief in her hands. "I guess I'd hoped you'd have some idea what to do, where the police might look. If he contacted you—"

"My dear, I assure you, if he contacts me, I will do everything in my power to lead the authorities to him. Perhaps his family knows something?"

She dried her tears and, calmer, shook her head. "The police have questioned them, I believe. I actually thought of going to see his mother myself, but I couldn't. I couldn't face that."

"I'll make some calls. Do whatever I can to help you."

"Thank you." She let out a shaky sigh followed by a shaky smile. "I feel better doing something. The worst is the waiting, the not knowing where he is or what he's planning. I'm afraid to go to sleep at night. If he came back—" She shuddered, sincerely. "I don't know what I'd do."

"You have no reason to think he will. Are you sure he gave you no idea why he chose your shop?"

"None. That's what's so terrifying. To be picked at random that way. Then Mrs. Lyle. He shot her housekeeper and left Mrs. Lyle for dead, all for some little statue." Her eyes, still wet, were guileless and trusting. "A man doesn't kill for that, does he?"

"I wish I knew." Finley heaved a heartfelt sigh. "Perhaps, as you say, he's gone mad. But I have every confidence in the authorities. I'll say, with full confidence, that you won't be bothered by Mr. DiCarlo again."

"I'm trying to hold on to that. You've been very kind, Mr. Finley."

"Edmund."

"Edmund." She smiled again, courageously. "Just talking it out has helped. I'd like to ask, if you find anything, anything at all, that you'd call me. The police aren't very free with information."

"I understand. And, of course, I'll keep in touch with you. We have an excellent security team on retainer. I'm going to put them on this. If there's a trace of DiCarlo, they'll find it."

"Yes." She closed her eyes, let her shoulders relax. "I knew I was right to come here. Thank you." When she rose, he took both her hands in his. "Thank you so much for listening to me."

"I only regret I can't do more. I'd consider it a favor if you'd agree to have dinner with me tonight."

"Dinner?" Her mind went sheet blank.

"I don't like to think of you alone, and upset. I feel responsible. DiCarlo is, after all, my man. Or was," he corrected, with a small smile.

"That's very kind of you."

"Then indulge me. Ease my conscience a bit. And, I admit, I would find it very pleasant to spend the evening with a lovely young woman who shares some of my interests."

"Your interests?"

"Collecting." Finley gestured toward a curio cabinet. "If you run an antique and collectibles shop, I think you'd be interested in some of my treasures."

"Yes, I am. I'm sure you're much more knowledgeable than I, but I've already admired several of your pieces. The horse's head?" She nodded toward a stone figure. "Han dynasty?"

"Precisely." He beamed, a professor to a prize student. "You have a good eye."

"I love things," she confessed. "Owning things."

"Ah, yes. I understand." He reached up to brush a fingertip lightly over her lapel pin. "A plique-à-jour—early nineteen hundreds."

She beamed back at him. "You, too, have a good eye."

"I have a brooch I'd like you to see." He thought of the sapphire, and the pleasure it would give him to taunt her with it. "I only recently acquired it, and I know you'd appreciate it. So it is decided. I'll have a car pick you up at your hotel. Say, seven-thirty."

"I..."

"Please, don't misunderstand. My home is fully staffed, so you'll be well chaperoned. But I don't often have the opportunity to show off my treasures to someone who recognizes their intrinsic worth. I'd love your opinion on my pomander collection."

"Pomanders?" Dora said, and sighed. If she hadn't been on a mission, she'd have agreed in any case. How could she resist a collection of pomanders? "I'd love to."

Dora strolled back into the hotel room filled with the warmth of success. She found Jed pacing, the air blue with smoke and rattled by an old war movie on television he wasn't watching.

"What the hell took you so long?"

"It was only an hour." She slipped out of her shoes as she walked to him. "I was brilliant," she said, and wrapped her arms around his neck.

"I'll tell you if you were brilliant." He put a hand on top of her head and pushed her into a chair. Snatching the remote, he ended the war with a fizzle. "You tell me about Finley. Everything, from the top."

"Is there any coffee left?" She picked up a room-service pot, sniffed the contents. "Let me savor the moment, will you?" She poured coffee and sipped it black and tepid. "I want some cheesecake," she decided. "Order us up some cheesecake, okay?"

"Don't push it, Conroy."

"You know how to take the fun out of things. All right." She took a last sip, sat back and told him.

"He really was nice," she concluded. "Very understanding, and properly shocked by my story. I, of course, played the part of the high-strung, spooked-at-every-shadow heroine to perfection. The police simply aren't doing enough to ease my mind, so he very gallantly offered to do whatever he could, down to hiring a private firm to track down DiCarlo."

"What about Winesap?"

"He wasn't there. I asked for him at first, but the receptionist told me he was out of the office today."

"If he's the one who's going to keep the appointment next Thursday, he couldn't afford having you see him."

"I thought of that. So I stopped to talk to the security guard in the lower lobby on the way out. I told him I'd seen Abel Winesap's name on the board, and that my father had worked with an Abel Winesap once, years ago, and had lost touch. So I asked if this guy was tall and heavyset with red hair. It turns out this Winesap is short and skinny, round-shouldered and balding."

"Good girl, Nancy."

"Thanks, Ned. Do you think Nancy and Ned ever made love? You know, in the back of her coupe after a particularly satisfying case."

"I like to think so. Get back on track, Conroy."

"Okay." Now came the hard part, Dora mused. She would have to work up to it carefully. "Finley's office is incredible—oh, I forgot to mention the monitors. He has a whole wall of them. Kind of creepy, you know? All these television shows running silently side by side with different parts of the building. I guess he has security cameras everywhere. But that's not why it's incredible. He had a Gallé lamp in his office that made me want to sit up and beg. And a Han horse. That barely touches on it. Anyway, I'll see his personal collection at dinner tonight."

Jed snatched her wrist before she could bound up. "Play that back, Conroy, slow speed."

"I'm having dinner with him."

"What makes you think so?"

"Because he asked me, and I accepted. And before you start listing all the reasons why I shouldn't, I'll tell you why I should." She'd worked it out point by point in the cab on the way back. "He was kind to me in the office—very concerned and avuncular. He believes I'm in town alone, and that I'm upset. He knows I have a rabid interest in collectibles and antiques. If I'd said no, it would have set the entirely wrong tone."

"If he's involved, the last place you should be is alone with him, at his house."

"If he's involved," she countered, "the last place he'd want anything to happen would be his own house. Especially when I tell him I called my parents to check in and told them I'd be having dinner with him."

"It's a stupid idea."

"It isn't. It will give me more time to cultivate him. He likes me," she added, and walked over to the closet. She'd brought a little black dress along, and had paired it with a glittery bolero jacket in red and gold stripes. Holding them in front of her, she turned to the mirror. "He doesn't like the idea of me spending the evening alone in LA while I'm upset."

Jed watched the sequins glimmer through narrowed eyes. "Did he come on to you?"

Dora paused in the act of unbuttoning her suit jacket. "Are you jealous, Skimmerhorn?" The laugh bubbled out, quick and delighted. "Isn't that cute?"

"I am not jealous." He'd never been jealous of a woman in his life. Never. He wasn't about to admit it now. "I asked you a simple question, and I'd like an answer."

She took off the jacket, revealing the creamy lace and silk of the camisole beneath. "You're going to put yourself in the awkward position of making me tell you I love you again. We wouldn't want that, would we?"

When his stomach clenched, he swore under his breath, grabbed another cigarette. "Maybe I'm fed up with watching you deck yourself out for another man."

"That's what I'm here for, isn't it? To meet him, gain his sympathy and confidence and to find out everything I can." With her head tilted to the side, she studied Jed's set face. "Would you feel better if I told you I didn't have any intention of sleeping with him?"

"Yeah, I'll rest easy now." He blew out a frustrated stream of smoke. "I don't like you going in there alone. I don't have enough on him, and I don't like it."

"You'll have more when I get back, won't you?" She walked over to hang up the jacket. He crossed the room so quietly she jumped when his hands touched her shoulders.

"I'm not used to being the one who waits."

She arranged the jacket meticulously on the hanger. "I guess I can understand that."

"I never had anyone to worry about before. I don't like it."

"I can understand that, too." She unzipped her skirt and clipped it neatly on another hanger. "I'll be fine."

"Sure you will." He lowered his cheek to the back of her head. "Dora . . ." What could he say? he wondered. Nothing that was churning inside him seemed right. "I'll miss you tonight. I guess I've gotten used to having you around."

Wonderfully touched, she smiled and lifted a hand to cover one of his. "You're such a sentimental slob, Skimmerhorn. It's always hearts and flowers with you."

"Is that what you want?" He turned her to face him. "Is that what you're looking for?"

Her smile didn't quite reach her eyes as she brushed her knuckles over his cheek. "I've got a heart, thanks, and I can buy flowers anytime I like." To comfort him, she nuzzled her lips to his. "I've also got an hour before I have to get ready. Why don't you take me to bed?"

It would have been a pleasure, and a relief, but both pleasure and relief would have to wait. "We've got work to do, Conroy. Put on your robe, and we'll go over the ground rules for your dinner."

Huffing, she stepped back. "I'm standing here in little more than a lace garter belt and you're telling me to put on a robe?"

"That's right."

"You have gotten used to me," she muttered.

26

Dora stepped off the curb and into a white Mercedes limo at precisely seven-thirty. There was a single white rosebud laid across the seat, and a Beethoven sonata playing softly on the stereo. A bottle of champagne was iced beside a crystal bowl of beluga.

Brushing the rose petals across her cheek, she looked up toward the window where she knew Jed would be watching.

Too bad, she mused as the car pulled smoothly away. It appeared that she did need hearts and flowers, and was unlikely to receive them from the man who mattered most.

Because she was looking back she noticed a man in a gray suit slip into a dark sedan and cruise out into traffic behind them.

Dora closed her eyes, slipped out of her shoes to run her bare feet luxuriously over the plush carpet and put all thoughts of Jed behind her.

For the next few hours, she was alone.

Armed with a glass of champagne and a toast point of caviar, she enjoyed the ride up into the hills. Though under other circumstances she might have struck up a conversation with the driver, she hugged the silence to her and prepared for Act Two.

After her impressions of his office, she'd expected Finley's house to be lavish. She wasn't disappointed. The sweeping drive up, the quick, teasing peeks of the building through screening trees. Then the full impact of stone and brick and glass simmering in the last fiery lights of the dying sun.

A well-set stage.

She took the rose with her.

There was only a moment to appreciate the Adam door knocker in the shape of a dolphin before the door was opened by a uniformed maid.

"Miss Conroy. Mr. Finley would like you to wait in the drawing room."

Dora didn't bother to disguise her open-mouthed admiration for the magnificence of the entrance hall. In the parlor she gave the maid a murmured assent at the offer of wine, and was grateful when she had the glass in hand and was alone to worship.

She felt as though she had entered some personal museum, one structured for her alone. Everything she saw was spectacular, and every piece her eyes feasted on seemed more glorious. So glorious it was impossible not to gorge.

She saw herself reflected in the George III mirror, ran her fingers delicately over a mahogany armchair of the same period, crooned over a Japanese Kakiemon tiger.

When Finley joined her she was mentally devouring a collection of netsukes.

"I see you're enjoying my toys."

"Oh yes." Eyes dark and brilliant with appreciation, she turned from the curios. "I feel like Alice, and I've just stumbled into the best corner of Wonderland."

He laughed and poured himself a glass of wine. He'd known he would enjoy her. "I was certain I'd find it pleasant to share my things with you. I'm afraid I spend too much time alone with them."

"You've made my trip very worthwhile, Mr. Finley."

"Then I'm content." He walked over, placed a light hand at the small of her back. It wasn't a suggestive move. She had no explanation as to why her skin crawled under the friendly pressure. "You were looking at the netsukes." He opened the curio and deliberately chose one of the pieces of erotica that had been smuggled in the mermaid bookends. "Not everyone can appreciate the humor and the sexuality, as well as the artistry of these pieces."

Chuckling, she took the figure of the man and woman into her palm. "But they look so pleased with themselves, trapped forever in that moment of anticipation. It's hard to imagine some stoic samurai with something like this dangling from his obi."

Finley merely smiled. "And yet that's precisely how I like to imagine it. Worn by a warlord, into bed and into battle. One of the Tokugawa family, perhaps. I enjoy giving a history to each of my possessions." He replaced the figure. "Shall I give you the tour before dinner?"

"Yes, please." Agreeably, she slipped a hand through his arm.

He was knowledgeable, erudite and entertaining, Dora thought. Why, before an hour was up, she was violently uncomfortable she couldn't have said.

He took a greedy delight in all that he'd acquired, yet she understood greed. He was unfailingly correct in his manner toward her, yet she felt increasingly as though she were being subtly violated. It took all of her skill and control to play out her prescribed role as they moved from room to room. By the time they were nearly finished, she'd begun to understand that one could have too much of even the beautiful and precious.

"This is the pin I mentioned earlier." Excited by the fact that he was showing her each and every one of the smuggled items, Finley offered her the sapphire brooch. "The stone is, of course, magnificent, but the workmanship of the setting, and again, the history, add intrigue."

"It's beautiful." It was, the gleaming blue eye winking up at her from its bed of delicate gold filigree and fiery diamonds, both beautiful and tragic. Tragic, she realized, because it would be forever behind glass, never again to grace a woman's silks or make her smile when she adorned herself with it.

Perhaps that was the difference between them. She passed her treasures on, gave them a new life. Finley locked his away.

"It was said to belong to a queen," Finley told her, waiting, watching her face for a sign of recognition. "Mary, Queen of Scots. I often wonder if she wore it when she was arrested for treason."

"I'd rather think of her wearing it when she was riding across the moors."

"And this." He chose the etui. "This belonged to another queen with a sad fate. Napoleon gave it to Josephine. Before he divorced her for being barren."

"You give your treasures a sad history, Edmund."

"I find poignancy increases their meaning for me. The trinkets of the rich and the royal, now a part of the collection of a commoner. Shall we dine?"

There was lobster bisque and Peking duck so delicate it all but melted on the tongue. The meal was served on Limoges and eaten with Georgian silver. Dom Perignon was poured into antique Waterford that glittered like crystal tears.

"Tell me about your shop," Finley invited. "It must be exciting for you to buy and sell every day, to handle lovely things time and again."

"I do love it." Dora fought to relax and enjoy the meal. "I'm afraid most of what I have falls far below your collections. What I stock is a mixture of antiques and estate items, along with . . ." Junk—she all but heard Jed's sneering and comforting voice. "Novelty items," she said a bit primly. "I love the foolish as well as the beautiful."

"And, like myself, you appreciate the having, the control. There's something innately satisfying about making your own business out of something you love. Not everyone has the opportunity, or the courage, to make it a success. I believe, Isadora, that you have a great deal of courage."

Her stomach fluttered, but she managed to swallow the bite of duck. "My family considers it stubbornness. I hate to confess, but I frighten very easily."

"You underestimate yourself. After all, you came here, to me." He smiled, watching her over the rim of his glass with eyes as sharp as carved jade. "For all you knew, DiCarlo might have been acting on my orders. After all, he is—was—an employee."

When she went pale and set down her fork with a rattle, he laughed, patted her hand. "Now I have frightened you. I apologize. It was merely said to illustrate my point. What sense would it make for me to have DiCarlo break into your shop and steal a few trinkets when I could so easily acquire them myself?"

"I doubt I'd have very much you'd find interesting."

"Oh, I disagree." He smiled and signaled for dessert. "I believe I'd find a great deal of what you have to offer of interest. Tell me," he said, "do you ever come across any Grueby?"

"I once had a statue of a boy—badly chipped, I'm afraid." She fisted and unfisted her hands in her lap as the creamy chocolate soufflé was served. "I noticed your vase in the library. It's lovely."

She relaxed into the discussion of pottery, and began to believe that she'd imagined he'd been baiting her.

Later, they had coffee and brandy before a sedate fire in the drawing room. The conversation was easy again, like that of old friends. All the while Dora's nerves drummed. She'd never wanted to escape so badly in her life.

"I'm sorry you can't extend your visit." Finley passed a small porcelain nude from hand to hand.

"Running a business doesn't give one as much flexible time as some people think. I'm sure you'd understand."

"Yes, indeed. There are times when I feel a prisoner of my own success. Do you?" He skimmed a fingertip over the nude's glossy breast. "Feel trapped?"

"No." But she couldn't shake the sensation that the walls of the room were shrinking in on her. "You must have marvelous contacts." Again she scanned the room. She couldn't watch the way he was fondling the nude. "Do you do much of the traveling and acquiring?"

"Not as much as I'd like. Over the years I've had to delegate that pleasure. But I take the occasional trip to the Orient, or Europe. I even get to the east coast from time to time."

"I hope you'll let me return your hospitality if you're ever in Philadelphia."

"I wouldn't think of taking the trip without paying you a call."

"Then I hope you find the time to come east soon. It was a wonderful meal, Edmund, a delightful evening." She rose to play her final scene, the contented guest taking a reluctant leave.

"Believe me, it was my pleasure." He stood, took her hand and kissed it gallantly at the knuckles. "I'd be happy to arrange for my car to take you to the airport tomorrow."

"That's so nice." It made her feel ashamed of the urge she had to rub her hand clean on her jacket. "But I've already arranged transportation. Please, call me if you—if there's any news about DiCarlo."

"I will. I have a feeling it will all be sorted out very soon."

When she returned to the Beverly Hills Hotel, Dora waited until the limo had driven away, then simply stood on the sidewalk breathing slowly and waiting to calm. She didn't want to face Jed until she had herself under control.

She felt idiotic to be shaken. Though she knew she would have to tell him how the evening had affected her, she wanted to be cool and precise when she did so.

Then she saw the dark sedan pull up across the street. And the man with the gray suit.

On a skidder of panic she bolted into the lobby.

Jumping at shadows, Conroy, she berated herself while her heartbeat roared in her ears. Chin up, she punched the button for the elevator. It was just jet lag. It helped a great deal to believe it. She was overtired and overstressed. Once she'd gotten through relaying everything to Jed, she'd get a good night's sleep and be fine again.

By the time she'd ridden up to her floor and slipped the key into the lock, she had herself back in line. She was even able to smile when she walked in and saw Jed scowling out of the window.

"Ah, you waited up for me."

"You're always good for a laugh, Conroy. You really ought to—" He broke off after he'd turned and gotten a look at her. He hadn't known anyone could appear so exhausted and still stand on both feet.

"What?" Such were her nerves that she groped at her throat and stepped back. "What is it?"

"Nothing. My mind was wandering. Have a seat."

"I'd just as soon get out of this dress first." Habit had her going to the closet for a hanger.

"Let me give you a hand." He tugged down the zipper for her. Casually, he gave her shoulders a quick massage and found them, as he'd suspected, knotted with tension. "You want a nightgown or something?"

"Or something." She sat tiredly on the edge of the bed to remove her hose. "You had something for dinner, didn't you?"

"I'm a big boy now, Conroy." He unhooked the black strapless bra, tossed it aside, then slipped the thin nightshirt over her head.

"We had duck."

"Beats the hell out of my cheeseburger."

"It was excellent. The house—really, you should see it. It's immense, with all these lofty rooms leading into other lofty rooms. I've never seen so many museum-quality pieces in one place."

When her eyes began to droop, she shook her head. "I need to wash my face. You should see if you can get some kind of financial report on E.F., Incorporated." In the bathroom she ran the water cold, scooping it up with both hands to splash on her face. "The butler served coffee out of a Meissen worth ten, twelve thousand." She yawned and splashed more water. "And a paperweight in the library—an Alméric Walter. I watched one go at Christie's a couple of years ago for fifteen big ones. Plus this—"

"I don't want an inventory."

"Sorry." After choosing a tube from the bathroom counter, she began creaming off her makeup. "I've never seen a collection to compare with it. Never heard of one to compare with it. You can't even call it a collection, really. It's more of a private little empire." Dutifully, she dabbed on moisturizer. "And there was something odd about the way he showed it to me."

"In what way?"

"Like he was waiting for me to do something, say something." She shook her head. "I don't know. I can't explain exactly, but the atmosphere was different than it had been in his office." Her eyes met his in the mirror. There were faint bruises of fatigue under hers and a fragility to her skin now that it was without the shield of cosmetics. "He spooked me, Jed. He was a perfect gentleman, a perfect host. And being alone with him terrified me."

"Tell me." He combed a hand through her hair. "It doesn't have to make sense."

Relieved, she nodded and walked back in to sit on the side of the bed. "He took me all through the house," she began. "And like I said, there was something off about the way he showed off his pieces. A handful of them in particular. I could feel him watching me when I looked at them, and it was . . . it was like watching someone masturbate. I kept telling myself I was imagining it because he was being so charming. We had dinner, this elegant dinner in this elegant room on elegant china. And we discussed art and music, and so forth. He never touched me in a way that wasn't perfectly correct, but . . ."

She laughed a little. "I'd really appreciate it if you wouldn't say I was being an overimaginative female when I tell you this, because that's exactly how I feel. But I felt as though he was seeing me naked. We're spooning up this incredibly delicate soufflé with Georgian silver and I felt as though he could see right through my dress. I have no explanation for it, just that unshakable and very creepy feeling."

"Maybe he was thinking of you that way. Men do, even elegant ones."

She could only shake her head. "No, it wasn't like that—not really sexual on either side. It was more like being defenseless."

"You were alone."

"Not really—or not often. He has an army of servants. I wasn't really afraid that he'd hurt me. I was afraid he wanted to. And there was that business in the bathroom."

"He took you into the bathroom?"

"No. I went into the powder room after dinner. I was freshening my makeup, and I kept feeling like he was right there, watching over my shoulder."

She blew out a breath, grateful that Jed didn't snort and tell her she was being a fool. "I honestly didn't think he had anything to do with this whole business after I'd left his office this afternoon. And now, I don't know what to think. I do know that I wouldn't want to go back into that house even if he offered me my pick of his pomanders. Which, I might add, were wonderful."

"You don't have to go back. We'll see if the IRS wants to poke a few fingers into Finley's pie."

"Good." There was a throbbing over her left eye she couldn't quite rub away. "You might see what you can find out about a sapphire brooch—possibly sixteenth-century. The stone looked to be about eight carats in a horizontal setting of gold filigree with some small, round-cut diamonds. He made a real issue of showing it to me."

"Fine. You did good."

"Yeah." She gave him a sleepy smile. "Do I get a detective's gold star?"

"That's gold shield, Nancy. And no. You're retiring."

"Good."

"You want something for that headache?"

She stopped rubbing her temple long enough to grimace. "Morphine, but I didn't bring any along. I do have something less effective in my makeup bag."

"I'll get it. Stretch out."

She took him up on it without bothering to crawl under the sheets. "I forgot. I saw this guy in a dark sedan—God, that sounds like a Charlie Chan movie. Anyway, I saw him pull out after the limo when we left. Then he drove up a few minutes after I got back. I don't know why Finley would have me followed to and from his house though."

"He didn't. I did. Where the hell do you keep pills? You've got all these little bottles."

"The pills aren't in a bottle, they're in a box. What we call a pillbox in the trade."

"Smartass."

"The little one with the enameled violets. What do you mean you had me followed?"

"I've had you tailed all day. Local PI."

She was smiling when he walked out with the pills. "Almost as good as flowers," she murmured. "You hired a bodyguard for me."

"I hired him for me," he said lightly.

After pillowing her head on her folded arms, she shut her eyes.

Straddling her, he began to rub her neck and shoulders. "Relax, Conroy, you don't get rid of a stress headache by tensing up."

But his fingers were already working their magic. "Jed?" Her voice was a thick murmur, hardly audible.

"Yeah."

"Mirrors. I forgot. He has dozens of them. You couldn't walk into a room without seeing yourself coming and going."

"So he's vain."

"I've got a cheval glass I could probably sell him."

"Shut up, Conroy. You're off the clock."

"Okay, but I don't think he just likes to watch himself. I think he likes to watch."

"Okay. He's a vain pervert." He ran the heels of his hands down the sides of her spine.

"I know. That doesn't make him a smuggler. I wish..."

"Wish what?"

But whatever she wished, it would remain unsaid. She was asleep.

Quietly, he turned down the covers and, lifting her, slipped her between the sheets. She never stirred. Jed studied her a moment before he turned off the lights, got in bed beside her. After a little while, he gathered her close to hold her while he joined her in sleep.

Because his arms were around her, her first shudders awakened him. Instinctively he tightened his grip, his hand soothing at her neck.

"Hey. Hey, Dora, come on. Pull out of it." He heard her gasping gulp of air, and her body trembled hard as she broke through the surface of the dream. "Bad one, huh?" he murmured.

She responded by pressing her face to his chest. "Can you reach the light? I need the light."

"Sure." Keeping an arm firm around her, he shifted to grope for the switch. The light flashed, cutting through the unrelieved dark. "Better?"

"Yeah." But she continued to shiver.

"Want some water?"

"No." The instant panic in the word had her biting down on her lip. "Just stay right here, okay?"

"Okay."

"And don't let go."

"I won't."

And because he didn't, her fluttering heart began to settle again. "That was the first nightmare I've had since I reread Stephen King's *The Shining*."

"Scary book." Though his eyes were far from calm, the kiss he brushed over her hair was light and easy. "Too bad about the movie."

"Yeah." Her laugh was shaky, but it was a laugh. "I didn't know you went in for horror stuff, Skimmerhorn."

"It relieves tension. It's tough to worry about life's little problems when you're reading about kiddie vampires or the walking dead."

"I've always been a sucker for the walking dead." Because he didn't ask, didn't press, she found herself able to tell him. "I was in that house, Finley's house—all those rooms and mirrors. All those things, those beautiful things. Did you ever read *Something Wicked?*"

"Bradbury. Sure."

"In the carnival, that house of mirrors? Remember, if you bought a ticket, they promised you you'd find what you wanted inside. But it was a very nasty trick. That's what it was like. I wanted to see all those beautiful things. Then I couldn't get out. DiCarlo was in there, too, and Finley. Every time I turned, one of them was there, reflected all around me. I kept running into walls of glass." Taking comfort in the heat of Jed's body, the press of muscle, she cuddled closer. "I feel like a jerk."

"You shouldn't. I've had some beauts."

"You have?" Intrigued, she tilted her head to study his face. "Really?"

"My rookie year I responded to a 'shots fired.' I was lucky enough to be first on the scene of a murder-suicide." He didn't add that what was left of a human head after a shotgun blast was not a pretty sight. "My subconscious pulled that little scene out on me in the middle of the night for weeks after. And after Elaine..." He hesitated, then continued. "I kept reliving that. Running across the lawn, through the roses. Watching her turn her head to look at me. The sound of the blast when she turned the key. I'll take the kiddie vampires any day."

"Yeah. Me too." They lay for a moment in silence. "Jed?"

"Hmmm?"

"You want to see if there's an old horror movie on TV?"

"Conroy, it's nearly six in the morning."

"It's too dark to be nearly six in the morning."

"The drapes are closed."

"Oh."

"Tell you what." He shifted, rolling on top of her and catching her chin between his teeth. "Why don't I show you something really scary?"

She chuckled, and slipped her arms around his neck just as the phone shrilled beside them. Her heart shot to her throat and pushed out a shriek.

"Hold that thought," he murmured, then lifted the receiver. "Skimmerhorn."

"Jed. Sorry to wake you." But the edge of excitement in Brent's voice had nothing to do with apology. "I've got something you might want to check out."

"Yeah?" Automatically Jed rolled over and picked up the pen from the nightstand.

"I just picked up a fax from the sheriff's department out there. A couple of hikers stumbled over a body a few days ago wedged in a shallow ravine in the hills. There was enough left for a couple of prints. We can stop looking for DiCarlo. He's real dead."

"How long?"

"They're having a tough time pinpointing it, given the exposure and the wildlife. Sometime around the first of the year. Since you're out there, I figured you might want to talk to the coroner, the investigating officers."

"Give me the names." Jed wrote down the information.

"I'm going to fax them back as soon as I hang up with you," Brent continued. "Tell them that you were on a related investigation out there. They'll be ready for you."

"Thanks. I'll be in touch."

Dora was sitting up in bed, her chin resting on her drawn-up knees, studying Jed when he hung up the phone. "You've got cop all over your face. It's an interesting metamorphosis to witness."

"Why don't you order up some breakfast?" He was already out of bed and on his way to the shower. "We're going to have to take a later flight."

"All right." She heard the water start. Her jaw clenched. Tossing back the covers, she marched into the bathroom, yanked back the shower curtain. "It's not enough to give orders, Captain. Some of us recruits require minimal information."

"I've got something to check on." He scooped up the soap. "In or out, Conroy, you're getting water all over the floor."

"What do you have to check on?"

He decided the issue himself by reaching out and tugging the nightshirt over her head. She didn't object when he lifted her up and into the tub with him. Saying nothing, she adjusted the hot water so that it wouldn't blister the skin. She dragged the wet hair out of her eyes. "What do you have to check on?" she repeated.

"DiCarlo," he said flatly. "They've found him."

27

Sheriff Curtis Dearborne harbored an innate distrust of outsiders. Since he considered any member of the LAPD an outsider, an east coast cop was an entity to be watched with extra care.

He was a towering, well-muscled man who wore his uniform proudly starched, kept his sandy moustache well trimmed and lightly waxed, and spit-polished his boots. Beneath his military sense of polish and style lurked a well of country-boy charm that he used cleverly and with great success.

He rose from his desk when Jed and Dora entered. His square, handsome face was set in serious lines, his handshake was dry and firm.

"Captain Skimmerhorn. Pretty handy you being out our way when we identify the John Doe."

Jed summed up his man instantly. Dearborne was going to be territorial. Jed's first move was to acknowledge Dearborne's authority.

"I appreciate your passing on the information, Sheriff. I'm sure Lieutenant Chapman filled you in on the mess we've got back home. This quick work on your part will be some comfort to Officer Trainor's widow."

It was exactly the right button. Dearborne's eyes frosted, his mouth thinned. "Your lieutenant told me the corpse was a cop killer. I'm only sorry the coyotes didn't take more of an interest in him. Sit down, Captain, Miss Conroy."

"Thanks." Stemming impatience, Jed took a seat. If he rushed Dearborne, it would probably cost him hours of time in diplomacy. "I was told there was no identification on the body."

"Not a lick." Dearborne's chair creaked comfortably as he sat back. "But we ruled out robbery right off. The wallet was gone, but the guy had a diamond on his pinkie and one of those gold chains around his neck." Dearborne sneered just enough to let Jed know he considered such trappings suspiciously unmasculine. "The body wasn't in such good shape, but I didn't need the coroner to tell me how he bought it. He'd been gut-shot. Not much blood on the tarp he'd been wrapped in though. Stands to reason the body had been moved after he bled to death. Probably took a good long nasty time. Begging your pardon, ma'am," he said for Dora's benefit. "Coroner confirmed it."

"I'd like a look at the coroner's report, if that's all right," Jed began. "And any physical evidence you've gathered. The more I go back with, the better."

Dearborne drummed his fingers on the desk as he considered. East Coast wasn't pushy, he decided. "I think we can accommodate you there. We've got the tarp and what's left of his clothes downstairs. I'll have the rest of the paperwork brought in after you've finished. If you want a look at the body, we'll take a run down to the coroner's."

"I'd appreciate that. If Miss Conroy could wait here?" he said as Dora started to rise.

"That's fine." Dearborne admired a woman who knew her place. "You just make yourself comfortable."

"Thank you, Sheriff. I wouldn't want to get in the way." The sarcasm was thinly veiled, but Dearborne wasn't a man for subtleties. "May I use my credit card to make a call?"

"Help yourself." Dearborne gestured toward the phone on his desk. "Use line one."

"Thank you." There was no use being annoyed with Jed, she mused. In any case, while he was off doing cop things, she could let her family know she was being delayed a few hours. After Jed and Dearborne trooped off, she settled behind Dearborne's desk. And she smiled. She wondered if Jed realized that Dearborne had called him "Captain"—and that Jed hadn't even winced at the title.

He'll have his badge back by spring, she predicted, and wondered what Jed Skimmerhorn would be like when he was completely happy.

"Good afternoon, Dora's Parlor."

"You've got a great voice, honey. Ever think about phone sex?"

Lea answered with a rich chuckle. "All the time. Hey, where are you? At thirty thousand feet?"

"No." Dora pushed back her hair and sent a smile to the officer who carried in a mug of coffee and a file folder. "Thank you, Sergeant," she said, deliberately mistaking his rank.

"Oh, it's just deputy, ma'am." But he flushed and grinned. "And you're welcome."

"Sergeant?" Lea demanded. "What, are you in jail or something? Do I have to post bond?"

"Not yet." She picked up the mug, tapping a finger idly against the file the deputy had set on the desk. "Just taking care of a little business Jed wanted to handle while we were here." No need to mention dead guys and gut shots, she mused. No need at all. "So we'll be taking a later plane. Everything there okay?"

"Everything's fine. We sold the Sherbourne desk this morning."

"Oh." As always with a particularly loved piece, Dora felt the twin tugs of pleasure and regret.

"No haggling either." The smug pride came through. "Oh, how did your meeting go?"

"Meeting?"

"With the import-export guy."

"Oh." Hedging, Dora thumbed at the file tab. "It went. I don't think we'll be doing business after all. He's out of my league."

"Well, I don't suppose you'd consider the trip a waste. See any movie stars?"

"Not a one, sorry."

"Oh well. You had Jed along to help you soak up the LA sunshine."

"There was that." She didn't add that she calculated she'd spent more time with Jed on the plane than she had since they'd landed.

"Call me when you get in so I'll know you're safe and sound."

"All right, Mommy. I don't imagine we'll make it much before ten your time, so don't start worrying until after eleven."

"I'll try to restrain myself. Oh, I should warn you, Mom's planning on having an informal gathering—so she can check Jed out on a more personal level. I thought you should know."

"Thanks a lot." Sighing, Dora idly flipped open the folder. "I'll try to prepare Jed for—" Her mouth went dust dry as she stared down at the photo. Through the buzzing in her head, she heard her sister's voice.

"Dora? Dory? Are you still there? Shoot. Did we get cut off?"

"No." With a herculean effort, Dora leveled her voice. Even when she lifted her gaze to stare at the wall, the photo's grim image remained imprinted on her mind. "Sorry, I have to go. I'll call you later."

"Okay. See you tomorrow, honey. Safe trip."

"Thanks. Bye." Very gently, very deliberately, Dora replaced the receiver. Her hands had gone icy cold beneath a sheer layer of sweat. Breathing shallowly, she looked back down.

It was DiCarlo. There was enough of his face left for her to be sure of that. She was also sure that he hadn't died well, that he hadn't died easy. With numb fingers she shifted the first police photo aside and stared at the second.

She knew now just how viciously cruel death could be to human flesh. No amount of Hollywood horror fantasies had prepared her for this ghastly reality. She could see where the bullet had ripped, where the animals had feasted. The desert sun had been every bit as merciless as the bullet and the carrion. The color photo was both lurid and dispassionate.

She couldn't stop looking, couldn't take her eyes away even when the buzzing in her head became a roar. She couldn't stop looking even when her vision blurred and grayed until the bloated body seemed to float off the surface of the photo toward her horrified eyes.

Jed let out one concise oath when he walked in and saw her white face and the open file. Even as he strode toward her he watched her eyes roll back. He had her chair pushed away from the desk and her head between her knees in two brisk moves.

"Just breathe slow." His voice was drum tight, but the hand on the back of her head was gentle as he reached up and slapped the file closed.

"I was calling Lea." Dora swallowed desperately as her stomach heaved. Bile tickled gleefully in the back of her throat. "I was just calling Lea."

"Keep your head down," he ordered. "And breathe."

"Try a little of this." Dearborne held out a glass of water to Jed. There was sympathy in his voice. He remembered his first murder victim. Most good cops did. "There's a cot in the back room if she wants to stretch out."

"She'll be all right." Jed kept the pressure light on Dora's head as he accepted the water. "Would you give us a minute, Sheriff?"

"Sure. Take your time," Dearborne added before he closed the door behind him.

"I want you to come up real slow," Jed told her. "If you feel faint again, put your head back down."

"I'm okay." But the trembling was worse than the nausea, and much more difficult to control. She let her head fall back against the chair and kept her eyes closed. "I guess I've made a lasting impression on the sheriff."

"Try some of this." He brought the cup to her lips, urging her to swallow. "I want you to feel better before I yell at you."

"You might have to wait awhile." She opened her eyes as she sipped. Yes, his were angry, she realized. Really angry. But she couldn't worry about that just yet. "How can you face that?" she said softly. "How can you possibly face that on a regular basis?"

He dipped his fingers in the cool water and rubbed them on the back of her neck. "Do you want to lie down?"

"No, I don't want to lie down." She looked away from him. "And if you have to yell, get it over with. But before you do, you should know I wasn't prying or playing detective. Believe me, I didn't want to see that. I didn't need to see that."

"Now you can start working on forgetting it."

"Is that what you do?" She made herself look at him again. "Do you just file this sort of thing away and forget it?"

"We're not talking about me. You have no business being this close, Dora."

"I have no business?" She moistened her dry lips and set the cup aside before she forced herself to stand. "The man inside that file tried to rape me. He would certainly have killed me. That brings me pretty Goddamn close. Even knowing that, knowing what he did and what he tried to do, I can't justify what I saw in those pictures. I just can't. I guess I want to know if you can."

He'd seen enough to know just what kind of afterimage she'd be carrying with her. He'd seen enough to know it was worse than most. "I don't justify, Dora. If you want to know if I can live with it, then yeah, I can. I can look at it. I can go down to the coroner's right now and take a good long look at the real thing. And I can live with it."

She nodded, then walked shakily to the door. "I'm going to wait in the car."

Jed waited until she was gone before he picked up the file and studied the photos. He swore, not at what he saw, but at what Dora had seen.

"She okay?" Dearborne asked as he came back in.

"She'll do." He handed the file over. "I'd like to take you up on your offer of talking to the coroner."

"Guess you want to see the stiff, too."

"I'd appreciate it."

"No problem." Dearborne picked up his hat, settled it on his head. "You can read the autopsy report on the way. It's interesting. Our pal had a hell of a last meal."

Dora refused the snack the flight attendant offered and stuck with icy ginger ale. Her system balked at even the thought of food. She did her best to ignore the scents of deli meat and mayo as the other passengers dug in.

She'd had a lot of time to think, stretched out on the front seat of the rental car while Jed had been with Dearborne. Time enough to realize that she'd taken her shock and revulsion out on him. And he hadn't taken his anger out on her.

"You haven't yelled at me yet."

Jed continued to work his crossword puzzle. He'd have preferred to read through Dearborne's reports again, but they would wait until he was alone. "It didn't seem worth it."

"I'd rather you did, so you'd stop being mad at me."

"I'm not mad at you."

"Could've fooled me." She wasn't certain what she was feeling herself, only knew it had to be put behind them. "You've hardly spoken since we left LA. And if I hadn't been making a fool of myself in the sheriff's office, you'd have torn into me." His eyes flicked up from his paper to meet her strained smile. "You wanted to."

"Yeah, I wanted to. But I wasn't mad at you. I was mad because you'd seen those pictures. Because I knew you'd walked through a door you wouldn't close easily, and never completely. There was nothing I could do about it."

She put a hand over his. "I can't go as far as saying I'm glad I opened that file. But you were right, it brings me closer. I think I'd handle it all better if you told me what you found out from Sheriff Dearborne and at the coroner's. Speculation can be even worse than reality."

"There isn't that much to tell." But he let the paper fall into his lap. "We know DiCarlo flew out to the coast on New Year's Eve, rented a car, booked a hotel room. He didn't sleep in the room that night, he didn't return the car. That hasn't turned up yet, either. Apparently he'd also booked a flight for Cancún, but he didn't use the ticket."

"So he didn't plan on coming back east anytime soon." She left her hand over his as she tried to think it through. "Do you think he came out to see Finley?"

"If he did, he didn't sign in. There's no record of him going to the offices on that date. If we go by the theory that he was working for himself, DiCarlo might have run into some bad luck on his way out of the country. Or he could have had a partner, a business disagreement."

"Makes me glad I'm in business for myself," Dora murmured.

"Or, choice number three, and my personal favorite, he worked for Finley, came out to report, and Finley killed him or had him killed."

"But why? DiCarlo hadn't finished the job, had he? I still had the painting."

"That might be the reason." Jed shrugged. "But there's no physical evidence to link Finley to any of it at this point. We know DiCarlo came to LA, and he died there. He was murdered sometime between December thirty-first and January second—as far as the coroner can pinpoint at this time. He died from a single gunshot wound to the abdomen, then, from the lack of blood on the tarp, was moved several hours later. Someone had the presence of mind to take his wallet to slow up the identification if and when his body was found. The bruises on the face were several days old. I put them there myself. Other traumas occurred after death."

He couldn't bring himself to tell her that DiCarlo had also been kneecapped.

"I see." To keep her voice clear and steady, she continued to sip the ginger ale like medicine. "That's like no signs of struggle, right?"

"That's right, Miss Drew." He gave her hand an approving squeeze. She was toughing it out, he thought, and admired her for it. "The condemned man had enjoyed a hearty last meal that had included pheasant, a considerable amount of wine and raspberries with white chocolate."

Nope, Dora thought as her stomach curdled, she definitely wouldn't be eating anytime soon. "Then one would assume," she began, pressing her free hand surreptitiously to her roiling stomach, "that the deceased was relaxed before he died."

"Kind of tough to put away a meal like that if you're tense. Dearborne's going to have his hands full checking restaurant menus. There were also some white stones and mulch found rolled up in the tarp. The kind you find in flower beds and around ornamental shrubs."

"I wonder how many flower beds there are in the LA area."

"I told you police work was tedious. Did Finley have gardens?"

"Extensive ones." She let out a shaky breath. "He's very proud of them, and was disappointed that there was a cloud cover so he couldn't show them to me properly in natural starlight. I admired part of them from his solarium." Her color had drained again when she turned to look at Jed, but her voice was level. "They were very neat and tidy, well mulched with narrow pathways of white stone."

"You've got good eyes, Conroy." He leaned over and kissed her. "Now close them for a while."

"I think I'd be better off watching the movie." She reached unsteadily for the headphone. "What did they say it was?"

"It's the new Costner flick." Jed plugged the cord in for her. "I think he plays a cop."

"Perfect." Dora sighed, slipped on the headphones and escaped.

In LA Winesap entered Finley's office. Timid men, like small dogs, often sense the mood of their master by the scent of the air. Winesap was wringing his hands.

"You wanted to see me, Mr. Finley?"

Without looking up from his paperwork, Finley gestured Winesap in. With a stroke of his pen he initialed changes in a contract that would eliminate nearly two hundred jobs. His eyes were blank when he sat back.

"How long have you worked for me, Abel?"

"Sir?" Winesap moistened his lips. "Eight years now."

"Eight years." Nodding slowly, Finley steepled his index fingers and tapped his top lip. "A fair amount of time. Are you happy in your work, Abel? You feel you're well treated, well compensated?"

"Oh, yes, sir. Absolutely, sir. You're very generous, Mr. Finley."

"I like to think so. And just, Abel. Do you find me a just man, as well?"

"Always." Unbidden, the image of DiCarlo's bloody body flashed into his brain. "Without exception, sir."

"I've been thinking of you this morning, Abel, all through the morning and into the afternoon. And as I did so, it occurred to me that over these—eight years, did you say?"

"Yes, eight." Winesap began to feel like a spider stunned by a hornet. "Eight years."

"That over these eight years," Finley continued, "I've had very little cause to criticize your work. You are prompt, you are efficient, you are—in most cases—thorough."

"Thank you, sir." But Winesap only heard the words "most cases." He felt fear. "I do my best."

"I believe you do. Which is why I find myself so disappointed today. I believe you did your best, and it wasn't quite enough."

"Sir?" Winesap's voice was a squeak.

"You perhaps haven't found the time in your busy schedule to read the morning paper?"

"I glanced at the headlines," Winesap said apologetically. "Things have been a bit hectic."

"One should always make time for current events." With his eyes glittering on Winesap's face, Finley stabbed a finger at the newspaper on his desk. "Such as this. Read it now, Abel, if you will."

"Yes, sir." All but shaking in terror, Winesap approached the desk and took the paper. The article Finley referred to was circled over and over again in blood-red ink. " 'Body discovered by hikers,' " Winesap began, and felt his bowels loosen. " 'An-an unidentified body was discovered several days ago in a r-ravine—' "

Finley snatched the paper away with a snap. "Your reading voice is weak, Abel. Let me do it for you." In flowing, melodious tones, Finley read the sketchy report, ending with the standard line about the police investigating. "Of course," he added, smoothing the paper out on his desk, "we would be able to identify the body, wouldn't we, Abel?"

"Mr. Finley. Sir. It was found miles from here. No one would possibly..." He cringed, lowering his eyes.

"I expected better from you, Abel. That was my mistake. You were not thorough," he said, spacing each word carefully. "They will, of course, identify the body sooner or later. And I will be forced to answer more questions. Naturally, I'm confident that I can handle the police, but the inconvenience, Abel. I really believe you should have spared me this inconvenience."

"Yes, sir. I'm terribly sorry." Winesap thought of the miserable drive into the mountains, the hideous trek with the body dragging behind him. His shoulders sagged. "I can't apologize enough."

"No, no, I don't believe you can. However, since I have considered your work record carefully and found no unsightly blemishes, I will try to overlook this one. You'll be leaving for the east in a day or two, Abel. I trust you'll handle Miss Conroy with more finesse than you handled Mr. DiCarlo."

"Yes, sir. Thank you. I'll be... thorough."

"I'm sure you will." Finley offered a glittering smile that made Winesap think of sharks feeding. "We'll put this unfortunate mistake out of our minds. I don't believe we need to discuss it again."

"That's very understanding of you, Mr. Finley." Cautious, Winesap backed out of the room. "Thank you."

"Oh, and Abel." Finley enjoyed watching the man stop on a dime and cringe. "I really think, under the circumstances, you should return the caddy spoon."

"Oh." Winesap's face fell. "Of course."

In much better spirits, Finley leaned back as the door closed respectfully. He'd been in a state of mental turmoil since reading the article, and now calmed himself by doing his deep-breathing exercises. There was nothing quite like yoga for soothing the soul.

He would have to keep a closer eye on Abel, he thought sadly. A much closer eye. If things got too sticky over DiCarlo, he would simply throw dear, devoted Abel to the wolves like so much dead meat.

But he sincerely hoped it wouldn't be necessary.

He wasn't worried for himself. When a man was rich enough, and powerful enough, Finley mused, he was above the common reach of the law.

The police couldn't touch him. No one could. And if, by some minor miracle, they came too close, there would always be small prey—like Abel—to throw off their scent.

But he was a forgiving man. Smiling, Finley took the etui he'd brought back to his office with him from his desk and fondled it. A very forgiving man—sometimes to a fault.

As long as Abel followed instructions carefully and managed Miss Conroy, there would be no need to kill him. No need at all.

28

It was good to be home in the simple routines of each day. Dora comforted herself with that and tried not to think of the meeting with Mr. Petroy she still had to face.

She hadn't realized she was ordinary enough, mundane enough, to wish for a lack of adventure. But the bald truth was, she wanted her simple life back. More, she wanted the chance to be bored.

At least Jed hadn't noticed her lack of appetite. Dora was certain he'd have made a few choice remarks if she hadn't covered it so well. The same held true for the female art of cosmetics. Her eyes might have been shadowed, her skin pale and drawn, but with facials and creams and powders, she presented a very competent mask.

She hoped it didn't slip until after Thursday.

She was rubbing at the throbbing between her eyes that the doses of aspirin seemed unable to ease when the shop door opened. Nothing could have made her happier than her father's smiling and slightly tipsy face.

"Izzy, my sweet."

"Dad, my own true love." She stepped away from the counter to kiss him, then found herself pressing her face against his shoulder and hugging him fiercely.

He returned the embrace. Though concern clouded his eyes, they were smiling again when he drew back. "All alone, little girl?"

"Not anymore. It's been a slow morning. Want some coffee?"

"Half a cup." He speculated, watching her move to the coffee service and pour. He knew his children—their faces, the tones of their voices, the subtleties of their body language. Isadora was hiding something, he mused. He would find out what easily enough.

"Your mother sends me as ambassador." He accepted the cup, then pulled out his flask to add a generous dollop of whiskey. "To extend an invitation to cocktails and conversation to you and your young man."

"If you're referring to Jed, I think he might object to the description, but accept the invitation. When?"

"Thursday night." His brow lifted as he saw something flicker over her face. "Pre-theater, of course."

"Of course. I'll be happy to check with him."

"I'll extend the invitation myself. Is he upstairs?"

"No, I think he's out." She sipped her coffee, grateful when a couple of window shoppers passed on without coming in. "You can check with him later, if you like."

Quentin watched her toy with the sugar bowl. "Have you had a lovers' tiff?"

"We don't tiff." She managed a smile. "We do fight now and then, but tiffing isn't part of our ritual." She picked up a cookie, put it down again. "You know, I'm feeling a little restless today. Do you want to take a walk?"

"With a beautiful woman? Always."

"Let me get my coat."

Quentin's eyes narrowed in speculation, wondering if his hand-picked partner was making his little girl so unsettled. But he was all smiles again when she returned, buttoning her coat. "I seem to recall someone who enjoys busman's holidays. Perhaps we should take a little ride over to NewMarket and check out some shop windows."

"My hero." Dora flipped the Closed sign over, then hooked her arm through her father's.

He bought her jelly beans, and she didn't have the heart not to eat them. They stayed outside, enjoying the cold and the cobblestones, the cosmopolitan air of the window displays. Dora knew she was feeling better when she was tempted by both a Limoges box and a cashmere sweater.

The wind whistled through the bare trees as they sat on a bench to enjoy more coffee. Quentin's was again stiffly laced.

"Shall I buy you a present?" he asked. "It always made you smile when you talked me into some little trinket."

"I've always been mercenary, haven't I?" Amused at herself, she leaned her head companionably on his shoulder.

"You've always loved pretty things—and appreciated them, as well. That's a gift, Izzy, not a flaw."

She felt foolish tears prick at her eyes. "I guess I'm having a mood. I always thought Will had the moods."

"All of my children had wonderful moods," Quentin said staunchly. "It's the theater in your blood. Artists are never easy, you know. We aren't meant to be."

"What about cops?"

He paused a moment to drink, to enjoy. "I see law enforcement as an art as well. Some would say science, of course. But the timing, the choreography, the drama. Yes, it's quite an art." He draped a comforting arm around her. "Tell me what you're feeling, Izzy."

And she could. She had always been able to tell him what she felt without fear of criticism or disapproval. "I'm so in love with him. I want to be happy about it. I nearly am, most of the time, but he doesn't trust those kind of emotions. He doesn't have any experience with them. His parents didn't give him anything of what you and Mom gave us."

She sighed and watched a young mother wheel a stroller over the stones. The toddler inside was rosy-cheeked and laughing. The yearning tug came quickly, with equal parts surprise and discomfort. I want to do that, she realized. I want to spend an hour pushing my child in the sunlight and smiling.

"I'm afraid we can't give each other what we need," she said carefully.

"First you have to discover what those needs are."

Wistfully, she watched mother and child roll away. "I think I have a pretty good handle on mine. How can you expect a man whose childhood was a study in misery to take the first step toward creating a family of his own? It isn't fair for me to push him toward that step, and it isn't fair for me to deny myself taking it."

"Do you think only people from happy families make happy families of their own?"

"I don't know."

"Jed's grandmother seems to think he's already taken that first step, and is cautiously debating over the second."

"I don't—" She stopped, straightened to frown at her father. "His grandmother? You've spoken to her?"

"Ria, your mother and I had a very nice visit while you were in California. A lovely woman," he added. "She's quite taken with you."

Dora's eyes slitted. "It appears I have to remind you that I'm a competent adult, and so is Jed. I don't think it's right that you would sit around discussing us as though we were slow-witted children."

"But you are our children." He smiled benignly and patted her flushed cheek. "When you have children of your own, you'll understand that the love never stops, and neither does the concern, the pride or the interference." He beamed at her. "I love you, Izzy, and I have great faith in you." He pinched her chin. "Now, tell me what else is worrying you?"

"I can't." And she was sorry for it. "But I can tell you it should be resolved in a few days."

"I won't pry," he said. At least not when she was so obviously on her guard. "But if you don't look happier soon, I'll sic your mother on you."

"I'm smiling." She bared her teeth. "See, couldn't be happier."

Satisfied for the moment, he rose. After tossing his empty cup in a wastebasket, he held out a hand. "Let's go shopping."

"She's a ball of nerves." Jed met Brent in the gym so that he could release some tension by pummeling the heavy bag. "She won't admit it, but she's tied up inside." More than a little tied up himself, Jed gave the bag a rapid series of sharp punches. As he'd been delegated to hold the bag steady, Brent grunted as the power sang up his arms. "I'm not helping."

"We're moving on it as fast as we can." Brent felt sweat trickle down his shirt and wished he'd talked Jed into meeting at some nice coffee shop. "After Thursday's meet, we should be able to keep her out of it."

"It's not just that." Jed moved from the heavy bag to the light, relieving Brent immeasurably. Eyes narrowed, Jed sent the bag flying into a blur. "She's in love with me."

Brent took off his glasses to clean the lenses of fog. "Is that supposed to be news?"

"She needs more than I can give her. She should have more."

"Maybe. Is she complaining?"

"No." Jed blinked sweat out of his eyes and kept his fists flying.

"Then relax and enjoy the ride."

Jed whirled on him so swiftly, so violently, that Brent braced for the blow. "It's not a fucking ride. It's not like that with Dora. It's—" He broke off, furious at the smug smile creasing Brent's face. "Don't play me," he said very softly.

"Just testing the waters, Captain." When Jed turned over his gloves, Brent obligingly unlaced them. "Speaking of which, the unofficial word is that you'll be back in command the first of the month. Goldman's sulking."

"He'll feel better when I sign his transfer papers."

"Oh, let me worship at your feet."

A grin tugged at Jed's mouth as he flexed his fist. "We'll make an official announcement on Monday. And if you try to kiss me in here, pal, I'll have to deck you." He picked up a towel to dry his face. "For now, Goldman's in charge. Is everything set for Thursday?"

"We'll have two men in the shop. Another pair outside, and a surveillance van a half block away. As long as Dora follows instructions, we'll pick up every word."

"She'll follow them."

Spending an hour with her father had given Dora a need for family. She indulged it by closing the shop an hour early and spending the evening at Lea's. The din from the family room soothed her soul.

"I think Richie's definitely improving on the trumpet," Dora commented.

Head cocked, Lea listened to the wet musical blats with a mixture of pride and resignation. "There's a band concert at school in three weeks. I'm saving you a front-row seat."

"God bless you." There was a series of muffled thumps from the next room, what was—if you had enough imagination—a stirring cavalry charge and an excellent rebel yell. "I needed this." Content, Dora slipped onto a stool by the counter.

"I'd be happy to leave you in charge for a couple hours." Lea added another touch of burgundy to the stew she had simmering.

"I don't need it that much." Dora drank a hurried sip of wine. "No. I spent some time with Dad this afternoon, and it made me think what it would be like if he wasn't so handy. That's all."

"Something's going on." Frowning, Lea tapped the spoon on the side of the pot, set it on a spoon rest shaped like a duck. "You've got that line between your eyebrows. And you're pale. You always get pale when you're worried about something."

"You'd be worried too if you had to find a new accountant right before end-of-January inventory."

"Not good enough." Lea leaned closer, probing. "You're edgy, Dory, and it has nothing to do with business. If you won't tell me, I'll have to turn Mom loose on you."

"Why does everyone threaten me with Mom?" she demanded. "I'm unsettled, okay? My life's taken a couple of odd turns. I'd like my family to respect my privacy enough to allow me to work out my own problems."

"Okay. I'm sorry. Really."

Passing a hand over her face, Dora took a cleansing breath. "No, I'm sorry. I shouldn't have snapped at you. I guess I'm still a little jet-lagged. I think I'll go home, take a hot bath and sleep for twelve hours."

"If you don't feel better tomorrow, I can come in early."

"Thanks. I'll let you know." She started to slide off the stool as the knock sounded on the back door.

"Hi." Mary Pat stuck in her head. "I came to pick up my share of the monsters." She listened a moment to the shouting and the blare of the trumpet. "Ah, the patter of little feet. Wonderful, isn't it?"

"Have a seat," Lea invited. "Unless you're in a hurry."

"I'd love a seat." She sighed as she took the one beside Dora. "I've been on my feet for eight straight hours. We had two codes back to back." She took a deep breath of air. "God, how do you manage to raise kids, hold down a job and cook like that?"

"I have an understanding boss." Smiling, Lea poured Mary Pat a glass of wine. "She gave me the day off."

"Speaking of work, terrific news about Jed, isn't it?"

"What news?"

"About him coming back on the job." With her eyes closed, she circled her neck and missed Dora's blank look. "Brent's really flying. He detested Goldman, of course. Who didn't? But it's more than that. The department needs Jed and Jed needs the department. Now that he's made the decision to come back, it's pretty clear he's got his head on straight again. I don't think he's going to wait until the first of the month to take command, either. Otherwise . . ." One look at Dora's face made Mary Pat stumble to a halt. "Oh, damn. Did I jump the gun? When Brent told me it would be official on Monday, I just assumed you knew."

"No, Jed didn't mention it." She fought to work a smile onto her lips, but couldn't make it reach her eyes. "It's good news, though. No, great news. I'm sure it's just what he needs. How long have you known?"

"A couple of days." Idiot, Mary Pat thought, but wasn't sure if she was referring to herself or to Jed. "I'm sure he planned to tell you himself. Once he, ah . . ." But she couldn't think of any handy excuses. "I'm sorry."

"Don't be. I really am glad to hear it." After sliding off the stool, Dora reached mechanically for her coat. "I've got to get going."

"Stay for dinner," Lea said quickly. "There's plenty."

"No, I have some things to do. Say hi to Brent," she told Mary Pat.

"Sure." When the door closed, Mary Pat lowered her forehead onto her fisted hands. "I feel like I ran over a puppy. Why the hell didn't he tell her?"

"Because he's a jerk." Lea's voice was low with fury. "All men are jerks."

"That's a given," Mary Pat agreed. "But this was major. And this was cold. Lea, I've known Jed a long time, and he's not cold. Careful, but not cold."

"Maybe he forgot the difference."

Odd things happen to the mind at two o'clock in the morning. Particularly to a man who's waiting for a woman. He begins to speculate, to project, to worry and to sweat. Jed paced his living room, strode through the door he'd propped open and paced the corridor.

As he had numerous times over the last four hours, he strode to the back door and stared out at the gravel lot. His car was as alone out there as he was alone inside. There was no sign of Dora.

Where the hell was she? He strode back to his apartment to look at the clock, to check its time with his watch. Two-oh-one. If she wasn't home in ten minutes, he promised himself, he would call in all his markers and put out an APB.

He stared at the phone. It wasn't until he'd picked up the receiver that he realized his hand was sweating. Swearing, he slammed the phone back on the cradle. No, he wasn't going to call the hospitals. He wasn't even going to let himself think that way.

But where the hell was she? What the hell could she have to do at two in the morning?

He started to reach for the phone again and stopped as a fresh idea sharpened in his brain. Unless she was paying him back. It was a safe, even a comforting thought, so he played with it. Was this how she'd felt when he'd come in late without leaving any word? Was she doing this to show him how it was to agonize over silence when the person who mattered was out of reach?

She wasn't going to get away with it, he decided. She damn well was going to pay for it. But he was reaching for the phone again when he heard her key in the outside lock.

He was out in the hall and at the door before she'd opened it.

"Where the hell have you been?" The demand burst out of him, ripe with worried fury. "Do you have any idea what time it is?"

"Yes." Very deliberately she closed the door and locked it. "Sorry. I didn't realize I had a curfew."

She walked past him only because he was too stunned to stop her. But he recovered quickly. He caught up with her at the door of her apartment and spun her around.

"Just a Goddamn minute, Conroy. We'll forget the personal stuff for now. The fact is you're a prime target, and it was incredibly irresponsible of you to be out of contact for half the night."

"I'm responsible to and for myself." She jammed the key in the lock and shoved the door open. "And as you can see, I'm perfectly fine."

He slapped a hand against the door before she could close it. "You had no right—"

"Don't tell me about rights," she interrupted, very cool, very calm. "I spent the evening as I chose to spend it."

Anger and resentment bubbled inside him. "And how was that?"

"Alone." She took off her coat and hung it in the closet.

"You did this to get under my skin, didn't you?"

"No." She walked past him toward the kitchen to pour a glass of water. "I did it because I wanted to. I'm sorry if you were worried. It didn't occur to me that you would be."

"It didn't occur to you." Incensed, hegrabbed the glass out of her hand and tossed it into the sink. It shattered effectively. "Fuck that, Conroy. You knew damn well I'd be half crazy. I was about to call out a Goddamn APB."

"Interesting, isn't it, the way those police terms slide right off your tongue? It's a good thing you're going back on, Skimmerhorn. You make a lousy civilian." Her eyes were as dull as her voice. "Are congratulations in order, Captain, or just best wishes?" When he didn't respond, she nodded. "Well, you can have both."

"It's not official until next week." He spoke carefully, studying her. He'd never seen her eyes that cold, or that detached. "How did you find out?"

"Does it matter? It's more to the point that I didn't find out from you. Excuse me." She brushed past him and into the living room.

He closed his eyes a moment and cursed himself for a fool. "So you're pissed. Okay. But that—"

"No," she interrupted. "It's not okay. And I'm not pissed." Because she was tired, unbearably so, she gave in and sat on the arm of a chair. "You could say I've been illuminated. You could even say that I'm devastated, but no, Jed, I'm not angry."

The quiet resignation in her voice reached him. "Dora, I didn't do it to hurt you."

"I know that. That's why I'm illuminated. You didn't tell me because you didn't think it was any of my concern. You didn't want it to be any of my concern is probably more accurate. It was a major decision in your life. Your life," she repeated with stinging emphasis. "Not mine. So why should you bother to tell me?"

She was slipping away from him. He was standing two feet away from her and watching the distance grow by leaps and bounds. It terrified him. "You make it sound as though I was keeping it from you. I needed to work it out, that's all. I didn't think you'd understand."

"You didn't give me the chance, Jed," she said quietly. "Did you think I could have felt the way I did about you and not understand how important your work was to you?"

Her use of the past tense had a quick skidder of panic sprinting up his spine. "It had nothing to do with you." As soon as the words were out of his mouth he knew they were ill chosen. Her eyes remained dry, but hurt filled them. "I didn't mean it that way."

"I think you did. I wish I didn't blame you for it, but I do. I know you had it rough, but you've been making your own choices for a long time. You chose not to accept my feelings for you, and you chose not to let yourself feel anything back. And I do blame you for that, Jed."

Her voice didn't waver, her eyes remained steady, but the hands in her lap were clenched tight. "I blame you very much for that, and for hurting me. I told you I don't handle pain very well, and I don't pretend it's not there when it is. Since you're the first man who's ever broken my heart, I think you should know it."

"For Christ's sake, Dora." He started toward her, but the way she jumped up and stepped back unmanned him.

"I don't want you to touch me now." She spoke very quietly, clinging to the slippery edge of control. "I really don't. It's humiliating for me to finally understand that's all we had."

"That's not true." He fisted his hands at his sides, but already knew he couldn't beat his way through the wall he'd thrown up between them. "You're blowing this out of proportion, Dora. It's just a job."

"I wish it were. But we both know it's not. It's the most important part of your life. You gave it up to punish yourself, and you're taking it back because you can't be happy without it—and maybe not even whole without it. I'm glad for you, Jed. I truly am."

"I don't need the analysis. I need you to stop this and be reasonable."

"I am being reasonable, believe me. So reasonable I'm going to make it easy for both of us. The day after tomorrow you should be able to tie up the loose ends about the painting. Or most of them. You shouldn't need me after that."

"Goddamn it, you know I need you."

Her eyes filled then, and she fought back tears like bitter enemies. "You can't imagine what I would have given to hear you say that before. Just once, for you to have been able to look at me and say that you needed me. But I'm not a courageous woman, Jed, and I have to protect myself."

No, he couldn't break through the wall she'd put between them, but her hurt could. It snuck through the cracks and battered at him. "What do you want, Dora?"

"When we're finished on Thursday, I intend to close the shop for a couple of weeks, take a trip someplace warm. That should give you plenty of time to find other accommodations and move out."

"That's no way to handle this."

"It's my way. And I figure I'm in the position of calling the shots. I'm sorry, but I don't want you here when I get back."

"Just like that?"

"Yes."

"Fine." He had his pride. He'd been rejected before. If it burned a hole in him this time, he'd find something to fill it with. But he wouldn't beg. He'd be damned if he'd beg. "I'll go as soon as things are wrapped up." Because it hurt, it hurt unbelievably, he covered the wounds with a professional shield. "There'll be a team in tomorrow after closing. They'll set up the wires. We'll go over procedure when they're done."

"All right. I'm very tired. I'd like you to go now." She walked to the door, held it open. "Please."

It wasn't until he'd reached her that he realized his hands were unsteady. When he heard the door close behind him he had the sick and certain feeling that he'd just been shut out of the best part of his life.

29

"What's with you two?" Brent asked as Jed climbed into the surveillance van.

Ignoring the question, Jed pulled out a cigarette. "How's the sound?"

"Loud and clear." Though Brent offered the headphones, he was far from finished. "Loud enough and clear enough to hear the two of you talking in there like polite strangers. Don't you think she could have used a little morale boost instead of a lecture on procedure?"

"Drop it." Jed slipped on the headphones and checked the rear window of the van to be sure he had a clear view of the shop. "Everybody in place?"

"We're set," Brent assured him. "Look, maybe you'd feel better if you were on the inside."

"She'll be more comfortable if I'm not. Look, I'll handle my end." Jed drew deeply on the cigarette. "You handle yours."

"You're not running the show yet, Captain." The edge of anger in Brent's voice sent off an answering ripple in Jed's blood. Before he could respond, the radio crackled.

"Base, this is Unit One. A man answering subject's description just got out of a cab on the corner of South and Front streets. He's walking west."

"Looks like it's show time," Brent murmured, but Jed was already reaching for the portable phone. Dora answered on the first ring.

"Good afternoon, Dora's Parlor."

"He's half a block away," Jed said flatly. "I've got him in view."

"All right. Everything's ready here."

"Keep loose, Conroy."

"Sure."

"Dora—" But she'd already broken the connection. "Fuck." He said it softly, finally, helplessly.

"She can handle it, Jed."

"Yeah. But I don't know if I can." He watched Winesap mince hurriedly down the sidewalk, shoulders hunched against the wind. "I just figured out I'm in love with her." Ignoring the throbbing at the back of his neck, he slipped on the headphones in time to hear the bells jingle as Winesap opened the shop door.

"Good afternoon." Dora stepped away from the counter and offered her best new-customer smile. "May I help you?"

"Miss Conroy? I'm Francis Petroy."

She let the smile broaden. "Yes, Mr. Petroy. I was expecting you." She walked to the door to flip the Closed sign around. Her eyes slashed to the van, then away. "I'm so glad you could make it. Can I get you some coffee? Tea?"

"I wouldn't want to trouble you."

"Not at all. I always keep both on hand for customers. It makes business so much more pleasant."

"I'd love some tea, then." It might soothe his stomach more than the Alka-Seltzer he'd downed an hour before. "Your shop is very impressive."

"Thank you." She saw, with satisfaction, that her hand was rock steady on the teapot. "I like to surround myself with beautiful things. But you'd understand that."

"Excuse me?"

"Being an art collector." She offered him a cup of tea and a smile. "Cream? Lemon?"

"No, no, nothing, thank you."

"You said you specialize in abstract, but you might find some of my nostalgia prints interesting." She gestured to a car manufacturer's sign for a Bugatti, which hung beside a Vargas girl.

"Yes, ah, very nice. Very nice indeed."

"I also have several good *Vanity Fair* caricatures in the other room." Watching him, she sipped her own tea. "But as an abstract buff, you'd be more interested in say, a Bothby or a Klippingdale," she said, making up names.

"Yes, of course. Exceptional talents." The tea soured like vinegar in Winesap's stomach. He'd tried, really tried to be thorough by studying book after book on the subject of abstract art. But all the names and pictures swam through his head. "My collection isn't extensive, you see. Which is why I concentrate on the emerging artist."

"Such as Billingsly."

"Exactly," he said on a sigh of relief. "I'm very anxious to see the work, Miss Conroy."

"Then, by all means." She led the way into the side room. Jed's artist friend had worked overtime to reproduce the painting. Now it stood, like a gaudy stripper among prim Victorian ladies, in the pretty sitting room.

"Ah." The sense of satisfaction was so great Winesap nearly wept with it. It was horrid, of course, he thought. Absolutely horrid, but it matched the description.

"Such a bold, arrogant style," Dora commented. "I was really taken with it."

"Yes, of course. It's everything I'd hoped for." He made a show of examining the brush strokes. "I'd very much like to add this to my collection."

"I'm sure you would." She let a touch of amusement color her voice. "Did you have an offer in mind, Mr. Petroy?"

"In mind, naturally," he said, trying to be coy. "I'd prefer if you'd set a price, for negotiation."

"I'd be happy to." Dora sat in a tufted-back chair and crossed her legs. "Why don't we start at two hundred and fifty thousand?"

Winesap's prim mouth fell open. He made a choked sound in the back of his throat before he managed to find his voice. "Miss Conroy, Miss Conroy, you can't be serious."

"Oh, but I am. You look as though you need to sit down, Mr. Petroy." She gestured to a petit-point stool. "Now, let's be frank," she began when he'd sunk onto the seat. "You don't know diddly about art, do you?"

"Well, really." He tugged at his strangling tie. "As I told you, I have a small collection."

"But you lied, Mr. Petroy," she said gently. "You haven't a clue about abstract. Wouldn't it be simpler, and more friendly, if we admitted that we're both more interested, at the moment, in Impressionism rather than Expressionism?"

For a moment he didn't follow her. Then his pasty face blanched. "You know about the painting."

"I bought it, didn't I?"

"Yes, but, that was a mistake." His frantic eyes widened. "No? You knew—knew all along about the Monet? You were working with DiCarlo? You—you cheated," he accused, miserably.

Dora merely chuckled and leaned forward. "You needn't sound so offended. After all, you sent DiCarlo here, didn't you?"

"It's been his fault." Disgusted, Winesap threw up his hands. "All this confusion is his fault. I can't imagine why I was sorry he died so badly."

The image in the police photo flashed obscenely in her mind. "So you killed him," she murmured. "For this."

But Winesap wasn't listening. "Now I have to clean up the entire mess, again. I'm not happy about the two hundred and fifty thousand, Miss Conroy. Not happy at all."

He rose. So did Dora. Even as he reached under his coat, two officers were bursting through the rear door.

"Freeze."

Winesap took one look at the guns pointing at him and fainted dead away. His checkbook slipped out of his hand and flapped onto the floor.

"He was going to pay me for it," Dora said dully. She watched, lightheaded, as two officers escorted a babbling and cuffed Winesap out of the shop. She hadn't needed to lower her head between her knees, but she remained sitting. It was an even bet as to whether or not her legs would support her. "He was going to write me a check." A laugh bubbled out, lightly tinted with hysteria. "Jesus Christ, I wonder if I'd have asked him for two forms of ID."

"Here." Jed shoved a cup into her hands.

"What is it?"

"That tea you drink—with a little brandy."

"Good idea." She knocked it back like water and felt it warm her jittery stomach. "I guess you guys got all you needed."

"We got plenty." He wanted to touch his fingertips to her hair, but he was afraid she'd cringe away. "You did good, Nancy."

"Yeah, I did." She lifted her eyes then, made herself meet his. "I guess on some level we didn't make such a bad team."

He stared down at her for a long time. "It's been hard on you."

"I come from pretty tough stock, Skimmerhorn. Conroys don't fold easily."

"You were brilliant." Brent swept in to lift Dora out of the chair by her elbows. He kissed her, hard. "A stand-up job, Dora. You want a job on the force, you've got my recommendation."

"Thanks. But I'm putting my magnifying glass and coupe in mothballs."

"Come again?"

"Nancy Drew," Jed muttered, and felt his heart sag. "I'm going down to Interrogation with Brent. Are you going to be all right?"

"I'm going to be fine. Terrific, in fact." Her smile was blinding, but she lowered herself carefully to the arm of the chair. "It's still tough for me to believe that pathetic little man engineered all this, and killed DiCarlo."

Brent opened his mouth, then shut it again at a swift, warning look from Jed. "We have enough on the tape to pry the rest out of him." Because they felt useless, Jed jammed his hands in his pockets. "Are you sure you'll be all right?"

"I said I would. Go be a cop." She softened the words with a smile. "It looks good on you." She pushed a hand through her hair. Jed watched as the strands fell beautifully back into place. "I'd appreciate it if you'd give me a call, let me know what the result of the interrogation is."

"You'll get a full report," Brent promised her.

"In the morning." Steadier, she rose again. "I'm going upstairs and sleep around the clock. If you're finished in here, I'll lock up behind you."

She followed them to the door. When he reached it Jed turned, closed his hand over hers on the knob. He couldn't help it. "I'd like to talk to you tomorrow, when you're feeling up to it."

She nearly gave in. Very nearly. There was as much hurt in his eyes as she was holding inside her. But a fast break was a clean one. "My schedule's a little tight, Jed. I've booked an early-morning flight to Aruba. I've got to pack."

There was nothing in her voice, nothing in her face that offered the slightest opening. "You move fast."

"It seemed best all around. I'll send you a postcard." Because she hated the bitter aftertaste of the statement, she turned her hand under his and gave it a quick squeeze. "Give 'em hell, Captain."

She closed the door quickly and turned the lock.

• • •

"Why didn't you tell her we've asked LAPD to move on Finley?" Brent demanded when Jed stood on the sidewalk.

He hurt, all over, as if someone had pounded him ruthlessly and methodically with foam-covered fists. "Do you think that would have made her sleep any better?"

"No," Brent murmured to Jed's retreating back. "Guess not."

And she was telling herself that sleep was exactly what she needed. She hadn't had a decent night of it in more than a week. Dora pulled the shade on the front door, then drummed up the energy to lift the coffee-and-tea tray.

Once she got to Aruba, she promised herself, she'd do nothing but sleep. She'd sleep in bed, on the beach, in the ocean. She'd bake this aching depression out of her body and mind with the Caribbean sunshine, beat those midwinter blues and come back tanned and revitalized.

She set the tray on her desk to carefully lock the storeroom door and engage the security alarm before heading up to her apartment.

It was habit more than desire that had her taking the tray into the kitchen to wash. When she turned from the sink, she was standing face-to-face with Finley.

He smiled and took her nerveless hand in his. "I've taken you up on your offer of hospitality, Isadora. And may I say you have a charming home."

"I really don't think I should make any sort of statement without a lawyer." Winesap chewed on his ragged nails and glanced fitfully at Brent and Jed. "I really don't."

"Suit yourself." Brent shrugged and straddled a chair. "We've got plenty of time. Do you want to call one, or do you want a PD?"

"A public defender?" That pricked the pride enough to have his sagging shoulders lift. "Oh no, I can afford counsel. I have a very good position." But his lawyer was in Los Angeles, he thought. "Perhaps if you could explain again why I'm here, we could dispense with the formality of an attorney."

"You're here on suspicion of theft, smuggling, conspiracy to murder a police officer and murder, among other things," Brent added.

"That's really absurd." Pride deflated again, Winesap hunched down in his seat. "I don't know where you could have gotten such a ridiculous idea."

"Maybe you'd like to listen to the tape of your conversation with Miss Conroy." Jed made the suggestion as he crossed to the recorder.

"That was a simple transaction—and a private one." Winesap tried to lever some indignation through the fear in his voice. But when Jed switched on the recorder, he said nothing at all. It was painfully clear after only a few moments that he hadn't been thorough at all—and that he'd been remarkably stupid.

While his mind worked, he began to suck on his knuckles. He didn't think he would care for prison. No indeed. Winesap thought of Finley and knew he would like his employer's brand of punishment a good deal less.

"Perhaps we can make an arrangement. Might I have a cup of water, please?"

"Sure." Agreeably, Brent went to the water cooler and pumped out a paper cupful.

"Thank you." Winesap sipped it slowly while he considered his options. "I think I would like immunity, and a place in the witness-protection program. I think that would suit me very well."

"I think it would suit me very well to see you rot in a cell for the next fifty years," Jed said pleasantly.

"Captain." Brent fell into the classic interrogation rhythm. "Let's give the guy a chance. Maybe he's got something to trade."

"I promise you, I do. If I have assurance that my cooperation will be rewarded, I'll give you everything you need to make a very big arrest."

Loyalty, a chain around his neck for eight long years, slipped easily off. "A very big one," he repeated.

Jed gave an imperceptible nod as Brent's eyes met his. "I'll call the DA."

"Why don't we sit down?" Finley kept his hand firm on Dora's arm as he pulled her into the living room. "And have a nice chat."

"How did you get in?"

"There was such a lot of confusion this evening, wasn't there?" He smiled as he pushed her into a chair. "I wasn't at all sure that Abel—Mr. Winesap—could handle this matter efficiently on his own. I came to supervise. A very good thing, too."

Finley took the chair beside her and folded his hands comfortably. He saw Dora's eyes cut toward the door and shook his head. "Please don't attempt to run, Isadora. I'm very strong and very fit. I'd hate to resort to physical violence."

She would hate it, too. Especially since she was certain she wouldn't get two feet. Her best bet was to play for time and wait for help. "It was you who sent DiCarlo."

"It's a long, sad tale. But I find you such good company." He settled back comfortably and began to talk. He told her of the carefully planned robberies in several different countries. The network of men and finances it required to operate a successful business—legally and illegally. When he reached DiCarlo's part in it, he paused, sighed.

"But I don't have to go into that with you, do I, dear? You're an excellent actress. One wonders why you decided to give it up. I realized quite soon after your visit to my office that you and DiCarlo had been in league together."

For a moment she was too stunned to speak. "You think I was his partner?"

"I'm sure you found him an adequate lover." Truly disappointed in her, Finley plucked at his cuffs. "And I can certainly see how you could have lured him into betraying me. A pity, too," Finley added softly. "He had potential."

"What I told you in your office was exactly the truth. He broke in here and attacked me."

"I'm quite sure you had some sort of falling out. Greed and sex working against one another, I would assume." His eyes narrowed, glinting dully. "Did you find another, more inventive man, Isadora, one you could maneuver and pit against poor Mr. DiCarlo so that he came to me with some feeble excuse for not returning my property?"

"The painting was not your property. You stole it. And I was never involved with DiCarlo."

"And when he didn't return," Finley continued as if she hadn't spoken, "you became concerned and decided to test the waters with me yourself. Oh, you were very clever.

So charming, so distressed. I very nearly believed you. There was just one niggling doubt in my mind, which proved sadly true once I witnessed the events of this afternoon. I'm disappointed that you turned to the police, Isadora. Settling for a finder's fee." He wagged a finger at her scoldingly. "I thought more of you than that. You've cost me two very good men, and a painting I wanted very much. Now how are we to reconcile?"

Too terrified to sit, she sprang to her feet. "They have your Mr. Winesap down at police headquarters. He'll be telling them all about you by now."

"Do you think he would have the nerve?" Finley considered it a moment, then moved his shoulders in elegant dismissal. "Perhaps. But don't be concerned. Mr. Winesap will very soon suffer a tragic and fatal accident. I would much rather talk about my painting, and how you think I can retrieve it."

"You can't."

"But surely, since you've been such a help, the police have told you where they've secured it."

She said nothing, only because it surprised her so much that she hadn't thought to ask.

"I thought so." Finley smiled broadly as he rose. "Just tell me where it is, Isadora, and leave the rest to me."

"I don't know where."

"Don't lie, please." He slipped his hand into the inside pocket of his Savile Row suit and pulled out a highly polished Luger. "Gorgeous, isn't it?" he asked when Dora's eyes fastened on the barrel. "A German make, used in World War II. I like to think that a Nazi officer killed quite efficiently with it. Now, Isadora, where is my painting?"

She looked helplessly into his eyes. "I don't know."

The force of the bullet slammed her back against the wall. Even as the fire erupted in her shoulder, she didn't believe he'd shot her. Couldn't believe it. Dazed, she touched a finger to the worst of the heat and stared blindly at her blood-smeared fingers. She was still staring at them when she slid limply down the wall.

"I really think you'd better tell me." All reason, Finley stepped up to where Dora lay in a boneless heap. "You're losing a great deal of blood." He crouched down, mindful not to stain his suit. "I don't want to cause you unnecessary distress. It took DiCarlo hours to die after I shot him. But there's no need for you to suffer like that." He sighed when she only whimpered. "We'll give you a little time to compose yourself, shall we?"

Leaving her bleeding, he began to methodically examine her treasures, one by one.

"The little bastard sure did sing." Brent felt like singing himself as he cut through traffic toward South Street.

"I don't like cutting deals with weasels," Jed muttered.

"Even for a big fat weasel like Finley?"

"Even for that." He checked his watch. "I'll feel better when I know that LAPD's picked him up."

"The warrant's in the works, pal. He won't be sleeping in his own bed tonight."

There was some comfort in that. Some small comfort. Jed would have been happier if he could have taken the man down himself. "You didn't have to come this far out of your way. I could have caught a cab."

"Nothing's too good for the captain. Not tonight. And if I were you, I wouldn't wait until morning to give a certain gorgeous brunette the good news."

"She needs to sleep."

"She needs some peace of mind."

"She ought to get plenty of it in Aruba."

"Come again?"

"Nothing." Jed turned to scowl at the light sleet that began to fall as they turned onto South.

"Now then." Finley sat down again, pleased when Dora found the strength to push herself to a sitting position against the wall. The blood seeping out of the wound on her shoulder had slowed to a sluggish ooze. "About the painting."

Her teeth were chattering. She'd never been so cold, so cold that even her bones felt like frigid sticks. While her arm and shoulder spurted fire, the rest of her seemed cased in ice. She tried to speak, but the words hitched one moment and slurred drunkenly the next. "The police . . . The police took it."

"I know that." The first sizzle of anger crept into his words. "I'm not a fool, Isadora, as you obviously believe. The police have the painting, and I intend to get it back. I paid for it."

"They took it away." Her head lolled on her shoulder, then rolled weakly against the wall. The room was losing its color, going gray. "To grandmother's house," she said, edging toward delirium. "Then away. I don't know."

"I can see you need incentive." He set the gun aside and loosened his tie. Dully, Dora watched him slip out of his jacket. When he reached for the gold buckle of his belt, slippery fingers of horror crept through the shock.

"Don't touch me." She tried to crawl away but the room revolved sickeningly so that she could only curl in a ball in a congealing puddle of her own blood. "Please, don't."

"No, no. Unlike DiCarlo, I have no plans to force myself on you. But a good whipping with this belt may loosen your tongue. It may be hard for you to believe, but I actually enjoy inflicting pain." He wrapped the end of the belt around his hand, the buckle loose to add bite to the beating. "Now, Isadora, where is the painting?"

She saw him pick up the gun and raise the belt at the same time. All she could do to try to block both weapons was close her eyes.

"You can drop me out front," Jed told Brent.

"Nope. Door-to-door service." He whipped into the parking lot, spitting gravel. "If you had any heart, you'd ask me up for a beer."

"I haven't got any heart." Jed pushed the door open and glanced back at Brent's engaging grin. "Sure, come ahead." If nothing else, it would put off the time he'd have to spend alone, waiting for morning."

"You got any of that imported stuff?" Brent slung a friendly arm over Jed's shoulders as they trooped toward the steps. "Mexican, maybe? I really feel like—"

When they heard the thin cry, they each slapped a weapon into their hands. They charged through the door in a dead run. Years of partnership clicked seamlessly into place. When Jed kicked open Dora's door, he went in high, Brent low.

The faintest flicker of irritation crossed Finley's face as he whirled. Two police issues fired simultaneously. Two 9mm bullets caught Finley high in the chest.

"God. Oh God." With terror singing in his head, Jed rushed to Dora. He said her name over and over like a prayer as he ripped off her blouse and used it to staunch the oozing blood. "Hang on, baby. You hang on."

There was so much blood, he thought frantically. Too much. And because it had begun to clot, he knew too much time had passed. When he looked at her still, white face he had one moment of unspeakable horror when he thought she was dead. But she was shaking. He could feel the racking trembles of shock even as he peeled off his jacket to cover her.

"You're going to be okay. Dora, baby, can you hear me?"

Her eyes were wide and dilated and remained unfocused. The second bullet had gone through the fleshy part of her upper arm. She hadn't even felt it.

"Use this." Brent pushed a towel into Jed's shaking hands and folded another to place under Dora's head. "Ambulance is on the way." He spared a glance at the body sprawled on the rug. "He's dead."

"Dora, listen to me. You listen to me, damn it." Jed worked quickly as he spoke to her, using the towel to pad the upper wound and what was left of her blouse to fashion a pressure bandage. "I want you to hold on. Just hold on." Then he could think of nothing else but to gather her close and rock her. "Please. Stay with me. I need you to stay with me."

He felt the light brush of her hand on his cheek. When he looked down at her face, her lips trembled open. "Don't—don't tell my parents," she whispered. "I don't want them to worry."

30

He would have wept if it would have helped. He'd tried everything else. Swearing, pacing, praying. Now he could only sit, his head in his hands, and wait.

The Conroys were there. Jed wondered if Dora would be surprised at how tough they were. He doubted it. There had been tears, and there had been terror, but they had all drawn together, a solid wall, in the hospital waiting room to count the minutes while Dora was in surgery.

He'd waited for recriminations. They had given him none. He'd wanted blame. But it hadn't come from them. Not even when he had stood, smeared with Dora's blood, and told them that he'd left her alone, left her defenseless, had they blamed him.

He wished to Christ they had.

Instead, John had gotten them all coffee, Lea had gone down to wait for Will to arrive from New York and Quentin and Trixie had sat side by side on the sofa, holding hands.

After the second hour had crawled by, Trixie murmured to her husband. When she received his nod of agreement, she rose and went to sit beside Jed.

"She was always a tough little girl," Trixie began. "She used to pick fights in school—well, not pick them, precisely, but she never would walk away from one without dignity.

It used to amaze me that she would scream like a banshee if she fell and banged her knee. But if she came home with a split lip or a swollen eye, you never heard a peep. A matter of pride, I suppose."

"This wasn't her fight." Jed kept the heels of his hands pressed hard against his eyes. "It shouldn't have been."

"That's for her to decide. She'll want lots of pampering, you know. She was never sick often, but when she was—" Trixie's voice broke, betraying her. She mopped quickly at her eyes and steadied it. "When she was, she expected everyone's devoted attention. Dora's never been one to suffer in silence."

Gently she touched the back of his hand. When he lowered it enough, she gripped it firmly. "It's so much harder to wait alone."

"Mrs. Conroy..." But he didn't have the words. He simply leaned against her and let himself be held.

They all rose to their feet at the quick slap of crepe-soled shoes on tile. Still in her scrubs, Mary Pat stepped through the doorway. "She's out of surgery," she said quickly. "It looks good. The doctor will be out soon."

It was then Trixie began to cry, with hard, racking sobs and hot tears that burned through Jed's shirt. His arms went around her automatically as he met Mary Pat's eyes.

"When can they see her?"

"The doctor will let you know. She's a tough one, I can tell you that."

"Didn't I say so?" Trixie managed. She stumbled blindly into Quentin's arms so they could weep out their relief together.

It wasn't until he was alone again that Jed started to shake. He'd gone outside, had fully intended on going home. It was a time for family, he'd told himself. Now that he knew she was going to pull through it, there was no need to hang around.

But he couldn't make it across the street to hail a cab, so he sat down on the steps and waited for the tremors to subside. The sleet had turned to snow that fell quick and light and damp. There was something otherworldly about the way it danced in the streetlights, something hypnotic. He stared at one beam of light as he smoked one cigarette, then another. Then he walked back in and rode the elevator to the floor where Dora lay sleeping.

"Figured you'd be back." Mary Pat smiled at him out of eyes red-rimmed with fatigue. "Damn it, Jed, you're soaked. Am I going to have to dig up a bed for you?"

"I just want to see her. I know she's sedated, I know she won't know I'm there. I just want to see her."

"Let me get you a towel."

"MP."

"You're going to dry off first," she told him. "Then I'll take you in."

She was as good as her word. When she was satisfied he was dry enough, she led him into Dora's room.

Dora lay, still and white as death. Jed's heart careered into his throat. "Are you sure she's going to be all right?"

"She's stabilized, and there were no complications. Dr. Forsythe's good. Believe me." She didn't want to think about the amount of blood they'd had to pump into Dora, or how long it had taken to get that feeble pulse to steady. "The bullet's out—and there's some tissue damage, but it'll heal. She's going to be weak as a baby for a while, and she's going to hurt."

"I don't want her to hurt." His control slipped a dangerous notch. "You make sure she gets whatever she needs so she isn't in pain."

"Why don't you just sit with her for a while?" Mary Pat ran a soothing hand up and down his back. "It'll make you feel better."

"Thanks."

"I go off duty in an hour. I'll check back."

But when she did, one look had her stepping back and leaving them alone.

He was still there in the morning.

She awakened slowly, as if swimming toward the surface of still, dark water. The air seemed too thick to breathe, and there was a whooshing sound in her head like waves lapping gently on the shore.

He watched her break through, every flicker of the eyelid. Her hand flexed once in his, then lay still again.

"Come on, Dora, don't go back yet." He brushed his fingers over her hair, over her cheek. She was still too pale, he thought, much too pale. But her lashes fluttered again, then her eyes opened. He waited for them to focus.

"Jed?" Her voice sounded hollow, lifeless, and the sound of it almost broke him.

"Yeah, baby. Right here."

"I had a nightmare." He pressed a kiss to her hand, fighting the need to simply lay his head on the bed and let go.

"It's all right now."

"It seemed awfully real. I—Oh God!" She shifted, sending an arrow of pain radiating through her arm.

"You've got to lie still."

Like the pain, memory burst back. "He shot me. Jesus." She started to move her hand to the fire blooming in her shoulder, but he clamped his fingers on hers. "It was Finley."

"It's all over now. You're going to be fine."

"I'm in the hospital." The panic came quickly, surging along with the pain. "How—how bad?"

"They fixed you all up. You just need to rest now." None of his fourteen years on the force had prepared him to deal with the terrified pain clouding her eyes. "I'm going to get a nurse."

"I remember." Her fingers trembled as she groped to hang onto his. "He was in the apartment, waiting for me. He wanted the painting back. I told him I didn't know where it was, and he shot me."

"He won't ever hurt you again. I swear it." He pressed his brow against their joined hands and felt himself crack. "I'm sorry, baby. I'm so sorry."

But she was swimming down through the dark water again, away from the pain. "Don't leave me alone here."

"I won't."

• • •

The next time he saw her conscious, she was surrounded by flowers, banks and bouquets of them from sweet little nosegays to towering exotic blooms. Rather than the drab hospital gown, she was wearing something frilly and pink. Her hair was washed and she was wearing makeup.

But to Jed she looked horribly frail.

"How you doing, Conroy?"

"Hi." She smiled and held out a hand. "How'd you break in? They're vicious about proper visiting hours around here."

"I pulled rank." He hesitated. The hand in his felt as fragile as bird wings. "If you're too tired, I can stop back by later."

"No, if you stay you can chase them away when they come in with their needles."

"Sure, my pleasure." Miserably awkward, he turned away to study the forest of flowers. "Looks like you ought to go into a different business."

"Great, isn't it? I love being fawned over." She shifted, winced and was grateful his back was to her. "You ratted on me, Skimmerhorn."

"What?"

"You told my family."

"I figured it was better than having them read it in the papers."

"You're probably right. So what's happening in your world? Mary Pat tells me you kicked Goldman out early and went back to work."

"Yeah." He'd had to have something filling his days, or go quietly mad.

"Can I see your badge?"

"What?"

"Really." She smiled again. "Can I see it?"

"Sure." He pulled out his shield as he crossed to the bed. She took it, studied it, opened and closed it a couple of times.

"Pretty cool. How does it feel?"

"Right," he told her as he slipped it back into his pocket. There was no possible way he could stand there and make small talk when he kept seeing the stark white bandage peeking out beneath that frilly pink nightgown. "Listen, I just stopped by to see how you were doing. I've got to go."

"Before you give me my present?" When he said nothing, she drummed up another smile, though it was becoming harder as her medication wore off. "That box you're holding? Isn't it for me?"

"Yeah, it's for you." He set it on her lap. "I've been by a couple of times when you were zonked out. After I saw the flower shop in here, I figured you wouldn't need any more posies."

"You can never have too many." She reached for the fussy bow, then sat back again. "Give me a hand, will you? I have a little trouble using my arm."

He didn't move, but his eyes were eloquent. "They told me there wouldn't be any permanent damage."

"Right." Her mouth moved into a pout. "Like a scar isn't permanent damage. I'm never going to look the same in a bikini."

He couldn't handle it, simply couldn't. Turning abruptly, he strode to the window and stared blindly out with the heavy scent of roses tormenting him.

"I should have been there," he managed after a moment. "You shouldn't have been alone."

His voice was so angry, his shoulders so stiff, that Dora waited for the storm. When it didn't come, she plucked at the bow with her good hand. "From what Brent tells me, Finley slipped right through LAPD. Nobody had a clue he'd left California. I don't see how anyone could have imagined he'd waltz right into my apartment and shoot me."

"It's my job to know."

"So, it's going to your head already. What do they call that super-cop thing—the John Wayne syndrome, right?" She'd managed to pull and tug the ribbon off and was lifting the top off the box when he turned. "Well, pilgrim," she said in a very poor Wayne imitation. "You just can't be everywhere at once." Though her arm was beginning to throb, she dug happily into the tissue paper. "I love presents, and I'm not ashamed to say so. I don't particularly care to get shot to . . . Oh, Jed, it's beautiful."

Stunned, really completely stunned, she lifted out the old wooden-and-gesso box, delicately painted and gilded with figures from mythology. When she opened the lid, it played "Greensleeves" softly.

"It was hanging around in storage." He dipped his hands into his pockets and felt like a fool. "I figured you'd get a kick out of it."

"It's beautiful," she said again, and the look she sent him was so sincerely baffled he felt even more foolish. "Thank you."

"It's no big deal. I figured you could put junk in it while you're stuck in here. I've really got to take off. You, ah, need anything?"

She continued to run her fingers over the box as she looked at him. "I could use a favor."

"Name it."

"Can you pull some strings, get me out of here?" It shamed her to feel tears pricking at her eyes. "I want to go home."

It took him several hours, and a great deal of negotiation, but Dora finally laid her head down on her own pillow, in her own bed.

"Thank you, God." Dora closed her eyes, sighed deeply, then opened them again to smile at Mary Pat. "Nothing against your workplace, MP, but personally, I hated it."

"You weren't exactly the ideal patient either, kiddo. Open up." She stuck a thermometer in Dora's mouth.

"I was a jewel," Dora muttered.

"A diamond in the rough, maybe. Very rough. But I'm not going to complain; a few days of private duty suits me just fine." Efficiently, she wrapped a blood-pressure cuff around Dora's uninjured arm. "Right on the money," she announced when she took the thermometer out to read. But Dora caught the quick frown over blood pressure.

"What's wrong?"

"Nothing that quiet and rest won't fix."

"I've been quiet. I never thought I'd hear myself say this, but I'm tired of being in bed."

"Live with it." Sitting on the edge of the bed, Mary Pat took her hand—and her pulse. "I'm going to be straight with you, Dora. You're going to be just fine with the proper rest and care. But this wasn't any skinned knee. If Jed hadn't gotten you in when he did, you wouldn't be here to complain. As it was, it was close."

"I know. I remember it all a bit too clearly for comfort."

"You're entitled to moan and bitch. I won't mind a bit. But you're also going to follow orders, to the letter, or I'll report you to the captain."

Dora smiled a little. "You nurses have ranks?"

"I'm talking about Jed, dimwit. He's financing this operation."

"What do you mean?"

"I mean you've got round-the-clock home care for as long as you need it, courtesy of Captain J. T. Skimmerhorn."

"But—I thought insurance was arranging it."

"Get real." Chuckling at the thought, Mary Pat plumped the pillows, smoothed the sheets. "Now, get some rest. I'm going to go fix you something to eat."

"He shouldn't feel guilty," Dora murmured when Mary Pat started out of the room.

Mary Pat stopped, looked back. "He feels a lot more than guilt where you're concerned. Did you know he didn't leave the hospital for the first forty-eight hours?"

"No." Dora looked down at her hands. "I didn't."

"Or that he checked on you every night."

Dora only shook her head.

"A lot of women wait their whole lives for someone to feel that guilty."

Alone, Dora reached for the music box. She opened the lid, closed her eyes and wondered what to do.

At the end of her shift, Mary Pat passed her patient's progress on to her replacement. But she didn't consider herself off duty yet. Marching across the hall, she rapped sharply on Jed's door. When Jed opened it, she jabbed a finger into his chest.

"Couldn't you find the energy to walk across the Goddamn hall and—" She broke off, scowling. "What are you doing?"

"I'm packing."

Darts of righteous fury shot out of her eyes. "The hell you are." Incensed, she stomped over and upended a box of books onto the floor. "You're not walking out on her when she's flat on her back and defenseless."

"I'm not walking out." He struggled for calm. He'd convinced himself, very logically, that what he was doing, he was doing for Dora. "She *asked* me to leave. It's only going to upset her if she finds out I haven't moved yet."

Mary Pat fisted her hands on her hips. "You're an idiot. I can almost accept that. But I never thought you were a coward."

"Back off, MP."

"Not a chance. Can you stand there and tell me you're not in love with her?"

He reached for a cigarette. Mary Pat snatched it out of his hand and broke it in two. He glared. She glared right back.

"No, I can't. But that's not the point. The doctor was real clear about keeping her free from stress. She doesn't need me hanging around upsetting her."

"Sit down. Sit down, damn it." She gave him a quick shove. "I'm going to tell you exactly what she needs."

"Fine." He slumped into a chair. "I'm sitting."

"Have you ever told her you loved her?"

"I don't see that that's any of your business."

"I didn't think so." Impatient, she took a quick turn around the room, barely preventing herself from kicking his weight bench. "Have you ever picked her wildflowers?"

"It's fucking February."

"You know exactly what I'm talking about." She turned on him, slapped both hands on the arm of his chair to cage him in. "I'll lay odds you never lit candles for her, or took her for a walk by the river, or brought her some silly present."

"I gave her a damn music box."

"Not enough. She needs to be wooed."

Incredibly, he felt a flush creeping up on his neck. "Give me a break."

"I'd like to break your butt, but I'm sworn to heal. You almost lost her."

His eyes whipped up, sharp as a sword. "Don't you think I know that? I wake up in a sweat every night remembering how close it was."

"Then do something positive. Show her what she means to you."

"I don't want to push myself on her when she's vulnerable."

Mary Pat rolled her eyes. "Then you are stupid." Feeling sorry for him, she kissed him. "Find some wildflowers, Jed. My money's on you."

The box arrived the following afternoon.

"More presents," Lea announced, struggling to shove the huge box across the living room to where Dora sat on the couch. "I'm thinking of getting shot myself—as long as it's a flesh wound."

"Believe me, it's not worth it. Get the scissors, will you? Let's get the baby open." She leaned down to study. "No return address."

"Ah, a secret admirer." Tongue caught in her teeth, Lea attacked the packing tape. "Oh," she said, deflating when she opened the lid. "It's just books."

"God. Oh my God. Carolyn Keene." She was down on her knees, rummaging. "Nancy Drew—it looks like the complete set. And first editions. Look, look. It's *The Clue of the Leaning Chimney, The Hidden Staircase*." All at once she clutched the books to her breasts and began to weep.

"Honey, oh, honey, did you hurt yourself? Let me help you to bed."

"No." She pressed *Passport to Larkspur Lane* against her cheek. "They're from Jed."

"I see," Lea said carefully, and sat back on her heels.

"He went to all this trouble just to be sweet. Why is he being so sweet? Look, a few days ago he sent me this bracelet." She held out her arm and continued babbling even when Lea oohed and aahed over it. "And that silly cow, and the watercolor. Why is he doing this? What's wrong with him?"

"Love sickness would be my guess."

Dora sniffled and rubbed tears away with the sleeve of her robe. "That's ridiculous."

"Honey, don't you know when you're being romanced?" Lea picked up a book, turned it over, shook her head. "I myself might prefer a slightly different style, but this certainly seems to have punched your buttons."

"He's just feeling sorry for me. And guilty." She hitched back tears, blinked them away. "Isn't he?"

"Honey, the man I saw haunting that hospital wasn't there out of guilt." She reached over to tuck her sister's hair behind her ear. "Are you going to give him a break?"

She laid a book on her lap, running her hands gently over the cover. "Before I was shot, I broke things off with him. I told him to move out. He hurt me, Lea. I don't want him to hurt me again."

"I can't tell you what to do, but it seems awfully unfair to make him keep suffering." She kissed Dora's forehead, then rose to answer the knock on the door. "Hi, Jed." Lea smiled and kissed him as well. "Your surprise hit the mark. She's in there right now crying over the books."

He stepped back automatically, but Lea took his hand and pulled him inside. "Look who's here."

"Hi." Dora brushed at tears and managed a shaky smile. "These are great." Her eyes overflowed again. "Really great."

"Their value's going to plummet if they're water-damaged," he warned her.

"You're right. But I always get sentimental over first editions."

"I was just on my way out." Lea grabbed her coat, but neither of them paid any attention to her departure.

"I don't know what to say." She continued to press *The Hidden Staircase* like a beloved child to her breast.

"Say thanks," he suggested.

"Thanks. But, Jed—"

"Listen, I've got the go-ahead to spring you for a while. You up for a drive?"

"Are you kidding?" She scrambled to her feet. "Outside? All the way outside and not to the hospital?"

"Get your coat, Conroy."

"I can't believe it," she said a few minutes later as she slid luxuriously down in the seat of Jed's car. "No nurses. No looming thermometers or blood-pressure cuffs."

"How's the shoulder doing?"

"It's sore." She opened the window just to feel the rush of air on her face and missed the way his fingers tightened on the wheel. "They make me do this physical therapy, which is—to put it mildly—unpleasant. But it's effective." She jockeyed her elbow to a right angle to prove it. "Not bad, huh?"

"That's great." There was such restrained violence in the statement she lifted a brow.

"Everything all right at work?"

"It's fine. You were right all along. I shouldn't have left."

"You just needed some time." She touched his arm, letting her hand fall away when he jerked. It was time, she thought, to clear the air. "Jed, I know that we were in a difficult position before—well, before I was hurt. I know I was unkind."

"Don't." He didn't think he could bear it. "You were right. Everything you said was right. I didn't want you to get too close, and I made certain you couldn't. You were one of the main reasons I went back on the job, but I didn't share it with you because I would have had to admit that it mattered. That what you thought of me mattered. It was deliberate."

She rolled up the window again, shutting out the wind. "There's no point in raking it up again."

"I guess it would sound pretty convenient if I told you that I was going to ask you to forgive me, that I'd have been willing to beg for another chance, before you got hurt." He shot her a look, caught her wide-eyed stare then scowled back through the windshield in disgust. "Yeah, that's what I thought you'd say."

"I'm not sure," she said cautiously, "what another chance might entail."

He was going to try to show her. He pulled up in the driveway, set the brake, then rounded the hood to help her out. Because she was staring at his house, she moved wrong and bumped her arm against the car door.

"Damn." Her gasp of helpless pain broke him.

"I can't stand to see you hurt." Shielding her arm, he gathered her close. "I just can't stand it. It rips at me, Dora, every time I think of it. Every time I remember what it was like to see you on the floor, to have your blood on my hands." He began to tremble, all those honed muscles quivering like plucked strings. "I thought you were dead. I looked at you and I thought you were dead."

"Don't." She soothed automatically. "I'm all right now."

"I didn't prevent it," he said fiercely. "I was too late."

"But you weren't. You saved my life. He'd have killed me. He wanted to, as much as he wanted the painting. You stopped him."

"It isn't enough." Fighting for control, he gentled his grip on her and stepped back.

"It suits me pretty well, Jed." She lifted a hand to his cheek. He grasped at it, pressed it hard to his lips.

"Just give me a minute." He stood there a moment, with the air cool and crisp, whispering through denuded trees and sleeping winter grass. "You shouldn't be standing out in the cold."

"It feels great."

"I want you to come inside. I want to finish this inside."

"All right." Though she no longer felt weak, she let him support her as they went up the walk. She thought he needed to.

But it was he who was unsteady as he unlocked the door, opened it, led her inside. His nerves jumped as she let out a quiet gasp of pleasure.

She stepped onto the welcoming Bokhara rug. "You've put things back."

"Some." He watched the way she ran her fingertips over the rosewood table, the curved back of a chair, the way she smiled at the fussy gilded mirror. "My landlord kicked me out, so I took a few things out of storage."

"The right things." She walked on into the front parlor. He'd put back a curvy pin-striped settee, a lovely Tiffany lamp on a satinwood table. There was a fire burning low in the hearth. She felt both a surge of pleasure and grief. "You're moving back in."

"That depends." He slipped her coat carefully off her shoulders, laid it on the arm of the settee. "I came back here last week. It wasn't the same. I could see you walking up the stairs, sitting on my window seat, looking out the kitchen window. You changed the house," he said as she turned slowly to face him. "You changed me. I want to move back in, and make it work. If you'll come with me."

Dora didn't think the sudden dizziness had anything to do with her healing injuries. "I think I want to sit down." She lowered herself to the striped cushions and took two careful breaths. "You're going to move back here? You *want* to move back here?"

"Yeah, that's right."

"And you want me to live with you?"

"If that's the best I can get." He took a small box out of his pocket and pushed it into her hands. "I'd like it better if you'd marry me."

"Can I—" Her voice came out in a squeak. "Can I have some water?"

Frustrated, he dragged a hand through his hair. "Damn it, Conroy—sure." He bit back on temper and a terrible fit of nerves. "Sure, I'll get it."

She waited until he was out of the room before she worked up the courage to open the box. She was glad she had because her mouth fell open. She was still staring dumbfounded at the ring when he came back in carrying a Baccarat tumbler filled with lukewarm tap water.

"Thanks." She took the glass, drank deeply. "It's a whopper."

Disgusted with himself, he fumbled out a cigarette. "I guess it's overstated."

"Oh no. There isn't a diamond in the world that's overstated." She laid the box in her lap, but kept a hand possessively around it. "Jed, I think these past few weeks have been as hard on you as they have on me. I might not have appreciated that, but—"

"I love you, Dora."

That stopped her cold. Before she could gather her wits, he was beside her on the settee, crunching several bones in her hand. "Goddamn it, don't ask me for another glass of water. If you don't want to answer yet, I'll wait. I just want a chance to make you love me again."

"Is that what all this has been about? The presents and the phone calls? You were trying to undermine my defenses when I was down."

He looked down at their joined hands. "That about sizes it up."

She nodded, then rose to walk to the window. She'd want tulips out there in the spring, she thought. And lots of sunny daffodils.

"Good job," she said quietly. "Damn good job, Skimmerhorn. It was the books that really did it, though. How could I possibly hold out against a complete set of first-edition Nancy Drew?" She looked down at the bold square-cut diamond still in her hand. "You exploited my weaknesses for nostalgia, romance and material gain."

"I'm not such a bad deal." Nerves screaming, he came up behind her to touch a hand to her hair. "I've got some flaws, sure, but I'm loaded."

Her lips curved. "That approach might have worked once, but I'm pretty well set myself, since I'll be awarded a fat finder's fee on the Monet. I might be greedy, Skimmerhorn, but I have my standards."

"I'm crazy about you."

"That's better."

"You're the only woman I've ever wanted to spend my life with." He brushed a light kiss at the curve of her shoulder and throat and made her sigh. "The only woman I've ever loved, or want to love."

"That's excellent."

"I don't think I can live without you, Dora."

Tears burned her throat, thickening her voice. "Direct hit."

"So does that mean you're going to fall in love with me again?"

"What makes you think I ever stopped?"

The hand he had in her hair fisted and made her wince. "And the marriage thing? You'll give it a shot?"

She grinned into the sunlight. It might not have been the world's most romantic proposal, but it suited her. It suited her just fine.

"We'll need lace at the curtains, Jed. And I have a Chippendale bench that's waiting to sit in front of that fire."

He turned her around, brushing her hair back so that his hands could frame her face. He only had to see her eyes for the nerves to vanish. "Kids?"

"Three."

"Good number." Overwhelmed, he rested his brow against hers. "There's a bed upstairs, in the master suite. I think it's a George the Third."

"Four-poster?"

"Tester. Stay here with me tonight."

She laughed her way into the kiss. "I thought you'd never ask."